ALSO BY

Tom Clancy

The Hunt for Red October
Red Storm Rising
Patriot Games
The Cardinal of the Kremlin
Clear and Present Danger
The Sum of All Fears
Without Remorse
Debt of Honor
Executive Orders
Rainbow Six

NONFICTION

Submarine:
A Guided Tour Inside a Nuclear Warship

Armored Cav:
A Guided Tour of an Armored Cavalry Regiment

Fighter Wing:
A Guided Tour of an Air Force Combat Wing

Marine:
A Guided Tour of a Marine Expeditionary Unit

Airborne:
A Guided Tour of an Airborne Task Force

Carrier:
A Guided Tour of an Aircraft Carrier

Into the Storm:
A Study in Command
(WITH GENERAL FRED FRANKS, JR. (RET.))

Every Man a Tiger
(WITH GENERAL CHUCK HORNER (RET.))

The Bear and the Dragon

The Bear and the Dragon

Tom Clancy

G. P. PUTNAM'S SONS
NEW YORK

This is a work of fiction. Names, characters, places, and incidents either are the product of the author's imagination or are used fictitiously, and any resemblance to actual persons, living or dead, business establishments, events, or locales is entirely coincidental.

G. P. Putnam's Sons
Publishers Since 1838
a member of
Penguin Putnam Inc.
375 Hudson Street
New York, NY 10014

Published simultaneously in Canada

Library of Congress Cataloging-in-Publication Data

Clancy, Tom, date.
The bear and the dragon / Tom Clancy.
p. cm.
ISBN 0-399-14563-X
ISBN 0-399-14640-7-(limited edition)
1. Ryan, Jack (Fictitious character)—Fiction. 2. International relations—Fiction.
3. World Politics—Fiction. 4. Presidents—Fiction. I. Title.
PS3553.L245 B42 2000b 00-056499
813'.54—dc21

Printed in the United States of America

1 3 5 7 9 10 8 6 4 2

This book is printed on acid-free paper. ♾

Book design by Deborah Kerner

Acknowledgments

As always, some friends were there to help:

Roland, the screw in Colorado,
for the superb language lesson—
good luck looking after your wayward children—

Harry, the kid in the ether world,
for some unexpected information,

John G., my gateway into
the world of technology,

And Charles, a fine teacher from long ago,
and probably a pretty good soldier, too.

History
admires
the wise,
but it
elevates
the brave.

—EDMUND MORRIS

The **Bear** and the **Dragon**

PROLOGUE

The White Mercedes

Going to work was the same everywhere, and the changeover from Marxism-Leninism to Chaos-Capitalism hadn't changed matters much—well, maybe things were now a little worse. Moscow, a city of wide streets, was harder to drive in now that nearly anyone could have a car, and the center lane down the wide boulevards was no longer tended by militiamen for the Politburo and used by Central Committee men who considered it a personal right of way, like Czarist princes in their troika sleds. Now it was a left-turn lane for anyone with a Zil or other private car. In the case of Sergey Nikolay'ch Golovko, the car was a white Mercedes 600, the big one with the S-class body and twelve cylinders of German power under the hood. There weren't many of them in Moscow, and truly his was an extravagance that ought to have embarrassed him . . . but didn't. Maybe there were no more *nomenklatura* in this city, but rank *did* have its privileges, and he was chairman of the SVR. His apartment was also large, on the top floor of a high-rise building on Kutusovskiy Prospekt, a structure relatively new and well-made, down to the German appliances which were a long-standing luxury accorded senior government officials.

He didn't drive himself. He had Anatoliy for that, a burly former Spetsnaz special-operations soldier who carried a pistol under his coat and who drove the car with ferocious aggression, while tending it with loving care. The windows were coated with dark plastic, which denied the casual onlooker the sight of the people inside, and the windows were thick, made of polycarbonate and specced to stop anything up to a 12.7-mm bullet, or so the company had told Golovko's purchasing agents sixteen months before. The armor made it nearly a ton heavier than was the norm for an S600 Benz, but the power and the ride didn't seem to suffer from that. It was the uneven streets that would ultimately destroy the car. Road-paving was a skill that his country had not yet mastered, Golovko thought as he turned the page in his morning paper. It was the American *International Herald Tribune,* always a good source of news since it was a joint venture of *The Washington Post* and *The New York Times,* which were together two of the most skilled intelligence services in the world, if a little too arrogant to be the true professionals Sergey Nikolay'ch and his people were.

He'd joined the intelligence business when the agency had been known as the KGB, the Committee for State Security, still, he thought, the best such government department the world had ever known, even if it had ultimately failed. Golovko sighed. Had the USSR not fallen in the early 1990s, then his place as Chairman would have put him as a full voting member of the Politburo, a man of genuine power in one of the world's *two* superpowers, a man whose mere gaze could make strong men tremble . . . but . . . no, what was the use of that? he asked himself. It was all an illusion, an odd thing for a man of supposed regard for objective truth to value. That had always been the cruel dichotomy. KGB had always been on the lookout for hard facts, but then reported those facts to people besotted with a dream, who then bent the truth in the service of that dream. When the truth had finally broken through, the dream had suddenly evaporated like a cloud of steam in a high wind, and reality had poured in like the flood following the breakup of an icebound river in springtime. And then the Politburo, those brilliant men who'd wagered their lives on the dream, had found that their theories had been only the thinnest of reeds, and reality was the swinging scythe, and the eminence bearing *that* tool didn't deal in salvation.

But it was not so for Golovko. A dealer in facts, he'd been able to continue his profession, for his government still needed them. In fact, his authority was broader now than it would have been, because as a man who well knew the surrounding world and some of its more important personalities intimately, he was uniquely suited to advising his president, and so he had a voice in foreign policy, defense, and domestic matters. Of them, the third was the trickiest lately, which had rarely been the case before. It was now also the most dangerous. It was an odd thing. Previously, the mere spoken (more often, shouted) phrase "State Security!" would freeze Soviet citizens in their stride, for KGB had been the most feared organ of the previous government, with power such as Reinhart Heydrich's *Sicherheitsdienst* had only dreamed about, the power to arrest, imprison, interrogate, and to kill any citizen it wished, with no recourse at all. But that, too, was a thing of the past. Now KGB was split, and the domestic-security branch was a shadow of its former self, while the SVR—formerly the First Chief Directorate—still gathered information, but lacked the immediate strength that had come with being able to enforce the *will,* if not quite the *law,* of the communist government. But his current duties were still vast, Golovko told himself, folding the paper.

He was only a kilometer away from Dzerzhinskiy Square. That, too, was no longer the same. The statue of Iron Feliks was gone. It had always been a chilling sight to those who'd known who the man was whose bronze image had stood alone in the square, but now it, too, was a distant memory. The building behind it was the same, however. Once the stately home office of the Rossiya Insurance Company, it had later been known as the Lubyanka, a fearsome word even in the fearsome land ruled by Iosef Vissarionovich Stalin, with its basement full of cells and interrogation rooms. Most of those functions had been transferred over the years to Lefortovo Prison to the east, as the KGB bureaucracy had grown, as all such bureaucracies grow, filling the vast building like an expanding balloon, as it claimed every room and corner until secretaries and file clerks occupied the (remodeled) spaces where Kamenev and Ordzhonikidze had been tortured under the eyes of Yagoda and Beriya. Golovko supposed that there hadn't been too many ghosts.

Well, a new working day beckoned. A staff meeting at 8:45, then the normal routine of briefings and discussions, lunch at 12:15, and with luck he'd be back in the car and on his way back home soon after six, before he had to change for the reception at the French Embassy. He looked forward to the food and wine, if not the conversation.

Another car caught his eye. It was a twin to his own, another large Mercedes S-class, iceberg white just like his own, complete down to the American-made dark plastic on the windows. It was driving purposefully in the bright morning, as Anatoliy slowed and pulled behind a dump truck, one of the thousand such large ugly vehicles that covered the streets of Moscow like a dominant life-form, this one's load area cluttered with hand tools rather than filled with earth. There was yet another truck a hundred meters beyond, driving slowly as though its driver was unsure of his route. Golovko stretched in his seat, barely able to see around the truck in front of his Benz, wishing for the first cup of Sri Lankan tea at his desk, in the same room that Beriya had once . . .

. . . the distant dump truck. A man had been lying in the back. Now he rose, and he was holding . . .

"Anatoliy!" Golovko said sharply, but his driver couldn't see around the truck to his immediate front.

. . . it was an RPG, a slender pipe with a bulbous end. The sighting bar was up, and as the distant truck was now stopped, the man came up to one knee and turned, aiming his weapon at the other white Benz—

—the other driver saw it and tried to swerve, but found his way blocked by the morning traffic and—

—not much in the way of a visual signature, just a thin puff of smoke from the rear of the launcher-tube, but the bulbous part leapt off and streaked into the hood of the other white Mercedes, and there it exploded.

It hit just short of the windshield. The explosion wasn't the fireball so beloved of Western movies, just a muted flash and gray smoke, but the sound roared across the square, and a wide, flat, jagged hole blew out of the trunk of the car, and that meant that anyone inside the vehicle would now be dead, Golovko knew without pausing to think on it. Then the gasoline ignited, and the car burned, along with a few square meters of asphalt. The Mercedes stopped almost at once, its left-side tires shredded and flattened by the explosion. The dump truck in front of Golovko's car panic-stopped, and Anatoliy swerved right, his eyes narrowed by the noise, but not yet—

"Govno!" Now Anatoliy saw what had happened and took action. He kept moving right, accelerating hard and swerving back and forth as his eyes picked holes in the traffic. The majority of the vehicles in sight had stopped, and Golovko's driver sought out the holes and darted through them, arriving at the vehicle entrance to Moscow Center in less than a minute. The armed guards there were already moving out into the square, along with the supplementary response force from its shack just

inside and out of sight. The commander of the group, a senior lieutenant, saw Golovko's car and recognized it, waved him inside and motioned to two of his men to accompany it to the drop-off point. The arrival time was now the only normal aspect of the young day. Golovko stepped out, and two young soldiers formed up in physical contact with his heavy topcoat. Anatoliy stepped out, too, his pistol in his hand and his coat open, looking back through the gate with suddenly anxious eyes. His head turned quickly.

"Get him inside!" And with that order, the two privates strong-armed Golovko through the double bronze doors, where more security troops were arriving.

"This way, Comrade Chairman," a uniformed captain said, taking Sergey Nikolay'ch's arm and heading off to the executive elevator. A minute later, he stumbled into his office, his brain only now catching up with what it had seen just three minutes before. Of course, he walked to the window to look down.

Moscow police—called militiamen—were racing to the scene, three of them on foot. Then a police car appeared, cutting through the stopped traffic. Three motorists had left their vehicles and approached the burning car, perhaps hoping to render assistance. Brave of them, Golovko thought, but an entirely useless effort. He could see better now, even at a distance of three hundred meters. The top had bulged up. The windshield was gone, and he looked into a smoking hole, which had minutes before been a hugely expensive vehicle, and which had been destroyed by one of the cheapest weapons the Red Army had ever mass-produced. Whoever had been inside had been shredded instantly by metal fragments traveling at nearly ten thousand meters per second. Had they even known what had happened? Probably not. Perhaps the driver had had time to look and wonder, but the owner of the car in the back had probably been reading his morning paper, before his life had ended without warning.

That was when Golovko's knees went weak. That could have been him . . . suddenly learning if there were an afterlife after all, one of the great mysteries of life, but not one which had occupied his thoughts very often . . .

But whoever had done the killing, who had been his target? As Chairman of the SVR, Golovko was not a man to believe in coincidences, and there were not all that many white Benz S600s in Moscow, were there?

"Comrade Chairman?" It was Anatoliy at the office door.

"Yes, Anatoliy Ivan'ch?"

"Are you well?"

"Better than he," Golovko replied, stepping away from the window. He needed to sit now. He tried to move to his swivel chair without staggering, for his legs were suddenly weak indeed. He sat and found the surface of his desk with both his hands, and looked down at the oaken surface with its piles of papers to be read—the routine sight of a day which was not now routine at all. He looked up.

Anatoliy Ivan'ch Shelepin was not a man to show fear. He'd served in Spetsnaz through his captaincy, before being spotted by a KGB talent scout for a place in the 8th "Guards" Directorate, which he'd accepted just in time for KGB to be broken apart. But Anatoliy had been Golovko's driver and bodyguard for years now, part of his official family, like an elder son, and Shelepin was devoted to his boss. He was a tall, bright man of thirty-three years, with blond hair and blue eyes that were now far larger than usual, because though Anatoliy had trained for much of his life to deal with and in violence, this was the first time he'd actually been there to see it when it happened. Anatoliy had often wondered what it might be like to take a life, but never once in his career had he contemplated losing his own, certainly not to an ambush, and most certainly not to an ambush within shouting distance of his place of work. At his desk outside Golovko's office, he acted like a personal secretary more than anything else. Like all such men, he'd grown casual in the routine of protecting someone whom no one would dare attack, but now his comfortable world had been sundered as completely and surely as that of his boss.

Oddly, but predictably, it was Golovko's brain that made it back to reality first.

"Anatoliy?"

"Yes, Chairman?"

"We need to find out who died out there, and then find out if it was supposed to be us instead. Call militia headquarters, and see what they are doing."

"At once." The handsome young face disappeared from the doorway.

Golovko took a deep breath and rose, taking another look out the window as he did so. There was a fire engine there now, and firefighters were spraying the wrecked car to extinguish the lingering flames. An ambulance was standing by as well, but that was a waste of manpower and equipment, Sergey Nikolay'ch knew. The first order of business was to get the license-plate number from the car and identify its owner, and from that knowledge determine if the unfortunate had died in Golovko's place, or perhaps had possessed enemies of his own. Rage had not yet supplanted the shock of the event. Perhaps that would come later, Golovko thought, as he took a step toward his private washroom, for suddenly his bladder was weak. It seemed a horrid display of frailty, but Golovko had never known immediate fear in his life, and, like many, thought in terms of the movies. The actors there were bold and resolute, never mind that their words were scripted and their reactions rehearsed, and none of it was anything like what happened when explosives arrived in the air without warning.

Who wants me dead? he wondered, after flushing the toilet.

The American Embassy a few miles away had a flat roof on which stood all manner of radio antennas, most of them leading to radio receivers of varying levels of sophistication, which were in turn attached to tape recorders that turned slowly in order to more efficiently use their tapes. In the room with the recorders were a dozen people, both civilian and military, all Russian linguists who reported to the National Security Agency at Fort Meade, Maryland, between Baltimore and Washington. It was early in the day, and these people were generally at work before the Russian officials whose communications they worked to monitor. One of the many radios in the room was a scanning monitor of the sort once used by American citizens to listen in on police calls. The local cops used the same bands and the exact same type of radios that their American counterparts had used in the 1970s, and monitoring them was child's play—they were not encrypted yet. They listened in on them for the occasional traffic accident, perhaps involving a big shot, and mainly to keep a finger on the pulse of Moscow, whose crime situation was bad and getting worse. It was useful for embassy personnel to know what parts of town to avoid, and to be able to keep track of a crime to one of the thousands of American citizens.

"Explosion?" an Army sergeant asked the radio. His head turned. "Lieutenant Wilson, police report an explosion right in front of Moscow Center."

"What kind?"

"Sounds like a car blew up. Fire department is on the scene now, ambulance . . ." He plugged in headphones to get a better cut on the voice traffic. "Okay, white Mercedes-Benz, tag number—" He pulled out a pad and wrote it down. "Three people dead, driver and two passengers and . . . oh, shit!"

"What is it, Reins?"

"Sergey Golovko . . ." Sergeant Reins's eyes were shut, and he had one hand pressing the headphones to his ears. "Doesn't he drive a white Benz?"

"Oh, shit!" Lieutenant Wilson observed for herself. Golovko was one of the people whom *her* people routinely tracked. "Is he one of the deaders?"

"Can't tell yet, ell-tee. New voice . . . the captain at the station, just said he's coming down. Looks like they're excited about this one, ma'am. Lotsa chatter coming up."

Lieutenant Susan Wilson rocked back and forth in her swivel chair. Make a call on this one or not? They couldn't shoot you for notifying your superiors of something, could they . . . ? "Where's the station chief?"

"On his way to the airport, ell-tee, he's flying off to St. Petersburg today, remember?"

"Okay." She turned back to her panel and lifted the secure phone, a STU-6 (for "secure telephone unit"), to Fort Meade. Her plastic encryption key was in its proper slot, and the phone was already linked and synchronized with another such phone at NSA headquarters. She punched the # key to get a response.

"Watch Room," a voice said half a world away.

"This is Station Moscow. We have an indication that Sergey Golovko may just have been assassinated."

"The SVR chairman?"

"Affirmative. A car similar to his has exploded in Dzerzhinskiy Square, and this is the time he usually goes to work."

"Confidence?" the disembodied male voice asked. It would be a middle-grade officer, probably military, holding down the eleven-to-seven watch. Probably Air Force. "Confidence" was one of their institutional buzzwords.

"We're taking this off police radios—the Moscow Militia, that is. We have lots of voice traffic, and it sounds excited, my operator tells me."

"Okay, can you upload it to us?"

"Affirmative," Lieutenant Wilson replied.

"Okay, let's do that. Thanks for the heads-up, we'll take it from here."

Okay, Station Moscow out," heard Major Bob Teeters. He was new in his job at NSA. Formerly a rated pilot who had twenty-one hundred hours in command of C-5s and C-17s, he'd injured his left elbow in a motorcycle accident eight months before, and the loss of mobility there had ended his flying career, much to his disgust. Now he was reborn as a spook, which was somewhat more interesting in an intellectual sense, but not exactly a happy exchange for an aviator. He waved to an enlisted man, a Navy petty officer first-class, to pick up on the active line from Moscow. This the sailor did, donning headphones and lighting up the word-processing program on his desktop computer. This sailor was a Russian linguist in addition to being a yeoman, and thus competent to drive the computer. He typed, translating as he listened in to the pirated Russian police radios, and his script came up on Major Teeters's computer screen.

I HAVE THE LICENSE NUMBER, CHECKING NOW, the first line read.

GOOD, QUICK AS YOU CAN.

WORKING ON IT, COMRADE. (TAPPING IN THE BACKGROUND, DO THRE RUSSKIES HAVE COMPUTERS FOR TIS STUFF NOW?)

I HAVE IT, WHITE MERCEDES BENZ, REGISTERED TO G. F. AVSYENKO, (NOT SURE OF SPELLING) 677 PROTOPOPOV PROSPEKT, FLAT 18A.

HIM? I KNOW THAT NAME!

Which was good for somebody, Major Teeters thought, but not all that great for Avsyenko. Okay, what next? The senior watch officer was another squid, Rear Admiral Tom Porter, probably drinking coffee in his office over in the main building and watching TV, maybe. Time to change that. He called the proper number.

"Admiral Porter."

"Sir, this is Major Teeters down in the watch center. We have some breaking news in Moscow."

"What's that, Major?" a tired voice asked.

"Station Moscow initially thought that somebody might have killed Chairman Golovko of the KG—the SVR, I mean."

"What was that, Major?" a somewhat more alert voice inquired.

"Turns out it probably wasn't him, sir. Somebody named Avsyenko—" Teeters spelled it out. "We're getting the intercepts off their police radio bands. I haven't run the name yet."

"What else?"

"Sir, that's all I have right now."

By this time, a CIA field officer named Tom Barlow was in the loop at the embassy. The third-ranking spook in the current scheme of things, he didn't want to drive over to Dzerzhinskiy Square himself, but he did the next best thing. Barlow called the CNN office, the direct line to a friend.

"Mike Evans."

"Mike, this is Jimmy," Tom Barlow said, initiating a prearranged and much-used lie. "Dzerzhinskiy Square, the murder of somebody in a Mercedes. Sounds messy and kinda spectacular."

"Okay," the reporter said, making a brief note. "We're on it."

At his desk, Barlow checked his watch. 8:52 local time. Evans was a hustling reporter for a hustling news service. Barlow figured there'd be a mini-cam there in twenty minutes. The truck would have its own Ku-band uplink to a satellite, down from there to CNN headquarters in Atlanta, and the same signal would be pirated by the DoD downlink at Fort Belvoir, Virginia, and spread around from there on government-owned satellites to interested parties. An attempt on the life of Chairman Golovko made it interesting as hell to a lot of people. Next he lit up his desktop Compaq computer and opened the file for Russian names that were known to CIA.

A duplicate of that file resided in any number of CIA computers at Langley, Virginia, and on one of those in the CIA Operations Room on the 7th floor of the Old Headquarters Building, a set of fingers typed A-V-S-Y-E-N-K-O . . . and came up with nothing other than:

ENTIRE FILE SEARCHED. THE SEARCH ITEM WAS NOT FOUND.

That evoked a grumble from the person on the computer. So, it wasn't spelled properly.

"Why does this name sound familiar?" he asked. "But the machine says no-hit."

"Let's see . . ." a co-worker said, leaning over and respelling the name. "Try this . . ." Again a no-hit. A third variation was tried.

"Bingo! Thanks, Beverly," the watch officer said. "Oh, yeah, we know who this guy is. Rasputin. Low-life bastard—sure as hell, look what happened when he went straight," the officer chuckled.

Rasputin?" Golovko asked. *"Nekulturniy* swine, eh?" He allowed himself a brief smile. "But who would wish *him* dead?" he asked his security chief, who, if anything, was taking the matter even more seriously than the Chairman. His job had just become far more complicated. For starters, he had to tell Sergey Nikolay'ch that the white Mercedes was no longer his personal conveyance. Too ostentatious. His next task of the day was to ask the armed sentries who posted the corners of the building's roof why they hadn't spotted a man in the load area of a dump truck with an RPG—*within three hundred meters of the building they were supposed to guard!* And not so much as a warning over their portable radios until the Mercedes of Gregoriy Filipovich Avseyenko had been blown to bits. He'd sworn many oaths already on this day, and there would be more to come.

"How long has he been out of the service?" Golovko asked next.

"Since '93, Comrade Chairman," Major Anatoliy Ivan'ch Shelepin said, having just asked the same question and received the answer seconds earlier.

The first big reduction-in-force, Golovko thought, but it would seem that the pimp had made the transition to private enterprise well. Well enough to own a Mercedes Benz S-600 . . . and well enough to be killed by enemies he'd made along the way . . . unless he'd unknowingly sacrificed his own life for that of another. That question still needed answering. The Chairman had recovered his self-control by this point, enough at any rate for his mind to begin functioning. Golovko was too bright a man to ask *Why would anyone wish to end* my *life?* He knew better than that. Men in positions like his made enemies, some of them deadly ones . . . but most of them were too smart to make such an attempt. Vendettas were dangerous things to begin at his level, and for that reason, they *never* happened. The business of international intelligence was remarkably sedate and civilized. People still died. Anyone caught spying for a foreign government against Mother Russia was in the deepest of trouble, new regime or not—state treason was still state treason—but those killings followed . . . what did the Americans call it? *Due process of law.* Yes, that was it. The Americans and their lawyers. If their lawyers approved of something, then it was civilized.

"Who else was in the car?" Golovko asked.

"His driver. We have the name, a former militiaman. And one of his women, it would seem, no name for her yet."

"What do we know of Gregoriy's routine? Why was he there this morning?"

"Not known at this time, Comrade," Major Shelepin replied. "The militia are working on it."

"Who is running the case?"

"Lieutenant Colonel Shablikov, Comrade Chairman."

"Yefim Konstantinovich—yes, I know him. Good man," Golovko allowed. "I suppose he'll need his time, eh?"

"It does require time," Shelepin agreed.

More than it took for Rasputin to meet his end, Golovko thought. Life was such a strange thing, so permanent when one had it, so fleeting when it was lost—and those who lost it could never tell you what it was like, could they? Not unless you believed in ghosts or God or an afterlife, things which had somehow been overlooked in Golovko's childhood. So, yet another great mystery, the spymaster told himself. It had come so close, for the first time in his life. It was disquieting, but on reflection, not so frightening as he would have imagined. The Chairman wondered if this was something he might call courage. He'd never thought of himself as a brave man, for the simple reason that he'd never faced immediate physical danger. It was not that he had avoided it, only that it had never come close until today, and after the outrage had passed, he found himself not so much bemused as curious. *Why* had this happened? *Who* had done it? Those were the questions he had to answer, lest it happen again. To be courageous once was enough, Golovko thought.

Dr. Benjamin Goodley arrived at Langley at 5:40, five minutes earlier than his customary time. His job largely denied him much of a social life, which hardly seemed fair to the National Intelligence Officer. Was he not of marriageable age, possessed of good looks, a man with good prospects both in the professional and business sense? Perhaps not the latter, Goodley thought, parking his car in a VIP slot by the cement canopy of the Old Headquarters Building. He drove a Ford Explorer because it was a nice car for driving in the snow, and there would be snow soon. At least winter was coming, and winter in the D.C. area was wholly unpredictable, especially now that some of the eco-nuts were saying that global warming would cause an unusually *cold* winter this year. The logic of that escaped him. Maybe he'd have a chat with the President's Science Adviser to see if that made any sense talking with someone who could explain things. The new one was pretty good, and knew how to use single-syllable words.

Goodley made his way through the pass-gate and into the elevator. He walked into the Operations Room at 5:50 A.M.

"Hey, Ben," one said.

"Morning, Charlie. Anything interesting happening?"

"You're gonna love this one, Ben," Charlie Roberts promised. "A big day in Mother Russia."

"Oh?" Narrowed eyes. Goodley had his worries about Russia, and so did his boss. "What's that?"

"No big deal. Just somebody tried to whack Sergey Nikolay'ch."

His head snapped around like an owl's. *"What?"*

"You heard me, Ben, but they hit the wrong car with the RPG and took out somebody else we know—well, used to know," Roberts corrected himself.

"Start from the beginning."

"Peggy, roll the videotape," Roberts commanded his watch officer with a theatrical wave of the arm.

"Whoa!" Goodley said after the first five seconds. "So, who was it really?"

"Would you believe Gregoriy Filipovich Avseyenko?"

"I don't know that name," Goodley admitted.

"Here." The watch officer handed over a manila folder. "What we had on the guy when he was KGB. A real sweetheart," she observed, in the woman's neutral voice of distaste.

"Rasputin?" Goodley said, scanning the first page. "Oh, okay, I have heard something about this one."

"So has the Boss, I bet."

"I'll know in two hours," Goodley imagined aloud. "What's Station Moscow saying?"

"The station chief is in St. Pete's for a trade conference, part of his cover duties. What we have is from his XO. The best bet to this point is that either Aveseyenko made a big enemy in the Russian Mafia, or maybe Golovko was the real target, and they hit the wrong car. No telling which at this point." Followed by the usual NIO damned-if-I-know shrug.

"Who would want to take Golovko out?"

"Their Mafia? Somebody got himself an RPG, and they don't sell them in hardware stores, do they? So, that means somebody deeply into their criminal empire, probably, made the hit—but who was the real target? Avseyenko must have had some serious enemies along the way, but Golovko must have enemies or rivals, too." She shrugged again. "You pays your money and you takes your choice."

"The Boss likes to have better information," Goodley warned.

"So do I, Ben," Peggy Hunter replied. "But that's all I got, and even the fuckin' Russians don't have better at this point."

"Any way we can look into their investigation?"

"The Legal Attaché, Mike Reilly, is supposed to be pretty tight with their cops. He got a bunch of them admitted to the FBI's National Academy post-grad cop courses down at Quantico."

"Maybe have the FBI tell him to nose around?"

Mrs. Hunter shrugged again. "Can't hurt. Worst thing anybody can say is no, and we're already there, right?"

Goodley nodded. "Okay, I'll recommend that." He got up. "Well," he observed on his way out the door, "the Boss won't bitch about how boring the world is today." He took the CNN tape with him and headed back to his SUV.

The sun was struggling to rise now. Traffic on the George Washington Parkway was picking up with eager-beaver types heading into their desks early, probably Pentagon people, most of them, Goodley thought, as he crossed over the Key Bridge, past Teddy Roosevelt Island. The Potomac was calm and flat, almost oily, like the pond behind a mill dam. The outside temperature, his dashboard said, was forty-four, and the forecast for the day was a high in the upper fifties, a few clouds, and calm winds. An altogether pleasant day for late fall, though he'd be stuck in his office for all of it, pleasant or not.

Things were starting early at The House, he saw on pulling in. The Blackhawk helicopter was just lifting off as he pulled into his reserved parking place, and the motorcade had already formed up at the West Entrance. It was enough to make him check his watch. No, he wasn't late. He hustled out of his car, bundling the papers and cassette into his arms as he hurried inside.

"Morning, Dr. Goodley," a uniformed guard said in greeting.

"Hi, Chuck." Regular or not, he had to pass through the metal detector. The papers and cassette were inspected by hand—as though he'd try to bring a gun in, Ben thought in passing irritation. Well, there had been a few scares, hadn't there? And these people were trained not to trust anybody.

Having passed the daily security test, he turned left, sprinted up the stairs, then left again to his office, where some helpful soul—he didn't know if it was one of the clerical staff or maybe one of the Service people—had his office coffee machine turning out some Gloria Jean's French Hazelnut. He poured himself a cup and sat down at his desk to organize his papers and his thoughts. He managed to down half of the cup before bundling it all up again for the ninety-foot walk. The Boss was already there.

"Morning, Ben."

"Good morning, Mr. President," replied the National Security Adviser.

"Okay, what's new in the world?" POTUS asked.

"It looks as though somebody might have tried to assassinate Sergey Golovko this morning."

"Oh?" President Ryan asked, looking up from his coffee. Goodley filled him in, then inserted the cassette in the Oval Office VCR and punched PLAY.

"Jeez," Ryan observed. What had been an expensive car was now fit only for the crushing machine. "Who'd they get instead?"

"One Gregoriy Filipovich Avseyenko, age fifty-two—"

"I know that name. Where from?"

"He's more widely known as Rasputin. He used to run the KGB Sparrow School."

Ryan's eyes went a little wider. "That cocksucker! Okay, what's the story on him?"

"He got RIF'd back in '93 or so, and evidently set himself up in the same business, and it would seem he's made some money at it, judging by his car, anyway. There was evidently a young woman in with him when he was killed, plus a driver. They were all killed."

Ryan nodded. The Sparrow School had been where for years the Soviets had trained attractive young women to be prostitutes in the service of their country both at home and abroad, because, since time immemorial, men with a certain weakness for women had often found their tongues loosened by the right sort of lubrication. Not a few secrets had been conveyed to the KGB by this method, and the women had also been useful in recruiting various foreign nationals for the KGB officers to exploit. So, on having his official office shut down, Rasputin—so called by the Soviets for his ability to get women to bend to his will—had simply plied his trade in the new free-enterprise environment.

"So, Avseyenko might have had 'business' enemies angry enough to take him out, and Golovko might not have been the target at all?"

"Correct, Mr. President. The possibility exists, but we don't have any supporting data one way or the other."

"How do we get it?"

"The Legal Attaché at the embassy is well connected with the Russian police," the National Security Adviser offered.

"Okay, call Dan Murray at FBI and have his man nose around," Ryan said. He'd already considered calling Golovko directly—they'd known each other for more than ten years, though one of their initial contacts had involved Golovko's pistol right in Jack's face on one of the runways of Moscow's Sheremetyevo Airport—and decided against it. He couldn't show that much immediate interest, though later, if they had a private moment together, he'd be able to ask a casual question about the incident. "Same for Ed and MP at CIA."

"Right." Goodley made a note.

"Next?"

Goodley turned the page. "Indonesia is doing some naval exercises that have the Aussies a little interested. . . ." Ben went on with the morning briefing for twenty more minutes, mainly covering political rather than military matters, because that's what national security had become in recent years. Even the international arms trade had diminished to the point that quite a few countries were treating their national military establishments as boutiques rather than serious instruments of statecraft.

"So, the world's in good shape today?" the President summarized.

"Except for the pothole in Moscow, it would seem so, sir."

The National Security Adviser departed, and Ryan looked at his schedule for the day. As usual, he had very little in the way of free time. About the only moments on his plan-of-the-day without someone in the office with him were those in which he'd have to read over briefing documents for the next meeting, many of which were planned literally weeks in advance. He took off his reading glasses—he hated them—and rubbed his eyes, already anticipating the morning headache that would come in about thirty minutes. A quick re-scan of the page showed no light moments today. No troop of Eagle Scouts from Wyoming, nor current World Series champs, nor Miss Plum Tomato from California's Imperial Valley to give him something to smile about. No. Today would be all work.

Shit, he thought.

The nature of the Presidency was a series of interlocking contradictions. The Most Powerful Man in the World was quite unable to use his power except under the most adverse circumstances, which he was supposed to avoid rather than to engage. In reality, the Presidency was about negotiations, more with the Congress than anyone else; it was a process for which Ryan had been unsuited until given a crash course by his chief of staff, Arnold van Damm. Fortunately, Arnie did a lot of the negotiations himself, then came into the Oval Office to tell the President what *his* (Ryan's) decision and/or position was on an issue, so that *he* (van Damm) could then do a press release or a statement in the Press Room. Ryan supposed that a lawyer treated his client that way much of the time, looking after his interests as best he could while *not* telling him what those interests were until they were already decided. The President, Arnie told everyone, had to be protected from direct negotiations with everyone—especially Congress. And, Jack reminded himself, he had a fairly tame Congress. What had it been like for presidents dealing with contentious ones?

And what the hell, he wondered, not for the first time, was he doing here?

The election process had been the purest form of hell—despite the fact that he'd had what Arnie invariably had called a cakewalk. Never less than five speeches per day, more often as many as nine, in as many different places before as many diverse groups—but *always* the same speech, delivered off file cards he kept in his pocket, changed only in minor local details by a frantic staff on the Presidential aircraft, trying to keep track of the flight plan. The amazing thing was that they'd never made a mistake that he'd caught. For variety, the President would alter the order of the cards. But the utility of that had faded in about three days.

Yes, if there were a hell in creation, a political campaign was its most tangible form, listening to yourself saying the same things over and over until your brain started rebelling and you started *wanting* to make random, crazy changes, which might amuse yourself, but it would make you appear crazy to the audience, and you couldn't do that, because a presidential candidate was expected to be a perfect automaton rather than a fallible man.

There had been an upside to it. Ryan had bathed in a sea of love for the ten weeks of the endurance race. The deafening cheers of the crowds, whether in a parking lot outside a Xenia, Ohio, shopping mall, or in Madison Square Garden in New York City, or Honolulu, or Fargo, or Los Angeles—it had all been the same. Huge crowds of ordinary citizens who both denied and celebrated the fact that John Patrick Ryan was one of them . . . kind of, sort of, something like that—but something else, too. From his first formal speech in Indianapolis, soon after his traumatic accession to the Presidency, he'd realized just how strong a narcotic that sort of adulation was, and sure enough, his continued exposure to it had given him the same sort of rush that a controlled substance might. With it came a desire to be perfect for them, to deliver his lines properly, to seem sincere—as indeed he was, but it would have been far easier doing it once or twice instead of three hundred and eleven times, as the final count had been reckoned.

The news media in every place asked the same questions, written down or taped the same answers, and printed them as new news in every local paper. In every city and town, the editorials had praised Ryan, and worried loudly that this election wasn't really an election at all, except on the congressional level, and there Ryan had stirred the pot by giving his blessing to people of both major parties, the better to retain his independent status, and therefore to risk offending everyone.

The love hadn't quite been universal, of course. There were those who'd protested, who got their heads on the nightly commentary shows, citing his professional background, criticizing his drastic actions to stop the terrorist-caused Ebola plague that had threatened the nation so desperately in those dark days—"Yes, it worked in this particular case, *but . . . !*"—and especially to criticize his politics, which, Jack said in his speeches, weren't politics at all, but plain common sense.

During all of this, Arnie had been a godsend, preselecting a response to every single objection. Ryan was wealthy, some said. "My father was a police officer" had been the answer. "I've *earned* every penny I have—and besides [going on with an engaging smile], now my wife makes a lot more money than I do."

Ryan knew nothing about politics: "Politics is one of those fields in which everybody knows what it is, but nobody can make it work. Well, maybe *I* don't know what it is, but I am *going* to make it work!"

Ryan had packed the Supreme Court: "I'm not a lawyer, either, sorry," he'd said to the annual meeting of the American Bar Association. "But I know the difference between right and wrong, and so do the justices."

Between the strategic advice of Arnie and the preplanned words of Callie Weston, he'd managed to parry every serious blow, and strike back with what was usually a soft and humorous reply of his own—leavened with strong words delivered with the fierce but quiet conviction of someone who had little left to prove. Mainly, with proper coaching and endless hours of preparation, he'd managed to present himself as Jack Ryan, regular guy.

Remarkably, his most politically astute move had been made entirely without outside expertise.

Morning, Jack," the Vice President said, opening the door unannounced.

"Hey, Robby." Ryan looked up from his desk with a smile. He still looked a little awkward in suits, Jack saw. Some people were born to wear uniforms, and Robert Jefferson Jackson was one of them, though the lapel of every suit jacket he owned sported a miniature of his Navy Wings of Gold.

"There's some trouble in Moscow," Ryan said, explaining on for a few seconds.

"That's a little worrisome," Robby observed.

"Get Ben to give you a complete brief-in on this. What's your day look like?" the President asked.

"Sierra-square, Delta-square." It was their personal code: SSDD—*same shit, different day.* "I have a meeting of the Space Council across the street in twenty minutes. Then tonight I have to fly down to Mississippi for a speech tomorrow morning at Ole Miss."

"You taking the wheel?" Ryan asked.

"Hey, Jack, the *one* good thing about this damned job is that I get to fly again." Jackson had insisted on getting rated on the VC-20B that he most often flew around the country on official trips under the code name "Air Force Two." It looked very good in the media, and it was also the best possible therapy for a fighter pilot who missed being in control of his aircraft, though it must have annoyed the Air Force flight crew. "But it's always to shit details you don't want," he added with a wink.

"It's the only way I could get you a pay raise, Robby. And nice quarters, too," he reminded his friend.

"You left out the flight pay," responded Vice Admiral R. J. Jackson, USN, retired. He paused at the door and turned. "What does that attack say about the situation over there in Russia?"

Jack shrugged. "Nothing good. They just can't seem to get ahead of things, can they?"

"I guess," the Vice President agreed. "Problem is, how the hell do we help them?"

"I haven't figured that one out yet," Jack admitted. "And we have enough potential economic problems on our horizon, with Asia sliding down the tubes."

"That's something I have to learn, this economic shit," Robby admitted.

"Spend some time with George Winston," Ryan suggested. "It's not all that hard, but you have to learn a new language to speak. Basis points, derivatives, all that stuff. George knows it pretty good."

Jackson nodded. "Duly noted, sir."

"'Sir'? Where the hell did that come from, Rob?"

"You still be the National Command Authority, oh great man," Robby told him with a grin and a lower-Mississippi accent. "I just be da XO, which means Ah gits all the shit details."

"So, think of this as PCO School, Rob, and thank God you have a chance to learn the easy way. It wasn't like that for me—"

"I remember, Jack. I was here as J-3, remember? And you did okay. Why do you think I allowed you to kill my career for me?"

"You mean it wasn't the nice house and the drivers?"

The Vice President shook his head. "And it wasn't to be a first-black, either. I couldn't say 'no' when my President asks, even if it's a turkey like you. Later, man."

"See ya at lunch, Robby," Jack said as the door closed.

"Mr. President, Director Foley on Three," the speakerphone announced.

Jack lifted the secure phone and punched the proper button. "Morning, Ed."

"Hi, Jack, we have some more on Moscow."

"How'd we get it?" Ryan asked first, just to have a way of evaluating the information he was about to receive.

"Intercepts," the Director of Central Intelligence answered, meaning that the information would be fairly reliable. Communications intelligence was the most trusted of all, because people rarely lied to one another over the radio or telephone. "It seems this case has a very high priority over there, and the militiamen are talking very freely over their radios."

"Okay, what do you got?"

"Initial thinking over there is that Rasputin was the main target. He was pretty big, making a ton of money with his female . . . employees," Ed Foley said delicately, "and trying to branch out into other areas. Maybe he got a little pushy with someone who didn't like being pushed."

You think so?" Mike Reilly asked.

"Mikhail Ivan'ch, I am not sure what I think. Like you, I am not trained to believe in coincidences," replied Lieutenant Oleg Provalov of the Moscow Militia. They were in a bar which catered to foreigners, which was obvious from the quality of the vodka being served.

Reilly wasn't exactly new to Moscow. He'd been there fourteen months, and before that had been the Assistant Special Agent in Charge of the New York office of the FBI—but not for Foreign Counter-Intelligence. Reilly was an OC—Organized Crime—expert who'd spent fifteen busy years attacking the Five Families of the New York Mafia, more often called LCN by the FBI, for La Cosa Nostra. The Russians knew this, and he'd established good relations with the local cops, especially since he'd arranged for some senior militia officers to fly to America to participate in the FBI's National Academy Program, essentially a Ph.D. course for senior cops, and a degree highly prized in American police departments.

"You ever have a killing like this in America?"

Reilly shook his head. "No, you can get regular guns pretty easy at home, but not anti-tank weapons. Besides, using them makes it an instant Federal case, and they've learned to keep away from us as much as they can. Oh, the wiseguys have used car bombs," he allowed, "but just to kill the people in the car. A hit like this is a little too spectacular for their tastes. So, what sort of guy was Avseyenko?"

A snort, and then Provalov almost spat the words out: "He was a pimp. He preyed on women, had them spread their legs, and then took their money. I will not mourn his passing, Mishka. Few will, but I suppose it leaves a vacuum that will be filled in the next few days."

"But you think he was the target, and not Sergey Golovko?"

"Golovko? To attack him would be madness. The chief of such an important state organ? I don't think any of our criminals have the balls for that."

Maybe, Reilly thought, *but you don't start off a major investigation by making assumptions of any kind, Oleg Gregoriyevich.* Unfortunately, he couldn't really say that. They were friends, but Provalov was thin-skinned, knowing that his police department did not measure up well against the American FBI. He'd learned that at Quantico. He was doing the usual right now, rattling bushes, having his investigators talk to Avseyenko's known associates to see if he'd spoken about enemies, disputes, or fights of one sort or another, checking with informants to see if anyone in the Moscow underworld had been talking about such things.

The Russians needed help on the forensic side, Reilly knew. At the moment they didn't even have the dump truck. Well, there were a few thousand of them, and that one might have been stolen without its owner/operator even knowing that it had been missing. Since the shot had been angled down, according to eyewitnesses, there would be little if any launch signature in the load area to help ID the truck, and they needed the right truck in order to recover hair and fibers. Of course, no one had gotten the tag number, nor had anyone been around with a camera during rush hour—well, so far. Sometimes a guy would show up a day or two later, and in major investigations you played for breaks—and usually the break was somebody who couldn't keep his mouth shut. Investigating people who knew how to stay silent was a tough way to earn a living. Fortunately, the criminal mind wasn't so circumspect—except for the smart ones, and Moscow, Reilly had learned, had more than a few of them.

There were two kinds of smart ones. The first was composed of KGB officers cut loose in the series of major reductions-in-force—known to Americans as RIFs—similar to what had happened in the American military. These potential criminals were frightening, people with real professional training and experience in black operations, who knew how to recruit and exploit others, and how to function invisibly—people, as Reilly thought of it, who'd played a winning game against the FBI despite the best efforts of the Bureau's Foreign Counter-Intelligence Division.

The other was a lingering echo of the defunct communist regime. They were called *tolkachi*—the word meant "pushers"—and under the previous economic system they'd been the grease that allowed things to move. They were facilitators whose relationships with everyone got things done, rather like guerrilla warriors who used unknown paths in the wilderness to move products from one place to another. With the fall of communism their skills had become genuinely lucrative because it was still the case that virtually no one understood capitalism, and the ability to get things done was more valuable than ever—and now it paid a *lot* better. Talent, as it always did, went where the money was, and in a country still learning what the rule of law meant, it was natural for men with this skill to break what laws there were, first in the service of whoever needed them, and then, almost instantly afterward, in the service of themselves. The former *tolkachi* were the most wealthy men in their country. With that wealth had come power. With power had come corruption, and with corruption had come crime, to the point that the FBI was nearly as active in Moscow as CIA had ever been. And with reason.

The union between the former KGB and the former *tolkachi* was creating the most powerful and sophisticated criminal empire in human history.

And so, Reilly had to agree, this Rasputin—the name meant literally "the debauched one"—might well have been part of that empire, and his death might well have been something related to that. Or something else entirely. This would be a very interesting investigation.

"Well, Oleg Gregoriyevich, if you need any help, I will do my best to provide it for you," the FBI agent promised.

"Thank you, Misha."

And they parted ways, each with his own separate thoughts.

CHAPTER 1

Echoes of the Boom

"So, who were his enemies?" Lieutenant Colonel Shablikov asked.

"Gregoriy Filipovich had many. He was overly free with his words. He insulted too many people and—"

"What else?" Shablikov demanded. "He was not blown up in the middle of the street for abusing some criminal's feelings!"

"He was beginning to think about importing narcotics," the informant said next.

"Oh? Tell us more."

"Grisha had contacts with Colombians. He met them in Switzerland three months ago, and he was working to get them to ship him cocaine through the port of Odessa. I heard whispers that he was setting up a pipeline to transport the drugs from there to Moscow."

"And how was he going to pay them for it?" The militia colonel asked. Russian currency was, after all, essentially valueless.

"Hard currency. Grisha made a lot of that from Western clients, and certain of his Russian clients. He knew how to make such people happy, for a price."

Rasputin, the colonel thought. And surely he'd been the debauched one. Selling the bodies of Russian girls—and some boys, Shablikov knew—for enough hard currency to purchase a large German car (for cash; his people had checked on the transaction already) and then planning to import drugs. That had to be for cash "up front," too, as the Americans put it, which meant that he planned to sell the drugs for hard currency, too, since the Colombians probably had little interest in rubles.

Avseyenko was no loss to his country. Whoever had killed him ought to get some reward . . . except someone new would certainly move into the vacuum and take control of the pimp's organization . . . and the new one might be smarter. That was the problem with criminals. There was a Darwinian process at work. The police caught some—even many—but they only caught the dumb ones, while the smart ones just kept getting smarter, and it seemed that the police were always trying to catch up, because those who broke the law always had the initiative.

"Ah, yes, and so, who else imports drugs?"

"I do not know who it is. There are rumors, of course, and I know some of the street vendors, but who actually organizes it, that I do not know."

"Find out," Shablikov ordered coldly. "It ought not to tax your abilities."

"I will do what I can," the informant promised.

"And you will do it quickly, Pavel Petrovich. You will also find out for me who takes over Rasputin's empire."

"Yes, Comrade Polkovnik Leytnant." The usual nod of submission.

There was power in being a senior policeman, Shablikov thought. Real human power, which you could impose on other men, and that made it pleasurable. In this case, he'd told a mid-level criminal what he had to do, and it would be done, lest his informant be arrested and find his source of income interrupted. The other side of the coin was protection of a sort. So long as this criminal didn't stray too far from what the senior cop found to be acceptable violations, he was safe from the law. It was the same over most of the world, Lieutenant Colonel Yefim Konstantinovich Shablikov of the Moscow Militia was sure. How else could the police collect the information they needed on people who did stray too far? No police agency in the world had the time to investigate everything, and thus using criminals against criminals was the easiest and least expensive method of intelligence-gathering.

The one thing to remember was that the informants *were* criminals, and hence unreliable in many things, too given to lying, exaggeration, to making up what they thought their master wanted to hear. And so Shablikov had to be careful believing anything this criminal said.

For his part, Pavel Petrovich Klusov had his own doubts, dealing as he did with this corrupted police colonel. Shablikov was not a former KGB officer, but rather a career policeman, and therefore not as smart as he believed himself to be, but more accustomed to bribes and informal arrangements with those he pursued. That was probably how he had achieved his fairly high rank. He knew how to get information by making deals with people like himself, Klusov thought. The informant wondered if the colonel had a hard-currency account somewhere. It would be interesting to find out where he lived, what sort of private car he or his wife drove. But he'd do what he was told, because his own "commercial" activities thrived under Shablikov's protection, and later that night he'd go out drinking with Irina Aganovna, maybe take her to bed later, and along the way find out how deeply mourned Avseyenko was by his . . . former . . . employees.

"Yes, Comrade Polkovnik Leytnant," Klusov agreed. "It will be as you say. I will try to be back with you tomorrow."

"You will not try. You will do it, Pasha," Shablikov told him, like a schoolmaster demanding homework from an underachieving child.

It is already under way," Zhang told his Premier.

"I trust this one will go more smoothly than its two predecessors," the Premier replied dryly. The risks attached to this operation were incomparably greater. Both previous times, with Japan's attempt to drastically alter the Pacific Rim equation, and Iran's effort to create a new nation from the ashes of the Soviet Union, the People's Republic had not *done* anything, just . . . encouraged, behind the scenes. This venture, though, was different. Well, one could not really expect great things to happen on the cheap, could one?

"I—we have been unlucky."

"Perhaps so." A casual nod as he switched papers on his desk.

Zhang Han San's blood went a little cold at that. The Premier of the People's Republic was a man known for his detachment, but he'd always regarded his Minister Without Portfolio with a certain degree of warmth. Zhang was one of the few whose advice the Premier usually heeded. As indeed today the advice would be heeded, but without any feeling on the part of the senior official.

"We have exposed nothing and we have lost nothing," Zhang went on.

The head didn't come up. "Except that there is now an American ambassador in Taipei." And now there was talk of a mutual-defense treaty whose only purpose was to place the American navy between the two countries, regular port visits, perhaps even a permanent base (to be built entirely, most certainly, from Taiwanese money) whose only purpose, the Americans would innocently say, was merely to be a replacement for Subic Bay in the Philippines. The economy on Taiwan had exploded after the renewal of full U.S. diplomatic recognition, with an influx of massive new capital investments from all over the world. Much of that money would—and *should*—have come to the PRC, except for the change in America's outlook.

But the American President Ryan had taken his action entirely on his own, so the intelligence services claimed, contrary to political and diplomatic advice in Washington—though the American Secretary of State, that Adler man, had reportedly supported Ryan's foolish decision.

Zhang's blood temperature dropped another degree or so. Both of his plans had gone almost as he'd calculated they should, hadn't they? In neither case had his country risked anything of consequence—oh, yes, they'd lost a few fighter aircraft the last time around, but those things and their pilots regularly crashed to no purpose anyway. Especially in the case of Taiwan, the People's Republic had acted responsibly, allowing Secretary Adler to shuttle directly back and forth between Beijing and its wayward province across the Formosa Strait, as though *giving* them legitimacy—something obviously *not* intended by the PRC, but rather as a convenience to aid the American in his peacemaking task, so as to appear more reasonable to the Americans . . . and so, why had Ryan done it? Had he guessed Zhang's play? That was possible, but it was more likely that there was a leak, an informer, a *spy* this close to the summit of political power in the People's Republic. The counterintelligence agencies were examining the possibility. There were few who knew what emerged from his mind and his office, and all of them would be questioned, while technical people checked his telephone lines and the very walls of his office. Had he, Zhang, been in error? Certainly not! Even if his Premier felt that way . . . Zhang next considered his standing with the Politburo. That could have been better. Too many of them regarded him as an adventurer with too great an access to the wrong ear. It was an easy thing to whisper, since they'd be delighted to reap the profits from his policy successes, and only slightly less delighted to pull away from him if things went awry. Well, such were the hazards of having reached the summit of policy-making in a country such as his.

"Even if we wished to crush Taiwan, unless we opted for nuclear weapons, it would require years and vast amounts of treasure to construct the means to make it possible, and then it would be a vast risk to little profit. Better that the People's Republic should grow so successful economically that they come begging to us to be let back into the family home. They are not powerful enemies, after all. They are scarcely even a nuisance on the world stage." But for some reason, they were a specific nuisance to his Premier, Zhang reminded himself, like some sort of personal allergy that marked and itched his sensitive skin.

"We have lost face, Zhang. That is enough for the moment."

"Face is not blood, Xu, nor is it treasure."

"They have ample treasure," the Premier pointed out, still not looking at his guest. And that was true. The small island of Taiwan was immensely rich from the industrious effort of its mainly ethnic-Chinese inhabitants, who traded nearly everything to nearly everywhere, and the restoration of American diplomatic recognition had increased both their commercial prosperity and their standing on the world stage. Try as he might, wish as he might, Zhang could not discount either of those things.

What had gone wrong? he asked himself again. Were not his plays brilliantly subtle ones? Had his country ever overtly threatened Siberia? No. Did even the People's Liberation Army's leadership know what the plans were? Well, yes, he had to admit to himself, some did, but only the most trusted people in the operations directorate, and a handful of senior field commanders—the ones who would have to execute the plans if the time ever came. But such people knew how to keep secrets, and if they talked to anyone . . . but they wouldn't, because they knew what happened to people who spoke of things best left unspoken in a society such as theirs, and they knew that the very air had ears at their level of "trust." They hadn't even commented on the draft plans to anyone, just made the usual adjustments in the technical arrangements, as senior officers always tended to do. And so, perhaps some file clerks had the ability to examine the plans, but that was exceedingly unlikely as well. Security in the PLA was excellent. The soldiers, from private to the lower general ranks, had no more freedom than a machine bolted to the factory floor, and by the time they reached senior rank they'd mainly forgotten how to think independently, except perhaps in some technical matters, like which sort of bridge to build over a particular river. No, to Zhang they might as well have been machines, and were just as trustworthy.

Back to the original question: *Why* had that Ryan fellow reestablished relations with the "Republic of China"? Had he guessed anything about the Japan and Iran initiatives? The incident with the airliner had certainly looked like the accident it was supposed to simulate, and afterward the PRC had invited the American navy to come to the area and "keep the peace," as they liked to put it, as though peace were something you could place in a metal box and guard. In reality it was the other way 'round. War was the animal you kept in a cage, and then released when the time suited.

Had this President Ryan guessed the PRC's intentions to begin the dismemberment of the former Soviet Union, and then decided to punish the People's Republic with his recognition of the renegades on Taiwan? It was possible. There were those who found Ryan to be unusually perceptive for an American political figure . . . he was a former intelligence officer, after all, and had probably been a good one, Zhang reminded himself. It was always a serious mistake to underrate an adversary, as the Japanese and the Iranians had learned to their considerable sorrow. This Ryan fellow had responded skillfully to both of Zhang's plans, and yet he hadn't so much as whispered his displeasure to the PRC. There had been no American military exercises aimed even indirectly at the People's Republic, no "leaks" to the American media, and nothing that his country's own intelligence officers operating out of the embassy in Washington had discovered. And so, he was again back to the original question: Why had Ryan taken that action? He just didn't know. Not knowing was a great annoyance to a man at his level of government. Soon his Premier might ask a question for which he needed to have the answer. But for now the leader of his government was flipping papers on his desk, ostensibly to tell him, Zhang, that he, the Premier, was displeased, but not at this moment doing anything about his emotions.

Ten meters away through a solid-core wood door, Lian Ming had her own emotions. The secretarial chair she sat in was an expensive one, purchased from Japan, the price of it equal to the wages of a skilled worker for, what? Four months? Five? Certainly more than the price of the new bicycle she could have used.

A university graduate in modern languages, she spoke English and French well enough to make herself understood in any city in the world, and as a result she found herself going over all manner of diplomatic and intelligence documents for her boss, whose language skills were considerably less than her own. The comfortable chair represented her boss's solicitude for the way in which she organized his work and his day. And a little more.

CHAPTER 2

The Dead Goddess

This was where it had all happened, Chester Nomuri told himself. The vast expanse of Tiananmen Square, the "Square of Heavenly Peace," with the massive walls to his right, was like . . . what? On reflection he realized that he had nothing with which to compare it. If there were another place in all the world like this place, he had neither visited nor even heard of it.

And yet the very paving stones seemed to drip with blood. It was almost as if he could smell it here, though that was more than ten years in the past, the massed students, not much younger than he had been at the time in California, rallying here to protest their government. They hadn't protested the form of their country's government so much as the corruption of those at its highest levels, and, predictably, such actions had been hugely offensive to the corrupted. Well, that's how it usually went. Only with discretion did one point out the nature of a powerful man to himself, Eastern or Western, but this was the most dangerous place of all, because of its long history of gross brutality. Here there was an *expectation* of it . . .

. . . but the first time it had been tried right here, the soldiers ordered to clear things up had balked. And *that* must have frightened the leadership in their plush and comfortable offices, because when the organs of the state refused to do the bidding of the state, *that* was when something called "Revolution" started (and in a place where there had already been a Revolution, enshrined on this very spot). And so, the initial troop formations had been pulled back and replaced with others, drawn from farther away, young soldiers (all soldiers were young,

Nomuri reminded himself). They had not yet been contaminated by the words and thoughts of their contemporaries demonstrating in the Square, not yet sympathetic with them, not yet willing to ask themselves *why* the government which gave them their weapons and uniforms wished for them to hurt these people instead of listening to what they had to say . . . and so, they'd acted like the mindless automatons they'd been trained to be.

There, just a few yards away, were some soldiers of the People's Liberation Army on parade, wearing the strange wax-doll look they tended to have, looking not quite human in their green wool uniforms, almost as though they used makeup, Chet thought, wanting to look more closely at their faces to see if maybe they really did. He turned away with a shake of his head. He hadn't flown JAL to China for that. Wangling this assignment for Nippon Electric Company had been difficult enough. It was a major drag working two jobs, as an upper-middle account executive for NEC *and* a field intelligence officer for CIA. To succeed in the second, he had also to succeed in the first, and to succeed in the first he had to simulate a true Japanese salaryman, one who subordinated everything short of his breathing to the good of the company. Well, at least he got to keep *both* of his salaries, and the Japanese one wasn't all that bad, was it? Not at the current exchange rate, anyway.

Nomuri supposed that this whole deal was a great sign of confidence in his abilities—he'd established a modestly productive network of agents in Japan who would now report to other CIA case officers—and also of desperation. The Agency had been singularly unsuccessful in getting a spy network operating over here in the PRC. Langley hadn't recruited many Chinese Americans into the fold . . . and one of those it had gotten was now in Federal prison after having developed a serious case of divided loyalties. It was a fact that certain federal agencies were allowed to be racist, and today Chinese ethnicity was strongly suspect at CIA headquarters. Well, there wasn't anything he could do about that—nor could he pretend to be Chinese himself, Nomuri knew. To some half-blind racist European types, everyone with crooked eyes looked the same, but here in Beijing, Nomuri, whose ancestry was a hundred percent Japanese (albeit entirely of the southern California variety), figured he stood out about as much as Michael Jordan would. It wasn't something to make an intelligence officer without diplomatic cover feel comfortable, especially since the Chinese Ministry of State Security was as active and well-supported as it was. MSS was every bit as powerful in this city as the Soviet KGB had ever been in Moscow, and was probably just as ruthless. China, Nomuri reminded himself, had been in the business of torturing criminals and other unloved ones for thousands of years . . . and *his* ethnicity would not be overly helpful. The Chinese did business with the Japanese because it was convenient—necessary was a more accurate term—but there was precisely zero love lost between the countries. Japan had killed far more Chinese in World War II than Hitler had killed Jews, a fact little appreciated anywhere in the world, except, of course, in China, and that set of facts only added to a racial/ethnic antipathy that went back at least as far as Kublai Khan.

He'd gotten too used to fitting in. Nomuri had joined CIA to serve his country, and to have a little fun, he'd thought at the time. Then he'd learned what a deadly serious business field-intelligence was, followed by the challenge of slipping into places he wasn't supposed to be, of obtaining information he wasn't supposed to get, and then giving it to people who weren't supposed to know it. It wasn't just serving his country that kept Nomuri in the business. There was also the thrill, the *rush* of knowing what others didn't know, of beating people at their own game, on their own turf.

But in Japan he looked like everyone else. Not here in Beijing. He was also a few inches taller than the average Chinese—that came from his childhood diet and American furniture—and better dressed in Western-style clothes. The clothes he could fix. His face he could not. For starters, he'd have to change his haircut, Chet thought. At least that way he could disappear from behind, and perhaps shake an MSS tail that way. He had a car to drive around, paid for by NEC, but he'd get a bicycle, too, a Chinese make rather than an expensive European one. If asked about it, he'd say it was good exercise—and besides, wasn't it a perfectly fine socialist bicycle? But such questions would be asked, and notice of his presence would be taken, and in Japan, Nomuri realized, he'd gotten slack and comfortable running his agents. He'd known that he could disappear in a place as intimate as a steaming bathhouse, and there talk about women and sports and many other things, but rarely business. In Japan every business operation was secret at some level or other, and even with the intimate friends with whom he discussed their wives' shortcomings, a Japanese salaryman would not discuss goings-on in the office until after they were overt and public. And that was good for operational security, wasn't it?

Looking around like any other tourist, he wondered how he would handle such things here. But most of all he noticed that eyes lingered on him as he walked from one side of this immense square to the other. How had this place sounded when the tanks were here? He stood still for a moment, remembering . . . it was right *there,* wasn't it? . . . the guy with the briefcase and shopping bag who'd held up a company of tanks, just by standing there . . . because even the private in the driver's seat of a Type 80 PRC tank didn't have the stones to run over the guy, despite whatever his captain might have been screaming at him over the interphones from his place on top of the turret. Yeah, it was right about here that had happened. Later on, of course, in about a week, the guy with the briefcase had been arrested by MSS, so said CIA's sources, and he'd been taken away and interrogated to see what had persuaded him to take so public and so foolish a political stand against both the government and the armed forces of his country. That had probably lasted a while, the CIA officer thought, standing here and looking around from the spot where one brave man had taken his stand . . . because the MSS interrogators just wouldn't have believed that it had been one man acting on his own . . . the concept of acting on one's own was not something encouraged in a communist regime, and was therefore entirely alien to those who enforced the will of the State on those who broke the State's rules. Whoever he'd been, the guy with the briefcase was dead now—the sources were pretty clear on that. An MSS official had commented on the matter with satisfaction later on, before someone whose ears were distantly connected to America. He'd taken the bullet in the back of the head, and his family—a wife and an infant son, the source believed—had been billed for the pistol round needed to execute the husband/father/counterrevolutionary/enemy-of-the-state in question. Such was justice in the People's Republic of China.

And what was it they called foreigners here? Barbarians. *Yeah,* Nomuri thought, *sure, Wilbur.* The myth of central position was as alive here as it had been on the Ku-Damm of Adolf Hitler's Berlin. Racism was the same all over the world. Dumb. That was one lesson his country had taught the world, Chester Nomuri thought, though America still had to absorb the lesson herself.

She was a whore, and a very expensive one, Mike Reilly thought from his seat behind the glass. Her hair had been unnaturally blonded by some expensive shop in Moscow—she needed another treatment, since there was a hint of dark brown at the roots—but it went well with her cheekbones and eyes, which were not quite any shade of blue he'd ever seen in a woman's eyes. That was probably a hook for her repeat customers, the color, he thought, but not the expression. Her body could have been sculpted by Phidias of Athens to be a goddess fit for public worship, ample curves everywhere, the legs thinner than normal for Russian tastes, but ones that would have gotten along well at the corner of Hollywood and Vine, if that were still a nice neighborhood in which to be spotted . . .

. . . but the *expression* in her lovely eyes could have stopped the heart of a marathon runner. What was it about prostitution that did this to women? Reilly shook his head. He hadn't worked that particular class of crime very often—it was mainly a violation for local cops—and not enough, he supposed, to understand its practitioners. The look in her eyes was frightening. Only men were supposed to be predators, so he and most men thought. But this woman belied that belief to a fare-thee-well.

Her name was Tanya Bogdanova. She was, she said, twenty-three years of age. She had the face of an angel, and the body of a movie star. It was her heart and soul the FBI agent was unsure of. Maybe she was just wired differently from normal people, as so many career criminals seemed to be. Maybe she'd been sexually abused in her youth. But even at twenty-three, her youth was a very distant thing, judging from the way her eyes looked at her interrogator. Reilly looked down at her dossier-folder from Militia headquarters. There was only one shot of her in it, a distant black-and-white of her with a john—well, probably an *ivan,* Reilly thought with a grunt—and in this photo her face was animated, youthful, and as alluring as the young Ingrid Bergman had been to Bogie in *Casablanca.* Tanya could act, Reilly thought. If this were the real Tanya in front of him, as it probably was, then the one in the photo was a construct, a role to be played, an illusion—a wonderful one, to be sure, but potentially a highly dangerous lie to anyone taken in by it. The girl on the other side of the one-way mirror could have dug a man's eyeballs out with her nail file, and then eaten them raw before going to her next appointment at the new Moscow Four Seasons Hotel and Convention Center.

"Who were his enemies, Tanya?" the militiaman asked in the interrogation room.

"Who were his friends?" she asked in bored reply. "He had none. Of enemies he had many." Her spoken language was literate and almost refined. Her English was supposed to be excellent as well. Well, she doubtless needed that for her customers . . . it was probably worth a few extra bucks, D-marks, pounds, or euros, a nice hard currency for whose printed notes she'd give a discount, doubtless smiling in a coquettish way when she told her john, jean, johannes, or ivan about it. Before or after? Reilly wondered. He'd never paid for it, though looking at Tanya, he understood why some men might . . .

"What's she charge?" he whispered to Provalov.

"More than I can afford," the detective lieutenant grunted. "Something like six hundred euros, perhaps more for an entire evening. She is medically clean, remarkably enough. A goodly collection of condoms in her purse, American, French, and Japanese brands."

"What's her background? Ballet, something like that?" the FBI agent asked, commenting implicitly on her grace.

Provalov grunted in amusement. "No, her tits are too big for that, and she's too tall. She weighs about, oh, fifty-five kilos or so, I would imagine. Too much for one of those little fairies in the Bolshoi to pick up and throw about. She could become a model for our growing fashion industry, but, no, on what you ask, her background is quite ordinary. Her father, deceased, was a factory worker, and her mother, also deceased, worked in a consumer-goods store. They both died of conditions consistent with alcohol abuse. Our Tanya drinks only in moderation. State education, undistinguished grades in that. No siblings, our Tanya is quite alone in the world—and has been so for some time. She's been working for Rasputin for almost four years. I doubt the Sparrow School ever turned out so polished a whore as this one. Gregoriy Filipovich himself used her many times, whether for sex or just for his public escort, we're not sure, and she is a fine adornment, is she not? But whatever affection he may have had for her, as you see, was not reciprocated."

"Anyone close to her?"

Provalov shook his head. "None known to us, not even a woman friend of note."

The interview was pure vanilla, Reilly saw, like fishing for bass in a well-stocked lake, one of twenty-seven interrogations to this point concerning the death of G. F. Avseyenko—everyone seemed to forget the fact that there had been two additional human beings in the car, but they probably hadn't been the targets. It wasn't getting any easier. What they really needed was the truck, something with physical evidence. Like most FBI agents, Reilly believed in tangibles, something you could hold in your hand, then pass off to a judge or jury, and have them *know* it was both evidence of a crime and proof of who had done it. Eyewitnesses, on the other hand, were often liars; at best they were easy for defense lawyers to confuse, and therefore they were rarely trusted by cops or juries. The truck might have blast residue from the RPG launch, maybe fingerprints on the greasy wrapping paper the Russians used for their weapons, maybe anything—best of all would be a cigarette smoked by the driver or the shooter, since the FBI could DNA-match the residual saliva on that to anyone, which was one of the Bureau's best new tricks (six-hundred-million-to-one odds were hard for people to argue with, even highly paid defense attorneys). One of Reilly's pet projects was to bring over the DNA technology for the Russian police to use, but for that the Russians would have to front the cash for the lab gear, which would be a problem—the Russians didn't seem to have the cash for anything important. All they had now was the remainder of the RPG warhead—it was amazing how much of the things actually did survive launch and detonation—which had a serial number that was being run down, though it was doubtful that this bit of information would lead anywhere. But you ran them all down because you never knew what was valuable and what was not until you got to the finish line, which was usually in front of a judge's bench with twelve people in a box off to your right. Things were a little different here in Russia, procedurally speaking, but the one thing he was trying to get through to the Russian cops he counseled was that the aim of every investigation was a conviction. They were getting it, slowly for most, quickly for a few, and also getting the fact that kicking a suspect's balls into his throat was not an effective interrogation technique. They had a constitution in Russia, but public respect for it still needed growing, and it would take time. The idea of the rule of law in this country was as foreign as a man from Mars.

The problem, Reilly thought, *was that neither he nor anyone else knew how much time there was for Russians to catch up with the rest of the world.* There was much here to admire, especially in the arts. Because of his diplomatic status, Reilly and his wife often got complimentary tickets to concerts (which he liked) and the ballet (which his wife loved), and that was still the class of the world . . . but the rest of the country had never kept up. Some at the embassy, some of the older CIA people who'd been here before the fall of the USSR, said that the improvements were incredible. But if that were true, Reilly told himself, then what had been here before must have been truly dreadful to behold, though the Bolshoi had probably still been the Bolshoi, even then.

"That is all?" Tanya Bogdanova asked in the interrogation room.

"Yes, thank you for coming in. We may call you again."

"Use this number," she said, handing over her business card. "It's for my cellular phone." That was one more Western convenience in Moscow for those with the hard currency, and Tanya obviously did.

The interrogator was a young militia sergeant. He stood politely and moved to get the door for her, showing Bogdanova the courtesy she'd come to expect from men. In the case of Westerners, it was for her physical attributes. In the case of her countrymen, it was her clothing that told them of her newfound worth. Reilly watched her eyes as she left the room. The expression was like that of a child who'd expected to be caught doing something naughty, but hadn't. *How stupid father was,* that sort of smile proclaimed. It seemed so misplaced on the angel-face, but there it was, on the other side of the mirror.

"Oleg?"

"Yes, Misha?" Provalov turned.

"She's dirty, man. She's a player," Reilly said in English. Provalov knew the cop-Americanisms.

"I agree, Misha, but I have nothing to hold her on, do I?"

"I suppose not. Might be interesting to keep an eye on her, though."

"If I could afford her, I would keep more than my eye on her, Mikhail Ivan'ch."

Reilly grunted amusement. "Yeah, I hear that."

"But she has a heart of ice."

"That's a fact," the FBI agent agreed. And the game in which she was a player was at best nasty, and at its worst, lethal.

So, what do we have?" Ed Foley asked, some hours later across the river from Washington.

"Gornischt so far," Mary Pat replied to her husband's question.

"Jack wants to be kept up to speed on this one."

"Well, tell the President that we're running as fast as we can, and all we have so far is from the Legal Attaché. He's in tight with the local cops, but they don't seem to know shit either. Maybe somebody tried to kill Sergey Nikolay'ch, but the Legat says he thinks Rasputin was the real target."

"I suppose he had his share of enemies," the Director of Central Intelligence conceded.

Thank you," the Vice President concluded to the packed house at the Ole Miss field house. The purpose of the speech was to announce that eight new destroyers would be built in the big Litton shipyard on the Mississippi Gulf Coast, which meant jobs and money for the state, always items of concern for the governor, who was now standing and applauding as though the Ole Miss football team had just knocked off Texas at the Cotton Bowl. They took their sports seriously down here. And their politics, Robby reminded himself, stifling a curse for this tawdry profession that was so much like medieval bargaining in a village square, three good pigs for a cow or something, toss in a mug of bitter ale. Was *this* how one governed a country? He grinned as he shook his head. Well, there had been politics in the Navy, too, and he'd scaled those heights, but he'd done it, by being one hell of a good naval officer, and the best fucking fighter pilot ever to catapult off a flattop. On the last score, of course he knew that *every* fighter pilot sitting and waiting for the cat shot felt exactly the same way . . . it was just that he was totally correct in his self-assessment.

There were the usual hands to shake coming off the platform, guided by his Secret Service detail in their dark, forbidding shades, then down the steps and out the back door to his car, where another squad of armed men waited, their vigilant eyes looking ever outward, like the gunners on a B-17 over Schweinfurt must have done, the Vice President thought. One of them held open the car door, and Robby slid in.

"TOMCAT is rolling," the chief of the VP detail told his microphone as the car headed off.

Robby picked up his briefing folder as the car got onto the highway for the airport. "Anything important happening in D.C.?"

"Not that they've told me about," the Secret Service agent answered.

Jackson nodded. These were good people looking after him. The detail chief, he figured, was a medium-to-senior captain, and the rest of his troops j.g.'s to lieutenant commanders, which was how Robby treated them. They were underlings, but good ones, well-trained pros who merited the smile and the nod when they did things right, which they nearly always did. They would have made good aviators, most of them—and the rest probably good Marines. The car finally pulled up to the VC-20B jet in an isolated corner of the general-aviation part of the airport, surrounded by yet more security troops. The driver stopped the car just twenty feet from the foot of the self-extending stairs.

"You going to drive us home, sir?" the detail chief asked, suspecting the answer.

"Bet your ass, Sam" was the smiling reply.

That didn't please the USAF captain detailed to be co-pilot on the aircraft, and it wasn't all that great for the lieutenant colonel supposed to be the pilot-in-command of the modified Gulfstream III. The Vice President liked to have the stick—in his case the yoke—in his hands at all times, while the colonel worked the radio and monitored the instruments. The aircraft spent most of its time on autopilot, of course, but Jackson, right seat or not, was determined to be the command pilot on the flight, and you couldn't very well say no to him. As a result, the captain would sit in the back and the colonel would be in the left seat, but jerking off. What the hell, the latter thought, the Vice President told good stories, and was a fairly competent stick for a Navy puke.

"Clear right," Jackson said, a few minutes later.

"Clear left," the pilot replied, confirming the fact from the plane-walker in front of the Gulfstream.

"Starting One," Jackson said next, followed thirty seconds later by "Starting Two."

The ribbon gauges came up nicely. "Looking good, sir," the USAF lieutenant colonel reported. The G had Rolls-Royce Spey engines, the same that had once been used on the U.K. versions of the F-4 Phantom fighter, but somewhat more reliable.

"Tower, this is Air Force Two, ready to taxi."

"Air Force Two, Tower, cleared to taxiway three."

"Roger, Tower AF-Two taxiing via three." Jackson slipped the brakes and let the aircraft move, its fighter engines barely above idle, but guzzling a huge quantity of fuel for all that. On a carrier, Jackson thought, you had plane handlers in yellow shirts to point you around. Here you had to go according to the map/diagram—clipped to the center of the yoke—to the proper place, all the while looking around to make sure some idiot in a Cessna 172 didn't stray into your path like a stray car in the supermarket parking lot. Finally, they reached the end of the runway, and turned to face down it.

"Tower, this is Spade requesting permission to take off." It just sort of came out on its own.

A laughing reply: "This ain't the *Enterprise,* Air Force Two, and we don't have cat shots here, but you are cleared to depart, sir."

You could hear the grin in the reply: "Roger, Tower, AF-Two is rolling."

"Your call sign was really 'Spade'?" the assigned command pilot asked as the VC-20B started rolling.

"Got hung on by my first CO, back when I was a new nugget. And it kinda stuck." The Vice President shook his head. "Jesus, that seems like a long time ago."

"V-One, sir," the Air Force officer said next, followed by "V-R."

At velocity-rotation, Jackson eased back on the yoke, bringing the aircraft off the ground and into the air. The colonel retracted the landing gear on command, while Jackson flipped the wheel half an inch left and right, rocking the wings a little as he always did to make sure the aircraft was willing to do what he told it. It was, and inside of three minutes, the G was on autopilot, programmed to turn, climb, and level out at thirty-nine thousand feet.

"Boring, isn't it?"

"Just another word for safe, sir," the USAF officer replied.

Fucking trash-hauler, Jackson thought. No fighter pilot would say something like that out loud. Since when was flying supposed to be . . . well, Robby had to admit to himself, he always buckled his seat belt before starting his car, and never did anything reckless, even with a fighter plane. But it offended him that this aircraft, like almost all of the new ones, did so much of the work that he'd been trained to do himself. It would even land itself . . . well, the Navy had such systems aboard its carrier aircraft, but *no* proper naval aviator ever used it unless ordered to, something Robert Jefferson Jackson had always managed to avoid. This trip would go into his logbook as time in command, but it really wasn't. Instead it was a microchip in command, and his real function was to be there to take proper action in case something broke. But nothing ever did. Even the damned engines. Once turbojets had lasted a mere nine or ten hours before having to be replaced. Now there were Spey engines on the G fleet that had twelve *thousand* hours. There was one out there with over *thirty* thousand that Rolls-Royce wanted back, offering a free brand-new replacement because its engineers wanted to tear that one apart to learn what they'd done so right, but the owner, perversely and predictably, refused to part with it. The rest of the Gulfstream airframe was about that reliable, and the electronics were utterly state-of-the-art, Jackson knew, looking down at the color display from the weather-radar. It was a clear and friendly black at the moment, showing what was probably smooth air all the way to Andrews. There was as yet no instrument that detected turbulence, but up here at flight level three-niner-zero, that was a pretty rare occurrence, and Jackson wasn't often susceptible to airsickness, and his hand was inches from the yoke in case something unexpected happened. Jackson occasionally hoped that something *would* happen, since it would allow him to show just how good an aviator he was . . . but it never did. Flying had become too routine since his childhood in the F-4N Phantom and his emerging manhood in the F-14A Tomcat. And maybe it was better that way. Yeah, he thought, sure.

"Mr. Vice President?" It was the voice of the USAF communications sergeant aboard the VC-20. Robby turned to see her with a sheaf of papers.

"Yeah, Sarge?"

"Flash traffic just came in on the printer." She extended her hand, and Robby took the paper.

"Colonel, your airplane for a while," the VP told the lieutenant colonel in the left seat.

"Pilot's airplane," the colonel agreed, while Robby started reading.

It was always the same, even though it was also always different. The cover sheet had the usual classification formatting. It had once impressed Jackson that the act of showing a sheet of paper to the wrong person could land him in Leavenworth Federal Penitentiary—at the time, actually, the since-closed Portsmouth Naval Prison in New Hampshire—but now as a senior government official in Washington, D.C., he knew he could show damned near anything to a reporter from *The Washington Post* and not be touched for it. It wasn't so much that he was above the law as he was one of the people who decided what the law meant. What was so damned secret and sensitive in this case was that CIA didn't know shit about the possible attempt on the life of Russia's chief spymaster . . . which meant nobody else in Washington did, either. . . .

CHAPTER 3

The Problems with Riches

The issue was trade, not exactly the President's favorite, but then, at this level, every issue took on sufficient twists that even the ones you thought you knew about became strange at best, unknown and alien at worst.

"George?" Ryan said to his Secretary of the Treasury, George Winston.

"Mr. Pres—"

"Goddammit, George!" The President nearly spilled his coffee with the outburst.

"Okay." SecTreas nodded submission. "It's hard to make the adjustment . . . *Jack.*" Ryan was getting tired of the Presidential trappings, and his rule was that here, in the Oval Office, his name was Jack, at least for his inner circle, of which Winston was one. After all, Ryan had joked a few times, after leaving this marble prison, he might be working *for* TRADER, as the Secret Service knew him, back in New York on The Street, instead of the other way 'round. After leaving the Presidency, something for which Jack prostrated himself before God every night—or so the stories went—he'd have to find gainful employment somewhere, and the trading business beckoned. Ryan had shown a rare gift for it, Winston reminded himself. His last such effort had been a California company called Silicon Alchemy, just one of many computer outfits, but the only one in which Ryan had taken an interest. So skillfully had he brought that firm to IPO that his own stock holdings in SALC—its symbol on the big board—were now valued at just over eighty million dollars, making Ryan by far the wealthiest American President in history. It was something his politically astute Chief of Staff, Arnold van Damm, did not advertise to the news media, who typically regarded every wealthy man as a robber baron, excepting, of course, the owners of the papers and TV stations themselves, who were, of course, the best of public-spirited citizens. None of this was widely known, even in the tight community of Wall Street big-hitters, which was remarkable enough. Should he ever return to The Street, Ryan's prestige would be sufficient to earn money while he slept in his bed at home. And that, Winston freely admitted, was something well and truly earned, and be damned to whatever the media hounds thought of it.

"It's China?" Jack asked.

"That's right, Boss," Winston confirmed with a nod. "Boss" was a term Ryan could stomach, as it was also the in-house term the Secret Service—which was part of Winston's Department of the Treasury—used to identify the man they were sworn to protect. "They're having a little cash-shortfall problem, and they're looking to make it up with us."

"How little?" POTUS asked.

"It looks as though it will annualize out to, oh, seventy billion or so."

"That is, as we say, real money."

George Winston nodded. "Anything that starts with a 'B' is real enough, and this is a little better than six 'Bs' a month."

"Spending it for what?"

"Not entirely sure, but a lot of it has to be military-related. The French arms industries are tight with them now, since the Brits kiboshed the jet-engine deal from Rolls-Royce."

The President nodded, looking down at the briefing papers. "Yeah, Basil talked the PM out of it." That was Sir Basil Charleston, chief of the British Secret Intelligence Service, sometimes called (erroneously) MI6. Basil was an old friend of Ryan's, going back to his CIA days. "It was a remarkably stand-up thing to do."

"Well, our friends in Paris don't seem to think the same way."

"They usually don't," Ryan agreed. The odd thing was the dichotomy inherent in dealing with the French. In some things, they weren't so much allies as blood brothers, but in others they were less than mere associates, and Ryan had trouble figuring out the logic by which the French changed their minds. Well, the President thought, that's what I have a State Department for. . . . "So, you think the PRC is building up its military again?"

"Big time, but not so much their navy, which makes our friends in Taiwan feel a little better."

That had been one of President Ryan's foreign-policy initiatives after concluding hostilities with the defunct United Islamic Republic, now restored to the separate nations of Iran and Iraq, which were at least at peace with each other. The real reasons for the recognition of Taiwan had never been made known to the public. It looked pretty clear to Ryan and his Secretary of State, Scott Adler, that the People's Republic of China had played a role in the Second Persian Gulf War, and probably in the preceding conflict with Japan, as well. Exactly why? Well, some in CIA thought that China lusted after the mineral riches in eastern Siberia—this was suggested by intercepts and other access to the electronic mail of the Japanese industrialists who'd twisted their nation's path into a not-quite-open clash with America. They'd referred to Siberia as the "Northern Resource Area," harkening back to when an earlier generation of Japanese strategists had called South Asia the "Southern Resource Area." That had been part of another conflict, one known to history as the Second World War. In any case, the complicity of the PRC with America's enemies had merited a countermove, Ryan and Adler had agreed, and besides, the Republic of China on Taiwan *was* a democracy, with government officials elected by the people of that nation island—and *that* was something America was supposed to respect.

"You know, it would be better if they started working their navy and threatening Taiwan. We are in a better position to forestall that than—"

"You really think so?" SecTreas asked, cutting his President off.

"The Russians do," Jack confirmed.

"They why are the Russians selling the Chinese so much hardware?" Winston demanded. "That doesn't make sense!"

"George, there is no rule demanding that the world has to make sense." That was one of Ryan's favorite aphorisms. "That's one of the things you learn in the intelligence business. In 1938, guess who was Germany's number one trading partner?"

SecTreas saw that sandbag coming before it struck. "France?"

"You got it." Ryan nodded. "Then, in '40 and '41, they did a lot of trade with the Russians. That didn't work out so well either, did it?"

"And everyone always told me that trade was a moderating influence," the Secretary observed.

"Maybe it is among people, but remember that governments don't have principles so much as interests—at least the primitive ones, the ones who haven't figured it all out yet . . ."

"Like the PRC?"

It was Ryan's turn to nod. "Yeah, George, like those little bastards in Beijing. They rule a nation of a billion people, but they do it as though they were the new coming of Caligula. Nobody ever told them that they have a positive duty to look after the interests of the people they rule—well, maybe that's not true," Ryan allowed, feeling a little generous. "They have this big, perfect theoretical model, promulgated by Karl Marx, refined by Lenin, then applied in their country by a pudgy sexual pervert named Mao."

"Oh? Pervert?"

"Yeah." Ryan looked up. "We had the data over at Langley. Mao liked virgins, the younger the better. Maybe he liked to see the fear in their cute little virginal eyes—that's what one of our pshrink consultants thought, kinda like rape, not so much sex as power. Well, I guess it could have been worse—at least they were girls," Jack observed rather dryly, "and their culture is historically a little more liberal than ours on that sort of thing." A shake of the head. "You should see the briefs I get whenever a major foreign dignitary comes over, the stuff we know about their personal habits."

A chuckle: "Do I really want to know?"

A grimace: "Probably not. Sometimes I wish they didn't give me the stuff. You sit them down right here in the office, and they're charming and businesslike, and you can spend the whole fucking meeting looking for horns and hooves." That could be a distraction, of course, but it was more generally thought that as in playing poker for high stakes, the more you knew about the guy on the other side of the table, the better, even if it might make you want to throw up during the welcoming ceremony on the White House South Lawn. But that was the business of being President, Ryan reminded himself. *And people actually fought like tigers to get there.* And would again, when he left, POTUS reminded himself. *And so, Jack, is it your job to protect your country from the kind of rat who lusts to be where all the really good cheese is stored?* Ryan shook his head again. So many doubts. It wasn't so much that they never went away. They just kept getting bigger all the time. How strange that he understood and could recount every small step that had led him to this office, and yet he still asked himself several times every hour how the *hell* he'd come to be in this place . . . and how the hell he'd ever get out. Well, he had no excuses at all this time. He'd actually run for election to the Presidency. If you could call it that—Arnie van Damm didn't, as a matter of fact—which you could, since he'd fulfilled the constitutional requirements, a fact on which just about every legal scholar in the nation had agreed, *and* talked about on every major news network *ad nauseam. Well,* Jack reminded himself, *I wasn't watching much TV back then, was I?* But it all really came down to one thing: The people you dealt with as President were very often people whom you would never willingly invite into your home, and it had nothing to do with any lack of manners or personal charm, which, perversely, they usually displayed in abundance. One of the things Arnie had told Jack early on was that the main requirement to enter the political profession was nothing more nor less than the ability to be pleasant to people whom you despised, and then to do business with them as if they were bosom friends.

"So, what do we know about our heathen Chinese friends?" Winston asked. "The current ones, that is."

"Not much. We're working on that. The Agency has a long way to go, though we are started on the road. We still get intercepts. Their phone system is leaky, and they use their cell phones too much without encrypting them. Some of them are men of commendable vigor, George, but nothing too terribly scandalous that we know about. Quite a few of them have secretaries who are very close to their bosses."

The Secretary of the Treasury managed a chuckle. "Well, a lot of that going around, and not just in Beijing."

"Even on Wall Street?" Jack inquired, with a theatrically raised eyebrow.

"I can't say for sure, sir, but I have heard the occasional rumor." Winston grinned at the diversion.

And even right here in this room, Ryan reminded himself. They'd changed the rug long since, of course, and all the furniture, except for the Presidential desk. One of the problems associated with holding this job was the baggage piled on your back by previous officeholders. They said the public had a short memory, but that wasn't true, was it? Not when you heard the whispers, followed by chuckles, and accompanied by knowing looks and the occasional gesture that made you feel dirty to be the subject of the chuckles. And all you could do about it was to live your life as best you could, but even then the best you could hope for was for people to think you were smart enough not to get caught, *because they* all *did it, right?* One of the problems with living in a free country was that anyone outside this palace/prison could think and say whatever he wished. And Ryan didn't even have the right that any other citizen might have to punch out whatever twit said something about his character that the twit was unwilling to back up. It hardly seemed fair, but as a practical matter, it would force Ryan to visit a lot of corner bars, and break a lot of knuckles, to little gain. And sending sworn cops or armed Marines out to handle matters wasn't exactly a proper use of Presidential power, was it?

Jack knew that he was far too thin-skinned to hold this job. Professional politicians typically had hides that made a rhinoceros's look like rose petals, because they expected to have things hurled at them, some true, some not. By cultivating that thick covering, they attenuated the pain somehow, until eventually people stopped hurling things at them, or such was the theory. Maybe it actually worked for some. Or maybe the bastards just didn't have consciences. You paid your money and you took your choice.

But Ryan did have a conscience. That was a choice he'd made long before. You still had to look in the mirror once a day, usually at shaving time, and there was no easy fix for not being able to like the face you saw there.

"Okay, back to the PRC's problems, George," the President commanded.

"They're going to juice up their trade—one way, that is. They're discouraging their own citizens from buying American, but all they can sell, they sell. Including some of Mao's young virgins, probably."

"What do we have to prove that?"

"Jack, I pay close attention to results, and I have friends in various businesses who shake the bushes and talk to people over drinks. What they learn frequently gets back to me. You know, a lot of ethnic Chinese have some weird medical condition. You get one drink into them, it's like four or five for us—and the second drink is like chugging a whole bottle of Jack Daniel's, but some of the dummies try to keep up anyway, some hospitality thing, maybe. Anyway, when that happens, well, the talk becomes freer, y'know? It's been going on quite a while, but lately Mark Gant set up a little program. Senior executives who go to certain special places, well, I *do* own the Secret Service now, and the Secret Service *does* specialize in economic crimes, right? And a lot of my old friends know who I am and what I do now, and they cooperate pretty nice, and so I get a lot of good stuff to write up. It mainly goes to my senior people across the street."

"I'm impressed, George. You cross-deck it to CIA?"

"I suppose I could, but I was afraid they'd get all pissy over turf rights and stuff."

Ryan rolled his eyes at that bit of information. "Not Ed Foley. He's a real pro from way back, and the bureaucracy over at Langley hasn't captured him yet. Have him over to your office for lunch. He won't mind what you're doing. Same thing with Mary Pat. She runs the Directorate of Operations. MP's a real cowgirl, and she wants results, too."

"Duly noted. You know, Jack, it's amazing how much people talk, and the things they talk about under the proper circumstances."

"How'd you make all that money on The Street, George?" Ryan asked.

"Mainly by knowing a little more than the guy across the street," Winston replied.

"Works the same way for me here. Okay, if our little friends go forward with this, what should we do?"

"Jack—no, now it's *Mr. President*—we've been financing Chinese industrial expansion for quite a few years now. They sell things to us, we pay cash for them, and then they either keep the money for their own purposes on the international money markets, or they purchase things they want from other countries, often things they could as easily buy from us, but maybe half a percent more expensive from an American manufacturer. The reason it's called 'trade' is that you theoretically exchange something of yours for something of the other guy's—just like kids with baseball cards, okay?—but they're not playing the game that way. They're also dumping some products just to get dollars, selling items here for less than what they sell them to their own citizens. Now, that is technically in violation of a couple federal statues. Okay," Winston shrugged, "it's a statute we enforce somewhat selectively, but it *is* on the books, and it *is* the law. Toss in the Trade Reform Act that we passed a few years ago because of the games the Japs were playing—"

"I remember, George. It kinda started a little shooting war in which some people got killed," POTUS observed dryly. Worst of all, perhaps, it had begun the process that had ended up with Ryan in this very room.

SecTreas nodded. "True, but it's still the law, and it was not a bill of attainder meant only to apply to Japan. Jack, if we apply the same trade laws to China that the Chinese apply to us, well, it'll put a major crimp in their foreign-exchange accounts. Is that a bad thing? No, not with the trade imbalance we have with them now. You know, Jack, if they start building automobiles and play the same game they're playing on everything else, our trade deficit could get real ugly real fast, and frankly I'm tired of having us finance their economic development, which they then execute with heavy equipment bought in Japan and Europe. If they want trade with the United States of America, fine, but let it be *trade.* We can hold our own in any truly fair trade war with any country, because American workers can produce as well as anybody in the world and better than most. But if we let them cheat us, we're being cheated, Jack, and I don't like that here any more than I do around a card table. And here, buddy, the stakes are a hell of a lot higher."

"I hear you, George. But we don't want to put a gun to their head, do we? You don't do that to a nation-state, especially a *big* nation-state, unless you have a solid reason for doing so. Our economy is chugging along rather nicely now, isn't it? We can afford to be a little magnanimous."

"Maybe, Jack. What I was thinking was a little friendly encouragement on our part, not a pointed gun exactly. The gun is always there in the holster—the big gun is most-favored-nation status, and they know it, and we know they know it. TRA is something we can apply to any country, and I happen to think the idea behind the law is fundamentally sound. It's been fairly useful as a club to show to a lot of countries, but we've never tried it on the PRC. How come?"

POTUS shrugged, with no small degree of embarrassment. "Because I haven't had the chance to yet, and before me too many people in this town just wanted to kiss their collective ass."

"Leaves a bad taste in your mouth when you do that, Mr. President, doesn't it?"

"It can," Jack agreed. "Okay, you want to talk this over with Scott Adler. The ambassadors all work for him."

"Who do we have in Beijing?"

"Carl Hitch. Career FSO, late fifties, supposed to be very good, and this is his sunset assignment."

"Payoff for all those years of holding coats?"

Ryan nodded. "Something like that, I suppose. I'm not entirely sure. State wasn't my bureaucracy." CIA, he didn't add, was bad enough.

It was a much nicer office, Bart Mancuso thought. And the shoulderboards on his undress whites were a little heavier now, with the four stars instead of the two he'd worn as ComSubPac. But no more. His former boss, Admiral Dave Seaton, had fleeted up to Chief of Naval Operations, and then the President (or someone close to him) had decided that Mancuso was the guy to be the next Commander in Chief, Pacific. And so he now worked in the same office once occupied by Chester Nimitz, and other fine—and some brilliant—naval officers since. It was quite a stretch since Plebe Summer at Annapolis, lo those many years before, especially since he'd had only a single command at sea, USS *Dallas,* though that command tour had been a noteworthy one, complete with two missions he could *still* tell no one about. And having been shipmates once and briefly with the sitting President probably hadn't hurt his career very much.

The new job came with a plush official house, a sizable team of sailors and chiefs to look after him and his wife—the boys were all away at college now—the usual drivers, official cars, and, now, armed bodyguards, because, remarkably enough, there were people about who didn't much care for admirals. As a theater commander Mancuso now reported directly to the Secretary of Defense, Anthony Bretano, who in turn reported directly to President Ryan. In return, Mancuso got a lot of new perks. Now he had direct access to all manner of intelligence information, including the holy of holies, sources and methods—where the information came from, and how we'd gotten it out—because as America's principal executor for a quarter of the globe's surface, he had to know it all, so that he'd know what to advise the SecDef, who would, in turn, advise the President of CINCPAC's views, intentions, and desires.

The Pacific, Mancuso thought, having just completed his first morning intel brief, looked okay. It hadn't always been like that, of course, including recently, when he'd fought a fairly major conflict—"war" was a word that had fallen very much out of favor in civilized discourse—with the Japanese, and that had included the loss of two of his nuclear submarines, killed with treachery and deceit, as Mancuso thought of it, though a more objective observer might have called the tactics employed by the enemy clever and effective.

Heretofore he'd been notified of the locations and activities of his various submarines, but now he also got told about his carriers, tin cans, cruisers, and replenishment ships, plus Marines, and even Army and Air Force assets, which were technically his as a theater commander-in-chief. All that meant that the morning intel brief lasted into a third cup of coffee, by the end of which he looked longingly to the executive head, just a few feet away from his desk. Hell, his intelligence coordinator, called a J-2, was, in fact, an Army one-star doing his "joint" tour, and, in fairness, doing it pretty well. This brigadier, named Mike Lahr, had taught political science at West Point, in addition to other assignments. Having to consider political factors was a new development in Mancuso's career, but it came with the increased command territory. CINCPAC had done his "joint" tour along the way, of course, and was theoretically conversant with the abilities and orientation of his brother armed services, but whatever confidence he'd had along those lines diminished in the face of having the command responsibility to utilize such forces in a professional way. Well, he had subordinate commanders in those other services to advise him, but it was his job to know more than just how to ask questions, and for Mancuso that meant he'd have to go out and get his clothes dirty seeing the practical side, because that was where the kids assigned to his theater would shed blood if he didn't do his job right.

The team was a joint venture of the Atlantic Richfield Company, British Petroleum, and the largest Russian oil exploration company. The last of the three had the most experience but the least expertise, and the most primitive methods. This was not to say that the Russian prospectors were stupid. Far from it. Two of them were gifted geologists, with theoretical insights that impressed their American and British colleagues. Better still, they'd grasped the advantages of the newest exploration equipment about as quickly as the engineers who'd designed it.

It had been known for many years that this part of eastern Siberia was a geological twin to the North Slope region of Alaska and Northern Canada, which had turned into vast oil fields for their parent countries to exploit. The hard part had been getting the proper equipment there to see if the similarity was more than just cosmetic.

Getting the gear into the right places had been a minor nightmare. Brought by train into southeastern Siberia from the port of Vladivostok, the "thumper trucks"—they were far too heavy to airlift—had then spent a month going cross-country, north from Magdagachi, through Aim and Ust Maya, finally getting to work east of Kazachye.

But what they had found had staggered them. From Kazachye on the River Yana all the way to Kolymskaya on the Kolyma was an oilfield to rival the Persian Gulf. The thumper trucks and portable computer-carrying seismic-survey vehicles had shown a progression of perfect underground dome formations in stunning abundance, some of them barely two thousand feet down, mere tens of vertical yards from the permafrost, and drilling through that would be about as hard as slicing a wedding cake with a cavalryman's saber. The scope of the field could not be ascertained without drilling test wells—over a hundred such wells, the chief American engineer thought, just from the sheer scope of the field—but no one had ever seen as promising or as vast a natural deposit of petroleum during his professional lifetime. The issues of exploitation would not be small ones, of course. Except for Antarctica itself, there was no place on the planet with a less attractive climate. Getting the production gear in here would take years of multistage investment, building airfields, probably building ports for the cargo ships that could alone deliver the heavy equipment—and then only in the brief summer months—needed to construct the pipeline which would be needed to get the oil out to market. Probably through Vladivostok, the Americans thought. The Russians could sell it from there, and supertankers, more precisely called VLCCs or ULCCs—for Very Large to Ultra-Large Crude Carriers—would move it out across the Pacific, maybe to Japan, maybe to America or elsewhere, wherever oil was needed, which was just about everywhere. From those users would come hard currency. It would take many more years until Russia could build the wherewithal needed for its own industries and consumers to use the oil, but, as such things happened, the cash generated from selling the Siberian crude could then be flipped and used to purchase oil from other sources, which would be much more easily transported to Russian ports and thence into existing Russian pipelines. The cash difference of selling and buying, as opposed to building a monstrous and monstrously expensive pipeline, was negligible in any case, and such decisions were usually made for political rather than economic reasons.

At precisely the same time, and only six hundred miles, or nine hundred sixty or so kilometers, away, another geology team was in the eastern extreme of the Sayan mountain range. Some of the seminomadic tribes in the area, who had made their living for centuries by herding reindeer, had brought into a government office some shiny yellow rocks. Few people in the world have been unaware of what such rocks mean, at least for the preceding thirty centuries, and a survey team had been dispatched from Moscow State University, still the nation's most prestigious school. They had been able to fly in, since their equipment was far lighter, and the last few hundred kilometers had been done on horseback, a wonderful anachronism for the survey team of academics, who were far more used to riding Moscow's fine subway system.

The first thing they'd found was an eighty-ish man living alone with his herd and a rifle to fend off wolves. This citizen had lived alone since the death of his wife, twenty years before, quite forgotten by the changing governments of his country, known to exist only by a few shopkeepers in a dreary village thirty kilometers to the south, and his mental state reflected his long-term isolation. He managed to shoot three or four wolves every year, and he kept the pelts as any hunter/herdsman might, but with a difference. First he took the pelts and, weighting them down with stones, set them in the small river that ran near his hut.

In Western literature there is the well-known story of Jason and the Argonauts, and their heroic quest for the Golden Fleece. It was not known until recently that the legend of the artifact sought was quite real: The tribesmen of Asia Minor had set the skins of sheep in their streams to catch the gold dust being washed down from deposits higher up, changing the pale wool fibers into something almost magical in appearance.

It was no different here. The wolf pelts the geologists found hanging inside the old soldier's hut looked on first inspection to be sculptures by Renaissance masters, or even artisans of the Pharaohs of dynastic Egypt, they were so evenly coated, and then the explorers found that each pelt weighed a good sixty kilograms, and there were thirty-four of them! Sitting down with him over the necessary bottle of fine vodka, they learned that his name was Pavel Petrovich Gogol, that he'd fought against the Fascisti in the Great Patriotic War as a sniper, and, remarkably, was twice a Hero of the Soviet Union for his marksmanship, mainly in the battles around Kiev and Warsaw. A somewhat grateful nation had allowed him to return to his ancestral lands—he was, it turned out, descended from the entrepreneurial Russians who'd come to Siberia in the early nineteenth century—where he'd been forgotten by the bureaucrats who never really wondered much where the reindeer meat eaten by the locals came from, or who might be cashing his pension checks to buy ammunition for his old bolt-action rifle. Pavel Petrovich knew the value of the gold he found, but he'd never spent any of it, as he found his solitary life quite satisfactory. The gold deposit a few kilometers upstream from the place where the wolves went for their last swim—as Pavel Petrovich described it with a twinkle in the eye and a snort of vodka—turned out to be noteworthy, perhaps as much as the South African strike of the mid–nineteenth century, and *that* had turned into the richest gold mine in the history of the world. The local gold had not been discovered for several reasons, mainly relating to the dreadful Siberian climate, which had, first, prevented a detailed exploratory survey, and, second, covered the local streams with ice so much of the time that the gold dust in the streambeds had never been noticed.

Both the oil and rock survey teams had traveled into the field with satellite phones, the more quickly to report what they found. This both teams did, coincidentally on the same day.

The Iridium satellite-communications system they used was a huge breakthrough in global communications. With an easily portable instrument, one could communicate with the low-altitude constellation of dedicated communications satellites which cross-linked their signals at the speed of light (which was *almost* instantaneous, but not quite) to conventional communications birds, and from there to the ground, which was where most people were most of the time.

The Iridium system was designed to speed communications worldwide. It was *not,* however, designed to be a secure system. There were ways to do that, but they all required the individual users to make their security arrangements. It was now theoretically possible to get commercially available 128-bit encryption systems, and these were extremely difficult to break even by the most sophisticated of nation-states and their black services . . . or so the salesmen said. But the remarkable thing was that few people bothered. Their laziness made life a lot easier for the National Security Agency, located between Baltimore and Washington at Fort Meade, Maryland. There, a computer system called ECHELON was programmed to listen in on every conversation that crossed the ether, and to lock in on certain codewords. Most of those words were nouns with national-security implications, but since the end of the Cold War, NSA and other agencies had paid more attention to economic matters, and so some of the new words were "oil," "deposit," "crude," "mine," "gold," and others, all in thirty-eight languages. When such a word crossed ECHELON's electronic ear, the continuing conversation was recorded onto electronic media and transcribed—and, where necessary, translated, all by computer. It was by no means a perfect system, and the nuances of language were still difficult for a computer program to unravel—not to mention the tendency of many people to mutter into the phone—but where a goof occurred, the original conversation would be reviewed by a linguist, of which the National Security Agency employed quite a few.

The parallel reports of the oil and gold strikes came in only five hours apart, and made their way swiftly up the chain of command, ending in a "flash" priority Special National Intelligence Estimate (called a

SNIE, and pronounced "snee") destined for the President's desk right after his next breakfast, to be delivered by his National Security Adviser, Dr. Benjamin Goodley. Before that, the data would be examined by a team from the Central Intelligence Agency's Directorate of Science and Technology, with a big assist from experts on the payroll of the Petroleum Institute in Washington, some of whose members had long enjoyed a cordial relationship with various government agencies. The preliminary evaluation—carefully announced and presented as such, *preliminary*, lest someone be charged for being wrong if the estimate proved to be incorrect someday—used a few carefully chosen superlatives.

Damn," the President observed at 8:10 EST. "Okay, Ben, how big are they really?"

"You don't trust our technical weenies?" the National Security Advisor asked.

"Ben, as long as I worked on the other side of the river, I never once caught them wrong on something like this, but damned if I didn't catch them *under*estimating stuff." Ryan paused for a moment. "But, Jesus, if these are lowball numbers, the implications are pretty big."

"Mr. President"—Goodley was not part of Ryan's inner circle—"we're talking billions, exactly how many nobody knows, but call it two hundred billion dollars in hard currency earnings over the next five to seven years at minimum. That's money they can use."

"And at maximum?"

Goodley leaned back for a second and took a breath. "I had to check. A trillion is a *thousand* billion. On the sunny side of that number. This is pure speculation, but the guys at the Petroleum Institute that CIA uses, the guys across the river tell me, spent most of their time saying 'Holy shit!' "

"Good news for the Russians," Jack said, flipping through the printed SNIE.

"Indeed it is, sir."

"About time they got lucky," POTUS thought aloud. "Okay, get a copy of this to George Winston. We want his evaluation of what this will mean to our friends in Moscow."

"I was planning to call some people at Atlantic Richfield. They were in on the exploration. I imagine they'll share in the proceeds. Their president is a guy named Sam Sherman. Know him?"

Ryan shook his head. "I know the name, but we've never met. Think I ought to change that?"

"If you want hard information, it can't hurt."

Ryan nodded. "Okay, maybe I'll have Ellen track him down." Ellen Sumter, his personal secretary, was located fifteen feet away through the sculpted door to his right. "What else?"

"They're still beating bushes for the people who blew up the pimp in Moscow. Nothing new to report on that, though."

"Would be nice to know what's going on in the world, wouldn't it?"

"Could be worse, sir," Goodley told his boss.

"Right." Ryan tossed the paper copy of the morning brief on his desk. "What else?"

Goodley shook his head. *"And that's the way it is* this morning, Mr. President." Goodley got a smile for that.

CHAPTER 4

Knob Rattling

It didn't matter what city or country you were in, Mike Reilly told himself. Police work was all the same. You talked to possible witnesses, you talked to the people involved, you talked to the victim.

But not the victim this time. Grisha Avseyenko would never speak again. The pathologist assigned to the case commented that he hadn't seen such a mess since his uniformed service in Afghanistan. But that was to be expected. The RPG was designed to punch holes in armored vehicles and concrete bunkers, which was a more difficult task than destroying a private-passenger automobile, even one so expensive as that stopped in Dzerzhinskiy Square. That meant that the body parts were very difficult to identify. It turned out that half the jaw had enough repaired teeth to say with great certainty that the decedent had indeed been Gregoriy Filipovich Avseyenko, and DNA samples would ultimately confirm this (the blood type also matched). There hadn't been enough of his body to identify—the face, for example, had been totally removed, and so had the left forearm, which had once borne a tattoo. The decedent's death had come instantaneously, the pathologist reported, after the processed remains had been packed into a plastic container, which in turn found its way into an oaken box for later cremation, probably—the Moscow Militia had to ascertain whether any family members existed, and what disposition for the body they might wish. Lieutenant Provalov assumed that cremation would be the disposal method of choice. It was, in its way, quick and clean, and it was easier and less expensive to find a resting place for a small box or urn than for a full-sized coffin with a cadaver in it.

Provalov took the pathology report back from his American colleague. He hadn't expected it to reveal anything of interest, but one of the things he'd learned from his association with the American FBI was that you checked everything thoroughly, since predicting how a criminal case would break was like trying to pick a ten-play football pool two weeks before the games were played. The human minds who committed crimes were simply too random in their operation for any sort of prediction.

And that had been the easy part. The pathology report on the driver had essentially been useless. The only data in it of any use at all had been blood and tissue types (which could be checked with his military-service records, if they could be located), since the body had been so thoroughly shredded as to leave not a single identifying mark or characteristic, though, perversely, his identity papers had survived in his wallet, and so, they probably knew who he had been. The same was true of the woman in the car, whose purse had survived virtually intact on the seat to the right of her, along with her ID papers . . . which was a lot more than could be said for her face and upper torso. Reilly looked at the photos of the other victims—well, one presumed they matched up, he told himself. The driver was grossly ordinary, perhaps a little fitter than was the average here. The woman, yet another of the pimp's high-priced hookers with a photo in her police file, had been a dish, worthy of a Hollywood screen test, and certainly pretty enough for a *Playboy* centerfold. Well, no more.

"So, Mishka, have you handled enough of these crimes that it no longer touches you?" Provalov asked.

"Honest answer?" Reilly asked, then shook his head. "Not really. We don't handle that many homicides, except the ones that happen on Federal property—Indian reservations or military bases. I have handled some kidnappings, though, and those you never get used to." Especially, Reilly didn't add, since kidnapping for money was a dead crime in America. Now children were kidnapped for their sexual utility, and most often killed in five hours, often before the FBI could even respond to the initial request for assistance from the local police department. Of all the crimes which Mike Reilly had worked, those were by far the worst, the sort after which you retired to the local FBI bar—every field division had one—and had a few too many as you sat quietly with equally morose and quiet colleagues, with the occasional oaths that you were going to get this mutt no matter what it took. And, mostly, the mutts were apprehended, indicted, and then convicted, and the lucky ones went to death row. Those convicted in states without a death penalty went into the general prison population, where they discovered what armed robbers thought of the abusers of children. "But I see what you mean, Oleg Gregoriyevich. It's the one thing you have trouble explaining to an ordinary citizen." It was that the worst thing about a crime scene or autopsy photo was the *sadness* of it, how the victim was stripped not merely of life, but of all dignity. And these photos were particularly grisly. Whatever beauty this Maria Ivanovna Sablin had once had was only a memory now, and then mainly memories held by men who'd rented access to her body. *Who mourned for a dead whore?* Reilly asked himself. Not the johns, who'd move on to a new one with scarcely a thought. Probably not even her own colleagues in the trade of flesh and desire, and whatever family she'd left behind would probably remember her not as the child who'd grown up to follow a bad path, but as a lovely person who'd defiled herself, pretending passion, but feeling no more than the trained physician who'd picked her organs apart on the dented steel table of the city morgue. Is that what prostitutes were, Reilly wondered, pathologists of sex? A victimless crime, some said. Reilly wished that such people could look at these photos and see just how "victimless" it was when women sold their bodies.

"Anything else, Oleg?" Reilly asked.

"We continue to interview people with knowledge of the deceased." Followed by a shrug.

He offended the wrong people," an informant said, with a shrug of his own that showed how absurdly obvious the answer to the preceding question was. How else could a person of Avseyenko's stature turn up dead in so spectacular a way?

"And what people are they?" the militiaman asked, not expecting a meaningful answer, but you asked the question anyway because you didn't know what the answer was until you did.

"His colleagues from State Security," the informant suggested.

"Oh?"

"Who else could have killed him in that way? One of his girls would have used a knife. A business rival from the street would have used a pistol or a larger knife, but an RPG . . . be serious, where does one get one of those?"

He wasn't the first to voice that thought, of course, though the local police did have to allow for the fact that all manner of weapons, heavy and light, had escaped one way or another from the coffers of what had once been called the Red Army into the active marketplace of criminal weapons.

"So, do you have any names for us?" the militia sergeant asked.

"Not a name, but I know the face. He's tall and powerfully built, like a soldier, reddish hair, fair skin, some freckles left over from his youth, green eyes." The informant paused. "His friends call him 'the boy,' because his appearance is so youthful. He was State Security once, but not a spy and not a catcher of spies. He was something else there, but I am not sure what."

The militia sergeant started taking more precise notes at this point, his pencil marks far more legible and much darker on the yellow page.

"And this man was displeased with Avseyenko?"

"So I have heard."

"And the reason for his displeasure?"

"That I do not know, but Gregoriy Filipovich had a way of offending men. He was very skilled at handling women, of course. For that he had a true gift, but the gift did not translate into his dealings with men. Many thought him a *zhopnik,* but he was not one of those, of course. He had a different woman on his arm every night, and none of them were ugly, but for some reason he didn't get along well with men, even those from State Security, where, he said, he was once a great national asset."

"Is that a fact," the militia sergeant observed, bored again. If there was anything criminals liked to do, it was boast. He'd heard it all a thousand times or more.

"Oh, yes. Gregoriy Filipovich claims to have supplied mistresses for all manner of foreigners, including some of ministerial rank, and says that they continue to supply valuable information to Mother Russia. I believe it," the informer added, editorializing again. "For a week with one of those angels, I would speak much."

And who wouldn't? the militiaman wondered with a yawn. "So, *how* did Avseyenko offend such powerful men?" the cop asked again.

"I have told you I do not know. Talk to 'the boy,' perhaps he will know."

"It is said that Gregoriy was beginning to import drugs," the cop said next, casting his hook into a different hole, and wondering what fish might lurk in the still waters.

The informant nodded. "That is true. It was said. But I never saw any evidence of it."

"Who would have seen evidence of it?"

Another shrug. "This I do not know. One of his girls, perhaps. I never understood how he planned to distribute what he thought about importing. To use the girls was logical, of course, but dangerous for them—and for him, because his whores would not have been loyal to him in the face of a trip to the camps. So, then, what does that leave?" the informant asked rhetorically. "He would have to set up an entirely new organization, and there were also dangers in doing that, were there not? So, yes, I believe he was thinking about importing drugs for sale, and making vast sums of money from it, but Gregoriy was not a man who wished to go to a prison, and I think he was merely thinking about it, perhaps talking a little, but not much. I do not think he had made his final decision. I do not think he actually imported anything before he met his end."

"Rivals with the same ideas?" the cop asked next.

"There are people who can find cocaine and other drugs for you, as you well know."

The cop looked up. In fact, the militia sergeant *didn't* know that for certain. He'd heard rumbles and rumors, but not statements of fact from informants he trusted (insofar as any cop in any city truly trusted *any* informant). As with many things, there was a buzz on the streets of Moscow, but like most Moscow cops he expected it to show up first in the Black Sea port of Odessa, a city whose criminal activity went back to the czars and which today, with the restoration of free trade with the rest of the world, tended to lead Russia in—well, led Russia *to* all forms of illicit activity. If there was an active drug trade in Moscow, it was so new and so small that he hadn't stumbled across it yet. He made a mental note to check with Odessa, to see what if anything was happening down there along those lines.

"And what people might they be?" the sergeant asked. If there was a growing distribution network in Moscow, he might as well learn about it.

Nomuri's job for Nippon Electric Company involved selling high-end desktop computers and peripherals. For him that meant the PRC government, whose senior bureaucrats had to have the newest and best of everything, from cars to mistresses, paid for in all cases by the government, which in turn took its money from the people, whom the bureaucrats represented and protected to the best of their abilities. As in many things, the PRC could have bought American brands, but in this case it chose to purchase the slightly less expensive (and less capable) computers from Japan, in the same way that it preferred to buy Airbus airlines from the European maker rather than Boeings from America—that had been a card played a few years before to teach the Americans a lesson. America had briefly resented it, then had quickly forgotten about it, in the way America seemed to handle all such slights, which was quite a contrast to the Chinese, who never forgot anything.

When President Ryan had announced the reestablishment of their official recognition of the Republic of China government on Taiwan, the repercussions had thundered through the corridors of power in Beijing like the main shocks of a major earthquake. Nomuri hadn't been here long enough yet to see the cold fury the move had generated, but the aftershocks were significant enough, and he'd heard echoes of it since his arrival in Beijing. The questions directed at himself were sometimes so direct and so demanding of an explanation that he'd momentarily wondered if his cover might have been blown, and his interlocutors had known that he was a CIA "illegal" field officer in the capital of the People's Republic of China, entirely without a diplomatic cover. But it hadn't been that. It was just a continuing echo of pure political rage. Paradoxically, the Chinese government was itself trying to shove that rage aside because they, too, had to do business with the United States of America, now their number-one trading partner, and the source of vast amounts of surplus cash, which their government needed to do the things which Nomuri was tasked to find out about. And so, here he was, in the outer office of one of the nation's senior officials.

"Good day," he said, with a bow and a smile to the secretary. She worked for a senior minister named Fang Gan, he knew, whose office was close by. She was surprisingly well dressed for a semi-ordinary worker, in a nation where fashion statements were limited to the color of the buttons one wore on the Mao jacket that was as much a part of the uniform of civilian government workers as was the gray-green wool of the soldiers of the People's Liberation Army.

"Good day," the young lady said in reply. "Are you Nomuri?"

"Yes, and you are . . . ?"

"Lian Ming," the secretary replied.

An interesting name, Chester thought. "Lian" in Mandarin meant "graceful willow." She was short, like most Chinese women, with a square-ish face and dark eyes. Her least attractive feature was her hair, short and cut in a manner that harkened back to the worst of the 1950s in America, and then only for children in Appalachian trailer parks. For all that, it was a classically Chinese face in its ethnicity, and one much favored in this tradition-bound nation. The look in her eyes, at least, suggested intelligence and education.

"You are here to discuss computers and printers," she said neutrally, having absorbed some of her boss's sense of importance and centrality of place in the universe.

"Yes, I am. I think you will find our new pin-matrix printer particularly appealing."

"And why is that?" Ming asked.

"Do you speak English?" Nomuri asked in that language.

"Certainly," Ming replied, in the same.

"Then it becomes simple to explain. If you transliterate Mandarin into English, the spelling, I mean, then the printer transposes into Mandarin ideographs automatically, like this," he explained, pulling a sheet of paper from his plastic folder and handing it to the secretary. "We are also working on a laser-printer system which will be even smoother in its appearance."

"Ah," the secretary observed. The quality of the characters was superb, easily the equal of the monstrous typewriting machine that secretaries had to use for official documents—or else have them hand-printed and then further processed on copying machines, mainly Canons, also of Japanese manufacture. The process was time-consuming, tedious, and much hated by the secretarial staff. "And what of inflection variations?"

Not a bad question, Nomuri noted. The Chinese language was highly dependent on inflection. The tone with which a word was delivered determined its actual meaning from as many as four distinct options, and it was also a determining factor in which ideograph it designated in turn.

"Do the characters appear on the computer screen in that way as well?" the secretary asked.

"They can, with just a click of the mouse," Nomuri assured her. "There may be a 'software' problem, insofar as you have to think simultaneously in two languages," he warned her with a smile.

Ming laughed. "Oh, we always do that here."

Her teeth would have benefited from a good orthodontist, Nomuri thought, but there weren't many of them in Beijing, along with the other bourgeois medical specialties, like reconstructive surgery. For all that, he'd gotten her to laugh, and that was something.

"Would you like to see me demonstrate our new capabilities?" the CIA field officer asked.

"Sure, why not?" She appeared a little disappointed that he wasn't able to do so right here and now.

"Excellent, but I will need you to authorize my bringing the hardware into the building. Your security people, you see."

How did I forget that? he saw her ask herself, blinking rather hard in a mild self-rebuke. Better to set the hook all the way.

"Do you have the authority for that, or must you consult someone more senior?" The most vulnerable point in any communist bureaucrat was their sense of importance-of-place.

A knowing smile: "Oh, yes, I can authorize that on my own authority."

A smile of his own: "Excellent. I can be here with my equipment at, say, ten in the morning."

"Good, the main entrance. They will be awaiting you."

"Thank you, Comrade Ming," Nomuri said with his best officious (short) bow to the young secretary—and, probably, mistress to her minister, the field officer thought. This one had possibilities, but he'd have to be careful with her both for himself and for her, he thought to himself while waiting for the elevator. That's why Langley paid him so much, not counting the princely salary from Nippon Electric Company that was his to keep. He needed it to survive here. The price of living was bad enough for a Chinese. For a foreigner, it was worse, because for foreigners everything was—had to be—special. The apartments were special—and almost certainly bugged. The food he bought in a special shop was more expensive—and Nomuri didn't object to that, since it was also almost certainly healthier.

China was what Nomuri called a thirty-foot country. Everything looked okay, even impressive, until you got within thirty feet of it. Then you saw that the parts didn't fit terribly well. He'd found it could be especially troublesome getting into an elevator, of all things. Dressed as he was in Western-made clothing (the Chinese thought of Japan as a Western country, which would have amused a lot of people, both in Japan and the West), he was immediately spotted as a *qwai*—a foreign devil—even before people saw his face. When that happened, the looks changed, sometimes to mere curiosity, sometimes to outright hostility, because the Chinese weren't like the Japanese; they weren't trained as thoroughly to conceal their feelings, or maybe they just didn't give a damn, the CIA officer thought behind his own blanked-out poker face. He'd learned the practice from his time in Tokyo, and learned it well, which explained both why he had a good job with NEC and why he'd never been burned in the field.

The elevator ran smoothly enough, but somehow it just didn't feel right. Maybe it was, again, because the pieces didn't quite seem to fit together. Nomuri hadn't had that feeling in Japan. For all their faults, the Japanese were competent engineers. The same was doubtless true of Taiwan, but Taiwan, like Japan, had a capitalist system which rewarded performance by giving it business and profits and comfortable salaries for the workers who turned out good work. The PRC was still learning how to do that. They exported a lot, but to this point the things exported were either fairly simple in design (like tennis shoes), or were manufactured mostly in strict accordance to standards established elsewhere and then slavishly copied here in China (like electronic gadgets).

This was already changing, of course. The Chinese people were as clever as any, and even communism could keep them down only so long. Yet the industrialists who were beginning to innovate and offer the world genuinely new products were treated by their government masters as . . . well, as unusually productive peasants at best. That was not a happy thought for the useful men who occasionally wondered over drinks why it was that they, the ones who brought wealth into their nation, were treated as . . . unusually productive peasants, by the ones who deemed themselves the masters of their country and their culture. Nomuri walked outside, toward his parked automobile, wondering how long *that* could last.

This whole political and economic policy was schizophrenic, Nomuri knew. Sooner or later, the industrialists would rise up and demand that they be given a voice in the political operation of their country. Perhaps—doubtless—such whispers had happened already. If so, word had gotten back to the whisperers that the tallest tree *is* quickly cut for lumber, and the well with the sweetest water *is* first to be drunk dry, and he who shouts too loudly *is* first to be silenced. So, maybe the Chinese industrial leaders were just biding their time and looking around the rooms where they gathered, wondering which of their number would be the first to take the risk, and maybe he would be rewarded with fame and honor and later memories of heroism—or maybe, more likely, his family would be billed for the 7.62×39 cartridge needed to send him into the next life, which Buddha had promised but which the government contemptuously denied.

So, they haven't made it public yet. That's a little odd," Ryan thought.

"It is," Ben Goodley agreed with a nod.

"Any idea why they're sitting on the news?"

"No, sir . . . unless somebody is hoping to cash in on it somehow, but exactly how . . ." CARDSHARP shrugged.

"Buy stock in Atlantic Richfield? Some mine-machine builder—"

"Or just buy options in some land in eastern Siberia," George Winston suggested. "Not that such a thing is ever done by the honorable servants of the people." The President laughed hard enough that he had to set his coffee down.

"Certainly not in this administration," POTUS pointed out. One of the benefits the media had with Ryan's team was that so many of them were plutocrats of one magnitude or another, not "working" men. It was as if the media thought that money just appeared in the hands of some fortunate souls by way of miracle . . . or some unspoken and undiscovered criminal activity. But never by work. It was the oddest of political prejudices that wealth didn't come from work, but rather from something else, a something never really described, but always implied to be suspect.

"Yeah, Jack," Winston said, with a laugh of his own. "We've got enough that we can afford to be honest. Besides, who the hell needs an oilfield or gold mine?"

"Further developments on the size of either?"

Goodley shook his head. "No, sir. The initial information is firming up nicely. Both discoveries are big. The oil especially, but the gold as well."

"The gold thing will distort the market somewhat," SecTreas opined. "Depending on how fast it comes on stream. It might also cause a shutdown of the mine we have operating in the Dakotas."

"Why?" Goodley asked.

"If the Russian strike is as good as the data suggests, they'll be producing gold for about twenty-five percent less than what it costs there, despite environmental conditions. The attendant reduction of the world price of gold will then make Dakota unprofitable to operate." Winston shrugged. "So, they'll mothball the site and sit until the price goes back up. Probably after the initial flurry of production, our Russian friends will scale things back so that they can cash in in a more, uh, orderly way. What'll happen is that the other producers, mainly South Africans, will meet with them and offer advice on how to exploit that find more efficiently. Usually the new kids listen to advice from the old guys. The Russians have coordinated diamond production with the De Beers people for a long time, back to when the country was called the Soviet Union. Business is business, even for commies. So, you going to offer our help to our friends in Moscow?" TRADER asked SWORDSMAN.

Ryan shook his head. "I can't yet. I can't let them know that we know. Sergey Nikolay'ch would start wondering how, and he'd probably come up with SIGINT, and that's a method of gathering information that we try to keep covert." Probably a waste of time, Ryan knew, but the game had rules, and everyone played by those rules. Golovko could guess at signals intelligence, but he'd never quite know. I'll probably never stop being a spook, the President admitted to himself. Keeping and guarding secrets was one of the things that came so easily to him—a little too easily, Arnie van Damm often warned. A modern democratic government was supposed to be more open, like a torn curtain on the bedroom window that allowed people to look in whenever they wished. That was an idea Ryan had never grown to appreciate. He was the one who decided what people were allowed to know and when they'd know it. It was a point of view he followed even when he knew it to be wrong, for no other reason than it was how he'd learned government service at the knee of an admiral named James Greer. Old habits were hard to break.

"I'll call Sam Sherman at Atlantic Richfield," Winston suggested. "If he breaks it to me, then it's in the open, or at least open enough."

"Can we trust him?"

Winston nodded. "Sam plays by the rules. We can't ask him to screw over his own board, but he knows what flag to salute, Jack."

"Okay, George, a discreet inquiry."

"Yes, sir, Mr. President, sir."

"God damn it, George!"

"Jack, when the hell are you going to learn to relax in this fucking job?" SecTreas asked POTUS.

"The day I move out of this goddamned museum and become a free man again," Ryan replied with a submissive nod. Winston was right. He had to learn to stay on a more even keel in the office of President. In addition to not being helpful to himself, it wasn't especially helpful to the country for him to be jumpy with the folderol of office-holding. That also made it easy for people like the Secretary of the Treasury to twist his tail, and George Winston was one of the people who enjoyed doing that . . . maybe because it ultimately helped him relax, Ryan thought. Backwards English on the ball or something. "George, why do you think I *should* relax in this job?"

"Jack, because you're here to be effective, and being tight all the time does not make you more effective. Kick back, guy, maybe even learn to like some aspect of it."

"Like what?"

"Hell." Winston shrugged, and then nodded to the secretaries' office. "Lots of cute young interns out there."

"There's been enough of that," Ryan said crossly. Then he did manage to relax and smile a little. "Besides, I'm married to a surgeon. Make that little mistake and I could wake up without something important."

"Yeah, I suppose it's bad for the country to have the President's dick cut off, eh? People might not respect us anymore." Winston stood. "Gotta go back across the street and look at some economic models."

"Economy looking good?" POTUS asked.

"No complaints from me or Mark Gant. Just so the Fed Chairman leaves the discount rate alone, but I expect he will. Inflation is pretty flat, and there's no upward pressure anywhere that I see happening."

"Ben?"

Goodley looked through his notes, as though he'd forgotten something. "Oh, yeah. Would you believe, the Vatican is appointing a Papal Nuncio to the PRC?"

"Oh? What's that mean, exactly?" Winston asked, stopping halfway to the door.

"The Nuncio is essentially an ambassador. People forget that the Vatican is a nation-state in its own right and has the usual trappings of statehood. That includes diplomatic representation. A nuncio is just that, an ambassador—and a spook," Ryan added.

"Really?" Winston asked.

"George, the Vatican has the world's oldest intelligence service. Goes back centuries. And, yeah, the Nuncio gathers information and forwards it to the home office, because people talk to him—who better to talk to than a priest, right? They're good enough at gathering information that we've made the occasional effort to crack their communications. Back in the '30s, a senior cryppie at the State Department resigned over it," Ryan informed his SecTreas, reverting back to history teacher.

"We still do that?" Winston directed this question at Goodley, the President's National Security Adviser. Goodley looked first to Ryan, and got a nod. "Yes, sir. Fort Meade still takes a look at their messages. Their ciphers are a little old-fashioned, and we can brute-force them."

"And ours?"

"The current standard is called TAPDANCE. It's totally random, and therefore it's theoretically unbreakable—unless somebody screws up and reuses a segment of it, but with approximately six hundred forty-seven million transpositions on every daily CD-ROM diskette, that's not very likely."

"What about the phone systems?"

"The STU?" Goodley asked, getting a nod. "That's computer-based, with a two-fifty-six-kay computer-generated encryption key. It *can* be broken, but you need a computer, the right algorithm, and a couple of weeks at least, and the shorter the message the harder it is to crack it, instead of the other way around. The guys at Fort Meade are playing with using quantum-physics equations to crack ciphers, and evidently they're having some success, but if you want an explanation, you're going to have to ask somebody else. I didn't even pretend to listen," Goodley admitted. "It's so far over my head I can't even see the bottom of it."

"Yeah, get your friend Gant involved," Ryan suggested. "He seems to know 'puters pretty well. As a matter of fact, you might want to get him briefed in on these developments in Russia. Maybe he can model the effects they'll have on the Russian economy."

"Only if everyone plays by the rules," Winston said in warning. "If they follow the corruption that's been gutting their economy the last few years, you just can't predict anything, Jack."

"We cannot let it happen again, Comrade President," Sergey Nikolay'ch said over a half-empty glass of vodka. This was still the best in the world, if the only such Russian product of which he could make that boast. *That* thought generated an angry frown at what his nation had become.

"Sergey Nikolay'ch, what do you propose?"

"Comrade President, these two discoveries are a gift from Heaven itself. If we utilize them properly, we can transform our country—or at least make a proper beginning at doing that. The earnings in hard currencies will be colossal, and we can use that money to rebuild so much of our infrastructure that we *can* transform our economy. *If,* that is"—he held up a cautionary finger—"if we don't allow a thieving few to take the money and bank it in Geneva or Liechtenstein. It does us no good there, Comrade President."

Golovko didn't add that a few people, a few well-placed individuals, would profit substantially from this. He didn't even add that he himself would be one of them, and so would his president. It was just too much to ask any man to walk away from such an opportunity. Integrity was a virtue best found among those able to afford it, and the press be damned, the career intelligence officer thought. What had they ever done for his country or any other? All they did was expose the honest work of some and the dishonest work of others, doing little actual work themselves—and besides, they were as easily bribed as anyone else, weren't they?

"And so, who gets the concession to exploit these resources?" the Russian president asked.

"In the case of the oil, our own exploration company, plus the American company, Atlantic Richfield. They have the most experience in producing oil in those environmental conditions anyway, and our people have much to learn from them. I would propose a fee-for-service arrangement, a generous one, but *not* an ownership percentage in the oil field itself. The exploration contract was along those lines, generous in absolute terms, but no share at all in the fields discovered."

"And the gold strike?"

"Easier still. No foreigners were involved in that discovery at all. Comrade Gogol will have an interest in the discovery, of course, but he is an old man with no heirs, and, it would seem, a man of the simplest tastes. A properly heated hut and a new hunting rifle will probably make him very happy, from what these reports tell us."

"And the value of this venture?"

"Upwards of seventy billions. And all we need do is purchase some special equipment, the best of which comes from the American company Caterpillar."

"Is that necessary, Sergey?"

"Comrade President, the Americans are our friends, after a fashion, and it will not hurt us to remain on good terms with their President. And besides, their heavy equipment is the world's finest."

"Better than the Japanese?"

"For these purposes, yes, but slightly more expensive," Golovko answered, thinking that people really were all the same, and despite the education of his youth, in every man there seemed to be a capitalist, looking for ways to cut costs and increase his profits, often to the point of forgetting the larger issues. Well, that was why Golovko was here, wasn't it?

"And who will want the money?"

A rare chuckle in this office: "Comrade President, *everyone* wants to have money. In realistic terms, our military will be at the front of the line."

"Of course," the Russian president agreed, with a resigned sigh. "They usually are. Oh, any progress in the attack on your car?" he asked, looking up from his briefing papers.

Golovko shook his head. "No notable progress, no. The current thinking is that this Avseyenko fellow was the actual target, and the automobile was just a coincidence. The militia continues to investigate."

"Keep me posted, will you?"

"Of course, Comrade President."

CHAPTER 5

Headlines

Sam Sherman was one of those whom age hadn't treated kindly, though he himself hadn't helped. An avid golfer, he moved from lie to lie via cart. He was much too overweight to walk more than a few hundred yards in a day. It was rather sad for one who'd been a first-string guard for the Princeton Tigers, once upon a time. Well, Winston thought, muscle just turned to blubber if you didn't use it properly. But the overweight body didn't detract from the sharpness of his brain. Sherman had graduated about fifth in a class not replete with dummies, double-majoring in geology and business. He'd followed up the first sheet of parchment with a Harvard MBA, and a Ph.D. from the University of Texas, this one in geology as well, and so Samuel Price Sherman could not only talk rocks with the explorers but finance with his board members, and that was one of the reasons why Atlantic Richfield stock was as healthy as any oil issue in the known world. His face was lined by a lot of low sun and field grit, and his belly swollen by a lot of beers with the roughnecks out in many godforsaken places, plus hot dogs and other junk food preferred by the men who drifted into such employment. Winston was surprised that Sam didn't smoke, too. Then he spotted the box on the man's desk. Cigars. Probably good ones. Sherman could afford the best, but he still had the Ivy League manners not to light up in front of a guest who might be offended by the blue cloud they generated.

Atlantic Richfield's home office was elsewhere, but as with most major corporations, it didn't hurt to have a set of offices in Washington, the better to influence members of Congress with the occasional lavish party. Sherman's personal office was in a corner on the top floor, and plush enough, with a thick beige carpet. The desk was either mahogany or well-seasoned oak, polished like glass, and probably cost more than his secretary made in a year or two.

"So, how do you like working for the government, George?"

"It's really a fun change of pace. Now I can play with all the things I used to bitch about—so, I guess I've kinda given up my right to bitch."

"That is a major sacrifice, buddy," Sherman replied with a laugh. "It's kinda like going over to the enemy, isn't it?"

"Well, sometimes you gotta pay back, Sam, and making policy the right way can be diverting."

"Well, I have no complaints with what you guys are doing. The economy seems to like it. Anyway," Sherman sat up in his comfortable chair. It was time to change subjects. Sam's time was valuable, too, as he wanted his guest to appreciate. "You didn't come here for small talk. What can I do for you, Mr. Secretary?"

"Russia."

Sherman's eyes changed a little, as they might when the last card was laid in a high-stakes game of stud. "What about it?"

"You have a high-powered exploration team working with the Russians . . . they find anything nice?"

"George, that's sensitive stuff you're asking. If you were still running Columbus, this would constitute insider-trading information stuff. Hell, *I* can't buy any more of our stock now, based on this stuff."

"Does that mean you'd like to?" TRADER asked with a smile.

"Well, it'll be public soon enough anyway. Yeah, George. Looks like we've found the biggest goddamned oil field ever, bigger 'n the Persian Gulf, bigger 'n Mexico, damned sight bigger than Prudhoe Bay and Western Canada combined. I'm talking big, *billions and billions* of barrels of what looks like the very best light-sweet crude, just sitting there and waiting for us to pump it out of the tundra. It's a field we'll measure in years of production, not just barrels."

"Bigger than the P.G.?"

Sherman nodded. "By a factor of forty percent, and that's a very conservative number. The only beef is where it is. Getting that crude out is going to be a mother-humper—to get started, anyway. We're talking twenty billion dollars just for the pipeline. It'll make Alaska look like a kindergarten project, but it'll be worth it."

"And your end of it?" the Secretary of the Treasury asked.

That question generated a frown. "We're negotiating that now. The Russians seem to want to pay us a flat consulting fee, like a billion dollars a year—they're talking a lot less than that now, but you know how the hog-tradin' works at this stage, right? They say a couple of hundred million, but they mean a billion a year, for seven to ten years, I'd imagine. And that isn't bad for what we'd have to do for the money, but I want a minimum of five percent of the find, and that's not at all an unreasonable request on our part. They have some good people in the geology business, but nobody in the world can sniff out oil in ice like my people can, and they've got a lot to learn about how to exploit something like this. We've been there and done that in these environmental conditions. Ain't nobody knows this like we do, even the guys at BP, and they're pretty good—but we're the best in the world, George. That's the barrel we have them over. They can do it without us, but with us helping, they'll make a ton more cash, and a hell of a lot faster, and they know that, and we know they know that. So, I got my lawyers talking to their lawyers—actually, they have diplomats doing the negotiating." Sherman managed a grin. "They're dumber than my lawyers."

Winston nodded. Texas turned out more good private-practice attorneys than most parts of America, and the excuse was that in Texas there were more men needin' killin' than horses needin' stealin'. And the oil business paid the best, and in Texas, like everyplace else, talent went where the money was.

"When will this go public?"

"The Russians are trying to keep a cork in it. One of the things we're getting from our lawyers is that they're worried about how to exploit this one—really who to keep out of it, you know, their Mafia and stuff. They do have some serious corruption problems over there, and I can sympathize—"

Winston knew he could ignore the next part. The oil industry did business all over the world. Dealing with corruption on the small scale (ten million dollars or less), or even the monstrous scale (ten *billion* dollars or more), was just part of the territory for such companies as Sam

Sherman ran, and the United States government had never probed too deeply into that. Though there were federal statutes governing how American companies handled themselves abroad, many of those laws were selectively enforced, and this was merely one such example. Even in Washington, business was business.

"—and so they're trying to keep it quiet until they can make the proper arrangements," Sherman concluded.

"You hearing anything else?"

"What do you mean?" Sherman asked in reply.

"Any other geological windfalls," Winston clarified.

"No, I'm not that greedy in what I pray for. George, I haven't made it clear enough, just how huge this oil field is. It's—"

"Relax, Sam, I can add and subtract with the best of 'em," SecTreas assured his host.

"Something I need to know about?" Sherman only saw hesitation. "Give and take, George. I played fair with you, remember?"

"Gold," Winston clarified.

"How much?"

"They're not sure. South Africa at least. Maybe more."

"Really? Well, that's not my area of expertise, but sounds like our Russian friends are having a good year for a change. Good for them," Sherman thought.

"You like them?"

"Yeah, as a matter of fact. They're a lot like Texans. They make good friends and fearsome enemies. They know how to entertain, and Jesus, do they know how to drink. About time they got some good luck. Christ knows they've had a lot of the other kind. This is going to mean a lot for their economy, and damned near all of it's going to be good news, 'specially if they can handle the corruption stuff and keep the money inside their borders where it'll do them some good, instead of finding its way onto some Swiss bank's computer. That new Mafia they have over there is smart and tough . . . and a little scary. They just got somebody I knew over there."

"Really? Who was that, Sam?"

"We called him Grisha. He took care of some high rollers in Moscow. Knew how to do it right. He was a good name to know if you had some special requirements," Sherman allowed. Winston recorded the information in his mind for later investigation.

"Killed him?"

Sherman nodded. "Yup, blew him away with a bazooka right there on the street—it made CNN, remember?" The TV news network had covered it as a crime story with no further significance except for its dramatic brutality, a story gone and forgotten in a single day.

George Winston vaguely remembered it, and set it aside. "How often you go over there?"

"Not too often, twice this year. Usually hop my G-V over direct out of Reagan or Dallas/Fort Worth. Long flight, but it's a one-hop. No, I haven't seen the new oil field yet. Expect I'll have to in a few months, but I'll try for decent weather. Boy, you don't know what cold means 'til you go that far north in the winter. Thing is, it's dark then, so you're better off waiting 'til summer anyway. But at best you can leave the sticks at home. Ain't no golf a' tall in that part of the world, George."

"So take a rifle and bag yourself a bear, make a nice rug," Winston offered.

"Gave that up. Besides, I got three polar bears. That one is number eight in the Boone and Crockett all-time book," Sherman said, pointing to a photo on the far wall. Sure enough, it showed a hell of a big polar bear. "I've made two kids on that rug," the president of Atlantic Richfield observed, with a sly smile. The pelt in question lay before his bedroom fireplace in Aspen, Colorado, where his wife liked to ski in the winter.

"Why'd you give it up?"

"My kids think there aren't enough polar bears anymore. All that ecology shit they learn in school now."

"Yeah," SecTreas said sympathetically, "and they do make such great rugs."

"Right, well, *that* rug was threatening some of our workers up at Prudhoe Bay back in . . . '75, as I recall, and I took him at sixty yards with my .338 Winchester. One shot," the Texan assured his guest. "I suppose nowadays you have to let the bear kill a human bein', and then all you're supposed to do is just cage him and transport him to another location so the bear doesn't get too traumatized, right?"

"Sam, I'm Secretary of the Treasury. I leave the birds and bees to EPA. I don't hug trees, not until they turn the wood chips into T-Bills, anyway."

A chuckle: "Sorry, George. I'm always hearing that stuff at home. Maybe it's Disney. All wild animals wear white gloves and talk to each other in good Midwestern Iowa English."

"Cheer up, Sam. At least they're laying off the supertankers out of Valdez now. How much of the eastern Alaska/Western Canada strike is yours?"

"Not quite half, but that'll keep my stockholders in milk and cookies for a long time."

"So, between that one and Siberia, how many options will they give you to exercise?" Sam Sherman got a nice salary, but at his level the way you earned your keep was measured in the number of options in the stock whose value your work had increased, invariably offered you by the board of directors, whose own holdings you inflated in value through your efforts.

A knowing smile, and a raised eyebrow: "A lot, George. Quite a lot."

Married life agrees with you, Andrea," President Ryan observed with a smile at his Principal Agent. She was dressing better, and there was a definite spring in her step now. He wasn't sure if her skin had a new glow, or maybe her makeup was just different. Jack had learned never to comment on a woman's makeup. He always got it wrong.

"You're not the only one to say that, sir."

"One hesitates to say such things to a grown adult female, especially if you're fashion-bereft, as I am," Jack said, his smile broadening somewhat. His wife, Cathy, still said she had to dress him because his taste was entirely, she said, in his mouth. "But the change is sufficiently marked that even a man such as myself can see it."

"Thank you, Mr. President. Pat is a very good man, even for a Bureau puke."

"What's he doing now?"

"He's up in Philadelphia right now. Director Murray sent him off on a bank robbery, two local cops got killed in that one."

"Caught that one on TV last week. Bad."

The Secret Service agent nodded. "The way the subjects killed the cops, both in the back of the head, that was pretty ruthless, but there's people out there like that. Anyway, Director Murray decided to handle that one with a Roving Inspector out of Headquarters Division, and that usually means Pat gets to go do it."

"Tell him to be careful," Ryan said. Inspector Pat O'Day had saved his daughter's life less than a year before, and that act had earned him undying Presidential solicitude.

"Every day, sir," Special Agent Price-O'Day made clear.

"Okay, what's the schedule look like?" His "business" appointments were on his desk already. Andrea Price-O'Day filled him in every morning, after his national-security briefing from Ben Goodley.

"Nothing unusual until after lunch. National Chamber of Commerce delegation at one-thirty, and then at three the Detroit Red Wings, they won the Stanley Cup this year. Photo op, TV pukes and stuff, take about twenty minutes or so."

"I ought to let Ed Foley do that one. He's the hockey fanatic—"

"He's a Caps fan, sir, and the Red Wings swept the Caps four straight in the finals. Director Foley might take it personally," Price-O'Day observed with half a smile.

"True. Well, last year we got the jerseys and stuff for his son, didn't we?"

"Yes, sir."

"Good game, hockey. Maybe I ought to catch a game or two. Trouble to arrange that?"

"No, sir. We have standing agreements with all the local sports facilities. Camden Yards even has that special box for us—they let us help design it, the protective stuff, that is."

Ryan grunted. "Yeah, I have to remember all the people who'd like to see me dead."

"My job to think about that, sir, not yours," Price-O'Day told him.

"Except when you won't let me go shopping or to a movie." Neither Ryan nor his family was entirely used to the restrictions imposed on the life of the President of the United States or his immediate family members. It was getting especially tough on Sally, who'd started dating (which was hard on her father), and dating was difficult with a lead car and a chase car (when the young gentleman drove himself) or an official car with a driver and a second armed agent up front (when he did not), and guns all over the place. It tended to restrain the young gentlemen in question—and Ryan hadn't told his daughter that this was just fine with him, lest she stop speaking to him for a week or so. Sally's Principal Agent, Wendy Merritt, had proven to be both a good Secret Service agent and a superb big sister of sorts. They spent at least two Saturdays per month shopping with a reduced detail—actually it wasn't reduced at all, but it appeared so to Sally Ryan when they went out to Tyson's Corner or the Annapolis Mall for the purpose of spending money, something for which all women seemed to have a genetic predisposition. That these shopping expeditions had been planned days in advance, with every site scouted by the Secret Service, and a supplementary detail of young agents selected for their relative invisibility who showed up there an hour before SHADOW's arrival, had never occurred to Sally Ryan. That was just as well, as the dating problems grated on her badly enough, along with being followed around St. Mary's School in Annapolis by the rifle squad, as she sometimes termed it. Little Jack, on the other hand, thought it was pretty neat, and had recently learned to shoot at the Secret Service Academy in Beltsville, Maryland, with his father's permission (and something he'd not allowed the press to learn, lest he get hammered on the front page of *The New York Times* for the social indiscretion of *encouraging* his own son to touch, much less actually to fire, something so inherently evil as a pistol!). Little Jack's Principal Agent was a kid named Mike Brennan, a South Boston Irishman, a third-generation Secret Service agent with fiery red hair and a ready laugh, who'd played baseball at Holy Cross and frequently played catch and pepper with the President's son on the South Lawn of the White House.

"Sir, we never don't let you do anything," Price said.

"No, you're pretty subtle about it," Ryan allowed. "You know that I'm too considerate of other people, and when you tell me about all the crap you people have to go through so that I can buy a burger at Wendy's, I usually back off . . . like a damned wimp." The President shook his head. Nothing frightened him more than the prospect that he'd somehow get used to all this panoply of "specialness," as he thought of it. As though he'd only recently discovered royal parentage, and was now to be treated like a king, hardly allowed to wipe his own ass after taking a dump. Doubtless some people who'd lived in this house *had* gotten used to it, but that was something John Patrick Ryan, Sr., wanted to avoid. He knew that *he* was *not* all that special, and not deserving of all this folderol . . . and besides, like every other man in the world, when he woke up in the morning the first thing he did was head to the bathroom. Chief Executive he might be, but he still had a working-class bladder. *And thank God for that,* the President of the United States reflected.

"Where's Robby today?"

"Sir, the Vice President is in California today, the Navy base at Long Beach, giving a speech at the shipyard."

Ryan grinned a little sideways. "I work him pretty hard, don't I?"

"That's the Vice President's job," Arnie van Damm said from the door. "And Robby's a big boy about it," added the President's Chief of Staff.

"Your vacation was good for you," Ryan observed. He had a very nice tan. "What did you do?"

"Mainly I laid on the beach and read all the books I haven't had time for. Thought I'd die of boredom," van Damm added.

"You actually thrive on this crap, don't you?" Jack asked, a little incredulous at the thought.

"It's what I do, Mr. President. Hey, Andrea," he added with a slight turn of the head.

"Good morning, Mr. van Damm." She turned to Jack. "That's all I have for you this morning. If you need me, I'll be in the usual place." Her office was in the Old Executive Office Building, just across the street, and upstairs from the new Secret Service command post, called JOC, for Joint Operations Center.

"Okay, Andrea, thanks." Ryan nodded, as she withdrew into the secretaries' room, from which she'd head down to the Secret Service Command Post. "Arnie, get some coffee?"

"Not a bad idea, boss." The Chief of Staff took his usual seat and poured a cup. The coffee in the White House was especially good, a rich blend, about half Colombian and half Jamaica Blue Mountain, the sort of thing that Ryan *could* get used to as President. There had to be *some* place he could buy this after escaping from his current job, he hoped.

"Okay, I've had my national security brief and my Secret Service brief. Now tell me about politics for the day."

"Hell, Jack, I've been trying to do that for over a year now, and you still aren't getting it very well."

Ryan allowed his eyes to flare at the simulated insult. "That's a cheap shot, Arnie. I've been studying this crap pretty hard, and even the damned newspapers say I'm doing fairly well."

"The Federal Reserve is doing a brilliant job of handling the economy, Mr. President, and that has damned little to do with you. But since you *are* the President, you get credit for all the good things that happen, and that's nice, but do remember, you will also get the blame for all the *bad* things that are going to happen—and some will, remember that—because you just happen to be here, and the citizens out there think you can make the rain fall on their flowers and the sun come out for their picnics just by wishing it so.

"You know, Jack," the Chief of Staff said after sipping his coffee. "We really haven't got past the idea of kings and queens. A lot of people really do think you have that sort of personal power—"

"But I don't, Arnie, how can that be?"

"It just is the truth, Jack. It doesn't have to make sense. It just is. Deal with it."

I do so love these lessons, Ryan thought to himself. "Okay, today is . . . ?"

"Social Security."

Ryan's eyes relaxed. "I've been reading up on that. The third rail of American political life. Touch it and die."

For the next half hour, they discussed what was wrong and why, and the irresponsibility of the Congress, until Jack sat back with a sigh.

"Why don't they learn, Arnie?"

"What do they need to learn?" Arnie asked, with the grin of a Washington insider, one of the anointed of God. "They've been *elected.* They must know it all already! How *else* do you think they got here?"

"Why the hell did I allow myself to stay in this damned place?" the President asked rhetorically.

"Because you had a conscience attack and decided to do the right thing for your country, you dumbass, that's why."

"Why is it you're the only person who can talk to me like that?"

"Besides the Vice President? Because I'm your teacher. Back to today's lesson. We *could* leave Social Security alone this year. It's in decent enough fiscal shape to last another seven to nine years without intervention, and that means you could leave it to your successor to handle—"

"That's not ethical, Arnie," Ryan snapped.

"True," the Chief of Staff agreed, "but it's good politics, and fairly Presidential. It's called letting sleeping dogs lie."

"You don't do that in the knowledge that as soon as it wakes up, it's going to rip the baby's throat out."

"Jack, you really ought to be a king. You'd be a good one," van Damm said, with what appeared to be genuine admiration.

"Nobody can handle that kind of power."

"I know: 'Power corrupts, and absolute power is actually pretty neat.' So said a staffer for one of your predecessors."

"And the bastard wasn't hanged for saying it?"

"We need to work on that sense of humor, Mr. President. That was meant as a joke."

"The scariest part of this job is that I do see the humor of it. Anyway, I told George Winston to start a quiet project to see what we can do with Social Security. Quiet project, I mean classified—black, this project doesn't exist."

"Jack, if you have one weakness as President, that's it. You're into this secrecy thing too much."

"But if you do something like this in the open, you get clobbered by ill-informed criticism before you manage to produce anything, and the press crawls up your ass demanding information you don't have yet, and so then they go make up stuff on their own, or they go to some yahoo who just makes up bullshit, and then *we* have to answer it."

"You are learning," Arnie judged. "That's exactly how it works in this town."

"That does not constitute 'working' by any definition I know of."

"This is Washington, a government town. Nothing is really supposed to function efficiently here. It would scare the hell out of the average citizen if the government started to function properly."

"How about I just fucking resign?" Jack asked the ceiling. "If I can't get this damned mess to start working, then why the hell am I here?"

"You're here because some Japanese 747 pilot decided to crash the party at the House Chamber fifteen months ago."

"I suppose, Arnie, but I still feel like a damned fraud."

"Well, by my old standards, you are a fraud, Jack."

Ryan looked up. "Old standards?"

"Even when Bob Fowler took over the statehouse in Ohio, Jack, even he didn't try as hard as you to play a fair game, and Bob got captured by the system, too. You haven't yet, and that's what I like about you. More to the point, that's what Joe Citizen likes about you. They may not like your positions, but everybody knows you try damned hard, and they're sure you're not corrupt. And you're not. Now: Back to Social Security."

"I told George to get a small group together, swear them to secrecy, and make recommendations—more than one—and at least one of them has to be completely outside the box."

"Who's running this?"

"Mark Gant, George's technical guy."

The Chief of Staff thought that one over for a moment. "Just as well you keep it quiet. The Hill doesn't like him. Too much of a smart-ass."

"And they're not?" SWORDSMAN asked.

"You were naïve with that, Jack. The people you tried to get elected, non-politicians, well, you semi-succeeded. A lot of them *were* regular people, but what you didn't allow for was the seductive nature of life in elected government service. The money isn't all that great, but the perks are, and a lot of people *like* being treated like a medieval prince. A lot of people *like* being able to enforce their will on the world. The people who used to be there, the ones that pilot fried in their seats, they started off as pretty good people, too, but the nature of the job is to seduce and capture. Actually, the mistake you made was to allow them to keep their staffs. Honestly, I think the problem down there is in the staffers, not the bosses. You have ten or more people around you all the time telling you how great you are, sooner or later you start believing that crap."

"Just so you don't do that to me."

"Not in this lifetime," Arnie assured him, as he stood to leave. "Make sure Secretary Winston keeps me in the loop on the Social Security project."

"No leaks," Ryan told his Chief of Staff forcefully.

"Me? Leak something? Me?" van Damm replied with open hands and an innocent face.

"Yeah, Arnie, you." As the door closed, the President wondered how fine a spook Arnie might have made. He lied with the plausibility one might associate with a trusted member of the clergy, and he could hold all manner of contradictory thoughts in his head at the same time, like the best of circus jugglers . . . and somehow they never quite crashed to earth. Ryan was the current president, but the one member of the administration who could not be replaced was the chief of staff he'd inherited from Bob Fowler, by way of Roger Durling . . .

And yet, Jack wondered, how much was he being manipulated by this staff employee? The truthful answer was that he couldn't tell, and that was somewhat troubling. He trusted Arnie, but he trusted Arnie because he had to trust him. Jack would not know what to do without him . . . but was that a good thing?

Probably not, Ryan admitted to himself, checking over his appointment list, but neither was being here in the Oval Office, and Arnie was at worst one more thing not to like about this job, and at best, he was a scrupulously honest, extremely hardworking, and utterly dedicated public servant . . .

. . . *just like everyone else in Washington, D.C.,* Ryan's cynicism added.

CHAPTER 6

Expansion

Moscow is eight hours ahead of Washington, a source of annoyance to diplomats who are either a day behind the times or too far out of synch with their body clocks to conduct business properly. This was more a problem for the Russians, as by five or six in the evening, most of them had had a few stiff drinks, and given the relative speed of all diplomatic exchange, it was well into the falling night in Moscow before American diplomats emerged from their "working lunches" to issue a démarche or communiqué, or a simple letter of reply to whatever the Russians had issued the previous working day. In both capitals, of course, there was always a night crew to read and evaluate things on a more timely basis, but these were underlings, or at best people on their way up but not quite there yet, who always had to judge which possibility was worse: waking up a boss with something unworthy of the nighttime phone call, or delaying until the post-breakfast morning something that the minister or secretary ought to have been informed of *right now!* And more than one career had been made or broken on such seeming trivialities.

In this particular case, it would not be a diplomat's hide at risk. It was six-fifteen on the Russian spring evening, the sun high in the sky still, in anticipation of the "White Nights" for which the Russian summer is justly famous.

"Yes, Pasha?" Lieutenant Provalov said. He'd taken over Klusov from Shablikov. This case was too important to leave in anyone else's hands—and besides, he'd never really trusted Shablikov: There was something a little too corrupt about him.

Pavel Petrovich Klusov was not exactly an advertisement for the quality of life in the new Russia. Hardly one hundred sixty-five centimeters or so in height, but close to ninety kilos, he was a man the bulk of whose calories came in liquid form, who shaved poorly when he bothered at all, and whose association with soap was less intimate than it ought to have been. His teeth were crooked and yellow from the lack of brushing and a surfeit of smoking cheap, unfiltered domestic cigarettes. He was thirty-five or so, and had perhaps a fifty-fifty chance of making forty-five, Provalov estimated. It was not as though he'd be much of a loss to society, of course. Klusov was a petty thief, lacking even the talent—or courage—to be a major violator of the law. But he knew those who were, and evidently scampered around them like a small dog, performing minor services, like fetching a bottle of vodka, the Militia lieutenant thought. But Klusov did have ears, which many people, especially criminals, had an odd inability to consider.

"Avseyenko was killed by two men from St. Petersburg. I do not know their names, but I think they were hired by Klementi Ivan'ch Suvorov. The killers are former Spetsnaz soldiers with experience in Afghanistan, in their late thirties, I think. One is blond, the other red-haired. After killing Grisha, they flew back north before noon on an Aeroflot flight."

"That is good, Pasha. Have you seen their faces?"

A shake of the head: "No, Comrade Lieutenant. I learned this from . . . someone I know, in a drinking place." Klusov lit a new cigarette with the end of its predecessor.

"Did your acquaintance say why our friend Suvorov had Avseyenko killed?" *And who the hell is Klementi Ivan'ch Suvorov?* the policeman wondered. He hadn't heard that name before, but didn't want Klusov to know that quite yet. Better to appear omniscient.

The informant shrugged. "Both were KGB, maybe there was bad blood between them."

"What exactly is Suvorov doing now?"

Another shrug: "I don't know. Nobody does. I am told he lives well, but the source of his income, no one knows."

"Cocaine?" the cop asked.

"It is possible, but I do not know." The one good thing about Klusov was that he didn't invent things. He told the (relatively) unvarnished truth . . . most of the time, the militia lieutenant told himself.

Provalov's mind was already spinning. Okay, a former KGB officer had hired two former Spetsnaz soldiers to eliminate another former KGB officer who'd specialized in running girls. Had this Suvorov chap approached Avseyenko for cooperation in a drug venture? Like most Moscow cops, he'd never grown to like the KGB. They'd been arrogant bullies most of the time, too besotted with their power to perform proper investigations, except against foreigners, for whom the niceties of civilized behavior were necessary, lest foreign nations treat Soviet citizens—worse, Soviet diplomats—the same way.

But so many KGB officers had been let go by their parent service, and few of them had drifted into menial labor. No, they had training in conspiracy, and many had done foreign travel, and there met all manner of people, most of whom, Provalov was sure, could be persuaded to undertake illegal operations for the right inducement, which invariably meant money. For money, people would do anything, a fact known by every police officer in every country in the world.

Suvorov. Must track that name down, the militia lieutenant told himself as he took a casual sip of his vodka. *Examine his background, determine his expertise, and get a photo.* Suvorov, Klementi Ivanovich.

"Anything else?" the lieutenant asked.

Klusov shook his head. "That is all I have uncovered."

"Well, not too bad. Get back to work, and call me when you discover more."

"Yes, Comrade Lieutenant." The informant stood up to leave. He left the bill with the cop, who'd pay it without much in the way of annoyance. Oleg Gregoriyevich Provalov had spent enough time in police work to understand that he might just have discovered something important. Of course, you couldn't tell at this stage, not until you ran it down, every single option and blind alley, which could take rather some time . . . but if it turned out to be something important, then it was worth it. And if not, it was just another blind alley, of which there were many in police work.

Provalov reflected on the fact that he hadn't asked his informant exactly who had given him this new flood of information. He hadn't forgotten, but perhaps had allowed himself to be a little gulled by the descriptions of the alleged former Spetsnaz soldiers who'd made the murder. He had their descriptions in his mind, and then removed his pad to write them down. Blond and red-haired, experience in Afghanistan, both living in St. Petersburg, flew back just before noon on the day Avseyenko was murdered. So, he would check for the flight number and run the names on the manifest through the new computers Aeroflot used to tie into the global ticketing system, then cross-check it against his own computer with its index of known and suspected criminals, and also with the army's records. If he got a hit, he'd have a man talk to the cabin crew of that Moscow–St. Petersburg flight to see if anyone remembered one or both of them. Then he'd have the St. Petersburg militia do a discreet check of these people, their addresses, criminal records if any, a normal and thorough background check, leading, possibly, to an interview. He might not conduct it himself, but he'd be there to observe, to get a feel for the suspects, because there was no substitute for that, for looking in their eyes, seeing how they talked, how they sat, if they fidgeted or not, if the eyes held those of the questioner, or traveled about the room. Did they smoke then, and if so, rapidly and nervously or slowly and contemptuously . . . or just curiously, as would be the case if they were innocent of this charge, if not, perhaps, of another.

The militia lieutenant paid the bar bill and headed outside.

"You need to pick a better place for your meets, Oleg," a familiar voice suggested from behind. Provalov turned to see the face.

"It is a big city, Mishka, with many drinking places, and most of them are poorly lit."

"And I found yours, Oleg Gregoriyevich," Reilly reminded him. "So, what have you learned?"

Provalov summarized what he'd found out this evening.

"Two shooters from Spetsnaz? I suppose that makes some sense. What would that cost?"

"It would not be inexpensive. As a guess . . . oh, five thousand euros or so," the lieutenant speculated as they walked up the street.

"And who would have that much money to throw around?"

"A Muscovite criminal . . . Mishka, as you well know, there are hundreds who could afford it, and Rasputin wasn't the most popular of men . . . and I have a new name, Suvorov, Klementi Ivan'ch."

"Who is he?"

"I do not know. It is a new name for me, but Klosov acted as though I ought to have known it well. Strange that I do not," Provalov thought aloud.

"It happens. I've had wise guys turn up from nowhere, too. So, check him out?"

"Yes, I will run the name. Evidently he, too, is former KGB."

"There are a lot of them around," Reilly agreed, steering his friend into a new hotel's bar.

"What will you do when CIA is broken up?" Provalov asked.

"Laugh," the FBI agent promised.

The city of St. Petersburg was known to some as the Venice of the North for the rivers and canals that cut through it, though the climate, especially in winter, could hardly have been more different. And it was in one of those rivers that the next clue appeared.

A citizen had spotted it on his way to work in the morning, and, seeing a militiaman at the next corner, he'd walked that way and pointed, and the policeman had walked back, and looked over the iron railing at the space designated by the passing citizen.

It wasn't much to see, but it only took a second for the cop to know what it was and what it would mean. Not garbage, not a dead animal, but the top of a human head, with blond or light brown hair. A suicide or a murder, something for the local cops to investigate. The militiaman walked to the nearest phone to make his call to headquarters, and in thirty minutes a car showed up, followed in short order by a black van. By this time, the militiaman on his beat had smoked two cigarettes in the crisp morning air, occasionally looking down into the water to make sure that the object was still there. The arriving men were detectives from the city's homicide bureau. The van that had followed them had a pair of people called technicians, though they had really been trained in the city's public-works department, which meant water-and-sewer workers, though they were paid by the local militia. These two men took a look over the rail, which was enough to tell them that recovering the body would be physically difficult but routine. A ladder was set up, and the junior man, dressed in waterproof coveralls and heavy rubber gauntlets, climbed down and grabbed the submerged collar, while his partner observed and shot a few frames from his cheap camera and the three policemen on the scene observed and smoked from a few feet away. That's when the first surprise happened.

The routine was to put a flexible collar on the body under the arms, like that used by a rescue helicopter, so that the body could be winched up. But when he worked to get the collar under the body, one of the arms wouldn't move at all, and the worker struggled for several unpleasant minutes, working to get the stiff dead arm upward . . . and eventually found that it was handcuffed to another arm.

That revelation caused both detectives to toss their cigarettes into the water. It was probably not a suicide, since that form of death was generally not a team sport. The sewer rat—that was how they thought of their almost-police comrades—took another ten minutes before getting the hoist collar in place, then came up the ladder and started cranking the winch.

It was clear in a moment. Two men, not old ones, not badly dressed. They'd been dead for several days, judging by the distortion and disfigurement of their faces. The water had been cold, and that had slowed the growth and hunger of the bacteria that devoured most bodies, but water itself did things to bodies that were hard on the full stomach to gaze upon, and these two faces looked like . . . like Pokémon toys, one of the detectives thought, just like perverse and horrible Pokémon toys, like those that one of his kids lusted after. The two sewer rats loaded the bodies into body bags for transport to the morgue, where the examinations would take place. As yet, they knew nothing except that the bodies were indeed dead. There were no obviously missing body parts, and the general dishevelment of the bodies prevented their seeing anything like a bullet or knife wound. For the moment, they had what Americans would call two John Does, one with blond or light brown hair, the other with what appeared to be reddish hair. From appearances, they'd been in the water for three or four days. And they'd probably died together, handcuffed as they were, unless one had murdered the other and then jumped to his own death, in which case one or both might have been homosexual, the more cynical of the two detectives thought. The beat cop was told to write up the proper reporting forms at his station, which, the militiaman thought, would be nice and warm. There was nothing like finding a corpse or two to make a cold day colder still.

The body-recovery team loaded the bags into their van for the drive to the morgue. The bags were not properly sealed because of the handcuffs, and they sat side by side on the floor of the van, perversely like the hands of lovers reaching out to each other in death . . . as they had in life? one of the detectives wondered aloud back in their car. His partner just growled at that one and continued his drive.

It was, agreeably, a slow day in the St. Petersburg morgue. The senior pathologist on duty, Dr. Aleksander Koniev, had been in his office reading a medical journal and well bored by the inactivity of the morning, when the call came in, a possible double homicide. Those were always interesting, and Koniev was a devotee of murder mysteries, most of them imported from Britain and America, which also made them a good way to polish up his language skills. He was waiting in the autopsy room when the bodies arrived, were transferred to gurneys at the loading ramp and rolled together into his room. It took a moment to see why the two gurneys were wheeled side by side.

"So," the pathologist asked with a sardonic grin, "were they killed by the militia?"

"Not officially," the senior detective replied, in the same emotional mode. He knew Koniev.

"Very well." The physician switched on the tape recorder. "We have two male cadavers, still fully dressed. It is apparent that both have been immersed in water—where were they recovered?" he asked, looking up at the cops. They answered. "Immersed in *fresh* water in the Neva. On initial visual inspection, I would estimate three to four days' immersion after death." His gloved hands felt around one head, and the other. "Ah," his voice said. "Both victims seem to have been shot. Both have what appear to be bullet holes in the center of the occipital region of both bodies. Initial impression is a small-caliber bullet hole in both victims. We'll check that later. Yevgeniy," he said, looking up again, this time at his own technician. "Remove the clothing and bag it for later inspection."

"Yes, Comrade Doctor." The technician put out his cigarette and came forward with cutting tools.

"Both shot?" the junior detective asked.

"In the same place in both heads," Koniev confirmed. "Oh, they were handcuffed after death, strangely enough. No immediately visible bruising on either wrist. Why do it afterwards?" the pathologist wondered.

"Keeps the bodies together," the senior detective thought aloud—*but why might that be important?* he wondered to himself. The killer or killers had an overly developed sense of neatness? But he'd been investigating homicides long enough to know that you couldn't fully explain all the crimes you solved, much less the ones you'd newly encountered.

"Well, they were both fit," Koniev said next, as his technician got the last of their clothes off. "Hmm, what's that?" He walked over and saw a tattoo on the left biceps of the blond one, then turned to see—"They both have the same tattoo."

The senior detective came over to see, first thinking that maybe his partner had been right and there was a sexual element to this case, but—

"Spetsnaz, the red star and thunderbolt, these two were in Afghanistan. Anatoliy, while the doctor conducts his examination, let's go through their clothing."

This they did, and in half an hour determined that both had been well dressed in fairly expensive clothing, but in both cases entirely devoid of identification of any kind. That was hardly unusual in a situation like this, but cops, like everyone else, prefer the easy to the hard. No wallet, no identity papers, not a banknote, key chain, or tie tack. Well, they could trace them through the labels on the clothes, and nobody had cut their fingertips off, and so they could also use fingerprints to identify them. Whoever had done the double murder had been clever enough to deny the police some knowledge, but not clever enough to deny them everything.

What did that mean? the senior detective wondered. The best way to prevent a murder investigation was to make the bodies disappear. Without a body there was no proof of death, and therefore, no murder investigation, just a missing person who could have run off with another woman or man, or just decided to go someplace to start life anew. And disposing of a body was not all *that* difficult, if you thought about it a little. Fortunately, most killings were, if not exactly impulse crimes, then something close to it, and most killers were fools who would later seal their own fates by talking too much.

But not this time. Had this been a sexual killing, he probably would have heard about it by now. Such crimes were virtually advertised by their perpetrators in some perverse desire to assure their own arrest and conviction, because no one who committed that kind of crime seemed able to keep his mouth shut about anything.

No, this double killing had every hallmark of professionalism. Both bodies killed in the same way, and only *then* handcuffed together . . . probably for better and/or lengthier concealment. No sign of a struggle on either body, and both were manifestly fit, trained, dangerous men. They'd been taken unawares, and that usually meant someone they both knew and trusted. Why criminals trusted anyone in their community was something neither detective quite understood. "Loyalty" was a word they could scarcely spell, much less a principle to which any of them adhered . . . and yet criminals gave strange lip-service to it.

As the detectives watched, the pathologist drew blood from both bodies for later toxicology tests. Perhaps both had been drugged as a precursor to the head shots, not likely, but possible, and something to be checked. Scrapings were taken from all twenty fingernails, and those, too, would probably be valueless. Finally, fingerprints were taken so that proper identification could be made. This would not be very fast. The central records bureau in Moscow was notoriously inefficient, and the detectives would beat their own local bushes in the hope of finding out who these two cadavers had once been.

"Yevgeniy, these are not men of whom I would have made enemies lightly."

"I agree, Anatoliy," the elder of the two said. "But someone either did not fear them at all . . . or feared them sufficiently to take very drastic action." The truth of the matter was that both men were accustomed to solving easy murders where the killer confessed almost at once, or had committed his crime in front of numerous witnesses. This one would challenge their abilities, and they would report that to their lieutenant, in the hope of getting additional assets assigned to the case.

As they watched, photos were taken of the faces, but those faces were so distorted as to be virtually unrecognizable, and the photos would then be essentially useless for purposes of identification. But taking them prior to opening the skull was procedure, and Dr. Koniev did everything by the book. The detectives stepped outside to make a few phone calls and smoke in a place with a somewhat more palatable ambience. By the time they came back, both bullets were in plastic containers, and Koniev told them that the presumptive cause of both deaths was a single bullet in each brain, with powder tattooing evident on both scalps. They'd both been killed at short range, less than half a meter, the pathologist told them, with what appeared to be a standard, light 2.6-gram bullet fired from a 5.45-mm PSM police pistol. That might have generated a snort, since this was the standard-issue police side arm, but quite a few had found their way into the Russian underworld.

"The Americans call this a professional job," Yevgeniy observed.

"Certainly it was accomplished with skill," Anatoliy agreed. "And now, first . . ."

"First we find out who these unlucky bastards were. Then, who the hell were their enemies."

The Chinese food in China wasn't nearly as good as that to be found in LA, Nomuri thought. Probably the ingredients, was his immediate analysis. If the People's Republic had a Food and Drug Administration, it had been left out of his premission briefing, and his first thought on entering this restaurant was that he didn't want to check the kitchen out. Like most Beijing restaurants, this one was a small mom-and-pop operation, operating out of the first floor of what was in essence a private home, and serving twenty people out of a standard Chinese communist home kitchen must have involved considerable acrobatics. The table was circular, small, and eminently cheap, and the chair was uncomfortable, but for all that, the mere fact that such a place existed was testimony to fundamental changes in the political leadership of this country.

But the mission of the evening sat across from him. Lian Ming. She wore the standard off-blue boiler suit that was virtually the uniform of low to mid-level bureaucrats in the various government ministries. Her hair was cut short, almost like a helmet. The fashion industry in this city must have been established by some racist son of a bitch who loathed the Chinese and tried his level best to make them as unattractive as he could. He'd yet to see a single local female citizen who dressed in a manner that anyone could call attractive—except, maybe, for some imports from Hong Kong. Uniformity was a problem with the Orient, the utter lack of variety, unless you counted the foreigners who were showing up in ever-increasing numbers, but they stuck out like roses in a junkyard, and that merely emphasized the plethora of junk. Back home, at USC, one could have—well, one could look at, the CIA officer corrected himself—any sort of female to be had on the planet. White, black, Jewish, gentile, yellow in various varieties, Latina, some real Africans, plenty of real Europeans—and there you had ample variety, too: the dark-haired, earthy Italians, the haughty French, the proper Brits, and the stiff Germans. Toss in some Canadians, and the Spanish (who went out of their way to be separated from the local Spanish speakers) and lots of ethnic Japanese (who were also separated from the local Japanese, though in this case at the will of the latter rather than the former), and you had a virtual deli of people. The only sameness there came from the Californian atmosphere, which commanded that every individual had to work hard to be presentable and attractive, for that was the One Great Commandment of life in California, home of Rollerblading and surfing, and the tight figures that went along with both pastimes.

Not here. Here everyone dressed the same, looked the same, talked the same, and largely acted the same way . . .

. . . except this one. There was something else to be had here, Nomuri thought, and that's why he'd asked her to dinner.

It was called seduction, which had been part of the spy's playbook since time immemorial, though it would be a first for Nomuri. He hadn't been quite celibate in Japan, where mores had changed in the past generation, allowing young men and young women to meet and . . . communicate on the most basic of levels—but there, in a savage, and for Chester Nomuri a rather cruel, irony, the more available Japanese girls had a yen for Americans. Some said it was because Americans had a reputation for being better equipped for lovemaking than the average Japanese male, a subject of much giggling for Japanese girls who have recently become sexually active. Part of it was also that American men were reputed to treat their women better than the Japanese variety, and since Japanese women were far more obsequious than their Western counterparts, it probably worked out as a good deal for both sides of the partnerships that developed. But Chet Nomuri was a spook covered as a Japanese salaryman, and had learned to fit in so well that the local women regarded him as just another Japanese male, and so his sex life had been hindered by his professional skills, which hardly seemed fair to the field officer, brought up, like so many American men, on the movies of 007 and his numerous conquests: Mr. Kiss-Kiss Bang-Bang, as he was known in the West Indies. Well, Nomuri hadn't handled a pistol either, not since his time at The Farm—the CIA's training school off Interstate 64 near Yorktown, Virginia—and hadn't exactly broken any records there in the first place.

But this one had possibilities, the field officer thought, behind his normal, neutral expression, and there was nothing in the manual against getting laid on the job—what a crimp on Agency morale *that* would have been, he considered. Such stories of conquest were a frequent topic of conversation at the rare but real field-officer get-togethers that the Agency occasionally held, usually at The Farm, for the field spooks to compare notes on techniques—the after-hour beer sessions often drifted in this direction. For Chet Nomuri since getting to Beijing, his sex life had consisted of prowling Internet pornography sites. For one reason or another, the Asian culture made for an ample collection of such things, and while Nomuri wasn't exactly proud of this addiction, his sexual drive needed *some* outlet.

With a little work, Ming might have been pretty, Nomuri thought. First of all she needed long hair. Then, perhaps, better frames on her eyeglasses. Those she wore had all the attraction of recycled barbed wire. Then some makeup. Exactly what sort Nomuri wasn't sure—he was no expert on such things, but her skin had an ivory-like quality to it that a little chemical enhancement might turn into something attractive. But in this culture, except for people on the stage (whose makeup was about as subtle as a Las Vegas neon sign), makeup meant washing your face in the morning, if that. It was her eyes, he decided. They were lively and . . . cute. There was life in them, or behind them, however that worked. She might even have had a decent figure, but it was hard to tell in that clothing.

"So, the new computer system works well?" he asked, after the lingering sip of green tea.

"It is magical," she replied, almost gushing. "The characters come out beautifully, and they print up perfectly on the laser printer, as though from a scribe."

"What does your minister think?"

"Oh, he is very pleased. I work faster now, and he is very pleased by that!" she assured him.

"Pleased enough to place an order?" Nomuri asked, reverting back to his salaryman cover.

"This I must ask the chief of administration, but I think you will be satisfied by the response."

That will make NEC happy, the CIA officer thought, again wondering briefly how much money he'd made for his cover firm. His boss in Tokyo would have gagged on his sake to know whom Nomuri really worked for, but the spook had won all of his promotions at NEC on merit, while moonlighting for his true country. It was a fortunate accident, Chet thought, that his real job and his cover one blended so seamlessly. That and the fact that he'd been raised in a very traditional home, speaking two native tongues . . . and more than that, the sense of *on,* the duty owed to his native land, far over and above that he pretended to owe to his parent culture. He'd probably gotten that from seeing his grandfather's framed plaque, the Combat Infantryman's Badge in the center on the blue velvet, surrounded by the ribbons and medallions that designated awards for bravery, the Bronze Star with combat "V," the Presidential Distinguished Unit Citation, and the campaign ribbons won as a grunt with the 442nd Regimental Combat team in Italy and Southern France. Fucked over by America, his grandfather had earned his citizenship rights in the ultimate and best possible way before returning home to the landscaping business that had educated his sons and grandsons, and taught one of them the duty he owed his country. And besides, this could be fun.

It was now, Nomuri thought, looking deeply into Ming's dark eyes, wondering what the brain behind them was thinking. She had two cute dimples at the sides of her mouth, and, he thought, a very sweet smile on an otherwise unremarkable face.

"This is such a fascinating country," he said. "By the way, your English is very good." And good that it was. His Mandarin needed a lot of help, and one doesn't seduce women with sign language.

A pleased smile. "Thank you. I do study very hard."

"What books do you read?" he asked with an engaging smile of his own.

"Romances, Danielle Steel, Judith Krantz. America offers women so many more opportunities than what we are used to here."

"America is an interesting country, but chaotic," Nomuri told her. "At least in this society one can know his place."

"Yes." She nodded. "There is security in that, but sometimes too much. Even a caged bird wishes to spread its wings."

"I will tell you one thing I find bad here."

"What is that?" Ming asked, not offended, which, Nomuri thought, was very good indeed. Maybe he'd get a Steele novel and read up on what she liked.

"You should dress differently. Your clothing is not flattering. Women should dress more attractively. In Japan there is much variety in clothing, and you can dress Eastern or Western as the spirit moves you."

She giggled. "I would settle for the underthings. They must feel so nice on the skin. That is not a very socialist thought," she told him, setting down her cup. The waiter came over, and with Nomuri's assent she ordered mao-tai, a fiery local liqueur. The waiter returned rapidly with two small porcelain cups and a flask, from which he poured daintily. The CIA officer nearly gasped with his first sip, and it went down hot, but it certainly warmed the stomach. Ming's skin, he saw, flushed from it, and there came the fleeting impression that a gate had just been opened and passed . . . and that it probably led in the right direction.

"Not everything can be socialist," Nomuri judged, with another tiny sip. "This restaurant is a private concern, isn't it?"

"Oh, yes. And the food is better than what I cook. That is a skill I do not have."

"Truly? Then perhaps you will allow me to cook for you sometime," Chet suggested.

"Oh?"

"Certainly." He smiled. "I can cook American style, and I am able to shop at a closed store to get the correct ingredients." Not that the ingredients would be worth a damn, shipped in as they were, but a damned sight better than the garbage you got here in the public markets, and a steak dinner was probably something she'd never had. Could he justify getting CIA to put a few Kobe beef steaks on his expense account? Nomuri wondered. Probably. The bean-counters at Langley didn't bother the field spooks all that much.

"Really?"

"Of course. There are some advantages to being a foreign barbarian," he told her with a sly smile. The giggling response was just right, he thought. Yeah. Nomuri took another careful sip of this rocket fuel. She'd just told him what she wanted to wear. Sensible, too, for this culture. However comfy it might be, it would also be quite discreet.

"So, what else can you tell me about yourself?" he asked next.

"There is little to tell. My job is beneath my education, but it carries prestige for . . . well, for political reasons. I am a highly educated secretary. My employer—well, technically I work for the state, as do most of us, but in fact I work for my minister as if he were in the capitalist sector and paid me from his own pocket." She shrugged. "I suppose it has always been so. I see and hear interesting things."

Don't want to ask about them now, Nomuri knew. Later, sure, but not now.

"It is the same with me, industrial secrets and such. Ahh," he snorted. "Better to leave such things at my official desk. No, Ming, tell me about you."

"Again, there is little to tell. I am twenty-four. I am educated. I suppose I am lucky to be alive. You know what happens to many girl babies here . . ."

Nomuri nodded. "I have heard the stories. They are distasteful," he agreed with her. It was more than that. It was not unknown for the father of a female toddler to drop her down a well in the hope that his wife would bear him a son on the next try. One-baby-per-family was almost a law in the PRC, and like most laws in a communist state, that one was ruthlessly enforced. An unauthorized baby was often allowed to come to term, but then as birth took place, when the baby "crowned," the top of the head appearing, the very moment of birth, the attending physician or nurse would take a syringe loaded with formaldehyde, and stab it into the soft spot at the crown of the almost-newborn's head, push the plunger, and extinguish its life at the moment of its beginning. It wasn't something the government of the PRC advertised as government policy, but government policy it was. Nomuri's one sister, Alice, was a physician, an obstetrician/gynecologist trained at UCLA, and he knew that his sister would take poison herself before performing such a barbarous act, or take a pistol to use on whoever demanded that she do it. Even so, some surplus girl babies somehow managed to be born, and these were often abandoned, and then given up for adoption, mainly to Westerners, because the Chinese themselves had no use for them at all. Had it been done to Jews, it would have been called genocide, but there were a lot of Chinese to go around. Carried to extremes, it could lead to racial extinction, but here it was just called population control. "In due course Chinese culture will again recognize the value of women, Ming. That is certain."

"I suppose it is," she allowed. "How are women treated in Japan?"

Nomuri allowed himself a laugh. "The real question is how well they treat us, and how well they *permit* us to treat them!"

"Truly?"

"Oh, yes. My mother ruled the house until she died."

"Interesting. Are you religious?"

Why that question? Chet wondered.

"I have never decided between Shinto and Zen Buddhism," he replied, truthfully. He'd been baptized a Methodist, but fallen away from his church many years before. In Japan he'd examined the local religions just to understand them, the better to fit in, and though he'd learned much about both, neither had appealed to his American upbringing. "And you?"

"I once looked into Falun Gong, but not seriously. I had a friend who got very involved. He's in prison now."

"Ah, a pity." Nomuri nodded sympathy, wondering how close the friend had been. Communism remained a jealous system of belief, intolerant of competition of any sort. Baptists were the new religious fad, springing up as if from the very ground itself, started off, he thought, from the Internet, a medium into which American Christians, especially Baptists and Mormons, had pumped a lot of resources of late. And so Jerry Falwell was getting some sort of religious/ideological foothold here? How remarkable—or not. The problem with Marxism-Leninism, and also with Mao it would seem, was that as fine as the theoretical model was, it lacked something the human soul craved. But the communist chieftains didn't and couldn't like that very much. The Falun Gong group hadn't even been a religion at all, not to Nomuri's way of thinking, but for some reason he didn't fully understand, it had frightened the powers that be in the PRC enough to crack down on it as if it had been a genuinely counterrevolutionary political movement. He heard that the convicted leaders of the group were doing seriously hard time in the local prisons. The thought of what constituted especially hard time in this country didn't bear much contemplation. Some of the world's most vicious tortures had been invented in this country, where the value of human life was a far less important thing than in the nation of his origin, Chet reminded himself. China was an ancient land with an ancient culture, but in many ways these people might as well have been Klingons as fellow human beings, so detached were their societal values from what Chester Nomuri had grown up with. "Well, I really don't have much in the way of religious convictions."

"Convictions?" Ming asked.

"Beliefs," the CIA officer corrected. "So, are there any men in your life? A fiancé, perhaps?"

She sighed. "No, not in some time."

"Indeed? I find that surprising," Nomuri observed with studied gallantry.

"I suppose we are different from Japan," Ming admitted, with just a hint of sadness in her voice.

Nomuri lifted the flask and poured some more mao-tai for both. "In that case," he said, with a smile and a raised eyebrow, "I offer you a friendly drink."

"Thank you, Nomuri-san."

"My pleasure, Comrade Ming." He wondered how long it would take. Perhaps not too long at all. Then the real work would begin.

CHAPTER 7

Developing Leads

It was the sort of coincidence for which police work is known worldwide. Provalov called militia headquarters, and since he was investigating a homicide, he got to speak with the St. Petersburg murder squad leader, a captain. When he said he was looking for some former Spetsnaz soldiers, the captain remembered his morning meeting in which two of his men had reported finding two bodies bearing possible Spetsnaz tattoos, and that was enough to make him forward the call.

"Really, the RPG event in Moscow?" Yevgeniy Petrovich Ustinov asked. "Who exactly was killed?"

"The main target appears to have been Gregoriy Filipovich Avseyenko. He was a pimp," Provalov told his colleague to the north. "Also his driver and one of his girls, but they appear to have been inconsequential." He didn't have to elaborate. You didn't use an antitank rocket to kill a chauffeur and a whore.

"And your sources tell you that two Spetsnaz veterans did the shooting?"

"Correct, and they flew back to St. Petersburg soon thereafter."

"I see. Well, we fished two such people from the River Neva yesterday, both in their late thirties or so, and both shot in the back of the head."

"Indeed?"

"Yes. We have fingerprints from both bodies. We're waiting for Central Army Records to match them up. But that will not be very fast."

"Let me see what I can do about that, Yevgeniy Petrovich. You see, also present at the murder was Sergey Nikolay'ch Golovko, and we have concerns that he might have been the true target of the killing."

"That would be ambitious," Ustinov observed coolly. "Perhaps your friends at Dzerzhinskiy Square can get the records morons moving?"

"I will call them and see," Provalov promised.

"Good, anything else?"

"Another name, Suvorov, Klementi Ivan'ch, reportedly a former KGB officer, but that is all I have at the moment. Does the name mean anything to you?" You could hear the man shaking his head over the phone, Provalov noted.

"*Nyet,* never heard that one," the senior detective replied as he wrote it down. "Connection?"

"My informant thinks he's the man who arranged the killing."

"I'll check our records here to see if we have anything on him. Another former 'Sword and Shield' man, eh? How many of those guardians of the state have gone bad?" the St. Petersburg cop asked rhetorically.

"Enough," his colleague in Moscow agreed, with an unseen grimace.

"This Avseyenko fellow, also KGB?"

"Yes, he reportedly ran the Sparrow School."

Ustinov chuckled at that one. "Oh, a state-trained pimp. Marvelous. Good girls?"

"Lovely," Provalov confirmed. "More than we can afford."

"A real man doesn't have to pay for it, Oleg Gregoriyevich," the St. Petersburg cop assured his Moscow colleague.

"That is true, my friend. At least not until long afterwards," Provalov added.

"That is the truth!" A laugh. "Let me know what you find out?"

"Yes, I will fax you my notes."

"Excellent. I will share my information with you as well," Ustinov promised. There is a bond among homicide investigators across the world. No country sanctions the private taking of human life. Nation-states reserve such power for themselves alone.

In his dreary Moscow office, Lieutenant Provalov made his notes for several minutes. It was too late to call the RVS about rattling the Central Army Records cage. First thing in the morning, he promised himself. Then it was time to leave. He picked his coat off the tree next to his desk and headed out to where his official car was parked. This he drove to a corner close to the American Embassy, and a place called Boris Godunov's, a friendly and warm bar. He'd only been there for five minutes when a familiar hand touched his shoulder.

"Hello, Mishka," Provalov said, without turning.

"You know, Oleg, it's good to see that Russian cops are like American cops."

"It is the same in New York?"

"You bet," Reilly confirmed. "After a long day of chasing bad guys, what's better than a few drinks with your pals?" The FBI agent waved to the bartender for his usual, a vodka and soda. "Besides, you get some real work done in a place like this. So, anything happening on the Pimp Case?"

"Yes, the two who did the killing may have shown up dead in St. Petersburg." Provalov tossed down the last of his straight vodka and filled the American in on the details, concluding, "What do you make of that?"

"Either it's revenge or insurance, pal. I've seen it happen at home."

"Insurance?"

"Yeah, had it happen in New York. The Mafia took Joey Gallo out, did it in public, and they wanted it to be a signature event, so they got a black hood to do the hit—but then the poor bastard gets shot himself about fifteen feet away. Insurance, Oleg. That way the subject can't tell anybody who asked him to take the job. The second shooter just walked away, never did get a line on him. Or it could have been a revenge hit: whoever paid them to do the job whacked them for hitting the wrong target. You pays your money and you takes your choice, pal."

"How do you say, wheels within wheels?"

Reilly nodded. "That's how we say it. Well, at least it gives you some more leads to run down. Maybe your two shooters talked to somebody. Hell, maybe they even kept a diary." It was like tossing a rock into a pond, Reilly thought. The ripples just kept expanding in a case like this. Unlike a nice domestic murder, where a guy whacked his wife for fucking around, or serving dinner late, and then confessed while crying his eyes out at what he'd done. But by the same token, it was an awfully loud crime, and those, more often than not, were the ones you broke because people commented on the noise, and some of those people knew things that you could use. It was just a matter of getting people out on the street, rattling doorknobs and wearing out shoes, until you got what you needed. These Russian cops weren't dumb. They lacked some of the training that Reilly took for granted, but for all that, they had the proper cop instincts, and the fact of the matter was that if you followed the proper procedures, you'd break your cases, because the other side wasn't all that smart. The smart ones didn't break the law in so egregious a way. No, the perfect crime was the one you never discovered, the murder victim you never found, the stolen funds missed by bad accounting procedures, the espionage never discovered. Once you knew a crime had been committed, you had a starting place, and it was like unraveling a sweater. There wasn't all that much holding the wool together if you just kept picking at it.

"Tell me, Mishka, how worthy were your Mafia adversaries in New York?" Provalov asked after sipping his second drink.

Reilly did the same. "It's not like the movies, Oleg. Except maybe *Goodfellas.* They're cheap hoods. They're not educated. Some of them are pretty damned dumb. Their cachet was that once upon a time they didn't talk, *omertà* they used to call it, the Law of Silence. I mean, they'd take the fall and never cooperate. But that changed over time. The people from the Old Country died out and the new generation was softer—and we got tougher. It's a lot easier to laugh your way through three years than it is to handle ten, and on top of that the organization broke down. They stopped taking care of the families while the dad was in the slammer, and that was real bad for morale. So, they started talking to us. And we got smarter, too, with electronic surveillance—now it's called 'special operations'; back then it was a 'black bag job'—and we weren't always very careful about getting a warrant. I mean, back in the '60s, a Mafia don couldn't take a leak without us knowing what color it was."

"And they never fought back?"

"You mean fuck with us? Mess with an FBI agent?" Reilly grinned at the very thought. "Oleg, *nobody ever* messes with the FBI. Back then, and still somewhat to this day, we are the Right Hand of God Himself, and if you mess with us, some really bad things are going to happen. The truth of the matter is that nothing like that has ever happened, but the bad guys worry that it might. The rules get bent some, but, no, we never really break them—at least not that I know about. But if you threaten a hood with serious consequences for stepping over the line, chances are he'll take you seriously."

"Not here. They do not respect us that much yet."

"Well, then you have to generate that respect, Oleg." And it really was about that simple in concept, though bringing it about, Reilly knew, would not be all that easy. Would it take having the local cops go off the reservation once in a while, to show the hoods the price of lèse-majesté? That was part of American history, Reilly thought. Town sheriffs like Wyatt Earp, Bat Masterson, and Wild Bill Hickock, Lone Wolf Gonzales of the Texas Rangers, Bill Tilghman and Billy Threepersons of the U.S. Marshal Service, the cops of their time who didn't so much enforce the law as embody it in the way they walked down the street. There was no corresponding Russian lawman of legend. Maybe they needed one. It was part of the heritage of every American cop, and from watching movies and TV westerns, American citizens grew up with the expectation that breaking the law would bring such a man into your life, and not to your personal profit. The FBI had grown up in an era of increased crime during the Great Depression, and had exploited the existing Western tradition with modern technology and procedures to create its own institutional mystique. To do that had meant convicting a lot of criminals, and killing a few on the street as well. In America there was the expectation that cops were heroic figures who didn't merely enforce the law, but who protected the innocent as well. There was no such tradition here. Growing it would solve many of the problems in the former Soviet Union, where the lingering tradition was of oppression rather than protection. No John Wayne, no Melvin Purvis in Russian movies, and this nation was the poorer for it. As much as Reilly liked working here, and as much as he'd come to like and respect his Russian counterparts, it was much like being dumped into a trash heap with instructions to make it as orderly as Bergdorf-Goodman's in New York. All the proper things were there, but organizing them made Hercules' task in the Augean stables seem trivial in comparison. Oleg had the right motivation, and the right set of skills, but it was some job he had ahead of him. Reilly didn't envy him the task, but he had to help as best he could.

"I do not envy you very much, Mishka, but your organization's status in your country is something I would like to have."

"It didn't just happen, Oleg. It's the product of many years and a lot of good men. Maybe I should show you a Clint Eastwood movie."

"*Dirty Harry*? I have seen it." *Entertaining,* the Russian thought, *but not overly realistic.*

"No, *Hang 'Em High,* about the Marshal Service, back in the Old West, when men were men and women were grateful. Actually it's not true in the usual sense. There wasn't much crime in the Old West."

That made the Russian look up from his drink in surprise. "Then why do all the movies say otherwise?"

"Oleg, movies have to be exciting, and there isn't much exciting about raising wheat or punching cattle. The American West was mainly settled by veterans of our Civil War. That was a hard and cruel conflict, but no man who'd survived the Battle of Shiloh was likely to be intimidated by some bozo on a horse, gun or not. A professor at Oklahoma State University did a book on this subject twenty or so years ago. He checked court records and such, and found out that except for saloon shootings—guns and whiskey make a crummy mix, right?—there wasn't a hell of a lot of crime in the West. The citizens could look after themselves, and the laws they had were pretty tough—not a hell of a lot of repeat offenders—but what it really came down to was that the citizens all had guns and all pretty much knew how to use them, and that is a big deterrent for the bad guys. A cop's less likely to shoot you than an aroused citizen, when you get down to it. He doesn't want to do all the paperwork if he can avoid it, right?" A sip and a chuckle from the American.

"In that we are the same, Mishka," Provalov agreed.

"And, by the way, all this quick-draw stuff in the movies. If it ever happened for real, I've never heard of such a case. No, that's all Hollywood bullshit. You can't draw and fire accurately that way. If you could, they would have trained us to do it that way at Quantico. But except for people who practice for special performances and tournaments and stuff, and that's always at the same angle and the same distance, it just can't be done."

"You're sure of that?" Legends die hard, especially for an otherwise pretty smart cop who had, however, seen his share of Westerns.

"I was a Principal Instructor in my Field Division, and damned if *I* can do it."

"You are good shot, eh?"

Reilly nodded with uncharacteristic modesty on this particular issue. "Fair," he allowed. "Pretty fair." There were less than three hundred names on the FBI Academy's "Possible Board," identifying those who'd fired a perfect qualifying course on graduating. Mike Reilly was one of them. He'd also been assistant head of the SWAT team in his first field division in Kansas City before moving over to the chess players in the OC—Organized Crime—department. It made him feel a little naked to walk around without his trusty S&W 1076 automatic, but that was life in the FBI's diplomatic service, the agent told himself. What the hell, the vodka was good here, and he was developing a taste for it. For that his diplomatic license plates helped. The local cops were pretty serious about giving tickets out. It was a pity they still had so much to learn about major criminal investigations.

"So, our pimp friend was probably the primary target, Oleg?"

"Yes, I think that is likely, but not entirely certain yet." He shrugged. "But we'll keep the Golovko angle open. After all," Provalov added, after a long sip of his glass, "it will get us lots of powerful cooperation from other agencies."

Reilly had to laugh at that. "Oleg Gregoriyevich, you know how to handle the bureaucratic part of the job. I couldn't do that better myself!" Then he waved to the bartender. He'd spring for the next round.

The Internet had to be the best espionage invention ever made, Mary Patricia Foley thought. She also blessed the day that she'd personally recommended Chester Nomuri to the Directorate of Operations. That little Nisei had some beautiful moves for an officer still on the short side of thirty. He'd done superb work in Japan, and had volunteered in a heartbeat for Operation GENGHIS in Beijing. His cover job at Nippon Electric Company could hardly have been better suited to the mission requirements, and it seemed that he'd waltzed into his niche like Fred Astaire on a particularly good day. The easiest part of all, it seemed, was getting the data out.

Six years before, CIA had gone to Silicon Valley—undercover, of course—and commissioned a modern manufacturer to set up a brief production run of a very special modem. In fact, it seemed to many to be a sloppy one, since the linkup time it used was four or five seconds longer than was the usual. What you couldn't tell was that the last four seconds weren't random electronic noise at all, but rather the mating of a special encryption system, which when caught on a phone tap sounded just like random noise anyway. So, all Chester had to do was set up his message for transmission and punch it through. To be on the safe side, the messages were super-encrypted with a 256-bit system specially made at the National Security Agency, and the double-encipherment was so complex that even NSA's own bank of supercomputers could only crack it with difficulty and after a lot of expensive time. After that, it was just a matter of setting up a www-dot-something domain through an easily available public vendor and a local ISP—Internet Service Provider—with which the world abounded. It could even be used on a direct call from one computer to another—in fact, that was the original application, and even if the opposition had a hardwire phone tap, it would take a mathematical genius *plus* the biggest and baddest supercomputer that Sun Microsystems made even to begin cracking into the message.

Lian Ming, Mary Pat read, secretary to . . . to him, eh? Not a bad potential source. The most charming part of all was that Nomuri included the sexual possibilities implicit in the recruitment. The kid was still something of an innocent; he'd probably blushed writing this, the Deputy Director (Operations) of the Central Intelligence Agency thought to herself, but he'd included it because he was so damned honest in everything he did. It was time to get Nomuri a promotion and a raise. Mrs. Foley made the appropriate note on a Post-it for attachment to his file. James Bond-san, she thought with an internal chuckle. The easiest part was the reply: *Approved, proceed.* She didn't even have to add the "with caution" part. Nomuri knew how to handle himself in the field, which was not always the rule for young field officers. Then she picked up the phone and called her husband on the direct line.

"Yeah, honey?" the Director of Central Intelligence said.

"Busy?"

Ed Foley knew that wasn't a question his wife asked lightly. "Not too busy for you, baby. Come on down." And hung up.

The CIA Director's office is relatively long and narrow, with floor-to-ceiling windows overlooking the woods and the special-visitors' parking lot. Beyond that are the trees overlooking the Potomac Valley and the

George Washington Parkway, and little else. The idea of anyone's having a direct line of sight into any part of this building, much less the Office of the Director, would have been the cause of serious heartburn for the security pukes. Ed looked up from his paperwork when his wife came in and took the leather chair across from his desk.

"Something good?"

"Even better than Eddie's marks at school," she replied with a soft, sexy smile she reserved for her husband alone. And that had to be pretty good. Edward Foley, Jr., was kicking ass up at Rensselaer Polytechnic in New York, and a starter on their hockey team, which damned near always kicked ass itself in the NCAA. Little Ed might earn a place on the Olympic team, though pro hockey was out. He'd make too much money as a computer engineer to waste his time in so pedestrian a pursuit. "I think we may have something here."

"Like what, honey?"

"Like the executive secretary to Fang Gan," she replied. "Nomuri's trying to recruit her, and he says the prospects are good."

"GENGHIS," Ed observed. They ought to have picked a different name, but unlike most CIA operations, the name for this one hadn't been generated by a computer in the basement. The fact of the matter was that this security measure hadn't been applied for the simple reason that nobody had ever expected anything to come of it. CIA had never gotten any kind of agent into the PRC government. At least not above the rank of captain in the People's Liberation Army. The problems were the usual ones. First, they had to recruit an ethnic Chinese, and CIA hadn't had much success at that; next, the officer in question had to have perfect language skills, and the ability to disappear into the culture. For a variety of reasons, none of that had ever happened. Then Mary Pat had suggested trying Nomuri. His corporation did a lot of business in China, after all, and the kid did have good instincts. And so, Ed Foley had signed off on it, not really expecting much to result. But again his wife's field instincts had proven superior to his. It was widely believed that Mary Pat Foley was the best field officer the Agency had had in twenty years, and it looked as if she was determined to prove that. "How exposed is Chet?"

His wife had to nod her concern at that one. "He's hanging out there, but he knows how to be careful, and his communications gear is the best we have. Unless they brute-force him, you know, just pick him up because they don't like his haircut, he ought to be pretty safe. Anyway—" She handed over the communication from Beijing.

The DCI read it three times before handing it back. "Well, if he wants to get laid—it's not good fieldcraft, honey. Not good to get that involved with your agent—"

"I *know* that, Ed, but you play the cards you're dealt, remember? And if we get her a computer like the one Chet's using, her security won't be all that bad either, will it?"

"Unless they have somebody pick it apart," Ed Foley thought aloud.

"Oh, Jesus, Ed, our best people would have a cast-iron motherfucker of a time figuring it all out. I ran that project myself, remember? It's *safe!*"

"Easy, honey." The DCI held up his hand. When Mary used that sort of language, she was really into the matter at hand. "Yeah, I know, it's secure, but I'm the worrier and you're the cowgirl, remember?"

"Okay, honey-bunny." The usual sweet smile that went with seduction and getting her way.

"You've already told him to proceed?"

"He's my officer, Eddie."

A resigned nod. It wasn't fair that he had to work with his wife here. He rarely won any arguments at the office, either. "Okay, baby. It's your operation, run with it, but—"

"But what?"

"But we change GENGHIS to something else. If this one pans out, then we go to a monthly name cycle. This one has some serious implications, and we've got to go max-security on it."

She had to agree with that. As case officers, the two of them had run an agent known in CIA legend as CARDINAL, Colonel Mikhail Semyonovich Filitov, who'd worked inside the Kremlin for more than thirty years, feeding gold-plated information on every aspect of the Soviet military, plus some hugely valuable political intelligence. For bureaucratic reasons lost in the mists of time, CARDINAL had not been handled as a regular agent-in-place, and that had saved him from Aldrich Ames and his treacherous betrayal of a dozen Soviet citizens who'd worked for America. For Ames it had worked out to roughly $100,000 per life given away. Both of the Foleys regretted the fact that Ames was allowed to live, but they weren't in the law-enforcement business.

"Okay, Eddie, monthly change-cycle. You're always so careful, honey. You call or me?"

"We'll wait until she gives us something useful before going to all the trouble, but let's change GENGHIS to something else. It's too obviously a reference to China."

"Okay." An impish smile. "How about SORGE for the moment?" she suggested. The name was that of Richard Sorge, one of the greatest spies who'd ever lived, a German national who'd worked for the Soviets, and just possibly the man who'd kept Hitler from winning his Eastern Front war with Stalin. The Soviet dictator, knowing this, hadn't lifted a hand to save him from execution. "Gratitude," Iosif Vissarionovich had once said, "is a disease of dogs."

The DCI nodded. His wife had a lively sense of humor, especially as applied to business matters. "When do you suppose we'll know if she'll play ball with us?"

"About as soon as Chet gets his rocks off, I suppose."

"Mary, did you ever . . . ?"

"In the field? Ed, that's a guy thing, not a girl thing," she told her husband with a sparkling grin as she lifted her papers and headed back out. "Except with you, honey-bunny."

The Alitalia DC-10 touched down about fifteen minutes early due to the favorable winds. Renato Cardinal DiMilo was pleased enough to think through an appropriate prayer of thanksgiving. A longtime member of the Vatican's diplomatic service, he was accustomed to long flights, but that wasn't quite the same as enjoying them. He wore his red—"cardinal"—and black suit that was actually more akin to an official uniform, and not a conspicuously comfortable one at that, despite the custom tailoring that came from one of Rome's better shops. One of the drawbacks to his clerical and diplomatic status was that he'd been unable to shed his suitcoat for the flight, but he'd been able to kick off his shoes, only to find that his feet had swollen on the flight, and getting them back on was more difficult than usual. That evoked a sigh rather than a curse, as the plane taxied to the terminal. The senior flight attendant ushered him to the forward door and allowed him to leave the aircraft first. One advantage to his diplomatic status was that all he ever had to do was wave his diplomatic passport at the control officers, and in this case a senior PRC government official was there to greet him at the end of the jetway.

"Welcome to our country," the official said, extending his hand.

"It is my pleasure to be here," the cardinal replied, noting that this communist atheist didn't kiss his ring, as was the usual protocol. Well, Catholicism in particular and Christianity in general were not exactly welcome in the People's Republic of China, were they? But if the PRC expected to live in the civilized world, then they'd have to accept representation with the Holy See, and that was that. And besides, he'd go to work on these people, and, who knew, maybe he could convert one or two. Stranger things had happened, and the Roman Catholic Church had handled more formidable enemies than this one.

With a wave and a small escort group, the demi-minister conducted his distinguished visitor through the concourse toward the place where the official car and escort waited.

"How was your flight?" the underling asked.

"Lengthy but not unpleasant" was the expected reply. Diplomats had to act as though they loved flying, though even the flight crews found journeys of this length tiresome. It was his job to observe the new ambassador of the Vatican, to see how he acted, how he looked out the car's windows, even, which, in this case, was not unlike all the other first-time diplomats who came to Beijing. They looked out at the differences. The shapes of the buildings were new and different to them, the color of the bricks, and how the brickwork looked close up and at a distance, the way in which things that were essentially the same became fascinating because of differences that were actually microscopic when viewed objectively.

It took a total of twenty-eight minutes to arrive at the residence/embassy. It was an old building, dating back to the turn of the previous century, and had been the largish home of an American Methodist missionary—evidently one who liked his American comforts, the official thought—and had passed through several incarnations, including, he'd learned the previous day, that of a bordello in the diplomatic quarter in the 1920s and '30s, because diplomats liked their comforts as well. Ethnic Chinese, he wondered, or Russian women who'd always claimed to be of the Czarist nobility, or so he'd heard. After all, Westerners enjoyed fucking noblewomen for some reason or other, as if their body parts were different somehow. He'd heard that one, too, at the office, from one of the archivists who kept track of such things at the Ministry. Chairman Mao's personal habits were not recorded, but his lifelong love for deflowering twelve-year-olds was well known in the Ministry of Foreign Affairs. Every national leader had something odd and distasteful about him, the young official knew. Great men had great aberrations.

The car pulled up to the old wooden frame house, where a uniformed policeman opened the door for the visiting Italian, and even saluted, earning himself a nod from the man wearing the ruby-red skullcap.

Waiting on the porch was yet another foreigner, Monsignor Franz Schepke, whose diplomatic status was that of DCM, or deputy chief of mission, which usually meant the person who was really in charge of things while the ambassador—mainly a man chosen for political reasons—reigned in the main office. They didn't know if that were the case here yet.

Schepke looked as German as his ancestry was, tall and spare with gray-blue eyes that revealed nothing at all, and a wonderful language gift that had mastered not only the complex Chinese language, but also the local dialect and accent as well. Over the phone this foreigner could pass for a party member, much to the surprise of local officials who were not in the least accustomed to foreigners who could even speak the language properly, much less master it.

The German national, the Chinese official saw, kissed his superior's ring. Then the Italian shook his hand and embraced the younger churchman. They probably knew each other. Cardinal DiMilo then led Schepke to the escort and introduced them—they'd met many times before, of course, and that made the senior churchman appear just a little backward to the local official. In due course, the luggage was loaded into the residence/embassy building, and the Chinese official got back in the official car for the ride to the Foreign Ministry, where he'd make his contact report. The Papal Nuncio was past his prime, he'd write, a pleasant enough old chap, perhaps, but no great intellect. A fairly typical Western ambassador, in other words.

No sooner had they gotten inside than Schepke tapped his right ear and gestured around the building.

"Everywhere?" the cardinal asked.

"Ja, doch," Monsignor Schepke replied in his native German, then shifted to Greek. Not modern, but Attic Greek, that spoken by Aristotle, similar to but different from the modern version of that language, a language perpetuated only by a handful of scholars at Oxford and a few more Western universities. "Welcome, Eminence."

"Even airplanes can take too long. Why can we not travel by ship? It would be a much gentler way to getting from point to point."

"The curse of progress," the German priest offered weakly. The Rome-Beijing flight was only forty minutes longer than the one between Rome and New York, after all, but Renato was a man from a different and more patient age.

"My escort. What can you tell me of him?"

"His name is Qian. He's forty, married, one son. He will be our point of contact with the Foreign Ministry. Bright, well educated, but a dedicated communist, son of another such man," Schepke said, speaking rapidly in the language learned long before in seminary. He and his boss knew that this exchange would probably be recorded, and would then drive linguists in the Foreign Ministry to madness. Well, it was not their fault that such people were illiterate, was it?

"And the building is fully wired, then?" DiMilo asked, heading over to a tray with a bottle of red wine on it.

"We must assume so," Schepke confirmed with a nod, while the cardinal poured a glass. "I could have the building swept, but finding reliable people here is not easy, and . . ." And those able to do a proper sweep would then use the opportunity to plant their own bugs for whatever country they worked for—America, Britain, France, Israel, all were interested in what the Vatican knew.

The Vatican, located in central Rome, is technically an independent country, hence Cardinal DiMilo's diplomatic status even in a country where religious convictions were frowned upon at best, and stamped into the earth at worst. Renato Cardinal DiMilo had been a priest for just over forty years, most of which time had been spent in the Vatican's foreign service. His language skills were not unknown within the confines of his own service, but rare even there, and damned rare in the outside world, where men and women took a great deal of time to learn languages. But DiMilo picked them up easily—so much so that it surprised him that others were unable to do so as well. In addition to being a priest, in addition to being a diplomat, DiMilo was also an intelligence officer—all ambassadors are supposed to be, but he was much more so than most. One of his jobs was to keep the Vatican—therefore the Pope—informed of what was happening in the world, so that the Vatican—therefore the Pope—could take action, or at least use influence in the proper direction.

DiMilo knew the current Pope quite well. They'd been friends for years before his election to the chair of the Pontifex Maximus ("maximus" in this context meaning "chief," and "pontifex" meaning "bridge-builder," as a cleric was supposed to be the bridge between men and their God). DiMilo had served the Vatican in this capacity in seven countries. Before the fall of the Soviet Union, he'd specialized in Eastern European countries, where he'd learned to debate the merits of communism with its strongest adherents, mostly to their discomfort and his own amusement. Here would be different, the cardinal thought. It wasn't just the Marxist beliefs. This was a very different culture. Confucius had defined the place of a Chinese citizen two millennia before, and that place was different from what Western culture taught. There was a place for the teachings of Christ here, of course, as there was everywhere. But the local soil was not as fertile for Christianity as it was elsewhere. Local citizens who sought out Christian missionaries would do so out of curiosity, and once exposed to the gospel would find Christian beliefs more curious still, since they were so different from the nation's more ancient teachings. Even the more "normal" beliefs that were in keeping, more or less, with Chinese traditions, like the Eastern Spiritualist movement known as Falun Gong, had been ruthlessly, if not viciously, repressed. Cardinal DiMilo told himself that he'd come to one of the few remaining pagan nations, and one in which martyrdom was still a possibility for the lucky or luckless, depending on one's point of view. He sipped his wine, trying to decide what time his body thought it was, as opposed to what time is was by his watch. In either case, the wine tasted good, reminding him as it did of his home, a place which he'd never truly left, even in Moscow or Prague. Beijing, though—Beijing might be a challenge.

CHAPTER 8

Underlings and Underthings

It wasn't the first time he'd done this. It was exciting in its way, and arousing, and marginally dangerous because of the time and place. Mainly it was an exercise in effective memory and the discerning eye. The hardest part was converting the English units to metric. The perfect female form was supposed to be 36-24-36, not 91.44-60.96-91.44.

The last time he'd been in a place like this had been in the Beverly Center Mall in Los Angeles, buying for Maria Castillo, a voluptuous Latina who'd been delighted at his error, taking her waist for twenty-four rather than its true twenty-seven. You wanted to err on the low side in numbers, but probably the big side in letters. If you took a 36B chest to be a 34C, she wouldn't be mad, but if you took a twenty-four-inch waist for a twenty-eight-inch, she'd probably be pissed. Stress, Nomuri told himself with a shake of the head, came in many shapes and sizes. He wanted to get this right because he wanted Ming as a source, but he wanted her as a mistress, too, and that was one more reason not to make a mistake.

The color was the easy part. Red. Of course, red. This was still a country in which red was the "good" color, which was convenient because red had always been the lively choice in women's underthings, the color of adventure and giggles and . . . looseness. And looseness served both his biological and professional purposes. He had other things to figure out, too. Ming was not tall, scarcely five feet—151 centimeters or so, Nomuri thought, doing the conversion in his head. She was short but not really petite. There was no real obesity in China. People didn't overeat here, probably because of the lingering memory of times when food had not been in abundance and overeating was simply not possible. Ming would have been considered overweight in California, Chester thought, but that was just her body type. She was squat because she was short, and no amount of dieting or working out or makeup could change it. Her waist wouldn't be much less than twenty-seven inches. For her chest, 34B was about the best he could hope for . . . well, maybe 34C—no, he decided, B+ at most. So, a 34B bra, and medium shorts—panties—red silk, something feminine . . . something on the wild, whorish side of feminine, something that she could look into the mirror alone with and giggle . . . and maybe sigh at how different she looked wearing such things, and maybe smile, that special inward smile women had for such moments. The moment when you knew you had them—and the rest was just dessert.

The best part of Victoria's Secret was the catalog, designed for men who really, and sensibly, wanted to buy the models themselves, despite the facial attitudes that sometimes made them look like lesbians on quaaludes—but with such bodies, a man couldn't have everything, could he? Fantasies, things of the mind. Nomuri wondered if the models really existed or were the products of computers. They could do anything with computers these days—make Rosie O'Donnell into Twiggy, or Cindy Crawford obsolete.

Back to work, he told himself. This might be a place for fantasies, but not that one, not yet. Okay, it had to be sexy. It had to be something that would both amuse and excite Ming, and himself, too: That was all part of it. Nomuri took the catalog off the pile because it was a lot easier for him to see what he wanted in a filled rather than an unfilled condition. He turned pages and stopped dead on page 26. There was a black girl modeling it, and whatever genetic stew she'd come from must have had some fine ingredients, as her face would have appealed to a member of Hitler's SS just as much as Idi Amin. It was that sort of face. Better yet, she wore something called a Racerback bra with matching string bikini panties, and the color was just perfect, a red-purple that the Romans had once called Tyrrian Scarlet, the color on the toga stripe of members of the senatorial order, reserved by price and custom to the richest of the Roman nobility, not quite red, not quite purple. The bra material was satin and Lycra, and it closed in front, the easier for a girl to put it on, and the more interesting for a guy to take it off, his mind thought, as he headed over to the proper rack of clothing. Thirty-four-B, he thought. If too small, it would be all the more flattering . . . small or medium on the string bikini? Shit, he decided, get one of each. Just to be sure, he also got a no-wire triangle-pattern bra and thong panties in an orange-red color that the Catholic Church would call a mortal sin just for looking at. On impulse he got several additional panties on the assumption that they soiled more quickly than bras did, something he wasn't sure of despite being a field intelligence officer of the Central Intelligence Agency. They didn't tell you about such things at The Farm. He'd have to do a memo on that. It might give MP a chuckle in her seventh-floor office at Langley.

One other thing, he thought. Perfume. Women liked perfume. You'd expect them to like it, especially here. The entire city of Beijing smelled like a steel mill, lots of coal dust and other pollutants in the air—as Pittsburgh had probably been at the turn of the last century—and the sad truth was that the Chinese didn't bathe as diligently as Californians did, and nowhere nearly as regularly as the Japanese. So, something that smelled nice . . .

"Dream Angels," the brand was called. It came in a perfume spray, lotion, and other applications that he didn't understand, but he was sure Ming would, since she was a girl, and this was a quintessential girl thing. So, he bought some of that, too, using his NEC credit card to pay for it—his Japanese bosses would understand. There were skillfully arranged and choreographed sex tours that took Japanese salarymen to various places in Asia that catered to the sex trade. That was probably how AIDS had gotten to Japan, and why Nomuri used a condom for everything there except urinating. The total came to about 300 euros. The salesclerk wrapped everything and commented that the lady in his life was very lucky.

She will be, Nomuri promised himself. The underthings he'd just bought her, well, the fabrics felt as smooth as flexible glass, and the colors would arouse a blind man. The only question was how they would affect a dumpy Chinese female secretary to a government minister. It wasn't as though he was trying to seduce Suzie Wong. Lian Ming was pretty ordinary rather than ordinarily pretty, but you never knew. Amy Irvin, his first conquest at the ripe old age of seventeen years and three months, had been pretty enough to inspire him—which meant, for a boy of that age, she had the requisite body parts, no beard like a Civil War general, and had showered in the previous month. At least Ming wouldn't be like so many American women now who'd visited the plastic surgeon to have their tummies tucked, tits augmented to look like cereal bowls, and lips pumped full of chemicals until they looked like some strange kind of two-part fruit. What women did to attract men . . . and what men did in the hope of seducing them. What a potential energy source, Nomuri thought, as he turned the key in his company Nissan.

"What is it today, Ben?" Ryan asked his National Security Adviser.

"CIA is trying to get a new operation underway in Beijing. For the moment it's called SORGE."

"As in Richard Sorge?"

"Correct."

"Somebody must be ambitious. Okay, tell me about it."

"There's an officer named Chester Nomuri, an illegal, he's in Beijing covered as a computer salesman for NEC. He's trying to make a move on a secretary, female, for a senior PRC minister, a guy named Fang Gan—"

"Who is?" Ryan asked over his coffee mug.

"Sort of a minister without portfolio, works with the Premier and the Foreign Minister."

"Like that Zhang Han San guy?"

"Not as senior, but yes. Looks like a very high-level go-fer type. Has contacts in their military and foreign ministries, good ideological credentials, sounding board for others in their Politburo. Anyway, Nomuri is trying to make a move on the girl."

"Bond," Ryan observed in a studiously neutral voice, "James Bond. I know Nomuri's name. He did some good work for us in Japan when I had your job. This is for information only, not my approval?"

"Correct, Mr. President. Mrs. Foley is running this one, and wanted to give you a heads-up."

"Okay, tell MP that I'm interested in whatever take comes out of this." Ryan fought off the grimace that came from learning of another person's private—well, if not private, then his sex—life.

"Yes, sir."

CHAPTER 9

Initial Results

Chester Nomuri had learned many things in his life, from his parents and his teachers and his instructors at The Farm, but one lesson he'd yet to learn was the value of patience, at least as it applied to his personal life. That didn't keep him from being cautious, however. That was why he'd sent his plans to Langley. It was embarrassing to have to inform a woman of his proposed sex life—MP was a brilliant field spook, but she still took her leaks sitting down, Nomuri reminded himself—but he didn't want the Agency to think that he was an alley cat on the government payroll, because the truth was, he liked his job. The excitement was at least as addictive as the cocaine that some of his college chums had played with.

Maybe that's why Mrs. Foley liked him, Nomuri speculated. They were of a kind. Mary Pat, they said in the Directorate of Operations, was The Cowgirl. She'd swaggered through the streets of Moscow during the last days of the Cold War like Annie Fucking Oakley packing heat, and though she'd been burned by KGB's Second Chief Directorate, she hadn't given the fuckers anything, and whatever operation she'd run—this was still very, very secret—it must have been a son of a bitch, because she'd never gone back in the field but had scampered up the CIA career ladder like a hungry squirrel up an oak tree. The President thought she was smart, and if you wanted a friend in this business, the President of the United States was right up there, because he knew the spook business. Then came the stories about what President Ryan had once done. Bringing out the chairman of the fucking KGB? MP must have been part of that, the boys and girls of the DO all thought. All they knew even within the confines of CIA—except, of course, for those who needed to know (both of them, the saying went)—was what had been published in the press, and while the media generally knew jack shit about black operations, a CNN TV crew *had* put a camera in the face of a former KGB chairman now living in Winchester, Virginia. While he hadn't spilled many beans, the face of a man the Soviet government had declared dead in a plane crash was bean enough to make a very rich soup indeed. Nomuri figured he was working for a couple of real pros, and so he let them know what he was up to, even if that meant causing a possible blush for Mary Patricia Foley, Deputy Director (Operations) of the Central Intelligence Agency.

He'd picked a Western-style restaurant. There were more than a few of them in Beijing now, catering both to the locals and to tourists who felt nostalgic for the taste of home (or who worried about their GI systems over here—not unreasonably, Nomuri thought). The quality wasn't anything close to a real American restaurant, but it was considerably more appealing than the deep-fried rat he suspected was on the menu of many Beijing eateries.

He'd arrived first, and was relaxing with a cheap American bourbon when Ming came through the door. Nomuri waved in what he hoped was not an overly boyish way. She saw him do so, and her resulting smile was just about right, he thought. Ming was glad to see him, and that was step one in the plan for the evening. She made her way to his corner table in the back. He stood, showing a degree of gentlemanliness unusual in China, where women were nowhere near as valued as they were back home. Nomuri wondered if that would change, if all the killing of female babies could suddenly make Ming a valuable commodity, despite her plainness. He still couldn't get over the casual killing of children; he kept it in the front of his mind, just to keep clear who the good guys were in the world, and who the bad guys were.

"It's so good to see you," he said with an engaging smile. "I was worried you might not meet me here."

"Oh, really? Why?"

"Well, your superior at work . . . I'm sure that he . . . well . . . needs you, I suppose is the polite way to put it," Nomuri said with a hesitant voice, delivering his rehearsed line pretty well, he thought. He had. The girl giggled a little.

"Comrade Fang is over sixty-five," she said. "He is a good man, a good superior, and a fine minister, but he works long hours, and he is no longer a young man."

Okay, so he fucks you, but not all that much, Nomuri interpreted that to mean. *And maybe you'd like a little more, from somebody closer to your age, eh?* Of course, if Fang was over sixty-five and still getting it on, then maybe he is worthy of some respect, Nomuri added to himself, then tossed the thought aside.

"Have you eaten here before?" The place was called Vincenzo's, and pretended to be Italian. In fact the owner/operator was a half-breed Italian-Chinese from Vancouver, whose spoken Italian would have gotten him hit by the Mafia had he tried it in Palermo, or even Mulberry Street in Manhattan, but here in Beijing it seemed genuinely ethnic enough.

"No," Ming replied, looking around at, to her, this most exotic of locations. Every table had an old wine bottle, its bottom wrapped in twine, and an old drippy red candle at the top. The tablecloth was checked white and red. Whoever had decorated this place had evidently seen too many old movies. That said, it didn't look anything like a local restaurant, even with the Chinese servers. Dark wood paneling, hooks near the door for hanging coats. It could have been in any East Coast city in America, where it would have been recognized as one of those old family Italian places, a mom-and-pop joint with good food and little flash. "What is Italian food like?"

"At its best, Italian cooking is among the very finest in the world," Nomuri answered. "You've never had Italian food? Never at all? Then may I select for you?"

Her response was girlish in its charm. Women were all the same. Treat them in the right way, and they turn into wax in your hand, to be kneaded and shaped to your will. Nomuri was starting to like this part of the job, and someday it might be useful in his *personal* personal life, too. He waved to the waiter, who came over with a subservient smile. Nomuri first of all ordered a genuine Italian white wine—strangely, the wine list here was actually first rate, and quite pricey to boot, of course—and, with a deep breath, fettuccine Alfredo, quintessential Italian heart-attack food. From looking at Ming, he figured that she'd not refuse rich food.

"So, the new computer and printer systems continue to work out?"

"Yes, and Minister Fang has praised me before the rest of the staff for choosing it. You have made me something of a hero, Comrade Nomuri."

"I am pleased to hear that," the CIA officer replied, wondering if being called "comrade" was a good thing for the current mission or a bad one. "We are bringing out a new portable computer now, one you could take home with you, but which has the same power as your office mainframe, with all the same features and software, of course, even a modem for accessing the Internet."

"Really? I get to do that so seldom. At work, you see, it is not encouraged for us to surf the 'Net, except when the Minister wants something specific."

"Is that so? What 'Net interests does Minister Fang have?"

"Mainly political commentary, and mainly in America and Europe. Every morning I print up various pieces from the newspapers, the *Times of London, New York Times, Washington Post,* and so on. The Minister especially likes to see what the Americans are thinking."

"Not very much," Nomuri observed, as the wine arrived.

"Excuse me?" Ming asked, getting him to turn back.

"Hmph, oh, the Americans, they don't think very much. The shallowest people I have ever encountered. Loud, poorly educated, and their women . . ." Chet let his voice trail off.

"What of their women, Comrade Nomuri?" Ming asked, virtually on command.

"Ahh." He took a sip of the wine and nodded for the waiter to serve it properly. It was a pretty good one from Tuscany. "Have you ever seen the American toy, the Barbie doll?"

"Yes, they are made here in China, aren't they?"

"That is what every American woman wishes to be, hugely tall, with massive bosoms, a waist you can put your hands around. That is not a woman. It's a toy, a mannequin for children to play with. And about as intelligent as your average American woman. Do you think they have language skills, as you do? Consider: We now converse in English, a language native to neither of us, but we converse well, do we not?"

"Yes," Ming agreed.

"How many Americans speak Mandarin, do you suppose? Or Japanese? No, Americans have no education, no sophistication. They are a backward nation, and their women are very backward. They even go to surgeons to have their bosoms made bigger, like that stupid child's doll. It's comical to see them, especially to see them nude," he concluded with a dangle.

"You have?" she asked, on cue.

"Have what—you mean seen American women nude?" He got a welcome nod for his question. This was going well. *Yes, Ming, I* am *a man of the world.* "Yes, I have. I lived there for some months, and it was interesting in a grotesque sort of way. Some of them can be very sweet, but not like a decent Asian woman with proper proportions, and womanly hair that doesn't come from some cosmetics bottle. And manners. Americans lack the manners of an Asian."

"But there are many of our people over there. Didn't you . . . ?"

"Meet one? No, the round-eyes keep them for themselves. I suppose their men appreciate real women, even while their own women turn into something else." He reached to pour some more wine into Ming's glass. "But in fairness, there are some things Americans are good at."

"Such as?" she asked. The wine was already loosening her tongue.

"I will show you later. Perhaps I owe you an apology, but I have taken the liberty of buying you some American things."

"Really?" Excitement in her eyes. This was *really* going well, Nomuri told himself. He'd have to go easier on the wine. Well, half a bottle, two of these glasses, wouldn't hurt him in any way. How did that song go . . . *It's okay to do it on the first date* . . . Well, he didn't have to worry about much in the way of religious convictions or inhibitions here, did he? That was one advantage to communism, wasn't it?

The fettuccine arrived right on time, and surprisingly it was pretty good. He watched her eyes as she took her first forkful. (Vincenzo's used silverware instead of chopsticks, which was a better idea for fettuccine Alfredo anyway.) Her dark eyes were wide as the noodles entered her mouth.

"This is fine . . . lots of eggs have gone into it. I love eggs," she confided.

They're your arteries, honey, the case officer thought. He watched her inhale the first bit of the fettuccine. Nomuri reached across the table to top off her wine glass once more. She scarcely noticed, she attacked her pasta so furiously.

Halfway through the plate of pasta, she looked up. "I have never had so fine a dinner," Ming told him.

Nomuri responded with a warm grin. "I am so pleased that you are enjoying yourself." *Wait'll you see the drawers I just got you, honey.*

"Attention to orders!"

Major General Marion Diggs wondered what his new command would bring him. The second star on his shoulder . . . well, he told himself that he could feel the additional weight, but the truth was that he couldn't, not really. His last five years in the uniform of his country had been interesting. The first commander of the reconstituted 10th Armored Cavalry Regiment—the Buffalo Soldiers—he'd made that ancient and honored regiment into the drill masters of the Israeli army, turning the Negev Desert into another National Training Center, and in two years he'd hammered every Israeli brigade commander into the ground, then built them up again, tripling their combat effectiveness by every quantifiable measure, so that now the Israeli troopers' swagger was actually justified by their skills. Then he'd gone off to the real NTC in the high California desert, where he'd done the same thing for his own United States Army. He'd been there when the Bio War had begun, with his own 11th ACR, the famous Blackhorse Cavalry, and a brigade of National Guardsmen, whose unexpected use of advanced battlefield-control equipment had surprised the hell out of the Blackhorse and their proud commander, Colonel Al Hamm. The whole bunch had deployed to Saudi, along with the 10th from Israel, and together they'd given a world-class bloody nose to the army of the short-lived United Islamic Republic. After acing his colonel-command, he'd really distinguished himself as a one-star, and that was the gateway to the second sparkling silver device on his shoulder, and also the gateway to his new command, known variously as "First Tanks," "Old Ironsides," or "America's Armored Division." It was the 1st Armored Division, based in Bad Kreuznach, Germany, one of the few remaining heavy divisions under the American flag.

Once there had been a lot of them. Two full corps of them right here in Germany, 1st and 3rd Armored, 3rd and 8th Infantry, plus a pair of Armored Cavalry Regiments, 2nd and 11th, and the POMCUS sites—monster equipment warehouses—for stateside units like the 2nd Armored, and the 1st Infantry, the Big Red One out of Fort Riley, Kansas, which could redeploy to Europe just as fast as the airlines could deliver them, there to load up their equipment and move out. All that force—and it was a whole shitload of force, Diggs reflected—had been part of NATO's commitment to defend Western Europe from a country called the Soviet Union and its mirror-image Warsaw Pact, huge formations whose objective was the Bay of Biscay, or so the operations and intelligence officers in Mons, Belgium, had always thought. And quite a clash it would have been. Who would have won? Probably NATO, Diggs thought, depending on political interference, and command skills on both sides of the equation.

But, now, the Soviet Union was no more. And with it was also gone the need for the presence of V and VII Corps in Western Germany, and so, 1st Armored was about the only vestige left of what had once been a vast and powerful force. Even the cavalry regiments were gone, the 11th to be the OpFor—"opposing force," or Bad Guys—at the National Training Center and the 2nd "Dragoon" Regiment essentially disarmed at Fort Polk, Louisiana, trying to make up new doctrine for weaponless troopers. That left Old Ironsides, somewhat reduced in size from its halcyon days, but still a formidable force. Exactly whom Diggs might fight in the event hostilities sprang unexpectedly from the ground, he had no idea at the moment.

That, of course, was the job of his G-2 Intelligence Officer, Lieutenant Colonel Tom Richmond, and training for it was the problem assigned to his G-3 Operations Officer, Colonel Duke Masterman, whom Diggs had dragged kicking and screaming from the Pentagon. It was not exactly unknown in the United States Army for a senior officer to collect about him younger men whom he'd gotten to know on the way up. It was his job to look after their careers, and their jobs to take care of their mentor—called a "rabbi" in the NYPD or a "Sea Daddy" in the United States Navy—in a relationship that was more father/son than anything else. Neither Diggs nor Richmond nor Masterman expected much more than interesting professional time in the 1st Armored Division, and that was more than enough. They'd seen the elephant—a phrase that went back in the United States Army to the Civil War to denote active participation in combat operations—and killing people with modern weapons wasn't exactly a trip to Disney World. A quiet term of training and sand-table exercises would be plenty, they all thought. Besides, the beer was pretty good in Germany.

"Well, Mary, it's all yours," outgoing Major General (promotable) Sam Goodnight said after his formal salute. "Mary" was a nickname for Diggs that went back to West Point, and he was long since past getting mad about it. But only officers senior to him could use that moniker, and there weren't all that many of them anymore, were there?

"Sam, looks like you have the kids trained up pretty well," Diggs told the man he'd just relieved.

"I'm especially pleased with my helicopter troops. After the hoo-rah with the Apaches down in Yugoslavia, we decided to get those people up to speed. It took three months, but they're ready to eat raw lion now—after they kill the fuckers with their pocket knives."

"Who's the boss rotor-head?"

"Colonel Dick Boyle. You'll meet him in a few minutes. He's been there and done that, and he knows how to run his command."

"Nice to know," Diggs allowed, as they boarded the World War II command car to troop the line, a goodbye ride for Sam Goodnight and welcome for Mary Diggs, whose service reputation was as one tough little black son of a bitch. His doctorate in management from the University of Minnesota didn't seem to count, except to promotion boards, and whatever private company might want to hire him after retirement, a possibility he had to consider from time to time now, though he figured two stars were only about half of what he had coming. Diggs had fought in two wars and comported himself well in both cases. There were many ways to make a career in the armed services, but none so effective as successful command on the field of battle, because when you got down to it, the Army was about killing people and breaking things as efficiently as possible. It wasn't fun, but it was occasionally necessary. You couldn't allow yourself to lose sight of that. You trained your soldiers so that if they woke up the next morning in a war, they'd know what to do and how to go about it, whether their officers were around to tell them or not.

"How about artillery?" Diggs asked, as they drove past the assembled self-propelled 155-mm howitzers.

"Not a problem there, Mary. In fact, no problems anywhere. Your brigade commanders all were there in 1991, mainly as company commanders or battalion S-3s. Your battalion commanders were almost all platoon leaders or company XOs. They're pretty well trained up. You'll see," Goodnight promised.

Diggs knew it would all be true. Sam Goodnight was a Major General (promotable), which meant he was going to get star number three as soon as the United States Senate got around to approving the next bill with all the flag officers on it, and that couldn't be rushed. Even the President couldn't do that. Diggs had screened for his second star six months earlier, just before leaving Fort Irwin, to spend a few months parked in the Pentagon—an abbreviated "jointness" tour, as it was called—before moving back to Germany. The division was slated to run a major exercise against the Bundeswehr in three weeks. First AD vs. four German brigades, two tanks, two mechanized infantry, and that promised to be a major test of the division. Well, that was something for Colonel Masterman to worry about. It was his neck on the line. Duke had come to Germany a week early to meet with his also-outgoing predecessor as divisional operations officer and go over the exercise's rules and assumptions. The German commander in the exercise was Generalmajor Siegfried Model. Siggy, as he was known to his colleagues, was descended from a pretty good Wehrmacht commander from the old-old days, and it was also said of him that he regretted the fall of the USSR, because part of him wanted to take the Russian Army on and rape it. Well, such things had been said about a lot of German, and a few American senior officers as well, and in nearly every case it was just that—talk, because nobody who'd seen one battlefield ever yearned to see another.

Of course, Diggs thought, there weren't many Germans left who had ever seen a battlefield.

"They look good, Sam," Diggs said, as they passed the last static display.

"It's a hell of a tough job to leave, Marion. Damn." The man was starting to fight back tears, which was one way of telling who the really tough ones were in this line of work, Diggs knew. Walking away from the command of soldiers was like leaving your kid in the hospital, or maybe even harder. They'd all been Sam's kids, and now they would be his kids, Diggs thought. On first inspection, they looked healthy and smart enough.

"Yeah, Arnie," President Ryan said. His voice betrayed his emotions more than a growl or a shout could have.

"Nobody ever said the job was fun, Jack. Hell, I don't know why you're complaining. You don't have to schmooze people to raise money for your reelection campaign, do you? You don't have to kiss ass. All you have to do is your work, and that saves you a good hour—maybe an hour and a half—per day to watch TV and play with your kids." If there was anything Arnie loved, Ryan thought, it was telling him (Ryan) how easy he had it in this fucking job.

"But I still spend half my day doing unproductive shit instead of doing what I'm paid to do."

"Only half, and still he complains," Arnie told the ceiling. "Jack, you'd better start liking this stuff, or it'll eat you up. This is the *fun* part of being President. And, hell, man, you were a government employee for fifteen years before you came here. You should *love* being unproductive!"

Ryan nearly laughed, but managed to contain himself. If there was anything Arnie knew how to do, it was to soften his lessons with humor. That could be annoying as hell.

"Fine, but exactly what do I promise them?"

"You promise that you'll support this dam and barge-canal scheme."

"But it's probably a waste of money."

"No, it is *not* a waste of money. It provides employment in this two-state area, which is of interest to not one, not two, but *three* United States Senators, all of whom support you steadfastly on the Hill, and whom you, therefore, must support in turn. You reward them for helping you by helping them get reelected. And you help them get reelected by allowing them to generate about fifteen thousand construction jobs in the two states."

"And screw with a perfectly good river for"—Ryan checked the briefing folder on his desk—"three and a quarter *billion* dollars . . . Jesus H. Christ," he finished with a long breath.

"Since when have you been a tree-hugger? Cutthroat trout don't vote, Jack. And even if the barge traffic up the river doesn't develop, you'll still have one hell of a recreation area for people to water-ski and fish, toss in a few new motels, maybe a golf course or two, fast-food places . . ."

"I don't like saying things and doing things I don't believe in," the President tried next.

"For a politician, that is like colorblindness or a broken leg: a serious handicap," van Damm noted. "That's part of the job, too. Nikita Khrushchev said it: 'Politicians are the same all over the world, we build bridges where there aren't any rivers.' "

"So wasting money is something we're *supposed* to do? Arnie, it isn't *our* money! It's the *people's* money. It belongs to them, and we don't have the right to piss it away!"

"Right? Who ever said this is about what's right?" Arnie asked patiently. "Those three senators who're"—he checked his watch—"on their way down here right now got you your defense appropriations bill a month ago, in case you didn't remember, and you may need their votes again. Now, that appropriations bill was important, wasn't it?"

"Yes, of course it was," President Ryan responded with guarded eyes.

"And getting that bill through was the right thing for the country, wasn't it?" van Damm asked next.

A long sigh. He could see where this was going. "Yes, Arnie, it was."

"And so, doing this little thing *does* help you to do the right thing for the country, doesn't it?"

"I suppose." Ryan hated conceding such things, but arguing with Arnie was like arguing with a Jesuit. You were almost always outgunned.

"Jack, we live in an imperfect world. You can't expect to be doing the *right thing* all the time. The best you can expect to do is to make the right thing happen most of the time—actually, you will do well to have the right things outbalance the not-so-right things over the long term. Politics is the art of compromise, the art of getting the important things you want, while giving to others the less important things they want, and doing so in such a way that you're the one doing the giving, not them doing the taking—because that's what makes you the boss. You must understand that." Arnie paused and took a sip of coffee. "Jack, you try hard, and you're learning pretty well—for a fourth-grader in graduate school—but you have to learn this stuff to the point that you don't even think about it. It has to become as natural as zipping your pants after you take a piss. You still have no idea how well you're doing." *And maybe that's a good thing,* Arnie added to himself alone.

"Forty percent of the people don't think I'm doing a good job."

"Fifty-nine percent do, and some of those forty percent voted for you anyway!"

The election had been a remarkable session for write-in candidates, and Mickey Mouse had done especially well, Ryan reminded himself.

"What am I doing to offend those others?" Ryan demanded.

"Jack, if the Gallup Poll had been around in ancient Israel, Jesus would probably have gotten discouraged and gone back to carpentry."

Ryan punched a button on his desk phone. "Ellen, I need you."

"Yes, Mr. President," Mrs. Sumter replied to their not-so-secret code. Thirty seconds later, she appeared through the door with her hand at her side. Approaching the President's desk, she extended her hand with a cigarette in it. Jack took it and lit it with a butane lighter, removing a glass ashtray from a desk drawer.

"Thanks, Ellen."

"Surely." She withdrew. Every other day Ryan would slip her a dollar bill to pay off his cigarette debt. He was getting better at this, mooching usually no more than three smokes on a stressful day.

"Just don't let the media catch you doing that," Arnie advised.

"Yeah, I know. I can get it on with a secretary right here in the Oval Office, but if I get caught smoking, that's like goddamned child abuse." Ryan took a long hit on the Virginia Slim, also knowing what his wife would say if she caught him doing this. "If I were king, then I'd make the goddamned rules!"

"But you're not, and you don't," Arnie pointed out.

"My job is to preserve, protect, and defend the country—"

"No, your job is to preserve, protect, and defend the *Constitution,* which is a whole lot more complicated. Remember, to the average citizen 'preserve, protect, and defend' means that they get paid every week, and they feed their families, get a week at the beach every year, or maybe Disney World, and football every Sunday afternoon in the fall. Your job is to keep them content and secure, not just from foreign armies, but from the general vicissitudes of life. The good news is that if you do that, you can be in this job another seven-plus years and retire with their love."

"You left out the legacy part."

That made Arnie's eyes flare a bit. "Legacy? Any president who worries too much about that is offending God, and that's almost as dumb as offending the Supreme Court."

"Yeah, and when the Pennsylvania case gets there—"

Arnie held up his hands as though protecting against a punch. "Jack, I'll worry about that when the time comes. You didn't take my advice on the Supreme Court, and so far you've been lucky, but if—no, *when* that blows up in your face, it won't be pretty." Van Damm was already planning the defense strategy for that.

"Maybe, but I won't worry about it. Sometimes you just let the chips fall where they may."

"And sometimes you look out to make sure the goddamned tree doesn't land on you."

Jack's intercom buzzed just as he put out the cigarette. It was Mrs. Sumter's voice. "The senators just came through the West Entrance."

"I'm out of here," Arnie said. "Just remember, you will support the dam and canal on that damned river, and you value their support. They'll be there when you need them, Jack. Remember that. And you *do* need them. Remember that, too."

"Yes, Dad," Ryan said.

You walked here?" Nomuri asked, with some surprise.

"It is only two kilometers," Ming replied airily. Then she giggled. "It was good for my appetite."

Well, you went through that fettuccine like a shark through a surfer, Nomuri thought. *I suppose your appetite wasn't hurt very much.* But that was unfair. He'd thought this evening through very carefully, and if she'd fallen into his trap, it was his fault more than hers, wasn't it? And she did have a certain charm, he decided as she got into his company car. They'd already agreed that they'd come to his apartment so that he could give her the present he'd already advertised. Now Nomuri was getting a little excited. He'd planned this for more than a week, and the thrill of the chase was the thrill of the chase, and that hadn't changed in tens of thousands of years of male humanity . . . and now he wondered what was going on in her head. She'd had two stiff glasses of wine with the meal—and she'd passed on dessert. She'd jumped right to her feet when he'd suggested going to his place. Either his trap had been superbly laid, or she was more than ready herself. . . . The drive was short, and it passed without words. He pulled into his numbered parking place, wondering if anyone would take note of the fact that he had company today. He had to assume that he was watched here. The Chinese Ministry of State Security probably had an interest in all foreigners who lived in Beijing, since all were potential spies. Strangely, his apartment was not in the same part of the building as the Americans and other Westerners. It wasn't overt segregation or categorization, but it had worked out that way, the Americans largely in one section, along with most of the Europeans . . . and the Taiwanese, too, Nomuri realized. And so, whatever surveillance existed was probably over on that end of the complex. A good thing now for Ming, and later, perhaps, a good thing for himself.

His place was a corner second-story walk-up in a Chinese interpretation of an American garden-apartment complex. The apartment was spacious enough, about a hundred square meters, and was probably not bugged. At least he'd found no microphones when he'd moved in and hung his pictures, and his sweep gear had discovered no anomalous signals—his phone had to be bugged, of course, but just because it was bugged didn't mean that there was somebody going over the tapes every day or even every week. MSS was just one more government agency, and in China they were probably little different from those in America, or France for that matter, lazy, underpaid people who worked as little as possible and served a bureaucracy that didn't encourage singular effort. They probably spent most of their time smoking the wretched local cigarettes and jerking off.

He had an American Yale lock on the door, with a pick-resistant tumbler and a sturdy locking mechanism. If asked about this, he'd explain that when living in California for NEC, he'd been burglarized—the Americans were such lawless and uncivilized people—and he didn't want that to happen again.

"So, this is the home of a capitalist," Ming observed, looking around. The walls were covered with prints, mainly movie posters.

"Yes, well, it's the home of a salaryman. I don't really know if I'm a capitalist or not, Comrade Ming," he added, with a smile and arched eyebrow. He pointed to his couch. "Please have a seat. Can I get you anything?"

"Another glass of wine, perhaps?" she suggested, spotting and then looking at the wrapped box on the chair opposite the couch.

Nomuri smiled. "That I can do." He headed off into the kitchen, where he had a bottle of California Chardonnay chilling in the fridge. Popping the cork was easy enough, and he headed back to the living room with two glasses, one of which he handed to his guest. "Oh," he said then. "Yes, this is for you, Ming." With that he handed over the box, wrapped fairly neatly in red—of course—gift paper.

"May I open it now?"

"Certainly." Nomuri smiled, in as gentlemanly a lustful way as he could manage. "Perhaps you would want to unwrap it, well . . ."

"Are you saying in your bedroom?"

"Excuse me. Just that you might wish some privacy when you open it. Please pardon me if I am too forward."

The mirth in her eyes said it all. Ming took a deep sip of her white wine and walked off into that room and closed the door. Nomuri took a small sip of his own and sat down on the couch to await developments. If he'd chosen unwisely, she might throw the box at him and storm out . . . not much chance of that, he thought. More likely, even if she found him too forward, she'd keep the present and the box, finish her wine, make small talk, and then take her leave in thirty minutes or so, just to show good manners—effectively the same result without the overt insult—and Nomuri would have to search for another recruitment prospect. No, the best outcome would be . . .

. . . the door opened, and there she stood with a small, impish smile. The boiler suit was gone. Instead she wore the red-orange bra and panties set, the one with the front closure. She stood there holding her wine glass in salute, and it looked as if she'd taken another sip of her drink, maybe to work up her courage . . . or to loosen her inhibitions.

Nomuri found himself suddenly apprehensive. He took another drink himself before standing, and he walked slowly, and a little uneasily, to the bedroom doorway.

Her eyes, he saw, were a little uneasy themselves, a little frightened, and with luck maybe his were, too, because women everywhere liked their men to be just a little vulnerable. Maybe John Wayne hadn't gotten all the action he wanted, Nomuri thought quickly. Then he smiled.

"I guessed right on the size."

"Yes, and it feels wonderful, like a second skin, smooth and silky." Every woman has it, Nomuri realized: the ability to smile and, regardless of the exterior, show the woman within, often a perfect woman, full of tenderness and desire, demureness and coquetry, and all you had to do . . .

. . . his hand came out and touched her face as gently as his slight shaking allowed. What the hell was this? he demanded of himself. *Shaking?* James Bond's hands never shook. This was the time when he was supposed to scoop her up in his arms and stride in a masterful way off to the bed, there to possess her like Vince Lombardi taking over a football team, like George Patton leading an attack. But for all his triumphal anticipation of this moment, things were different from what he'd expected. Whoever or whatever Ming was, she was giving herself to him. There was no more in her than that—that was all she had. And she was giving it to him.

He bent his head down to kiss her, and there he caught the scent of the Dream Angel perfume, and somehow it suited the moment perfectly. Her arms came around him sooner than he'd expected. His hands replicated her gesture, and he found that her skin was smooth, like oiled silk, and his hands rubbed up and down of their own accord. He felt something strange on his chest and looked down to see her small hands undoing his buttons, and then her eyes looked into his, and her face was no longer plain. He unbuttoned his own cuffs, and she forced his shirt off, down his back, then lifted his T-shirt over his head—or tried to, for her arms were too short to make it quite all the way—and then he hugged her tighter, feeling the silklike artificial fibers of her new bra rub on his hairless chest. It was then that his hug became harder, more insistent, and his kiss harder on her mouth, and he took her face in his hands and looked hard into her dark, suddenly deep eyes, and what he saw was woman.

Her hands moved and unfastened his belt and slacks, which fell to his ankles. He nearly fell himself when he moved one leg, but Ming caught him and both laughed a little as he lifted his feet clear of his loafers and the slacks, and with that they both took a step toward the bed. Ming took another and turned, displaying herself for him. He'd underestimated the girl. Her waist was a full four inches slimmer than he'd thought—must be the damned boiler suit she wore to work, Nomuri thought at once—and her breasts filled the bra to perfection. Even the awful haircut seemed right just now, somehow fitting the amber skin and slanted eyes.

What came next was both easy and very, very hard. Nomuri reached out to her side, pulling her close, but not too close. Then he let his hand wander across her chest, for the first time feeling her breast through the gossamer fabric of the bra, at the same time watching her eyes closely for a reaction. There was little of that, though her eyes did seem to relax, perhaps even smile just a little at his touch, and then came the obligatory next step. With both hands, he unfastened the front closure of the bra. Instantly Ming's hands dropped to cover herself. *What did that mean?* the CIA officer wondered, but then her hands dropped and she pulled him to her, and their bodies met and his head came down to kiss her again, and his hands slid the bra straps off her arms and onto the floor. There was little left to be done, and both, so it seemed, advanced with a combination of lust and fear. Her hands went down and loosened the elastic band of his briefs, with her eyes now locked on his, and this time she smiled, a for-real smile that made him blush, because he was as ready as he needed to be, and then her hands pushed down on the briefs, and all that left was his socks, and then it was his turn to kneel and pull down on the red silklike panties. She kicked them loose and each stood apart to inspect the other. Her breasts were about a large B, Nomuri thought, the nipples brown as potting soil. Her waist was not nearly model-thin, but a womanly contrast with both the hips and upper body. Nomuri took a step and then took her hand and walked her to the bed, laying her down with a gentle kiss, and for this moment he was not an intelligence officer for his country.

CHAPTER 10

Lessons of the Trade

The pathway started in Nomuri's apartment, and from there went to a web site established in Beijing, notionally for Nippon Electric Company, but the site had been designed for NEC by an American citizen who worked for more than one boss, one of whom was a front operated by and for the Central Intelligence Agency. The precise address point for Nomuri's e-mail was then accessible to the CIA's Beijing station chief, who, as a matter of fact, didn't know anything about Nomuri. That was a security measure to which he would probably have objected, but which he would have understood as a characteristic of Mary Patricia Foley's way of running the Directorate of Operations—and besides which, Station Beijing hadn't exactly covered itself with glory in recruiting senior PRC officials to be American agents-in-place.

The message the station chief downloaded was just gibberish to him, scrambled letters that might as easily have been typed by a chimpanzee in return for a bunch of bananas at some research university, and he took no note of it, just super-encrypting on his own in-house system called TAPDANCE and cross-loading it to an official government communications network that went to a communications satellite, to be downloaded at Sunnyvale, California, then uploaded yet again, and downloaded at Fort Belvoir, Virginia, across the Potomac River from Washington, D.C. From there the message went by secure fiber-optic landline to CIA headquarters at Langley, and then first of all into Mercury, the Agency's communications center, where the Station Beijing super-encryption was stripped away, revealing the original gibberish, and then cross-loaded one last time to Mrs. Foley's personal computer terminal, which was the only one with the encryption system and daily key-selection algorithm for the counterpart system on Chet Nomuri's laptop, which was called INTERCRYPT. MP was doing other things at the time, and took twenty minutes to log into her own system and note the arrival of a SORGE message. That piqued her interest at once. She executed the command to decrypt the message, and got gibberish, then realized (not for the first time) that Nomuri was on the other side of the date line, and had therefore used a different key sequence. *So, adjust the date for tomorrow . . .* and, yes! She printed a hard copy of the message for her husband, and then saved the message to her personal hard drive, automatically encrypting it along the way. From there, it was a short walk to Ed's office.

"Hey, baby," the DCI said, without looking up. Not too many people walked into his office without announcement. The news had to be good. MP had a beaming smile as she handed the paper over.

"Chet got laid last night!" the DDO told the DCI.

"Am I supposed to break out a cigar?" the Director of Central Intelligence asked. His eyes scanned the message.

"Well, it's a step forward."

"For him, maybe," Ed Foley responded with a twinkling eye. "I suppose you can get pretty horny on that sort of assignment, though I never had that problem myself." The Foleys had always worked the field as a married couple, and had gone through The Farm together. It had saved the senior Foley from all the complications that James Bond must have encountered.

"Eddie, you can be such a mudge!"

That made the DCI look up. "Such a what?"

"Curmudgeon!" she growled. "This could be a real breakthrough. This little chippy is personal secretary to Fang Gan. She knows all sorts of stuff we want to know."

"And Chet got to try her out last night. Honey, that's not the same thing as recruitment. We don't have an agent-in-place quite yet," he reminded his wife.

"I know, I know, but I have a feeling about this."

"Woman's intuition?" Ed asked, scanning the message again for any sordid details, but finding only cold facts, as though *The Wall Street Journal* had covered the seduction. Well, at least Nomuri had a little discretion. No rigid quivering rod plunging into her warm moist sheath—though Nomuri was twenty-nine, and at that age the rod tended to be pretty rigid. *Chet was from California, wasn't he?* the DCI wondered. So, probably not a virgin, maybe even a competent lover, though on the first time with anybody you mainly wanted to see if the pieces fit together properly—they always did, at least in Ed Foley's experience, but you still wanted to check and see. He remembered Robin Williams's takeoff on Adam and Eve, "Better stand back, honey. I don't know how big this thing gets!" The combination of careful conservatism and out-of-control wishful thinking common to the male of the species. "Okay, so, what are you going to reply? 'How many orgasms did the two of you have'?"

"God damn it, Ed!" The pin in the balloon worked, the DCI saw. He could almost see steam coming out of his wife's pretty ears. "You know damned well what I'm going to suggest. Let the relationship blossom and ease her into talking about her job. It'll take a while, but if it works it'll be worth the wait."

And if it doesn't work, it's not a bad deal for Chester, Ed Foley thought. There weren't many professions in the world in which getting sex was part of the job that earned you promotions, were there?

"Mary?"

"Yes, Ed?"

"Does it strike you as a little odd that the kid's reporting his sex life to us? Does it make you blush a little?"

"It would if he were telling me face-to-face. The e-mail method is best for this, I think. Less human content."

"You're happy with the security of the information transfer?"

"Yeah, we've been through this. The message could just be sensitive business information, and the encryption system is very robust. The boys and girls at Fort Meade can break it, but it's brute force every time, and it takes up to a week, even after they make the right guesses on how the encryption system works. The PRC guys would have to go from scratch. The trapdoor in the ISP was very cleverly designed, and the way we tap into it should also be secure—and even then, just because an embassy phone taps into an ISP doesn't mean anything. We have a consular official downloading pornography from a local Web site through that ISP as another cover, in case anybody over there gets real clever." That had been carefully thought through. It would be something that one would wish to be covert, something the counterintelligence agency in Beijing would find both understandable and entertaining in its own right, if and when they cracked into it.

"Anything good?" Ed Foley asked, again, just to bedevil his wife.

"Not unless you're into child abuse. Some of the subjects for this site are too young to vote. If you downloaded it over here, the FBI might come knocking on your door."

"Capitalism really has broken out over there, eh?"

"Some of the senior Party officials seem to like this sort of thing. I guess when you're pushing eighty, you need something special to help jump-start the motor." Mary Pat had seen some of the photographs, and once had been plenty. She was a mother, and all of those photographic subjects had been infants once, strange though that might seem to a subscriber to that Web site. The abusers of girls must have thought that they all sprang into life with their legs spread and a welcoming look in their doll-child faces. Not quite, the DDO thought, but her job wasn't to be a clergyman. Sometimes you had to do business with such perverts, because they had information which her country needed. If you were lucky, and the information was really useful, then you often arranged for them to defect, to live in the United States, where they could live and enjoy their perversions to some greater or lesser degree, after being briefed on the law, and the consequences of breaking it. Afterward there was always a bathroom and soap to wash your hands. It was a need of which she'd availed herself more than once. One of the problems with espionage was that you didn't always do business with the sort of people whom you'd willingly invite into your home. But it wasn't about Miss Manners. It was about getting information that your country needed to guard its strategic interests, and even to prevail in war, if it came to that. Lives were often at stake, either directly or indirectly. And so, you did business with anyone who had such information, even if he or she wasn't exactly a member of the clergy.

"Okay, babe. Keep me posted," Foley told his wife.

"Will do, honey-bunny." The DDO headed back to her own office. There she drew up her reply to Nomuri: MESSAGE RECEIVED. KEEP US POSTED ON YOUR PROGRESS. MP. ENDS.

The reply came as a relief to Nomuri when he woke and checked his e-mail. It was a disappointment that he didn't wake up with company, but to expect that would have been unrealistic. Ming would have been ill-advised to spend the night anywhere but in her own bed. Nomuri couldn't even drive her back. She'd just left, carrying her presents—well, wearing some of them—for the walk back to her own shared flat where, Nomuri fervently hoped, she wouldn't discuss her evening's adventures with her roommates. You never knew about women and how they talked. It wasn't all that dissimilar with some men, Nomuri remembered from college, where some of his chums had talked at length about their conquests, as though they'd slain a dragon with a Popsicle stick. Nomuri had never indulged in this aural spectator sport. Either he'd had a spy's mentality even then, or he'd been somehow imbued with the dictum that a gentleman didn't kiss and tell. But did women? That was a mystery to him, like why it was that women seemed to go to the bathroom in pairs—he'd occasionally joked that that was when they'd held their "union meetings." Anyway, women talked more than men did. He was sure of that. And while they kept many secrets from men, how many did they keep from other women? Jesus, all that had to happen was for her to tell a roomie that she'd had her brains fucked out by a Japanese salaryman, and if that roomie was an informant to the MSS, Ming would get a visit from a security officer, who at the very least would counsel her never to see Nomuri again. More likely, the counseling would involve a demand to send that degenerate American bourgeois trash (the Victoria's Secret underthings) back to him, plus a threat to lose her ministry job if she ever appeared on the same street with him again. And that also meant that he'd be tailed and observed and investigated by the MSS, and that was something he had to take seriously. They didn't have to catch him committing espionage. This was a communist country, where due process of law was a bourgeois concept unworthy of serious consideration, and civil rights were limited to doing what one was told. As a foreigner doing business in the PRC, he might get some easiness of treatment, but not all that much.

So, he hadn't just gotten his rocks off, Nomuri told himself, past the delightful memories of a passionate evening. He'd crossed a wide red line in the street, and his safety depended entirely upon on how discreet Ming was. He hadn't—could not have—warned her to keep her mouth shut about their time together. Such things weren't said, because they added a level of gravity to what was supposed to have been a time of joy and friendship . . . or even something potentially bigger than friendship. Women thought in such terms, Chester reminded himself, and for that reason he might see a pointed nose and whiskers the next time he looked in the mirror, but this was *business,* not *personal,* he told himself as he shut down his computer.

Except for one small thing. He'd had sexual relations with an intelligent and not entirely unattractive young female human being, and the problem was that when you gave a little bit of your heart away, you never really got it back. And his heart, Nomuri belatedly realized, was distantly connected to his dick. He wasn't James Bond. He could not embrace a woman as a paid whore embraced a man. It just wasn't in him to be that sort of heartless swine. The good news was that for this reason he could stand to look in a mirror for the time being. The bad news was that this ability might be short-lived, if he treated Ming as a thing and not a person.

Nomuri needed advice on how to feel about this operation, and he didn't have a place to get it. It wasn't the sort of thing to e-mail to Mary Pat or to one of the pshrinks the Agency employed for counseling DO people who needed a little guidance with their work. This sort of thing had to be handled face-to-face with a real person, whose body language you could read and whose tone of voice would deliver its own content. No, e-mail wasn't the medium he needed right now. He needed to fly to Tokyo and meet a senior officer of the Directorate of Operations who could counsel him on how to handle things. But if the guy told him to cut himself off from intimate contact with Ming, then what would he do? Nomuri asked himself. It wasn't as though he had a girlfriend of any kind, and he had his needs for intimacy, too—and besides, if he cut her off, what effect would that have on his potential, prospective agent? You didn't check your humanity by the door when you joined up with the Agency, despite what all the books said and the public expectations were. All the chuckles over beer during the nights after training sessions seemed a distant thing now, and all the expectations he and his colleagues had had back then. They'd been so far off the mark, in spite of what their training officers had told them. He'd been a child then, and to some extent even in Japan, but suddenly he was a man, alone in a country that was at best suspicious, and at worst hostile to him and his country. Well, it was in her hands now, and that was something he couldn't change.

Her co-workers noted a slight difference in their colleague. She smiled a little more, and in a somewhat different way. Something good must have happened to her, some of them thought, and for this they rejoiced, albeit in a reserved and private way. If Ming wished to share the experience with them, all well and good, and if not, that, too, was okay with them, because some things were private, even among a group of women who shared virtually everything, including stories of their minister and his fumbling, lengthy, and occasionally futile efforts at lovemaking. He was a wise man, and usually a gentle one, though as a boss he had his bad points. But Ming would notice none of those today. Her smile was sweeter than ever, and her eyes twinkled like little diamonds, the rest of the admin/secretarial staff all thought. They'd all seen it before, though not with Ming, whose love life had been an abbreviated one, and whom the minister liked a little too much, but whom he serviced imperfectly and too seldom. She sat at her computer to do her correspondence and translations of Western news articles that might be of interest to the Minister. Ming had the best English skills of anyone in this corner of the building, and the new computer system worked superbly. The next step, so the story went, was a computer into which you'd just speak, making the characters appear by voice command, sure to become the curse of every executive secretary in the world, because it would largely make them obsolete. Or maybe not. The boss couldn't fuck a computer, could he? Not that Minister Fang was all *that* intrusive in his demands. And the perks he delivered in return weren't bad at all.

Her first morning assignment took the customary ninety minutes, after which she printed up the resulting copy and stapled the pages together by article. This morning she'd translated pieces by the *Times of London,* and *The New York Times,* plus *The Washington Post,* so that her Minister would know what the barbarians around the world thought of the enlightened policy of the People's Republic.

In his private office, Minister Fang was going over other things. The MSS had a double report on the Russians: both oil and gold, the reports said. So, he thought, Zhang had been right all along, even more right than he knew. Eastern Siberia was indeed a treasure-house, full of things everyone needed. Oil, because petroleum was the very blood of modern society, and gold, because in addition to its negotiable value as an old but still very real medium of exchange, it still had industrial and scientific uses as well. And each had a cache of its own. What a pity that such riches should fall to a people without the wit to make proper use of them. It was so strange, the Russians who had given the world the gift of Marxism but then failed to exploit it properly, and then abandoned it, only to fail also in their transition to a bourgeois capitalist society. Fang lit a cigarette, his fifth of the day (he was trying to cut back as his seventieth birthday approached), and set the MSS report down on his desk before leaning back in his chair to puff on his unfiltered smoke and consider the information this morning had brought. Siberia, as Zhang had been saying for some years now, had so much that the PRC needed, timber, minerals in abundance—even greater abundance, so these intelligence documents said—and *space,* which China needed above all things.

There were simply too many people in China, and that despite population-control measures that could only be called draconian both in their content, and in their ruthless application. Those measures were an affront to Chinese culture, which had always viewed children as a blessing, and now the social engineering was having an unexpected result. Allowed only one child per married couple, the people often chose to have boys instead of girls. It was not unknown for a peasant to take a female toddler of two years and drop her down a well—the merciful ones broke their necks first—to dispose of the embarrassing encumbrance. Fang understood the reasons for this. A girl child grew up to marry, to join her life to a man, while a boy child could always be depended upon to support and honor his parents, and provide security. But a girl child would merely spread her legs for some other couple's boy child, and where was the security for her parents in that?

It had been true in Fang's case. As he'd grown to a senior party official, he'd made sure that his own mother and father had found a comfortable place to live out their lives, for such were the duties of a child for those who had given him life. Along the way, he'd married, of course—his wife was long dead of cardiovascular disease—and he'd given some lip service to his wife's parents . . . but not as much as he'd done for his own. Even his wife had understood that, and used her shadow-influence as the wife of a party official to make her own special but lesser arrangements. Her brother had died young, at the hands of the American army in Korea, and was therefore just a memory without practical value.

But the problem for China that no one really talked about, even at Politburo level, was that their population policy was affecting the demographics of their country. In elevating the value of boy children over girls, the PRC was causing an imbalance that was becoming statistically significant. In fifteen years or so, there would be a shortage of women—some said that this was a good thing, because they would achieve the overarching national objective of population stability faster but it also meant that for a generation, millions of Chinese men would have no women to marry and mate with. Would this turn into a flood of homosexuality? PRC policy still frowned upon that as a bourgeois degeneracy, though sodomy had been decriminalized in 1998. But if there were no women to be had, what was a man to do? And in addition to killing off surplus girl babies, those abandoned by their parents were often given away, to American and European couples unable to have children of their own. This happened by the hundreds of thousands, with the children disposed of as readily and casually as Americans sold puppies in shopping malls. Something in Fang's soul bridled at that, but his feelings were mere bourgeois sentimentality, weren't they? National policy dictated what must be, and policy was the means to achieving the necessary goal.

His was a life as comfortable as privilege could make it. In addition to a plush office as pleasant as any capitalist's, he had an official car and driver to take him to his residence, an ornate apartment with servants to look after his needs, the best food that his country could provide, good beverages, a television connected to a satellite service so that he could receive all manner of entertainment, even including Japanese pornographic channels, for his manly drives had not yet deserted him. (He didn't speak Japanese, but you didn't need to understand the dialogue in such movies, did you?)

Fang still worked long hours, rising at six-thirty, and was at his desk before eight every morning. His staff of secretaries and assistants took proper care of him, and some of the female ones were agreeably compliant, once, occasionally twice per week. Few men of his years had his vigor, Fang was sure, and unlike Chairman Mao, he didn't abuse children, which he'd known of at the time and found somewhat distasteful. But great men had their flaws, and you overlooked them because of the greatness that made them who they were. As for himself and people like him, they were entitled to the proper environments in which to rest, good nourishment to sustain their bodies through their long and grueling workdays, and the opportunities for relaxation and recreation that men of vigor and intelligence needed. It was *necessary* that they live better than most other citizens of their country, and it was also *earned.* Giving direction to the world's most populous country was no easy task. It demanded their every intellectual energy, and such energy needed to be conserved and restored. Fang looked up as Ming entered with her folder of news articles.

"Good morning, Minister," she said with proper deference.

"Good morning, child." Fang nodded with affection. This one shared his bed fairly well, and for that reason merited more than a grunt. Well, he'd gotten her a very comfortable office chair, hadn't he? She withdrew, bowing proper respect for her father figure, as she always did. Fang noticed nothing particularly different about her demeanor, as he lifted the folder and took out the news articles, along with a pencil for making notations. He'd compare these with MSS estimates of the mood of other countries and their governments. It was Fang's way of letting the Ministry of State Security know that the Politburo members still had minds of their own with which to think. The MSS had signally failed to predict America's diplomatic recognition of Taiwan, though in fairness, the American news media didn't seem to predict the actions of this President Ryan all that well, either. What an odd man he was, and certainly no friend of the People's Republic. A peasant, the MSS analysts called him, and in many ways that seemed both accurate and appropriate. He was strangely unsophisticated in his outlook, something *The New York Times* commented upon rather frequently. Why did they dislike him? Was he not capitalist enough, or was he too capitalist? Understanding the American news media was beyond Fang's powers of analysis, but he could at least digest the things they said, and that was something the intelligence "experts" at the MSS Institute for American

Studies were not always able to do. With that thought, Fang lit another cigarette and settled back in his chair.

It was a miracle, Provalov thought. Central Army Records had gotten the files, fingerprints, and photographs of the two bodies recovered in St. Petersburg—but perversely sent the records to him rather than to Abramov and Ustinov, doubtless because he was the one who had invoked the name of Sergey Golovko. Dzerzhinskiy Square still inspired people to do their jobs in a timely fashion. The names and vital statistics would be taxed at once to St. Petersburg so that his northern colleagues might see what information could be developed. The names and photographs were only a start—documents nearly twenty years old showing youthful, emotionless faces. The service records were fairly impressive, though. Once upon a time, Pyotr Alekseyevich Amalrik and Pavel Borissovich Zimyanin had been considered superior soldiers, smart, fit . . . and highly reliable, politically speaking, which was why they'd gone to Spetsnaz school and sergeant school. Both had fought in Afghanistan, and done fairly well—they'd survived Afghanistan, which was not the usual thing for Spetsnaz troops, who'd drawn all of the dirtiest duty in an especially dirty war. They'd not reenlisted, which was not unusual. Hardly anyone in the Soviet Army had ever reenlisted voluntarily. They they'd returned to civilian life, both working in the same factory outside Leningrad, as it had been called then. But Amalrik and Zimyanin had both found ordinary civilian life boring, and both, he gathered, had drifted into something else. He'd have to let the investigators in St. Petersburg find out more. He pulled a routing slip from his drawer and rubber-banded it to the records package. It would be couriered to St. Petersburg, where Abramov and Ustinov would play with the contents.

A Mr. Sherman, Mr. Secretary," Winston's secretary told him over the intercom. "Line three."

"Hey, Sam," SecTreas said, as he picked up the phone. "What's new?"

"Our oil field up north," the president of Atlantic Richfield replied.

"Good news?"

"You might say that. Our field people say the find is about fifty percent bigger than our initial estimates."

"How solid is that information?"

"About as reliable as one of your T-bills, George. My head field guy is Ernie Beach. He's as good at finding oil as you used to be playing up on The Street." *Maybe even better,* Sam Sherman didn't add. Winston was known to have something of an ego on the subject of his own worth. The addendum got through anyway.

"So, summarize that for me," the Secretary of the Treasury commanded.

"So, when this field comes on line, the Russians will be in a position to purchase Saudi Arabia outright, plus Kuwait and maybe half of Iran. It makes east Texas look like a fart in a tornado. It's *huge,* George."

"Hard to get out?"

"It won't be easy, and it won't be inexpensive, but from an engineering point of view it's pretty straightforward. If you want to buy a hot stock, pick a Russian company that makes cold-weather gear. They're going to be real busy for the next ten years or so," Sherman advised.

"Okay, and what can you tell me of the implications for Russia in economic terms?"

"Hard to say. It will take eight to twelve years to bring this field fully on line, and the amount of crude this will dump on the market will distort market conditions quite a bit. We haven't modeled all that out—but it's going to be *huge,* like in the neighborhood of one hundred billion dollars per year, current-year dollars, that is."

"For how long?" Winston could almost hear the shrug that followed.

"Twenty years, maybe more. Our friends in Moscow still want us to sit on this, but word's perking out in our company, like trying to hide a sunrise, y'know? I give it a month before it breaks out into the news media. Maybe a little longer'n that, but not much."

"What about the gold strike?"

"Hell, George, they're not telling *me* anything about that, but my guy in Moscow says the cat's gobbled down some kind of canary, or that's how it appears to him. That will probably depress the world price of gold about five, maybe ten percent, but our models say it'll rebound before Ivan starts selling the stuff he pulls out of the ground. Our Russian friends—well, their rich uncle just bit the big one and left them the whole estate, y'know?"

"And no adverse effects on us," Winston thought.

"Hell, no. They'll have to buy all sorts of hardware from our people, and they'll need a lot of expertise that only we have, and after that's over, the world price of oil goes down, and that won't hurt us either. You know, George, I like the Russians. They've been unlucky sonsabitches for a long time, but maybe this'll change that for 'em."

"No objections here or next door, Sam," TRADER assured his friend. "Thanks for the information."

"Well, you guys still collect my taxes." *You bastards,* he didn't add, but Winston heard it anyway, including the chuckle. "See you around, George."

"Right, have a good one, Sam, and thanks." Winston killed one button on his phone, selected another line, and hit his number nine speed-dial line.

"Yeah?" a familiar voice responded. Only ten people had access to this number.

"Jack, it's George, just had a call from Sam Sherman, Atlantic Richfield."

"Russia?"

"Yeah. The field is fifty percent bigger than they initially thought. That makes it pretty damned big, biggest oil strike ever, as a matter of fact, bigger than the whole Persian Gulf combined. Getting the oil out will be a little expensive, but Sam says it's all cookbook stuff—hard, but they know how it's done, no new technology to invent, just a matter of spending the money—and not even all that much, 'cause labor is a lot cheaper there than it is here. The Russians are going to get rich."

"How rich?" the President asked.

"On the order of a hundred billion dollars per year once the field is fully on line, and that's good for twenty years, maybe more."

Jack had to whistle at that. "Two *trillion* dollars. That's real money, George."

"That's what we call it on The Street, Mr. President," Winston agreed. "Sure as hell, that's real money."

"And what effect will it have on the Russian economy?"

"It won't hurt them very much," SecTreas assured him. "It gets them a ton of hard currency. With that money they can buy the things they'd like to have, and buy the tools to build the things they can make on their own. This will re-industrialize their country, Jack, jump-start them into the new century, assuming they have the brains to make proper use of it and not let it all bug out to Switzerland and Liechtenstein."

"How can we help them?" POTUS asked.

"Best answer to that, you and I and two or three others sit down with our Russian counterparts and ask them what they need. If we can get a few of our industrialists to build some plants over there, it won't hurt, and it'll damned sure look good on TV."

"Noted, George. Get me a paper on that by the beginning of next week, and then we'll see if we can figure out a way to let the Russians know what we know."

It was the end of another overlong day for Sergey Golovko. Running the SVR was job enough for any man, but he also had to back up Eduard Petrovich Grushavoy, President of the Russian Republic. President Grushavoy had his own collection of ministers, some of them competent, the others selected for their political capital, or merely to deny them to the political opposition. They could still do damage on the inside of Grushavoy's administration, but less than on the outside. On the inside they had to use small-caliber weapons, lest they be killed by their own shots.

The good news was that the Economics Minister, Vasily Konstantinovich Solomentsev, was intelligent and seemingly honest as well, as rare a combination in the Russian political spectrum as anywhere else in the known world. He had his ambitions—it was a rare minister who did not—but mainly, it seemed, he wanted his nation to prosper, and didn't want to profit himself all that much. A little self-enrichment was all right with Golovko, just so that a man wasn't a pig about it. The line, for Sergey Nikolay'ch, was about twenty million euros. More than that was hoggish, but less was understandable. After all, if a minister was successful at helping his country, he or she was entitled to get a proper reward for doing so. The ordinary working people out there wouldn't mind, if the result was a better life for them, would they? Probably not, the spymaster thought. This wasn't America, overrun with pointless and counterproductive "ethics" laws. The American President, whom Golovko knew well, had an aphorism that the Russian admired: *If you have to write your ethics rules down, you've already lost.* No fool, that Ryan, once a deadly enemy, and now a good friend, or seemingly so. Golovko had cultivated that friendship by providing help to America in two serious international crises. He'd done it because it had, first of all, been in his nation's interest, and secondly, because Ryan was a man of honor, and unlikely to forget such favors. It had also amused Golovko, who'd spent most of his adulthood in an agency devoted to the destruction of the West.

But what about himself? Was someone intent on his own destruction? Had someone desired to end his life in a loud and spectacular manner on the paving stones of Dzerzhinskiy Square? The more his mind dwelt on that question, the more frightening it became. Few healthy men could contemplate the end of their lives with equanimity, and Golovko wasn't one of them. His hands never shook, but he didn't argue at all with Major Shelepin's increasingly invasive measures to keep him alive. The car changed every day in color, and sometimes in make, and the routes to his office shared only the starting place—the SVR building was sufficiently large that the daily journey to work had a total of five possible end points. The clever part, which Golovko admired, was that he himself occasionally rode in the front seat of the lead vehicle, while some functionary sat in the back seat of the putative guarded car. Anatoliy was no fool, and even showed the occasional spark of creativity.

But none of that now. Golovko shook his head and opened his last folder of the day, scanning first of all the executive summary—and his mind skidded to an almost instant halt, his hand reaching for a phone and dialing a number.

"This is Golovko," he told the male voice who answered. He didn't have to say anything else.

"Sergey Nikolay'ch," the minister's voice greeted him pleasantly five seconds later. "What can I do for you?"

"Well, Vasily Konstantinovich, you can confirm these numbers to me. Are they possible?"

"They are more than possible, Sergey. They are as real as the sunset," Solomentsev told the intelligence chief *cum* chief minister and advisor to President Grushavoy.

"Solkin syn," the intelligence chief muttered. *Son of a bitch!* "And this wealth has been there for how long?" he asked incredulously.

"The oil, perhaps five hundred thousand years; the gold, rather longer, Sergey."

"And we never knew," Golovko breathed.

"No one really looked, Comrade Minister. Actually, I find the gold report the more interesting. I must see one of these gold-encrusted wolf pelts. Something for Prokofiev, eh? Peter and the *Golden* Wolf."

"An entertaining thought," Golovko said, dismissing it immediately. "What will it mean to our country?"

"Sergey Nikolay'ch, I would have to be a fortune-teller to answer that substantively, but it could be the salvation of our country in the long term. Now we have something that all nations want—two somethings, as a matter of fact—and it belongs to us, and for it those foreigners will pay vast sums of money, and do so with a smile. Japan, for example. We will answer their energy needs for the next fifty years, and along the way we will save them vast sums in transportation costs—ship the oil a few hundred kilometers instead of ten *thousand.* And perhaps America, too, though they've made their own big strike on the Alaskan-Canadian border. The question becomes how we move the oil to market. We'll build a pipeline from the field to Vladivostok, of course, but maybe another one to St. Petersburg so that we can sell oil more easily to Europe as well. In fact, we can probably have the Europeans, especially the Germans, build the pipeline for us, just to get a discount on the oil. Serge, if we'd found this oil twenty years ago, we—"

"Perhaps." It wasn't hard to imagine what would come next: The Soviet Union would not have fallen but grown strong instead. Golovko had no such illusions. The Soviet government would have managed to fuck up these new treasures as it had fucked up everything else. The Soviet government had *owned* Siberia for seventy years but had never even gone looking for what might have been there. The country had lacked the proper experts to do the looking, but was too proud to let anyone else do it, lest they think less of the Motherland. If any one thing had killed the USSR, it wasn't communism, or even totalitarianism. It was that perverse *amour propre* that was the most dangerous and destructive aspect of the Russian character, created by a sense of inferiority that went back to the House of Romanov and beyond. The Soviet Union's death had been as self-inflicted as any suicide's, just slower and therefore far deadlier in coming. Golovko endured the next ninety seconds of historical speculation from a man who had little sense of history, then spoke: "All this is good, Vasily Konstantinovich, but what of the future? That is the time in which we will all live, after all."

"It will do us little harm. Sergey, this is the salvation of our country. It will take ten years to get the full benefit from the outfields, but then we shall have a steady and regular income for at least one whole generation, and perhaps more besides."

"What help will we need?"

"The Americans and the British have expertise which we need, from their own exploitation of the Alaskan fields. They have knowledge. We shall learn it and make use of it. We are in negotiations now with Atlantic Richfield, the American oil company, for technical support. They are being greedy, but that's to be expected. They know that only they have what we need, and paying them for it is cheaper than having to replicate it ourselves. So, they will get most of what they now demand. Perhaps we will pay them in gold bricks," Solomentsev suggested lightly.

Golovko had to resist the temptation to inquire too deeply into the gold strike. The oil field was far more lucrative, but gold was prettier. He, too, wanted to see one of those pelts that this Gogol fellow had used to collect the dust. And this lonely forest-dweller would have to be properly taken care of—no major problem, as he lived alone and was childless. Whatever he got, the state would soon get back, old as he was. And there'd be a TV show, maybe even a feature film, about this hunter. He'd once hunted Germans, after all, and the Russians still made heroes of such men. That would make Pavel Petrovich Gogol happy enough, wouldn't it?

"What does Eduard Petrovich know?"

"I've been saving the information until I had a full and reliable reading on it. I have that now. I think he will be pleased at the next cabinet meeting, Sergey Nikolay'ch."

As well he should, Golovko thought. President Grushavoy had been as busy as a one-armed, one-legged paperhanger for three years. No, more like a stage magician or conjurer, forced to produce real things from nothing, and his success in keeping the nation moving often seemed nothing short of miraculous. Perhaps this was God's own way of rewarding the man for his efforts, though it would not be an entirely unmixed blessing. Every government agency would want its piece of the gold-and-oil pie, each with its needs, all of them presented by its own minister as vital to the security of the state, in white papers of brilliant logic and compelling reasoning. Who knew, maybe some of them would even be telling the truth, though truth was so often a rare commodity in the cabinet room. Each minister had an empire to build, and the better he built it, the closer he would come to the seat at the head of the table that was occupied, for now, by Eduard Petrovich Grushavoy. Golovko wondered if it had been this way under the czars. Probably, he decided at once. Human nature didn't change very much. The way people had acted in Babylon or Byzantium was probably little different from the way they'd act at the next cabinet meeting, three days hence. He wondered how President Grushavoy would handle the news.

"How much has leaked out?" the spymaster asked.

"There are doubtless some rumors," Minister Solomentsev answered, "but the current estimates are less than twenty-four hours old, and it usually takes longer than that to leak. I will have these documents messengered to you—tomorrow morning?"

"That will be fine, Vasily. I'll have some of my own analysts go over the data, so that I can present my own independent estimate of the situation."

"I have no objection to that," the economics minister responded, surprising Golovko more than a little. But then this wasn't the USSR anymore. The current cabinet might be the modern counterpart to the old Politburo, but nobody there told lies . . . well, at least not big lies. And that was a measure of progress for his country, wasn't it?

CHAPTER 11

Faith of the Fathers

His name was Yu Fa An, and he said he was a Christian. That was rare enough that Monsignor Schepke invited him in at once. What he saw was a Chinese national of fifty-plus years and stooped frame, with hair a curious mix of black and gray that one saw only rarely in this part of the world.

"Welcome to our embassy. I am Monsignor Schepke." He bowed quickly and then shook the man's hand.

"Thank you. I am the Reverend Yu Fa An," the man replied with the dignity of truth, one cleric to another.

"Indeed. Of what denomination?"

"I am a Baptist."

"Ordained? Is that possible?" Schepke motioned the visitor to follow him, and in a moment they stood before the Nuncio. "Eminence, this is the Reverend Yu Fa An—of Beijing?" Schepke asked belatedly.

"Yes, that is so. My congregation is mainly northwest of here."

"Welcome." Cardinal DiMilo rose from his chair for a warm handshake, and guided the man to the comfortable visitor's chair. Monsignor Schepke went to fetch tea. "It is a pleasure to meet a fellow Christian in this city."

"There are not enough of us, and that is a fact, Eminence," Yu confirmed.

Monsignor Schepke swiftly arrived with a tray of tea things, which he set on the low coffee table.

"Thank you, Franz."

"I thought that some local citizens should welcome you. I expect you've had the formal welcome from the Foreign Ministry, and that it was correct . . . and rather cold?" Yu asked.

The Cardinal smiled as he handed a cup to his guest. "It was correct, as you say, but it could have been warmer."

"You will find that the government here has ample manners and good attention to protocol, but little in the way of sincerity," Yu said, in English, with a very strange accent.

"You are originally from . . . ?"

"I was born in Taipei. As a youth, I traveled to America for my education. I first attended the University of Oklahoma, but the call came, and I transferred to Oral Roberts University in the same state. There I got my first degree—in electrical engineering—and went on for my doctor of divinity and my ordination," he explained.

"Indeed, and how did you come to be in the People's Republic?"

"Back in the 1970s, the government of Chairman Mao was ever so pleased to have Taiwanese come here to live—rejecting capitalism and coming to Marxism, you see," he added with a twinkling eye. "It was hard on my parents, but they came to understand. I started my congregation soon after I arrived. That was troublesome for the Ministry of State Security, but I also worked as an engineer, and at the time the state needed that particular skill. It is remarkable what the State will accept if you have something it needs, and back then their need for people with my degree was quite desperate. But now I am a minister on a full-time basis." With the announcement of his triumph, Yu lifted his own teacup for a sip.

"So, what can you tell us about the local environment?" Renato asked.

"The government is truly communist. It trusts and tolerates no loyalty to anything except itself. Even the Falun Gong, which was not truly a religion—that is, not really a belief system as you or I would understand the term—has been brutally suppressed, and my own congregation has been persecuted. It is a rare Sunday on which more than a quarter of my congregation comes to attend services. I must spend much of my time traveling from home to home to bring the gospel to my flock."

"How do you support yourself?" the Cardinal asked.

Yu smiled serenely. "That is the least of my problems. American

Baptists support me most generously. There is a group of churches in Mississippi that is particularly generous—many are black churches, as it turns out. I just received some letters from them yesterday. One of my classmates at Oral Roberts University has a large congregation near Jackson, Mississippi. His name is Gerry Patterson. We were good friends then, and he remains a friend in Christ. His congregation is large and prosperous, and he still looks after me." Yu almost added that he had far more money than he knew how to spend. In America, such prosperity would have translated into a Cadillac and a fine parsonage. In Beijing, it meant a nice bicycle and gifts to the needy of his flock.

"Where do you live, my friend?" the Cardinal asked.

The Reverend Yu fished in his pocket for a business card and handed it over. Like many such Chinese cards, it had a sketch-map on the back. "Perhaps you would be so kind as to join my wife and myself for dinner. Both of you, of course," he added.

"We should be delighted. Do you have children?"

"Two," Yu replied. "Both born in America, and so exempt from the bestial laws the communists have in place here."

"I know of these laws," DiMilo assured his visitor. "Before we can make them change, we need more Christians here. I pray on this subject daily."

"As do I, Eminence. As do I. I presume you know that your dwelling here is, well . . ."

Schepke tapped his ear and pointed his finger around the room. "Yes, we know."

"You have a driver assigned to you?"

"Yes, that was very kind of the ministry," Schepke noted. "He's a Catholic. Isn't that remarkable?"

"Is that a fact?" Yu asked rhetorically, while his head shook emphatically from side to side. "Well, I am sure he's loyal to his country as well."

"But of course," DiMilo observed. It wasn't much of a surprise. The Cardinal had been in the Vatican's diplomatic service a long time, and he'd seen most of the tricks at least once. Clever though the Chinese communists were, the Catholic Church had been around a lot longer, loath though the local government might be to admit that fact.

The chitchat went on for another thirty minutes before the Reverend Yu took his leave, with another warm handshake to send him on his way.

"So, Franz?" DiMilo asked outside, where a blowing breeze would impede any microphones installed outside the dwelling itself.

"First time I've seen the man. I've heard his name since I arrived here. The PRC government has indeed given him a bad time, and more than once, but he is a man of strong faith and no small courage. I hadn't known of his educational background. We could check on this."

"Not a bad idea," the Papal Nuncio said. It wasn't that he distrusted or disbelieved Yu, just that it was good to be sure of things. Even the name of a classmate, now an ordained minister, Gerry Patterson. Somewhere in Mississippi, USA. That would make it easy. The message to Rome went out an hour later, over the Internet, a method of communication that lent itself so readily to intelligence operations.

In this case, the time differences worked for them, as sometimes happened when the inquiries went west instead of east. In a few hours, the dispatch was received, decrypted, and forwarded to the proper desk. From there, a new dispatch, also encrypted, made its way to New York, where Timothy Cardinal McCarthy, Archbishop of New York and the chief of the Vatican's intelligence operations in the United States of America, received his copy immediately after breakfast. From there, it was even easier. The FBI remained a bastion of Irish-Catholic America, though not so much as in the 1930s, with a few Italians and Poles tossed in. The world was an imperfect place, but when the Church needed information, and as long as the information was not compromising to American national security, it was gotten, usually very quickly.

In this case, particularly so. Oral Roberts University was a very conservative institution, and therefore ready to cooperate with the FBI's inquiries, official or not. A clerk there didn't even consult her supervisor, so innocuous was the phoned inquiry from Assistant Special Agent in Charge Jim Brennan of the FBI's Oklahoma City office. It was quickly established via computer records that one Yu Fa An had graduated the university, first with a bachelor of science degree in electrical engineering, and then spent an additional three years in the university for his doctor of divinity, both degrees attained "with distinction," the clerk told Brennan, meaning nothing lower than a B+. The alumni office added that the Reverend Yu's current address was in Beijing, China, where he evidently preached the gospel courageously in the land of the pagans. Brennan thanked the clerk, made his notes, and replied to the e-mail inquiry from New York, then went off to his morning meeting with the SAC to review the Field Division's activities in enforcing federal law in the Sooner State.

It was a little different in Jackson, Mississippi. There it was the SAC—Special Agent in Charge—himself who made the call on Reverend Gerry Patterson's First Baptist Church, located in an upscale suburb of the Mississippi state capital. The church was three-quarters of the way into its second century, and among the most prosperous of such congregations in the region. The Reverend Patterson could scarcely have been more impressive, impeccably turned out in a white button-down shirt and a striped blue tie. His dark suit coat was hung in a corner in deference to the local temperature. He greeted the visiting FBI official with regal manners, conducted him to his plush office, and asked how he could be of service. On hearing the first question, he replied, "Yu! Yes, a fine man, and a good friend from school. We used to call him Skip—Fa sounded too much like something from *The Sound of Music,* you know? A good guy, and a *fine* minister of the gospel. He could give lessons in faith to Jerry Falwell. Correspond with him? You bet I do! We send him something like twenty-five thousand dollars a year. Want to see a picture? We have it in the church itself. We were both a lot younger then," Patterson added with a smile. "Skip's got real guts. It can't be much fun to be a Christian minister in China, you know? But he never complains. His letters are always upbeat. We could use a thousand more men like him in the clergy."

"So, you are that impressed with him?" SAC Mike Leary asked.

"He was a good kid in college, and he's a good man today, and a fine minister of the gospel who does his work in a very adverse environment. Skip is a hero to me, Mr. Leary." Which was very powerful testimony indeed from so important a member of the community. First Baptist Church hadn't had a mortgage in living memory, despite its impressive physical plant and amply cushioned pews.

The FBI agent stood. "That's about all I need. Thank you, sir."

"Can I ask why you came here to ask about my friend?"

Leary had expected that question, and so had preframed his answer.

"Just a routine inquiry, sir. Your friend isn't in any trouble at all—at least not with the United States government."

"Good to know," the Reverend Patterson responded, with a smile and a handshake. "You know, we're not the only congregation that looks after Skip."

Leary turned. "Really?"

"Of course. You know Hosiah Jackson?"

"Reverend Jackson, the Vice President's dad? Never met him, but I know who he is."

Patterson nodded. "Yep. Hosiah's as good as they come." Neither man commented on how unusual it would have been a mere forty years earlier for a white minister to comment so favorably on a black one, but Mississippi had changed over time, in some ways even faster than the rest of America. "I was over at his place a few years ago and we got talking about things, and this subject came up. Hosiah's congregation sends Skip five or ten thousand dollars a year also, and he organized some of the other black congregations to help us look after Skip as well."

Mississippi whites and blacks looking after a Chinese preacher, Leary thought. *What was the world coming to?* He supposed that Christianity might really mean something after all, and headed back to his office in his official car, content at having done some actual investigative work for a change, if not exactly for the FBI.

Cardinal McCarthy learned from his secretary that his two requests for information had been answered before lunch, which was impressive even by the standards of the FBI–Catholic Church alliance. Soon after his midday meal, Cardinal McCarthy personally encrypted both of the replies and forwarded them back to Rome. He didn't know why the inquiry had come, but figured that he'd find out in due course if it were important, and if not, then not. It amused the churchman to be the Vatican's master spy in America.

It would have amused him less to know that the National Security Agency at Fort Meade, Maryland, was interested in this sideshow activity also, and that their monster Thinking Machines, Inc. supercomputer in the cavernous basement under the main building in the sprawling complex was on the case. This machine, whose manufacturer had gone bankrupt some years before, had been both the pride and joy and the greatest disappointment in the huge collection of computers at NSA, until quite recently, when one of the agency's mathematicians had finally figured out a way to make use of it. It was a massive parallel-processing machine and supposedly operated much as the human brain did, theoretically able to attack a problem from more than one side simultaneously, just as the human brain was thought to do. The problem was that no one actually knew how the human brain worked, and as a result drafting the software to make full use of the hugely powerful computer had been impossible for some years. This had relegated the impressive and expensive artifact to no more practical utility than an ordinary workstation. But then someone had recognized the fact that quantum mechanics had become useful in the cracking of foreign ciphers, wondered *why* this should be the case, and started looking at the problems from the programming unit. Seven months later, that intellectual sojourn had resulted in the first of three new operating systems for the Thinking Machines Super-Cruncher, and the rest was highly classified history. NSA was now able to crack any book or machine cipher in the world, and its analysts, newly rich with information, had pitched in to have a woodworker construct a sort of pagan altar to put before the Cruncher for the notional sacrifice of goats before their new god. (To suggest the sacrifice of virgins would have offended the womenfolk at the agency.) NSA had long been known for its eccentric institutional sense of humor. The only real fear was that the world would learn about the TAPDANCE system NSA had come up with, which was totally random, and therefore totally unbreakable, plus easy to manufacture—but it was also an administrative nightmare, and that would prevent most foreign governments from using it.

The Cardinal's Internet dispatches were copied, illegally but routinely, by NSA and fed into the Cruncher, which spat out the clear text, which found its way quickly to the desk of an NSA analyst, who, it had been carefully determined beforehand, wasn't Catholic.

That's interesting, the analyst thought. *Why is the Vatican interested in some Chink minister? And why the hell did they go to New York to find out about him? Oh, okay, educated over here, and friends in Mississippi . . . what the hell is* this *all about?* He was supposed to know about such things, but that was merely the theory under which he operated. He frequently didn't know beans about the information he looked at, but was honest enough to tell his superiors that. And so, his daily report was forwarded electronically to his supervisor, who looked it over, coded it, and then forwarded it to CIA, where three more analysts looked it over, decided that they didn't know what to make of it either, and then filed it away, electronically. In this case, the data went onto VHS-sized tape cassettes, one of which went into storage container Doc, and the other into Grumpy—there are seven such storage units in the CIA computer room, each named after one of Disney's Seven Dwarfs—while the reference names went into the mainframe so that the computer would know where to look for the data for which the United States government as yet had no understanding. That situation was hardly unknown, of course, and for that reason CIA had every bit of information it generated in a computerized and thoroughly cross-referenced index, instantly accessible, depending on classification, to anyone in either the New or Old Headquarters Buildings located one ridgeline away from the Potomac River. Most of the data in the Seven Dwarfs just sat there, forevermore to be untouched, footnotes to footnotes, never to be of interest even to the driest of academics.

And so?" Zhang Han San asked.

"And so, our Russian neighbors have the luck of the devil," Fang Gan replied, handing the folder over to the senior Minister Without Portfolio. Zhang was seven years older than Fang, closer to his country's Premier. But not that much, and there was little competition between the two ministers. "What we could do with such blessings . . ." His voice trailed off.

"Indeed." That any country could have made constructive use of oil and gold was an obvious truth left unsaid. What mattered here and now was that China would not, and Russia would.

"I had planned for this, you know."

"Your plans were masterful, my friend," Fang said from his seat, reaching inside his jacket for a pack of cigarettes. He held it up to seek approval from his host, who'd quit the habit five years before. The response was a dismissive wave of the hand, and Fang tapped one out and lit it from a butane lighter. "But anyone can have bad luck."

"First the Japanese failed us, and then that religious fool in Tehran,"

Zhang groused. "Had either of our supposed allies performed as promised, the gold and the oil would now be ours . . ."

"Useful, certainly, for our own purposes, but I am somewhat doubtful on the subject of world acceptance of our notionally prosperous status," Fang said, with a lengthy puff.

The response was yet another wave of the hand. "You think the capitalists are governed by principle? They need oil and gold, and whoever can provide it cheaply gets to sell the most of it. Look whom they buy from, my old friend, anyone who happens to have it. With all the oil in Mexico, the Americans can't even work up the courage to seize it. How cowardly of them! In our case, the Japanese, as we have learned to our sorrow, have no principles at all. If they could buy oil from the company which made the bombs dropped on Hiroshima and Nagasaki, they would. They call it realism," Zhang concluded scornfully. The real cite came from Vladimir Il'ych Ulyanov, Lenin himself, who'd predicted, not unreasonably, that capitalist nations would compete among themselves to sell the Soviet Union the rope with which the Russians would later hang them all. But Lenin had never planned for Marxism to fail, had he? Just as Mao hadn't planned for his perfect political/economic vision to fail in the People's Republic, as evidenced by such slogans as "The Great Leap Forward," which, among other things, had encouraged ordinary peasants to smelt iron in their backyards. That the resulting slag hadn't been useful even to make andirons with was a fact not widely advertised in the East or West.

"Alas, fortune did not smile upon us, and so, the oil and gold are not ours."

"For the moment," Zhang murmured.

"What was that?" Fang asked, not having quite caught the comment.

Zhang looked up, almost startled from his internal reverie. "Hmph? Oh, nothing, my friend." And with that the discussion turned to domestic matters. It lasted a total of seventy-five minutes before Fang went back to his office. There began another routine. "Ming," Fang called, gesturing on the way to his inner office.

The secretary stood and scampered after him, closing the door behind before finding her seat.

"New entry," Fang said tiredly, for it had been a lengthy day. "Regular afternoon meeting with Zhang Han San, and we discussed . . ." His voice went on, relating the substance and contents of the meeting. Ming duly took her notes for her minister's official diary. The Chinese were inveterate diarists, and besides that, members of the Politburo felt both an obligation (for scholarly history) and a personal need (for personal survival) to document their every conversation on matters political and concerning national policy, the better to document their views and careful judgment should one of their number make an error of judgment. That this meant his personal secretary, as, indeed, all of the Politburo members' personal secretaries, had access to the most sensitive secrets of the land was not a matter of importance, since these girls were mere robots, recording and transcription machines, little more than that—well, a little more, Fang and a few of his colleagues thought with the accompanying smile. You couldn't have a tape machine suck on your penis, could you? And Ming was especially good at it. Fang was a communist, and had been for all of his adult life, but he was not a man entirely devoid of heart, and he had the affection for Ming that another man, or even himself, might have had for a favored daughter . . . except that you usually didn't fuck your own daughter. . . . His diary entry droned on for twenty minutes, his trained memory recounting every substantive part of his exchange with Zhang, who was doubtless doing the same with his own private secretary right at this moment—unless Zhang had succumbed to the Western practice of using a tape machine, which would not have surprised Fang. For all of Zhang's pretended contempt for Westerners, he emulated them in so many ways.

They'd also tracked down the name of Klementi Ivan'ch Suvorov. He was yet another former KGB officer, part then of the Third Chief Directorate, which had been a hybrid department of the former spy agency, tasked to overseeing the former Soviet military, and also to overseeing certain special operations of the latter force, like the Spetsnaz, Oleg Provalov knew. He turned a few more pages in Suvorov's package, found a photograph and fingerprints, and also discovered that his first assignment had been in the First Chief Directorate, known as the Foreign Directorate because of its work in gathering intelligence from other nations. Why the change? he wondered. Usually in KGB, you stayed where you were initially put. But a senior officer in the Third had drafted him by name from the First . . . why? Suvorov, K. I., asked for by name by General Major Pavel Konstantinovich Kabinet. The name made Provalov pause. He'd heard it somewhere, but exactly where, he couldn't recall, an unusual state of affairs for a long-term investigator. Provalov made a note and set it aside.

So, they had a name and a photo for this Suvorov fellow. Had he known Amalrik and Zimyanin, the supposed—and deceased—killers of Avseyenko the pimp? It seemed possible. In the Third Directorate he would have had possible access to the Spetsnaz, but that could have been a mere coincidence. The KGB's Third Directorate had been mainly concerned with political control of the Soviet military, but that was no longer something the State needed, was it? The entire panoply of political officers, the *zampoliti* who had so long been the bane of the Soviet military, was now essentially gone.

Where are you now? Provalov asked the file folder. Unlike Central Army Records, KGB records were usually pretty good at showing where former intelligence officers lived, and what they were doing. It was a carryover from the previous regime that worked for the police agencies, but not in this case. *Where are you? What are you doing to support yourself? Are you a criminal? Are you a murderer?* Homicide investigations by their nature created more questions than answers, and frequently ended with many such questions forever unanswered because you could never look inside the mind of a killer, and even if you could, what you might find there didn't have to make any sort of sense.

This murder case had begun as a complex one, and was only becoming more so. All he knew for certain was that Avseyenko was dead, along with his driver and a whore. And now, maybe, he knew even less. He'd assumed almost from the beginning that the pimp had been the real target, but if this Suvorov fellow had hired Amalrik and Zimyanin to do the killing, why would a former—he checked—lieutenant colonel in the Third Chief Directorate of the KGB go out of his way to kill a pimp? Was not Sergey Golovko an equally likely target for the killing, and would that not also explain the murder of the two supposed killers, for eliminating the wrong target? The detective lieutenant opened a desk drawer for a bottle of aspirin. It wasn't the first headache this case had developed, and it didn't seem likely that this would be the last. Whoever Suvorov was, if Golovko had been the target, he had not made the decision to kill the man himself. He'd been a contract killer, and therefore someone else had made the decision to do the killing.

But who?

And why?

Cui bonuo was the ancient question—old enough that the adage was in a dead language. *To whom the good?* Who profited from the deed?

He called Abramov and Ustinov. Maybe they could run Suvorov down, and then he'd fly north to interview the man. Provalov drafted the fax and fired it off to St. Petersburg, then left his desk for the drive home. He checked his watch. Only two hours late. Not bad for this case.

General Lieutenant Gennady Iosifovich Bondarenko looked around his office. He'd had his three stars for a while, and sometimes he wondered if he'd get any farther. He'd been a professional soldier for thirty-one years, and the job to which he'd always aspired was Commanding General of the Russian Army. Many good men, and some bad ones, had been there. Gregoriy Zhukov, for one, the man who'd saved his country from the Germans. There were many statues to Zhukov, whom Bondarenko had heard lecture when he was a wet-nosed cadet all those years before, seeing the blunt, bulldog face and ice-blue determined eyes of a killer, a true Russian hero whom politics could not demean, and whose name the Germans had come to fear.

That Bondarenko had come this far was no small surprise even to himself. He'd begun as a signals officer, seconded briefly to Spetsnaz in Afghanistan, where he'd cheated death twice, both times taking command of a panic-worthy situation and surviving with no small distinction. He'd taken wounds, and killed with his own hands, something few colonels do, and few colonels relished, except at a good officers' club bar after a few stiff ones with their comrades.

Like many generals before him, Bondarenko was something of a "political" general. He'd hitched his career-star to the coattails of a quasi-minister, Sergey Golovko, but in truth he'd never have gone to general-lieutenant's stars without real merit, and courage on the battlefield went as far in the Russian army as it did in any other. Intelligence went farther still, and above all came accomplishment. His job was what the Americans called J-3, Chief of Operations, which meant killing people in war and training them in peace. Bondarenko had traveled the globe, learning how other armies trained their men, sifted through the lessons, and applied them to his own soldiers. The only difference between a soldier and a civilian was training, after all, and Bondarenko wanted no less than to bring the Russian army to the same razor-sharp and granite-hard condition with which it had kicked in the gates of Berlin under Zhukov and Koniev. That goal was still off in the future, but the general told himself that he'd laid the proper foundation. In ten years, perhaps, his army would be at that goal, and he'd be around to see it, retired by then, of course, honorably so, with his decorations framed and hanging on the wall, and grandchildren to bounce on his knee . . . and occasionally coming in to consult, to look things over and offer his opinion, as retired general officers often did.

For the moment, he had no further work to do, but no particular desire to head home, where his wife was hosting the wives of other senior officers. Bondarenko had always found such affairs tedious. The military attaché in Washington had sent him a book, *Swift Sword,* by a Colonel Nicholas Eddington of the American Army National Guard. Eddington, yes, he was the colonel who'd been training with his brigade in the desert of California when the decision had come to deploy to the Persian Gulf, and his troops—civilians in uniform, really—had performed well: Better than well, the Russian general told himself. They'd exercised the Medusa Touch, destroying everything they'd touched, along with the regular American formations, the 10th and 11th cavalry regiments. Together that one division-sized collection of forces had smashed a full four corps of mechanized troops like so many sheep in the slaughter pen. Even Eddington's guardsmen had performed magnificently. Part of that, Gennady Iosifovich knew, was their motivation. The biological attack on their homeland had understandably enraged the soldiers, and such rage could make a poor soldier into an heroic one as easily as flipping a light switch. "Will to combat" was the technical term. In more pedestrian language, it was the reason a man put his life at risk, and so it was a matter of no small importance to the senior officers whose job it was to lead those men into danger.

Paging through the book, he saw that this Eddington—also a professor of history, the flap said; wasn't that interesting?—paid no small attention to that factor. Well, maybe he was smart in addition to being lucky. He'd had the good fortune to command reserve soldiers with many years of service, and while they'd only had part-time practice for their training, they'd been in highly stable units, where every soldier knew every other, and that was a virtually unknown luxury for regular soldiers. And they'd also had the revolutionary new American IVIS gear, which let all the men and vehicles in the field know exactly what their commander knew, often in great detail . . . and in turn told their commander exactly what his men saw. Eddington said that had made his job a lot easier than any mechanized-force commander had ever had it.

The American officer also talked about knowing not only what his subordinate commanders were saying, but also the importance of knowing what they were *thinking,* the things they didn't have the time to say. The implicit emphasis was on the importance of continuity within the officer corps, and *that,* Bondarenko thought as he made a marginal note, was a most important lesson. He'd have to read this book in detail, and maybe have Washington purchase a hundred or so for his brother officers to read . . . even get reprint rights in Russia for it? It was something the Russians had done more than once.

CHAPTER 12

Conflicts of the Pocket

"Okay, George, let's have it," Ryan said, sipping his coffee. The White House had many routines, and one that had evolved over the past year was that, after the daily intelligence briefing, the Secretary of the Treasury was Ryan's first appointment two or three days of the week. Winston most often walked across—actually under—15th Street via a tunnel between the White House and Treasury Building that dated back to the time of FDR. The other part of the routine was that the President's Navy messmen laid out coffee and croissants (with butter) in which both men indulged to the detriment of their cholesterol numbers.

"The PRC. The trade negotiations have hit the wall pretty hard. They just don't want to play ball."

"What are the issues?"

"Hell, Jack, what *aren't* the friggin' issues?" TRADER took a bite of croissant and grape jelly. "That new computer company their government started up is ripping off a proprietary hardware gadget that Dell has patented—that's the new doohickey that kicked their stock up twenty percent, y'know? They're just dropping the things into the boxes they make for their own market *and* the ones they just started selling in Europe. That's a goddamned violation of all sorts of trade *and* patent treaties, but when we point that out to them over the negotiating table, they just change the subject and ignore it. That could cost Dell something like four hundred million dollars, and that's real money for one company to lose, y'know? If I was their corporate counsel, I'd be flipping through the Yellow Pages for Assassins 'R Us. Okay, that's one. Next, they've told us that if we make too big a deal of these 'minor' disagreements, Boeing can forget the 777 order—twenty-eight aircraft they've optioned—in favor of Airbus."

Ryan nodded. "George, what's the trade balance with the PRC now?"

"Seventy-eight billion, and it's their way, not ours, as you know."

"Scott's running this over at Foggy Bottom?"

SecTreas nodded. "He's got a pretty fair team in place, but they need a little more in the way of executive direction."

"And what's this doing to us?"

"Well, it gets our consumers a lot of low-cost goods, about seventy percent of which is in low-tech stuff, lots of toys, stuffed animals, like that. But, Jack, thirty percent is upscale stuff. That amount's almost doubled in two and a half years. Pretty soon that's going to start costing us jobs, both in terms of production for domestic consumption and lost exports. They're selling a lot of laptops domestically—in their country, I mean—but they don't let us into the market, even though we've got 'em beat in terms of performance and price. We know for sure they're taking part of their trading surplus with us and using it to subsidize their computer industries. They want to build that up for strategic reasons, I suppose."

"Plus selling weapons to people we'd prefer not to have them," POTUS added. *Which they also do for strategic reasons.*

"Well, doesn't everybody need an AK-47 to take care of his gophers?" A shipment of fourteen hundred true—that is, fully automatic—assault rifles had been seized in the Port of Los Angeles two weeks before, but the PRC had denied responsibility, despite the fact that U.S. intelligence services had tracked the transaction order back to a particular Beijing telephone number. That was something Ryan knew, but it had not been allowed to leak, lest it expose methods of intelligence collection—in this case to the National Security Agency at Fort Meade. The new Beijing telephone system hadn't been built by an American firm, but much of the design work had been contracted to a company that had made a profitable arrangement with an agency of the United States government. It wasn't strictly legal, but different rules were attached to national security matters.

"They just don't play by the rules, do they?"

Winston grunted. "Not hardly."

"Suggestions?" President Ryan asked.

"Remind the little slant-eyed fucks that they need us a shitload more than we need them."

"You have to be careful talking like that to nation-states, especially ones with nuclear weapons," Ryan reminded his Treasury Secretary. "Plus the racial slur."

"Jack, either it's a level playing field or it isn't. Either you play fair or you don't. If they keep that much more of our money than we do of theirs, then it means they've got to start playing fair with us. Okay, I know"—he held his hands up defensively—"their noses are a little out of joint over Taiwan, but that was a good call, Jack. You did the right thing, punishing them. Those little fucks killed people, and they probably had complicity in our last adventure in the Persian Gulf—*and* the Ebola attack on us—and so they had it coming. But *nooooo,* we can't punish them for murder and complicity in an act of war on the United States, can we? We have to be too big and strong to be so petty. Petty, my ass, Jack! Directly or indirectly, those little bastards helped that Daryaei guy kill seven thousand of our citizens, and establishing diplomatic relations with Taiwan was the price they paid for it—and a damned small price that was, if you ask me. They ought to understand that. They've got to learn that the world has rules. So, what we have to do is show them that there's pain when you break the rules, and we have to make the pain stick. Until they understand that, there's just going to be more trouble. Sooner or later, they have to learn. I think it's been long enough to wait."

"Okay, but remember their point of view: Who are we to tell them the rules?"

"Horseshit, Jack!" Winston was one of the very few people who had the ability—if not exactly the right—to talk that way in the Oval Office. Part of it came from his own success, part of it from the fact that Ryan respected straight talk, even if the language was occasionally off-color. "Remember, they're the ones sticking it to us. We *are* playing fair. The world *does* have rules, and those rules are honored by the community of nations, and if Beijing wants to be part of that community, well, then they have to abide by the same rules that everyone else does. If you want to join the club, you have to pay the cost of admittance, *and* even then you still can't drive your golf cart on the greens. You can't have it both ways."

The problem, Ryan reflected, was that the people who ran entire nations—especially large, powerful, important nations—were not the sort to be told how or why to do anything at all. This was all the more true of despotic countries. In a liberal democracy the idea of the rule of law applied to just about everyone. Ryan was President, but he couldn't rob a bank just because he needed pocket change.

"George, okay. Sit down with Scott and work something out that I can agree to, and we'll have State explain the rules to our friends in Beijing." *And who knows, maybe it might even work this time.* Not that Ryan would bet money on it.

This would be the important evening, Nomuri thought. Yeah, sure, he'd banged Ming the night before, and she seemed to have liked it, but now that she'd had time to think it over, would her reaction be the same? Or would she reflect that he'd plied her with liquor and taken advantage of her? Nomuri had dated and bedded his share of women, but he didn't confuse amorous successes with any sort of understanding of the female psyche.

He sat at the bar of the medium-sized restaurant—different from the last one—smoking a cigarette, which was new for the CIA officer. He wasn't coughing, though his first two had made the room seem to spin around some. Carbon monoxide poisoning, he thought. Smoking reduced the oxygen supply to your brain, and was bad for you in so many ways. But it also made waiting a lot easier. He'd bought a Bic lighter, blue, with a facsimile of the PRC flag on it, so that it appeared like their banner was waving in a clear sky. *Yeah,* he thought, *sure, and here I am wondering if my girl will show up, and she's already*—he checked his watch—*nine minutes late.* Nomuri waved to the bartender and ordered another Scotch. It was a Japanese brand, drinkable, not overly expensive, and when you got down to it, booze was booze, wasn't it?

Are you coming, Ming? the case officer's mind asked the air around him. Like most bars around the world, this one had a mirror behind the glasses and bottles, and the California native examined his face quizzically, pretending it was someone else's, wondering what someone else might see in it. Nervousness? Suspicion? Fear? Loneliness? Lust? There could be someone making that evaluation right now, some MSS counterintelligence officer doing his stakeout, careful not to look toward Nomuri too much of the time. Maybe using the mirror as an indirect surveillance tool. More likely sitting at an angle so that his posture naturally pointed his eyes to the American, whereas Nomuri would have to turn his head to see him, giving the surveillance agent a chance to avert his glance, probably toward his partner—you tended to do this with teams rather than an individual—whose head would be on the same line of sight, so that he could survey his target without seeming to do so directly. Every nation in the world had police or security forces trained in this, and the methods were the same everywhere because human nature was the same everywhere, whether your target was a drug dealer or a spook. That's just the way it was, Nomuri said to himself, checking his watch again. Eleven minutes late. *It's cool, buddy, women are* always *late. They do it because they can't tell time, or it takes them fucking forever to get dressed and do their makeup, or because they don't remember to wear a watch . . . or most likely of all, because it gives them an advantage.* Such behavior, perhaps, made women appear more valuable to men—after all, men waited for *them,* right? Not the other way around. It put a premium on their affection, which if *not* waited for, might *not* appear one day, and that gave men something to fear.

Chester Nomuri, behavioral anthropologist, he snorted to himself, looking back up in the mirror.

For Christ's sake, dude, maybe she's working late, or the traffic is heavy, or some friend at the office needed her to come over and help her move the goddamned furniture. Seventeen minutes. He fished out another Kool and lit it from his ChiComm lighter. *The East is Red,* he thought. And maybe this was the last country in the world that really was red . . . wouldn't Mao be proud . . . ?

Where are you?

Well, whoever from the MSS might be watching, if he had any doubts about what Nomuri was doing, they'd damned sure know he was waiting for a woman, and if anything his stress would look like that of a guy bewitched by the woman in question. And spooks weren't supposed to be bewitched, were they?

What are you worrying about that *for, asshole, just because you might not get laid tonight?*

Twenty-three minutes late. He stubbed out one cigarette and lit another. If this was a mechanism women used to control men, then it was an effective one.

James Bond never had these problems, the intelligence officer thought. Mr. Kiss-Kiss Bang-Bang was always master of his women—*and if anyone needed proof that Bond was a character of fiction, that was sure as hell it!*

As it turned out, Nomuri was so entranced with his thoughts that he didn't see Ming come in. He felt a gentle tap on his back, and turned rapidly to see—

—she wore the radiant smile, pleased with herself at having surprised him, the beaming dark eyes that crinkled at the corners with the pleasure of the moment.

"I am so sorry to be late," she said rapidly. "Fang needed me to transcribe some things, and he kept me in the office late."

"I must talk to this old man," Nomuri said archly, hauling himself erect on the barstool.

"He is, as you say, an old man, and he does not listen very well. Perhaps age has impeded his hearing."

No, the old fucker probably doesn't want to listen, Nomuri didn't say. Fang was probably like bosses everywhere, well past the age when he looked for the ideas of others.

"So, what do you want for dinner?" Nomuri asked, and got the best possible answer.

"I'm not hungry." With sparkles in the dark eyes to affirm what she did want. Nomuri tossed off the last of his drink, stubbed out his cigarette, and walked out with her.

So?" Ryan asked.

"So, this is not good news," Arnie van Damm replied.

"I suppose that depends on your point of view. When will they hear arguments?"

"Less than two months, and that's a message, too, Jack. Those good 'strict-constructionist' justices you appointed are going to hear this case, and if I had to bet, I'd wager they're hot to overturn *Roe.*"

Jack settled back in his chair and smiled up at his Chief of Staff. "Why is that bad, Arnie?"

"Jack, it's bad because a lot of the citizens out there like to have the option to choose between abortion or not. That's why. 'Pro choice' is what they call it, and so far it's the law."

"Maybe that'll change," the President said hopefully, looking back down at his schedule. The Secretary of the Interior was coming in to talk about the national parks.

"That is *not* something to look forward to, damn it! And it'll be blamed on you!"

"Okay, if and when that happens, I will point out that *I* am not a justice of the United States Supreme Court, and stay away from it entirely. If they decide the way I—and I guess you—think they will, abortion becomes a legislative matter, and the legislature of the 'several states,' as the Constitution terms them, will meet and decide for themselves if the voters want to be able to kill their unborn babies or not—but, Arnie, I've got four kids, remember. I was there to see them all born, and be damned if you are going to tell me that abortion is okay!" The fourth little Ryan, Kyle Daniel, had been born during Ryan's Presidency, and the cameras had been there to record his face coming out of the delivery room, allowing the entire nation—and the world, for that matter—to share the experience. It had bumped Ryan's approval rating a full fifteen points, pleasing Arnie very greatly at the time.

"God damn it, Jack, I never said that, did I?" van Damm demanded. "But you and I do objectionable things every so often, don't we? And we don't deny other people the right to do such things, too, do we? Smoke, for example?" he added, just to twist Ryan's tail a little.

"Arnie, you use words as cleverly as any man I know, and that was a good play. I'll give you that. But there's a qualitative difference between lighting up a goddamned cigarette and killing a living human being."

"True, if a fetus is a living human being, which is something for theologians, not politicians."

"Arnie, it's like this. The pro-abortion crowd says that whether or not a fetus is human is beside the point because it's inside a woman's body, and therefore her property to do with as she pleases. Fine. It was the law in the Roman Republic and Empire that a wife and children were property of the *paterfamilias,* the head of the family, and he could kill them anytime he pleased. You think we should go back to that?"

"Obviously not, since it empowers men and dis-empowers women, and we don't do things like that anymore."

"So, you've taken a moral issue and degraded it to what's good politically and what's bad politically. Well, Arnie, I am not here to do that. Even the President is allowed to have some moral principles, or am I supposed to check my ideas of right and wrong outside the door when I show up for work in the morning?"

"But he's not allowed to impose it on others. Moral principles are things you keep on the inside, for yourself."

"What we call law is nothing more or less than the public's collective belief, their conviction of what right and wrong is. Whether it's about murder, kidnapping, or running a red light, society decides what the rules are. In a democratic republic, we do that through the legislature by electing people who share our views. That's how laws happen. We also set up a constitution, the supreme law of the land, which is very carefully considered because it decides what the other laws may and may not do, and therefore it protects us against our transitory passions. The job of the judiciary is to interpret the laws, or in this case the constitutional principles embodied in those laws, as they apply to reality. In *Roe versus Wade,* the Supreme Court went too far. It legislated; it changed the law in a way not anticipated by the drafters, and that was an error. All a reversal of *Roe* will do is return the abortion issue to the state legislatures, where it belongs."

"How long have you been thinking about that speech?" Arnie asked. Ryan's turn of phrase was too polished for extemporaneous speech.

"A little while," the President admitted.

"Well, when that decision comes through, be ready for a firestorm," his Chief of Staff warned. "I'm talking demonstrations, TV coverage, and enough newspaper editorials to paper the walls of the Pentagon, and your Secret Service people will worry about the additional danger to your life, and your wife's life, and your kids. If you think I'm kidding, ask them."

"That doesn't make any sense."

"There's no law, federal, state, or local, which compels the world to be logical, Jack. The people out there depend on you to keep the fucking weather pleasant, and they blame you when you don't. Deal with it." With that, an annoyed Chief of Staff headed out and west toward his corner office.

"Crap," Ryan breathed, as he flipped to the briefing papers for the Secretary of the Interior. Smokey Bear's owner. Also custodian of the national parks, which the President only got to see on the Discovery Channel, on such nights as he had free time to switch the TV on.

There wasn't much to be said for the clothing people wore in this place, Nomuri thought again, except for one thing. When you undid the buttons and found the Victoria's Secret stuff underneath, well, it was like having a movie switch from black-and-white to Technicolor. This time Ming allowed him to do her buttons, then slide the jacket down her arms, and then get her trousers off. The panties looked particularly inviting, but then, so did her entire body. Nomuri scooped her up in his arms and kissed her passionately before dropping her on the bed. A minute later, he was beside her.

"So, why were you late?"

She made a face. "Every week Minister Fang meets with other ministers, and when he comes back, he has me transcribe the notes of the meetings so that he has a record of everything that was said."

"Oh, do you use my new computer for that?" The question concealed the quivering *Jesus!* he felt throughout his body on hearing Ming's words. This girl could be one hell of a source! Nomuri took a deep breath and resumed his poker face of polite disinterest.

"Of course."

"Excellent. It's equipped with a modem, yes?"

"Of course, I use it every day to retrieve Western news reports and such from their media web sites."

"Ah, that is good." So, he'd taken care of business for the day, and with that job done, Nomuri leaned over for a kiss.

"Before I came into the restaurant, I put the lipstick on," Ming explained. "I don't wear it at work."

"So I see," the CIA officer replied, repeating the initial kiss, and extending it in time. Her arms found their way around his neck. The reason for her lateness had nothing to do with a lack of affection. That was obvious now, as his hands started to wander also. The front-closure on the bra was the smartest thing he'd done. Just a flick of thumb and forefinger and it sprang open, revealing both of her rather cute breasts, two more places for his hand to explore. The skin there was particularly silky . . . and, he decided a few seconds later, tasty as well.

This resulted in an agreeable moan and squirm of pleasure from his . . . what? Friend? Well, okay, but not enough. Agent? Not yet. Lover would do for the moment. They'd never talked at The Farm about this sort of thing, except the usual warnings not to get too close to your agent, lest you lose your objectivity. But if you didn't get a little bit close, you'd never recruit the agent, would you? Of course, Chester knew that he was far more than a *little bit* close at the moment.

Whatever her looks, she had delightful skin, and his fingertips examined it in great detail as his eyes smiled into hers, with the occasional kiss. And her body wasn't bad at all. A nice shape even when she stood. A little too much waist, maybe, but this wasn't Venice Beach, and the hourglass figure, however nice it might look in pictures, was just that, a picture look. Her waist was smaller than her hips, and that was enough for the moment. It wasn't as though she'd be walking down the ramp at some New York fashion show, where the models looked like boys anyway. *So, Ming is not now and would never be a supermodel—deal with it, Chet,* the officer told himself. Then it was time to put all the CIA stuff aside. He was a man, dressed only in boxer shorts, next to a woman, dressed only in panties. Panties large enough maybe to make a handkerchief, though orange-red wouldn't be a good color for a man to pull from his back pocket, especially, he added to himself with a smile, in some artificial silk fabric.

"Why do you smile?" Ming asked.

"Because you are pretty," Nomuri replied. And so she was, now, with that particular smile on her face. No, she'd never be a model, but inside every woman was the look of beauty, if only they would let it out. And her skin was first-class, especially her lips, coated with after-work lipstick, smooth and greasy, yet making his lips linger even so. Soon their bodies touched almost all over, and a warm, comfortable feeling it was, so nicely she fit under one arm, while his left hand played and wandered. Ming's hair didn't tangle much. She could evidently brush it out very easily, it was so short. Her underarms, too, were hairy, like many Chinese women's, but that only gave Nomuri something else to play with, teasing and pulling a little. That evidently tickled her. Ming giggled playfully and hugged him tighter, then relaxed to allow his hand to wander more. As it passed her navel, she lay suddenly still, relaxing herself in some kind of invitation. Time for another kiss as his fingertips wandered farther, and there was humor in her eyes now. What game could this be . . . ?

As soon as his hands found her panties, her bottom lifted off the mattress. He sat up halfway and pulled them down, allowing her left foot to kick them into the air, where the red-orange pants flew like a mono-colored rainbow, and then—

"Ming!" he said in humorous accusation.

"I've heard that men like this," she said with a sparkle and a giggle.

"Well, it *is* different," Nomuri replied, as his hands traced over skin even smoother than the rest of her body. "Did you do this at work?"

A riotous laugh now: "No, fool! This morning at my apartment! In my own bathroom, with my own razor."

"Just wanted to make sure," the CIA officer assured her. *Damn, isn't* this *something!* Then her hand moved to do to him much the same as he was doing to her.

"You are different from Fang," her voice told him in a playful whisper.

"Oh? How so?"

"I think the worst thing a woman can say to a man is 'Are you in yet?' One of the other secretaries said that to Fang once. He beat her. She came into work the next day with black eyes—he made her come in—and then the next night . . . well, he had me to bed," she admitted, not so much with shame as embarrassment. "To show what a man he still is. But I knew better than to say *that* to him. We all do, now."

"Will you say that to me?" Nomuri asked with a smile and another kiss.

"Oh, no! You are a sausage, not a string bean!" Ming told him enthusiastically.

It wasn't the most elegant compliment he'd ever had, but it sufficed for the moment, Nomuri thought.

"Do you think it's time for the sausage to find a home?"

"Oh, yes!"

As he rolled on top, Nomuri saw two things under him. One was a girl, a young woman with the usual female drives, which he was about to answer. The other was a potential agent, with access to political intelligence such as an experienced case officer only dreamed about. But Nomuri wasn't an experienced case officer. He was still a little wet behind the ears, and so he didn't know what was impossible. He'd have to worry about his potential agent, because if he ever recruited her successfully, her life would be in the gravest danger . . . he thought about what would happen, how her face would change as the bullet entered her brain . . . but, no, it was too ugly. With an effort, Nomuri forced the thought aside as he slipped into her. If he were to recruit her at all, he had to perform this function well. And if it made him happy, too, well, that was just a bonus.

I'll think about it," POTUS promised the Secretary of the Interior, walking him to the door that led to the corridor, to the left of the fireplace. *Sorry, buddy, but the money isn't there to do all that.* His SecInterior was by no means a bad man, but it seemed he'd been captured by his departmental bureaucracy, which was perhaps the worst danger of working in Washington. He sat back down to read the papers the Secretary had handed over. Of course he wouldn't have time to read it all over himself. On a good day, he'd be able to skim through the Executive Summary of the documents, while the rest went to a staffer who'd go through it all and draft a report to the President—in effect, *another* Executive Summary of sorts, and from that document, typed up by a White House staff member of maybe twenty-eight years, policy would actually be made.

And that was crazy! Ryan thought angrily. *He* was supposed to be the chief executive of the country. *He* was the only one who was supposed to make policy. But the President's time was valuable. So valuable, in fact, that others guarded it for him—and really those others guarded his time from himself, because ultimately it was they who decided what Ryan saw and didn't see. Thus, while Ryan *was* the Chief Executive, and *did* alone make executive policy, he made that policy often based solely on the information presented to him by others. And sometimes it worried him that he was controlled by the information that made it to his desk, rather as the press decided what the public saw, and thus had a hand in deciding what the public thought about the various issues of the day.

So, Jack, have you been captured by your *bureaucracy, too?* It was hard to know, hard to tell, and hard to decide how to change the situation, if the situation existed in the first place.

Maybe that's why Arnie likes me to get out of this building to where the real people are, Jack realized.

The more difficult problem was that Ryan was a foreign-policy and national-security expert. In those areas he felt the most competent. It was on domestic stuff that he felt disconnected and dumb. Part of that came from his personal wealth. He'd never worried about the cost of a loaf of bread or a quart of milk—all the more so in the White House, where you never saw milk in a quart container anyway, but only in a chilled glass on a silver tray, carried by a Navy steward's mate right to your hands while you sat in your easy chair. There were people out there who did worry about such things, or at least worried about the cost of putting little Jimmy through college, and Ryan, as President, had to concern himself with their worries. He had to try to keep the economy in balance so that they could earn their decent livings, could go to Disney World in the summer, and the football games in the fall, and splurge to make sure there were plenty of presents under the Christmas tree every year.

But *how* the hell was he supposed to do that? Ryan remembered a lament attributed to the Roman Emperor Caesar Augustus. On learning that he'd been declared a god, and that temples had been erected to him, and that people sacrificed to the statues of himself in those temples, Augustus angrily inquired: *When someone prays to me to cure his gout, what am I supposed to* do? The fundamental issue was how much government policy really had to do with reality. That was a question seldom posed in Washington even by conservatives who ideologically despised the government and everything it did in domestic terms, though they were often in favor of showing the flag and rattling the national saber overseas—exactly why they enjoyed this Ryan had never thought about. Perhaps just to be different from liberals who flinched from the exercise of force like a vampire from the cross, but who, like vampires, liked to extend government as far as they could get away with into the lives of everyone, and so suck their blood—in reality, use the instrument of taxation to take more and more to pay for the more and more they would have the government do.

And yet the economy seemed to move on, regardless of what government did. People found their jobs, most of them in the private sector, providing goods and services for which people paid voluntarily with their after-tax money. And yet "public service" was a phrase used almost exclusively by and about political figures, almost always the elected sort. Didn't everyone out there serve the public in one way or another? Physicians, teachers, firefighters, pharmacists. Why did the media say it was just Ryan and Robby Jackson, and the 535 elected members of the Congress? He shook his head.

Damn. Okay, I know how I got here, but why the hell did I allow myself to run for election? Jack asked himself. It had made Arnie happy. It had even made the media happy—*perhaps because they loved him as a target?* the President asked himself—and Cathy had not been cross with him about it. But *why* the hell had he ever allowed himself to be stampeded into this? He fundamentally didn't know what he was supposed to do as President. He had no real agenda, and sort of bumped along from day to day. Making tactical decisions (for which he was singularly unqualified) instead of large strategic ones. There was nothing important he really wanted to change about his country. Oh, sure, there were a few problems to be fixed. Tax policy needed rewriting, and he was letting George Winston ramrod that. And Defense needed firming up, and he had Tony Bretano working on that. He had a Presidential Commission looking at health-care policy, which his wife, actually, was overseeing in a distant way, along with some of her Hopkins colleagues, and all of that was kept quiet. And there was that very black look at Social Security, being guided by Winston and Mark Gant.

The "third rail of American politics," he thought again. Step on it and die. But Social Security was something the American people really cared about, not for what it was, but for what they wrongly thought it to be—and, actually, they knew that their thoughts were wrong, judging by the polling data. As thoroughly mismanaged as any financial institution could possibly be, it was still part of a government promise made by the representatives *of* the people *to* the people. And somehow, despite all the cynicism out there—which was considerable—the average Joe Citizen really did trust his government to keep its word. The problem was that union chiefs and industrialists who'd dipped into pension funds and gone to federal prison for it had done nothing compared to what succeeding Congresses had done to Social Security—but the advantage of a crook in Congress was that he or she was not a crook, not legally. After all, Congress made the *law.* Congress made *government policy,* and those things couldn't be *wrong,* could they? Yet another proof that the drafters of the Constitution had made one simple but far-reaching error. They'd assumed that the people selected by The People to manage the nation would be as honest and honorable as they'd been. One could almost hear the "Oops!" emanating from all those old graves. The people who'd drafted the Constitution had sat in a room dominated by George Washington himself, and whatever honor they'd lacked he'd probably provided from his own abundant supply, just by sitting there and looking at them. *The current Congress had no such mentor/living god to take George's place, and more was the pity,* Ryan thought. The mere fact that Social Security had shown a profit up through the 1960s had meant that—well, Congress couldn't let a *profit* happen, could it? *Profits* were what made rich people (who had to be bad people, because no one grew rich without having exploited someone or other, right?, which never stopped members of the Congress from going to those people for campaign contributions, of course) rich, and so profits had to be spent, and so Social Security taxes (properly called premiums, because Social Security was actually called OASDI, for Old Age, Survivors, and Disability *Insurance*) were transformed into general funds, to be spent along with everything else. One of Ryan's students from his days of teaching history at the Naval Academy had sent him a small plaque to keep on his White House desk. It read: *THE AMERICAN REPUBLIC WILL ENDURE UNTIL THE DAY CONGRESS DISCOVERS THAT IT CAN BRIBE THE PUBLIC WITH THE PUBLIC'S MONEY—ALEXIS DE TOCQUEVILLE.* Ryan paid heed to it. There were times when he wanted to grab Congress by its collective neck and throttle it, but there was no single such neck, and Arnie never tired of telling him how tame a Congress he had, the House of Representatives especially, which was the reverse of how things usually went.

The President grumbled and checked his daily schedule for his next appointment. As with everything else, the President of the United

States lived a schedule determined by others, his appointments made weeks in advance, the daily briefing pages prepared the day before so that he'd know who the hell was coming in, and what the hell he, she, or they wanted to talk about, and also what his considered position (mainly drafted by others) was. The President's position was usually a friendly one so that the visitor(s) could leave the Oval Office feeling good about the experience, and the rules were that you couldn't change the agenda, lest the Chief Executive say, "What the hell are you asking me for now!" This would alarm both the guest and the Secret Service agents standing right behind them, hands close to their pistols—just standing there like robots, faces blank but scanning, ears taking everything in. After their shift ended, they probably headed off to whatever cop bar they frequented to chuckle over what the City Council President of Podunk had said in the Oval Office that day—"Jesus, did you see the Boss's eyes when that dumb bastard . . . ?"—because they were bright, savvy people who in many ways understood his job better than he did, Ryan reflected. Well they should. They had the double advantage of having seen it all, and not being responsible for any of it. *Lucky bastards,* Jack thought, standing for his next appointment.

If cigarettes were good for anything, it was for this, Nomuri thought. His left arm was curled around Ming, his body snuggled up against her, staring at the ceiling in the lovely, relaxed, deflationary moment, and puffing gently on his Kool as an accent to the moment, feeling Ming's breathing, and feeling very much like a man. The sky outside the windows was dark. The sun had set.

Nomuri stood, stopping first in the bathroom and then heading to the kitchenette. He returned with two wine glasses. Ming sat up in bed and took a sip from hers. For his part, Nomuri couldn't resist reaching over to touch her. Her skin was just so smooth and inviting.

"My brain is still not working," she said, after her third sip.

"Darling, there are times when men and women don't need their brains."

"Well, your sausage doesn't need one," she responded, reaching down to fondle it.

"Gently, girl! He's run a long hard race!" the CIA officer warned her with an inner smile.

"Oh, so he has." Ming bent down to deliver a gentle kiss. "And he won the race."

"No, but he did manage to catch up with you." Nomuri lit another cigarette. Then he was surprised to see Ming reach into her purse and pull out one of her own. She lit it with grace and took a long puff, finally letting the smoke out her nose.

"Dragon girl!" Nomuri announced with a laugh. "Do flames come next? I didn't know you smoked."

"At the office, everyone does."

"Even the minister?"

Another laugh: *"Especially* the minister."

"Someone should tell him that smoking is dangerous to the health, and not good for the yang."

"A smoked sausage is not a firm sausage," Ming said, with a laugh. "Maybe that's his problem, then."

"You do not like your minister?"

"He is an old man with what he thinks is a young penis. He uses the office staff as his personal bordello. Well, it could be worse," Ming admitted. "It's been a long time since I was his favorite. Lately he's fixed on Chai, and she is engaged, and Fang knows it. That is not a civilized act on the part of a senior minister."

"The laws do not apply to him?"

She snorted with borderline disgust. "The laws apply to none of them. Nomuri-san, these are government *ministers.* They *are* the law in this country, and they care little for what others think of them or their habits—few enough find out in any case. They are corrupt on a scale that shames the emperors of old, and they say they are the guardians of the common people, the peasants and workers they claim to love as their own children. Well, I suppose sometimes I am one of those peasants, eh?"

"And I thought you liked your minister," Nomuri responded, goading her on. "So, what does he talk about?"

"What do you mean?"

"The late work that kept you away from here," he answered, waving at the bedclothes with a smile.

"Oh, talk between the ministers. He keeps an extensive personal political diary—in case the president might want to oust him, that is his defense, you see, something he could present to his peers. Fang doesn't want to lose his official residence and all the privileges that come along with it. So, he keeps records of all he does, and I am his secretary, and I transcribe all his notes. Sometimes it can take forever."

"On your computer, of course."

"Yes, the new one, in perfect Mandarin ideographs now that you've given us the new software."

"You keep it on your computer?"

"On the hard drive, yes. Oh, it's encrypted," she assured him. "We learned that from the Americans, when we broke into their weapons records. It's called a robust encryption system, whatever that means. I select the file I wish to open and type in the decryption key, and the file opens. Do you want to know what key I use?" She giggled. "YELLOW SUBMARINE. In English because of the keyboard—it was before your new software—and it's from a Beatles song I heard on the radio once. 'We all live in a yellow submarine,' something like that. I listened to the radio a lot back then, when I was first studying English. I spent half an hour looking up submarines in the dictionary and then the encyclopedia, trying to find out why a ship was painted yellow. Ahh!" Her hands flew up in the air.

The encryption key! Nomuri tried to hide his excitement. "Well, it must be a lot of folders. You've been his secretary for a lot of time," he said casually.

"Over four hundred documents. I keep them by number instead of making up new names for them. Today was number four hundred eighty-seven, as a matter of fact."

Holy shit, Nomuri thought, *four hundred eighty-seven computer documents of inside-the-Politburo conversations. This makes a gold mine look like a toxic waste dump.*

"What exactly do they talk about? I've never met a senior government functionary," Nomuri explained.

"Everything!" she answered, finishing her own cigarette. "Who's got ideas in the Politburo, who wants to be nice to America, who wants to hurt them—everything you can imagine. Defense policy. Economic policy. The big one lately is how to deal with Hong Kong. 'One Country, Two Systems' has developed problems with some industrialists around Beijing and Shanghai. They feel they are treated with less respect than they deserve—less than they get in Hong Kong, that is—and they are unhappy about it. Fang's one of the people trying to find a compromise to make them happy. He might. He's very clever at such things."

"It must be fascinating to see such information—to really know what's going on in your country!" Nomuri gushed. "In Japan, we never know what the *zaibatsu* and the MITI people are doing—ruining the economy, for the most part, the fools. But because nobody knows, no action is ever taken to fix things. Is it the same here?"

"Of course!" She lit another smoke, getting into the conversation, and hardly noticing that it wasn't about love anymore. "Once I studied my Marx and my Mao. Once I believed in it all. Once I even trusted the senior ministers to be men of honor and integrity, and totally believed the things they taught me in school. But then I saw how the army has its own industrial empire, and that empire keeps the generals rich and fat and happy. And I saw how the ministers use women, and how they furnish their apartments. They've become the new emperors. They have too much power. Perhaps a woman could use such power without being corrupted, but not a man."

Feminism's made it over here, too? Nomuri reflected. Maybe she was too young to remember Mao's wife, Jiang Qing, who could have given corruption lessons to the court of Byzantium.

"Well, that is not a problem for people like us. And at least you get to see such things, and at least *you* get to know it. That makes you even more unique, Ming-chan," Nomuri suggested, tracing the palm of his hand over her left nipple. She shivered right on command.

"You think so?"

"Of course." A kiss this time, a nice lingering one, while his hand stroked her body. He was so close. She had told him of all the information she had—she'd even given him the fucking encryption key! So her 'puter was wired into the phone system—that meant he could call in to it, and with the right software he could go snooping around her hard drive, and with the encryption key he could lift things right off, and cross-load them right to Mary Pat's desk. *Damn, first I get to fuck a Chinese citizen, and then I can fuck their whole country.* It didn't get much better than this, the field spook decided, with a smile at the ceiling.

CHAPTER 13

Penetration Agent

Well, he left the prurient parts out this time, Mary Pat saw when she lit up her computer in the morning. Operation SORGE was moving right along. Whoever this Ming girl was, she talked a little too much. Odd. Hadn't the MSS briefed all the executive secretaries about this sort of thing? Probably—it would have been a remarkable oversight if they hadn't—but it also seemed likely that of the well-known reasons for committing treason and espionage (known as MICE: Money, Ideology, Conscience, and Ego), this one was Ego. Young Miss Ming was being used sexually by her Minister Fang, and she didn't much like it, and that made perfect sense to Mary Patricia Foley. A woman only had so much to give, and to have it taken coercively by a man of power wasn't something calculated to make a woman happy—though ironically the powerful man in question probably thought he was honoring her with his biological attention. After all, was he not a great man, and was she not a peasant? The thought was good for a snort as she took a sip of morning seventh-floor coffee. It didn't matter what culture or race, men were all the same, weren't they? So many of them thought from the dick instead of the brain. Well, it was going to cost this one dearly, the Deputy Director (Operations) concluded.

Ryan saw and heard the PDB, the President's Daily Brief, every day. It covered intelligence information developed by CIA, was prepared late every night and printed early every morning, and there were less than a hundred copies, almost all of which were shredded and burned later in the day of delivery. A few copies, maybe three or four, were kept as archives, in case the electronic files somehow got corrupted, but even President Ryan didn't know where the secure-storage site was. He hoped it was carefully guarded, preferably by Marines.

The PDB didn't contain everything, of course. Some things were so secret that even the President couldn't be trusted. That was something Ryan accepted with remarkable equanimity. Sources' names had to remain secret, even from him, and methods were often so narrowly technical that he'd have trouble understanding the technology used anyway. But even some of the "take," the information obtained by the CIA through nameless sources and overly intricate methods, was occasionally hidden from the Chief Executive, because some information *had* to come from a certain limited number of sources. The intelligence business was one in which the slightest mistake could end the life of a priceless asset, and while such things had happened, nobody had ever felt good about it—though to some politicians, it had been a matter of infuriating indifference. A good field spook viewed his agents as his own children, whose lives were to be protected against all hazards. Such a point of view was necessary. If you didn't care that much, then people died—and with their lost lives went lost information, which was the whole point of having a clandestine service in the first place.

"Okay, Ben," Ryan said, leaning back in his chair and flipping through the PDB pages. "What's interesting?"

"Mary Pat has something happening in China. Not sure what it is, though. She's keeping these cards pretty close. The rest of today's document you can get on CNN."

Which was, depressingly, not infrequently the case. On the other hand, the world was fairly sedate, and penetrating information wasn't all that necessary . . . or apparently so, Ryan corrected himself. You could never tell. He'd learned that one at Langley, too.

"Maybe I'll call her about it," POTUS said, flipping the page. "Whoa!"

"The Russian oil and gas?"

"Are these numbers for real?"

"It appears so. They track with what TRADER's been feeding us from his sources, step for step."

"Ummhmm," Ryan breathed, looking over the resulting forecasts for the Russian economy. Then he frowned with some disappointment. "George's people did a better evaluation of results."

"Think so? CIA's economics troops have a pretty decent track record."

"George lives in that business. That's better than being an academic observer of events, Ben. Academia is fine, but the real world is the *real* world, remember."

Goodley nodded. "Duly noted, sir."

"Throughout the '80s, CIA overestimated the Soviet economy. Know why?"

"No, I don't. What went wrong?"

Jack smiled wryly. "It wasn't what was wrong. It was what was *right.* We had an agent back then who fed us the same information the Soviet Politburo got. It just never occurred to us that the system was lying to itself. The Politburo based its decisions on a chimera. Their numbers were almost never right because the underlings were covering their own asses. Oops."

"Same thing in China, you suppose?" Goodley asked. "They're the last really Marxist country, after all."

"Good question. Call Langley and ask. You'll get an answer from the same sort of bureaucrat the Chinese have in Beijing, but to the best of my knowledge we don't have a penetration agent in Beijing who can give us the numbers we want." Ryan paused and looked at the fireplace opposite his desk. He'd have to have the Secret Service put a real fire in it someday . . . "No, I expect the Chinese have better numbers. They can afford to. Their economy is working, after a fashion. They probably deceive themselves in other ways. But they *do* deceive themselves. It's a universal human characteristic, and Marxism doesn't ameliorate it very much." Even in America, with its free press and other safeguards, reality often slapped political figures in the face hard enough to loosen some teeth. Everywhere, people had theoretical models based on ideology rather than facts, and those people usually found their way into academia or politics, because real-world professions punished that sort of dreamer more than politics ever did.

"Morning, Jack," a voice said from the corridor door.

"Hey, Robby." POTUS pointed to the coffee tray. Vice President

Jackson got himself a cup, but passed on the croissants. His waistline looked a little tight. Well, Robby had never looked like a marathoner. So many fighter pilots tended to have thick waists. Maybe it was good for fighting g-forces, Jack speculated.

"Read the PDB this morning. Jack, this Russian oil and gold thing. Is it really that big?"

"George says it's even bigger. You ever sit down with him to learn economics?"

"End of the week, we're going to play a round at Burning Tree, and I'm reading Milton Friedman and two other books to bone up for it. You know, George comes across as pretty smart."

"Smart enough to make a ton of money on The Street—and I mean if you put his money in hundred dollar bills and weigh them, it *is* a fucking ton of money."

"Must be nice," breathed a man who'd never made more than $130,000 in a year before taking on his current job.

"Has its moments, but the coffee here's still pretty good."

"It was better on *Big John,* once upon a time."

"Where?"

"John F. Kennedy, back when I was an O-3, and doing fun work, like driving Tomcats off the boat."

"Robby, hate to tell you, my friend, but you're not twenty-six anymore."

"Jack, you have such a way of brightening up my days for me. I've walked past death's door before, but it's safer and a hell of a lot more fun to do it with a fighter plane strapped to your back."

"What's your day look like?"

"Believe it or not, I have to drive down to the Hill and preside at the Senate for a few hours, just to show I know what the Constitution says I'm supposed to do. Then a dinner speech in Baltimore about who makes the best brassieres," he added with a smile.

"What?" Jack asked, looking up from the PDB. The thing about Robby's sense of humor was that you never really knew when he was kidding.

"National meeting of artificial fiber manufacturers. They also make bulletproof vests, but bras get most of their fibers, or so my research staff tells me. They're trying to make a few jokes for the speech."

"Work on your delivery," the President advised the Vice President.

"You thought I was funny enough way back when," Jackson reminded his old friend.

"Rob, I thought *I* was funny enough way back when, but Arnie tells me I'm not sensitive enough."

"I know, no Polish jokes. Some Polacks learned to turn on their TVs last year, and there's six or seven who know how to read. That doesn't count the Polish gal who doesn't use a vibrator because it chips her teeth."

"Jesus, Robby!" Ryan almost spilled his coffee laughing. "We're not even allowed to *think* things like that anymore."

"Jack, I'm not a politician. I'm a fighter jock. I got the flight suit, the hackwatch, and the dick to go along with the job title, y'dig?" the Vice President asked with a grin. "And I am allowed to tell a joke once in a while."

"Fine, just remember this isn't the ready room on the *Kennedy.* The media lacks the sense of humor enjoyed by naval aviators."

"Yeah, unless they catch us in something. Then it's funnier 'n hell," the retired Vice Admiral observed.

"Rob, you're finally catching on. Glad to see it." Ryan's last sight of the departing subordinate was the back of a nicely tailored suit, accompanied by a muttered vulgarity.

So, Misha, any thoughts?" Provalov asked.

Reilly took a sip of his vodka. It was awfully smooth here. "Oleg, you just have to shake the tree and see what falls out. It could be damned near anything, but 'don't know' means 'don't know.' And at the moment, we don't know." Another sip. "Does it strike you that two former Spetsnaz guys are a lot of firepower to go after a pimp?"

The Russian nodded. "Yes, of course, I've thought of that, but he was a very prosperous pimp, wasn't he, Misha? He had a great deal of money, and very many contacts inside the criminal establishment. He had power of his own. Perhaps he'd had people killed as well. We never had his name come up in a serious way in any murder investigations, but that doesn't mean that Avseyenko was not a dangerous man in his own right, and therefore worthy of such high-level attention."

"Any luck with this Suvorov guy?"

Provalov shook his head. "No. We have a KGB file for him and a photograph, but even if that is for the right person, we haven't found him yet."

"Well, Oleg Gregoriyevich, it looks as though you have a real head-scratcher on your hands." Reilly lifted his hand to order another round.

"You are supposed to be the expert on organized crime," the Russian lieutenant reminded his FBI guest.

"That's true, Oleg, but I ain't no gypsy fortune-teller, and I ain't the Oracle of Delphi either. You don't know who the real target was yet, and until you learn that, you don't know jack shit. Problem is, to find out who the target was, you have to find somebody who knows something about the crime. The two things are wrapped up together, bro. Get one, get both. Get neither, get nothing." The drinks arrived. Reilly paid and took another hit.

"My captain is not pleased."

The FBI agent nodded. "Yeah, bosses are like that in the Bureau, too, but he's supposed to know what the problems are, right? If he does, he knows he has to give you the time and the resources to play it out. How many men you have on it now?"

"Six here, and three more in St. Petersburg."

"May want to get some more, bro." In the FBI's New York OC office, a case like this could have as many as twenty agents working it, half of them on a full-time basis. But the Moscow Militia was stretched notoriously thin. For as much crime as there was now in Moscow, the local cops were still sucking hind tit when it came to government support. But it could have been worse. Unlike much of Russian society, the militiamen were getting paid.

You tire me out," Nomuri protested.

"There is always Minister Fang," Ming replied with a playful look.

"Ah!" was the enraged reply. "You compare me with an old man?"

"Well, both of you are men, but better a sausage than a string bean," she answered, grasping the former in her soft left hand.

"Patience, girl, allow me to recover from the first race." With that he lifted her body over his and let it down. *She must really like me,* Nomuri reflected. *Three nights in a row. I suppose Fang isn't the man he thinks he is. Well, can't win 'em all, Charlie.* Plus the advantage of being forty years younger. There was probably something to that, the CIA officer admitted to himself.

"But you run so fast!" Ming protested, rubbing her body on his.

"There is something I want you to do."

A very playful smile. "What might that be?" she asked while her hand wandered a little.

"Not that!"

"Oh . . ." The disappointment in her voice was noteworthy.

"Something for work," Nomuri explained on. Just as well she couldn't feel the shaking inside his body, which, remarkably enough, didn't show.

"For work? I can't bring you into the office for this!" she said with a laugh, followed by a warm, affectionate kiss.

"Yes, something to upload onto your computer." Nomuri reached into the night-table drawer and pulled out a CD-ROM. "Here, you just load this into your machine, click INSTALL, and then dispose of it when you're done."

"And what will it do?" she asked.

"Do you care?"

"Well . . ." Hesitation. She didn't understand. "I must care."

"It will allow me to look at your computer from time to time."

"But why?"

"Because of Nippon Electric—we make your computer, don't you see?" He allowed his body to relax. "It is useful for my company to know how economic decisions are made in the People's Republic," Nomuri explained, with a well-rehearsed lie. "This will allow us to understand that process a little better, so that we can do business more effectively. And the better I do for them, the more they will pay me—and the more I can spend on my darling Ming."

"I see," she thought, wrongly.

He bent down to kiss a particularly nice spot. Her body shuddered in just the right way. Good, she wasn't resisting the idea, or at least wasn't letting it get in the way of this activity, which was good for Nomuri in more than one way. The intelligence officer wondered if someday his conscience would attack him for using this girl in such a way. But business, he told himself, was business.

"No one will know?"

"No, that is not possible."

"And it will not get me into trouble?"

With that question he rolled over, finding himself on top. He held her face in both hands. "Would I ever do something to get Ming-chan in trouble? Never!" he announced, with a deep and passionate kiss.

Afterward there was no talk about the CD-ROM, which she tucked into her purse before leaving. It was a nice-looking purse, a knockoff of something Italian that you could buy on the street here, rather like the genuine ones in New York that "fell off the back of the truck," as the euphemism went.

Every time they parted, it was a little hard. She didn't want to leave, and truly he didn't want her to depart, but it was necessary. For them to share an apartment would be commented upon. Even in her dreams, Ming couldn't think of that, actually sleeping at the apartment of a foreigner, because she *did* have a security clearance, and she *had* been given her security brief by a bored MSS officer, along with all the other senior secretaries, and she *hadn't* reported this contact to her superiors or the office security chief as she ought to have done—why? Partly because she'd forgotten the rules, because she'd never broken them or known someone who had done so, and partly because like many people she drew a line between her private life and her professional one. That the two were not allowed to be separate in her case was something that the MSS briefing had covered, but in so clumsy a way as to have been disregarded even upon its delivery. And so here she was, not even knowing where and what *here* was. With luck, she'd never have to find out, Nomuri thought, watching her turn the corner and disappear from view. Luck would help. What the MSS interrogators did to young women in the Beijing version of the Lubyanka didn't really bear much contemplation, certainly not when one had just made love to her twice in two hours.

"Good luck, honey," Nomuri whispered, as he closed the door and headed to the bathroom for a shower.

CHAPTER 14

(dot)com

It was a sleepless night for Nomuri. Would she do it? Would she do what she was told? Would she tell a security officer about it, and then about him? Might she be caught with the CD-ROM going into work and questioned about it? If so, a casual inspection would show it to be a music CD, Bill Conti's musical score for *Rocky*—a poorly marked knockoff of an American intellectual property that was quite common in the PRC. But a more careful examination would have revealed that the first—outermost—data line on the metallic surface told the computer CD-ROM reader to skip to a certain place where the content was not music, but binary code, and very efficient binary code at that.

The CD-ROM didn't contain a virus per se, because a virus circulates mainly across computer networks, entering a computer surreptitiously the way a disease organism enters a living host (hence the term virus). But this one came in the front door, and on being read by the CD-ROM reader, a single prompt came up on the screen, and Ming, after a quick look-around in her office, moved her mouse to put the pointer on the prompt, clicked the INSTALL command, and everything immediately disappeared. The program thus implanted searched her hard drive at nearly the speed of light, categorizing every file and setting up its own index, then compressing it into a small file that hid in plain sight, as it were, identified by any disk-sorting program with a wholly innocent name that referred to a function carried out by another program entirely. Thus only a very careful and directed search by a skilled computer operator could even detect that something was even there. Exactly what the program did could only be determined by a one-by-zero reading of the program itself, something difficult to accomplish at best. It would be like trying to find what was wrong with a single leaf on a single tree in a vast forest where all the trees and all the leaves looked pretty much alike, except that this one leaf was smaller and humbler than most. CIA and NSA could no longer attract the best programmers in America. There was just too much money in the consumer electronics industry for government to compete effectively in that marketplace. But you could still hire them, and the work that came out was just as good. And if you paid them enough—strangely, you could pay lots more to a contractor than to an employee—they wouldn't talk to anyone about it. And besides, they never really knew what it was all about anyway, did they?

In this case, there was an additional level of complexity that went back over sixty years. When the Germans had overrun the Netherlands in 1940, they'd created a strange situation. In Holland the Germans had found both the most cooperative of their conquered nations and the most fiercely resistant. More Dutchmen per capita had joined the Germans than any other nationality—enough to form their own SS division, SS Nordland. At the same time, the Dutch resistance became the most effective in Europe, and one of their number was a brilliant mathematician/engineer working for the national telephone company. In the second decade of the twentieth century, the telephone had reached a developmental roadblock. When you lifted a phone, you were immediately connected with an operator to whom you gave the destination you were trying to call, and she then physically moved a plug into the proper hole. This system had been workable when only a few telephones were in use, but the appliance had rapidly proved too useful for limited applications. The solution to the problem, remarkably enough, had come from a mortician in the American South. Vexed by the fact that the local operator in his town referred the bereaved to a competing undertaker, he had invented the stepping switch, which enabled people to reach their own phone destinations merely by turning a rotary dial. That system served the world well, but also required the development of a whole body of new mathematical knowledge called "complexity theory," which was systematized by the American company AT&T in the 1930s.

Ten years later, merely by adding additional digits to be dialed, the

Dutch engineer in the resistance had applied complexity theory to covert operations by creating theoretical pathways through the switching gear, thus enabling resistance fighters to call others without knowing whom they called, or even the actual telephone numbers they were calling.

This bit of electronic skullduggery had first been noticed by an officer for the British Special Operations Executive, the SOE, and, finding it very clever indeed, he'd discussed it over a beer with an American colleague in a London pub. The American OSS officer, like most of the men Wild Bill Donovan had chosen, was an attorney by profession, and in his case, a very thorough one, who wrote everything down and forwarded it up the line. The report on the Dutch engineer had made its way to the office of Colonel William Friedman, then America's foremost code-breaker. Though not himself a hardware expert, Friedman had known something useful when he saw it, and he knew there would be an after-the-war, during which his agency—later reborn as the National Security Agency—would still be busy cracking other countries' codes and ciphers and producing codes and ciphers itself. The ability to develop covert communications links through a relatively simple mathematical trick had seemed a gift from God's own hand.

In the 1940s and '50s, NSA *had* been able to hire American's finest mathematicians, and one of the tasks assigned them had been to work with AT&T to create a universal telephone operating system that could be used covertly by American intelligence officers. Back then, AT&T was the only real rival NSA had had in the hiring of skilled mathematicians, and beyond that, AT&T had always been a prime contractor for just about every executive agency of the government. By 1955, it was done, and for a surprisingly modest fee AT&T provided the entire world with a model for telephone systems that most of the world adopted—the modest cost was explained by the desire of AT&T to make its systems compatible with every other country's to ease international communications. With the 1970s had come push-button phones, which directed calls electronically by frequency-controlled codes even easier for electronic systems to use, and infinitely easier to maintain than the former electro-mechanical stepping switches that had made the mortician hugely rich. They also proved even easier for AT&T to rig for NSA. The operating systems first given the world's telephone companies by AT&T's Parsippany, New Jersey, research laboratory had been upgraded yearly at least, giving further improvements to the efficiency of the world's phone systems—so much so that scarcely any telephone system in the world didn't use it. And tucked into that operating system were six lines of binary code whose operational concept traced back to the Nazi occupation of Holland.

Ming finished the installation and ejected the disk, discarding it into her waste can. The easy way to dispose of secret material was to have your adversary do it, through the front door, not the back one.

Nothing really happened for some hours, while Ming did her usual office tasks and Nomuri visited three commercial businesses to sell his high-powered desktop computers. All that changed at 7:45 P.M.

By this time, Ming was at her own home. Nomuri would get a night off; Ming had to do some things with her roommate to avoid too much suspicion—watching local television, chatting with her friend, and thinking about her lover, while the whole reason for the wispy smiles on her face played out entirely outside her consciousness. Strangely, it never occurred to her that her roomie had it all figured out in an instant, and was merely polite enough not to broach the subject.

Her NEC desktop computer had long since gone into auto-sleep mode, leaving the monitor screen dark and blank, and the indicator light in the lower right position of the plastic frame amber instead of the green that went with real activity. The software she'd installed earlier in the day had been custom-designed for the NEC machines, which like all such machines had proprietary source-code unique to the brand. The source-code, however, was known to the National Security Agency.

Immediately upon installation, the Ghost program—as it had been christened at Fort Meade, Maryland—had buried itself in a special niche in the NEC's operating system, the newest version of Microsoft Windows. The niche had been created by a Microsoft employee whose favorite uncle had died over North Vietnam while flying an F-105 fighter-bomber, and who did his patriotic work entirely without the knowledge of his parent company. It also dovetailed exactly with the NEC code, with the effect of making it virtually invisible even to a line-by-line inspection of all the code within the machine by an expert software engineer.

The Ghost had gone immediately to work, creating a directory that sorted the documents on Ming's computer first by date of creation/modification, and then by file type. Some files, like the operating system, it ignored. It similarly ignored the NEC-created transcription program that converted Roman characters, actually the English phonemes of the spoken Mandarin language, into the corresponding ideographs, but the Ghost did not ignore the graphic-text files that resulted from that program. Those it copied, along with telephone indexes and every other text file on the five-gigabyte hard drive. This entire procedure took the machine, guided by the Ghost, seventeen-point-one-four seconds, leaving a large file that sat by itself.

The machine did nothing for a second and a half, then new activity started. The NEC desktop machines had built-in high-speed modems. The Ghost activated these, but also turned off their internal mini-speakers so that no evidence of the transmission would be heard by anyone. (Leaving the speakers on was a primary security measure. The flashing lights that told of their activity were hidden because the modem was inside the box for this model.) The computer then dialed (this term had somehow survived the demise of rotary dials on telephones) a twelve-digit number rather than the usual seven used by the Beijing telephone system. The additional five digits sent the seeker-signal on a round-robin adventure through the hardware of the central switching computer, and it came out in the place designated two weeks before by the engineers at Fort Meade, who, of course, never had an idea what this was all for, or where it would happen, or who might be involved. The number that rang—actually there wasn't a mechanical or electronic ringer of any sort—was the dedicated modem line that exited the wall by Chester Nomuri's desk and ended in the back of his very high-end laptop—which was not an NEC, because here, as with most computer applications, the best was still American.

Nomuri was also watching TV at the moment, though in his case it was the CNN international news, so that he could know what was going on at home. After that he'd switch to a Japanese satellite channel, because it was part of his cover. A samurai show he liked was on tonight, in theme and simplicity rather like the Westerns that had polluted American TV in the 1950s. Though an educated man and a professional intelligence officer, Nomuri liked mindless entertainment as much as anyone else. The *beep* made him turn his head. Though his computer had software similar to that running in Ming's office, he'd allowed the aural prompt to tell him that something was coming in, and a three-key code lit up his screen to show exactly what it was and where it was coming from.

Yes! the CIA officer exulted, his right fist slamming into his open left hand hard enough to sting. Yes. He had his agent in fucking place, and here was the take from Operation SORGE. A bar at the top of the screen showed that the data was coming it at a rate of 57,000 bits per second. That was pretty fast. Now, just hope that the local commie phone system didn't develop a bad connection somewhere between Ming's office and the switching center, and from the switching center to his flat, Chester thought. Shouldn't be much of a problem. The outbound leg from Ming's office would be first-rate, tasked as it was to the service of the Party nobility. And from the switching center to his place would be okay, because he'd gotten numerous messages that way, most of them from NEC in Tokyo to congratulate him on exceeding his sales quota already.

Yeah, well, Chet, you are pretty good at making a sale, aren't you? he asked himself on the way to the kitchen. He figured he owed himself a drink for this bit of performance. On returning, he saw that the download wasn't finished yet.

Damn. How much shit is she sending me? Then he realized that the text files he was getting were actually graphics files, because Ming's computer didn't store ideographs as letters, but rather as the pictures that they actually were. That made the files memory-intensive. Exactly how memory-intensive they were, he saw forty minutes later when the download ended.

At the far end of the electronic chain, the Ghost program appeared to shut itself down, but in fact it slept rather as a dog did, one ear always cocked up, and always aware of the time of day. On finishing the transmission, the Ghost made a notation on its inside index of the files. It had sent everything up until this day. From now on, it would only send new ones—which would make for much shorter and faster transmissions—but only in the evening, and only after ninety-five minutes of total inactivity on the computer, and only when it was outwardly in auto-sleep mode. Tradecraft and caution had been programmed in.

"Fuck," Nomuri breathed on seeing the size of the download. In pictures this could be the porno shots of damned near every hooker in

Hong Kong. But his job was only half done. He lit up a program of his own and selected the "Preferences" folder that controlled it. Already checked was the box for autoencryption. Virtually everything on his computer was encrypted anyway, which was easily explainable as trade and business secrets—Japanese companies are renowned for the secrecy of their operations—but with some files more encrypted than others. The ones that arrived from the Ghost got the most robust scrambling, from a mathematically derived transcription system, fully 512 bits in the key, plus an additional random element which Nomuri could not duplicate. That was in addition to his numeric password, 51240, the street number of his first "score" in East LA. Then it was time to transmit his take.

This program was a close cousin to the Ghost he'd given Ming. But this one dialed the local Internet Service Provider, or ISP, and sent off a lengthy e-mail to a destination called patsbakery@brownienet.com. The "brownienet" was putatively a network established for bakeries and bakers, professional and amateur, who liked to swap recipes, often posting photos of their creations for people to download, which explained the occasional large file transferred. Photographs are notoriously rapacious in their demands for bytes and disk space.

In fact, Mary Patricia Foley had posted her own highly satisfactory recipe for French apple pie, along with a photo her elder son had taken with his Apple electronic camera. Doing so hadn't been so much a case of establishing a good cover as womanly pride in her own abilities as a cook, after spending an hour one night looking over the recipes others had put on this bulletin board. She'd tried one from a woman in Michigan a few weeks previously and found it okay, but not great. In coming weeks she wanted to try some of the bread recipes, which did look promising.

It was morning when Nomuri uploaded his e-mail to Pat's Bakery, an entirely real and legitimate business three blocks from the statehouse in Madison, Wisconsin, as a matter of fact, owned by a former CIA officer in the Science and Technology Directorate, now retired and a grandmother who was, however, too young for knitting. She'd created this Internet domain, paying the nominal fee and then forgetting about it, just as she'd forgotten nearly everything she'd ever done at Langley.

"You've got mail," the computer said when MP switched on her Internet mail service, which used the new Pony Express e-mail program. She keyed the download command and saw the originator was cgood-jadecastle.com. The username was from *Gunsmoke.* Marshal Dillon's crippled sidekick had been named Chester Good.

DOWNLOADING, the prompt-box on the screen said. It also gave an estimate for how long the download would take. 47 MINUTES . . . !

"Son of a bitch," the DDO breathed, and lifted her phone. She pressed a button, waiting a second for the right voice to answer. "Ed, better come see this . . ."

"Okay, honey, give me a minute."

The Director of Central Intelligence came in, holding his morning mug of coffee, to see his wife of twenty-three years leaning back, away from her computer screen. Rarely in that time had Mary Pat ever backed away from anything. It just wasn't her nature.

"From our Japanese friend?" Ed asked his wife.

"So it would seem," MP replied.

"How much stuff is this?"

"Looks like a lot. I suppose Chester is pretty good in the sack."

"Who trained him?"

"Whoever it was, we need to get his ass down to The Farm and pass all that knowledge along. For that matter," she added, with a changed voice and an upward look to catch her husband's eye, "maybe you could audit the course, honey-bunny."

"Is that a complaint?"

"There's always room for improvement—and, okay, yes, I need to drop fifteen pounds, too," she added, to cut the DCI off before he could reply in kind. He hated when she did that. But not now. Now his hand touched her face quite tenderly, as the prompt screen said another thirty-four minutes to complete the download.

"Who's the guy at Fort Meade who put the Ghost programs together?"

"They contracted a game place—a guy at a game company, I guess," Mrs. Foley corrected herself. "They paid him four hundred fifty big ones for the job." Which was more than the Director of Central Intelligence and the Deputy Director (Operations) made together, what with the federal pay caps, which didn't allow any federal employee to make more than a member of Congress—and they feared raising their own salaries, lest they offend the voters.

"Call me when you have it downloaded, baby."

"Who's the best guy we have for China?"

"Joshua Sears, Ph.D. from U-Cal Berkley, runs the China desk in the DI. But the guy at NSA is better for linguistic nuances, they say. His name's Victor Wang," the DCI said.

"Can we trust him?" MP asked. Distrust of ethnic Chinese in the American national-security apparatus had reached a considerable level.

"Shit, I don't know. You know, we have to trust somebody, and Wang's been on the box twice a year for the last eight years. The ChiComms can't compromise every Chinese-American we have, you know. This Wang guy's third-generation American, was an officer in the Air Force—ELINT guy, evidently worked out of Wright-Patterson—and just made super-grade at NSA. Tom Porter says he's very good."

"Okay, well, let me see what all this is, then we'll have Sears check it out, and then, maybe, if we have to, we'll talk to this Wang guy. Remember, Eddie, at the end of this is an officer named Nomuri and a foreign national who has two eyes—"

Her husband cut her off with a wave. "And two ears. Yeah, baby, I know. We've been there. We've done that. And we both have the T-shirts to prove it." And he was about as likely to forget that as his wife was. Keeping your agents alive was as important to an intelligence agency as capital preservation was to an investor.

Mary Pat ignored her computer for twenty minutes, and instead went over routine message traffic hand-carried up from MERCURY down in the basement of the Old Headquarters Building. That was not especially easy, but necessary nonetheless, because CIA's Clandestine Service was running agents and operations all over the world—or trying to, Mary Pat corrected herself. It was her job to rebuild the Directorate of Operations, to restore the human-intelligence—HUMINT—capability largely destroyed in the late 1970s, and only slowly being rebuilt. That was no small task, even for an expert in the field. But Chester Nomuri was one of her pets. She'd spotted him at The Farm some years before and seen in him the talent, the gift, and the motivation. For him espionage was as much a vocation as the priesthood, something important to his country, and *fun,* as much fun as dropping a fifty-footer at Augusta was for Jack Nicklaus. Toss in his brains and street sense, and, Mary Pat had thought at the time, she had a winner there. Now Nomuri was evidently living up to her expectations. Big time. For the first time, CIA had an agent-in-place inside the ChiComm Politburo, and that was about as good as it got. Perhaps even the Russians didn't have one of those, though you could never be sure, and you could lose a lot of money betting against the Russian intelligence services.

"File's done," the computer's electronic voice finally said. That occasioned a turn in her swivel chair. The DDO first of all backed up her newly downloaded file to a second hard drive, and then to a "toaster" disk, so called because the disk went in and out of the drive box like a slice of bread. With that done, she typed in her decryption code, 51240. She had no idea why Nomuri had specified that number, but knowing was not necessary, just so long as nobody else knew either. After typing in the five digits and hitting RETURN, the file icons changed. They were already aligned in list form, and MP selected the oldest. A page full of Chinese ideographs came up. With that bit of information, MP lifted her office phone and punched the button for her secretary. "Dr. Joshua Sears, DI, Chinese Section. Please ask him to come see me right away."

That took six endless minutes. It took rather a lot to make Mary Patricia Kaminsky Foley shiver, but this was one such occasion. The image on her screen looked like something one might get from inking the feet of several drunken roosters, then making them loiter on a piece of white paper, but within the imagery were words and thoughts. Secret words and hidden thoughts. On her screen was the ability to read the minds of adversaries. It was the sort of thing that could win the World Series of Poker in Las Vegas, but infinitely more important. It was the sort of thing that had won wars and altered history from the expected path determined by the most important of players, and in that was the value of espionage, the whole point of having an intelligence community, because the fates of nations really did ride on such things—

—and therefore, the fates of nations rode on Chet Nomuri's schwantz and how well he used it, Mrs. Foley reflected. What a crazy fucking world it was. How the hell could an historian ever get that right? How did you communicate the importance of seducing some nameless secretary, an underling, a modern-day peasant who merely transcribed the thoughts of the important, but in being compromised made those thoughts available to others, and in doing so, altered the course of history as surely as turning the rudder changed the course of a mighty ship. For Mary Pat, Deputy Director (Operations) of the Central Intelligence Agency, it was a moment of fulfillment to place alongside the birth of her children. Her entire *raison d'être* lay in black-and-white ideographs on her computer monitor—and she couldn't read the fucking things. She had the language skills to teach Russian literature at Moscow State University, but all she knew of Chinese was chop suey and moo goo gai pan.

"Mrs. Foley?" A head appeared at her door. "I'm Josh Sears." He was fifty, tall, losing his hair, most of it gray. Brown eyes. He hit the cafeteria line downstairs a little too hard, the DDO thought.

"Please come in, Dr. Sears. I need you to translate some things for me."

"Sure," he replied, picking a seat and relaxing into it. He watched the DDO take some pages off her laser printer and hand them across.

"Okay, it says the date is last March twenty-first, and the place is Beijing—hmph, the Council of Ministers Building, eh? Minister Fang is talking to Minister Zhang." Sears ran his eyes down the page. "Mrs. Foley, this is hot stuff. They're talking about the possibilities of Iran—no, the old UIR—taking over the entire Persian Gulf oil fields, and what effect it would have on China. Zhang appears to be optimistic, but guarded. Fang is skeptical . . . oh, this is an *aide-memoir,* isn't it? It's Fang's notes from a private conversation with Zhang."

"The names mean anything to you?"

"Both are Ministers Without Portfolio. They're both full Politburo members without direct ministerial duties. That means they're both trusted by the chairman, the PRC premier, Xu Kun Piao. They go back thirty years plus, well into the time of Mao and Chou. As you know, the Chinese are really into lengthy relationships. They develop—well, not friendships as we understand them, but associations. It's a comfort-level thing, really. Like at a card table. You know what the other guy's mannerisms and capabilities are, and that makes for a long, comfortable game. Maybe you won't win big, but you won't lose your shirt either."

"No, they don't gamble, do they?"

"This document demonstrates that. As we suspected, the PRC backed the Ayatollah Daryaei in his play, but they never allowed their support to be public. From skimming this, it appears that this Zhang guy is the one who ramrodded this—and the play the Japanese made. We've been trying to build a book on this Zhang guy—and Fang as well—without a whole lot of success. What do I need to know about this?" he asked, holding the page up.

"It's code word," MP replied. By federal statute, "top secret" was as high as it went, but in reality there were more secret things than that, called "special-access programs," which were designated by their controlling code words. "This one's called SORGE." She didn't have to say that he could not discuss this information with anyone, and that even dreaming in bed about it was forbidden. Nor did she have to say that in SORGE was Sears's path to a raise and much greater personal importance within the CIA's pantheon of bureaucrats.

"Okay." Sears nodded. "What can you tell me?"

"What we have here is a digest of conversations between Fang and Zhang, and probably other ministers as well. We've found a way to crash into their documents storage. We believe the documents are genuine," MP concluded. Sears would know that he was being misled on sources and methods, but that was to be expected. As a senior member of the DI—the Directorate of Intelligence—it was his job to evaluate information provided to him by various sources, in this case the DO. If he got bad information, his evaluation would be bad as well, but what Mrs. Foley had just told him was that he would not be held at fault for bad information. But he'd also question the authenticity of the documents in an internal memo or two, just to cover his own ass, of course.

"Okay, ma'am. In that case, what we have here is pure nitroglycerine. We've suspected this, but here's confirmation. It means that President Ryan did the right thing when he granted diplomatic recognition to Taiwan. The PRC had it coming. They conspired to wage aggressive war, and since we got involved, you can say that they conspired against us. Twice, I bet. We'll see if another of these documents refers to the Japanese adventure. You'll recall that the Japanese industrialists implicated this Zhang guy by name. That's not a hundred percent, but if it's confirmed by this, then it's almost something you could take before a judge. Mrs. Foley, this is some source we have here."

"Evaluation?"

"It feels right," the analyst said, reading over the page again. "It sounds like conversation. I mean, it's unguarded, not official diplomatic-speak or even inside-minister-speak. So, it sounds like what it purports to be, the notes of a private, informal policy discussion between two senior colleagues."

"Any way to cross-check it?" MP asked next.

An immediate shake of the head. "No. We don't know much about either one of these guys. Zhang, well, we have the evaluation from Secretary Adler—you know, from the shuttle diplomacy after the Airbus shoot-down, which pretty well confirms what that Yamata guy told the Japanese police and our FBI guys about how the Chinese nudged them into the conflict with us, and what for. The PRC looks on eastern Siberia with covetous eyes," Sears reminded her, showing his knowledge of the PRC policies and objectives. "For Fang Gan, we have photos of him sipping mao-tai at receptions in his Mao jacket and smiling benignly, like they all do. We know he's tight with Xu, there are stories that he likes to play with the office help—but a lot of them do that—and that's about it."

It was good of Sears not to remind her that playing with the office help wasn't a character defect limited to China.

"So, what do we think about them?"

"Fang and Zhang? Well, both are Ministers Without Portfolio. So, they're utility infielders, maybe even assistant coaches. Premier Xu trusts their judgment. They get to sit in at the Politburo as full voting members. They get to hear everything and cast votes on everything. They influence policy not so much by making it as shaping it. Every minister knows them. These two know all the others. They've both been around a long time. Both are well into their sixties or seventies, but people over there don't mellow with age like they do in America. Both will be ideologically sound, meaning they're both probably solid communists. That implies a certain ruthlessness, and you can add to that their age. At seventy-five, death starts being a very real thing. You don't know how much time you have left, and these guys don't believe in an afterlife. So, whatever goals they have, they have to address pretty quick at that age, don't they?"

"Marxism doesn't mix well with humanity, does it?"

Sears shook his head. "Not hardly, and toss in a culture that places a much lower value on human life than ours does."

"Okay. Good brief. Here," she said, handing over ten printed pages. "I want a written evaluation after lunch. Whatever you might be working on now, SORGE is more important."

That meant a "seventh-floor tasking" to Dr. Sears. He'd be working directly for the Directors. Well, he had a private office already, and a computer that wasn't hooked into any telephone lines, even a local area network, as many of the CIA's 'puters were. Sears tucked the papers into a coat pocket and departed, leaving Mary Pat to look out her floor-to-ceiling windows and contemplate her next move. Really it was Ed's call, but things like this were decided collegially, especially when the DCI was your husband. This time she'd wander over to see him.

The DCI's office is long and relatively narrow, with the director's office near the door, well away from the sitting area. Mary Pat took the easy chair across from the desk.

"How good is it?" Ed asked, knowing the reason for her visit.

"Calling this SORGE was unusually prescient for us. It's at least that good."

Since Richard Sorge dispatches from Tokyo to Moscow might have saved the Soviet Union in 1941, that got Ed Foley's eyes to widen some. "Who looked at it?"

"Sears. He seems pretty smart, by the way. I've never really talked to him before."

"Harry likes him," Ed noted, referring to Harry Hall, the current Deputy Director (Intelligence), who was in Europe at the moment. "Okay, so he says it looks pretty good, eh?"

A serious nod. "Oh, yeah, Eddie."

"Take it to see Jack?" They could not *not* take this to the President, could they?

"Tomorrow, maybe?"

"Works for me." Just about any government employee can find space in his or her day for a drive to the White House. "Eddie, how far can this one spread?"

"Good question. Jack, of course. *Maybe* the Vice President. I like the guy," the DCI said, "but usually the veep doesn't get into stuff like this. SecState, SecDef, both are maybes. Ben Goodley, again a maybe. Mary, you know the problem with this."

It was the oldest and most frequent problem with really valuable high-level intelligence information. If you spread it too far, you ran the risk of compromising the information—which also meant getting the source killed—and that killed the goose laying the golden eggs. On the other hand, if you didn't make *some* use of the information, then you might as well not have the eggs anyway. Drawing the line was the most delicate operation in the field of intelligence, and you never knew where the right place was to draw it. You also had to worry about methods of spreading it around. If you sent it encrypted from one place to another, what if the bad guys had cracked your encryption system? NSA swore that its systems, especially TAPDANCE, could not be broken, but the Germans had thought ENIGMA crack-proof, too.

Almost as dangerous was giving the information, even by hand, to a senior government official. The bastards talked too much. They lived by talking. They lived by leaking. They lived by showing people how important they were, and importance in D.C. meant knowing what other people didn't know. Information was the coin of the realm in this part of America. The good news here was that President Ryan understood about that. He'd been CIA, as high as Deputy Director, and so he knew about the value of security. The same was probably true of Vice President Jackson, former naval aviator. He'd probably seen lives lost because of bad intelligence. Scott Adler was a diplomat, and he probably knew as well. Tony Bretano, the well-regarded SecDef, worked closely with CIA, as all Secretaries of Defense had to do, and he could probably be trusted as well. Ben Goodley was the President's National Security Advisor, and thus couldn't easily be excluded. So, what did that total up to? Two in Beijing. At Langley, the DCI, DDCI, DDI, and DDO, plus Sears from inside the DI. That made seven. Then the President, Vice President, SecState, SecDef, and Ben Goodley. That made twelve. And twelve was plenty for the moment, especially in a town where the saying went, *If two people know it, it's not a secret.* But the entire reason for having CIA was this sort of information.

"Pick a name for the source," Foley instructed his wife.

"SONGBIRD will do for now." It was a sentimental thing for MP, naming agents for birds. It dated back to CARDINAL.

"Fair enough. Let me see the translations you get, okay?"

"You bet, honey-bunny." Mary Pat leaned over her husband's desk to deliver a kiss, before heading back to her own office.

On arriving there, MP checked her computer for the SORGE file. She'd have to change that, MP realized. Even the name of this special-access compartment would be classified top secret or higher. Then she did a page count, making a note on a paper pad next to the screen.

ALL 1,349 PAGES OF RECIPES RECEIVED, she wrote as a reply to cgood@jadecastle.com. WILL LOOK THE RECIPES OVER. THANKS A BUNCH. MARY. She hit the RETURN key, and off the letter went, through the electronic maze called the Internet. *One thousand, three hundred and forty-nine pages,* the DDO thought. It would keep the analysts busy for quite a while. Inside the Old Headquarters Building, analysts would see bits and pieces of SORGE material, covered under other transitory code names randomly chosen by a computer in the basement, but only Sears would know the whole story—and, in fact, he didn't even know that, did he? What he knew might—probably would—be enough to get this Ming woman killed, once the MSS realized who'd had access to the information. They could do some things in Washington to protect her, but not much.

Nomuri rose early in his Beijing apartment, and the second thing he did was to log on to check his e-mail. There it was, number seven in the list, one from patsbakery@brownienet.com. He selected the decryption system and typed in the key . . . so, the pages had all been received. That was good. Nomuri dragged the message he'd dispatched to the "wipe-info" bin, where Norton Utilities not only deleted the file, but also five times electronically scrubbed the disk segments where they'd briefly resided, so that the files could never be recovered by any attempt, no matter how skilled. Next he eliminated the record of having sent any e-mail to brownienet. Now there was no record whatever of his having done anything, unless his telephone line were tapped, which he didn't really suspect. And even then the data was scrambled, fully encrypted, and thus not recoverable. No, the only dangers in the operation now attached to Ming. His part of it, being the spymaster, was protected by the method in which her desktop computer called him, and from now on those messages would be sent out to brownienet automatically, and erased the same way, in a matter of seconds. It would take a very clever counterintelligence operation to hurt Nomuri now.

CHAPTER 15

Exploitation

"What's this mean, Ben?" Ryan asked, seeing a change in his morning schedule.

"Ed and Mary Pat want to talk something over with you. They didn't say what it was," Goodley replied. "The Vice President can be here, too, and me, but that's it, they requested."

"Some new kind of toilet paper in the Kremlin, I suppose," POTUS said. It was a long-standing CIA joke from Ryan's time in the Bad Old Days of the Cold War. He stirred his coffee and leaned back in his comfortable chair. "Okay, what else is happening in the world, Ben?"

"So, this is mao-tai?" Cardinal DiMilo asked. He didn't add that he'd been given to understand that Baptists didn't drink alcoholic beverages. Odd, considering that Jesus' first public miracle had been to change water into wine at the marriage feast at Cana. But Christianity had many faces. In any case, the mao-tai was vile, worse than the cheapest grappa. With advancing years, the Cardinal preferred gentler drinks. It was much easier on the stomach.

"I should not drink this," Yu admitted, "but it is part of my heritage."

"I know of no passage in Holy Scripture that prohibits this particular human weakness," the Catholic said. And besides, wine was part of the Catholic liturgy. He saw that his Chinese host barely sipped at his tiny cup. Probably better for his stomach, too, the Italian reasoned.

He'd have to get used to the food, too. A gourmet like many Italians, Renato Cardinal DiMilo found that the food in Beijing was not as good as he'd experienced in Rome's numerous Chinese restaurants. The problem, he thought, was the quality of the ingredients rather than the cook. In this case, the Reverand Yu's wife was away in Taiwan to see her sick mother, he'd said, apologizing on the Catholic's arrival. Monsignor Schepke had taken over the serving, rather like a young lieutenant-aide serving the needs of his general, Yu had thought, watching the drama play out with some amusement. The Catholics certainly had their bureaucratic ways. But this Renato fellow was a decent sort, clearly an educated man, and a trained diplomat from whom Yu realized he might learn much.

"So, you cook for yourself. How did you learn?"

"Most Chinese men know how. We learn from our parents as children."

DiMilo smiled. "I, as well, but I have not cooked for myself in years. The older I get the less they allow me to do for myself, eh, Franz?"

"I have my duties also, Eminence," the German answered. He was drinking the mao-tai with a little more gusto. Must be nice to have a young stomach lining, both the older men thought.

"So, how do you find Beijing?" Yu asked.

"Truly fascinating. We Romans think that our city is ancient and redolent with history, but Chinese culture was old before the Romans set one stone upon another. And the art we saw yesterday . . ."

"The jade mountain," Schepke explained. "I spoke with the guide, but she didn't know about the artists involved, or the time required to carve it."

"The names of artisans and the time they needed—these were not matters of importance to the emperors of old. There was much beauty then, yes, but much cruelty as well."

"And today?" Renato asked.

"Today as well, as you know, Eminence," Yu confirmed with a long sigh. They spoke in English, and Yu's Oklahoma accent fascinated his visitors. "The government lacks the respect for human life, which you and I would prefer."

"Changing that will not be simple," Monsignor Schepke added. The problem wasn't limited to the communist PRC government. Cruelty had long been part of Chinese culture, to the point that someone had once said that China was too vast to be governed with kindness, an aphorism picked up with indecent haste by the left wings of the world, ignoring the explicit racism in such a statement. Perhaps the problem was that China had always been crowded, and in crowds came anger, and in anger came a callous disregard for others. Nor had religion helped. Confucius, the closest thing China had developed to a great religious leader, preached conformity as a person's best action. While the Judeo-Christian tradition talked of transcendent values of right and wrong, and the human rights that devolved from them, China saw authority as Society, not God. For that reason, Cardinal DiMilo thought, communism had taken root here. Both societal models were alike in their absence of an absolute rule of right and wrong. And that was dangerous. In relativism lay man's downfall, because, ultimately, if there were no absolute values, what difference was there between a man and a dog? And if there were no such difference, where was man's fundamental dignity? Even a thinking atheist could mark religion's greatest gift to human society: human dignity, the value placed on a single human life, the simple idea that man *was* more than an animal. *That* was the foundation of all human progress, because without it, human life was doomed to Thomas Hobbes's model, "nasty, brutish, and short."

Christianity—and Judaism, and Islam, which were also religions of The Book—required merely that man believe in that which was self-evident: There *was* order in the universe, and that order came from a source, and that source was called God. Christianity didn't even require that a man believe in that idea—not anymore, anyway—just that he accept the sense of it, and the result of it, which was human dignity and human progress. Was that so hard?

It was for some. Marxism, in condemning religion as "the opiate of the people," merely prescribed another, less effective drug—"the radiant future," the Russians had called it, but it was a future they'd never been able to deliver. In China, the Marxists had shown the good sense to adopt some of the forms of capitalism to save their country's economy, but not to adopt the principle of human freedom that usually came along with it. That had worked to this point, DiMilo thought, only because Chinese culture had a preexisting model of conformity and acceptance of authority from above. But how long would that last? And how long could China prosper without some idea of the difference between what was *right* and what was *wrong*? Without that information,

China and the Chinese were doomed to perdition. Someone had to bring the Good News of Jesus to the Chinese, because with that came not only eternal salvation, but temporal happiness as well. Such a fine bargain, and yet there were those too stupid and too blind to accept it. Mao had been one. He'd rejected all forms of religion, even Confucius and the Lord Buddha. But when he'd lain dying in his bed, what had Chairman Mao thought? To what Radiant Future had he looked forward then? What did a communist think on his deathbed? The answer to that question was something none of the three clergymen wanted to know, or to face.

"I was disappointed to see the small number of Catholics here—not counting foreigners and diplomats, of course. How bad is the persecution?"

Yu shrugged. "It depends on where you are, and the political climate, and the personality of the local party leadership. Sometimes they leave us alone—especially when foreigners are here, with their TV cameras. Sometimes they can become very strict, and sometimes they can harass us directly. I have been questioned many times, and been subjected to political counseling." He looked up and smiled. "It's like having a dog bark at you, Eminence. You need not answer back. Of course, you will be spared any of that," the Baptist pointed out, noting DiMilo's diplomatic status, and his resulting personal inviolability.

The cardinal caught that reference, somewhat to his discomfort. He didn't see his life as any more valuable than anyone else's. Nor did he wish his faith to appear less sincere than this Chinese Protestant's, who'd been educated at some pretentious pseudo-university in the American prairie, whereas he had acquired his knowledge in some of the most ancient and honored institutions of higher learning on the planet, whose antecedents went back to the Roman empire, and beyond that, to the chambers of Aristotle himself. If there was one vanity Renato Cardinal DiMilo possessed, it was in his education. He'd been superbly educated, and he knew it. He could discuss Plato's *Republic* in Attic Greek, or the law cases of Marcus Tullius Cicero in Imperial Latin. He could debate a committed Marxist on the attributes of that political philosophy in the same language the German Marx himself had spoken—and win, because Marx had left a lot of unfilled holes in the walls of his political theories. He'd forgotten more about human nature than some psychologists knew. He was in the Vatican's diplomatic service because he could read minds—better than that, he could read the minds of politicians and diplomats highly skilled in concealing their thoughts. He could have been a gambler of talent and riches with these skills, but instead he applied them for the Greater Glory of God.

His only failing was that, like all men, he could not predict the future, and thus could not see the world war that this meeting would ultimately bring about.

"So, does the government harass you?" the Cardinal asked his host.

A shrug. "Occasionally. I propose to hold a prayer service in public to test their willingness to interfere with my human rights. There is some danger involved, of course."

It was a challenge skillfully delivered, and the elderly Catholic cleric rose to it: "Keep Franz and me informed, if you would."

SONGBIRD?" Ryan asked. "What can you tell me about him?"

"Do you really want to know, Jack?" Ed Foley asked, somewhat pointedly.

"You telling me I ought not to know?" Ryan responded. Then he realized that Robby Jackson and Ben Goodley were here as well, and he could know things which they could not. Even at this level, there were rules of classification. The President nodded. "Okay, we'll let that one go for now."

"The overall operation is called SORGE. That'll change periodically," Mary Pat told the assembled audience. Unusually, the Secret Service had been hustled out of the Oval Office for this briefing—which told the USSS a lot more than CIA would have liked—and also a special jamming system had been switched on. It would interfere with any electronic device in the room. You could see that from the TV set to the left of the President's desk, tuned to CNN. The screen was now full of snow, but with the sound turned all the way down, there was no annoying noise to disturb the meeting. The possibility of a bug in this most secure of rooms was slight, but so great was the value of SORGE that this card was being played as well. The briefing folders had already been passed out. Robby looked up from his.

"Notes from the Chinese Politburo? Lordy," Vice President Jackson breathed. "Okay, no sources and methods. That's cool with me, guys. Now, how reliable is it?"

"For the moment, reliability is graded 'B+' " Mary Pat answered. "We expect to upgrade that later on. The problem is that we don't grade 'A' or higher without outside confirmation, and this stuff is so deep inside that we have no other asset to verify what we have here."

"Oops," Jackson observed. "So it could all be a false flag. Pretty one, I admit, but false even so."

"Perhaps, but unlikely. There's stuff here that is awfully sensitive to let out voluntarily, even for a major sting operation."

"So I see," Ryan partially agreed. "But I remember what Jim Greer used to say: Ain't nothing too crazy to be true. Our fundamental problem with these guys is that their culture is so different in so many ways that they might as well be Klingons."

"Well, they don't display much love for us in this," Ben Goodley observed, flipping halfway through the briefing folder. "Jesus, this is interesting material. We going to show it to Scott Adler?"

"That's our recommendation," the DCI agreed. "Adler is pretty good at figuring people out, and his take on some of this—especially page five—will be very interesting. Tony Bretano, too."

"Okay, that's EAGLE and THUNDER. Who else?" Ryan asked.

"That's all for now," Ed Foley said, with a nod from his wife. "Mr. Pres—"

Ryan's eyes flared a little. "My name is . . ."

The DCI held up his hand. "Okay. *Jack,* let's keep this one real close for a while. We'll figure a way to launder the information so that some others can know what we've learned. But *not* how. Not ever that. SONGBIRD's too precious an asset to lose."

"This is potentially right up there with CARDINAL, isn't it?"

"Maybe even better, Jack," Mary Pat said. "This is like having a bug in the boardroom, and we've streamlined our methods on this one. We're being very, very careful with this source."

"Okay, what about analysts?" Ben Goodley asked. "Our best guy with the PRC is Professor Weaver up at Brown University. You know him, Ed."

Foley nodded. "Yeah, I know him, but let's hold off for a while. We have a pretty good guy in-house. Let me see what he can develop for us before we start farming things out. By the way, we're looking at something like a total of fifteen hundred printed pages from this source, plus daily information from now on."

Ryan looked up at that one. *Daily* information. How the hell had they arranged that? *Back to business,* he told himself. "Okay, for one thing, I want an evaluation of the Zhang Han San character," Ryan said. "I've seen this bastard's name before. He started two wars we got pulled into. What the hell is he all about?"

"We have a psychiatrist on staff to work on that," Mary Foley replied. *After,* she didn't say, *we scrub this information clean of source-related material.* "He does our profiling."

"Okay, yeah, I remember him." Ryan nodded agreement on this point. "Anything else?"

"Just the usual," Ed Foley said as he stood. "Don't leave these documents on your desk, okay?"

They all nodded agreement. They all had personal safes for that purpose, and every one was wired into the Secret Service command center, and was on round-the-clock TV surveillance. The White House was a good place to store documents, and besides, the secretaries were cleared higher than God. Mary Pat left the office with a special spring in her step. Ryan waved for his Vice President to stay as the rest walked toward the West Entrance.

"What do you think?" SWORDSMAN asked TOMCAT.

"This looks pretty damned hot, Jack. Jesus, boy, how the *hell* do they get stuff like this?"

"If they ever get around to telling me, I can't tell you, Rob, and I'm not sure I want to know. It isn't always pretty."

The retired fighter pilot agreed. "I believe it. Not quite the same as catapulting off the boat and shooting the bastard in the lips, is it?"

"But just as important."

"Hey, Jack, I know. Battle of Midway, like. Joe Rochefort and his band of merry men at FRUPAC back in '42 saved our country a lot of hassles with our little yellow friends in WestPac when they told Nimitz what was coming."

"Yeah, Robby, well, looks like we have more of the same sort of friends. If there's operational stuff in here, I want your opinion of it."

"I can do that already. Their army and what passes for a navy are talking in the open about how they take us on, how to counter carriers and stuff like that. It's mostly pipe dreams and self-delusion, but my question is, why the hell are they putting this in the open? Maybe to impress the unwashed of the world—reporters and the other idiots who don't know shit about war at sea—and maybe to impress their own people with how smart and how tough they are. Maybe to put more heat on the ROC government on Taiwan, but if they want to invade, they have something to do first, like building a real navy with real amphibious capability. But that would take ten years, and we'd probably notice all the big gray canoes in the water. They've got some submarines, and the Russians, of all people, are selling them hardware—just forked over a Sovremenny-class DDG, complete with Sunburn missiles, supposedly. Exactly what they want to do with them, I have no idea. It's not the way I'd build up a navy, but they didn't ask me for advice. What freaks me is, the Russians sold them the hardware, and they're selling some other stuff, too. Crazy," the Vice President concluded.

"Tell me why," POTUS commanded.

"Because once upon a time a guy named Genghis Khan rode all the way to the Baltic Sea—like, all the way across Russia. The Russkies have a good sense of history, Jack. They ain't forgot that. If I'm a Russian, what enemies do I have to worry about? NATO? The Poles? Romania? I don't think so. But off to my southeast is a great big country with a shitload of people, a nice large collection of weapons, and a long history of killing Russians. But I was just an operations guy, and sometimes I get a little paranoid about what my counterparts in other countries might be thinking." Robby didn't have to add that the Russians had invented paranoia once upon a time.

This is *madness!*" Bondarenko swore. "There are many ways to prove Lenin was right, but *this* is not the one I would choose!" Vladimir Il'ych Ulyanov had once said that the time would come when the capitalist countries would bid among themselves to sell to the Soviet Union the rope with which the Soviet Union would later hang them. He hadn't anticipated the death of the country he'd founded, and certainly not that the next Russia might be the one doing what he had predicted.

Golovko could not disagree with his guest. He'd made a similar argument, though with fewer decibels, in the office of President Grushavoy. "Our country needs the hard currency, Gennady Iosifovich."

"Indeed. And perhaps someday we will also need the oil fields and the gold mines of Siberia. What will we do when the Chinks take those away from us?" Bondarenko demanded.

"The Foreign Ministry discounts that possibility," Sergey Nikolay'ch replied.

"Fine. Will those foreign-service pansies take up arms if they are proven wrong, or will they wring their hands and say it isn't their fault? I am spread too thin for this. I cannot stop a Chinese attack, and so now we sell them the T-99 tank design . . ."

"It will take them five years to bring about series production, and by that time we will have the T-10 in production at Chelyabinsk, will we not?"

That the People's Liberation Army had four thousand of the Russian-designed T-80/90 tanks was not discussed. That had happened years earlier. But the Chinese had not used the Russian-designed 115-mm gun, opting instead for the 105-mm rifled gun sold to them by Israel Defense Industries, known to America as the M-68. They came complete with three million rounds of ammunition made to American specifications, down to the depleted uranium projectiles, probably made with uranium depleted by the same reactors that made plutonium for their nuclear devices. What was it about politicians? Bondarenko wondered. You could talk and talk and talk to them, but they *never listened!* It had to be a *Russian* phenomenon, the general thought, rather than a political one. Stalin had executed the intelligence officer who'd predicted—correctly, as it turned out—the German attack of June 1941 on the Soviet Union. And *that* one had come within sight of Moscow. Executed him, why? Because his prediction was less pleasing than that of Levrenti Beriya, who'd had the good sense to say what Stalin had wanted to hear. And Beriya had survived being completely wrong. So much for the rewards of patriotism.

"If we have the money for it, and if Chelyabinsk hasn't been retooled to make fucking washing machines!" Russia had cannibalized its defense infrastructure even more quickly than America had. Now there was talk of converting the MiG airplane plants to automobile production. Would this never stop? Bondarenko thought. He had a potentially hostile nation next door, and he was years away from rebuilding the Russian Army into the shape he wished. But to do that meant asking President Grushavoy for something that he knew he couldn't have. To build a proper army, he had to pay the soldiers a living wage, enough to attract the patriotic and adventurous boys who wanted to wear their country's uniform for a few years, and most particularly those who found that they enjoyed uniformed life enough to make a career of it, to become sergeants, the middle-level professional soldiers without whom an army simply could not function, the sinews that held the muscles to the bone. To make that happen, a good platoon sergeant had to make almost as much money as a skilled factory worker, which was only fair, since the demands of such a man were on the same intellectual level. The rewards of a uniformed career could not be duplicated in a television plant. The comradeship, and the sheer joy of soldiering, was something to which a special sort of man responded. The Americans had such men, as did the British and the Germans, but these priceless professionals had been denied the Russian Army since the time of Lenin, the first of many Soviet leaders who'd sacrificed military efficiency in favor of the political purity the Soviet Union had insisted upon. Or something like that, Bondarenko thought. It all seemed so distant now, even to one who'd grown up within the misbegotten system.

"General, please remember that I am your friend in the government," Golovko reminded him. Which was just as well. The Defense Minister was—well, he spoke the right words, but he wasn't really able to think the right thoughts. He could repeat what others told him, and that was about it. In that sense, he was the perfect politician.

"Thank you, Sergey Nikolay'ch." The general inclined his head with the proper respect. "Does that mean that I can count upon some of these riches that Fate has dropped into our lap?"

"At the proper time I will make the proper recommendation to the president."

By that time, I will be retired, writing my memoirs, or whatever the hell a Russian general is supposed to do, Bondarenko told himself. *But at least I can try to get the necessary programs drafted for my successors, and perhaps help choose the right man to follow me into the operations directorate.* He didn't expect to go any farther than he already had. He was chief of operations (which included training) for his army, and that was as fine a goal as any man could ask for his career.

"Thank you, Comrade Minister. I know your job is also difficult. So, is there anything I need to know about the Chinese?"

Minister Golovko wished he could tell this general that SVR didn't have a decent pipeline into the PRC anymore. Their man, a second-deputy minister, long in the employ of the KGB, had retired on grounds of ill health.

But he could not make the admission that the last Russian source inside the Forbidden City was no longer operational, and with him had gone all the insights they needed to evaluate the PRC's long-term plans and intentions. Well, there was still the Russian ambassador in Beijing, and he was no one's fool, but a diplomat saw mainly what the host government wanted him to see. The same was true of the military, naval, and air attachés, trained intelligence officers all, but also limited to what the Chinese military wished them to see, and even that had to be reciprocated every step of the way in Moscow, as though in some elegant international waltz. No, there was no substitute for a trained intelligence officer running agents who looked inside the other government, so that he, Golovko, could know exactly what was going on and report on it to his president. It wasn't often that Golovko had to report that he did not know enough, but it had happened in this case, and he would not confess his shortcomings to this soldier, senior one or not.

"No, Gennady Iosifovich, I have nothing to indicate that the Chinese seek to threaten us."

"Comrade Minister, the discoveries in Siberia are too vast for them not to consider the advantage to be had from seizing them. In their place, *I* would draw up the necessary plans. They import oil, and these new fields would obviate that necessity, and make them rich in the foreign exchange they seek. And the gold, Comrade, speaks for itself, does it not?"

"Perhaps." Golovko nodded. "But their economy seems healthy at the moment, and wars are not begun by those already rich."

"Hitler was prosperous enough in 1941. That did not prevent him from driving his army to within sight of this building," the chief of operations for the Russian army pointed out. "If your neighbor has an apple tree, sometimes you will pick an apple even if your belly is full. Just for the taste, perhaps," Bondarenko suggested.

Golovko couldn't deny the logic of that. "Gennady Iosifovich, we are of a kind. We both look out for dangers even when they are not obvious. You would have made a fine intelligence officer."

"Thank you, Comrade Minister." The three-star toasted his host with his almost empty vodka glass. "Before I leave my office, it is my hope to lay before my successor a plan, the accomplishment of which will make our country invulnerable to attack from any country. I know I will not be able myself to make that happen, but I will be grateful for the ability to set a firm plan in place, if our political leadership can see the merit of our ideas." And that was the real problem, wasn't it? The Russian army might be able to deal with external enemies. It was the internal ones which formed the really intractable problem. You usually knew where your enemy stood, because you faced them. Where your friends stood was more difficult, because they were usually behind you.

"I will make sure you present the case yourself to the cabinet. But"—Golovko held up his hand—"you must wait for the right moment."

"I understand, and let us hope the Chinese allow us the time for that moment." Golovko tossed off the last of his drink and rose. "Thanks for letting me come in to bare my heart to you, Comrade Chairman."

So, where is he?" Provalov demanded.

"I do not know," Abramov replied tiredly. "We've identified one person who claims to know him, but our informant has no idea where he lives."

"Very well. What *do* you know?" Moscow asked St. Petersburg.

"Our informant says that Suvorov is former KGB, RIF'd in 1996 or so, that he lives, probably, in St. Petersburg—but if that is true, he docs so under an assumed name and false documents, or 'Suvorov' is itself a false name. I have a description. Male, fifty or so, average height and build. Thinning blond hair. Regular features. Blue eyes. Physically fit. Unmarried. Thought to frequent prostitutes. I have some people asking around those women for more information. Nothing yet," the St. Petersburg investigator replied.

This is amazing, Lieutenant Provalov thought. *All the resources we have, and we can't develop a single reliable piece of information.* Was he chasing ghosts? Well, he had five of those already. Avseyenko, Maria Ivanovna Sablin, a driver whose name he couldn't remember at the moment, and the two putative Spetsnaz killers, Pyotr Alekseyevich Amalrik and Pavel Borissovich Zimyanin. Three blown up spectacularly during a morning rush hour, and two murdered in St. Petersburg after having done the job—but killed for succeeding or failing?

"Well, let me know when you develop anything."

"I will do that, Oleg Gregoriyevich," Abramov promised.

The militia lieutenant hung up his phone and cleared his desk, putting all his "hot" files into the locked drawer, then he walked downstairs to his official car and drove to his favorite bar. Reilly was inside, and waved when he came through the door. Provalov hung up his coat on a hook and walked over to shake hands. He saw that a drink was waiting for him.

"You are a true comrade, Mishka," the Russian said to his American friend as he took his first slug.

"Hey, I know the problem, pal," the FBI agent said sympathetically.

"It is this way for you as well."

"Hell, when I was a brand-new brick agent, I started working the Gotti case. We busted our asses bagging that lowlife. Took three juries to put him in Marion. He's never coming back. Marion is a particularly nasty prison." Though "nasty" in American terms was different from the Russian. Russian prisons didn't really bear thinking about, though Reilly didn't worry much about that. People who broke the law in any society knew about the possible consequences going in, and what happened when they got caught was their problem, not his. "So, what's the story?"

"This Suvorov. We can't find him. Mishka, it is as if he doesn't exist."

"Really?" It both was and was not a surprise to Reilly. The former, because Russia, like many European societies, kept track of people in ways that would have started a Second American Revolution. The cops here were supposed to know where everybody lived, a carryover from the Bad Old Days when KGB had kept a third of the population as informers on the other two-thirds. It was an uncommon situation for the local cops not to be able to find someone.

The situation was *not* surprising, however, because if this Suvorov mutt really was a former KGB officer, then he'd been expertly trained to disappear, and that sort of adversary didn't just die of the dumbs, like most American and Russian hoods did. Nor would he die from talking too much. Your average criminals acted—well, like criminals. They bragged too much, and to the wrong people, other criminals for the most part, who had the loyalty of rattlesnakes and would sell out a "friend" as readily as taking a piss. No, this Suvorov guy, if he was who and what the informants said he was, was a pro, and they made interesting game for interesting hunts, and usually long hunts at that. But you always got them in the end, because the cops never stopped looking, and sooner or later, he'd make a mistake, maybe not a big one, but big enough. He wouldn't be hanging with his former buds in KGB, people who would help keep him hidden, and would only talk among themselves and then not much. No, he was in a different milieu now, not a friendly one, not a safe one, and that was just too damned bad. Reilly had occasionally felt a certain sympathy for a criminal, but never for a killer. There were some lines you just couldn't cross.

"He has dived into a hole and then covered it up from inside," the Russian said, with some frustration.

"Okay, what do we know about him?"

Provalov related what he'd just learned. "They say they will be asking whores if they might know him."

"Good call." Reilly nodded. "I bet he likes the high-end ones. Like our Miss Tanya, maybe. You know, Oleg, maybe he knew Avseyenko. Maybe he knows some of his girls."

"That is possible. I can have my men check them out as well."

"Can't hurt," the FBI agent agreed, waving to the bartender for a couple of refills. "You know, buddy, you've got yourself a real investigation happening here. I kinda wish I was on your force to help out."

"You enjoy this?"

"Bet your ass, Oleg. The harder the case, the more thrilling the chase. And it feels real good at the end when you bag the bastards. When we convicted Gotti, damn if we didn't have one big party in Manhattan. The Teflon Don," Reilly said, hoisting his glass, and telling the air, "Hope you like it in Marion, boy."

"This Gotti, he killed people, yes?" Provalov asked.

"Oh, yeah, some himself, and others he gave the orders. His number one boy, Salvatore Gravano—Sammy the Bull, they called him—turned government witness and helped make the case for us. So then we put Sammy in the witness-protection program, and the mutt starts dealing drugs again down in Arizona. So, Sammy's back inside. The dummy."

"They all are, as you say, criminals," Provalov pointed out.

"Yeah, Oleg, they are. They're too stupid to go straight. They think they can outsmart us. And y'know, for a while they do. But sooner or later . . ." Reilly took a sip and shook his head.

"Even this Suvorov, you think?"

Reilly smiled for his new friend. "Oleg, do you ever make a mistake?"

The Russian grunted. "At least once a day."

"So, why do you think they're any smarter than you are?" the FBI agent asked. "Everybody makes mistakes. I don't care if he's driving a garbage truck or President of the fucking United States. We all fuck up every so often. It's just part of being human. Thing is, if you recognize that fact, you can make it a lot farther. Maybe this guy's been well trained, but we all have weaknesses, and we're not all smart enough to acknowledge them, and the smarter we are, the less likely we are to acknowledge them."

"You are a philosopher," Provalov said with a grin. He liked this American. They were of a kind, as though the gypsies had switched babies at birth or something.

"Maybe, but you know the difference between a wise man and a fool?"

"I am sure you will tell me." Provalov knew how to spot pontification half a block away, and the one approaching had flashing red lights on the roof.

"The difference between a wise man and a fool is the magnitude of his mistakes. You don't trust a fool with anything important." *The vodka was making him wax rhapsodic,* Reilly thought. "But a wise man you *do,* and so the fool doesn't have the chance to make a big screwup, while a wise man does. Oleg, a private can't lose a battle, but a general can. Generals are smart, right? You have to be real smart to be a doc, but docs kill people by accident all the time. It is the nature of man to make mistakes, and brains and training don't matter a rat-fuck. I make 'em. You make 'em." Reilly hoisted his glass again. "And so does Comrade Suvorov." *It'll be his dick,* Reilly thought. *If he likes to play with hookers, it'll be his dick that does him in. Tough luck, bro.* But he wouldn't be the first to follow his dick into trouble, Reilly knew. He probably wouldn't be the last, either.

So, did it all work?" Ming asked.

"Hmph?" Nomuri responded. This was strange. She was supposed to be in the afterglow period, his arm still around her, while they both smoked the usual after-sex cigarette.

"I did what you wished with my computer. Did it work?"

"I'm not sure," Nomuri tried as a reply. "I haven't checked."

"I do not believe that!" Ming responded, laughing. "I have thought about this. You have made me a spy!" she said, followed by a giggle.

"I did *what?*"

"You want me to make my computer accessible to you, so you can read all my notes, yes?"

"Do you care?" He'd asked her that once before, and gotten the right answer. Would it be true now? She'd sure as hell seen through his cover story. Well, that was no particular surprise, was it? If she weren't smart, she'd be useless as a penetration agent. But knowing what she was . . . how patriotic was she? Had he read her character right? He didn't let his body tense next to hers, remarkably enough. Nomuri congratulated himself for mastering another lesson in the duplicity business.

A moment's contemplation, then: "No."

Nomuri tried not to let his breath out in too obvious an expression of relief.

"Well, then you need not concern yourself. From now on, you will do nothing at all."

"Except this?" she asked with yet another giggle.

"As long as I continue to please you, I suppose!"

"Master Sausage!"

"Huh?"

"Your sausage pleases me greatly," Ming explained, resting her head on his chest.

And that, Chester Nomuri thought, was sufficient to the moment.

CHAPTER 16

The Smelting of Gold

Pavel Petrovich Gogol could believe his eyes, but only because he'd seen the whole Red Army armored corps on the move in the Western Ukraine and Poland, when he was a younger man. The tracked vehicles he saw now were even bigger and knocked down most of the trees, those that weren't blown down by engineers with explosives. The short season didn't allow the niceties of tree-felling and road-laying they used in the effete West. The survey team had found the source of the gold dust with surprising ease, and now a team of civil and military engineers was pushing a road to the site, slashing a path across the tundra and through the trees, dropping tons of gravel on the path which might someday be properly paved, though such roads were a problem in these weather conditions. Over the roads would come heavy mining equipment, and building materials for the workers who would soon make their homes in what had been "his" woods. They told him that the mine would be named in his honor. That hadn't been worth much more than a spit. And they'd taken most of his golden wolf pelts—after paying for them and probably paying most generously, he allowed. The one thing they'd given him that he liked was a new rifle, an Austrian Steyr with a Zeiss scope in the American .338 Winchester Magnum caliber, more than ample for local game. The rifle was brand new—he'd fired only fifteen rounds through it to make sure it was properly sighted in. The blued steel was immaculate, and the walnut stock was positively sensuous in its honeyed purity. *How many Germans might he have killed with this!* Gogol thought. And how many wolves and bear might he take now.

They wanted him to leave his river and his woods. They promised him weeks on the beaches at Sochi, comfortable apartments anywhere in the country. Gogol snorted. Was he some city pansy? No, he was a *man* of the woods, a man of the mountains, a man feared by the wolves and the bear, and even the tigers to the south had probably heard of him. This land was *his* land. And truth be told, he knew no other way to live, and was too old to learn one in any case. What other men called comforts he would call annoyances, and when his time came to die, he would be content to die in the woods and let a wolf or a bear pick over his corpse. It was only fair. He'd killed and skinned enough of them, after all, and good sport was good sport.

Well, the food they'd brought in—flown in, they'd told him—was pretty good, especially the beef, which was richer than his usual reindeer, and he had fresh tobacco for his pipe. The television reporters loved the pipe, and encouraged him to tell his story of life in the Siberian forests, and his best bear and wolf stories. But he'd never see the TV story they were doing on him; he was too far away from what they occasionally called "civilization" to have his own TV set. Still, he was careful to tell his stories carefully and clearly, so that the children and grandchildren he'd never had would see what a great man he'd been. Like all men, Gogol had a proper sense of self-worth, and he would have made a fine storyteller for any children's school, which hadn't occurred to any of the bureaucrats and functionaries who'd come to disturb his existence. Rather, they saw him as a TV personality, and an example of the rugged individualist whom the Russians had always worshipped on the one hand and brutally suppressed on the other.

But the real subject of the forty-minute story that was being put together by Russian national television wasn't really here. It was seventeen kilometers away, where a geologist tossed a gold nugget the size of his fist up and down like a baseball, though it weighed far more than the equivalent volume of iron. That was merely the biggest nugget they'd found. This deposit, the geology team explained to the cameras, was worthy of a tale from mythology, the garden, perhaps, of Midas himself. Exactly how rich it was they'd learn only from tunneling into the ground, but the chief of the geology team was willing to wager his professional reputation that it would beggar the South African mine, by far the richest found to date on the planet. Every day the tapes the cameras made were uploaded to the Russian communications satellite that spent most of its time hanging over the North Pole—much of the country is too far north to make proper use of the geosynchronous birds used by the rest of the world.

This was not a problem for the National Security Agency. NSA has stations worldwide, and the one located at Chicksands in England took the feed of the Russian satellite and instantly cross-loaded it to an American military-communications satellite, which dispatched the signal to Fort Meade, Maryland. Agreeably, the signal was not encrypted and so could be immediately forwarded to Russian linguists for translation, and then off it went to CIA and other national assets for evaluation. As it played out, the President of the United States would see the footage a week before the average Russian citizen.

"Damn, who is that guy, Jim Bridger?" Jack asked.

"His name is Pavel Petrovich Gogol. He's the guy credited with discovering the gold deposit. See," Ben Goodley said. The camera took in the row of gilded wolf pelts.

"Damn, those could be hung in the Smithsonian . . . like something out of a George Lucas movie . . ." SWORDSMAN observed.

"Or you could buy one for your wife," Goodley suggested.

POTUS shook his head. "Nah . . . but . . . maybe if it was a gilded sable coat . . . you think the voters could handle it?"

"I think I defer on such questions to Mr. van Damm," the National Security Adviser said after a moment's consideration.

"Yeah, might be fun to see him have a cow right here in the Oval Office. This tape isn't classified, is it?"

"Yes, it is, but only 'confidential.' "

"Okay, I want to show this one to Cathy tonight." That level of classification wouldn't faze anybody, not even a major city newspaper.

"You want one with subtitles or a voice-over translation?"

"We both *hate* subtitles," Jack informed his aide, with a look.

"I'll have Langley get it done for you, then," Goodley promised.

"She'll flip out when she sees that pelt." With the money from his investment portfolio, Ryan had become a connoisseur of fine jewelry and furs. For the former, he had an arrangement with Blickman's, a very special firm in Rockefeller Center. Two weeks before the previous Christmas, one of their salespeople had come by train to Washington, accompanied by two armed guards, who hadn't been allowed into the White House proper—the outside guards had gone slightly nuts on learning that armed men were on campus, but Andrea Price-O'Day had smoothed that over—and shown the President about five million dollars' worth of estate jewelry, and some pieces newly made just across the street from their office, some of which Ryan had purchased. His reward had been to see Cathy's eyes pop nearly out of her head under the Christmas tree, and lament the fact that all she'd gotten him was a nice set of Taylor golf clubs. But that was fine with SWORDSMAN. To see his wife smile on Christmas morning was as fine a prize as he expected in life. Besides, it was proof that he had taste in jewelry, one of the better things for a man to have—at least in his woman's eyes. But damn, if he could have gotten her one of those wolf-fur coats . . . could he cut a deal with Sergey Golovko? Jack wondered briefly. But where the hell could you wear such a thing? He had to be practical.

"Would look nice in the closet," Goodley agreed, seeing the distant look in his boss's eyes.

Color would go so nice with her butter-blond hair. Ryan mused on for a few more seconds, then shook his head to dismiss the thought.

"What else today?"

"SORGE has developed new information. It's being couriered down even as we speak."

"Important?"

"Mrs. Foley didn't say so, but you know how it works."

"Oh, yeah, even the minor stuff fits together into a real pretty picture when you need it." The major download still sat in his private safe. The sad truth was that while he did, technically, have the time to read it, that would have entailed taking time away from his family, and it would have had to have been *really* important for the President to do that.

So, what will the Americans do?" Fang asked Zhang.

"On the trade issue? They will, finally, bow to the inevitable, and grant us most-favored-nation status *and* remove their objection to our full entry into into the World Trade Organization," the minister replied.

"None too soon," Fang Gan observed.

"That is true," Zhang Han San agreed. The financial conditions in the PRC had been well concealed to this point, which was one advantage of the communist form of government, both ministers would have agreed, if they had ever considered another form of government. The cold truth of the matter was that the PRC was nearly out of foreign exchange, having spent it mainly on armaments and arms-related technology all over the world. Only incidental goods had come from America—mainly computer chips, which could be used in nearly any sort of mechanical contrivance. The overtly military material they'd purchased came most often from Western Europe, and sometimes from Israel. America sold what arms it released to this part of the world to the renegades on Taiwan, who paid cash, of course. That was like a mosquito bite to the mainland regime, not large, not life-threatening, but an annoyance that they continuously scratched at, in the process making it worse instead of better. There were over a billion—a *thousand* million—people in mainland China, and less than thirty million on the island across the strait. The misnamed Republic of China used its people well, producing more than a quarter of the goods and services the PRC turned out in a given year with forty times as many workers and peasants. However, while the mainland coveted the goods and services and the riches that resulted, they did not covet the political and economic system that made it possible. Their system was far superior, of course, because theirs was the better ideology. Mao himself had said so.

Neither of these two Politburo members, nor any of the others, reflected much on the objective realities at hand. They were as certain in their beliefs as any Western clergyman was in his. They even ignored the self-evident fact that what prosperity the People's Republic possessed came from capitalist enterprise allowed by previous rulers, often over the screams and howls of other ministerial-rank politicians. The latter contented themselves by denying political influence to the people who were enriching their country, confident that this situation would go on forever, and that those businessmen and industrialists would be satisfied to make their money and live in relative luxury while they, the political theorists, continued to manage the nation's affairs. After all, the weapons and the soldiers belonged to *them*, didn't they? And power still grew out of the barrel of a gun.

"You are certain of this?" Fang Gan asked.

"Yes, Comrade, I am quite certain. We have been 'good' for the Yankees, haven't we? We have not rattled our saber at the Taiwanese bandits lately, have we?"

"What of American trade complaints?"

"Do they not understand business?" Zhang asked grandly. "We sell goods to them because of their quality and price. We shop the same way. Yes, I admit, their Boeing airplane company makes fine airplanes, but so does Airbus in Europe, and the Europeans have been more . . . accommodating to us politically. America rants on about opening our markets to their goods, and we do this—slowly, of course. We need to keep the surplus they so kindly give us, and spend it on items of importance to us. Next, we will expand our automobile production and enter their auto market, as the Japanese once did. In five years, Fang, we will be taking another ten billion dollars from America annually—and that, my friend, is a very conservative estimate."

"You think so?"

An emphatic nod. "Yes! We will not make the mistake the Japanese made early on, selling ugly little cars. We are already looking for American styling engineers who will help us design automobiles which are aesthetically pleasing to the white devils."

"If you say so."

"When we have the money we need to build up our military, we will be the world's leading power in every respect. Industrially, we will lead the world. Militarily, we are at the center of the world."

"I fear these plans are too ambitious," Fang said cautiously. "They will take more years than we have to implement in any case, *but* what legacy will we leave to our country if we point her on a erroneous path?"

"What error is this, Fang?" Zhang asked. "Do you doubt our ideas?"

Always that question, Fang thought with an inward sigh. "I remember when Deng said, 'It doesn't matter if the cat is black or white, so long as it catches mice.' To which Mao responded with a livid snarl: 'What *emperor* said that?'"

"But it *does* matter, my old friend, and well you know it."

"That is true," Fang agreed with a submissive nod, not wanting a confrontation this late in the day, not when he had a headache. Age had made Zhang even more ideologically pure than he'd been in his youth, and it hadn't tempered his imperial ambition. Fang sighed once more. He was of a mind to set the issue aside. It wasn't worth the trouble. Though he'd mention it just once more, to cover his political backside.

"What if they don't?" Fang asked finally.

"What?"

"What if they don't go along? What if the Americans are troublesome on the trade issue?"

"They will not be," Zhang assured his old friend.

"But if they are, Comrade, what then will we do? What are our options?"

"Oh, I suppose we could punish with one hand and encourage with the other, cancel some purchases from America and then inquire about making some other ones. It's worked before many times," Zhang assured his guest. "This President Ryan is predictable. We need merely control the news. We will give him nothing to use against us."

Fang and Zhang continued their discussion into other issues, until the latter returned to his office, where, again, he dictated his notes of the discussion to Ming, who then typed them into her computer. The minister considered inviting her to his apartment, but decided against it. Though she'd become somewhat more attractive in the preceding weeks, catching his eye with her gentle smiles in the outer office, it had been a long day for him, and he was too tired for it, enjoyable though it often was with Ming. Minister Fang had no idea that his dictation would be in Washington, D.C., in less than three hours.

"What do you think, George?"

"Jack," TRADER began, "what the hell is this, and how the hell did we get it?"

"George, this is an internal memorandum—well, of sorts—from the government of the People's Republic of China. How we got it, you do not, repeat, *not* need to know."

The document had been laundered—scrubbed—better than Mafia income. All the surnames had been changed, as had the syntax and adjectives, to disguise patterns of speech. It was thought—hoped would be a better term—that even those whose discourse was being reported would not have recognized their own words. But the content had been protected—even improved, in fact, since the nuances of Mandarin had been fully translated in to American English idiom. That had been the hardest part. Languages do not really translate into one another easily or well. The denotations of words were one thing. The connotations were another, and these never really paralleled from one tongue to another. The linguists employed by the intelligence services were among the best in the country, people who regularly read poetry, and sometimes published journal pieces, under their own names, so that they could communicate their expertise in—and indeed, love of—their chosen foreign language with others of a similar mind. *What resulted were pretty good translations,* Ryan thought, but he was always a little wary of them.

"These cocksuckers! They're talking about how they plan to fuck us over." For all his money, George Winston retained the patois of his working-class origins.

"George, it's business, not personal," the President tried as a tension-release gambit.

The Secretary of the Treasury looked up from the briefing document. "Jack, when I ran Columbus Group, I had to regard all of my investors as my family, okay? *Their* money had to be as important to me as *my* money. That was my professional obligation as an investment counselor."

Jack nodded. "Okay, George. That's why I asked you into the cabinet. You're honest."

"Okay, but now, I'm Sec-fucking-Treas, okay? *That* means that every citizen in our country is part of my family, and these Chink bastards are planning to fuck with my county—all those people out there"—Secretary Winston waved toward the thick windows of the Oval Office—"the ones who trust *us* to keep the economy leveled out. So, they want MFN, do they? They want into the WTO, do they? Well, *fuck* them!"

President Ryan allowed himself an early-morning laugh, wondering if the Secret Service detail had heard George's voice, and might now be looking through the spy holes in the door to see what the commotion was. "Coffee and croissants, George. The grape jelly is Smuckers, even."

TRADER stood and walked around the couch, tossing his head forcefully like a stallion circling a mare in heat. "Okay, Jack, I'll cool down, but you're used to this shit, and I'm not." He paused and sat back down. "Oh, okay, up on The Street we trade jokes and stories, and we even plot a little bit, but deliberately fucking people over—no! I've *never* done that! And you know what's worst?"

"What's that, George?"

"They're stupid, Jack. They think they can mess with the marketplace according to their little political theories, and it'll fall into line like a bunch of soldiers right out of boot camp. These little bastards couldn't run a Kmart and show a profit, but they let them dick around with a whole national economy—and then they want to dick with ours, too."

"Got it all out of your system?"

"Think this is funny?" Winston asked crossly.

"George, I've never seen you get this worked up. I'm surprised by your passion."

"Who do you think I am, Jay Gould?"

"No," Ryan said judiciously. "I was thinking more of J. P. Morgan." The remark had the desired effect. SecTreas laughed.

"Okay, you got me there. Morgan was the first actual Chairman of the Fed, and he did it as a private citizen, and did it pretty well, but that's probably an institutional function, 'cuz there ain't that many J. P. Morgans waiting around on deck. Okay, Mr. President, sir, I am calmed down. Yes, this is business, not personal. And our reply to this miserable *business* attitude will be *business,* too. The PRC will *not* get MFN. They will not get into the WTO—as a practical matter, they don't deserve it yet anyway, based on the size of their economy. And, I think we rattle the Trade Reform Act at them nice and hard. Oh, there's one other thing, and I'm surprised it's not in here," Winston said, pointing down at the briefing sheet.

"What's that?"

"We can get 'em by the short hairs pretty easy, I think. CIA doesn't agree, but Mark Gant thinks their foreign-exchange account's a little thin."

"Oh?" the President asked, stirring his coffee.

Winston nodded emphatically. "Mark's my tech-weenie, remember. He's very good at modeling stuff on the computers. I've set him up with his own little section to keep an eye on various things. Pulled the professor of economics out of Boston University to work there, Morton Silber, another good man with the microchips. Anyway, Mark's been looking at the PRC, and he thinks they're driving off the edge of the Grand Canyon because they've been pissing away their money, mainly on military hardware and heavy-manufacturing equipment, like to make tanks and things. It's a repeat of the old communist stuff, they have a fixation on heavy industry. They are really missing the boat on electronics. They have little companies manufacturing computer games and stuff, but they're not applying it at home, except for that new computer factory they set up that's ripping off Dell."

"So you think we ought to shove that up their ass at the trade negotiations?"

"I'm going to recommend it to Scott Adler at lunch this afternoon, as a matter of fact," SecTreas agreed. "They've been warned, but this time we're going to press it hard."

"Back to their foreign exchange account. How bad is it?"

"Mark thinks they're down to negative reserves."

"In the hole? For how much?" POTUS asked.

"He says at least fifteen billion, floated with paper out of German banks for the most part, but the Germans have kept it quiet—and we're not sure why. It could be a normal transaction, but either the Germans or the PRC wants to keep it under wraps."

"Wouldn't be the Germans, would it?" Ryan asked next.

"Probably not. It makes their banks look good. And, yeah, that leaves the Chinese covering it up."

"Any way to confirm that?"

"I have some friends in Germany. I can ask around, or have a friend do it for me. Better that way, I guess. Everybody knows I'm a government employee now, and that makes me sinister," Winston observed with a sly grin. "Anyway, I am having lunch with Scott today. What do I tell him about the trade negotiations?'

Ryan thought about that for several seconds. This was one of those moments—the frightening ones, as he thought of them—when his words would shape the policy of his own country, and, possibly, others as well. It was easy to be glib or flip, to say the first thing that popped into his mind, but, no, he couldn't do that. Moments like this were too important, too vast in their potential consequences, and he couldn't allow himself to make government policy on a whim, could he? He had to think the matter through, quickly perhaps, but through.

"We need China to know that we want the same access to their markets that we've given them to ours, and that we won't tolerate their stealing products from American companies without proper compensation. George, I want the playing field level and fair for everyone. If they don't want to play that way, we start hurting them."

"Fair enough, Mr. President. I will pass that message along to your Secretary of State. Want I should deliver this, too?" Winston asked, holding up his SORGE briefing sheet.

"No, Scott gets his own version of it. And, George, be very, very careful with that. If the information leaks, a human being will lose his life," SWORDSMAN told TRADER, deliberately disguising the source as a man, and therefore deliberately misleading his Secretary of the Treasury. But that, too, was business, and not personal.

"It goes into my confidential files." Which was a pretty secure place, they both knew. "Nice reading the other guy's mail, isn't it?"

"Just about the best intelligence there is," Ryan agreed.

"The guys at Fort Meade, eh? Tapping into somebody's cell phone via satellite?"

"Sources and methods—you really don't want to know that, George. There's always the chance that you'll spill it to the wrong person by mistake, and then you have some guy's life on your conscience. Something to be avoided, trust me."

"I hear you, Jack. Well, I have a day to start. Thanks for the coffee and the pastry, boss."

"Any time, George. Later." Ryan turned to his appointment calendar as the Secretary walked out the corridor door, from which he'd go downstairs, cross outside because the West Wing wasn't directly connected to the White House proper, dart back inside, and head off into the tunnel leading to Treasury.

Outside Ryan's office, the Secret Service detail went over the appointment list also, but their copy also included the results of a National Crime Information Computer check, to make sure that no convicted murderer was being admitted into the Sanctum Sanctorum of the United States of America.

CHAPTER 17

The Coinage of Gold

Scott Adler was regarded as too young and inexperienced for the job, but that judgment came from would-be political appointees who'd schemed their way to near-the-top, whereas Adler had been a career foreign-service officer since his graduation from Tufts University's Fletcher School of Law and Diplomacy twenty-six years earlier. Those who'd seen him work regarded him as a very astute diplomatic technician. Those who played cards with him—Adler liked to play poker before a major meeting or negotiation—thought he was one very lucky son of a bitch.

His seventh-floor office at the State Department building was capacious and comfortable. Behind his desk was a credenza covered with the usual framed photographs of spouse, children, and parents. He didn't like wearing his suit jacket at his desk, as he found it too confining for comfort. In this he'd outraged some of the senior State Department bureaucrats, who thought this an entirely inappropriate informality. He did, of course, don the jacket for important meetings with foreign dignitaries, but he didn't think internal meetings were important enough to be uncomfortable for.

That suited George Winston, who tossed his coat over a chair when he came in. Like himself, Scott Adler was a working guy, and those were the people with whom Winston was most comfortable. He might be a career government puke, but the son of a bitch had a work ethic, which was more than he could say for too many of the people in his own department. He was doing his best to weed the drones out, but it was no easy task, and civil-service rules made firing unproductive people a nontrivial exercise.

"Have you read the Chinese stuff?" Adler asked, as soon as the lunch tray was on the table.

"Yeah, Scott. I mean, holy shit, fella," TRADER observed to EAGLE.

"Welcome to the club. The intelligence stuff we get can be very interesting." The State Department had its own spook service, called Intelligence and Research, or I&R, which, while it didn't exactly compete with CIA and the other services, occasionally turned up its own rough little diamonds from the thick diplomatic mud. "So, what do you think of our little yellow brothers?"

Winston managed not to growl. "Buddy, I might not even eat their goddamned food anymore."

"They make our worst robber barons look like Mother Teresa. They're conscienceless motherfuckers, George, and that's a fact." Winston immediately started liking Adler more. A guy who talked like this had real possibilities. Now it was his turn to be coldly professional to counterpoint Adler's working-class patois.

"They're ideologically driven, then?"

"Totally—well, maybe with a little corruption thrown in, but remember, they figure that their political astuteness entitles them to live high on the hog, and so to them it's not corruption at all. They just collect tribute from the peasants, and 'peasant' is a word they still use over there."

"In other words, we're dealing with dukes and earls?"

The Secretary of State nodded. "Essentially, yes. They have an enormous sense of personal entitlement. They are not used to hearing the word 'no' in any form, and as a result they don't always know what to do when they do hear it from people like me. That's why they're often at a disadvantage in negotiations—at least, when we play hardball with them. We haven't done much of that, but last year, after the Airbus shoot-down I came on a little strong, and then we followed up with official diplomatic recognition of the ROC government on Taiwan. That really put the PRC noses seriously out of joint, even though the ROC government hasn't officially declared its independence."

"What?" Somehow SecTreas had missed that.

"Yeah, the people on Taiwan play a pretty steady and reasonable game. They've never really gone out of their way to offend the mainland. Even though they have embassies all over the world, they've never actually proclaimed the fact that they're an independent nation. That would flip the Beijing Chinese out. Maybe the guys in Taipei think it would be bad manners or something. At the same time, we have an understanding that Beijing knows about. If somebody messes with Taiwan, Seventh Fleet comes over to keep an eye on things, and we will not permit a direct military threat to the Republic of China government. The PRC doesn't have enough of a navy to worry our guys that much, and so all that flies back and forth, really, is words." Adler looked up from his sandwich. "Sticks and stones, y'know?"

"Well, I had breakfast with Jack this morning, and we talked about the trade talks."

"And Jack wants to play a little rougher?" SecState asked. It wasn't much of a surprise. Ryan had always preferred fair play, and that was often a rare commodity in the intercourse among nation-states.

"You got it," Winston confirmed around a bite of his sandwich. One thing about working-class people like Adler, the SecTreas thought, they knew what a proper lunch was. He was so tired of fairyfied French food for lunch. Lunch was supposed to be a piece of meat with bread wrapped around it. French cuisine was just fine, but for dinner, not for lunch.

"How rough?"

"We get what we want. We need them to get accustomed to the idea that they need us a hell of a lot more than we need them."

"That's a tall order, George. If they don't want to listen?"

"Knock louder on the door, or on their heads. Scott, you read the same document this morning I did, right?"

"Yeah," SecState confirmed.

"The people they're cheating out of their jobs are American citizens."

"I know that. But what you have to remember is that we can't dictate to a sovereign country. The world doesn't work that way."

"Okay, fine, but we can tell them that they can't dictate trade practices to us, either."

"George, for a long time America has taken a very soft line on these issues."

"Maybe, but the Trade Reform Act is now law—"

"Yeah, I remember. I also remember how it got us into a shooting war," Adler reminded his guest.

"We won. I remember that, too. Maybe other people will as well. Scott, we're running a huge trade deficit with the Chinese. The President says that has to stop. I happen to agree. If we can buy from them, then they damned well have to buy from us, or we buy our chopsticks and teddy bears elsewhere."

"There are jobs involved," Adler warned. "They know how to play that card. They cancel contracts and stop buying our finished goods, and then some of our people lose their jobs, too."

"Or, if we succeed, then we sell more finished goods to them, and our factories have to hire people to make them. Play to win, Scott," Winston advised.

"I always do, but this isn't a baseball game with rules and fences. It's like racing a sailboat in the fog. You can't always see your adversary, and you can damned near never see the finish line."

"I can buy you some radar, then. How about I give you one of my people to help out?"

"Who?"

"Mark Gant. He's my computer whiz. He really knows the issues from a technical, monetary point of view."

Adler thought about that. State Department had always been weak in that area. Not too many business-savvy people ended up in the Foreign Service, and learning it from books wasn't the same as living it out in the real world, a fact that too many State Department "professionals" didn't always appreciate as fully as they should.

"Okay, send him over. Now, just how rough are we supposed to play this?"

"Well, I guess you'll need to talk that one over with Jack, but from what he told me this morning, we want the playing field leveled out."

An easy thing to say, Adler thought, but less easy to accomplish. He liked and admired President Ryan, but he wasn't blind to the fact that SWORDSMAN was not the most patient guy in the world, and in diplomacy, patience was everything—hell, patience was just about the only thing. "Okay," he said, after a moment's reflection. "I'll talk it over with him before I tell my people what to say. This could get nasty. The Chinese play rough."

"Life's a bitch, Scott," Winston advised.

SecState smiled. "Okay, duly noted. Let me see what Jack says. So, how's the market doing?"

"Still pretty healthy. Price/earnings ratios are still a little outrageous, but profits are generally up, inflation is under control, and the investment community is nice and comfy. The Fed Chairman is keeping a nice, even strain on monetary policy. We're going to get the changes we want in the tax code. So, things look pretty good. It's always easier to steer the ship in calm seas, y'know?"

Adler grimaced. "Yeah, I'll have to try that sometime." But he had marching orders to lay on a typhoon. This would get interesting.

So, how's readiness?" General Diggs asked his assembled officers.

"Could be better," the colonel commanding 1st Brigade admitted. "We've been short lately on funds for training. We have the hardware, and we have the soldiers, and we spend a lot of time in the simulators, but that's not the same as going out in the dirt with our tracks." There was general nodding on that point.

"It's a problem for me, sir," said Lieutenant Colonel Angelo Giusti, who commanded 1st Squadron, 4th Armored Cavalry Regiment. Known within the Army as the Quarter Horse for the 1st/4th unit designator, it was the division reconnaissance screen, and its commander reported directly to the commanding general of First Tanks instead of through a brigade commander. "I can't get my people out, and it's hard to train for reconnaissance in the *kazerne.* The local farmers get kinda irate when we crunch through their fields, and so we have to pretend we can do recon from hard-surface roads. Well, sir, we can't, and that bothers me some."

There was no denying the fact that driving armored vehicles across a cornfield was tough on the corn, and while the U.S. Army trailed every tactical formation with a Hummer whose passengers came with a big checkbook to pay for the damage, the Germans were a tidy people, and Yankee dollars didn't always compensate for the suddenly untidy fields. It had been easier when the Red Army had been right on the other side of the fence, threatening death and destruction on West Germany, but Germany was now one sovereign country, and the Russians were now on the far side of Poland, and a lot less threatening than they'd once been. There were a few places where large formations could exercise, but those were as fully booked as the prettiest debutante's dance card at the cotillion, and so the Quarter Horse spent too much time in simulators, too.

"Okay," Diggs said. "The good news is that we're going to profit from the new federal budget. We have lots more funds to train with, and we can start using them in twelve days. Colonel Masterman, do you have some ways for us to spend it?"

"Well, General, I think I might come up with something. Can we pretend that it's 1983 again?" At the height of the Cold War, Seventh Army had trained to as fine an edge as any army in history, a fact ultimately demonstrated in Iraq rather than in Germany, but with spectacular effect. Nineteen eighty-three had been the year the increased funding had first taken real effect, a fact noted fully by the KGB and GRU intelligence officers, who'd thought until that time that the Red Army might have had a chance to defeat NATO. By 1984, even the most optimistic Russian officers fell off that bandwagon for all time. If they could reestablish that training regimen, the assembled officers all knew they'd have a bunch of happy soldiers, because, though training is hard work, it is what the troops had signed up for. A soldier in the field is most often a happy soldier.

"Colonel Masterman, the answer to your question is, Yes. Back to my original question. How's readiness?"

"We're at about eighty-five percent," 2nd Brigade estimated. "Probably ninety or so for the artillery—"

"Thank you, Colonel, and I agree," the colonel commanding divisional artillery interjected.

"But we all know how easy life is for the cannon-cockers," 2nd Brigade added as a barb.

"Aviation?" Diggs asked next.

"Sir, my people are within three weeks of being at a hundred percent. Fortunately, we don't squash anybody's corn when we're up practicing. My only complaint is that it's too easy for my people to track tanks on the ground if they're road-bound, and a little more realistic practice wouldn't hurt, but, sir, I'll put my aviators up against anyone in this man's army, especially my Apache drivers." The "snake" drivers enjoyed a diet of raw meat and human babies. The problems they'd had in Yugoslavia a few years earlier had alarmed a lot of people, and the aviation community had cleaned up its act with alacrity.

"Okay, so you're all in pretty good shape, but you won't mind sharpening the edge up a little, eh?" Diggs asked, and got the nods he expected. He'd read up on all his senior officers on the flight across the pond. There was little in the way of dead wood here. The Army had less trouble than the other services in holding on to good people. The airlines didn't try to hire tank commanders away from 1st Armored, though they were always trying to steal fighter and other pilots from the Air Force, and while police forces loved to hire experienced infantrymen, his division had only about fifteen hundred of them, which was the one structural weakness in an armored division: not enough people with rifles and bayonets. An American tank division was superbly organized to take ground—to immolate everyone who happened to be on real estate they wanted—but not so well equipped to hold the ground they overran. The United States Army had never been an army of conquest. Indeed, its ethos has always been liberation, and part and parcel of that was the expectation that the people who lived there would be of assistance, or at least show gratitude for their deliverance, rather than hostility. It was so much a part of the American military's history that its senior members rarely, if ever, thought about other possibilities. Vietnam was too far in the past now. Even Diggs had been too young for that conflict, and though he'd been told how lucky he was to have missed it, it was something he almost never thought about. Vietnam had not been his war, and he didn't really want to know about light infantry in the jungle. He was a cavalryman, and his idea of combat was tanks and Bradleys on open ground.

"Okay, gentlemen. I'll want to meet with all of you individually in the next few days. Then I need to come out and see your outfits. You will find that I'm a fairly easy guy to work for"—by which he meant that he wasn't a screamer, as some general officers were; he demanded excellence as much as anyone else, but he didn't think ripping a man's head off in public was a good way to achieve it—"and I know you're all pretty good.

In six months or less, I want this division ready to deal with anything that might come down the road. I mean anything at all."

Who might that be, Colonel Masterman mused to himself, *the Germans?* It might be a little harder to motivate the troops, given the total absence of a credible threat, but the sheer joy of soldiering was not all that much different from the kick associated with football. For the right guy, it was just plain fun to play in the mud with the big toys, and after a while, they started wondering what the real thing might be like. There was a leavening of troops in First Tanks from the 10th and 11th Cavalry Regiments who'd fought the previous year in Saudi Arabia, and like all soldiers, they told their stories. But few of the stories were unhappy ones. Mainly they expounded on how much like training it had been, and referred to their then-enemies as "poor, dumb raghead sunsabitches" who'd been, in the final analysis, unworthy of their steel. But that just made them swagger a little more. A winning war leaves only good memories for the most part, especially a short winning war. Drinks would be hoisted, and the names of the lost would be invoked with sadness and respect, but the overall experience had not been a bad one for the soldiers involved.

It wasn't so much that soldiers lusted for combat, just that they often felt like football players who practiced hard but never actually got to play for points. Intellectually, they knew that combat was the game of death, not football, but that was too theoretical for most of them. The tankers fired their practice rounds, and if the pop-up targets were steel, there was the satisfaction of seeing sparks from the impact, but it wasn't quite the same as seeing the turret pop off the target atop a column of flame and smoke . . . and knowing that the lives of three or four people had been extinguished like a birthday-cake candle in front of a five-year-old. The veterans of the Second Persian Gulf War did occasionally talk about what it was like to see the results of their handiwork, usually with a "Jesus, it was really something awful to see, bro," but that was as far as it went. For soldiers, killing wasn't really murder once you stepped back from it; they'd been the enemy, and both had played the game of death on the same playing field, and one side had won, and the other side had lost, and if you weren't willing to run that risk, well, don't put the uniform on, y'know? Or, "Train better, asshole, cuz we be serious out here." And that was the other reason soldiers liked to train. It wasn't just interesting and fairly enjoyable hard work. It was life insurance if the game ever started for real, and soldiers, like gamblers, like to hold good cards.

Diggs adjourned the meeting, waving for Colonel Masterman to stay behind.

"Well, Duke?"

"I've been nosing around. What I've seen is pretty good, sir. Giusti is especially good, and he's always bitching about training time. I like that."

"So do I," Diggs agreed at once. "What else?"

"Like the man said, artillery is in very good shape, and your maneuver brigades are doing okay, considering the lack of field time. They might not like using the sims all that much, but they are making good use of them. They're about twenty percent off where we were in the Tenth Cav down in the Negev playing with the Israelis, and that isn't bad at all. Sir, you give me three or four months in the field, and they'll be ready to take on the world."

"Well, Duke, I'll write you the check next week. Got your plans ready?"

"Day after tomorrow. I'm taking some helicopter rides to scout out the ground we can use and what we can't. There's a German brigade says they're eager to play aggressor for us."

"They any good?"

"They claim to be. I guess we'll just have to see. I recommend we send Second Brigade out first. They're a little sharper than the other two. Colonel Lisle is our kind of colonel."

"His package looks pretty good. He'll get his star next go-round."

"About right," Masterman agreed. *And what about my star?* he couldn't ask. He figured himself a pretty good bet, but you never really knew. Oh, well, at least he was working for a fellow cavalryman.

"Okay, show me your plans for Second Brigade's next adventure in the farmland . . . tomorrow?"

"The broad strokes, yes, sir." Masterman bobbed his head and walked off toward his office.

How rough?" Cliff Rutledge asked.

"Well," Adler replied, "I just got off the phone with the President, and he says he wants what he wants and it's our job to get it for him."

"That's a mistake, Scott," the Assistant Secretary of State warned.

"Mistake or not, we work for the President."

"I suppose so, but Beijing's been pretty good about not tearing us a new asshole over Taiwan. This might not be the right time for us to press on them so hard."

"Even as we speak, American jobs are being lost because of their trade policy," Adler pointed out. "When does enough become too much?"

"I guess Ryan decides that, eh?"

"That's what the Constitution says."

"And you want me to meet with them, then?"

SecState nodded. "Correct. Four days from now. Put your position paper together and run it past me before we deliver it, but I want them to know we're not kidding. The trade deficit has to come down, and it has to come down soon. They can't make that much money off us and spend it somewhere else."

"But they can't buy military hardware from us," Rutledge observed.

"What do they need all that hardware for?" Scott Adler asked rhetorically. "What external enemies do they have?"

"They'll say that their national security is their affair."

"And we reply that our economic security is our affair, and they're not helping." That meant observing to the PRC that it looked as though they were preparing to fight a war—but against whom, and was that a good thing for the world? Rutledge would ask with studied sangfroid.

Rutledge stood. "Okay, I can present our case. I'm not fully comfortable with it, but, well, I suppose I don't have to be, do I?"

"Also correct." Adler didn't really like Rutledge all that much. His background and advancement had been more political than properly earned. He'd been very tight with former Vice President Kealty, for example, but after that incident had settled out, Cliff had dusted off his coattails with admirable speed. He would probably not get another promotion. He'd gone as far as one could go without really serious political ties—say a teaching position at the Kennedy School at Harvard, where one taught and became a talking head on the PBS evening news hour and waited to be noticed by the right political hopeful. But that was pure luck. Rutledge had come farther than actual merit could justify, but with it came a comfortable salary and a lot of prestige on the Washington cocktail-party circuit, where he was on most of the A lists. And that meant that when he left government service, he'd increase his income by an order of magnitude or so with some consulting firm or other. Adler knew he could do the same, but probably wouldn't. He'd probably take over the Fletcher School at Tufts and try to pass along what he'd learned to a new generation of would-be diplomats. He was too young for real retirement, though there was little in the way of a government afterlife from being Secretary of State, and academia wouldn't be too bad. Besides, he'd get to do the odd consulting job, and do op-ed pieces for the newspapers, where he would assume the role of elder-statesman sage.

"Okay, let me get to work." Rutledge walked out and turned left to head to his seventh-floor office.

Well, this was a plum, the Assistant Secretary thought, even if it was the wrong plum. The Ryan guy was not what he thought a president should be. He thought international discourse was about pointing guns at people's heads and making demands, instead of reasoning with them. Rutledge's way took longer, but was a lot safer. You had to give something to get something. Well, sure, there wasn't much left to give the PRC, except maybe renouncing America's diplomatic recognition of Taiwan. It wasn't hard to understand the reason they'd done it, but it had still been a mistake. It made the PRC unhappy, and you couldn't let some damned-fool "principle" get in the way of international reality. Diplomacy, like politics—another area in which Ryan was sadly lacking—was a practical business. There were a *billion* people in the People's Republic, and you had to respect that. Sure, Taiwan had a democratically elected government and all that, but it was *still* a breakaway province of China, and that made it an internal matter. Their civil war was a fifty-plus-year affair, but Asia was a place where people took the long-term view.

Hmm, he thought, sitting down at his desk. *We want what we want, and we're going to get what we want . . .* Rutledge took out a legal pad and leaned back in his chair to make some notes. It might be the wrong policy. It might be dumb policy. It might be policy he disagreed with. But it *was* policy, and if he ever wanted to be kicked upstairs—actually to a different office on the same floor—to Undersecretary of State, he had to present the policy as though it were his own personal passion. It was like being a lawyer, Rutledge thought. They had to argue dumb cases all the time, didn't they? That didn't make them mercenaries. It made them professionals, and he was a professional.

And besides, he'd never been caught. One thing about Ed Kealty, he'd never told anybody how Rutledge had tried to help him be President. Duplicitous he might have been toward the President, but he'd been loyal to his own people about it, as a politician was supposed to be. And that Ryan guy, smart as he might have been, he'd never caught on. *So there, Mr. President,* Rutledge thought. *You may be smart, you think, but you need* me *to formulate your policy for you.* Ha!

This is a pleasant change, Comrade Minister," Bondarenko observed on coming in. Golovko waved him to a chair, and poured him a small glass of vodka, the fuel of a Russian business meeting. The visiting general-lieutenant took the obligatory sip and expressed his thanks for the formal hospitality. He most often came here after normal working hours, but this time he'd been summoned officially, and right after lunch. It would have made him uneasy—once upon a time, such an invitation to KGB headquarters would involve a quick trip to the men's room—except for his cordial relationship with Russia's chief spy.

"Well, Gennady Iosifovich, I've talked you and your ideas over with President Grushavoy, and you've had three stars for a long time. It is time, the president and I agreed, for you to have another, and a new assignment."

"Indeed?" Bondarenko wasn't taken aback, but he became instantly wary. It wasn't always pleasant to have one's career in others' hands, even others one liked.

"Yes. As of Monday next, you will be General-Colonel Bondarenko, and soon after that you will travel to become commander-in-chief of the Far East Military District."

That got his eyebrows jolting upward. This was the award of a dream he'd held in his own mind for some time. "Oh. May I ask, why there?"

"I happen to agree with your concerns regarding our yellow neighbors. I've seen some reports from the GRU about the Chinese army's continuing field exercises, and to be truthful, our intelligence information from Beijing is not all we would wish. Therefore, Eduard Petrovich and I feel that our eastern defenses might need some firming up. That becomes your job, Gennady. Do it well, and some additional good things might happen for you."

And that could only mean one thing, Bondarenko thought, behind an admirable poker face. Beyond the four stars of a general-colonel lay only the single large star of a marshal, and that was as high as any Russian soldier could go. After that, one could be commander-in-chief of the entire army, or defense minister, or one could retire to write memoirs.

"There are some people I'd like to take out to Chabarsovil with me, some colonels from my operations office," the general said contemplatively.

"That is your prerogative, of course. Tell me, what will you wish to do out there?"

"Do you really want to know?" the newly frocked four-star asked.

Golovko smiled broadly at that. "I see. Gennady, you wish to remake the Russian army in your image?"

"Not my image, Comrade Minister. A winning image, such as we had in 1945. There are images one wishes to deface, and there are images one dares not touch. Which, do you think, ought we to have?"

"What will the costs be?"

"Sergey Nikolay'ch, I am not an economist, nor am I an accountant, but I can tell you that the cost of doing this will be far less than the cost of not doing it." And now, Bondarenko thought, he'd get wider access to whatever intelligence his country possessed. It'd have been better if Russia had spent the same resources on what the Americans delicately called National Technical Means—strategic reconnaissance satellites—that the Soviet Union had once done. But he'd get such as there was, and maybe he could talk the air force into making a few special flights . . .

"I will tell that to President Grushavoy." Not that it would do all that much good. The cupboard was still bare of funding, though that could change in a few years.

"Will these new mineral discoveries in Siberia give us a little more money to spend?"

Golovko nodded. "Yes, but not for some years. Patience, Gennady."

The general took a final shot of the vodka. "I can be patient, but will the Chinese?"

Golovko had to grant his visitor's concern. "Yes, they are exercising their military forces more than they used to." What had once been a cause for concern had become, with its continuance, a matter of routine, and Golovko, like many, tended to lose such information in the seemingly random noise of daily life. "But there are no diplomatic reasons for concern. Relations between our countries are cordial."

"Comrade Minister, I am not a diplomat, nor am I an intelligence officer, but I do study history. I recall that the Soviet Union's relations with Hitler's Germany were cordial right up until June 23, 1941. The leading German elements passed Soviet trains running westbound with oil and grain to the *fascisti.* I conclude from this that diplomatic discourse is not always an indicator of a nation's intentions."

"That is true, and that is why we have an intelligence service."

"And then you will also recall that the People's Republic has in the past looked with envy on the mineral riches of Siberia. That envy has probably grown with the discoveries we have made. We have not publicized them, but we may assume that the Chinese have intelligence sources right here in Moscow, yes?"

"It is a possibility not to be discounted," Golovko admitted. He didn't add that those sources would most probably be true-believing communists from Russia's past, people who lamented the fall of their nation's previous political system, and saw in China the means, perhaps, to restore Russia to the true faith of Marxism-Leninism, albeit with a little Mao tossed in. Both men had been Communist Party members in their day: Bondarenko because advancement in the Soviet Army had absolutely demanded it, and Golovko because he would never have been entrusted with a post in KGB without it. Both had mouthed the words, and kept their eyes mostly open during party meetings, in both cases while checking out the women in the meetings or just daydreaming about things of more immediate interest. But there were those who had listened and thought about it, who had actually believed all that political rubbish. Both Bondarenko and Golovko were pragmatists, interested mainly in a reality they could touch and feel rather than some model of words that might or might not come to pass someday. Fortunately for both, they'd found their way into professions more concerned with reality than theory, where their intellectual explorations were more easily tolerated, because men of vision were always needed, even in a nation where vision was supposed to be controlled. "But you will have ample assets to act upon your concerns."

Not really, the general thought. He'd have—what? Six motor-rifle divisions, a tank division, and a divisional formation of artillery, all regular-army formations at about seventy percent nominal strength and dubious training—that would be his first task, and not a minor one, to crack those uniformed boys into Red Army soldiers of the sort who had crushed the Germans at Kursk, and moved on to capture Berlin. *That would be a major feat to accomplish, but who was better suited to this task?* Bondarenko asked himself. There were some promising young generals he knew of, and maybe he'd steal one, but for his own age group Gennady Iosifovich Bondarenko felt himself to be the best brain in his nation's armed forces. Well, then, he'd have an active command and a chance to prove it. The chance of failure was always there, but men such as he are the kind who see opportunities where others see dangers.

"I presume I will have a free hand?" he asked, after some final contemplation.

"Within reason." Golovko nodded. "We'd prefer that you did not start a war out there."

"I have no desire to drive to Beijing. I have never enjoyed their cooking," Bondarenko replied lightly. And Russians should be better soldiers. The fighting ability of the Russian male had never been an issue for doubt. He just needed good training, good equipment, and proper leadership. Bondarenko thought he could supply two of those needs, and that would have to do. Already, his mind was racing east, thinking about his headquarters, what sort of staff officer he would find, whom he'd have to replace, and where the replacements would come from. There'd be drones out there, careerist officers just serving their time and filling out their forms, as if that were what it meant to be a field-grade officer. Those men would see their careers aborted—well, he'd give everyone thirty days to straighten up, and if he knew himself, he'd inspire some to rediscover their vocations. His best hope was in the individual soldiers, the young boys wearing their country's uniform indifferently because no one had told them exactly what they were and how important that thing was. But he'd fix *that.* They were *soldiers,* those boys. Guardians of their country, and they deserved to be proud guardians. With proper training, in nine months they'd wear the uniforms better, stand straighter, and swagger a bit on leave, as soldiers were supposed to do. He'd show them how to do it, and he'd become their surrogate father, pushing and cajoling his new crop of sons toward manhood. It was as worthy a goal as any man could wish, and as Commander-in-Chief Far East, he just might set a standard for his country's armed forces to emulate.

"So, Gennady Iosifovich, what do I tell Eduard Petrovich?" Golovko asked, as he leaned across the desk to give his guest a little more of the fine Starka vodka.

Bondarenko lifted the glass to salute his host. "Comrade Minister, you will please tell our president that he has a new CINC–Far East."

CHAPTER 18

Evolutions

The interesting part for Mancuso in his new job was that he now commanded aircraft, which he could fairly well understand, but also ground troops, which he hardly understood at all. This latter contingent included the 3rd Marine Division based on Okinawa, and the Army's 25th Light Infantry Division at Schofield Barracks on Oahu. Mancuso had never directly commanded more than one hundred fifty or so men, all of whom had been aboard his first and last real—as he thought of it—command, USS *Dallas.* That was a good number, large enough that it felt larger than even an extended family, and small enough that you knew every face and name. Pacific Command wasn't anything like that. The *square* of *Dallas*'s crew didn't begin to comprise the manpower which he could direct from his desk.

He'd been through the Capstone course. That was a program designed to introduce new flag officers to the other branches of the service. He'd walked in the woods with Army soldiers, crawled in the mud with Marines, even watched an aerial refueling from the jump seat of a C-5B transport (the most unnatural act he ever expected to see, two airplanes mating in midair at three hundred knots), and played with the Army's heavy troops at Fort Irwin, California, where he'd tried his hand at driving and shooting tanks and Bradleys. But seeing it all and playing with the kids, and getting mud on his clothing, wasn't really the same as knowing it. He had some very rough ideas of what it looked and sounded and smelled like. He'd seen the confident look on the faces of men who wore uniforms of different color, and told himself about a hundred times that they were, really, all the same. The sergeant commanding an Abrams tank was little different in spirit from a leading torpedoman on a fast-attack boat, just not recently showered, and a Green Beret was little different from a fighter pilot in his godlike self-confidence. But to command such people effectively, he ought to know more, CINCPAC told himself. He ought to have had more "joint" training. But then he told himself that he could take the best fighter jock in the Air Force or the Navy, and even then it would take months for them to understand what he'd done on *Dallas.* Hell, just getting them to understand the importance of reactor safety would take a year—about what it had taken him to learn all those things once upon a time, and Mancuso wasn't a "nuc" by training. He'd always been a front-end guy. The services were all different in their *feel* for the mission, and that was because the missions were all as different in nature as a sheepdog was from a pit bull.

But he had to command them all, and do so effectively, lest he make a mistake that resulted in a telegram coming to Mrs. Smith's home to announce the untimely death of her son or husband because some senior officer had fucked up. Well, Admiral Bart Mancuso told himself, that was why he had such a wide collection of staff officers, including a surface guy to explain what that sort of target did (to Mancuso any sort of surface ship was a target), an Airedale to explain what naval aircraft did, a Marine and some soldiers to explain life in the mud, and some Air Force wing-wipers to tell him what their birds were capable of. All of them offered advice, which, as soon as he took it, became his idea alone, because he was in command, and command meant being responsible for everything that happened in or near the Pacific Ocean, including when some newly promoted E-4 petty officer commented lustily on the tits of another E-4 who happened to have them—a recent development in the Navy, and one which Mancuso would just as soon have put off for another decade. They were even letting women on submarines now, and the admiral didn't regret having missed that one little bit. What the hell would Mush Morton and his crop of WWII submarines have made of *that?*

He figured he knew how to set up a naval exercise, one of those grand training evolutions in which half of 7th Fleet would administratively attack and destroy the other half, followed by the simulated forced-entry landing of a Marine battalion. Navy fighters would tangle with Air Force ones, and after it was all over, computer records would show who'd won and who'd lost, and bets of various sorts would be paid off in various bars—and there'd be some hard feelings, because fitness reports (and with them, careers) could ride on outcomes of simulated engagements.

Of all his services, Mancuso figured his submarine force was in the best shape, which made sense, since his previous job had been COMSUBPAC, and he'd ruthlessly whipped his boats into shape. And, besides, the little shooting war they'd engaged in two years before had given everyone the proper sense of mission, to the point that the crews of the boomers who'd laid on a submarine ambush worthy of Charlie Lockwood's best day still swaggered around when on the beach. The boomers remained in service as auxiliary fast-attacks because Mancuso had made his case to the CNO, who was his friend, Dave Seaton, and Seaton had made his case to Congress to get some additional funding, and Congress was nice and tame, what with two recent conflicts to show them that people in uniform did have more purposes than opening and closing doors for the people's elected representatives. Besides, the Ohio-class boats were just too expensive to throw away, and they were mainly off doing valuable oceanographic missions in the North Pacific, which appealed to the tree- (actually fish- and dolphin- in this case) huggers, who had far too much political power in the eyes of this white-suited warrior.

With every new day came his official morning briefing, usually run by Brigadier General Mike Lahr, his J-2 Intelligence Officer. This was particularly good news. On the morning of 7 December, 1941, the United States had learned the advantage of providing senior area commanders with the intelligence they might need, and so this CINCPAC, unlike Admiral Husband E. Kimmel, got to hear a lot.

"Morning, Mike," Mancuso said in greeting, while a chief steward's mate set up morning coffee.

"Good morning, sir," the one-star replied.

"What's new in the Pacific?"

"Well, top of the news this morning, the Russians have appointed a new guy to head their Far Eastern Military District. His name is Gennady Bondarenko. His last job was J-3 operations officer for the Russian army. His background's pretty interesting. He started off in signals, not a combat arm, but he distinguished himself in Afghanistan toward the end of that adventure on their part. He's got the Order of the Red Banner and he's a Hero of the Soviet Union—got both of those as a colonel. He moved rapidly up from there. Good political connections. He's worked closely with a guy named Golovko—he's a former KGB officer who's still in the spook business and is personally known to the President—ours, that is. Golovko is essentially the operational XO for the Russian President Grushavoy—like a chief minister or something. Grushavoy listens to him on a lot of issues, and he's a pipeline into the White House on matters 'of mutual interest.' "

"Great. So the Russians have Jack Ryan's ear via this guy. What sort of mensch is he?" CINCPAC asked.

"Very smart and very capable, our friends at Langley say. Anyway, back to Bondarenko. The book on the guy says he's also very smart and also very capable, a contender for further advancement. Brains and personal bravery can be career-enhancing in their military, just like ours."

"What sort of shape is his new command in?"

"Not very good at all, sir. We see eight division-sized formations, six motor-rifle divisions, one tank, and one artillery division. All appear to be under strength on our overheads, and they don't spend much time in the field. Bondarenko will change that, if he goes according to the form card."

"Think so?"

"As their J-3, he agitated for higher training standards—and he's a bit of an intellectual. He published a lengthy essay last year on the Roman legions. It was called 'Soldiers of the Caesars.' It had that great quote from Josephus, 'Their drills are bloodless battles and their battles are bloody drills.' Anyway, it was a straight historical piece, sources like Josephus and Vegetius, but the implication was clear. He was crying out for better training in the Russian army, and also for career NCOs. He spent a lot of time with Vegetsius's discussion of how you build centurions. The Soviet army didn't really have sergeants as we understand the term, and Bondarenko is one of the new crop of senior officers who's saying that the new *Russian* army should reintroduce that institution. Which makes good sense," Lahr thought.

"So, you think he's going to whip his people into shape. What about the Russian navy?"

"They don't belong to him. He's got Frontal Aviation tactical aircraft and ground troops, but that's all."

"Well, their navy's so far down the shitter they can't see where the paper roll is," Mancuso observed. "What else?"

"A bunch of political stuff you can read up on at your leisure. The Chinese are still active in the field. They're running a four-division exercise now south of the Amur River."

"That big?"

"Admiral, they've been on an increased training regimen for almost three years now. Nothing frantic or anything, but they've been spending money to get the PLA up to speed. This one's heavy with tanks and APCs. Lots of artillery live-fire exercises. That's a good training area for them, not much in the way of civilians, kinda like Nevada but not as flat. At first when they started this we kept a close eye on it, but it's fairly routine now."

"Oh, yeah? What do the Russians think about it?"

Lahr stretched in his chair. "Sir, that's probably why Bondarenko drew this assignment. This is backwards from how the Russians trained to fight. The Chinese have them heavily outnumbered in theater, but nobody sees hostilities happening. The politics are pretty smooth at the moment."

"Uh-huh," CINCPAC grunted behind his desk. "And Taiwan?"

"Some increased training near the strait, but those are mainly infantry formations, and nothing even vaguely like amphibious exercises. We keep a close eye on that, with help from our ROC friends."

Mancuso nodded. He had a filing cabinet full of plans to send 7th Fleet west, and there was almost always one of his surface ships making a "courtesy call" to that island. For his sailors, the Republic of China was one hell of a good liberty port, with lots of women whose services were subject to commercial negotiations. And having a gray U.S. Navy warship tied alongside pretty well put that city off-limits for a missile attack. Even scratching an American warship was classified delicately as a *casus belli,* a reason for war. And nobody thought the ChiComms were ready for that sort of thing yet. To keep things that way, Mancuso had his carriers doing constant workups, exercising their interceptor and strike-fighter forces in the manner of the 1980s. He always had at least one fast-attack or boomer slow-attack submarine in the Formosa Strait, too, something that was advertised only by casual references allowed to leak to the media from time to time. Only very rarely would a submarine make a local port call, however. They were more effective when not seen. But in another filing cabinet he had lots of periscope photos of Chinese warships, and some "hull shots," photos made from directly underneath, which was mainly good for testing the nerve of his submarine drivers.

He also occasionally had his people track ChiComm submarines, much as he'd done in *Dallas* against the former Soviet navy. But this was much easier. The Chinese nuclear-power plants were so noisy that fish avoided them to prevent damage to their ears, or so his sonarmen joked. As much as the PRC had rattled its saber at Taiwan, an actual attack, if opposed by his 7th Fleet, would rapidly turn into a bloody shambles, and he hoped Beijing knew that. If they didn't, finding out would be a messy and expensive exercise. But the ChiComms didn't have much in the way of amphibious capability yet, and showed no signs of building it.

"So, looks like a routine day in theater?" Mancuso asked, as the briefing wound down.

"Pretty much," General Lahr confirmed.

"What sort of assets do we have tasked to keep an eye on our Chinese friends?"

"Mainly overheads," the J-2 replied. "We've never had much in the way of human intelligence in the PRC—at least not that I ever heard about."

"Why is that?"

"Well, in simplest terms it would be kind of hard for you or me to disappear into their society, and most of our Asian citizens work for computer-software companies, last time I checked."

"Not many of them in the Navy. How about the Army?"

"Not many, sir. They're pretty underrepresented."

"I wonder why."

"Sir, I'm an intelligence officer, not a demographer," Lahr pointed out.

"I guess that job is hard enough, Mike. Okay, if anything interesting happens, let me know."

"You bet, sir." Lahr headed out the door, to be replaced by Mancuso's J-3 operations officer, who would tell him what all his theater assets were up to this fine day, plus which ships and airplanes were broken and needed fixing.

She hadn't gotten any less attractive, though getting her here had proven difficult. Tanya Bogdanova hadn't avoided anything, but she'd been unreachable for several days.

"You've been busy?" Provalov asked.

"Da, a special client," she said with a nod. "We spent time together in St. Petersburg. I didn't bring my beeper. He dislikes interruptions," she explained, without showing much in the way of remorse.

Provalov could have asked the cost of several days in this woman's company, and she would probably have told him, but he decided that he didn't need to know all that badly. She remained a vision, lacking only the white feathery wings to be an angel. Except for the eyes and the heart, of course. The former cold, and the latter nonexistent.

"I have a question," the police lieutenant told her.

"Yes?"

"A name. Do you know it? Klementi Ivan'ch Suvorov."

Her eyes showed some amusement. "Oh, yes. I know him well." She didn't have to elaborate on what "well" meant.

"What can you tell me about him?"

"What do you wish to know?"

"His address, for starters."

"He lives outside Moscow."

"Under what name?"

"He does not know that I know, but I saw his papers once. Ivan Yurievich Koniev."

"How do you know this?" Provalov asked.

"He was asleep, of course, and I went through his clothes," she replied, as matter-of-factly as if she'd told the militia lieutenant where she shopped for bread.

So, he fucked you, and you, in turn, fucked him, Provalov didn't say. "Do you remember his address?"

She shook her head. "No, but it's one of the new communities off the outer ring road."

"When did you last see him?"

"It was a week before Gregoriy Filipovich died," she answered at once.

It was then that Provalov had a flash: "Tanya, the night before Gregoriy died, whom did you see?"

"He was a former soldier or something, let me think . . . Pyotr Alekseyevich . . . something . . ."

"Amalrik?" Provalov asked, almost coming off his seat.

"Yes, something like that. He had a tattoo on his arm, the Spetsnaz tattoo a lot of them got in Afghanistan. He thought very highly of himself, but he wasn't a very good lover," Tanya added dismissively.

And he never will be, Provalov could have said then, but didn't. "Who set up that, ah, appointment?"

"Oh, that was Klementi Ivan'ch. He had an arrangement with Gregoriy. They knew each other, evidently for a long time. Gregoriy often made special appointments for Klementi's friends."

Suvorov had one or both of his killers fuck the whores belonging to the man they would kill the next day . . . ? Whoever Suvorov was, he had an active sense of humor . . . or the real target actually had been Sergey Nikolay'ch. Provalov had just turned up an important piece of information, but it didn't seem to illuminate his criminal case at all. Another fact which only made his job harder, not easier. He was back to the same two possibilities: This Suvorov had contracted the two Spetsnaz soldiers to kill Rasputin, and then had them killed as "insurance" to avoid repercussions. Or he'd contracted them to eliminate Golovko, and then killed them for making a serious error. Which? He'd have to find this Suvorov to find out. But now he had a name and a probable location. And that was something he could work on.

CHAPTER 19

Manhunting

Things had quieted down at Rainbow headquarters in Hereford, England, to the point that both John Clark and Ding Chavez were starting to show the symptoms of restlessness. The training regimen was as demanding as ever, but nobody had ever drowned in sweat, and the targets, paper and electronic were—well, if not as *satisfying* as a real human miscreant wasn't the best way to put it, then maybe not as *exciting* was the right phrase. But the Rainbow team members didn't say that, even among themselves, for fear of appearing bloodthirsty and unprofessional. To them the studied mental posture was that it was all the same. Practice *was* bloodless battle, and battle *was* bloody drill. And certainly by taking their training so seriously, they were still holding a very fine edge. Fine enough to shave the fuzz off a baby's face.

The team had never gone public, at least not per se. But the word had leaked out somehow. Not in Washington, and not in London, but somewhere on the continent, the word had gotten out that NATO now had a very special and very capable counterterrorist team that had raped and pillaged its way through several high-profile missions, and only once taken any lumps, at the hands of Irish terrorists who had, however, paid a bitter price for their misjudgment. The European papers called them the "Men of Black" for their assault uniforms, and in their relative ignorance the European newsies had somehow made Rainbow even more fierce than reality justified. Enough so that the team had deployed to the Netherlands for a mission seven months before, a few weeks after the first news coverage had broken, and when the bad guys at the grammar school had found there were new folks in the neighborhood, they'd stumbled through a negotiating session with Dr. Paul Bellow and cut a deal before hostilities had to be initiated, which was pleasing for everyone. The idea of a shoot-out in a school full of kids hadn't even appealed to the Men of Black.

Over the last several months, some members had been hurt or rotated back to their parent services, and new members had replaced them. One of these was Ettore Falcone, a former member of the Carabinieri sent to Hereford as much for his own protection as to assist the NATO team. Falcone had been walking the streets of Palermo in Sicily with his wife and infant son one pleasant spring evening when a shoot-out had erupted right before his eyes. Three criminals were hosing a pedestrian, his wife, and their police bodyguard with submachine guns, and in an instant Falcone had pulled out his Beretta and dropped all three with head shots from ten meters away. His action had been too late to save the victims, but not too late to incur the wrath of a *capo mafioso,* two of whose sons had been involved in the hit. Falcone had publicly spat upon the threat, but cooler heads had prevailed in Rome—the Italian government did not want a blood feud to erupt between the Mafia and its own federal police agency—and Falcone had been dispatched to Hereford to be the first Italian member of Rainbow. He had quickly proven himself to be the best pistol shot anyone had ever seen.

"Damn," John Clark breathed, after finishing his fifth string of ten shots. This guy had beaten him again! They called him Big Bird. Ettore—Hector—was about six-three and lean like a basketball player, the wrong size and shape for a counterterror trooper, but, Jesus, could this son of a bitch shoot!

"Grazie, General," the Italian said, collecting the five-pound note that had accompanied *this* blood feud.

And John couldn't even bitch that he'd done it for real, whereas Big Bird had only done it with paper. This spaghetti-eater had dropped three guys armed with SMGs, and done it with his wife and kid next to him. Not just a talented shooter, this guy had two big brass ones dangling between his legs. And his wife, Anna-Maria, was reputed to be a dazzling cook. In any case, Falcone had bested him by one point in a fifty-round shootoff. And John had practiced for a week before this grudge match.

"Ettore, where the hell did you learn to shoot?" Rainbow Six demanded.

"At the police academy, General Clark. I never fired a gun before that, but I had a good instructor, and I learned well," the sergeant said, with a friendly smile. He wasn't the least bit arrogant about his talent, and somehow that just made it worse.

"Yeah, I suppose." Clark zippered his pistol into the carrying case and walked away from the firing line.

"You, too, sir?" Dave Woods, the rangemaster, said, as Clark made for the door.

"So I'm not the only one?" Rainbow Six asked.

Woods looked up from his sandwich. "Bloody hell, that lad's got a fookin' letter of credit at the Green Dragon from besting me!" he announced. And Sergeant-Major Woods really *had* taught Wyatt Earp everything he knew. And at the SAS/Rainbow pub he'd probably taught the new boy how to drink English bitter. Beating Falcone would not be easy. There just wasn't much room to take a guy who often as not shot a "possible," or perfect score.

"Well, Sergeant-Major, then I guess I'm in good company." Clark punched him on the shoulder as he headed out the door, shaking his head. Behind him, Falcone was firing another string. He evidently liked being Number One, and practiced hard to stay there. It had been a long time since anyone had bested him on a shooting range. John didn't like it, but fair was fair, and Falcone had won within the rules.

Was it just one more sign that he was slowing down? He wasn't running as fast as the younger troops at Rainbow, of course, and that bothered him, too. John Clark wasn't ready to be old yet. He wasn't ready to be a grandfather either, but he had little choice in that. His daughter and Ding had presented him with a grandson, and he couldn't exactly ask that they take him back. He was keeping his weight down, though that often required, as it had today, skipping lunch in favor of losing five paper-pounds at the pistol range.

"Well, how did it go, John?" Alistair Stanley asked, as Clark entered the office building.

"The kid's real good, Al," John replied, as he put his pistol in the desk drawer.

"Indeed. He won five pounds off me last week."

A grunt. "I guess that makes it unanimous." John settled in his swivel chair, like the "suit" he'd become. "Okay, anything come in while I was off losing money?"

"Just this from Moscow. Ought not to have come here anyway," Stanley told his boss, as he handed over the fax.

They want what?" Ed Foley asked in his seventh-floor office.

"They want us to help train some of their people," Mary Pat repeated for her husband. The original message had been crazy enough to require repetition.

"Jesus, girl, how ecumenical are we supposed to get?" the DCI demanded.

"Sergey Nikolay'ch thinks we owe him one. And you know . . ."

He had to nod at that. "Yeah, well, maybe we do, I guess. This has to go up the line, though."

"It ought to give Jack a chuckle," the Deputy Director (Operations) thought.

Shit," Ryan said in the Oval Office, when Ellen Sumter handed him the fax from Langley. Then he looked up. "Oh, excuse me, Ellen."

She smiled like a mother to a precocious son. "Yes, Mr. President."

"Got one I can . . . ?"

Mrs. Sumter had taken to wearing dresses with large slash pockets. From the left one, she fished out a flip-top box of Virginia Slims and offered it to her President, who took one out and lit it from the butane lighter also tucked in the box.

"Well, ain't this something?"

"You know this man, don't you?" Mrs. Sumter asked.

"Golovko? Yeah." Ryan smiled crookedly, again remembering the pistol in his face as the VC-137 thundered down the runway at Moscow's Sheremetyevo airport all those years before. He could smile now. At the time, it hadn't seemed all that funny. "Oh, yeah, Sergey and I are old friends."

As a Presidential secretary, Ellen Sumter was cleared for just about everything, even the fact that President Ryan bummed the occasional smoke, but there were some things she didn't and would never know. She was smart enough to have curiosity, but also smart enough not to ask.

"If you say so, Mr. President."

"Thanks, Ellen." Ryan sat back down in his chair and took a long puff on the slender cigarette. Why was it that stress of any sort made him gravitate back to these damned things that made him cough? The good news was that they also made him dizzy. *So, that meant he wasn't a smoker, not really,* POTUS told himself. He read over the fax again. It had two pages. One was the original fax from Sergey Nikolay'ch to Langley—unsurprisingly, he had Mary Pat's direct fax line, and wanted to show off that fact—and the second was the recommendation from Edward Foley, his CIA director.

For all the official baggage, it was pretty simple stuff. Golovko didn't even have to explain *why* America had to accede to his request. The Foleys and Jack Ryan would know that KGB had assisted the CIA and the American government in two very sensitive and important missions, and the fact that both of them had also served Russian interests was beside the point. Thus Ryan had no alternative. He lifted the phone and punched a speed-dial button.

"Foley," the male voice at the other end said.

"Ryan," Jack said in turn. He then heard the guy at the other end sit up straighter in his chair. "Got the fax."

"And?" the DCI asked.

"And what the hell else can we do?"

"I agree." Foley could have said that he personally liked Sergey Golovko. Ryan did, too, as he knew. But this wasn't about like or don't-like. They were making government policy here, and that was bigger than personal factors. Russia had helped the United States of America, and now Russia was asking the United States of America for help in return. In the regular intercourse among nations, such requests, if they had precedents, had to be granted. The principle was the same as lending your neighbor a rake after he had lent you a hose the previous day, just that at this level, people occasionally got killed from such favors. "You handle it or do I?"

"The request came to Langley. You do the reply. Find out what the parameters are. We don't want to compromise Rainbow, do we?"

"No, Jack, but there's not much chance of that. Europe's quieted down quite a bit. The Rainbow troopers are mainly exercising and punching holes in paper. That news story that ran—well, we might actually want to thank the putz who broke it." The DCI rarely said anything favorable about the press. And in this case some government puke had talked far too much about something he knew, but the net effect of the story had had the desired effect, even though the press account had been replete with errors, which was hardly surprising. But some of the errors had made Rainbow appear quite superhuman, which appealed to their egos and gave their potential enemies pause. And so, terrorism in Europe had slowed down to a crawl after its brief (and somewhat artificial, they knew now) rebirth. The Men of Black were just too scary to mess with. Muggers, after all, went after the little old ladies who'd just cashed their Social Security checks, not the armed cop on the corner. In this, criminals were just being rational. A little old lady can't resist a mugger very effectively, but a cop carries a gun.

"I expect our Russian friends will keep a lid on it."

"I think we can depend on that, Jack," Ed Foley agreed.

"Any reason not to do it?"

Ryan could hear the DCI shift in his seat. "I never have been keen on giving 'methods' away to anybody, but this isn't an intelligence operation per se, and most of it they could get from reading the right books. So, I guess we can allow it."

"Approved," the President said.

Ryan imagined he could see the nod at the other end. "Okay, the reply will go out today."

With a copy to Hereford, of course. It arrived on John's desk before closing time. He summoned Al Stanley and handed it to him.

"I suppose we're becoming famous, John."

"Makes you feel good, doesn't it?" Clark asked distastefully. Both were former clandestine operators, and if there had been a way to keep their own supervisors from knowing their names and activities, they would have found it long before.

"I presume you will go yourself. Whom will you take to Moscow with you?"

"Ding and Team-2. Ding and I have been there before. We've both met Sergey Nikolay'ch. At least this way he doesn't see all that many new faces."

"Yes, and your Russian, as I recall, is first-rate."

"The language school at Monterey is pretty good," John said, with a nod.

"How long do you expect to be gone?"

Clark looked back down at the fax and thought it over for a few seconds. "Oh, not more than . . . three weeks," he said aloud. "Their Spetsnaz people aren't bad. We'll set up a training group for them, and after a while, we can probably invite them here, can't we?"

Stanley didn't have to point out that the SAS in particular, and the British Ministry of Defense in general, would have a conniption fit over that one, but in the end they'd have to go along with it. It was called diplomacy, and its principles set policy for most of the governments in the world, whether they liked it or not.

"I suppose we'll have to, John," Stanley said, already hearing the screams, shouts, and moans from the rest of the camp, and Whitehall.

Clark lifted his phone and hit the button for his secretary, Helen Montgomery. "Helen, could you please call Ding and ask him to come over? Thank you."

"His Russian is also good, as I recall."

"We had some good teachers. But his accent is a little southern."

"And yours?"

"Leningrad—well, St. Petersburg now, I guess. Al, do you believe all the changes?"

Stanley took a seat. "John, it is all rather mad, even today, and it's been well over ten years since they took down the red flag over the Spaskiy gate."

Clark nodded. "I remember when I saw it on TV, man. Flipped me out."

"Hey, John," a familiar voice called from the door. "Hi, Al."

"Come in and take a seat, my boy."

Chavez, simulated major in the SAS, hesitated at the "my boy" part. Whenever John talked that way, something unusual was about to happen. But it could have been worse. "Kid" was usually the precursor to danger, and now that he was a husband and a father, Domingo no longer went too far out of his way to look for trouble. He walked to Clark's desk and took the offered sheets of paper.

"Moscow?" he asked.

"Looks like our Commander-in-Chief has approved it."

"Super," Chavez observed. "Well, it's been a while since we met Mr. Golovko. I suppose the vodka's still good."

"It's one of the things they do well," John agreed.

"And they want us to teach them to do some other things?"

"Looks that way."

"Take the wives with us?"

"No." Clark shook his head. "This one's all business."

"When?"

"Have to work that out. Probably a week or so."

"Fair enough."

"How's the little guy?"

A grin. "Still crawling. Last night he started pulling himself up, standing, like. Imagine he'll start walking in a few days."

"Domingo, you spend the first year getting them to walk and talk. The next twenty years you spend getting them to sit down and shut up," Clark warned.

"Hey, pop, the little guy sleeps all the way through the night, and he wakes up with a smile. Damned sight better than I can say for myself, y'know?" Which made sense. When Domingo woke up, all he had to look forward to was the usual exercises and a five-mile run, which was both strenuous and, after a while, boring.

Clark had to nod at that. It was one of the great mysteries of life, how infants always woke up in a good mood. He wondered where, in the course of years, one lost that.

"The whole team?" Chavez asked.

"Yeah, probably. Including Big Bird," Rainbow Six added.

"Did he clean your clock today, too?" Ding asked.

"Next time I shoot against that son of a bitch, I want it right after the morning run, when he's a little shaky," Clark said crossly. He just didn't like to lose at much of anything, and certainly not something so much a part of his identity as shooting a handgun.

"Mr. C, Ettore just isn't human. With the MP, he's good, but not spectacular, but with that Beretta, he's like Tiger Woods with a pitching wedge. He just lays 'em dead."

"I didn't believe it until today. I think maybe I ought to have eaten lunch over at the Green Dragon."

"I hear you, John," Chavez agreed, deciding not to comment on his father-in-law's waist. "Hey, I'm pretty good with a pistol, too, remember. Ettore blew my ass away by three whole points."

"The bastard took me by one," John told his Team-2 commander. "First man-on-man match I've lost since Third SOG." And that was thirty years in the past, against his command-master-chief, for beers. He'd lost by two points, but beat the master-chief three straight after that, Clark remembered with pride.

Is that him?" Provalov asked.

"We don't have a photograph," his sergeant reminded him. "But he fits the general description." And he was walking to the right car. Several cameras would be snapping now to provide the photos.

They were both in a van parked half a block from the apartment building they were surveilling. Both men were using binoculars, green, rubber-coated military-issue.

The guy looked about right. He'd come off the building's elevator, and had left the right floor. It had been established earlier in the evening that one Ivan Yurievich Koniev lived on the eighth floor of this upscale apartment building. There had not been time to question his neighbors, which had to be done carefully, in any case. There was more than the off-chance that this Koniev/Suvorov's neighbors were, as he was reputed to be, former KGB, and thus asking them questions could mean alerting the subject of their investigation. This was not an ordinary subject, Provalov kept reminding himself.

The car the man got into was a rental. There was a private automobile registered to one Koniev, Ian Yurievich, at this address, a Mercedes C-class, and who was to say what other cars he might own under another identity? Provalov was sure he'd have more of those, and they'd all be very carefully crafted. The Koniev ID certainly was. KGB had trained its people thoroughly.

The sergeant in the driver's seat started up the van's motor and got on the radio. Two other police cars were in the immediate vicinity, both manned by pairs of experienced investigators.

"Our friend is moving. The blue rental car," Provalov said over the radio. Both of his cars radioed acknowledgments.

The rental car was a Fiat—a real one made in Turin rather than the Russian copy made at Togliattistad, one of the few special economic projects of the Soviet Union that had actually worked, after a fashion. Had it been selected for its agility, Provalov wondered, or just because it was a cheap car to rent? There was no knowing that right now. Koniev/Suvorov pulled out, and the first tail car formed up with him, half a block behind, while the second was half a block in front, because even a KGB-trained intelligence officer rarely looked for a tail *in front of* himself. A little more time and they might have placed a tracking device on the Fiat, but they hadn't had it, nor the darkness required. If he returned to his apartment, they'd do it late tonight, say about four in the morning. A radio beeper with a magnet to hold it onto the inside of the rear bumper; its antenna would hang down like a mouse's tail, virtually invisible. Some of the available technology Provalov was using had originally been used to track suspected foreign spies around Moscow, and that meant it was pretty good, at least by Russian standards.

Following the car was easier than he'd expected. Three trail cars helped. Spotting a single-car tail was not overly demanding. Two could also be identified, since the same two would switch off every few minutes. But three shadow cars broke up the pattern nicely, and, KGB-trained or not, Koniev/Suvorov was not superhuman. His real defense lay in concealing his identity, and cracking that had been a combination of good investigation and luck—but cops knew about luck. KGB, on the other hand, didn't. In their mania for organization, their training program had left it out, perhaps because trusting to luck was a weakness that could lead to disaster in the field. That told Provalov that Koniev/Suvorov hadn't spent that much time in field operations. In the real world of working the street, you learned such things in a hurry.

The tailing was conducted at extreme range, over a block, and the city blocks were large ones here. The van had been specially equipped for it. The license-plate holders were triangular in cross-section, and at the flip of a switch one could switch from among three separate pairs of tags. The lights on the front of the vehicle were paired as well, and so one could change the light pattern, which was what a skilled adversary would look for at night. Switch them once or twice when out of sight of his rearview mirror, and he'd have to be a genius to catch on. The most difficult job went with the car doing the front-tail, since it was hard to read Koniev/Suvorov's mind, and when he made an unexpected turn, the lead car then had to scurry about under the guidance of the trailing shadow cars to regain its leading position. All of the militiamen on this detail, however, were experienced homicide investigators who'd learned how to track the most dangerous game on the planet: human beings who'd displayed the willingness to take another life. Even the stupid murderers could have animal cunning, and they learned a lot about police operations just from watching television. That made some of his investigations more difficult than they ought to have been, but in a case like this, the additional difficulty had served to train his men more thoroughly than any academy training would have done.

"Turning right," his driver said into his radio. "Van takes the lead." The leading trail car would proceed to the next right turn, make it, and then race to resume its leading position. The trailing car would drop behind the van, falling off the table for a few minutes before resuming its position. The trail car *was* a Fiat-clone from Togliattistad, by far the most common private-passenger auto in Russia, and therefore fairly anonymous, with its dirty off-white paint job.

"If that's his only attempt at throwing us off, he's very confident of himself."

"True," Provalov agreed. "Let's see what else he does."

The "what else" took place four minutes later. The Fiat took another right turn, this one not onto a cross-street, but into the underpass of another apartment building, one that straddled an entire block. Fortunately, the lead trail car was already on the far side of the building, trying to catch up with the Fiat, and had the good fortune to see Koniev/Suvorov appear thirty meters in front.

"We have him," the radio crackled. "We'll back off somewhat."

"Go!" Provalov told his driver, who accelerated the van to the next corner. Along the way, he toggled the switch to flip the license plates and change the headlight pattern, converting the van into what at night would seem a new vehicle entirely.

"He is confident," Provalov observed five minutes later. The van was now in close-trail, with the lead trail car behind the van, and the other surveillance vehicle close behind that one. Wherever he was going, they were on him. He'd run his evasion maneuver, and a clever one it had been, but only one. Perhaps he thought that one such SDR—surveillance-detection run—was enough, that if he were being trailed it would only be a single vehicle, and so he'd run that underpass, eyes on the rearview mirror, and spotted nothing. Very good, the militia lieutenant thought. It was a pity he didn't have his American FBI friend along. The FBI could scarcely have done this better, even with its vast resources. It didn't hurt that his men knew the streets of Moscow and its suburbs as well as any taxi driver.

"He's getting dinner and a drink somewhere," Provalov's driver observed. "He'll pull over in the next kilometer."

"We shall see," the lieutenant said, thinking his driver right. This area had ten or eleven upscale eateries. Which would his quarry choose . . . ?

It turned out to be the Prince Michael of Kiev, a Ukrainian establishment specializing in chicken and fish, known also for its fine bar. Koniev/Suvorov pulled over and allowed the restaurant's valet to park his vehicle, then walked in.

"Who's the best dressed among us?" Provalov asked over the radio.

"You are, Comrade Lieutenant." His other two teams were attired as working-class people, and that wouldn't fly here. Half of the Prince Michael of Kiev's clientele were foreigners, and you had to dress well around such people—the restaurant saw to that. Provalov jumped out half a block away and walked briskly to the canopied entrance. The doorman admitted him after a look—in the new Russia, clothing made the man more than in most European nations. He could have flashed his police ID, but that might not be a good move. Koniev/Suvorov might well have some of the restaurant staff reporting to him. That was when he had a flash of imagination. Provalov immediately entered the men's lavatory and pulled out his cellular phone.

"Hello?" a familiar voice said on picking up the receiver.

"Mishka?"

"Oleg?" Reilly asked. "What can I do for you?"

"Do you know a restaurant called the Prince Michael of Kiev?"

"Yeah, sure. Why?"

"I need your help. How quickly can you get here?" Provalov asked, knowing that Reilly lived only two kilometers away.

"Ten or fifteen minutes."

"Quickly, then. I'll be at the bar. Dress presentably," the militiaman added.

"Right," Reilly agreed, wondering how he'd explain it to his wife, and wondering why he'd had his quiet evening in front of the TV interrupted.

Provalov headed back to the bar, ordered a pepper vodka, and lit a cigarette. His quarry was seven seats away, also having a solitary drink, perhaps waiting for his table to become available. The restaurant was full. A string quartet was playing some Rimsky-Korsakov on the far side of the dining room. The restaurant was far above anything Provalov could afford as a regular part of his life. So, Koniev/Suvorov was well set financially. That was no particular surprise. A lot of ex–KGB officers were doing very well indeed in the economic system of the new Russia. They had worldly ways and knowledge that few of their fellow citizens could match. In a society known for its burgeoning corruption, they had a corner on the market, and a network of fellow-travelers to call upon, with whom they could, for various considerations, share their gains, ill-gotten or not.

Provalov had finished his first drink, and had motioned to the bartender for another when Reilly appeared.

"Oleg Gregoriyevich," the American said in greeting. He was no fool, the Russian militia lieutenant realized. The American's Russian was manifestly American and overloud, a fine backwards stealth for this environment. He was well dressed also, proclaiming his foreign origin to all who saw him.

"Mishka!" Provalov said in response, taking the American's hand warmly and waving to the bartender.

"Okay, who we looking for?" the FBI agent asked more quietly.

"The gray suit, seven seats to my left."

"Got him," Reilly said at once. "Who is he?"

"He is currently under the name Koniev, Ivan Yurievich. In fact we believe him to be Suvorov, Klementi Ivan'ch."

"Aha," Reilly observed. "What else can you tell me?"

"We trailed him here. He used a simple but effective evasion method, but we have three cars tracking him, and we picked him right back up."

"Good one, Oleg," the FBI agent said. Inadequately trained and poorly equipped or not, Provalov was a no-shit copper. In the Bureau, he'd be at least a supervisory special agent. Oleg had fine cop instincts. Tracking a KGB type around Moscow was no trivial exercise, like following a paranoid button-man in Queens. Reilly sipped his pepper vodka and turned sideways in his seat. On the far side of the subject was a dark-haired beauty wearing a slinky black dress. She looked like another of those expensive hookers to Reilly, and her shingle was out. Her dark eyes were surveying the room as thoroughly as his. The difference was that Reilly was a guy, and looking at a pretty girl—or seeming to—was not the least bit unusual. In fact, his eyes were locked not on the woman, but the man. Fifty-ish, well turned out, nondescript in overall appearance, just as a spy was supposed to be, looked to be waiting for a table, nursing his drink and looking studiously in the bar's mirror, which was a fine way to see if he were being watched. The American and his Russian friend he dismissed, of course. What interest could an American businessman have in him, after all? And besides, the American was eyeing the whore to his left. For that reason, the subject's eyes did not linger on the men to his right, either directly or in the mirror. Oleg *was* smart, Reilly thought, using *him* as camouflage for his discreet surveillance.

"Anything else turn lately?" the FBI agent asked. Provalov filled in what he'd learned about the hooker and what had happened the night before the murders. "Damn, that *is* swashbuckling. But you still don't know who the target was, do you?"

"No," Provalov admitted, with a sip of his second drink. He'd have to go easy on the alcohol, he knew, lest he make a mistake. His quarry was too slick and dangerous to take any sort of risk at all. He could always bring the guy in for questioning, but he knew that would be a fruitless exercise. Criminals like this one had to be handled as gently as a cabinet minister. Provalov allowed his eyes to look into the mirror, where he got a good look at the profile of a probable multiple murderer. Why was it that there was no black halo around such people? Why did they look normal?

"Anything else we know about the mutt?"

The Russian had come to like that American term. He shook his head. "No, Mishka. We haven't checked with SVR yet."

"Worried that he might have a source inside the building?" the American asked. Oleg nodded.

"That is a consideration." And an obvious one. The fraternity of former KGB officers was probably a tight one. There might well be someone inside the old headquarters building, say someone in personnel records, who'd let people know if the police showed interest in any particular file.

"Damn," the American noted, thinking, *You son of a bitch, fucking the guy's hookers before you waste him.* There was a disagreeable coldness to it, like something from a Mafia movie. But in real life, La Cosa Nostra members didn't have the stones for such a thing. Formidable as they might be, Mafia button-men didn't have the training of a professional intelligence officer, and were tabby cats next to panthers in this particular jungle. Further scrutiny of the subject. The girl beyond him was a distraction, but not that much.

"Oleg?"

"Yes, Mikhail?"

"He's looking at somebody over by the musicians. His eyes keep coming back to the same spot. He isn't scanning the room like he was at first." The subject did check out everyone who came into the restaurant, but his eyes kept coming back to one part of the mirror, and he'd probably determined that nobody in the place was a danger to him. Oops. Well, Reilly thought, even training has its limitations, and sooner or later your own expertise could work against you. You fell into patterns, and you made assumptions that could get you caught. In this case, Suvorov assumed that no American could be watching him. After all, he'd done nothing to any Americans in Moscow, and maybe not in his entire career, and he was on friendly, not foreign ground, and he'd dusted off his tail on the way over in the way he always did, looking for a single tail car. Well, the smart ones knew their limitations. How did it go? The difference between genius and stupidity was that genius knew that it had limits. This Suvorov guy thought himself a genius . . . but whom was he looking at? Reilly turned a little more on his bar stool and scanned that part of the room.

"What do you see, Mishka?"

"A lot of people, Oleg Gregoriyevich, mainly Russians, some foreigners, all well-dressed. Some Chinese, look like two diplomats dining with two Russians—they look like official types. Looks cordial enough," Reilly thought. He'd eaten here with his wife three or four times. The food was pretty good, especially the fish. And they had a good source of caviar at the Prince Michael of Kiev, which was one of the best things you could get over here. His wife loved it, and would have to learn that getting it at home would be a lot more expensive than it was here. . . . Reilly'd done discreet surveillance for so many years that he had trained himself to be invisible. He could fit in just about anyplace but Harlem, and the Bureau had black agents to handle that.

Sure as hell, that Suvorov guy was looking in the same place. Casually, perhaps, and using the bar's mirror to do it. He even sat so that his eyes naturally looked at the same place as he sat on his bar stool. But people like this subject didn't do anything by accident or coincidence. They were trained to think through everything, even taking a leak . . . it was remarkable, then, that he'd been turned so stupidly. By a hooker who'd gone through his things while he was sleeping off an orgasm. Well, some men, no matter how smart, thought with their dicks. . . . Reilly turned again. . . . one of the Chinese men at the distant table excused himself and stood, heading for the men's room. Reilly thought to do the same at once, but . . . no. If it were prearranged, such a thing could spook it . . . *Patience, Mishka,* he told himself, turning back to look at the principal subject. Koniev/Suvorov set down his drink and stood.

"Oleg. I want you to point me toward the men's room," the FBI agent said. "In fifteen seconds."

Provalov counted out the time, then extended his arm toward the main entrance. Reilly patted him on the shoulder and headed that way.

The Prince Michael of Kiev restaurant was nice, but it didn't have a bathroom attendant, as many European places did, perhaps because Americans were uneasy with the custom, or maybe because the management thought it an unnecessary expense. Reilly entered and saw three urinals, two of them being used. He unzipped and urinated, then rezipped and turned to wash his hands, looking down as he did so . . . and just out of the corner of his eye, he saw the other two men share a sideways look. The Russian was taller. The men's room had the sort of pull-down roller towel that America had largely done away with. Reilly pulled it down and dried his hands, unable to wait too much longer. Heading toward the door, he reached in his pocket and pulled his car keys part of the way out. These he dropped just as he pulled the door open, with a muttered, "Damn," as he bent down to pick them up, shielded from their view by the steel divider. Reilly picked them off the tile floor and stood back up.

Then he saw it. It was well done. They could have been more patient, but they probably both discounted the importance of the American, and both were trained professionals. They scarcely touched each other, and what touching and bumping there was happened below the waist and out of sight to the casual observer. Reilly wasn't a casual observer, however, and even out of the corner of his eyes, it was obvious to the initiated. It was a classic brush-pass, so well done that even Reilly's experience couldn't determine who had passed what to whom. The FBI agent continued out, heading back to his seat at the bar, where he waved to the barkeep for the drink he figured he'd just earned.

"Yes?"

"You want to identify that Chinaman. He and our friend traded something in the shitter. Brush-pass, and nicely done," Reilly said, with a smile and a gesture at the brunette down the bar. Good enough, in fact, that had Reilly been forced to sit in a witness stand and describe it to a jury, a week-old law-school graduate could make him admit that he hadn't actually seen anything at all. But that told him much. That degree of skill was either the result of a totally chance encounter between two entirely innocent people—the purest of coincidences—or it had been the effort of two trained intelligence officers applying their craft at a perfect place in a perfect way. Provalov was turned the right way to see the two individuals leave the men's room. They didn't even notice each other, or didn't appear to acknowledge the presence of the other any more than they would have greeted a stray dog—exactly as two unrelated people would act after a happenstance encounter with a total stranger in any men's room anywhere. But this time as Koniev/Suvorov resumed his seat at the bar, he tended to his drink and didn't have his eyes interrogate the mirror regularly. In fact, he turned and greeted the girl to his left, then waved for the bartender to get her another drink, which she accepted with a warm, commercial smile. Her face proclaimed the fact that she'd found her trick for the night. The girl could act, Reilly thought.

"Well, our friend's going to get laid tonight," he told his Russian colleague.

"She is pretty," Provalov agreed. "Twenty-three, you think?"

"Thereabouts, maybe a little younger. Nice hooters."

"Hooters?" the Russian asked.

"Tits, Oleg, tits," the FBI agent clarified. "That Chinaman's a spook. See any coverage on him around?"

"No one I know," the lieutenant replied. "Perhaps he is not known to be an intelligence officer."

"Yeah, sure, your counterintelligence people have all retired to Sochi, right? Hell, guy, they trail me every so often."

"That means I am one of your agents, then?" Provalov asked.

A chuckle. "Let me know if you want to defect, Oleg Gregoriyevich."

"The Chinese in the light blue suit?"

"That's the one. Short, about five-four, one fifty-five, pudgy, short hair, about forty-five or so."

Provalov translated that to about 163 centimeters and seventy kilos, and made a mental note as he turned to look at the face, about thirty meters away. He looked entirely ordinary, as most spies did. With that done, he headed back to the men's room to make a phone call to his agents outside.

And that pretty much ended the evening. Koniev/Suvorov left the restaurant about twenty minutes later with the girl on his arm, and drove straight back to his apartment. One of the men who'd stayed behind walked with the Chinese to his car, which had diplomatic plates. Notes were written down, and the cops all headed home after an overtime day, wondering what they'd turned up and how important it might be.

CHAPTER 20

Diplomacy

Well?" Rutledge took his notes back from Secretary Adler.

"It looks okay, Cliff, assuming that you can deliver the message in an appropriate way," SecState told his subordinate.

"Process is something I understand." Then he paused. "The President wants this message delivered in unequivocal terms, correct?"

Secretary Adler nodded. "Yep."

"You know, Scott, I've never really landed on people this hard before."

"Ever want to?"

"The Israelis a few times. South Africa," he added thoughtfully.

"But never the Chinese or Japanese?"

"Scott, I've never been a trade guy before, remember?" But he was this time, because the mission to Beijing was supposed to be high-profile, requiring a higher-level diplomat instead of someone of mere ambassadorial rank. The Chinese knew this already. In their case negotiations would be handled publicly by their Foreign Minister, though they would actually be run by a lesser-ranked diplomat who was a foreign-trade specialist, and who had experienced a good run of luck dealing with America. Secretary Adler, with President Ryan's permission, was slowly leaking to the press that the times and the rules might have changed a little bit. He worried that Cliff Rutledge wasn't exactly the right guy to deliver the message, but Cliff was the on-deck batter.

"How are you working out with this Gant guy from Treasury?"

"If he were a diplomat, we'd be at war with the whole damned world, but I suppose he does know numbers and computers, probably," Rutledge allowed, not troubling to hide his distaste for the Chicago-born Jew with his nouveau-riche ways. That Rutledge had been of modest origins himself was long forgotten. A Harvard education and a diplomatic passport help one forget such distasteful things as having grown up in a row house, eating leftovers.

"Remember that Winston likes him, and Ryan likes Winston, okay?" Adler warned his subordinate gently. He decided not to concern himself with Cliff's WASP-ish anti-Semitism. Life was too short for trivialities, and Rutledge knew that his career rested in Scott Adler's hands. He might make more money as a consultant after leaving the State Department, but being fired out of Foggy Bottom would not enhance his value on the free-agent market.

"Okay, Scott, and, yeah, I need backup on the monetary aspects of this trade stuff." The accompanying nod was almost respectful. Good. He did know how to grovel when required. Adler didn't even consider telling Rutledge about the intelligence source in his pocket, courtesy of POTUS. There was something about the career diplomat that failed to inspire trust in his superior.

"What about communications?"

"The Embassy in Beijing has TAPDANCE capability. Even the new phone kind, same as the airplane." But there were problems with it, recently fielded by Fort Meade. The instruments had trouble linking up with each other, and using a satellite lash-up didn't help at all. Like most diplomats, Rutledge rarely troubled himself with such trivialities. He often expected the intelligence to appear as if by magic, rarely wondering how it had been obtained, but *always* questioning the motives of the source, whoever that might be. All in all, Clifford Rutledge II was the perfect diplomat. He believed in little beyond his own career, some vague notions of international amity, and his personal ability to make it come about and to avoid war through the sheer force of his brilliance.

But on the plus side, Adler admitted to himself, Rutledge was a competent diplomatic technician who knew how the banter worked, and how to present a position in the gentlest possible but still firm terms. The State Department never had enough of those. As someone had once remarked of Theodore Roosevelt, "The nicest gentleman who ever slit a throat." But Cliff would never do that, even to advance his own career. He probably shaved with an electric razor, not for fear of cutting himself so much as fear of actually seeing blood.

"When's your plane leave?" EAGLE asked his subordinate.

Barry Wise was already packed. He was an expert at it, as well he might be, because he traveled about as much as an international airline pilot. At fifty-four, the black ex-Marine had worked for CNN since its beginnings more than twenty years before, and he'd seen it all. He'd covered the contras in Nicaragua, and the first bombing missions in Baghdad. He'd been there when mass graves were excavated in Yugoslavia, and done live commentary over Rwanda's roads of death, simultaneously wishing that he could and thanking God that he could not broadcast the ghastly smells that still haunted his dreams. A news professional, Wise regarded his mission in life to be this: to transmit the truth from where it happened to where people were interested in it—and helping them to become interested if they were not. He didn't have much of a personal ideology, though he was a great believer in justice, and one of the ways to make justice happen was to give the correct information to the jury—in his case, the television-watching public. He and people like him had changed South Africa from a racist state into a functioning democracy, and he'd also played a role in destroying world communism. The truth, he figured, was about the most powerful weapon in the world, if you had a way of getting it to the average Joe. Unlike most members of his business, Wise respected Joe Citizen, at least the ones who were smart enough to watch him. They wanted the truth, and it was his job to deliver it to them to the best of his abilities, which he often doubted, as he constantly asked himself how well he was doing.

He kissed his wife on the way out the door, promising to bring back things for the kids, as he always did, and lugging his travel bag out to his one personal indulgence, a red Mercedes two-seater, which he then drove south to the D.C. Beltway and south again toward Andrews Air Force Base. He had to arrive early, because the Air Force had gotten overly security-conscious. Maybe it was from that dumb-ass movie that had had terrorists getting past all the armed guards—even though they were merely Air Force, not Marines, they did carry rifles, and they did at least *appear* to be competent—and aboard one of the 89th Military Airlift Wing's aircraft, which, Wise figured, was about as likely as having a pickpocket walk into the Oval Office and lift the President's wallet. But the military followed its own rules, senseless though they might be—that was something he remembered well from his time in the Corps. So, he'd drive down, pass through all the checkpoints, whose guards knew him better than they knew their own CO, and wait in the plush Distinguished Visitors' lounge at the end of Andrews' Runway Zero-One Left for the official party to arrive. Then they'd board the venerable VC-137 for the endless flight to Beijing. The seats were as comfortable as they could be on an airplane, and the service was as good as any airline's first class, but flights this long were never fun.

Never been there before," Mark Gant said, answering George Winston's question. "So—what's the score on this Rutledge guy?"

The SecTreas shrugged. "Career State Department puke, worked his way pretty far up the ladder. Used to have good political connections—he was tight with Ed Kealty once upon a time."

The former stock trader looked up. "Oh? Why hasn't Ryan fired his ass?"

"Jack doesn't play that sort of game," Winston replied, wondering if in this case principle was getting in the way of common sense.

"George, he's still pretty naïve, isn't he?"

"Maybe so, but he's a straight shooter, and I can live with that. He sure as hell backed us up on tax policy, and that's going to pass through Congress in another few weeks."

Gant wouldn't believe that until he saw it. "Assuming every lobbyist in town doesn't jump in front of the train."

That engendered an amused grunt. "So, the wheels get greased a little better. You know, wouldn't it be nice to close all those bastards down . . . ?"

George, Gant couldn't say in this office, *if you believe that, you've been hanging out with the President too long.* But idealism wasn't all that bad a thing, was it?

"I'll settle for squeezing those Chinese bastards on the trade balance. Ryan's going to back us up?"

"All the way, he says. And I believe him, Mark."

"I guess we'll see. I hope this Rutledge guy can read numbers."

"He went to Harvard," Secretary Winston observed.

"I know," Gant said back. He had his own academic prejudice, having graduated from the University of Chicago twenty years earlier. What the hell was Harvard except a name and an endowment?

Winston chuckled. "They're not all dumb."

"I suppose we'll see, boss. Anyway"—he lifted his suitcase up on its rollers; his computer bag went over his shoulder—"my car's waiting downstairs."

"Good trip, Mark."

Her name was Yang Lien-Hua. She was thirty-four, nine months pregnant, and very frightened. It was her second pregnancy. Her first had been a son whom they had named Ju-Long, a particularly auspicious given name, which translated roughly as Large Dragon. But the youngster had died at the age of four, bumped by a bicycle off the sidewalk into the path of a passenger bus. His death had devastated his parents, and even saddened the local Communist Party officials who'd officiated at the inquest, which had absolved the bus driver of guilt and never identified the careless bicyclist. The loss has been sufficiently hard on Mrs. Yang that she'd sought comfort in a way that this country's government did not especially approve.

That way was Christianity, the foreign religion despised in fact if not exactly in law. In another age she might have found solace in the teachings of Buddha or Confucius, but these, too, had been largely erased from the public consciousness by the Marxist government, which still regarded all religion as a public narcotic. A co-worker had quietly suggested that she meet a "friend" of hers, a man named Yu Fa An. Mrs. Yang had sought him out, and so had begun her first adventure in treason.

Reverend Yu, she found, was a well-educated and -traveled man, which added to his stature in her eyes. He was also a fine listener, who attended to her every word, occasionally pouring her some sympathetic tea, and gently touching her hand when tears streamed down her face. Only when she had finished her tale of woe had he begun his own lessons.

Ju-Long, he told her, was with God, because God was especially solicitous to the needs of innocent children. While she could not see her son at this moment, her son could see her, looking down from Heaven, and while her sorrow was completely understandable, she should believe that the God of the Earth was a God of Mercy and Love who had sent his Only Begotten Son to earth to show mankind the right path, and to give His own life for the sins of humanity. He handed her a Bible printed in the *Gouyu,* the national language of the PRC (also called Mandarin), and helped her find appropriate passages.

It had not been easy for Mrs. Yang, but so deep was her grief that she kept returning for private counseling, finally bringing along her husband, Quon. Mr. Yang proved a harder sell on any religion. He'd served his time in the People's Liberation Army, where he'd been thoroughly indoctrinated in the politics of his nation, and done sufficiently well in his test answers to be sent off to sergeant school, for which political reliability was required. But Quon had been a good father to his little Large Dragon, and he, too, found the void in his belief system too large to bridge easily. This bridge the Reverend Yu provided, and soon both of the Yangs came to his discreet church services, and gradually they'd come to accept their loss with confidence in the continued life of Ju-Long, and the belief that they would someday see him again in the presence of an Almighty God, whose existence became increasingly real to both of them.

Until then, life had to go on. Both worked at their jobs, as factory workers in the same factory, with a working-class apartment in the Di'Anmen district of Beijing near Jingshan—Coal Hill—Park. They labored at their factory during the day, watched state-run television at night, and in due course, Lien-Hua became pregnant again.

And ran afoul of the government's population-control policy that was well to the left of draconian. It had long since been decreed that any married couple could have but one child. A second pregnancy required official government permission. Though this was not generally denied to those whose first child had died, pro forma permission had to be obtained, and in the case of politically unacceptable parents, this permission was generally withheld as a method of controlling the living population, as well. *That* meant that an unauthorized pregnancy had to be terminated. Safely, and at state expense in a state hospital—but terminated.

Christianity translated exactly into political unreliability for the communist government, and unsurprisingly the Ministry of State Security had inserted intelligence officers into Reverend Yu's congregation. This individual—actually there were three, lest one be corrupted by religion and become unreliable himself—had entered the names of the Yangs on a master list of political unreliables. For that reason, when Mrs. Yang Lien-Hua had duly registered her pregnancy, an official letter had appeared in her box, instructing her to go to the Longfu Hospital located on Meishuguan Street for a therapeutic abortion.

This Lien-Hua was unwilling to do. Her given name translated as "Lotus Flower," but inside she was made of much sterner stuff. She wrote a week later to the appropriate government agency, telling them that her pregnancy had miscarried. Given the nature of bureaucracies, her lie was never checked out.

That lie had merely won Lotus Flower six months of ever-increasing stress. She never saw a physician, not even one of the "barefoot medics" that the PRC had invented a generation earlier, much to the admiration of political leftists all over the world. Lien-Hua was healthy and strong, and the human body had been designed by Nature to produce healthy offspring long before the advent of obstetricians. Her swelling belly she was able to hide, mostly, in her ill-fitting clothing. What she could not hide—at least from herself—was her inward fear. She carried a new baby in her belly. She wanted it. She wanted to have another chance at motherhood. She wanted to feel her child suckling at her breast. She wanted to love it and pamper it, watch it learn to crawl and stand and walk and talk, to see it grow beyond four years, enter school, learn and grow into a good adult of whom she could be proud.

The problem was politics. The state enforced its will with ruthlessness. She knew what could happen, the syringe filled with formaldehyde stabbed into the baby's head at the very moment of birth. In China, it was state policy. For the Yangs, it was premeditated, cold-blooded murder, and they were determined not to lose a second child, who, the Reverend Yu had told them, was a gift from God Himself.

And there was a way. If you delivered the baby at home without medical assistance, and if the baby took its first breath, then the state would not kill it. There were some things even the government of the

People's Republic quailed at, and the killing of a living, breathing human infant was one of them. But until it took that breath, it was of no more consequence than a piece of meat in a market. There were even rumors that the Chinese government was selling organs from the aborted newborns on the world's tissue market, to be used for medical purposes, and that was something the Yangs were able to believe.

So, their plan was for Lien-Hua to deliver the child at home, after which they would present their state with a *fait accompli*—and eventually have it baptized by Reverend Yu. To this end, Mrs. Yang had kept herself in good physical shape, walking two kilometers every day, eating sensibly, and generally doing all the things the government-published booklets told expectant mothers to do. And if anything went badly wrong, they'd go to Reverend Yu for counsel and advice. The plan enabled Lien-Hua to deal with the stress—in fact it was a heart-rending terror—of her unauthorized condition.

Well?" Ryan asked.

"Rutledge has all the right talents, and we've given him the instructions he needs. He ought to carry them out properly. Question is, will the Chinese play ball."

"If they don't, things become harder for them," the President said, if not coldly, then with some degree of determination. "If they think they can bully us, Scott, it's time they found out who the big kid in the playground is."

"They'll fight back. They've taken out options on fourteen Boeing 777s—just did that four days ago, remember? That's the first thing they'll chop if they don't like us. That's a lot of money and a lot of jobs for Boeing in Seattle," SecState warned.

"I never have been real big on blackmail, Scott. Besides, that's a classic case of penny-wise, pound-foolish. If we cave because of that, then we lose ten times the money and ten times the jobs elsewhere—okay, they won't be all in one place, and so the TV news guys won't be able to point their cameras, and so they won't do the real story, just the one that can fit on half-inch tape. But I'm not in here to keep the goddamned media happy. I'm here to serve the people to the best of my ability, Scott. And that's by-God going to happen," POTUS promised his guest.

"I don't doubt it, Jack," Adler responded. "Just remember that it won't play out quite the way you want it to."

"It never does, but if they play rough, it's going to cost them seventy billion dollars a year. We can afford to do without their products. Can they afford to do without our money?" Ryan asked.

Secretary Adler was not totally comfortable with the way the question was posed. "I suppose we'll have to wait and see."

CHAPTER 21

Simmering

"So, what did you develop last night?" Reilly asked. He'd be late to his embassy office, but his gut told him that things were breaking loose in the RPG Case—that was how he thought of it—and Director Murray had a personal interest in the case, because the President did, and *that* made it more important than the routine bullshit on Reilly's desk.

"Our Chinese friend—the one in the men's room, that is—is the Third Secretary at their mission. Our friends across town at SVR have suspected that he is a member of their Ministry for State Security. He's not regarded as a particularly bright diplomat by the Foreign Ministry—ours, that is."

"That's how you cover a spook," Reilly agreed. "A dumb cookie-pusher. Okay, so he's a player."

"I agree, Mishka," Provalov said. "Now, it would be nice to know who passed what to whom."

"Oleg Gregoriyevich"—Reilly liked the semiformal Russian form of address—"if I'd been standing right there and staring, I might not have been able to tell." That was the problem dealing with real professionals. They were as good at that maneuver as a Vegas dealer was with a deck of Bicycles. You needed a good lens and a slow-motion camera to be sure, and that was a little bulky for work in the field. But they'd just proved, to their satisfaction at least, that both men were active in the spook business, and that was a break in the case any way you sliced it. "ID the girl?"

"Yelena Ivanova Dimitrova." Provalov handed the folder across. "Just a whore, but, of course, a very expensive one."

Reilly flipped it open and scanned the notes. Known prostitute specializing in foreigners. The photo of her was unusually flattering.

"You came in early this morning?" Reilly asked. He must have, to have all this work done already.

"Before six," Oleg confirmed. The case was becoming more exciting for him as well. "In any case, Klementi Ivan'ch kept her all night. She left his apartment and caught a taxi home at seven-forty this morning. She looked happy and satisfied, according to my people."

That was good for a chuckle. She didn't leave her trick until after Oleg hit the office? *That* must have affected his attitude somewhat, Reilly thought, with an inward grin. It sure as hell would have affected his. "Well, good for our subject. I expect he won't be getting too much of that in a few months," the FBI agent thought aloud, hoping it would make his Russian colleague a little happier about life.

"One can hope," Provalov agreed coldly. "I have four men watching his apartment. If he leaves and appears to be heading away for a while, I will try to get a team into his apartment to plant some electronic surveillance."

"They know how to be careful?" Reilly asked. If this Suvorov mutt was as trained as they thought, he'd leave telltales in his apartment that could make breaking in dicey.

"They are KGB-trained also. One of them helped catch a French intelligence officer back in the old times. Now, I have a question for you," the Russian cop said.

"Shoot."

"What do you know of a special counterterrorist group based in England?"

"The 'Men of Black,' you mean?"

Provalov nodded. "Yes. Do you know anything about them?"

Reilly knew he had to watch his words, even though he knew damned little. "Really, I don't know anything more than what I've seen in the papers. It's some sort of multinational NATO group, part military and part police, I think. They had a good run of luck last year. Why do you ask?"

"A request from on high, because I know you. I've been told that they are coming to Moscow to assist in training our people—Spetsnaz groups with similar tasks," Oleg explained.

"Really? Well, I've never been in the muscle end of the Bureau, just in a local SWAT team once. Gus Werner probably knows a lot about them. Gus runs the new Counter-Terrorism Division at Headquarters. Before that, Gus ran HRT and had a field command—a field division, that is, a big-city field office. I've met him once, just to say hello. Gus has a very good service rep."

"Rep?"

"Reputation, Oleg. He's well regarded by the field agents. But like I said, that's the muscle end of the Bureau. I've always been with the chess players."

"Investigations, you mean."

Reilly nodded. "That's right. It's what the FBI is supposed to be all about, but the outfit's mutated a bit over the years." The American paused. "So, you're covering this Suvorov/Koniev guy real tight?" Reilly asked, to recenter the discussion.

"My men have orders to be discreet, but yes, we will keep a close eye on him, as you say."

"You know, if he really is working with the Chinese spooks . . . do you think they might want to kill that Golovko guy?"

"I do not know, but we must regard that as a real possibility."

Reilly nodded, thinking this would make an interesting report to send to Washington, and maybe discuss with the CIA station chief as well.

I want the files for everyone who ever worked with him," Sergey Nikolay'ch ordered. "And I want *you* to get me his personal file."

"Yes, Comrade Chairman," Major Shelepin replied, with a bob of the head.

The morning briefing, delivered by a colonel of the militia, had pleased neither the SVR Chairman nor his principal bodyguard. In this case, for a change, the legendarily slow Russian bureaucracy had been circumvented, and the information fast-tracked to those interested in it. That included the man whose life might have been spared accidentally after all.

"And we will set up a special-action group to work with this Provalov child."

"Of course, Comrade Chairman."

It was strange, Sergey Nikolay'ch thought, how rapidly the world could change. He vividly remembered the morning of the murder—it was not the sort of thing a man could forget. But after the first few days of shock and attendant fear, he'd allowed himself to relax, to believe that this Avseyenko had been the real target of an underworld rub out—an archaic American term he liked—and that his own life had never been directly threatened. With the acceptance of that belief, the entire thing had become like driving past an ordinary traffic accident. Even if some unfortunate motorist had been killed there at the side of the road, you just dismissed it as an irrelevance, because that sort of thing couldn't happen to you in your own expensive official car, not with Anatoliy driving. But now he'd begun to wonder if perhaps his life had been *spared* by accident. Such things were not supposed to occur—there shouldn't have been any need for them.

Now he was more frightened than he'd been that bright Moscow morning, looking down from his window at the smoking wreck on the pavement. It meant that he might be in danger still, and he dreaded that prospect as much as the next man.

Worse still, his hunter might well be one of his own, a former KGB officer with connections to Spetsnaz, and if he were in contact with the Chinese . . .

. . . But why would the Chinese wish to end his life? For that matter, why would the Chinese wish to perform any such crime in a foreign land? It was beyond imprudent.

None of this made any sense, but as a career intelligence officer, Golovko had long since shed the illusion that the world was supposed to make sense. What he did know was that he needed more information, and at least he was in a very good place to seek it out. If he wasn't as powerful as he might once have been, he was still powerful enough for his own purposes, Golovko told himself.

Probably.

He didn't try to come to the ministry very often. It was just a routine security measure, but a sensible one. Once you recruited an agent, you didn't want to hang out with him or her for fear of compromise. That was one of the things they taught you at The Farm. If you compromised one of your agents, you might have trouble sleeping at night, because CIA was usually active in countries where the Miranda warning was delivered by a gun or knife or fist, or something just as bad—as unpleasant as a police state could make it, and that, the instructors had told his class, could be pretty fuckin' unpleasant. Especially in a case like this, he was intimate with this agent, and breaking away from her could cause her to stop her cooperation, which, Langley had told him, was pretty damned good, and they wanted more of it. Erasing the program he'd had her input on her machine would be difficult for a CalTech-trained genius, but you could accomplish the same thing by clobbering the whole hard drive and reinstalling new files over the old ones, because the valuable little gopher file was hidden in the system software, and a write-over would destroy it as surely as the San Francisco Earthquake.

So, he didn't want to be here, exactly, but he was a businessman, in addition to being a spook, and the client had called him in. The girl two desks away from Ming had a computer problem, and he was the NEC rep for the ministry offices.

It turned out to be a minor problem—you just couldn't turn some women loose on computers. It was like loosing a four-year-old in a gun shop, he thought, but didn't dare say such things aloud in these liberated times, even here. Happily, Ming hadn't been in sight when he'd come in. He'd walked over to the desk with the problem and fixed it in about three minutes, explaining the error to the secretary in simple terms she was sure to understand, and which would now make her the office expert for an easily replicated problem. With a smile and a polite Japanese bow, he'd made his way to the door, when the door to the inner office opened, and Ming came out with her Minister Fang behind her, looking down at some papers.

"Oh, hello, Nomuri-san," Ming said in surprise, as Fang called the name "Chai," and waved to another of the girls to follow him in. If Fang saw Nomuri there, he didn't acknowledge it, simply disappeared back into his private office.

"Hello, Comrade Ming," the American said, speaking in English. "Your computer operates properly?" he asked formally.

"Yes, it does, thank you."

"Good. Well, if you experience a problem, you have my card."

"Oh, yes. You are well settled in to Beijing now?" she asked politely.

"Yes, thank you, I am."

"You should try Chinese food instead of sticking to the food of your homeland, though, I admit, I have developed a taste lately for Japanese sausage," she told him, and everyone else in the room, with a face that would have done Amarillo Slim proud.

For his part, Chester Nomuri felt his heart not so much skip a beat as stop entirely for about ten seconds, or so it seemed. "Ah, yes," he had to say in reply, as soon as he got breath back in his lungs. "It can be very tasty."

Ming just nodded and went to her desk and back to work. Nomuri nodded and bowed politely to the office and made his departure as well, then headed down the corridor immediately for a men's room, the need to urinate urgent. Sweet Jesus. But that was one of the problems with agents. They sometimes got off on their work the way a drug addict got off on the immediate rush when the chemical hit his system, and they'd tickle the dragon with their new and playful enthusiasm just to experience a little more of the rush, forgetting that the dragon's tail was a lot closer to its mouth than it appeared. It was foolish to enjoy danger. Zipping himself back up, he told himself that he hadn't broken training, hadn't stumbled on his reply to her playful observation. But he had to warn her about dancing in a minefield. You never really knew where to put your feet, and discovering the wrong places was usually painful.

That's when he realized why it had happened, and the thought stopped him dead in his tracks. Ming loved him. She was playful because . . . well, why else would she have said that? As a game? Did she regard the whole thing as a game? No, she wasn't the right personality type to be a hooker. The sex had been good, maybe too good—if such a thing were possible, Nomuri thought as he resumed walking toward the elevator. She'd surely be over tonight after saying that. He'd have to stop by the liquor store on the way home and get some more of that awful Japanese scotch for thirty bucks a liter. A working man couldn't afford to get drunk here unless he drank the local stuff, and that was too vile to contemplate.

But Ming had just consecrated their relationship by risking her life in front of her minister and her co-workers, and that was far more frightening to Nomuri than her ill-considered remark about his dick and her fondness for it. *Jesus,* he thought, *this is getting too serious.* But what could he do now? He'd seduced her and made a spy of her, and she'd fallen for him for no better reason, probably, than that he was younger than the old fucker she worked for, and was far nicer to her. Okay, so he was pretty good in the sack, and that was excellent for his male ego, and he was a stranger in a strange land and he had to get his rocks off, too, and doing it with her was probably safer to his cover than picking up some hooker in a bar—and he didn't even want to consider getting seriously involved with a real girl in his real life—

—but how was *this* so different from *that?* he asked himself. Aside from the fact that while she was loving him, her computer was sending her transcribed notes off into the etherworld. . . .

It was doing it again soon after the close of regular business hours, and the eleven-hour differential pretty much guaranteed that it arrived on the desks of American officials soon after their breakfasts. In the case of Mary Patricia Foley, mornings were far less hectic than they'd once been. Her youngest was not yet in college, but preferred to fix her own oatmeal from the Quaker envelopes, and now drove herself to school, which allowed her mother an extra twenty-five minutes or so of additional sleep every morning. Twenty years of being a field spook and mother should have been enough to drive her to distracted insanity, but it was, actually, a life she'd enjoyed, especially her years in Moscow, doing her business right there in the belly of the beast, and giving the bastard quite an ulcer at the time, she remembered with a smile.

Her husband could say much the same. The first husband-wife team to rise so high at Langley, they drove together to work every morning—in their own car rather than the "company" one to which they were entitled, but with lead and chase cars full of people with guns, because any terrorist with half a brain would regard them as targets more valuable than rubies. This way they could talk on the way in—and the car was swept for bugs on a weekly basis.

They took their usual reserved and oversized place in the basement of the Old Headquarters Building, then rode up in the executive elevator, which somehow was always waiting for them, to their seventh-floor offices.

Mrs. Foley's desk was always arrayed just so. The overnight crew had all her important papers arranged just so, also. But today, as she had for the last week, instead of looking over the striped-border folders full of Top Secret Codeworded material, she first of all flipped on her desktop computer and checked her special e-mail. This morning was no disappointment. She copied the file electronically to her hard drive, printed up a hard copy, and when that was off her printer, deleted the e-mail from her system, effectively erasing it from electronic existence. Then she reread the paper copy and lifted the phone for her husband's office.

"Yeah, baby?"

"Some egg-drop soup," she told the Director of Central Intelligence. It was a Chinese dish he found especially vile, and she enjoyed teasing her husband.

"Okay, honey. Come on in." It had to be pretty good if she was trying to turn his stomach over this early in the friggin' morning, the DCI knew.

More Sorge?" the President asked, seventy-five minutes later.

"Yes, sir," Ben Goodley replied, handing the sheet over. It wasn't long, but it was interesting.

Ryan skimmed through it. "Analysis?"

"Mrs. Foley wants to go over it with you this afternoon. You have a slot at two-fifteen."

"Okay. Who else?"

"The Vice President, since he's around." Goodley knew that Ryan liked to have Robby Jackson in for strategically interesting material. "He's fairly free this afternoon as well."

"Good. Set it up," POTUS ordered.

Six blocks away, Dan Murray was just arriving at his capacious office (considerably larger than the President's, as a matter of fact) with his own security detail, because he, as the country's principal counterintelligence and counterterrorist officer, had all manner of information that others were interested in. This morning only brought in some more.

"Morning, Director," one of the staff said—she was a sworn agent carrying a side arm, not just a secretary.

"Hey, Toni," Murray responded. This agent had very nice wheels, but the FBI Director realized that he'd just proven to himself that his wife, Liz, was right: He was turning into a dirty old man.

The piles on the desk were arranged by the overnight staff, and there was a routine for this. The rightward-most pile was for intelligence-related material, the leftward-most for counterintelligence operations, and the big one in the middle was for ongoing criminal investigations requiring his personal attention or notification. That tradition went back to "Mr. Hoover," as he was remembered at the FBI, who seemingly went over every field case bigger than the theft of used cars off the government parking lot.

But Murray had long worked the "black" side of the Bureau, and that meant he attacked the rightward pile first. There wasn't much there. The FBI was running some of its own pure intelligence operations at the moment, somewhat to the discomfort of CIA—but those two government agencies had never gotten along terribly well, even though Murray rather liked the Foleys. What the hell, he thought, a little competition was good for everybody, so long as CIA didn't mess with a criminal investigation, which would be a very different kettle of fish. The top report was from Mike Reilly in Moscow. . . .

"Damn . . ." Murray breathed. Then an inward smile. Murray had personally selected Reilly for the Moscow slot, over the objections of some of his senior people, who had all wanted Paul Landau out of the Intelligence Division. But no, Murray had decided, Moscow needed help with cop work, not spy-chasing, at which they had lots of good experience, and so he'd sent Mike, a second-generation agent who, like his father, Pat Reilly, had given the Mafia in New York City a serious case of indigestion. Landau was now in Berlin, playing with the German Bundeskriminalamt, the BKA, doing regular crime liaison stuff, and doing it pretty well. But Reilly was a potential star. His dad had retired an ASAC. Mike would do better than that.

And the way he'd bonded with this Russian detective, Provalov, wouldn't hurt his career one bit. So. They'd uncovered a link between a former KGB officer and the Chinese MSS, eh? And this was part of the investigation into the big ka-boom in Moscow . . . ? Jesus, could the Chinese have had a part in that? If so, what the hell did *that* mean? Now, *this* was something the Foleys had to see. To that end, Director Murray lifted his phone. Ten minutes later, the Moscow document slid into his secure fax machine to Langley—and just to make sure that CIA didn't take credit for an FBI job, a hard copy was hand-carried to the White House, where it was handed to Dr. Benjamin Goodley, who'd surely show it to the President before lunch.

It had gotten to the point that he recognized her knock at the door. Nomuri set his drink down and jumped to answer, pulling it open less than five seconds after the first sexy *tap tap.*

"Ming," Chet said.

"Nomuri-san," she greeted in turn.

He pulled her in the door, closed, and locked it. Then he lifted her off the floor with a passionate hug that was less than three percent feigned.

"So, you have a taste for Japanese sausage, eh?" he demanded, with a smile and a kiss.

"You didn't even smile when I said it. Wasn't it funny?" she asked, as he undid a few of her buttons.

"Ming—" Then he hesitated and tried something he'd learned earlier in the day. *"Bau-bei,"* he said instead. It translated to "beloved one."

Ming smiled at the words and made her own reply: *"Shing-gan,"* which literally meant "heart and liver," but in context meant "heart and soul."

"Beloved one," Nomuri said, after a kiss, "do you advertise our relationship at your office?"

"No, Minister Fang might not approve, but the other girls in the office probably would not object if they found out," she explained, with a coquettish smile. "But you never know."

"Then why risk exposing yourself by making such a joke, unless you wish *me* to betray you?"

"You have no sense of humor," Ming observed. But then she ran her hands under his shirt and up his chest. "But that is all right. You have the other things I need."

Afterward, it was time to do business.

"Bau-bei?"

"Yes?"

"Your computer still works properly?"

"Oh, yes," she assured him in a sleepy voice.

His left hand stroked her body gently. "Do any of the other girls in the office use their computers to surf the 'Net?"

"Only Chai. Fang uses her as he uses me. In fact, he likes her better. He thinks she has a better mouth."

"Oh?" Nomuri asked, softening the question with a smile.

"I told you, Minister Fang is an old man. Sometimes he needs special encouragement, and Chai doesn't mind so much. Fang reminds her of her grandfather, she says," Ming told him.

Which was good in the American's mind for a *Yuck!* and little else. "So, all the girls in the office trade notes on your minister?"

Ming laughed. It was pretty funny. "Of course. We all do."

Damn, Nomuri thought. He'd always thought that women would be more . . . discreet, that it was just the men who bragged in the locker room over their sweat socks.

"The first time he did me," she went on, "I didn't know what to do, so I talked with Chai for advice. She's been there the longest, you see. She just said to enjoy it, and try to make him happy, and I might get a nice office chair out of it, like she did. Chai must be very good to him. She got a new bicycle last November. Me, well, I think he only likes me because I'm a little different to look at. Chai has bigger breasts than I do, and I think I'm prettier, but she has a sweet disposition, and she likes the old man. More than I do, anyway." She paused. "I don't want a new bicycle enough for that."

What does this mean?" Robby Jackson asked.

"Well, we're not sure," the DCI admitted. "This Fang guy had a long talk with our old friend Zhang Han San. They're talking about the meeting with our trade team that starts tomorrow. Hell"—Ed Foley looked at his watch—"call that fourteen hours from now. And it looks as though they want concessions from us instead of offering any to us. They're even angrier over our recognition of Taiwan than we'd anticipated."

"Tough shit," Ryan observed.

"Jack, I agree with your sentiment, but let's try not to be overcavalier about their opinions, shall we?" Foley suggested.

"You're starting to sound like Scott," the President said.

"So? You want a yes-man handling Langley, you got the wrong guy," the DCI countered.

"Fair enough, Ed," Jack conceded. "Go on."

"Jack, we need to warn Rutledge that the PRC isn't going to like what he has to say. They may not be in a mood to make many trade concessions."

"Well, neither is the United States of America," Ryan told his Director of Central Intelligence. "And we come back to the fact that they need our money more than we need their trade goods."

"What's the chance that this is a setup, this information I mean?" Vice President Jackson asked.

"You mean that they're using this source as a conduit to get back-channel information to us?" Mary Patricia Foley asked. "I evaluate that chance as practically zero. As close to zero as something in the real world can be."

"MP, how can you be that confident?" President Ryan asked.

"Not here, Jack, but I *am* that confident," Mary Pat said, somewhat to the discomfort of her husband, Ryan saw. It was rare in the intelligence community for anyone to feel that confident about anything, but Ed had always been the careful one, and Mary Pat had always been the cowgirl. She was as loyal to her people as a mother was to her infant, and Ryan admired that, even though he also had to remind himself that it wasn't always realistic.

"Ed?" Ryan asked, just to see.

"I back Mary up on this one. This source appears to be gold-plated and copper-bottomed."

"So, this document represents the view of their government?" TOMCAT asked.

Foley surprised the Vice President by shaking his head. "No, it represents the view of this Zhang Han San guy. He's a powerful and influential minister, but he doesn't speak for their government per se. Note that the text here doesn't say what their official position is. Zhang probably does represent a view, and a powerful view, inside their Politburo. There are also moderates whose position this document does not address."

"Okay, great," Robby said, shifting in his seat, "so why are you taking up our time with this stuff, then?"

"This Zhang guy is tight with their Defense Minister—in fact he has a major voice in their entire national-security establishment. If he's expanding his influence into trade policy, we have a problem, and our trade negotiations team needs to know that up front," the DCI informed them.

"So?" Ming asked tiredly. She hated getting dressed and leaving, and it meant a night of not-enough sleep.

"So, you should get in early and upload this on Chai's computer. It's just a new system file, the new one, six-point-eight-point-one, like the one I uploaded on your computer." In fact, the newest real system file was 6.3.2, and so there was at least a year until a write-over would actually be necessary.

"Why do you have me do this?"

"Does it matter, *Bau-Bei?*" he asked.

She actually hesitated, thinking it over a bit, and the second or so of uncertainty chilled the American spy. "No, I suppose not."

"I need to get you some new things," Nomuri whispered, taking her in his arms.

"Like what?" she asked. All his previous gifts had been noteworthy.

"It will be a surprise, and a good one," he promised.

Her dark eyes sparkled with anticipation. Nomuri helped her on with her dreadful jacket. Dressing her back up was not nearly as fun as undressing her, but that was to be expected. A moment later, he gave her the final goodbye kiss at the door, and watched her depart, then went back to his computer to tell patsbakery@brownienet.com that he'd arranged for a second recipe that he hoped she might find tasty.

CHAPTER 22

The Table and the Recipe

"Minister, this is a pleasure," Cliff Rutledge said in his friendliest diplomatic voice, shaking hands. Rutledge was glad the PRC had adopted the Western custom—he'd never learned the exact protocol of bowing.

Carl Hitch, the U.S. Ambassador to the People's Republic, was there for the opening ceremony. He was a career foreign service officer who'd always preferred working abroad to working at Foggy Bottom. Running day-to-day diplomatic relations wasn't especially exciting, but in a place like this, it did require a steady hand. Hitch had that, and he was apparently well liked by the rest of the diplomatic community, which didn't hurt.

It was all new for Mark Gant, however. The room was impressive, like the boardroom of a major corporation—designed to keep the board members happy, like noblemen from medieval Italy. It had high ceilings and fabric-covered walls—Chinese silk, in this case, red, of course, so that the effect was rather like crawling inside the heart of a whale, complete with chandeliers, cut crystal, and polished brass. Everyone had a tiny glass of mao-tai, which really was like drinking flavored lighter fluid, as he'd been warned.

"It is your first time in Beijing?" some minor official asked him.

Gant turned to look down at the little guy. "Yes, it is."

"Too soon for first impressions, then?"

"Yes, but this room is quite stunning . . . but then silk is something with which your people have a long and fruitful history," he went on, wondering if he sounded diplomatic or merely awkward.

"This is so, yes," the official agreed with a toothy grin and a nod, neither of which told the visiting American much of anything, except that he didn't waste much money on toothbrushes.

"I have heard much of the imperial art collection."

"You will see it," the official promised. "It is part of the official program."

"Excellent. In addition to my duties, I would like to play tourist."

"I hope you will find us acceptable hosts," the little guy said. For his part, Gant was wondering if this smiling, bowing dwarf would hit his knees and offer a blow job, but diplomacy was an entirely new area for him. These were not investment bankers, who were generally polite sharks, giving you good food and drink before sitting you down and trying to bite your dick off. But they never concealed the fact that they were sharks. These people—he just wasn't sure. This degree of politeness and solicitude was a new experience for Gant, but given his pre-mission brief, he wondered if the hospitality only presaged an unusually hostile meeting when they got to business. If the two things had to balance out, then the downside of this seesaw was going to be a son of a bitch, he was sure.

"So, you are not from the American State Department?" the Chinese man asked.

"No. I'm in the Department of the Treasury. I work directly for Secretary Winston."

"Ah, then you are from the trading business?"

So, the little bastard's been briefed . . . But that was to be expected. At this level of government you didn't freelance things. Everyone would be thoroughly briefed. Everyone would have read the book on the Americans. The State Department members of the American crew had done the same. Gant, however, had not, since he wasn't really a player per se, and had only been told what he needed to know. That gave him an advantage over the Chinese assigned to look after him. He was not State Department, hence should not have been regarded as important—but he was the personal representative of a very senior American official, known to be part of that man's inner circle, and that made him very important indeed. Perhaps he was even a principal adviser to the Rutledge man—and in a Chinese context, that might even mean that he, Gant, was the man actually running the negotiations rather than the titular chief diplomat, because the Chinese often ran things that way. It occurred to Gant that maybe he could fuck with their minds a little bit . . . but how to go about it?

"Oh, yes, I've been a capitalist all my life," Gant said, deciding to play it cool and just talk to the guy as though he were a human being and not a fucking communist diplomat. "So has Secretary Winston, and so has our President, you know."

"But he was mainly an intelligence officer, or so I have been told."

Time to stick the needle: "I suppose that's partly true, but his heart is in business, I think. After he leaves government service, he and George will probably go into business together and really take the world over." Which was almost true, Gant thought, remembering that the best lies usually were.

"And you have worked some years with Secretary Winston." A statement rather than a question, Gant noted. How to answer it? How much did they really know about him . . . or was he a man of mystery to the ChiComms? If so, could he make that work for him . . . ?

A gentle, knowing smile. "Well, yeah, George and I made a little money together. When Jack brought him into the cabinet, George decided that he wanted me to come down with him and help make a little government policy. Especially tax policy. That's been a real mess, and George turned me loose on it. And you know? We just might get all of that changed. It looks as though Congress is going to do what we told them to do, and that's not bad, making those idiots do what we want them to do," Gant observed, looking rather deliberately at the carved ivory fixture on the wooden display cabinet. Some craftsman with a sharp knife had spent a lot of time to get that thing just right . . . *So, Mr. Chinaman, do I look important now?* One thing about this guy. He would have been a pretty good poker player. His eyes told you nothing at all. Not a fucking thing. Gant looked down at the guy again. "Excuse me. I talk too much."

The official smiled. "There is much of that at times like this. Why do you suppose everyone gets something to drink?" Amusement in his voice, letting Gant know, perhaps, who was really running this affair . . . ?

"I suppose," Gant observed diffidently and wandered off with the junior—or was he?—official in tow.

For his part, Rutledge was trying to decide if the opposition knew what his instructions were. There had been a few leaked hints in the media, but Adler had arranged the leaks with skill, so that even a careful observer—and the PRC ambassador in Washington was one of those—might have trouble deciding who was leaking what, and to what purpose. The Ryan administration had utilized the press with a fair degree of skill, probably, Rutledge thought, because the cabinet officers mainly took their lead from Ryan's chief of staff, Arnie van Damm, who was a very skillful political operator. The new cabinet didn't have the usual collection of in-and-out political figures who needed to stroke the press to further their own agendas. Ryan had chiefly selected people with no real agenda at all, which was no small feat—especially since most of them seemed to be competent technicians who, like Ryan, only seemed to want to escape Washington with their virtue intact and return to their real lives as soon as they finished serving their country for a short period of time. The career diplomat had not thought it possible that his country's government could be so transformed. He assigned credit for all this to that madman Japanese pilot who'd killed so much of official Washington in that one lunatic gesture.

It was then that Xu Kun Piao showed up, sweeping in to the greeting room with his official entourage. Xu was General Secretary of the Communist Party of the People's Republic of China, and Chairman of the Chinese Politburo, though referred to in the media as the country's "Premier," which was something of a misnomer, but one adopted even in the diplomatic community. He was a man of seventy-one years, one of the second generation of Chinese leaders. The Long March survivors had long since died out—there were some senior officials who claimed to have been there, but a check of the numbers showed that if they had, they'd been sucking their mothers' nipples at the time, and those men were not taken seriously. No, the current crop of Chinese political leaders were mainly the sons or nephews of the original set, raised in privilege and relative comfort, but always mindful of the fact that their place in life was a precarious one. On one side were the other political children who craved advancement beyond their parents' places, and to achieve that they'd been more Catholic than the local communist pope. They'd carried their *Little Red Book*s high as adults during the Cultural Revolution, and before that they'd kept their mouths shut and ears open during the abortive and predatory "Hundred Flowers" campaign of the late '50s, which had trapped a lot of intellectuals who'd thought to keep hidden for the first decade of Maoist rule. They'd been enticed into the open by Mao's own solicitation for their ideas, which they'd foolishly given out, and in the process only extended their necks over the broad block for the axe that fell a few years later in the brutal, cannibalistic Cultural Revolution.

The current Politburo members had survived in two ways. First, they'd been secured by their fathers and the rank that attached to such lofty parentage. Second, they'd been carefully warned about what they could say and what they could not say, and so all along they'd observed cautiously, always saying out loud that Chairman Mao's ideas were those which China really needed, and that the others, while interesting, perhaps, in a narrow intellectual sense, were dangerous insofar as they distracted the workers and peasants from The True Way of Mao. And so when the axe had fallen, borne as it had been by the *Little Red Book,* they'd been among the first to carry and show that book to others, and so escaped the destruction for the most part—a few of their number had been sacrificed, of course, but none of the really smart ones who now shared the seats on the Politburo. It had been a brutal Darwinian process that they had all gotten through by being a little smarter than those around them, and now, at the peak of the power won for them by brains and caution, it was time for them to enjoy that which they'd earned.

The new crop of leaders accepted communism as truly as other men believed in God, because they'd learned nothing else, and had not exercised their intellectual agility to seek another faith, or even to seek solutions to the questions that Marxism could not answer. Theirs was a faith of resignation rather than enthusiasm. Raised within a circumscribed intellectual box, they never ventured out of it, for they feared what they might find out there. In the past twenty years, they'd been forced to allow capitalism to blossom within the borders of their country, because that country needed money to grow into something more powerful than the failed experiment in the Democratic Republic of Korea. China had experienced its own killer famine around 1960, and slowly learned from it and the Chinese also used it as a launching point for the Cultural Revolution, thus gaining political capital from a self-imposed disaster.

They wanted their nation to be great. In fact, they already regarded it as such, but recognized the fact that other nations lacked this appreciation, and so they had to seek out the means to correct the misimpression foolishly held by the rest of the world. That had meant money, and money had meant industry, and industry required capitalists. It was something they had figured out before the foolish Soviets to their north and west. And so the Soviet Union had fallen, but the People's Republic of China remained.

Or so they all believed. They looked out, when they bothered themselves to do so, at a world that they pretended to understand and to which they felt superior for no better reason than their skin and their language—ideology came second in their self-reckoning; *amour propre* starts from within. They expected people to defer to them, and the previous years of interactive diplomacy with the surrounding world had not altered their outlook very much.

But in this, they suffered from their own illusions. Henry Kissinger had come to China in 1971 at the behest of President Richard Nixon not so much from his perceived need to establish normal relations with the world's most populous nation as to use the PRC as a stick with which to beat the Soviet Union into submission. In fact Nixon had begun a process so lengthy as to be considered beyond Western capabilities—it was more the sort of thing that Westerners thought the Chinese themselves capable of conceiving. With such ideas, people merely show ethnic prejudices of one sort or another. The typical chief of a totalitarian government is far too self-centered to think much beyond his own lifetime, and men all over the world live roughly the same number of years. For that simple reason, they all think in terms of programs that can be completed in their own living sight, and little beyond, because they were all men who'd torn down the statues of others, and such men had few illusions over the fate of their own monuments. It was only as they faced death that they considered what they had done, and Mao had conceded bleakly to Henry Kissinger that all he'd accomplished had been to change the lives of peasants within a few miles of Beijing.

But the men in this ceremonial room were not yet close enough to death to think in such terms. They were the magisters of their land. They made the rules that others followed. Their words were law. Their whims were granted with alacrity. People looked upon them as they once looked upon the emperors and princes of old. All a man could wish to have, they had. Most of all, they had the power. It was their wishes that ruled their vast and ancient land. Their communist ideology was merely the magic that defined the form their wishes took, the rules of the game they had all agreed to play all those years before. The power was the thing. They could grant life or take it with the stroke of a pen—or more realistically, a dictated word, taken down by a personal secretary, for transmission to the underling who squeezed the trigger.

Xu was a man of average everything—height, weight, eyes, and face . . . and intellect, some said. Rutledge had read all this in his briefing documents. The real power was elsewhere. Xu was a figurehead of sorts, chosen for his looks, partially; his ability to give a speech, certainly; and his ability to front the occasional idea of others on the Politburo, to simulate conviction. Like a Hollywood actor, he didn't so much have to be smart as to play smart.

"Comrade Premier," Rutledge said in greeting, holding out his hand, which the Chinese man took.

"Mr. Rutledge," Xu replied in passable English. There was an interpreter there, too, for the more complex thoughts. "Welcome to Beijing."

"It is my pleasure, and my honor, to visit your ancient country again," the American diplomat said, showing proper respect and subservience, the Chinese leader thought.

"It is always a pleasure to welcome a friend," Xu went on, as he'd been briefed to do. Rutledge had been to China before in his official capacity, but never before as a delegation leader. He was known to the Chinese Foreign Ministry as a diplomat who'd climbed his way up the ladder of his bureaucracy, much as they did in their own—a mere technician, but a high-ranking one. The Politburo chief raised his glass. "I drink to successful and cordial negotiations."

Rutledge smiled and hoisted his glass as well. "As do I, sir."

The cameras got it. The news media people were circulating around, too. The cameramen were doing mainly what they called "locator" shots, like any amateur would do with his less expensive minicam. They showed the room at an artificial distance, so that the viewers could see the colors, with a few close-ups of the furniture on which no one was supposed to sit, with somewhat closer shots of the major participants drinking their drinks and looking pleasant to one another—this was called "B-roll," intended to show viewers what it was like to be at a large, formal, and not overly pleasant cocktail party. The real news coverage for the event would be by people like Barry Wise and the other talking heads, who would tell the viewer what the visuals could not.

Then the coverage would shift back to CNN's Washington studio, down the hill from Union Station, where other talking heads would discuss what had been leaked or not leaked to them, then discuss what they in their personal sagacious wisdom thought the proper course for the United States of America ought to be. President Ryan would see all this over breakfast, as he read the papers and the government-produced *Early Bird* clipping service. Over breakfast, Jack Ryan would make his own terse comments to be noted by his wife, who might discuss it over lunch with her colleagues at Johns Hopkins, who might discuss it with their spouses, from whom it would go no farther. In this way, the President's thoughts often remained a mystery.

The party broke up at the predetermined hour, and the Americans headed back to the embassy in their official cars.

"So, what can you tell us off the record?" Barry asked Rutledge, in the sanctity of the stretch Lincoln's back seat.

"Not much, really," the Assistant Secretary of State for Policy replied. "We'll listen to what they have to say, and they'll listen to what we have to say, and it'll go from there."

"They want MFN. Will they get it?"

"That's not for me to decide, Barry, and you know that." Rutledge was too tired and jet-lagged for intelligent conversation at the moment. He didn't trust himself to speak under these circumstances, and figured Wise knew that. The reporter was leaning on him for just that reason.

"So, what are you going to talk about?"

"Obviously, we'd like the Chinese to open their markets more, and also to take a closer look at some issues we have, like patent and copyright violations that American business has complained about."

"The Dell Computer issue?"

Rutledge nodded. "Yes, that's one." Then he yawned. "Excuse me. The long flight . . . you know how it is."

"I was on the same airplane," Barry Wise pointed out.

"Well, maybe you're just better at this than I am," Rutledge offered. "Can we postpone this discussion a day or so?"

"If you say so," the CNN reporter agreed. He didn't much like this preppy asshole, but he was a source of information, and Wise was in the information business. The ride was a brief one in any case. The official delegation hopped out at the embassy, and the embassy cars took the newsies back to their hotels.

The embassy had sleeping accommodations for the entire official party, mainly to ensure that anything they said wouldn't be recorded by the MSS bugs in every hotel room in the city. This was not to say that the accommodations were palatial, though Rutledge had a comfortable room. Here protocol failed Mark Gant, but he did have a comfortable single bed in his small private room and a shared bathroom with a shower. He opted instead for a hot bath and one of the sleeping pills the physician who accompanied the official party had issued him. It was supposed to give him a solid eight hours or so, which would just about synchronize him with local time by the morning. There would then be a big working breakfast, much like the astronauts got before a shuttle launch, and as much of an American tradition as the Stars and Stripes over Fort McHenry.

Nomuri caught the arrival of the trade delegation on Chinese TV, which he watched mainly to hone his language skills. These were improving, though the tonal nature of Mandarin drove him slightly nuts. He'd once thought Japanese was hard, but it was a walk in the park compared to Guoyu. He looked at the faces, wondering who they were. The Chinese narrator helped, stumbling badly over "Rutledge," however. Well, Americans murdered Chinese names, too, except for simple ones like Ming and Wang, and listening to an American businesman try to make himself understood to a local was enough to make Nomuri gag. The commentator went on to talk about the Chinese position on the trade talks, how America owed the PRC all manner of concessions—after all, was not China generous in allowing Americans to spend their worthless dollars for the valuable products of the People's Republic? In this, China sounded a lot like Japan had once done, but the new Japanese government had opened up their markets. While there was still a trade deficit in Japan's favor, fair competition on the playing field had muted American criticism, though Japanese cars were still less welcome in America than they had been. But that would pass, Nomuri was sure. If America had a weakness it was in forgiving and forgetting too rapidly. In this, he greatly admired the Jews. They still hadn't forgotten Germany and Hitler. As well they shouldn't, he thought. His last thought before retiring was to wonder how the new software was working on Chai's computer, and if Ming had actually installed it or not. Then he decided to check.

Rising from bed, he switched his laptop on and . . . yes! Chai's system lacked Ming's transcription software, but it was transmitting what it had. Okay, fine, they had linguists at Langley to fiddle with that. He didn't have the desire to do so, and just uploaded it and headed back to bed.

Damn!" Mary Pat observed. Nearly all of it was unreadable, but this was a second SORGE source. That was evident from the pathway it had taken through the 'Net. She wondered if Nomuri was showing off, or had somehow managed to get in the pants of a second high-ranking Chinese government secretary. It wouldn't exactly be a first for a field officer to have that active a sex life, but it wasn't all that common, either. She printed it up, saved it to disk, and called for a linguist to come up and translate. Then she downloaded SONGBIRD's current take. It was becoming as regular as *The Washington Post,* and a lot more interesting. She settled back in her chair and started reading the translation of Ming's latest notes from Minister Fang Gan. He'd be talking about the trade negotiations, she hoped, then to see that, sure enough, he was . . . This would be important, the DDO thought. She'd soon be surprised to find out how wrong that impression was.

CHAPTER 23

Down to Business

Bacon and eggs, toast and hash-brown potatoes, plus some Colombian-bean coffee. Gant was Jewish but not observant, and he loved his bacon. Everyone was up and looking pretty good, he thought. The government-issued black capsule (they all called it that, evidently some sort of tradition that he didn't know about) had worked for all of them, and the cookie-pushers were all bright-eyed and bushy-tailed. Most of the talk, he noted, was about the NBA. The Lakers were looking tough again. Rutledge, Gant saw, was at the head of the table chatting amiably with Ambassador Hitch, who seemed a solid citizen. Then a more ruffled employee of the embassy came in with a manila folder whose borders were lined with striped red-and-white tape. This he handed to Ambassador Hitch, who opened it at once.

Gant realized at once that it was classified material. There wasn't much of that to be seen at Treasury, but there was some, and he'd been screened for a Top Secret/Special Access clearance as part of his employment on Secretary Winston's personal staff. So, there was intel coming in from Washington for the negotiations. Exactly what it was about, he couldn't see, and didn't know if he would see it. He wondered if he could flex his institutional muscles on this one, but Rutledge would be the one who decided if he got to see it or not, and he didn't want to give the State Department puke the excuse to show who was the he-bull in this herd. Patience was a virtue he'd long had, and this was just one more chance to exercise it. He returned to his breakfast, then decided to stand and get more off the buffet. Lunch in Beijing probably wouldn't be very appealing, even at their Foreign Ministry Building, where they would feel constrained to show off their most exotic national dishes, and Fried Panda Penis with candied bamboo roots wasn't exactly to his taste. At least the tea they served was acceptable, but even at its best, tea wasn't coffee.

"Mark?" Rutledge looked up from his seat and waved the Treasury guy over. Gant walked over with his refilled plate of eggs and bacon.

"Yeah, Cliff?"

Ambassador Hitch made room for Gant to sit down, and a steward arrived with fresh silverware. The government could make one comfortable when it wanted. He asked the guy for more hash browns and toast. Fresh coffee arrived seemingly of its own volition.

"Mark, this just came in from Washington. This is code-word material—"

"Yeah, I know. I can't even see it now, and I am not allowed to have any memory of it. So, can I see it now?"

Rutledge nodded and slipped the papers across. "What do you make of these foreign-exchange figures?"

Gant took a bite of bacon and stopped chewing almost at once. "Damn, they're *that* low? What have they been pissing their money away on?"

"What does this mean?"

"Cliff, once upon a time, Dr. Samuel Johnson put it this way: 'Whatever you have, spend less.' Well, the Chinese didn't listen to that advice." Gant flipped the pages. "It doesn't say what they've been spending it on."

"Mainly military stuff, so I am told," Ambassador Hitch replied. "Or things that can be applied to military applications, especially electronics. Both finished goods and the machinery with which to make electronic stuff. I gather it's expensive to invest in such things."

"It can be," Gant agreed. He turned the pages back to start from the beginning. He saw it was transmitted with the TAPDANCE encryption system. That made it hot. TAPDANCE was only used for the most sensitive material because of some technical inconveniences in its use . . . so this was some really hot intelligence, TELESCOPE thought. Then he saw why. Somebody must have bugged the offices of some *very* senior Chinese officials to get *this* stuff . . . "Jesus."

"What does this mean, Mark?"

"It means they've been spending money faster than it's coming in, and investing it in noncommercial areas for the most part. Hell, it means they're acting like some of the idiots we have in our government. They think money is just something that appears when you snap your fingers, and then you can spend it as fast as you want and just snap your fingers to get some more . . . These people don't live in the real world, Cliff. They have no idea how and why the money appears." He paused. He'd gone too far. A Wall Street person would understand his language, but this Rutledge guy probably didn't. "Let me rephrase. They know that the money comes from their trade imbalance with the United States, and it appears that they believe the imbalance to be a natural phenomenon, something they can essentially dictate because of who they are. They think the rest of the world owes it to them. In other words, if they believe that, negotiating with them is going to be hard."

"Why?" Rutledge asked. Ambassador Hitch, he saw, was already nodding. He must have understood these Chinese barbarians better.

"People who think this way do not understand that negotiations mean give and take. Whoever's talking here thinks that he just gets whatever the hell he wants because everybody owes it to him. It's like what Hitler must have thought at Munich. I want, you give, and then I am happy. We're not going to cave for these bastards, are we?"

"Those are not my instructions," Rutledge replied.

"Well, guess what? Those are the instructions your Chinese counterpart has. Moreover, their economic position is evidently a lot more precarious than what we've been given to expect. Tell CIA they need better people in their financial-intelligence department," Gant observed. Then Hitch shifted his glance across the table to the guy who must have run the local CIA office.

"Do they appreciate how serious their position is?" Rutledge asked.

"Yes and no. Yes, they know they need the hard currency to do the business they want to do. No, they think they can continue this way indefinitely, that an imbalance is natural in their case because—because why? Because they think they're the fucking master race?" Gant asked.

Again it was Ambassador Hitch who nodded. "It's called the Middle Kingdom Complex. Yes, Mr. Gant, they really do think of themselves in those terms, and they expect people to come to them and give, not for themselves to go to other people as supplicants. Someday that will be their downfall. There's an institutional . . . maybe a racial arrogance here that's hard to describe and harder to quantify." Then Hitch looked over to Rutledge. "Cliff, you're going to have an interesting day."

Gant realized at once that this was not a blessing for the Assistant Secretary of State for Policy.

They should be eating breakfast right about now," Secretary Adler said over his Hennessey in the East Room.

The reception had gone well—actually Jack and Cathy Ryan found these things about as boring as reruns of *Gilligan's Island,* but they were as much a part of the Presidency as the State of the Union speech. At least the dinner had been good—one thing you could depend on at the White House was the quality of the food—but the people had been Washington people. Even that, Ryan did not appreciate, had been greatly improved from previous years. Once Congress had largely been populated with people whose life's ambition was "public service," a phrase whose noble intent had been usurped by those who viewed $130,000 per year as a princely salary (it was far less than a college dropout could earn doing software for a computer-game company, and a hell of a lot less than one could make working on Wall Street), and whose real ambition was to apply their will to the laws of their nation. Many of them now, mainly because of speeches the President had made all over the country, were people who actually had *served* the public by doing useful work until, fed up with the machinations of government, they had decided to take a few years off to repair the train wreck Washington had become, before escaping back to the real world of productive work. The First Lady had spent much of the evening talking with the junior senator from Indiana, who in real life was a pediatric surgeon of good reputation and whose current efforts were centered on straightening out government health-care programs before they killed too many of the citizens they supposedly wanted to assist. His greatest task was to persuade the media that a physician might know as much about making sick people well as Washington lobbyists did, something he'd been bending SURGEON's ear about most of the night.

"That stuff we got from Mary Pat ought to help Rutledge."

"I'm glad that Gant guy is there to translate it for him. Cliff is going to have a lively day while we sleep off the food and the booze, Jack."

"Is he good enough for the job? I know he was tight with Ed Kealty. That does not speak well for the guy's character."

"Cliff's a fine technician," Adler said, after another sip of brandy. "And he has clear instructions to carry out, and some awfully good intelligence to help him along. This is like the stuff Jonathan Yardley gave our guys during the Washington Naval Treaty negotiations. We're not exactly reading their cards, but we are seeing how they think, and that's damned near as good. So, yes, I think he's good enough for this job, or I wouldn't have sent him out."

"How's the ambassador we have there?" POTUS asked.

"Carl Hitch? Super guy. Career pro, Jack, ready to retire soon, but he's like a good cabinetmaker. Maybe he can't design the house for you, but the kitchen will be just fine when he's done—and you know, I'll settle for that in a diplomat. Besides, designing the house is your job, Mr. President."

"Yeah," Ryan observed. He waved to an usher, who brought over some ice water. He'd pushed the booze enough for one night, and Cathy was starting to razz him about it again. *Damn, being married to a doctor,* Jack thought. "Yeah, Scott, but who the hell do I go to for advice when I don't know what the hell I'm doing?"

"Hell, I don't know," EAGLE replied. Maybe some humor, he thought: "Try doing a séance and call up Tom Jefferson and George Washington." He turned with a chuckle and finished his Hennessey. "Jack, just take it easy on yourself and do the fuckin' job. You're doing just fine. Trust me."

"I hate this job," SWORDSMAN observed with a friendly smile at his Secretary of State.

"I know. That's probably why you're doing it pretty well. God protect us all from somebody who *wants* to hold high public office. Hell, look at me. Think I ever wanted to be SecState? It was a lot more fun to eat lunch in the cafeteria with my pals and bitch about the dumb son of a bitch who was. But now—shit, they're down there saying that about *me!* It ain't fair, Jack. I'm a working guy."

"Tell me about it."

"Well, look at it this way: When you do your memoirs, you'll get a great advance from your publisher. *The Accidental President?"* Adler speculated for the title.

"Scott, you get funny when you're drunk. I'll settle for working on my golf game."

"Who spoke the magic word?" Vice President Jackson asked as he joined the conversation.

"This guy whips my ass so bad out there," Ryan complained to Secretary Adler, "that sometimes I wish I had a sword to fall on. What's your handicap now?"

"Not playing much, Jack, it's slipped to six, maybe seven."

"He's going to turn pro—Senior Tour," Jack advised.

"Anyway, Jack, this is my father. His plane was late and he missed the receiving line," Robby explained.

"Reverend Jackson, we finally meet." Jack took the hand of the elderly black minister. For the inauguration he'd been in the hospital with kidney stones, which probably had been even less fun than the inauguration.

"Robby's told me a lot of good things about you."

"Your son is a fighter pilot, sir, and they exaggerate a lot."

The minister had a good laugh at that. "Oh, that I know, Mr. President. That I know."

"How was the food?" Ryan asked. Hosiah Jackson was a man on the far side of seventy, short like his son, and rotund with increasing years, but he was a man possessed of the immense dignity that somehow attached to black men of the cloth.

"Much too rich for an old man, Mr. President, but I ate it anyway."

"Don't worry, Jack. Pap doesn't drink," TOMCAT advised. On the lapel of his tuxedo jacket was a miniature of his Navy Wings of Gold. Robby would never stop being a fighter pilot.

"And you shouldn't either, boy! That Navy taught you lots of bad habits, like braggin' on yourself too much."

Jack had to jump to his friend's defense. "Sir, a fighter pilot who doesn't brag isn't allowed to fly. And besides, Dizzy Dean said it best—if you can do it, it isn't bragging. Robby can do it . . . or so he claims."

"They started talking over in Beijing yet?" Robby asked, checking his watch.

"Another half hour or so," Adler replied. "It's going to be interesting," he added, referring to the SORGE material.

"I believe it," Vice President Jackson agreed, catching the message. "You know, it's hard to love those people."

"Robby, you are not allowed to say such things," his father retorted. "I have a friend in Beijing."

"Oh?" His son didn't know about that. The answer came rather as a papal pronouncement.

"Yes, Reverend Yu Fa An, a fine Baptist preacher, educated at Oral Roberts University. My friend Gerry Patterson went to school with him."

"Tough place to be a priest—or minister, I guess," Ryan observed.

It was as though Jack had turned the key in the minister's dignity switch. "Mr. President, I envy him. To preach the Gospel of the Lord anywhere is a privilege, but to preach it in the land of the heathen is a rare blessing."

"Coffee?" a passing usher asked. Hosiah took a cup and added cream and sugar.

"This is fine," he observed at once.

"One of the fringe bennies here, Pap," Jackson told his dad with considerable affection. "This is even better than Navy coffee—well, we have navy stewards serving it. Jamaica Blue Mountain, costs like forty bucks a pound," he explained.

"Jesus, Robby, don't say that too loud. The media hasn't figured that one out yet!" POTUS warned. "Besides, I asked. We get it wholesale, thirty-two bucks a pound if you buy it by the barrel."

"Gee, that's a real bargoon," the VP agreed with a chuckle.

With the welcoming ceremony done, the plenary session began without much in the way of fanfare. Assistant Secretary Rutledge took his seat, greeted the Chinese diplomats across the table, and began. His statement started off with the usual pleasantries that were about as predictable as the lead credits for a feature film.

"The United States," he went on, getting to the meat of the issue, "has concerns about several disturbing aspects of our mutual trading relationship. The first is the seeming inability of the People's Republic to abide by previous agreements to recognize international treaties and conventions on trademarks, copyrights, and patents. All of these items have been discussed and negotiated at length in previous meetings like this one, and we had thought that the areas of disagreement were successfully resolved. Unfortunately, this seems not to be the case." He went on to cite several specific items, which he described as being illustrative but in no way a comprehensive listing of his areas of "concern."

"Similarly," Rutledge continued, "commitments to open the Chinese market to American goods have not been honored. This has resulted in an imbalance in the mercantile exchange which ill serves our overall relationship. The current imbalance is approaching seventy *billion* U.S. dollars, and that is something the United States of America is not prepared to accept.

"To summarize, the People's Republic's commitment to honor international treaty obligations and private agreements with the United States has not been carried out. It is a fact of American law that our country has the right to adopt the trade practices of other nations in its own law. This is the well-known Trade Reform Act, enacted by the American government several years ago. It is my unpleasant obligation, therefore, to inform the government of the People's Republic that America will enforce this law with respect to trade with the People's Republic forthwith, unless these previously agreed-upon commitments are met immediately," Rutledge concluded. *Immediately* is a word not often used in international discourse. "That concludes my opening statement."

For his part, Mark Gant halfway wondered if the other side might leap across the polished oak table with swords and daggers at the end of Rutledge's opening speech. The gauntlet had been cast down in forceful terms not calculated to make the Chinese happy. But the diplomat handling the other side of the table—it was Foreign Minister Shen Tang—reacted no more than he might on getting the check in a restaurant and finding that he'd been overcharged about five bucks' worth. Not even a look up. Instead the Chinese minister continued to look down at his own notes, before finally lifting his eyes as he felt the end of Rutledge's opening imminent, with no more feeling or emotion than that of a man in an art gallery looking over some painting or other that his wife wanted him to purchase to cover a crack in the dining room wall.

"Secretary Rutledge, thank you for your statement," he began in his turn.

"The People's Republic first of all welcomes you to our country and wishes to state for the record its desire for a continued friendly relationship with America and the American people.

"We cannot, however, reconcile America's stated desire for friendly relations with her action to recognize the breakaway province on the island of Taiwan as the independent nation it is not. Such action was calculated to inflame our relationship—to fan the flames instead of helping to extinguish them. The people of our country will not accept this unconscionable interference with Chinese internal affairs and—" The diplomat looked up in surprise to see Rutledge's hand raised in interruption. He was sufficiently shocked by this early breach of protocol that he actually stopped talking.

"Minister," Rutledge intoned, "the purpose of this meeting is to discuss trade. The issue of America's diplomatic recognition of the Republic of China is one best left to another venue. The American delegation has no desire to detour into that area today." Which was diplo-speak for "Take that issue and shove it."

"Mr. Rutledge, you cannot dictate to the People's Republic what our concerns and issues are," Minister Shen observed, in a voice as even as one discussing the price of lettuce in the street market. The rules of a meeting like this were simple: The first side to show anger lost.

"Do go on, then, if you must," Rutledge responded tiredly. *You're wasting my time, but I get paid whether I work or not,* his demeanor proclaimed.

Gant saw that the dynamic for the opening was that both countries had their agendas, and each was trying to ignore that of the other in order to take control of the session. This was so unlike a proper business meeting as to be unrecognizable as a form of verbal intercourse—and in terms of other intercourse, it was like two naked people in bed, purportedly for the purpose of sex, starting off their foreplay by fighting over the TV remote. Gant had seen all manner of negotiations before, or so he thought. This was something entirely new and, to him, utterly bizarre.

"The renegade bandits on Taiwan are part of China in their history and heritage, and the People's Republic cannot ignore this deliberate insult to our nationhood by the Ryan Regime."

"Minister Shen, the government of the United States of America has a long history of supporting democratically elected governments throughout the world. That has been part of our nation's ethos for over two hundred years. I would remind the People's Republic that the United States of America has the longest-lived government in the world. We have lived under our constitutional form of government for well over two hundred years. That is a small number in terms of Chinese history, but I would remind you further that when America elected her first President and first Congress, China was ruled by a hereditary monarch. The government of your country has changed many times since then, but the government of the United States of America has not. Thus it is well within our power both as an independent nation under recognized international law, and also as a *moral* right as a long-lived and therefore legitimate form of government, both to act as we choose and to foster governments like our own. The government of the Republic of China is democratically elected, and therefore it commands the respect of similarly chosen governments of the people, like our own. In any case, Minister, the purpose of this meeting is to discuss trade. Shall we do that, or shall we fritter away our time discussing irrelevancies?"

"Nothing could be more relevant to this discussion than the fundamental lack of respect shown by your government—by the Ryan Regime, shall I say?—for the government of our country. The Taiwan issue is one of fundamental importance to . . ." He droned on for another four minutes.

"Minister Shen, the United States of America is not a 'regime' of any sort. It is an independent nation with a freely elected government chosen by its people. That experiment in government which we undertook when your country was ruled by the Manchu Dynasty is one which you might consider imitating at some future date, for the benefit of your own people. Now, shall we return to the issue at hand, or do you wish to continue wasting your own time and mine by discussing a topic for which I have neither instructions nor much in the way of interest?"

"We will not be brushed aside so cavalierly as that," Shen responded, earning Rutledge's brief and irrelevant respect for his unexpected command of the English language.

The American chief diplomat settled back in his chair and looked politely across the table while he thought over his wife's plans for redecorating the kitchen of their Georgetown town house. Was green and blue the right color scheme? He preferred earth tones, but he was far more likely to win this argument in Beijing than that one in Georgetown. A lifetime spent in diplomacy didn't enable him to win arguments with Mrs. Rutledge over items like decorating . . .

So it went for the first ninety minutes, when there came time for the first break. Tea and finger food was served and people wandered out the French doors—a strange place to find *those,* Gant thought—into the garden. It was Gant's first adventure in diplomacy, and he was about to learn how these things really worked. People paired off, American and Chinese. You could tell who was who from a distance. Every single one of the Chinese smoked, a vice shared by only two of the American delegation, both of whom looked grateful for the chance to enjoy their habit *indoors* in this country. They might be trade nazis, the Treasury Department official reflected, but they weren't health nazis.

"What do you think?" a voice asked. Gant turned to see the same little guy who'd bugged him at the reception. His name was Xue Ma, Gant remembered, all of five-foot-nothing, with poker-player's eyes and some acting ability. Smarter than he appeared to be, the American reminded himself. So, how was he supposed to handle this? When in doubt, Gant decided, fall back on the truth.

"It's my first time observing diplomatic negotiations. It's intensely boring," Gant replied, sipping his (dreadful) coffee.

"Well, this is normal," Xue answered.

"Really? It's not that way in business. How do you get anything done?"

"Every endeavor has its process," the Chinese man told him.

"I suppose. Can you tell me something?" TELESCOPE asked.

"I can try."

"What's the big deal about Taiwan?"

"What was the big deal when your Civil War began?" Xue replied, with a clever question of his own.

"Well, okay, but after fifty years, why not call it even and start over?"

"We do not think in such short terms," Xue answered with a superior smile.

"Okay, but in America we call that living in the past." *Take* that, *you little Chink!*

"They are our countrymen," Xue persisted.

"But they have chosen not to be. If you want them back, then make it advantageous for them. You know, by achieving the same prosperity here that they've achieved there." *You backward commie.*

"If one of your children ran away from home, would you not work for his return?"

"Probably, but I would entice him, not threaten him, especially if I didn't have the ability to threaten him effectively." *And your military is for shit, too.* So the briefings had told them before flying over.

"But when others encourage our child to abscond and defy their father, are we not to object?"

"Look, pal," Gant responded, not quite showing the inward heat he felt—or so he thought. "If you want to do business, then do business. If you want to chat, we can chat. But my time is valuable, and so is the time of our country, and we can save the chat for another time." And then Gant realized that, no, he wasn't a diplomat, and this was not a game he could play and win. "As you see, I am not gifted at this sort of exchange. We have people who are, but I am not one of them. I am the kind of American who does real work and earns real money. If you enjoy this game, that's fine, but it's not my game. Patience is a good thing, I suppose, but not when it impedes the objective, and I think your minister is missing something."

"What is that, Mr. Gant?"

"It is we who will have what we wish to have out of these meetings," Gant told the little Chinese man, and realized instantly that he'd stuck his own foot into his mouth about to the knee. He finished his coffee and excused himself, then headed unnecessarily for the bathroom, where he washed his hands before heading back outside. He found Rutledge standing alone, examining some spring flowers.

"Cliff, I think I fucked something up," Gant confessed quietly.

"What's that?" the Assistant Secretary asked, then listened to the confession. "Don't sweat it. You didn't tell them anything I haven't already told them. You just don't understand the language."

"But they'll think we're impatient, and that makes us vulnerable, doesn't it?"

"Not with me doing the talking inside," Rutledge answered, with a gentle smile. "Here I am Jimmy Connors at the U.S. Open, Mark. This is what I do."

"The other side thinks so, too."

"True, but we have the advantage. They need us more than we need them."

"I thought you didn't like taking this sort of line with people," Gant observed, puzzled by Rutledge's attitude.

"I don't have to like it. I just have to do it, and winning is always fun." He didn't add that he'd never met Minister Shen before, and therefore had no personal baggage to trip over, as often happened with diplomats who had been known to put personal friendship before the interest of their countries. They usually justified it by telling themselves that the bastard would owe them one next time, which would serve their country's interest. Diplomacy had always been a personal business, a fact often lost on observers, who thought of these verbose technicians as robots.

Gant found all of this puzzling, but he would play along with Rutledge because he had to, and because the guy at least acted as though he knew what the hell he was doing. Whether he did or not . . . Gant wondered how he'd be able to tell. Then it was time to go back indoors.

The ashtrays had been cleaned and the water bottles replenished by the domestic help, who were probably all politically reliable functionaries of one sort or another, or more likely professional intelligence officers, who were here because their government took no chances with anything, or at least tried not to. It was, in fact, a waste of trained personnel, but communists had never been overly concerned with utilizing manpower in an efficient way.

Minister Shen lit a smoke and motioned for Rutledge to lead off. For his part, the American remembered that Bismarck had counseled the use of a cigar in negotiations, because some found the thick tobacco smoke irritating and that gave the smoker the advantage.

"Minister, the trade policies of the People's Republic are set in place by a small number of people, and those policies are set in place for political reasons. We in America understand that. What you fail to understand is that ours truly is a government of the people, and our people demand that we address the trade imbalance. The People's Republic's inability to open markets to American goods costs the jobs of American citizens. Now, in our country it is the business of the government to serve the people, not to rule them, and for that reason, we must address the trade imbalance in an effective way."

"I fully agree that it is the business of government to serve the interests of the people, and for that reason, we must consider also the agony that the Taiwan issue imposes on the citizens of my country. Those who should be our countrymen have been separated from us, and the United States has assisted in the estrangement of our kinsmen . . ." The remarkable thing, Rutledge thought, was that this droning old fart hadn't died from smoking those damned things. They looked and smelled like the Lucky Strikes his grandfather had died of, at age eighty. It had not been a death to please a physician, however. Grandpa Owens had been driving his great-grandson to South Station in Boston when, lighting one, he'd dropped it into his lap and, in retrieving it, strayed onto the wrong side of the road. Grandpa hadn't believed in seat belts, either . . . the bastard actually chain-smoked, lighting a new one with the butt of the previous one, like Bogie in a '30s movie. Well, maybe it was a way for the Chinese to pursue their population-control policy . . . but in rather an ugly way . . .

"Mr. Foreign Minister," Rutledge started off, when it was next his turn, "the government of the Republic of China is one elected in free and fair elections by the people who live in that country. In America's eyes, that makes the government of the Republic of China legitimate"—he didn't say that the government of the People's Republic was, therefore, illegitimate, but the thought hung in the room like a dark cloud—"and that makes the government in question worthy of international recognition, as you may have noticed has been the case in the last year.

"It is the policy of our government to recognize such governments. We will not change policies based upon firm principles to suit the wishes of other countries which do not share those principles. We can talk until you run out of cigarettes, but my government's position in this case is set in stone. So, you can recognize this fact and allow the meeting to move on to productive areas, or you can beat this dead horse until nothing is left of it. The choice is yours, of course, but is it not better to be productive than not?"

"America cannot dictate to the People's Republic that which concerns us. You claim to have your principles, and surely we have our own, and one of ours is the importance of our country's territorial integrity."

For Mark Gant, the hard part was keeping an impassive face. He had to pretend that this all made sense and was important, when he'd much prefer to set up his computer to review stock prices, or for that matter read a paperback book under the rim of the table. But he couldn't do that. He had to pretend that this was all interesting, which, if successfully done, could get him nominated for the next Academy Award ceremonies for Best Actor in a Supporting Role: "For keeping awake during the most boring contest since the Iowa grass-growing championships, the winner is . . ." He concentrated on not shifting in his seat, but that just made his ass tired, and these seats hadn't been designed to fit his ass. Maybe one of those skinny Chinese ones, but not that of a Chicago-raised professional who liked having a beer and a corned-beef sandwich for lunch at least once a week and didn't work out enough. His ass required a broader and softer seat for comfort, but he didn't have one. He tried to find something interesting. He decided that Foreign Minister Shen had terrible skin, as though his face had once been on fire and a friend had tried to extinguish the flames with an ice pick. Gant tried to conjure up the image of that supposed event without smiling. Then came the fact that Shen was smoking so much, lighting his smokes from cheap paper matches instead of a proper lighter. Perhaps he was one of those people who set things down and forgot where they were, which would also explain why he used cheap throwaway pens instead of something in keeping with his rank and status. So, this important son of a bitch had suffered from terminal acne as a kid and was a butterfingers. . . . ? It was something worthy of an inward smile as the minister droned on in passable English. That engendered a new thought. He had access to an earphone for simultaneous translation . . . could he get one tuned to a local station? They had to have a radio station in Beijing that played music of some sort or other, didn't they?

When Rutledge's turn came, it was almost as bad. The stated American position was as repetitive as the Chinese one, perhaps more reasonable but no less boring. Gant imagined that lawyers talking over a divorce settlement probably went through bullshit like this. Like diplomats, they were paid by the hour and not by the product. Diplomats and lawyers. What a pair, Gant thought. He was unable even to look at his watch. The American delegation had to present a united front of solid stone, Gant thought, to show the Heathen Chinese that the Forces of Truth and Beauty were firm in their resolve. Or something like that. He wondered if it would feel different negotiating with the British, for example, everyone speaking much the same language, but those negotiations were probably handled with phone calls or e-mails rather than this formalistic crap. . . .

Lunch came at the expected hour, about ten minutes late because the Shen guy ran over, which was hardly unexpected. The American team all headed to the men's room, where no talking was done for fear of bugs. Then they went back outside, and Gant went to Rutledge.

"This is how you earn your living?" the stock trader asked with no small degree of incredulity.

"I try to. These talks are going pretty well," the Assistant Secretary of State observed.

"What?" Gant inquired with total amazement.

"Yeah, well, their Foreign Minister is doing the negotiating, so we're playing with their varsity," Rutledge explained. "That means that we'll be able to reach a real agreement instead of a lot of back-and-forth between lower-level people and the Politburo—the additional layer of people can really mess things up. There'll be some of that, of course. Shen will have to talk over his positions with them every evening, maybe even right now—he's nowhere to be seen. I wonder who he reports to, exactly. We don't think he really has plenipotentiary powers, that the rest of the big boys second-guess him a lot. Like the Russians used to be. That's the problem with their system. Nobody really trusts anybody else."

"You serious?" TELESCOPE asked.

"Oh, yeah, it's how their system works."

"That's a clusterfuck," Gant observed.

"Why do you thing the Soviet Union went belly-up?" Rutledge asked with amusement. "They never had their act together on any level because they fundamentally didn't know how properly to exercise the power they had. It was rather sad, really. But they're doing a lot better now."

"But how are the talks going, well?"

"If all they have to throw at us is Taiwan, their counterarguments on trade won't be all that impressive. Taiwan's a settled issue, and they know it. We may have a mutual-defense treaty with them in ten or eleven months, and they probably know that. They have good intelligence sources in Taipei."

"How do we know *that?*" Gant demanded.

"Because our friends in Taipei make sure they do. You want your adversaries to know a lot of things. It makes for better understandings, cuts down on mistakes and stuff." Rutledge paused. "I wonder what's for lunch . . . ?"

Jesus, Gant thought. Then he thanked God that he was just here to offer economic backup for this diplomat. They were playing a game so different from anything he'd ever encountered before that he felt like a truck driver doing some day-trading on his laptop at a highway phone booth.

The newsies showed up for lunch so that they could get more B-roll tape of diplomats chatting amiably about such things as the weather and the food—the viewers would think they were handling matters of state, of course, when in fact at least half of the talks between diplomats at such affairs were limited to the problems of raising children or killing the crabgrass in your lawn. It was all, in fact, a kind of gamesmanship with few parallels in other forms of endeavor, Gant was only beginning to understand. He saw Barry Wise approach Rutledge without a microphone or camera in attendance.

"So, how's it going, Mr. Secretary?" the reporter asked.

"Pretty well. In fact, we had a fine opening session," Rutledge replied in Gant's earshot. It was a shame, TELESCOPE decided, that the people couldn't see what really happened. It would be the funniest thing this side of Chris Rock. It made *Laverne & Shirley* look like *King Lear* in its lunacy, and the world chess championship look like a heavyweight-championship fight in its torpor. But every field of human endeavor had its rules, and these were just different ones.

There's our friend," the cop observed, as the car pulled out. It was Suvorov/Koniev in his Mercedes C-class. The license tag number checked, as did the face in the binoculars.

Provalov had gotten the local varsity to handle this case, with even some help now from the Federal Security Service, formerly the Second Chief Directorate of the former KGB, the professional spy-chasers who'd made life in Moscow difficult for foreign intelligence operations. They remained superbly equipped, and though not so well funded as in the past, there was little to criticize in their training.

The problem, of course, was that they knew all that themselves, and took on a degree of institutional arrogance that had gotten the noses of his homicide investigators severely out of joint. Despite all that, they were useful allies. There were a total of seven vehicles to handle the surveillance. In America, the FBI would have arranged a helicopter as well, but Michael Reilly wasn't here to make that condescending observation, somewhat to Provalov's relief. The man had become a friend, and a gifted mentor in the business of investigation, but enough was sometimes enough. There were trucks containing TV cameras to tape the business of the morning, and every automobile had two people in it so that driving wouldn't interfere with watching. They followed Suvorov/Koniev into central Moscow.

Back at his apartment, another team had already defeated his lock and was inside his flat. What happened there was as graceful as any performance by the Bolshoi Ballet. Once inside, the investigative team stood still at first, scanning for telltales, left-behind items as innocuous as a human hair stuck in place across a closet door to show if someone had opened it. Suvorov's KGB file was finally in Provalov's possession now, and he knew all the things the man had been trained in—it turned out that his training had been quite thorough, and Suvorov's grades had been, well, "C" class most of the time: not outstanding enough to earn him the chance to operate in the field as an "illegal" officer on the home ground of the "Main Enemy," meaning the United States, but good enough that he'd become a diplomatic-intelligence specialist, mainly going over information brought in by others, but spending some time in the field, trying to recruit and "run" agents. Along the way, he'd established contact with various foreign diplomats, including three from China—those three he'd used to gather low-level diplomatic information, mainly chitchat-level stuff, but it was all regarded as useful. Suvorov's last field assignment had been from 1989 to '91 in the Soviet

Embassy in Beijing, where he'd again tried to gather diplomatic intelligence, and, they saw, with some success this time. The accomplishments had not been questioned at the time, Provalov saw, probably because he'd had some minor victories against the same country's diplomatic service while in Moscow. His file said that he could both speak and write Chinese, skills learned at the KGB Academy that had militated in favor of making him a China specialist.

One of the problems with intelligence operations was that what looked suspicious was often innocuous, and what looked innocuous could well be suspicious. An intelligence officer was *supposed* to establish contact with foreign nationals, often foreign intelligence officers, and then the foreign spy could execute a maneuver that the Americans called a "flip," turning an enemy into an asset. The KGB had done the same thing many times, and part of the price of doing such business was that it could happen to your own people, not so much while you were not looking as when you *were.* Nineteen eighty-nine to '91 had been the time of *glasnost,* the "openness" that had destroyed the Soviet Union as surely as smallpox had annihilated primitive tribesmen. *At that time, KGB was having problems of its own,* Provalov reminded himself, *and what if the Chinese had recruited Suvorov?* The Chinese economy had just been starting to grow back then, and so they'd had the money to toss around, not as much as the Americans always seemed to have, but enough to entice a Soviet civil servant looking at the prospect of losing his job soon.

But what had Suvorov been doing since then? He was now driving a Mercedes-Benz automobile, and those didn't appear in your mailbox. The truth was that they didn't know, and finding out would not be very easy. They knew that neither Klementi Ivan'ch Suvorov nor Ivan Yurievich Koniev had paid his income taxes, but that merely put him at the same level as most Russian citizens, who didn't want to be bothered with such irrelevancies. And, again, they hadn't wanted to question his neighbors. Those names were now being checked to see if any were former KGB, and perhaps, therefore, allies of their suspect. No, they didn't want to alert him in any way.

The apartment looked "clean" in the police sense. With that, they began looking around. The bed was mussed up. Suvorov/Koniev was a man and therefore not terribly neat. The contents of the apartment were, however, expensive, much of them of foreign manufacture. West German appliances, a common affectation of the Russian well-to-do. The searchers wore latex surgical gloves as they opened the refrigerator door (refrigerator-freezers are well-regarded hiding places) for a visual examination. Nothing obvious. Then dresser drawers. The problem was that their time was limited and any residence just had too many places to hide things, whether rolled up in a pair of socks or inside the toilet-paper tube. They didn't really expect to find much, but making the effort was *de rigueur*—it was too hard to explain to one's superiors why one didn't do it than it was to send the search team in to waste their expensively trained time. Elsewhere, people were tapping the apartment's phone. They'd thought about installing some pinhole-lens cameras. These were so easy to hide that only a paranoid genius was likely to find them, but putting them in took time—the hard part was running the wires to the central monitoring station—and time was an asset they didn't have. As it was, their leader had a cell phone in his shirt pocket, waiting for it to vibrate with the word that their quarry was driving back home, in which case they'd tidy up and leave in a hurry.

He was twelve kilometers away. Behind him, the trail cars were switching in and out of visual coverage as deftly as the Russian national football team advancing the soccer ball into tied-game opposition. Provalov was in the command vehicle, watching and listening as the KGB/FSS team leader used a radio and a map to guide his people in and out. The vehicles were all dirty, middle-aged, nondescript types that could be owned by the Moscow city government or gypsy-cab operators, expected to dart around, concealing themselves among the numerous twins they all had. In most cases, the second vehicle occupant was in the back seat, not the front, to simulate a taxi's passenger, and they even had cell phones to complete the disguise, which allowed them to communicate with their base station without looking suspicious. That, the FSS leader remarked to the cop, was one advantage of new technology.

Then came the call that the subject had pulled over, stopped, and parked his car. The two surveillance vehicles in visual contact continued past, allowing new ones to close in and stop.

"He's getting out," a Federal Security Service major reported. "I'm getting out to follow on foot." The major was young for his rank, usually a sign of a precocious and promising young officer on the way up, and so it was in this case. He was also handsome with his twenty-eight years, and dressed in expensive clothing like one of the new crop of Moscovite business entrepreneurs. He was talking into his phone in a highly animated fashion, the very opposite of what someone conducting a surveillance would do. That enabled him to get within thirty meters of the subject, and to watch his every move with hawk's eyes. Those eyes were needed to catch the most elegant of maneuvers. Suvorov/Koniev sat on a bench, his right hand already in his overcoat pocket while his left fiddled with the morning paper he'd brought out from the car—and that is what tipped the FSS major that he was up to no good. A newspaper was the main disguise used by a spy, something to cover the actions of the working hand, just as a stage magician kept one hand ostentatiously busy while the other performed the actual illusion. And so it was here, so beautifully done that had he been an untrained man, he would never have caught it. The major took a seat on another bench and dialed up another false number on his cell phone and started talking to a fictitious business associate, then watched his surveillance subject stand and walk with studied casualness back to his parked Mercedes.

Major Yefremov called a real number when his subject was a hundred meters away. "This is Pavel Georgiyevich. I am staying here to see what he left behind," he told his base station. He crossed his legs and lit a cigarette, watching the figure get back into his car and drive off. When he was well out of sight, Yefremov walked over to the other bench and reached under. Oh, yes. A magnetic holder. Suvorov had been using this one for some time. He'd glued a metal plate to the bottom of the green-painted wood, and to this he could affix a magnetic holder . . . about a centimeter in thickness, his hand told him. Their subject was a "player" after all. He'd just executed a dead-drop.

On hearing it, Provalov experienced the thrill of seeing a crime committed before his very eyes. Now they had their man committing a crime against the state. Now he was theirs. Now they could arrest him at any time. But they wouldn't, of course. The operation's commander next to him ordered Yefremov to retrieve the container for examination. That would be done very speedily, because the container would have to be returned. They only had half of the spy team. The other half would come to pick it up.

It was the computer. It had to be. On turning it on, they found a maze of folders, but one of them, they quickly saw, had encrypted contents. The encryption program was one they hadn't come across before. It was American, and its name was written down. They could do no more now. They lacked the proper disks to copy the covert file. That they could fix, and they could also copy the encryption program. Next, they'd have to plant a bugging device on the keyboard. In that way, they could use Sovorov's own password code to crack the encrypted file. With that decision made, the burglary team left the premises.

The next part was virtually preordained. They followed the Mercedes using the same multi-car drill, but the break came when a dump truck—still the dominant form of life on the Moscow streets—was closest. The subject parked the German sedan and jumped out, took just enough time to affix a strip of paper tape to a lamppost, and hopped back into his car. He didn't even bother to look around, as though he'd only done something routine.

But he hadn't. He'd just posted a flag, a notice to someone unknown that the dead-drop had something in it. That someone would walk or drive past and see the tape and know where to go. So, they had to examine the capsule quickly and replace it, lest they warn the enemy spy that their little operation had been compromised. No, you didn't do that until you had to, because things like this were like an unraveling sweater on a pretty woman. You didn't stop pulling the yarn until the tits were exposed, the FSS commander told Provalov.

CHAPTER 24

Infanticide

"What's this?" the President asked at his morning intelligence briefing.

"A new SORGE source, this one's called WARBLER. I'm afraid it's not as good from an intelligence point of view, though it does tell us things about their ministers," Dr. Goodley added with some feigned delicacy.

Whoever WARBLER was, Ryan saw, she—it was definitely a she—kept a very intimate diary. She, too, worked with this Minister Fang Gan, and, it appeared, he was enamored of her, and she, if not exactly enamored of him, certainly kept records of his activities. All of them, Ryan saw. It was enough to make his eyes go a little wide this early in the morning.

"Tell Mary Pat that she can sell this stuff to *Hustler* if she wants, but I really don't need it at eight in the goddamned morning."

"She included it to give you a feel for the source," Ben explained. "The material isn't as narrowly political as we're getting from SONGBIRD, but MP thinks it tells us a lot about the guy's character, which is useful, and also there's some political content to go along with the information on Fang's sex life. It would appear he's a man of, uh . . . well, commendable vigor, I guess, though the girl in question would clearly prefer a younger lover. It appears that she had one, but this Fang guy scared him off."

"Possessive bastard," Ryan saw, skimming that section. "Well, I guess at that age you hold on to what you need. Does this tell us anything?"

"Sir, it tells us something about the kind of people who make decisions over there. Here we call them sexual predators."

"Of which we have a few in government service ourselves," Ryan observed. The papers had just broken a story on a member of the Senate.

"At least not in this office," Goodley told his President. He didn't add *anymore.*

"Well, this President is married to a surgeon. She knows how to use sharp instruments," Ryan said, with a wry grin. "So, the Taiwan stuff yesterday was just a ploy because they haven't figured out how to address the trade issues yet?"

"So it would appear, and yes, that does seem a little odd. Also, MP thinks that they might have a low-level source in State. They know a little more than they could have gotten from the press, she thinks."

"Oh, great," Jack noted. "So what happened? The Japanese corporations sold their old sources to the Chinese?"

Goodley shrugged. "No telling at this time."

"Have Mary Pat call Dan Murray about this. Counterespionage is the FBI's department. Is this something we want to move on at once, or will this compromise SONGBIRD?"

"That's for somebody else to judge, sir," Goodley said, reminding the President that he was good, but not quite *that* good at this business.

"Yeah, somebody other than me, too. What else?"

"The Senate Select Intelligence Committee wants to look into the Russian situation."

"That's nice. What's the beef?"

"They seem to have their doubts about how trustworthy our friends in Moscow are. They're worried that they're going to use the oil and gold money to become the USSR again, and maybe threaten NATO."

"NATO's moved a few hundred miles east, last time I looked. The buffer zone will not hurt our interests."

"Except that we *are* obligated to defend Poland now," Goodley reminded his boss.

"I remember. So, tell the Senate to authorize funds to move a tank brigade east of Warsaw. We can take over one of the old Soviet laagers, can't we?"

"If the Poles want us to. They don't seem overly concerned, sir."

"Probably more worried by the Germans, right?"

"Correct, and there is a precedent for that concern."

"When will Europe get the word that peace has finally broken out for good and all?" Ryan asked the ceiling.

"There's a lot of history, some of it pretty recent, for them to remember, Mr. President. And much of it militates in the other direction."

"I've got a trip to Poland scheduled, don't I?"

"Yes, not too far off, and they're working out the itinerary right now."

"Okay, I'll tell the Polish president personally that he can depend on us to keep the Germans under control. If they step out of line—well, we'll take Chrysler back." Jack sipped his coffee and checked his watch. "Anything else?"

"That should do it for today."

The President looked up slyly. "Tell Mary Pat if she sends me more of this WARBLER stuff, I want the pictures to go with it."

"Will do, sir." Goodley had himself a good hoot at that.

Ryan picked up the briefing papers again and read through them more slowly this time, between sips of coffee and snorts, with a few grumbles thrown in. Life had been much easier when he was the guy who prepared these briefing papers than it was now that he was the guy who had to read them. Why was that? Shouldn't it have been the other way around? Before, he'd been the one to find the answers and anticipate the questions, but now that other people had done all that stuff for him . . . it was harder. That didn't make any sense at all, damn it. Maybe, he decided, it was because, after him, the information stopped. He had to make the decisions, and so whatever other decisions and analyses had been made at lower levels, the process came to one place and stopped cold. It was like driving a car: Someone else could tell him to turn right at the corner, but he was the guy at the wheel who had to execute the turn, and if somebody clobbered the car, he was the guy who'd get the blame. For a moment, Jack wondered if he was better suited to being a step or two down in the process, able to do the analysis work and make his recommendations with confidence . . . but always knowing that someone else would always get the credit for making the right move, or the blame for making the wrong one. In that insulation from consequence, there was safety and security. But that was cowardice talking, Ryan reminded himself. If there were anyone in Washington better suited for making decisions, he hadn't met the guy yet, and if that was arrogance talking, then so be it.

But there ought to be someone better, Jack thought, as the clock wound to his first appointment of the day, and it wasn't his fault that there wasn't. He checked his appointment sheet. The whole day was political bullshit . . . except it wasn't bullshit. Everything he did in this office affected the lives of American citizens in one way or another, and that made it important, to them and to him. But who had decided to make him the national *daddy?* What the hell made *him* so damned smart? The people behind his back, as he thought of it, outside the overly thick windows of the Oval Office, all expected him to know how to do the right thing, and over the dinner table or a low-stakes card game, they'd bitch and moan and complain about the decisions he'd made that they didn't like, as though they knew better—which was easy to say out there. In here it was different. And so, Ryan had to apply himself to every little decision, even menus for school lunches—that one was a real son of a bitch. If you gave kids what they liked to eat, nutritionists would complain that they really ought to eat healthy twigs and berries, but for the most part, parents would probably opt for burgers and fries, because that's what the kids *would* eat, and even healthy food, uneaten, did them little good. He'd talked that one over with Cathy once or twice, but he really didn't need to. She let their own kids eat pizza whenever they wished, claiming that pizza was high in protein, and that a kid's metabolism could eat almost anything without ill effect, but when cornered, she'd admit *that* put her at odds with some of her fellow professors at Johns Hopkins. And so what was Jack Ryan, President of the United States, Doctor of Philosophy in History, Bachelor of Arts in Economics, *and* a Certified Public Accountant (Ryan couldn't even remember why he had bothered taking that exam), supposed to think, when experts—including the one he was married to—disagreed? That was worth another snort, when his desk buzzer went off and Mrs. Sumter announced that his first appointment of the day was here. Already Jack was wishing for a bummed cigarette, but he couldn't do that until he had a break in his schedule, because only Mrs. Sumter and a few of his Secret Service detail were allowed to know that the President of the United States suffered, intermittently, from *that* vice.

Jesus, he thought, as he did so often when the work day began, *how did I ever get stuck in here?* Then he stood and faced the door, conjuring up his welcoming Presidential smile as he tried to remember who the hell was coming in first to discuss farm subsidies in South Dakota.

The flight, as usual, was out of Heathrow, this one in a Boeing 737, because it wasn't all that long a hop to Moscow. The Rainbow troopers filled the entire first-class section, which would please the cabin staff, though they didn't know it yet, because the passengers would be unusually polite and undemanding. Chavez sat with his father-in-law, politely watching the safety-briefing video, though both knew that if the airplane hit the ground at four hundred knots, it really wouldn't help all that much to know where the nearest emergency exit was. But such things were rare enough to be ignored. Ding grabbed the magazine from the pocket in front and flipped through it in the hope of finding something interesting. He'd already bought all the useful items from the "flying mall" magazine, some to his wife's pitying amusement.

"So, the little guy's walking better?" Clark asked.

"You know, the enthusiasm he has for it is kinda funny, the big grin every time he makes it from the TV to the coffee table, like he's won the marathon, got a big gold medal, and a kiss from Miss America on his way to Disney World."

"The big things are made up of a lot of little things, Domingo," Clark observed, as the aircraft started its takeoff run. "And the horizon's a lot closer when you're that short."

"I suppose, Mr. C. Does seem kinda amusing, though . . . and kinda cute," he allowed.

"Not bad duty being the father of a little guy, is it?"

"I got no complaints," Chavez agreed, leaning his seat back now that the gear was up.

"How's Ettore working out?" Back to business, Clark decided. This grandpa stuff had its limitations.

"He's in better shape now. Needed about a month to get caught up.

He took some razzing, but he handled it just fine. You know, he's smart. Good tactical instincts, considering he's a cop and not a soldier."

"Being a cop in Sicily isn't like walking a beat on Oxford Street in London, you know?"

"Yeah, guess so," Chavez agreed. "But on the simulator he hasn't made a single shoot/no-shoot mistake yet, and that's not bad. The only other guy who hasn't blown one is Eddie Price." The computerized training simulator back at Hereford was particularly ruthless in its presentation of possible tactical scenarios, to the point that in one a twelve-year-old picked up an AK-74 and hosed you if you didn't pay close enough attention. The other nasty one was the woman holding the baby who'd just happened to pick up a pistol from a dead terrorist and turn innocently to face the incoming Men of Black. Ding had taken her down once, to find a Cabbage Patch doll on his desk the next morning with a packet of McDonald's ketchup spread across the face. The RAINBOW troopers had a lively, if somewhat perverse, institutional sense of humor.

"So, what exactly are we supposed to be doing?"

"The old Eighth Chief Directorate of the KGB, their executive protective service," John explained. "They've got worries about domestic terrorists—from the Chechens, I guess, and other internal nationalities who want out of the country. They want us to help train up their boys to deal with them."

"How good are they?" Ding asked.

RAINBOW SIX shrugged. "Good question. The personnel are former KGB types, but with Spetsnaz training, so, probably career people as opposed to two-year in-and-outs in the Red Army. All probably titular commissioned officers, but with sergeants' duties. I expect they'll be smart, properly motivated, probably in decent physical shape, and they'll understand the mission. Will they be as good as they need to be? Probably not," John thought. "But in a few weeks we ought to be able to point them in the right direction."

"So mainly we're going to be training up their instructors?"

Clark nodded. "That's how I read it, yeah."

"Fair enough," Chavez agreed, as the lunch menu appeared. Why was it, he wondered, that airline food never seemed to have what you wanted? This was dinner food, not lunch food. What the hell was wrong with a cheeseburger and fries? Oh, well, at least he could have a decent beer. The one thing he'd come to love about life in the UK was the beer. There wouldn't be anything like it in Russia, he was sure.

Sunrise in Beijing was as drab as the polluted air could make it, Mark Gant thought. For some reason he'd slipped out of synch with the local time, despite the black capsule and planned sleep. He'd found himself awake just at first light, which fought through air that was as bad as Los Angeles on its worst-ever day. Certainly there was no EPA in the PRC, and this place didn't even have much in the way of automobiles yet. If that ever happened, China might solve its local population problem with mass gassing. He hadn't been around enough to recognize this as a problem of Marxist nations—but there weren't many of them left to be examples, were there? Gant had never smoked—it was a vice largely removed from the stock-trading community, where the normal working stress was enough of a killer that they needed few others—and this degree of air pollution made his eyes water.

He had nothing to do and lots of time in which to do it—once awake he was never able to escape back into sleep—so he decided to flip on his reading light and go over some documents, most of which he'd been given without any particular expectation that he would read them. The purpose of diplomacy, Commander Spock had once said on *Star Trek,* was to *prolong* a crisis. Certainly the discourse meandered enough to make the Mississippi River look like a laser beam, but like the Father of Waters, it eventually had to get downstream, or downhill, or wherever the hell it was that rivers went. But this morning—what had awakened him? He looked out the window, seeing the orange-pink smudge beginning to form at the horizon, backlighting the buildings. Gant found them ugly, but he knew he just wasn't used to them. The tenements of Chicago weren't exactly the Taj Mahal, and the wood-frame house of his youth wasn't Buckingham Palace. Still, the sense of different-ness here was overpowering. Everywhere you looked, things seemed alien, and he wasn't cosmopolitan enough to overcome that feeling. It was like a background buzz in the Muzak, never quite there, but never gone away either. It was almost a sense of foreboding, but he shook it off. There was no reason to feel anything like that. He didn't know that he would be proven wrong very soon.

Barry Wise was already up in his hotel room, with breakfast coming—the hotel was one of an American chain, and the breakfast menu approximately American as well. The local bacon would be different, but even Chinese chickens laid real eggs, he was sure. His previous day's experiment with waffles hadn't worked out very well, and Wise was a man who needed a proper breakfast to function throughout the day.

Unlike most American TV correspondent/reporters, Wise looked for his own stories. His producer was a partner, not a boss-handler. He credited that fact for his collection of Emmy awards, though his wife just grumbled about dusting the damned things behind the basement bar.

He needed a fresh new story for today. His American audience would be bored with another talking-head-plus-B-roll piece on the trade negotiations. He needed some local color, he thought, something to make the American people feel as one with the Chinese people. It wasn't easy, and there'd been enough stories on Chinese restaurants, which was the only Chinese thing with which most Americans were familiar. What, then? What did Americans have in common with the citizens of the People's Republic of China? *Not a hell of a lot,* Wise told himself, but there had to be *something* he could use. He stood when breakfast arrived, looking out the picture windows as the waiter wheeled the cart close to the bed. It turned out that they'd goofed on his order, ham instead of bacon, but the ham looked okay and he went with it, tipping the waiter and sitting back down.

Something, he thought, pouring his coffee, *but what?* He'd been through this process often enough. The writers of fiction often chided reporters for their own sort of "creativity," but the process was real. Finding stuff of interest was doubly hard for reporters, because, unlike novelists, they couldn't make things up. They had to use reality, and reality could be a son of a bitch, Barry Wise thought. He reached for his reading glasses in the drawer of the night table and was surprised to see . . .

Well, it wasn't all *that* surprising. It was a matter of routine in any

American hotel, a Bible left there by the Gideon Society. It was only here, probably, because the hotel was American-owned and -operated, and they had a deal with the Gideon people . . . but what a strange place to find a Bible. The People's Republic wasn't exactly overrun with churches. Were there Christians here? Hmph. Why not find out? Maybe there was a story in that. . . . Better than nothing, anyway. With that semi-decided, he went back to breakfast. His crew would be waking up about now. He'd have his producer look around for a Christian minister, maybe even a Catholic priest. A rabbi was too much to hope for. That would mean the Israeli embassy, and that was cheating, wasn't it?

How was your day, Jack?" Cathy asked.

The night was an accident. They had nothing to do, no political dinner, no speech, no reception, no play or concert at the Kennedy Center, not even an intimate party of twenty or thirty on the bedroom level of the residence portion of the White House, which Jack hated and Cathy enjoyed, because they could invite people they actually knew and liked to those, or at least people whom they wanted to meet. Jack didn't mind the parties as such, but he felt that the bedroom level of The House (as the Secret Service called it, as opposed to the other *House,* sixteen blocks down the street) was the only private space he had left—even the place they owned at Peregrine Cliff on Chesapeake Bay had been redone by the Service. Now it had fire-protection sprinklers, about seventy phone lines, an alarm system like they used to protect nuclear-weapon storage sites, and a new building to house the protective detail who deployed there on the weekends when the Ryans decided to see if they still had a house to retreat to when this official museum got to be too much.

But tonight there was none of that. Tonight they were almost real people again. The difference was that if Jack wanted a beer or drink, he couldn't just walk to the kitchen and get it. That wasn't allowed. No, he had to order it through one of the White House ushers, who'd either take the elevator down to the basement-level kitchen, or to the upstairs bar. He could, of course, have insisted and walked off to make his own, but that would have meant insulting one of the ushers, and while these men, mainly black (some said they traced their lineage back to Andrew Jackson's personal slaves), didn't mind, it seemed unnecessarily insulting to them. Ryan had never been one to have others do his work, however.

Oh, sure, it was nice to have his shoes shined every night by some guy who didn't have anything else to do, and who drew a comfortable government salary to do it, but it just seemed unmanly to be fussed over as if he were some sort of nobleman, when in fact his father had been a hardworking homicide detective on the Baltimore city police force, and he'd needed a government scholarship (courtesy of the United States Marine Corps) to get through Boston College without having his mom take a job. Was it his working-class roots and upbringing? Probably, Ryan thought. Those roots also explained what he was doing now, sitting in an easy chair with a drink in his hand, watching TV, as though he were a normal person for a change.

Cathy's life was actually the least changed in the family, except that every morning she flew to work on a Marine Corps VH-60 Blackhawk helicopter, to which the taxpayers and the media didn't object—not after SANDBOX, also known as Katie Ryan, had been attacked in her daycare center by some terrorists. The kids were off watching televisions of their own, and Kyle Daniel, known to the Secret Service as SPRITE, was asleep in his crib. And so, *that* Dr. Ryan—code name SURGEON—was sitting in her own chair in front of the TV, going over her patient notes and checking a medical journal as part of her never-ending professional education.

"How are things at work, honey?" SWORDSMAN asked SURGEON.

"Pretty good, Jack. Bernie Katz has a new granddaughter. He's all bubbly about it."

"Which kid?"

"His son Mark—got married two years ago. We went, remember?"

"That's the lawyer?" Jack asked, remembering the ceremony, in the good old days, before he'd been cursed into the Presidency.

"Yeah, his other son, David, is the doctor—up at Yale, on the faculty, thoracic surgeon."

"Have I met that one?" Jack couldn't remember.

"No. He went to school out west, UCLA." She turned the page in the current *New England Journal of Medicine,* then decided to dog-ear it. It was an interesting piece on a new discovery in anesthesia, something worth remembering. She'd talk about it at lunch with one of the professors. It was her custom to lunch with her colleagues in different fields, to keep current on what was going on in medicine. The next big breakthrough, she thought, would be in neurology. One of her Hopkins colleagues had discovered a drug that seemed to make damaged nerve cells regrow. If it panned out, that was a Nobel Prize. It would be the ninth hanging on the trophy wall of the Johns Hopkins University School of Medicine. Her work with surgical lasers had won her a Lasker Public Service Award—the highest such award in American medicine—but it hadn't been fundamental enough for a trip to Stockholm. That was fine with her. Ophthalmology wasn't that sort of field, but fixing people's sight was pretty damned rewarding. Maybe the one good thing about Jack's elevation and her attendant status as First Lady was that she'd have a real shot at the Directorship of the Wilmer Institute if and when Bernie Katz ever decided to hang it up. She'd still be able to practice medicine—that was something she never wanted to give up—and also be able to oversee research in her field, decide who got the grants, where the really important exploratory work was, and that, she thought, was something she might be good at. So, maybe this President stuff wasn't a total loss.

Her only real beef was that people expected her to dress like a supermodel, and while she had always dressed well, being a clotheshorse had never appealed to her. It was enough, she figured, to wear nice formal gowns at all the damned formal affairs she had to attend (and not get charged for it, since the gowns were all donated by the makers). As it was, *Women's Wear Daily* didn't like her normal choice of clothing, as though her white lab coat was a fashion statement—no, it was her uniform, like the Marines who stood at the doors to the White House, and one she wore with considerable pride. Not many women, or men, could claim to be at the very pinnacle of their profession. But she could. As it was, this had turned into a nice evening. She didn't even mind Jack's addiction to The History Channel, even when he grumbled at some minor mistake in one of their shows. Assuming, she chuckled to herself, that he was right, and the show was wrong. . . . Her wineglass was empty, and since she didn't have any procedures scheduled for the next day, she waved to the usher for a refill. Life could have been worse. Besides, they'd had their big scare with those damned terrorists, and with good luck and that wonderful FBI agent Andrea Price had married, they'd survived, and she didn't expect anything like that to happen again. Her own Secret Service detail was her defense against that. Her own Principal

Agent, Roy Altman, inspired the same sort of confidence at his job that she did at hers, Cathy judged.

"Here you go, Dr. Ryan," the usher said, delivering the refilled glass.

"Thank you, George. How are the kids?"

"My oldest just got accepted to Notre Dame," he answered proudly.

"That's wonderful. What's she going to major in?"

"Premed."

Cathy looked up from her journal. "Great. If there's any way I can help her, you let me know, okay?"

"Yes, ma'am, I sure will." And the nice thing, George thought, was that she wasn't kidding. The Ryans were very popular with the staff, despite their awkwardness with all the fussing. There was one other family the Ryans looked after, the widow and kids of some Air Force sergeant whose connection with the Ryans nobody seemed to understand. And Cathy had personally taken care of two kids of staff members who'd had eye problems.

"What's tomorrow look like, Jack?"

"Speech to the VFW convention in Atlantic City. I chopper there and back after lunch. Not a bad speech Callie wrote for me."

"She's a little weird."

"She's different," the President agreed, "but she's good at what she does."

Thank God, Cathy didn't say aloud, *that* I *don't have to do much of that!* For her, a speech was telling a patient how she was going to fix his or her eyes.

There's a new Papal Nuncio in Beijing," the producer said.

"That's an ambassador, like, isn't it?"

The producer nodded. "Pretty much. Italian guy, Cardinal Renato DiMilo. Old guy, don't know anything about him."

"Well, maybe we can drive over and meet the guy," Barry thought as he knotted his tie. "Got an address and phone number?"

"No, but our contact at the American Embassy can get 'em quick enough."

"Give the guy a call," Wise ordered gently. He and the producer had been together for eleven years, and together they'd dodged bullets and won those Emmys, which wasn't bad for a couple of ex–Marine sergeants.

"Right."

Wise checked his watch. The timing worked just fine. He could get a report at his leisure, upload it on the satellite, and Atlanta could edit it and show it to people for breakfast in America. That would pretty much take care of his day in this heathen country. Damn, why couldn't they do trade conferences in Italy? He remembered Italian food fondly from his time in the Mediterranean Fleet Marine Force. And the Italian women. They'd like the United States Marine uniform. Well, lots of women did.

One thing neither Cardinal DiMilo nor Monsignor Schepke had learned to like was Chinese breakfast food, which was totally alien from anything Europeans had ever served for the early-morning meal. And so Schepke fixed breakfast every morning before their Chinese staff came in—they'd do the dishes, which was enough for both churchmen. Both had already said their morning mass, which necessitated their rising before six every morning, rather like soldiers did, the elderly Italian had often remarked to himself.

The morning paper was the *International Herald Tribune,* which was too American-oriented, but the world was an imperfect place. At least the paper showed the football scores, and European football was a sport of interest to both of them, and one which Schepke could still go out and play when the opportunity arose. DiMilo, who'd been a pretty good midfielder in his day, had to content himself with watching and kibitzing now.

The CNN crew had their own van, an American make that had been shipped into the PRC ages ago. It had its own miniature satellite transceiver rig, a small technical miracle of sorts that enabled instant contact with any place in the world via orbiting communications satellites. It could do anything but operate when the vehicle was moving, and someone was working on that feature, which would be the next major breakthrough, because then the mobile crews could work with little threat of interference from the gomers in whatever country they happened to be operating.

They also had a satellite-navigation system, which was a genuine miracle that allowed them to navigate anywhere, in any city for which they had a CD-ROM map. With it, they could find any address faster than a local taxi driver. And with a cell phone, they could get the address itself, in this case from the U.S. embassy, which had the street addresses for all foreign legations, of which the Papal Nuncio's house was just one more. The cell phone also allowed them to call ahead. The call was answered by a Chinese voice at first, then one that sounded German, of all things, but which said, sure, come on over.

Barry Wise was dressed in his usual coat and tie—his neatness was another leftover from the Marines—and he knocked on the door, finding the expected local—he was tempted to call them "natives," but that was too English, and distantly racist—at the door to conduct them in. The first Westerner they met was clearly not a Cardinal. Too young, too tall, and far too German.

"Hello, I am Monsignor Schepke," the man greeted him.

"Good day, I am Barry Wise of CNN."

"Yes," Schepke acknowledged with a smile. "I have seen you many times on the television. What brings you here?"

"We're here to cover the trade meeting between America and China, but we decided to look for other items of interest. We were surprised to see that the Vatican has a diplomatic mission here."

Schepke ushered Wise into his office and motioned him to a comfortable chair. "I've been here for several months, but the Cardinal just arrived recently."

"Can I meet him?"

"Certainly, but His Eminence is on the phone to Rome at the moment. Do you mind waiting a few minutes?"

"No problem," Wise assured him. He looked the monsignor over. He looked athletic, tall, and very German. Wise had visited that country many times, and always felt somewhat uneasy there, as if the racism that had occasioned the Holocaust was still there somewhere, hiding close by but out of sight. In other clothing, he would have taken Schepke for a soldier, even a Marine. He looked physically fit and very smart, clearly a keen observer.

"What order are you in, if I may ask?" Wise said.

"The Society of Jesus," Schepke replied.

A Jesuit, Wise thought at once. That explained it. "From Germany?"

"Correct, but I'm based in Rome now at Robert Bellarmine University, and I was asked to accompany His Eminence here because of my language skills." His English was about halfway between English and American, but not Canadian, grammatically perfect and remarkably precise in his pronunciations.

And because you're smart, Wise added to himself. He knew that the Vatican had a respected intelligence-gathering service, probably the oldest in the world. So, this Monsignor was a combination diplomat and spook, Wise decided.

"I won't ask how many languages you speak. I'm sure you have me beat," Wise observed. He'd never met or even heard of a dumb Jesuit.

Schepke offered a friendly smile. "It is my function." Then he looked at his desk phone. The light had gone out. Schepke excused himself and headed to the inner office, then returned. "His Eminence will see you now."

Wise rose and followed the German priest in. The man he saw was corpulent and clearly Italian, dressed not in priestly robes, but rather a coat and trousers, with a red shirt (or was it a vest?) underneath his Roman collar. The CNN correspondent didn't remember if the protocol was for him to kiss the man's ring, but hand-kissing wasn't his thing anyway, and so he just shook hands in the American custom.

"Welcome to our legation," Cardinal DiMilo said. "You are our first American reporter. Please—" The Cardinal gestured him to a chair.

"Thank you, Your Eminence." Wise did remember that part of the protocol.

"How may we serve you this day?"

"Well, we're in town to cover the trade talks—America and China—and we're just looking for a story about life in Beijing. We just learned last night that the Vatican has an embassy here, and we thought we might come over to talk to you, sir."

"Marvelous," DiMilo observed with a gracious priestly smile. "There are a few Christians in Beijing, though this is not exactly Rome."

Wise felt a light bulb go off. "What about Chinese Christians?"

"We've only met a few. We're going over to see one this afternoon, as a matter of fact, a Baptist minister named Yu."

"Really?" That was a surprise. A *local* Baptist?

"Yes," Schepke confirmed. "Good chap, he was even educated in America, at Oral Roberts University."

"A Chinese citizen from Oral Roberts?" Wise asked somewhat incredulously, as the STORY! light flashed in his head.

"Yes, it is somewhat unusual, isn't it?" DiMilo observed.

It was unusual enough that a Baptist and a Cardinal of the Roman Catholic Church were on speaking terms, Wise thought, but to have it happen here seemed about as likely as a live dinosaur strolling up the Mall in Washington. Atlanta would sure as hell like this one.

"Could we go over with you?" the CNN correspondent asked.

The terror began soon after she arrived at her workplace. For all the waiting and all the anticipation, it still came as a surprise, and an unwelcome one, the first twinge in her lower abdomen. The last time, now nearly six years before, it had presaged the birth of Ju-Long, and been a surprise as well, but that pregnancy had been authorized, and this one was not. She'd hoped that it would begin in the morning, but on a weekend, in their apartment, where she and Quon could handle things without external complications, but babies came at their own time in China, as they did elsewhere in the world, and this one would be no exception. The question was whether or not the State would allow it to take his first breath, and so the first muscle twinge, the first harbinger of the contractions of frank labor, brought with it the fear that murder would be committed, that her own body would be the scene of the crime, that she would be there to see it, to feel the baby stop moving, to feel death. The fear was the culmination of all the sleepless nights and the nightmares which had caused her to sweat in her bed for weeks. Her co-workers saw her face and wondered. A few of the women on the shop floor had guessed her secret, though they'd never discussed it with her. The miracle was that no one had informed on her, and that had been Lien-Hua's greatest fear of all—but that just wasn't the sort of thing one woman could do to another. Some of them, too, had given birth to daughters who had "accidentally" died a year or two later to satisfy their husbands' desire for a male heir. That was one more aspect of life in the People's Republic that was rarely the subject of conversation, even among women in private.

And so Yang Lien-Hua looked around the factory floor, feeling her muscles announce what was to come, and all she could hope was that it would stop, or delay itself. Another five hours, and she could pedal her bicycle home and deliver the baby there, and maybe that wasn't as good as on a weekend, but it was better than having an emergency here. "Lotus Flower" told herself that she had to be strong and resolute. She closed her eyes, and bit her lip, and tried to concentrate on her job, but the twinges soon grew into discomfort. Then would come mild pain, followed by the real contractions that would deny her the ability to stand, and then . . . what? It was her inability to see just a few hours beyond where she stood that contorted her face worse than pain ever could. She feared death, and while that fear is known to all humans, hers was for a life still part of herself, but not really her own. She feared seeing it die, feeling it die, feeling an unborn soul depart, and while it would surely go back to God, that was not God's intention. She needed her spiritual counselor now. She needed her husband, Quon. She needed Reverend Yu even more. But how would she make that happen?

The camera setup went quickly. Both of the churchmen watched with interest, since neither had seen this happen before. Ten minutes later, both were disappointed with the questions. Both had seen Wise on television, and both had expected better of him. They didn't realize that the story he really wanted was a few miles and an hour or so away.

"Good," Wise said, when the vanilla questions were asked and answered. "Can we follow you over to your friend's place?"

"Certainly," His Eminence replied, standing. He excused himself, because even Cardinals have to visit the bathroom before motoring off—at least they did at DiMilo's age. But he reappeared and joined Franz for the walk to the car, which the Monsignor would drive, to the continuing disappointment of their own servant/driver who was, as they suspected, a stringer for the Ministry of State Security. The CNN van followed, twisting through the streets until they arrived at the modest house of the Reverend Yu Fa An. Parking was easy enough. The two Catholic churchmen walked to Yu's door, carrying a large package, Wise noted.

"Ah!" Yu observed with a surprised smile, on opening the door. "What brings you over?"

"My friend, we have a gift for you," His Eminence replied, holding up the package. It was clearly a large Bible, but no less pleasing for the obvious nature of the gift. Yu waved them in, then saw the Americans.

"They asked if they could join us," Monsignor Schepke explained.

"Certainly," Yu said at once, wondering if maybe Gerry Patterson might see the story, and even his distant friend Hosiah Jackson. But they didn't get the cameras set up before he unwrapped the package.

Yu did this at his desk, and on seeing it, he looked up in considerable surprise. He'd expected a Bible, but this one must have cost hundreds of American dollars . . . It was an edition of the King James version in beautifully literate Mandarin . . . and magnificently illustrated. Yu stood and walked around the desk to embrace his Italian colleague.

"May the Lord Jesus bless you for this, Renato," Yu said, with no small emotion.

"We both serve Him as best we can. I thought of it, and it seemed something you might wish to have," DiMilo replied, as he might to a good parish priest in Rome, for that was what Yu was, wasn't it? Close enough, certainly.

For his part, Barry Wise cursed that he hadn't quite gotten his camera running for that moment. "We don't often see Catholics and Baptists this friendly," the reporter observed.

Yu handled the answer, and this time the camera was rolling. "We are allowed to be friends. We work for the same boss, as you say in America." He took DiMilo's hand again and shook it warmly. He rarely received so sincere a gift, and it was so strange to get it here in Beijing from what some of his American colleagues called papists, and an Italian one at that. Life really did have purpose after all. Reverend Yu had sufficient faith that he rarely doubted that, but to have it confirmed from time to time was a blessing.

The contractions came too fast, and too hard. Lien-Hua withstood it as long as she could, but after an hour, it felt as though someone had fired a rifle into her belly. Her knees buckled. She did her best to control it, to remain standing, but it was just too much. Her face turned pasty-white, and she collapsed to the cement floor. A co-worker was there at once. A mother herself, she knew what she beheld.

"It is your time?" she asked.

"Yes." Delivered with a gasp and a painful nod.

"Let me run and get Quon." And she was off at once. That bit of help was when things went bad for Lotus Flower.

Her supervisor noted one running employee, and then turned his head to see another prostrate one. He walked over, as one might to see what had happened after an automobile accident, more with curiosity than any particular desire to intervene. He'd rarely taken note of Yang Lien-Hua. She performed her function reliably, with little need for chiding or shouting, and was popular with her co-workers, and that was all he knew about her, really, and all that he figured he needed to know. There was no blood about. She hadn't fallen from some sort of accident or mechanical malfunction. How strange. He stood over her for a few seconds, seeing that she was in some discomfort and wondering what the problem was, but he wasn't a doctor or a medic, and didn't want to interfere. Oh, if she'd been bleeding he might have tried to slap a bandage over the wound or something, but this wasn't such a situation and so he just stood there, as he figured a manager should, showing that he was there, but not making things worse. There was a medical orderly in the first-aid room two hundred meters away. The other girl had probably run that way to fetch her, he thought.

Lien-Hua's face contorted after a few minutes' relative peace, as another contraction began. He saw her eyes screw closed and her face go pale, and her breathing change to a rapid pant. *Oh,* he realized, *that's it.* How odd. He was supposed to know about such things, so that he could schedule substitutions on the line. Then he realized something else. This was not an authorized pregnancy. Lien-Hua had broken the rules, and that wasn't supposed to happen, and it could reflect badly on his department, and on *him* as a supervisor . . . and he wanted to own an automobile someday.

"What is happening here?" he asked her.

But Yang Lien-Hua was in no shape to reply at the moment. The contractions were accelerating much faster than they'd done with Ju-Long. *Why couldn't this have waited until Saturday?* she demanded of Destiny. *Why does God wish my child to die aborning?* She did her best to pray through the pain, doing her utmost to concentrate, to entreat God for mercy and help in this time of pain and trial and terror, but all she saw around her was more cause for fear. There was no help in the face of her shop supervisor. Then she heard running feet again and looked to see Quon approaching, but before he got to her, the supervisor intercepted him.

"What goes on here?" the man demanded, with all the harshness of petty authority. "Your woman makes a baby here? An unauthorized baby?" the most minor of officials asked and accused in the same breath. *"Ju hai,"* he added: *Bitch!*

For his part, Quon wanted this baby as well. He hadn't told his wife of the fears that he'd shared with her, because he felt that it would have been unmanly, but that last statement from the shop supervisor was a little much for a man under two kinds of simultaneous stress. Recalling his army training, Quon struck out with his fist, following his hand with an imprecation of his own:

"Pok gai," literally, fall down in the street, but in context, *Get the fuck out of my way!* The shop supervisor gashed his head when he went down, giving Quon the satisfaction of seeing an injury to avenge the insult to his wife. But he had other things to do.

With the words said, and the blow struck, he lifted Lien-Hua to her feet and supported her as best he could on the way to where their bicycles were parked. But, now what to do? Like his wife, Quon had wanted this all to happen at home, where at the worst she could call in sick. But he had no more power to stop this process than he did to stop the world from turning on its axis. He didn't even have time or energy to curse fate. He had to deal with reality as it came, one shaky second at a time, and help his beloved wife as best he could.

You were educated in America?" Wise asked, in front of the rolling camera.

"Yes," Yu replied over tea. "At Oral Roberts University in Oklahoma. My first degree was in electrical engineering, then my divinity degree and my ordination came later."

"I see you are married," the reporter observed, pointing to a picture on the wall.

"My wife is away in Taiwan, looking after her mother, who is sick at the moment," he explained.

"So, how did you two meet?" Wise asked, meaning Yu and the Cardinal.

"That was Fa An's doing," the Cardinal explained. "It was he who came to us to extend a greeting to a newcomer in the same—same line of work, one could say." DiMilo was tempted to say that they enjoyed drinks together, but refrained for fear of demeaning the man before his fellow Baptists, some of whom objected to alcohol in any form. "As you might imagine, there are not so many Christians in this city, and what few there are need to stick together."

"Do you find it odd, a Catholic and a Baptist to be so friendly?"

"Not at all," Yu replied at once. "Why should it be odd? Are we not united by faith?" DiMilo nodded agreement at this perfect, if unanticipated, statement of belief.

"And what of your congregation?" Wise asked the Chinese minister next.

The bicycle lot outside was a confused mass of metal and rubber, for few of the Chinese workers owned automobiles, but as Quon helped Lien-Hua to the far corner, the two of them were spotted by someone who did have access to one. He was a factory security guard who drove about the perimeter of the plant very importantly in his three-wheel motorized cart, an accessory more important to his sense of status than his uniform and badge. Like Quon, a former sergeant in the People's Liberation Army, he'd never lost his feeling of personal authority, and this communicated itself in the way he spoke to people.

"Stop!" he called from the driver's seat in his cart. "What goes on here?"

Quon turned. Lien-Hua had just been hit with another contraction, with buckled knees and gasping breath, and he was almost dragging her to their bikes. Suddenly, he knew that this wasn't going to work. There was just no way that she could pedal her own bike. It was eleven blocks to their apartment. He could probably drag her up the three flights of steps, but how the hell was he going to get her to the front door?

"My wife is . . . she's hurt," Quon said, unwilling—afraid—to explain what the problem really was. He knew this guard—his name was

Zhou Jingjin—and he seemed a decent enough chap. "I'm trying to get her home."

"Where do you live, Comrade?" Zhou asked.

"Great Long March Apartments, number seventy-four," Quon replied. "Can you help us?"

Zhou looked them over. The woman seemed to be in some distress. His was not a country which placed great value on personal initiative, but she was a comrade in difficulty, and there was supposed to be solidarity among the people, and their apartment was only ten or eleven blocks, hardly fifteen minutes even in this slow and awkward cart. He made his decision, based on socialist worker solidarity.

"Load her on the back, Comrade."

"Thank you, Comrade." And Quon got his wife there, lifted her bottom up, and set her on the rusted steel deck behind the driver's compartment. With a wave, he signaled Zhou to head west. This contraction proved a difficult one. Lien-Hua gasped and then cried out, to the distress of her husband, and worse, the distress of the driver, who turned and saw what ought to have been a healthy woman grasping her abdomen in great pain. It was not a pretty thing to see by any stretch of the imagination, and Zhou, having taken one leap of initiative, decided that maybe he ought to take another. The path to Great Long March Apartments led down Meishuguan Street, past the Longfu Hospital, and like most Beijing teaching hospitals, this one had a proper emergency-receiving room. This woman was in distress, and she was a comrade, like himself a member of the working class, and she deserved his help. He looked back. Quon was doing his best to comfort his woman as a man should, far too busy to do much of anything as the security cart bumped along the uneven streets at twenty kilometers per hour.

Yes, Zhou decided, he had to do it. He turned the steering tiller gently, pulled up to the loading dock designed more for delivery trucks than ambulances, and stopped.

It took Quon a few seconds to realize that they'd stopped. He looked around, ready to help his wife off the cart, until he saw that they weren't at the apartment complex. Disoriented by the previous thirty minutes of unexpected emergency and chaos, he didn't understand, didn't grasp where they were, until he saw someone in a uniform emerge from the door. She wore a white bandanna-hat on her head—a nurse? Were they at the hospital? No, he couldn't allow that.

Yang Quon stood off the cart and turned to Zhou. He started to object that they'd come to the wrong place, that he didn't want to be here, but the hospital workers had an unaccustomed sense of industry at the moment—the emergency room was perversely idle at the moment—and a wheeled gurney emerged from the door with two men in attendance. Yang Quon tried to object, but he was merely pushed aside by the burly attendants as Lien-Hua was loaded on the gurney and wheeled inside before he could do much more than flap his mouth open and closed. He took a breath and rushed in, only to be intercepted by a pair of clerks asking for the information they needed to fill out their admitting forms, stopping him dead in his tracks as surely as a man with a loaded rifle, but far more ignominiously.

In the emergency room itself, a physician and a nurse watched as the orderlies loaded Lien-Hua onto an examining table. It didn't take more than a few seconds for their trained eyes to make the first guess, which they shared with a look. Only a few seconds more and her work clothes had been removed, and the pregnant belly was as obvious as a sunrise. It was similarly obvious that Yang Lien-Hua was in frank labor, and that this was no emergency. She could be wheeled to the elevator and taken to the second floor, where there was a sizable obstetrics staff. The physician, a woman, beckoned to the orderlies and told them where to move the patient. Then she walked to the phone to call upstairs and tell them that a delivery was on the way up. With that "work" done, the doctor went back to the physicians' lounge for a smoke and a magazine.

Comrade Yang?" another clerk, a more senior one, said.

"Yes?" the worried husband replied, still stuck in the waiting room, held prisoner by clerks.

"Your wife is being taken upstairs to obstetrics. But," the clerk added, "there's one problem."

"What is that?" Quon asked, knowing the answer, but hoping for a miracle, and utterly trapped by the bureaucratic necessities of the moment.

"We have no record of your wife's pregnancy in our files. You are in our health district—we show you at Number Seventy-two Great Long March Flats. Is that correct?"

"Yes, that's where we live," Quon sputtered out, trying to find a way out of this trap, but not seeing one anywhere.

"Ah." The clerk nodded. "I see. Thank you. I must now make a telephone call."

It was the way the last statement was delivered that frightened Quon: Ah, yes, I have to see that the trash is removed properly. Ah, yes, the glass is broken, and I'll try to find a repairman. Ah, yes, an unauthorized pregnancy, I'll call upstairs so that they'll know to kill the baby when it crowns.

Upstairs, Lien-Hua could see the difference in their eyes. When Ju-Long had been on his way, there'd been joy and anticipation in the eyes of the nurses who oversaw her labor. You could see their eyes crinkle with smiles at the corners of their masks . . . but not this time. Someone had come over to where she was in labor room #3 and said something to the nurse, and her head had turned rapidly to where Lien-Hua lay, and her eyes had turned from compassionate to . . . something else, and while Mrs. Yang didn't know what other thing it was, she knew the import. It might not be something the nurse particularly liked, but it was something she would assist in doing, because she had to. China was a place where people did the things they had to do, whether they approved it or liked it or not. Lien-Hua felt the next contraction. The baby in her uterus was trying to be born, not knowing that it was racing to its own destruction at the hands of the State. But the hospital staffers knew. Before, with Ju-Long, they'd been close by, not quite hovering, but close enough to watch and see that things were going well. Not now. Now they withdrew, desiring not to hear the sounds of a mother struggling to bring forth death in a small package.

On the first floor, it was equally plain to Yang Quon. What came back to him now was his firstborn son, Ju-Long, the feel of his small body in his arms, the little noises he made, the first smile, sitting up, crawling, the first step in their small apartment, the first words he'd spoken . . . but their little Large Dragon was dead now, never to be seen again, crushed by the wheel of a passenger bus. An uncaring fate had ripped that child from his arms and cast him aside like a piece of blowing trash on the street—and now the State was going to slay his second child. And it would all happen upstairs, less than ten meters away, and he couldn't do a thing about it. . . . It was a feeling not unknown to citizens of the People's Republic, where rule from above *was* the rule, but opposed to it now was the most fundamental of human drives. The two forces battled within the mind of factory worker Yang Quon. His hands shook at his sides as his mind struggled with the dilemma. His eyes strained, staring at nothing closer than the room's wall, but straining even so . . . something, there had to be *something* . . .

There *was* a pay telephone, and he *did* have the proper coins, and he *did* remember the number, and so Yang Quon lifted the receiver and dialed the number, unable to find the ability within himself to change fate, but hoping to find that ability in another.

I'll get it," Reverend Yu said in English, rising and walking to where it was ringing.

"A remarkable guy, isn't he?" Wise asked the two Catholics.

"A fine man," Cardinal DiMilo agreed. "A good shepherd for his flock, and that is all a man can hope to be."

Monsignor's Schepke's head turned when he caught the tone of Yu's voice. Something was wrong here, and by the sound, something serious. When the minister returned to the sitting room, his face told the tale.

"What is amiss?" Schepke asked in his perfect Mandarin. Perhaps this was not something for the American reporters.

"One of my congregation," Yu replied, as he reached for his jacket. "She is pregnant, in labor even now—but her pregnancy is unauthorized, and her husband fears the hospital will try to kill it. I must go to help."

"Franz, *was gibt's hier?"* DiMilo asked in German. The Jesuit then replied in Attic Greek to make damned sure the Americans wouldn't get it.

"You've been told about this, Eminence," Monsignor Schepke explained in the language of Aristotle. "The abortionists here commit what is virtually murder in any civilized country in the world, and the decision to do so, in this case, is purely political and ideological. Yu wishes to go and help the parents prevent this vile act."

DiMilo needed less than a second. He stood, and turned his head. "Fa An?"

"Yes, Renato?"

"May we come with you and assist? Perhaps our diplomatic status will have practical value," His Eminence said, in badly accented but comprehensible Mandarin.

It didn't take long for Reverend Yu either: "Yes, a fine idea! Renato, I cannot allow this child to die!"

If the desire to procreate is the most fundamental known to mankind, then there are few more powerful calls to action for an adult than *child-in-danger.* For this, men race into burning buildings and jump into rivers. For this now, three clergymen would go to a community hospital to challenge the power of the world's most populous nation.

"What's happening?" Wise asked, surprised by the sudden shifts in language and the way the three churchmen had leapt to their feet.

"A pastoral emergency. A member of Yu's congregation is in the hospital. She needs him, and we will go with our friend to assist in his pastoral duties," DiMilo said. The cameras were still running, but this was the sort of thing that got edited out. *But what the hell,* Wise thought.

"Is it far? Can we help? Want us to run you over?"

Yu thought it over and quickly decided that he couldn't make his bike go as fast as the American news van. "That is very kind. Yes."

"Well, let's go, then." Wise stood and motioned to the door. His crew broke down their gear in a matter of seconds and beat them all out the door.

Longfu Hospital turned out to be less than two miles away, facing a north-south street. It was, Wise thought, a place designed by a blind architect, so lacking in aesthetic as to be a definite government-owned building even in this country. The communists had probably killed off anyone with a sense of style back in 1950 or so, and no one had attempted to take his place. Like most reporters, the CNN team came in the front door in the manner of a police SWAT team. The cameraman's tool was up on his shoulder, with the soundman beside him, Barry Wise and the producer trailing while they looked for good establishing shots.

To call the lobby dreary was generous. A Mississippi state prison had a better atmosphere than this, to which was added the disinfectant smell that makes dogs cringe in the vet's office and made kids hug your neck harder for fear of the coming needle.

For his part, Barry Wise was unnaturally alert. He called it his Marine training, though he'd never seen combat operations. But one January night in Baghdad, he'd started looking out the windows forty minutes before the first bombs had fallen from the Stealth fighters, and kept looking until what U.S. Air Force planners had called the AT&T Building took the first spectacular hit. He took the producer's arm and told him to keep his head up. The other ex-Marine nodded agreement. For him it was the suddenly grim looks on the faces of the three clergymen, who'd been so genial until the phone had rung. For that old Italian guy to look this way—it had to be something, they both were sure, and whatever it was, it wouldn't be pleasant, and that often made for a good news story, and they were only seconds from their satellite uplink. Like hunters hearing the first rustle of leaves in the forest, the four CNN men looked alertly for the game and the shot.

"Reverend Yu!" Yang Quon called, walking—almost running—to where they were.

"Eminence, this is my parishioner, Mr. Yang."

"Buon giorno," DiMilo said in polite greeting. He looked over to see the newsies taking their pictures and keeping out of the way, more politely than he'd expected them to do. While Yu spoke with Yang, he walked over to Barry Wise to explain the situation.

"You are right to observe that relations between the Catholics and the Baptists are not always as friendly as they ought to be, but on this issue we stand as one. Upstairs, the officials of this government wish to kill a human baby. Yu wants to save that child. Franz and I will try to help."

"This could get messy, sir," Wise warned. "The security personnel in this country can play rough. I've seen it before."

DiMilo was not an imposing man in physical terms. He was short and a good thirty pounds overweight, the American figured. His hair was thinning. His skin was sagging with age. He probably went out of breath going up two flights of stairs. But for all that, the Cardinal summoned what manhood he had and transformed himself before the American's eyes. The genial smile and gentle disposition evaporated like steam in cold air. Now he looked more like a general on a battlefield.

"The life of an innocent child is at risk, Signore Wise" was all DiMilo said, and it was all he had to say. The Cardinal walked back to his Chinese colleague.

"Get that?" Wise asked his cameraman, Pete Nichols.

"Fuckin' A, Barry!" the guy said behind his eyepiece.

Yang pointed. Yu headed that way. DiMilo and Schepke followed. At the reception desk, the head clerk lifted a phone and made a call. The CNN crew followed the others into the stairwell and headed up to the second floor.

If anything, the obstetrics and gynecology floor was even more drab than the first. They heard the shouts, cries, and moans of women in labor, because in China, the public-health system did not waste drugs on women giving birth. Wise caught up to see that Yang guy, the father of the baby, standing still in the corridor, trying to identify the cries of his own wife from all the others. Evidently, he failed. Then he walked to the nurse's desk.

Wise didn't need to understand Chinese to get what the exchange was all about. Yang was supported by Reverend Yu and demanded to know where his wife was. The head nurse asked that the hell they were doing here, and told them all that they had to leave at once! Yang, his back straight with dignity and fear, refused and repeated his question. Again the head nurse told him to get lost. Then Yang seriously broke the rules by reaching across the high countertop and grabbing the nurse. You could see it in her eyes. It shocked her at a very fundamental level that anyone could defy her state-issued authority so blatantly. She tried to back away, but his grip was too strong, and for the first time she saw that his eyes were no longer a display of fear. Now they showed pure killing rage, because for Yang human instincts had cast aside all the societal conditioning he'd absorbed in his thirty-six years. His wife and child were in danger, and for them, right here and right now, he'd face a fire-breathing dragon barehanded and be damned to the consequences! The nurse took the easy way out and pointed to the left. Yang headed that way, Yu and the other two clergy with him, and the CNN crew trailing.

The nurse felt her neck and coughed to get her breath back, still too surprised to be fearful, trying to understand how and why her orders had been disregarded.

Yang Lien-Hua was in Labor Room #3. The walls were of yellow glazed brick, the floor tile of some color that had been overcome by years of use, and was now a brown-gray.

For "Lotus Flower," it had been a nightmare without end. Alone, all alone in this institution of life and death, she'd felt the contractions strengthen and merge into one continuous strain of her abdominal muscles, forcing her unborn child down the birth canal, toward a world that didn't want it. She'd seen that in the nurses' faces, the sorrow and resignation, what they must have seen and felt elsewhere in the hospital when death came to take a patient. They'd all learned to accept it as inevitable, and they tried to step away from it, because what had to be done was so contrary to all human instincts that the only way they could be there and see it happen was to—to be somewhere else. Even that didn't work, and though they scarcely admitted it even to one another, they'd go home from work and lie in their beds and weep bitterly at what they as women had to do to newborns. Some would cradle the dead children who never were, who never got to take that first life-affirming breath, trying to show womanly gentleness to someone who would never know about it, except perhaps the spirits of the murdered babies who might have lingered close by. Others went the other way, tossing them into bins like the trash the state said they were. But even they never joked about it—in fact, never talked about it, except perhaps to note it had been done, or, maybe, "There's a woman in Number Four who needs *the shot.*"

Lien-Hua felt the sensations, but worse, knew the thoughts, and her mind cried out to God for mercy. Was it so wrong to be a mother, even if she attended a Christian church? Was it so wrong to have a second child to replace the first that Fate had ripped from her arms? Why did the State deny to her the blessing of motherhood? Was there no way out? She hadn't killed the first child, as many Chinese families did. She hadn't murdered her little Large Dragon, with his sparkling black eyes and comical laugh and grasping little hands. Some other force had taken that away from her, and she *wanted,* she *needed* another. Just one other.

She wasn't being greedy. She didn't want to raise two more children. Only one. Only one to suckle at her breasts and smile at her in the mornings. She *needed* that. She worked hard for the State, asked little in return, but she did ask for *this!* It was her *right* as a human being, wasn't it?

But now she knew only despair. She tried to reverse the contractions, to stop the delivery from happening, but she might as well have tried to stop the tide with a shovel. Her little one was coming out. She could feel it. She could see the knowledge of it in the face of the delivery nurse. She checked her watch and leaned out of the room, waving her arm just as Lien-Hua fought the urge to push and complete the process, and so offer up her child to Death. She fought, controlled her breathing, struggled with her muscles, panted instead of breathing deeply, fought and fought and fought, but it was all for nothing. She knew that now. Her husband was nowhere near to protect her. He'd been man enough to put her here, but not enough to protect her and his own child from what was happening now. With despair came relaxation. It was time. She recognized the feeling from before. She could not fight anymore. It was time to surrender.

The doctor saw the nurse wave. This one was a man. It was easier on the men, and so they gave most of the "shots" in this hospital. He took the 50-cc syringe from stores and then went to the medication closet, unlocking it and withdrawing the big bottle of formaldehyde. He filled the syringe, not bothering to tap out the bubbles, because the purpose of this injection was to kill, and any special care was superfluous. He walked down the corridor toward Labor #3. He'd been on duty for nine hours that day. He'd performed a difficult and successful Caesarian section a few hours before, and now he'd end his working day with this. He didn't like it. He did it because it was his job, part of the State's policy. The foolish woman, having a baby without permission. It really was *her* fault, wasn't it? She knew what the rules were. Everyone did. It was impossible *not* to know. But she'd broken the rules. And she wouldn't be punished for it. Not really *her.* She wouldn't go to prison or lose her job or suffer a monetary fine. She'd just get to go home with her uterus the way it had been nine months before—empty. She'd be a little older, and a little wiser, and know that if this happened again, it was a lot better to have the abortion done in the second or third month, before you got too attached to the damned thing. Damned sure it was a lot more comfortable than going through a whole labor for nothing. That was sad, but there was much sadness in life, and for this part of it they'd all volunteered. The doctor had chosen to become a doctor, and the woman in #3 had chosen to become pregnant.

He came into #3, wearing his mask, because he didn't want to give the woman any infection. That was why he used a clean syringe, in case he should slip and stick her by mistake.

So.

He sat on the usual stool that obstetricians used both for delivering babies and for aborting the late-term ones. The procedure they used in America was a little more pleasant. Just poke into the baby's skull, suck the brains out, crush the skull and deliver the package with a lot less trouble than a full-term fetus, and a lot easier on the woman. He wondered what the story was on this one, but there was no sense in knowing, was there? No sense knowing that which you can't change.

So.

He looked. She was fully dilated and effaced, and, yes, there was the head. Hairy little thing. Better give her another minute or two, so that after he did his duty she could expel the fetus in one push and be done with it. Then she could go off and cry for a while and start getting over it. He was concentrating a little too much to note the commotion in the corridor outside the labor room.

Yang pushed the door open himself. And there it all was, for all of them to see. Lien-Hua was on the delivery table. Quon had never seen one of them before, and the way it held a woman's legs up and apart, it looked for all the world like a device to make women easier to rape. His wife's head was back and down, not up and looking to see her child born, and then he saw why.

There was the . . . doctor, was he? And in his hand a large needle full of—

—they were in time! Yang Quon pushed the doctor aside, off his stool. He darted right to his wife's face.

"I am here! Reverend Yu came with me, Lien." It was like a light coming on in a darkened room.

"Quon!" Lien-Hua cried out, feeling her need to push, and finally wanting to.

But then things became more complicated still. The hospital had its own security personnel, but on being alerted by the clerk in the main lobby, one of them called for the police, who, unlike the hospital's own personnel, were armed. Two of them appeared in the corridor, surprised first of all to see foreigners with TV equipment right there in front of them. Ignoring them, they pushed into the delivery room to find a pregnant woman about to deliver, a doctor on the floor, and four men, two of *them* foreigners as well!

"What goes on here!" the senior one bellowed, since intimidation was a major tool for controlling people in the PRC.

"These people are interfering with my duties!" the doctor answered, with a shout of his own. If he didn't act fast, the damned baby would be born and breathe, and then he couldn't . . .

"What?" the cop demanded of him.

"This woman has an unauthorized pregnancy, and it is my duty to terminate the fetus now. These people are in my way. Please remove them from the room."

That was enough for the cops. They turned to the obviously unauthorized visitors. "You will leave now!" the senior one ordered, while the junior one kept his hand on his service pistol.

"No!" was the immediate reply, both from Yang Quon and Yu Fa An.

"The doctor has given his order, you must leave," the cop insisted. He was unaccustomed to having ordinary people resist his orders. "You will go now!"

The doctor figured this was the cue for him to complete his distasteful duty, so that he could go home for the day. He set the stool back up and slid it to where he needed to be.

"You will not do this!" This time it was Yu, speaking with all the moral authority his education and status could provide.

"Will you get him out of here?" the doctor growled at the cops, as he slid the stool back in place.

Quon was ill-positioned to do anything, standing as he was by his wife's head. To his horror, he saw the doctor lift the syringe and adjust his glasses. Just then his wife, who might as well have been in another city for the past two minutes, took a deep breath and pushed.

"Ah," the doctor said. The fetus was fully crowned now, and all he had to do was—

Reverend Yu had seen as much evil in his life as most clergymen, and they see as much as any seasoned police officer, but to see a human baby murdered before his eyes was just too much. He roughly shoved the junior of the two policemen aside and struck the doctor's head from behind, flinging him to the right and jumping on top of him.

"Getting this?" Barry Wise asked in the corridor.

"Yep," Nichols confirmed.

What offended the junior policeman was not the attack on the doctor, but rather the fact that this—this citizen had laid hands on a uniformed member of the Armed People's Police. Outraged, he drew his pistol from its holster, and what had been a confused situation became a deadly one.

"No!" shouted Cardinal DiMilo, moving toward the young cop. He turned to see the source of the noise and saw an elderly *gwai,* or foreigner in very strange clothes, moving toward him with a hostile expression. The cop's first response was a blow to the foreigner's face, delivered with his empty left hand.

Renato Cardinal DiMilo hadn't been physically struck since his childhood, and the affront to his personhood was all the more offensive for his religious and diplomatic status, and to be struck by this child! He turned back from the force of the blow and pushed the man aside, wanting to go to Yu's aid, and to help him keep this murderous doctor away from the baby about to be born. The doctor was wavering on one foot, holding the syringe up in the air. This the Cardinal seized in his hand and hurled against the wall, where it didn't break, because it was plastic, but the metal needle bent.

Had the police better understood what was happening, or had they merely been better trained, it would have stopped there. But they hadn't, and it didn't. Now the senior cop had his Type 77 pistol out. This he used to club the Italian on the back of the head, but his blow was poorly delivered, and all it managed to do was knock him off balance and split his skin.

Now it was Monsignor Schepke's turn. His Cardinal, the man whom it was his duty to serve and protect, had been attacked. He was a priest. He couldn't use deadly force. He couldn't attack. But he could defend. That he did, grasping the older officer's gun hand and twisting it up, in a safe direction, away from the others in the room. But there it went off, and though the bullet merely flattened out in the concrete ceiling, the noise inside the small room was deafening.

The younger policeman suddenly thought that his comrade was under attack. He wheeled and fired, but missed Schepke, and struck Cardinal DiMilo in the back. The .30 caliber bullet transited the body back to front, damaging the churchman's spleen. The pain surprised DiMilo, but his eyes were focused on the emerging baby.

The crash of the shot had startled Lien-Hua, and the push that followed was pure reflex. The baby emerged, and would have fallen headfirst to the hard floor but for the extended hands of Reverend Yu, who stopped the fall and probably saved the newborn's life. He was lying on his side, and then he saw that the second shot had gravely wounded his Catholic friend. Holding the baby, he struggled to his feet and looked vengefully at the youthful policeman.

"Huai dan!" he shouted: *Villain!* Oblivious of the infant in his arms, he lurched forward toward the confused and frightened policeman.

As automatically as a robot, the younger cop merely extended his arm and shot the Baptist preacher right in the forehead.

Yu twisted and fell, bumping into Cardinal DiMilo's supine form and landing on his back, so that his chest cushioned the newborn's fall.

"Put that away!" the older cop screamed at his young partner. But the damage had been done. The Chinese Reverend Yu was dead, the back of his head leaking brain matter and venting blood at an explosive rate onto the dirty tile floor.

The doctor was the first to take any intelligent action. The baby was out now, and he couldn't kill it. He took it from Yu's dead arms, and held it up by the feet, planning to smack it on the rump, but it cried out on its own. *So,* the doctor thought as automatically as the second policeman's shot, *this lunacy has one good result.* That he'd been willing to kill it sixty seconds before was another issue entirely. Then, it had been unauthorized tissue. Now, it was a breathing citizen of the People's Republic, and his duty as a physician was to protect it. The dichotomy did not trouble him because it never even occurred to him.

There followed a few seconds in which people tried to come to terms with what had happened. Monsignor Schepke saw that Yu was dead. He couldn't be alive with that head wound. His remaining duty was to his Cardinal.

"Eminence," he said, kneeling down to lift him off the bloody floor.

Renato Cardinal DiMilo thought it strange that there was so little pain, for he knew that his death was imminent. Inside, his spleen was lacerated, and he was bleeding out internally at a lethal rate. He had not the time to reflect on his life or what lay in his immediate future, but despite that, his life of service and faith reasserted itself one more time.

"The child, Franz, the child?" he asked in a gasping voice.

"The baby lives," Monsignor Schepke told the dying man.

A gentle smile: *"Bene,"* Renato said, before closing his eyes for the last time.

The last shot taken by the CNN crew was of the baby lying on her mother's chest. They didn't know her name, and the woman's face was one of utter confusion, but then she felt her daughter, and the face was transformed as womanly instincts took over completely.

"We better get the fuck out of here, Barry," the cameraman advised, with a hiss.

"I think you're right, Pete." Wise stepped back and started to his left to get down the corridor to the stairs. He had a potential Emmy-class story in his hands now. He'd seen a human drama with few equals, and it had to go out, and it had to go out fast.

Inside the delivery room, the senior cop was shaking his head, his ears still ringing, trying to figure out what the hell had happened here, when he realized that the light level was lower—the TV camera was gone! He had to do something. Standing erect, he darted from the room and looked right, and saw the last American disappear into the stairwell. He left his junior in the delivery room and ran that way, turned into the fire stairs and ran downstairs as fast as gravity could propel him.

Wise led his people into the main lobby and right toward the main door, where their satellite van was. They'd almost made it, when a shout made them turn. It was the cop, the older one, about forty, they thought, and his pistol was out again, to the surprise and alarm of the civilians in the lobby.

"Keep going," Wise told his crew, and they pushed through the doors into the open air. The van was in view, with the mini–satellite dish lying flat on the roof, and that was the key to getting this story out.

"Stop!" the cop called. He knew some English, so it would seem.

"Okay, guys, let's play it real cool," Wise told the other three.

"Under control," Pete the cameraman advised. The camera was off his shoulder now, and his hands were out of casual view.

The cop holstered his pistol and came close, with his right hand up and out flat. "Give me tape," he said. "Give me tape." His accent was crummy, but his English was understandable enough.

"That tape is my property!" Wise protested. "It belongs to me and my company."

The cop's English wasn't that good. He just repeated his demand: "Give me tape!"

"Okay, Barry," Pete said. "I got it."

The cameraman—his name was Peter Nichols—lifted the camera up and hit the EJECT button, punching the Beta-format tape out of the Sony camera. This he gave to the police officer with a downcast and angry expression. The cop took it with his own expression of satisfaction and turned on his heel to go back into the hospital.

There was no way he could have known that, like any news cameraman, Pete Nichols could deal seconds as skillfully as any Las Vegas poker dealer. He winked at Barry Wise, and the four headed off to the van.

"Send it up now?" the producer asked.

"Let's not be too obvious about it," Wise thought. "Let's move a few blocks."

This they did, heading west toward Tiananmen Square, where a news van doing a satellite transmission wasn't out of the ordinary. Wise was already on his satellite phone to Atlanta.

"This is Wise Mobile in Beijing with an upload," the correspondent said into the phone.

"Hey, Barry," a familiar voice said in reply. "This is Ben Golden. What you got for us?"

"It's hot," Wise told his controller half a world away. "A double murder and a childbirth. One guy who got whacked is a Catholic cardinal, the Vatican ambassador to Beijing. The other one's a Chinese Baptist minister. They were both shot on camera. You might want to call Legal about it."

"Fuck!" Atlanta observed.

"We're uploading the rough-cut now, just so you get it. I'll stand by to do the talking. But let's get the video uploaded first."

"Roger that. We're standing by on Channel Zero Six."

"Zero Six, Pete," Wise told his cameraman, who also ran the uplink.

Nichols was kneeling by the control panels. "Standing by . . . tape's in . . . setting up for Six . . . transmitting . . . *now!"* And with that, the Ku-band signal went racing upward through the atmosphere to the satellite hovering 22,800 miles directly over the Admiralty Islands in the Bismarck Sea.

CNN doesn't bother encrypting its video signals. To do so is technically inconvenient, and few people bother pirating signals they could just as easily get off their cable systems for free in a few minutes, or even get live just four seconds later.

But this one was coming in at an awkward hour, which was, however, good for CNN Atlanta, because some headquarters people would want to go over it. A shooting death was not what the average American wanted with his Rice Krispies in the morning.

It was also downloaded by the American intelligence community, which holds CNN in very high regard, and doesn't distribute its news coverage very far in any case. But this one did go to the White House Office of Signals, a largely military operation located in the basement of the West Wing. There a watch officer had to decide how important it was. If it ranked as a CRITIC priority, the President had to know about it in fifteen minutes, which meant waking him up *right now,* which was not something to be done casually to the Commander-in-Chief. A mere FLASH could wait a little longer, like—the watch officer checked the wall clock—yeah, like until breakfast. So, instead, they called the President's National Security Adviser, Dr. Benjamin Goodley. They'd let him make the call. He was a carded National Intelligence Officer.

"Yeah?" Goodley snarled into the phone while he checked the clock radio next to his bed.

"Dr. Goodley, this is Signals. We just copied something off CNN from Beijing that the Boss is going to be interested in."

"What is it?" CARDSHARP asked. Then he heard the reply. "How certain are you of this?"

"The Italian guy looks like he might possibly have survived, from the video—I mean if there was a good surgeon close—but the Chinese minister had his brains blowed right out. No chance for him at all, sir."

"What was it all about?"

"We're not sure of that. NSA might have the phone conversation between this Wise guy and Atlanta, but we haven't seen anything about it yet."

"Okay, tell me what you got again," Goodley ordered, now that he was approximately awake.

"Sir, we have a visual of two guys getting shot and a baby being born in Beijing. The video comes from Barry Wise of CNN. The video shows three gunshots. One is upwards into the ceiling of what appears to be a hospital delivery room. The second shot catches a guy in the back. That guy is identified as the Papal Nuncio to Beijing. The third shot goes right into the head of a guy identified as a Baptist minister in Beijing. That one appears to be a Chinese national. In between, we have a baby being born. Now we—stand by a minute, Dr. Goodley, okay, I have FLASH traffic from Fort Meade. Okay, they got it, too, and they got a voice transmission via their ECHELON system, reading it now. Okay, the Catholic cardinal is dead, according to this, says Cardinal Renato Di-Milo—can't check the spelling, maybe State Department for that—and the Chinese minister is a guy named Yu Fa An, again no spelling check. They were there to, oh, okay, they were there to prevent a late-term abortion, and looks like they succeeded, but these two clergy got their asses killed doing it. Third one, a monsignor named Franz Schepke—that sounds pretty German to me—was there, too, and looks like he survived—oh, okay, he must be the tall one you see on the tape. You gotta see the tape. It's a hell of a confused mess, sir, and when this Yu guy gets it, well, it's like that video from Saigon during the Tet Offensive. You know, where the South Vietnamese police colonel shot the North Vietnamese spy in the side of the head with a Smith Chief's Special, you know, like a fountain of blood coming out the head. Ain't something to watch with your Egg McMuffin, y'know?" the watch officer observed.

The reference came across clearly enough. The news media had celebrated the incident as an example of the South Vietnamese government's bloodthirstiness. They had never explained—probably never even knew—that the man shot had been an officer of the North Vietnamese army captured in a battle zone wearing civilian clothing, therefore, under the Geneva Protocols was a spy liable to summary execution, which was exactly what he'd received.

"Okay, what else?"

"Do we wake the Boss up for this? I mean, we got a diplomatic team over there, and this has some serious implications."

Goodley thought about that for a second or two. "No. I'll brief him in in a few hours."

"Sir, it's sure as hell going to be on CNN's seven o'clock morning report," the watch officer warned.

"Well, let me brief him when he have more than just pictures."

"Your call, Dr. Goodley."

"Thanks. Now, I think I'll try to get one more hour before I drive over to Langley." The phone went down before Goodley heard a reaction. His job carried a lot of prestige, but it denied him sleep and much of a social or sex life, and at moments like this he wondered what the hell was so goddamned prestigious about it.

CHAPTER 25

Fence Rending

The speed of modern communications makes for curious disconnects. In this case, the American government knew what had happened in Beijing long before the government of the People's Republic did. What appeared in the White House Office of Signals appeared also in the State Department's Operations Center, and there the senior officer present had decided, naturally enough, to get the information immediately to the U.S. Embassy in Beijing. There Ambassador Carl Hitch took the call at his desk on the encrypted line. He forced the caller from Foggy Bottom to confirm the news twice before making his first reaction, a whistle. It wasn't often that an accredited ambassador of any sort got killed in a host country, much less *by* a host country. What the hell, he wondered, was Washington going to do about this?

"Damn," Hitch whispered. He hadn't even met Cardinal DiMilo yet. The official reception had been planned for two weeks from now in a future that would never come. What was *he* supposed to do? First, he figured, get off a message of condolence to the Vatican mission. (Foggy Bottom would so notify the Vatican through the Nuncio in Washington, probably. Maybe even Secretary Adler would drive over himself to offer official condolences. Hell, President Ryan was Catholic, and maybe *he* would go himself, Hitch speculated.) Okay, Hitch told himself, things to do here. He had his secretary call the Nuncio's residence, but all he got there was a Chinese national answering the phone, and that wasn't worth a damn. That would have to go on the back burner . . . what about the Italian Embassy? he thought next. The Nuncio was an Italian citizen, wasn't he? Probably. Okay. He checked his card file and dialed up the Italian ambassador's private line.

"Paulo? This is Carl Hitch. Thanks, and you? I have some bad news, I'm afraid . . . the Papal Nuncio, Cardinal DiMilo, he's been shot and killed in some Beijing hospital by a Chinese policeman . . . it's going to be on CNN soon, not sure how soon . . . we're pretty certain of it, I'm afraid . . . I'm not entirely sure, but what I've been told is that he was there trying to prevent the death of a child, or one of those late-term abortions they do here . . . yeah . . . say, doesn't he come from a prominent family?" Then Hitch started taking notes. "Vincenzo, you said? I see . . . Minister of Justice two years ago? I tried to call over there, but all I got was some local answering the phone. German? Schepke?" More notes. "I see. Thank you, Paulo. Hey, if there's anything we can help you with over here . . . right. Okay. Bye." He hung up. "Damn. Now what?" he asked the desk. He could spread the bad news to the German Embassy, but, no, he'd let someone else do that. For now . . . he checked his watch. It was still short of sunrise in Washington, and the people there would wake up to find a firestorm. His job, he figured, was to verify what had happened so that he could make sure Washington had good information. But how the hell to do that? His best potential source of information was this Monsignor Schepke, but the only way to get him was to stake out the Vatican Embassy and wait for him to come home. Hmm, would the Chinese be holding him somewhere? No, probably not. Once their Foreign Ministry found out about this, they'd probably fall all over themselves trying to apologize. So, they'd put extra security on the Nuncio's place, and that would keep newsies away, but they're not going to mess with accredited diplomats, not after killing one. This was just so bizarre. Carl Hitch had been a foreign-service officer since his early twenties. He'd never come across anything like this before, at least not since Spike Dobbs had been held hostage in Afghanistan by guerrillas, and the Russians had screwed up the rescue mission and gotten him killed. Some said that had been deliberate, but even the Soviets weren't that dumb, Hitch thought. Similarly, this hadn't been a deliberate act either. The Chinese were communists, and communists didn't gamble that way. It just wasn't part of their nature or their training.

So, how had this happened? And what, exactly, *had* happened?

And when would he tell Cliff Rutledge about it? And what effect might this have on the trade talks? Carl Hitch figured he'd have a full evening.

The People's Republic will not be dictated to," Foreign Minister Shen Tang concluded.

"Minister," Rutledge replied, "it is not the intention of the United States to dictate to anyone. You make your national policy to suit your nation's needs. We understand and respect that. We require, however, that you understand and respect our right to make *our* national policy as well, to suit *our* country's needs. In this case, that means invoking the provisions of the Trade Reform Act."

That was a big, sharp sword to wave, and everyone in the room knew it, Mark Gant thought. The TRA enabled the Executive Branch to replicate any nation's trade laws as applied to American goods, and mirror-image them against that nation's own goods. It was international proof of the adage that the shoe could sure pinch if it was on the other foot. In this case, everything China did to exclude American manufactured goods from the Chinese marketplace would simply be invoked in order to do the same to Chinese goods, and with a trade surplus of seventy billion dollars per year, that could well mean seventy billion dollars—all of it hard currency. The money to buy the things the PRC government wanted from America or elsewhere wouldn't be there anymore. Trade would become *trade,* one of mine for one of yours, which was the theory that somehow never became reality.

"If America embargoes Chinese trade, China can and will do the same to America," Shen shot back.

"Which serves neither your purposes nor our own," Rutledge responded. *And that dog ain't gonna hunt,* he didn't have to say. The Chinese knew that well enough without being told.

"And what of most-favored-nation status for our country? What of entry into the World Trade Organization?" the Chinese foreign minister demanded.

"Mr. Minister, America cannot look favorably upon either so long as your country expects open export markets while closing your import markets. Trade, sir, means *trade,* the even exchange of your goods for ours," Rutledge pointed out again—about the twelfth time since lunch, he reckoned. Maybe the guy would get it this time. But that was unfair. He already got it. He just wasn't acknowledging the fact. It was just domestic Chinese politics projected into the international arena.

"And again you dictate to the People's Republic!" Shen replied, with enough anger, real or feigned, to suggest that Rutledge had usurped his parking place.

"No, Minister, we do no such thing. It is you, sir, who tried to dictate to the United States of America. You say that we must accept your trade terms. In that, sir, you are mistaken. We see no more need to buy your goods than you do to buy ours." *Just that you need our hard cash a damned sight more than we need your chew toys for our fucking dogs!*

"We can buy our airliners from Airbus just as easily as from Boeing."

This really was getting tiresome. Rutledge wanted to respond: *But without our dollars, what will you pay for them with, Charlie?* But Airbus had excellent credit terms for its customers, one more way in which a European government-subsidized enterprise played "fair" in the marketplace with a private American corporation. So, instead he said:

"Yes, Mr. Minister, you can do that, and we can buy trade goods from Taiwan, or Korea, or Thailand, or Singapore, just as easily as we can buy them here." *And they'll fucking well buy their airplanes from Boeing!* "But that does not serve the needs of your people, or of ours," he concluded reasonably.

"We are a sovereign nation and a sovereign people," Shen retorted, continuing on as he had before, and Rutledge figured that the rhetoric was all about taking command of the verbiage. It was a strategy that had worked many times before, but Rutledge had instructions to disregard all the diplomatic theatrics, and the Chinese just hadn't caught on yet. Maybe in a few more days, he thought.

"As are we, Minister," Rutledge said, when Shen concluded. Then he ostentatiously checked his watch, and here Shen took the cue.

"I suggest we adjourn until tomorrow," the PRC foreign minister said.

"Good. I look forward to seeing you in the morning, Minister," Rutledge responded, rising and leaning across the table to shake hands. The rest of the party did the same, though Mark Gant didn't have a counterpart to be nice to at the moment. The American party shuffled out, downstairs toward their waiting cars.

"Well, that was lively," Gant observed, as soon as they were outside.

Rutledge actually had himself a nice grin. "Yeah, it was kind of diverting, wasn't it?" A pause. "I think they're exploring how far bluster can take them. Shen is actually rather a sedate kind of guy. He likes it nice and gentle most of the time."

"So, he has his instructions, too?" Gant wondered.

"Of course, but he reports to a committee, their Politburo, whereas we report to Scott Adler, and he reports to President Ryan. You know, I was a little mad about the instructions I had coming over here, but this is actually turning into fun. We don't get to snarl back at people very often. We're the U.S. of A., and we're supposed to be nice and calm and accommodating to everybody. That's what I'm used to doing. But this—this feels good." That didn't mean that he approved of President Ryan, of course, but switching over from canasta to poker made an interesting change. Scott Adler liked poker, didn't he? Maybe that explained why he got along so well with that yahoo in the White House.

It was a short drive back to the embassy. The Americans in the delegation rode mainly in silence, blessing the few minutes of quiet. The hours of precise diplomatic exchange had had to be attended to in the same way a lawyer read a contract, word by goddamned word, seeking meaning and nuance, like searching for a lost diamond in a cesspool. Now they sat back in their seats and closed their eyes or looked mutely at the passing drab scenery with no more than an unstifled yawn, until they pulled through the embassy gate.

About the only thing to complain about was the fact that the limousines here, like those everywhere, were hard to get in and out of, unless you were six years old. But as soon as they alighted from their official transport, they could see that something was wrong. Ambassador Hitch was right there, and he hadn't bothered with that before. Ambassadors have high diplomatic rank and importance. They do not usually act as doormen for their own countrymen.

"What's the matter, Carl?" Rutledge asked.

"A major bump in the road," Hitch answered.

"Somebody die?" the Deputy Secretary of State asked lightly.

"Yeah," was the unexpected answer. Then the ambassador waved them inside. "Come on."

The senior delegation members followed Rutledge into the ambassador's conference room. Already there, they saw, were the DCM—the Deputy Chief of Mission, the ambassador's XO, who in many embassies was the real boss—and the rest of the senior staff, including the guy Gant had figured was the CIA station chief. *What the hell?* TELESCOPE thought. They all took their seats, and then Hitch broke the news.

"Oh, shit," Rutledge said for them all. "Why did this happen?"

"We're not sure. We have our press attaché trying to track this Wise guy down, but until we get more information, we really don't know the cause of the incident." Hitch shrugged.

"Does the PRC know?" Rutledge asked next.

"Probably they're just finding out," the putative CIA officer opined. "You have to assume the news took a while to percolate through their bureaucracy."

"How do we expect them to react?" one of Rutledge's underlings asked, sparing his boss the necessity of asking the obvious and fairly dumb question.

The answer was just as dumb: "Your guess is as good as mine," Hitch said.

"So, this could be a minor embarrassment or a major whoopsie," Rutledge observed. "Whoopsie" is a term of art in the United States Department of State, usually meaning a massive fuckup.

"I'd lean more toward the latter," Ambassador Hitch thought. He couldn't come up with a rational explanation for why this was so, but his instincts were flashing a lot of bright red lights, and Carl Hitch was a man who trusted his instincts.

"Any guidance from Washington?" Cliff asked.

"They haven't woken up yet, have they?" And as one, every member of the delegation checked his watch. The embassy people already had, of course. The sun had not yet risen on their national capital. What decisions would be made would happen in the next four hours. Nobody here would be getting much sleep for a while, because once the decisions were made, then they'd have to decide how to implement them, how to present the position of their country to the People's Republic.

"Ideas?" Rutledge asked.

"The President won't like this very much," Gant observed, figuring he knew about as much as anyone else in the room. "His initial reaction will be one of disgust. Question is, will that spill over into what we're here for? I think it might, depending on how our Chinese friends react to the news."

"How will the Chinese react?" Rutledge asked Hitch.

"Not sure, Cliff, but I doubt we'll like it. They will regard the entire incident as an intrusion—an interference with their internal affairs—and their reaction will be somewhat crass, I think. Essentially they're going to say, 'Too damned bad.' If they do, there's going to be a visceral reaction in America and in Washington. They don't understand us as well as they'd like to think they do. They misread our public opinion at every turn, and they haven't showed me much sign of learning. I'm worried," Hitch concluded.

"Well, then it's our job to walk them through this. You know," Rutledge thought aloud, "this could work in favor of our overall mission here."

Hitch bristled at that. "Cliff, it would be a serious mistake to try to play this one that way. Better to let them think it through for themselves. The death of an ambassador is a big deal," the American ambassador told the people in the room, in case they didn't know. "All the more so if the guy was killed by an agent of their government. But, Cliff, if you try to shove this down their throats, they're going to choke, and I don't think we want that to happen either. I think our best play is to ask for a break of a day or two in the talks, to let them get their act together."

"That's a sign of weakness for our side, Carl," Rutledge replied, with a shake of the head. "I think you're wrong on that. I think we press forward and let them know that the civilized world has rules, and we expect them to abide by them."

What lunacy is this?" Fang Gan asked the ceiling.

"We're not sure," Zhang Han San replied. "Some troublesome churchman, it sounds like."

"And some foolish policeman with more gun than brains. He'll be punished, of course," Fang suggested.

"Punished? For what? For enforcing our population-control laws, for protecting a doctor against an attack by some *gwai?"* Zhang shook his head. "Do we allow foreigners to spit upon our laws in this way? No, Fang, we do not. I will not see us lose face in such a way."

"Zhang, what is the life of one insignificant police officer next to our country's place in the world?" Fang demanded. "The man he killed was an *ambassador,* Zhang, a foreigner accredited to our country by another—"

"Country?" Zhang spat. "A *city,* my friend, no, not even that—a *district* in Rome, smaller than Qiong Dao!" He referred to Jade Island, home of one of the many temples built by the emperors, and not much larger than the building itself. Then he remembered a quote from Iosef Stalin. "How big an army does that Pope have, anyway? Ahh!" A dismissive wave of the hand.

"He *does* have a country, whose ambassador *we* accredited, in the hope of improving *our* position in the diplomatic world," Fang reminded his friend. "His death is to be regretted, at the least. Perhaps he was merely one more troublesome foreign devil, Zhang, but for the purposes of diplomacy we must *appear* to regret his passing." And if that meant executing some nameless policeman, they had plenty of policemen, Fang didn't add.

"For what? For interfering with our laws? An *ambassador* may not do such a thing. *That* violates diplomatic protocol, does it not? Fang, you have become overly solicitous to the foreign devils," Zhang concluded, using the term from history to identify the lesser people from those lesser lands.

"If we want their goods in trade, and we want them to pay for our goods so that we might have their hard currency, then we must treat them like guests in our home."

"A guest in your home does not spit on the floor, Fang."

"And if the Americans do not react kindly to this incident?"

"Then Shen will tell them to mind their own affairs," Zhang replied, with the finality of one who had long since made up his mind.

"When does the Politburo meet?"

"To discuss this?" Zhang asked in surprise. "Why? The death of some foreign troublemaker and a Chinese . . . churchman? Fang, you are too cautious. I have already discussed the incident with Shen. There will be no full meeting of the Politburo for this trivial incident. We will meet the day after tomorrow, as usual."

"As you say," Fang responded, with a nod of submission. Zhang had him ranked on the Politburo. He had much influence with the foreign and defense ministries, and the ear of Xu Kun Piao. Fang had his own political capital—mainly for internal matters—but less such capital than Zhang, and so he had to spend it carefully, when it could profit himself. This was not such a case, he thought. With that, he went back to his office and called Ming to transcribe his notes. Then, later, he thought, he'd have Chai come in. She was so useful in easing the tension of his day.

He felt better on waking this morning than was usually the case, probably because he'd gotten to sleep at a decent hour, Jack told himself, on the way to the bathroom for the usual morning routine. You never got a day off here, at least not in the sense that most people understood the term. You never really got to sleep late—8:25 was the current record dating all the way back to that terrible winter day when this had begun—and every day you had to have the same routine, including the dreaded national security briefing, which told you that some people really did believe that the world couldn't get on without you. The usual look in the mirror. He needed a haircut, Jack saw, but for that the barber came here, which wasn't a bad deal, really, except that you lost the fellowship of sitting in a male place and discussing male things. Being the most powerful man in the world insulated you from so many of the things that mattered. The food was good, and the booze was just fine, and if you didn't like the sheets they were changed at the speed of light, and people jumped to the sound of your voice. Henry VIII never had it so good . . . but Jack Ryan had never thought to become a crowned monarch. That whole idea of kingship had died across the world except in a few distant places, and Ryan didn't live in one of them. But the entire routine at the White House seemed designed to make him feel like a king, and that was disturbing on a level that was like grasping a cloud of cigarette smoke. It was there, but every time you tried to hold it, the damned stuff just vanished. The staff was just so eager to serve, grimly—but pleasantly—determined to make everything easy for them. The real worry was the effect this might have on his kids. If they started thinking they were princes and princesses, sooner or later their lives would go to hell in one big hurry. But that was his problem to worry about, Jack thought as he shaved. His and Cathy's. Nobody else could raise their kids for them. That was their job. Just that all of this White House *crap* got in the way practically all the time.

The worst part of all, however, was that he had to be dressed all the time. Except in bed or in the bathroom, the President had to be properly dressed—*or what would the staff think?* So, Ryan couldn't walk out into the corridor without pants and at least some kind of shirt. At home, a normal person would have padded around barefoot in his shorts, but while a truck driver might have that freedom in his own home, the President of the United States did not have that freedom in *his.*

Then he had to smile wryly at the mirror. He bitched to himself about the same things every morning, and if he *really* wanted to change them, he could. But he was afraid to, afraid to take action that would cause people to lose their jobs. Aside from the fact that it would really look shitty in the papers—and practically everything he did made it into the news—it would feel bad to him, here, shaving every morning. And he didn't really need to walk out to the box and get the paper in the morning, did he?

And if you factored out the dress code, it wasn't all that bad. The breakfast buffet was actually quite nice, though it wasted at least five times the food it actually served. His cholesterol was still in the normal range, and so Ryan enjoyed eggs for his morning meal two or even three times a week, somewhat to his wife's distaste. The kids opted mainly for cereal or muffins. These were still warm from the downstairs kitchen and came in all sorts of healthy—and tasty—varieties.

The *Early Bird* was the clipping service the government provided for senior officials, but for breakfast SWORDSMAN preferred the real paper, complete with cartoons. Like many, Ryan lamented the retirement of Gary Larson and the attendant loss of the morning *Far Side,* but Jack understood the pressure of enforced daily output. There was also a sports page to be read, something the *Early Bird* left out completely. And there was CNN, which started in the White House breakfast room promptly at seven.

Ryan looked up when he heard the warning that kids should not see what they were about to show. His kids, like all other kids, stopped what they were doing to look.

"Eww, gross!" Sally Ryan observed, when some Chinese guy got shot in the head.

"Head wounds do that," her mother told her, wincing even so. Cathy did surgery, but not that sort. "Jack, what's this all about?"

"You know as much as I do, honey," the President told the First Lady.

Then the screen changed to some file tape showing a Catholic Cardinal. Then Jack caught "Papal Nuncio" off the audio, leaning to reach for the controller to turn the sound up.

"Chuck?" Ryan said, to the nearest Secret Service agent. "Get me Ben Goodley on the phone, if you could."

"Yes, Mr. President." It took about thirty seconds, then Ryan was handed the portable phone. "Ben, what the hell's this thing out of Beijing?"

In Jackson, Mississippi, Reverend Gerry Patterson was accustomed to rising early in preparation for his morning jog around the neighborhood, and he turned on the bedroom TV while his wife went to fix his hot chocolate (Patterson didn't approve of coffee any more than he did of alcohol). His head turned at the words "Reverend Yu," then his skin went cold when he heard, "a Baptist minister here in Beijing . . ." He came back into the bedroom just in time to see a Chinese face go down, and shoot out blood as from a garden hose. The tape didn't allow him to recognize a face.

"My God . . . Skip . . . God, no . . ." the minister breathed, his morning suddenly and utterly disrupted. Ministers deal with death on a daily basis, burying parishioners, consoling the bereaved, entreating God to look after the needs of both. But it was no easier for Gerry Patterson than it would have been for anyone else this day, because there had been no warning, no "long illness" to prepare the mind for the possibility, not even the fact of age to reduce the surprise factor. Skip was—what? Fifty-five? No more than that. Still a young man, Patterson thought, young and vigorous to preach the Gospel of Jesus Christ to his flock. Dead? Killed, was it? Murdered? By whom? Murdered by that *communist* government? A Man of God, *murdered* by the godless heathen?

"Oh, shit," the President said over his eggs. "What else do we know, Ben? Anything from SORGE?" Then Ryan looked around the room, realizing he'd spoken a word that was itself classified. The kids weren't looking his way, but Cathy was. "Okay, we'll talk about it when you get in." Jack hit the kill button on the phone and set it down.

"What's the story?"

"It's a real mess, babe," SWORDSMAN told SURGEON. He explained what he knew for a minute or so. "The ambassador hasn't gotten to us with anything CNN didn't just show."

"You mean with all the money we spend on CIA and stuff, CNN is the best source of information we have?" Cathy Ryan asked, somewhat incredulously.

"You got it, honey," her husband admitted.

"Well, that doesn't make any sense!"

Jack tried to explain: "CIA can't be everywhere, and it would look a little funny if all our field spooks carried video-cams everywhere they went, you know?"

Cathy made a face at being shut down so cavalierly. "But—"

"But it's not that easy, Cathy, and the news people are in the same business, gathering information, and occasionally they get there first."

"But you have other ways of finding things out, don't you?"

"Cathy, you don't need to know about things like that," POTUS told FLOTUS.

That was a phrase she'd heard before, but not one she'd ever learned to love. Cathy went back to her morning paper while her husband graduated to the *Early Bird.* The Beijing story, Jack saw, had happened too late for the morning editions, one more thing to chuff up the TV newsies and annoy the print ones. Somehow the debate over the federal education budget didn't seem all that important this morning, but he'd learned to scan the editorials, because they tended to reflect the questions the reporters would ask at the press conferences, and that was one way for him to defend himself.

By 7:45, the kids were about ready for their drive to school, and

Cathy was ready for her flight to Hopkins. Kyle Daniel went with her, with his own Secret Service detail, composed exclusively of women who would look after him at the Hopkins daycare center rather like a pack of she-wolves. Katie would head back to her daycare center, the rebuilt Giant Steps north of Annapolis. There were fewer kids there now, but a larger protective detail. The big kids went to St. Mary's. On cue, the Marine VH-60 Blackhawk helicopter eased down on the South Lawn helipad. The day was about to start for real. The entire Ryan family took the elevator downstairs. First Mom and Dad walked the kids to the west entrance of the West Wing, where, after hugs and kisses, three of the kids got into their cars to drive off. Then Jack walked Cathy to the helicopter for the kiss goodbye, and the big Sikorsky lifted off under the control of Colonel Dan Malloy for the hop to Johns Hopkins. With that done, Ryan walked back to the West Wing, and inside to the Oval Office. Ben Goodley was waiting for him.

"How bad?" Jack asked his national security adviser.

"Bad," Goodley replied at once.

"What was it all about?"

"They were trying to stop an abortion. The Chinese do them late-term if the pregnancy is not government-approved. They wait until just before the baby pops out and zap it in the top of the head with a needle before it gets to take a breath. Evidently, the woman on the tape was having an unauthorized baby, and her minister—that's the Chinese guy who gets it in the head, a Baptist preacher educated, evidently, at Oral Roberts University in Oklahoma, would you believe? Anyway, he came to the hospital to help. The Papal Nuncio, Renato Cardinal DiMilo, evidently knew the Baptist preacher pretty well and came to offer assistance. It's hard to tell exactly what went wrong, but it blew up real bad, as the tape shows."

"Any statements?"

"The Vatican deplores the incident and has requested an explanation. But it gets worse. Cardinal DiMilo is from the DiMilo family. He has a brother, Vincenzo DiMilo, who's in the Italian parliament—he was a cabinet minister a while back—and so the Italian government has issued its own protest. Ditto the German government, because the Cardinal's aide is a German monsignor named Schepke, who's a Jesuit, and he got a little roughed up, and the Germans aren't very happy either. This Monsignor Schepke was arrested briefly, but he was released after a few hours when the Chinese remembered he had diplomatic status. The thinking at State is that the PRC might PNG the guy, just to get him the hell out of the country and make the whole thing all go away."

"What time is it in Beijing?"

"Us minus eleven, so it's nine at night there," CARDSHARP answered.

"The trade delegation will need instructions of some sort about this. I need to talk to Scott Adler as soon as he gets in this morning."

"You need more than that, Jack." It was the voice of Arnold van Damm, at the door to the office.

"What else?"

"The Chinese Baptist who got killed, I just heard he has friends over here."

"Oral Roberts University," Ryan said. "Ben told me."

"The churchgoers are not going to like this one, Jack," Arnie warned.

"Hey, guy, *I* don't goddamn like it," the President pointed out. "Hell, *I* don't like abortion under the best of circumstances, remember?"

"I remember," van Damm said, recalling all the trouble Ryan had gotten into with his first Presidential statement on the issue.

"And this kind of abortion is especially barbaric, and so, two guys go to the fucking hospital and try to save the baby's life, and they get *killed* for it! Jesus," Ryan concluded, "and we have to do business with people like this."

Then another face showed up at the door. "You've heard, I suppose," Robby Jackson observed.

"Oh, yeah. Hell of a thing to see over breakfast."

"My Pap knows the guy."

"What?" Ryan asked.

"Remember at the reception last week? He told you about it. Pap and Gerry Patterson both support his congregation out of Mississippi—some other congregations, too. It's a Baptist thing, Jack. Well-off churches look after ones that need help, and this Yu guy sure as hell needed help, looks like. I haven't talked to him yet, but Pap is going to raise pure fucking hell about this one, and you can bet on it," the Vice President informed his Boss.

"Who's Patterson?" van Damm asked.

"White preacher, got a big air-conditioned church in the suburbs of Jackson. Pretty good guy, actually. He and Pap have known each other forever. Patterson went through school with this Yu guy, I think."

"This is going to get ugly," the Chief of Staff observed.

"Arnie, baby, it's *already* ugly," Jackson pointed out. The CNN cameraman had been a little too good, or had just been standing in a good place, and had caught both shots in all their graphic majesty.

"What's your dad going to say?" Ryan asked.

TOMCAT made them wait for it. "He's going to call down the Wrath of Almighty God on those murdering cocksuckers. He's going to call Reverend Yu a martyr to the Christian faith, right up there with the Maccabees of the Old Testament, and those courageous bastards the Romans fed to the lions. Arnie, have you ever seen a Baptist preacher calling down the Vengeance of the Lord? It beats the hell out of the Super Bowl, boy," Robby promised. "Reverend Yu is standing upright and proud before the Lord Jesus right now, and the guys who killed him have their rooms reserved in the Everlasting Fires of Hell. Wait till you hear him go at it. It's impressive, guys. I've seen him do it. And Gerry Patterson won't be far behind."

"And the hell of it is, I can't disagree with any of it. Jesus," Ryan breathed. "Those two men died to save the life of a baby. If you gotta die, that's not a bad reason for it."

They both died like men, Mr. C," Chavez was saying in Moscow. "I wish I was there with a gun." It had hit Ding especially hard. Fatherhood had changed his perspective on a lot of things, and this was just one of them. The life of a child was sacrosanct, and a threat against a child was an invitation to immediate death in his ethical universe. And in the real universe, he was known to have a gun a lot of the time, and the training to use it efficiently.

"Different people have different ways of looking at things," Clark told his subordinate. But if he'd been there, he would have disarmed both of the Chinese cops. On the videotape, they hadn't looked all that formidable. And you didn't kill people to make a fashion statement. Domingo still had the Latin temperament, John reminded himself. And that wasn't so bad a thing, was it?

"What are you saying, John?" Ding asked in surprise.

"I'm saying two good men died yesterday, and I imagine God'll look after both of them."

"Ever been to China?"

He shook his head. "Taiwan once, for R and R, long time ago. That was okay, but aside from that, no closer than North Vietnam. I don't speak the language and I can't blend in." Both factors were distantly frightening to Clark. The ability to disappear into the surroundings was the *sine qua non* of being a field-intelligence officer.

They were in a hotel bar in Moscow after their first day of lecturing their Russian students. The beer on tap was acceptable. Neither of them was in a mood for vodka. Life in Britain had spoiled them. This bar, which catered to Americans, had CNN on a large-screen TV next to the bar, and this was CNN's lead story around the globe. The American government, the report concluded, hadn't reacted to the incident yet.

"So, what's Jack going to do?" Chavez wondered.

"I don't know. We have that negotiations team in Beijing right now for trade talks," Clark reminded him.

"The diplomatic chatter might get a little sharp," Domingo thought.

Scott, we can't let this one slide," Jack said. A call from the White House had brought Adler's official car here instead of Foggy Bottom.

"It is not, strictly speaking, pertinent to trade talks," the Secretary of State pointed out.

"Maybe you want to do business with people like that," Vice President Jackson responded, "but the people outside the Beltway might not."

"We have to consider public opinion on this, Scott," Ryan said. "And, you know, we have to damn well consider *my* opinion. The murder of a diplomat is not something we can ignore. Italy is a NATO member. So is Germany. And we have diplomatic relations with the

Vatican and about seventy million Catholics in the country, plus millions more Baptists."

"Okay, Jack," EAGLE said, with raised, defensive hands. "I am not defending them, okay? I'm talking about the foreign policy of the United States of America here, and we're not supposed to manage that on the basis of emotions. The people out there pay us to use our heads, not our dicks."

Ryan let out a long breath. "Okay, maybe I had that coming. Go on."

"We issue a statement deploring this sorry incident in strong language. We have Ambassador Hitch make a call on their foreign ministry and say the same thing, maybe even stronger, but in more informal language. We give them a chance to think this mess through before they become an international pariah, maybe discipline those trigger-happy cops—hell, maybe shoot them, given how the law works over there. We let common sense break out, okay?"

"And what do I say?"

Adler thought that one over for a few seconds. "Say whatever you want. We can always explain to them that we have a lot of churchgoers here and you have to assuage their sensibilities, that they have inflamed American public opinion, and in our country, public opinion counts for something. They know that on an intellectual level, but deep down in the gut they don't get it. That's okay," SecState went on. "Just so they get it in the brain, because the brain talks to the gut occasionally. They have to understand that the world doesn't like this sort of thing."

"And if they don't?" the Vice President asked.

"Well, then we have a trade delegation to show them the consequences of uncivilized behavior." Adler looked around the room. "Are we okay on that?"

Ryan looked down at the coffee table. There were times when he wished he were a truck driver, able to scream out bloody murder when certain things happened, but that was just one more freedom the President of the United States didn't have. *Okay, Jack, you have to be sensible and rational about all this.* He looked up. "Yes, Scott, we're sort of okay on that."

"Anything from our, uh, new source on this issue?"

Ryan shook his head. "No, MP hasn't sent anything over yet."

"If she does . . ."

"You'll get a copy real fast," the President promised. "Get me some talking points. I'll have to make a statement—when, Arnie?"

"Eleven-ish ought to be okay," van Damm decided. "I'll talk to some media guys about this."

"Okay, if anybody has ideas later today, I want to hear them," Ryan said, standing, and adjourning the meeting.

CHAPTER **26**

Glass Houses and Rocks

Fang Gan had worked late that day because of the incident that had Washington working early. As a result, Ming hadn't transcribed his discussion notes and her computer hadn't gotten them out on the 'Net as early as usual, but Mary Pat got her e-mail about 9:45. This she read over, copied to her husband, Ed, and then shot via secure fax line to the White House, where Ben Goodley walked it to the Oval Office. The cover letter didn't contain Mary Pat's initial comment on reading the transmission: "Oh, shit . . ."

"Those *cocksuckers!"* Ryan snarled, to the surprise of Andrea Price, who happened to be in the room just then.

"Anything I need to know about, sir?" she asked, his voice had been so furious.

"No, Andrea, just that thing on CNN this morning." Ryan paused, blushing that she'd heard his temper let go again—and in that way. "By the way, how's your husband doing?"

"Well, he bagged those three bank robbers up in Philadelphia, and they did it without firing a shot. I was a little worried about that."

Ryan allowed himself a smile. "That's one guy I wouldn't want to have a shoot-out with. Tell me, you saw CNN this morning, right?"

"Yes, sir, and we replayed it at the command post."

"Opinion?"

"If I'd've been there, my weapon would have come out. That was cold-blooded murder. Looks bad on TV when you do dumb stuff like that, sir."

"Sure as hell does," the President agreed. He nearly asked her opinion on what he ought to do about it. Ryan respected Mrs. O'Day's (she still went by Price on the job) judgment, but it wouldn't have been fair to ask her to delve into foreign affairs, and, besides, he already had his mind pretty well made up. But then he speed-dialed Adler's direct line on his phone.

"Yes, Jack?" Only one person had *that* direct line.

"What do you make of the SORGE stuff?"

"It's not surprising, unfortunately. You have to expect them to circle wagons."

"What do we do about it?" SWORDSMAN demanded.

"We say what we think, *but* we try not to make it worse than it already is," SecState replied, cautious as ever.

"Right," Ryan growled, even though it was exactly the good advice he'd expected from his SecState. Then he hung up. He reminded himself that Arnie had told him a long time ago that a president wasn't allowed to have a temper, but that was asking a hell of a lot, and at what point was he allowed to react the way a man needed to react? When was he supposed to stop acting like a goddamned robot?

"You want Callie to work up something for you in a hurry?" Arnie asked over the phone.

"No," Ryan replied, with a shake of the head. "I'll just wing it."

"That's a mistake," the Chief of Staff warned.

"Arnie, just let me be me once in a while, okay?"

"Okay, Jack," van Damm replied, and it was just as well the President didn't see his expression.

Don't make things worse than they already are, Ryan told himself at his desk. *Yeah, sure, like that's possible . . .*

Hi, Pap," Robby Jackson was saying in his office at the northwest corner of the West Wing.

"Robert, have you seen—"

"Yes, we've all seen it," the Vice President assured his father.

"And what are y'all going to do about it?"

"Pap, we haven't figured that out yet. Remember that we have to do business with these people. The jobs of a lot of Americans depend on trade with China and—"

"Robert"—the Reverend Hosiah Jackson used Robby's proper name mainly when he was feeling rather stern—"those people *murdered* a man of God—no, excuse me, they murdered *two* men of God, doing their duty, trying to save the life of an innocent child, and one does not do business with murderers."

"I know that, and I don't like it any more than you do, and, trust me, Jack Ryan doesn't like it any more than you do, either. But when we make foreign policy for our country, we have to think things through, because if we screw it up, people can lose their lives."

"Lives have already been lost, Robert," Reverend Jackson pointed out.

"I know that. Look, Pap, I know more about this than you do, okay? I mean, we have ways of finding out stuff that doesn't make it on CNN," the Vice President told his father, with the latest SORGE report right in his hand. Part of him wished that he could show it to his father, because his father was easily smart enough to grasp the importance of the secret things that he and Ryan knew. But there was no way he could even approach discussing that sort of thing with anyone without a TS/SAR clearance, and that included his wife, just as it included Cathy Ryan. Hmm, Jackson thought—maybe that was something he should discuss with Jack. You had to be able to talk this stuff over with someone you trusted, just as a reality check on what was right and wrong. Their wives weren't security risks, were they?

"Like what?" his father asked, only halfway expecting an answer.

"Like I can't discuss some things with you, Pap, and you know that. I'm sorry. The rules apply to me just like they do to everybody else."

"So, what are we going to do about this?"

"We're going to let the Chinese know that we are pretty damned angry, and we expect them to clean their act up, and apologize, and—"

"Apologize!" Reverend Jackson shot back. "Robert, they *murdered* two people!"

"I know that, Pap, but we can't send the FBI over to arrest their government for this, can we? We're very powerful here, but we are not God, and as much as I'd like to hurl a thunderbolt at them, I can't."

"So, we're going to do *what?*"

"We haven't decided yet. I'll let you know when we figure it out," TOMCAT promised his father.

"Do that," Hosiah said, hanging up far more abruptly than usual.

"Christ, Pap," Robby breathed into the phone. Then he wondered how representative of the religious community his father was. The hardest thing to figure was public reaction. People reacted on a subintellectual level to what they saw on TV. If you showed some chief of state tossing a puppy dog out the window of his car, the ASPCA might demand a break in diplomatic relations, and enough people might agree to send a million telegrams or e-mails to the White House. Jackson remembered a case in California where the killing of a *dog* had caused more public outrage than the kidnap-murder of a little girl. But at least the bastard who'd killed the girl had been caught, tried, and sentenced to death, whereas the asshole who'd tossed the little dog into traffic had never been identified, despite the ton of reward money that had been raised. Well, it had all happened in the San Francisco area. Maybe that explained it. America wasn't supposed to make policy on the basis of emotion, but America was a democracy, and therefore her elected officials had to pay attention to what the *people* thought—and it wasn't easy, especially for rational folk, to predict the emotions of the public at large. Could the television image they'd just seen, theoretically upset international trade? Without a doubt, and *that* was a very big deal.

Jackson got up from his desk and walked to Arnie's office. "Got a question," he said, going in.

"Shoot," the President's Chief of Staff replied.

"How's the public going to react to this mess in Beijing?"

"Not sure yet," van Damm answered.

"How do we find out?"

"Usually you just wait and see. I'm not into this focus-group stuff. I prefer to gauge public opinion the regular way: newspaper editorials, letters to the editor, and the mail we get here. You're worried about this?"

"Yep." Robby nodded.

"Yeah, so am I. The Right-to-Lifers are going to be on this like a lion on a crippled gazelle, and so are the people who don't like the PRC. Lots of them in Congress. If the Chinese think they're going to get

MFN this year, they're on drugs. It's a public relations nightmare for the PRC, but I don't think they're capable of understanding what they started. And I don't see them apologizing to anybody."

"Yeah, well, my father just tore me a new asshole over this one," Vice President Jackson said. "If the rest of the clergy picks this one up, there's going to be a firestorm. The Chinese have to apologize loud and fast if they want to cut their losses."

Van Damm nodded agreement. "Yeah, but they won't. They're too damned proud."

"Pride goeth before the fall," TOMCAT observed.

"Only *after* you feel the pain from the broken assbone, Admiral," van Damm corrected the Vice President.

Ryan entered the White House press room feeling tense. The usual cameras were there. CNN and Fox would probably be running this news conference live, and maybe C-SPAN as well. The other networks would just tape it, probably, for use in their news feeds to the local stations and their own flagship evening news shows. He came to the lectern and took a sip of water before staring into the faces of the assembled thirty or so reporters.

"Good morning," Jack began, grasping the lectern tightly, as he tended to do when angry. He didn't know that reporters knew about it, too, and could see it from where they sat.

"We all saw those horrible pictures on the television this morning, the deaths of Renato Cardinal DiMilo, the Papal Nuncio to the People's Republic of China, and the Reverend Yu Fa An, who, we believe, was a native of the Republic of China and educated at Oral Roberts University in Oklahoma. First of all, the United States of America extends our condolences to the families of both men. Second, we call upon the government of the People's Republic to launch an immediate and full investigation of this horrible tragedy, to determine who, if anyone, was at fault, and if someone was at fault, for such person or persons to be prosecuted to the full extent of the law.

"The death of a diplomat at the hands of an agent of a government is a gross violation of international treaty and convention. It is a quintessentially uncivilized act that must be set right as quickly and definitively as possible. Peaceful relations between nations cannot exist without diplomacy, and diplomacy cannot be carried out except through men and women whose personal safety is sacrosanct. That has been the case for literally thousands of years. Even in time of war, the lives of diplomats have always been protected by all sides for this very reason. We require that the government of the PRC explain this tragic event and take proper action to see to it that nothing of this sort will *ever* happen again. That concludes my statement. Questions?" Ryan looked up, trying not to brace too obviously for the storm that was about to break.

"Mr. President," the Associated Press said, "the two clergymen who died were there to prevent an abortion. Does that affect your reaction to this incident?"

Ryan allowed himself to show surprise at the stupid question: "My views on abortion are on the public record, but I think everyone, even the pro-choice community, would respond negatively to what happened here. The woman in question did *not* choose to have an abortion, but the Chinese government tried to impose its will on her by killing a full-term fetus about to be born. If anyone did that in the United States, that person would be guilty of a felony—probably more than one—yet that is government policy in the People's Republic. As you know, I personally object to abortion on moral grounds, but what we saw attempted on TV this morning is worse even than that. It's an act of incomprehensible barbarism. Those two courageous men tried to stop it, and they were killed for their efforts, but, thank God, the baby appears to have survived. Next question?" Ryan pointed next to a known troublemaker.

"Mr. President," the *Boston Globe* said, "the government's action grew out of the People's Republic's population-control policy. Is it our place to criticize a country's internal policy?"

Christ, Ryan thought, *another one?* "You know, once upon a time, a fellow named Hitler tried to manage the population of his country—in fact, of a lot of Europe—by killing the mentally infirm, the socially undesirable, and those whose religions he didn't like. Now, yes, Germany was a nation-state, and we even had diplomatic relations with Hitler until December 1941. But are you saying that America does not have the right to object to a policy we consider barbaric just because it is the official policy of a nation-state? Hermann Göring tried that defense at the Nürnberg Trials. Do you want the United States of America to recognize it?" Jack demanded.

The reporter wasn't as used to answering questions as to asking them. Then she saw that the cameras were pointed her way, and she was having a bad-hair day. Her response, therefore, could have been a little better: "Mr. President, is it possible that your views of abortion have affected your reaction to this event?"

"No, ma'am. I've disapproved of murder even longer than I've objected to abortion," Ryan replied coldly.

"But you've just compared the People's Republic of China to Hitler's Germany," the *Globe* reporter pointed out. *You can't say* that *about* them!

"Both countries shared a view of population control that is antithetical to American traditions. Or do you approve of imposing late-term abortions on women who choose *not* to have one?"

"Sir, I'm not the President," the *Globe* replied, as she sat down, avoiding the question, but not the embarrassed blush.

"Mr. President," began the *San Francisco Examiner*, "whether we like it or not, China has decided for itself what sort of laws it wants to have, and the two men who died this morning were interfering with those laws, weren't they?"

"The Reverend Doctor Martin Luther King interfered with the laws of Mississippi and Alabama back when I was in high school. Did the *Examiner* object to his actions then?"

"Well, no, but—"

"But we regard the personal human conscience as a sovereign force, don't we?" Jack shot back. "The principle goes back to St. Augustine, when he said that an unjust law is *no* law. Now, you guys in the media agree with that principle. Is it only when you happen to agree with the person operating on that principle? Isn't that intellectually dishonest? I do not personally approve of abortion. You all know that. I've taken a considerable amount of heat for that personal belief, some of which has been laid on me by you good people. Fine. The Constitution allows us all to feel the way we choose. But the Constitution does not allow me *not* to enforce the law against people who blow up abortion clinics. I can sympathize with their overall point of view, but I cannot agree or sympathize with the use of violence to pursue a political position. We call that terrorism, and it's against the law, and I have sworn an oath to enforce the law fully and fairly in all cases, regardless of how I may or may not feel on a particular issue.

"Therefore, if *you* do not apply it evenhandedly, ladies and gentlemen, it is not a principle at all, but ideology, and it is not very helpful to the way we govern our lives and our country.

"Now, on the broader question, you said that China has chosen its laws. Has it? Has it really? The People's Republic is not, unfortunately, a democratic country. It is a place where the laws are imposed by an elite few. Two courageous men died yesterday objecting to those laws, and in the successful attempt to save the life of an unborn child. Throughout history, men have given up their lives for worse causes than that. Those men are heroes by any definition, but I do not think anyone in this room, or for that matter anyone in our country, believes that they deserved to die, heroically or not. The penalty for civil disobedience is not supposed to be death. Even in the darkest days of the 1960s, when black Americans were working to secure their civil rights, the police in the southern states did not commit wholesale murder. And those local cops and members of the Ku Klux Klan who *did* step over that line were arrested and convicted by the FBI and the Justice Department.

"In short, there are fundamental differences between the People's Republic of China and America, and of the two systems, I much prefer ours."

Ryan escaped the press room ten minutes later, to find Arnie standing at the top of the ramp.

"Very good, Jack."

"Oh?" The President had learned to fear that tone of voice.

"Yeah, you just compared the People's Republic of China to Nazi Germany and the Ku Klux Klan."

"Arnie, why is it that the media feel such great solicitude for communist countries?"

"They *don't,* and—"

"The *hell* they don't! I just compared the PRC to Nazi Germany and they damned near wet their pants. Well, guess what? Mao murdered more people than Hitler did. That's public knowledge—I remember when CIA released the study that documented it—but they ignore it. Is some Chinese citizen killed by Mao less dead than some poor Polish bastard killed by Hitler?"

"Jack, they have their sensibilities," van Damm told his President.

"Yeah? Well, just once in a while, I wish they'd display something I can recognize as a principle." With that, Ryan strode back to his office, practically trailing smoke from his ears.

"Temper, Jack, temper," Arnie said to no one in particular. The President still had to learn the first principle of political life, the ability to treat a son of a bitch like your best friend, because the needs of your nation depended on it. The world would be a better place if it were as simple as Ryan wished, the Chief of Staff thought. But it wasn't, and it showed no prospect of becoming so.

A few blocks away at Foggy Bottom, Scott Adler had finished cringing and was making notes on how to mend the fences that his President had just kicked over. He'd have to sit down with Jack and go over a few things, like the principles he held so dear.

What did you think of that, Gerry?"

"Hosiah, I think we have a real President here. What does your son think of him?"

"Gerry, they've been friends for twenty years, back to when they both taught at the Naval Academy. I've met the man. He's a Catholic, but I think we can overlook that."

"We have to." Patterson almost laughed. "So was one of the guys who got shot yesterday, remember?"

"Italian, too, probably drank a lot of wine."

"Well, Skip was known to have the occasional drink," Patterson told his black colleague.

"I didn't know," Reverend Jackson replied, disturbed at the thought.

"Hosiah, it is an imperfect world we live in."

"Just so he wasn't a dancer." That was almost a joke, but not quite.

"Skip? No, I've never known him to dance," Reverend Patterson assured his friend. "By the way, I have an idea."

"What's that, Gerry?"

"How about this Sunday you preach at my church, and I preach at yours? I'm sure we're both going to speak on the life and martyrdom of a Chinese man."

"And what passage will you base your sermon on?" Hosiah asked, surprised and interested by the suggestion.

"Acts," Patterson replied at once.

Reverend Jackson considered that. It wasn't hard to guess the exact passage. Gerry was a fine biblical scholar. "I admire your choice, sir."

"Thank you, Pastor Jackson. What do you think of my other suggestion?"

Reverend Jackson hesitated only a few seconds. "Reverend Patterson, I would be honored to preach at your church, and I gladly extend to you the invitation to preach at my own."

Forty years earlier, when Gerry Patterson had been playing baseball in the church-sponsored Little League, Hosiah Jackson had been a young Baptist preacher, and the mere idea of preaching in Patterson's church could have incited a lynching. But, by the Good Lord, they *were* men of God, and they *were* mourning the death—the *martyrdom*—of another man of God of yet another color. Before God, all men were equal, and that was the whole point of the Faith they shared. Both men were thinking quickly of how they might have to alter their styles, because though both were Baptists, and though both preached the Gospel of Jesus Christ to Baptist congregations, their communities were a little bit different and required slightly different approaches. But it was an accommodation both men could easily make.

"Thank you, Hosiah. You know, sometimes we have to acknowledge that our faith is bigger than we are."

For his part, Reverend Jackson was impressed. He never doubted the sincerity of his white colleague, and they'd chatted often on matters of religion and scripture. Hosiah would even admit, quietly, to himself, that Patterson was his superior as a scholar of the Holy Word, due to his somewhat lengthier formal education, but of the two, Hosiah Jackson was marginally the better speaker, and so their relative talents played well off each other.

"How about we get together for lunch to work out the details?" Jackson asked.

"Today? I'm free."

"Sure. Where?"

"The country club? You're not a golfer, are you?" Patterson asked hopefully. He felt like a round, and his afternoon was free today for a change.

"Never touched a golf club in my life, Gerry." Hosiah had a good laugh at that. "Robert is, learned at Annapolis and been playing ever since. Says he kicks the President's backside every time they go out." He'd never been to the Willow Glen Country Club either, and wondered if the club had any black members. Probably not. Mississippi hadn't changed quite *that* much yet, though Tiger Woods had played at a PGA tournament there, and so *that* color line had been breached, at least.

"Well, he'd probably whip me, too. Next time he comes down, maybe we can play a round." Patterson's membership at Willow Glen was complimentary, another advantage to being pastor of a well-to-do congregation.

And the truth of the matter was that, white or not, Gerry Patterson was not the least bit bigoted, Reverend Jackson knew. He preached the Gospel with a pure heart. Hosiah was old enough to remember when that had not been so, but that, too, had changed once and for all. Praise God.

For Admiral Mancuso, the issues were the same, and a little different. An early riser, he'd caught CNN the same as everyone else. So had Brigadier General Mike Lahr.

"Okay, Mike, what the hell is this all about?" CINCPAC asked when his J-2 arrived for his morning intel brief.

"Admiral, it looks like a monumental cluster-fuck. Those clergy stuck their noses in a tight crack and paid the price for it. More to the point, NCA is seriously pissed." NCA was the code-acronym for National Command Authority, President Jack Ryan.

"What do I need to know about this?"

"Well, things are likely to heat up between America and China, for starters. The trade delegation we have in Beijing is probably going to catch some heat. If they catch too much, well . . ." His voice trailed off.

"Give me worst case," CINCPAC ordered.

"Worst case, the PRC gets its collective back up, and we recall the trade delegation *and* the ambassador, and things get real chilly for a while."

"Then what?"

"Then—that's more of a political question, but it wouldn't hurt for us to take it a little seriously, sir," Lahr told his boss, who took just about everything seriously.

Mancuso looked at his wall map of the Pacific. *Enterprise* was back at sea doing exercises between Marcus Island and the Marianas. *John Stennis* was alongside in Pearl Harbor. *Harry Truman* was en route to Pearl Harbor after taking the long way around Cape Horn—modern aircraft carriers are far too beamy for the Panama Canal. *Lincoln* was finishing up a bobtail refit in San Diego and about to go back to sea. *Kitty Hawk* and *Independence,* his two old, oil-fired carriers, were both in the Indian Ocean. At that, he was lucky. First and Seventh Fleets had six carriers fully operational for the first time in years. So, if he needed to project power, he had the assets to give people something to think about. He also had a lot of Air Force aircraft at his disposal. The 3rd Marine Division and the Army's 25th Light based right there in Hawaii wouldn't play in this picture. The Navy might bump heads with the ChiComms, and the Air Force, but he lacked the amphibious assets to invade China, and besides, he wasn't insane enough to think that was a rational course of action under any circumstances.

"What do we have in Taiwan right now?"

"Mobile Bay, Milius, Chandler, and *Fletcher* are showing the flag. Frigates *Curtis* and *Reid* are doing operations with the ROC navy. The submarines *La Jolla, Helena,* and *Tennessee* are trolling in the Formosa Strait or along the Chinese coast looking at their fleet units."

Mancuso nodded. He usually kept some high-end SAM ships close to Taiwan. *Milius* was a Burke-class destroyer, and *Mobile Bay* was a cruiser, both of them with the Aegis system aboard to make the ROC feel a little better about the putative missile threat to their island. Mancuso didn't think the Chinese were foolish enough to launch an attack against a city with some U.S. Navy ships tied alongside, and the Aegis ships had a fair chance of stopping anything that flew their way. But you never knew, and if this Beijing incident blew up any more . . . He lifted the phone for SURFPAC, the three-star who administratively owned Pacific Fleet's surface ships.

"Yeah," answered Vice Admiral Ed Goldsmith.

"Ed, Bart. What material shape are those ships we have in Taipei harbor in?"

"You're calling about the thing on CNN, right?"

"Correct," CINCPAC confirmed.

"Pretty good. No material deficiencies I know about. They're doing the usual port-visit routine, letting people aboard and all. Crews are spending a lot of time on the beach."

Mancuso didn't have to ask what they were doing on the beach. He'd been a young sailor once, though never on Taiwan.

"Might not hurt for them to keep their ears perked up some."

"Noted," SURFPAC acknowledged. Mancuso didn't have to say more. The ships would now stand alternating Condition-Three on their combat systems. The SPY radars would be turned on aboard one of the Aegis ships at all times. One nice thing about Aegis ships was that they could go from half-asleep to fully operational in about sixty seconds; it was just a matter of turning some keys. They'd have to be a little careful. The SPY radar put out enough power to fry electronic components for miles around, but it was just a matter of how you steered the electronic beams, and that was computer-controlled. "Okay, sir, I'll get the word out right now."

"Thanks, Ed. I'll get you fully briefed in later today."

"Aye, aye," SURFPAC replied. He'd put a call to his squadron commanders immediately.

"What else?" Mancuso wondered.

"We haven't heard anything directly from Washington, Admiral," BG Lahr told his boss.

"Nice thing about being a CINC, Mike. You're allowed to think on your own a little."

What a fucking mess," General-Colonel Bondarenko observed to his drink. He wasn't talking about the news of the day, but about his command, even though the officers' club in Chabarsovil was comfortable. Russian general officers have always liked their comforts, and the building dated back to the czars. It had been built during the Russo-Japanese war at the beginning of the previous century and expanded several times. You could see the border between pre-revolution and post-revolution workmanship. Evidently, German POWs hadn't been trained this far east—they'd built most of the dachas for the party elite of the old days. But the vodka was fine, and the fellowship wasn't too bad, either.

"Things could be better, Comrade General," Bondarenko's operations officer agreed. "But there is much that can be done the right way, and little bad to undo."

That was a gentle way of saying that the Far East Military District was less of a military command than it was a theoretical exercise. Of the five motor-rifle divisions nominally under his command, only one, the 265th, was at eighty-percent strength. The rest were at best regimental-size formations, or mere cadres. He also had theoretical command of a tank division—about a regiment and a half—plus thirteen reserve divisions that existed not so much on paper as in some staff officer's dreams. The one thing he did have was huge equipment stores, but a lot of that equipment dated back to the 1960s, or even earlier. The best troops in his area of command responsibility were not actually his to command. These were the Border Guards, battalion-sized formations once part of the KGB, now a semi-independent armed service under the command of the Russian president.

There was also a defense line of sorts, which dated back to the 1930s and showed it. For this line, numerous tanks—some of them actually *German* in origin—were buried as bunkers. In fact, more than anything else the line was reminiscent of the French Maginot Line, also a thing of the 1930s. It had been built to protect the Soviet Union against an attack by the Japanese, and then upgraded halfheartedly over the years to protect against the People's Republic of China—a defense never forgotten, but never fully remembered either. Bondarenko had toured parts of it the previous day. As far back as the czars, the engineering officers of the Russian Army had never been fools. Some of the bunkers were sited with shrewd, even brilliant appreciation for the land, but the problem with bunkers was explained by a recent American aphorism: *If you can see it, you can hit it, and if you can hit it, you can kill it.* The line had been conceived and built when artillery fire had been a chancy thing, and an aircraft bomb was fortunate to hit the right county. Now you could use a fifteen-centimeter gun as accurately as a sniper rifle, and an aircraft could select which windowpane to put the bomb through on a specific building.

"Andrey Petrovich, I am pleased to hear your optimism. What is your first recommendation?"

"It will be simple to improve the camouflage on the border bunkers. That's been badly neglected over the years," Colonel Aliyev told his commander-in-chief. "That will reduce their vulnerability considerably."

"Allowing them to survive a serious attack for . . . sixty minutes, Andrushka?"

"Maybe even ninety, Comrade General. It's better than five minutes, is it not?" He paused for a sip of vodka. Both had been drinking for half an hour. "For the 265th, we must begin a serious training program at once. Honestly, the division commander did not impress me greatly, but I suppose we must give him a chance."

Bondarenko: "He's been out here so long, maybe he likes the idea of Chinese food."

"General, I was out here as a lieutenant," Aliyev said. "I remember the political officers telling us that the Chinese had increased the length of the bayonets on their AK-47s to get through the extra fat layer we'd grown after discarding true Marxism-Leninism and eating too much."

"Really?" Bondarenko asked.

"That is the truth, Gennady Iosifovich."

"So, what do we know of the PLA?"

"There are a lot of them, and they've been training seriously for about four years now, much harder than we've been doing."

"They can afford to," Bondarenko observed sourly. The other thing he'd learned on arriving was how thin the cupboard was for funds and training equipment. But it wasn't totally bleak. He had stores of consumable supplies that had been stocked and piled for three generations. There was a virtual mountain of shells for the 100-mm guns on his many—and long-since obsolete—T-54/55 tanks, for example, and a sea of diesel fuel hidden away in underground tanks too numerous to count. The one thing he had in the Far East Military District was infrastructure, built up by the Soviet Union over generations of institutional paranoia. But that wasn't the same as an army to command.

"What about aviation?"

"Mainly grounded," Aliyev answered glumly. "Parts problems. We used up so much in Chechnya that there isn't enough to go around, and the Western District still has first call."

"Oh? Our political leadership expects the Poles to invade us?"

"That's the direction Germany is in," the G-3 pointed out.

"I've been fighting that out with the High Command for three years," Bondarenko growled, thinking of his time as chief of operations for the entire Russian army. "People would rather listen to themselves than to others with the voice of reason." He looked up at Aliyev. "And if the Chinese come?"

The theater operations officer shrugged. "Then we have a problem."

Bondarenko remembered the maps. It wasn't all that far to the new gold strike . . . and the ever-industrious army engineers were building the damned roads to it . . .

"Tomorrow, Andrey Petrovich. Tomorrow we start drawing up a training regimen for the whole command," CINC–FAR EAST told his own G-3.

CHAPTER 27

Transportation

Diggs didn't entirely like what he saw, but it wasn't all that unexpected. A battalion of Colonel Lisle's 2nd Brigade was out there, maneuvering through the exercise area—clumsily, Diggs thought. He had to amend his thoughts, of course. This wasn't the National Training Center at Fort Irwin, California, and Lisle's 2nd Brigade wasn't the 11th ACR, whose troopers were out there training practically every day, and as a result knew soldiering about as well as a surgeon knew cutting. No, 1st Armored Division had turned into a garrison force since the demise of the Soviet Union, and all that wasted time in what was left of Yugoslavia, trying to be "peacekeepers," hadn't sharpened their war-fighting skills. That was a term Diggs hated. Peacekeepers be damned, the general thought, they were supposed to be *soldiers,* not policemen in battle dress uniform. The opposing force here was a German brigade, and by the looks of it, a pretty good one, with their Leopard-II tanks. Well, the Germans had soldiering in their genetic code somewhere, but they weren't any better trained than Americans, and *training* was the difference between some ignorant damned civilian and a soldier. Training meant knowing where to look and what to do when you saw something there. Training meant knowing what the tank to your left was going to do without having to look. Training meant knowing how to fix your tank or Bradley when something broke. Training eventually meant pride, because with training came confidence, the sure knowledge that you were the baddest motherfucker in the Valley of the Shadow of Death, and you didn't have to fear no evil at all.

Colonel Boyle was flying the UH-60A in which Diggs was riding.

Diggs was in the jump seat immediately aft and between the pilots' seats. They were cruising about five hundred feet over the ground.

"Oops, that platoon down there just walked into something," Boyle reported, pointing. Sure enough the lead tank's blinking yellow light started flashing the *I'm dead* signal.

"Let's see how the platoon sergeant recovers," General Diggs said.

They watched, and sure enough, the sergeant pulled the remaining three tanks back while the crew bailed out of the platoon leader's M1A2 main battle tank. As a practical matter, both it and its crew would probably have survived whatever administrative "hit" it had taken from the Germans. Nobody had yet come up with a weapon to punch reliably through the Chobham armor, but someone might someday, and so the tank crews were not encouraged to think themselves immortal and their tanks invulnerable.

"Okay, that sergeant knows his job," Diggs observed, as the helicopter moved to another venue. The general saw that Colonel Masterman was making notes aplenty on his pad. "What do you think, Duke?"

"I think they're at about seventy-five percent efficiency, sir," the G-3 operations officer replied. "Maybe a little better. We need to put everybody on the SimNet, to shake 'em all up a little." That was one of the Army's better investments. SimNet, the simulator network, comprised a warehouse full of M1 and Bradley simulators, linked by supercomputer and satellite with two additional such warehouses, so that highly complex and realistic battles could be fought out electronically. It had been hugely expensive, and while it could never fully simulate training in the field, it was nevertheless a training aid without parallel.

"General, all that time in Yugoslavia didn't help Lisle's boys," Boyle said from the chopper's right seat.

"I know that," Diggs agreed. "I'm not going to kill anybody's career just yet," he promised.

Boyle's head turned to grin. "Good, sir. I'll spread that word around."

"What do you think of the Germans?"

"I know their boss, General Major Siegfried Model. He's damned smart. Plays a hell of a game of cards. Be warned, General."

"Is that a fact?" Diggs had commanded the NTC until quite recently, and had occasionally tried his luck at Las Vegas, a mere two hours up I-15 from the post.

"Sir, I know what you're thinking. Think again," Boyle cautioned his boss.

"Your helicopters seem to be doing well."

"Yep, Yugoslavia was fairly decent training for us, and long as we have gas, I can train my people."

"What about live-fire?" the commanding general of First Tanks asked.

"We haven't done that in a while, sir, but again, the simulators are almost as good as the real thing," Boyle replied over the intercom. "But I think you'll want your track toads to get some in, General." And Boyle was right on that one. Nothing substituted for live-fire in an Abrams or a Bradley.

The stakeout on the park bench turned out to be lengthy and boring. First of all, of course, they'd pulled the container, opened it, and discovered that the contents were two sheets of paper, closely printed with Cyrillic characters, but encrypted. So the sheet had been photographed and sent off to the cryppies for decryption. This had not proven to be easy. In fact, it had thus far proven to be impossible, leading the officers from the Federal Security Service to conclude that the Chinese (if that was who it was) had adopted the old KGB practice of using one-time pads. These were unbreakable in theoretical terms because there was no pattern, formula, or algorithm to crack.

The rest of the time was just a matter of waiting to see who came to pick up the package.

It ended up taking days. The FSS put three cars on the case. Two of them were vans with long-lens cameras on the target. In the meanwhile, Suvorov/Koniev's apartment was as closely watched as the Moscow Stock Exchange ticker. The subject himself had a permanent shadow of up to ten trained officers, mainly KGB-trained spy-chasers instead of Provalov's homicide investigators, but with a leavening of the latter because it was technically still their case. It would remain a homicide case until some foreign national—they hoped—picked up the package under the bench.

Since it was a park bench, people sat on it regularly. Adults reading papers, children reading comic books, teenagers holding hands, people chatting amiably, even two elderly men who met every afternoon for a game of chess played on a small magnetic board. After every such visit, the stash was checked for movement or disturbance, always without result. By the fourth day, people speculated aloud that it was all some sort of trick. This was Suvorov/Koniev's way of seeing if he were being trailed or not. If so, he was a clever son of a bitch, the surveillance people all agreed. But they already knew that.

The break came in the late afternoon of day five, and it was the man they wanted it to be. His name was Kong Deshi, and he was a minor diplomat on the official list, age forty-six, a man of modest dimensions, and, the form card at the Foreign Ministry said, modest intellectual gifts—that was a polite way of saying he was considered a dunce. But as others had noted, that was the perfect cover for a spy, and one which wasted a lot of time for counterintelligence people, making them trail dumb diplomats all over the world who turned out to be nothing more than just that—dumb diplomats—of which the global supply was ample. The man was walking casually with another Chinese national, who was a businessman of some sort, or so they'd thought. Sitting, they'd continued to chat, gesturing around until the second man had turned to look at something Kong had pointed at. Then Kong's right hand had slipped rapidly and almost invisibly under the bench and retrieved the stash, possibly replacing it with another before his hand went back in his lap. Five minutes later, after a smoke, they'd both walked off, back in the direction of the nearest Metro station.

"Patience," the head FSS officer had told his people over the radio circuit, and so they'd waited over an hour, until they were certain that there were no parked cars about keeping an eye on the dead-drop. Only then had an FSS man walked to the bench, sat down with his afternoon paper, and pulled the package. The way he flicked his cigarette away told the rest of the team that there had been a substitution.

In the laboratory, it was immediately discovered that the package had a key lock, and that got everyone's attention. The package was x-rayed immediately and found to contain a battery and some wires, plus a semi-opaque rectangle that collectively represented a pyrotechnic device. Whatever was inside the package was therefore valuable. A skilled locksmith took twenty minutes picking the lock, and then the holder was opened to reveal a few sheets of flash paper. These were removed and photographed, to show a solid collection of Cyrillic letters—and they were all random. It was a one-time-pad key sheet, the best thing they could have hoped to find. The sheets were refolded exactly as they had been replaced in the holder, and then the thin metal container—it looked like a cheap cigarette case—was returned to the bench.

"So?" Provalov asked the Federal Security Service officer on the case.

"So, the next time our subject sends a message, we'll be able to read it."

"And then we'll know," Provalov went on.

"Perhaps. We'll know something more than we know now. We'll have proof that this Suvorov fellow is a spy. That I can promise you," the counterintelligence officer pronounced.

Provalov had to admit to himself that they were no closer to solving his murder case than they'd been two weeks before, but at least things were moving, even if the path merely led them deeper into the fog.

So, Mike?" Dan Murray asked, eight time zones away.

"No nibbles yet, Director, but now it looks like we're chasing a spook. The subject's name is Klementi Ivan'ch Suvorov, currently living as Ivan Yurievich Koniev." Reilly read off the address. "The trail leads to him, or at least it seems to, and we spotted him making probable contact with a Chinese diplomat."

"And what the hell does all this mean?" FBI Director Murray wondered aloud into the secure phone.

"You got me there, Director, but it sure has turned into an interesting case."

"You must be pretty tight with this Provalov guy."

"He's a good cop, and yes, sir, we get along just fine."

That was more than Cliff Rutledge could say about his relationship with Shen Tang.

"Your news coverage of this incident was bad enough, but your President's remarks on our domestic policy is a violation of Chinese sovereignty!" the Chinese foreign minister said almost in a shout, for the seventh time since lunch.

"Minister," Cliff Rutledge replied. "None of this would have happened but for your policeman shooting an accredited diplomat, and that is not, strictly speaking, an entirely civilized act."

"Our internal affairs are our internal affairs," Shen retorted at once.

"That is so, Minister, but America has her own beliefs, and if you ask us to honor yours, then we may request that you show some respect for ours."

"We grow weary of America's interference with Chinese internal affairs. First you recognize our rebellious province on Taiwan. Then you encourage foreigners to interfere with our internal policies. Then you send a spy under the cover of religious beliefs to violate our laws with a diplomat from yet another country, then you photograph a Chinese policeman doing his duty, and then your President condemns *us* for *your* interference with our internal affairs. The People's Republic will not tolerate this uncivilized activity!"

And now you're going to demand most-favored-nation trade status, eh? Mark Gant thought in his chair. Damn, this *was* like a meeting with investment bankers—the pirate kind—on Wall Street.

"Minister, you call us uncivilized," Rutledge replied. "But there is no blood on our hands. Now, we are here, as I recall, to discuss trade issues. Can we return to that agenda?"

"Mr. Rutledge, America does not have the right to dictate to the People's Republic on one hand and to deny us our rights on the other," Shen retorted.

"Minister, America has made no such intrusion on China's internal affairs. If you kill a diplomat, you must expect a reaction. On the question of the Republic of China—"

"There is no Republic of China!" the PRC's Foreign Minister nearly screamed. "They are a renegade province, and *you* have violated our sovereignty by recognizing them!"

"Minister, the Republic of China is an independent nation with a freely elected government, and we are not the only country to recognize this fact. It is the policy of the United States of America to encourage the self-determination of peoples. At such time as the people in the ROC elect to become part of the mainland, that is their choice. But since they have freely chosen to be what they are, America chooses to recognize them. As we expect others to recognize America as a legitimate government because it represents the will of her people, so it is incumbent upon America to recognize the will of other peoples." Rutledge sat back in his chair, evidently bored with the course the afternoon had taken. The morning he'd expected. The PRC had to blow off some steam, but one morning was enough for that. This was getting tiresome.

"And if another of our provinces rebels, will you recognize that?"

"Is the Minister telling me of further political unrest in the People's Republic?" Rutledge inquired at once, a little too fast and too glibly, he told himself a moment later. "In any case, I have no instructions for that eventuality." It was supposed to have been a (semi) humorous response to rather a dumb question, but Minister Shen evidently didn't have his sense of humor turned on today. His hand came up, finger extended, and now he shook it at Cliff Rutledge and the United States.

"You cheat us. You interfere with us. You insult us. You blame us for the inefficiency of your economy. You deny us fair access to your markets. And you sit there as though you are the seat of the world's virtue. We will have none of this!"

"Minister, we have opened our doors to trade with your country, and you have closed your door in our face. It is your door to open or close," he conceded, "but we have our doors to close as well if you so force us. We have no wish to do this. We wish for fair and free trade between the great Chinese people and the American people, but the impediments to that trade are not to be found in America."

"You insult us, and then you expect us to invite you into our home?"

"Minister, America insults no one. A tragedy happened in the People's Republic yesterday. It was probably something you would have preferred to avoid, but even so, it happened. The President of the United States has asked for you to investigate the incident. That is not an unreasonable request. What do you condemn us for? A journalist reported the facts. Does China deny the facts we saw on television? Do you claim that a private American company fabricated this event? I think not. Do you say that those two men are not dead? Regrettably, this is not the case. Do you say that your policeman was justified in killing an accredited diplomat and a clergyman holding a newborn child?" Rutledge asked in his most reasonable voice. "Minister, all you have said for the past three and a half hours is that America is wrong for objecting to what appears to be cold-blooded murder. And our objection was merely a request for your government to investigate the incident. Minister, America has neither done nor said anything unreasonable, and we grow weary of the accusation. My delegation and I came here to discuss trade. We would like the People's Republic to open up its markets more so that trade can become *trade,* the free exchange of goods across international borders. You request a most-favored-nation trading relationship with the United States. That will not happen until such time as your markets are as open to America as America's are open to China, but it *can* happen at such time as you make the changes we require."

"The People's Republic is finished with acceding to America's insulting demands. We are finished with tolerating your insults to our sovereignty. We are finished with your interference in our internal affairs. It is time for America to consider our reasonable requests. China desires to have a fair trading relationship with the United States. We ask no more than what you give other nations: most favored nation."

"Minister, that will not happen until such time as you open your markets to our goods. Trade is not free if it is not fair. We object also to the PRC's violation of copyright and trademark treaties and agreements. We object to having industries fully owned by agencies of the government of the People's Republic to violate patent treaties, even to the point of manufacturing proprietary American products without permission or compensation and—"

"So now you call us thieves?" Shen demanded.

"Minister, I point out that such words have not escaped my lips. It is a fact, however, that we have examples of products made in China by factories owned by agencies of your government, which products appear to contain American inventions for which the inventors have not been compensated, and from whom permission to manufacture the copies has not been obtained. I can show you examples of those products if you wish." Shen's reaction was an angry wave of the hand, which Rutledge took to mean *No, thank you.* Or something like that.

"I have no interest in seeing physical evidence of American lies and distortions."

Gant just sat back in his chair while Rutledge made his injured reply, like a spectator at a prizefight, wondering if anyone would land the knockdown punch. Probably not, he thought. Neither had a glass chin, and both were too light on their feet. What resulted was a lot of flailing about, but no serious result. It was just a new kind of boring for him, exciting in its form, but dull in its result. He made some notes, but those were merely memory aids to help him remember how this had gone. It might make a fun chapter in his autobiography. What title, he wondered. *Trader and Diplomat,* maybe?

Forty-five minutes later, it broke up, with the usual handshakes, as cordial as the meeting had been contentious, which rather amazed Mark Gant.

"It's all business, not personal," Rutledge explained. "I'm surprised they're dwelling on this so much. It's not as though we've actually accused them of anything. Hell, even the President just asked for an investigation. Why are they so touchy?" he wondered aloud.

"Maybe they're worried they won't get what they want out of the talks," Gant speculated.

"But why are they *that* worried?" Rutledge asked.

"Maybe their foreign-exchange reserves are even lower than my computer model suggests." Gant shrugged.

"But even if they are, they're not exactly following a course that would ameliorate it." Rutledge slammed his hands together in frustration. "They're not behaving logically. Okay, sure, they're allowed to have a conniption fit over this shooting thing, and, yeah, maybe President Ryan pushed it a little too far saying some of the things he said—and Christ knows he's a real Neanderthal on the abortion issue. But all of that does not justify the time and the passion in their position."

"Fear?" Gant wondered.

"Fear of what?"

"If their cash reserves are that low, or maybe even lower, then they could be in a tight crack, Cliff. Tighter than we appreciate."

"Assume that they are, Mark. What makes it something to be fearful about?"

"A couple of things," Gant said, leaning forward in his limo seat. "It means they don't have the cash to buy things, or to meet the payments on the things they've already bought. It's an embarrassment, and like you said, these are proud people. I don't see them admitting they're wrong, or wanting to show weakness."

"That's a fact," Rutledge agreed.

"Pride can get people into a lot of trouble, Cliff," Gant thought aloud. He remembered a fund on Wall Street that had taken a hundred-million-dollar hit because its managing director wouldn't back off a position that he'd thought was correct a few days earlier, but then stayed with after it was manifestly clear that he was wrong. Why? Because he hadn't wanted to look like a pussy on The Street. And so instead of appearing to be a pussy, he'd proclaimed to the whole world that he was an ass. But how did one translate that into foreign affairs? A chief of state was smarter than that, wasn't he?

"It's not going well, my friend," Zhang told Fang.

"That foolish policeman is to blame. Yes, the Americans were wrong to react so strongly, but that would not have taken place at all if not for the overzealous police officer."

"President Ryan—why does he hate us so?"

"Zhang, twice you have plotted against the Russians, and twice you've played your intrigue against America. Is it not possible that the Americans know of this? Is it not possible that they guessed it was the case? Has it not occurred to you that this is why they recognized the Taiwan regime?"

Zhang Han San shook his head. "This is not possible. Nothing was ever written down." *And our security was perfect in both cases,* he didn't trouble himself to add.

"When things are said around people with ears, Zhang, they remember them. There are few secrets in the world. You can no more keep the affairs of state secret than you can conceal the sunrise," Fang went on, thinking that he'd make sure that this phrase went into the record of the talk that Ming would write up for him. "They spread too far. They reach too many people, and each of them has a mouth."

"Then what would you have us do?"

"The American has requested an investigation, so, we give him one. The facts we discover will be whatever facts we wish them to be. If a policeman must die, there are many others to take his place. Our trading relationship with America is more important than this trivial matter, Zhang."

"We cannot afford to abase ourselves before the barbarian."

"We cannot not afford *not* to in this case. We cannot allow false pride to put the country at risk." Fang sighed. His friend Zhang had always been a proud one. A man able to see far, certainly, but too aware of himself and the place he wanted. Yet the one he'd chosen was difficult. He'd never wanted the *first* place for himself, but instead to be the man who influenced the man at the top, to be like the court eunuchs who had directed the various emperors for over a thousand years. Fang almost smiled, thinking that no amount of power was worth becoming a eunuch, at the royal court or not, and that Zhang probably didn't wish to go that far, either. But to be the man of power behind the curtain was probably more difficult than to be the man in the first chair . . . and yet, Fang remembered, Zhang had been the prime mover behind Xu's selection to general secretary. Xu was an intellectual nonentity, a pleasant enough man with regal looks, able to speak in public well, but not himself a man of great ideas . . .

. . . and that explained things, didn't it? Zhang had helped make Xu the chief of the Politburo precisely *because* he was an empty vessel, and Zhang was the one to fill the void of ideas with his own thoughts. Of course. He ought to have seen it sooner. Elsewhere, it was believed that Xu had been chosen for his middle-of-the-road stance on everything—a conciliator, a consensus-maker, they called him outside the PRC. In fact, he was a man of few convictions, able to adopt those of anyone else, if that someone—Zhang—looked about first and decided where the Politburo should go.

Xu was not a complete puppet, of course. That was the problem with people. However useful they might be on some issues, on others they held to the illusion that they thought for themselves, and the most foolish of them *did* have ideas, and those ideas were rarely logical and almost never helpful. Xu had embarrassed Zhang on more than one occasion, and since he *was* chairman of the Politburo, Xu *did* have real personal power, just not the wit to make proper use of it. But—what? Sixty percent of the time, maybe a little more?—he was merely Zhang's mouthpiece. And Zhang, for his part, was largely free to exert his own influence, and to make his own national policy. He did so mostly unseen and unknown outside the Politburo itself, and not entirely known inside, either, since so many of his meetings with Xu were private, and most of the time Zhang never spoke of them, even to Fang.

His old friend was a chameleon, Fang thought, hardly for the first time. But if he showed humility in not seeking prominence to match his influence, then he balanced that with the fault of pride, and, worse, he didn't seem to know what weakness he displayed. He thought either that it wasn't a fault at all, or that only he knew of it. All men had their weaknesses, and the greatest of these were invariably those unknown to their practitioners. Fang checked his watch and took his leave. With luck, he'd be home at a decent hour, after he transcribed his notes through Ming. What a novelty, getting home on time.

CHAPTER 28

Collision Courses

"Those sonsabitches," Vice President Jackson observed with his coffee.

"Welcome to the wonderful world of statecraft, Robby," Ryan told his friend. It was 7:45 A.M. in the Oval Office. Cathy and the kids had gotten off early, and the day was starting fast. "We've had our suspicions, but here's the proof, if you want to call it that. The war with Japan and that little problem we had with Iran started in Beijing—well, not exactly, but this Zhang guy, acting for Xu, it would seem, aided and abetted both."

"Well, he may be a nasty son of a bitch, but I wouldn't give him points for brains," Robby said, after a moment's reflection. Then he thought some more. "But maybe that's not fair. From his point of view, the plans were pretty clever, using others to be his stalking horse. He risked nothing himself, then he figured to move in and profit on the risks of others. It certainly looked efficient, I suppose."

"Question is, what's his next move?"

"Between this and what Rutledge reports from Beijing, I'd say we have to take these people a little seriously," Robby reflected. Then his head perked up some more. "Jack, we have to get more people in on this."

"Mary Pat will flip out if we even suggest it," Ryan told him.

"Too damned bad. Jack, it's the old problem with intelligence information. If you spread it out too much, you risk compromising it, and then you lose it—*but* if you don't use it at all, you might as well not even have it. Where do you draw the line?" It was a rhetorical question. "If you err, you err on the side of safety—but the safety of the country, not the source."

"There's a real, live person on the other end of this sheet of paper, Rob," Jack pointed out.

"I'm sure there is. But there are two hundred fifty million people outside this room, Jack, and the oath we both swore was to them, not some Chinese puke in Beijing. What this tells us is that the guy making policy in China is willing to start wars, and twice now we've sent our people to fight wars he's had a part in starting. Jesus, man, war is supposed to be a thing of the past, but this Zhang guy hasn't figured that one out yet. What's he doing that we don't know about?"

"That's what SORGE's all about, Rob. The idea is that we find out beforehand and have a chance to forestall it."

Jackson nodded. "Maybe so, but once upon a time, there was a source called MAGIC that told us a lot about an enemy's intentions, but when that enemy launched the first attack, we were asleep—because MAGIC was so important we never told CINCPAC about it, and he ended up not preparing for Pearl Harbor. I know intel's important, but it has its operational limitations. All this really tells us is that we have a potential adversary with little in the way of inhibitions. We know his mindset, but not his intentions or current operations. Moreover, SORGE's giving us recollections of private conversations between one guy who makes policy and another guy who tries to influence policy. A lot of stuff is being left out. This looks like a cover-your-ass diary, doesn't it?"

Ryan told himself that this was a particularly smart critique. Like the people at Langley, he'd allowed himself to wax a little too euphoric about a source they'd never even approached before. SONGBIRD was good, but not without limitations. Big ones.

"Yeah, Rob, that's probably just what it is. This Fang guy probably keeps the diary just to have something to pull out of the drawer if one of his colleagues on the Chinese Politburo tries to butt-fuck him."

"So, it isn't Sir Thomas More whose words we're reading," TOMCAT observed.

"Not hardly," Ryan conceded. "But it's a good source. All the people who've looked at this for us say it feels very real."

"I'm not saying it isn't *true,* Jack, I'm saying it isn't *all,*" the Vice President persisted.

"Message received, Admiral." Ryan held up his hands in surrender. "What do you recommend?"

"SecDef for starters, and the Chiefs, and J-3 and J-5, and probably CINCPAC, your boy Bart Mancuso," Jackson added, with a hint of distaste.

"Why don't you like the guy?" SWORDSMAN asked.

"He's a bubblehead," the career fighter pilot answered. "Submariners don't get around all that much . . . but I grant you he's a pretty good operator." *The submarine operation he'd run on the Japs using old boomers had been pretty swift,* Jackson admitted to himself.

"Specific recommendations?"

"Rutledge tells us that the ChiComms are talking like they're real torqued over the Taiwan thing. What if they act on that? Like a missile strike into the island. Christ knows they have enough missiles to toss, and we have ships in harbor there all the time."

"You really think they'd be dumb enough to launch an attack on a city with one of our ships tied alongside?" Ryan asked. Nasty or not, this Zhang guy wasn't going to risk war with America quite that foolishly, was he?

"What if they don't know the ship's there? What if they get bad intel? Jack, the shooters don't always get good data from the guys in the back room. Trust me. Been there, done that, got the fucking scars, y'know?"

"The ships can take care of themselves, can't they?"

"Not if they don't have all their systems turned on, and can a Navy SAM stop a ballistic inbound?" Robby wondered aloud. "I don't know. How about we have Tony Bretano check it out for us?"

"Okay, give him a call." Ryan paused. "Robby, I have somebody coming in in a few minutes. We need to talk some more about this. With Adler and Bretano," the President added.

"Tony's very good on hardware and management stuff, but he needs a little educating on operations."

"So, educate him," Ryan told Jackson.

"Aye, aye, sir." The Vice President headed out the door.

They got the container back to its magnetic home less than two hours after removing it, thanking God—Russians were allowed to do that now—that the lock mechanism wasn't one of the new electronic ones.

Those could be very difficult to break. But the problem with all such security measures was that they all too often ran the chance of going wrong and destroying that which they were supposed to protect, which only added complexity to a job with too much complexity already. The world of espionage was one in which everything that could go wrong invariably did, and so over the years, every way of simplifying operations had been adopted by all the players. The result was that since what worked for one man worked for all, when you saw someone following the same procedures as your own intelligence officers and agents, you knew you had a player in your sights.

And so the stakeout on the bench was renewed—of course it had never been withdrawn, in case Suvorov/Koniev should appear unexpectedly while the transfer case was gone off to the lab—with an ever-changing set of cars and trucks, plus coverage in a building with a line-of-sight to the bench. The Chinese subject was being watched, but no one saw him set a telltale for the dead-drop. But that could be as simple as calling a number for Suvorov/Koniev's beeper . . . but probably no, since they'd assume that every phone line out of the Chinese embassy was bugged, and the number would be captured and perhaps traced to its owner. Spies had to be careful, because those who chased after them were both resourceful and unrelenting. That fact made them the most conservative of people. But difficult to spot though they might be, once spotted they were usually doomed. And that, the FSS men all hoped, would be the case with Suvorov/Koniev.

In this case, it took until after nightfall. The subject left his apartment building and drove around for forty minutes, following a path identical to one driven two days before—probably checking to see if he had a shadow, and also to check for some telltale alert the FSS people hadn't spotted yet. But this time, instead of driving back to his flat, he came by the park, parked his car two blocks from the bench, and walked there by an indirect route, pausing on the way twice to light a cigarette, which gave him ample opportunity to turn and check his back. Everything was right out of the playbook. He saw nothing, though three men and a woman were following him on foot. The woman was pushing a baby carriage, which gave her the excuse to stop every so often to adjust the infant's blanket. The men just walked, not looking at the subject or, so it seemed, anything else.

"There!" one of the FSS people said. Suvorov/Koniev didn't sit on the bench this time. Instead he rested his left foot on it, tied his shoelace, and adjusted his pants cuff. The pickup of the holder was accomplished so skillfully that no one actually saw it, but it seemed rather a far-fetched coincidence that he would pick that particular spot to tie his shoes—and besides, one of the FSS men would soon be there to see if he'd replaced one holder with another. With that done, the subject walked back to his car, taking a different circuitous route and lighting two more American Marlboros on the way.

The amusing part, Lieutenant Provalov thought, was how obvious it was once you knew whom to look at. What had once been anonymous was now as plain as an advertising billboard.

"So, now what do we do?" the militia lieutenant asked his FSS counterpart.

"Not a thing," the FSS supervisor replied. "We wait until he places another message under the bench, and then we get it, decode it, and find out what exactly he's up to. Then we make a further decision."

"What about my murder case?" Provalov demanded.

"What about it? This is an espionage case now, Comrade Lieutenant, and that takes precedence."

Which was true, Oleg Gregoriyevich had to admit to himself. The murder of a pimp, a whore, and a driver was a small thing compared to state treason.

His naval career might never end, Admiral Joshua Painter, USN (Ret.), thought to himself. And that wasn't so bad a thing, was it? A farm boy from Vermont, he'd graduated the Naval Academy almost forty years earlier, made it through Pensacola, then gotten his life's ambition, flying jets off aircraft carriers. He'd done it for the next twenty years, plus a stint as a test pilot, commanded a carrier air wing, then a carrier, then a group, and finally topped out as SACLANT/CINCLANT/CINCLANTFLT, three very weighty hats that he'd worn comfortably enough for just over three years before removing the uniform forever. Retirement had meant a civilian job paying about four times what the government had, mainly consulting with admirals he'd watched on the way up and telling them how he would have done it. In fact, it was something he would have done for free in any officers' club on any

Navy base in America, maybe for the cost of dinner and a few beers and a chance to smell the salt air.

But now he was in the Pentagon, back on the government payroll, this time as a civilian supergrade and special assistant to the Secretary of Defense. Tony Bretano, Josh Painter thought, was smart enough, a downright brilliant engineer and manager of engineers. He was prone to look for mathematical solutions to problems rather than human ones, and he tended to drive people a little hard. All in all, Bretano might have made a decent naval officer, Painter thought, especially a nuc.

His Pentagon office was smaller than the one he'd occupied as OP-05—Assistant Chief of Naval Operations for Air—ten years earlier, a job since de-established. He had his own secretary and a smart young commander to look after him. He was an entry-port to the SecDef's office for a lot of people, one of whom, oddly enough, was the Vice President.

"Hold for the Vice President," a White House operator told him on his private line.

"You bet," Painter replied.

"Josh, Robby."

"Good morning, sir," Painter replied. This annoyed Jackson, who'd served under Painter more than once, but Josh Painter wasn't a man able to call an elected official by his Christian name. "What can I do for you?"

"Got a question. The President and I were going over something this morning, and I didn't have the answer to his question. Can an Aegis intercept and kill a ballistic inbound?"

"I don't know, but I don't think so. We looked at that during the Gulf War and—oh, okay, yeah, I remember now. We decided they could probably stop one of those Scuds because of its relatively slow speed, but that's the top end of their ability. It's a software problem, software on the SAM itself." Which was the same story for the Patriot missiles as well, both men then remembered. "Why did that one come up?"

"The President's worried that if the Chinese toss one at Taiwan and we have a ship alongside, well, he'd prefer that the ship could look after herself, y'know?"

"I can look into that," Painter promised. "Want me to bring it up with Tony today?"

"That's affirmative," TOMCAT confirmed.

"Roger that, sir. I'll get back to you later today."

"Thanks, Josh," Jackson replied, hanging up.

Painter checked his watch. It was about time for him to head in anyway. The walk took him out into the busy E-Ring corridor, then right again into the SecDef's office, past the security people and the various private secretaries and aides. He was right on time, and the door to the inner office was open.

"Morning, Josh," Bretano greeted.

"Good morning, Mr. Secretary."

"Okay, what's new and interesting in the world today?"

"Well, sir, we have an inquiry from the White House that just came in."

"And what might that be?" THUNDER asked. Painter explained. "Good question. Why is the answer so hard to figure out?"

"It's something we've looked at on and off, but really Aegis was set up to deal with cruise-missile threats, and they top out at about Mach Three or so."

"But the Aegis radar is practically ideal for that sort of threat, isn't it?" The Secretary of Defense was fully briefed in on how the radar-computer system worked.

"It's a hell of a radar system, sir, yes," Painter agreed.

"And making it capable for this mission is just a question of software?"

"Essentially yes. Certainly it involves software in the missile's seekerhead, maybe also for the SPY and SPG radars as well. That's not exactly my field, sir."

"Software isn't all that difficult to write, and it isn't that expensive either. Hell, I had a world-class guy at TRW who's an expert on this stuff, used to work in SDIO downstairs. Alan Gregory, retired from the Army as a half-colonel, Ph.D. from Stony Brook, I think. Why not have him come in to check it out?"

It amazed Painter that Bretano, who'd run one major corporation and had almost been headhunted away to head Lockheed-Martin before President Ryan had intercepted him, had so little appreciation for procedure.

"Mr. Secretary, to do that, we have to—"

"My ass," THUNDER interrupted. "I have discretionary authority over small amounts of money, don't I?"

"Yes, Mr. Secretary," Painter confirmed.

"And I've sold all my stock in TRW, remember?"

"Yes, sir."

"So, I am not in violation of any of those fucking ethics laws, am I?"

"No, sir," Painter had to agree.

"Good, so call TRW in Sunnyvale, get Alan Gregory, I think he's a junior vice president now, and tell him we need him to fly here right away and look into this, to see how easy it would be to upgrade Aegis to providing a limited ballistic-missile-defense capability."

"Sir, it won't make some of the other contractors happy." *Including,* Painter did not add, *TRW.*

"I'm not here to make them happy, Admiral. Somebody told me I was here to defend the country efficiently."

"Yes, sir." It was hard not to like the guy, even if he did have the bureaucratic sensibilities of a pissed-off rhinoceros.

"So let's find out if Aegis has the technical capabilities do this particular job."

"Aye, aye, sir."

"What time do I have to drive up to the Hill?" the SecDef asked next.

"About thirty minutes, sir."

Bretano grumbled. Half his working time seemed to be spent explaining things to Congress, talking to people who'd already made up their minds and who only asked questions to look good on C-SPAN. For Tony Bretano, an engineer's engineer, it seemed like a hellishly unproductive way to spend his time. But they called it public service, didn't they? In a slightly different context, it was called slavery, but Ryan was even more trapped than he was, leaving THUNDER with little room to complain. And besides, he'd volunteered, too.

They were eager enough, these Spetsnaz junior officers, and Clark remembered that what makes elite troops is often the simple act of telling them that they are elite—then waiting for them to live up to their own self-image. There was a little more to it, of course. The Spetsnaz were special in terms of their mission. Essentially they'd been copies of the British Special Air Service. As so often happened in military life, what one country invented, other countries tended to copy, and so the Soviet Army had selected troops for unusually good fitness tests and a high degree of political reliability—Clark never learned exactly how one tested for that characteristic—and then assigned them a different training regimen, turning them into commandos. The initial concept had failed for a reason predictable to anyone but the political leadership of the Soviet Union: The great majority of Soviet soldiers were drafted, served two years, then went back home. The average member of the British SAS wasn't even considered for membership until he'd served four years and had corporal's stripes, for the simple reason that it takes more than two years to learn to be a competent soldier in ordinary duties, much less the sort that required thinking under fire—yet another problem for the Soviets, who didn't encourage independent thought for any of those in uniform, much less conscripted non-officers. To compensate for this, some clever weapons had been thought up. The spring-loaded knife was one with which Chavez had played earlier in the day. At the push of a button, it shot off the blade of a serious combat knife with a fair degree of accuracy over a range of five or six meters. But the Soviet engineer who'd come up with this idea must have been a movie watcher, because only in the movies do men fall silently and instantly dead from a knife in the chest. Most people find this experience painful, and most people respond to pain by making noise. As an instructor at The Farm, Clark had always warned, "Never cut a man's throat with a knife. They flop around and make noise when you do that."

By contrast, after all the thought and good engineering that had gone into the spring-knife, their pistol silencers were garbage, cans loaded with steel wool that self-destructed after less than ten shots, when manufacturing a decent suppressor required only about fifteen minutes of work from a semi-skilled machinist. John sighed to himself. There was no understanding these people.

But the individual troopers were just fine. He'd watched them run with Ding's Team-2, and not one of the Russians fell out of the formation. Part of that had been pride, of course, but most of it had been ability. The shoot-house experience had been less impressive. They weren't as carefully trained as the boys from Hereford, and not nearly so well equipped. Their supposedly suppressed weapons were sufficiently noisy to make John and Ding both jump . . . but for all that, the eagerness of these kids was impressive. Every one of the Russians was a senior lieutenant in rank, and each was airborne-qualified. They all were pretty good with light weapons—and the Russian snipers *were* as good as Homer Johnston and Dieter Weber, much to the surprise of the latter. The Russian sniper rifles looked a little clunky, but they shot pretty well—at least out to eight hundred meters.

"Mr. C, they have a ways to go, but they got spirit. Two weeks, and they'll be right on line," Chavez pronounced, looking skeptically at the vodka. They were in a Russian officers' club, and there was plenty of the stuff about.

"Only two?" John asked.

"In two weeks, they'll have all their skills down pat, and they'll master the new weapons." Rainbow was transferring five complete team-sets of weapons to the Russian Spetsnaz team: MP-10 submachine guns, Beretta .45 pistols, and most important, the radio gear that allowed the team to communicate even when under fire. The Russians were keeping their own Dragunov long-rifles, which was partly pride, but the things could shoot, and that was sufficient to the mission. "The rest is just experience, John, and we can't really give 'em that. All we can really do is set up a good training system for 'em, and the rest they'll do for themselves."

"Well, nobody ever said Ivan couldn't fight." Clark downed a shot. The working day was over, and everybody else was doing it.

"Shame their country's in such a mess," Chavez observed.

"It's their mess to clean up, Domingo. They'll do it if we keep out of their way." *Probably,* John didn't add. The hard part for him was thinking of them as something other than the enemy. He'd been here in the Bad Old Days, operating briefly on several occasions in Moscow as an "illegal" field officer, which in retrospect seemed like parading around Fifth Avenue in New York stark naked holding up a sign saying he hated Jews, blacks, and NYPD cops. At the time, it had just seemed like part of the job, John remembered. But now he was older, a grandfather, and evidently a lot more chicken than he'd been back in the '70s and '80s. Jesus, the chances he'd taken back then! More recently, he'd been in KGB—to him it would *always* be KGB—headquarters at #2 Dzerzhinskiy Square as a guest of the Chairman. Sure, Wilbur, and soon he'd hop in the alien spacecraft that landed every month in his backyard and accept their invitation for a luncheon flight to Mars. It felt about that crazy, John thought.

"Ivan Sergeyevich!" a voice called. It was Lieutenant General Yuriy Kirillin, the newly selected chief of Russian special forces—a man defining his own job as he went along, which was not the usual thing in this part of the world.

"Yuriy Andreyevich," Clark responded. He'd kept his given name and patronymic from his CIA cover as a convenience that, he was sure, the Russians knew all about anyway. So, no harm was done. He lifted a vodka bottle. It was apple vodka, flavored by some apple skins at the bottom of the bottle, and not bad to the taste. In any case, vodka was the fuel for any sort of business meeting in Russia, and since he was in Rome it was time to act Italian.

Kirillin gunned down his first shot as though he'd been waiting all week for it. He refilled and toasted John's companion: "Domingo Stepanovich," which was close enough. Chavez reciprocated the gesture. "Your men are excellent, comrades. We will learn much from them."

Comrades, John thought. *Son of a* bitch*!* "Your boys are eager, Yuriy, and hard workers."

"How long?" Kirillin asked. His eyes didn't show the vodka one little bit. *Perhaps they were immune,* Ding thought. He had to go easy on the stuff, lest John have to guide him home.

"Two weeks," Clark answered. "That's what Domingo tells me."

"That fast?" Kirillin asked, not displeased by the estimate.

"They're good troops, General," Ding said. "Their basic skills are there. They're in superb physical condition, and they're smart. All they need is familiarization with their new weapons, and some more directed training that we'll set up for them. And after that, they'll be training the rest of your forces, right?"

"Correct, Major. We will be establishing regional special-operations and counterterror forces throughout the country. The men you train this week will be training others in a few months. The problem with the Chechens came as a surprise to us, and we need to pay serious attention to terrorism as a security threat."

Clark didn't envy Kirillin the mission. Russia was a big country containing too many leftover nationalities from the Soviet Union—and for that matter from the time of the czars—many of whom had never particularly liked the idea of being part of Russia. America had had the problem once, but never to the extent that the Russians did, and here it wouldn't be getting better anytime soon. Economic prosperity was the only sure cure—prosperous people don't squabble; it's too rough on the china and the silverware—but prosperity was a way off in the future yet.

"Well, sir," Chavez went on, "in a year you'll have a serious and credible force, assuming you have the funding support you're going to need."

Kirillin grunted. "That is the question here, and probably in your country as well, yes?"

"Yeah." Clark had himself a laugh. "It helps if Congress loves you."

"You have many nationalities on your team," the Russian general observed.

"Yeah, well, we're mainly a NATO service, but we're used to working together. Our best shooter now is Italian."

"Really? I saw him, but—"

Chavez cut him off. "General, in a previous life, Ettore was James Butler Hickock. Excuse me, Wild Bill Hickock to you. That son of a bitch can sign his name with a handgun."

Clark refilled the vodka glasses. "Yuriy, he's won money off all of us at the pistol range. Even me."

"Is that a fact?" Kirillin mused, with the same look in his eyes that Clark had had a few weeks earlier. John punched him on the arm.

"I know what you're thinking. Bring money when you have your match with him, Comrade General," John advised. "You'll need it to pay off his winnings."

"This I must see," the Russian announced.

"Hey, Eddie!" Chavez waved his number-two over.

"Yes, sir?"

"Tell the general here how good Ettore is with a pistol."

"That fucking Eyetalian!" Sergeant Major Price swore. "He's even taken twenty pounds off Dave Woods."

"Dave's the range-master at Hereford, and he's pretty good, too,"

Ding explained. "Ettore really ought to be in the Olympics or something—maybe Camp Perry, John?"

"I thought of that, maybe enter him in the President's Cup match next year . . ." Clark mused. Then he turned. "Go ahead, Yuriy. Take him on. Maybe you will succeed where all of us failed."

"All of you, eh?"

"Every bloody one of us," Eddie Price confirmed. "I wonder why the Italian government gave him to us. If the Mafia want to go after him, I wish the bastards luck."

"This I must see," Kirillin persisted, leading his visitors to wonder how smart he was.

"Then you will see it, *Tovarisch General,"* Clark promised.

Kirillin, who'd been on the Red Army pistol team as a lieutenant and a captain, couldn't conceive of being beaten in a pistol match. He figured these NATO people were just having fun with him, as he might do if the situation were reversed. He waved to the bartender and ordered pepper vodka for his own next round. But all that said, he liked these NATO visitors, and their reputation spoke forcefully for itself. This Chavez, a major—he was really CIA, Kirillin knew, and evidently a good spy at that, according to his briefing from the SVR—had the look of a good soldier, with confidence won in the field, the way a soldier ought to win his confidence. Clark was much the same—and also very capable, so the book on him read—with his own ample experience both as a soldier and a spy. And his spoken Russian was superb and very literate, his accent of St. Petersburg, where he probably could—and probably once or twice *had,* Kirillin reflected—pass for a native. It was so strange that such men as these had once been his sworn enemies. Had battle happened, it would have been bloody, and its outcome very sad. Kirillin had spent three years in Afghanistan, and had learned firsthand just how horrid a thing combat was. He'd heard the stories from his father, a much-decorated infantry general, but hearing them wasn't the same as seeing, and besides, you never told the really awful parts because you tended to edit them out of your memory. One did not discuss seeing a friend's face turn to liquid from a rifle bullet over a few drinks in a bar, because it was just not the sort of thing you could describe to one who didn't understand, and you didn't need to describe it to one who did. You just lifted your glass to toast the memory of Grisha or Mirka, or one of the others, and in the community of arms, that was enough. Did these men do it? Probably. They'd lost men once, when Irish terrorists had attacked their own home station, to their ultimate cost, but not without inflicting their own harm on highly trained men.

And that was the essence of the profession of arms right there. You trained to skew the odds your way, but you could never quite turn them all the way in the direction you wished.

Yu Chun had experienced a thoroughly vile day. In the city of Taipei to look after her aged and seriously ill mother, she'd had a neighbor call urgently, telling her to switch on her TV, then seen her husband shot dead before her blinking eyes. And that had just been the first hammer blow of the day.

The next one involved getting to Beijing. The first two flights to Hong Kong were fully booked, and that cost her fourteen lonely and miserable hours sitting in the terminal as an anonymous face in a sea of such faces, alone with her horror and additional loneliness, until she finally boarded a flight to the PRC capital. That flight had been bumpy, and she had cowered in her last-row window seat, hoping that no one could see the anguish on her face, but hiding it as well as she might conceal an earthquake. In due course, that trial had ended, and she managed to leave the aircraft, and actually made it through immigration and customs fairly easily because she carried virtually nothing that could conceal contraband. Then it started all over again with the taxi to her home.

Her home was hidden behind a wall of policemen. She tried to pass through their line as one might wiggle through a market checkout, but the police had orders to admit no one into the house, and those orders did not include an exception for anyone who might actually live there. That took twenty minutes and three policemen of gradually increasing rank to determine. By this time, she'd been awake for twenty-six hours and traveling for twenty-two of them. Tears did not avail her in the situation, and she staggered her way to the nearby home of a member of her husband's congregation, Wen Zhong, a man who operated a small restaurant right in his home, a tall and rotund man, ordinarily jolly, liked by all who met him. Seeing Chun, he embraced her and took her into his home, at once giving her a room in which to sleep and a few drinks to help her relax. Yu Chin was asleep in minutes, and would remain that way for some hours, while Wen figured he had his own things to do. About the only thing Chun had managed to say before collapsing from exhaustion was that she wanted to bring Fa An's body home for proper burial. That Wen couldn't do all by himself, but he called a number of his fellow parishioners to let them know that their pastor's widow was in town. He understood that the burial would be on the island of Taiwan, which was where Yu had been born, but his congregation could hardly bid their beloved spiritual leader farewell without a ceremony of its own, and so he called around to arrange a memorial service at their small place of worship. He had no way of knowing that one of the parishioners he called reported directly to the Ministry of State Security.

Barry Wise was feeling pretty good about himself. While he didn't make as much money as his colleagues at the other so-called "major" networks—CNN didn't have an entertainment division to dump money into news—he figured that he was every bit as well known as their (white) talking heads, and he stood out from them by being a serious newsie who went into the field, found his own stories, and wrote his own copy. Barry Wise did the news, and that was all. He had a pass to the White House press room, and was considered in just about every capital city in the world not only as a reporter with whom you didn't trifle, but also as an honest conveyor of information. He was by turns respected and hated, depending on the government and the culture. *This* government, he figured, had little reason to love him. To Barry Wise, they were fucking barbarians. The police here had delusions of godhood that evidently devolved from the big shots downtown who must have thought their dicks were pretty big because they could make so many people dance to their tune. To Wise, that was the sign of a little one, instead, but you didn't tell them that out loud, because, small or not, they had cops with guns, and the guns were certainly big enough.

But these people had huge weaknesses, Wise also knew. They saw the world in a distorted way, like people with astigmatism, and assumed that was its real shape. They were like scientists in a lab who couldn't see past their own theories and kept trying to twist the experimental data into the proper result—or ended up ignoring the data which their theory couldn't explain.

But that was going to change. Information was getting in. In allowing free-market commerce, the government of the PRC had also allowed the installation of a forest of telephone lines. Many of them were connected to fax machines, and even more were connected to computers, and so *lots* of information was circulating around the country now. Wise wondered if the government appreciated the implications of *that.* Probably not. Neither Marx nor Mao had really understood how powerful a thing information was, because it was the place where one found the Truth, once you rooted through it a little, and Truth wasn't Theory. Truth was the way things really *were,* and that's what made it a son of a bitch. You could deny it, but only at your peril, because sooner or later the son of a bitch would bite you on the ass. Denying it just made the inevitable bite worse, because the longer you put it off, the wider its jaws got. The world had changed quite a bit since CNN had started up. As late as 1980, a country *could* deny anything, but CNN's signals, the voice *and* the pictures, came straight down from the satellite. You couldn't deny pictures worth a damn.

And that made Barry Wise the croupier in the casino of Information and Truth. He was an honest dealer—he had to be in order to survive in the casino, because the customers demanded it. In the free marketplace of ideas, Truth always won in the end, because it didn't need anything else to prop it up. Truth stood by itself, and sooner or later the wind would blow the props away from all the bullshit.

It was a noble enough profession, Wise thought. His mission in life was reporting history, and along the way, he got to make a little of it himself—or at least to help—and for that reason he was feared by those who thought that defining history was their exclusive domain. The thought often made him smile to himself. He'd helped a little the other day, Wise thought, with those two churchmen. He didn't know where it would lead. That was the work of others.

He still had more work of his own to do in China.

CHAPTER 29

Billy Budd

"So, what else is going to go wrong over there?" Ryan asked.

"Things will quiet down if the other side has half a brain," Adler said hopefully.

"Do they?" Robby Jackson asked, just before Arnie van Damm could.

"Sir, that's not a question with an easy answer. Are they stupid? No, they are not. But do they see things in the same way that we do? No, they do not. That's the fundamental problem dealing with them—"

"Yeah, Klingons," Ryan observed tersely. "Aliens from outer space. Jesus, Scott, how do we predict what they're going to do?"

"We don't, really," SecState answered. "We have a bunch of good people, but the problem is in getting them all to agree on something when we need an important call. They *never* do," Adler concluded. He frowned before going on. "Look, these guys are kings from a different culture. It was already very different from ours long before Marxism arrived, and the thoughts of our old friend Karl only made things worse. They're kings because they have absolute power. There *are* some limitations on that power, but we don't fully understand what they are, and therefore it's hard for us to enforce or to exploit them. They are Klingons. So, what we need is a Mr. Spock. Got one handy, anyone?"

Around the coffee table, there were the usual half-humorous snorts that accompany an observation that is neither especially funny nor readily escapable.

"Nothing new from SORGE today?" van Damm asked.

Ryan shook his head. "No, the source doesn't produce something every day."

"Pity," Adler said. "I've discussed the take from SORGE with some of my I and R people—always as my own theoretical musings . . ."

"And?" Jackson asked.

"And they think it's decent speculation, but not something to bet the ranch on."

There *was* amusement around the coffee table at that one.

"That's the problem with good intelligence information. It doesn't agree with what your own people think—assuming they really think at all," the Vice President observed.

"Not fair, Robby," Ryan told his VP.

"I know, I know." Jackson held up surrendering hands. "I just can't forget the motto of the whole intelligence community: 'We bet *your* life.' It's lonely out there with a fighter plane strapped to your back, risking your life on the basis of a piece of paper with somebody's opinion typed on it, when you never know the guy it's from or the data it's based on." He paused to stir his coffee. "You know, out in the fleet we used to think—well, we used to *hope*—that decisions made in this room here were based on solid data. It's quite a disappointment to learn what things are really like."

"Robby, back when I was in high school, I remember the Cuban Missile Crisis. I remember wondering if the world was going to blow up. But I still had to translate half a page of Caesar's goddamned Gallic Wars, and I saw the President on TV, and I figured things were okay, because he was the President of the United Goddamned States, and he had to know what was really going on. So, I translated the battle with the Helvetii and slept that night. The President knows, because he's the President, right? Then I become President, and I don't know a damned thing more than I knew the month before, but everybody out there"—Ryan waved his arm at the window—"thinks I'm fucking omniscient. . . . *Ellen!*" he called loudly enough to get through the door.

The door opened seven seconds later. "Yes, Mr. President?"

"I think you know, Ellen," Jack told her.

"Yes, sir." She fished in her pocket and pulled out a fliptop box of Virginia Slims. Ryan took one out, along with the pink butane lighter stashed inside. He lit the smoke and took a long hit. "Thanks, Ellen."

Her smile was downright motherly. "Surely, Mr. President." And she headed back to the secretaries' room, closing the curved door behind her.

"Jack?"

"Yeah, Rob?" Ryan responded, turning.

"That's disgusting."

"Okay, I am not omniscient, and I'm not perfect," POTUS admitted crossly after the second puff. "Now, back to China."

"They can forget MFN," van Damm said. "Congress would impeach you if you asked for it, Jack. And you can figure that the Hill will offer Taiwan any weapons system they want to buy next go-round."

"I have no problems with that. And there's no way I was going to offer them MFN anyway, unless they decide to break down and start acting like civilized people."

"And that's the problem," Adler reminded them all. "They think we're the uncivilized ones."

"I see trouble," Jackson said, before anyone else could. Ryan figured it was his background as a fighter pilot to be first in things. "They're just out of touch with the rest of the world. The only way to get them back in touch will involve some pain. Not to their people, especially, but sure as hell to the guys who make the decisions."

"And they're the ones who control the guns," van Damm noted.

"Roger that, Arnie," Jackson confirmed.

"So, how can we ease them the right way?" Ryan asked, to center the conversation once more.

"We stick to it. We tell them we want reciprocal trade access, or they will face reciprocal trade barriers. We tell them that this little flare-up with the Nuncio makes any concessions on our part impossible, and that's just how things are. If they want to trade with us, they have to back off," Adler spelled out. "They don't like being told such things, but it's the real world, and they have to acknowledge objective reality. They do understand that, for the most part," SecState concluded.

Ryan looked around the room and got nods. "Okay, make sure Rutledge understands what the message is," he told EAGLE.

"Yes, sir," SecState agreed, with a nod. People stood and started filing out. Vice President Jackson allowed himself to be the last in the line of departure.

"Hey, Rob," Ryan said to his old friend.

"Funny thing, watched some TV last night for a change, caught an old movie I hadn't seen since I was a kid."

"Which one?"

"Billy Budd, Melville's story about the poor dumb sailor who gets himself hanged. I'd forgot the name of Billy's ship."

"Yeah?" So had Ryan.

"It was *The Rights of Man.* Kind of a noble name for a ship. I imagine Melville made that up with malice aforethought, like writers do, but that's what we fight for, isn't it? Even the Royal Navy, they just didn't fight as well as we did back then. *The Rights of Man,"* Jackson repeated. "It *is* a noble sentiment."

"How does it apply to the current problem, Rob?"

"Jack, the first rule of war is the mission: First, why the hell are you out there, and then what are you proposing to do about it. The Rights of Man makes a pretty good starting point, doesn't it? By the way, CNN's going to be at Pap's church tomorrow and at Gerry Patterson's. They're switching off, preaching in each other's pulpit for the memorial ceremonies, and CNN decided to cover it as a news event in and of itself. Good call, I think," Jackson editorialized. "Wasn't like that in Mississippi back when I was a boy."

"It's going to be like you said?"

"I'm only guessing," Robby admitted, "but I don't see either one of them playing it cool. It's too good an opportunity to teach a good lesson about how the Lord doesn't care a rat's ass what color we are, and how all men of faith should stand together. They'll both probably fold in the abortion thing—Pap ain't real keen on abortion rights, and neither's Patterson—but mainly it'll be about justice and equality and how two good men went to see God after doing the right thing."

"Your dad's pretty good with a sermon, eh?"

"If they gave out Pulitzers for preaching, he'd have a wall covered in the things, Jack, and Gerry Patterson ain't too bad for a white boy either."

"Ah," Yefremov observed. He was in the building perch instead of one of the vehicles. It was more comfortable, and he was senior enough to deserve and appreciate the comforts. There was Suvorov/Koniev, sitting back on the bench, an afternoon newspaper in his hands. They didn't have to watch, but watch they did, just to be sure. Of course, there were thousands of park benches in Moscow, and the probability that their subject would sit in the same one this many times was genuinely astronomical. That's what they would argue to the judge when the time came for the trial . . . depending on what was in the subject's right hand. (His KGB file said that he was right-handed, and it seemed to be the case.) He was so skillful that you could hardly see what he did, but it was done, and it was seen. His right hand left the paper, reached inside his jacket, and pulled out something metallic. Then the hand paused briefly, and as he turned pages in the paper—the fluttering of the paper was a fine distraction to anyone who might be watching, since the human eye is always drawn to movement—the right hand slid down and affixed the metal transfer case to the magnetic holder, then returned for the paper, all in one smooth motion, done so quickly as to be invisible. Well, almost, Yefremov thought. He'd caught spies before—four of them, in fact, which explained his promotion to a supervisory position—and every one had a thrill attached to it, because he was chasing and catching the most elusive of game. And this one was Russian-trained, the most elusive of all. He'd never bagged one of them before, and there was the extra thrill of catching not just a spy but a traitor as well . . . and perhaps a traitor guilty of murder? he wondered. That was another first. Never in his experience had espionage involved the violation of that law. No, an intelligence operation was about the transfer of information, which was dangerous enough. The inclusion of murder was an additional hazard that was not calculated to please a trained spy. It made noise, as they said, and noise was something a spy avoided as much as a cat burglar, and for much the same reason.

"Call Provalov," Yefremov told his subordinate. Two reasons for that. First, he rather owed it to the militia lieutenant, who'd presented him with both the case and the subject. Second, the civilian cop might know something useful to his part of this case. They continued to watch Suvorov/Koniev for another ten minutes. Finally, he stood and walked back to his car for the drive back to his apartment, during which he was duly followed by the ever-changing surveillance team. After the requisite fifteen minutes, one of Yefremov's people crossed the street and retrieved the case from the bench. It was the locked one again, which told them that the item inside was perhaps more important. You had to get past the anti-tamper device to keep the contents from being destroyed, but the FSS had people well skilled in that, and the key for this transfer case had already been struck. That was confirmed twenty minutes later, when the case was opened and the contents extracted, unfolded, photographed, refolded, reinserted, and, finally, relocked in the container, which was immediately driven back to the bench.

Back at FSS headquarters, the decryption team typed the message into a computer into which the one-time-pad had already been inputted. After that, it was a matter of mere seconds before the computer performed a function not unlike sliding a document over a printed template. The clear-text message was, agreeably, in Russian. The content of the message was something else.

"Yob tvoyu maht!" the technician breathed, in one of his language's more repulsive imprecations: *Fuck your mother.* Then he handed the page to one of the supervising inspectors, whose reaction was little different. Then he walked to the phone and dialed Yefremov's number.

"Pavel Georgeyevich, you need to see this."

Provalov was there when the chief of the decryption section walked in. The printout was in a manila folder, which the head cryppie handed over without a word.

"Well, Pasha?" the homicide investigator asked.

"Well, we have answered our first question."

The motorcar was even purchased at the same dealership in central Moscow, the sheet read. *There is no fault to be found here. The men who performed the mission are both dead in St. P. Before I can make another attempt, I need an indication from you on the timeline, and also on the payment to my contractors.*

"Golovko was the target, then," Provalov observed. *And the head of our country's intelligence service owes his life to a pimp.*

"So it would appear," Yefremov agreed. "Note that he doesn't ask payment for himself. I would imagine he's somewhat embarrassed at having missed his target on the first attempt."

"But he's working for the Chinese?"

"So that would appear as well," the FSS man observed, with an inward chill. *Why,* he asked himself, *would the Chinese wish to do such a thing? Isn't that nearly an act of war?* He sat back in his chair and lit up a smoke, looking into the eyes of his police colleague. Neither man knew what to say at the moment, and both kept silent. It would all soon be out of and far beyond their hands. With that decided, both men headed home for dinner.

The morning broke more brightly than usual in Beijing. Mrs. Yu had slept deeply and well, and though she awoke with a slight headache, she was grateful for Wen's insistence on a couple of drinks before retiring. Then she remembered why she was in Beijing, and any good feelings departed from her mind. Breakfast was mainly green tea and was spent looking down, remembering the sound of her husband's voice in the bleak acceptance of the fact that she'd never hear it again. He'd always been in a good mood over breakfast, never forgetting, as she had just done, to say grace over the morning meal and thank God for another day in which to serve Him. No more. *No more would he do that,* she reminded herself. But she had duties of her own to perform.

"What can we do, Zhong?" she asked, when her host appeared.

"I will go with you to the police post and we will ask for Fa An's body, and then I will help you fly our friend home, and we will have a memorial prayer service at the—"

"No, you can't, Zhong. There are police there to keep everyone out. They wouldn't even let me in, even though I had my papers in order."

"Then we will have it outside, and they will watch us pray for our friend," the restaurateur told his guest with gentle resolve.

Ten minutes later, she'd cleaned up and was ready to leave. The police station was only four blocks away, a simple building, ordinary in all respects except for the sign over the door.

"Yes?" the desk officer said when his peripheral vision noted the presence of people by his desk. He looked up from the paper forms that had occupied his attention for the past few minutes to see a woman and a man of about the same age.

"I am Yu Chun," Mrs. Yu answered, seeing some recognition in the desk officer's eyes result from her words.

"You are the wife of Yu Fa An?" he asked.

"That is correct."

"Your husband was an enemy of the people," the cop said next, sure of that but not sure of much else in this awkward case.

"I believe he was not, but all I ask is for his body, so that I might fly it home for burial with his family."

"I do not know where his body is," the cop said.

"But he was shot by a policeman," Wen put in, "and the disposal of his body is therefore a police matter. So, might you be so kind, comrade, as to call the proper number so that we can remove our friend's body?" His manners did not allow anger on the part of the desk officer.

But the desk cop really didn't know what number to call, and so he called someone inside the building, in the large administration division. He found this embarrassing to do with two citizens standing by his desk, but there was no avoiding that.

"Yes?" a voice answered on his third internal call.

"This is Sergeant Jiang at the desk in the public lobby. I have Yu Chun here, seeking the body of her husband, Yu Fa An. I need to tell her where to go."

The reply took a few seconds for the man on the other end of the phone, who had to remember. . . . "Ah, yes, tell her she can go to the Da Yunhe River. His body was cremated and the ashes dumped in the water last evening."

And, enemy of the people or not, it would not be a pleasant thing to tell his widow, who'd probably had feelings for him. Sergeant Jiang set the phone down and decided to give her the news.

"The body of Yu Fa An was cremated and the ashes scattered in the river, comrade."

"That is cruel!" Wen said at once. Chun was too stunned to say anything at the moment.

"I cannot help you more than that," Jiang told his visitors and looked back down at his paperwork to dismiss them.

"Where is my husband?" Yu Chun managed to blurt, after thirty seconds or so of silence.

"Your husband's body was cremated and the ashes scattered," Jiang said, without looking up, because he really didn't wish to see her eyes under these circumstances. "I cannot help you further. You may leave now."

"I want my husband back!" she insisted.

"Your husband is dead and his body has been cremated. Be gone now!" Sergeant Jiang insisted in return, wishing she'd just go away and allow him to get back to his paperwork.

"I want my husband," she said louder now, causing a few eyes to turn her way in the lobby.

"He is gone, Chun," Wen Zhong told her, taking her arm and steering her to the door. "Come, we will pray for him outside."

"But why did they—I mean, why is he—and why did they—" It had just been too much for one twenty-four-hour period. Despite the night's sleep, Yu Chun was still too disoriented. Her husband of over twenty years had vanished, and now she could not even see the urn containing his ashes? It was a lot to absorb for a woman who'd never so much as bumped into a policeman on the street, who'd never done a single thing to offend the state—except, perhaps, to marry a Christian—but what did *that* hurt, anyway? Had either of them, had any of their congregation ever plotted treason against the state? No. Had any of them so much as violated the criminal or civil law? No. And so why had this misfortune fallen upon her? She felt as though she'd been struck by an invisible truck while crossing the street, then had it decided that her injuries were all her fault. Behind one invisible truck was just another, and all the more merciless at that.

There was nothing left for her to do, no recourse, legal or otherwise. They couldn't even go into her home, whose living room had so often served as their church, there to pray for Yu's soul and entreat God for mercy and help. Instead they'd pray . . . where? she wondered. One thing at a time. She and Wen walked outside, escaping the eyes of the lobby, which had zoomed in on them with almost physical impact. The eyes and the weight they'd carried were soon left behind, but the sun outside was just one more thing that intruded on what ought to have been, and what needed to be, a day of peace and lonely prayer to a God whose mercy was not very evident at the moment. Instead, the brightness of the sun defeated her eyelids, bringing unwanted brilliance into the darkness that might have simulated, if not exactly granted, peace. She had a flight booked back to Hong Kong, and from there back to Taipei, where she could at least weep in the presence of her mother, who was awaiting her death as well, for the woman was over ninety and frail.

For Barry Wise, the day had long since begun. His colleagues in Atlanta had praised him to the heavens in an e-mail about his earlier story. Maybe another Emmy, they said. Wise liked getting the awards, but they weren't the reason for his work. It was just what he did. He wouldn't even say he enjoyed it, because the news he reported was rarely pretty or pleasant. It was just his job, the work he'd chosen to do. If there was an aspect of it that he actually liked, it was the newness of it. Just as people awoke wondering what they'd see on CNN every day, from baseball scores to executions, so he awoke every day wondering what he'd report. He often had some idea of where the story would be and roughly what it would contain, but you were never really sure, and in the newness was the adventure of his job. He'd learned to trust his instincts, though he never really understood where they came from or how they seemed to know what they did, and today his instincts reminded him that one of the people he'd seen shot the other day had said he was married, and that his wife was on Taiwan. Maybe she'd be back now? It was worth trying out. He'd tried to get Atlanta to check with the Vatican, but that story would be handled by the Rome bureau. The aircraft containing Cardinal DiMilo's body was on its way back to Italy, where somebody would be making a big deal about it for CNN to cover live and on tape to show to the entire world ten times at least.

The hotel room had a coffeemaker, and he brewed his own from beans stolen from the CNN Beijing bureau office. Sipping coffee, for him as for so many others, helped him think.

Okay, he thought, the Italian guy, the Cardinal, his body was gone, boxed and shipped out on an Alitalia 747, probably somewhere over Afghanistan right now. But what about the Chinese guy, the Baptist minister who took the round in the head? He had to have left a body behind, too, and he had a congregation and—he said he was married, didn't he? Okay, if so, he had a wife somewhere, and she'd want the body back to bury. So, at the least he could try to interview her . . . it would be a good followup, and would allow Atlanta to play the tape of the killings again. He was sure the Beijing government had written him onto their official shitlist, but fuck 'em, Wise thought with a sip of the Starbucks, it was hardly a disgrace to be there, was it? These people were racist as hell. Even folks on the street cringed to see him pass, with his dark skin. Even Birmingham under Bull Connor hadn't treated black Americans like aliens from another goddamned planet. Here, everyone looked the same, dressed the same, talked the same. Hell, they *needed* some black people just to liven up the mix some. Toss in a few blond Swedes and maybe a few Italians to set up a decent restaurant. . . .

But it wasn't his job to civilize the world, just to tell people what was going on in it. The trade talks were not where it was happening, not today, Wise thought. Today he and his satellite truck would head back to the home of Reverend Yu Fa An. Wise was playing a hunch. No more than that. But they'd rarely failed him before.

Ryan was enjoying another night off. The following night would be different. He had to give another goddamned speech on foreign policy. Why he couldn't simply announce policy in the press room and be done with it, nobody had yet told him—and he hadn't asked, for fear of looking the fool (again) before Arnie. This was just how it was done. The speech and the subject had nothing to do with the identity of the group he was addressing. Surely there had to be an easier way to tell the world what he thought. This way, too, Cathy had to come with him, and she hated these things even more than he did, because it took her away from her patient notes, which she guarded about as forcefully as a lion over the wildebeests he'd just killed for lunch. Cathy often complained that this First Lady stuff was hurting her performance as a surgeon. Jack didn't believe that. It was more likely that like most women, Cathy needed something to bitch about, and this subject was worthier than her more pedestrian complaints, like being unable to cook dinner once in a while, which she missed a lot more than the women's lib people would have cared to learn. Cathy had spent over twenty years learning to be a gourmet cook, and when time allowed (rarely) she'd sneak down to the capacious White House kitchen to trade ideas and recipes with the head chef. For the moment, however, she was curled up in a comfortable chair making notes on her patient files and sipping at her wineglass, while Jack watched TV, for a change *not* under the eyes of the Secret Service detail and the domestic staff.

But the President wasn't really watching TV. His eyes were pointed in that direction, but his mind was looking at something else. It was a look his wife had learned to understand in the past year, almost like open-eyed sleep while his brain churned over a problem. In fact, it was something she did herself often enough, thinking about the best way to treat a patient's problem while eating lunch at the Hopkins doctors' cafeteria, her brain creating a picture as though in a Disney cartoon, simulating the problem and then trying out theoretical fixes. It didn't happen all that much anymore. The laser applications she'd helped to develop were approaching the point that an auto mechanic could perform them—which was not something she or her colleagues advertised, of course. There had to be a mystique with medicine, or else you lost your power to tell your patients what to do in a way that ensured that they might actually do it.

For some reason, that didn't translate to the Presidency, Cathy thought. With Congress, well, most of the time they went along with him—as well they ought, since Jack's requests were usually as reasonable as they could be—but not always, and often for the dumbest reasons. "It may be good for the country, but it's not so good for my district, and . . ." And they all forgot the fact that when they had arrived in Washington, they'd sworn an oath to the country, not to their stupid little districts. When she'd said that to Arnie, he'd had a good laugh and lectured her on how the real world worked—*as though a* physician *didn't know that!* she fumed. And so Jack had to balance what was real with what wasn't but ought to be—as opposed to what wasn't and never would be. Like foreign affairs. It made a lot more sense for a married man to have an affair with some floozy than it did to try to reason with some foreign countries. At least you could tell the floozy that it was all over after three or four times, but these damned foreign chiefs of state would stay around forever with their stupidity.

That was one nice thing about medicine, Professor Ryan thought. Doctors all over the world treated patients pretty much the same way because the human body was the same everywhere, and a treatment regimen that worked at Johns Hopkins in east Baltimore worked just as well in Berlin or Moscow or Tokyo, even if the people looked and talked different—and if that was true, why couldn't people all over the world think the same way? Their damned brains were the same, weren't they? Now it was her turn to grumble, as her husband did often enough.

"Jack?" she said, as she put her notebook down.

"Yeah, Cathy?"

"What are you thinking about now?"

Mainly how I wish Ellen Sumter was here with a cigarette, he couldn't say. If Cathy knew he was sneaking smokes in the Oval Office, she didn't let on, which was probably the case, since she didn't go around looking for things to fight over, and he never ever smoked in front of her or the kids anymore. Cathy allowed him to indulge his weaknesses, as long as he did so in the utmost moderation. But her question was about the cause for his yearning for some nicotine.

"China, babe. They really stepped on the old crank with the golf shoes this time, but they don't seem to know how bad it looked."

"Killing those two people—how could it *not* look bad?" SURGEON asked.

"Not everybody values human life in the same way that we do, Cath."

"The Chinese doctors I've met are—well, they're doctors, and we talk to each other like doctors."

"I suppose." Ryan saw a commercial start on the TV show he was pretending to watch, and stood to walk off to the upstairs kitchen for another whiskey. "Refill, babe?"

"Yes, thank you." With her Christmas-tree smile.

Jack lifted his wife's wineglass. So, she had no procedures scheduled for the next day. She'd come to love the Chateau Ste. Michelle Chardonnay they'd first sampled at Camp David. For him tonight, it was Wild Turkey bourbon over ice. He loved the pungent smell of the corn and rye grains, and tonight he'd dismissed the upstairs staff and could enjoy the relative luxury of fixing his own—he could even have made a peanut butter sandwich, had he been of such a mind. He walked the drinks back, touching his wife's neck on the way, and getting the cute little shiver she always made when he did so.

"So, what's going to happen in China?"

"We'll find out the same way as everybody else, watching CNN. They're a lot faster than our intelligence people on some things. And our spooks can't predict the future any better than the traders on Wall Street." *You'd be able to identify such a man at Merrill Lynch easily if he existed,* Jack didn't bother saying aloud. *He'd be the guy with all the millionaires lined up outside his office.*

"So, what do you think?"

"I'm worried, Cath," Ryan admitted, sitting back down.

"About what?"

"About what we'll have to do if they screw things up again. But we can't warn them. That only makes it certain that bad things are going to happen, because then they'll do something really dumb just to show us how powerful they are. That's how nation-states are. You can't talk to them like real people. The people who make the decisions over there think with their . . ."

". . . dicks?" Cathy offered with a half giggle.

"Yep," Jack confirmed with a nod. "A lot of them follow their dicks everywhere they go, too. We know about some foreign leaders who have habits that would get them tossed out of any decent whorehouse in the world. They just love to show everybody how tough and manly they are, and to do that, they act like animals in a goddamned barnyard."

"Secretaries?"

"A lot of that." Ryan nodded. "Hell, Chairman Mao liked doing twelve-year-old virgins, like changing shirts. I guess old as he was, it was the best he could do—"

"No Viagra back then, Jack," Cathy pointed out.

"Well, you suppose that drug will help civilize the world?" he asked, turning to grin at his physician wife. It didn't seem a likely prospect.

"Well, maybe it'll protect a lot of twelve-year-olds."

Jack checked his watch. Another half hour and he'd be turning in. Until then, maybe he could actually watch the TV for a little while.

Rutledge was just waking up. Under his door was an envelope, which he picked up and opened, to find an official communiqué from Foggy Bottom, his instructions for the day, which weren't terribly different from those of the previous day. Nothing in the way of concessions to offer, which were the grease of dealing with the PRC. You had to give them something if you wanted to get anything, and the Chinese never seemed to realize that such a procedure could and occasionally *should* work the other way as well. Rutledge headed to his private bathroom and wondered if it had been like this chatting with German diplomats in May 1939. Could anyone have prevented *that* war from breaking out? he wondered. Probably not, in retrospect. Some chiefs of state were just too damned stupid to grasp what their diplomats told them, or maybe the idea of war just appealed to one sort of mind. Well, even diplomacy had its limitations, didn't it?

Breakfast was served half an hour later, by which time Rutledge was showered and shaved pink. His staff were all there in the dining room, looking over the papers for the most part, learning what was going on back home. They already knew, or thought they knew, what was going to happen here. A whole lot of nothing. Rutledge agreed with that assessment. He was wrong, too.

CHAPTER 30

And the Rights of Men

"Got the address?" Wise asked his driver. He was also the team's cameraman, and drew the driving duty because of his steady hands and genius for anticipating traffic clogs.

"Got it, Barry," the man assured him. Better yet, it had been inputted into the satellite-navigation system, and the computer would tell them how to get there. *Hertz was going to conquer the world someday,* Wise reflected with a chuckle. Just so they didn't bring back the O.J. commercials.

"Going to rain, looks like," Barry Wise thought.

"Could be," his producer agreed.

"What do you suppose happened to the gal who had the baby?" the cameraman asked from the driver's seat.

"Probably home with her kid now. I bet they don't keep mothers in the hospital very long here," Wise speculated. "Trouble is, we don't know her address. No way to do a follow-up on her and the kid." And that was too bad, Wise could have added. They had the surname, Yang, on their original tape, but the given names of the husband and wife were both garbled.

"Yeah, I bet there's a lot of Yangs in the phone book here."

"Probably," Wise agreed. He didn't even know if there was such a thing as a Beijing phone book—or if the Yang family had a phone—and none of his crew could read the ideographic characters that constituted the Chinese written language. All of those factors combined to make a stone wall.

"Two blocks," the cameraman reported from the front seat. "Just have to turn left . . . here . . ."

The first thing they saw was a crowd of khaki uniforms, the local police, standing there like soldiers on guard duty, which was essentially what they were, of course. They parked the van and hopped out, and were immediately scrutinized as though they were alighting from an alien spacecraft. Pete Nichols had his camera out and up on his shoulder, and that didn't make the local cops any happier, because they'd all been briefed on this CNN crew at the Longfu hospital and what they'd done to damage the People's Republic. So the looks they gave the TV crew were poisonous—Wise and his crew could not have asked for anything better for their purposes.

Wise just walked up to the cop with the most rank-stuff on his uniform.

"Good day," Barry said pleasantly.

The sergeant in command of the group just nodded. His face was entirely neutral, as though he were playing cards for modest stakes.

"Could you help us?" Wise asked.

"Help you do what?" the cop asked in his broken English, suddenly angry at himself for admitting he could speak the language. Better if he'd played dumb, he realized a few seconds too late.

"We are looking for Mrs. Yu, the wife of the Reverend Yu, who used to live here."

"No here," the police sergeant replied with a wave of the hands. "No here."

"Then we will wait," Wise told him.

Minister," Cliff Rutledge said in greeting.

Shen was late, which was a surprise to the American delegation. It could have meant that he was delivering a message to his guests, telling them that they were not terribly important in the great scheme of things; or he might have been delayed by new instructions from the Politburo; or maybe his car hadn't wanted to start this morning. Personally, Rutledge leaned toward option number two. The Politburo would want to have input into these talks. Shen Tang had probably been a moderating influence, explaining to his colleagues that the American position, however unjust, would be difficult to shake in this series of talks, and so the smart long-term move would be to accommodate the American position for now, and make up for the losses in the next go-around the following year—the American sense of fair play, he would have told them, had cost them more negotiations than any other single factor in history, after all.

That's what Rutledge would have done in his place, and he knew Shen was no fool. In fact, he was a competent diplomatic technician, and pretty good at reading the situation quickly. He had to know—no, Rutledge corrected himself, he *should know* or *ought to know*—that the American position was being driven by public opinion at home, and that that public opinion was against the interests of the PRC, because the PRC had fucked up in public. So, if he'd been able to sell his position to the rest of the Politburo, he'd start off with a small concession, one which would show the course the day would take, allowing Rutledge to beat him back a few steps by the close of the afternoon session. Rutledge hoped for that, because it would get him what his country wanted with little further fuss, and would, by the way, make him look pretty good at Foggy Bottom. So he took a final sip of the welcoming tea and settled back in his chair, motioning for Shen to begin the morning's talks.

"We find it difficult to understand America's position in this and other matters—"

Uh-oh . . .

"America has chosen to affront our sovereignty in many ways. First, the Taiwan issue . . ."

Rutledge listened to the earphone which gave him the simultaneous translation. So, Shen hadn't been able to persuade the Politburo to take a reasonable tack. That meant another unproductive day at these talks, and maybe—possible but not likely as yet—failed talks entirely. If America was unable to get concessions from China, and was therefore forced to impose sanctions, it would be ruinous to both sides, and not calculated to make the world a safer or better place. The tirade lasted twenty-seven minutes by his watch.

"Minister," Rutledge began when it was his turn, "I find it difficult as well to understand your intransigence—" He went on along his own well-grooved path, varying only slightly when he said, "We put you *on notice* that unless the PRC allows its markets to be opened to American trade goods, the government of the United States will enact the provisions of the Trade Reform Act—"

Rutledge saw Shen's face coloring up some. Why? He had to know the rules of the new game. Rutledge had said this half a hundred times in the previous few days. Okay, fine, he'd never said "put on notice," which was diplo-speak for *no shit, Charlie, we're not fuckin' kidding anymore,* but the import of his earlier statements had been straightforward enough, and Shen was no fool . . . was he? Or had Cliff Rutledge misread this whole session?

Hello," a female voice said.

Wise's head turned sharply. "Hi. Have we met?"

"You met my husband briefly. I am Yu Chun," the woman said, as Barry Wise came to his feet. Her English was pretty good, probably from watching a lot of TV, which was teaching English (the American version, anyway) to the entire world.

"Oh." Wise blinked a few times. "Mrs. Yu, please accept our condolences for the loss of your husband. He was a very courageous man."

Her head nodded at the good wishes, but they made her choke up a little, remembering what sort of man Fa An had been. "Thank you," she managed to say, struggling not to show the emotions that welled up within her, held back, however, as though by a sturdy dam.

"Is there going to be a memorial service for your husband? If so, ma'am, we would ask your permission to make a record of it." Wise had never grown to like the oh-your-loved-one-is-dead, what's-it-feel-like? school of journalism. He'd seen far more death as a reporter than as a Marine, and it was all the same all over the world. The guy on the pale horse came to visit, always taking away something precious to somebody, most of the time more than one somebody, and the vacuum of feelings it left behind could only be filled by tears, and that language was universal. The good news was that people all over the world understood. The bad news was that getting it out did further harm to the living victims, and Wise had trouble stomaching his occasional obligation to do that, however relevant it was to the all-important story.

"I do not know. We used to worship there in our house, but the police will not let me inside," she told him.

"Can I help?" Wise offered, truly meaning it. "Sometimes the police will listen to people like us." He gestured to them, all of twenty meters away. Quietly, to Pete Nichols: "Saddle up."

How it looked to the cops was hard for the Americans to imagine, but the widow Yu walked toward them with this American black man in attendance and the white one with the camera close behind.

She started talking to the senior cop, with Wise's microphone between the two of them, speaking calmly and politely, asking permission to enter her home.

The police sergeant shook his head in the universal *No, you cannot* gesture that needed no translation.

"Wait a minute. Mrs. Yu, could you please translate for me?" She nodded. "Sergeant, you know who I am and you know what I do, correct?" This generated a curt and none too friendly nod. "What is the reason for not allowing this lady to enter her own home?"

" 'I have my orders,' " Chun translated the reply.

"I see," Wise responded. "Do you know that this will look bad for your country? People around the world will see this and feel it is improper." Yu Chun duly translated this for the sergeant.

" 'I have my orders,' " he said again, through her, and it was plain that further discussion with a statue would have been equally productive.

"Perhaps if you called your superior," Wise suggested, and to his surprise the Chinese cop leaped on it, lifting his portable radio and calling his station.

" 'My lieutenant come,' " Yu Chun translated. The sergeant was clearly relieved, now able to dump the situation on someone else, who answered directly to the captain at the station.

"Good, let's go back to the truck and wait for him," Wise suggested. Once there, Mrs. Yu lit up an unfiltered Chinese cigarette and tried to retain her composure. Nichols let the camera down, and everyone relaxed for a few minutes.

"How long were you married, ma'am?" Wise asked, with the camera shut off.

"Twenty-four years," she answered.

"Children?"

"One son. He is away at school in America, University of Oklahoma. He study engineering," Chun told the American crew.

"Pete," Wise said quietly, "get the dish up and operating."

"Right." The cameraman ducked his head to go inside the van. There he switched on the uplink systems. Atop the van, the mini-dish turned fifty degrees in the horizontal and sixty degrees in the vertical, and saw the communications satellite they usually used in Beijing. When he had the signal on his indicator, he selected Channel Six again and used it to inform Atlanta that he was initiating a live feed from Beijing. With that, a home-office producer started monitoring the feed, and saw nothing. He might have succumbed to immediate boredom, but he knew Barry Wise was usually good for something, and didn't go live unless there was a good reason for it. So, he leaned back in his comfortable swivel chair and sipped at his coffee, then notified the duty director in Master Control that there was a live signal inbound from Beijing, type and scope of story unknown. But the director, too, knew that Wise and his crew had sent in a possible Emmy-class story just two days earlier, and to the best of anyone's knowledge, none of the majors was doing anything at all in Beijing at the moment—CNN tracked the communications-satellite traffic as assiduously as the National Security Agency, to see what the competition was doing.

More people started showing up at the Wen house/church. Some were startled to see the CNN truck, but when they saw Yu Chun there, they relaxed somewhat, trusting her to know what was happening. Showing up in ones and twos for the most part, there were soon thirty or so people, most of them holding what had to be Bibles, Wise thought, getting Nichols up and operating again, but this time with a live signal going up and down to Atlanta.

"This is Barry Wise in Beijing. We are outside the home of the Reverend Yu Fa An, the Baptist minister who died just two days ago along with Renato Cardinal DiMilo, the Papal Nuncio, or Vatican Ambassador to the People's Republic. With me now is his widow, Yu Chun. She and the reverend were married for twenty-four years, and they have a son now studying at the University of Oklahoma at Norman. As you can imagine, this is not a pleasant time for Mrs. Yu, but it is all the more unpleasant since the local police will not allow her to enter her own home. The house also served as the church for their small congregation, and as you can see, the congregation has come together to pray for their departed spiritual leader, the Reverend Yu Fa An.

"But it does not appear that the local government is going to allow them to do so in their accustomed place of worship. I've spoken personally with the senior police official here. He has orders, he says, not to admit anyone into the house, not even Mrs. Yu, and it appears that he intends to follow those orders." Wise walked to where the widow was.

"Mrs. Yu, will you be taking your husband's body back to Taiwan for burial?" It wasn't often that Wise allowed his face to show emotion, but the answer to this question grabbed him in a tender place.

"There will be no body. My husband—they take his body and burn it, and scatter the ashes in river," Chun told the reporter, and saying it cracked both her composure and her voice.

"What?" Wise blurted. He hadn't expected that any more than she had, and it showed on his face. "They cremated his body without your permission?"

"Yes," Chun gasped.

"And they're not even giving you the ashes to take home with you?"

"No, they scatter ashes in river, they tell me."

"Well" was all Wise could manage. He wanted to say something stronger, but as a reporter he was supposed to maintain some degree of objectivity, and so he couldn't say what he might have preferred to say. *Those barbarian cocksuckers.* Even the differences in culture didn't explain this one away.

It was then that the police lieutenant arrived on his bicycle. He walked at once to the sergeant, spoke to him briefly, then walked to where Yu Chun was.

"What is this?" he asked in Mandarin. He recoiled when the TV camera and microphone entered the conversation. *What is THIS?* his face demanded of the Americans.

"I wish to enter my house, but he won't let me," Yu Chun answered, pointing at the sergeant. "Why can't I go in my house?"

"Excuse me," Wise put in. "I am Barry Wise. I work for CNN. Do you speak English, sir?" he asked the cop.

"Yes, I do."

"And you are?"

"I am Lieutenant Rong."

He could hardly have picked a better name for the moment, Wise thought, not knowing that the literal meaning of this particular surname actually was *weapon.*

"Lieutenant Rong, I am Barry Wise of CNN. Do you know the reason for your orders?"

"This house is a place of political activity which is ordered closed by the city government."

"Political activity? But it's a private residence—a house, is it not?"

"It is a place of political activity," Rong persisted. "Unauthorized political activity," he added.

"I see. Thank you, Lieutenant." Wise backed off and started talking directly to the camera while Mrs. Yu went to her fellow church members. The camera traced her to one particular member, a heavyset person whose face proclaimed resolve of some sort. This one turned to the other parishioners and said something loud. Immediately, they all opened their Bibles. The overweight one flipped his open as well and started reading a passage. He did so loudly, and the other members of the congregation looked intently into their testaments, allowing the first man to take the lead.

Wise counted thirty-four people, about evenly divided between men and women. All had their heads down into their own Bibles, or those next to them. That's when he turned to see Lieutenant Rong's face. It twisted into a sort of curiosity at first, then came comprehension and outrage. Clearly, the "political" activity for which the home had been declared off-limits was religious worship, and that the local government called it "political" activity was a further affront to Barry Wise's sense of right and wrong. He reflected briefly that the news media had largely forgotten what communism really had been, but now it lay right here in front of him. The face of oppression had never been a pretty one. It would soon get uglier.

Wen Zhong, the restaurateur, was leading the ad-hoc service, going through the Bible but doing so in Mandarin, a language which the CNN crew barely comprehended. The thirty or so others flipped the pages in their Bibles when he did, following his scriptural readings very carefully, in the way of Baptist, and Wise started wondering if this corpulent chap might be taking over the congregation right before his eyes. If so, the guy seemed sincere enough, and that above all was the quality a clergyman needed. Yu Chun headed over to him, and he reached out to put his arm around her shoulder in a gesture that didn't seem Chinese at all. That was when she lost it and started weeping, which hardly seemed shameful. Here was a woman married over twenty years who'd lost her husband in a particularly cruel way, then doubly insulted by a government which had gone so far as to destroy his body, thus denying her even the chance to look upon her beloved's face one last time, or the chance to have a small plot of ground to visit.

These people are *barbarians,* Wise thought, knowing he couldn't say such a thing in front of the camera, and angry for that reason, but his profession had rules and he didn't break them. But he did have a camera, and the camera showed things that mere words could not convey.

Unknown to the news crew, Atlanta had put their feed on live, with voice-over commentary from CNN headquarters because they hadn't managed to get Barry Wise's attention on the side-band audio circuit. The signal went up to the satellite, then down to Atlanta, and back up to a total of four orbiting birds, then it came down all over the world, and one of the places it came to was Beijing.

The members of the Chinese Politburo all had televisions in their offices, and all of them had access to the American CNN, which was for them a prime source of political intelligence. It came down also to the various hotels in the city, crowded as they were with businessmen and other visitors, and even some Chinese citizens had access to it, especially business people who conducted their affairs both within and without the People's Republic and needed to know what was happening in the outside world.

In his office, Fang Gan looked up from his desk to the TV that was always kept on while he was there. He lifted the controller to get the sound, and heard English, with some Chinese language in the background that he could not quite understand. His English wasn't very good, and he called Ming into his office to translate.

"Minister, this is coverage of something right here in Beijing," she told him first of all.

"I can see that, girl!" he snapped back at her. "What is being said?"

"Ah, yes. It is associates of the man Yu who was shot by the police two days ago . . . also his widow . . . this is evidently a funeral ceremony of some sort—oh, they say that Yu's body was cremated and scattered, and so his widow has nothing to bury, and that explains her added grief, they say."

"What lunatic did that?" Fang wondered aloud. He was not by nature a very compassionate man, but a wise man did not go out of his way to be cruel, either. "Go on, girl!"

"They are reading from the Christian Bible, I can't make out the words, the English speaker is blanking them out . . . the narrator is mainly repeating himself, saying . . . ah, yes, saying they are trying to establish contact with their reporter Wise here in Beijing but they are having technical difficulties . . . just repeating what he has already said, a memorial ceremony for the man Yu, friends . . . no, members of his worship group, and that is all, really. They are now repeating what happened before at the Longfu hospital, commenting also on the Italian churchman whose body will soon arrive back in Italy."

Fang grumbled and lifted his phone, calling for the Interior Minister.

"Turn on your TV!" he told his Politburo colleague at once. "You need to get control of this situation, but do so intelligently! This could be ruinous for us, the worst since those foolish students at Tiananmen Square."

Ming saw her boss grimace before setting the phone down and mutter, *"Fool!"* after he did so, then shake his head with a mixture of anger and sorrow.

"That will be all, Ming," he told her, after another minute.

His secretary went back to her desk and computer, wondering what was happening with the aftermath of the man Yu's death. Certainly it had seemed sad at the time, a singularly pointless pair of deaths which had upset and offended her minister for their stupidity. He'd even advocated punishing the trigger-happy policemen, but that suggestion had come to nothing, for fear of losing face for their country. With that thought, she shrugged and went back to her daily work.

The word from the Interior Minister went out fast, but Barry Wise couldn't see that. It took another minute for him to hear the voices from Atlanta on his IFB earphone. Immediately thereafter, he went live on audio and started again to do his own on-the-scene commentary for a global audience. He kept turning his head while Pete Nichols centered the video on this rump religious meeting in a narrow, dirty street. Wise saw the police lieutenant talk into his portable radio—it looked like a Motorola, just like American cops used. He talked, listened, talked again, then got something confirmed. With that, he holstered the radio and came walking directly to the CNN reporter. There was determination on his face, a look Wise didn't welcome, all the more so that on the way over, this Lieutenant Rong spoke discreetly with his men, who turned in the same direction, staying still but with a similar look of determination on their faces as they flexed their muscles in preparation for something.

"You must turn camera off," Rong told Wise.

"Excuse me?"

"Camera, turn off," the police lieutenant repeated.

"Why?" Wise asked, his mind going immediately into race mode.

"Orders," Rong explained tersely.

"What orders?"

"Orders from police headquarter," Rong said further.

"Oh, okay," Wise replied. Then he held out his hand.

"Turn off camera now!" Lieutenant Rong insisted, wondering what the extended hand was all about.

"Where is the order?"

"What?"

"I cannot turn my camera off without a written order. It is a rule for my company. Do you have a written order?"

"No," Rong said, suddenly nonplussed.

"And the order must be signed by a captain. A major would be better, but it must be a captain at least to sign the order," Wise went on. "It is a rule of my company."

"Ah," Rong managed to say next. It was as if he'd walked headfirst into an invisible wall. He shook his head, as though to shake off the force of a physical impact, and walked five meters away, pulling out his radio again to report to someone elsewhere. The exchange took about a minute, then Rong came back. "Order come soon," the lieutenant informed the American.

"Thank you," Wise responded, with a polite smile and half bow.

Lieutenant Rong went off again, looking somewhat confused until he grouped his men together. He had instructions to carry out now, and they were instructions he and they understood, which was usually a good feeling for citizens of the PRC, especially those in uniform.

"Trouble, Barry," Nichols said, turning the camera toward the cops. He'd caught the discussion of the written order, and managed to keep his face straight only by biting his tongue hard. Barry had a way of confounding people. He'd even done it to presidents more than once.

"I see it. Keep rolling," Wise replied off-mike. Then to Atlanta: "Something's going to happen here, and I don't like the looks of it. The police appear to have gotten an order from someone. As you just heard, they asked us to turn our camera off and we managed to refuse the request until we get a written order from a superior police official, in keeping with CNN policy," Wise went on, knowing that someone in Beijing was watching this. The thing about communists, he knew, was that they were maniacally organized, and found a request in writing to be completely reasonable, however crazy it might appear to an outsider. The only question now, he knew, was whether they'd follow their verbal radioed order before the draft for the CNN crew came. Which priority came first . . . ?

The immediate priority, of course, was maintaining order in their own city. The cops took out their batons and started heading toward the Baptists.

"Where do I stand, Barry?" Pete Nichols asked.

"Not too close. Make sure you can sweep the whole playing field," Wise ordered.

"Gotcha," the cameraman responded.

They tracked Lieutenant Rong right up to Wen Zhong, where a verbal order was given, and just as quickly rejected. The order was given again. The shotgun mike on the camera just barely caught the reply for the third iteration:

"Diao ren, chou ni ma di be!" the overweight Chinese shouted into the face of the police official. Whatever the imprecation meant, it made a few eyes go wide among the worshippers. It also earned Wen a smashed cheekbone from Rong's personal baton. He fell to his knees, blood already streaming from the ripped skin, but then Wen struggled back to

his feet, turned his back on the cop, and turned to yet another page in his Bible. Nichols changed position so that he could zoom in on the testament, and the blood dripping onto the pages.

Having the man turn his back to him only enraged Lieutenant Rong more. His next swing came down on the back of Wen's head. That one buckled his knees, but amazingly failed to drop him. This time, Rong grabbed his shoulder with his left hand and spun him about, and the third blow from the baton rammed directly into the man's solar plexus. That sort of blow will fell a professional boxer, and it did so to this restaurateur. A blink later, he was on his knees, one hand holding his Bible, the other grasping at his upper abdomen.

By this time, the other cops were moving in on the remainder of the crowd, swinging their own nightsticks at people who cringed but didn't run. Yu Chun was the first of them. Not a tall woman even by Chinese standards, she took the full force of a blow squarely in the face, which broke her nose and shot blood out as though from a garden sprinkler.

It didn't take long. There were thirty-four parishioners and twelve cops, and the Christians didn't resist effectively, not so much because of their religious beliefs as because of their societal conditioning not to resist the forces of order in their culture. And so, uniformly they stood, and uniformly they took the blows with no more defense than a cringe, and uniformly they collapsed to the street with bleeding faces. The policemen withdrew almost immediately, as though to display their work to the CNN camera, which duly took the shots and transmitted them around the world in a matter of seconds.

"You getting this?" Wise asked Atlanta.

"Blood and all, Barry," the director replied, from his swivel chair at CNN headquarters. "Tell Nichols I owe him a beer."

"Roger that."

"It seems that the local police had orders to break up this religious meeting, which they regard as something of a political nature, and politically threatening to their government. As you can see, none of these people are armed, and none resisted the attack by the police in any way. Now—" He paused on seeing another bicycle speed its way up the street to where they were. A uniformed cop jumped off and handed something to Lieutenant Rong. This the lieutenant carried to Barry Wise.

"Here order. Turn camera off!" he demanded.

"Please, allow me to look at the order," Wise replied, so angry at what he'd just seen that he was willing to risk a cracked head of his own, just so Pete got it up to the satellite. He scanned the page and handed it back. "I cannot read this. Please excuse me," he went on, deliberately baiting the man and wondering exactly where the limits were, "but I cannot read your language."

It looked as though Rong's eyes would pop out of his head. "It say here, turn camera off!"

"But I can't read it, and neither can my company," Wise responded, keeping his voice entirely reasonable.

Rong saw the camera and microphone were both pointed his way, and now he realized that he was being had, and had badly. But he also knew he had to play the game. "It say here, must turn camera off now." Rong's fingers traced the page from one symbol to another.

"Okay, I guess you're telling me the truth." Wise stood erect and turned to face the camera. "Well, as you have just seen, we've been ordered by the local police to cease transmission from this place. To summarize, the widow of the Reverend Yu Fa An and members of his congregation came here today to pray for their departed pastor. It turns out that Reverend Yu's body was cremated and his ashes scattered. His widow, Yu Chun, was denied access to her home by the police because of alleged improper 'political' activity, by which I guess they mean religious worship, and as you just saw, the local police attacked and clubbed members of the congregation. And now we're being chased away, too. Atlanta, this is Barry Wise, reporting live from Beijing." Five seconds later, Nichols dropped the camera off his shoulder and turned to stow it in the truck. Wise looked back down at the police lieutenant and smiled politely, thinking, *You can shove this up your skinny little ass, Gomer!* But he'd done his job, getting the story out. The rest was in the hands of the world.

CHAPTER 31

The Protection of Rights

CNN transmits its news coverage twenty-four hours a day to satellite dishes all over the world, and so the report from the streets of Beijing was noted not only by the American intelligence services, but by accountants, housewives, and insomniacs. Of the last group, a goodly number had access to personal computers, and being insomniacs, many of them also knew the e-mail address for the White House. E-mail had almost overnight replaced telegrams as the method of choice for telling the U.S. government what you thought, and was a medium which they appeared to heed, or at least to read, count, and catalog. The latter was done in a basement office in the Old Executive Office Building, the OEOB, the Victorian monstrosity immediately to the west of The House. The people who ran this particular office reported directly to Arnold van Damm, and it was actually rather a thorough and well-organized measure of American public opinion, since they also had electronic access to every polling organization in the country—and, indeed, the entire world. It saved money for the White House not to conduct its own polling, which was useful, since this White House didn't really have a political office per se, somewhat to the despair of the Chief of Staff. Nevertheless, he ran that part of White House operations himself, and largely uncompensated. Arnie didn't mind. For him, politics was as natural as breathing, and he'd decided to serve this President faithfully long before, especially since serving him so often meant protecting him from himself and his frequently stunning political ineptitude.

The data which started arriving just after midnight, however, didn't require a political genius to understand it. Quite a few of the e-mails had actual names attached—not mere electronic "handles"—and a lot of them were DEMANDING!!! action. Arnie would remark later in the day that he hadn't known that so many Baptists were computer-literate, something he reproached himself for even thinking.

In the same building, the White House Office of Signals duly made a high-quality tape of the report and had it walked to the Oval Office. Elsewhere in the world, the CNN report from Beijing arrived at breakfast time, causing more than a few people to set their coffee (or tea) cups down immediately before a groan of anger. *That* occasioned brief dispatches from American embassies around the world, informing the Department of State that various foreign governments had reacted adversely to the story on CNN, and that various PRC embassies had found demonstrators outside their gates, some of them quite vociferous. This information rapidly found its way to the Diplomatic Protection Service, the State Department agency tasked with the job of securing foreign diplomats and their embassies. Calls went out from there to the D.C. police to increase the uniformed presence near the PRC's various missions to America, and to arrange a rapid backup should any similar problems develop right here in Washington.

By the time Ben Goodley awoke and drove over to Langley for his morning briefing, the American intelligence community had pretty well diagnosed the problem. As Ryan had so colorfully said it himself, the PRC had stepped very hard on the old crank with the golf shoes, and even they would soon feel the pain. This would prove to be a gross understatement.

The good news for Goodley, if you could call it that, was that Ryan invariably had his breakfast-room TV tuned to CNN, and was fully aware of the new crisis before putting on his starched white button-down shirt and striped tie. Even kissing his wife and kids on their way out of The House that morning couldn't do much to assuage his anger at the incomprehensible stupidity of those people on the other side of the world.

"God damn it, Ben!" POTUS snarled when Goodley came into the Oval Office.

"Hey, Boss, *I* didn't do it!" the National Security Adviser protested, surprised at the President's vehemence.

"What do we know?"

"Essentially, you've seen it all. The widow of the poor bastard who got his brains blown out the other day came to Beijing hoping to bring his body back to Taiwan for burial. She found out that the body had been cremated, and the ashes disposed of. The local cops would not let her back into her house, and when some members of the parish came by to hold a prayer service, the local cops decided to break it up." He didn't have to say that the attack on the widow had been caught with particular excellence by the CNN cameraman, to the point that Cathy Ryan had commented upstairs that the woman definitely had a broken nose, and possibly worse, and would probably need a good maxillary surgeon to put her face back together. Then she'd asked her husband why the cops would hate anyone so much.

"She believes in God, I suppose," Ryan had replied in the breakfast room.

"Jack, this is like something out of Nazi Germany, something from that History Channel stuff you like to watch." And doctor or not, she'd cringed at the tape of the attacks on Chinese citizens armed only with Bibles.

"I've seen it, too," van Damm said, arriving in the Oval Office. "And we're getting a flood of responses from the public."

"Fuckin' barbarians," Ryan swore, as Robby Jackson came in to complete the morning's intelligence-briefing audience.

"You can hang a big roger on that one, Jack. Damn, I know Pap's going to see this, too, and today's the day for him to do the memorial service at Gerry Patterson's church. It's going to be epic, Jack. Epic," the Vice President promised.

"And CNN's going to be there?"

"Bet your bippy, My Lord President," Robby confirmed.

Ryan turned to his Chief of Staff. "Okay, Arnie, I'm listening."

"No, *I'm* the one listening, Jack," van Damm replied. "What are you thinking?"

"I'm thinking I have to talk to the public about this. Press conference, maybe. As far as action goes, I'll start by saying that we have a huge violation of human rights, all the more so that they had the fucking arrogance to do it in front of world opinion. I'll say that America has trouble doing business with people who act in this way, that commercial ties do not justify or cancel out gross violations of the principles on which our country is founded, that we have to reconsider all of our relations with the PRC."

"Not bad," the Chief of Staff observed, with a teacher's smile to a bright pupil. "Check with Scott for other options and ideas."

"Yeah." Jack nodded. "Okay, broader question, how will the country react to this?"

"The initial response will be outrage," Arnie replied. "It looks bad on TV, and that's how most people will respond, from the gut. If the Chinese have the good sense to make some kind of amends, then it'll settle down. If not"—Arnie frowned importantly—"I have a bad feeling. The church groups are going to raise hell. They've offended the Italian and German governments—so our NATO allies are also pissed off at this—and smashing that poor woman's face isn't going to win them any friends in the women's rights movement. This whole business is a colossal loser for them, but I'm not sure they understand the implications of their actions."

"Then they're going to learn, the easy way or the hard way," Goodley suggested to the group.

Dr. Alan Gregory always seemed to stay at the same Marriott overlooking the Potomac, under the air approach to Reagan National Airport. He'd again taken the red-eye in from Los Angeles, a flight which hadn't exactly improved with practice over the years. Arriving, he took a cab to the hotel for a shower and a change of clothes, which would enable him to feel and look vaguely human for his 10:15 with the SecDef. For this at least, he would not need a taxi. Dr. Bretano was sending a car for him. The car duly arrived with an Army staff sergeant driving, and Gregory hopped in the back, to find a newspaper. It took only ten minutes to pull up to the River Entrance, where an Army major waited to escort him through the metal detector and onto the E-ring.

"You know the Secretary?" the officer asked on the way in.

"Oh, yeah, from a short distance, anyway."

He had to wait half a minute in an anteroom, but only half a minute.

"Al, grab a seat. Coffee?"

"Yes, thank you, Dr. Bretano."

"Tony," the SecDef corrected. He wasn't a formal man most of the time, and he knew the sort of work Gregory was capable of. A Navy steward got coffee for both men, along with croissants and jam, then withdrew. "How was the flight?"

"The red-eye never changes, sir—Tony. If you get off alive, they haven't done it right."

"Yeah, well, one nice thing about this job, I have a G waiting for me all the time. I don't have to walk or drive very much, and you saw the security detail outside."

"The guys with the knuckles dragging on the floor?" Gregory asked.

"Be nice. One of them went to Princeton before he became a SEAL."

That must be the one who reads the comic books to the others, Al didn't observe out loud. "So, Tony, what did you want me here for?"

"You used to work downstairs in SDIO, as I recall."

"Seven years down there, working in the dark with the rest of the mushrooms, and it never really worked out. I was in the free-electron-laser project. It went pretty well, except the damned lasers never scaled up the way we expected, even after we stole what the Russians were doing. They had the best laser guy in the world, by the way. Poor bastard got killed in a rock-climbing accident back in 1990, or that's what we heard in SDIO. He was bashing his head against the same wall our guys were. The 'wiggle chamber,' we called it, where you lase the hot gasses to extract the energy for your beam. We could never get a stable magnetic containment. They tried everything. I helped for nineteen months. There were some really smart guys working that problem, but we all struck out. I think the guys at Princeton will solve the fusion-containment problem before this one. We looked at that, too, but the problems were too different to copy the theoretical solutions. We ended up giving them a lot of our ideas, and they've been putting it to good use. Anyway, the Army made me a lieutenant colonel, and three weeks later, they offered me an early out because they didn't have any more use for me, and so I took the job at TRW that Dr. Flynn offered, and I've been working for you ever since." And so Gregory was getting eighty percent of his twenty-year Army pension, plus half a million a year from

TRW as a section leader, with stock options, and one hell of a retirement package.

"Well, Gerry Flynn sings your praises about once a week."

"He's a good man to work for," Gregory replied, with a smile and a nod.

"He says you can do software better than anyone in Sunnyvale."

"For some things. I didn't do the code for 'Doom,' unfortunately, but I'm still your man for adaptive optics."

"How about SAMs?"

Gregory nodded. "I did some of that when I was new in the Army. Then later they had me in to play with Patriot Block-4, you know, intercepting Scuds. I helped out on the warhead software." It had been three days too late to be used in the Persian Gulf War, he didn't add, but his software was now standard on all Patriot missiles in the field.

"Excellent. I want you to look over something for me. It'll be a direct contract for the Office of the Secretary of Defense—me—and Gerry Flynn won't gripe about it."

"What's that, Tony?"

"Find out if the Navy's Aegis system can intercept a ballistic inbound."

"It can. It'll stop a Scud, but that's only Mach three or so. You mean a *real* ballistic inbound?"

The SecDef nodded. "Yeah, an ICBM."

"There's been talk about that for years . . ." Gregory sipped his coffee. "The radar system is up to it. May be a slight software issue there, but it would not be a hard one, because you'll be getting raid-warning from other assets, and the SPY radar can see a good five hundred miles, and you can do all sorts of things with it electronically, like blast out seven million watts of RF down half a degree of bearing. That'll fry electronic components out to, oh, seven or eight thousand meters. You'll end up having two-headed kids, and have to buy a new watch.

"Okay," he went on, a slightly spacey look in his eyes. "The way Aegis works, the big SPY radar gives you a rough location for your target-interception, so you can loft your SAMs into a box. That's why Aegis missiles get such great range. They go out on autopilot and only do actual maneuvering for the last few seconds. For that, you have the

SPG radars on the ships, and the seeker-head on the missile tracks in on the reflected RF energy off the target. It's a killer system against airplanes, because you don't know you're being illuminated until the last couple of seconds, and it's hard to eyeball the missile and evade in so short a time.

"Okay, but for an ICBM, the terminal velocity is way the hell up there, like twenty-five thousand feet per second, like Mach eleven. That means your targeting window is very small . . . in all dimensions, but especially depth. Also you're talking a fairly hard, robust target. The RV off an ICBM is fairly sturdy, not tissue paper like the boosters are. I'll have to see if the warhead off a SAM will really hurt one of those." The eyes cleared and he looked directly into Bretano's eyes. "Okay, when do I start?"

"Commander Matthews," THUNDER said into his intercom phone. "Dr. Gregory is ready to talk to the Aegis people. Keep me posted, Al" was Bretano's final order.

"You bet."

The Reverend Doctor Hosiah Jackson donned his best robe of black silk, a gift handmade by the ladies of his congregation, the three stripes on the upper arms designating his academic rank. He was in Gerry Patterson's study, and a nice one it was. Outside the white wooden door was his congregation, all of them well-dressed and fairly prosperous white folks, some of whom would be slightly uncomfortable with having a black minister talk to them—Jesus was white, after all (or Jewish, which was almost the same thing). This was a little different, though, because this day they were remembering the life of someone only Gerry Patterson had ever met, a Chinese Baptist named Yu Fa An, whom their minister had called Skip, and whose congregation they had supported and supported generously for years. And so to commemorate the life of a yellow minister, they would sit through the sermon of a black one while their own pastor preached the gospel in a black church. *It was a fine gesture on Gerry's part,* Hosiah Jackson thought, hoping it wouldn't get him into any trouble with this congregation. *There'd be a few out there, their bigoted thoughts invisible behind their self-righteous faces, but,* the Reverend Jackson admitted to himself, *they'd be tortured souls because of it.* Those times had passed. He remembered them better than white Mississippians did because he'd been the one walking in the streets—he'd been arrested seven times during his work with the Southern Christian Leadership Conference—and getting his parishioners registered to vote. That had been the real problem with the rednecks. Riding in a municipal bus was no big deal, but voting meant power, real civic power, the ability to elect the people who made the laws which would be enforced on black and white citizens alike, and the rednecks hadn't liked that at all. But times had changed, and now they accepted the inevitable—*after* it had come to pass—and they'd learned to deal with it, and they'd also learned to vote Republican instead of Democrat, and the amusing part of *that* to Hosiah Jackson was that his own son Robert was more conservative than these well-dressed rednecks were, and *he'd* gone pretty far for the son of a colored preacherman in central Mississippi. But it was time. Patterson, like Jackson, had a large mirror on the back of the door so that he could check his appearance on the way out. Yes, he was ready. He looked solemn and authoritative, as the Voice of God was supposed to look.

The congregation was already singing. They had a fine organ here, a real hundred-horsepower one, not the electronic kind he had at his church, but the singing . . . they couldn't help it. They sang white, and there was no getting around it. The singing had all the proper devotion, but not the exuberant passion that he was accustomed to . . . but he'd love to have that organ, Hosiah decided. The pulpit was finely appointed, with a bottle of ice water, and a microphone provided by the CNN crew, who were discreetly in both back corners of the church and not making any trouble, *which was unusual for news crews,* Reverend Jackson thought. His last thought before beginning was that the only other black man to stand in this pulpit before this moment was the man who'd painted the woodwork.

"Ladies and gentlemen, good morning. I am Hosiah Jackson. You all probably know where my church is. I am here today at the invitation of my good friend and colleague, your pastor, Gerry Patterson.

"Gerry has the advantage over me today, because, unlike me, and I gather unlike any person in the church, he actually knew the man whom we are here to remember.

"To me, Yu Fa An was just a pen pal. Some years ago, Gerry and I had occasion to talk about the ministry. We met in the chapel at the local hospital. It'd been a bad day for both of us. We'd both lost good people that day, at about the same time, and to the same disease, cancer, and both of us needed to sit in the hospital chapel. I guess we both needed to ask God the same question. It's the question all of us have asked—why is there such cruelty in the world, why does a loving and merciful God permit it?

"Well, the answer to that question is found in Scripture, and in many places. Jesus Himself lamented the loss of innocent life, and one of his miracles was the raising of Lazarus from the dead, both to show that He was indeed the Son of God, and also to show His humanity, to show how much He cared about the loss of a good man.

"But Lazarus, like our two parishioners that day in the hospital, had died from disease, and when God made the world, He made it in such a way that there were, and there still are, things that need fixing. The Lord God told us to take dominion over the world, and part of that was God's desire for us to cure disease, to fix *all* the broken parts and so to bring perfection to the world, even as, by following God's Holy Word, we can bring perfection to ourselves.

"Gerry and I had a good talk that day, and that was the beginning of our friendship, as all ministers of the Gospel ought to be friends, because we preach the same Gospel from the same God.

"The next week we were talking again, and Gerry told me about his friend Skip. A man from the other side of the world, a man from a place where the religious traditions do not know Jesus. Well, Skip learned about all that at Oral Roberts University in Oklahoma, the same as many others, and he learned it so well that he thought long and hard and decided to join the ministry and preach the Gospel of Jesus Christ . . ."

Skip's skin was a different color than mine," Gerry Patterson was saying in another pulpit less than two miles away. "But in God's eyes, we are all the same, because the Lord Jesus looks through our skin into our hearts and our souls, and He always knows what's in there."

"That's right," a man's voice agreed in the congregation.

"And so, Skip became a minister of the Gospel. Instead of returning to his native land, where freedom of religion is something their government protects, Skip decided to keep flying west, into communist

China. Why there?" Patterson asked. "Why there indeed! The other China does not have freedom of religion. The other China refuses to admit that there is such a thing as God. The other China is like the Philistines of the Old Testament, the people who persecuted the Jews of Moses and Joshua, the enemies of God Himself. Why did Skip do this? Because he knew that no other place needed to hear the Word of God more than those people, and that Jesus wants us to preach to the heathen, to bring His Holy Word to those whose souls cry out for it, and this he did. No United States Marine storming the shores of Iwo Jima showed more courage than Skip did, carrying his Bible into Red China and starting to preach the Gospel in a land where religion is a crime."

And we must not forget that there was another man there, a Catholic cardinal, an old unmarried man from a rich and important family who long ago decided on his own to join the clergy of his church," Jackson reminded those before him. "His name was Renato, a name as foreign to us as Fa An, but despite that, he was a man of God who also took the Word of Jesus to the land of the heathen.

"When the government of that country found out about Reverend Yu, they took Skip's job away. They hoped to *starve* him out, but the people who made that decision didn't know Skip. They didn't know Jesus, and they didn't know about the faithful, did they?"

"Hell, no!" replied a white male voice from the pews, and that's when Hosiah knew he had them.

"No, sir! That's when your Pastor Gerry found out and that's when you good people started sending help to Skip Yu, to support the man his godless government was trying to destroy, because they didn't know that people of faith share a *commitment* to justice!"

Patterson's arm shot out. "And Jesus pointed and said, see that woman there, she gives from her *need,* not from her riches. It takes more for a poor man or a poor woman to give than it does for a rich man to do it. *That* was when you good people began helping my congregation to support my friend Skip. And Jesus also said that which you do for the least of My brethren you do also unto Me. And so your church and my church helped this man, this lonely minister of the Gospel in the land of the pagans, those people who *deny* the Name and Word of God, those people who worship the corpse of a monster named Mao, who put his embalmed body on display as though it were the body of a saint! He was no saint. He was no man of God. He was hardly a man at all. He was a mass murderer worse than anything our country has ever seen. He was like the Hitler that our fathers fought to destroy sixty years ago. But to the people who run that country, that killer, that murderer, that destroyer of life and freedom is the new god. That 'god' is *false,"* Patterson told them, with passion entering his voice. "That 'god' is the voice of Satan. That 'god' is the mouthpiece for the fires of Hell. That 'god' was the incarnation of evil—and that 'god' is dead, and now he's a stuffed animal, like the dead bird you might see over the bar in a saloon, or the deer head a lot of you have in your den—and they still worship him. They *still* honor his word, and they *still* revere his beliefs—the beliefs that *killed* millions of people just because their false god didn't like them." Patterson stood erect and brushed his hair back.

"There are those who say that what evil we see in the world is just the absence of good. But we know better than that. There is a devil in creation, and that devil has agents among us, and some of those agents run countries! Some of those agents start wars. Some of those agents take innocent people from their homes and put them in camps and murder them there like cattle in a slaughterhouse. Those are the agents of Satan! Those are the devotees of the Prince of Darkness. They are those among us who take the lives of the innocent, even the lives of innocent little babies . . ."

And so, those three men of God went to the hospital. One of them, our friend Skip, went to assist his parishioner in her time of need. The other two, the Catholics, went because they, too, were men of God, and they, too, stood for the same things that we do, *because the Word of Jesus IS THE SAME FOR ALL OF US*!" Hosiah Jackson's voice boomed out.

"Yes, sir," the same white voice agreed, and there were nods in the congregation.

"And so those three men of God went to the hospital to save the life of a little baby, a little baby that the government of that heathen land wanted to kill—and why? They wanted to kill it because its mother and father believe in God—and, oh, no, they couldn't allow people like *that* to bring a child into the world! Oh, no, they couldn't allow people of faith to bring a child into their country, because that was like inviting in a spy. That was a *danger* to their godless government. And why is it a danger?

"It's a *danger* because they *know* that they are godless pagans! It's a *danger* because they *know* that God's Holy Word is the most powerful force in the world! And their only response to that kind of danger is to kill, to take the life that God Himself gives to each of us, because in denying God, they can also deny life, and you know, those pagans, those unbelievers, those killers *love* to have that kind of power. They *love* pretending that *they* are gods. They love their power, and they love using it in the service of Satan! They know they are destined to spend eternity in Hell, and they want to share their Hell with us here on earth, and they want to deny to us the only thing that can liberate us from the destiny they have chosen for themselves. *That* is why they condemned that innocent little baby to death.

"And when those three men went to the hospital to preserve the life of that innocent baby, they stood in God's own place. They took God's place, but they did so in humility and in the strength of their faith. They stood in *God's* place to fulfill *God's* will, not to get power for themselves, not to be false heroes. They went there to serve, not to rule. To serve, as the Lord Jesus Himself served. As his apostles served. They went there to protect an innocent life. They went there to do the Lord God's work!"

"You people probably don't know this, but when I was first ordained I spent three years in the United States Navy, and I served as a chaplain to the Marines. I was assigned to the Second Marine Division at Camp Lejeune, North Carolina. When I was there, I got to know people we call heroes, and for sure a lot of Marines fall into that category. I was there to minister to the dead and dying after a terrible helicopter crash, and it was one of the great honors of my life to be there and to comfort dying young Marines—because I *knew* they were going to see God. I remember one, a sergeant, the man had just gotten married a month before, and he died while he was saying a prayer to God for his wife. He was a veteran of Vietnam, that sergeant, and he had lots of decorations. He was what we call a tough guy," Patterson told the black congregation, "but the toughest thing about that Marine was that when he knew he was going to die, he prayed not for himself, but for his young wife, that God would comfort her. That Marine died as a Christian man, and he went from this world to stand proud before his God as a man who did his duty in every way he could.

"Well, so did Skip, and so did Renato. They sacrificed their lives to save a baby. God sent them. God gave those men their orders. And they heard the orders, and they followed them without flinching, without hesitating, without thinking except to be sure that they were doing the right thing.

"And today, eight thousand miles from here there is a new life, a new little baby, probably asleep now. That baby will never know all the hubbub that came just before she was born, but with parents like that, that baby will know the Word of God. And all that happened because three brave men of God went to that hospital, and two of them died there to do the Lord's Work.

"Skip was a Baptist. Renato was a Catholic.

"Skip was yellow. I'm white. You people are black.

"But Jesus doesn't care about any of that. We have all heard His words. We have all accepted Him as our Savior. So did Skip. So did Renato. Those two brave men sacrificed their lives for The Right. The Catholic's last words—he asked if the baby was okay, and the other Catholic, the German priest, said 'yes,' and Renato said, *'Bene.'* That's Italian. It means, 'That's good, that's all right.' He died knowing that he did the right thing, And that's not a bad thing, is it?"

"That's right!" three voices called out.

There is so much to learn from their example," Hosiah Jackson told his borrowed congregation.

"We must learn, first of all, that God's Word is the same for all of us. I'm a black man. You folks are white. Skip was Chinese. In that we are all different, but in God's Holy Word we are all the same. Of all the things we have to learn, of all the things we have to keep in our hearts every day we live, that is the most important. Jesus is Savior to us all, if only we accept Him, if only we take Him into our hearts, if only we listen when He talks to us. That is the first lesson we need to learn from the death of those two brave men.

"The next lesson we need to learn is that Satan is still alive out there, and while we must listen to the words of God, there are those out there who prefer to listen to the words of Lucifer. We need to recognize those people for what they are.

"Forty years ago, we had some of those people among us. I remember it, and probably you do, too. We got over all that. The reason we got over it is that we have all heard the Word of God. We've all remembered that our God is a God of Mercy. Our God is a God of Justice. If we remember that, we remember a lot more besides. God does not measure us by what we are against. Jesus looks into our hearts and measures us by what we are *for.*

"But we cannot be *for* justice except by being against *in*justice. We must remember Skip and Renato. We must remember Mr. and Mrs. Yang, and all like them, those people in China who've been denied the chance to hear the Word of God. The sons of Lucifer are *afraid* of God's Holy Word. The sons of Lucifer are *afraid* of us. The sons of Satan are *afraid* of God's Will, because in God's Love and in the Way of the Lord lies their destruction. They may hate God. They may hate God's word—but they *fear,* they *FEAR* the consequences of their own actions. They *fear* the damnation that awaits them. They may *deny* God, but they know the *righteousness* of God, and they know that every human soul cries out for knowledge of our Lord.

"*That's* why they feared Reverend Yu Fa An. That's why they feared Cardinal DiMilo, and that's why they fear us. Me and you good people. Those sons of Satan are *afraid* of us because they know that their words and their false beliefs can no more stand up to the Word of God than a house trailer can stand before a springtime tornado! And they know that all men are born with some knowledge of God's Holy Word. That's why they fear us.

"Good!" Reverend Hosiah Jackson exclaimed. "Then let's give them another reason to fear us! Let God's faithful show them the power and the conviction of our faith!"

But we can be sure that God was there with Skip, and with Cardinal DiMilo. God directed their brave hands, and through them God saved that innocent little child," Patterson told his black congregation. "And God welcomed to his bosom the two men He sent there to do His work, and today our friend Skip and Cardinal DiMilo stand proudly before the Lord God, those good and faithful servants of His Holy Word.

"My friends, they did their job. They did the Lord's work that day. They saved the life of an innocent child. They showed the whole world what the power of faith can be.

"But what of our job?" Patterson asked.

It is *not* the job of the faithful to encourage Satan," Hosiah Jackson told the people before him. He'd captured their attention as surely as Lord Olivier on his best day—and why not? These were not the words of Shakespeare. These were the words of one of God's ministers. "When Jesus looks into our hearts, will He see people who support the sons of Lucifer? Will Jesus see people who give their money to support the godless killers of the innocent? Will Jesus see people who give their money to the new *Hitler?"*

"No!" A female voice shouted in reply. *"No!"*

"What is it that we, we the people of God, the people of faith—what is it that we stand for? When the sons of Lucifer kill the faithful, where do *you* stand? Will you stand for justice? Will you stand for your faith? Will you stand with the holy martyrs? Will you stand with Jesus?" Jackson demanded of his borrowed white congregation.

And as one voice, they answered him: *"Yes!"*

Jesus H. Christ," Ryan said. He'd walked over to the Vice President's office to catch the TV coverage.

"Told you my Pap was good at this stuff. Hell, I grew up with it over the dinner table, and he still gets inside my head," said Robby Jackson, wondering if he'd allow himself a drink tonight. "Patterson is probably doing okay, too. Pap says he's an okay guy, but my Pap is the champ."

"Did he ever think of becoming a Jesuit?" Jack asked with a grin.

"Pap's a preacherman, but he ain't quite a saint. The celibacy would be kinda hard on him," Robby answered.

Then the scene changed to Leonardo di Vinci International Airport outside Rome, where the Alitalia 747 had just landed and was now pulling up to the jetway. Below it was a truck, and next to the truck some cars belonging to the Vatican. It had already been announced that

Renato Cardinal DiMilo would be getting his own full state funeral at St. Peter's Basilica, and CNN would be there to cover all of it, joined by SkyNews, Fox, and all the major networks. They'd been late getting onto the story at the beginning, but that only made this part of the coverage more full.

Back in Mississippi, Hosiah Jackson walked slowly down from the pulpit as the last hymn ended. He walked with grace and dignity to the front door, so as to greet all of the congregation members on the way out.

That took much longer than he'd expected. It seemed that every single one of them wanted to take his hand and thank him for coming—the degree of hospitality was well in excess of his most optimistic expectations. And there was no doubting their sincerity. Some insisted on talking for a few moments, until the press of the departing crowd forced them down the steps and onto the parking lot. Hosiah counted six invitations to dinner, and ten inquiries about his church, and if it needed any special work. Finally, there was just one man left, pushing seventy, with scraggly gray hair and a hooked nose that had seen its share of whiskey bottles. He looked like a man who'd topped out as assistant foreman at the sawmill.

"Hello," Jackson said agreeably.

"Pastor," the man replied, uneasily, as though wanting to say more.

It was a look Hosiah had seen often enough. "Can I help you, sir?"

"Pastor . . . years ago . . ." And his voice choked up again. "Pastor," he began again. "Pastor, I sinned."

"My friend, we all sin. God knows that. That's why he sent His Son to be with us and conquer our sins." The minister grabbed the man's shoulder to steady him.

"I was in the Klan, Pastor, I did . . . sinful things . . . I . . . hurt nigras just cuz I hated them, and I—"

"What's your name?" Hosiah asked gently.

"Charlie Picket," the man replied. And then Hosiah knew. He had a good memory for names. Charles Worthington Picket had been the Grand Kleegle of the local Klavern. He'd never been convicted of a major crime, but his name was one that came up much of the time.

"Mr. Picket, those things all happened many years ago," he reminded the man.

"I ain't never—I mean, I ain't never *killed* nobody. Honest, Pastor, I ain't never done that," Picket insisted, with real desperation in his voice. "But I know'd thems that did, and I never told the cops. I never told them not to do it . . . sweet Jesus, I don't know what I was back then, Pastor. I was . . . it was . . ."

"Mr. Picket, are you sorry for your sins?"

"Oh, yes, oh Jesus, yes, Pastor. I've prayed for forgiveness, but—"

"There is no 'but,' Mr. Picket. God has forgiven you your sins," Jackson told him in his gentlest voice.

"Are you sure?"

A smile and a nod. "Yes, I'm sure."

"Pastor, you need help at your church, roofing and stuff, you call me, y'hear? That's the house of God, too. Maybe I didn't always know it, but by damn I know it now, sir."

He'd probably never called a black man "sir" in his life, unless there'd been a gun to his head. So, the minister thought, at least one person had listened to his sermon, and learned something from it. And that wasn't bad for a man in his line of work.

"Pastor, I gots to apologize for all the evil words and thoughts I had. Ain't never done that, but I gots to do it now." He seized Hosiah's hand. "Pastor, I am sorry, sorry as a man can be for all the things I done back then, and I beg your forgiveness."

"And the Lord Jesus said, 'Go forth and sin no more.' Mr. Picket, that's all of scripture in one sentence. God came to forgive our sins. God has already forgiven you."

Finally, their eyes met. "Thank you, Pastor. And God bless you, sir."

"And may the Lord bless you, too." Hosiah Jackson watched the man walk off to his pickup truck, wondering if a soul had just been saved. If so, Skip would be pleased with the black friend he'd never met.

CHAPTER 32

Coalition Collision

It was a long drive from the airport to the Vatican, every yard of it covered by cameras in the high-speed motorcade, until finally the vehicles entered the Piazza San Pietro, St. Peter's Square. There, waiting, was a squad of Swiss Guards wearing the purple-and-gold uniforms designed by Michelangelo. Some of the Guards pulled the casket containing a Prince of the Church, martyred far away, and carried it through the towering bronze doors into the cavernous interior of the church, where the next day a Requiem Mass would be celebrated by the Pope himself.

But it wasn't about religion now, except to the public. For the President of the United States, it was about matters of state. It turned out that Tom Jefferson had been right after all. The power of government devolved directly from the people, and Ryan had to act now, in a way that the people would approve, because when you got down to it, the nation wasn't his. It was theirs.

And one thing made it worse. SORGE had coughed up another report that morning, and it was late coming in only because Mary Patricia Foley wanted to be doubly sure that the translation was right.

Also in the Oval Office were Ben Goodley, Arnie van Damm, and the Vice President. "Well?" Ryan asked them.

"Cocksuckers," Robby said, first of all. "If they really think this way, we shouldn't sell them shit in a paper bag. Even at Top Gun after a long night of boilermakers, even Navy fighter pilots don't talk like this."

"It is callous," Ben Goodley agreed.

"They don't issue consciences to the political leaders, I guess," van Damm said, making it unanimous.

"How would your father react to information like this, Robby?" Ryan asked.

"His immediate response will be the same as mine: Nuke the bastards. Then he'll remember what happens in a real war and settle down some. Jack, we have to punish them."

Ryan nodded. "Okay, but if we shut down trade to the PRC, the first people hurt are the poor schlubs in the factories, aren't they?"

"Sure, Jack, but who's holding them hostage, the good guys or the bad guys? Somebody can *always* say that, and if fear of hurting them prevents you from taking any action, then you're only making sure that things *never* get better for them. So, you can't allow yourself to be limited that way," TOMCAT concluded, "or *you* become the hostage."

Then the phone rang. Ryan got it, grumbling at the interruption.

"Secretary Adler for you, Mr. President. He says it's important."

Jack leaned across his desk and punched the blinking button. "Yeah, Scott."

"I got the download. It's not unexpected, and people talk differently inside the office than outside, remember."

"That's great to hear, Scott, and if they talk about taking a few thousand Jews on a train excursion to Auschwitz, is that supposed to be funny, too?"

"Jack, I'm the Jew here, remember?"

Ryan let out a long breath and pushed another button. "Okay, Scott, you're on speaker now. Talk," POTUS ordered.

"This is just the way the bastards talk. Yes, they're arrogant, but we already knew that. Jack, if other countries knew how *we* talk inside the White House, we'd have a lot fewer allies and a lot more wars. Sometimes intelligence can be too good."

Adler really was a good SecState, Ryan thought. His job was to look for simple and safe ways out of problems, and he worked damned hard at it.

"Okay, suggestions?"

"I have Carl Hitch lay a note on them. We demand a statement of apology for this fuckup."

"And if they tell us to shove it?"

"Then we pull Rutledge and Hitch back for 'consultations,' and let them simmer for a while."

"The note, Scott?"

"Yes, Mr. President."

"Write it on asbestos paper and sign it in blood," Jack told him coldly.

"Yes, sir," SecState acknowledged, and the line went dead.

It was a lot later in the day in Moscow when Pavel Yefremov and Oleg Provalov came into Sergey Golovko's office.

"I'm sorry I couldn't have you in sooner," the SVR chairman told his guests. "We've been busy with problems—the Chinese and that shooting in Beijing." He'd been looking into it just like every other person in the world.

"Then you have another problem with them, Comrade Chairman."

"Oh?"

Yefremov handed over the decrypt. Golovko took it, thanking the man with his accustomed good manners, then settled back in his chair and started reading. In less than five seconds, his eyes widened.

"This is not possible," his voice whispered.

"Perhaps so, but it is difficult to explain otherwise."

"*I* was the target?"

"So it would appear," Provalov answered.

"But *why?*"

"That we do not know," Yefremov said, "and probably nobody in the city of Moscow knows. If the order was given through a Chinese intelligence officer, the order originated in Beijing, and the man who forwarded it probably doesn't know the reasoning behind it. Moreover, the operation is set up to be somewhat deniable, since we cannot even prove that this man is an intelligence officer, and not an assistant or what the Americans call a 'stringer.' In fact, their man was identified for us by an American," the FSS officer concluded.

Golovko's eyes came up. "How the hell did *that* happen?"

Provalov explained. "A Chinese intelligence officer in Moscow is unlikely to be concerned by the presence of an American national, whereas any Russian citizen is a potential counterintelligence officer.

Mishka was there and offered to help, and I permitted it. Which leads me to a question."

"What do you tell this American?" Golovko asked for him.

The lieutenant nodded. "Yes, Comrade Chairman. He knows a good deal about the murder investigation because I confided in him and he offered some helpful suggestions. He is a gifted police investigator. And he is no fool. When he asks how this case is going, what can I say?"

Golovko's initial response was as predictable as it was automatic: *Say nothing.* But he restrained himself. If Provalov said nothing, then the American would have to be a fool not to see the lie, and, as he said, the American was no fool. On the other hand, did it serve Golovko's—or Russia's—purposes for America to know that his life was in danger? That question was deep and confusing. While he pondered it, he'd have his bodyguard come in. He beeped his secretary.

"Yes, Comrade Chairman," Major Shelepin said, coming in the door.

"Something new for you to worry about, Anatoliy Ivan'ch," Golovko told him. It was more than that. The first sentence turned Shelepin pale.

It started in America with the unions. These affiliations of working people, which had lost power in the preceding decades, were in their way the most conservative organizations in America, for the simple reason that their loss of power had made them mindful of the importance of what power they retained. To hold on to that, they resisted any change that threatened the smallest entitlement of their humblest member.

China had long been a *bête noir* for the labor movement, for the simple reason that Chinese workers made less in a day than American union automobile workers made during their morning coffee break. That tilted the playing field in favor of the Asians, and *that* was something the AFL/CIO was not prepared to approve.

So much the better that the government that ruled those underpaid workers disregarded human rights. That just made them easier to oppose.

American labor unions are nothing if not organized, and so every single member of Congress started getting telephone calls. Most of them were taken by staffers, but those from senior union officials in a member's state or district usually made it all the way through, regardless of which side the individual member stood on. Attention was called to the barbaric action of that godless state which also, by the way, shit on its workers *and* took American jobs through its unfair labor practices. The size of the trade surplus came up in every single telephone call, which would have made the members of Congress think that it was a carefully orchestrated phone campaign (which it was) had they compared notes on the telephone calls with one another (which they didn't).

Later in the day, demonstrations were held, and though they were about as spontaneous as those held in the People's Republic of China, they were covered by the local and/or national media, because it was a place to send cameras, and the newsies belonged to a union, too.

Behind the telephone calls and in front of the TV coverage of the demonstrations came the letters and e-mails, all of which were counted and cataloged by the members' staffers.

Some of them called the White House to let the President know what was happening on the Hill. Those calls *all* went to the office of Arnold van Damm, whose own staff kept a careful count of the calls, their position, and their degree of passion, which was running pretty high.

On top of that came the notices from the religious communities, virtually all of which China had managed to offend at once.

The one unexpected but shrewd development of the day didn't involve a call or letter to anyone in the government. Chinese manufacturers located on the island of Taiwan all had lobbying and public-relations agencies in America. One of these came up with an idea that caught on as rapidly as the powder inside a rifle cartridge. By midday, three separate printers were turning out peel-off stickers with the flag of the Republic of China and the caption "We're the good guys." By the following morning, clerks at retail outlets all over America were affixing them to items of Taiwanese manufacture. The news media found out about it even before the process had begun, and thus aided the Republic of China industrialists by letting the public know of their "them not us" campaign even before it had properly begun.

The result was that the American public was reacquainted with the fact that there were indeed *two* countries called China, and that only one of them killed people of the clergy and then beat up on those who tried to say a few prayers on a public street. The other one even played Little League baseball.

It wasn't often that union leaders and the clergy both cried out so vociferously, and together they were being heard. Polling organizations scrambled to catch up, and were soon framing their questions in such a way that the answers were defined even before they were given.

The draft note arrived in the Beijing embassy early in the morning. When decrypted by an NS employee, it was shown to the embassy's senior watch officer, who managed not to throw up and decided to awaken Ambassador Hitch at once. Half an hour later, Hitch was in the office, sleepy and crabby at being awakened two hours before his accustomed time. The content of the note wasn't contrived to brighten his day. He was soon on the phone to Foggy Bottom.

"Yes, that's what we want you to say," Scott Adler told him on the secure phone.

"They're not going to like it."

"That doesn't surprise me, Carl."

"Okay, just so you know," Hitch told the SecState.

"Carl, we do think about these things, but the President is seriously pissed about—"

"Scott, I live here, y'know? I *know* what happened."

"What are they going to do?" EAGLE asked.

"Before or after they take my head off?" Hitch asked in return. "They'll tell me where to stick this note—a little more formally, of course."

"Well, make it clear to them that the American people demand some sort of amends. And that killing diplomats cannot be done with impunity."

"Okay, Scott. I know how to handle it. I'll get back to you later."

"I'll be awake," Adler promised, thinking of the long day in the office he was stuck with.

"See ya." Hitch broke the connection.

CHAPTER 33

Square One

"You may not talk to us this way," Shen Tang observed.

"Minister, my country has principles which we do not violate. Some of those are respect for human rights, the right of free assembly, the right to worship God as one wishes, the right to speak freely. The government of the People's Republic has seen fit to violate those principles, hence America's response. Every other great power in the world recognizes those rights. China must as well."

"Must? You tell us what we *must* do?"

"Minister, if China wishes to be a member of the community of nations, then, yes."

"America will *not* dictate to us. You are not the rulers of the world!"

"We do not claim to be. But we can choose those nations with whom we have normal relations, and we would prefer them to recognize human rights as do all other civilized nations."

"Now you say we are uncivilized?" Shen demanded.

"I did not say that, Minister," Hitch responded, wishing he'd not let his tongue slip.

"America does not have the right to impose its wishes on us or any other nation. You come here and dictate trade terms to us, and now also you demand that we conduct our internal affairs so as to suit you. Enough! We will not kowtow to you. We are not your servants. I reject this note." Shen even tossed it back in Hitch's direction to give further emphasis to his words.

"That is your reply, then?" Hitch asked.

"That is the reply of the People's Republic of China," Shen answered imperiously.

"Very well, Minister. Thank you for the audience." Hitch bowed politely and withdrew. Remarkable, he thought, that normal—if not exactly friendly—relations could come unglued this fast. Only six weeks before, Shen had been over to the embassy for a cordial working dinner, and they'd toasted each other's country in the friendliest manner possible. But Kissinger had said it: Countries do not have friends; they have interests. And the PRC had just shit on some of America's most closely felt principles. And that was that. He walked back out to his car for the drive to the embassy.

Cliff Rutledge was waiting there. Hitch waved him into his private office.

"Well?"

"Well, he told me to shove it up my ass—in diplo-speak," Hitch told his visitor. "You might have a lively session this morning."

Rutledge had seen the note already, of course. "I'm surprised Scott let it go out that way."

"I gather things at home have gotten a little firm. We've seen CNN and all, but maybe it's even worse than it appears."

"Look, I don't condone anything the Chinese did, but all this over a couple of shot clergymen . . ."

"One was a diplomat, Cliff," Hitch reminded him. "If you got your ass shot off, you'd want them to take it seriously in Washington, wouldn't you?"

The reprimand made Rutledge's eyes flare a little. "It's President Ryan who's driving this. He just doesn't understand how diplomacy works."

"Maybe, maybe not, but he *is* the President, and it's our job to represent him, remember?"

"Hard to forget it," Rutledge groused. He'd never be Undersecretary of State while that yahoo sat in the White House, and Undersecretary was the job he'd had his eye on for the last fifteen years. But neither would he get the job if he allowed his private feelings, however justified, to cloud his professional judgment. "We're going to be called home or sent home," he estimated.

"Probably," Hitch agreed. "Be nice to catch some baseball. How do the Sox look this season?"

"Forget it. A rebuilding year. Once again."

"Sorry about that." Hitch shook his head and checked his desk for new dispatches, but there were none. Now he had to let Washington know what the Chinese Foreign Minister had said. Scott Adler was probably sitting in his seventh-floor office waiting for the secure direct line to ring.

"Good luck, Cliff."

"Thanks a bunch," Rutledge said on his way out the door.

Hitch wondered if he should call home and tell his wife to start packing for home, but no, not yet. First he had to call Foggy Bottom.

So, what's going to happen?" Ryan asked Adler from his bed. He'd left orders to be called as soon as they got word. Now, listening to Adler's reply, he was surprised. He'd thought the wording of the note rather wimpy, but evidently diplomatic exchange had even stricter rules than he'd appreciated. "Okay, now what, Scott?"

"Well, we'll wait and see what happens with the trade delegation, but even money we call them and Carl Hitch home for consultations."

"Don't the Chinese realize they could take a trade hit from all this?"

"They don't expect that to happen. Maybe if it does, it'll make them think over the error of their ways."

"I wouldn't bet much on that card, Scott."

"Sooner or later, common sense has to break out. A hit in the wallet usually gets a guy's attention," SecState said.

"I'll believe that when I see it," POTUS replied. "'Night, Scott."

"'Night, Jack."

"So what did they say?" Cathy Ryan asked.

"They told us to stick it up our ass."

"Really?"

"Really," Jack replied, flipping the light off.

The Chinese thought they were invincible. It must be nice to believe that. Nice, but dangerous.

The 265th Motor Rifle Division was composed of three regiments of conscripts—Russians who hadn't chosen to avoid military service, which made them patriotic, or stupid, or apathetic, or sufficiently bored with life that the prospect of two years in uniform, poorly fed and largely unpaid, didn't seem that much of a sacrifice. Each regiment was composed of about fifteen hundred soldiers, about five hundred fewer than full authorized strength. The good news was that each regiment had an organic tank battalion, and that all of the mechanized equipment was, if not new, then at least recently manufactured, and reasonably well maintained. The division lacked its organic tank regiment, however, the fist which gave a motor-rifle division its offensive capabilities. Also missing was the divisional antitank battalion, with its Rapier antitank cannons. These were anachronistic weapons which Bondarenko nonetheless liked because he'd played with them as an officer cadet nearly forty years before. The new model of the BMP infantry carrier had been modified to carry the AT-6 antitank missile, the one NATO called "Spiral," actually a Russian version of the NATO Milan, courtesy of some nameless KGB spy of the 1980s. The Russian troops called it the Hammer for its ease of use, despite a relatively small warhead. Every BMP had ten of these, which more than made up for the missing battalion of towed guns.

What worried Bondarenko and Aliyev most was the lack of artillery. Historically the best trained and best drilled part of the Russian army, the artillery was only half present in the Far East's maneuver forces, battalions taking the place of regiments. The rationale for this was the fixed defense line on the Chinese border, which had a goodly supply of fixed and fortified artillery positions, albeit of obsolete designs, though with trained crews and massive stocks of shells to pour into predetermined positions.

The general scowled in the confines of his staff car. It was what he got for being smart and energetic. A properly prepared and trained military district didn't *need* a man like him, did it? No, his talents were needed by a shithole like this one. Just once, he thought, might a good officer get a reward for good performance instead of another "challenge," as they called it? He grunted. Not in this lifetime. The dunces and dolts drew the comfortable districts with no threats and lots of equipment to deal with them.

His worst worry was the air situation. Of all the Russian military arms, the air forces had suffered the most from the fall of the Soviet

Union. Once Far East had had its own fleets of tactical fighters, poised to deal with a threat from American aircraft based in Japan or on aircraft carriers of their Pacific Fleet, that *plus* what was needed to face off the Chinese. No more. Now he had perhaps fifty usable aircraft in theater, and the pilots for those got perhaps seventy flight hours per year, barely enough to make sure they could take off and land safely. Fifty modern fighter-class aircraft, mainly for air-to-air combat, not air-to-ground. There were several hundred more, rotting at their bases, mainly in hardened shelters to keep them dry, their tires dry-rotted and internal seals cracked from lack of use because of the spare-parts shortage that grounded nearly the entire Russian air force.

"You know, Andrey, I can remember when the world shook with fear of our country's army. Now, they shake with laughter, those who bother to take note of us." Bondarenko took a sip of vodka from a flask. It had been a long time since he'd drunk alcohol on duty, but it was cold—the heater in the car was broken—and he needed the solace.

"Gennady Iosifovich, it is not as bad as it appears—"

"I agree! It is worse!" CINC–FAR EAST growled. "If the Chinks come north, I shall learn to eat with chopsticks. I've always wondered how they do that," he added with a wry smile. Bondarenko was always one to see the humor in a situation.

"But to others we appear strong. We have thousands of tanks, Comrade General."

Which was true. They'd spent the morning inspecting monstrous sheds containing of all things T-34/85 tanks manufactured at Chelyabinsk in 1946. Some had virgin guns, never fired. The Germans had shaken in their jackboots to see these tanks storm over the horizon, but that's what they were, World War II tanks, over nine hundred of them, three complete division sets. And there were even troops to maintain them! The engines still turned over, serviced as they were by the *grand*children of the men who'd used them in combat operations against the *fascisti.* And in the same sheds were shells, some made as recently as 1986, for the 85-mm guns. The world was mad, and surely the Soviet Union had been mad, first to store such antiques, then to spend money and effort maintaining them. And even now, more than ten years after the demise of that nation-state, the sheer force of bureaucratic inertia *still* sent conscripts into the sheds to maintain the antique collection. For what purpose? No one knew. It would take an archivist to find the documents, and while that might be of interest to some historian of a humorous bent, Bondarenko had better things to do.

"Andrey, I appreciate your willingness to see the lighter side of every situation, but we do face a practical reality here."

"Comrade General, it will take months to get permission to terminate this operation."

"That is probably true, Andruska, but I remember a story about Napoleon. He wished to plant trees by the side of the French roads to shade his marching troops. A staff officer said, but, Marshal, it will take twenty years for the trees to grow enough to accomplish that. And Napoleon said, yes, indeed, so we must start at once! And so, Colonel, we will start with that at once."

"As you say, Comrade General." Colonel Aliyev knew that it was a worthwhile idea. He only wondered if he would have enough time to pursue all of the ideas that needed accomplishing. Besides, the troops at the tank sheds seemed happy enough. Some even took the tanks out into the open to play with them, drive them about the nearby test range, even shoot the guns occasionally. One young sergeant had commented to him that it was good to use them, because it made the war movies he'd seen as a child seem even more real. Now *that,* Colonel Aliyev thought, was something to hear from a soldier. It made the movies better. Damn.

Who does that slant-eyed motherfucker think he is?" Gant demanded out in the garden.

"Mark, we laid a rather firm note on them this morning, and they're just reacting to it."

"Cliff, explain to me why it's okay for other people to talk like that to us, but it's not okay for us to talk that way to them, will you?"

"It's called diplomacy," Rutledge explained.

"It's called horseshit, Cliff," Gant hissed back. "Where I come from, if somebody disses you like that, you punch him right in the face."

"But we don't do that."

"Why not?"

"Because we're above it, Mark," Rutledge tried to explain. "It's the little dogs that yap at you. The big powerful dogs don't bother. They know they can rip your head off. And we know we can handle these people if we have to."

"Somebody needs to tell *them* that, Cliffy," Gant observed. "Because I don't think they got the word yet. They're talking like they own the world, and they think they can play tough-guy with us, Cliff, and until they find out they can't, we're going to have a lot more of their shit to deal with."

"Mark, this is how it's done, that's all. It's just how the game is played at this level."

"Oh, yeah?" Gant countered. "Cliff, it's not a game to them. I see that, but you don't. After this break, we're going back in there, and they're going to threaten us. What do we do then?"

"We brush it off. How can they threaten us?"

"The Boeing order."

"Well, Boeing will have to sell its airplanes to somebody else this year," Rutledge said.

"Really? What about the interests of all those workers we're supposed to represent?"

"Mark, at this level, we deal with the big picture, not the little one, okay?" Rutledge was actually getting angry with this stock trader.

"Cliffy, the big picture is made up of a lot of little ones. You ought to go back in there and ask if they like selling things to us. Because if they do, then they have to play ball. Because they need us a fucking lot more than we need them."

"You don't talk that way to a great power."

"Are we a great power?"

"The biggest," Rutledge confirmed.

"Then how come they talk that way to us?"

"Mark, this is my job. You're here to advise me, but this is your first time to this sort of ball game, okay? I know how to play the game. It's my job."

"Fine." Gant let out a long breath. "But when we play by the rules and they don't, the game gets a little tedious." Gant wandered off on his own for a moment. The garden was pretty enough. He hadn't done this sort of thing enough to know that there was usually a garden of some sort for diplomats to wander in after two or three hours of talking at each other in a conference room, but he had learned that the garden was where a lot of the real work got done.

"Mr. Gant?" He turned to see Xue Ma, the diplomat/spook he'd chatted with before.

"Mr. Xue," TELESCOPE said in his own greeting.

"What do you think of the progress of the talks?" the Chinese diplomat asked.

Mark was still trying to understand this guy's use of language. "If this is progress, I'd hate to see what you call an adverse development."

Xue smiled. "A lively exchange is often more interesting than a dull one."

"Really? I'm surprised by all this. I always thought that diplomatic exchange was more polite."

"You think this impolite?"

Gant again wondered if he was being baited or not, but decided *the hell with it.* He didn't really need his government job anyway, did he? And taking it had involved a considerable personal sacrifice, hadn't it? Like a few million bucks. Didn't that entitle him to say what the hell he thought?

"Xue, you accuse us of threatening your national identity because we object to the murders your government—or its agents, I suppose—committed in front of cameras. Americans don't like it when people commit murder."

"Those people were breaking our laws," Xue reminded him.

"Maybe so," Gant conceded. "But in America when people break the law, we arrest them and give them a trial in front of a judge and jury, with a defense lawyer to make sure the trial is fair, and we damned sure don't shoot people in the head when they're holding a goddamned newborn infant!"

"That was unfortunate," Xue almost admitted, "but as I said, those men *were* breaking the law."

"And so your cops did the judge/jury/executioner number on them. Xue, to Americans that was the act of a barbarian."

The "B" word finally got through. "America cannot talk to China in that way, Mr. Gant."

"Look, Mr. Xue, it's your country, and you can run your country as you wish. We're not going to declare war on you for what you do inside your own borders. But there's no law that says we have to do business with you either, and so we *can* stop buying your goods—and I have news for you: The American people *will* stop buying your stuff if you continue to do stuff like that."

"Your people? Or your government?" Xue asked, with a knowing smile.

"Are you really *that* stupid, Mr. Xue?" Gant fired back.

"What do you mean?" The last insult had actually cracked through the shell, Gant saw.

"I mean America is a democracy. Americans make a lot of decisions entirely on their own, and one of them is what they spend their money on, and the average American will not buy something from a fucking barbarian." Gant paused. "Look, I'm a Jew, okay? Sixty-some years ago, America fucked up. We saw what Hitler and the Nazis were doing in Germany, and we didn't act in time to stop it. We really blew the call and a lot of people got killed unnecessarily, and we've been seeing things on TV about that since I was in short pants, and it ain't *never* going to happen again on our watch, and when people like you do stuff like what we just saw, it just sets off the Holocaust light in American heads. Do you get it now?"

"You cannot talk to us in that way."

Again with the broken record! The doors were opening. It was time to head back inside for the next round of confrontational diplo-speak.

"And if you persist in attacking our national sovereignty, we will buy elsewhere," Xue told him with some satisfaction.

"Fine, and we can do the same. And you need our cash a lot more than we need your trade goods, Mr. Xue." He must have finally understood, Gant thought. His face actually showed some emotion now. So did his words:

"We will never kowtow to American attacks on our country."

"We're not attacking your country, Xue."

"But you threaten our economy," Xue said, as they got to the door.

"We threaten nothing. I am telling you that my fellow citizens will not buy goods from a country that commits barbarities. That is not a threat. It is a statement of fact." Which was an even greater insult, Gant did not fully appreciate.

"If America punishes us, we will punish America."

Enough was goddamned enough. Gant pulled the door open halfway and stopped to face the diplomat/spook:

"Xue, your dicks aren't big enough to get in a pissing contest with us." And with that, he walked on inside. A half-hour later, he was on his way out again. The words had been sharp and heated, and neither side had seen any purpose in continuing that day—though Gant strongly suspected that once Washington heard about that morning's exchanges, there wouldn't *be* any other day.

In two days, he'd be totally jet-lagged but back at his office on 15th Street. He was surprised that he was looking forward to *that.*

Anything from WestPac?" Mancuso asked.

"They just put three submarines to sea, a Song and two of the Kilos the Russians sold them," BG Lahr answered. "We're keeping an eye on them. *La Jolla* and *Helena* are close by. *Tennessee* is heading back to Pearl as of midday." The former boomer had been on patrol for fifty days, and that was about enough. "Our surface assets are all back to sea. Nobody's scheduled to get back into Taipei for twelve days."

"So, the Taipei hookers get two weeks off?" CINCPAC asked with a chuckle.

"And the bartenders. If your sailors are like my soldiers, they may need the relaxation," the J-2 replied, with a smile of his own.

"Oh, to be young and single again," Bart observed. "Anything else out there?"

"Routine training on their side, some combined air and ground stuff, but that's up north by the Russian border."

"How good do they look?"

Lahr shrugged. "Good enough to give the Russians something to think about, sir. On the whole, the PLA is trained up as good as I've ever known them to be, but they've been working hard for the past three or four years."

"How many of them?" Bart asked, looking at his wall map, which was a lot more useful for a sailor than a soldier. China was just a beige shape on the left border.

"Depends on where. Like, if they go north into Russia, it'd be like cockroaches in some ghetto apartment in New York. You'd need a lot o' Raid to deal with it."

"And you said the Russians are thin in their East?"

Lahr nodded. "Yep. Admiral, if I was that Bondarenko guy, I'd sweat it some. I mean, it's all theoretical as a threat and all, but as theoretical threats go, that's one that might keep me awake at night."

"And what about reports of gold and oil in eastern Siberia?"

Lahr nodded. "Makes the threat less theoretical. China's a net importer of oil, and they're going to need a lot more to expand their economy the way they plan to—and on the gold side, hell, everybody's wanted that for the last three thousand years. It's negotiable and fungible."

"Fungible?" That was a new word for Mancuso.

"Your wedding band might have been part of Pharaoh Ramses II's double-crown once," Lahr explained. "Or Caligula's necklace, or Napoleon's royal scepter. You take it, hammer it, and it's just raw material again, and it's *valuable* raw material. If the Russian strike's as big as our intel says, it'll be sold all over the world. Everybody'll use it for all sorts of purposes, from jewelry to electronics."

"How big's the strike supposed to be?"

Lahr shrugged. "Enough to buy you a new Pacific Fleet, and then some."

Mancuso whistled. That was real money.

It was late in Washington, and Adler was up late, again, working in his office. SecState was usually a busy post, and lately it had been busier than usual, and Scott Adler was getting accustomed to fourteen-hour days. He was reading over post reports at the moment, waiting for the other shoe to drop in Beijing. On his desk was a STU-6 secure telephone. The "secure telephone unit" was a sophisticated encryption device grafted onto an AT&T-made digital telephone. This one worked on a satellite-communications channel, and though its signal therefore sprinkled down all over the world from its Defense Department communications satellite, all the casual listener would get was raspy static, like the sound of water running out of a bathroom faucet. It had a randomized 512-bit scrambling system that the best computers at Fort Meade could break about a third of the time after several days of directed effort. And that was about as secure as things got. They were trying to make the TAPDANCE encryption system link into the STU units to generate a totally random and hence unbreakable signal, but that was proving difficult, for technical reasons that nobody had explained to the Secretary of State, and that was just as well. He was a diplomat, not a mathematician. Finally, the STU rang in its odd trilling warble. It took eleven seconds for the two STU units on opposite sides of the world to synchronize.

"Adler."

"Rutledge here, Scott," the voice said on the other side of the world. "It didn't go well," he informed SecState at once. "And they're canceling the 777 order with Boeing, as we thought they would."

Adler frowned powerfully into the phone. "Super. No concessions at all on the shootings?"

"Zip."

"Anything to be optimistic about?"

"Nothing, Scott, not a damned thing. They're stonewalling like we're the Mongols and they're the Chin Dynasty."

Somebody needs to remind them that the Great Wall ultimately turned out to be a waste of bricks, EAGLE didn't bother saying aloud. "Okay, I need to discuss this with the President, but you're probably going to be flying home soon. Maybe Carl Hitch, too."

"I'll tell him. Any chance that we can make some concession, just to get things going?"

"Cliff, the likelihood that Congress will roll over on the trade issue is right up there with Tufts making the Final Four. Maybe less." Tufts University *did* have a basketball team, after all. "There's nothing we can give them that they would accept. If there's going to be a break, they're the ones who'll have to bend this time. Any chance of that?"

"Zero" was the reply from Beijing.

"Well, then, they'll just have to learn the hard way." The good news, Adler thought, was that the hard lessons were the ones that really did teach you something. Maybe even the Chinese.

What did that capitalist *diao ren* say?" Zhang asked. Shen told him what Xue had relayed, word-for-word. "And what does he represent?"

"He is personal assistant to the American Treasury Minister. Therefore we think he has the ear of both his minister and the American president," Shen explained. "He has not taken an active part in the talks, but after every session he speaks privately with Vice Minister Rutledge. Exactly what their relationship is, we do not know for certain, and clearly he is not an experienced diplomat. He talks like an arrogant capitalist, to insult us in so crude a way, but I fear he represents the American position more forthrightly than Rutledge does. I think he gives Rutledge the policy he must follow. Rutledge is an experienced diplomat, and the positions he takes are not his own, obviously. He wants to give us some concessions. I am sure of that, but Washington is dictating his words, and this Gant fellow is probably the conduit to Washington."

"Then you were right to adjourn the talks. We will give them a chance to reconsider their position. If they think they can dictate to us, then they are mistaken. You canceled the airplane order?"

"Of course, as we agreed last week."

"Then *that* will give them something to think about," Zhang observed smugly.

"If they do not walk out of the talks."

"They wouldn't dare." *Walk away from the Middle Kingdom? Absurd.*

"There is one other thing that Gant man said. He said, not in so many words, that we need them—their money, that is—more than they need us. And he is not entirely wrong in that, is he?"

"We do not need their dollars more than we need our sovereignty. Do they really think they can dictate our domestic laws to us?"

"Yes, Zhang, they do. They apply an astounding degree of importance to this incident."

"Those two policemen ought to be shot for what they did, but we cannot allow the Americans to dictate that sort of thing to us." The embarrassment of the incident was one thing—and embarrassing the state was often a capital offense in the People's Republic—but China had to make such a decision on its own, not at the order of an outsider.

"They call it barbaric," Shen added.

"Barbaric? They say *that* to *us?"*

"You know that Americans have tender sensibilities. We often forget that. And their religious leaders have some influence in their country. Our ambassador in Washington has cabled some warnings to us about this. It would be better if we had some time to let things settle down, and truly it would be better to punish those two policemen just to assuage American sensibilities, but I agree we cannot allow them to dictate domestic policy to us."

"And this Gant man says his *ji* is bigger than ours, does he?"

"So Xue tells me. Our file on him says that he's a stock trader, that he's worked closely with Minister Winston for many years. He's a Jew, like lots of them are—"

"Their Foreign Minister is also a Jew, isn't he?"

"Minister Adler? Yes, he is," Shen confirmed after a moment's thought.

"So, this Gant really does tell us their position, then?"

"Probably," Foreign Minister Shen said.

Zhang leaned forward in his chair. "Then you will make them clear on ours. The next time you see this Gant, tell him *chou ni ma de bi."* Which was rather a strong imprecation, best said to someone in China if you had a gun already in your hand.

"I understand," Shen replied, knowing that he'd never say anything like that except to a particularly humble underling in his own office.

Zhang left. He had to talk this one over with his friend Fang Gan.

CHAPTER 34

Hits

Over the last week Ryan had come to expect bad news upon waking up, and as a result so had his family. He knew that he was taking it too seriously when his children started asking him about it over breakfast.

"What's happening with China, Dad?" Sally asked, giving Ryan one more thing to lament. Sally didn't say "daddy" anymore, and that was a title far more precious to Jack than "Mr. President." You expected it from your sons, but not from your daughter. He'd discussed it with Cathy, but she'd told him that he just had to roll with the punch.

"We don't know, Sally."

"But you're supposed to know everything!" And besides, her friends asked her about it at school.

"Sally, the President doesn't know everything. At least I don't," he explained, looking up from the morning *Early Bird.* "And if you never noticed, the TVs in my office are tuned to CNN and the other news networks because they frequently tell me more than CIA does."

"Really?" Sally observed. She watched too many movies. In Hollywood, CIA was a dangerous, lawbreaking, antidemocratic, fascist, and thoroughly evil government agency that nonetheless knew everything about everybody, and had really killed President Kennedy for its own purposes, whatever they were (Hollywood never quite got around to that). But it didn't matter, because whoever the star was always managed to thwart the nasty old CIA before the credits, or the last commercial, depending on the format.

"Really, honey. CIA has some good people in it, but basically it's just one more government agency."

"What about the FBI and Secret Service?" she asked.

"They're cops. Cops are different. My dad was a cop, remember?"

"Oh, yeah," and then she went back to the "Style" section of *The Washington Post,* which had both the comics and the stories that interested her, mainly ones having to do with the sort of music that her father put quotation marks around.

Then there was a discreet knock at the door, and Andrea came in. At this time of day, she also acted as his private secretary, in this case delivering a dispatch from the State Department. Ryan took it, looked at it, and managed not to pound on the table, because his children were present.

"Thanks, Andrea," he told her.

"Yes, Mr. President." And Special Agent Price-O'Day went back out to the corridor.

Jack saw his wife looking at him. The kids couldn't read all his facial expressions, but his wife could. To Cathy, Ryan couldn't lie worth a damn, which was also why she didn't worry about his fidelity. Jack had the dissimulation ability of a two-year-old, despite all the help and training he got from Arnie. Jack caught the look and nodded. Yeah, it was China again. Ten minutes later, breakfast was fully consumed and the TV was turned off, and the Ryan family headed downstairs to work, to school, or to the day-care center at Johns Hopkins, depending on age, with the requisite contingent of Secret Service bodyguards. Jack kissed them all in their turn, except for little Jack—SHORTSTOP to the Secret Service—because John Patrick Ryan, Jr., didn't go in for that sissy stuff. *There was something to be said for having daughters,* Ryan thought, as he headed for the Oval Office. Ben Goodley was there, waiting with the President's Daily Brief.

"You have the one from SecState?" CARDSHARP asked.

"Yeah, Andrea delivered it." Ryan fell into his swivel chair and lifted the phone, punching the proper speed-dial button.

"Good morning, Jack," SecState said in greeting, despite a short night's sleep gotten on the convertible sofa in his own office. Fortunately, his private bathroom also had a shower.

"Approved. Bring them all back," SWORDSMAN told EAGLE.

"Who handles the announcement?" Secretary Adler asked.

"You do it. We'll try to low-key it," the president said, with forlorn hope in his voice.

"Right," Adler thought. "Anything else?"

"That's it for now."

"Okay, see ya, Scott." Ryan replaced the phone. "What about China?" he asked Goodley. "Are they doing anything unusual?"

"No. Their military is active, but it's routine training activity only. Their most active sectors are up in their northeast and opposite Taiwan. Lesser activity in their southwest, north of India."

"With all the good luck the Russians are having with oil and gold, are the Chinese looking north with envy?"

"It's not bad speculation, but we have no positive indications of that from any of our sources." Everybody envied rich neighbors, after all. That's what had encouraged Saddam Hussein to invade Kuwait, despite having lots of oil under his own sand.

"Any of our sources" includes SORGE, the President reminded himself. He pondered that for a second. "Tell Ed I want a SNIE on Russia and China."

"Quick?" Goodley asked. A Special National Intelligence Estimate could take months to prepare.

"Three or four weeks. And I want to be able to hang my hat on it."

"I'll tell the DCI," Goodley promised.

"Anything else?" Ryan asked.

"That's it for now, sir."

Jack nodded and checked his calendar. He had a fairly routine day, but the next one would largely be spent on Air Force One flying hither and yon across America, and he was overnighting in—he flipped the page on the printout—Seattle, before flying home to Washington and another full day. It was just as easy for him to use the VC-25A as a red-eye . . . oh, yeah, he had a breakfast speech in Seattle to the local Jaycees. He'd be talking about school reform. That generated a grunt. There just weren't enough nuns to go around. The School Sisters of Notre Dame had taught him at St. Matthew's Elementary School in northeast Baltimore back forty-plus years earlier—and taught him well, because the penalty for not learning or for misbehaving did not bear contemplation for a seven-year-old. But the truth of the matter was that he'd been a good, and fairly obedient—*dull,* Jack admitted to himself with a wry smile—child who'd gotten good marks because he'd had a good mom and a good dad, which was a lot more than too many contemporary American kids could say—*and how the hell was he supposed to fix* that? Jack asked himself. How could he bring back the ethos of his parents' generation, the importance of religion, and a world in which engaged people went to the altar as virgins? Now they were talking about telling kids that homosexual and lesbian sex was okay. *What would Sister Frances Mary have said about* that? Jack wondered. A pity she wasn't around to crack some senators and representatives over the knuckles with her ruler. It had worked on him and his classmates at St. Matthew's . . .

The desk speaker buzzed. "Senator Smithers just arrived at the West Entrance." Ryan stood and went to his right, the door that came in from the secretaries' anteroom. For some reason, people preferred that one to the door off the corridor opposite the Roosevelt Room. Maybe it was more businesslike. But mainly they liked to see the President standing when the door opened, his hand extended and a smile on his face, as though he really was glad to see them. Sure, Wilbur.

Mary Smithers from Iowa, matronly, three kids and seven grandkids, he thought, *more talk about the Farm Bill.* What the hell was he supposed to know about farms? the President wondered. On those rare occasions that he purchased food, he did it at the supermarket—because that's where it all came from, wasn't it? One of the things on the briefing pages for his political appearances was always the local price for bread and milk in case some local reporter tested him. And chocolate milk came from brown cows.

Accordingly, Ambassador Hitch and Assistant Secretary Rutledge will be flying back to Washington for consultations," the spokesman told the audience.

"Does this signal a break in relations with China?" a reporter asked at once.

"Not at all. 'Consultations' means just that. We will discuss the recent developments with our representatives so that our relations with China can more speedily be brought back to what they ought to be," the spokesman replied smoothly.

The assembled reporters didn't know what to make of that and so three more questions of virtually identical content were immediately asked, and answers of virtually identical content repeated for them.

"He's good," Ryan said, watching the TV, which was pirating the CNN (and other) coverage off the satellites. It wasn't going out live, oddly enough, despite the importance of the news being generated.

"Not good enough," Arnie van Damm observed. "You're going to get hit with this, too."

"I figured. When?"

"The next time they catch you in front of a camera, Jack."

And he had as much chance of ducking a camera as the leadoff hitter at opening day at Yankee Stadium, the President knew. Cameras at the White House were as numerous as shotguns during duck season, and there was no bag limit here.

Christ, Oleg!" It took a lot to make Reilly gasp, but this one crossed the threshold. "Are you serious?"

"So it would appear, Mishka," Provalov answered.

"And why are you telling me?" the American asked. Information like this was a state secret equivalent to the inner thoughts of President Grushavoy.

"There is no hiding it from you. I assume you tell everything we do together to Washington, and it was you who identified the Chinese diplomat, for which I and my country are in your debt."

The amusing part of that was that Reilly had darted off to track Suvorov/Koniev without a thought, just as a cop thing, to help out a brother cop. Only afterward—about a nanosecond afterward, of course—had he thought of the political implications. And he'd thought this far ahead, but only as speculation, not quite believing that it could possibly have gone this far forward.

"Well, yes, I have to keep the Bureau informed of my operations here," the legal attaché admitted, not that it was an earthshaking revelation.

"I know that, Mishka."

"The Chinese wanted to kill Golovko," Reilly whispered into his vodka. *"Fuck."*

"My word exactly," Provalov told his American friend. "The question is—"

"Two questions, Oleg. First, why? Second, now what?"

"Third, who is Suvorov, and what is he up to?"

Which was obvious, Reilly thought. Was Suvorov merely a paid agent of a foreign country? Or was he part of the KGB wing of the Russian Mafia being paid by the Chinese to do something—but what, and to what purpose?

"You know, I've been hunting OC guys for a long time, but it never got anywhere near this big. This is right up there with all those bullshit stories about who 'really' killed Kennedy."

Provalov's eyes looked up. "You're not saying . . ."

"No, Oleg. The Mafia isn't that crazy. You don't go around looking to make enemies that big. You can't predict the consequences, and it isn't good for business. The Mafia is a business, Oleg. They try to make money for themselves. Even their political protection is aimed only at that, and that has limits, and they know what the limits are."

"So, if Suvorov is Mafia, then he is only trying to make money?"

"Here it's a little different," Reilly said slowly, trying to help his brain keep up with his mouth. "Here your OC guys think more politically than they do in New York." And the reason for that was that the KGB types had all grown up in an intensely political environment. Here politics really was power in a more direct sense than it had ever been in America, where politics and commerce had always been somewhat separate, the former protecting the latter (for a fee) but also controlled by it. Here it had always been, and still remained, the other way around. Business needed to rule politics because business was the source of prosperity, from which the citizens of a country derived their comforts. Russia had never prospered, because the cart kept trying to pull the horse. The recipient of the wealth had always tried to generate that wealth—and political figures are always pretty hopeless in that department. They are only good at squandering it. Politicians live by their political theories. Businessmen use reality and have to perform in a world defined by reality, not theory. That was why even in America they understood one another poorly, and never really trusted one another.

"What makes Golovko a target? What's the profit in killing him?" Reilly asked aloud.

"He is the chief adviser to President Grushavoy. He's never wanted to be an elected official, and therefore cannot be a minister per se, but he has the president's ear because he is both intelligent and honest—and he's a patriot in the true sense."

Despite his background, Reilly didn't add. Golovko was KGB, formerly a deadly enemy to the West, and an enemy to President Ryan, but somewhere along the line they'd met each other and they'd come to respect each other—even *like* each other, so the stories in Washington went. Reilly finished off his second vodka and waved for another. He was turning into a Russian, the FBI agent thought. It was getting to the point that he couldn't hold an intelligent conversation without a drink or two.

"So, get him and thereby hurt your president, and thereby hurt your entire country. Still, it's one hell of a dangerous play, Oleg Gregoriyevich."

"A *very* dangerous play, Mishka," Provalov agreed. "Who would do such a thing?"

Reilly let out a long and speculative breath. "One very ambitious motherfucker." He had to get back to the embassy and light up his STU-6 in one big fucking hurry. He'd tell Director Murray, and Murray would tell President Ryan in half a New York minute. Then what? It was way the hell over his head, Mike Reilly thought.

"Okay, you're covering this Suvorov guy."

"We and the Federal Security Service now," Provalov confirmed.

"They good?"

"Very," the militia lieutenant admitted. "Suvorov can't fart without us knowing what he had to eat."

"And you have his communications penetrated."

Oleg nodded. "The written kind. He has a cell phone—maybe more than one, and covering them can be troublesome."

"Especially if he has an encryption system on it. There's stuff commercially available now that our people have a problem with."

"Oh?" Provalov's head came around. He was surprised for two reasons: first, that there was a reliable encryption system available for cell phones, and second, that the Americans had trouble cracking it.

Reilly nodded. "Fortunately, the bad guys haven't found out yet." Contrary to popular belief, the Mafia wasn't all that adept at using technology. Microwaving their food was about as far as they went. One Mafia don had thought his cell phone secure because of its frequency-hopping abilities, and then had entirely canceled that supposed advantage out by standing still while using it! The dunce-don had never figured that out, even after the intercept had been played aloud in Federal District Court.

"We haven't noticed any of that yet."

"Keep it that way," Reilly advised. "Anyway, you have a national-security investigation."

"It's still murder and conspiracy to commit murder," Provalov said, meaning it was still his case.

"Anything I can do?"

"Think it over. You have good instincts for Mafia cases, and that is probably what it is."

Reilly tossed off his last drink. "Okay. I'll see you tomorrow, right here?"

Oleg nodded. "That is good."

The FBI agent walked back outside and got into his car. Ten minutes later, he was at his desk. He took the plastic key from his desk drawer and inserted it into the STU, then dialed Washington.

All manner of people with STU phones had access to Murray's private secure number, and so when the large system behind his desk started chirping, he just picked it up and listened to the hiss of static for thirty seconds until the robotic voice announced, "Line is secure."

"Murray," he said.

"Reilly in Moscow," the other voice said.

The FBI Director checked his desk clock. It was pretty damned late there. "What's happening, Mike?" he asked, then got the word in three fast-spoken minutes.

"Yeah, Ellen?" Ryan said when the buzzer went off.

"The AG and the FBI Director want to come over, on something important, they said. You have an opening in forty minutes."

"Fair enough." Ryan didn't wonder what it was about. He'd find out quickly enough. When he realized what he'd just thought, he cursed the Presidency once more. He was becoming jaded. In *this* job?

"What the hell?" Ed Foley observed.

"Seems to be solid information, too," Murray told the DCI.

"What else do you know?"

"The fax just came in, only two pages, and nothing much more than what I just told you, but I'll send it over to you. I've told Reilly to offer total cooperation. Anything to offer from your side?" Dan asked.

"Nothing comes to mind. This is all news to us, Dan. My congrats to your man Reilly for turning it." Foley was an information whore, after all. He'd take from anybody.

"Good kid. His father was a good agent, too." Murray knew better than to be smug about it, and Foley didn't deserve the abuse. Things like this were not, actually, within CIA's purview, and not likely to be tumbled to by one of their operations.

For his part, Foley wondered if he'd have to tell Murray about SORGE. If this was for real, it had to be known at the very highest levels of the Chinese government. It wasn't a free-lance operation by their Moscow station. People got shot for fucking around at this level, and such an operation would not even occur to communist bureaucrats, who were not the most inventive people in the world.

"Anyway, I'm taking Pat Martin over with me. He knows espionage operations from the defensive side, and I figure I'll need the backup."

"Okay, thanks. Let me go over the fax and I'll be back to you later today."

He could hear the nod at the other end. "Right, Ed. See ya."

His secretary came in thirty seconds later with a fax in a folder. Ed Foley checked the cover sheet and called his wife in from her office.

CHAPTER 35

Breaking News

Shit," Ryan observed quietly when Murray handed him the fax from Moscow. "Shit!" he added on further reflection. "Is this for real?"

"We think so, Jack," the FBI Director confirmed. He and Ryan went back more than ten years, and so he was able to use the first name. He filled in a few facts. "Our boy Reilly, he's an OC expert, that's why we sent him over there, but he has FCI experience, too, also in the New York office. He's good, Jack," Murray assured his President. "He's going places. He's established a very good working relationship with the local cops—helped them out on some investigations, held their hands, like we do with local cops over here, y'know?"

"And?"

"And this looks gold-plated, Jack. Somebody tried to put a hit on Sergey Nikolay'ch, and it looks as though it was an agency of the Chinese government."

"Jesus. Rogue operation?"

"If so, we'll find out when some Chinese minister dies of a sudden cerebral hemorrhage—induced by a bullet in the back of the head," Murray told the President.

"Has Ed Foley seen this yet?"

"I called it in, and sent the fax over. So, yeah, he's seen it."

"Pat?" Ryan turned to the Attorney General, the smartest lawyer Ryan had yet met, and that included all of his Supreme Court appointees.

"Mr. President, this is a stunning revelation, again, if we assume it's true, and not some sort of false-flag provocation, or a play by the Russians to make something happen—problem is, I can't see the rationale for such a thing. We appear to be faced with something that's too crazy to be true, and too crazy to be false as well. I've worked foreign counterintelligence operations for a long time. I've never seen nothing like this before. We've always had an understanding with the Russians that they wouldn't hit anybody in Washington, and we wouldn't hit anybody in Moscow, and to the best of my knowledge that agreement was never violated by either side. But this thing here. If it's real, it's tantamount to an act of war. That doesn't seem like a very prudent thing for the Chinese to do either, does it?"

POTUS looked up from the fax. "It says here that your guy Reilly turned the connection with the Chinese . . . ?"

"Keep reading," Murray told him. "He was there during a surveillance and just kinda volunteered his services, and—bingo."

"But can the Chinese really be this crazy . . ." Ryan's voice trailed off. "This isn't the Russians messing with our heads?" he asked.

"What would be the rationale behind that?" Martin asked. "If there is one, I don't see it."

"Guys, nobody is *this* crazy!" POTUS nearly exploded. It was penetrating all the way into his mind now. The world wasn't rational yet.

"Again, sir, that's something you're better equipped to evaluate than we are," Martin observed. It had the effect of calming Jack down a few notches.

"All the time I spent at Langley, I saw a lot of strange material, but this one really takes the prize."

"What do we know about the Chinese?" Murray asked, expecting to hear a reply along the lines of *jack shit,* because the Bureau had not experienced conspicuous success in its efforts to penetrate Chinese intelligence operations in America, and figured that the Agency had the same problem and for much the same reason—Americans of Chinese ethnicity weren't thick in government service. But instead he saw that President Ryan instantly adopted a guarded look and said nothing. Murray had interviewed thousands of people during his career and along the way had picked up the ability to read minds a little bit. He read Ryan's right then and wondered about what he saw there.

"Not enough, Dan. Not enough," Ryan replied tardily. His mind was still churning over this report. Pat Martin had put it right. It was too crazy to be true, and too crazy to be false. He needed the Foleys to go over this for him, and it was probably time to get Professor Weaver down from Brown University, assuming Ed and Mary Pat wouldn't throw a complete hissy-fit over letting him into both SORGE and this FBI bombshell. SWORDSMAN wasn't sure of much right now, but he was sure that he needed to figure this stuff out, and do it damned fast. American relations with China had just gone down the shitter, and now he had information to suggest they were making a direct attack on the Russian government. Ryan looked up at his guests. "Thanks for this, guys. If you have anything else to tell me, let me know quick as you can. I have to ponder this one."

"Yeah, I believe it, Jack. I've told Reilly to offer all the assistance he can and report back. They know he's doing that, of course. So, your pal Golovko wants you to know this one. How you handle that one's up to you, I suppose."

"Yeah, I get all the simple calls." Jack managed a smile. The worst part was the inability to talk things over with people in a timely way. Things like this weren't for the telephone. You wanted to see a guy's face and body language when you picked his brain—her brain, in MP's case—on a topic like this one. He hoped George Weaver was as smart as everyone said. Right now he needed a witch.

The new security pass was entirely different from his old SDI one, and he was heading for a different Pentagon office. This was the Navy section of the Pentagon. You could tell by all the blue suits and serious looks. Each of the uniformed services had a different corporate mentality. In the U.S. Army, everyone was from Georgia. In the Air Force, they were all from southern California. In the Navy, they all seemed to be swamp Yankees, and so it was here in the Aegis Program Office.

Gregory had spent most of the morning with a couple of serious commander-rank officers who seemed smart enough, though both were praying aloud to get the hell back on a ship and out to sea, just as Army officers always wanted to get back out in the field where there was mud to put on your boots and you had to dig a hole to piss in—but that's where the soldiers were, and any officer worth his salt wanted to be where the soldiers were. For sailors, Gregory imagined, it was salt water and fish, and probably better food than the MREs inflicted on the guys in BDUs.

But from his conversations with the squids, he'd learned much of what he'd already known. The Aegis radar/missile system had been developed to deal with the Russian airplane and cruise-missile threat to the Navy's aircraft carriers. It entailed a superb phased-array radar called the SPY and a fair-to-middlin' surface-to-air missile originally called the Standard Missile, because, Gregory imagined, it was the only one the Navy had. The Standard had evolved from the SM-1 to the SM-2, actually called the SM-2-MR because it was a "medium-range" missile instead of an ER, or extended-range, one, which had a booster stage to kick it out of the ships' launch cells a little faster and farther. There were about two hundred of the ER versions sitting in various storage sheds for the Atlantic and Pacific fleets, because full production had never been approved—because, somebody thought, the SM-2-ER might violate the 1972 Anti-Ballistic Missile Treaty, which had, however, been signed with a country called the Union of Soviet Socialist Republics, which country, of course, no longer existed. But after the 1991 war in the Persian Gulf, the Navy had looked at using the Standard Missile and Aegis system that shot it off against theater-missile threats like the Iraqi Scud. During that war, Aegis ships had actually been deployed into Saudi and other Gulf ports to protect them against the ballistic inbounds, but no missiles had actually been aimed that way, and so the system had never been combat-tested. Instead, Aegis ships periodically sailed out to Kwajalein Atoll, where their theater-missile capabilities were tested against ballistic target drones, and where, most of the time, they worked. But that wasn't quite the same, Gregory saw. An ICBM reentry vehicle had a maximum speed of about seventeen thousand miles per hour, or twenty-five thousand feet per second, which was almost ten times the speed of a rifle bullet.

The problem here was, oddly enough, one of both hardware and software. The SM-2-ER-Block-IV missile had indeed been designed with a ballistic target in mind, to the point that its terminal guidance system was infrared. You could, theoretically, stealth an RV against radar, but anything plunging through the atmosphere at Mach 15-plus would heat up to the temperature of molten steel. He'd seen Minuteman warheads coming into Kwajalein from California's Vandenberg Air Force

Base; they came in like man-made meteors, visible even in daylight, screaming in at an angle of thirty degrees or so, slowing down, but not visibly so, as they encountered thicker air. The trick was hitting them, or rather, hitting them hard enough to destroy them. In this, the new ones were actually easier to kill than the old ones. The original RVs had been metallic, some actually made of beryllium copper, which had been fairly sturdy. The new ones were lighter—therefore able to carry a heavier and more powerful nuclear warhead—and made from material like the tiles on the space shuttle. This was little different in feel from Styrofoam and not much stronger, since it was designed only to insulate against heat, and then only for a brief span of seconds. The space shuttles had suffered damage when their 747 ferry had flown through rainstorms, and some in the ICBM business referred to large raindrops as "hydro meteors" for the damage they could do to a descending RV. On rare occasions when an RV had come down through a thunderstorm, relatively small hailstones had damaged them to the point that the nuclear warhead might not have functioned properly.

Such a target was almost as easy a kill as an aircraft—shooting airplanes down is easy if you hit them, not unlike dropping a pigeon with a shotgun. The trick remained hitting the damned things.

Even if you got close with your interceptor, close won you no cigars. The warhead on a SAM is little different from a shotgun shell. The explosive charge destroys the metal case, converting it into jagged fragments with an initial velocity of about five thousand feet per second. These are ordinarily quite sufficient to rip into the aluminum skin that constitutes the lift and control surfaces of the strength-members of an airplane's internal framing, turning an aircraft into a ballistic object with no more ability to fly than a bird stripped of its wings.

But hitting one necessitates exploding the warhead far enough from the target that the cone formed of the flying fragments intersects the space occupied by the target. For an aircraft, this is not difficult, but for a missile warhead traveling *faster* than the explosive-produced fragments, it is—which explained the controversy over the Patriot missiles and the Scuds in 1991.

The gadget telling the SAM warhead where and when to explode is generically called the "fuse." For most modern missiles, the fusing system is a small, low-powered laser, which "nutates," or turns in a circle to project its beam in a cone forward of its flight path, until the beam hits and reflects off the target. The reflected beam is received by a receptor in the laser assembly, and *that* generates the signal telling the warhead to explode. But quick as it is, it takes a finite amount of time, and the inbound RV is coming in very fast. So fast, in fact, that if the laser beam lacks the power for more than, say, a hundred meters of range, there isn't enough time for the beam to reflect off the RV in time to tell the warhead to explode soon enough to form the cone of destruction to engulf the RV target. Even if the RV is immediately next to the SAM warhead when the warhead explodes, the RV is going faster than the fragments, which cannot hurt it because they can't catch up.

And there's the problem, Gregory saw. The laser chip in the Standard Missile's nose wasn't very powerful, and the nutation speed was relatively slow, and that combination could allow the RV to slip right past the SAM, maybe as much as half the time, even if the SAM came within three meters of the target, and that was no good at all. They might actually have been better off with the old VT proximity fuse of World War II, which had used a non-directional RF emitter, instead of the new high-tech gallium-arsenide laser chip. But there was room for him to play. The nutation of the laser beam was controlled by computer software, as was the fusing signal. That was something he could fiddle with. To that end, he had to talk to the guys who made it, "it" being the current limited-production test missile, the SM-2-ER-Block-IV, and they were the Standard Missile Company, a joint venture of Raytheon and Hughes, right up the street in McLean, Virginia. To accomplish that, he'd have Tony Bretano call ahead. Why not let them know that their visitor was anointed by God, after all?

My God, Jack," Mary Pat said. The sun was under the yardarm. Cathy was on her way home from Hopkins, and Jack was in his private study off the Oval Office, sipping a glass of whiskey and ice with the DCI and his wife, the DDO. "When I saw this, I had to go off to the bathroom."

"I hear you, MP." Jack handed her a glass of sherry—Mary Pat's favorite relaxing drink. Ed Foley picked a Samuel Adams beer in keeping with his working-class origins. "Ed?"

"Jack, this is totally fucking crazy," the Director of Central Intelligence blurted. "Fucking" was not a word you usually used around the President, even this one. "I mean, sure, it's from a good source and all that, but, Jesus, you just don't *do* shit like this."

"Pat Martin was in here, right?" the Deputy Director (Operations) asked. She got a nod. "Well, then he told you this is damned near an act of war."

"Damned near," Ryan agreed, with a small sip of his Irish whiskey. Then he pulled out his last cigarette of the day, stolen from Mrs. Sumter, and lit it. "But it's a hard one to deny, and we have to fit this into government policy somehow or other."

"We have to get George down," Ed Foley said first of all.

"And show him SORGE, too?" Ryan asked. Mary Pat winced immediately. "I know we have to guard that one closely, MP, but, damn it, if we can't use it to figure out these people, we're no better off than we were before we had the source."

She let out a long breath and nodded, knowing that Ryan was right, but not liking it very much. "And our internal pshrink," she said. "We need a doc to check this out. It's crazy enough that we probably need a medical opinion."

"Next, what do we say to Sergey?" Jack asked. "He knows we know."

"Well, start off with 'keep your head down,' I suppose," Ed Foley announced. "Uh, Jack?"

"Yeah?"

"You give this to your people yet, the Secret Service, I mean?"

"No . . . oh, yeah."

"If you're willing to commit one act of war, why not another?" the DCI asked rhetorically. "And they don't have much reason to like you at the moment."

"But why Golovko?" MP asked the air. "He's no enemy of China. He's a pro, a king-spook. He doesn't *have* a political agenda that I know about. Sergey's an *honest* man." She took another sip of sherry.

"True, no political ambitions that I know of. But he is Grushavoy's tightest adviser on a lot of issues—foreign policy, domestic stuff, defense. Grushavoy likes him because he's smart and honest—"

"Yeah, that's rare enough in this town, too," Jack acknowledged.

That wasn't fair. He'd chosen his inner circle well, and almost exclusively of people with no political ambition, which made them an endangered species in the environs of Washington. The same was true of Golovko, a man who preferred to serve rather than to rule, in which he was rather like the American President. "Back to the issue at hand. Are the Chinese making some sort of play, and if so, what?"

"Nothing that I see, Jack," Foley replied, speaking for his agency in what was now an official capacity. "But remember that even with SORGE, we don't see that much of their inner thinking. They're so different from us that reading their minds is a son of a bitch, and they've just taken one in the teeth, though I don't think they really know that yet."

"They're going to find out in less than a week."

"Oh? How's that?" the DCI asked.

"George Winston tells me a bunch of their commercial contracts are coming up due in less than ten days. We'll see then what effect this has on their commercial accounts—and so will they."

The day started earlier than usual in Beijing. Fang Gan stepped out of his official car and hurried up the steps into the building, past the uniformed guard who always held the door open for him, and this time did not get a thank-you nod from the exalted servant of the people. Fang walked to his elevator, into it, then stepped off after arriving at his floor. His office door was only a few more steps. Fang was a healthy and vigorous man for his age. His personal staff leaped to their feet as he walked in—an hour early, they all realized.

"Ming!" he called on the way to his inner office.

"Yes, Comrade Minister," she said, on going through the still-open door.

"What items have you pulled off the foreign media?"

"One moment." She disappeared and then reappeared with a sheaf of papers in her hand. *"London Times, London Daily Telegraph, Observer, New York Times, Washington Post, Miami Herald, Boston Globe.* The Western American papers are not yet available." She hadn't included Italian or other European papers because she couldn't speak or read those languages well enough, and for some reason Fang only seemed interested in the opinions of English-speaking foreign devils. She handed over the translations. Again, he didn't thank her even peremptorily, which was unusual for him. Her minister was exercised about something.

"What time is it in Washington?" Fang asked next.

"Twenty-one hours, Comrade Minister," she answered.

"So, they are watching television and preparing for bed?"

"Yes, Comrade Minister."

"But their newspaper articles and editorials are already prepared."

"That is the schedule they work, Minister. Most of their stories are done by the end of a normal working day. At the latest, news stories—aside from the truly unusual or unexpected ones—are completely done before the reporters go home for their dinner."

Fang looked up at that analysis. Ming was a clever girl, giving him information on something he'd never really thought about. With that realization, he nodded for her to go back to her desk.

For their part, the American trade delegation was just boarding their plane. They were seen off by a minor consular official who spoke plastic words from plastic lips, received by the Americans through plastic ears. Then they boarded their USAF aircraft, which started up at once and began rolling toward the runway.

"So, how do we evaluate this adventure, Cliff?" Mark Gant asked.

"Can you spell 'disaster'?" Rutledge asked in return.

"That bad?"

The Assistant Secretary of State for Policy nodded soberly. Well, it wasn't his fault, was it? That stupid Italian clergyman gets in the way of a bullet, and then the widow of that other minister-person had to pray for him in public, *knowing* that the local government would object. And, of course, CNN had to be there for both events to stir the pot at home . . . How was a diplomat supposed to make peace happen if people kept making things worse instead of better?

"That bad, Mark. China may never get a decent trade agreement if this crap keeps going on."

"All they have to do is change their own policies a little," Gant offered.

"You sound like the President."

"Cliffy, if you want to join a club, you have to abide by the club rules. Is that so hard to understand?"

"You don't treat great nations like the dentist nobody likes who wants to join the country club."

"Why is the principle different?"

"Do you really think the United States can govern its foreign policy by *principle?"* Rutledge asked in exasperation. So much so, in fact, that he'd let his mind slip a gear.

"The President does, Cliff, and so does your Secretary of State," Gant pointed out.

"Well, if we want a trade agreement with China, we have to consider their point of view."

"You know, Cliff, if you'd been in the State Department back in 1938, maybe Hitler could have killed all the Jews without all that much of a fuss," Gant observed lightly.

It had the desired effect. Rutledge turned and started to object: "Wait a minute—"

"It was just his internal policy, Cliff, wasn't it? So what, they go to a different church—gas 'em. Who cares?"

"Now look, Mark—"

"You look, Cliff. A country has to stand for certain things, because if you don't, who the fuck are you, okay? We're in the club—hell, we pretty much run the club. Why, Cliff? Because people know what we stand for. We're not perfect. You know it. I know it. They all know it. But they also know what we will and won't do, and so, we can be trusted by our friends, and by our enemies, too, and so the world makes a little sense, at least in our parts of it. And *that* is why we're respected, Cliff."

"And all the weapons don't matter, and all the commercial power we have, what about them?" the diplomat demanded.

"How do you think we got them, Cliffy?" Gant demanded, using the diminutive of Rutledge's name again, just to bait him. "We are what we are because people from all over the world came to America to work and live out their dreams. They worked hard. My grandfather came over from Russia because he didn't like getting fucked over by the czar, and he worked, and he got his kids educated, and they got *their* kids educated, and so now I'm pretty damned rich, but I haven't forgotten what Grandpa told me when I was little either. He told me this was the best place the world ever saw to be a Jew. Why, Cliff? Because the dead white European men who broke us away from England and wrote the Constitution had some good ideas and they lived up to them, for the most part. That's who we are, Cliff. And that means we have to *be* what we are, and *that* means we have to stand for certain things, and the world has to see us do it."

"But we have so many flaws ourselves," Rutledge protested.

"Of course we do! Cliff, we don't have to be perfect to be the best around, and we never stop trying to be better. My dad, when he was in college, he marched in Mississippi, and got his ass kicked a couple of times, but you know, it all worked out, and so now we have a black guy in the Vice Presidency. From what I hear, maybe he's good enough to take one more step up someday. Jesus, Cliff, how can you represent America to other nations if you don't get it?"

Diplomacy is business, Rutledge wanted to reply. *And I know how to do the business.* But why bother trying to explain things to this Chicago Jew? So, he rocked his seat back and tried to look dozy. Gant took the cue and stood for a seventy-foot walk. The Air Force sergeants who pretended to be stewardesses aboard served breakfast, and the coffee was pretty decent. He found himself in the rear of the aircraft looking at all the reporters, and that felt a little bit like enemy territory, but not, on reflection, as much as it did sitting next to that diplo-jerk.

The morning sun that lit up Beijing had done the same to Siberia even earlier in the day.

"I see our engineers are as good as ever," Bondarenko observed. As he watched, earthmoving machines were carving a path over a hundred meters wide through the primeval forests of pine and spruce. This road would serve both the gold strike and the oil fields. And this wasn't the only one. Two additional routes were being worked by a total of twelve crews. Over a third of the Russian Army's available engineers were on these projects, and that was a lot of troops, along with more than half of the heavy equipment in the olive-green paint the Russian army had used for seventy years.

"This is a 'Hero Project,' " Colonel Aliyev said. And he was right.

The "Hero Project" idea had been created by the Soviet Union to indicate something of such great national importance that it would draw the youth of the nation in patriotic zeal—and besides, it was a good way to meet girls and see a little more of the world. This one was moving even faster than that, because Moscow had assigned the military to it, and the military was no longer worrying itself about an invasion from (or into) NATO. For all its faults, the Russian army still had access to a lot of human and material resources. Plus, there was real money in this project. Wages were very high for the civilians. Moscow wanted both of these resource areas brought on line—and quickly. And so the gold-field workers had been helicoptered in with light equipment, with which they'd built a larger landing area, which allowed still heavier equipment to be air-dropped, and with that a small, rough airstrip had been built. That had allowed Russian air force cargo aircraft to lift in truly heavy equipment, which was now roughing in a proper air-landing strip for when the crew extending the railroad got close enough to deliver the cement and rebar to create a real commercial-quality airport. Buildings were going up. Some of the first things that had been sent in were the components of a sawmill, and one thing you didn't have to import into this region was wood. Large swaths were being cleared, and the trees cut down to clear them were almost instantly transformed into lumber for building. First, the sawmill workers set up their own rough cabins. Now, administrative buildings were going up, and in four months, they expected to have dormitories for over a thousand of the miners who were already lining up for the highly paid job of digging this gold out of the ground. The Russian government had decided that the workers here would have the option of being paid in gold coin at world-price, and that was something few Russian citizens wanted to walk away from. And so expert miners were filling out their application forms in anticipation of the flights into the new strike. Bondarenko wished them luck. There were enough mosquitoes there to carry off a small child and suck him dry of blood like mini-vampires. Even for gold coin, it was not a place he'd want to work.

The oil field was ultimately more important to his country, the general knew. Already, ships were fighting their way through the late-spring ice, shepherded by navy icebreakers like the *Yamal* and *Rossiya,* to deliver the drilling equipment needed to commence proper exploration for later production. But Bondarenko had been well briefed on this subject. This oil field was no pipe dream. It was the economic salvation of his country, a way to inject *huge* quantities of hard currency into Russia, money to buy the things it needed to smash its way into the twenty-first century, money to pay the workers who'd striven so hard and so long for the prosperity they and their country deserved.

And it was Bondarenko's job to guard it. Meanwhile, army engineers were furiously at work building harbor facilities so that the cargo ships would be able to land what cargo they had. The use of amphibious-warfare ships, so that the Russian navy could land the cargo on the beaches as though it were battle gear, had been examined but discarded. In many cases, the cargo to be landed was larger than the main battle tanks of the Russian army, a fact which had both surprised and impressed the commanding general of the Far East Military District.

One consequence of all this was that most of Bondarenko's engineers had been stripped away for one project or another, leaving him with a few battalions organically attached to his fighting formations. And he had uses of his own for those engineers, the general grumbled. There were several places on the Chinese border where a couple of regiments could put together some very useful obstacles against invading mechanized forces. But they'd be visible, and too obviously intended to be used against Chinese forces, Moscow had told him, not caring, evidently, that the only way they could be used against the People's Liberation Army was if that army decided to come north and *liberate* Russia!

What was it about politicians? Bondarenko thought. Even the ones in America were the same, so he'd been told by American officers he'd met. Politicians didn't really care much about what something did, but they cared a great deal about what it *appeared* to do. *In that sense, all politicians of whatever political tilt all over the world were communists,* Bondarenko thought with an amused grunt, *more interested in show than reality.*

"When will they be finished?" the general-colonel asked.

"They've made amazing progress," Colonel Aliyev replied. "The routes will be fully roughed in—oh, another month or six weeks, depending on weather. The finishing work will take much longer."

"You know what worries me?"

"What is that, Comrade General?" the operations officer asked.

"We've built an invasion route. For the first time, the Chinese could jump across the border and make good time to the north Siberian coast." Before, the natural obstacles—mainly the wooded nature of the terrain—would have made that task difficult to the point of impossibility. But now there was a way to get there, and a reason to go there as well. Siberia now truly *was* something it had often been thought to be, a treasure house of cosmic proportions. *Treasure house,* Bondarenko thought. *And I am the keeper of the keys.* He walked back to his helicopter to complete his tour of the route being carved out by army engineers.

CHAPTER 36

Sorge Reports

President Ryan awoke just before six in the morning. The Secret Service preferred that he keep the shades closed, thus blocking the windows, but Ryan had never wanted to sleep in a coffin, even a large one, and so when he awoke momentarily at such times as 3:53 he preferred to see some sort of light outside the window, even if only the taillights of a patrolling police car or a lonely taxicab. Over the years, he'd become accustomed to waking early. That surprised him. As a boy, he'd always preferred to sleep late, especially on weekends. But Cathy had been the other way, like most doctors, and especially most surgeons: early to rise, and get to the hospital, so that when you worked on a patient you had all day to see how he or she tolerated the procedure.

So, maybe he'd picked it up from her, and in some sort of perverse one-upmanship he'd come to open his eyes even earlier. Or maybe it was a more recently acquired habit in this damned place, Jack thought, as he slid off the bed and padded off to the bathroom as another damned day started, this one like so many others, too damned early. What the hell was the matter? the President wondered. Why was it that he didn't need sleep as much anymore? Hell, sleep was one of the very few pure pleasures given to man on earth, and all he wanted was just a little more of it . . .

But he couldn't have it. It was just short of six in the morning, Jack told himself as he looked out the window. Milkmen were up, as were paperboys. Mailmen were in their sorting rooms, and in other places people who had worked through the night were ending their working days.

That included a lot of people right here in the White House: protective troops in the Secret Service, domestic staff, some people Ryan knew by sight but not by name, which fact shamed him somewhat. They were *his* people, after all, and he was supposed to know about them, know their names well enough to speak them when he saw the owners thereof—but there were just too many of them for him to know. Then there were the uniformed people in the White House Military Office—called *Wham-o* by insiders—who supplemented the Office of Signals. There was, in fact, a small army of men and women who existed only to serve John Patrick Ryan—and through him the country as a whole, or that was the theory. What the hell, he thought, looking out the window. It was light enough to see. The streetlights were clicking off as their photoelectric sensors told them the sun was coming up. Jack pulled on his old Naval Academy robe, stepped into his slippers—he'd only gotten them recently; at home he just walked around barefoot, but a President couldn't do that in front of the troops, could he?—and moved quietly into the corridor.

There must have been some sort of bug or motion sensor close to the bedroom door, Jack thought. He never managed to surprise anyone when he came out into the upstairs corridor unexpectedly. The heads always seemed to be looking in his direction and there was the instant morning race to see who could greet him first.

The first this time was one of the senior Secret Service troops, head of the night crew. Andrea Price-O'Day was still at her home in Maryland, probably dressed and ready to head out the door—what shitty hours these people worked on his behalf, Jack reminded himself—for the hourlong drive into D.C. And with luck she'd make it home—when? Tonight? That depended on his schedule for today, and he couldn't remember offhand what he had happening.

"Coffee, boss?" one of the younger agents asked.

"Sounds like a winner, Charlie." Ryan followed him, yawning. He ended up in the Secret Service guard post for this floor, a walk-in closet, really, with a TV and a coffeepot—probably stocked by the kitchen staff—and some munchies to help the people get through the night.

"When did you come on duty?" POTUS asked.

"Eleven, sir," Charlie Malone answered.

"Boring duty?"

"Could be worse. At least I'm not working the bad-check detail in Omaha anymore."

"Oh, yeah," agreed Joe Hilton, another one of the young agents on the deathwatch.

"I bet you played ball," Jack observed.

Hilton nodded. "Outside linebacker, sir. Florida State University. Not big enough for the pros, though."

Only about two-twenty, and it's all lean meat, Jack thought. Young Special Agent Hilton looked like a fundamental force of nature.

"Better off playing baseball. You make a good living, work fifteen years, maybe more, and you're healthy at the end of it."

"Well, maybe I'll train my boy to be an outfielder," Hilton said.

"How old?" Ryan asked, vaguely remembering that Hilton was a recent father. His wife was a lawyer at the Justice Department, wasn't she?

"Three months. Sleeping through the night now, Mr. President. Good of you to ask."

I wish they'd just call me Jack. I'm not God, *am I?* But that was about as likely as his calling his commanding general Bobby-Ray back when he'd been Second Lieutenant John P. Ryan, USMC.

"Anything interesting happen during the night?"

"Sir, CNN covered the departure of our diplomats from Beijing, but that just showed the airplane taking off."

"I think they just send the cameras down halfway hoping the airplane'll blow up so that they'll have tape of it—you know, like when the chopper comes to lift me out of here." Ryan sipped his coffee. These junior Secret Service agents were probably a little uneasy to have "The Boss," as he was known within the Service, talking with them as if he and they were normal people. If so, Jack thought, tough shit. He wasn't going to turn into Louis XIV just to make *them* happy. Besides, he wasn't as good-looking as Leonardo DiCaprio, at least according to Sally, who thought that young actor was the cat's ass.

Just then, a messenger arrived with the day's copies of the morning's *Early Bird.* Jack took one along with the coffee and headed back to read it over. A few editorials bemoaning the recall of the trade delegation—maybe it was the lingering liberalism in the media, the reason they were not, never had been, and probably never would be entirely comfortable with the amateur statesman in the White House. Privately, Ryan knew, they called him other things, some rather less polite, but the average Joe out there, Arnie van Damm told Jack once a week or so, still liked him a lot. Ryan's approval rating was still very high, and the reason for it, it seemed, was that Jack was perceived as a regular guy who'd gotten lucky—if they called *this* luck, POTUS thought with a stifled grunt.

He returned to reading the news articles, wandering back to the breakfast room, as he did so, where, he saw, people were hustling to get things set up—notified, doubtless, by the Secret Service that SWORDSMAN was up and needed to be fed. Yet more of the *His Majesty Effect,* Ryan groused. But he was hungry, and food was food, and so he wandered in, picked what he wanted off the buffet, and flipped the TV on to see what was happening in the world as he attacked his eggs Benedict. He'd have to devour them quickly, before Cathy appeared to yell at him about the cholesterol intake. All around him, to a radius of thirty miles or so, the government was coming to consciousness, or what passed for it, dressing, getting in their cars, and heading in, just as he was, but not as comfortably.

"Morning, Dad," Sally said, coming in next and walking to the TV, which she switched to MTV without asking. It was a long way since that bright afternoon in London when he'd been shot, Jack thought. He'd been "daddy" then.

In Beijing, the computer on Ming's desk had been in auto-sleep mode for just the right number of minutes. The hard drive started turning again, and the machine began its daily routine. Without lighting up the monitor, it examined the internal file of recent entries, compressed them, and then activated the internal modem to shoot them out over the 'Net. The entire process took about seventeen seconds, and then the computer went back to sleep. The data proceeded along the telephone lines in the city of Beijing until it found its destination server, which was, actually, in Wisconsin. There it waited for the signal that would call it up, after which it would be dumped out of the server's memory, and soon thereafter written over, eliminating any trace that it had ever existed.

In any case, as Washington woke up, Beijing was heading for sleep, with Moscow a few hours behind. The earth continued its turning, oblivious of what transpired in the endless cycle of night and day.

Well?" General Diggs looked at his subordinate.

"Well, sir," Colonel Giusti said, "I think the cavalry squadron is in pretty good shape." Like Diggs, Angelo Giusti was a career cavalryman. His job as commander of 1st Armored's cavalry squadron (actually a battalion, but the cav had its own way of speaking) was to move out ahead of the division proper, locating the enemy and scouting out the land, being the eyes of Old Ironsides, but with enough combat power of its own to look after itself. A combat veteran of the Persian Gulf War, Giusti had smelled the smoke and seen the elephant. He knew what his job was, and he figured he had his troopers trained up about as well as circumstances in Germany allowed. He actually preferred the free-form play allowed by simulators to the crowded training fields of the Combat Maneuver Training Center, which was barely seventy-five square kilometers. It wasn't the same as being out there in your vehicles, but neither was it restricted by time and distance, and on the global SimNet system you could play against a complete enemy battalion, even a brigade if you wanted your people to get some sweat in their play. Except for the bumpy-float sensation of driving your Abrams around (some tankers got motion sickness from that), it conveyed the complexity better than any place except the NTC at Fort Irwin in the California desert, or the comparable facility the Army had established for the Israelis in the Negev.

Diggs couldn't quite read the younger officer's mind, but he'd just watched the Quarter Horse move around with no lack of skill. They'd played against some Germans, and the Germans, as always, were pretty good at the war business—but not, today, as good as First Tanks' cavalry troopers, who'd first outmaneuvered their European hosts, and then (to the surprise and distaste of the German brigadier who'd supervised the exercise) set an ambush that had cost them half a battalion of their Leos, as the Americans called the Leopard-II main battle tanks. Diggs would be having dinner with the brigadier later today. Even the Germans didn't know night-fighting as well as the Americans did—which was odd, since their equipment was roughly comparable, and their soldiers pretty well trained . . . but the German army was still largely a conscript army, most of whose soldiers didn't have the time-in-service the Americans enjoyed.

In the wider exercise—the cavalry part had just been the "real" segment of a wider command post exercise, or CPX—Colonel Don Lisle's 2nd Brigade was handling the fuller, if theoretical, German attack quite capably. On the whole, the Bundeswehr was not having a good day. Well, it no longer had the mission of protecting its country against a Soviet invasion, and with that had gone the rather furious support of the citizenry that the West German army had enjoyed for so many years. Now the Bundeswehr was an anachronism with little obvious purpose, and the occupier of a lot of valuable real estate for which Germans could think up some practical uses. And so the former West German army had been downsized and mainly trained to do peacekeeping duty, which, when you got down to it, was heavily armed police work. The New World Order was a peaceful one, at least so far as Europeans were concerned. The Americans had engaged in combat operations to the rather distant interest of the Germans, who, while they'd always had a healthy interest in war-fighting, were now happy enough that their interest in it was entirely theoretical, rather like a particularly intricate Hollywood production. It also forced them to respect America a little more than they would have preferred. But some things couldn't be helped.

"Well, Angelo, I think your troopers have earned themselves a beer or two at the local Gasthauses. That envelopment you accomplished at zero-two-twenty was particularly adroit."

Giusti grinned and nodded his appreciation. "Thank you, General. I'll pass that one along to my S-3. He's the one who thought it up."

"Later, Angelo."

"Roger that one, sir." Lieutenant Colonel Giusti saluted his divisional commander on his way.

"Well, Duke?"

Colonel Masterman pulled a cigar out of his BDU jacket and lit it up. One nice thing about Germany was that you could always get good Cuban ones here. "I've known Angelo since Fort Knox. He knows his stuff, and he had his officers particularly well trained. Even had his own book on tactics and battle-drill printed up."

"Oh?" Diggs turned. "Is it any good?"

"Not bad at all," the G-3 replied. "I'm not sure that I agree with it all, but it doesn't hurt to have everyone singing out of the same hymnal. His officers all think pretty much the same way. So, Angelo's a good football coach. Sure enough he kicked the Krauts' asses last night." Masterman closed his eyes and rubbed his face. "These night exercises take it out of you."

"How's Lisle doing?"

"Sir, last time I looked, he had the Germans well contained. Our friends didn't seem to know what he had around them. They were putzing around trying to gather information—short version, Giusti won the reconnaissance battle, and that decided things—again."

"Again," Diggs agreed. If there was any lesson out of the National Training Center, it was that one. Reconnaissance and counter-reconnaissance. Find the enemy. Don't let the enemy find you. If you pulled that off, it was pretty hard to lose. If you didn't, it was very hard to win.

"How's some sleep grab you, Duke?"

"It's good to have a CG who looks after his troopers, *mon Général.*" Masterman was sufficiently tired that he didn't even want a beer first.

And so with that decided, they headed for Diggs's command UH-60 Blackhawk helicopter for the hop back to the divisional kazerne. Diggs particularly liked the four-point safety belt. It made it a lot easier to sleep sitting up.

O*ne of the things I have to do today,* Ryan told himself, *is figure out what to do about the Chinese attempt on Sergey.* He checked his daily briefing sheet. Robby was out west again. That was too bad. Robby was both a good sounding board and a source of good ideas. So, he'd talk it over with Scott Adler, if he and Scott both had holes in their day, and the Foleys. *Who else?* Jack wondered. Damn, whom else could he trust with this? If this one leaked to the press, there'd be hell to pay. Okay, Adler had to be there. He'd actually met that Zhang guy, and if some Chinese minister-type had owned a piece of this, then he'd be the one, wouldn't he?

Probably. Not *certainly,* however. Ryan had been in the spook business too long to make that mistake. When you made *certainty* assumptions about things you weren't really sure about, you frequently walked right into a stone wall headfirst, and that could hurt. Ryan punched a button on his desk. "Ellen?"

"Yes, Mr. President."

"Later today, I need Scott Adler and the Foleys in here. It'll take about an hour. Find me a hole in the schedule, will you?"

"About two-thirty, but it means putting off the Secretary of Transportation's meeting about the air-traffic-control proposals."

"Make it so, Ellen. This one's important," he told her.

"Yes, Mr. President."

It was by no means perfect. Ryan preferred to work on things as they popped into his mind, but as President you quickly learned that you served the schedule, not the other way around. Jack grimaced. So much for the illusion of power.

Mary Pat Foley strolled into her office, as she did nearly every morning, and as always turned on her computer—if there was one thing she'd learned from SORGE, it was to turn the damned thing all the way off when she wasn't using it. There was a further switch on her phone line that manually blocked it, much as if she'd pulled the plug out of the wall. She flipped that, too. It was an old story for an employee of an intelligence service. Sure, she was paranoid, but was she paranoid *enough?*

Sure enough, there was another e-mail from cgood@jadecastle.com. Chet Nomuri was still at work, and this download took a mere twenty-three seconds. With the download complete, she made sure she'd backed it up, then clobbered it out of her in-box so that no copies remained even in the ether world. Next, she printed it all up and called down for Joshua Sears to do the translations and some seat-of-the-pants analysis. SORGE had become routine in handling if not in importance, and by a quarter to nine she had the translation in hand.

"Oh, Lord. Jack's just going to love this one," the DDO observed at her desk. Then she walked the document to Ed's larger office facing the woods. That's when she found out about the afternoon trip to the White House.

Mary Abbot was the official White House makeup artist. It was her job to make the President look good on TV, which meant making him look like a cheap whore in person, but that couldn't be helped. Ryan had learned not to fidget too much, which made her job easier, but she knew he was fighting the urge, which both amused and concerned her.

"How's your son doing at school?" Ryan asked.

"Just fine, thank you, and there's a nice girl he's interested in."

Ryan didn't comment on that. He knew that there had to be some boy or boys at St. Mary's who found his Sally highly interesting (she was pretty, even to disinterested eyes), but he didn't want to think about that. It did make him grateful for the Secret Service, however. Whenever Sally went on a date, there would be at least a chase car full of armed agents close by, and *that* would take the starch out of most teenaged boys. So, the USSS did have its uses, eh? *Girl children,* Jack thought, *were God's punishment on you for being a man.* His eyes were scanning his briefing sheets for the mini–press conference. The likely questions and the better sorts of answers to give to them. It seemed very dishonest to do it this way, but some foreign heads of government had the question prescreened so that the answers could be properly canned. Not a bad idea in the abstract, Jack thought, but the American media would spring for that about as quickly as a coyote would chase after a whale.

"There," Mrs. Abbot said, as she finished touching up his hair. Ryan stood, looked in the mirror, and grimaced as usual.

"Thank you, Mary," he managed to say.

"You're welcome, Mr. President."

And Ryan walked out, crossing the hall from the Roosevelt Room to the Oval Office, where the TV equipment was set up. The reporters stood when he entered, as the kids at St. Matthew's had stood when the priest came into class. But in third grade, the kids asked easier questions. Jack sat down in a rocking swivel chair. Kennedy had done something similar to that, and Arnie thought it a good idea for Jack as well. The gentle rocking that a man did unconsciously in the chair gave him a homey look, the spin experts all thought—Jack didn't know that, and knowing it would have caused him to toss the chair out the window, but Arnie did and he'd eased the President into it merely by saying it looked good, and getting Cathy Ryan to agree. In any case, SWORDSMAN sat down, and relaxed in the comfortable chair, which was the other reason Arnie had foisted it on him, and the real reason why Ryan had agreed. It was comfortable.

"We ready?" Jack asked. When the President asked that, it usually meant *Let's get this fucking show on the road!* But Ryan thought it was just a question.

Krystin Matthews was there to represent NBC. There were also reporters from ABC and Fox, plus a print reporter from the *Chicago Tribune.* Ryan had come to prefer these more intimate press conferences, and the media went along with it because the reporters were assigned by lot, which made it fair, and everyone had access to the questions and answers. The other good thing from Ryan's perspective was that a reporter was less likely to be confrontational in the Oval Office than in the raucous locker-room atmosphere of the pressroom, where the reporters tended to bunch together in a mob and adopt a mob mentality.

"Mr. President," Krystin Matthews began. "You've recalled both the trade delegation and our ambassador from Beijing. Why was that necessary?"

Ryan rocked a little in the chair. "Krystin, we all saw the events in Beijing that so grabbed the conscience of the world, the murder of the cardinal and the minister, followed by the roughing-up—to use a charitable term for it—of the minister's widow and some members of the congregation."

He went on to repeat the points he'd made in his previous press conference, making particular note of the Chinese government's indifference to what had happened.

"One can only conclude that the Chinese government doesn't care. Well, we care. The American people care. And this administration cares. You cannot take the life of a human being as casually as though you are swatting an insect. The response we received was unsatisfactory, and so, I recalled our ambassador for consultations."

"But the trade negotiations, Mr. President," the *Chicago Tribune* broke in.

"It is difficult for a country like the United States of America to do business with a nation which does not recognize human rights. You've seen for yourself what our citizens think of all this. I believe you will find that they find those murders as repellent as I do, and, I would imagine, as you do yourself."

"And so you will not recommend to Congress that we normalize trading relations with China?"

Ryan shook his head. "No, I will not so recommend, and even if I did, Congress would rightly reject such a recommendation."

"At what time might you change your position on this issue?"

"At such time as China enters the world of civilized nations and recognizes the rights of its common people, as all other great nations do."

"So you are saying that China today is not a civilized country?"

Ryan felt as though he'd been slapped across the face with a cold, wet fish, but he smiled and went on. "Killing diplomats is not a civilized act, is it?"

"What will the Chinese think of that?" Fox asked.

"I cannot read their minds. I do call upon them to make amends, or at least to consider the feelings and beliefs of the rest of the world, and then to reconsider their unfortunate action in that light."

"And what about the trade issues?" This one came from ABC.

"If China wants normalized trade relations with the United States, then China will have to open its markets to us. As you know, we have a law on the books here called the Trade Reform Act. That law allows us to mirror-image other countries' trade laws and practices, so that whatever tactics are used against us, we can then use those very same tactics with respect to trade with them. Tomorrow, I will direct the Department of State and the Department of Commerce to set up a working group to implement TRA with respect to the People's Republic," President Ryan announced, making the story for the day, and a bombshell it was.

Christ, Jack," the Secretary of the Treasury said in his office across the street. He was getting a live feed from the Oval Office. He lifted his desk phone and punched a button. "I want a read of the PRC's current cash accounts, global," he told one of his subordinates from New York. Then his phone rang.

"Secretary of State on Three," his secretary told him over the intercom. SecTreas grunted and picked up the phone.

"Yeah, I saw it too, Scott."

So, Yuriy Andreyevich, how did it go?" Clark asked. It had taken over a week to set up, and mainly because General Kirillin had spent a few hours on the pistol range working on his technique. Now he'd just stormed into the officers' club bar looking as though he'd taken one in the guts.

"Is he a Mafia assassin?"

Chavez had himself a good laugh at that. "General, he came to us because the Italian police wanted to get him away from the Mafia. He got in the way of a mob assassination, and the local chieftain made noises about going after him and his family. What did he get you for?"

"Fifty euros," Kirillin nearly spat.

"You were confident going in, eh?" Clark asked. "Been there, done that."

"Got the fuckin' T-shirt," Ding finished the statement with a laugh. And fifty euros was a dent even in the salary of a Russian three-star.

"Three points, in a five-hundred-point match. I scored four ninety-three!"

"Ettore only got four ninety-six?" Clark asked. "Jesus, the boy's slowing down." He slid a glass in front of the Russian general officer.

"He's drinking more over here," Chavez observed.

"That must be it." Clark nodded. The Russian general officer was not, however, the least bit amused.

"Falcone is not human," Kirillin said, gunning down his first shot of vodka.

"He could scare Wild Bill Hickok, and that's a fact. And you know the worst part about it?"

"What is that, Ivan Sergeyevich?"

"He's so goddamned humble about it, like it's fucking normal to shoot like that. Jesus, Sam Snead was never that good with a five-iron."

"General," Domingo said after his second vodka of the evening. The problem with being in Russia was that you tended to pick up the local customs, and one of those was drinking. "Every man on my team is an expert shot, and by expert, I mean close to being on his country's Olympic team, okay? Big Bird's got us all beat, and none of us are used to losing any more'n you are. But I'll tell you, I'm goddamned glad he's on my team." Just then, Falcone walked through the door. "Hey, Ettore, come on over!"

He hadn't gotten any shorter. Ettore towered over the diminutive Chavez, and still looked like a figure from an El Greco painting. "General," he said in greeting to Kirillin. "You shoot extremely well."

"Not so good as you, Falcone," the Russian responded.

The Italian cop shrugged. "I had a lucky day."

"Sure, guy," Clark reacted, as he handed Falcone a shot glass.

"I've come to like this vodka," Falcone said on gunning it down. "But it affects my aim somewhat."

"Yeah, Ettore." Chavez chuckled. "The general told us you blew four points in the match."

"You mean you have done better than this?" Kirillin demanded.

"He has," Clark answered. "I watched him shoot a possible three weeks ago. That was five hundred points, too."

"That was a good day," Falcone agreed. "I had a good night's sleep beforehand and no hangover at all."

Clark had himself a good chuckle and turned to look around the room. Just then, another uniform entered the room and looked around. He spotted General Kirillin and walked over.

"Damn, who's this recruiting poster?" Ding wondered aloud as he approached.

"Tovarisch General," the man said by way of greeting.

"Anatoliy Ivan'ch," Kirillin responded. "How are things at the Center?"

Then the guy turned. "You are John Clark?"

"That's me," the American confirmed. "Who are you?"

"This is Major Anatoliy Shelepin," General Kirillin answered. "He's chief of personal security for Sergey Golovko."

"We know your boss." Ding held out his hand. "Howdy. I'm Domingo Chavez."

Handshakes were exchanged all around.

"Could we speak in a quieter place?" Shelepin asked. The four men took over a corner booth in the club. Falcone remained at the bar.

"Sergey Nikolay'ch sent you over?" the Russian general asked.

"You haven't heard," Major Shelepin answered. It was the way he said it that got everyone's attention. He spoke in Russian, which Clark and Chavez understood well enough. "I want my people to train with you."

"Haven't heard what?" Kirillin asked.

"We found out who tried to kill the Chairman," Shelepin announced.

"Oh, he was the target? I thought they were after the pimp," Kirillin objected.

"You guys want to tell us what you're talking about?" Clark asked.

"A few weeks ago, there was an assassination attempt in Dzerzhinskiy Square," Shelepin responded, explaining what they'd thought at the time. "But now it appears they hit the wrong target."

"Somebody tried to waste Golovko?" Domingo asked. "Damn."

"Who was it?"

"The man who arranged it was a former KGB officer named Suvorov—so we believe, that is. He used two ex–Spetsnaz soldiers. They have both been murdered, probably to conceal their involvement, or at least to prevent them from discussing it with anyone." Shelepin didn't add anything else. "In any case, we have heard good things about your Rainbow troops, and we want you to help train my protective detail."

"It's okay with me, so long as it's okay with Washington." Clark stared hard into the bodyguard's eyes. He looked damned serious, but not very happy with the world at the moment.

"We will make the formal request tomorrow."

"They are excellent, these Rainbow people," Kirillin assured him. "We're getting along well with them. Anatoliy used to work for me, back when I was a colonel." The tone of voice told what he thought of the younger man.

There was more to this, Clark thought. A senior Russian official didn't just ask a former CIA officer for help with something related to his personal safety out of the clear blue. He caught Ding's eye and saw the same thought. Suddenly both were back in the spook business.

"Okay," John said. "I'll call home tonight if you want." He'd do that from the American Embassy, probably on the STU-6 in the station chief's office.

CHAPTER **37**

Fallout

The VC-137 landed without fanfare at Andrews Air Force Base. The base lacked a proper terminal and the attendant jetways, and so the passengers debarked on stairs grafted onto a flatbed truck. Cars waited at the bottom to take them into Washington. Mark Gant was met by two Secret Service agents who drove him at once to the Treasury Department building across the street from the White House. He'd barely gotten used to being on the ground when he found himself in the Secretary's office.

"How'd it go?" George Winston asked.

"Interesting, to say the least," Gant said, his mind trying to get used to the fact that his body didn't have a clue where it was at the moment. "I thought I'd be going home to sleep it off."

"Ryan's invoking the Trade Recovery Act against the Chinese."

"Oh? Well, that's not all that much of a surprise, is it?"

"Look at this," SecTreas commanded, handing over a recently produced printout. "This" was a report on the current cash holdings of the People's Republic of China.

"How solid is this information?" TELESCOPE asked TRADER.

The report was an intelligence estimate in all but name. Employees within the Treasury Department routinely kept track of international monetary transactions as a means of determining the day-to-day strength of the dollar and other internationally traded currencies. That included the Chinese yuan, which had been having a slightly bad time of late.

"They're this thin?" Gant asked. "I thought they were running short of cash, but I didn't know it was quite this bad . . ."

"It surprised me, too," SecTreas admitted. "It appears that they've been purchasing a lot of things on the international market lately, especially jet engines from France, and because they're late paying for the last round, the French company has decided to take a harder line—they're the only game in town. We won't let GE or Pratt and Whitney bid on the order, and the Brits have similarly forbidden Rolls-Royce. That makes the French the sole source, which isn't so bad for the French, is it? They've jacked up the price about fifteen percent, and they're asking for cash up front."

"The yuan's going to take a hit," Gant predicted. "They've been trying to cover this up, eh?"

"Yeah, and fairly successfully."

"That's why they were hitting us so hard on the trade deal. They saw this one coming, and they wanted a favorable announcement to bail them out. But they sure didn't play it very smart. Damn, you have this sort of a problem, you learn to crawl a little."

"I thought so, too. Why, do you think?"

"They're proud, George. Very, very proud. Like a rich family that's lost its money but not its social position, and tries to make up for the one with the other. But it doesn't work. Sooner or later, people find out that you're not paying your bills, and then the whole world comes crashing in on you. You can put it off for a while, which makes sense if you have something coming in, but if the ship don't dock, you sink." Gant flipped some pages, thinking: The other problem is that countries are run by politicians, people with no real understanding of money, who figure they can always maneuver their way out of whatever comes up. They're so used to having their own way that they never really think they can't have it that way all the time. One of the things Gant had learned working in D.C. was that politics was just as much about illusion as the motion-picture business was, which perhaps explained the affinity the two communities had for each other. But even in Hollywood you had to pay the bills, and you had to show a profit. Politicians always had the option of using T-bills to finance their accounts, and they also printed the money. Nobody expected the government to show a profit, and the board of directors was the voters, the people whom politicians conned as a way of life. It was all crazy, but that was the political game.

That's probably what the PRC leaders were thinking, Gant surmised.

But sooner or later, reality raised its ugly head, and when it did all the time spent trying to avoid it was what really bit you on the ass. That was when the whole world said *gotcha.* And then you were well and truly got. In this case, the *gotcha* could be the collapse of the Chinese economy, and it would happen virtually overnight.

"George, I think State and CIA need to see this, and the President, too."

Lord." The President was sitting in the Oval Office, smoking one of Ellen Sumter's Virginia Slims and watching TV. This time it was C-SPAN. Members of the United States House of Representatives were speaking in the well about China. The content of the speeches was not complimentary, and the tone was decidedly inflammatory. All were speaking in favor of a resolution to condemn the People's Republic of China. C-SPAN2 was covering much the same verbiage in the Senate. Though the language was a touch milder, the import of the words was not. Labor unions were united with churches, liberals with conservatives, even free-traders with protectionists.

More to the point, CNN and the other networks showed demonstrations in the streets, and it appeared that Taiwan's "We're the Good Guys" campaign had taken hold. Somebody (nobody was sure who yet) had even printed up stickers of the Red Chinese flag with the caption "We Kill Babies and Ministers." They were being attached to products imported from China, and the protesters were also busy identifying the American firms that did a lot of business on the Chinese mainland, with the aim of boycotting them.

Ryan's head turned. "Talk to me, Arnie."

"This looks serious, Jack," van Damm said.

"Gee, Arnie, I can see that. How serious?"

"Enough that I'd sell stock in those companies. They're going to take a hit. And this movement may have legs . . ."

"What?"

"I mean it might not go away real soon. Next you're going to see posters with stills from the TV coverage of those two clerics being murdered. That's an image that doesn't go away. If there's any product the Chinese sell here that we can get elsewhere, then a lot of Americans will start buying it elsewhere."

The picture on CNN changed to live coverage of a demonstration outside the PRC Embassy in Washington. The signs said things like MURDERERS, KILLERS, and BARBARIANS!

"I wonder if Taiwan is helping to organize this . . ."

"Probably not—at least not yet," van Damm thought. "If I were they, I wouldn't exactly mind, but I wouldn't need to play with this. They'll probably increase their efforts to distinguish themselves from the mainland—and that amounts to the same thing. Look for the networks to do stories about the Republic of China, and how upset *they* are with all this crap in Beijing, how they don't want to be tarred with the same brush and all that," the Chief of Staff said. "You know, 'Yes, we are Chinese, but *we* believe in human rights and freedom of religion.' That sort of thing. It's the smart move. They have some good PR advisers here in D.C. Hell, I probably know some of them, and if I were on the payroll, that's what I would advise."

That's when the phone rang. It was Ryan's private line, the one that usually bypassed the secretaries. Jack lifted it. "Yeah?"

"Jack, it's George across the street. Got a minute? I want to show you something, buddy."

"Sure. Come on over." Jack hung up and turned to Arnie. "SecTreas," he explained. "Says it's important." The President paused. "Arnie?"

"Yeah?"

"How much maneuvering room do I have with this?"

"The Chinese?" Arnie asked, getting a nod. "Not a hell of a lot, Jack. Sometimes the people themselves decide what our policy is. And the people will be making policy now by voting with their pocketbooks. Next we'll see some companies announce that they're suspending their commercial contracts with the PRC. The Chinese already fucked Boeing over, and in the full light of day, which wasn't real smart. Now the people out there will want to fuck them back. You know, there are times when the average Joe Citizen stands up on his hind feet and gives the world the finger. When that happens, it's your job mainly to follow them, not to lead them," the Chief of Staff concluded. His Secret Service code name was CARPENTER, and he'd just constructed a box for his President to stay inside.

Jack nodded and stubbed out the smoke. He might be the Most

Powerful Man in the World, but his power came from the people, and as it was theirs to give, it was also sometimes theirs to exercise.

Few people could simply open the door to the Oval Office and walk in, but George Winston was one of them, mainly because the Secret Service belonged to him. Mark Gant was with him, looking as though he'd just run a marathon chased by a dozen armed and angry Marines in jeeps.

"Hey, Jack."

"George. Mark, you look like hell," Ryan said. "Oh, you just flew in, didn't you?"

"Is this Washington or Shanghai?" Gant offered, as rather a wan joke.

"We took the tunnel. Jesus, have you seen the demonstrators outside? I think they want you to nuke Beijing," SecTreas observed. The President just pointed at his bank of television sets by way of an answer.

"Hell, why are they demonstrating here? I'm on *their* side—at least I think I am. Anyway, what brings you over?"

"Check this out." Winston nodded to Gant.

"Mr. President, these are the PRC's current currency accounts. We keep tabs on currency trading worldwide to make sure we know where the dollar is—which means we pretty much know where all the hard currency is in the world."

"Okay." Ryan knew about that—sort of. He didn't worry much about it, since the dollar was in pretty good shape, and the nonsqueaky wheel didn't need any grease. "So?"

"So, the PRC's liquidity situation is in the shitter," Gant reported. "Maybe that's why they were so pushy in the trade talks. If so, they picked the wrong way to approach us. They demanded instead of asked."

Ryan looked down the columns of numbers. "Damn, where have they been dumping all their money?"

"Buying military hardware. France and Russia, mostly, but a lot went to Israel, too." It was not widely known that the PRC had spent a considerable sum of money in Israel, mainly paid to IDI—Israel Defense Industries—to buy American-designed hardware manufactured under license in Israel. It was stuff the Chinese could not purchase directly from America, including guns for their tanks and air-to-air missiles for their fighter aircraft. America had winked at the transactions for years. In conducting this business, Israel had turned its back on Taiwan, despite the fact that both countries had produced their nuclear weapons as a joint venture, back when they'd stuck together—along with South Africa—as international pariahs with no other friends in that particular area. In polite company, it was called *realpolitik.* In other areas of human activity, it was called *fuck your buddy.*

"And?" Ryan asked.

"And they've spent their entire trade surplus this way," Gant reported. "All of it, mainly on short-term purchase items, but some long-term as well, and for the long-term stuff they had to pay cash up front because of the nature of the transactions. The producers need the cash to run the production, and they don't want to get stuck holding the bag. Not too many people need five thousand tank guns," Gant explained. "The market is kinda exclusive."

"So?"

"So, China is essentially out of cash. And they have real short-term cash needs. Like oil," TELESCOPE went on. "China's a net importer of oil. Production in their domestic fields falls well short, even though their needs are not really that great. Not too many Chinese citizens own cars. They have enough cash for three months' worth of oil, and then they come up short. The international oil market demands prompt payment. They can skate for a month, maybe six weeks, but after that, the tankers will turn around in mid-ocean and go somewhere else—they can do that, you know—and then the PRC runs out. It'll be like running into a wall, sir. *Smack.* No more oil, and then their country starts coming to a stop, including their military, which is their largest oil consumer. They've been running unusually high for some years because of increased activity in their maneuvers and training and stuff. They probably have strategic reserves, but we don't know exactly how much. And that can run out, too. We've been expecting them to make a move on the Spratly Islands. There's oil there, and they've been making noises about it off and on for about ten years, but the Philippines and other countries in the area have made claims, too, and they probably expect us to side with the Philippines for historical reasons. Not to mention, Seventh Fleet is still the biggest kid on the block in that part of the world."

"Yeah." Ryan nodded. "If it came to a showdown, the Philippines appear to have the best claim on the islands, and we would back them up. We've shed blood together in the past, and that counts. Go on."

"So, John Chinaman is short of oil, and he may not have the cash to pay for it, especially if our trade with them goes down the toilet. They need our dollars. The yuan isn't very strong anyway. International trading is also done in dollars, and as I just told you, sir, they've spent most of them."

"What are you telling me?"

"Sir, the PRC is just about bankrupt. In a month or so, they're going to find that out, and it's going to be a bit of a shock for them."

"When did *we* find this out?"

"That's my doing, Jack," the Secretary of the Treasury said. "I called up these documents earlier today, and then I had Mark go over them. He's our best man for economic modeling, even whacked out with jet lag."

"So, we can squeeze them on this?"

"That's one option."

"What if these demonstrations take hold?"

Gant and Winston shrugged simultaneously. "That's where psychology enters into the equation," said Winston. "We can predict it to some extent on Wall Street—that's how I made most of my money—but psychoanalyzing a country is beyond my ken. That's your job, pal. I just run your accounting office across the street."

"I need more than that, George."

Another shrug. "If the average citizen boycotts Chinese goods, and/or if American companies who do business over there start trimming their sails—"

"That's damned likely," Gant interjected. "This has got to have a lot of CEOs shitting their pants."

"Well, if that happens, the Chinese get one in the guts, and it's going to hurt, big time," TRADER concluded.

And how will they react to that? Ryan wondered. He punched his phone button. "Ellen, I need one." His secretary appeared in a flash and handed him a cigarette. Ryan lit it and thanked her with a smile and a nod.

"Have you talked this one over with State yet?"

A shake of the head. "No, wanted to show it to you first."

"Hmm. Mark, what did you make of the negotiations?"

"They're the most arrogant sons of bitches I've ever seen. I mean, I've met all sorts of big shots in my time, movers and shakers, but even the worst of them know when they need my money to do business, and when they know that, their manners get better. When you shoot a gun, you try to make sure you don't have it aimed at your own dick."

That made Ryan laugh, while Arnie cringed. You weren't supposed to talk that way to the President of the United States, but some of these people knew that you could talk that way to John Patrick Ryan, the man.

"By the way, along those lines, I liked what you told that Chinese diplomat."

"What's that, sir?"

"Their dicks aren't big enough to get in a pissing contest with us. Nice turn of phrase, if not exactly diplomatic."

"How did you know that?" Gant asked, the surprise showing on his face. "I never repeated that to anybody, not even to that jerk Rutledge."

"Oh, we have ways," Jack answered, suddenly realizing that he'd revealed something from a compartment named SORGE. *Oops.*

"Sounds like something you say at the New York Athletic Club," SecTreas observed. "But only if you're four feet or so away from the guy."

"But it appears it's true. At least in monetary terms. So, we have a gun we can point at their heads?"

"Yes, sir, we sure do," Gant answered. "It might take them a month to figure it out, but they won't be able to run away from it for very long."

"Okay, make sure State and the Agency find this out. And, oh, tell CIA that they're supposed to get this stuff to me first. Intelligence estimates are their job."

"They have an economics unit, but they're not all that good," Gant told the others. "No surprise. The smart people in this area work The Street, or maybe academia. You can make more money at Harvard Business School than you can in government service."

"And talent goes where the money is," Jack agreed. Junior partners at medium-sized law firms made more than the President, which sometimes explained the sort of people who ended up here. Public service was supposed to be a sacrifice. It was for him—Ryan had proven his ability to make money in the trading business, but for him service to his country had been learned from his father, and at Quantico, long before he'd been seduced into the Central Intelligence Agency and then later tricked into the Oval Office. And once here, you couldn't run away from it. At least, not and keep your manhood. That was always the trap. Robert Edward Lee had called duty the most sublime of words. And he would have known, Ryan thought. Lee had felt himself trapped into fighting for what was at best a soiled cause because of his perceived duty to his place of birth, and therefore many would curse his name for all eternity, despite his qualities as a man and a soldier. *So, Jack,* he asked himself, *in* your *case, where do talent and duty and right and wrong and all that other stuff lie? What the hell are* you *supposed to do now?* He was supposed to know. All those people outside the White House's campuslike grounds expected him to know all the time where the right thing was, right for the country, right for the world, right for every working man, woman, and innocent little kid playing T-ball. *Yeah,* the President thought, *sure. You're anointed by the wisdom fairy when you walk in here every day, or kissed on the ear by the muse, or maybe Washington and Lincoln whisper to you in your dreams at night.* He sometimes had trouble picking his tie in the morning, especially if Cathy wasn't around to be his fashion adviser. But he was supposed to know what to do with taxes, defense, and Social Security—why? Because it was his job to know. Because he happened to live in government housing at One Thousand Six Hundred Pennsylvania Avenue and had the Secret goddamned Service protect him everywhere he went. At the Basic School at Quantico, the officers instructing newly commissioned Marine second lieutenants had told them about the loneliness of command. The difference between that and what he had here was like the difference between a fucking firecracker and a nuclear weapon. This kind of situation had started wars in the past. That wouldn't happen now, of course, but it had once. It was a sobering thought. Ryan took a last puff on his fifth smoke of the day and killed it in the brown glass ashtray he kept hidden in a desk drawer.

"Thanks for bringing me this. Talk it over with State and CIA," he told them again. "I want a SNIE on this, and I want it soon."

"Right," George Winston said, standing for the underground walk back to his building across the street.

"Mr. Gant," Jack added. "Get some sleep. You look like hell."

"I'm allowed to sleep in this job?" TELESCOPE asked.

"Sure you are, just like I am," POTUS told him with a lopsided smile. When they left, he looked at Arnie: "Talk to me."

"Speak to Adler, and have him talk to Hitch and Rutledge, which you ought to do, too," Arnie advised.

Ryan nodded. "Okay, tell Scott what I need, and that I need it fast."

Good news," Professor North told her, as she came back into the room.

Andrea Price-O'Day was in Baltimore, at the Johns Hopkins Hospital, seeing Dr. Madge North, Professor of Obstetrics and Gynecology.

"Really?"

"Really," Dr. North assured her with a smile. "You're pregnant."

Before anything else could happen, Inspector Patrick O'Day leapt to his feet and lifted his wife in his arms for a powerful kiss and a rib-cracking hug.

"Oh," Andrea said almost to herself. "I thought I was too old."

"The record is well into the fifties, and you're well short of that," Dr. North said, smiling. It was the first time in her professional career that she'd given this news to *two* people carrying guns.

"Any problems?" Pat asked.

"Well, Andrea, you are prime-ep. You're over forty and this is your first pregnancy, isn't it?"

"Yes." She knew what was coming, but she didn't invite it by speaking the word.

"That means that there is an increased likelihood of Down's syndrome. We can establish that with an amniocentesis. I'd recommend we do that soon."

"How soon?"

"I can do it today if you wish."

"And if the test is . . . ?"

"Positive? Well, then you two have to decide if you want to bring a Down's child into the world. Some people do, but others don't. It's your decision to make, not mine," Madge North told them. She'd done abortions in her career, but like most obstetricians, she much preferred to deliver babies.

"Down's—how and . . . I mean . . ." Andrea said, squeezing her husband's hand.

"Look, the odds are very much in your favor, like a hundred to one or so, and those are betting odds. Before you worry about it, the smart thing is to find out if there's anything to worry about at all, okay?"

"Right now?" Pat asked for his wife.

Dr. North stood. "Yes, I have the time right now."

"Why don't you take a little walk, Pat?" Special Agent Price-O'Day suggested to her husband. She managed to keep her dignity intact, which didn't surprise her husband.

"Okay, honey." A kiss, and he watched her leave. It was not a good moment for the career FBI agent. His wife was pregnant, but now he had to wonder if the pregnancy was a good one or not. If not—then what? He was an Irish Catholic, and his church forbade abortion as murder, and murders were things he'd investigated—and even witnessed once. Ten minutes later, he'd killed the two terrorists responsible for it. That day still came back to him in perverse dreams, despite the heroism he'd displayed and the kudos he'd received for all of it.

But now, he was afraid. Andrea had been a fine stepmother for his little Megan, and both he and she wanted nothing in all the world more than this news—if it was, really, good news. It would probably take an hour, and he knew he couldn't spend it sitting down in a doctor's outer office full of pregnant women reading old copies of *People* and *US Weekly*. But where to go? Whom to see?

Okay. He stood and walked out, and decided to head over to the Maumenee Building. It ought not be too hard to find. And it wasn't.

Roy Altman was the telltale. The big former paratrooper who headed the SURGEON detail didn't stand in one place like a potted plant, but rather circulated around, not unlike a lion in a medium-sized cage, always checking, looking with highly trained and experienced eyes for something that wasn't quite right. He spotted O'Day in the elevator lobby and waved.

"Hey, Pat! What's happening?" All the rivalry between the FBI and the USSS stopped well short of this point. O'Day had saved the life of SANDBOX and avenged the deaths of three of Altman's fellow agents, including Roy's old friend, Don Russell, who'd died like a man, gun in hand and three dead assassins in front of him. O'Day had finished Don's work.

"My wife's over being checked out," the FBI inspector answered.

"Nothing serious?" Altman asked.

"Routine," Pat responded, and Altman caught the scent of a lie, but not an important one.

"Is she around? While I'm here, I thought I'd stop over and say hi."

"In her office." Altman waved. "Straight down, second on the right."

"Thanks."

"Bureau guy coming back to see SURGEON," he said into his lapel mike.

"Roger," another agent responded.

O'Day found the office door and knocked.

"Come in," the female voice inside said. Then she looked up. "Oh, Pat, how are you?"

"No complaints, just happened to be in the neighborhood, and—"

"Did Andrea see Madge?" Cathy Ryan asked. FLOTUS had helped make the appointment, of course.

"Yeah, and the little box doodad has a plus sign in it," Pat reported.

"Great!" Then Professor Ryan paused. "Oh, you're worried about something." In addition to being an eye doctor, she knew trouble when she saw it.

"Dr. North is doing an amniocentesis. Any idea how long it takes?"

"When did it start?"

"Right about now, I think."

Cathy knew the problem. "Give it an hour. Madge is very good, and very careful in her procedures. They tap into the uterus and withdraw some of the amniotic fluid. That will give them some of the tissue from the embryo, and then they examine the chromosomes. She'll have the lab people standing by. Madge is senior staff, and when she talks, people listen."

"She seems pretty competent."

"She's a wonderful doc. She's *my* OB. You're worried about Down's, right?"

A nod. "Yep."

"Nothing you can do but wait."

"Dr. Ryan, I'm—"

"My name's Cathy, Pat. We're friends, remember?" There was nothing like saving the life of a woman's child to get on her permanent good side.

"Okay, Cathy. Yeah, I'm scared. It's not—I mean, Andrea's a cop, too, but—"

"But being good with a gun or just being tough doesn't help much right now, does it?"

"Not worth a damn," Inspector O'Day confirmed quietly. He was about as used to being frightened as he was of flying the Space Shuttle, but potential danger to his wife and/or kid—*kids* now, maybe—the kind of danger in which he was utterly helpless—well, that was one of the buttons a capricious Fate could push while she laughed.

"The odds are way in your favor," Cathy told him.

"Yeah, Dr. North said so . . . but . . ."

"Yeah. And Andrea's younger than I am."

O'Day looked down at the floor, feeling like a total fucking wimp. More than once in his life, he'd faced down armed men—criminals with violent pasts—and intimidated them into surrender. Once in his life he'd had to use his Smith & Wesson 1076 automatic in anger, and both times he'd double-tapped the heads of the terrorists, sending them off to Allah—so they'd probably believed—to answer for the murder of the innocent woman. It hadn't been easy, exactly, but neither had it been all that hard. The endless hours of practice had made it nearly as routine as the working of his service automatic. But this wasn't danger to himself. He could deal with that. The worst danger, he was just learning, was to those you loved.

"Pat, it's okay to be scared. John Wayne was just an actor, remember?"

But that was it. The code of manhood to which most Americans subscribed was that of the Duke, and that code did not allow fear. In truth it was about as realistic as *Who Framed Roger Rabbit,* but foolish or not, there it was.

"I'm not used to it."

Cathy Ryan understood. Most doctors did. When she'd been a straight ophthalmic surgeon, before specializing in lasers, she'd seen the patients and the patients' families, the former in pain, but trying to be brave, the latter just scared. You tried to repair the problems of one and assuage the fears of the other. Neither task was easy. The one was just skill and professionalism; the other involved showing them that, although this was a horrid emergency which they'd never experienced before, for Cathy Ryan, M.D., FACS, it was just another day at the office. She was the Pro from Dover. She could handle it. SURGEON was blessed with the demeanor that inspired confidence in all she met.

But even that didn't apply here. Though Madge North was a gifted physician, she was testing for a predetermined condition. Maybe someday it could be fixed—genetic therapy offered that hope, ten years or so down the line—but not today. Madge could merely determine what already was. Madge had great hands, and a good eye, but the rest of it was in God's hands, and God had already decided one way or the other. It was just a matter of finding out what His decision had been.

"This is when a smoke comes in handy," the inspector observed, with a grimacing smirk.

"You smoke?"

He shook his head. "Gave it up a long time ago."

"You should tell Jack."

The FBI agent looked up. "I didn't know he smokes."

"He bums them off his secretary every so often, the wimp," Cathy told the FBI agent, with almost a laugh. "I'm not supposed to know."

"That's very tolerant for a doc."

"His life's hard enough, and it's only a couple a day, and he doesn't do it around the kids, or Andrea'd have to shoot me for ripping his face off."

"You know," O'Day said, looking down again and speaking from the cowboy boots he liked to wear under his blue FBI suit, "if it comes back that it's a Down's kid, what the hell do we do then?"

"That's not an easy choice."

"Hell, under the law I don't get a choice. I don't even have a say in it, do I?"

"No, you don't." Cathy didn't venture that this was an inequity. The law was firm on the point. The woman—in this case, the wife—alone could choose to continue the pregnancy or terminate it. Cathy knew her husband's views on abortion. Her own views were not quite identical, but she did regard that choice as distasteful. "Pat, why are you borrowing trouble?"

"It's not under my control."

Like most men, Cathy saw, Pat O'Day was a control freak. She could understand that, because so was she. It came from using instruments to change the world to suit her wishes. But this was an extreme case. This tough guy was deeply frightened. He really ought not to be, but it was a question of the unknown for him. She knew the odds, and they were actually pretty good, but he was not a doctor, and all men, even the tough ones, she saw, feared the unknown. Well, it wasn't the first time she'd baby-sat an adult who needed his hand held—and this one had saved Katie's life.

"Want to walk over to the day-care center?"

"Sure." O'Day stood.

It wasn't much of a walk, and her intention was to remind O'Day what this was all about—getting a new life into the world.

"SURGEON's on the way to the playpen," Roy Altman told his detail. Kyle Daniel Ryan—SPRITE—was sitting up now, and playing very simply with very rudimentary toys under the watchful eyes of the lionesses, as Altman thought of them, four young female Secret Service agents who fawned over SPRITE like big sisters. But these sisters all carried guns, and they all remembered what had nearly happened to SANDBOX. A nuclear-weapons-storage site was hardly as well-guarded as this particular day-care center.

Outside the playroom was Trenton "Chip" Kelley, the only male agent on the detail, a former Marine captain who would have frightened the average NFL lineman with a mere look.

"Hey, Chip."

"Hi, Roy. What's happening?"

"Just strolling over to see the little guy."

"Who's the muscle?" Kelley saw that O'Day was carrying heat, but decided he looked like a cop. But his left thumb was still on the button of his "crash alarm," and his right hand was within a third of a second of his service automatic.

"Bureau. He's cool," Altman assured his subordinate.

" 'Kay." Kelley opened the door.

"Who'd he play for?" O'Day asked Altman, once inside.

"The Bears drafted him, but he scared Ditka too much." Altman laughed. "Ex-Marine."

"I believe it." Then O'Day walked up behind Dr. Ryan. She'd already scooped Kyle up, and his arms were around her neck. The little boy was babbling, still months away from talking, but he knew how to smile when he saw his mommy.

"Want to hold him?" Cathy asked.

O'Day cradled the infant somewhat like a football. The youngest Ryan examined his face dubiously, especially the Zapata mustache, but Mommy's face was also in sight, and so he didn't scream.

"Hey, buddy," O'Day said gently. Some things came automatically. When holding a baby, you don't stand still. You move a little bit, rhythmically, which the little ones seemed to like.

"It'll ruin Andrea's career," Cathy said.

"Make for a lot better hours for her, and be nice to see her every night, but, yeah, Cathy, be kinda hard for her to run alongside the car with her belly sticking out two feet." The image was good enough for a laugh. "I suppose they'll put her on restricted duty."

"Maybe. Makes for a great disguise, though, doesn't it?"

O'Day nodded. This wasn't so bad, holding a kid. He remembered the old Irish adage: *True strength lies in gentleness.* But what the hell, taking care of kids was also a man's duty. There was a lot more to being a man than just having a dick.

Cathy saw the display and had to smile. Pat O'Day had saved Katie's life, and done it like something out of a John Woo movie, except that Pat was a real tough guy, not the movie kind. His scenes weren't scripted; he'd had to do it for real, making it up as he'd gone along. He was a lot like her husband, a servant of the law, a man who'd sworn an oath to Do the Right Thing every time, and like her husband, clearly a man who took his oaths seriously. One of those oaths concerned Pat's relationship with Andrea, and they all came down to the same thing: preserve, protect, defend. And now, this tiger with a tie was holding a baby and smiling and swaying back and forth, because that's what you did with a baby in your arms.

"How's your daughter?" Cathy asked.

"She and your Katie are good friends. And she's got a thing going with one of the boys at Giant Steps."

"Oh?"

"Jason Hunt. I think it's serious. He gave Megan one of his Hot Wheels cars." O'Day laughed. That's when his cell phone went off. "Right side coat pocket," he told the First Lady.

Cathy fished in his pocket and pulled it out. She flipped it open. "Hello?"

"Who's this?" a familiar voice asked.

"Andrea? It's Cathy. Pat's right here." Cathy took Kyle and handed off the phone, watching the FBI agent's face.

"Yeah, honey?" Pat said. Then he listened, and his eyes closed for two or three seconds, and that told the tale. His tense face relaxed. A long breath came out slowly, and the shoulders no longer looked like a man anticipating a heavy blow. "Yeah, baby, I came over to see Dr. Ryan, and we're in the nursery. Oh, okay." Pat looked over and handed over the phone. Cathy cradled it between her shoulder and ear.

"So, what did Madge say?" Cathy asked, already knowing most of it.

"Normal—and it's going to be a boy."

"So, Madge was right, the odds were in your favor." And they still were. Andrea was very fit. She wouldn't have any problems, Cathy was sure.

"Seven months from next Tuesday," Andrea said, her voice already bubbling.

"Well, listen to what Madge says. I do," Cathy assured her. She knew all the stuff Dr. North believed in. Don't smoke. Don't drink. Do your exercises. Take the classes on prepared delivery along with your husband. Come see me in five weeks for your next checkup. Read *What to Expect When You're Expecting.* Cathy handed the phone back. Inspector O'Day had taken a few steps and turned away. When he turned back to take the phone, his eyes were unusually moist.

"Yeah, honey, okay. I'll be right over." He killed the phone and dumped it back in his pocket.

"Feel better?" she asked with a smile. One of the lionesses came over to take Kyle back. The little guy loved them all, and smiled up at her.

"Yes, ma'am. Sorry to bother you. I feel like a wuss."

"Oh, bullcrap." Rather a strong imprecation for Mrs. Dr. Ryan.

"Like I said, life isn't a movie, and this isn't the Alamo. I know you're a tough guy, Pat, and so does Jack. What about you, Roy?"

"Pat can work with me any day. Congratulations, buddy," Altman added, turning back from the lead.

"Thanks, pal," O'Day told his colleague.

"Can I tell Jack, or does Andrea want to?" SURGEON asked.

"I guess you'll have to ask her about that one, ma'am."

Pat O'Day was transformed, enough spring in his step now to make him collide with the ceiling. He was surprised to see that Cathy was heading off to the OB-GYN building, but five minutes later it was obvious why. This was to be girl-girl bonding time. Even before he could embrace his wife, Cathy was there.

"Wonderful news, I'm so happy for you!"

"Yeah, well, I suppose the Bureau is good for something after all," Andrea joked.

Then the bear with the Zapata mustache lifted her off the floor with a hug and a kiss. "This calls for a small celebration," the inspector observed.

"Join us for dinner tonight at the House?" SURGEON asked.

"We can't," Andrea replied.

"Says who?" Cathy demanded. And Andrea had to bow to the situation.

"Well, maybe, if the President says it's okay."

"*I* say it's okay, girl, and there are times when Jack doesn't count," Dr. Ryan told them.

"Well, yes, then, I guess."

"Seven-thirty," SURGEON told them. "Dress is casual." It was a shame they were no longer regular people. This would have been a good chance for Jack to do steaks on the grill, something he remained very good at, and she hadn't made her spinach salad in months. Damn the Presidency anyway! "And, Andrea, you *are* allowed two drinks tonight to celebrate. After that, one or two a week."

Mrs. O'Day nodded. "Dr. North told me."

"Madge is a real stickler on the alcohol issue." Cathy wasn't sure about the data on that, but then, she wasn't an OB-GYN, and she'd followed Dr. North's rules with Kyle and Katie. You just didn't fool around when you were pregnant. Life was too precious to risk.

CHAPTER 38

Developments

It's all handled electronically. Once a country's treasury was in its collection of gold bricks, which were kept in a secure, well-guarded place, or else traveled in a crate with the chief of state wherever he went. In the nineteenth century, paper currency had gained wide acceptance. At first, it had to be redeemable for gold or silver—something whose weight told you its worth—but gradually this, too, was discarded, because precious metals were just too damned heavy to lug around. But soon enough even paper currency became too bulky to drag about, as well. For ordinary citizens, the next step was plastic cards with magnetic strips on the back, which moved your *theoretical* currency from your account to someone else's when you made a purchase. For major corporations and nations, it meant something even more theoretical. It became an electronic expression. A nation determined the value of its currency by estimating what quantity of goods and services its citizens generated with their daily toil, and that became the volume of its monetary wealth, which was generally agreed upon by the other nations and citizens of the world. Thus it could be traded across national boundaries by fiber-optic or copper cables, or even by satellite transmissions, and so billions of dollars, pounds, yen, or the new euros moved from place to place via simple keystrokes. It was a lot easier and faster than shipping gold bricks, but, for all the convenience, the system that determined a person's or a nation's wealth was no less rigid, and at certain central banks of the world, a country's net collection of those monetary units was calculated down to a fraction of a percentage point. There was some leeway built into the system, to account for trades in process and so forth, but that leeway was also closely calculated electronically. What resulted was no different in its effect from the numbering of the bricks of King Croesus of Lydia. In fact, if anything, the new system that depended on the movement of electrons or photons from one computer to another was even more exact, and even less forgiving. Once upon a time, one could paint lead bricks yellow and so fool a casual inspector, but lying to a computerized accounting system required a lot more than that.

In China, the lying was handled by the Ministry of Finance, a bastard orphan child in a Marxist country peopled by bureaucrats who struggled on a daily basis to do all manner of impossible things. The first and easiest impossibility—because it had to be done—was for its senior members to cast aside everything they'd learned in their universities and Communist Party meetings. To operate in the world financial system, they had to understand and play by—and within—the world monetary rules, instead of the Holy Writ of Karl Marx.

The Ministry of Finance, therefore, was placed in the unenviable position of having to explain to the communist clergy that their god was a false one, that their perfect theoretical model just didn't play in the real world, and that therefore they had to bend to a reality which they had rejected. The bureaucrats in the ministry were for the most part observers, rather like children playing a computer game that they didn't believe in but enjoyed anyway. Some of the bureaucrats were actually quite clever, and played the game well, sometimes even making a profit on their trades and transactions. Those who did so won promotions and status within the ministry. Some even drove their own automobiles to work and were befriended by the new class of local industrialists who had shed their ideological straitjackets and operated as capitalists within a communist society. That brought wealth into their nation, and earned the tepid gratitude, if not the respect, of their political masters, rather as a good sheepdog might. This crop of industrialists worked closely with the Ministry of Finance, and along the way influenced the bureaucracy that managed the income that they brought into their country.

One result of all this activity was that the Ministry of Finance was surely and not so slowly drifting away from the True Faith of Marxism into the shadowy in-between world of socialist capitalism—a world with no real name or identity. In fact, every Minister of Finance had drifted away from Marxism to some greater or lesser extent, whatever his previous religious fervor, because one by one they had all seen that their country needed to play on this particular international playground, and to do that, had to play by the rules, and, oh, by the way, this game was bringing prosperity to the People's Republic in a way that fifty years of Marx and Mao had singularly failed to do.

As a direct result of this inexorable process, the Minister of Finance was a candidate, not a full member of the Politburo. He had a voice at the table, but not a vote, and his words were judged by those who had never really troubled themselves to understand his words or the world in which he operated.

This minister was surnamed Qian, which, appropriately, meant coins or money, and he'd been in the job for six years. His background was in engineering. He'd built railroads in the northeastern part of his country for twenty years, and done so well enough to merit a change in posting. He'd actually handled his ministerial job quite well, the international community judged, but Qian Kun was often the one who had to explain to the Politburo that the Politburo couldn't do everything it wanted to do, which meant he was often about as welcome in the room as a plague rat. This would be one more such day, he feared, sitting in the back of his ministerial car on the way to the morning meeting.

Eleven hours away, on Park Avenue in New York, another meeting was under way. Butterfly was the name of a burgeoning chain of clothing stores which marketed to prosperous American women. It had combined new microfiber textiles with a brilliant young designer from Florence, Italy, into fully a six percent share of its market, and in America that was big money indeed.

Except for one thing. Its textiles were all made in the People's Republic, at a factory just outside the great port city of Shanghai, and then cut and sewn into clothing at yet another plant in the nearby city of Yancheng.

The chairman of Butterfly was just thirty-two, and after ten years of hustling, he figured he was about to cash in on a dream he'd had from all the way back in Erasmus Hall High School in Brooklyn. He'd spent nearly every day since graduating Pratt Institute conceiving and building up his business, and now it was *his* time. It was time to buy that G so that he could fly off to Paris on a whim, get that house in the hills of Tuscany, and another in Aspen, and really live in the manner he'd earned.

Except for that one little thing. His flagship store at Park and 50th today had experienced something as unthinkable as the arrival of men from Mars. People had demonstrated there. People wearing Versace clothing had shown up with cardboard placards stapled to wooden sticks proclaiming their opposition to trade with BARBARIANS! and condemning Butterfly for doing business with such a country. Someone had even shown up with an image of the Chinese flag with a swastika on it, and if there was *anything* you didn't want associated with your business in New York, it was Hitler's odious logo.

"We've got to move fast on this," the corporate counsel said. He was Jewish and smart, and had steered Butterfly through more than one minefield to bring it to the brink of ultimate success. "This could kill us."

He wasn't kidding, and the rest of the board knew it. Exactly four customers had gone past the protesters into the store today, and one of them had been returning something which, she said, she no longer wanted in her closet.

"What's our exposure?" the founder and CEO asked.

"In real terms?" the head of accounting asked. "Oh, potentially four hundred." By which he meant four hundred *million* dollars. "It could wipe us out in, oh, twelve weeks."

Wipe us out was not what the CEO wanted to hear. To bring a line of clothing this far was about as easy as swimming the Atlantic Ocean during the annual shark convention. This was his moment, but he found himself standing in yet another minefield, one for which he'd had no warning at all.

"Okay," he responded as coolly as the acid in his stomach allowed. "What can we do about it?"

"We can walk on our contracts," the attorney advised.

"Is that legal?"

"Legal enough." By which he meant that the downside exposure of shorting the Chinese manufacturers was less onerous than having a shop full of products that no person would buy.

"Alternatives?"

"The Thais," Production said. "There's a place outside Bangkok that would love to take up the slack. They called us today, in fact."

"Cost?"

"Less than four percent difference. Three-point-six-three, to be exact, and they will be off schedule by, oh, maybe four weeks max. We have enough stock to keep the stores open through that, no problem," Production told the rest of the board with confidence.

"How much of that stock is Chinese in origin?"

"A lot comes from Taiwan, remember? We can have our people start putting the Good Guys stickers on them . . . and we can fudge that some, too." Not all that many consumers knew the difference between one Chinese place name and another. A flag was much easier to differentiate.

"Also," Marketing put in, "we can start an ad campaign tomorrow. 'Butterfly doesn't do business with dragons.' " He held up an illustration that showed the corporate logo escaping a dragon's fiery breath. That it looked terminally tacky didn't matter for the moment. They had to take action, and they had to do it fast.

"Oh, got a call an hour ago from Frank Meng at Meng, Harrington, and Cicero," Production announced. "He says he can get some ROC textile houses on the team in a matter of days, and he says they have the flexibility to retool in less than a month—and if we greenlight it, the ROC ambassador will officially put us on their good-guy list. In return, we just have to guarantee five years' worth of business, with the usual escape clauses."

"I like it," Legal said. The ROC ambassador would play fair, and so would his country. They knew when they had the tiger by the balls.

"We have a motion on the table," the chairman and CEO announced. "All in favor?"

With this vote, Butterfly was the first major American company to walk out on its contracts with the People's Republic. Like the first goose to leave Northern Canada in the fall, it announced that a new and chilly season was coming. The only potential problem was legal action from the PRC businesses, but a federal judge would probably understand that a signed contract wasn't quite the same thing as a suicide note, and perhaps even regard the overarching political question sufficient to make the contract itself void. After all, counsel would argue in chambers—and in front of a New York jury if necessary—when you find out you're doing business with Adolf Hitler, you *have* to take a step back. Opposing counsel would argue back, but he'd know his position was a losing one, and he'd tell his clients so before going in.

"I'll tell our bankers tomorrow. They're not scheduled to cut the money loose for another thirty-six hours." This meant that one hundred forty million dollars would not be transferred to a Beijing account as scheduled. And now the CEO could contemplate going ahead with his order for the G. The corporate logo of a monarch butterfly leaving its cocoon, he thought, would look just great on the rudder.

"We don't know for sure yet," Qian told his colleagues, "but I am seriously concerned."

"What's the particular problem today?" Xu Kun Piao asked.

"We have a number of commercial and other contracts coming due in the next three weeks. Ordinarily I would expect them to proceed normally, but our representatives in America have called to warn my office that there might be a problem."

"Who are these representatives?" Shen Tang asked.

"Mainly lawyers whom we employ to manage our business dealings for us. Almost all are American citizens. They are not fools, and their advice is something a wise man attends carefully," Qian said soberly.

"Lawyers are the curse of America," Zhang Han San observed. "And all civilized nations." *At least here* we *decide the law,* he didn't have to explain.

"Perhaps so, Zhang, but if you do business with America you need such people, and they are very useful in explaining conditions there. Shooting the messenger may get you more pleasant news, but it won't necessarily be accurate."

Fang nodded and smiled at that. He liked Qian. The man spoke the truth more faithfully than those who were supposed to listen for it. But Fang kept his peace on this. He, too, was concerned with the political developments caused by those two overzealous policemen, but it was too late to discipline them now. Even if Xu suggested it, Zhang and the others would talk him out of it.

Secretary Winston was at home watching a movie on his DVD player. It was easier than going to the movies, and he could do it without four Secret Service agents in attendance. His wife was knitting a ski sweater—she did her important Christmas presents herself, and it was something she could do while watching TV or talking, and it brought the same sort of relaxation to her that sailing his big offshore yacht did for her husband.

Winston had a multiline phone in the family room—and every other room in his Chevy Chase house—and the private line had a different ring so that he knew which one he had to answer himself.

"Yeah?"

"George, it's Mark."

"Working late?"

"No, I'm home. Just got a call from New York. It may have just started."

"What's that?" TRADER asked TELESCOPE.

"Butterfly—the ladies' clothing firm?"

"Oh, yeah, I know the name," Winston assured his aide. Well he might: His wife and daughter loved the place.

"They're going to bail on their contracts with their PRC suppliers."

"How big?"

"About a hundred forty."

Winston whistled. "That much?"

"That big," Gant assured him. "And they're a trend-setter. When this breaks tomorrow, it's going to make a lot of people think. Oh, one other thing."

"Yeah?"

"The PRC just terminated its options with Caterpillar—equipment to finish up the Three Gorges project. That's about three-ten million, switching over to Kawa in Japan. That's going to be in the *Journal* tomorrow morning."

"That's real smart!" Winston grumbled.

"Trying to show us who's holding the whip, George."

"Well, I hope they like how it feels going up their ass," SecTreas observed, causing his wife to look over at him.

"Okay, when's the Butterfly story break?"

"It's too late for the *Journal* tomorrow, but it'll be on CNN-FN and CNBC for damned sure."

"And what if other fashion houses do the same?"

"Over a billion, right away, and you know what they say, George, a billion here, a billion there, pretty soon you're talking real money." It had been one of Everett McKinley Dirksen's better Washington observations.

"How much before their currency account goes in the tank?"

"Twenty, and it starts hurting. Forty, and they're in the shitter. Sixty, and they're fuckin' broke. Never seen a whole country sleeping over a steam vent, y'know? George, they also import food, wheat mainly, from Canada and Australia. That could *really* hurt."

"Noted. Tomorrow."

"Right." The phone clicked off.

Winston picked up the controller to un-pause the DVD player, then had another thought. He picked up the mini–tape machine he used for notes and said, "Find out how much of the PRC military purchases have been executed financially—especially Israel." He clicked the STOP button, set it down, and picked the DVD controller back up to continue his movie, but soon found he couldn't concentrate on it very well. Something big was happening, and experienced as he was in the world of commerce, and now in the business of international transactions, he realized that he didn't have a handle on it. That didn't happen to George Winston very often, and it was enough to keep him from laughing at *Men in Black*.

Her minister didn't look very happy, Ming saw. The look on his face made her think that he might have lost a family member to cancer. She found out more when he called her in to dictate his notes. It took fully ninety minutes this time, and then two entire hours for her to transcribe them into her computer. She hadn't exactly forgotten what her computer probably did with them every night, but she hadn't thought about it in weeks. She wished she had the ability to discuss the notes' content with Minister Fang. Over the years of working for him, she'd acquired rather a sophisticated appreciation for the politics of her country, to the point that she could anticipate not only the thoughts of her master, but also those of some of his colleagues. She was in effect, if not in fact, a confidant of her minister, and while she could not counsel him on his job, if he'd had the wit to appreciate the effect of her education and her time inside his head, he might have used her far more efficiently than as a mere secretary. But she was a woman in a land ruled by men, and therefore voiceless. Orwell had been right. She'd read *Animal Farm* some years ago. Everyone *was* equal, but some *were* more equal than others. If Fang were smart, he'd use her more intelligently, but he wasn't, and he didn't. She'd talk to Nomuri-san about that tonight.

For his part, Chester was just finalizing an order for one thousand six hundred sixty-one high-end NEC desktops at the China Precision Machine Import and Export Corporation, which, among other things, made guided missiles for the People's Liberation Army. That would make Nippon Electric Company pretty happy. The sad part was that he couldn't rig these machine to talk as glibly as the two in the Council of Ministers, but that would have been too dangerous, if a good daydream over a beer and a smoke. Chester Nomuri, cyber-spy. Then his beeper started vibrating. He reached down and gave it a look. The number was 745-4426. Applied to the keys on a phone, and selecting the right letters, that translated in personal code to *shin gan,* "heart and soul," Ming's private endearment for her lover and an indication that she wanted to come over to his place tonight. That suited Nomuri just fine. So, he'd turned into James Bond after all. Good enough for a private smile, as he walked out to his car. He flipped open his shoephone, dialed up his e-mail access, and sent his own message over the 'Net, 226-234: *bao bei,* "beloved one." She liked to hear him say that, and he didn't mind saying it. So, something other than TV for tonight. Good. He hoped he had enough of the Japanese scotch for the *après*-sex.

You knew you had a bad job when you welcomed a trip to the dentist. Jack had been going to the same one for nineteen years, but this time it involved a helicopter flight to a Maryland State Police barracks with its own helipad, followed by five minutes in a car to the dentist's office. He was thinking about China, but his principal bodyguard mistook his expression.

"Relax, boss," Andrea told the President. "If he makes you scream, I'll cap him."

"You shouldn't be up so early," Ryan responded crossly.

"Dr. North said I could work my regular routine until further notice, and I just started the vitamins she likes."

"Well, Pat looks rather pleased with himself." It had been a pleasant evening at the White House. It was always good to entertain guests who had no political agenda.

"What is it about you guys? You strut like roosters, but *we* have to do all the work!"

"Andrea, I would *gladly* switch jobs with you!" Ryan joked. He'd had this discussion with Cathy often enough, claiming that having a baby couldn't be all that hard—men had to do almost all of the tough work in life. But he couldn't joke with someone else's wife that way.

Nomuri heard his computer beep in the distance, meaning it had received and was now automatically encrypting and retransmitting the date e-mailed from Ming's desktop. It made an entertaining interruption to his current activity. It had been five days since their last tryst, and that was a long enough wait for him . . . and evidently for her as well, judging by the passion in her kisses. In due course, it was over, and they both rolled over for a smoke.

"How is the office?" Nomuri asked, with the answer to his question now residing in a server in Wisconsin.

"The Politburo is debating great finance. Qian, the minister in charge of our money, is trying to persuade the Politburo to change its ways, but they're not listening as Minister Fang thinks they ought."

"Oh?"

"He's rather angry with his old comrades for their lack of flexibility." Then Ming giggled. "Chai said the minister was very flexible with her two nights ago."

"Not a nice thing to say about a man, Ming," Nomuri chided.

"I would never say it about you and your jade sausage, *shin gan,*" she said, turning for a kiss.

"Do they argue often there? In the Politburo, I mean?"

"There are frequent disagreements, but this is the first time in months that the matter has not been resolved to Fang's satisfaction. They are usually collegial, but this is a disagreement over ideology. Those can be violent—at least in intellectual terms." Obviously, the Politburo members were too old to do much more than smack an enemy over the head with their canes.

"And this one?"

"Minister Qian says the country may soon be out of money. The other ministers say that is nonsense. Qian says we must accommodate the Western countries. Zhang and the others like him say we cannot show weakness after all they—especially the Americans—have done to us lately."

"Don't they see that killing that Italian priest was a bad thing?"

"They see it as an unfortunate accident, and besides, he was breaking our laws."

Jesus, Nomuri thought, *they really do think they're god-kings, don't they? "Bao bei,* that is a mistake on their part."

"You think so?"

"I have been to America, remember? I lived there for a time. Americans are very solicitous to their clergy, and they place a high value on religion. Spitting on it angers them greatly."

"You think Qian is right, then?" she asked. "You think America will deny us money for this foolish action?"

"I think it is possible, yes. Very possible, Ming."

"Minister Fang thinks we should take a more moderate course, to accommodate the Americans somewhat, but he did not say so at the meeting."

"Oh? Why?"

"He does not wish to depart too greatly from the path of the other ministers. You say that in Japan people fear not being elected. Here, well, the Politburo elects its own, and it can expel those who no longer fit in. Fang does not wish to lose his own status, obviously, and to make sure that doesn't happen, he takes a cautious line."

"This is hard for me to understand, Ming. How do they select their members? How do the 'princes' choose the new 'prince'?"

"Oh, there are party members who have distinguished themselves ideologically, or sometimes from work in the field. Minister Qian, for example, used to be chief of railroad construction, and was promoted for that reason, but mainly they are picked for political reasons."

"And Fang?"

"My minister is an old comrade. His father was one of Mao's faithful lieutenants, and Fang has always been politically reliable, but in recent years he has taken note of the new industries and seen how well they function, and he admires some of the people who operate them. He even has some into his office from time to time for tea and talk."

So, the old pervert is a progressive *here?* Nomuri wondered. Well, the bar for that was pretty low in China. You didn't have to jump real high, but that put him in advance of the ones who dug a trench under it, didn't it?

"Ah, so the people have no voice at all, do they?"

Ming laughed at that. "Only at party meetings, and there you guard your voice."

"Are you a member?"

"Oh, yes. I go to meetings once a month. I sit in the back. I nod when others nod, and applaud when they applaud, and I pretend to listen. Others probably listen better. It is not a small thing to be a party member, but my membership is because of my job at the ministry. I am here because they needed my language and computer skills—and besides, the ministers like to have young women under them," she added.

"You're never on top of him, eh?"

"He prefers the ordinary position, but it is hard on his arms." Ming giggled.

Ryan was glad to see that he was brushing enough. The dentist told him to floss, as he always did, and Ryan nodded, as he always did, and he'd never bought floss in his life and wasn't going to start now. But at least he'd undergone nothing more invasive than a couple of X rays, for which, of course, he'd gotten the leather apron. On the whole, it had been ninety minutes torn off the front of his day. Back in the Oval Office, he had the latest SORGE, which was good enough for a whispered "damn." He lifted the phone for Mary Pat at Langley.

"They're dense," Ryan observed.

"Well, they sure as hell don't know high finance. Even I know better than this."

"TRADER has to see this. Put him on the SORGE list," POTUS ordered.

"With your day-to-day approval only," the DDO hedged. "Maybe he has a need-to-know on economics, but nothing else, okay?"

"Okay, for now," Jack agreed. But George was coming along nicely on strategic matters, and might turn into a good policy adviser. He understood high-stress psychology better than most, and that was the name of the game. Jack broke the connection and had Ellen Sumter call the SecTreas over from across the street.

So, what else do they worry about?" Chester asked.

"They're concerned that some of the workers and peasants are not as happy as they should be. You know about the riots they had in the coal region."

"Oh?"

"Yes, the miners rioted last year. The PLA went in to settle things down. Several hundred people were shot, and three thousand arrested." She shrugged while putting her bra back on. "There is unrest, but that is nothing especially new. The army keeps control of things in the outlying regions. That's why they spend so much money, to keep the army reliable. The generals run the PLA's economic empire—all the factories and things—and they're good at keeping a lid on things. The ordinary soldiers are just workers and peasants, but the officers are all party members, and they are reliable, or so the Politburo thinks. It's probably true," Ming concluded. She hadn't seen her minister worry all that much about it. Power in the People's Republic decidedly grew from the barrel of a gun, and the Politburo owned all the guns. That made things simple, didn't it?

For his part, Nomuri had just learned things he'd never thought about before. He might want to make his own report on this stuff. Ming probably knew a lot of things that didn't go out as SONGBIRD material, and he'd be remiss not to send that to Langley, too.

It's like a five-year-old in a gun store," Secretary Winston observed. "These people have no business making economic decisions for a city government, much less a major country. I mean, hell, as stupid as the Japanese were a few years ago, at least they know to listen to the coaches."

"And?"

"And when they run into the brick wall, their eyes'll still be closed. That can smart some, Jack. They're going to get bit on the ass, and they don't see it coming." Winston could mix metaphors with the best of 'em, Ryan saw.

"When?" SWORDSMAN asked.

"Depends on how many companies do what Butterfly did. We'll know more in a few days. The fashion business will be the lead indicator, of all things."

"Really?"

"Surprised me, too, but this is the time for them to commit to the next season, and there's a *ton* of money in that business going on over there, man. Toss in all the toys for next Christmas. There's seventeen billion–plus just in that, Mark Gant tells me."

"Damn."

"Yeah, I didn't know Santa's reindeer had slanted eyes either, Jack. At least not to that extent."

"What about Taiwan?" Ryan wondered.

"You're not kidding. They're jumping into the growing gap with both feet. Figure they pick up a quarter, maybe a third, of what the PRC is going to lose. Singapore's going to be next. And the Thais. This little bump in the road will go a long way to restore the damage done to their economy a few years back. In fact, the PRC's troubles might rebuild the whole South Asian economy. It could be a swing of fifty billion dollars out of China, and it has to go somewhere. We're starting to take bids, Jack. It won't be a bad deal for our consumers, and I'll bet those countries learn from Beijing's example, and kick their doors open a notch or so. So, our workers will profit from it, too—somewhat, anyway."

"Downside?"

"Boeing's squealing some. They wanted that triple-seven order, but you wait an' see. Somebody's going to take up that slack, too. One other thing."

"Yeah?" Ryan asked.

"It's not just American companies bailing out on them. Two big Italian places, and Siemens in Germany, they've announced termination of some business with their Chinese partners," TRADER said.

"Will it turn into a general movement . . . ?"

"Too soon to say, but if I were these guys"—Winston shook the fax from CIA—"I'd be thinking about fence-mending real soon."

"They won't do it, George."

"Then they're going to learn a nasty lesson."

CHAPTER 39

The Other Question

"No action with our friend?" Reilly asked.

"Well, he continues his sexual adventures," Provalov answered.

"Talk to any of the girls yet?"

"Earlier today, two of them. He pays them well, in euros or d-marks, and doesn't request any, uh, 'exotic' services from them."

"Nice to know he's normal in his tastes," the FBI agent observed, with a grunt.

"We have numerous photos of him now. We've put an electronic tracker on his cars, and we've also planted a bug on his computer keyboard. That'll allow us to determine his encryption password, next time he makes use of it."

"But he hasn't done anything incriminating yet," Reilly said. He didn't even make it a question.

"Not under our observation," Oleg confirmed.

"Damn, so, he was really trying to whack Sergey Golovko. Hard to believe, man."

"That is so, but we cannot deny it. And on Chinese orders."

"That's like an act of war, buddy. It's a big fucking deal." Reilly took a sip of his vodka.

"So it is, Mishka. Rather more complex than any case I've handled this year." It was, Provalov thought, an artful understatement. He'd gladly go back to a normal homicide, a husband killing his wife for fucking a neighbor, or the other way around. Such things, nasty as they were, were far less nasty than this one was.

"How's he pick the girls up, Oleg?" Reilly asked.

"He doesn't call for them on the phone. He seems to go to a good restaurant with a good bar and wait until a likely prospect appears at his elbow."

"Hmm, plant a girl on him?"

"What do you mean?"

"I mean get yourself a pretty girl who does this sort of thing for a living, brief her on what she ought to say, and set her in front of him like a nice fly on your fishhook. If he picks her up, maybe she can get him to talk."

"Have you ever done such a thing?"

"We got a wiseguy that way in Jersey City three years ago. Liked to brag in front of women how tough he was, and the guys he whacked, that sort of thing. He's in Rahway State Prison now on a murder rap. Oleg, a lot more people have talked their way into prison than you'll ever catch on your own. Trust me. That's how it is for us, even."

"I wonder if the Sparrow School has any graduates working . . . ?" Provalov mused.

It wasn't fair to do it at night, but nobody had ever said war was marked by fairness in its execution. Colonel Boyle was in his command post monitoring the operation of 1st Armored's Aviation Brigade. It was mainly his Apaches, though some Kiowa Warriors were up, too, as scouts for the heavy shooters. The target was a German heavy battalion, simulating a night's laagering after a day on the offense. In fact, they were pretending to be Russians—it was a NATO scenario that went back thirty years to the introduction of the first Huey Cobras, back in the 1970s, when the value of a helicopter gunship had first been noticed in Vietnam. And a revelation it had been. Armed for the first time in 1972 with TOW missiles, they'd proven to the tanks of the North Vietnamese just how fearsome a foe a missile-armed chopper could be, and that had been before night-vision systems had come fully on line. Now the Apache turned combat operations into sport shooting, and the Germans were still trying to figure a counter for it. Even their own night-vision gear didn't compensate for the huge advantage held by the airborne hunters. One idea that had almost worked was to lay a thermal-insulating blanket over the tanks so as to deny the helicopters the heat signature by which they hunted their motionless prey, but the problem there was the tank's main gun tube, which had proved impractical to conceal, and the blankets had never really worked properly, any more than a twin-bed coverlet could be stretched over a king-size bed. And so, now, the Apaches' laser-illumination systems were "painting" the Leos for enough seconds to guarantee hits from the Hellfire missiles, and while the German tanks tried to shoot back, they couldn't seem to make it work. And now the yellow "I'm dead" lights were blinking, and yet another tank battalion had fallen victim to yet another administrative attack.

"They should have tried putting SAM teams outside their perimeter," Colonel Boyle observed, watching the computer screen. Instead, the German colonel had tried IR lures, which the Apache gunners had learned to distinguish from the real thing. Under the rules of the scenario, proper tank decoys had not been allowed. They were a little harder to discriminate—the American-made ones almost exactly replicated the visual signature of an M1 tank, and had an internal heat source for fooling infrared gear at night—*and* fired off a Hoffman pyrotechnic charge to simulate a return shot when they took a hit. But they were made so well for their mission that they could not be mistaken for anything other than what they were, either a real M1 main battle tank, and hence friendly, or a decoy, and thus not really useful in a training exercise, all in all a case of battlefield technology being too good for a training exercise.

"Pegasus Lead to Archangel, over," the digital radio called. With the new radios, it was no longer a static-marred crackle.

"Archangel to Pegasus," Colonel Boyle answered.

"Sir, we are Winchester and just about out of targets. No friendly casualties. Pegasus is RTB, over."

"Roger, Pegasus. Looks good from here. Out."

And with that, the Apache battalion of attack choppers and their Kiowa bird-dogs turned back for their airfield for the mission debrief and post-game beers.

Boyle looked over at General Diggs. "Sir, I don't know how to do it much better than that."

"Our hosts are going to be pissed."

"The Bundeswehr isn't what it used to be. Their political leadership thinks peace has broken out all the way, and their troopers know it. They could have put some of their own choppers up to run interference, but my boys are pretty good at air-to-air—we train for it, and my pilots really like the idea of making ace on their own—but their chopper drivers aren't getting all the gas they need for operational training. Their best chopper drivers are down in the Balkans doing traffic observation."

Diggs nodded thoughtfully. The problems of the Bundeswehr were not, strictly speaking, his problems. "Colonel, that was well done. Please convey my pleasure to your people. What's next for you?"

"General, we have a maintenance stand-down tomorrow, and two days later we're going to run a major search-and-rescue exercise with my Blackhawks. You're welcome to come over and watch."

"I just might, Colonel Boyle. You done good. Be seeing you."

"Yes, sir." The colonel saluted, and General Diggs walked out to his HMMWV, with Colonel Masterman in attendance.

"Well, Duke?"

"Like I told you, sir, Boyle's been feeding his boys and girls a steady diet of nails and human babies."

"Well, his next fitness report's going to get him a star, I think."

"His Apache commander's not bad either."

"That's a fact," the divisional G-3 agreed. "Pegasus" was his call sign, and he'd kicked some serious ass this night.

"What's next?"

"Sir, in three days we have a big SimNet exercise against the Big Red One at Fort Riley. Our boys are pretty hot for it."

"Divisional readiness?" Diggs asked.

"We're pushing ninety-five percent, General. Not much slack left to take up. I mean, sir, to go any farther, we gotta take the troops out to Fort Irwin or maybe the Negev Training Area. Are we as good as the Tenth Cav or the Eleventh? No, we don't get to play in the field as much as they do." And, he didn't have to add, no division in any army in the world got the money to train that hard. "But given the limitations we have to live with, there's not a whole lot more we can do. I figure we play hard on SimNet to keep the kids interested, but we're just about as far as we can go, sir."

"I think you're right, Duke. You know, sometimes I kinda wish the Cold War could come back—for training purposes, anyway. The Germans won't let us play the way we used to back then, and that's what we need to take the next step."

"Unless somebody springs for the tickets to fly a brigade out to California." Masterman nodded.

"That ain't gonna happen, Duke," Diggs told his operations officer. And more was the pity. First Tanks' troops were almost ready to give the Blackhorse a run for their money. Close enough, Diggs thought, that he'd pay to watch. "How's a beer grab you, Colonel?"

"If the General is buying, I will gladly assist him in spending his money," Duke Masterman said graciously, as their sergeant driver pulled up to the *kazerne*'s O-Club.

Good morning, Comrade General," Gogol said, pulling himself to attention.

Bondarenko had felt guilt at coming to see this old soldier so early in the morning, but he'd heard the day before that the ancient warrior was not one to waste daylight. And so he wasn't, the general saw.

"You kill wolves," Gennady Iosifovich observed, seeing the gleaming pelts hanging on the wall of this rough cabin.

"And bear, but when you gild the pelts, they grow too heavy," the old man agreed, fetching tea for his guests.

"These are amazing," Colonel Aliyev said, touching one of the remaining wolf pelts. Most had been carried off.

"It's an amusement for an old hunter," Gogol said, lighting a cigarette.

General Bondarenko looked at his rifles, the new Austrian-made one, and the old Russian M1891 Mosin-Nagant sniper rifle.

"How many with this one?" Bondarenko asked.

"Wolves, bears?"

"Germans," the general clarified, with coldness in his voice.

"I stopped counting at thirty, Comrade General. That was before Kiev. There were many more after that. I see we share a decoration," Gogol observed, pointing to his visitor's gold star, for Hero of the Soviet Union, which he'd won in Afghanistan. Gogol had two, one from Ukraine and the other in Germany.

"You have the look of a soldier, Pavel Petrovich, and a good one." Bondarenko sipped his tea, served properly, a clear glass in a metal—was it silver?—holder.

"I served in my time. First at Stalingrad, then on the long walk to Berlin."

I bet you did walk all the way, too, the general thought. He'd met his share of Great Patriotic War veterans, now mostly dead. This wizened old bastard had stared death in the face and spat at it, trained to do so, probably, by his life in these woods. He'd grown up with bears and wolves as enemies—as nasty as the German fascists had been, at least they didn't eat you—and so had been accustomed to wagering his life on his eye and his nerve. There was no real substitute for that, the kind of training you couldn't institute for an army. A gifted few learned how the hard way, and of those the lucky ones survived the war. Pavel Petrovich hadn't had an easy time. Soldiers might admire their own snipers, might value them for their skills, but you could never say "comrade" to a man who hunted men as though they were animals—because on the other side of the line might be another such man who wanted to hunt *you.* Of all the enemies, that was the one you loathed and feared the most, because it became personal to see another man through a telescopic sight, to see his face, and take his life as a deliberate act against *one* man, even gazing at his face when the bullet struck. Gogol had been one of those, Gennady thought, a hunter of individual men. And he'd probably never lost a minute's sleep over it. Some men were just born to it, and Pavel Petrovich Gogol was one of them. With a few hundred thousand such men, a general could conquer the entire world, but they were too rare for that . . .

. . . and maybe that was a good thing, Bondarenko mused.

"Might you come to my headquarters some night? I would like to feed you dinner and listen to your stories."

"How far is it?"

"I will send you my personal helicopter, Sergeant Gogol."

"And I will bring you a gilded wolf," the hunter promised his guest.

"We will find an honored place for it at my headquarters," Bondarenko promised in turn. "Thank you for your tea. I must depart and see to my command, but I *will* have you to headquarters for dinner,

Sergeant Gogol." Handshakes were exchanged, and the general took his leave.

"I would not want him on the other side of a battlefield," Colonel Aliyev observed, as they got into their helicopter.

"Do we have a sniper school in the command?"

"Yes, General, but it's mainly inactive."

Gennady turned. "Start it up again, Andrushka! We'll get Gogol to come and teach the children how it's done. He's a priceless asset. Men like that are the soul of a fighting army. It's our job to command our soldiers, to tell them where to go and what to do, but those are the men who do the fighting and the killing, and it's *our* job to make sure they're properly trained and supplied. And when they're too old, we use them to teach the new boys, to give them heroes they can touch and talk to. How the *hell* did we ever forget that, Andrey?" The general shook his head as the helicopter lifted off.

Gregory was back in his hotel room, with three hundred pages of technical information to digest as he sipped his Diet Coke and finished off his french fries. Something was wrong with the whole equation, but he couldn't put his finger on it. The Navy had tested its Standard-2-ER missile against all manner of threats, mainly on computer, but also against live targets at Kwajalein Atoll. It had done pretty well, but there'd never been a full-up live test against a for-real ICBM reentry vehicle. There weren't enough of them to go around. Mainly they used old Minuteman-II ICBMs, long since retired from service and fired out of test silos at Vandenberg Air Force Base in California, but those were mostly gone. Russia and America had retired all of their ballistic weapons, chiefly as a reaction to the nuclear terrorist explosion at Denver and the even more horrific aftermath that had barely been averted. The negotiations to draw the numbers down to zero—the last ones had been eliminated in public just before the Japanese had launched their sneak attack on the Pacific Fleet—had gone so rapidly that a lot of the minor ancillary points had scarcely been considered, and only later had it been decided to take the "spare" launchers whose disposition had somehow been overlooked and retain them for ABM testing (every month a Russian officer checked the American ones at Vandenberg, and an American officer counted the Russian ones outside Plesetsk). The ABM tests were also monitored, but that entire area of effort was now largely theoretical. Both America and Russia retained a goodly number of nuclear warheads, and these could easily be affixed to cruise missiles, which, again, both sides had in relative abundance and no country could stop. It might take five hours instead of thirty-four minutes, but the targets would be just as dead.

Anti-missile work had been relegated to theater missiles, such as the ubiquitous Scuds, which the Russians doubtless regretted ever having built, much less sold to jerkwater countries that couldn't even field a single decent mechanized division, but who loved to parade those upgraded V-2-class ballistic stovepipes because they looked impressive as hell to the people on the sidewalks. But the new upgrades on Patriot and its Russian counterpart SAM largely negated that threat, and the Navy's Aegis system had been tested against them, with pretty good success. Like Patriot, though, Standard was really a point-defense weapon with damned little cross-range ability to cover an area instead of maybe twenty square miles of important sea-estate.

All in all, it was a pity that they'd never solved the power-throughput problem with his free-electron lasers. *Those* could have defended whole coastlines, if only . . . and if only his aunt had balls, Gregory thought, she'd be his uncle. There was talk of building a chemical laser aboard a converted 747 that could sure as hell clobber a ballistic launch during boost phase, but to do *that*, the 747 had to be fairly close to the launch point, and so *that* was just one more version of theater defense, and of little strategic use.

The Aegis system had real possibilities. The SPY radar system was first-rate, and though the computer that managed the information was the flower of 1975 technology—a current Apple Macintosh had it beat by a good three orders of magnitude in all categories of performance—intercepting a ballistic warhead wasn't a question of computing speed so much as kinetic energy—getting the kill vehicle to the right place at the right time. Even that wasn't so great a feat of engineering. The real work had been done as far back as 1959, with the Nike Zeus, which had turned into Spartan and shown great promise before being shitcanned by the 1972 treaty with the Soviet Union, which was, belatedly, just as dead as the Safeguard system, which had been aborted at half-built.

Well, the fact of the matter was that MIRV technology had negated that entire defense concept. No, you had to kill the ICBM in boost phase to kill all the MIRVs at once, and do it over the enemy's territory so that if he had a primitive arming system he'd only fry his own turf. The method for doing that was the Brilliant Pebbles system developed at Lawrence-Livermore National Laboratory, and though it had never been given a full-up test, the technology was actually pretty straightforward. Being hit by a matchstick traveling at fifteen thousand miles per hour would ruin your entire day. But that would never happen. The drive to fund and deploy such a system had died with all the ballistic launchers. In a way, it was a pity, Gregory thought. Such a system would have been a really cool engineering accomplishment—but it had little practical application today. The PRC retained its land-based ballistic launchers, but there were only ten or so of them, and that was a long way from the fifteen hundred the Soviets had once pointed at America. The Chinese had a missile submarine, too, but Gregory figured that CINCPAC could make that go away if he had to. Even if it was just tied alongside the pier, one two-thousand-pound smart bomb could take it out of play, and the Navy had a lot of those.

So, he thought, *figure the PRC gets really pissed at Taiwan, and figure the Navy has an Aegis cruiser tied alongside so that its sailors can get drunk and laid in the city, and those folks in Beijing pick that moment to push the button on one of their ICBMs, how can the Navy keep its cruiser from turning into slag, and oh, by the way, keep the city of Taipei alive . . . ?*

The SM-2-ER had almost enough of the right ingredients to handle such a threat. If the missile was targeted on where the cruiser was, cross-range was not an issue. You just had to put the interceptor on the same line of bearing, because in essence the inbound rack wasn't moving at all, and you just had to put the SAM in the same place—Spot X—that the RV was going to be, at Time Y. The Aegis computer could figure where and when that was, and you weren't really hitting a bullet with a bullet. The RV would be about a meter across, and the kill-zone of the SAM's warhead would be about, what? Three meters across? Five? Maybe even eight or ten?

Call it eight, Al Gregory thought. Was the SM-2 *that* accurate? In absolute terms, probably yes. It had ample-sized control surfaces, and getting into the line of a jet aircraft—what the SM-2 had been designed to kill—had to take into account the maneuverability of the aircraft (pilots would do their damnedest to avoid the things), and so the eight-meter globe of destruction could probably be made to intercept the in-bound RV in terms of pure geometry.

The issue was speed. Gregory popped open another Diet Coke from the room's minibar and sat back on the bed to consider how troublesome that issue was. The inbound RV, at a hundred thousand feet, would be traveling at about sixteen thousand miles per hour, 23,466 feet per second, eight times the speed of a rifle bullet, 7,150 meters per second. That was pretty damned fast. It was about the same speed as a high-explosive detonation. You could have the RV sitting next to a ton of TNT at the moment the explosive went off, and the explosion couldn't catch up with the RV. *That was FAST.*

So, the SAM's warhead has to go off well before it gets to where the RV is. Figuring out how much was a simple mathematical exercise. That meant that the proximity fuse on the SM-2 was the important variable in the equation, Gregory decided. He didn't know that he was wrong on this, didn't see what he was missing, and went on with his calculations. The software fix for the proximity laser fusing system looked less difficult than he'd imagined. Well, wasn't that good news?

It was another early day for Minister Fang Gan. He'd gotten a phone call at his home the previous night, and decided he had to arrive early for the appointment made then. This was a surprise for his staff, who were just setting up for the day when he breezed in, not looking as cross as he felt for the disturbance of his adamantine routine. It wasn't their fault, after all, and they had the good sense not to trouble him, and thus generate artificial wrath.

Ming was just printing up her downloads from the Web. She had pieces that she thought would be of interest, especially one from *The Wall Street Journal,* and another from *Financial Times.* Both commented on what she thought might be the reason for the minister's early arrival. His 9:20 appointment was with Ren He-Ping, an industrialist friendly with her boss. Ren arrived early. The slender, elderly man looked unhappy—no, she thought, worried—about something. She lifted her phone to get permission, then stood and walked him into the inner office, racing back outside to fetch morning tea, which she hadn't had a chance to serve her boss yet.

Ming was back inside in less than five minutes, with the fine porcelain cups on a decorated serving tray. She presented the morning drinks to both men with an elegance that earned her a thank-you from her boss, and then she took her leave. Ren, she saw, wasn't any happier to be in with her minister.

"What is the problem, Ren?"

"In two weeks, I will have a thousand workers with nothing to do, Fang."

"Oh? What is the reason for that, my friend?"

"I do much business with an American business. It is called Butterfly. They sell clothing to wealthy American women. My factory outside Shanghai makes the cloth, and my tailoring plant at Yancheng turns the fabric into clothing, which we ship to America and Europe. We've been doing business with Butterfly for three years now, very satisfactorily for all concerned."

"Yes? So, what, then, is the difficulty?"

"Fang, Butterfly just canceled an order worth one hundred forty million American dollars. They did it without any warning. Only last week they told us how happy they were with our products. We've invested a fortune into quality control to make sure they would stay with us—but they've left us like a dog in the street."

"Why did this happen, Ren?" Minister Fang asked, fearing he knew the answer.

"Our representative in New York tells us that it's because of the deaths of the two clergymen. He tells us that Butterfly had no choice, that Americans demonstrated outside his establishment in New York and prevented people from going inside to buy his wares. He says that Butterfly cannot do business with me for fear of having their own business collapse."

"Do you not have a contract with them? Are they not obligated to honor it?"

Ren nodded. "Technically, yes, but business is a practical thing, Minister. If they cannot sell our goods, then they will not buy them from us. They cannot get the financing to do so from their bankers—bankers loan money in the expectation that it will be paid back, yes? There is an escape clause in the contract. We could dispute it in court, but it would take years, and we would probably not succeed, and it would also offend others in the industry, and thus prevent us from *ever* doing business in New York again. So, in practical terms there is no remedy."

"Is this a temporary thing? Surely this difficulty will pass, will it not?"

"Fang, we also do business in Italy, with the House of d'Alberto, a major trend-setter in European fashion. They also canceled their relationship with us. It seems that the Italian man our police killed comes from a powerful and influential family. Our representative in Italy says that no Chinese firm will be able to do business there for some time. In other words, Minister, that 'unfortunate incident' with the churchmen is going to have grave consequences."

"But these people have to purchase their cloth somewhere," Fang objected.

"Indeed they do. And they will do so in Thailand, Singapore, and Taiwan."

"Is that possible?"

Ren nodded quickly and sadly. "It is very possible. Sources have told me that they are busily contacting our former business partners to 'take up the slack,' as they put it. You see, the Taiwan government has launched an aggressive campaign to distinguish themselves from us, and it would appear that their campaign is, for the moment, highly successful."

"Well, Ren, surely you can find other customers for your goods," Fang suggested with confidence.

But the industrialist shook his head. He hadn't touched his tea and his eyes looked like wounds in a stone head. "Minister, America is the world's largest such market, and it appears it will soon be closed to us. After that is Italy, and that door, also, has been slammed shut. Paris, London, even the avant-garde marketers in Denmark and Vienna will not even return our phone calls. I've had my representatives contact all potential markets, and they all say the same thing: No one wants to do business with China. Only America could save us, but America will not."

"What will this cost you?"

"As I told you, one hundred forty million dollars just from the

Butterfly account alone, and another similar amount from our other American and European businesses."

Fang didn't have to think long to calculate the take the PRC's government got from that.

"Your colleagues?"

"I have spoken with several. The news is the same. The timing could hardly be worse. *All* of our contracts are coming due at the same time. We are talking *billions* of dollars, Minister. *Billions,"* he repeated.

Fang lit a cigarette. "I see," he said. "What would it take to fix this?"

"Something to make America happy, not just the government, but the citizens, too."

"Is that truly important?" Fang asked, somewhat tiredly. He'd heard this rubbish so many times from so many voices.

"Fang, in America people can buy their clothing from any number of stores and manufacturers, any number of marketers. The people choose which succeeds and which fails. Women's clothing in particular is an industry as volatile as vapor. It does not take much to make such a company fail. As a result, those companies will not assume additional and unnecessary risks. To do business with the People's Republic, now, today, is something they see as an unnecessary risk."

Fang took a drag and thought about that. It was, actually, something he'd always known, intellectually, but never quite appreciated. America *was* a different place, and it *did* have different rules. And since China wanted American money, China had to abide by those rules. That wasn't politics. That was practicality.

"So, you want me to do what?"

"Please, tell your fellow ministers that this could mean financial ruin for us. Certainly for my industry, and we are a valuable asset for our country. We bring wealth into China. If you want that wealth to spend on other things, then you must pay attention to what we need in order to get you that wealth." What Ren could not say was that he and his fellow industrialists were the ones who made the Politburo's economic (and therefore, also political) agenda possible, and that therefore the Politburo needed to listen to them once in a while. But Fang knew what the Politburo would say in reply. A horse may pull the cart, but you do not ask the horse where it wishes to go.

Such was political reality in the People's Republic of China. Fang knew that Ren had been around the world, that he had a sizable personal fortune which the PRC had graciously allowed him to accumulate, and that, probably more important, he had the intelligence and personal industry to thrive anywhere he chose to live. Fang knew also that Ren could fly to Taiwan and get financing to build a factory there, where he could employ others who looked and spoke Chinese, and he'd make money there *and* get some political influence in the bargain. Most of all, he knew that Ren knew this. Would he act upon it? Probably not. He was Chinese, a citizen of the mainland. This was *his* land, and he had no desire to leave it, else he would not be here now, pleading his case to the one minister—well, probably Qian Kun would listen also—whose ear might be receptive to his words. Ren was a patriot, but not a communist. What an odd duality that was . . .

Fang stood. This meeting had gone far enough. "I will do this, my friend," he told his visitor. "And I will let you know what develops."

"Thank you, Comrade Minister." Ren bowed and took his leave, not looking better, but pleased that someone had actually listened to him. Listening was not what one expected of Politburo members.

Fang sat back down and lit another cigarette, then reached for his tea. He thought for a minute or so. "Ming!" he called loudly. It took seven seconds by his watch.

"Yes, Minister?"

"What news articles do you have for me?" he asked. His secretary disappeared for another few seconds, then reappeared, holding a few pages.

"Here, Minister, just printed up. This one may be of particular interest."

'This one" was a cover story from *The Wall Street Journal.* "Major Shift in China Business?" it proclaimed. The question mark was entirely rhetorical, he saw in the first paragraph. Ren was right. He had to discuss this with the rest of the Politburo.

The second major item in Bondarenko's morning was observing tank gunnery. His men had the newest variant of the T-80UM main battle tank. It wasn't quite the newest T-99 that was just coming into production. This UM *did,* however, have a decent fire-control system, which was novel enough. The target range was about as simple as one could ask, large white cardboard panels with black tank silhouettes painted on them, and they were set at fixed, known ranges. Many of his gunners had never fired a live round since leaving gunnery school—such was the current level of training in the Russian Army, the general fumed.

Then he fumed some more. He watched one particular tank, firing at a target an even thousand meters away. It should have been mere spitting distance, but as he watched, first one, then two more, of the tracer rounds missed, all falling short, until the fourth shot hit high on the painted turret shape. With that feat accomplished, the tank shifted aim to a second target at twelve hundred meters and missed that one twice, before achieving a pinwheel in the geometric center of the target.

"Nothing wrong with that," Aliyev said next to him.

"Except that the tank and the crew were all dead ninety seconds ago!" Bondarenko observed, followed by a particularly vile oath. "Ever see what happens when a tank blows up? Nothing left of the crew but sausage! Expensive sausage."

"It's their first time in a live-fire exercise," Aliyev said, hoping to calm his boss down. "We have limited practice ammunition, and it's not as accurate as warshots."

"How many live rounds do we have?"

Aliyev smiled. "Millions." They had, in fact, warehouses full of the things, fabricated back in the 1970s.

"Then issue them," the general ordered.

"Moscow won't like it," the colonel warned. Warshots were, of course, far more expensive.

"I am not here to *please* them, Andrey Petrovich. I am here to *defend* them." And someday he'd meet the fool who'd decided to replace the tank's loader crewman with a machine. It was slower than a soldier, and removed a crewman who could assist in repairing damage. Didn't engineers ever consider that tanks were actually supposed to go into *battle?* No, this tank had been designed by a committee, as all Soviet weapons had been, which explained, perhaps, why so many of them didn't work—or, just as badly, didn't protect their users. Like putting the gas tank inside the *doors* of the BTR armored personnel carrier. Who ever thought that a crewman might want to bail out of a damaged vehicle and perhaps even survive to fight afoot? The tank's vulnerability had been the very first thing the Afghans had learned about Soviet mobile equipment . . . and how many Russian boys had burned to death because of it? *Well,* Bondarenko thought, *I have a new country now, and Russia* does *have talented engineers, and in a few years perhaps we can start building weapons worthy of the soldiers who carry them.*

"Andrey, is there anything in our command which does work?"

"That's why we're training, Comrade General." Bondarenko's service reputation was of an upbeat officer who looked for solutions rather than problems. His operations officer supposed that Gennady Iosifovich was overwhelmed by the scope of the difficulties, not yet telling himself that however huge a problem was, it had to be composed of numerous small ones which *could* be addressed one at a time. Gunnery, for example. Today, it was execrable. But in a week it would be much better, especially if they gave the troops real rounds instead of the practice ones. Real "bullets," as soldiers invariably called them, made you feel like a man instead of a schoolboy with his workbook. There was much to be said for that, and like many of the things his new boss was doing, it made good sense. In two weeks, they'd be watching more tank gunnery, and seeing more hits than misses.

CHAPTER 40

Fashion Statements

So, George?" Ryan asked.

"So, it's started. Turns out there are a ton of similar contracts coming due for the next season or something, plus Christmas toy contracts," SecTreas told his President. "And it's not just us. Italy, France, England, *everybody's* bugging out on them. The Chinese have made huge inroads into that industry, and they pissed off a lot of people in the process. Well, the chicken hasn't so much come home to roost as it's flown the coop, and that leaves our friends in Beijing holding the bag. It's a big bag, Jack. We're talking billions here."

"How badly will that hurt them?" SecState asked.

"Scott, I grant you it seems a little odd that the fate of a nation could ride on Victoria's Secret brassieres, but money is money. They need it, and all of a sudden there's a big hole in their current account. How big? Billions. It's going to make a hell of a bellyache for them."

"Any actual harm?" Ryan asked.

"Not my department, Jack," Winston answered. "That's Scott."

"Okay." Ryan turned his head to look at his other cabinet member.

"Before I can answer that, I need to know what net effect this will have on the Chinese economy."

Winston shrugged. "Theoretically, they could ride this out with minimal difficulties, but that depends on how they make up the shortfall. Their national industrial base is an incredibly muddled hodgepodge of private- and state-owned industries. The private ones are the efficient ones, of course, and the worst of the state-owned industries belong to their army. I've seen analyses of PLA operations that look like something out of *MAD magazine,* just impossible to credit on first reading. Soldiers don't generally know much about making things—they're better at breaking them—and tossing Marxism into the mix doesn't exactly help the situation. So, those 'enterprises' piss away vast quantities of cash. If they shut those down, or just cut them back, they could kiss this little shortfall off and move on—but they won't."

"That's right," Adler agreed. "The Chinese People's Liberation Army has a lot of political clout over there. The party controls it, but the tail wags the dog to a considerable extent. There's quite a bit of political and economic unrest over there. They need the army to keep things under control, and the PLA takes a big cut off the top of the national treasure because of that."

"The Soviets weren't like that," POTUS objected.

"Different country, different culture. Keep that in mind."

"Klingons," Ryan muttered, with a nod. "Okay, go on."

Winston took the lead. "We can't predict the impact this will have on their society without knowing how they're going to react to the cash shortfall."

"If they squeal when it starts to hurt, what do we do?" Ryan asked next.

"They're going to have to make nice, like reinstating the Boeing and Caterpillar orders, and doing it publicly."

"They won't—they can't," Adler objected. "Too much loss of face. Asian mind-set. That won't happen. They might offer us concessions, but they'll have to be hidden ones."

"Which is not politically acceptable to us. If I try to take *that* to Congress, first they'll laugh at me, then they'll crucify me." Ryan took a sip of his drink.

"And they won't understand why you can't tell Congress what to do. They think you're a strong leader, and therefore you're supposed to make decisions on your own," EAGLE informed his President.

"Don't they know *anything* about how our government works?" POTUS asked.

"Jack, I'm sure they have all sorts of experts who know more about the constitutional process than I do, but the Politburo members are not required to listen to them. They come from a very different political environment, and that's the one they understand. For us 'the people' means popular opinion, polls, and ultimately elections. For them, it means the peasants and workers who are supposed to do what they're told."

"We do business with these people?" Winston asked the ceiling.

"It's called realpolitik, George," Ryan explained.

"But we can't pretend they don't exist. There's over a billion of them, and, oh, by the way, they also have nuclear weapons, on ballistic launchers, even." Which added a decidedly unpleasant element to the overall equation.

"Twelve of them, according to CIA, and we can turn their country into a parking lot if we have to, just it'll take twenty-four hours instead of forty minutes," Ryan told his guests, managing not to get a chill when he said it. The possibility was too remote to make him nervous. "And they know that, and who wants to be the king of a parking lot? They *are* that rational, Scott, aren't they?"

"I think so. They rattle their saber at Taiwan, but not even much of that lately, not when we have Seventh Fleet there all the time." Which, however, burned up a lot of fuel oil for the Navy.

"Anyway, this cash problem won't actually cripple their economy?" Jack asked.

"I don't think so, unless they're pretty damned dumb."

"Scott, are they dumb?" Ryan asked State Department.

"Not that dumb—at least I don't think so," State told the President.

"Good, then I can go upstairs and have another drink." Ryan rose, and his guests did the same.

This is lunacy!" Qian Kun growled at Fang half a world away, discussing what turned out to be the same set of issues.

"I will not disagree with you, Qian, but we must make our case to the rest of our colleagues."

"Fang, this could mean ruin for us. With what shall we buy wheat and oil?"

"What are our reserves?"

The Finance Minister had to sit back and think about that one. He closed his eyes and tried to remember the numbers on which he got briefed the first Monday of every month. The eyes opened. "The harvest from last year was better than average. We have food for about a year—assuming an average harvest this year, or even a slightly short one. The immediate problem is oil. We've been using a lot of that lately, with the PLA's constant exercises up north and on the coast. In oil, we have perhaps four months in reserve, and the money to purchase another two months. After that, we will have to cut back our uses. Now, we are self-sufficient in coal, and so we'll have all the electricity we need. The lights will burn. The trains will run, but the PLA will be crippled." *Not that this is an entirely bad thing,* he didn't add. Both men acknowledged the value of the People's Liberation Army, but today it was really more of a domestic security service, like a large and well-armed police force, than a real guarantor of their national security, which had, really, no external threats to deal with.

"The army won't like that," Fang warned.

"I am not overly concerned with their likes and dislikes, Fang," the Finance Minister countered. "We have a country to bring out of the nineteenth century. We have industries to grow, and people to feed and employ. The ideology of our youth has not been as successful in bringing this about as we were educated to expect."

"Do you say that . . . ?"

Qian shifted in his chair. "Remember what Deng said? It doesn't matter if the cat is black or white as long as it catches mice. And Mao exiled him soon thereafter, and so today we have two hundred million more mouths to feed, but the only additional funds with which we do it came to us from the black cat, not the white one. We live in a practical world, Fang. I, too, have my copy of *The Little Red Book,* but I've never tried to eat it."

This former railroad engineer had been captured by his bureaucracy and his job, just like the last one had been—he'd died at the relatively young age of seventy-eight, before he could be expelled from his Politburo chair. Qian, a youthful sixty-six, would have to learn to watch his words, and his thoughts, more carefully. He was about to say so when Qian started speaking again.

"Fang, people like you and me, we must be able to speak freely to one another. We are not college students full of revolutionary zeal. We are men of years and knowledge, and we *must* have the ability to discuss issues frankly. We waste too much time in our meetings kneeling before Mao's cadaver. The man is *dead,* Fang. Yes, he was a great man, yes, he was a great leader for our people, but *no,* he *wasn't* the Lord Buddha, or

Jesus, or whatever. He was only a man, and he had ideas, and most of them were right, but some of them were wrong, some of them don't work. The Great Leap Forward accomplished nothing, and the Cultural Revolution, in addition to killing off undesirable intellectuals and troublemakers, also starved millions of our people to death, and that is not desirable, is it?"

"That is true, my young friend, but it is important how you present your ideas," Fang warned his junior, non-voting member of the Politburo. *Present them stupidly, and you'll find yourself counting rice bags on a collective farm.* He was a little old to go barefoot into the paddies, even as punishment for ideological apostasy.

"Will you support me?" Qian asked.

"I will try," was the halfhearted answer. He had to plead Ren He-Ping's case as well this day, and it wouldn't be easy.

They'd counted on the funds transfer at Qian's ministry. They had contracts to pay for. The tanker had long since been scheduled, because they were booked well in advance, and this carrier was just now coming alongside the loading pier off the coast of Iran. She'd load four hundred and fifty-six thousand tons of crude oil over a period of less than a day, then steam back out of the Persian Gulf, turn southeast for the passage around India, then transit the crowded Malacca Strait past Singapore and north to the huge and newly built oil terminal at Shanghai, where she'd spend thirty or forty hours offloading the cargo, then retrace her journey back to the Gulf for yet another load in an endless procession.

Except that the procession wasn't quite endless. It would end when the money stopped, because the sailors had to be paid, the debt on the tanker serviced, and most of all, the oil had to be bought. And it wasn't just one tanker. There were quite a few of them on the China run. A satellite focused on just that one segment of the world's oil trade would have seen them from a distance, looking like cars on a highway going to and from the same two points continuously. And like cars, they didn't have to go merely between those two places. There were other ports at which to load oil, and others at which to offload it, and to the crews of the tankers, the places of origin and destination didn't really matter very much, because almost all of their time was spent at sea, and the sea was always the same. Nor did it matter to the owners of the tankers, or the agents who did the chartering. What mattered was that they got paid for their time.

For this charter, the money had been wire-transferred from one account to another, and so the crew stood at their posts watching the loading process—monitoring it mainly by watching various dials and gauges; you couldn't see the oil going through the pipes, after all. Various crew members were on the beach to see to the victualing of their ship, and to visit the chandlers to get books and magazines to read, videocassette movies, and drink to go with the food, plus whatever consumable supplies had been used up on the inbound trip. A few crewmen looked for women whose charms might be rented, but that was an iffy business in Iran. None of them knew or thought very much about who paid for their services. Their job was to operate the ship safely and efficiently. The ship's officers mainly had their wives along, for whom the voyages were extended, if rather boring, pleasure cruises: Every modern tanker had a swimming pool and a deck for tanning, plus satellite TV for news and entertainment. And none of them particularly cared where the ship went, because for the women shopping was shopping, and any new port had its special charms.

This particular tanker, the *World Progress,* was chartered out of London, and had five more Shanghai runs scheduled until the charter ran out. The charter was paid, however, on a per-voyage basis, and the funds for this trip had been wired only seven days before. That was hardly a matter of concern for the owners or the ship's agent. After all, they were dealing with a nation-state, whose credit tended to be good. In due course, the loading was completed. A computerized system told the ship's first officer that the ship's trim was correct, and he so notified the master, who then told the chief engineer to wind up the ship's gas-turbine engines. This engine type made things easy, and in less than five minutes, the ship's power plant was fully ready for sea. Twenty minutes after that, powerful harbor tugs eased the ship away from the loading dock. This evolution is the most demanding for a tanker's crew, because only in confined waters is the risk of collision and serious damage quite so real. But within two hours, the tanker was under way under her own power, heading for the narrows at Bandar Abbas, and then the open sea.

"Yes, Qian," Premier Xu said tiredly. "Proceed."

"Comrades, at our last meeting I warned you of a potential problem of no small proportions. That problem is with us now, and it is growing larger."

"Are we running out of money, Qian?" Zhang Han San asked, with a barely concealed smirk. The answer amused him even more.

"Yes, Zhang, we are."

"How can a nation run out of money?" the senior Politburo member demanded.

"The same way a factory worker can, by spending more than he has. Another way is to offend his boss and lose his job. We have done both," Qian replied evenly.

"What 'boss' do we have?" Zhang inquired, with a disarming and eerie gentleness.

"Comrades, that is what we call trade. We sell our goods to others in return for money, and we use that money to purchase goods from those others. Since we are not peasants from ancient times bartering a pig for a sheep, we must use money, which is the means of international exchange. Our trade with America has generated an annual surplus on the order of seventy billion American dollars."

"Generous of the foreign devils," Premier Xu observed to Zhang *sotto voce.*

"Which we have almost entirely spent for various items, largely for our colleagues in the People's Liberation Army of late. Most of these are long-term purchase items for which advance payment was necessary, as is normal in the international arms business. To this, we must add oil and wheat. There are other things which are important to our economy, but we will concentrate on these for the moment." Qian looked around the table for approval. He got it, though Marshal Luo Cong, Defense Minister, and commander-in-chief of the People's Liberation Army—*and* lord of the PLA's sizable industrial empire—was now looking on with a gimlet eye. The expenditures of his personal empire had been singled out, and that was not calculated to please him.

"Comrades," Qian continued, "we now face the loss of much, perhaps most, of that trade surplus with America, and other foreign countries as well. You see these?" He held up a fistful of telexes and e-mail printouts. "These are cancellations of commercial business orders and funds transfers. Let me clarify. *These* are *billions* of lost dollars, money which in some cases we have already spent—but money we will never have because we have angered those with whom we do business."

"Do you tell me that they have such power over us? Rubbish!" another member observed.

"Comrade, they have the power to buy our trade goods for cash, or *not* buy them for cash. If they choose *not* to buy them, we do *not* get the money we need to spend for Marshal Luo's expensive toys." He used that word deliberately. It was time to explain the facts of life to these people, and a slap across the face was sure to get their attention. "Now, let us consider wheat. We use wheat to make bread and noodles. If you have no wheat, you have no noodles.

"Our country does not grow enough wheat to feed our people. We know this. We have too many mouths to feed. In a few months, the great producing countries, America, Canada, Australia, Argentina, and so forth, they will all have wheat to sell—but with what shall we buy it? Marshal Luo, your army needs oil to refine into diesel fuel and jet fuel, does it not? We need the same things for our diesel trains, and our airlines. But we cannot produce all the oil we need for our domestic needs, and so we must buy it from the Persian Gulf and elsewhere—again, with what shall we buy it?"

"So, sell our trade goods to someone else?" a member asked, *with rather surprising innocence,* Qian thought.

"Who else might there be, comrade? There is only one America. We have also offended all of Europe. Whom does that leave? Australia? They are allied to Europe and America. Japan? They also sell to America, and *they* will move to replace our lost markets, not to buy from us. South America, perhaps? Those are all Christian countries, and we just killed a senior Christian churchman, didn't we? Moreover, in *their* ethical world, he died heroically. We have not just killed. We have created a holy martyr to their faith!

"Comrades, we have deliberately structured our industry base to sell to the American market. To sell elsewhere, we would first have to determine what they need that we can make, and then enter the market. You don't just show up with a boatload of products and exchange it for cash on the dock! It takes time and patience to become a force in such a market. Comrades, we have cast away the work of *decades.* The money we are losing will not come back for years, and until then, we must learn to live our national life differently."

"What are you saying?" Zhang shot back.

"I am saying that the People's Republic faces economic ruin because two of our policemen killed those two meddling churchmen."

"That is not possible!"

"It is not possible, Zhang? If you offend the man who gives you money, then he will give you no more. Can you understand that? We've gone far out of our way to offend America, and then we offended all of Europe as well. We have made ourselves outcasts—they call *us* barbarians because of that unhappy incident at the hospital. I do not defend them, but I must tell you what *they* say and think. And as long as they say those things and think those things, it is we who will pay for the error."

"I refuse to believe this!" Zhang insisted.

"That is fine. You may come to my ministry and add up the numbers yourself." Qian was feeling full of himself, Fang saw. Finally, he had them listening to him. Finally, he had them thinking about his thoughts and his expertise. "Do you think I make this story up to tell in some country inn over rice wine?"

Then it was Premier Xu leaning forward and thinking aloud. "You have our attention, Qian. What can we do to avert this difficulty?"

Having delivered his primary message quickly and efficiently, Qian Kun didn't know what to say now. There *wasn't* a way to avert it that these men would accept. But having given them a brief taste of the harsh truth, now he had to give them some more:

"We need to change the perception of American minds. We need to show them that we are not what they consider barbarians. We have to transform our image in their eyes. For starters, we must make amends for the deaths of those two priests."

"Abase ourselves before the foreign devils? *Never!"* Zhang snarled.

"Comrade Zhang," Fang said, coming carefully to Qian's defense. "Yes, we are the Middle Kingdom, and no, we are not the barbarians. They are. But sometimes one must do business with barbarians, and that might mean understanding their point of view, and adapting to it somewhat."

"Humble ourselves before *them?"*

"Yes, Zhang. We need what they have, and to get it, we must be acceptable to them."

"And when they next demand that we make political changes, then what?" This was the premier, Xu, getting somewhat agitated, which was unusual for him.

"We face such decisions when and if they come," Qian answered, pleasing Fang, who didn't want to risk saying *that* himself.

"We cannot risk that," the Interior Minister, Tong Jie, responded, speaking for the first time. The police of the nation belonged to him, and he was responsible for civil order in the country—only if he failed would he call upon Marshal Luo, which would cause him both loss of face and loss of power at this table. In a real sense, the deaths of the two men had been laid at his place, for he had generated the formal orders on the suppression of religious activity in the PRC, increasing the harshness of law enforcement in order to increase the relative influence of his own ministry. "If the foreigners insist upon internal political changes, it could bring us all down."

And that was the core issue, Fang saw at once. The People's Republic rested absolutely upon the power of the party and its leaders, these men before him in this room. Like noblemen of old, each was attended by a trusted servant, sitting in the chairs against the wall, around the table, waiting for the order to fetch tea or water. Each had his rationale for power, whether it was Defense, or Interior, or Heavy Industry, or in his particular case, friendship and general experience. Each had labored long and hard to reach this point, and none of them relished the thought of losing what he had, any more than a provincial governor under the Ching Dynasty would have willingly reverted to being a mere mandarin, because that meant at least ignominy, and just as likely, death. These men knew that if a foreign country demanded and got internal political concessions, then their grip on power would loosen, and that was the one thing they dared not risk. They ruled the workers and peasants, and because of that, they also feared them. The noblemen of old could fall back upon the teachings of Confucius, or Buddha; on a spiritual foundation for their temporal power. But Marx and Mao had swept all that away, leaving only force as their defense. And if to maintain their country's prosperity they had to diminish that force, what would then happen? They didn't know, and these men feared the unknown as a child feared the evil monsters under his bed at night, but with far more reason. It had happened, right here in Beijing, not all that many years before. Not one of these men had forgotten it. To the public, they'd always shown steadfast determination. But each of them, alone in his bathroom before the mirror, or lying in bed at night before sleep came, had shown fear. Because though they basked in the devotion of the peasants and workers, somehow each of them knew that the peasants and workers might fear them, but also hated them. Hated them for their arrogance, their corruption, for their privilege, their better food, their luxurious housing, their personal servants. Their servants, they all knew, loathed them as well, behind smiles and bows of obeisance, which could just as easily conceal a dagger, because that's how the peasants and workers had felt about the nobles of a hundred years before. The revolutionaries had made use of that hatred against the class enemies of that age, and new ones, they all knew, could make use of the same silent rage against themselves. And so they would cling to power with the same desperation as the nobles of old, except they would show even more ruthlessness, because unlike the nobles of old, they had no place to run to. Their ideology had trapped them in their golden cages more surely than any religion could.

Fang had never before considered all of these thoughts *in toto.* Like the others, he'd worried a lot when the college students had demonstrated, building up their "goddess of liberty" out of plaster or papier-mâché—Fang didn't remember, though he did remember his sigh of relief when the PLA had destroyed it. It came as a surprise to him, the realization of how snared he was here in this place. The power he and his colleagues exercised was like something shown before a mirror that could be turned on them all instantly under the proper circumstances. They had immense power over every citizen in their country, but that power was all an illusion—

—and, no, they couldn't allow another country to dictate political practices to them, because their lives all depended on that illusion. It was like smoke on a calm day, seemingly a pillar to hold up the heavens, but the slightest wind could blow it all away, and then the heavens would fall. On them all.

But Fang also saw that there was no way out. If they didn't change to make America happy, then their country would run out of wheat and oil, and probably other things as well, and they would risk massive social change in a groundswell from below. But if to prevent that, they allowed some internal changes, they would just be inviting the same thing on themselves.

Which would kill them the more surely?

Did it matter? Fang asked himself. Either way, they'd be just as dead. He wondered idly how it would come, the fists of a mob, or bullets before a wall, or a rope. No, it would be bullets. That was how his country executed people. Probably preferable to the beheading sword of old. What if the swordsman missed his aim, after all? It must have been a horrid mess. He only had to look around the table to see that everyone here had similar thoughts, at least those with *enough* wit. All men feared the unknown, but now they had to choose which unknown to fear, and the choice was yet another thing to dread.

"So, Qian, you say we risk running out of things because we can no longer get the money we need to purchase them?" Premier Xu asked.

"That is correct," the Finance Minister confirmed.

"In what other ways could we get money and oil?" Xu asked next.

"That is not within my purview, Chairman," Qian answered.

"Oil is its own currency," Zhang said. "And there is ample oil to our north. There is also gold, and many other things we need. Timber in vast quantities. And that which we need most of all—space, living space for our people."

Marshal Luo nodded. "We have discussed this before."

"What do you mean?" Fang asked.

"The Northern Resource Area, our Japanese friends once called it," Zhang reminded them all.

"*That* adventure ended in disaster," Fang observed at once. "We were fortunate not to have been damaged by it."

"But we were not damaged at all," Zhang replied lightly. "We were not even implicated. We can be sure of that, can we not, Luo?"

"This is so. The Russians have never strengthened their southern defenses. They even ignore our exercises that have raised our forces to a high state of readiness."

"Can we be sure of that?"

"Oh, yes," the Defense Minister told them all. "Tan?" he asked.

Tan Deshi was the chief of the Ministry of State Security, in charge of the PRC's foreign and domestic intelligence services. One of the younger men here at seventy, he was probably the healthiest of them all, a nonsmoker and a very light imbiber of alcohol. "When we first began our increased exercises, they watched with concern, but after the first two years, they lost interest. We have over a million of our citizens living in eastern Siberia—it's illegal, but the Russians do not make much issue of it. A goodly number of them report to me. We have good intelligence of the Russian defenses."

"And what is their state of readiness?" Tong Jie asked.

"Generally, quite poor. They have one full-strength division, one at two-thirds, and the rest are hardly better than cadre-strength. Their new Far East commander, a General-Colonel Bondarenko, despairs of making things better, our sources tell us."

"Wait," Fang objected. "Are we discussing the possibility of war with Russia here?"

"Yes," Zhang Han San replied. "We have done this before."

"That is true, but on the first such occasion, we would have had Japan as an ally, and America neutralized. On the second, we assumed that Russia would have been broken up beforehand along religious lines. Who are our allies in this case? How has Russia been crippled?"

"We've been a little unlucky," Tan answered. "The chief minister—well, the chief adviser to their President Grushavoy is still alive."

"What do you mean?" Fang asked.

"I mean that our attempt to kill him misfired." Tan explained on for two minutes. The reaction around the table was one of mild shock.

"Tan had my approval," Xu told them calmly.

Fang looked over at Zhang Han San. That's where the idea must have originated. His old friend might have hated capitalists, but that didn't stop him from acting like the worst pirate when it suited his goals. And he had Xu's ear, and Tan as his strong right arm. Fang thought he knew all of these men, but now he saw that his assumption had been in error. In each was something hidden, and sinister. They were far more ruthless than he, Fang saw.

"That is an act of war," Fang objected.

"Our operational security was excellent. Our Russian agent, one Klementi Suvorov, is a former KGB officer we recruited ages ago when he was stationed here in Beijing. He's performed various functions for us for a long time and he has superb contacts within both their intelligence and military communities—that is, those segments of it that are now in the new Russian underworld. In fact he's a common criminal—a lot of the old KGB people have turned into that—but it works for us. He likes money, and for enough of it, he will do anything. Unfortunately in this case, a pure happenstance prevented the elimination of this Golovko person," Tan concluded.

"And now?" Fang asked. Then he cautioned himself. He was asking too many questions, taking too much of a personal position here. Even in this room, even with these old comrades, it didn't pay to stand out too far.

"And now, that is for the Politburo to decide," Tan replied blandly. It had to be affected, but was well acted in any case.

Fang nodded and leaned back, keeping his peace for the moment.

"Luo?" Xu asked. "Is this feasible?"

The Marshal had to guard his words as well, not to appear too confident. You could get in trouble around this table by promising more than you could deliver, though Luo was in the unique position—somewhat shared by Interior Minister Tong—of having guns behind him and his position.

"Comrades, we have long examined the strategic issue here. When Russia was the Soviet Union, this operation was not possible. Their military was much larger and better supported, and they had numerous intercontinental and theater ballistic missiles tipped with thermonuclear warheads. Now they have none, thanks to their bilateral agreement with America. Today, the Russian military is a shadow of what it was only ten or twelve years ago. Fully half of their draftees do not even report when called for service—if that happened here, we all know what would happen to the miscreants, do we not? They squandered much of their remaining combat power with their Chechen religious minority—and so, you might say that Russia is *already* splitting up along religious lines. In practical terms, the task is straightforward, if not entirely easy. The real difficulty facing us is distance and space, not actual military opposition. It's many kilometers from our border to their new oil field on the Arctic Ocean—much fewer to the new gold field. The best news of all is that the Russian army is itself building the roads we need to make the approach. It reduces our problems by two thirds right there. Their air force is a joke. We should be able to cope with it—they sell us their best aircraft, after all, and deny them to their own flyers. To make our task easier, we would do well to disrupt their command and control, their political stability and so forth. Tan, can you accomplish that?"

"That depends on what, exactly, is the task," Tan Deshi replied.

"To eliminate Grushavoy, perhaps," Zhang speculated. "He is the only person of strength in Russia at the moment. Remove him, and their country would collapse politically."

"Comrades," Fang had to say, taking the risk, "what we discuss here is bold and daring, but also fraught with danger. What if we fail?"

"Then, my friend, we are no worse off than we appear to be already," Zhang replied. "But if we succeed, as appears likely, we achieve the position for which we have striven since our youth. The People's Republic will become the foremost power in all the world." *As is our right,* he didn't have to add. "Chairman Mao never considered failing to destroy Chiang, did he?"

There was no arguing with that, and Fang didn't attempt it. The switchover from fear to adventurousness had been as abrupt as it was now becoming contagious. Where was the caution these men exercised so often? They were men on a floundering ship, and they saw a means of saving themselves, and having accepted the former proposition, they were catapulted into the latter. All he could do was lean back and watch the talk evolve, waiting—hoping—that reason would break out and prevail.

But from whom would it come?

CHAPTER 41

Plots of State

"Yes, Minister?" Ming said, looking up from her almost-completed notes.

"You are careful with these notes, aren't you?"

"Certainly, Comrade Minister," she replied at once. "I never even print these documents up, as you well know. Is there a concern?"

Fang shrugged. The stresses of today's meeting were gradually bleeding off. He was a practical man of the world, and he was an elderly man. If there was a way to deal with the current problem, he would find it. If there wasn't, then he would endure. He always had. He was not the one taking the lead here, and his notes would show that he was one of the few cautious skeptics at the meeting. One of the others, of course, was Qian Kun, who'd walked out of the room shaking his head and muttering to his senior aide. Fang then wondered if Qian was keeping notes. It would have been a good move. If things went badly, those could be his only defense. At this level of risk, the hazard wasn't relegation to a menial job, but rather having one's ashes scattered in the river.

"Ming?"

"Yes, Minister?"

"What did you think of the students in the square all those years ago?"

"I was only in school then myself, Minister, as you know."

"Yes, but what did you think?"

"I thought they were reckless. The tallest tree is always the first to be cut down." It was an ancient Chinese adage, and therefore a safe thing to say. Theirs was a culture that discouraged taking such action—

but perversely, their culture also lionized those who'd had the courage to do so. As with every human tribe, the criterion was simple. If you succeeded, then you were a hero, to be remembered and admired. If you failed, nobody would remember you anyway, except, perhaps, as a negative example. And so safety lay always in the middle course, and in safety was life.

The students had been too young to know all that. Too young to accept the idea of death. The bravest soldiers were always the young ones, those spirits of great passions and beliefs, those who had not lived long enough to reflect on what shape the world took when it turned against you, those too foolish to know fear. For children, the unknown was something you spent almost all your time exploring and finding out. Somewhere along the line, you discovered that you'd learned all that was safe to learn, and that's where most men stopped, except for the very few upon whom progress depended, the brave ones and the bold ones who walked with open eyes into the unknown, and humanity remembered those few who came back alive . . .

. . . and soon enough forgot those who did not.

But it was the substance of history to remember those who did, and the substance of Fang's society to remind them of those who didn't. Such a strange dichotomy. *What societies,* he wondered, *encourage people to seek out the unknown? How did they do? Did they thrive, or did they blunder about in the darkness and lose their substance in aimless, undirected wanderings?* In China, everyone followed the words and thoughts of Marx, as modified by Mao, because he had boldly walked into the darkness and returned with revolution, and changed the path of his nation. But there things had stopped, because no one was willing to proceed beyond the regions Mao had explored and illuminated—and proclaimed to be all that China and the world in general needed to know about. *Mao was like some sort of religious prophet, wasn't he?* Fang reflected.

. . . Hadn't China just killed a couple of those?

"Thank you, Ming," he told her, waiting there for his next order. He didn't see her close the door as she went to her desk to transcribe the notes of this Politburo meeting.

Dear God," Dr. Sears whispered at his desk. As usual, the SORGE document had been printed up on the DDO's laser jet and handed over to him, and he'd walked back to his office to do the translation. Sometimes the documents were short enough to translate standing in front of her desk, but this one was pretty long. It was, in fact, going to take eight line-and-a-half-spaced pages off *his* laser printer. He took his time on this because of its content. He rechecked his translation. Suddenly he had doubts about his understanding of the Chinese language. He couldn't afford to mistranslate or misrepresent this sort of thing. It was just too hot. All in all, he took two and a half hours, more than double what Mrs. Foley probably expected, before he walked back.

"What took so long?" MP asked when he returned.

"Mrs. Foley, this is hot."

"How hot?"

"Magma," Sears said, as he handed the folder across.

"Oh?" She took the pages and leaned back in her comfortable chair to read it over. SORGE, source SONGBIRD. Her eyes cataloged the heading, yesterday's meeting of the Chinese Politburo. Then Sears saw it. Saw her eyes narrow as her hand reached for a butterscotch. Then her eyes shifted to him. "You weren't kidding. Evaluation?"

"Ma'am, I can't evaluate the accuracy of the source, but if this is for real, well, then we're looking in on a process I've never seen before outside history books, and hearing words that nobody has ever heard in this building—not that I've ever heard about, anyway. I mean, every minister in their government is quoted there, and most of them are saying the same thing—"

"And it's not something we want them to say," Mary Patricia Foley concluded his statement. "Assuming this is all accurately reported, does it feel real?"

Sears nodded. "Yes, ma'am. It sounds to me like real conversation by real people, and the content tracks with the personalities as I know them. Could it be fabricated? Yes, it could. If so, the source has been compromised in some way or other. However, I don't see that this could be faked without their wanting to produce a specific effect, and that would be an effect which would not be overly attractive to them."

"Any recommendations?"

"It might be a good idea to get George Weaver down from Providence," Sears replied. "He's good at reading their minds. He's met a lot of them face-to-face, and he'll be a good backup for my evaluation."

"Which is?" Mary Pat asked, not turning to the last page, where it would be printed up.

"They're considering war."

The Deputy Director (Operations) of the Central Intelligence Agency stood and walked out her door, with Dr. Joshua Sears right behind her. She took the short walk to her husband's office and went through the door without even looking at Ed's private secretary.

Ed Foley was having a meeting with the Deputy Director (Science and Technology) and two of his senior people when MP walked in. He looked up in surprise, then saw the blue folder in her hand. "Yeah, honey?"

"Excuse me, but this can't wait even one minute." Her tone of voice told as much as her words did.

"Frank, can we get together after lunch?"

"Sure, Ed." DDS&T gathered his documents and his people and headed out.

When they were gone and the door closed, the DCI asked, "SORGE?"

Mary Pat just nodded and handed the folder across, taking a seat on the couch. Sears remained standing. It was only then that he realized his hands were a little moist. That hadn't happened to him before. Sears, as head of the DI's Office of China Assessments, worked mainly on political evaluations: who was who in the PRC's political hierarchy, what economic policies were being pursued—the Society Page for the People's Republic, as he and his people thought of it, and joked about it over lunch in the cafeteria. He'd never seen anything like this, nothing hotter than handling internal dissent, and while their methods for handling such things tended to be a little on the rough side, as he often put it—mainly it meant summary execution, which was more than a *little* on the rough side for those affected—the distances involved helped him to take a more detached perspective. But not on this.

"Is this for real?" the DC asked.

"Dr. Sears thinks so. He also thinks we need to get Weaver down from Brown University."

Ed Foley looked over at Sears. "Call him. Right now."

"Yes, sir." Sears left the room to make the call.

"Jack has to see this. What's he doing now?"

"He's leaving for Warsaw in eight hours, remember? The NATO meeting, the photo opportunity at Auschwitz, stopping off at London on the way home for dinner at Buckingham Palace. Shopping on Bond Street," Ed added. There were already a dozen Secret Service people in London working with the Metropolitan Police and MI-5, properly known as the Security Service. Twenty more were in Warsaw, where security concerns were not all that much of an issue. The Poles were very happy with America right now, and the leftover police agencies from the communist era still kept files on everyone who might be a problem. Each would have a personal baby-sitter for the entire time Ryan was in country. The NATO meeting was supposed to be almost entirely ceremonial, a basic feel-good exercise to make a lot of European politicians look pretty for their polyglot constituents.

"Jesus, they're talking about making a move on Grushavoy!" Ed Foley gasped, getting to page three. "Are they totally off their fuckin' rockers?"

"Looks like they found themselves in a corner unexpectedly," his wife observed. "We may have overestimated their political stability."

Foley nodded and looked up at his wife. "Right now?"

"Right now," she agreed.

Her husband lifted his phone and punched speed-dial #1.

"Yeah, Ed, what is it?" Jack Ryan asked.

"Mary and I are coming over."

"When?"

"Now."

"That important?" the President asked.

"This is CRITIC stuff, Jack. You'll want Scott, Ben, and Arnie there, too. Maybe George Winston. The foundation of the issue is his area of expertise."

"China?"

"Yep."

"Okay, come on over." Ryan switched phones. "Ellen, I need SecState, SecTreas, Ben, and Arnie in my office, thirty minutes from right now."

"Yes, Mr. President," his secretary acknowledged. This sounded hot, but Robby Jackson was on his way out of town again, to give a speech in Seattle, at the Boeing plant of all places, where the workers and the management wanted to know about the 777 order to China. Robby didn't have much to say on that point, and so he'd talk about the importance of human rights and America's core beliefs and principles, and all that wave-the-flag stuff. The Boeing people would be polite about it, and it was hard to be impolite to a black man, especially one with Navy Wings of Gold on his lapel, and learning to handle this political bullshit was Robby's main task. Besides, it took pressure off Ryan, and that was Jackson's primary mission in life, and oddly enough, one which he accepted with relative equanimity. So, his VC-20B would be over Ohio right about now, Jack thought. Maybe Indiana. Just then Andrea came in.

"Company coming?" Special Agent Price-O'Day asked. She looked a little pale, Jack thought.

"The usual suspects. You feeling okay?" the President asked.

"Stomach is a little upset. Too much coffee with breakfast."

Morning sickness? Ryan wondered. If so, too bad. Andrea tried so hard to be one of the boys. Admitting this female failing would scar her soul as though from a flamethrower. He couldn't say anything about it. Maybe Cathy could. It was a girl thing.

"Well, the DCI's coming over with something he says is important. Maybe they've changed the toilet paper in the Kremlin, as we used to say at Langley back when I worked there."

"Yes, sir." She smiled. Like most Secret Service agents, she'd seen the people and the secrets come and go, and if there were important things for her to know, she'd find out in due course.

General-Lieutenant Kirillin liked to drink as much as most Russians, and that was quite a lot by American standards. The difference between Russians and Brits, Chavez had learned, was that the Brits drank just as much, but they did it with beer, while the Russians made do with vodka. Ding was neither a Mormon nor a Baptist, but he was over his capacity here. After two nights of keeping up with the local Joneses, he'd nearly died on the morning run with his team, and only avoided falling out for fear of losing face before the Russian Spetsnaz people they were teaching to come up to Rainbow standards. Somehow he'd managed not to puke, though he had allowed Eddie Price to take charge of the first two classes that day while he'd wandered off to drink a gallon of water to chase down three aspirins. Tonight, he'd decided, he'd cut off the vodkas at two . . . maybe three.

"How are our men doing?" the general asked.

"Just fine, sir," Chavez answered. "They like their new weapons, and they're picking up on the doctrine. They're smart. They know how to think before they act."

"Does this surprise you?"

"Yes, General, it does. It was the same for me once, back when I was a squad sergeant in the Ninjas. Young soldiers tend to think with their dicks rather than their brains. I learned better, but I had to learn it the hard way in the field. It's sometimes a lot easier to get yourself into trouble than it is to think yourself out of it. Your Spetsnaz boys started off that way, but if you show them the right way, they listen pretty good. Today's exercise, for example. We set it up with a trap, but your captain stopped short on the way in and thought it through before he committed, and he passed the test. He's a good team leader, by the way. I'd say bump him to major." Chavez hoped he hadn't just put the curse of hell on the kid, realizing that praise from a CIA officer wasn't calculated to be career-enhancing for a Russian officer.

"He's my nephew. His father married my sister. He's an academician, a professor at Moscow State University."

"His English is superb. I'd take him for a native of Chicago." And so Captain Leskov had probably been talent-scouted by KGB or its successor agency. Language skills of that magnitude didn't just happen.

"He was a parachutist before they sent him to Spetsnaz," Kirillin went on, "a good light-infantryman."

"That's what Ding was, once upon a time," Clark told the Russian.

"Seventh Light Infantry. They de-established the division after I left. Seems like a long time now."

"How did you go from the American army into CIA?"

"His fault," Chavez answered. "John spotted me and foolishly thought I had potential."

"We had to clean him up and send him to school, but he's worked out pretty well—even married my daughter."

"He's still getting used to having a Latino in the family, but I made him a grandfather. Our wives are back in Wales."

"So, how did you emerge from CIA into Rainbow?"

"My fault, again," Clark admitted. "I did a memo, and it perked to the top, and the President liked it, and he knows me, and so when they set the outfit up, they put me in charge of it. I wanted Domingo here to be part of it, too. He's got young legs, and he shoots okay."

"Your operations in Europe were impressive, especially at the park in Spain."

"Not our favorite. We lost a kid there."

"Yeah," Ding confirmed with a tiny sip of his drink. "I was fifty yards away when that bastard killed Anna. Homer got him later on. Nice shot it was."

"I saw him shoot two days ago. He's superb."

"Homer's pretty good. Went home last fall on vacation and got himself a Dall sheep at eight hundred–plus yards up in Idaho. Hell of a trophy. He made it into the Boone and Crockett book in the top ten."

"He should go to Siberia and hunt tiger. I could arrange that," Kirillin offered.

"Don't say that too loud." Chavez chuckled. "Homer will take you up on it."

"He should meet Pavel Petrovich Gogol," Kirillin went on.

"Where'd I hear that name?" Clark wondered at once.

"The gold mine," Chavez handled the answer.

"He was a sniper in the Great Patriotic War. He has two gold stars for killing Germans, and he's killed hundreds of wolves. There aren't many like him left."

"Sniper on a battlefield. The hunting must get real exciting."

"Oh, it is, Domingo. It is. We had a guy in Third SOG who was good at it, but he damned near got his ass killed half a dozen times. You know—" John Clark had a satellite beeper, and it started vibrating in his belt. He picked it up and checked the number. "Excuse me," he said and looked for a good place. The Moscow officers' club had a courtyard, and he headed for it.

What does this mean?" Arnie van Damm asked. The executive meeting had started with copies of the latest SORGE/SONGBIRD being passed out. Arnie was the fastest reader of the group, but not the best strategic observer.

"It doesn't mean anything good, pal," Ryan observed, turning to the third page.

"Ed," Winston asked, looking up from page two. "What can you tell me about the source? This looks like the insider-trading document from hell."

"A member of the Chinese Politburo keeps notes on his conversations with the other ministers. We have access to those notes, never mind how."

"So, this document and the source are both genuine?"

"We think so, yes."

"How reliable?" TRADER persisted.

The DCI decided to take a long step out on a thin limb. "About as reliable as one of your T-bills."

"Okay, Ed, you say so." And Winston's head went back down. In ten seconds, he muttered, "Shit . . ."

"Oh, yeah, George," POTUS agreed. " 'Shit' about covers it."

"Concur, Jack," SecState agreed.

Of those present, only Ben Goodley managed to get all the way through it without a comment. For his part, Goodley, for all the status and importance that came from his job as the President's National Security Adviser, felt particularly junior and weak at the moment. Mainly he knew that he was far the President's inferior in knowledge of national-security affairs, that he was in his post mainly as a high-level secretary. He was a carded National Intelligence Officer, one of whom, by law and custom, accompanied the President everywhere he went. His job was to convey information to the President. Former occupants of his corner office in the West Wing of the White House had often told their presidents what to think and what to do. But he was just an information-conveyor, and at the moment, he felt weak even in that diminished capacity.

Finally, Jack Ryan looked up with blank eyes and a vacant face. "Okay. Ed, Mary Pat, what do we have here?"

"It looks as if Secretary Winston's predictions on the financial consequences of the Beijing Incident might be coming true."

"They're talking about precipitous consequences," Scott Adler observed coolly. "Where's Tony?"

"Secretary Bretano's down at Fort Hood, Texas, looking at the heavy troopers at Third Corps. He gets back late tonight. If we yank him back in a hurry, people will notice," van Damm told the rest.

"Ed, will you object if we get this to him, secure?"

"No."

"Okay." Ryan nodded and reached across his desk for his phone. "Send Andrea in, please." That took less than five seconds.

"Yes, Mr. President?"

"Could you walk this over to Signals, and have them TAPDANCE it to THUNDER?" He handed her the document. "Then please bring it back here?"

"Yes, sir."

"Thanks, Andrea," Ryan told the disappearing form. Then he took a drink of water and turned to his guests. "Okay, it looks pretty serious. How serious is it?"

"We're bringing Professor Weaver down from Brown to evaluate it for us. He's about the best guy in the country for reading their minds."

"Why the hell doesn't he work for me?" Jack asked.

"He likes it at Brown. He comes from Rhode Island. We've offered him a job across the river half a dozen times that I know of," DCI Foley told Ryan, "but he always says the same thing."

"Same at State, Jack. I've known George for fifteen years or more. He doesn't want to work for the government."

"Your kind of man, Jack," Arnie added for a little levity.

"Besides, he can make more money as a contractor, can't he? Ed, when he comes down, make sure he comes in to see me."

"When? You're flying out in a few hours," Ed pointed out.

"Shit." Ryan remembered it now. Callie Weston was just finishing up the last of his official speeches in her office across the street. She was even coming across on Air Force One with the official party. Why was it that you couldn't deal with things one at a time? Because at this level, they just didn't arrive that way.

"All right," Jack said next. "We need to evaluate how serious this is, and then figure a way to forestall it. That means—what?"

"One of several things. We can approach them quietly," SecState Adler said. "You know, tell them that this has gone too far, and we want to work with them on the sly to ameliorate the situation."

"Except Ambassador Hitch is over here now, consulting, remember? Where's he doing it today, Congressional or Burning Tree?" POTUS asked. Hitch enjoyed golf, a hobby he could hardly pursue in Beijing. Ryan could sympathize. He was lucky to get in one round a week, and what swing he'd once had was gone with the wind.

"The DCM in Beijing is too junior for something like this. No matter what we said through him, they wouldn't take it seriously enough."

"And what, exactly, could we give them?" Winston asked. "There's nothing big enough to make them happy that we could keep quiet. They'd have to give us something so that we could justify giving them anything, and from what I see here, they don't want to give us anything but a bellyache. We're limited in our action by what the country will tolerate."

"You think they'd tolerate a shooting war?" Adler snapped.

"Be cool, Scott. There are practical considerations. Anything juicy enough to make these Chinese bastards happy has to be approved by Congress, right? To get such a concession through Congress would mean giving them the justification for it." Winston waved the secret document in his hand. "But we can't do that because Ed here would have a fit, and even if we did, somebody on the Hill would leak it to the papers in a New York minute, and half of them would call it danegeld, and say fuck the Chinks, millions for defense but not one penny for tribute. Am I right?"

"Yes," Arnie answered. "The other half would call it responsible statesmanship, but the average Joe out there wouldn't much like it. The average citizen would expect you to call Premier Xu on the phone and say, 'Better not do this, buddy,' and expect it to stick."

"Which would, by the way, kill SONGBIRD," Mary Pat added as a warning, lest they take that option seriously. "That would end a human life, and deny us further information that we need to have. And from my reading of this report, Xu would deny everything and just keep going forward. They really think they're in a corner, but they can't see a way to smart themselves out of it."

"The danger is . . . ?" TRADER asked.

"Internal political collapse," Ryan explained. "They're afraid that if anything upsets the political or economic conditions inside the country, the whole house of cards comes tumbling down. With serious consequences for the current royal family of the PRC."

"Called the chop." Ben Goodley had to say something, and that was an easy one. "Actually a rifle bullet today." It didn't help him feel much better. He was out of his depth and he knew it.

That's when the President's STU rang. It was SecDef Tony Bretano, THUNDER. "Yeah," Ryan said. "Putting you on speaker, Tony. Scott, George, Arnie, Ed, Mary Pat, and Ben are here, and we just read what you got."

"I presume this is real?"

"Real as hell," Ed Foley told the newest member of the SORGE/SONGBIRD chorus.

"This is worrisome."

"On that we are agreed, Tony. Where are you now?"

"Standing on top of a Bradley in the parking lot. Never seen so many tanks and guns in my life. Feels like real power here."

"Yeah, well, what you just read shows you the limits of our power."

"So I gather. If you want to know what I think we should do about it—well, make it clear to them somehow that this would be a really bad play for them."

"How do we do that, Tony?" Adler asked.

"Some animals—the puffer fish, for example. When threatened, it swallows a gallon of water and expands its size—makes it look too big to eat."

Ryan was surprised to hear that. He'd no idea that Bretano knew anything about animals. He was a physics and science guy. Well, maybe he watched the Discovery Channel like everyone else.

"Scare them, you mean?"

"Impress them, better way of putting it."

"Jack, we're going to Warsaw—we can let Grushavoy know about this . . . how about we invite him into NATO? The Poles are there already. It would commit all of Europe to come to Russia's defense in the event of an invasion. I mean, that's what alliances and mutual-defense treaties are all about. 'You're not just messing with me, Charlie. You're messing with all my friends, too.' It's worked for a long time."

Ryan considered that one, and looked around the room. "Thoughts?"

"It's something," Winston thought.

"But what about the other NATO counties? Will they buy into this? The whole purpose of NATO," Goodley reminded them, "was to protect them from the Russians."

"The Soviets," Adler corrected. "Not the same thing anymore, remember?"

"The same people, the same language, sir," Goodley persisted. He felt pretty secure on this one. "What you propose is an elegant possible solution to the present problem, but to make it happen we'd have to share SORGE with other countries, wouldn't we?" The suggestion made the Foleys both wince. There were few things on the planet as talkative as a chief of government.

"What the hell, we've been watching their military with overheads for a long time. We can say that we're catching stuff there that makes us nervous. Good enough for the unwashed," the DCI offered.

"Next, how do we persuade the Russians?" Jack wondered aloud. "This could be seen in Moscow as a huge loss of face."

"We have to explain the problem to them. The danger is to their country, after all," Adler pronounced.

"But they're not unwashed. They'll want to know chapter and verse, and it is *their* national security we're talking about here," Goodley added.

"You know who's in Moscow now?" Foley asked POTUS.

"John?"

"RAINBOW SIX. John and Ding both know Golovko, and he's Grushavoy's number-one boy. It's a nice, convenient back channel. Note that this also confirms that the Moscow rocket was aimed at him. Might not make Sergey Nikolay'ch feel better, but he'd rather know than guess."

"Why can't those stupid fucking people just say they're sorry they shot those two people?" Ryan wondered crossly.

"Why do you think pride is one of the Seven Deadly Sins?" the DCI asked in reply.

Clark's portable phone was a satellite type with a built-in encryption system, really just a quarter-inch-thick plastic pad that actually made the phone easier to cradle against his shoulder. Like most such phones, it took time to synchronize with its companion on the other end, the task made harder by the delay inherent in the use of satellites.

"Line is secure," the synthetic female voice said finally.

"Who's this?"

"Ed Foley, John. How's Moscow?"

"Pleasant. What gives, Ed?" John asked. The DCI didn't call from D.C. on a secure line to exchange pleasantries.

"Get over to the embassy. We have a message we want you to deliver."

"What sort?"

"Get to the embassy. It'll be waiting. Okay?"

"Roger. Out." John killed the phone and walked back inside.

"Anything important?" Chavez asked.

"We have to go to the embassy to see somebody," Clark replied, simulating anger at the interruption of his quiet time of the day.

"See you tomorrow then, Ivan and Domingo," Kirillin saluted them with his glass.

"What gives?" Chavez asked from thirty feet away.

"Not sure, but it was Ed Foley who paged me."

"Something important?"

"I guess we'll just have to wait and see."

"Who drives?"

"Me." John knew Moscow fairly well, having learned it first on missions in the 1970s that he was just as happy to forget about, when his daughters had been the age of his new grandson.

The drive took twenty minutes, and the hard part turned out to be persuading the Marine guard that they really were entitled to come inside after normal business hours. To this end, the man waiting for them, Tom Barlow, proved useful. The Marines knew him, and he knew them, and that made everything okay, sort of.

"What's the big deal?" Jack asked, when they got to Barlow's office.

"This." He handed the fax across, a copy to each. "Might want to take a seat, guys."

"Madre de Dios," Chavez gasped thirty seconds later.

"Roger that, Domingo," his boss agreed. They were reading a hastily laundered copy of the latest SORGE dispatch.

"We got us a source in Beijing, 'mano."

"Hang a big roger on that one, Domingo. And we're supposed to share the take with Sergey Nikolay'ch. Somebody back home is feeling real ecumenical."

"Fuck!" Chavez observed. Then he read on a little. "Oh, yeah, I see. This does make some sense."

"Barlow, we have a phone number for our friend?"

"Right here." The CIA officer handed over a Post-it note and pointed to a phone. "He'll be out at his dacha, out in the Lenin Hills. They haven't changed the name yet. Since he found out he was the target, he's gotten a little more security-conscious."

"Yeah, we've met his baby-sitter, Shelepin," Chavez told Barlow. "Looks pretty serious."

"He'd better be. If I read this right, he might be called up to bat again, or maybe Grushavoy's detail."

"Is this for real?" Chavez had to wonder. "I mean, this is *casus belli* stuff."

"Well, Ding, you keep saying that international relations is two countries fucking each other." Then he dialed the phone. "Tovarisch Golovko," he told the voice that answered it, adding in Russian, "It's Klerk, Ivan Sergeyevich. That'll get his attention," John told the other two.

"Greetings, Vanya," a familiar voice said in English. "I will not ask how you got this number. What can I do for you?"

"Sergey, we need to see you at once on an important matter."

"What sort of matter?"

"I am the mailman, Sergey. I have a message to deliver to you. It is worthy of your attention. Can Domingo and I see you this evening?"

"Do you know how to get here?"

Clark figured he'd find his way out to the woods. "Just tell the people at the gate to expect two capitalist friends of Russia. Say about an hour from now?"

"I will be waiting."

"Thank you, Sergey." Clark replaced the phone. "Where's the piss-parlor, Barlow?"

"Down the hall on the right."

The senior field intelligence officer folded the fax and tucked it into his coat pocket. Before having a talk about something like this, he needed a bathroom.

CHAPTER 42

Birch Trees

They drove into the sunset, west from the Russian capital. Traffic had picked up in Moscow since his last real adventure here, and you could use the center lane in the wide avenues. Ding handled navigation with a map, and soon they were beyond the ring roads around the Russian capital and entering the hills that surrounded the city. They passed a memorial which neither had ever seen before, three huge—

"What the hell is that?" Ding asked.

"This is as close as the Germans got in 1941," John explained. "This is where they stopped 'em."

"What do you call those things?" "Those things" were immense steel I-beams, three of them welded at ninety-degree angles to look like enormous jacks.

"Hedgehogs, but in the SEALs we called 'em horned scullies. Hard to drive a tank over one," Clark told his younger partner.

"They take their history serious here, don't they?"

"You would, too, if you stopped somebody who wanted to erase your country right off the map, sonny. The Germans were pretty serious back then, too. It was a very nasty war, that one."

"Guess so. Take the next right, Mr. C."

Ten minutes later, they were in a forest of birch trees, as much a part of the Russian soul as vodka and borscht. Soon thereafter they came to a guard shack. The uniformed guard held an AK-74 and looked surprisingly grim. *Probably briefed on the threat to Golovko and others,* John imagined. But he'd also been briefed on who was authorized to pass, and they only had to show their passports to get cleared, the guard also giving them directions about which country lane to take.

"The houses don't look too bad," Chavez observed.

"Built by German POWs," John told him. "Ivan doesn't exactly like the Germans very much, but he does respect their workmanship. These were built for the Politburo members, mainly after the war, probably. There's our place."

It was a wood-frame house, painted brown and looking like a cross between a German country house and something from an Indiana farm, Clark thought. There were guards here, too, armed and walking around. *They'd been called from the first shack,* John figured. One of them waved. The other two stood back, ready to cover the first one if something untoward happened.

"You are Klerk, Ivan Sergeyevich?"

"Da," John answered. "This is Chavez, Domingo Stepanovich."

"Pass, you are expected," the guard told them.

It was a pleasant evening. The sun was down now, and the stars were making their appearance in the sky. There was also a gentle westerly breeze, but Clark thought he could hear the ghosts of war here. Hans von Kluge's panzer grenadiers, men wearing the *feldgrau* of the Wehrmacht. World War II on this front had been a strange conflict, like modern TV wrestling. No choice between good and bad, but only between bad and worse, and on that score it had been six-five and pick 'em. But their host probably wouldn't see history that way, and Clark had no intention of bringing up the subject.

Golovko was there, standing on the sheltered porch by the furniture, dressed casually. Decent shirt, but no tie. He wasn't a tall man, about halfway between Chavez and himself in height, but the eyes always showed intelligence, and now they also showed interest. He was curious about the purpose of this meeting, as well he might be.

"Ivan Sergeyevich," Golovko said in greeting. Handshakes were exchanged, and the guests conducted inside. Mrs. Golovko, a physician, was nowhere in evidence. Golovko first of all served vodka, and directed them to seats.

"You said you had a message for me." The language for this meeting was to be English, John saw.

"Here it is." Clark handed the pages across.

"Spasiba." Sergey Nikolay'ch sat back in his chair and started to read.

He would have been a fine poker player, John thought. His face changed not at all through the first two pages. Then he looked up.

"Who decided that I needed to see this?" he asked.

"The President," Clark answered.

"Your Ryan is a good comrade, Vanya, and an honorable man." Golovko paused. "I see you have improved your human-intelligence capabilities at Langley."

"That's probably a good supposition, but I know nothing of the source here, Chairman Golovko," Clark answered.

"This is, as you say, hot."

"It is all of that," John agreed, watching him turn another page.

"Son of a bitch!" Golovko observed, finally showing some emotion.

"Yeah, that's about what I said," Chavez entered the conversation.

"They are well-informed. This does not surprise me. I am sure they have ample espionage assets in Russia," Golovko observed, with anger creeping into his voice. "But this is—this is naked aggression they discuss."

Clark nodded. "Yep, that's what it appears to be."

"This is genuine information?" Golovko asked.

"I'm just the mailman, Chairman," Clark replied. "I vouch for nothing here."

"Ryan is too good a comrade to play agent provocateur. This is madness." And Golovko was telling his guests that he had no good intelligence assets in the Chinese Politburo, which actually surprised John. It wasn't often that CIA caught the Russians short at anything. Golovko looked up. "We once had a source for such information, but no longer."

"I've never worked in that part of the world, Chairman, except long ago when I was in the Navy." And the Chinese part of that, he didn't explain, was mainly getting drunk and laid in Taipei.

"I've traveled to Beijing several times in a diplomatic capacity, not recently. I cannot say that I've ever really understood those people." Golovko finished reading the document and set it down. "I can keep this?"

"Yes, sir," Clark replied.

"Why does Ryan give us this?"

"I'm just the delivery boy, Sergey Nikolay'ch, but I should think the motive is in the message. America does not wish to see Russia hurt."

"Decent of you. What concessions will you require?"

"None that I am aware of."

"You know," Chavez observed, "sometimes you just want to be a good neighbor."

"At this level of statecraft?" Golovko asked skeptically.

"Why not? It does not serve American interests to see Russia crippled and robbed. How big are these mineral finds, anyway?" John asked.

"Immense," Golovko replied. "I'm not surprised you've learned of them. Our efforts at secrecy were not serious. The oil field is one to rival the Saudi reserves, and the gold mine is very rich indeed. Potentially, these finds could save our economy, could make us a truly wealthy nation and a fit partner for America."

"Then you know why Jack sent this over. It's a better world for both of us if Russia prospers."

"Truly?" Golovko was a bright man, but he'd grown up in a world in which both America and Russia had often wished each other dead. Such thoughts died hard, even in so agile a mind as his.

"Truly," John confirmed. "Russia is a great nation, and you are great people. You *are* fit partners for us." He didn't add that, this way, America wouldn't have to worry about bailing them out. Now they'd have the wherewithal to see to their own enrichment, and America needed only offer expertise and advice about how to enter the capitalist world with both feet, and open eyes.

"This from the man who helped arrange the defection of the KGB chairman?" Golovko asked.

"Sergey, as we say at home, that was business, not personal. I don't have a hard-on for Russians, and you wouldn't kill an American just for entertainment purposes, would you?"

Indignation: "Of course not. That would be *nekulturniy.*"

"It is the same with us, Chairman."

"Hey, man," Chavez added. "From when I was a teenager, I was trained to kill your people, back when I was an Eleven-Bravo carrying a rifle, but, guess what, we're not enemies anymore, are we? And if we're not enemies, then we can be friends. You helped us out with Japan and Iran, didn't you?"

"Yes, but we saw that we were the ultimate target of both conflicts, and it was in our national interest."

"And perhaps the Chinese have us as *their* ultimate target. Then this is in our interest. They probably don't like us any more than they like you."

Golovko nodded. "Yes, one thing I do know about them is their sense of racial superiority."

"Dangerous way for people to think, man. Racism means your enemies are just insects to be swatted," Chavez concluded, impressing Clark with the mixture of East LA accent and master's-degree analysis of the situation at hand. "Even Karl Marx didn't say that he was better than anybody else 'cuz of his skin color, did he?"

"But Mao did," Golovko added.

"Doesn't surprise me," Ding went on. "I read his *Little Red Book* in graduate school. He didn't want to be just a political leader. Hell, he wanted to be God. Let his ego get in the way of his brain—not an uncommon affliction for people who take countries over, is it?"

"Lenin was not such a man, but Stalin was," Golovko observed. "So, then Ivan Emmetovich is a friend of Russia. What shall I do with this?"

"That's up to you, pal," Clark told him.

"I must speak to my president. Yours comes to Poland tomorrow, doesn't he?"

"I think so."

"I must make some phone calls. Thank you for coming, my friends. Perhaps another time I will be able to entertain you properly."

"Fair enough." Clark stood and tossed off the end of his drink. More handshakes, and they left the way they'd come.

"Christ, John, what happens now?" Ding asked, as they drove back out.

"I suppose everybody tries to beat some sense into the Chinese."

"Will it work?"

A shrug and arched eyebrows: "News at eleven, Domingo."

Packing for a trip isn't easy, even with a staff to do it all for you. This was particularly true for SURGEON, who was not only concerned about what she wore in public while abroad, but was also the Supreme

Authority on her husband's clothes, a status which her husband tolerated rather than entirely approved. Jack Ryan was still in the Oval Office trying to do business that couldn't wait—actually it mostly could, but there were fictions in government that had to be honored—and also waiting for the phone to ring.

"Arnie?"

"Yeah, Jack?"

"Tell the Air Force to have another G go over to Warsaw in case Scott has to fly to Moscow on the sly."

"Not a bad idea. They'll probably park it at some air force base or something." Van Damm went off to make the phone call.

"Anything else, Ellen?" Ryan asked his secretary.

"Need one?"

"Yeah, before Cathy and I wing off into the sunset." Actually, they were heading east, but Mrs. Sumter understood. She handed Ryan his last cigarette of the day.

"Damn," Ryan breathed with his first puff. He'd be getting a call from Moscow sure as hell—wouldn't he? That depended on how quickly they digested the information, or maybe Sergey would wait for the morning to show it to President Grushavoy. Would he? In Washington, something that hot would be graded CRITIC and shoved under the President's nose inside twenty minutes, but different countries had different rules, and he didn't know what the Russians did. For damned sure he'd be hearing from one of them before he stepped off the plane at Warsaw. But for now . . . He stubbed the smoke out, reached inside his desk for the breath spray, and zapped his mouth with the acidic stuff before leaving the office and heading outside—the West Wing and the White House proper are not connected by an indoor corridor, due to some architectural oversight. In any case, inside six minutes he was on the residential level, watching the ushers organize his bags. Cathy was there, trying to supervise, under the eyes of the Secret Service as well, who acted as though they worried about having a bomb slipped in. But paranoia was their job. Ryan walked over to his wife. "You need to talk to Andrea."

"What for?"

"Stomach trouble, she says."

"Uh-oh." Cathy had suffered from queasiness with Sally, but that was ages ago, and it hadn't been severe. "Not really much you can do about it, you know."

"So much for medical progress," Jack commented. "She probably could use some girl-girl support anyway."

Cathy smiled. "Oh, sure, womanly solidarity. So, you're going to bond with Pat?"

Jack grinned back at her. "Yeah, maybe he'll teach me to shoot a pistol better."

"Super," SURGEON observed dryly.

"Which dress for the big dinner?" POTUS asked FLOTUS.

"The light-blue one."

"Slinky," Jack said, touching her arm.

The kids showed up then, shepherded up to the bedroom level by their various detail leaders, except for Kyle, who was carried by one of his lionesses. Leaving the kids was never particularly easy, though all concerned were somewhat accustomed to it. The usual kisses and hugs took place, and then Jack took his wife's hand and led her to the elevator.

It let them off at the ground level, with a straight walk out to the helicopter pad. The VH-3 was there, with Colonel Malloy at the controls. The Marines saluted, as they always did. The President and First Lady climbed inside and buckled into the comfortable seats, under the watchful eyes of a Marine sergeant, who then went forward to report to the pilot in the right-front seat.

Cathy enjoyed helicopter flight more than her husband did, since she flew in one twice a day. Jack was no longer afraid of it, but he did prefer driving a car, which he hadn't been allowed to do in months. The Sikorsky lifted up gently, pivoted in the air, and headed off to Andrews. The flight took about ten minutes. The helicopter alighted close to the VC-25A, the Air Force's version of the Boeing 747; it was just a few seconds to the stairs, with the usual TV cameras to mark the event.

"Turn and wave, honey," Jack told Cathy at the top of the steps. "We might make the evening news."

"Again?" Cathy grumped. Then she waved and smiled, not at people, but at cameras. With this task completed, they went inside the aircraft and forward to the presidential compartment. There they buckled in, and were observed to do so by an Air Force NCO, who then told the pilot it was okay to spool up the engines and taxi to the end of Runway

Zero-one-right. Everything after that was ordinary, including the speech from the pilot, followed by the usual, stately takeoff roll of the big Boeing, and the climb out to thirty-eight thousand feet. Aft, Ryan was sure, everyone was comfortable, because the worst seat on this aircraft was as good as the best first-class seat on any airline in the world. On the whole this seemed a serious waste of the taxpayers' money, but to the best of his knowledge no taxpayer had ever complained very loudly.

The expected happened off the coast of Maine.

"Mr. President?" a female voice asked.

"Yeah, Sarge?"

"Call for you, sir, on the STU. Where do you want to take it?"

Ryan stood. "Topside."

The sergeant nodded and waved. "This way, sir."

"Who is it?"

"The DCI."

Ryan figured that made sense. "Let's get Secretary Adler in on this, too."

"Yes, sir," she said as he started up the spiral stairs.

Upstairs, Ryan settled into a working-type seat vacated for him by an Air Force NCO who handed him the proper phone. "Ed?"

"Yeah, Jack. Sergey called."

"Saying what?"

"He thinks it's a good idea you coming to Poland. He requests a high-level meeting, on the sly if possible."

Adler took the chair next to Ryan and caught the comment.

"Scott, feel like a hop to Moscow?"

"Can we do it quietly?" SecState asked.

"Probably."

"Then, yes. Ed, did you field the NATO suggestion?"

"Not my turf to try that, Scott," the Director of Central Intelligence replied.

"Fair enough. Think they'll spring for it?"

"Three-to-one, yes."

"I'll agree with that," Ryan concurred. "Golovko will like it, too."

"Yeah, he will, once he gets over the shock," Adler observed, with irony in his voice.

"Okay, Ed, tell Sergey that we are amenable to a covert meeting.

SecState flying into Moscow for consultations. Let us know what develops."

"Will do."

"Okay, out." Ryan set the handset down and turned to Adler. "Well?"

"Well, if they spring for it, China will have something to think about." This statement was delivered with a dollop of hope.

The problem, Ryan thought once again as he stood, *is that Klingons don't think quite the same way we do.*

The bugs had them all smirking. Suvorov/Koniev had picked up another expensive hooker that night, and her acting abilities had played out in the proper noises at the proper moments. *Or maybe he was really that good in bed,* Provalov wondered aloud, to the general skepticism of the others in the surveillance van. *No,* the others thought, *this girl was too much of a professional to allow herself to get into it that much.* They all thought that was rather sad, lovely as she was to look at. But they knew something their subject didn't know. This girl had been a "dangle," pre-briefed to meet Suvorov/Koniev.

Finally the noise subsided, and they heard the distinctive *snap* of an American Zippo lighter, and the usual post-sex silence of a sated man and a (simulatedly) satisfied woman.

"So, what sort of work do you do, Vanya?" the female voice asked, showing the expected professional interest of an expensive hooker in a wealthy man she might wish to entertain again.

"Business" was the answer.

"What sort?" Again, just the right amount of interest. The good news, Provalov thought, was that she didn't need coaching. The Sparrow School must have been fairly easy to operate, he realized. Women did this sort of thing from instinct.

"I take care of special needs for special people," the enemy spy answered. His revelation was followed by a feminine laugh.

"I do that, too, Vanya."

"There are foreigners who need special services which I was trained to handle under the old regime."

"You were KGB? Really?" Excitement in her voice. This girl was good.

"Yes, one of many. Nothing special about it."

"To you, perhaps, but not to me. Was there really a school for women like me? Did KGB train women to . . . to take care of the needs of men?"

A man's laugh this time: "Oh, yes, my dear. There was such a school. You would have done well there."

Now the laugh was coquettish. "As well as I do now?"

"No, not at what you charge."

"But am I worth it?" she asked.

"Easily" was the satisfied answer.

"Would you like to see me again, Vanya?" Real hope, or beautifully simulated hope, in the question.

"Da, I would like that very much, Maria."

"So, you take care of people with special needs. What needs are those?" She could get away with this because men so enjoyed to be found fascinating by beautiful women. It was part of their act of worship at this particular altar, and men *always* went for it.

"Not unlike what I was trained to do, Maria, but the details need not concern you."

Disappointment: "Men always say that," she grumped. "Why do the most interesting men have to be so mysterious?"

"In that is our fascination, woman," he explained. "Would you prefer that I drove a truck?"

"Truck drivers don't have your . . . your manly abilities," she replied, as if she'd learned the difference.

"A man could get hard just listening to this bitch," one of the FSS officers observed.

"That's the idea," Provalov agreed. "Why do you think she can charge so much?"

"A real man need not pay for it."

"Was I that good?" Suvorov/Koniev asked in their headphones.

"Any better and I would have to pay you, Vanya," she replied, with joy in her voice. Probably a kiss went along with the proclamation.

"No more questions, Maria. Let it lie for now," Oleg Gregoriyevich urged to the air. She must have heard him.

"You know how to make a man feel like a man," the spy/assassin told her. "Where did you learn this skill?"

"It just comes naturally to a woman," she cooed.

"To some women, perhaps." Then the talking stopped, and in ten minutes, the snoring began.

"Well, that's more interesting than our normal cases," the FSS officer told the others.

"You have people checking out the bench?"

"Hourly." There was no telling how many people delivered messages to the dead-drop, and they probably weren't all Chinese nationals. No, there'd be a rat-line in this chain, probably not a long one, but enough to offer some insulation to Suvorov's handler. That would be good fieldcraft, and they had to expect it. So, the bench and its dead-drop would be checked out regularly, and in *that* surveillance van would be a key custom-made to fit the lock on the drop-box, and a photocopier to make a duplicate of the message inside. The FSS had also stepped up surveillance of the Chinese Embassy. Nearly every employee who came outside had a shadow now. To do this properly meant curtailing other counterespionage operations in Moscow, but this case had assumed priority over everything else. It would soon become even more important, but they didn't know that yet.

How many engineers do we have available?" Bondarenko asked Aliyev in the east Siberian dawn.

"Two regiments not involved with the road-building," the operations officer answered.

"Good. Get them all down here immediately to work on the camouflage on these bunkers, and to set up false ones on the other side of these hills. Immediately, Andrey."

"Yes, General, I'll get them right on it."

"I love the dawn, the most peaceful time of day."

"Except when the other fellow uses it for his attack." Dawn was the universal time for a major offensive, so that one had all the light of the day to pursue it.

"If they come, it will be right up this valley."

"Yes, it will."

"They will shoot up the first line of defenses—what they think they are, that is," Bondarenko predicted, pointing. The first line was composed of seemingly real bunkers, made of rebarred concrete, but the gun tubes sticking out of them were fake. Whatever engineer had laid out these fortifications had been born with an eye for terrain worthy of Alexander of Macedon. They *appeared* to be beautifully sited, but a little too much so. Their positioning was a little too predictable, and they were visible, if barely so, to the other side, and something *barely* visible would be the first target hit. There were even pyrotechnic charges in the false bunkers, so that after a few direct hits they'd explode, and really make the enemy feel fine for having hit them. Whoever had come up with *that* idea had been a genius of a military engineer.

But the real defenses on the front of the hills were tiny observation posts whose buried phone lines led back to the real bunkers, and beyond them to artillery positions ten or more kilometers back. Some of these were old, also pre-sited, but the rockets they launched were just as deadly today as they'd been in the 1940s, design progeny of the Katushka artillery rockets the Germans had learned to hate. Then came the direct-fire weapons. The first rank of these were the turrets of old German tanks. The sights and the ammunition still worked, and the crewmen knew how to use them, and they had escape tunnels leading to vehicles that would probably allow them to survive a determined attack. The engineers who had laid this line out were probably all dead now, and General Bondarenko hoped they'd been buried honorably, as soldiers deserved. This line wouldn't stop a determined attack—no fixed line of defenses could accomplish that—but it would be enough to make an enemy wish he'd gone somewhere else.

But the camouflage needed work, and that work would be done at night. A high-flying aircraft tracing over the border with a side-looking camera could see far into his country and take thousands of useful, pretty pictures, and the Chinese probably had a goodly collection of such pictures, plus whatever they could get from their own satellites, or from the commercial birds that anyone could employ now for money—

"Andrey, tell intelligence to see if we can determine if the Chinese have accessed commercial photo satellites."

"Why bother? Don't they have their own—"

"We don't know how good their reconsats are, but we do know that the new French ones are as good as anything the Americans had up until 1975 or so, and that's good enough for most purposes."

"Yes, General." Aliyev paused. "You think something is going to happen here?"

Bondarenko paused, frowning as he stared south over the river. He could see into China from this hilltop. The ground looked no different, but for political reasons it was alien land, and though the inhabitants of that land were no different ethnically from the people native to *his* land, the political differences were enough to make the sight of them a thing of concern, even fear, for him. He shook his head.

"Andrey Petrovich, you've heard the same intelligence briefings I've heard. What concerns me is that their army has been far more active than ours. They have the ability to attack us, and we do not have the ability to defeat them. We have less than three full-strength divisions, and the level of their training is inadequate. We have much to do before I will begin to feel comfortable. Firming up this line is the easiest thing to do, and the easiest part of firming it up is hiding the bunkers. Next, we'll start rotating the soldiers back to the training range and have them work on their gunnery. That will be easy for them to do, but it hasn't been done in ten months! So much to do, Andrushka, so much to do."

"That is so, Comrade General, but we've made a good beginning."

Bondarenko waved his hand and growled, "Ahh, a good beginning will be a year from now. We've taken the first morning piss in what will be a long day, Colonel. Now, let's fly east and see the next sector."

General Peng Xi-Wang, commander of the Red Banner 34th Shock Army, only sixteen kilometers away, looked through powerful spotting glasses at the Russian frontier. Thirty-fourth Shock was a Type A Group Army, and comprised about eighty thousand men. He had an armored division, two mechanized ones, a motorized infantry division, and other attachments, such as an independent artillery brigade under his direct command. Fifty years of age, and a party member since his twenties, Peng was a long-term professional soldier who'd enjoyed the last ten years of his life. Since commanding his tank regiment as a senior colonel, he'd been able to train his troops incessantly on what had become his home country.

The Shenyang Military District comprised the northeasternmost part of the People's Republic. It was composed of hilly, wooded land,

and had warm summers and bitter winters. There was a touch of early ice on the Amur River below Peng now, but from a military point of view, the trees were the real obstacle. Tanks could knock individual trees down, but not every ten meters. No, you had to drive between and around them, and while there was room for that, it was hard on the drivers, and it ate up fuel almost as efficiently as tipping the fuel drum over on its side and just pouring it out. There were some roads and railroad rights-of-way, and if he ever went north, he'd be using them, though that made for good ambush opportunities, if the Russians had a good collection of antitank weapons. But the Russian doctrine, going back half a century, was that the best antitank weapon was a better tank. In their war with the fascists, the Soviet army had enjoyed possession of a superb tank in the T-34. They'd built a lot of the Rapier antitank guns, and duly copied NATO guided antitank weapons, but you dealt with those by blanketing an area with artillery fire, and Peng had lots of guns and mountains of shells to deal with the unprotected infantrymen who had to steer the missiles into their targets. He wished he had the Russian-designed Arena anti-missile system, which had been designed to protect their tanks from the swarm of NATO's deadly insects, but he didn't, and he heard it didn't work all that well anyway.

The spotting glasses were Chinese copies of a German Zeiss model adopted for use by the Soviet Army of old. They zoomed from twenty- to fifty-power, allowing him an intimate view of the other side of the river. Peng came up here once a month or so, which allowed him to inspect his own border troops, who stood what was really a defensive watch, and a light one at that. He had little concern about a Russian attack into his country. The People's Liberation Army taught the same doctrine as every army back to the Assyrians of old: The best defense is a good offense. If a war began here, better to begin it yourself. And so Peng had cabinets full of plans to attack into Siberia, prepared by his operations and intelligence people, because that was what operations people did.

"Their defenses look ill-maintained," Peng observed.

"That is so, Comrade," the colonel commanding the border-defense regiment agreed. "We see little regular activity there."

"They are too busy selling their weapons to civilians for vodka," the army political officer observed. "Their morale is poor, and they do not train anything like we do."

"They have a new theater commander," the army's intelligence chief countered. "A General-Colonel Bondarenko. He is well regarded in Moscow as an intellect and as a courageous battlefield commander from Afghanistan."

"That means he survived contact once," Political observed. "Probably with a Kabul whore."

"It is dangerous to underestimate an adversary," Intelligence warned.

"And foolish to overestimate one."

Peng just looked through the glasses. He'd heard his intelligence and political officer spar before. Intelligence tended to be an old woman, but many intelligence officers were like that, and Political, like so many of his colleagues, was sufficiently aggressive to make Genghis Khan seem womanly. As in the theater, officers played the roles assigned to them. His role, of course, was to be the wise and confident commander of one of his country's premier striking arms, and Peng played that role well enough that he was in the running for promotion to General First Class, and if he played his cards very carefully, in another eight years or so, maybe Marshal. With that rank came real political power and personal riches beyond counting, with whole factories working for his own enrichment. Some of those factories were managed by mere colonels, people with the best of political credentials who knew how to kowtow to their seniors, but Peng had never gone that route. He enjoyed soldering far more than he enjoyed pushing paper and screaming at worker-peasants. As a new second lieutenant, he'd fought the Russians, not very far from this very spot. It had been a mixed experience. His regiment had enjoyed initial success, then had been hammered by a storm of artillery. That had been back when the Red Army, the real Soviet Army of old, had fielded whole artillery *divisions* whose concentrated fire could shake the very earth and sky, and that border clash had incurred the wrath of the nation the Russians had once been. But no longer. Intelligence told him that the Russian troops on the far side of this cold river were not even a proper shadow of what had once been there. Four divisions, perhaps, and not all of them at full strength. So, however clever this Bondarenko fellow was, if a clash came, he'd have his hands very full indeed.

But that was a political question, wasn't it? Of course. All the really important things were.

"How are the bridging engineers?" Peng asked, surveying the watery obstacle below.

"Their last exercise went very well, Comrade General," Operations replied. Like every other army in the world, the PLA had copied the Russian "ribbon" bridge, designed by Soviet engineers in the 1960s to force crossings of all the streams of Western Germany in a NATO/Warsaw Pact war so long expected, but never realized. Except in fiction, mainly Western fiction that had had the NATO side win in every case. Of course. Would capitalists spend money on books that ended their culture? Peng chuckled to himself. Such people enjoyed their illusions . . .

. . . almost as much as his own country's Politburo members. That's the way it was all over the world, Peng figured. The rulers of every land held images in their heads, and tried to make the world conform to them. Some succeeded, and those were the ones who wrote the history books.

"So, what do we expect here?"

"From the Russians?" Intelligence asked. "Nothing that I have heard about. Their army is training a little more, but nothing to be concerned about. If they wanted to come south across that river, I hope they can swim in the cold."

"The Russians like their comforts too much for that. They've grown soft with their new political regime," Political proclaimed.

"And if we are ordered north?" Peng asked.

"If we give them one hard kick, the whole rotten mess will fall down," Political answered. He didn't know that he was exactly quoting another enemy of the Russians.

CHAPTER 43

Decisions

The colonel flying Air Force One executed an even better landing than usual. Jack and Cathy Ryan were already awake and showered to alertness, helped by a light breakfast heavy on fine coffee. The President looked out the window to his left and saw troops formed up in precise lines, as the aircraft taxied to its assigned place.

"Welcome to Poland, babe. What do you have planned?"

"I'm going to spend a few hours at their big teaching hospital. Their chief eye-cutter wants me to look at his operation." It was always the same for FLOTUS, and she didn't mind. It came from being an academic physician, treating patients, but also teaching young docs, and observing how her counterparts around the world did their version of her job. Every so often, you saw something new that was worth learning from, or even copying, because smart people happened everywhere, not just at the Johns Hopkins University School of Medicine. It was the one part of the First Lady folderol that she actually enjoyed, because she could learn from it, instead of just being a somewhat flat-chested Barbie doll for the world to gawk at. To this end she was dressed in a beige business suit, whose jacket she would soon exchange for a doc's proper white lab coat, which was always her favorite item of apparel. Jack was wearing one of his dark-blue white-pinstriped President-of-the-United-States suits, with a maroon striped tie because Cathy liked the color combination, and she really did decide what Jack wore, except for the shirt. SWORDSMAN wore only white cotton shirts with button-down collars, and despite Cathy's lobbying for something different, on that issue he stood firm. This had caused Cathy to observe more than once that he'd wear the damned things with his tuxedos if convention didn't demand otherwise.

The aircraft came to a halt, and the stagecraft began. The Air Force sergeant—this one always a man—opened the door on the left side of the aircraft to see that the truck-mounted stairs were already in place. Two more non-coms scurried down so that they could salute Ryan when he walked down. Andrea Price-O'Day was talking over her digital radio circuit to the chief of the Secret Service advance team to make sure it was safe for the President to appear in the open. She'd already heard that the Poles had been as cooperative as any American police force, and had enough security deployed here to defend against an attack by space aliens or Hitler's Wehrmacht. She nodded to the President and Mrs. Ryan.

"Showtime, babe," Jack told Cathy, with a dry smile.

"Knock 'em dead, Movie Star," she said in reply. It was one of their inside jokes.

John Patrick Ryan, President of the United States of America, stood in the door to look out over Poland, or at least as much of it as he could see from this vantage. The first cheers erupted then, for although he'd never even been close to Poland before, he was a popular figure here, for what reason Jack Ryan had no idea. He walked down, carefully, telling himself not to trip and spill down the steps. It looked bad to do so, as one of his antecedents had learned the hard way. At the bottom, the two USAF sergeants snapped off their salutes, which Ryan unconsciously returned, and then he was saluted again by a Polish officer. They did it differently, Jack saw, with ring and little finger tucked in, like American Cub Scouts. Jack nodded and smiled to this officer, then followed him to the receiving line. There was the U.S. ambassador to introduce him to the Polish president. Together they walked down a red carpet to a small lectern, where the Polish president welcomed Ryan, and Ryan make remarks to demonstrate his joy at visiting this ancient and important new American ally. Ryan had a discordant memory of the "Polack" jokes so popular when he'd been in high school, but managed not to relate any to the assembled throng. This was followed by a review past the honor guard of soldiers, about three companies of infantrymen, all spiffed up for this moment; Jack walked past them, looking in each face for a split second and figuring they just wanted to go back to barracks to change into their more comfortable fatigues, where they'd say that this Ryan guy looked okay for a damned American chief of state, and wasn't it good that this pain-in-the-ass duty was over. Then Jack and Cathy (carrying flowers given to her by two cute Polish kids, a boy and a girl, age six or so, because that was the best age to greet an important foreign woman) got into the official car, an American limo from the U.S. Embassy, for the drive into town. Once there, Jack looked over to the ambassador.

"What about Moscow?"

Ambassadors had once been Very Important People, which explained why each still had to be approved by vote of the United States Senate. When the Constitution had been drafted, world travel had been done by sailing ship, and an ambassador in a foreign land *was* the United States of America, and had to be able to speak for his country entirely without guidance from Washington. Modern communications had transformed ambassadors into glorified mailmen, but they still, occasionally, had to handle important matters with discretion, and this was such a case.

"They want the Secretary to come over as soon as possible. The backup aircraft is at a fighter base about fifteen miles from here. We can get Scott there within the hour," Stanislas Lewendowski reported.

"Thanks, Stan. Make it happen."

"Yes, Mr. President," the ambassador, a native of Chicago, agreed with a curt nod.

"Anything we need to know?"

"Aside from that, sir, no, everything's pretty much under control."

"I hate it when they say that," Cathy observed quietly. "That's when I look up for the falling sandbag."

"Not here, ma'am," Lewendowski promised. "Here things *are* under control."

That's nice to hear, President Ryan thought, *but what about the rest of the fucking world?*

Eduard Petrovich, this is not a happy development," Golovko told his president.

"I can see that," Grushavoy agreed tersely. "Why did we have to learn this from the Americans?"

"We had a very good source in Beijing, but he retired not long ago. He's sixty-nine years old and in ill health, and it was time to leave his post in their Party Secretariat. Sadly, we had no replacement for him," Golovko admitted. "The American source appears to be a man of similar placement. We are fortunate to have this information, regardless of its source."

"Better to have it than not to have it," Eduard Petrovich admitted. "So, now what?"

"Secretary of State Adler will be joining us in about three hours, at the Americans' request. He wishes to consult with us directly on a 'matter of mutual interest.' That means the Americans are as concerned with this development as we are."

"What will they say?"

"They will doubtless offer us assistance of some sort. Exactly what kind, I cannot say."

"Is there anything I don't already know about Adler and Ryan?"

"I don't think so. Scott Adler is a career diplomat, well regarded everywhere as an experienced and expert diplomatic technician. He and Ryan are friends, dating back to when Ivan Emmetovich was Deputy Director of CIA. They get along well and do not have any known disagreements in terms of policy. Ryan I have known for over ten years. He is bright, decisive, and a man of unusually fine personal honor. A man of his word. He was the enemy of the Soviet Union, and a skilled enemy, but since our change of systems he has been a friend. He evidently wishes us to succeed and prosper economically, though his efforts to assist us have been somewhat disjointed and confused. As you know, we have assisted the Americans in two black operations, one against China and one against Iran. This is important, because Ryan will see that he owes us a debt. He is, as I said, an honorable man, and he will wish to repay that debt, as long as it does not conflict with his own security interests."

"Will an attack on China be seen that way?" President Grushavoy asked.

Golovko nodded decisively. "Yes, I believe so. We know that Ryan has said privately that he both likes and admires Russian culture, and that he would prefer that America and Russia should become strategic partners. So, I think Secretary Adler will offer us substantive assistance against China."

"What form will it take?"

"Eduard Petrovich, I am an intelligence officer, not a gypsy fortune-teller . . ." Golovko paused. "We will know more soon, but if you wish me to make a guess . . ."

"Do so," the Russian president commanded. The SVR Chairman took a deep breath and made his prediction:

"He will offer us a seat on the North Atlantic Council." That startled Grushavoy:

"Join NATO?" he asked, with an open mouth.

"It would be the most elegant solution to the problem. It allies us with the rest of Europe, and would face China with a panoply of enemies if they attack us."

"And if they make this offer to us . . . ?"

"You should accept it at once, Comrade President," the chief of the RSV replied. "We would be fools not to."

"What will they demand in return?"

"Whatever it is, it will be far less costly than a war against China."

Grushavoy nodded thoughtfully. "I will consider this. Is it really possible that America can recognize Russia as an ally?"

"Ryan will have thought this idea through. It conforms to his strategic outlook, and, as I said, I believe he honestly admires and respects Russia."

"After all his time in CIA?"

"Of course. That is why he does. He knows us. He ought to respect us."

Grushavoy thought about that one. Like Golovko, he was a Russian patriot who loved the very smell of Russian soil, the birch forests, the vodka and the borscht, the music and literature of his land. But he was not blind to the errors and ill fortune his country had endured over the centuries. Like Golovko, Grushavoy had come to manhood in a nation called the Union of Soviet Socialist Republics, and had been educated to be a believer in Marxism-Leninism, but he'd gradually come to see that, although the path to political power had required worshiping at that godless altar, the god there had been a false one. Like many, he'd seen that the previous system simply didn't work. But unlike all but a small and courageous few, he'd spoken out about the system's shortcomings. A lawyer, even under the Soviet system when law had been subordinated to political whim, he'd crusaded for a rational system of laws which would allow people to predict the reaction of the state to their actions with something akin to confidence. He'd been there when the old system had fallen, and had embraced the new system as a teenager embraced his first love. Now he was struggling to bring order—lawful order, which was harder still—to a nation which had known only dictatorial rule for centuries. If he succeeded, he knew he'd be remembered as one of the giants of human political history. If he failed, he'd just be remembered as one more starry-eyed visionary unable to turn his dream into reality. The latter, he thought in quiet moments, was the more likely outcome.

But despite that concern, he was playing to win. Now he had the gold and oil discoveries in Siberia, which had appeared as if gifts from the merciful God his education had taught him to deny. Russian history predicted—nay, demanded—that such gifts be taken from his country, for such had always been their hateful ill luck. Did God hate Russia? Anyone familiar with the past in his ancient country would think so. But today hope appeared as a golden dream, and Grushavoy was determined not to let this dream evaporate as all the others had. The land of Tolstoy and Rimsky-Korsakov had given much to the world, and now it deserved something back. Perhaps this Ryan fellow would indeed be a friend of his country and his people. His country needed friends. His country had the resources to exist alone, but to make use of those resources, he needed assistance, enough to allow Russia to enter the world as a complete and self-sufficient nation, ready to be a friend to all, ready to give and to take in honor and amity. The wherewithal was within his reach, if not quite within his hand. To take it would make him an Immortal, would make Eduard Petrovich Grushavoy the man who raised up his entire country. To do that he'd need help, however, and while that abraded his sense of *amour propre,* his patriotism, his duty to his country required that he set self aside.

"We shall see, Sergey Nikolay'ch. We shall see."

The time is ripe," Zhang Han San told his colleagues in the room of polished oak. "The men and weapons are in place. The prize lies right before our eyes. That prize offers us economic salvation, economic security such as we have dreamed of for decades, the ability," he went on, "to make China the world's preeminent power. That is a legacy to leave our people such as no leader has ever granted his descendants. We need only take it. It lies almost in our hands, like a peach upon a tree."

"It is feasible?" Interior Minister Tong Jie asked cautiously.

"Marshal?" Zhang handed the inquiry off to the Defense Minister.

Luo Cong leaned forward. He and Zhang had spent much of the previous evening together with maps, diagrams, and intelligence estimates. "From a military point of view, yes, it is possible. We have four Type A Group armies in the Shenyang Military District, fully trained and poised to strike north. Behind them are six Type B Group armies with sufficient infantry to support our mechanized forces, and four more Type C Group armies to garrison the land we take. From a strictly military point of view, the only issues are moving our forces into place and then supplying them. That is mainly a question of railroads, which will move supplies and men. Minister Qian?" Luo asked. He and Zhang had considered this bit of stage-managing carefully, hoping to co-opt a likely opponent of their proposed national policy early on.

The Finance Minister was startled by the question, but pride in his former job and his innate honesty compelled him to respond truthfully: "There is sufficient rolling stock for your purposes, Marshal Luo," he replied tersely. "The concern will be repairing damage done by enemy air strikes on our rights-of-way and bridges. That is something the Railroad Ministry has examined for decades, but there is no precise answer to it, because we cannot predict the degree of damage the Russians might inflict."

"I am not overly worried about that, Qian," Marshal Luo responded. "The Russian air force is in miserable shape due to all their activity against their Muslim minorities. They used up a goodly fraction of their best weapons and spare parts. We estimate that our air-defense groups should preserve our transportation assets with acceptable losses. Will we be able to send railroad-construction personnel into Siberia to extend our railheads?"

Again Qian felt himself trapped. "The Russians have surveyed and graded multiple rights-of-way over the years in their hopes for extending the Trans-Siberian Railroad and settling people into the region. Those efforts date back to Stalin. Can we lay track rapidly? Yes. Rapidly enough for your purposes? Probably not, Comrade Marshal," Qian replied studiously. If he didn't answer honestly, his seat at this table would evaporate, and he knew it.

"I am not sanguine on this prospect, comrades," Shen Tang spoke for the Foreign Ministry.

"Why is that, Shen?" Zhang asked.

"What will other nations do?" he asked rhetorically. "We do not know, but I would not be optimistic, especially with the Americans. They become increasingly friendly with the Russians. President Ryan is well known to be friendly with Golovko, chief advisor to President Grushavoy."

"A pity that Golovko still lives, but we were unlucky," Tan Deshi had to concede.

"Depending on luck is dangerous at this level," Fang Gan told his colleagues. "Fate is no man's friend."

"Perhaps the next time," Tan responded.

"Next time," Zhang thought aloud, "better to eliminate Grushavoy and so throw their country into total chaos. A country without a president is like a snake without a head. It may thrash about, but it harms no one."

"Even a severed head can bite," Fang observed. "And who is to say that Fate will smile upon this enterprise?"

"A man can wait for fate to decide for him, or he can seize the foul woman by the throat and take her by force—as we have all done in our time," Zhang added with a cruel smile.

Much more easily done with a docile secretary than with Destiny herself, Zhang, Fang didn't say aloud. He could go only so far in this forum, and he knew it. "Comrades, I counsel caution. The dogs of war have sharp teeth, but any dog may turn and bite his master. We have all seen *that* happen, have we not? Some things, once begun, are less easily halted. War is such a thing, and it is not to be undertaken so lightly."

"What would you have us do, Fang?" Zhang asked. "Should we wait until we run out of oil and wheat? Should we wait until we need troops to quell discord among our own people? Should we wait for Fate to decide for us, or should we choose our own destiny?"

The only reply to that came from Chinese culture itself, the ancient beliefs that came to all of the Politburo members almost as genetic knowledge, unaffected by political conditioning: "Comrades, Destiny awaits us all. It chooses us, not we it. What you propose here, my old friend, could merely accelerate what comes for us in any case, and who among us can say if it will please or displease us?" Minister Fang shook his head. "Perhaps what you propose is necessary, even beneficial," he allowed, "but only after the alternatives have been examined fully and discarded."

"If we are to decide," Luo told them, "then we must decide soon. We have good campaigning weather before us. That season will only last so long. If we strike soon—in the next two weeks—we can seize our objectives, and then time works *for* us. Then winter will set in and make offensive campaigning virtually impossible against a determined defense. Then we can depend upon Shen's ministry to safeguard and consolidate what we have seized, perhaps to share our winnings with the Russians . . . for a time," he added cynically. China would never share such a windfall, they all knew. It was merely a ploy fit to fool children and mushy-headed diplomats, which the world had in abundance, they all knew.

Through all this, Premier Xu had sat quietly, observing how the sentiments went, before making his decision and calling for a vote whose outcome would, of course, be predetermined. There was one more thing that needed asking. Not surprisingly, the question came from Tan Deshi, chief of the Ministry of State Security:

"Luo, my friend, how soon would the decision have to be made to ensure success? How easily could the decision be called back if circumstances warrant?"

"Ideally, the 'go' decision would be made today, so that we can start moving our forces to their preset jumping-off places. To stop them—well, of course, you can stop the offensive up to the very moment the artillery is to open fire. It is much harder to advance than it is to stay in place. Any man can stand still, no matter where he is." The preplanned answer to the preplanned question was as clever as it was misleading. Sure, you could always stop an army poised to jump off, about as easily as you could stop a Yangtze River flood.

"I see," Tan said. "In that case, I propose that we vote on *conditional* approval of a 'go' order, subject to change at any time by majority vote of the Politburo."

Now it was Xu's turn to take charge of the meeting: "Comrades, thank you all for your views on the issue before us. Now we must decide what is best for our country and our people. We shall vote on Tan's proposal, a conditional authorization for an attack to seize and exploit the oil and gold fields in Siberia."

As Fang had feared, the vote was already decided, and in the interests of solidarity, he voted with the rest. Only Qian Kun wavered, but like all the others, he sided with the majority, because it was dangerous to stand alone in any group in the People's Republic, most of all this one. And besides, Qian was only a candidate member, and didn't have a vote at this most democratic of tables.

The vote turned out to be unanimous.

Long Chun, it would be called: Operation SPRING DRAGON.

Scott Adler knew Moscow as well as many Russian citizens did, he'd been here so many times, including one tour in the American Embassy as a wet-behind-the-ears new foreign-service officer, all those years before, during the Carter Administration. The Air Force flight crew delivered him on time, and they were accustomed to taking people on covert missions to odd places. This mission was less unusual than most. His aircraft rolled to a stop at the Russian fighter base, and the official car rolled up even before the mechanical steps unfolded. Adler hustled out, unaccompanied even by an aide. A Russian official shook hands with him and got him into the car for the drive into Moscow. Adler was at ease. He knew that he was offering Russia a gift fit for the world's largest Christmas tree, and he didn't think they were stupid enough to reject it. No, the Russians were among the world's most skillful diplomats and geopolitical thinkers, a trait that went back sixty years or more. It had struck him as sad, back in 1978, that their adroit people had been chained to a doomed political system—even back then, Adler had seen the demise of the Soviet Union coming. Jimmy Carter's "human rights" proclamation had been that president's best and least appreciated foreign-policy play, for it had injected the virus of rot into their political empire, begun the process of eating away their power in Eastern Europe, and also of letting their own people start to ask questions. It was a pot that Ronald Reagan had sweetened—upping the ante with his defense buildup that had stretched the Soviet economy to the breaking point and beyond, allowing George Bush to be there when they'd tossed in their cards and cast off from the political system that stretched back to Vladimir Il'ych Ulyanov, Lenin himself, the founding father, even the god of Marxism-Leninism. It was usually sad when a god died . . .

. . . but not in this case, Adler thought as the buildings flashed by.

Then he realized that there was one more large but false god out there, Mao Zedong, awaiting final interment in history's rubbish heap. When would that come? Did this mission have a role to play in that funeral? Nixon's opening to China had played a role in the destruction of the Soviet Union, which historians still had not fully grasped. Would its final echo be found in the fall of the People's Republic itself? That remained to be seen.

The car pulled into the Kremlin through the Spaskiy Gate, then proceeded to the old Council of Ministers Building. There Adler alighted and hurried inside, into an elevator to a third-floor meeting room.

"Mr. Secretary." The greeting came from Golovko. Adler should have found him an *eminence gris,* he thought. But Sergey Nikolay'ch was actually a man of genuine intellect and the openness that resulted directly from it. He was not even a pragmatist, but a man who sought what was best for his country, and would search for it everywhere his mind could see. *A seeker of truth,* SecState thought. That sort of man he and America could live with.

"Chairman. Thank you for receiving us so quickly."

"Please come with me, Mr. Adler." Golovko led him through a set of high double doors into what almost appeared to be a throne room. EAGLE couldn't remember if this building went back to the czars. President Eduard Petrovich Grushavoy was waiting for him, already standing politely, looking serious but friendly.

"Mr. Adler," the Russian president said, with a smile and an extended hand.

"Mr. President, a pleasure to be back in Moscow."

"Please." Grushavoy led him to a comfortable set of chairs with a low table. Tea things were already out, and Golovko handled the serving like a trusted earl seeing to the needs of his king and guest.

"Thank you. I've always loved the way you serve your tea in Russia." Adler stirred his and took a sip.

"So, what do you have to say to us?" Grushavoy asked in passable English.

"We have shown you what has become for us a cause for great concern."

"The Chinese," the Russian president observed. Everyone knew all of this, but the beginning of the conversation would follow the conventions of high-level talk, like lawyers discussing a major case in chambers.

"Yes, the Chinese. They seem to be contemplating a threat to the peace of the world. America has no wish to see that peace threatened. We've all worked very hard—your country and mine—to put an end to conflict. We note with gratitude Russia's assistance in our most recent conflicts. Just as we were allies sixty years ago, so Russia has acted again lately. America is a country that remembers her friends."

Golovko let out a breath slowly. Yes, his prediction was about to come true. Ivan Emmetovich was a man of honor, and a friend of his country. What came back to him was the time he'd held a pistol to Ryan's head, the time Ryan had engineered the defection of KGB chairman Gerasimov all those years before. Sergey Nikolay'ch had been enraged back then, as furious as he had ever been in a long and stressful professional life, but he'd held back from firing the pistol because it would have been a foolish act to shoot a man with diplomatic status. Now he blessed his moderation, for now Ivan Emmetovich Ryan offered to Russia what he had always craved from America: predictability. Ryan's honor, his sense of fair play, the personal honesty that was the most crippling aspect of his newly acquired political persona, all combined to make him a person upon whom Russia could depend. And at this moment, Golovko could do that which he'd spent his life trying to do: He could see the future that lay only a few short minutes away.

"This Chinese threat, it is real, you think?" Grushavoy asked.

"We fear it is," the American Secretary of State answered. "We hope to forestall it."

"But how will we accomplish that? China knows of our military weakness. We have de-emphasized our defense capabilities of late, trying to shift the funds into areas of greater value to our economy. Now it seems we might pay a bitter price for that," the Russian president worried aloud.

"Mr. President, we hope to help Russia in that respect."

"How?"

"Mr. President, even as we speak, President Ryan is also speaking with the NATO chiefs of state and government. He is proposing to them that we invite Russia to sign the North Atlantic Treaty. That will ally the Russian Federation with all of Europe. It ought to make China take a step back to consider the wisdom of a conflict with your country."

"Ahh," Grushavoy breathed. "So, America offers Russia a full alliance of state?"

Adler nodded. "Yes, Mr. President. As we were allies against Hitler, so today we can again be allies against all potential enemies."

"There are many complications in this, talks between your military and ours, for example—even talks with the NATO command in Belgium. It could take months to coordinate our country with NATO."

"Those are technical matters to be handled by diplomatic and military technicians. At this level, however, we offer the Russian Federation our friendship in peace and in war. We place the word and the honor of our countries at your disposal."

"What of the European Union, their Common Market of economic alliances?"

"That, sir, is something left to the EEC, but America will encourage our European friends to welcome you completely into the European community, and offer all influence we can muster to that end."

"What do you ask in return?" Grushavoy asked. Golovko hadn't offered that prediction. This could be the answer to many Russian prayers, though his mind made the leap to see that Russian oil would be a major boon to Europe, and hence a matter of mutual, not unilateral, profit.

"We ask for nothing special in return. It is in the American interest to help make a stable and peaceful world. We welcome Russia into that world. Friendship between your people and ours is desirable to everyone, is it not?"

"And in our friendship is profit also for America," Golovko pointed out.

Adler sat back and smiled agreement. "Of course. Russia will sell things to America, and America will sell things to Russia. We will become neighbors in the global village, friendly neighbors. We will compete economically, giving and taking from each other, as we do with many other countries."

"The offer you make is this simple?" Grushavoy asked.

"Should it be more complicated?" the SecState asked. "I am a diplomat, not a lawyer. I prefer simple things to complex ones."

Grushavoy considered all this for half a minute or so. Usually, diplomatic negotiations lasted weeks or months to do even the simplest of things, but Adler was right: Simple was better than complex, and the fundamental issue here was simple, though the downstream consequences might be breathtaking. America offered salvation to Russia, not just a military alliance, but the opening of all doors to economic development. America and Europe would partner with the Russian Federation, creating what could become both an open and integrated community to span the northern hemisphere. It stood to make Eduard Petrovich Grushavoy the Russian who brought his country a full century into the present/future of the world, and for all the statues of Lenin and Stalin that had been toppled, well, maybe some of his own likeness would be erected. It was a thought to appeal to a Russian politician. And after a few minutes, he extended his hand across the low table of tea things.

"The Russian Federation gladly accepts the offer of the United States of America. Together we once defeated the greatest threat to human culture. Perhaps we can do so again—better yet, together we may forestall it."

"In that case, sir, I will report your agreement to my president."

Adler checked his watch. It had taken twenty minutes. Damn, you could make history in a hurry when you had your act together, couldn't you? He stood. "I must be off then to make my report."

"Please convey my respects to President Ryan. We will do our best to be worthy allies to your country."

"He and I have no doubts of that, Mr. President." Adler shook hands with Golovko and walked to the door. Three minutes after that, he was back in his car and heading back to the airport. Once there, the aircraft had barely begun to taxi when he got on the secure satellite phone.

Mr. President?" Andrea said, coming up to Ryan just as the plenary session of the NATO chiefs was about to begin. She handed over the secure portable phone. "It's Secretary Adler."

Ryan took the phone at once. "Scott? Jack here. What gives?"

"It's a done deal, Jack."

"Okay, now I have to sell it to these guys. Good job, Scott. Hurry back."

"We're rolling now, sir." The line went dead. Ryan tossed the phone to Special Agent Price-O'Day.

"Good news?" she asked.

"Yep." Ryan nodded and walked into the conference room.

"Mr. President." Sir Basil Charleston came up to him. The chief of the British Secret Intelligence Service, he'd known Ryan longer than anyone else in the room had. One odd result of Ryan's path to the Presidency was that the people who knew him best were all spooks, mainly NATO ones, and these found themselves advising their chiefs of government on how to deal with America. Sir Basil had served no less than five Prime Ministers of Her Majesty's Government, but now he was in rather a higher position than before.

"Bas, how are you?"

"Doing quite well, thank you. May I ask a question?"

"Sure." *But I don't have to answer it,* Jack's smile added in reply.

"Adler is in Moscow now. Can we know why?"

"How will your PM react to inviting Russia into NATO?"

That made Basil blink, Ryan saw. It wasn't often that you could catch this guy unawares. Instantly, his mind went into overdrive to analyze the new situation. "China?" he asked after about six seconds.

Jack nodded. "Yeah. We may have some problems there."

"Not going north, are they?"

"They're thinking about it," Ryan replied.

"How good is your information on that question?"

"You know about the Russian gold strike, right?"

"Oh, yes, Mr. President. Ivan's been bloody lucky on both scores."

"Our intel strike in Beijing is even better."

"Indeed?" Charleston observed, letting Jack know that the SIS had also been pretty much shut out there.

"Indeed, Bas. It's class-A information, and it has us worried. We're hoping that pulling Russia into NATO can scare them off. Grushavoy just agreed on it. How do you suppose the rest of these folks will react to it?"

"They'll react cautiously, but favorably, after they've had a chance to consider it."

"Will Britain back us on this play?" Ryan asked.

"I must speak with the PM. I'll let you know." With that, Sir Basil walked over to where the British Prime Minister was chatting with the German Foreign Minister. Charleston dragged him off and spoke quietly into his ear. Instantly, the Prime Minister's eyes, flaring a little wide, shot over to Ryan. The British PM was somewhat trapped, somewhat unpleasantly because of the surprise factor, but the substance of the trap was that Britain and America *always* supported each other. The "special relationship" was as alive and well today as it had been under the governments of Franklin Roosevelt and Winston Churchill. It was one of the few constants in the diplomatic world for both countries, and it belied Kissinger's dictum that great nations didn't have friendships, but rather interests. Perhaps it was the exception proving the rule, but if so, exception it was. Both Britain and America would hurl themselves in front of a train for the other. The fact that in England, President Ryan was Sir John Ryan, KCVO, made the alliance even more firm. In acknowledgment of that, the Prime Minister of the United Kingdom walked over to the American chief of state.

"Jack, will you let us in on this development?"

"Insofar as I can. I may give Basil a little more on the side, but, yeah, Tony, this is for real, and we're damned worried about it."

"The gold and the oil?" the PM asked.

"They seem to think they're in an economic box. They're just about out of hard currency, and they're hurting for oil and wheat."

"You can't make an arrangement for that?"

"After what they did? Congress would hang me from the nearest lamppost."

"Quite," the Brit had to agree. BBC had run its own news miniseries on human rights in the PRC, and the Chinese hadn't come off very well. Indeed, despising China was the new European sport, which hadn't helped their foreign-currency holdings at all. As China had trapped themselves, so the Western nations had been perversely co-opted into building the wall. The citizens of these democracies wouldn't stand for economic or trade concessions any more than the Chinese Politburo could see its way to making the political sort. "Rather like Greek tragedy, isn't it, Jack?"

"Yeah, Tony, and our tragic flaw is adherence to human rights. Hell of a situation, isn't it?"

"And you're hoping that bringing Russia into NATO will give them pause?"

"If there's a better card to play, I haven't seen it in my deck, man."

"How set are they on the path?"

"Unknown. Our intelligence on this is very good, but we have to be careful making use of it. It could get people killed, and deny us the information we need."

"Like our chap Penkovskiy in the 1960s." One thing about Sir Basil, he knew how to educate his bosses on how the business of intelligence worked.

Ryan nodded, then proceeded with a little of his own disinformation. It was business, and Basil would understand: "Exactly. I can't have that man's life on my conscience, Tony, and so I have to treat this information very carefully."

"Quite so, Jack. I understand fully."

"Will you support us on this?"

The PM nodded at once. "Yes, old boy, we must, mustn't we?"

"Thanks, pal." Ryan patted him on the shoulder.

CHAPTER 44

The Shape of a New World Order

It took all day, lengthening what was supposed to have been a pro forma meeting of the NATO chiefs into a minor marathon. It took all of Scott Adler's powers of persuasion to smooth things over with the various foreign ministers, but with the assistance of Britain, whose diplomacy had always been of the Rolls-Royce class, after four hours there was a head-nod-and-handshake agreement, and the diplomatic technicians were sent off to prepare the documents. All this was accomplished behind closed doors, with no opportunity for a press leak, and so when the various government leaders made it outside, the media learned of it like a thunderbolt from a clear sky. What they did not learn was the real reason for the action. They were told it had to do with the new economic promise in the Russian Federation, which seemed reasonable enough, and when you came down to it, was the root cause in any case.

In fact most of the NATO partners didn't know the whole story, either. The new American intelligence was directly shared only with Britain, though France and Germany were given some indications of America's cause for concern. For the rest, the simple logic of the situation was enough to offer appeal. It would look good in the press, and for most politicians all over the world, that was sufficient to make them doff their clothes and run about a public square naked. Secretary Adler cautioned his President about the dangers of drawing sovereign nations into treaty obligations without telling them all the reasons behind them, but even he agreed that there was little other choice in the matter. Besides, there *was* a built-in escape clause that the media wouldn't see at first, and hopefully, neither would the Chinese.

The media got the story out in time for the evening news broadcasts in America and the late-night ones in Europe, and the TV cameras showed the arrival of the various VIPs at the official dinner in Warsaw.

"I owe you one, Tony," Ryan told the British Prime Minister with a salute of his wineglass. The white wine was French, from the Loire Valley, and excellent. The hard liquor of the night had been an equally fine Polish vodka.

"Well, one can hope that it gives our Chinese friends pause. When will Grushavoy arrive?"

"Tomorrow afternoon, followed by more drinking. Vodka again, I suppose." The documents were being printed up at this very moment, and then would be bound in fine leather, as such important documents invariably were, after which they'd be tucked away in various dusty basement archives, rarely to be seen by the eyes of men again.

"Basil tells me that your intelligence information is unusually good, and rather frightening," the PM observed, with a sip of his own.

"It is all of that, my friend. You know, we're supposed to think that this war business is a thing of the past."

"So they thought a hundred years ago, Jack. It didn't quite work out that way, did it?"

"True, but that was then, and this is now. And the world really has changed in the past hundred years."

"I hope that is a matter of some comfort to Franz Ferdinand, and the ten million or so chaps who died as an indirect result of his demise, not to mention Act Two of the Great European Civil War," the Prime Minister observed.

"Yeah, day after tomorrow, I'm going down to Auschwitz. That ought to be fun." Ryan didn't really want to go, but he figured it was something of an obligation under the circumstances, and besides, Arnie thought it would look good on TV, which was why he did a lot of the things he did.

"Do watch out for the ghosts, old boy. I should think there are a number of them there."

"I'll let you know," Ryan promised. Would it be like Dickens's *A*

Christmas Carol? he wondered. The ghost of horrors past, accompanied by the ghost of horrors present, and finally the ghost of horrors yet to be? But he was in the business of preventing such things. That's what the people of his country paid him for. Maybe $250,000 a year wasn't much for a guy who'd twice made a good living in the trading business, but it was a damned sight more than most of the taxpayers made, and they gave it to him in return for his work. That made the obligation as sacred as a vow sworn to God's own face. Auschwitz had happened because other men hadn't recognized their obligation to the people whom *they* had been supposed to serve. Or something like that. Ryan had never quite made the leap of imagination necessary to understand the thought processes of dictators. Maybe Caligula had really figured that the lives of the Roman people were his possessions to use and discard like peanut shells. Maybe Hitler had thought that the German people existed only to serve his ambition to enter the history books—and if so, sure enough it had happened, just not quite the way he'd hoped it would. Jack Ryan knew objectively that he'd be in various history books, but he tried to avoid thinking about what future generations would make of him. Just surviving in his job from day to day was difficult enough. The problem with history was that you couldn't transport yourself into the future so that you could look back with detachment and see what the hell you were supposed to do. No, making history was a damned sight harder than studying it, and so he'd decided to avoid thinking about it altogether. He wouldn't be around to know what the future thought anyway, so there was no sense in worrying about it, was there? He had his own conscience to keep him awake at night, and that was hard enough.

Looking around the room, he could see the chiefs of government of more than fifteen countries, from little Iceland to the Netherlands to Turkey. He was President of the United States of America, by far the largest and most powerful country of the NATO alliance—until tomorrow, anyway, he corrected himself—and he wanted to take them all aside and ask each one how the hell he (they were all men at the moment) reconciled his self and his duties. How did you do the job honorably? How did you look after the needs of every citizen? Ryan knew that he couldn't reasonably expect to be universally loved. Arnie had told him that—that he only needed to be liked, not loved, by half-plus-one of the voters in America—but there had to be more to the job than that, didn't there? He knew all of his fellow chief executives by name and sight, and he'd been briefed in on each man's character. That one there, he had a mistress only nineteen years old. That one drank like a fish. That one had a little confusion about his sexual preference. And that one was a crook who'd enriched himself hugely on the government payroll. But they were all allies of his country, and therefore they were officially his friends. And so Jack had to ignore what he knew of them and treat them like what they appeared to be rather than what they really were, and the really funny part of that was that they felt themselves to be his superiors because they were better politicians than he was. And the funniest part of all was that they were right. They *were* better politicians than he was, Ryan thought, sipping his wine. The British Prime Minister walked off to see his Norwegian counterpart, as Cathy Ryan rejoined her husband.

"Well, honey, how did it go?"

"The usual. Politics. Don't any of these women have a real job?" she asked the air.

"Some do," Jack remembered from his briefings. "Some even have kids."

"Mainly grandkids. I'm not old enough for that yet, thank God."

"Sorry, babe. But there are advantages to being young and beautiful," POTUS told FLOTUS.

"And you're the best-looking guy here," Cathy replied with a smile.

"But I'm too tired. Long day at the bargaining table."

"Why are you bringing Russia into NATO?"

"To stop a war with China," Jack replied honestly. It was time she knew. The answer to her question got her attention.

"What?"

"I'll fill you in later, babe, but that's the short version."

"A war?"

"Yeah. It's a long story, and we hope that what we agreed to do today will prevent it."

"You say so," Cathy Ryan observed dubiously.

"Meet anybody you like?"

"The French president is very charming."

"Oh, yeah? He was a son of a bitch in the negotiating session today. Maybe he's just trying to get in your knickers," Jack told his wife. He'd been briefed in on the French president, and he was reputed to be a man of "commendable vigor," as the State Department report delicately put it. Well, the French had a reputation as great lovers, didn't they?

"I'm spoke for, Sir John," she reminded him.

"And so am I, my lady." He could have Roy Altman shoot the Frenchman for making a move on his wife, Ryan thought with amusement, but that would cause a diplomatic incident, and Scott Adler always got upset about those. . . . Jack checked his watch. It was about time to call this one a day. Soon some diplomat would make a discreet announcement that would end the evening. Jack hadn't danced with his wife. The sad truth was that Jack couldn't dance a lick, which was a source of minor contention with his wife, and a shortcoming he planned to correct someday . . . maybe.

The party broke up on time. The embassy had comfortable quarters, and Ryan found his way to the king-sized bed brought in for his and Cathy's use.

Bondarenko's official residence at Chabarsovil was a very comfortable one, befitting a four-star resident and his family. But his wife didn't like it. Eastern Siberia lacked the social life of Moscow, and besides, one of their daughters was nine months pregnant, and his wife was in St. Petersburg to be there when the baby arrived. The front of the house overlooked a large parade ground. The back, where his bedroom was, looked into the pine forests that made up most of this province. He had a large personal staff to look after his needs. That included a particularly skilled cook, and communications people. It was one of the latter who knocked on his bedroom door at three in the local morning.

"Yes, what is it?"

"An urgent communication for you, Comrade General," the voice answered.

"Very well, wait a minute." Gennady Iosifovich rose and donned a cloth robe, punching on a light as he went to open the door. He grumbled as any man would at the loss of sleep, but generals had to expect this sort of thing. He opened the door without a snarl at the NCO who handed over the telex.

"Urgent, from Moscow," the sergeant emphasized.

"Da, spasiba," the general replied, taking it and walking back to-

ward his bed. He sat in the comfortable chair that he usually dumped his tunic on and picked up the reading glasses that he didn't actually need, but which made reading easier in the semidarkness. It was something urgent—well, urgent enough to wake him up in the middle of the fucking—

"My God," CINC–FAR EAST breathed to himself, halfway down the cover sheet. Then he flipped it over to read the substance of the report.

In America it would be called a Special National Intelligence Estimate. Bondarenko had seen them before, even helped draft some, but never one like this.

It is believed that there is an imminent danger of war between Russia and the People's Republic of China. The Chinese objective in offensive operations will be to seize the newly-discovered gold and oil deposits in eastern Siberia by rapid mechanized assault north from their border west of Khabarovsk. The leading elements will include the 34th Shock Army, a Type A Group Army . . .

This intelligence estimate is based upon national intelligence assets with access to the political leaders of the PRC, and the quality of the intelligence is graded "1A," the report went on, meaning that the SVR regarded it as Holy Writ. Bondarenko hadn't seen that happen very much.

Far East Command is directed to make all preparations to meet and repel such an attack . . .

"With what?" the general asked the papers in his hand. "With what, comrades?" With that he lifted the bedside phone. "I want my staff together in forty minutes," he told the sergeant who answered. He would not take the theatrical step of calling a full alert just yet. That would follow his staff meeting. Already his mind was examining the problem. It would continue to do so as he urinated, then shaved, his mind running in small circles, a fact which he recognized but couldn't change, and the fact that he couldn't change it didn't slow the process one small bit. The problem he faced as he scraped the whiskers from his face was not an easy one, perhaps an impossible one, but his four-star rank made it *his* problem, and he didn't want to be remembered by future Russian military students as the general who'd not been up to the task of defending his country against a foreign invasion. He was here, Bondarenko told himself, because he was the best operational thinker his country had. He'd faced battle before, and comported himself well enough not only to live but to wear his nation's highest decorations for bravery. He'd studied military history his whole life. He'd even spent time with the Americans at their battle laboratory in California, something he lusted to copy and re-create in Russia as the best possible way to prepare soldiers for battle, but which his country couldn't begin to afford for years. He had the knowledge. He had the nerve. What he lacked were the assets. But history was not made by soldiers who had what they needed, but by those who did not. When the soldiers had enough, the political leaders went into the books. Gennady Iosifovich was a soldier, and a *Russian* soldier. His country was *always* taken by surprise, because for whatever reason her political leaders didn't ever see war coming, and because of that soldiers had to pay the price. A distant voice told him that at least he wouldn't be shot for failure. Stalin was long dead, and with him the ethos of punishing those whom he had failed to warn or prepare. But Bondarenko didn't listen to that voice. Failure was too bitter an alternative for him to consider while he lived.

The Special National Intelligence Estimate made its way to American forces in Europe and the Pacific even more quickly than to Chabarsovil. For Admiral Bartolomeo Vito Mancuso, it came before a scheduled dinner with the governor of Hawaii. His Public Affairs Officer had to knock that one back a few hours while CINCPAC called his staff together.

"Talk to me, Mike," Mancuso commanded his J-2, BG Michael Lahr.

"Well, it hasn't come totally out of left field, sir," the theater intelligence coordinator replied. "I don't know anything about the source of the intelligence, but it looks like high-level human intelligence, probably with a political point of origin. CIA says it's highly reliable, and Director Foley is pretty good. So, we have to take this one very seriously." Lahr paused for a sip of water.

"Okay, what we know is that the PRC is looking with envious eyes at the Russian mineral discoveries in the central and northern parts of eastern Siberia. That plays into the economic problems they got faced with after the killings in Beijing caused the break in trade talks, and it also appears that their other trading partners are backing away from them as well. So, the Chinese now find themselves in a really tight economic corner, and that's been a *casus belli* as far back as we have written history."

"What can we do to scare them off?" asked the general commanding Pacific Fleet Marine Force.

"What we're doing tomorrow is to make the Russian federation part of NATO. Russian President Grushavoy will be flying to Warsaw in a few hours to sign the North Atlantic Treaty. *That* makes Russia an ally of the United States of America, and of *all* the NATO members. So, the thinking is that if China moves, they're not just taking on Russia, but all the rest of the North Atlantic Council as well, and *that* ought to give them pause."

"And if it doesn't?" Mancuso asked. As a theater commander-in-chief, he was paid to consider diplomatic failure rather than success.

"Then, sir, if the Chinese strike north, we have a shooting war on the Asian mainland between the People's Republic of China and an American ally. That means we're going to war."

"Do we have any guidance from Washington along those lines?" CINCPAC asked.

Lahr shook his head. "Not yet, Admiral. It's developing a little fast for that, and Secretary Bretano is looking to us for ideas."

Mancuso nodded. "Okay. What can we do? What kind of shape are we in?"

The four-star commanding Seventh Fleet leaned forward: "I'm in pretty decent shape. My carriers are all available or nearly so, but my aviators could use some more training time. Surface assets—well, Ed?"

Vice Admiral Goldsmith looked over to his boss. "We're good, Bart."

ComSubPac nodded. "It'll take a little time to surge more of my boats west, but they're trained up, and we can give their navy a major bellyache if we have to."

Then eyes turned to the Marine. "I hope you're not going to tell me to invade the Chinese mainland with one division," he observed. Besides, all of Pacific Fleet didn't have enough amphibious-warfare ships to land more than a brigade landing force, and they knew that. Good as the Marines were, they couldn't take on the entire People's Liberation Army.

"What sort of shape are the Russians in?" Seventh Fleet asked General Lahr.

"Not good, sir. Their new Commander Far East is well regarded, but he's hurting for assets. The PLA has him outnumbered a good eight to one, probably more. So, the Russians don't have much in the way of deep-strike capabilities, and just defending themselves against air attack is going to be a stretch."

"That's a fact," agreed the general commanding the Air Force assets in the Pacific Theater. "Ivan's pissed away a lot of his available assets dealing with the Chechens. Most of their aircraft are grounded with maintenance problems. That means his drivers aren't getting the stick time they need to be proficient airmen. The Chinese, on the other hand, have been training pretty well for several years. I'd say their air force component is in pretty good shape."

"What can we move west with?"

"A lot," the USAF four-star answered. "But will it be enough? Depends on a lot of variables. It'll be nice to have your carriers around to back us up." Which was unusually gracious of the United States Air Force.

"Okay," Mancuso said next. "I want to see some options. Mike, let's firm up our intelligence estimates on what the Chinese are capable of, first of all, and second, what they're thinking."

"The Agency is altering the tasking of its satellites. We ought to be getting a lot of overheads soon, plus our friends on Taiwan—they keep a pretty good eye on things for us."

"Are they in on this SNIE?" Seventh Fleet asked.

Lahr shook his head. "No, not yet. This stuff is being held pretty close."

"Might want to tell Washington that they have a better feel for Beijing's internal politics than we do," the senior Marine observed. "They ought to. They speak the same language. Same thought processes and stuff. Taiwan ought to be a prime asset to us."

"Maybe, maybe not," Lahr countered. "If a shooting war starts, they won't jump in for the fun of it. Sure, they're our friends, but they don't really have a dog in this fight yet, and the smart play for them is to play it cautious. They'll go to a high alert status, but they will not commence offensive operations on their own hook."

"Will we really back the Russians if it comes to that? More to the point, will the Chinese regard that as a credible option on our part?" ComAirPac asked. He administratively "owned" the carriers and naval air wings. Getting them trained was his job.

"Reading their minds is CIA's job, not ours," Lahr answered. "As far as I know, DIA has no high-quality sources in Beijing, except what we get from intercepts out of Fort Meade. If you're asking me for a personal opinion, well, we have to remember that their political assessments are made by Maoist politicians who tend to see things their own way rather than with what we would term an objective outlook. Short version, I don't know, and I don't know anyone who does, but the asset that got us this information tells us that they're serious about this possible move. Serious enough to bring Russia into NATO. You could call that rather a desperate move towards deterring the PRC, Admiral."

"So, we regard war as a highly possible eventuality?" Mancuso summarized.

"Yes, sir," Lahr agreed.

"Okay, gentlemen. Then we treat it that way. I want plans and options for giving our Chinese brethren a bellyache. Rough outlines after lunch tomorrow, and firm options in forty-eight hours. Questions?" There were none. "Okay, let's get to work on this."

Al Gregory was working late. A computer-software expert, he was accustomed to working odd hours, and this was no exception. At the moment he was aboard USS *Gettysburg,* an Aegis-class cruiser. The ship was not in the water, but rather in dry dock, sitting on a collection of wooden blocks while undergoing propeller replacement. *Gettysburg* had tangled with a buoy that had parted its mooring chain and drifted into the fairway, rather to the detriment of the cruiser's port screw. The yard was taking its time to do the replacement because the ship's engines were about due for programmed maintenance anyway. This was good for the crew. Portsmouth Naval Shipyard, part of the Norfolk Naval Base complex, wasn't exactly a garden spot, but it was where most of the crew's families lived, and that made it attractive enough.

Gregory was in the ship's CIC, or Combat Information Center, the compartment from which the captain "fought" the ship. All the weapons systems were controlled from this large space. The SPY radar display was found on three side-by-side displays about the size of a good big-screen TV. The problem was the computers that drove the systems.

"You know," Gregory observed to the senior chief who maintained the systems, "an old iMac has a ton more power than this."

"Doc, this system is the flower of 1975 technology," the senior chief protested. "And it ain't all that hard to track a missile, is it?"

"Besides, Dr. Gregory," another chief put it, "that radar of mine is still the best fucking system ever put to sea."

"That's a fact," Gregory had to agree. The solid-state components could combine to blast six *megawatts* of RF power down a one-degree line of bearing, enough to make a helicopter pilot, for example, produce what cruel physicians called FLKs: funny-looking kids. And more than enough to track a ballistic reentry vehicle at a thousand miles or more. The limitation there also was computer software, which was the new gold standard in just about every weapons system in the world.

"So, when you want to track an RV, what do you do?"

"We call it 'inserting the chip,' " the senior chief answered.

"What? It's hardware?" Al asked. He had trouble believing that. This wasn't a computer that you slid a board into.

"No, sir, it's software. We upload a different control program."

"Why do you need a second program for that? Can't your regular one track airplanes and missiles?" the TRW vice president demanded.

"Sir, I just maintain and operate the bitch. I don't design the things. RCA and IBM do that."

"Shit," Gregory observed.

"You could talk to Lieutenant Olson," the other chief thought aloud. "He's a Dartmouth boy. Pretty smart for a j.g."

"Yeah," the first chief agreed. "He writes software as sort of a hobby."

"Dennis the Menace. Weps and the XO get annoyed with him sometimes."

"Why?" Gregory asked.

"Because he talks like you, sir," Senior Chief Leek answered. "But he ain't in your pay grade."

"He's a good kid, though," Senior Chief Matson observed. "Takes good care of his troops, and he knows his stuff, doesn't he, Tim?"

"Yeah, George, good kid, going places if he stays in."

"He won't. Computer companies are already trying to recruit him. Shit, Compaq offered him three hundred big ones last week."

"That's a living wage," Chief Leek commented. "What did Dennis say?"

"He said no. I told him to hold out for half a mil." Matson laughed as he reached for some coffee.

"What d'ya think, Dr. Gregory? The kid worth that kinda money in the 'puter business?"

"If he can do really good code, maybe," Al replied, making a mental note to check out this Lieutenant Olson himself. TRW always had room for talent. Dartmouth was known for its computer science department. Add field experience to that, and you had a real candidate for the ongoing SAM project. "Okay, if you insert the chip, what happens?"

"Then you change the range of the radar. You know how it works, the RF energy goes out forever on its own, but we only accept signals that bounce back within a specific time gate. This"—Senior Chief Leek held up a floppy disk with a hand-printed label on it—"changes the gate. It extends the effective rage of the SPY out to, oh, two thousand kilometers. Damned sight farther than the missiles'll go. I was on *Port Royal* out at Kwajalein five years ago doing a theater-missile test, and we were tracking the inbound from the time it popped over the horizon all the way in."

"You hit it?" Gregory asked with immediate interest.

Leek shook his head. "Guidance-fin failure on the bird, it was an early Block-IV. We got within fifty meters, but that was a cunt hair outside the warhead's kill perimeter, and they only allowed us one shot, for some reason or other nobody ever told me about. *Shiloh* got a kill the next year. Splattered it with a skin-skin kill. The video of that one is a son of a bitch," the senior chief assured his guest.

Gregory believed it. When an object going one way at fourteen thousand miles per hour got hit by something going the other way at two thousand miles per hour, the result could be quite impressive. "First-round hit?" he asked.

"You bet. The sucker was coming straight at us, and this baby doesn't miss much."

"We always clean up with Vandal tests off Wallops Island," Chief Matson confirmed.

"What are those exactly?"

"Old Talos SAMs," Matson explained. "Big stovepipes, ramjet engines, they can come in on a ballistic track at about twenty-two hundred miles per hour. Pretty hot on the deck, too. That's what we worry about. The Russians came out with a sea-skimmer we call Sunburn—"

"Aegis-killer, some folks call it," Chief Leek added. "Low and fast."

"But we ain't missed one yet," Matson announced. "The Aegis system's pretty good. So, Dr. Gregory, what exactly are you checking out?"

"I want to see if your system can be used to stop a ballistic inbound."

"How fast?" Matson asked.

"A for-real ICBM. When you detect it on radar, it'll be doing about seventeen thousand miles per hour, call it seventy-six hundred meters per second."

"That's real fast," Leek observed. "Seven, eight times the speed of a rifle bullet."

"Faster'n a theater ballistic weapon like a Scud. Not sure we can do it," Matson worried.

"This radar system'll track it just fine. It's very similar to the Cobra Dane system in the Aleutians. Question is, can your SAMs react fast enough to get a hit?"

"How hard's the target?" Matson asked.

"Softer than an aircraft. The RV's designed to withstand heat, not an impact. Like the space shuttle. When you fly it through a rainstorm, it plays hell with the tiles."

"Oh, yeah?"

"Yep." Gregory nodded. "Like Styrofoam coffee cups."

"Okay, so then the problem's getting the SM2 close enough to have the warhead pop off when the target's in the fragmentation cone."

"Correct." They might be enlisted men, Gregory thought, but that didn't make them dumb.

"Software fix in the seeker head, right?"

"Also correct. I've rewritten the code. Pretty easy job, really. I reprogrammed the way the laser mutates. Ought to work okay if the infrared homing system works as advertised. At least it did in the computer simulations up in Washington."

"It worked just fine on *Shiloh,* Doc. We got the videotape aboard somewhere," Leek assured him. "Wanna see it?"

"You bet," Dr. Gregory said with enthusiasm.

"Okay." Senior Chief Leek checked his watch. "I'm free now. Let me head aft for a smoke, and then we'll *roll the videotape,"* he said, sounding like Warner Wolf on WCBS New York.

"You can't smoke in here?"

Leek grunted annoyance. "It's the New Navy, Doc. The cap'n's a health Nazi. You gotta go aft to light up. Not even in chief's quarters," Leek groused.

"I quit," Matson said. "Not a pussy like Tim here."

"My ass," Leek responded. "There's a few real men left aboard."

"How come you sit sideways here?" Gregory asked, rising to his feet to follow them aft. "The important displays go to the right side of the ship instead of fore and aft. How come?"

" 'Cuz it helps you puke if you're in a seaway." Matson laughed. "Whoever designed these ships didn't like sailors much, but at least the air-conditioning works." It rarely got above sixty degrees in the CIC, causing most of the men who worked there to wear sweaters. Aegis cruisers were decidedly not known for their comforts.

This is serious?" Colonel Aliyev asked. It was a stupid question, and he knew it. But it just had to come out anyway, and his commander knew that.

"We have orders to treat it that way, Colonel," Bondarenko replied crossly. "What do we have to stop them?"

"The 265th Motor-Rifle Division is at roughly fifty percent combat efficiency," the theater operations officer replied. "Beyond that, two tank regiments at forty percent or so. Our reserve formations are mostly theoretical," Aliyev concluded. "Our air assets—one regiment of fighter-interceptors ready for operations, another three who don't have even half their aircraft fit to fly."

Bondarenko nodded at the news. It was better than it had been upon his arrival in theater, and he'd done well to bring things that far, but that wouldn't impress the Chinese very much.

"Opposition?" he asked next. Far East's intelligence officer was another colonel, Vladimir Konstantinovich Tolkunov.

"Our Chinese neighbors are in good military shape, Comrade General. The nearest enemy formation is Thirty-fourth Shock Army, a Type A Group Army commanded by General Peng Xi-Wang," he began, showing off what he knew. "That one formation has triple or more our mechanized assets, and is well trained. Chinese aircraft—well, their tactical aircraft number over two thousand, and we must assume they will commit everything to this operation. Comrades, we do not have anything like the assets we need to stop them."

"So, we will use space to our advantage," the general proposed. "Of that we have much. We will fight a holding action and await reinforcements from the west. I'll be talking with Stavka later today. Let's draw up what we'll need to stop these barbarians."

"All down one line of railroad," Aliyev observed. "And our fucking engineers have been busily clearing a route for the Chinks to take to the oil fields. General, first of all, we need to get our engineers working on minefields. We have millions of mines, and the route the Chinese will take is easily predicted."

The overall problem was that the Chinese had strategic, if not tactical, surprise. The former was a political exercise, and like Hitler in 1941, the Chinese had pulled it off. At least Bondarenko would have tactical warning, which was more than Stalin had allowed his Red Army. He also expected to have freedom of maneuver, because also unlike Stalin, his President Grushavoy would be thinking with his brain instead of his balls. With freedom of maneuver Bondarenko would have the room to play a mobile war with his enemy, denying the Chinese a chance at decisive engagement, allowing hard contact only when it served his advantage. Then he'd be able to wait for reinforcements to give him a chance to fight a set-piece battle on his own terms, at a place and time of his choosing.

"How good are the Chinese, really, Pavel?"

"The People's Liberation Army has not engaged in large-scale combat operations for over fifty years, since the Korean War with the Americans, unless you cite the border clashes we had with them in the late '60s and early '70s. In that case, the Red Army dealt with them well, but to do that we had massive firepower, and the Chinese were only fighting for limited objectives. They are trained largely on our old model. Their soldiers will not have the ability to think for themselves. Their discipline is worse than draconian. The smallest infraction can result in summary execution, and that makes for obedience. At the operational level, their general officers are well-trained in theoretical terms. Qualitatively, their weapons are roughly the equal of ours. With their greater funding, their training levels mean that their soldiers are intimately familiar with their weapons and rudimentary tactics," Zhdanov told the assembled staff. "But they are probably not our equal in operational-maneuver thinking. Unfortunately, they do have numbers going for them, and quantity has a quality all its own, as the NATO armies used to say of us. What they will want to do, and what I fear they will, is try to roll over us quickly—just crush us and move on to their political and economic objectives as quickly as possible."

Bondarenko nodded as he sipped his tea. This was mad, and the maddest part of all was that he was playing the role of a NATO commander from 1975—maybe a German one, which was truly insane—faced with adverse numbers, but blessed, as the Germans had not been, with space to play with, and Russians had always used space to their advantage. He leaned forward:

"Very well. Comrades, we will *deny* them the opportunity for decisive engagement. If they cross the border, we will fight a maneuver war. We will sting and move. We will hurt them and withdraw before they can counterattack. We will give them land, but we will *not* give them blood. The life of every single one of our soldiers is precious to us. The Chinese have a long way to go to their objectives. We will let them go a lot of that way, and we will bide our time and husband our men and equipment. We will make them pay for what they take, but we will not—we must not—give them the chance to catch our forces in decisive battle. Are we understood on that?" he asked his staff. "When in doubt, we will run away and deny the enemy what he wants. When we have what we need to strike back, we will make him wish he never heard of Russia, but until then, let him chase his butterflies."

"What of the border guards?" Aliyev asked.

"They will hurt the Chinese, and then they will pull out. Comrades, I cannot emphasize this enough: the life of every single private soldier is important to us. Our men will fight harder if they know we care about them, and more than that, they *deserve* our care and solicitude. If we ask them to risk their lives for their country, their country *must* be loyal to them in return. If we achieve that, they will fight like tigers. The Russian soldier knows how to fight. We must all be worthy of him. You are all skilled professionals. This will be the most important test of our lives. We must all be equal to our task. Our nation depends on us. Andrey Petrovich, draw up some plans for me. We are authorized to call up reserves. Let us start doing that. We have hectares of equipment for them to use. Unlock the gates and let them start drawing gear, and God permit the officers assigned to those cadres are worthy of their men. Dismissed." Bondarenko stood and walked out, hoping his declamation had been enough for the task.

But wars were not won by speeches.

CHAPTER 45

Ghosts of Horrors Past

President Grushavoy arrived in Warsaw with the usual pomp and circumstance. A good actor, Ryan saw, watching the arrival on TV. You never would have guessed from his face that his country was looking at a major war. Grushavoy passed the same receiving line, doubtless composed of the same troops Ryan had eyeballed on his arrival, made a brief but flowery arrival speech citing the long and friendly history shared by Poland and Russia (conveniently leaving out the equally long and less-than-friendly parts), then got into a car for the city, accompanied, Ryan was glad to see, by Sergey Nikolay'ch Golovko.

In the President's hand was a fax from Washington outlining what the Chinese had in the way of war assets to turn loose on their northern neighbors, along with an estimate from the Defense Intelligence Agency on what they called the "correlation of forces," which, Jack remembered, was a term of art used by the Soviet army of old. Its estimate of the situation was not especially favorable. Almost as bad, America didn't have much with which to help the Russians. The world's foremost navy was of little direct use in a land war. The United States Army had a division and a half of heavy troops in Europe, but that was thousands of miles from the expected scene of action. The Air Force had all the mobility it needed to project force anywhere on the globe, and that could give anyone a serious headache, but airplanes could not by themselves defeat an army. No, this would be largely a Russian show, and the Russian army, the fax said, was in terrible shape. The DIA had some good things to say about the senior Russian commander in theater, but a smart guy with a .22 against a dumb one with a machine gun was still at a disadvantage. So, he hoped the Chinese would be taken aback by this day's news, but CIA and State's estimate of that possibility was decidedly iffy.

"Scott?" Ryan asked his Secretary of State.

"Jack, I can't say. This ought to discourage them, but we can't be sure how tight a corner they think they are in. If they think they're trapped, they might still lash out."

"God damn it, Scott, is this the way nations do business?" Jack demanded. "Misperceptions? Fears? Outright stupidity?"

Adler shrugged. "It's a mistake to think a chief of government is any smarter than the rest of us, Jack. People make decisions the same way, regardless of how big and smart they are. It comes down to how they perceive the question, and how best they can serve their own needs, preserve their own personal well-being. Remember that we're not dealing with clergymen here. They don't have much in the way of consciences. Our notion of right and wrong doesn't play in that sort of mind. They translate what's good for their country into what's good for themselves, just like a king in the twelfth century, but in this case there isn't any bishop around to remind them that there may be a God looking down at them with a notebook." They'd gone out of their way, Adler didn't have to say, to eliminate a cardinal-archbishop just to get themselves into this mess.

"Sociopaths?" the President asked.

Secretary Adler shrugged. "I'm not a physician, just a diplomat. When you negotiate with people like this, you dangle what's good for their country—them—in front of their eyes and hope they reach for it. You play the game without entirely understanding them. These people do things neither one of us would ever do. And they run a major country, complete with nuclear weapons."

"Great," Ryan breathed. He stood and got his coat. "Well, let's go watch our new ally sign up, shall we?"

Ten minutes later, they were in the reception room of the Lazienski Palace. There was the usual off-camera time for the various chiefs of government to socialize over Perrier-and-a-twist before some nameless protocol official opened the double doors to the table, chairs, documents, and TV cameras.

The speech from President Grushavoy was predictable in every detail. The NATO alliance had been established to protect Western Europe against what his country had once been, and his former country had established its own mirror-image alliance called the Warsaw Pact right here in this very city. But the world had turned, and now Russia was pleased to join the rest of Europe in an alliance of friends whose only wish was peace and prosperity for all. Grushavoy was pleased indeed to be the first Russian in a very long time to be a real part of the European community, and promised to be a worthy friend and partner of his newly close neighbors. (The military ramifications of the North Atlantic Treaty were not mentioned at all.) And everyone present applauded. And Grushavoy pulled out an ancient fountain pen borrowed from the collection at The Hermitage in St. Petersburg to sign in the name of his country, and so bring membership in NATO up by one. And everyone applauded again as the various chiefs of state and government walked over to shake their new ally's hand. And the shape of the world changed yet again.

"Ivan Emmetovich," Golovko said, as he approached the American President.

"Sergey Nikolay'ch," Ryan said in quiet reply.

"What will Beijing think of this?" the chief of the Russian intelligence service asked.

"With luck, we'll know in twenty-four hours," Ryan answered, knowing that this ceremony had gone out on CNN's live global feed, and positive that it was being watched in China.

"I expect the language will be profane."

"They've said nasty things about me lately," Jack assured him.

"That you should have carnal relations with your mother, no doubt."

"Actually, that I should have oral sex with her," the President confirmed distastefully. "I suppose everybody says things like that in private."

"In person, it can get a man shot."

Ryan grunted grim semi-amusement. "Bet your ass, Sergey."

"Will this work?" Golovko asked.

"I was going to ask you that. You're closer to them than we are."

"I do not know," the Russian said, with a tiny sip of his vodka glass. "And if it does not . . ."

"In that case, you have some new allies."

"And what of the precise wording of Articles Five and Six of the treaty?"

"Sergey, you may tell your president that the United States will regard an attack on any part of the territory of the Russian Federation as operative under the North Atlantic Treaty. On that, Sergey Nikolay'ch, you have the word and the commitment of the United States of America," SWORDSMAN told his Russian acquaintance.

"Jack, if I may address you in this way, I have told my president more than once that you are a man of honor, and a man of your word." The relief on his face was obvious.

"Sergey, from you those words are flattering. It's simple, really. It's your land, and a nation like ours cannot just stand by and watch a robbery of this scale taking place. It corrupts the foundations of international peace. It's our job to remake the world into a peaceful place. There's been enough war."

"I fear there will be another," Golovko said, with characteristic honesty.

"Then together your country and mine will make it the very last."

"Plato said, 'Only the dead have seen the end of war.' "

"So, are we to be bound by the words of a Greek who lived twenty-five centuries ago? I prefer the words of a Jew who lived five centuries later. It's time, Sergey. It's fucking time," Ryan said forcefully.

"I hope you are right. You Americans, always so madly optimistic . . ."

"There's a reason for that."

"Oh? What would that be?" the Russian asked.

Jack fixed his eyes on his Russian colleague. "In my country, all things *are* possible. They will be in your country, too, if you just allow it. Embrace democracy, Sergey. Embrace freedom. Americans are not genetically different from the rest of the world. We're mongrels. We have the blood of every country on earth in our veins. The only thing different between us and the rest of the world is our Constitution. Just a set of rules. That's all, Sergey, but it has served us well. You've been studying us for how long?"

"Since I joined KGB? Over thirty-five years."

"And what have you learned of America and how it works?" Ryan asked.

"Obviously not enough," Golovko answered honestly. "The spirit of your country has always puzzled me."

"Because it's too simple. You were looking for complexity. We allow people to pursue their dreams, and when the dreams succeed, we reward them. Others see that happen and chase after their own dreams."

"But the class issues?"

"What class issues? Sergey, not everybody goes to Harvard. I didn't, remember? My father was a cop. I was the first guy in my family to finish college. Look how I turned out. Sergey, we do not have class distinctions in America. You can be what you choose to be, if you are willing to work at it. You can succeed or you can fail. Luck helps," Ryan admitted, "but it comes down to work."

"All Americans have stars in their eyes," the Chairman of the SVR observed tersely.

"The better to see the heavens," Ryan responded.

"Perhaps. Just so they don't come crashing down on us."

So, what does this mean for us?" Xu Kun Piao asked, in an entirely neutral voice.

Zhang Han San and his premiere had been watching the CNN feed in the latter's private office, complete with simultaneous translation through headphones now discarded. The senior Minister Without Portfolio made a dismissive wave of the hand.

"I've read the North Atlantic Treaty," he said. "It does not apply to us at all. Articles Five and Six limit its military application to events in Europe and North America only—all right, it includes Turkey, and, as originally written, Algeria, which was part of France in 1949. For incidents at sea, it applies only to the Atlantic Ocean and the Mediterranean Sea, and then only north of the Tropic of Cancer. Otherwise, the NATO countries would have been compelled to join in the Korean War and Vietnam on the American side. Those things did not happen because the treaty did not apply outside its defined area. Nor does it apply to us. Treaty documents have discrete language and discrete application," he reminded his party chief. "They are not open-ended."

"I am concerned even so," Xu responded.

"Hostilities are not activities to be undertaken lightly," Zhang admitted. "But the real danger to us is economic collapse and the resulting social chaos. *That,* comrade, could bring down our entire social order, and *that* is something we cannot risk. But, when we succeed in seizing the oil and gold, we need not worry about such things. With our own abundant oil supply, we will not face an energy crisis, and with gold we can buy anything we require from the rest of the world. My friend, you must understand the West. They worship money, and they base their economies on oil. With those two things they must do business with us. Why did America intervene in the Kuwait affair? Oil. Why did Britain, France, and all the other nations join in? Oil. He who has oil is their friend. We shall have oil. It is that simple," Zhang concluded.

"You are very confident."

The minister nodded. "Yes, Xu, I am, because I have studied the West for many years. The way they think is actually very predictable. The purpose of this treaty might be to frighten us, I suppose, but it is at most a paper tiger. Even if they wished to provide military assistance to Russia, they do not have the ability to do so. And I do not believe that they have that wish. They cannot know our plans, because if they did, they would have pressed their advantage over us in terms of currency reserves at the trade talks, but they did not, did they?" Zhang asked.

"Is there no way they could know?"

"It is most unlikely. Comrade Tan has no hint of foreign espionage in our country at anything approaching a high level, and his sources in Washington and elsewhere have not caught a sniff of such information being available to them."

"Then why did they just broaden NATO?" Xu demanded.

"Is it not obvious? Russia is becoming rich with oil and gold, and the capitalist states wish to partake in the Russians' good fortune. That is what they said in the press, isn't it? It is fully in keeping with the capitalist ethos: mutual greed. Who can say, perhaps in five years they will invite us into NATO for the same reason," Zhang observed with an ironic leer.

"You are confident that our plans have not been compromised?"

"As we come to a higher alert level and begin moving troops, we may expect some reaction from the Russians. But the rest of them? Bah! Tan and Marshal Luo are confident as well."

"Very well," Xu said, not entirely persuaded, but agreeing even so.

It was morning in Washington. Vice President Jackson was de facto boss of the crisis-management team, a place assured by his previous job, Director of Operations—J-3—for the Joint Chiefs of Staff. One nice thing about the White House was the good security, made better still by bringing people in via helicopter and car, and by the fact that the Joint Chiefs could teleconference in from their meeting room—"the Tank"—over a secure fiber-optic link.

"Well?" Jackson asked, looking at the large television on the wall of the Situation Room.

"Mancuso has his people at work in Hawaii. The Navy can give the Chinese a bad time, and the Air Force can move a lot of assets to Russia if need be," said Army General Mickey Moore, Chairman of the Joint Chiefs. "It's the land side of the equation that has me worried. We could theoretically move one heavy division—First Armored—from Germany east, along with some attachments, and maybe NATO will join in with some additional stuff, but the Russian army is in miserable shape at the moment, especially in the Far East, and there's also the additional problem that China has twelve CSS-4 intercontinental ballistic missiles. We figure eight or more of them are aimed at us."

"Tell me more," TOMCAT ordered.

"They're Titan-II clones. Hell," Moore went on, "I just found out the background earlier today. They were designed by a CalTech-educated Air Force colonel of Chinese ethnicity who defected over there in the 1950s. Some bonehead trumped up some security charges against him—turned out they were all bullshit, would you believe—and he bugged out with a few suitcases' worth of technical information right out of JPL, where he was working at the time. So, the ChiComms built what were virtually copies of the old Martin-Marietta missile, and, like I said, we figure eight of them are aimed back at us."

"Warheads?"

"Five-megaton is our best guess. City-busters. The birds are bitches to maintain, just like ours were. We figure they're kept defueled most of the time, and they probably need two to four hours to bring them up to launch readiness. That's the good news. The bad news is that they upgraded the protection on the silos over the last decade, probably as a result of what we did in the Iraq bombing campaign and also the B-2 strikes into Japan on their SS-19 clones. The current estimate is that the covers are fifteen feet of rebarred concrete plus three feet of armor-class steel. We don't have a conventional bomb that'll penetrate that."

"Why not?" Jackson demanded in considerable surprise.

"Because the GBU-29 we cobbled together to take out that deep bunker in Baghdad was designed to hang on the F-111. It's the wrong dimensions for the B-2's bomb bay, and the 111s are all at the boneyard in Arizona. So, we have the bombs, okay, but nothing to deliver them with. Best option to take those silos out would be air-launched cruise missiles with W-80 warheads, assuming the President will authorize a nuclear strike on them."

"What warning will we have that the Chinese have prepared the missiles for launch?"

"Not much," Moore admitted. "The new silo configuration pretty well prevents that. The silo covers are massive beasts. We figure they plan to blow them off with explosives, like we used to do."

"Do we have nuke-tipped cruise missiles?"

"No, the President has to authorize that. The birds and the warheads are co-located at Whiteman Air Force Base along with the B-2s. It would take a day or so to mate them up. I'd recommend that the President authorize that if this Chinese situation goes any farther," Moore concluded.

And the best way to deliver nuclear-tipped cruise missiles—off Navy submarines or carrier-based strike aircraft—was impossible because the Navy had been completely stripped of its nuclear weapons inventory, and fixing that would not be especially easy, Jackson knew. The fallout of the nuclear explosion in Denver, which had brought the world to the brink of a full-scale nuclear exchange, had caused Russia and America to take a deep breath and then to eliminate all of their ballistic launchers. Both sides still had nuclear weapons, of course. For America they were mostly B-61 and -83 gravity bombs and W-80 thermonuclear warheads that could be affixed to cruise missiles. Both systems could be delivered with a high degree of confidence and accuracy, and stealth. The B-2A bomber was invisible to radar (and hard enough to spot visually unless you were right next to it) and the cruise missiles smoked in so low that they merged not merely with ground clutter but with highway traffic as well. But they lacked the speed of ballistic weapons. That was the trouble with the fearsome weapons, but that was also their advantage.

Twenty-five minutes from turning the "enable-launch" key to impact—even less for the sea-launched sort, which usually flew shorter distances. But those were all gone, except for the ones kept for ABM tests, and those had been modified to make them difficult to fit with warheads.

"Well, we just try to keep this one conventional. How many nuclear weapons could we deliver if we had to?"

"First strike, with the B-2s?" Moore asked. "Oh, eighty or so. If you figure two per target, enough to turn every major city in the PRC into a parking lot. It would kill upwards of a hundred million people," the Chairman added. He didn't have to say that he had no particular desire to do that. Even the most bloodthirsty soldiers were repelled by the idea of killing civilians in such numbers, and those who made four-star rank got there by being thoughtful, not psychotic.

"Well, if we let them know that, they ought to think hard about pissing us off that big," Jackson decided.

"They ought to be *that* rational, I suppose," Mickey Moore agreed. "Who wants to be the ruler of a parking lot?" But the problem with that, he didn't add, was that people who started wars of aggression were never completely rational.

"How do we go about calling up reserves?" Bondarenko asked.

Theoretically, almost every Russian male citizen was liable to such a call-up, because most of them had served in their country's military at one time or another. It was a tradition that dated back to the czars, when the Russian army had been likened to a steamroller because of its enormous mass.

The practical problem today, however, was that the state didn't know where they all lived. The state required that the veterans of uniformed service tell the army when they moved from one residence to another, but the men in question, since until recently they'd needed the state's permission to move anywhere, assumed that the state knew where they were and rarely bothered, and the country's vast and cumbersome bureaucracy was too elephantine to follow up on such things. As a result, neither Russia, nor the Soviet Union before it, had done much to test its ability to call up trained soldiers who'd left their uniforms behind. There were whole reserve divisions that had the most modern of equipment, but it had never been moved after being rolled into their warehouses, and was attended only by cadres of active-duty mechanics who actually spent the time to maintain it, turning over the engines in accordance with written schedules which they followed as mindlessly as the orders that had been drafted and printed. And so, the general commanding the Far East Military Theater had access to thousands of tanks and guns for which he had no soldiers, along with mountains of shells and virtual lakes of diesel fuel.

The word "camouflage," meaning a trick to be played or a ruse, is French in origin. It really ought to be Russian, however, because Russians were the world's experts at this military art. The storage sites for the real tanks that formed the backbone of Bondarenko's theoretical army were so skillfully hidden that only his own staff knew where they were. A good fraction of the sites had even evaded American spy satellites that had searched for years for the locations. Even the roads leading to the storage sites were painted with deceptive colors, or planted with false conifer trees. This was all one more lesson of World War II, when the Soviet Army had totally befuddled the Germans so often that one wondered why the Wehrmacht even bothered employing intelligence officers, they had been snookered so frequently.

"We're getting orders out now," Colonel Aliyev replied. "With luck, half of them ought to find people who've worn the uniform. We could do better if we made a public announcement."

"No," Bondarenko replied. "We can't let them know we're getting ready. What about the officer corps?"

"For the reserve formations? Well, we have an ample supply of lieutenants and captains, just no privates or NCOs for them to command. I suppose if we need to we can field a complete regiment or so of junior officers driving tanks," Aliyev observed dryly.

"Well, such a regiment ought to be fairly proficient," the general observed with what passed for light humor. "How fast to make the call-up happen?"

"The letters are already addressed and stamped. They should all be delivered in three days."

"Mail them at once. See to it yourself, Andrey," Bondarenko ordered.

"By your command, Comrade General." Then he paused. "What do you make of this NATO business?"

"If it brings us help, then I am for it. I'd love to have American aircraft at my command. I remember what they did to Iraq. There are a lot of bridges I'd like to see dropped into the rivers they span."

"And their land forces?"

"Do not underestimate them. I've seen how they train, and I've driven some of their equipment. It's excellent, and their men know how to make use of it. One company of American tanks, competently led and supported, can hold off a whole regiment. Remember what they did to the army of the United Islamic Republic. Two active-duty regiments and a brigade of territorials crushed two heavy corps as if it were a sand-table exercise. That's why I want to upgrade our training. Our men are as good as theirs, Andrey Petrovich, but their training is the best I have ever seen. Couple that to their equipment, and there you have their advantage."

"And their commanders?"

"Good, but no better than ours. Shit, they copy our doctrine time and again. I've challenged them on this face-to-face, and they freely admit that they admire our operational thinking. But they make better use of our doctrine than we do—because they train their men better."

"And they train better because they have more money to spend."

"There you have it. They don't have tank commanders painting rocks around the motor pool, as we do," Bondarenko noted sourly. He'd just begun to change that, but just-begun was a long way from mission-accomplished. "Get the call-up letters out, and remember, we must keep this quiet. Go. I have to talk to Moscow."

"Yes, Comrade General." The G-3 made his departure.

Well, ain't that something?" Major General Diggs commented after watching the TV show.

"Makes you wonder what NATO is for," Colonel Masterman agreed.

"Duke, I grew up expecting to see T-72 tanks rolling through the Fulda Gap like cockroaches on a Bronx apartment floor. Hell, now they're our friends?" He had to shake his head in disbelief. "I've met a few of their senior people, like that Bondarenko guy running the Far East Theater. He's pretty smart, serious professional. Visited me at Fort

Irwin. Caught on real fast, really hit it off with Al Hamm and the Blackhorse. Our kind of soldier."

"Well, sir, I guess he really is now, eh?"

That's when the phone rang. Diggs lifted it. "General Diggs. Okay, put him through. . . . Morning, sir. . . . Just fine, thanks, and—yes? What's that? . . . This is serious, I presume. . . . Yes, sir. Yes, sir, we're ready as hell. Very well, sir. Bye." He set the phone back down. "Duke, good thing you're sitting down."

"What gives?"

"That was SACEUR. We got alert orders to be ready to entrain and move east."

"East where?" the divisional operations officer asked, surprised. An unscheduled exercise in Eastern Germany, maybe?

"Maybe as far as Russia, the eastern part. Siberia, maybe," Diggs added in a voice that didn't entirely believe what it said.

"What the hell?"

"NCA is concerned about a possible dust-up between the Russians and the Chinese. If it happens, we may have to go east to support Ivan."

"What the hell?" Masterman observed yet again.

"He's sending his J-2 down to brief us in on what he's got from Washington. Ought to be here in half an hour."

"Who else? Is this a NATO tasking?"

"He didn't say. Guess we'll have to wait and see. For the moment just you and the staff, the ADC, and the brigade sixes are in on the brief."

"Yes, sir," Masterman said, there being little else he could say.

The Air Force sends a number of aircraft when the President travels. Among these were C-5B Galaxies. Known to the Navy as "the aluminum cloud" for its huge bulk, the transport is capable of carrying whole tanks in its cavernous interior. In this case, however, they carried VC-60 helicopters, larger than a tank in dimensions, but far lighter in weight.

The VH-60 is a version of the Sikorsky Blackhawk troop-carrier, somewhat cleaned up and appointed for VIP passengers. The pilot was Colonel Dan Malloy, a Marine with over five thousand hours of stick time in rotary-ring aircraft, whose radio call-sign was "Bear." Cathy

Ryan knew him well. He usually flew her to Johns Hopkins in the morning in a twin to this aircraft. There was a co-pilot, a lieutenant who looked impossibly young to be a professional aviator, and a crew chief, a Marine staff sergeant E-6 who saw to it that everyone was properly strapped in, something that Cathy did better than Jack, who was not used to the different restraints in this aircraft.

Aside from that the Blackhawk flew superbly, not at all like the earthquake-while-sitting-on-a-chandelier sensation usually associated with such contrivances. The flight took almost an hour, with the President listening in on the headset/ear protectors. Overhead, all aerial traffic was closed down, even commercial flights in and out of every commercial airport to which they came close. The Polish government was concerned with his safety.

"There it is," Malloy said over the intercom. "Eleven o'clock."

The aircraft banked left to give everyone a good look out the polycarbonate windows. Ryan felt a sudden sense of enforced sobriety come over him. There was a rudimentary railroad station building with two tracks, and another spur that ran off through the arch in yet another building. There were a few other structures, but mainly just concrete pads to show where there had been a large number of others, and Ryan's mind could see them from the black-and-white movies shot from aircraft, probably Russian ones, in World War II. They'd been oddly warehouse-like buildings, he remembered. But the wares stored in them had been human beings, though the people who'd built this place hadn't seen it that way; they had regarded them as vermin, insects or rats, something to be eliminated as efficiently and coldly as possible.

That's when the chill hit. It was not a warm morning, the temperature in the upper fifties or so, Jack thought, but his skin felt colder than that number indicated. The chopper landed softly, and the sergeant got the door open and the President stepped out onto the landing pad that had recently been laid for just this purpose. An official of the Polish government came up and shook his hand, introducing himself, but Ryan missed it all, suddenly a tourist in Hell itself, or so it felt. The official who would be serving as guide led them to a car for the short drive closer to the facility. Jack slid in beside his wife.

"Jack . . ." she whispered.

"Yeah," he acknowledged. "Yeah, babe, I know." And he spoke not another word, not even hearing the well-prepared commentary the Pole was giving him.

"Arbeit Macht Frei" the wrought-iron arch read. *Work makes free* was the literal meaning, perhaps the most callously cynical motto ever crafted by the twisted minds of men calling themselves civilized. Finally, the car stopped, and they got out into the air again, and again the guide led them from place to place, telling them things they didn't hear but rather felt, because the very air seemed heavy with evil. The grass was wonderfully green, almost like a golf course from the spring rain . . . from the nutrients in the soil? Jack wondered. Lots of those. More than two million people had met death in this place. Two million. Maybe three. After a while, counting lost its meaning, and it became just a number, a figure on a ledger, written in by some accountant or other who'd long since stopped considering what the digits represented.

He could see it in his mind, the human shapes, the bodies, the heads, but thankfully not the faces of the dead. He presently found himself walking along what the German guards had called *Himmel Straße,* the Road to Heaven. But why had they called it that? Was it pure cynicism, or did they really believe there was a God looking down on what they did, and if so, what had they thought He thought of this place and their activity? What kind of men could they have been? Women and children had been slaughtered immediately upon arrival here because they had little value as workers in the industrial facilities that I. G. Farben had built, so as to take the last measure of utility from the people sent here to die—to make a little profit from their last months. Not just Jews, of course; the Polish aristocracy and the Polish priesthood had been killed here. Gypsies. Homosexuals. Jehovah's Witnesses. Others deemed undesirable by Hitler's government. Just insects to be eliminated with Zyklon-B gas, a derivative of pesticide research by the German chemical industries.

Ryan had not expected this to be a pleasant side-trip. What he'd anticipated was an educational experience, like visiting the battlefield at Antietam, for example.

But this hadn't been a battlefield, and it didn't feel like at all like one.

What must it have been like for the men who'd liberated this place in 1944? Jack wondered. Even hardened soldiers, men who'd faced death every day for years, must have been taken aback by what they'd found here. For all its horrors, the battlefield remained a place of honor, where men tested men in the most fundamental way—it was cruel and final, of course, but there was the purity of fighting men contesting with other fighting men, using weapons, but—but that was rubbish, Jack thought. There was little nobility to be found in war . . . and far less in this place. On a battlefield, for whatever purpose and with whatever means, men fought against *men,* not women and kids. There was some honor to be had in the former, but not . . . this. This was crime on a vast scale, and as evil as war was, at the human level it stopped short of what men called crime, the deliberate infliction of harm upon the innocent. How could men do such a thing? Germany was today, as it had been then, a Christian country, the same nation that had brought forth Martin Luther, Beethoven, and Thomas Mann. Did it all come down to their leader? Adolf Hitler, a nebbish of a man, born to a middle-grade civil servant, a failure at everything he'd tried . . . except demagoguery. He'd been a fucking genius at that . . .

. . . But why had Hitler hated anyone so much as to harness the industrial might of his nation not for conquest, which was bad enough, but for the base purpose of cold-blooded extermination? That, Jack knew, was one of history's most troublesome mysteries. Some said Hitler had hated the Jews because he'd seen one on the streets of Vienna and simply disliked him. Another expert in the field, a Jew himself, had posed the proposition that a Jewish prostitute had given the failed Austrian painter gonorrhea, but there was no documentary evidence upon which to base that. Yet another school of thought was more cynical still, saying that Hitler hadn't really cared about the Jews one way or another, but needed an enemy for people to hate so that he could become leader of Germany, and had merely seized upon the Jews as a target of opportunity, just something against which to mobilize his nation. Ryan found this alternative unlikely, but the most offensive of all. For whatever reason, he'd taken the power his country had given him and turned it to this purpose. In doing so, Hitler had cursed his name for all time to come, but that was no consolation to the people whose remains fertilized the grass. Ryan's wife's boss at Johns Hopkins was a Jewish doc named Bernie

Katz, a friend of many years. How many such men had died here? How many potential Jonas Salks? Maybe an Einstein or two? Or poets, or actors, or just ordinary workers who would have raised ordinary kids . . .

. . . and when Jack had sworn the oath of office mandated by the United States Constitution, he'd really sworn to protect such people as those, and maybe such people as these, too. As a man, as an American, and as President of the United States, did he not have a duty to prevent such things from ever happening again? He actually believed that the use of armed force could only be justified to protect American lives and vital American security interests. But was that all America was? What about the principles upon which his nation was founded? Did America only apply them to specific, limited places and goals? What about the rest of the world? Were these not the graves of real people?

John Patrick Ryan stood and looked around, his face as empty right now as his soul, trying to understand what had taken place here, and what he could—what he *had to* learn from this. He had immense power at his fingertips every day he lived in the White House. How to use it? How to apply it? What to fight against? More important, what to fight *for?*

"Jack," Cathy said quietly, touching his hand.

"Yeah, I've seen enough, too. Let's get the hell away from this place." He turned to the Polish guide and thanked him for words he'd scarcely heard and started walking back to where the car was. Once more they passed under the wrought-iron arch of a lie, doing what two or three million people had never done.

If there were such a thing as ghosts, they'd spoken to him without words, but done it in one voice: *Never again.* And silently, Ryan agreed. Not while he lived. Not while America lived.

CHAPTER 46

Journey Home

They waited for SORGE, and rarely had anyone waited more expectantly even for the arrival of a firstborn child. There was a little drama to it, too, because SORGE didn't deliver every day, and they could not always see a pattern in when it appeared and when it didn't. Ed and Mary Pat Foley both awoke early that morning, and lay in bed for over an hour with nothing to do, then finally arose to drink their breakfast coffee and read the papers in the kitchen of their middle-class home in suburban Virginia. The kids went off to school, and then the parents finished dressing and walked out to their "company" car, complete with driver and escort vehicle. The odd part was that their car was guarded but their house was not, and so a terrorist only had to be smart enough to attack the house, which was not all that hard. The *Early Bird* was waiting for them in the car, but it had little attraction for either of them this morning. The comic strips in the *Post* had been more interesting, especially "Non Sequitur," their favorite morning chuckle, and the sports pages.

"What do you think?" Mary Pat asked Ed. That managed to surprise him, since his wife didn't often ask his opinion of a field-operations question.

He shrugged as they passed a Dunkin' Donuts box. "Coin toss, Mary."

"I suppose. I sure hope it comes up heads this time."

"Jack's going to ask us in . . . an hour and a half, I suppose."

"Something like that," the DDO agreed in a breathy voice.

"The NATO thing ought to work, ought to make them think things over," the DCI thought aloud.

"Don't bet the ranch on it, honey bunny," Mary Pat warned.

"I know." Pause. "When does Jack get on the airplane to come home?"

She checked her watch. "About two hours."

"We should know by then."

"Yeah," she agreed.

Ten minutes later, informed of the shape of the world en route by National Public Radio's *Morning Edition,* they arrived at Langley, again parking in the underground garage, and again taking the elevator up to the seventh floor, where, again, they split up, going to their separate offices. In this, Ed surprised his wife. She'd expected him to hover over her shoulder as she flipped on her office computer, looking for another brownie recipe, as she called it. This happened at seven-fifty-four.

"You've got mail," the electronic voice announced as she accessed her special Internet account. Her hand wasn't quite shaking when she moved the mouse to click on the proper icon, but nearly so. The letter came up, went through the descrambling process, and came up as cleartext she couldn't read. As always, MP saved the document to her hard drive, confirmed that it was saved, then printed up a hard copy, and finally deleted the letter from her electronic in-box, completely erasing it off the Internet. Then she lifted her phone.

"Please have Dr. Sears come up right away," she told her secretary.

Joshua Sears had also come in early this morning, and was sitting at his desk reading *The New York Times* financial page when the call came. He was in the elevator in under a minute, and then in the office of the Deputy Director (Operations).

"Here," Mary Pat said, handing over the six pages of ideographs. "Take a seat."

Sears sat in a comfortable chair and started his translation. He could see that the DDO was a little exercised about this, and his initial diagnosis came as he turned to page two.

"This isn't good news," he said, without looking up. "Looks like Zhang is guiding Premier Xu in the direction he wants. Fang is uneasy about it, but he's going along, too. Marshal Luo is fully on the team. I guess that's to be expected. Luo's always been a hardball guy," Sears commented. "Talk here's about operational security, concern that we might know what they're up to—but they think they're secure," Sears assured the DDO.

As many times as she'd heard that sort of thing, it never failed to give her a severe case of the chills, hearing the enemy (to Mary Pat nearly everyone was an enemy) discuss the very possibility that she'd devoted her entire professional life to realizing. And almost always you heard their voices saying that, no, there wasn't anyone like her out there hearing them. She'd never really left her post in Moscow, when she'd been control officer for Agent CARDINAL. He'd been old enough to have been her grandfather, but she'd thought of him as her own newborn, as she gave him taskings, and collected his take, forwarding it back to Langley, always worried for his safety. She was out of that game now, but it came down to the same thing. Somewhere out there was a foreign national sending America information of vital interest. She knew the person's name, but not her face, not her motivation, just that she liked to share her bed with one of her officers, and she kept the official diary for this Minister Fang, and her computer sent it out on the Web, on a path that ended at her seventh-floor desk.

"Summary?" she asked Dr. Sears.

"They're still on the warpath," the analyst replied. "Maybe they'll turn off it at some later date, but there is no such indication here."

"If we warn them off . . . ?"

Sears shrugged. "No telling. Their real concern is internal political dissension and possible collapse. This economic crisis has them worried about political ruin for them all, and that's all they're worried about."

"Wars are begun by frightened men," the DDO observed.

"That's what history tells us," Sears agreed. "And it's happening again, right before our eyes."

"Shit," Mrs. Foley observed. "Okay, print it up and get it back to me, fast as you can."

"Yes, ma'am. Half hour. You want me to show this to George Weaver, right?"

"Yeah." She nodded. The academic had been going over the SORGE data for several days, taking his time to formulate his part of the SNIE slowly and carefully, which was the way he worked. "You mind working with him?"

"Not really. He knows their heads pretty well, maybe a little better than I do—he has a master's in psychology from Yale. Just he's a little slow formulating his conclusions."

"Tell him I want something I can use by the end of the day."

"Will do," Sears promised, rising for the door. Mary Pat followed him out, but took a different turn.

"Yeah?" Ed Foley said, when she came into his office.

"You'll have the write-up in half an hour or so. Short version: They are not impressed by the NATO play."

"Oh, shit," the DCI observed at once.

"Yeah," his wife agreed. "Better find out how quick we can get the information to Jack."

"Okay." The DCI lifted his secure phone and punched the speed-dial button for the White House.

There was one last semi-official meeting at the American Embassy before departure, and again it was Golovko speaking for his president, who was away schmoozing with the British Prime Minister.

"What did you make of Auschwitz?" the Russian asked.

"It ain't Disney World," Jack replied, taking a sip of coffee. "Have you been there?"

"My uncle Sasha was part of the force that liberated the camp," Sergey replied. "He was a tank commander—a colonel—in the Great Motherland War."

"Did you talk to him about it?"

"When I was a boy. Sasha—my mother's brother, he was—was a true soldier, a hard man with hard rules for life, and a committed communist. That must have shaken him, though," Golovko went on. "He didn't really talk about what effect it had on him. Just that it was ugly, and proof to him of the correctness of his cause. He said he had an especially good war after that—he got to kill more Germans."

"And what about the things—"

"Stalin did? We never spoke of that in my family. My father was NKVD, as you know. He thought that whatever the state did was correct. Not unlike what the *fascisti* thought at Auschwitz, I admit, but he would not have seen it that way. Those were different times, Ivan Emmetovich. Harder times. Your father served in the war as well, as I recall."

"Paratrooper, One-Oh-First. He never talked much about it, just the funny things that happened. He said the night drop into Normandy was pretty scary, but that's all—he never said what it was like running around in the dark with people shooting at him."

"It cannot be very enjoyable, to be a soldier in combat."

"I don't suppose it is. Sending people out to do it isn't fun, either. God damn it, Sergey! I'm supposed to protect people, not risk their lives."

"So, you are not like Hitler. And not like Stalin," the Russian added graciously. "And neither is Eduard Petrovich. It is a gentler world we live in, gentler than that of our fathers and our uncles. But not gentle enough yet. When will you know how our Chinese friends reacted to yesterday's events?"

"Soon, I hope, but we're not exactly sure. You know how that works."

"Da." You depended on the reports of your agents, but you were never sure when they would come in, and in the expectation came frustration. Sometimes you wanted to wring their necks, but that was both foolish and morally wrong, as they both knew.

"Any public reaction?" Ryan asked. The Russians would have seen it sooner than his own people.

"A nonreaction, Mr. President. No public comment at all. Not unexpected, but somewhat disappointing."

"If they move, can you stop them?"

"President Grushavoy has asked that very question of Stavka, his military chiefs, but they have not yet answered substantively. We are concerned with operational security. We do not wish the PRC to know that we know anything."

"That can work against you," Ryan warned.

"I said that very thing this morning, but soldiers have their own ways, don't they? We are calling up some reserves, and warning orders have gone out to some mechanized troops. The cupboard, however, as you Americans say, is somewhat bare at the moment."

"What have you done about the people who tried to kill you?" Ryan asked, changing the subject.

"The main one is under constant observation at the moment. If he tries something else, we will then speak to him," Golovko promised. "The connection, again, is Chinese, as you know."

"I've heard."

"Your FBI agent in Moscow, that Reilly fellow, is very talented. We could have used him in Second Directorate."

"Yeah, Dan Murray thinks a lot of him."

"If this Chinese matter goes further, we need to set up a liaison group between your military and ours."

"Work through SACEUR," Ryan told him. He'd already thought that one through. "He has instructions to cooperate with your people."

"Thank you, Mr. President. I will pass that along. So, your family, it is well?" You couldn't have this sort of meeting without irrelevant pleasantries.

"My oldest, Sally, is dating. That's hard on Daddy," Ryan admitted.

"Yes." Golovko allowed himself a smile. "You live in fear that she will come upon such a boy as you were, yes?"

"Well, the Secret Service helps keep the little bastards under control."

"There is much to be said for men with guns, yes," the Russian agreed with some amusement, to lighten the moment.

"Yeah, but I think daughters are God's punishment on us for being men." That observation earned Ryan a laugh.

"Just so, Ivan Emmetovich, just so." And Sergey paused again. Back to business: "It is a hard time for both of us, is it not?"

"Yeah, it is that."

"Perhaps the Chinese will see us standing together and reconsider their greed. Together our fathers' generation killed Hitler, after all. Who can stand against the two of us?"

"Sergey, wars are not rational acts. They are not begun by rational men. They're begun by people who don't care a rat-fuck about the people they rule, who're willing to get their fellow men killed for their own narrow purposes. This morning I saw such a place. It was Satan's amusement park, I suppose, but not a place for a man like me. I came away angry. I wouldn't mind having a chance to see Hitler, long as I have a gun in my hand when I do." It was a foolish thing to say, but Golovko understood.

"With luck, together we will prevent this Chinese adventure."

"And if not?"

"Then together we will defeat them, my friend. And perhaps that will be the last war of all."

"I wouldn't bet on it," the President replied. "I've had that thought before myself, but I suppose it's a worthy goal."

"When you find out what the Chinese say . . . ?"

"We'll get the word to you."

Golovko rose. "Thank you. I will convey that to my president."

Ryan walked the Russian to the door, then headed off to the ambassador's office.

"This just came in." Ambassador Lewendowski handed over the fax. "Is this as bad as it looks?" The fax was headed EYES-ONLY PRESIDENT, but it had come into *his* embassy.

Ryan took the pages and started reading. "Probably. If the Russians need help via NATO, will the Poles throw in?"

"I don't know. I can ask."

The President shook his head. "Too soon for that."

"Did we bring the Russians into NATO with the knowledge of this?" The question showed concern that stopped short of outrage at the violation of diplomatic etiquette.

Ryan looked up. "What do you think?" He paused. "I need your secure phone."

Forty minutes later, Jack and Cathy Ryan walked up the steps into their airplane for the ride home. SURGEON was not surprised to see her husband disappear into the aircraft's upper communications level, along with the Secretary of State. She suspected that her husband might have stolen a smoke or two up there, but she was asleep by the time he came back down.

For his part, Ryan wished he had, but couldn't find a smoker up there. The two who indulged had left their smokes in their luggage to avoid the temptation to violate USAF regulations. The President had a single drink and got into his seat, rocking it back for a nap, during which he found himself dreaming of Auschwitz, mixing it up with scenes remembered from *Schindler's List.* He awoke over Iceland, sweating, to see his wife's angelic sleeping face, and to remind himself that, bad as the world was, it wasn't quite that bad anymore. And his job was to keep it that way.

"Okay, is there any way to make them back off?" Robby Jackson asked the people assembled in the White House Situation Room.

Professor Weaver struck him as just one more academic, long of wind and short of conclusion. Jackson listened anyway. This guy knew more about the way the Chinese thought. He must. His explanation was about as incomprehensible as the thought processes he was attempting to make clear.

"Professor," Jackson said finally, "that's all well and good, but what the hell does something that happened nine centuries ago tell us about today? These are Maoists, not royalists."

"Ideology is usually just an excuse for behavior, Mr. Vice President, not a reason for it. Their motivations are the same today as they would have been under the Chin Dynasty, and they fear exactly the same thing: the revolt of the peasantry if the economy goes completely bad," Weaver explained to this pilot, a technician, he thought, and decidedly not an intellectual. At least the President had some credentials as a historian, though they weren't impressive to the tenured Ivy League department chairman.

"Back to the real question here: What can we do to make them back off, short of war?"

"Telling them that we know of their plans might give them pause, but they will make their decision on the overall correlation of forces, which they evidently believe to be fully in their favor, judging from what I've been reading from this SORGE fellow."

"So, they won't back off?" the VP asked.

"I cannot guarantee that," Weaver answered.

"And blowing our source gets somebody killed," Mary Pat Foley reminded the assembly.

"Which is just one life against many," Weaver pointed out.

Remarkably, the DDO didn't leap across the table to rip his academic face off. She respected Weaver as an area specialist/consultant. But fundamentally he was one more ivory-tower theoretician who didn't consider the human lives that rode on decisions like that one. Real people had their lives end, and that was a big deal to those real people, even if it wasn't to this professor in his comfortable office in Providence, Rhode Island.

"It also cancels out a vital source of information in the event that they go forward anyway—which could adversely affect our ability to deal with the real-world military threat, by the way."

"There is that, I suppose," Weaver conceded diffidently.

"Can the Russians stop them?" Jackson asked. General Moore took the question.

"It's six-five and pick 'em," the Chairman of the Joint Chiefs answered. "The Chinese have a lot of combat power to unleash. The Russians have a lot of room to absorb it, but not the combat power to repel it per se. If I had to bet, I'd put my money on the PRC—unless we come in. Our airpower could alter the equation somewhat, and if NATO comes in with ground forces, the odds change. It depends on what reinforcements we and the Russians can get into the theater."

"Logistics?"

"A real problem," Mickey Moore conceded. "It all comes down one railway line. It's double-tracked and electrified, but that's the only good news about it."

"Does anybody know how to run an operation like that down a railroad? Hell, we haven't done it since the Civil War," Jackson thought aloud.

"Just have to wait and see, sir, if it comes to that. The Russians have doubtless thought it over many times. We'll depend on them for that."

"Great," the Vice President muttered. A lifelong USN sailor, he didn't like depending on anything except people who spoke American and wore Navy Blue.

"If the variables were fully in our favor, the Chinese wouldn't be thinking about this operation as seriously as they evidently are." Which was about as obvious as the value of a double play with the bases loaded and one out in the bottom of the ninth.

"The problem," George Winston told them, "is that the prize is just too damned inviting. It's like the bank doors have been left open over a three-day weekend, and the local cops are on strike."

"Jack keeps saying that a war of aggression is just an armed robbery writ large," Jackson told them.

"That's not far off," SecTreas agreed. Professor Weaver thought the comparison overly simplistic, but what else could you expect of people like these?

"We can warn them off when we start seeing preparations on our overheads," Ed Foley proposed. "Mickey, when will we start seeing that?"

"Conceivably, two days. Figure a week for them to get ramped up. Their forces are pretty well in theater already, and it's just a matter of getting them postured—putting them all near their jump-off points. Then doing the final approach march will happen, oh, thirty-six hours before they start pulling the strings on their field guns."

"And Ivan can't stop them?"

"At the border? Not a chance," the general answered, with an emphatic shake of the head. "They'll have to play for time, trading land for time. The Chinese have a hell of a long trip to get the oil. That's their weakness, a huge flank to protect and a god-awful vulnerable logistics train. I'd look out for an airborne assault on either the gold or the oil fields. They don't have much in the way of airborne troops or airlift capacity, but you have to figure they'll try it anyway. They're both soft targets."

"What can we send in?"

"First thing, a lot of air assets, fighters, fighter-bombers, and every aerial tanker we can scrape up. We may not be able to establish air superiority, but we can quickly deny it to them, make it a fifty-fifty proposition almost at once, and then start rolling their air force back. Again it's a question of numbers, Robby, and a question of how well their flyers are trained. Probably better than the Russians, just because they have more hours on the stick, but technically the Russians actually have generally better aircraft, and probably better doctrine—except they haven't had the chance to practice it."

Robby Jackson wanted to grumble that the situation had too many unknowns, but if there hadn't been, as Mickey Moore had just told him, the Chinese wouldn't be leaning on their northern border. Muggers went after little old ladies with their Social Security money, not cops who had just cashed their paychecks on the way home from work. There was much to be said for carrying a gun on the street, and as irrational as street crime or war-starting might be, those who did it were *somewhat* reflective in their choices.

Scott Adler hadn't slept at all on the flight, as he'd played over and over in his mind the question of how to stop a war from starting. That was the primary mission of a diplomat, wasn't it? Mainly he considered his shortcomings. As the prime foreign-affairs officer of his country, he was supposed to know—he was *paid* to know—what to say to people to deflect them from irrational actions. At base that could mean telling them, *Do this and the full power and fury of America will descend on you and ruin your whole day.* Better to cajole them into being reasonable, because in reasonableness was their best salvation as a nation in the global village. But the truth was that the Chinese thought in ways that he could not replicate within his own mind, and so he wasn't sure what to say to make them see the light. The worst part of all was that he'd met this Zhang guy in addition to Foreign Minister Shen, and all he knew for sure was that they did not look upon reality as he did. They saw blue where he saw green, and he couldn't understand their strange version of green well enough to explain it into blue. A small voice chided him for possible racism, but this situation was too far gone for political correctness. He had a war to stop, and he didn't know how. He ended up staring at the bulkhead in front of his comfortable glove-leather seat and wishing it was a movie screen. He felt like seeing a movie now, something to get his mind off the hamster wheel that just kept turning and turning. Then he felt a tap on his shoulder, and turned to see his President, who motioned him to the circular staircase to the upper level. Again they chased two Air Force communicators off their seats.

"Thinking over the newest SORGE?"

"Yep." EAGLE nodded.

"Any ideas?"

The head moved in a different plane now. "No. Sorry, Jack, but it just isn't there. Maybe you need a new SecState."

Ryan grunted. "No, just different enemies. The only thing I see is to tell them we know what they're up to, and that they'd better stop."

"And when they tell us to shove it up our collective ass, then what?"

"You know what we need right now?" SWORDSMAN asked.

"Oh, yeah, a couple hundred Minuteman or Trident missiles would work just fine to show them the light. Unfortunately . . ."

"Unfortunately, we did away with them to make the world a safer place. Oops," Ryan concluded.

"Well, we have the bombs and the aircraft to deliver them, and—"

"No!" Ryan hissed. "No, God damn it, I will not initiate a nuclear war in order to stop a conventional one. How many people do you want me to kill?"

"Easy, Jack. It's my job to present options, remember? Not to advocate them—not that one anyway." He paused. "What did you think of Auschwitz?"

"It's the stuff of nightmares—wait a minute, your parents, right?"

"My father—Belzec in his case, and he lucked out and survived."

"Does he talk about it?"

"Never. Not a single word, even to his rabbi. Maybe a pshrink. He went to one for a few years, but I never knew what for."

"I can't let anything like that happen again. To stop that—yeah, to stop that," Ryan speculated aloud, "yeah, I might drop a B-83."

"You know the lingo?"

"A little. I got briefed in a long time ago, the names for the hardware stuck in my mind. Funny thing, I've never had nightmares about *that.* Well, I've never read into the SIOP—Single Integrated Operation Plan, the cookbook for ending the world. I think I'd eat a gun before I did that."

"A whole lot of presidents had to think those things over," Adler pointed out.

"Before my time, Scott, and they never expected them to happen anyway. They all figured they'd smart their way through it. 'Til Bob Fowler came along and damned near stumbled into calling in the codes. That was some wild Sunday night," Ryan said, remembering.

"Yeah, I know the story. You kept your head screwed on straight. Not many others did."

"Yeah. And look where it got me," POTUS observed with a grim chuckle. He looked out a window. They were over land now, probably Labrador, lots of green and lakes, and few straight lines to show the hand of man on the land. "What do we do, Scott?"

"We try to warn them off. They'll do things we can see with satellites, and then we can call them on it. Our last play will be to tell them that Russia is an American ally now, and messing with Ivan means messing with Uncle Sam. If that doesn't stop them, nothing else will."

"Offer some danegeld to buy them off?" the President wondered.

"A waste of time. I don't think it would work, but I'd be for-damned sure they'd see it as a sign of weakness and be encouraged by it. No, they respect strength, and we have to show them that. Then they'll react one way or another."

"They're going to go," Jack thought.

"Coin toss. Hope it comes up tails, buddy."

"Yeah." Ryan checked his watch. "Early morning in Beijing."

"They'll be waking up and heading in for work," Adler agreed. "What exactly can you tell me about this SORGE source?"

"Mary Pat hasn't told me much, probably best that way. One of the things I learned at Langley. You can know too much sometimes. Better not to know their faces, and especially their names."

"In case something bad happens?"

"When it does, it's pretty bad. Don't want to think what these people would do. Their version of the Miranda warning is, 'You can scream all you want. We don't mind.' "

"Funny," SecState thought.

"Actually it's not all that effective as an interrogation technique. They end up telling you exactly what you want to hear, and you end up dictating it to them instead of getting what they really know."

"What about the appeals process?" Scott asked, with a yawn. Finally, belatedly, he was getting sleepy.

"In China? That's when the shooter asks if you prefer the left ear or the right ear." Ryan stopped himself. Why was he making bad jokes on *this* subject?

The busy place in the Washington, D.C., area was the National Reconnaissance Office. A joint venture of CIA and the Pentagon, NRO ran the reconsats, the big camera birds circling the earth at low-medium altitude, looking down with their hugely expensive cameras that rivaled the precision and expense of the Hubble space telescope. There were three photo-birds up, circling the earth every two hours or so, and passing over the same spot twice a day each. There was also a radar-reconnaissance satellite that had much poorer resolution than the Lockheed- and TRW-made KH-11s, but which could see through clouds. This was important at the moment, because a cold front was tracing across the Chinese-Siberian border, and the clouds at its forward edge blanked out all visual light, much to the frustration of the

NRO technicians and scientists whose multibillion-dollar satellites were useful only for weather forecasting at the moment. Cloudy with scattered showers, and chilly, temperature in the middle forties, dropping to just below freezing at night.

The intelligence analysts, therefore, closely examined the "take" from the Lacrosse radar-intelligence bird because that was the only game in town at the moment.

"The clouds go all the way down to six thousand feet or so. Even a Blackbird wouldn't be much use at the moment," one of the photo-interpreters observed. "Okay, what do we have here . . . ? Looks like a higher level of railroad activity, looks like flatcars mostly. Something on them, but too much clutter to pick out the shapes."

"What do they move on flatcars?" a naval officer asked.

"Tracked vehicles," an Army major answered, "and heavy guns."

"Can we confirm that supposition from this data?" the Navy guy asked.

"No," the civilian answered. "But . . . there, that's the yard. We see six long trains sitting still in the yard. Okay, where's the . . ." He accessed his desktop computer and called up some visual imagery. "Here we go. See these ramps? They're designed to offload rolling equipment from the trains." He turned back to the Lacrosse "take." "Yeah, these here look like tank shapes coming off the ramps, and forming up right here in the assembly areas, and that's the shape of an armored regiment. That's three hundred twenty-two main battle tanks, and about a buck and a quarter of APCs, and so . . . yeah, I'd estimate that this is a full armored division detraining. Here's the truck park . . . and this grouping here, I'm not sure. Looks bulky . . . square or rectangular shapes. Hmm," the analyst concluded. He turned back to his own desktop and queried some file images. "You know what this looks like?"

"You going to tell us?"

"Looks like a five-ton truck with a section of ribbon bridge on it. The Chinese copied the Russian bridge design—hell, everybody did. It's a beautiful little design Ivan cobbled together. Anyway, on radar, it looks like this and"—he turned back to the recent satellite take—"that's pretty much what these look like, isn't it? I'll call that eighty percent likelihood. So, this group here I'll call two engineer regiments accompanying this tank division."

"Is that a lot of engineers to back up a single division?" the naval officer asked.

"Sure as hell," the Army major confirmed.

"I'd say so," the photo-interpreter agreed. "The normal TO and E is one battalion per division. So, this is a corps or army vanguard forming up, and I'd have to say they plan to cross some rivers, guys."

"Go on," the senior civilian told him.

"They're postured to head north."

"Okay," the Army officer said. "Have you ever seen this before?"

"Two years ago, they were running an exercise, but that was one engineer regiment, not two, and they left this yard and headed southeast. That one was a pretty big deal. We got a lot of visual overheads. They were simulating an invasion or at least a major assault. That one used a full Group A army, with an armored division and two mechanized divisions as the assault force, and the other mech division simulating a dispersed defense force. The attacking team won that one."

"How different from the way the Russians are deployed on their border?" This was the Navy intelligence officer.

"Thicker—I mean, for the exercise the Chinese defenders were thicker on the ground than the Russians are today."

"And the attacking force won?"

"Correct."

"How realistic was the exercise?" the major asked.

"It wasn't Fort Irwin, but it was as honest as they can run one, and probably accurate. The attackers had the usual advantages in numbers and initiative. They punched through and started maneuvering in the defender's trains area, had themselves a good old time."

The naval officer looked at his colleague in green. "Just what they'd be thinking if they wanted to head north."

"Concur."

"Better call this one in, Norm."

"Yep." And both uniformed officers headed to the phones.

"When's the weather clear?" the lingering civilian asked the tech.

"Call it thirty-six hours. It'll start to clear tomorrow night, and we have the taskings already programmed in." He didn't have to say that the nighttime capabilities on the KH-11 satellites weren't all that different from in the daylight—you just didn't get much in the way of color.

CHAPTER 47

Outlooks and All-Nighters

Westbound jet lag, or travel-shock, as President Ryan preferred to call it, is always easier than eastbound's, and he'd gotten sleep on the airplane. Jack and Cathy walked off Air Force One and to the waiting helicopter, which got them to the landing pad on the South Lawn in the usual ten minutes. This time FLOTUS walked directly into the White House while POTUS walked left toward the West Wing, but to the Situation Room rather than the Oval Office. Vice President Jackson was waiting for him there, along with the usual suspects.

"Hey, Robby."

"How was the flight, Jack?"

"Long." Ryan stretched to get his muscles back under control. "Okay, what's happening?"

"Ain't good, buddy. We have Chinese mechanized troops heading for the Russian border. Here's what we got in from NRO." Jackson personally spread out the printouts from the photo-intelligence troops. "We got mechanized forces here, here, and here, and these are engineers with bridging equipment."

"How long before they're ready?" Ryan asked.

"Potentially as little as three days," Mickey Moore answered. "More likely five to seven."

"What are we doing?"

"We have a lot of warning orders out, but nobody's moving yet."

"Do they know we're onto this?" the President asked next.

"Probably not, but they must know we're keeping an eye on things, and they must know our reconnaissance capabilities. It's been in the open media for twenty-some years," Moore answered.

"Nothing from them to us over diplomatic channels?"

"Bupkis," Ed Foley said.

"Don't tell me they don't care. They have to care."

"Maybe they care, Jack," the DCI responded. "But they're not losing as much sleep over it as they are over internal political problems."

"Anything new from SORGE?"

Foley shook his head. "Not since this morning."

"Okay, who's our senior diplomat in Beijing?"

"The DCM at the embassy, but he's actually fairly junior, new in the post," the DCI said.

"Okay, well, the note we're going to send won't be," Ryan said. "What time is it over there?"

"Eight-twelve in the morning," Jackson said, pointing to a wall clock set on Chinese time.

"So, SORGE didn't report anything from their working day yesterday?"

"No. That happens two or three days per week. It's not unusual," Mary Pat pointed out. "Sometimes that means the next one will be extra meaty."

Everyone looked up when Secretary Adler came in; he had driven instead of helicoptered in from Andrews. He quickly came up to speed.

"That bad?"

"They look serious, man," Jackson told SecState.

"Sounds like we have to send them that note."

"They're too far gone down this road to stop," another person said. "It's not likely that any note will work."

"Who are you?" Ryan asked.

"George Weaver, sir, from Brown. I consult to the Agency on China."

"Oh, okay. I've read some of your work. Pretty good stuff, Dr. Weaver. So, you say they won't turn back. Tell us why," the President commanded.

"It's not because they fear revelation of what they're up to. Their people don't know, and won't find out until Beijing tells them. The problem, as you know, is that they fear a potential economic collapse.

If their economy goes south, sir, then you get a revolt of the masses, and that's the one thing they really fear. They don't see a way to avoid that other than getting rich, and the way for them to get rich is to seize the newly discovered Russian assets."

"Kuwait writ large?" Ryan asked.

"Larger and more complex, but, yes, Mr. President, the situation is fundamentally similar. They regard oil both as a commodity and as an entry card into international legitimacy. They figure that if they have it, the rest of the world will have to do business with them. The gold angle is even more obvious. It's the quintessential trading commodity. If you have it, you can sell it for anything you care to purchase. With those assets and the cash they can buy with them, they figure to bootstrap their national economy to the next level, and they just assume that the rest of the world will play along with them because they're going to be rich, and capitalists are only interested in money."

"They're really that cynical, that shallow?" Adler asked, somewhat shocked at the thought, even after all he'd already been through.

"Their reading of history justifies that outlook, Mr. Secretary. Their analysis of our past actions, and those of the rest of the world, lead them to this conclusion. I grant you that they fail to appreciate what we call our reasons for the actions we took, but in strictly and narrowly factual terms, that's how the world looks to them."

"Only if they're idiots," Ryan observed tiredly. "We're dealing with idiots."

"Mr. President, you're dealing with highly sophisticated political animals. Their outlook on the world is different from ours, and, true, they do not understand us very well, but that does not make them fools," Weaver told the assembly.

Fine, Ryan thought for what seemed the hundredth time, *but then they're Klingons.* There was no sense saying that to Weaver. He'd simply launch into a long-winded rebuttal that wouldn't take the discussion anywhere. And Weaver would be right. Fools or geniuses, you only had to understand *what* they were doing, not *why.* The *what* might not make sense, but if you knew it, you also knew what had to be stopped.

"Well, let's see if they understand this," Ryan said. "Scott, tell the PRC that if they attack into Russia, America will come to Russia's aid, as required by the North Atlantic Treaty, and—"

"The NATO Treaty doesn't actually say that," Adler warned.

"I say it does, Scott, and more to the point, I told the Russians it does. If the Chinese realize we're not kidding, will it make a difference?"

"That opens up a huge can of worms, Jack," Adler warned. "We have thousands of Americans in China, thousands. Businessmen, tourists, a lot of people."

"Dr. Weaver, how will the Chinese treat foreign nationals in time of war?"

"I would not want to be there to find out. The Chinese can be fine hosts, but in time of war, if, for example, they think you're a spy or something, it could get very difficult. The way they treat their own citizens—well, we've seen that on TV, haven't we?"

"Scott, we also tell them that we hold their government leaders *personally* responsible for the safety and well-being of American citizens in their country. I mean that, Scott. If I have to, I'll sign the orders to track them down and bury their asses. Remind them of Tehran and our old friend Daryaei. That Zhang guy met him once, according to the former Indian Prime Minister, and I had him taken all the way out," Ryan announced coldly. "Zhang would do well to consider that."

"They will not respond well to such threats," Weaver warned. "It's just as easy to say we have a lot of their citizens here, and—"

"We can't do that, and they know it," Ryan shot back.

"Mr. President, I just told you, our concept of laws is alien to them. That sort of threat is one they *will* understand, and they will take it seriously. The question then is how valuable they regard the lives of their own citizens."

"And that is?"

"Less than we do," Weaver answered.

Ryan considered that. "Scott, make sure they know what the Ryan Doctrine means," he ordered. "If necessary, I *will* put a smart bomb through their bedroom windows, even if it takes us ten years to find them."

"The DCM will make that clear. We can also alert our citizens to get the next bird out."

"Yeah, I'd want to get the hell out of Dodge City," Robby Jackson observed. "And you can get that warning out over CNN."

"Depending on how they respond to our note. It's eight-thirty in the morning over there. Scott, that note has to be in their hands before lunch."

SecState nodded. "Right."

"General Moore, we have warning orders cut to the forces we can deploy?"

"Yes, sir. We can have Air Force units in Siberia in less than twenty-four hours. Twelve hours after that, they'll be ready to launch missions."

"What about bases, Mickey?" Jackson asked.

"Tons of 'em, from when they worried about splashing B-52s. Their northern coast is lousy with airstrips. We have our Air Attaché in Moscow sitting down with their people right now," General Moore said. The colonel in question was pulling a serious all-nighter. "The Russians, he says, are being very cooperative."

"How secure will the bases be?" the Vice President asked next.

"Their main protection will be distance. The Chinese will have to reach the best part of a thousand miles to hit them. We've tagged ten E-3B AWACS out of Tinker Air Force Base to go over and establish continuous radar coverage, plus a lot of fighters to do BARCAP. Once that's done, we'll think about what missions we'll want to fly. Mainly defensive at first, until we get firmly established."

Moore didn't have to explain to Jackson that there was more to moving an Air Force than just the aircraft. With each fighter squadron went mechanics, ordnancemen, and even air-traffic controllers. A fighter plane might have only one pilot, but it needed an additional twenty or more personnel to make it a functioning weapon. For more complex aircraft, the numbers just went higher.

"What about CINCPAC?" Jackson asked.

"We can give their navy a serious headache. Mancuso's moving his submarines and other ships."

"These images aren't all that great," Ryan observed, looking down at the radar overheads.

"We'll have visuals late tomorrow," Ed Foley told him.

"Okay, when we do, we'll have to show them to NATO, see what they'll do to help us out."

"First Armored has orders to stand by to entrain. The German railroads are in better shape today than they were in 1990 for DESERT SHIELD," the Chairman of the Joint Chiefs informed them. "We can change trains just east of Berlin. The Russian railroads have a different gauge. It's wider. That actually helps us, wider cars for our tracks to ride on. We figure we can move First Armored to the far side of the Urals in about seven days."

"Who else?" Ryan asked.

"Not sure," Moore answered.

"The Brits'll go with us. Them we can depend on," Adler told them all. "And Grushavoy was talking to their Prime Minister. We need to talk to Downing Street to see what developed from that."

"Okay, Scott, please look into that. But first let's get that note drafted for Beijing."

"Right," SecState agreed, and headed for the door.

"Jesus, I hope we can get them to see sense," Ryan said to the maps and imagery before his eyes.

"Me, too, Jack," the Vice President agreed. "But don't bet the farm on it."

What Adler had said to him on the flight from Warsaw came back to him. If only America still had ballistic missiles, deterrence would have been far easier. But Ryan had played a role in eliminating the damned things, and it seemed a very strange thing for him to regret now.

The note was generated and sent to the embassy in Beijing in less than two hours. The Deputy Chief of Mission, or DCM, in the embassy was a career foreign-service officer named William Kilmer. The formal note arrived as e-mail, and he had a secretary print it up in proper form and on expensive paper, which was folded into an envelope of creamy texture for hand delivery. He called the Chinese Foreign Ministry, requesting an urgent meeting with Foreign Minister Shen Tang. This was granted with surprising alacrity, and Kilmer walked to his own automobile, a Lincoln Town Car, and drove himself to the Ministry.

Kilmer was in his middle thirties, a graduate of the College of William and Mary in Virginia and Georgetown University in Washington. A man on his way up, his current position was rather ahead of his years, and the only reason he'd gotten it was that Ambassador Carl Hitch had been expected to be a particularly good mentor for bringing him along from AAA ball into the bigs. This mission, delivering *this* note, made him think about just how junior he was. But he couldn't very well run from the job, and career-wise he was taking a big step. Assuming he didn't get shot. Unlikely, but . . .

The walk to Shen's office was a lonely one. The corridor seemed to stretch into infinity as he stepped down it in his best suit and shiny black shoes. The building and its appointments were supposed to be imposing, to show representatives of foreign countries just how impressive the People's Republic of China was. Every country did it this way, some better than others. In this case the architect had earned his money, Kilmer thought. Finally—but sooner than he'd expected when he'd begun—he found the door and turned right to enter the secretaries' anteroom. Shen's male executive assistant led the American into a more comfortable waiting room and fetched water for him. Kilmer waited for the expected five minutes, because you didn't just barge in to see a senior government minister of a major power, but then the high doors—they were always double doors at this level of diplomacy—opened and he was beckoned in.

Shen was wearing a Mao jacket today instead of the usual Western-style business suit, a dark blue in color. He approached his guest and extended his hand.

"Mr. Kilmer, a pleasure to see you again."

"Thank you for allowing this impromptu audience, Minister."

"Please have a seat." Shen waved to some chairs surrounding the usual low table. When both of them were seated, Shen asked, "What can I do for you this day?"

"Minister, I have a note from my government to place into your hand." With that, Kilmer pulled the envelope from his coat pocket and handed it across.

The envelope was not sealed. Shen withdrew the two-page diplomatic message and leaned back to read it. His face didn't alter a dot before he looked up.

"This is a most unusual communication, Mr. Kilmer."

"Minister, my government is seriously concerned with recent deployments of your military."

"The last note delivered from your embassy was an insulting interference with our internal affairs. Now you threaten us with war?"

"Sir, America makes no threats. We remind you that since the Russian Federation is now a signatory of the North Atlantic Treaty, any hostilities directed at Russia will compel America to honor her treaty commitments."

"And you threaten the senior members of our government if something untoward should happen to Americans in our country? What do you take us for, Mr. Kilmer?" Shen asked in an even, unexcited voice.

"Minister, we merely point out that, as America extends to all of our visitors the protection of our laws, we hope that the People's Republic will do the same."

"Why should we treat American citizens any differently from the way we treat our own?"

"Minister, we merely request your assurance that this will be the case."

"Why should it not be the case? Do you accuse us of plotting a war of aggression against our neighbor?"

"We take note of recent military actions by the People's Republic and request clarification."

"I see." Shen folded the papers back up and set them on the table. "When do you request a reply?"

"As soon as you find it convenient to do so, Minister," Kilmer answered.

"Very well. I will discuss this matter with my colleagues on the Politburo and reply to you as quickly as we can."

"I will convey that good news to Washington, Minister. I will not take more time from your day, sir. Thank you very much indeed for your time." Kilmer stood and shook hands one more time. Kilmer walked through the anteroom without a glance left or right, turned left in the corridor, and headed toward the elevators. The corridor seemed just as long for this little walk, he thought, and the clicking of his heels on the tile floor seemed unusually loud. Kilmer had been an FSO long enough to know that Shen should have reacted more irately to the note. Instead he had received it like an invitation to an informal dinner at the embassy. That meant something, but Kilmer wasn't sure what. Once in his car, he started composing his dispatch to Foggy Bottom, then quickly realized that this was something he'd better report by voice first over the STU.

How good is he, Carl?" Adler asked the ambassador.

"He's an okay kid, Scott. Photographic memory, talent I wish

I had. Maybe he was promoted a little fast, but he's got the brains he needs, just a little short on field experience. I figure in another three years or so, he'll be ready to run his own embassy and start his way up the ladder."

In a place like Lesotho, SecState thought, which was a place to make "backwater" seem a compliment. Well, you had to start somewhere. "How will Shen react?"

"Depends. If they're just maneuvering troops on routine training, they might be a little angry. If it's for real and we've caught them with their hands in the cookie jar, they'll act hurt and surprised." Hitch paused for a yawn. "Excuse me. The real question is whether it'll make them think things over."

"Will it? You know most of 'em."

"I don't know," Hitch admitted uncomfortably. "Scott, I've been there a while, sure, but I can't say that I fully understand them. They make decisions on political considerations that Americans have a hard time comprehending."

"The President calls them Klingons," Adler told the ambassador.

Hitch smiled. "I wouldn't go that far, but there is logic in the observation." Then Adler's intercom buzzed.

"Call from William Kilmer in Beijing on the STU, Mr. Secretary," the secretary's voice said.

"This is Scott Adler," SecState said when he lifted the phone. "Ambassador Hitch is here with me. You're on speaker."

"Sir, I made the delivery. Minister Shen hardly blinked. He said he'd get back to us soon, but not exactly when, after he talked it over with his Politburo colleagues. Aside from that, not much of a reaction at all. I can fax you the transcript in about half an hour. The meeting didn't last ten minutes."

Adler looked over at Hitch, who shook his head and didn't look happy at the news.

"Bill, how was his body language?" Hitch asked.

"Like he was on Prozac, Carl. No physical reaction at all."

"Shen tends to be a little hyperactive," Hitch explained. "Sometimes he has trouble sitting still. Conclusions, Bill?"

"I'm worried," Kilmer replied at once. "I think we have a problem here."

"Thank you, Mr. Kilmer. Send the fax quick as you can." Adler punched the phone button and looked at his guest. "Oh, shit."

"Yeah. How soon will we know how they're going to react to this?"

"Tomorrow morning, I hope, we—"

"We have a source inside their government?" Hitch asked. The blank look he got in reply was answer enough.

"Thanks, Scott," Ryan said, hanging up the phone. He was back in the Oval Office now, sitting in his personally-fitted swivel chair, which was about as comfortable as any artifact could make him. It didn't help much at the moment, but he supposed it was one less thing to worry about.

"So?"

"So, we wait to see if SORGE tells us anything."

"SORGE?" Professor Weaver asked.

"Dr. Weaver, we have a sensitive source of information that sometimes gives us information on what their Politburo is thinking," Ed Foley told the academic. "And that information does not leave this room."

"Understood." Academic or not, Weaver played by the rules. "That's the name for the special stuff you've been showing me?"

"Correct."

"It's a hell of a source, whoever it is. It reads like a tape of their meetings, captures their personalities, especially Zhang. He's the real bad actor here. He's got Premier Xu pretty well wrapped around his little finger."

"Adler's met him, during the shuttle talks after the Airbus shootdown at Taipei," Ryan said.

"And?" Weaver asked. He knew the name and the words, but not the man.

"And he's powerful and not a terribly nice chap," the President answered. "He had a role in our conflict with Japan, and also the fracas with the UIR last year."

"Machiavelli?"

"That's pretty close, more a theoretician than a lead actor, the man-behind-the-throne sort of guy. Not an ideologue per se, but a guy who likes to play in the real world—patriot, Ed?" Ryan asked the DCI.

"We've had our pshrink profile him." Foley shrugged. "Part sociopath, part political operator. A guy who enjoys the exercise of power. No known personal weaknesses. Sexually active, but a lot of their Politburo members are. Maybe it's a cultural thing, eh, Weaver?"

"Mao was like that, as we all know. The emperors used to have rather large stables of concubines."

"That's what people did before TV, I suppose," Arnie van Damm observed.

"Actually that's not far from the truth," Weaver agreed. "The carryover to today is cultural, and it's a fundamental form of personal power that some people like to exercise. Women's lib hasn't made it into the PRC yet."

"I must be too Catholic," the President thought aloud. "The idea of Mao popping little girls makes my skin crawl."

"They didn't mind, Mr. President," Weaver told him. "Some would bring their little sisters over after they got in bed with the Great Leader. It's a different culture, and it has different rules from ours."

"Yeah, just a little different," observed the father of two daughters, one just starting to date. What would the fathers of those barely nubile little girls have thought? Honored to have their daughters deflowered by the great Mao Zedong? Ryan had a minor chill from the thought, and dismissed it. "Do they care about human life at all? What about their soldiers?"

"Mr. President, the Judeo-Christian Bible wasn't drafted in China, and efforts by missionaries to get Christianity going over there were not terribly successful—and when Mao came along, he suppressed it fairly effectively, as we saw again recently. Their view of man's place in nature is different from ours, and, no, they do not value a single human life as we do. We're talking here about communists who view everything through a political lens, and that is over and above a culture in which a human life had little import. So, you could say it's a very infelicitous confluence of belief systems from our point of view."

Infelicitous, Ryan thought, *there's a delicate turn of phrase. We're talking about a government that killed off twenty million-plus of its own people along the way, just in a few months, in pursuit of political perfection.* "Dr. Weaver, best guess: What's their Politburo going to say?"

"They will continue on the path they're on," Weaver answered quickly. He was surprised at the reaction.

"God damn it, doesn't anybody think common sense is going to break out?" Ryan snarled. He looked around the room, to see people suddenly looking down at the royal-blue rug.

"Mr. President, they fear war less than they fear the alternatives to war," Weaver answered, rather courageously, Arnie van Damm thought. "To repeat, if they don't enrich their country in oil and gold, they fear an economic collapse that will destroy their entire political order, and that, to them, is more frightening than the prospect of losing a hundred thousand soldiers in a war of conquest."

"And I can stop it only by dropping a nuclear bomb on their capital—which will, by the way, kill a couple of million ordinary people. God damn it!" Ryan swore again.

"More like five million, maybe as many as ten," General Moore pointed out, earning him a withering look from his Commander in Chief. "Yes, sir, that would work, but I agree the price of doing it's a little high."

"Robby?" Jack turned to his Vice President in hope of hearing something encouraging.

"What do you want me to say, Jack? We can hope they realize that this is going to cost them more than they expect, but it would appear the odds are against it."

"One other thing we need to do is prepare the people for this," Arnie said. "Tomorrow we should alert the press, and then you'll have to go on TV and tell everybody what's happening and why."

"You know, I really don't like this job very much—excuse me. That's rather a puerile thing to say, isn't it?" SWORDSMAN apologized.

"Ain't supposed to be fun, Jack," van Damm observed. "You've played the game okay to this point, but you can't always control the other people at the card table."

The President's phone rang. Jack answered it. "Yes? Okay." He looked up. "Ed, it's for you."

Foley stood and walked to take the phone. "Foley . . . Okay, good, thanks." He replaced the phone. "Weather's clearing over Northeast China. We'll have some visual imagery in half an hour."

"Mickey, how fast can we get aerial recon assets in place?" Jackson asked.

"We have to fly them in. We have things we can stage out of California, but it's a lot more efficient to fly them over in a C-17 and lift them off from a Siberian airfield. We can do that in, oh . . . thirty-six hours from your order."

"The order is given," Ryan said. "What sort of aircraft are they?"

"They're UAVs, sir. Unmanned Aerial Vehicles, used to call them drones. They're stealthy and they stay up a long time. We can download real-time video from them. They're fabulous for battlefield reconnaissance, the best new toys the Air Force has fielded, so far as the Army is concerned. I can get them going right now."

"Do it," Ryan told him.

"Assuming we have a place to land them. But we could stage them out of Elmendorf in Alaska if we have to." Moore lifted the phone and made his call to the National Military Command Center, the NMCC, in the Pentagon.

For General Peng, things were getting busy. The operation order was topped with the ideographs Long Chun, SPRING DRAGON. The "dragon" part sounded auspicious, since for thousands of years the dragon had been the symbol of imperial rule and also good fortune. There was still plenty of daylight. That suited Peng, and he hoped it would suit his soldiers. Daylight made for good hunting, and made it harder for large bodies of men to hide or move unseen, and that suited his mission.

He was not without misgivings. He was a general officer with orders to fight a war, and nothing makes such a man reflective like instructions to perform the things he'd claimed the ability to do. He would have preferred more artillery and air support, but he had a good deal of the former, and probably enough of the latter. At the moment, he was going over intelligence estimates and maps. He'd studied the Russian defenses on the far side of the border for years, to the point of occasionally putting reconnaissance specialists across the river to scout out the bunkers that had faced south for fifty years. The Russians were good military engineers, and those fixed defenses would take some dealing with.

But his attack plan was a simple one. Behind a massive artillery barrage, he'd put infantry across the Amur River in assault boats to deal with the Russian bunkers, simultaneously bringing up engineers to span the river with ribbon bridges in order to rush his mechanized forces across, up the hills on the far side, then farther north. He had helicopters, though not enough of the attack kind to suit his needs. He'd complained about this, but so had every other senior officer in the People's Liberation Army. The only thing about the Russian Army that worried him were their Mi-24 attack helicopters. They were clumsy machines but dangerous in their capabilities, if wisely used.

His best intelligence came from reams of Humint from Chinese citizens living illegally but comfortably in Russia—shopkeepers and workers, a fair number of whom were officers or stringers for the Ministry for State Security. He would have preferred more photographs, but his country had only a single orbiting reconnaissance satellite, and the truth was that the imagery purchased from the French SPOT commercial satellite company was better, at one-meter resolution, than his own country could manage. It was also easier to acquire over the Internet, and for that his intelligence coordinator had a blank check. They showed the nearest Russian mechanized formation over a hundred kilometers away. That confirmed the human intelligence that had said only things within artillery range were garrison units assigned to the border defenses. It was interesting that the Russian high command had not surged forces forward, but they didn't have many to surge, and defending a border, with its numerous crenellations and meanders, used up manpower as a sponge used up water—and they didn't have that many troops to squander. He also possessed information that this General-Colonel Bondarenko was training his troops harder than his predecessor had, but that was not much cause for concern. The Chinese had been training hard for years, and Ivan would take time to catch up.

No, his only concern was distance. His army and its neighbors had a long way to go. Keeping them supplied would be a problem, because as Napoleon said that an army marched on its stomach, so tanks and tracked vehicles floated on a sea of diesel oil. His intelligence sources gave locations for large Russian stocks, but he couldn't count on seizing them intact, desirable though that might be, and even though he had plans for helicopter assaults on every one he had charted.

Peng put out his sixtieth cigarette of the day and looked up at his operations officer. "Yes?"

"The final order has arrived. Jump off at 0330 in three days."

"Will you have everything in place by then?" Peng asked.

"Yes, Comrade General, with twenty-four hours to spare."

"Good. Let's make sure that all our men are well fed. It may be a long time between meals for the next few weeks."

"That order has already been given, Comrade General," the colonel told him.

"And total radio silence."

"Of course, Comrade General."

Not a whisper," the sergeant said. "Not even carrier waves."

The RC-135 Rivet Joint aircraft was the first USAF bird to deploy, flying out of Anderson Air Force base on the island of Guam. It had refueled over the Sea of Okhotsk and entered Russian airspace over the port city of Ayan, and now, two hours later, was just east of Skovorodino on the Russian side of the border. The Rivet Joint was an extensively modified windowless version of the old Boeing 707, crammed with radio-receiving equipment and crewed with experienced ferret personnel, one of only two USAF crews who spoke passable Chinese.

"Sergeant, what's it mean when you have a lot of soldiers in the field and no radios?" the colonel in command of the mission asked. It was a rhetorical question, of course.

"Same thing it means when your two-year-old isn't making any noise, sir. He's crayoning the wall, or doing something else to get his bottom smacked." The sergeant leaned back in the pilot-type seat, looking at the numerous visual scans tuned to known PLA frequencies. The screen was blank except for mild static. Maybe there'd been some chatter as the PLA had moved units into place, but now there was nothing but some commercial FM traffic, mainly music that was as alien to the American flight crew as Grand Ol' Opry would have been in Beijing. Two crewmen listening to the civilian stations noted that the lyrics of the Chinese love ballads were as mindless as those of their Nashville counterparts, though the stations were leaning more heavily to patriotic songs at the moment.

The same was noted at Fort Meade, Maryland. The National Security Agency had a lot of ferret satellites up and circling the globe, including two monster Rhyolite-types in geosynchronous orbit over the equator, and all were tuned to Chinese military and government channels. The FM-radio chatter associated with military formations had trended down to zero in the last twelve hours, and to the uniformed and civilian analysts alike that meant just one thing: A quiet army is an army planning to do something.

The people at the National Reconnaissance Office had the main tasking in finishing up a Special National Intelligence Estimate, because people tended to believe photographs more than mere words. The imagery had been computer-matched with the radar-imaging satellites' "take," but surprisingly to no one, the assembly areas were mostly empty now. The tanks and other tracked vehicles had lingered only long enough to get reorganized after the train trip, and had moved out north, judging by the ruts they'd left in the mainly dirt roads of the region. They'd taken the time to spread their camouflage nets over the redeployed tanks, but that, too, had been a pro forma waste of time, because they could as little hide the track marks of hundreds of such vehicles as they could hide a mountain range. And scarcely any such effort had been taken with the hundreds of supply trucks, which, they saw, were still moving in tight little convoys, at about thirty kilometers per hour, heading for assembly areas just a few klicks south of where the shooters were. The imagery was printed up on six of the big laser printers custom-made for the NRO, and driven to the White House, where people were mainly sitting around in the Oval Office pulling a Presidential all-nighter, which was rather more special than those done by the deliveryman, an Army sergeant E-5 in this case. The civilian analyst who'd come with him stayed inside while the NCO walked back out to the government Ford sedan, having left behind a Newport hundred-millimeter cigarette for the President.

"Jack, you're bad," Jackson observed. "Bumming a smoke off that innocent young boy."

"Stick it, Robby," POTUS replied with a grin. The smoke made him cough, but it helped him stay awake as much as the premium coffee did. "You handle the stress your way, I'll handle it my way. Okay, what do we have here?" the President asked the senior analyst.

"Sir, this is as many armored vehicles in one area as I have ever seen in China, plus all their equipment. They're going north, and soon, in less than three days, I'd say."

"What about air?" Jackson asked.

"Right here, sir." The analyst's finger traced over one of the photos. "Dedicated fighter base at Jinxi is a good example. Here's a squadron of Russian-made Su-27s, plus a whole regiment of J-7s. The Sukhoi's a pretty good fighter plane, similar in mission and capabilities to an early F-15. The -7's a day-fighter knockoff of the old MiG-21, modified for ground attack as well as mixing up in the furball. You can count sixty-eight aircraft. Probably at least four were in the air when the satellite went overhead. Note the fueling trucks right on the ramp, and this aircraft has ground crew tinkering with it. We estimate that this base was stood-down for five days—"

"—getting everything ready?" Jackson asked. That's how people did it.

"Yes, sir. You will also note missile noses peeking out under the wings of all these aircraft. They appear to be loaded for combat."

"White ones on the rails," Robby observed. "They're planning to go do some work."

"Unless our note gets them to calm down," Ryan said, with a minor degree of hope in his voice. A very minor note, the others in the room thought. The President got one last puff off the purloined Newport and stubbed it out. "Might it help for me to make a direct personal call to Premier Xu?"

"Honest answer?" It was Professor Weaver, rather the worse for wear at four in the Washington morning.

"The other sort isn't much use to me at the moment," Ryan replied, not quite testily.

"It will look good in the papers and maybe the history books, but it is unlikely to affect their decision-making process."

"It's worth a try," Ed Foley said in disagreement. "What do we have to lose?"

"Wait until eight, Jack," van Damm thought. "We don't want him to think we've been up all night. It'll inflate his sense of self-worth."

Ryan turned to look at the windows on his south wall. The drapes hadn't been closed, and anyone passing by could have noted that the lights had been on all night. But, strangely, he didn't know if the Secret Service ever turned them off at night.

"When do we start moving forces?" Jack asked next.

"The Air Attaché will call from Moscow when his talks have been concluded. Ought to be any time."

The President grunted. "Longer night than ours."

"He's younger than we are," Mickey Moore observed. "Just a colonel."

"If this goes, what are our plans like?" van Damm asked.

"Hyperwar," Moore answered. "The world doesn't know the new weapons we've been developing. It'll make DESERT STORM look like slow motion."

CHAPTER 48

Opening Guns

While others were pulling all-nighters, Gennady Iosifovich Bondarenko was forgetting what sleep was supposed to have been. His teleprinter was running hot with dispatches from Moscow, reading that occupied his time, and not always to his profit. Russia had still not learned to leave people alone when they were doing their jobs, and as a result, his senior communications officer cringed when he came in with new "FLASH" traffic.

"Look," the general said to his intelligence officer. "What I need is information on what equipment they have, where they are, and how they are postured to move north on us. Their politics and objectives are not as important to me as where they are right now!"

"I expect to have hard information from Moscow momentarily. It will be American satellite coverage, and—"

"God damn it! I remember when we had our own fucking satellites. What about aerial reconnaissance?"

"The proper aircraft are on their way to us now. We'll have them flying by tomorrow noon, but do we dare send them over Chinese territory?" Colonel Tolkunov asked.

"Do we dare not to?" CINC–FAR EAST demanded in reply.

"General," the G-2 said, "the concern is that we would be giving the Chinese a political excuse for the attack."

"Who said that?"

"Stavka."

Bondarenko's head dropped over the map table. He took a breath and closed his eyes for three blissful seconds, but all that achieved was to make him wish for an hour—no, just thirty minutes of sleep. That's all, he thought, just thirty minutes.

"A political excuse," the general observed. "You know, Vladimir Konstantinovich, once upon a time, the Germans were sending high-flying reconnaissance aircraft deep into Western Russia, scouting us out prior to their invasion. There was a special squadron of fighters able to reach their altitude, and their regimental commander asked for permission to intercept them. He was relieved of his command on the spot. I suppose he was lucky that he wasn't shot. He ended up a major ace and a Hero of the Soviet Union before some German fighter got him. You see, Stalin was afraid of provoking Hitler, too!"

"Comrade Colonel?" Heads turned. It was a young sergeant with an armful of large-format photographs.

"Here, quickly!"

The sergeant laid them on the table, obscuring the topographical maps that had occupied the previous four hours. The quality wasn't good. The imagery had been transmitted over a fax machine instead of a proper photographic printer, but it was good enough for their purposes. There were even inserts, small white boxes with legends typed in, in English, to tell the ignorant what was in the pretty little pictures. The intelligence officer was the first to make sense of it all.

"Here they come," the colonel breathed. He checked the coordinates and the time indicated in the lower-right corner of the top photo. "That's a complete tank division, and it's right"—he turned back to the printed map—"right here, just as we expected. Their marshaling point is Harbin. Well, it had to be. All their rail lines converge there. Their first objective will be Belogorsk."

"And right up the valley from there," Bondarenko agreed. "Through this pass, then northwest." One didn't need to be a Nobel laureate to predict a line of advance. The terrain was the prime objective condition to which all ambitions and plans had to bend. Bondarenko could read the mind of the enemy commander well enough, because any trained soldier would see the contour lines on the map and analyze them the same way. Flat was better than sloped. Clear was better than wooded. Dry was better than wet. There was a lot of sloped terrain on the border, but it smoothed out, and there were too many valleys inviting speedy advance. With enough troops, he could have made every one of those valleys a deathtrap, but if he'd had enough troops, the Chinese wouldn't be lined up on his border. They'd be sitting in their own prepared defenses, fearing him. But that was not the shape of the current world for Commander-in-Chief Far East.

The 265th Motor Rifle was a hundred kilometers back from the border. The troops were undergoing frantic gunnery training now, because that would generate the most rapid return for investment. The battalion and regimental officers were in their command posts running map-table exercises, because Bondarenko needed them thinking, not shooting. He had sergeants for that. The good news for Bondarenko was that his soldiers enjoyed shooting live rounds, and their skill levels were improving rapidly. The bad news was that for every trained tank crew he had, the Chinese had over twenty.

"What an ambush we could lay, if we only had the men," Tolkunov breathed.

"When I was in America, watching them train, I heard a good if-only joke. If only your aunt had balls, then she'd be your uncle, Vladimir Konstantinovich."

"Quite so, Comrade General." They both turned back to the maps and the photos.

So, they know what we're doing," Qian Kun observed. "This is not a good development."

"You can know what a robber will do, but if he has a pistol and you don't, what difference does it make?" Zhang Han San asked in return. "Comrade Marshal?"

"One cannot hide so large a movement of troops," Marshal Luo said blandly. "Tactical surprise is always hard to achieve. But we do have strategic surprise."

"That is true," Tan Deshi told the Politburo. "The Russians have alerted some of their divisions for movement, but they are all in the west, and days away, and all will approach down this rail line, and our air force can close it, can't you, Luo?"

"Easily," the Defense Minister agreed.

"And what of the Americans?" Fang Gan asked. "In that note we just got, they have told us that they regard the Russians as allies. How many times have people underestimated the Americans, Zhang? Including yourself," he added.

"There are objective conditions which apply even to the Americans, for all their magic," Luo assured the assembly.

"And in three years we will be selling them oil and gold," Zhang assured them all in turn. "The Americans have no political memory. They always adapt to the changing shape of the world. In 1949, they drafted the NATO Treaty, which included their bitter enemies in Germany. Look at what they did with Japan, after dropping atomic bombs on them. The only thing we should consider: though few Americans will be deployed, and they will have to take their chances along with everyone else, perhaps we should avoid inflicting too many casualties. We would also do well to treat prisoners and captured civilians gently—the world does have sensibilities we must regard somewhat, I suppose."

"Comrades," Fang said, summoning up his courage for one last display of his inner feelings. "We still have the chance to stop this from happening, as Marshal Luo told us some days ago. We are not fully committed until shots are fired. Until then, we can say we were running a defense exercise, and the world will go along with that explanation, for the reasons my friend Zhang has just told us. But once hostilities are begun, the tiger is out of the cage. Men defend what is theirs with tenacity. You will recall that Hitler underestimated the Russians, to his ultimate sorrow. Iran underestimated the Americans just last year, causing disaster for them and the death of their leader. Are we *sure* that we can prevail in this adventure?" he asked. "Sure? We gamble with the life of our country here. We ought not to forget that."

"Fang, my old comrade, you are wise and thoughtful as ever," Zhang responded graciously. "And I know you speak on behalf of our nation and our people, but as we must not underestimate our enemies, so we ought not to underestimate ourselves. We fought the Americans once before, and we gave them the worst military defeat in their history, did we not?"

"Yes, we did surprise them, but in the end we lost a *million* men, including Mao's own son. And why? Because we *over*estimated our own abilities."

"Not this time, Fang," Luo assured them all. "Not this time. We will do to the Russians the same thing we did to the Americans at the Yalu River. We will strike with power and surprise. Where they are weak, we will rush through. Where they are strong, we will encircle and surround. In 1950, we were a peasant army with only light weapons. Today," Luo went on, "we are a fully modern army. We can do things today such as even the Americas could not dream of back then. We *will* prevail," the Defense Minister concluded with firm conviction.

"Comrades, do we wish to stop now?" Zhang asked, to focus the debate. "Do we wish to doom our country's economic and political future? For that is the issue at hand. If we stand still, we risk national death. Who among us wishes to stand still then?"

Predictably no one, not even Qian, moved to pick up that gauntlet. The vote was entirely pro forma, and unanimous. As always, the Politburo achieved collegiality for its own sake. The ministers returned to their various offices. Zhang buttonholed Tan Deshi for several minutes before heading back to his. An hour after that, he dropped in on his friend, Fang Gan.

"You are not cross with me?" Fang asked.

"The voice of caution is something that does not offend me, my old friend," Zhang said, graciously taking his seat opposite the other's desk. He could afford to be gracious. He had won.

"I am afraid of this move, Zhang. We *did* underestimate the Americans in 1950, and it cost us many men."

"We have the men to spare," the senior Minister Without Portfolio pointed out. "And it will make Luo feel valuable."

"As if he needs that." Fang gestured his displeasure with that strutting martinet.

"Even a dog has his uses," his visitor pointed out.

"Zhang, what if the Russians are more formidable than you think?"

"I've taken care of that. We will create instability in their country in two days, the very day our attack begins."

"How?"

"You'll recall we had that failed attempt against Grushavoy's senior advisor, that Golovko fellow."

"Yes, and I counseled against that, too," Fang reminded his visitor.

"And there, perhaps, you were right," Zhang acknowledged, to smooth his host's feathers. "But Tan has developed the capability, and what better way to destabilize Russia than to eliminate their president? This we can do, and Tan has his orders."

"You assassinate a government chief in a foreign land?" Fang asked, surprised at this level of boldness. "What if you fail?"

"We commit an act of war against Russia anyway. What have we to lose by this? Nothing—but there is much to gain."

"But the political implications . . ." Fang breathed.

"What of them?"

"What if they turn the tables on us?"

"You mean attempt to attack Xu personally?" The look on his face provided the real answer to the question: *China would be better off without the nonentity.* But even Zhang would not say that aloud, even in the privacy of this room. "Tan assures me that our physical security is perfect. Perfect, Fang. There are no foreign intelligence operations of consequence in our country."

"I suppose every nation says such a thing—right before the roof caves in on them. We've done well with our spying in America, for example, and for that our good Comrade Tan is to be congratulated, but arrogance falls before the blow, and such blows are never anticipated. We would do well to remember that."

Zhang dismissed the thought: "One cannot fear everything."

"That is true, but to fear nothing is also imprudent." Fang paused to mend fences. "Zhang, you must think me an old woman."

That made the other minister smile. "Old woman? No, Fang, you are a comrade of many years' standing, and one of our most thoughtful thinkers. Why, do you suppose, I brought you onto the Politburo?"

To get my votes, of course, Fang didn't answer. He had the utmost respect for his senior colleague, but he wasn't blind to his faults. "For that I am grateful."

"For that the *people* ought to be grateful, you are so solicitous to their needs."

"Well, one must remember the peasants and workers out there. We serve them, after all." The ideological cant was just perfect for the moment. "This is not an easy job we share."

"You need to relax a little. Get that girl Ming out there, take her to your bed. You've done it before." It was a weakness both men shared. The tension of the moment abated, as Zhang wished it to.

"Chai sucks better," Fang replied, with a sly look.

"Then take her to your flat. Buy her some silk drawers. Get her drunk. They all like that."

"Not a bad idea," Fang agreed. "It certainly helps me sleep."

"Then do it by all means! We'll need our sleep. The next few weeks will be strenuous for us—but more so for our enemies."

"One thing, Zhang. As you said, we must treat the captives well. One thing the Americans do not forgive rapidly is cruelty to the helpless, as we have seen here in Beijing."

"Now, *they* are old women. They do not understand the proper use of strength."

"Perhaps so, but if we wish to do business with them, as you say, why offend them unnecessarily?"

Zhang sighed and conceded the point, because he knew it to be the smart play. "Very well. I will tell Luo." He checked his watch. "I must be off. I've having dinner with Xu tonight."

"Give him my best wishes."

"Of course." Zhang rose, bowed to his friend, and took his leave. Fang took a minute or so before rising and walking to the door. "Ming," he called, on opening it. "Come here." He lingered at the door as the secretary came in, allowing his eyes to linger on Chai. Their eyes met and she winked, adding a tiny feminine smile. Yes, he needed his sleep tonight, and she would help.

"The Politburo meeting ran late this day," Fang said, settling into his chair and doing his dictation. It took twenty-five minutes, and he dismissed Ming to do her daily transcription. Then he had Chai come in, gave her an order, and dismissed her. In another hour, the working day ended. Fang walked down to his official car, with Chai in trail. Together they rode to his comfortable apartment, and there they got down to business.

Ming met her lover at a new restaurant called the Jade Horse, where the food was better than average.

"You look troubled," Nomuri observed.

"Busy time at the office," she explained. "There is big trouble to come."

"Oh? What sort of trouble?"

"I cannot say," she demurred. "It will probably not affect your company."

And Nomuri saw that he'd taken his agent to the next—actually the last—step. She no longer thought about the software on her office computer. He never brought the subject up. Better that it should happen below the visible horizon. Better that she should forget what she was doing. Your conscience doesn't worry about things you've forgotten. After dinner, they walked back to Nomuri's place, and the CIA officer tried his best to relax her. He was only partially successful, but she was properly appreciative and left him at quarter to eleven. Nomuri had himself a nightcap, a double, and checked to make sure his computer had relayed her almost-daily report. Next week he hoped to have software he could cross-load to hers over the 'Net, so that she'd be transmitting the reports directly out to the recipe network. If Bad Things were happening in Beijing, NEC might call him back to Japan, and he didn't want SONGBIRD's reports to stop going to Langley.

As it happened, this one was already there, and it had generated all manner of excitement.

It was enough to make Ed Foley wish he'd lent a STU to Sergey Golovko, but America didn't give away its communications secrets that readily, and so the report had been redrafted and sent by secure fax to the U.S. Embassy in Moscow, then hand-carried to SVR headquarters by a consular officer not associated with the CIA. Of course, now they'd assume that he was a spook, which would cause the Russians to shadow him everywhere he went, and use up trained personnel of the FSS. Business was still business, even in this New World Order.

Golovko, predictably, bounced hard off his high office ceiling.

John Clark got the news over his secure satellite phone.

"What the hell?" RAINBOW SIX asked, sitting still in his personal car not far from Red Square.

"You heard me," Ed Foley explained.

"Okay, now what?"

"You're tight with their special-operations people, right?"

"Somewhat," Clark allowed. "We're training them."

"Well, they might come to you for advice of some sort. You have to know what's happening."

"Can I tell Ding?"

"Yes," the DCI agreed.

"Good. You know, this proves the Chavez Premise."

"What's that?" Foley asked.

"He likes to say that international relations is largely composed of one nation fucking another."

It was enough to make Foley laugh, five thousand miles and eight time zones away. "Well, our Chinese friends are sure playing rough."

"How good is the information?"

"It's Holy Writ, John. Take it to the bank," Ed assured his distant field officer.

We have some *source in Beijing,* Clark didn't observe aloud. "Okay, Ed. If they come to me, I'll let you know. We cooperate, I presume."

"Fully," the DCI assured him. "We're allies now. Didn't you see CNN?"

"I thought it was the Sci-Fi Channel."

"You ain't the only one. Have a good one, John."

"You, too, Ed. Bye." Clark thumbed the END button and went on just to himself: "Holy jumpin' Jesus." Then he restarted the car and headed off to his rendezvous with Domingo Chavez.

Ding was at the bar that RAINBOW had adopted during its stay in the Moscow area. The boys congregated in a large corner booth, where they complained about the local beer, but appreciated the clear alcohol preferred by the natives.

"Hey, Mr. C," Chavez said in greeting.

"Just got a call from Ed on my portable."

"And?"

"And John Chinaman is planning to start a little war with our hosts, and that's the good news," Clark added.

"What the fuck is the bad news?" Chavez asked, with no small incredulity in his voice.

"Their Ministry of State Security just put a contract out on Eduard Petrovich," John went on.

"Are they fuckin' crazy?" the other CIA officer asked the booth.

"Well, starting a war in Siberia isn't exactly a rational act. Ed let us in because he thinks the locals might want our help soon. Supposedly they know the local contact for the ChiComms. You have to figure a hot takedown's going to evolve from this, and we've been training their troopies. I figure we might be invited in to watch, but they probably won't want us to assist."

"Agreed."

That's when General Kirillin came in, with a sergeant at his side. The sergeant stood by the door with his overcoat unbuttoned and his right hand close to the opening. The senior officer spotted Clark and came directly over.

"I don't have your cell-phone number."

"What do you want us for today, General?" Clark asked.

"I need for you to come with me. We have to see Chairman Golovko."

"Do you mind if Domingo comes along?"

"That is fine," Kirillin replied.

"I've talked to Washington recently. How much do you know?" Clark asked his Russian friend.

"Much, but not all. That's why we need to see Golovko." Kirillin waved them to the door, where his sergeant was doing his best Doberman imitation.

"Something happening?" Eddie Price asked. No one was guarding his expression, and Price knew how to read faces.

"Tell you when we get back," Chavez told him. The staff car waiting outside had a chase car with four men in it, and the sergeant/bodyguard accompanying the general was one of the few enlisted men who'd been let into the cross-training that RAINBOW had been running. The Russians, they knew, were coming along very well. It didn't hurt to draw people hand-selected from an already elite unit.

The cars moved through Moscow traffic with less than the usual regard for traffic and safety laws, then pulled into the main gate at #2 Dzerzhinskiy Square. The elevator was held for them, and they made the top floor in a hurry.

"Thank you for coming so quickly. I assume you've spoken with Langley," Golovko observed.

Clark held up his cell phone.

"The encryption unit is so small?"

"Progress, Chairman," Clark observed. "I'm told this intelligence information is to be taken seriously."

"Foleyeva has a fine source in Beijing. I've seen some of the 'take' from him. It would appear, first, that a deliberate attempt was made on my life, and now another is planned for President Grushavoy. I've already notified him. His security people are fully alerted. The Chinese lead agent in Moscow has been identified and is under surveillance. When he receives his instructions, we will arrest him. But we do not know who his contacts are. We assume they are former Spetsnaz people loyal to him, criminals, of course, doing special work for the underworld we've grown up here."

That made sense, John thought. "Some people will do anything for money, Sergey Nikolay'ch. How can we help you?"

"Foley has instructed you to assist? Good of him. Given the nature of how the intelligence came to us, an American observer seems appropriate. For the takedown, we will use police, with cover from General Kirillin's people. As RAINBOW commander, this will be your task."

Clark nodded. It wasn't all that demanding. "Fair enough."

"We'll keep you safe," the general assured him.

"And you expect the Chinese to launch a war on Russia?"

"Within the week," Golovko nodded.

"The oil and the gold?" Chavez asked.

"So it would seem."

"Well, that's life in the big city," Ding observed.

"We will make them regret this barbaric act," Kirillin told everyone present.

"That remains to be seen," Golovko cautioned. He knew what Bondarenko was saying to Stavka.

"And with you guys in NATO, we're coming to help out?" Clark asked.

"Your President Ryan is a true comrade," the Russian agreed.

"That means RAINBOW, too, then," John thought aloud. "We're all NATO troopers."

"Ain't never fought in a real war before," Chavez thought aloud. But now he was a simulated major, and he might just get drafted into this one. His life insurance, he remembered, was fully paid up.

"It's not exactly fun, Domingo," Clark assured him. *And I'm getting a little old for this shit.*

The Chinese embassy was under continuous and expert surveillance by a large team of officers from the Russian Federal Security Service. Almost all of them were formerly of the KGB's Second Chief Directorate. Reconstituted under a new agency's aegis, they performed the same function as the FBI's Intelligence Division, and they gave away little to their American counterparts. No fewer than twenty of them were assigned to this task. They comprised all physical types, male and female, prosperous- and impoverished-looking, middle-aged and old—but no really young ones, because this case was too important for inexperienced officers. The vehicles assigned to the task included everything from dump trucks to motorbikes, and every mobile group had at least one radio, of types so advanced that the Russian Army didn't have them yet.

Kong Deshi emerged from the PRC embassy at seven-forty. He walked to the nearest Metro station and took the escalator down. This was entirely routine. At the same time, another minor consular officer left and headed in a different direction, but the FSS officers didn't know to watch him. He walked three blocks to the second lamppost on a busy street and, passing it, he pulled a strip of white paper tape from his coat pocket and stuck it vertically on the metal post. Then he walked on to a restaurant and had dinner alone, having fulfilled a mission whose purpose he didn't know. He was the flagman for the MSS in the embassy, but was not a trained intelligence officer.

Third Secretary Kong rode the train for the proper number of stops and got off, with four FSS officers in trail, another one waiting in the station, and two more at the top of the long escalator to the surface. Along the way, he purchased a newspaper from one of the kiosks on the street. Twice he stopped, once to light a cigarette and the other time to look around as if lost and trying to get his bearings. Both efforts, of course, were to spot a tail, but the FSS people were too numerous, some too near, and the close ones studiously, but not too studiously, looking elsewhere. The truth of the matter, as known to the FBI and the British Security Service as well, is that once a contact is identified, he is as naked and helpless as a newborn in the jungle, as long as those shadowing him are not total fools. These KGB-trained professionals were anything but fools. The only thing they didn't know was the identity of the flagman, but that, as usual, was something you might never get. The problem there was that you never knew how quickly to get the dead-drop that was about to be made.

The other problem for the control agent, Kong Deshi, was that once the location of the dead-drop was identified, it was as easily watched as the single cloud in an otherwise clear sky. The size of the surveillance troop was just to make sure there wasn't another drop. And there wasn't. Kong sat down on the expected bench. Here he violated fieldcraft by acting as though he could read a newspaper in the diminishing light, but as there was a streetlamp close by, it wouldn't tip off the casual onlooker.

"There," one of the FSS men observed. Kong's right hand made the emplacement. Three minutes later, he folded his paper and strolled off, in the same direction he'd been heading. The FSS detail let him go a long way before they moved in.

Again it was done from a van, and again the locksmith was inside and waiting with the custom-made key. Also in the van was a high-end American laptop computer with the onetime cipher pad preprogrammed in, an exact copy of Suvorov/Koniev's desktop machine in his upscale flat on the ring road. And so, the senior FSS officer on the case thought, their quarry was like a tiger prowling through the jungle with ten unknown rifles aimed at it, powerful, and dangerous, perhaps, but utterly doomed.

The transfer case was delivered. The locksmith popped it open. The contents were unfolded and photocopied, then replaced, and the case was resealed and returned to its spot on the metal plate under the bench. Already a typist was keying in the random letters of the message, and inside of four minutes, the clear-text came up.

"Yob tvoyu mat!" the senior officer observed. "They want him to kill President Grushavoy!"

"What is that?" a junior officer asked. The case-leader just handed over the laptop computer and let him read the screen.

"This is an act of war," the major breathed. The colonel nodded.

"It is that, Gregoriy." And the van pulled away. He had to report this, and do it immediately.

Lieutenant Provalov was home when the call came. He grumbled the usual amount as he re-dressed and headed to FSS headquarters. He hadn't grown to love the Federal Security Service, but he had come to respect it. With such resources, he thought, he could end crime in Moscow entirely, but they didn't share resources, and they retained the above-the-law arrogance their antecedent agency had once displayed. Perhaps it was necessary. The things they investigated were no less serious than murder, except in scale. Traitors killed not individuals, but entire regions. Treason was a crime that had been taken seriously in his country for centuries, and one that his nation's long-standing institutional paranoia had always feared as much as it had hated.

They were burning more than the usual amount of midnight oil here, Provalov saw. Yefremov was standing in his office, reading a piece of paper with the sort of blank look on his face that frequently denoted something monstrous.

"Good evening, Pavel Georgiyevich."

"Lieutenant Provalov. Here." Yefremov handed over the paper. "Our subject grows ambitious. Or at least his controllers do."

The militia lieutenant took the page and read it quickly, then returned to the top to give it a slower redigestion.

"When did this happen?"

"Less than an hour ago. What observations do you make?"

"We should arrest him at once!" the cop said predictably.

"I thought you'd say that. But instead we will wait and see whom he contacts. Then we will snatch him up. But first, I want to see the people he notifies."

"What if he does it from a cell phone or a pay phone?"

"Then we will have the telephone company identify them for us. But I want to see if he has a contact within an important government office. Suvorov had many colleagues where he was in KGB. I want to know which of them have turned mercenary, so that we can root all of them out. The attack on Sergey Nikolay'ch displayed a frightening capability. I want to put an end to it, to scoop that all up, and send them all to a labor camp of strict regime." The Russian penal system had three levels of camps. Those of "mild" regime were unpleasant. The "medium" ones were places to avoid. But those of "strict" regime were hell on earth. They were particularly useful for getting the recalcitrant to speak of things they preferred to keep quiet about in ordinary circumstances. Yefremov had the ability to control which scale of punishment a man earned. Suvorov already merited death, in Russia, usually delivered by a bullet . . . but there were worse things than death.

"The president's security detail has been warned?"

The FSS officer nodded. "Yes, though that was a tender one. How can we be sure that one of them is not compromised? That nearly happened to the American president last year, you may have heard, and it is a possibility we have to consider. They are all being watched. But Suvorov had few contacts with the Eighth Directorate when he was KGB, and none of the people he knew ever switched over to there."

"You are sure of that?"

"We finished the cross-check three days ago. We've been busy checking records. We even have a list of people Suvorov might call. Sixteen of them, in fact. All of their phones have been tapped, and all are being watched." But even the FSS didn't have the manpower to put full surveillance details on those potential suspects. This had become the biggest case in the history of the FSS, and few of the KGB's investigations had used up this much manpower, even back to Oleg Penkovskiy.

"What about the names Amalrik and Zimyanin?"

"Zimyanin came up in our check, but not the other. Suvorov didn't know him, but Zimyanin did—they were comrades in Afghanistan—and presumably recruited the other himself. Of the sixteen others, seven are prime suspects, all Spetsnaz, three officers and four non-coms, all of them people who've put their talent and training on the open market. Two are in St. Petersburg, and might have been implicated in the elimination of Amalrik and Zimyanin. It would appear that their comradeship was lacking," Yefremov observed dryly. "So, Provalov, do you have anything to add?"

"No, it would seem that you have covered all likely investigative avenues."

"Thank you. Since it remains a murder case, you will accompany us when we make the arrest."

"The American who assisted us . . . ?"

"He may come along," Yefremov said generously. "We'll show him how we do things here in Russia."

Reilly was back in the U.S. Embassy on the STU, talking to Washington.

"Holy shit," the agent observed.

"That about covers it," Director Murray agreed. "How good's their presidential-protective detail?"

"Pretty good. As good as the Secret Service? I don't know what their investigative support is like, but on the physical side, I'd have to say they're okay."

"Well, they've certainly been warned by now. Whatever they have is going to be perked up a notch or two. When will they do the takedown on this Suvorov guy?"

"Smart move is to sit on it until he makes a move. Figure the Chinese will get the word to him soon—like now, I suppose—and then he'll make some phone calls. That's when I'd put the arm on him, and not before."

"Agreed," Murray observed. "We want to be kept informed on all this. So, stroke your cop friend, will ya?"

"Yes, sir." Reilly paused. "This war scare is for real?"

"It looks that way," Murray confirmed. "We're ramping up to help them out, but I'm not sure how it's going to play out. The President's hoping that the NATO gig will scare them off, but we're not sure of that either. The Agency's running in circles trying to figure the PRC out. Aside from that, I don't know much."

That surprised Reilly. He'd thought Murray was tight with the President, but supposed now that this information was too compartmentalized.

I'll take that," Colonel Aliyev said to the communications officer.

"It's for the immediate attention of—"

"He needs sleep. To get to him, you must go through me," the operations officer announced, reading through the dispatches. "This one can wait . . . this one I can take care of. Anything else?"

"This one's from the president!"

"President Grushavoy needs a lucid general more than he needs an answer to this, Pasha." Aliyev could use some sleep, too, but there was a sofa in the room, and its cushions were calling out to him.

"What's Tolkunov doing?"

"Updating his estimate."

"Is it getting better in any way?" Comms asked.

"What do you think?" Ops replied.

"Shit."

"That's about right, comrade. Know where we can purchase chopsticks for us to eat with?"

"Not while I have my service pistol," the colonel replied. At nearly two meters in height, he was much too tall to be a tanker or an infantryman. "Make sure he sees these when he wakes. I'll fix it with Stavka."

"Good. I'm going to get a few hours, but wake me, not him," Aliyev told his brother officer.

"Da."

They were small men in the main. They started arriving at Never, a small railroad town just east of Skovorodino, on day coaches tacked onto the regular rail service on the Trans-Siberian Railroad. Getting off, they found officers in uniform directing them to buses. These headed down a road paralleling the railroad right-of-way southeast toward a tunnel drilled ages before in the hills over the diminutive Urkan River. Beside the tunnel was an opening which appeared to the casual viewer to be a siding for service equipment for the railroad. And so it was, but this service tunnel went far into the hillside, and branching off it were many more, all constructed in the 1930s by political prisoners, part of Iosef Stalin's gulag labor empire. In these man-made caverns were three hundred T-55 tanks, built in the mid-1960s and never used, but rather stored here to defend against an invasion from China, along with a further two hundred BTR-60 wheeled infantry carriers, plus all the other rolling stock for a Soviet-pattern tank division. The post was garrisoned by a force of four hundred conscripts who, like generations before them, served their time servicing the tanks and carriers, mainly moving from one to another, turning over the diesel engines and cleaning the metal surfaces, which was necessary because of water seepage through the stone roof. The "Never Depot," it was called on classified maps, one of several such places close to the main rail line that went from Moscow to Vladivostok. Cunningly hidden, partially in plain sight, it was one of the aces that General-Colonel Bondarenko had hidden up his sleeve.

As were the men. They were mostly in their thirties, confused, and more than a little angry at having been called away from their homes. However, like good Russians, or indeed good citizens in any land, they got their notices, figured that their country had a need, and it *was* their country, and so about three-fourths of them went as summoned. Some saw familiar faces from their time in the conscript army of the Soviet Union—these men were mainly from that time—and greeted old friends, or ignored those less happily remembered. Each was given a preprinted card telling him where to go, and so the tank crews and infantry squads formed up, the latter finding their uniforms and light weapons, plus ammunition, waiting in the assigned motor-carrier. The tank crewmen were all small men, about 167 centimeters in height—about five feet six inches to an American—because the interiors of the old Russian tanks did not permit tall men to fit inside.

The tankers returning to the steeds of their youth knew the good and bad points of the T-55s. The engines were made of roughly machined parts and would grind off a full kilogram of metal shavings into the oil sumps during the first few hours of running, but, they all figured, that would have been taken care of by the routine turning-over of the engines in the depot. The tanks were, in fact, in surprisingly good shape, better than the ones they'd used on active duty. This seemed both strange and unsurprising to the returning soldiers, because the Red Army had made little logical sense when they'd been in it, but that, for a Soviet citizen of the 1970s and '80s, was not unexpected either. Most remembered their service with some fondness, and for the usual reasons, the chance to travel and see new, different things, and the comradeship of men their own age—a time of life in which young men seek out the new and the exciting. The poor food, miserable pay, and strenuous duty were largely forgotten, though exposure to the rolling equipment brought back some of it with the instant memory that accompanied smells and feels from the past. The tanks all had full internal fuel tanks, plus the oil drums affixed to the rear that had made all of the men cringe when thinking about a battlefield—one live round could turn every tank into a pillar of fire, and so that was the fuel you burned off first, just so you could pull the handle to dump the damned things off when the first bullet flew.

Most agreeably of all, those who pressed the start buttons felt and heard the familiar rumble after only a few seconds of cranking. The benign environment of this cavern had been kind to these old, but essentially unused, tanks. They might have been brand new, fresh from the assembly lines of the massive factory at Nizhnyi Tagil, for decades the armory of the Red Army. The one thing that had changed, they all saw, was that the red star was gone from the glacis plate, replaced with an all-too-visible representation of their new white-blue-red flag, which, they all thought, was far too good an aiming point. Finally they were all called away from their vehicles by the young reserve officers, who, they saw, looked a little worried. Then the speeches began, and the reservists found out why.

Damn, isn't she a lovely one," the FSS officer said, getting into the car. They'd followed their subject to yet another expensive restaurant, where he'd dined alone, then walked into the bar, and within five minutes fixed upon a woman who'd also arrived alone, pretty in her black, red-striped dress that looked to have been copied from some Italian designer. Suvorov/Koniev was driving back toward his flat, with a total of six cars in trail, three of them with light-change switches on their dashboards to alter their visual appearance at night. The cop riding in the number-two car thought that was an especially clever feature.

He was taking his time, not racing his car to show his courage, but instead dazzling the girl with his man-of-the-world demeanor, the investigators thought. The car slowed as it passed one corner, a street with old iron lampposts, then changed direction, if not abruptly, then unexpectedly.

"Shit, he's going to the park," the senior FSS guy said, picking up his radio microphone to say this over the air. "He must have spotted a flag somewhere."

And so he did, but first he dropped off what appeared to be a very disappointed woman, holding some cash in her hand to ease the pain. One of the FSS cars paused to pick her up for questioning, while the others continued their distant pursuit, and five minutes later, it happened. Suvorov/Koniev parked his car on one side of the park and walked across the darkened grass to the other, looking about as he did so, not noticing the fact that five cars were circling.

"That's it. He picked it up." He'd done it skillfully, but that didn't matter if you knew what to look for. Then he walked back to his car. Two of the cars headed directly over to his flat, and the three in trail just kept going when he pulled in.

He said he felt suddenly ill. I gave him my card," she told the interrogators. "He gave me fifty euros for my trouble." Which was fair payment, she thought, for wasting half an hour of her valuable time.

"Anything else? Did he look ill?"

"He said that the food suddenly disagreed with him. I wondered if he'd gotten cold feet as some men do, but not this one. He is a man of some sophistication. You can always tell."

"Very well. Thank you, Yelena. If he calls you, please let us know."

"Certainly." It had been a totally painless interview, which came as rather a surprise for her, and for that reason she'd cooperated fully, wondering what the hell she'd stumbled into. A criminal of some sort? Drug trafficker, perhaps? If he called her, she'd call these people and to hell with him. Life for a woman of her trade was difficult enough.

He's on the computer," an electronics specialist said at FSS headquarters. He read the keystrokes off the keyboard bug they'd planted, and they not only showed up on his screen, but also ran live on a duplicate of the subject desktop system. "There, there's the clear-text. He's got the message."

There was a minute or so of thoughtful pause, and then he began typing again. He logged onto his e-mail service and started typing up messages. They all said some variant of "contact me as soon as you can," and that told them what he was up to. A total of four letters had gone out, though one suggested forwarding to one or more others. Then he logged off and shut his computer down.

"Now, let's see if we can identify his correspondents, shall we?" the senior investigator told his staff. That took all of twenty minutes. What had been routine drudgery was now as exciting as watching the World Cup football final.

The Myasishchev M-5 reconnaissance aircraft lifted off from Taza just before dawn. An odd-looking design with its twin booms, it was a forty-years-too-late Russian version of the venerable Lockheed U-2, able to cruise at seventy thousand feet at a sedate five hundred or so knots and take photographs in large numbers with high resolution. The pilot was an experienced Russian air force major with orders not to stray within ten kilometers of the Chinese border. This was to avoid provoking his country's potential enemies, and that order was not as easy to execute as it had been to write down in Moscow, because the borders between countries are rarely straight lines. So, the major programmed his autopilot carefully and sat back to monitor his instruments while the camera systems did all the real work. The main instrument he monitored was his threat-receiver, essentially a radio scanner programmed to note the energy of radar transmitters. There were many such transmitters on the border, most of the low- to-mid-frequency search types, but then a new one came up. This was on the X-band, and it came from the south, and that meant that a Chinese surface-to-air missile battery was illuminating him with a tracking-and-targeting radar. *That* got his attention, because although seventy thousand was higher than any commercial aircraft could fly, and higher than many fighters could reach, it was well within the flight envelope of a SAM, as an American named Francis Gary Powers had once discovered over Central Russia. A fighter could outmaneuver most SAMs, but the M-5 was not a fighter and had trouble outmaneuvering clouds on a windless day. And so he kept his eye on the threat-receiver's dials while his ears registered the shrill *beep-beep* of the aural alert. The visual display showed that the pulse-repetition rate was in the tracking rather than the lock-up mode. So, a missile was probably not in the air, and the sky was clear enough that he'd probably see the smoke trail that such missiles always left, and today—no, no smoke coming up from the ground. For defensive systems, he had only a primitive chaff dispenser and prayer. Not even a white-noise jammer, the major groused. But there was no sense in worrying. He *was* ten kilometers inside his own country's airspace, and whatever SAM systems the Chinese possessed were probably well inside their own borders. It would be a stretch for them to reach him, and he could always turn north and run while punching loose a few kilos of shredded aluminum foil to give the inbound missile something else to chase. As it played out, the mission involved four complete sweeps of the border region, and that required ninety otherwise boring minutes before he reprogrammed the M-5 back to the old fighter base outside Taza.

The ground crew supporting the mission had also been deployed from the Moscow area. As soon as the M-5 rolled to a stop, the film cassettes were unloaded and driven to the portable film lab for development, then forwarded, still wet, to the interpreters. They saw few tanks, but lots of tracks in the ground, and that was all they needed to see.

CHAPTER 49

Disarming

"I know, Oleg. I understand that we developed the intelligence in Washington and forwarded it to your people immediately," Reilly said to his friend.

"You must be proud of that," Provalov observed.

"Wasn't the Bureau that did it," Reilly responded. The Russians would be touchy about having Americans provide them with such sensitive information. Maybe Americans would have reacted the same way. "Anyway, what are you going to do about it?"

"We're trying to locate his electronic correspondents. We have their addresses, and they are all on Russian-owned ISPs. FSS probably has them all identified by now."

"Arrest them when?"

"When they meet Suvorov. We have enough to make the arrests now."

Reilly wasn't sure about that. The people Suvorov wanted to meet could always say that they came to see him by invitation without having a clue as to the purpose of the meeting, and a day-old member of the bar could easily enough sell the "reasonable doubt" associated with that to a jury. Better to wait until they all did something incriminating, and then squeeze one of them real hard to turn state's evidence on the rest. But the rules and the juries were different here.

"Anatoliy, what are you thinking about?" Golovko asked.

"Comrade Chairman, I am thinking that Moscow has suddenly become dangerous," Major Shelepin replied. "The idea of former Spetsnaz men conspiring to commit treason on this scale sickens me. Not just the threat, but also the infamy of it. These men were my comrades in the army, trained as I was to be guardians of the State." The handsome young officer shook his head.

"Well, when this place was the KGB, it happened to us more than once. It is unpleasant, yes, but it is reality. People are corruptible. It is human nature," Golovko said soothingly. *Besides, the threat isn't against me now,* he didn't add. An unworthy thought, perhaps, but that also was human nature. "What is President Grushavoy's detail doing now?"

"Sweating, I should imagine. Who can say that this is the only threat? What if this Kong bastard has more than one such agent in Moscow? We should pick him up, too."

"So we shall, when the time comes. He's been observed to do only one dead-drop over the past week, and we control that one—yes, yes, I know," Sergey added, when he saw the beginnings of Anatoliy's objections. "He isn't the only MSS operative in Moscow, but he's probably the only one on this case. Security considerations are universal. They must worry that one of their officers might be in *our* employ, after all. There are many wheels in such an operation, and they don't all turn in the same direction, my young friend. You know what I miss?"

"I should imagine it is having the second chief directorate under the same roof. That way the operation would be run cooperatively."

Golovko smiled. "Correct, Anatoliy Ivan'ch. For now, we can only do our job and wait for others to do theirs. And, yes, waiting is never an entertaining way to spend one's time." With that observation, both men resumed staring at the desk phones, waiting for them to ring.

The only reason that surveillance hadn't been tightened any more was that there wasn't enough room for the additional personnel, and Suvorov might take note of the thirty people who followed him everywhere. That day he awoke at his normal hour, washed up, had coffee and kasha for breakfast, left the apartment building at 9:15, and drove his car into the city, with a good deal of elusive company. He parked his car two blocks from Gor'kiy Park and walked the rest of the way there.

So did four others, also under surveillance. They met at a magazine kiosk at precisely 9:45 and walked together toward a coffee shop that was disagreeably crowded, too much so for any of the watchers to get close enough to listen in, though the faces were observed. Suvorov/Koniev did most of the talking, and the other four listened intently, and nods started.

Yefremov of the Federal Security Service kept his distance. He was senior enough that he could no longer guarantee that his face was unknown, and had to trust the more junior men to get in close, their earpieces removed and radio transmitters turned off, wishing they could read lips like the people in spy movies.

For Pavel Georgiyevich Yefremov, the question was, what to do now? Arrest them all and risk blowing the case—or merely continue to shadow, and risk having them go forward . . . and perhaps accomplish the mission?

The question would be answered by one of the four contacts. He was the oldest of them, about forty, a Spetsnaz veteran of Afghanistan with the Order of the Red Banner to his name. His name was Igor Maximov. He held up his hand, rubbing forefinger and thumb, and, getting the answer to his question, he shook his head and politely took his leave. His departure was a cordial one, and his personal two-man shadow team followed him to the nearest Metro station while the others continued talking.

On learning this, Yefremov ordered him picked up. That was done when he got off the Metro train five kilometers away at the station near his flat, where he lived with his wife and son. The man did not resist and was unarmed. Docile as a lamb, he accompanied the two FSS officers to their headquarters.

"Your name is Maximov, Igor Il'ych," Yefremov told him. "You met with your friend Suvorov, Klementi Ivan'ch, to discuss participation in a crime. We want to hear your version of what was discussed."

"Comrade Yefremov, I met some old friends for coffee this morning and then I left. Nothing in particular was discussed. I do not know what you are talking about."

"Yes, of course," the FSS man replied. "Tell me, do you know two former Spetsnaz men like yourself, Amalrik and Zimyanin?"

"I've heard the names, but I don't know the faces."

"Here are the faces." Yefremov handed over the photos from the Leningrad Militia. "They are not pleasant to look upon."

Maximov didn't blanch, but he didn't look at the photos with affection either. "What happened to them?"

"They did a job for your comrade, Suvorov, but he was evidently displeased with how they went about it, and so, they went swimming in the River Neva. Maximov, we know that you were Spetsnaz. We know that you earn your living today doing illegal things, but that is not a matter of concern to us at the moment. We want to know exactly what was said at the coffee shop. You will tell us this, the easy way or the hard way. The choice is yours." When he wanted to, Yefremov could come on very hard to his official guests. In this case, it wasn't difficult. Maximov was not a stranger to violence, at least on the giving side. The receiving side was something he had no wish to learn about.

"What do you offer me?"

"I offer you your freedom in return for your cooperation. You left the meeting before any conclusions were reached. That is why you are here. So, do you wish to speak now, or shall we wait a few hours for you to change your mind?"

Maximov was not a coward—Spetsnaz didn't have many of those, in Yefremov's experience—but he was a realist, and realism told him that he had nothing to gain by noncooperation.

"He asked me and the others to participate in a murder. I presume it will be a difficult operation, otherwise why would he need so many men? He offers for this twenty thousand euros each. I decided that my time is more valuable than that."

"Do you know the name of the target?"

Maximov shook his head. "No. He did not say. I did not ask."

"That is good. You see, the target is President Grushavoy." That got a reaction, as Maximov's eyes flared.

"That is state treason," the former Spetsnaz sergeant breathed, hoping to convey the idea that he'd never do such a thing. He learned fast.

"Yes. Tell me, is twenty thousand euros a good price for a murder?"

"I would not know. If you want me to tell you that I have killed for money, no, Comrade Yefremov, I will not say that."

But you have, and you'd probably participate in this one if the price went high enough. In Russia, E20,000 was a considerable sum. But Yefremov had much bigger fish to fry. "The others at the meeting, what do you know of them?"

"All are Spetsnaz veterans. Ilya Suslov and I served together east of Qandahar. He's a sniper, a very good one. The others, I know them casually, but I never served with them."

Sniper. Well, those were useful, and President Grushavoy appeared in public a lot. He was scheduled to have an outdoor rally the very next day, in fact. It was time to wrap this up.

"So, Suvorov spoke of a murder for hire?"

"Yes, he did."

"Good. We will take your statement. You were wise to cooperate, Igor Il'ych." Yefremov had a junior officer lead him away. Then he lifted his phone. "Arrest them all," he told the field commander.

"The meeting broke up. We have all of them under surveillance. Suvorov is en route back to his flat with one of the three."

"Well, assemble the team and arrest them both."

Feeling better?" Colonel Aliyev asked.

"What time is it?"

"Fifteen-forty, Comrade General," Colonel Aliyev replied. "You slept for thirteen hours. Here are some dispatches from Moscow."

"You let me sleep that long?" the general demanded, instantly angry.

"The war has not begun. Our preparations, such as they are, are progressing, and there seemed no sense in waking you. Oh, we have our first set of reconnaissance photos. Not much better than the American ones we had faxed to us. Intelligence has firmed up its estimate. It's not getting any better. We have support now from an American ELINT aircraft, but they tell us that the Chinese aren't using their radios, which is not a surprise."

"God damn it, Andrey!" the general responded, rubbing his unshaven face with both hands.

"So, court-martial me after you've had your coffee. I got some sleep, too. You have a staff. I have a staff, and I decided to let them do their jobs while we slept," the operations officer said defiantly.

"What of the Never Depot?"

"We have a total of one hundred eighty tanks operating with full crews. Shorter on the infantry component and artillery, but the reservists seem to be functioning with some degree of enthusiasm, and the 265th

Motor Rifle is starting to act like a real division for the first time." Aliyev walked over a mug of coffee with milk and sugar, the way Bondarenko preferred it. "Drink, Gennady Iosifovich." Then he pointed to a table piled with buttered bread and bacon.

"If we live, I will see you promoted, Colonel."

"I've always wanted to be a general officer. But I want to see my children enter university, too. So, let's try to stay alive."

"What of the border troops?"

"I have transport assigned to each post—where possible, two sets of transport. I've sent some of the reservists in BTRs to make sure they have a little protection against the artillery fire when they pull out. We have a lot of guns in the photos from the M-5, Comrade General. And fucking mountains of shells. But the border troops have ample protection, and the orders have gone out so that they will not need permission to leave their posts when the situation becomes untenable—at the company-officer level, that is," Aliyev added. Commissioned officers were less likely to bug out than enlisted men.

"No word on when?"

The G-3 shook his head. "Nothing helpful from Intelligence. The Chinese are still moving trucks and such around, from what we can tell. I'd say another day, maybe as many as three."

So?" Ryan asked.

"So, the overheads show they're still moving the chess pieces on the board," Foley answered. "But most of them are in place."

"What about Moscow?"

"They're going to arrest their suspects soon. Probably going to pick up the control officer in Moscow, too. They'll sweat him some, but he does have diplomatic immunity, and you can't squeeze him much." Ed Foley remembered when KGB had arrested his wife in Moscow. It hadn't been pleasant for her—and less so for him—but they hadn't roughed her up, either. Messing with people who traveled on diplomatic passports didn't happen often, despite what they'd seen on TV a few weeks before. And the Chinese probably regretted that one a lot, pronouncements on the SORGE feeds to the contrary notwithstanding.

"Nothing from inside to encourage us?"

"Nope." The DCI shook his head.

"We ought to start moving the Air Force," Vice President Jackson urged.

"But then it could be seen as a provocation," Secretary Adler pointed out. "We can't give them any excuse."

"We can move First Armored into Russia, say it's a joint training exercise with our new NATO allies," TOMCAT said. "That could buy us a few days."

Ryan weighed that and looked over at the Chairman of the Joint Chiefs. "Well, General?"

"It can't hurt all that much. They're already working with Deutsche Rail to get the move organized."

"Then do it," the President ordered.

"Yes, sir." General Moore moved to make the call.

Ryan checked his watch. "I have a reporter to talk to."

"Have fun," Robby told his friend.

Zhigansk, on the west side of the Lena River, had once been a major regional air-defense center for the old Soviet PVO Strany, the Russian air-defense command. It had a larger-than-average airfield with barracks and hangars, and had been largely abandoned by the new Russian military, with just a caretaker staff to maintain the facility in case it might be needed someday. This turned out to be a piece of lucky foresight, because the United States Air Force started moving in that day, mainly transport aircraft from the central part of America that had staged through Alaska and flown over the North Pole to get there. The first of thirty C-5 Galaxy transports landed at ten in the morning local time, taxiing to the capacious but vacant ramps to offload their cargo under the direction of ground crewmen who'd ridden in the large passenger area aft of the wing box in the huge transports. The first things wheeled off were the Dark Star UAVs. They looked like loaves of French bread copulating atop slender wings, and were long-endurance, stealthy reconnaissance drones that took six hours to assemble for flight. The crews got immediately to work, using mobile equipment shipped on the same aircraft.

Fighter and attack aircraft came into Suntar, far closer to the Chinese border, with tankers and other support aircraft—including the American E-3 Sentry AWACS birds—just west of there at Mirnyy. At these two air bases, the arriving Americans found their Russian counterparts, and immediately the various staffs started working together. American tankers could not refuel Russian aircraft, but to everyone's relief the nozzles for ground fueling were identical, and so the American aircraft could make use of the take fuel from the Russian JP storage tanks, which, they found, were huge, and mainly underground to be protected against nuclear airbursts. The most important element of cooperation was the assignment of Russian controllers to the American AWACS, so that Russian fighters could be controlled from the American radar aircraft. Almost at once, some E-3s lifted off to test this capability, using arriving American fighters as practice targets for controlled intercepts. They found immediately that the Russian fighter pilots reacted well to the directions, to the pleased surprise of the American controllers.

They also found almost immediately that the American attack aircraft couldn't use Russian bombs and other ordnance. Even if the shackle points had been the same (they weren't), the Russian bombs had different aerodynamics from their American counterparts, and so the computer software on the American aircraft could not hit targets with them—it would have been like trying to jam the wrong cartridge into a rifle: even if you could fire the round, the sights would send it to the wrong point of impact. So, the Americans would have to fly in the bombs to be dropped, and shipping bombs by air was about as efficient as flying in gravel to build roads. Bombs came to fighter bases by ship, train, truck, and forklift, not by air. For this reason, the B-1s and other heavy-strike aircraft were sent to Andersen Air Force Base on Guam, where there *were* some bomb stores to be used, even though they were a long way from the supposed targets.

The air forces of the two sides established an immediate and friendly rapport, and in hours—as soon as the American pilots had gotten a little mandated crew rest—they were planning and flying missions together with relative ease.

The Quarter Horse went first. Under the watchful eyes of Lieutenant Colonel Angelo Giusti, the M1A2 main battle tanks and M3 Bradley cavalry scout vehicles rolled onto the flatcars of Deutsche Rail, accompanied by the fuel and other support trucks. Troops went into coaches at the head end of the train "consists" and were soon heading east to Berlin, where they'd change over to the Russian-gauge cars for the further trip east. Oddly, there were no TV cameramen around at the moment, Giusti saw. That couldn't last, but it was one less distraction for the unit that was the eyes of First Tanks. The division's helicopter brigade was sitting at its own base, awaiting the availability of Air Force transports to ferry them east. Some genius had decided against having the aircraft fly themselves, which, Giusti thought, they were perfectly able to do, but General Diggs had told him not to worry about it. Giusti would worry about it, but not out loud. He settled into a comfortable seat in the lead passenger coach, along with his staff, and went over maps just printed up by the division's cartography unit, part of the intelligence shop. The maps showed the terrain they might be fighting for. Mostly they predicted where the Chinese would be going, and that wasn't overly demanding.

So, what are we going to do?" Bob Holtzman asked.

"We're beginning to deploy forces to support our allies," Ryan answered. "We hope that the PRC will see this and reconsider the activities that now appear to be under way."

"Have we been in contact with Beijing?"

"Yes." Ryan nodded soberly. "The DCM of our embassy in Beijing, William Kilmer, delivered a note from us to the Chinese government, and we are now awaiting a formal reply."

"Are you telling us that you think there will be a shooting war between Russia and China?"

"Bob, our government is working very hard to forestall that possibility, and we call on the Chinese government to think very hard about its position and its actions. War is no longer a policy option in this world. I suppose it once was, but no longer. War only brings death and ruin to people. The world has turned a corner on this thing. The lives of people—including the lives of soldiers—are too precious to be thrown away. Bob, the reason we have governments is to serve the needs and the interests of *people,* not the ambitions of rulers. I hope the leadership of the PRC will see that." Ryan paused. "A couple of days ago, I was at Auschwitz. Bob, that was the sort of experience to get you thinking. You could *feel* the horror there. You could hear the screams, smell the death smell, you could *see* the lines of people being led off under guns to where they were murdered. Bob, all of a sudden it wasn't just black-and-white TV anymore.

"It came to me then that there is no excuse at all for the government of a country, any country, to engage in killing for profit. Ordinary criminals rob liquor stores to get money. Countries rob countries to get oil or gold or territory. Hitler invaded Poland for *Lebensraum,* for room for Germany to expand—but, damn it, there were already people living there, and what he tried to do was to steal. That's all. Not statecraft, not vision. Hitler was a *thief* before he was a murderer. Well, the United States of America will not stand by and watch that happen again." Ryan paused and took a sip of water.

"One of the things you learn in life is that there's only one thing really worth having, and that's love. Well, by the same token there's only one thing worth fighting for, and that is justice. Bob, that's what America fights for, and if China launches a war of aggression—a war of robbery—America will stand by her ally and stop it from happening."

"Many say that your policy toward China has helped to bring this situation about, that your diplomatic recognition of Taiwan—" Ryan cut him off angrily.

"Bob, I will not have any of that! The Republic of China's government is a freely elected one. America *supports* democratic governments. Why? Because we stand *for* freedom and self-determination. Neither I nor America had anything to do with the cold-blooded murders we saw on TV, the death of the Papal Nuncio, Cardinal DiMilo, and the killing of the Chinese minister Yu Fa An. We had nothing to do with that. The revulsion of the entire civilized world came about because of the PRC's actions. Even then, China could have straightened it out by investigating and punishing the killers, but they chose not to, and the world reacted—to what they did all by themselves."

"But what is this all about? Why are they massing troops on the Russian border?"

"It appears that they want what the Russians have, the new oil and gold discoveries. Just as Iraq once invaded Kuwait. It was for oil, for money, really. It was an armed robbery, just like a street thug does, mugging an old lady for her Social Security check, but somehow, for some reason, we sanctify it when it happens at the nation-state level. Well, no more, Bob. The world will no longer tolerate such things. And America will not stand by and watch this happen to our ally. Cicero once said that Rome grew great not through conquest, but rather through defending her allies. A nation acquires respect from acting *for* things, not *against* things. You measure people not by what they are against, but by what they are *for.* America stands *for* democracy, *for* the self-determination of people. We stand *for* freedom. We stand *for* justice. We've told the People's Republic of China that if they launch a war of aggression, then America will stand with Russia and against the aggressor. We believe in a peaceful world order in which nations compete on the economic battlefield, not with tanks and guns. There's been enough killing. It's time for that to stop, and America will be there to make it stop."

"The world's policeman?" Holtzman asked. Immediately, the President shook his head.

"Not that, but we will defend our allies, and the Russian Federation is an ally. We stood with the Russian people to stop Hitler. We stand with them again," Ryan said.

"And again we send our young people off to war?"

"There need be no war, Bob. There is no war today. Neither America nor Russia will start one. That question is in the hands of others. It isn't hard, it isn't demanding, for a nation-state to stand its military down. It's a rare professional soldier who relishes conflict. Certainly no one who's seen a battlefield will voluntarily rush to see another. But I'll tell you this: If the PRC launches a war of aggression, and if because of them American lives are placed at risk, then those who make the decision to set loose those dogs are putting their own lives at risk."

"The Ryan Doctrine?" Holtzman asked.

"Call it anything you want. If it's acceptable to kill some infantry private for doing what his government tells him, then it's also acceptable to kill the people who tell the government what to do, the ones who send that poor, dumb private out in harm's way."

Oh, shit, Arnie van Damm thought, hovering in the doorway of the Oval Office. *Jack, did you have to say* that*?*

"Thank you for your time, Mr. President," Holtzman said. "When will you address the nation?"

"Tomorrow. God willing, it'll be to say that the PRC has backed off. I'll be calling Premier Xu soon to make a personal appeal to him."

"Good luck."

We are ready," Marshal Luo told the others. "The operation commences early tomorrow morning."

"What have the Americans done?"

"They've sent some aircraft forward, but aircraft do not concern me," the Defense Minister replied. "They can sting, as a mosquito does, but they cannot do real harm to a man. We will make twenty kilometers the first day, and then fifty per day thereafter—maybe more, depending on how the Russians fight. The Russian Air Force is not even a paper tiger. We can destroy it, or at least push it back out of our way. The Russians are starting to move mechanized troops east on their railroad, but we will pound on their marshaling facility at Chita with our air assets. We can dam them up and stop them to protect our left flank until we move troops in to wall that off completely."

"You are confident, Marshal?" Zhang asked—rhetorically, of course.

"We'll have their new gold mine in eight days, and then it's ten more to the oil," the marshal predicted, as though describing how long it would take to build a house.

"Then you are ready?"

"Fully," Luo insisted.

"Expect a call from President Ryan later today," Foreign Minister Shen warned the premier.

"What will he say?" Xu asked.

"He will give you a personal plea to stop the war from beginning."

"If he does, what ought I to say?"

"Have your secretary say you are out meeting the people," Zhang advised. "Don't talk to the fool."

Minister Shen wasn't fully behind his country's policy, but nodded anyway. It seemed the best way to avoid a personal confrontation, which Xu would not handle well. His ministry was still trying to get a feel for how to handle the American President. He was so unlike other governmental chiefs that they still had difficulty understanding how to speak with him.

"What of our answer to their note?" Fang asked.

"We have not given them a formal answer," Shen told him.

"It concerns me that they should not be able to call us liars," Fang said. "That would be unfortunate, I think."

"You worry too much, Fang," Zhang commented, with a cruel smile.

"No, in that he is correct," Shen said, rising to his colleague's defense. "Nations must be able to trust the words of one another, else no intercourse at all is possible. Comrades, we must remember that there will be an 'after the war,' in which we must be able to reestablish normal relations with the nations of the world. If they regard us as outlaw, that will be difficult."

"That makes sense," Xu observed, speaking his own opinion for once. "No, I will not accept the call from Washington, and no, Fang, I will not allow America to call us liars."

"One other development," Luo said. "The Russians have begun high-altitude reconnaissance flights on their side of the border. I propose to shoot down the next one and say that their aircraft intruded on our airspace. Along with other plans, we will use that as a provocation on their part."

"Excellent," Zhang observed.

So?" John asked.

"So, he is in this building," General Kirillin clarified. "The takedown team is ready to go up and make the arrest. Care to observe?"

"Sure," Clark agreed with a nod. He and Chavez were both dressed in their RAINBOW ninja suits, black everything, plus body armor, which struck them both as theatrical, but the Russians were being overly solicitous to their hosts, and that included official concern for their safety. "How is it set up?"

"We have four men in the apartment next door. We anticipate no difficulties," Kirillin sold his guests. "So, if you will follow me."

"Waste of time, John," Chavez observed in Spanish.

"Yeah, but they want to do a show-and-tell." The two of them followed Kirillin and a junior officer to the elevator, which whisked them up to the proper floor. A quick, furtive look showed that the corridor was clear, and they moved like cats to the occupied apartment.

"We are ready, Comrade General," the senior Spetsnaz officer, a major, told his commander. "Our friend is sitting in his kitchen discussing matters with his guest. They're looking at how to kill President Grushavoy tomorrow on his way to parliament. Sniper rifle," he concluded, "from eight hundred meters."

"You guys make good ones here," Clark observed. Eight hundred was close enough for a good rifleman, especially on a slow-moving target like a walking man.

"Proceed, Major," Kirillin ordered.

With that, the four-man team walked back out into the corridor. They were dressed in their own RAINBOW suits, black Nomex, and carrying the equipment Clark and his people had brought over, German MP-10 submachine guns, and .45 Beretta sidearms, plus the portable radios from E-Systems. Clark and Chavez were wearing identical gear, but not carrying weapons. Probably the real reason Kirillin had brought them over, John thought, was to show them how much his people had learned, and that was fair enough. The Russian troopers looked ready. Alert and pumped up, but not nervous, just the right amount of tenseness.

The officer in command moved down the corridor to the door. His explosives man ran a thin line of det-cord explosive along the door's edges and stepped aside, looking at his team leader for the word.

"Shoot," the major told him—

—and before Clark's brain could register the single-word command, the corridor was sundered with the crash of the explosion that sent the solid-core door into the apartment at about three hundred feet per second. Then the Russian major and a lieutenant tossed in flashbangs sure to disorient anyone who might have been there with a gun of his own. It was hard enough for Clark and Chavez, and they'd known what was coming and had their hands over their ears. The Russians darted into the apartment in pairs, just as they'd been trained to do, and there was no other sound, except for a scream down the hall from a resident who hadn't been warned about the day's activities. That left John Clark and Domingo Chavez just standing there, until an arm appeared and waved them inside.

The inside was a predictable mess. The entry door was now fit only for kindling and toothpicks, and the pictures that decorated the wall did so without any glass in the frames. The blue sofa had a ruinous scorch mark on the right side, and the carpet was cratered by the other flash-bang.

Suvorov and Suslov had been sitting in the kitchen, always the heart of any Russian home. That had placed them far enough away from the explosion to be unhurt, though both looked stunned by the experience, and well they might be. There were no weapons in evidence, which was surprising to the Russians but not to Clark, and the two supposed miscreants were now facedown on the tile floor, their hands manacled behind them and guns not far behind their heads.

"Greetings, Klementi Ivan'ch," General Kirillin said. "We need to talk."

The older of the two men on the floor didn't react much. First, he was not really able to, and second, he knew that talking would not improve his situation. Of all the spectators, Clark felt the most sympathy for him. To run a covert operation was tense enough. To have one blown—it had never happened to John, but he'd thought about the possibility often enough—was not a reality that one wished to contemplate. Especially in this place, though since it was no longer the Soviet Union, Suvorov could take comfort in the fact that things might have been a little worse. But not that much worse, John was sure. It was time for him to say something.

"Well executed, Major. A little heavy on the explosives, but we all do that. I say that to my own people almost every time."

"Thank you, General Clark." The senior officer of the strike team beamed, but not too much, trying to look cool for his subordinates. They'd just done their first real-life mission, and pleased as they all were, the attitude they had to adopt was *of course we did it right.* It was a matter of professional pride.

"So, Yuriy Andreyevich, what will happen with them now?" John asked in his best Leningrad Russian.

"They will be interrogated for murder and conspiracy to commit murder, plus state treason. We picked up Kong half an hour ago, and he's talking," Kirillin added, lying. Suvorov might not believe it, but the statement would get his mind wandering in an uncomfortable direction. "Take them out!" the general ordered. No sooner had that happened than an FSS officer came in to light up the desktop computer to begin a detailed check of its contents. The protection program Suvorov had installed was bypassed because they knew the key to it, from the keyboard bug they'd installed earlier. Computers, they all agreed, must have been designed with espionage in mind—but they worked both ways.

"Who are you?" a stranger in civilian clothes asked.

"John Clark" was the surprising answer in Russian. "And you?"

"Provalov. I am a lieutenant-investigator with the militia."

"Oh, the RPG case?"

"Correct."

"I guess that's your man."

"Yes, a murderer."

"Worse than that," Chavez said, joining the conversation.

"There is nothing worse than murder," Provalov responded, always the cop.

Chavez was more practical in his outlook. "Maybe, depends on if you need an accountant to keep track of all the bodies."

"So, Clark, what do you think of the operation?" Kirillin asked, hungry for the American's approval.

"It was perfect. It was a simple operation, but flawlessly done. They're good kids, Yuriy. They learn fast and they work hard. They're ready to be trainers for your special-operations people."

"Yeah, I'd take any of them out on a job," Ding agreed. Kirillin beamed at the news, unsurprising as it was.

CHAPTER 50

Thunder and Lightning

"They got him," Murray told Ryan. "Our friend Clark was there to watch. Damned ecumenical of the Russkies."

"Just want to be an ally back to us, I suppose, and RAINBOW is a NATO asset. You suppose he'll sing?"

"Like a canary, probably," the FBI Director predicted. "The Miranda Rule never made it to Russia, Jack, and their interrogation techniques are a little more—uh, enthusiastic than ours are. Anyway, it's something to put on TV, something to get their public seriously riled up. So, boss, this war going to stop or go?"

"We're trying to stop it, Dan, but—"

"Yeah, I understand," Murray said. "Sometimes big shots act just like street hoods. Just with bigger guns."

This bunch has H-bombs, Jack didn't say. It wasn't something you wanted to talk about right after breakfast. Murray hung up and Ryan checked his watch. It was time. He punched the intercom button on his phone.

"Ellen, could you come in, please?"

It took the usual five seconds. "Yes, Mr. President."

"I need one, and it's time to call Beijing."

"Yes, sir." She handed Ryan a Virginia Slim and went back to the anteroom.

Ryan saw one of the phone lights go on and waited, lighting his smoke. He had his speech to Premier Xu pretty well canned, knowing that the Chinese leader would have a good interpreter nearby. He also knew that Xu would still be in the office. He'd been working pretty late over the past few days—it wasn't hard to figure out why. Starting a potential world war had to be a time-consuming business. So, it would be less than thirty seconds to make the guy's phone ring, then Ellen Sumter would talk to the operator on the far end—the Chinese had full-time switchboard operators rather than secretary-receptionists as in the White House—and the call would be put through. So, figure another thirty seconds, and then Jack would get to make his case to Xu: *Let's reconsider this one, buddy, or something bad will happen. Bad for our country. Bad for yours. Probably worse for yours.* Mickey Moore had promised something called Hyperwar, and that would be seriously bad news for someone unprepared for it. The phone light stayed on, but Ellen wasn't beeping him to get on the line . . . why? Xu was still in his office. The embassy in Beijing was supposed to be keeping an eye on the guy. Ryan didn't know how, but he was pretty sure they knew their job. It might have been as easy as having an embassy employee—probably an Agency guy—stand on the street with a cell phone and watch a lit-up office window, then report to the embassy, which would have an open line to Foggy Bottom, which had many open lines to the White House. But then the light on the phone blinked out, and the intercom started:

"Mr. President, they say he's out of the office," Mrs. Sumter said.

"Oh?" Ryan took a long puff. "Tell State to confirm his location."

"Yes, Mr. President." Then forty seconds of silence. "Mr. President, the embassy says he's in his office, as far as they can tell."

"And his people said . . . ?"

"They said he's out, sir."

"When will he be back?"

"I asked. They said they didn't know."

"Shit," Ryan breathed. "Please get me Secretary Adler."

"Yeah, Jack," SecState said a few seconds later.

"He's dodging my call, Scott."

"Xu?"

"Yeah."

"Not surprising. They—the Chinese Politburo—don't trust him to talk on his own without a script."

Like Arnie and me, Ryan thought with a mixture of anger and humor. "Okay, what's it mean, Scott?"

"Nothing good, Jack," Adler replied. "Nothing good."

"So, what do we do now?"

"Diplomatically, there's not much we can do. We've sent them a stiff note, and they haven't answered. Your position vis-à-vis them and the Russian situation is as clear as we can make it. They know what we're thinking. If they don't want to talk to us, it means they don't care anymore."

"Shit."

"That's right," the Secretary of State agreed.

"You're telling me we can't stop it?"

"Correct." Adler's tone was matter-of-fact.

"Okay, what else?"

"We tell our civilians to get the hell out of China. We're set up to do that here."

"Okay, do it," Ryan ordered, with a sudden flip of his stomach.

"Right."

"I'll get back to you." Ryan switched lines and punched the button for the Secretary of Defense.

"Yeah," Tony Bretano answered.

"It looks like it's going to happen," Ryan told him.

"Okay, I'll alert all the CINCs."

In a matter of minutes, FLASH traffic was dispatched to each of the commanders-in-chief of independent commands. There were many of them, but at the moment the most important was CINCPAC, Admiral Bart Mancuso in Pearl Harbor. It was just after three in the morning when the STU next to his bed started chirping.

"This is Admiral Mancuso," he said, more than half asleep.

"Sir, this is the watch officer. We have a war warning from Washington. China. 'Expect the commencement of hostilities between the PRC and the Russian Federation to commence within the next twenty-four hours. You are directed to take all measures consistent with the safety of your command.' Signed Bretano, SecDef, sir," the lieutenant commander told him.

Mancuso already had both feet on the floor of the bedroom. "Okay, get my staff together. I'll be in the office in ten minutes."

"Aye, aye, sir."

The chief petty officer assigned to drive him was already outside the front door, and Mancuso noted the presence of four armed Marines in plain sight. The senior of them saluted while the others studiously looked outward at a threat that probably wasn't there . . . but might be. Minutes later, he walked into his hilltop headquarters overlooking the naval base. Brigadier General Lahr was there, waiting for him.

"How'd you get in so fast?" CINCPAC asked him.

"Just happened to be in the neighborhood, Admiral," the J-2 told him. He followed Mancuso into the inner office.

"What's happening?"

"The President tried to phone Premier Xu, but he didn't take the call. Not a good sign from our Chinese brethren," the theater intelligence officer observed.

"Okay, what's John Chinaman doing?" Mancuso asked, as a steward's mate brought in coffee.

"Not much in our area of direct interest, but he's got a hell of a lot of combat power deployed in the Shenyang Military District, most of it right up on the Amur River." Lahr set up a map stand and started moving his hand on the acetate overlay, which had a lot of red markings on it. For the first time in his memory, Mancuso saw Russian units drawn in blue, which was the "friendly" color. It was too surprising to comment on.

"What are we doing?"

"We're moving a lot of air assets into Siberia. The shooters are here at Suntar. Reconnaissance assets back here at Zhigansk. The Dark Stars ought to be up and flying soon. It'll be the first time we've deployed 'em in a real shooting war, and the Air Force has high hopes for them. We have some satellite overheads that show where the Chinese are. They've camouflaged their heavy gear, but the Lacrosse imagery sees right through the nets."

"And?"

"And it's over half a million men, five Group-A mechanized armies. That's one armored division, two mechanized infantry, and one motorized infantry each, plus attachments that belong directly to the army commander. The forces deployed are heavy in tanks and APCs, fair in artillery, but light in helicopters. The air assets belong to somebody else. Their command structure for coordinating air and ground isn't as streamlined as it ought to be, and their air forces aren't very good by our standards, but their numbers are better than the Russians'. Manpower-wise, the Chinese have a huge advantage on the ground. The Russians have space to play with, but if it comes down to a slugging match, bet your money on the People's Liberation Army."

"And at sea?"

"Their navy doesn't have much out of port at the moment, but overheads show they're lighting up their boilers alongside. I would expect them to surge some ships out. Expect them to stay close in, defensive posture, deployment just to keep their coast clear."

Mancuso didn't have to ask what he had out. Seventh Fleet was pretty much out to sea after the warnings from previous weeks. His carriers were heading west. He had a total of six submarines camped out on the Chinese coast, and his surface forces were spun up. If the People's Liberation Army Navy wanted to play, they'd regret it.

"Orders?"

"Self-defense only at this point," Lahr said.

"Okay, we'll close to within two hundred fifty miles of their coast minimum for surface ships. Keep the carriers an additional hundred back for now. The submarines can close in and shadow any PLAN forces at will, but no shooting unless attacked, and I don't want anyone counter-detected. The Chinese have that one reconsat up. I don't want it to see anything painted gray." Dodging a single reconnaissance satellite wasn't all that difficult, since it was entirely predictable in course and speed. You could even keep out of the way of two. When the number got to three, things became difficult.

In the Navy, the day never starts because the day never ends, but that wasn't true for a ship sitting in wooden blocks. Then things changed, if not to an eight-hour day, then at least to a semi-civilian job where most of the crew lived at home and drove in every morning (for the most part) to do their jobs. That was principally preventive maintenance, which is one of the U.S. Navy's religions. It was the same for Al Gregory; in his case, he drove his rented car in from the Norfolk motel and blew a kiss at the rent-a-cop at the guard shack, who waved everyone in. Once there had been armed Marines at the gates, but they'd gone away when the Navy had been stripped of its tactical nuclear weapons. There were still some nukes at the Yorktown ordnance station, because the Trident warheads hadn't yet all been disassembled out at Pantex in Texas, and some still occupied their mainly empty bunkers up on the York River, awaiting shipment west for final disposal. But not at Norfolk, and the ships that had guards mainly depended on sailors carrying Beretta M9 pistols which they might, or might not, know how to use properly. That was the case on USS *Gettysburg,* whose sailors recognized Gregory by sight and waved him aboard with a smile and a greeting.

"Hey, Doc," Senior Chief Leek said, when the civilian came into CIC. He pointed to the coffee urn. The Navy's real fuel was coffee, not distillate fuel, at least as far as the chiefs were concerned.

"So, anything good happening?"

"Well, they're going to put a new wheel on today."

"Wheel?"

"Propeller," Leek explained. "Controllable pitch, reversible screw, made of high-grade manganese-bronze. They're made up in Philadelphia, I think. It's interesting to watch how they do it, long as they don't drop the son of a bitch."

"What about your toy shop?"

"Fully functional, Doc. The last replacement board went in twenty minutes ago, didn't it, Mr. Olson?" The senior chief addressed his assistant CIC officer, who came wandering out of the darkness and into view. "Mr. Olson, this here's Dr. Gregory from TRW."

"Hello," the young officer said, stretching his hand out. Gregory took it.

"Dartmouth, right?"

"Yep, physics and mathematics. You?"

"West Point and Stony Brook, math," Gregory said.

"Hudson High?" Chief Leek asked. "You never told me that."

"Hell, I even did Ranger School between second- and first-class years," he told the surprised sailors. People looked at him and often thought "pussy." He enjoyed surprising them. "Jump School, too. Did nineteen jumps, back when I was young and foolish."

"Then you went into SDI, I gather," Olson observed, getting himself some CIC coffee. The black-gang coffee, from the ship's engineers, was traditionally the best on any ship, but this wasn't bad.

"Yeah, spent a lot of years in that, but it all kinda fizzled out, and TRW hired me away before I made bird. When you were at Dartmouth, Bob Jastrow ran the department?"

"Yeah, he was involved in SDI, too, wasn't he?"

Gregory nodded. "Yeah, Bob's pretty smart." In his lexicon, *pretty smart* meant doing the calculus in your head.

"What do you do at TRW?"

"I'm heading up the SAM project at the moment, from my SDI work, but they lend me out a lot to other stuff. I mainly do software and the theoretical engineering."

"And you're playing with our SM-2s now?"

"Yeah, I've got a software fix for one of the problems. Works on the 'puter, anyway, and the next job's reprogramming the seeker heads on the Block IVs."

"How you going to do that?"

"Come on over and I'll show you," Gregory said. He and Olson wandered to a desk, with the chief in tow. "The trick is fixing the way the laser nutates. Here's how the software works . . ." This started an hour's worth of discussion, and Senior Chief Leek got to watch a professional software geek explaining his craft to a gifted amateur. Next they'd have to sell all this to the Combat Systems Officer—"Weps"—before they could run the first computer simulations, but it looked to Leek as though Olson was pretty well sold already. Then they'd have to get the ship back in the water to see if all this bullshit actually worked.

The sleep had worked, Bondarenko told himself. Thirteen hours, and he hadn't even awakened to relieve his bladder—so, he must have really needed it. Then and there he decided that Colonel Aliyev would screen successfully for general's stars.

He walked into his evening staff meeting feeling pretty good, until he saw the looks on their faces.

"Well?" he asked, taking his seat.

"Nothing new to report," Colonel Tolkunov reported for the intelligence staff. "Our aerial photos show little, but we know they're there, and they're still not using their radios at all. Presumably they have a lot of phone lines laid. There are scattered reports of people with binoculars on the southern hilltops. That's all. But they're ready, and it could start at any time—oh, yes, just got this from Moscow," the G-2 said. "The Federal Security Service arrested one K. I. Suvorov on suspicion of conspiring to assassinate President Grushavoy."

"What?" Aliyev asked.

"Just a one-line dispatch with no elaboration. It could mean many things, none of them good," the intelligence officer told them. "But nothing definite either."

"An attempt to unsettle our political leadership? That's an act of war," Bondarenko said. He decided he had to call Sergey Golovko himself about that one!

"Operations?" he asked next.

"The 265th Motor Rifle is standing-to. Our air-defense radars are all up and operating. We have interceptor aircraft flying combat air patrol within twenty kilometers of the border. The border defenses are on full alert, and the reserve formation—"

"Have a name for it yet?" the commanding general asked.

"Boyar," Colonel Aliyev answered. "We have three companies of motorized infantry deployed to evacuate the border troops if necessary, the rest are out of their depot and working up north of Never. They've done gunnery all day."

"And?"

"And for reservists they did acceptably," Aliyev answered. Bondarenko didn't ask what that meant, partly because he was afraid to.

"Anything else we can do? I want ideas, comrades," General Bondarenko said. But all he saw were headshakes. "Very well. I'm going to get some dinner. If anything happens, I want to know about it. Anything at all, comrades." This generated nods, and he walked back to his quarters. There he got on the phone.

"Greetings, General," Golovko said. It was still afternoon in Moscow. "How are things at your end?"

"Tense, Comrade Chairman. What can you tell me of this attempt on the president?"

"We arrested a chap named Suvorov earlier today. We're interrogating him and one other right now. We believe that he was an agent of the Chinese Ministry of State Security, and we believe also that he was conspiring to kill Eduard Petrovich."

"So, in addition to preparing an invasion, they also wish to cripple our political leadership?"

"So it would seem," Golovko agreed gravely.

"Why weren't we given fuller information?" Far East demanded.

"You weren't?" The chairman sounded surprised.

"No!" Bondarenko nearly shouted.

"That was an error. I am sorry, Gennady Iosifovich. Now, you tell me: Are you ready?"

"All of our forces are at maximum alert, but the correlation of forces is adverse in the extreme."

"Can you stop them?"

"If you give me more forces, probably yes. If you do not, probably no. What help can I expect?"

"We have three motor-rifle divisions on trains at this moment crossing the Urals. We have additional air power heading to you, and the Americans are beginning to arrive. What is your plan?"

"I will not try to stop them at the border. That would merely cost me all of my troops to little gain. I will let the Chinese in and let them march north. I will harass them as much as possible, and then when they are well within our borders, I will kill the body of the snake and watch the head die. *If,* that is, you give me the support I need."

"We are working on it. The Americans are being very helpful. One of their tank divisions is now approaching Poland on trains. We'll send them right through to where you are."

"What units?"

"Their First Tank division, commanded by a Negro chap named Diggs."

"Marion Diggs? I know him."

"Oh?"

"Yes, he commanded their National Training Center and also commanded the force they deployed to the Saudi kingdom last year. He's excellent. When will he arrive?"

"Five days, I should imagine. You'll have three Russian divisions well before then. Will that be enough, Gennady?"

"I do not know," Bondarenko replied. "We have not yet taken the measure of the Chinese. Their air power worries me most of all. If they attack our railhead at Chita, deploying our reinforcements could be very difficult." Bondarenko paused. "We are well set up to move forces laterally, west to east, but to stop them we need to move them northeast from their drop-off points. It will be largely a race to see who can go north faster. The Chinese will also be using infantry to wall off the western flank of their advance. I've been training my men hard. They're getting better, but I need more time and more men. Is there any way to slow them down politically?"

"All political approaches have been ignored. They pretend nothing untoward is happening. The Americans have approached them as well, in hope of discouraging them, but to no avail."

"So, it comes to a test of arms?"

"Probably," Golovko agreed. "You're our best man, Gennady Iosifovich. We believe in you, and you will have all the support we can muster."

"Very well," the general replied, wondering if it would be enough. "I will let you know of any developments here."

General Bondarenko knew that a proper general—the sort they had in movies, that is—would now eat the combat rations his men were having, but no, he'd eat the best food available because he needed his strength, and false modesty would not impress his men at all. He did refrain from alcohol, which was probably more than his sergeants and privates were doing. The Russian soldier loves his vodka, and the reservists had probably all brought their own bottles to ease the chill of the nights—such would be the spoken excuse. He could have issued an order forbidding it, but there was little sense in drafting an order that his men would ignore. It only undermined discipline, and discipline was something he needed. That would have to come from within his men. The great unknown, as Bondarenko thought of it. When Hitler had struck Russia in 1941—well, it was part of Russian mythology, how the ordinary men of the land had risen up with ferocious determination. From the first day of the war, the courage of the Russian soldier had given the Germans pause. Their battlefield skills might have been lacking, but never their courage. For Bondarenko, both were needed; a skillful man need not be all that brave, because skill would defeat what bravery would only defy. Training. It was always training. He yearned to train the Russian soldier as the Americans trained their men. Above all, to train them to think—to encourage them to think. A thinking *German* soldier had nearly destroyed the Soviet Union—how close it had been was something the movies never admitted, and it was hard enough to learn about it at the General Staff academies, but three times it had been devilishly close, and for some reason the gods of war had sided with Mother Russia on all three occasions.

What would those gods do now? That was the question. Would his men be up to the task? Would *he* be up to the task? It was his name that would be remembered, for good or ill, not those of the private soldiers carrying the AK-74 rifles and driving the tanks and infantry carriers. Gennady Iosifovich Bondarenko, general-colonel of the Russian Army, commander-in-chief Far East, hero or fool? Which would it be? Would future military students study his actions and cluck their tongues at his stupidity or shake their heads in admiration of his brilliant maneuvers?

It would have been better to be a colonel again, close to the men of his regiment, even carrying a rifle of his own as he'd done at Dushanbe all those years before, to take a personal part in the battle, and take direct fire at enemies he could see with his own eyes. That was what came back to him now, the battle against the Afghans, defending that missited apartment block in the snow and the darkness. He'd earned his medals that day, but medals were always things of the past. People respected him for them, even his fellow soldiers, the pretty ribbons and metal stars and medallions that hung from them, but what did they mean, really? Would he find the courage he needed to be a commander? He was sure here and now that that sort of courage was harder to find than the sort that came from mere survival instinct, the kind that was generated in the face of armed men who wished to steal your life away.

It was so easy to look into the indeterminate future with confidence, to know what had to be done, to suggest and insist in a peaceful conference room. But today he was in his quarters, in command of a largely paper army that happened to be facing a real army composed of men and steel, and if he failed to deal with it, his name would be cursed for all time. Historians would examine his character and his record and say, well, yes, he was a brave colonel, and even an adequate theoretician, but when it came to a real fight, he was unequal to the task. And if he failed, men would die, and the nation he'd sworn to defend thirty years before would suffer, if not by his hand, then by his responsibility.

And so General Bondarenko looked at his plate of food and didn't eat, just pushed the food about with his fork, and wished for the tumbler of vodka that his character denied him.

General Peng Xi-Wang was finishing up what he expected to be his last proper meal for some weeks. He'd miss the long-grain rice that was not part of combat rations—he didn't know why that was so: The general who ran the industrial empire that prepared rations for the front-line soldiers had never explained it to him, though Peng was sure that he never ate those horrid packaged foods himself. He had a staff to taste-test, after all. Peng lit an after-dinner smoke and enjoyed a small sip of rice wine. It would be the last of those for a while, too. His last pre-combat meal completed, Peng rose and donned his tunic. The gilt shoulderboards showed his rank as three stars and a wreath.

Outside his command trailer, his subordinates waited. When he came out, they snapped to attention and saluted as one man, and Peng saluted back. Foremost was Colonel Wa Cheng-Gong, his operations officer. Wa was aptly named. Cheng-Gong, his given name, meant "success."

"So, Wa, are we ready?"

"Entirely ready, Comrade General."

"Then let us go and see." Peng led them off to his personal Type 90 command-post vehicle. Cramped inside, even for people of small size, it was further crowded by banks of FM radios, which fed the ten-meter-tall radio masts at the vehicle's four corners. There was scarcely room for the folding map table, but his battle staff of six could work in there, even when on the move. The driver and gunner were both junior officers, not enlisted men.

The turbocharged diesel caught at once, and the vehicle lurched toward the front. Inside, the map table was already down, and the operations officer showed their position and their course to men who already knew it. The large roof hatch was opened to vent the smoke. Every man aboard was smoking a cigarette now.

Hear that?" Senior Lieutenant Valeriy Mikhailovich Komanov had his head outside the top hatch of the tank turret that composed the business end of his bunker. It was the turret of an old—ancient—JS-3 tank. Once the most fearsome part of the world's heaviest main-battle tank, this turret had never gone anywhere except to turn around, its already thick armor upgraded by an additional twenty centimeters of appliqué steel. As part of a bunker, it was only marginally slower than the original tank, which had been underpowered at best, but the monster 122-mm gun still worked, and worked even better here, because underneath it was not the cramped confines of a tank hull, but rather a spacious concrete structure which gave the crewmen room to move and turn around. That arrangement cut the reloading speed of the gun by more than half, and didn't hurt accuracy either, because this turret had better optics. Lieutenant Komanov was, notionally, a tanker, and his platoon here was twelve tanks instead of the normal three, because these didn't move. Ordinarily, it was not demanding duty, commanding twelve six-man crews, who didn't go anywhere except to the privy, and they even got to practice their gunnery at a duplicate of this emplacement at a range located twenty kilometers away. They'd been doing that lately, in fact, at the orders of their new commanding general, and neither Komanov nor his men minded, because for every soldier in the world, shooting is fun, and the bigger the gun, the greater the enjoyment. Their 122-mms had a relatively slow muzzle velocity, but the shell was large enough to compensate for it. Lately, they'd gotten to shoot at worn-out old T-55s and blown the turret off each one with a single hit, though getting the single hit had taken the crews, on the average, 2.7 shots fired.

They were on alert now, a fact which their eager young lieutenant was taking seriously. He'd even had his men out running every morning for the last two weeks, not the most pleasant of activities for soldiers detailed to sit inside concrete emplacements for their two years of conscripted service. It wasn't easy to keep their edge. One naturally felt secure in underground concrete structures capped with thick steel and surrounded with bushes which made their bunker invisible from fifty meters away. Theirs was the rearmost of the platoons, sitting on the south slope of Hill 432—its summit was 432 meters high—facing the north side of the first rank of hills over the Amur Valley. Those hills were a lot shorter than the one they were on, and also had bunkers on them, but those bunkers were fakes—not that you could tell without going inside, because they'd also been made of old tank turrets—in their case from truly ancient KV-2s that had fought the Germans before rusting in retirement—set in concrete boxes. The additional height of their hill meant that they could see into China, whose territory started less than four kilometers away. And that was close enough to hear things on a calm night.

Especially if the thing they heard was a few hundred diesel engines starting up at once.

"Engines," agreed Komanov's sergeant. "A fucking lot of them."

The lieutenant hopped down from his perch inside the turret and walked the three steps to the phone switchboard. He lifted the receiver and punched the button to the regimental command post, ten kilometers north.

"This is Post Five Six Alfa. We can hear engines to our south. It sounds like tank engines, a lot of them."

"Can you see anything?" the regimental commander asked.

"No, Comrade Colonel. But the sound is unmistakable."

"Very well. Keep me informed."

"Yes, comrade. Out." Komanov set the phone back in its place. His most-forward bunker was Post Five Nine, on the south slope of the first rank of hills. He punched that button.

"This is Lieutenant Komanov. Can you see or hear anything?"

"We see nothing," the corporal there answered. "But we hear tank engines."

"You see nothing?"

"Nothing, Comrade Lieutenant," Corporal Vladimirov responded positively.

"Are you ready?"

"We are fully ready," Vladimirov assured him. "We are watching the south."

"Keep me informed," Komanov ordered, unnecessarily. His men were alert and standing-to. He looked around. He had a total of two hundred rounds for his main gun, all in racks within easy reach of the turret. His loader and gunner were at their posts, the former scanning the terrain with optical sights better than his own officer's binoculars. His reserve crewmen were just sitting in their chairs, waiting for someone to die. The door to the escape tunnel was open. A hundred meters through that was a BTR-60 eight-wheeled armored personnel carrier ready to get them the hell away, though his men didn't expect to make use of it. Their post was impregnable, wasn't it? They had the best part of a meter of steel on the gun turret, and three meters of reinforced concrete, with a meter of dirt atop it—and besides, they were hidden in a bush. You couldn't hit what you couldn't see, could you? And the Chinks had slitty little eyes and couldn't see very well, could they? Like all the men in this crew, Komanov was a European Russian, though there were Asians under his command. This part of his country was a mishmash of nationalities and languages, though all had learned Russian, if not at home, then in school.

"Movement," the gunner said. "Movement on Rice Ridge." That was what they called the first ridge line in Chinese territory. "Infantrymen."

"You're sure they're soldiers?" Komanov asked.

"I suppose they might be shepherds, but I don't see any sheep, Comrade Lieutenant." The gunner had a wry sense of humor.

"Move," the lieutenant told the crewman who'd taken his place in the command hatch. He reclaimed the tank commander's seat. "Get me the headset," he ordered next. Now he'd be connected to the phone system with a simple push-button microphone. With that, he could talk to his other eleven crews or to regiment. But Komanov didn't don the earphones just yet. He wanted his ears clear. The night was still, the winds calm, just a few gentle breezes. They were a good distance from any real settlement, and so there were no sounds of traffic to interfere. Then he leveled his binoculars on the far ridge. Yes, there was the ghostly suggestion of movement there, almost like seeing someone's hair blowing in the wind. But it wasn't hair. It could only be people. And as his gunner had observed, they would not be shepherds.

For ten years, the officers in the border bunkers had cried out for low-light goggles like those issued to the Spetsnaz and other elite formations, but, no, they were too expensive for low-priority posts, and so such things were only seen here when some special inspection force came through, just long enough for the regular troops to drool over them. No, they were supposed to let their eyes adapt to the darkness . . . *as though they think we're cats,* Komanov thought. But all the interior battle lights in the bunkers were red, and that helped. He'd forbidden the use of white lights inside the post for the past week.

Brothers of this tank turret had first been produced in late 1944—the JS-3 had stayed in production for many years, *as though no one had summoned the courage to stop producing something with the name Iosif Stalin on it*, he thought. Some of them had rolled into Germany, invulnerable to anything the Fritzes had deployed. And the same tanks had given serious headaches to the Israelis, with their American- and English-built tanks, as well.

"This is Post Fifty. We have a lot of movement, looks like infantry, on the north slope of Rice Ridge. Estimate regimental strength," his earphones crackled.

"How many high-explosive shells do we have?" Komanov asked.

"Thirty-five," the loader answered.

And that was a goodly amount. And there were fifteen heavy guns within range of Rice Ridge, all of them old ML-20 152-mm howitzers, all sitting on concrete pads next to massive ammo bunkers. Komanov checked his watch. Almost three-thirty. Ninety minutes to first light. The sky was cloudless. He could look up and see stars such as they didn't have in Moscow, with all its atmospheric pollution. No, the Siberian sky was clear and clean, and above his head was an ocean of light made brighter still by a full moon still high in the western sky. He focused his eyes through his binoculars again. Yes, there *was* movement on Rice Ridge.

So?" Peng asked.

"At your command," Wa replied.

Peng and his staff were forward of their guns, the better to see the effect of their fire.

But seventy thousand feet over General Peng's head was Marilyn Monroe. Each of the Dark Star drones had a name attached to it, and given the official name of the platform, the crews had chosen the names of movie stars, all of them, of course, of the female persuasion. This one even had a copy of the movie star's *Playboy* centerfold from 1953 skillfully painted on the nose, but the eyes looking down from the stealthy UAV were electronic and multi-spectrum rather than china blue. Inside the fiberglass nosecone, a directional antenna cross-linked the "take" to a satellite, which then distributed it to many places. The nearest was Zhigansk. The farthest was Fort Belvoir, Virginia, within spitting distance of Washington, D.C., and that one sent its feed via fiberoptic cable to any number of classified locations. Unlike most spy systems, this one showed real-time movie-type imagery.

"Looks like they're getting ready, sir," an Army staff sergeant observed to his immediate boss, a captain. And sure enough, you could see soldiers ramming shells into the breeches of their field pieces, followed by the smaller cloth bags that contained the propellant. Then the breeches were slammed shut, and the guns elevated. The 30-30-class blank cartridges were inserted into the firing ports of the breechblocks, and the guns were fully ready. The last step was called "pulling the string," and was fairly accurate. You just jerked the lanyard rope to fire the blank cartridge and that ignited the powder bags, and then the shell went north at high speed.

"How many guns total, Sergeant?" the captain asked.

"A whole goddamned pisspot full, sir."

"I can see that. What about a number?" the officer asked.

"North of six hundred, and that's just in this here sector, Cap'n. Plus four hundred mobile rocket launchers."

"We spotted air assets yet?"

"No, sir. The Chinese aren't nighttime flyers yet, least not for bombing."

Eagle Seven to Zebra, over," the AWACS senior controller radioed back to Zhigansk.

"Zebra to Seven, reading you five-by-five," the major running the ground base replied.

"We got bogies, call it thirty-two coming north out of Siping, estimate they're Sierra-Uniform Two-Sevens."

"Makes sense," the major on the ground told his wing commander. "Siping's their 667th Regiment. That's their best in terms of aircraft, and stick-time. That's their varsity, Colonel."

"Who do we have to meet them?"

"Our Russian friends out of Nelkan. Nearest American birds are well north and—"

"—and we haven't got orders to engage anybody yet," the colonel agreed. "Okay, let's get the Russians alerted."

"Eagle Seven to Black Falcon Ten, we have Chinese fighters three hundred kilometers bearing one-nine-six your position, angels thirty, speed five hundred knots. They're still over Chinese territory, but not for much longer."

"Understood," the Russian captain responded. "Give me a vector."

"Recommend intercept vector two-zero-zero," the American controller said. His spoken Russian was pretty good. "Maintain current speed and altitude."

"Roger."

On the E-3B's radar displays, the Russian Su-27s turned to head for the Chinese Su-27s. The Russians would have radar contact in about nine minutes.

Sir, this don't look real nice," another major in Zhigansk said to his general.

"Then it's time to get a warning out," the USAF two-star agreed. He lifted a phone that went to the Russian regional command post. There hadn't as yet been time to get a proper downlink to them.

General, a call from the American technical mission at Zhigansk," Tolkunov said.

"This is General Bondarenko."

"Hello, this is Major General Gus Wallace. I just set up the reconnaissance shop here. We just put up a stealthy recon-drone over the Russian Chinese border at . . ." He read off the coordinates. "We show people getting ready to fire some artillery at you, General."

"How much?" Bondarenko asked.

"Most I've ever seen, upwards of a thousand guns total. I hope your people are hunkered down, buddy. The whole damned world's about to land on 'em."

"What can you do to help us?" Bondarenko asked.

"My orders are not to take action until they start shooting," the American replied. "When that happens, I can start putting fighters up, but not much in the way of bombs. We hardly have any to drop," Wallace reported. "I have an AWACS up now, supporting your fighters in the Chulman area, but that's all for now. We have a C-130 ferrying you a downlink tomorrow so that we can get you some intelligence directly. Anyway, be warned, General, it looks here as though the Chinese are going to launch their attack momentarily."

"Thank you, General Wallace." Bondarenko hung up and looked at his staff. "He says it's going to start at any moment."

And so it did. Lieutenant Komanov saw it first. The line of hills his men called Rice Ridge was suddenly backlit by yellow flame that could only be the muzzle flashes of numerous field guns. Then came the upward-flying meteor shapes of artillery rockets.

"Here it comes," he told his men. Unsurprisingly, he kept his head up so that he could see. His head, he reasoned, was a small target. Before the shells landed, he felt the impact of their firing; the rumble came through the ground like a distant earthquake, causing his loader to mutter, "Oh, shit," probably the universal observation of men in their situation.

"Get me regiment," Komanov ordered.

"Yes, Lieutenant," the voice answered.

"We are under attack, Comrade Colonel, massive artillery fire to the south. Guns and rockets car coming our—"

Then the first impacts came, mainly near the river, well to his south. The exploding shells were not bright, but like little sparks of light that fountained dirt upward, followed by the noise. That *did* sound like an earthquake. Komanov had heard artillery fire before, and seen what the shells do at the far end, but this was as different from that as an exploding oil tank was from a cigarette lighter.

"Comrade Colonel, our country is at war," Post Five Six Alfa reported to command. "I can't see enemy troop movement yet, but they're coming."

"Do you have any targets?" regiment asked.

"No, none at this time." He looked down into the bunker. His various positions could just give a direction to a target, and when another confirmed it and called in its own vector, they'd have a pre-plotted artillery target for the batteries in the rear—

—but those were being hit already. The Chinese rockets were targeted well behind him, and that's what their targets had to be. He turned his head to see the flashes and hear the booms from ten kilometers back.

A moment later, there was a fountaining explosion skyward. One of the first flight of Chinese rockets had gotten lucky and hit one of the artillery positions in the rear. *Bad news for that gun crew,* Komanov thought. The first casualties in this war. There would be many more . . . perhaps including himself. Surprisingly, that thought was a distant one. Someone was attacking *his* country. It wasn't a supposition or a possibility anymore. He could see it, and feel it. This was *his* country they were attacking. He'd grown up in this land. His parents lived here. His grandfather had fought the Germans here. His grandfather's two brothers had, too, and both had died for their country, one west of Kiev and the other at Stalingrad. And now these Chink bastards were attacking his country, too? More than that, they were attacking *him,* Senior Lieutenant Valeriy Mikhailovich Komanov. These *foreigners* were trying to kill him, his men, *and* trying to steal part of his country.

Well, fuck that! he thought.

"Load HE!" he told his loader.

"Loaded!" the private announced. They all heard the breech clang shut.

"No target, Comrade Lieutenant," the gunner observed.

"There will be, soon enough."

"Post Five Nine, this is Five Six Alfa. What can you see?"

"We just spotted a boat, a rubber boat, coming out of the trees on the south bank . . . more, more, more, many of them, maybe a hundred, maybe more."

"Regiment, this is Fifty-six Alfa, fire mission!" Komanov called over the phone.

The gunners ten kilometers back were at their guns, despite the falling Chinese shells and rockets that had already claimed three of the fifteen gun crews. The fire mission was called in, and the preset concentration dialed in from range books so old they might as well have been engraved in marble. In each case, the high-explosive projectile was rammed into the breech, followed by the propellant charge, and the gun cranked up and trained to the proper elevation and azimuth, and the lanyards pulled, and the first Russian counterstrokes in the war just begun were fired.

Unknown to them, fifteen kilometers away a fire-finder radar was trained on their positions. The millimeter-wave radar tracked the shells in flight and a computer plotted their launch points. The Chinese knew that the Russians had guns covering the border, and knew roughly where they would be—the performance of the guns told that tale—but not exactly where, because of the skillful Russian efforts at camouflage. In this case, those efforts didn't matter too greatly. The calculated position of six Russian howitzers was instantly radioed to rocket launchers that were dedicated counter-battery weapons. One Type-83 launcher was detailed to each target, and each of them held four monster 273-mm rockets, each with a payload of 150 kilograms of submunitions, in this case eighty hand grenade–sized bomblets. The first rocket launched three minutes after the first Russian counter-fire salvo, and required less than two minutes of flight time from its firing point ten kilometers inside Chinese territory. Of the first six fired, five destroyed their targets, and then others, and the Russian gunfire died in less than five minutes.

Why did it stop?" Komanov asked. He'd seen a few rounds hit among the Chinese infantry just getting out of their boats on the Russian side of the river. But the shriek of shells overhead passing south had just stopped after a few minutes. "Regiment, this is Five Six Alfa, why has our fire stopped?"

"Our guns were taking counter-battery fire from the Chinese. They're trying to get set back up now," was the encouraging reply. "What is your situation?"

"Position Five-Zero has taken a little fire, but not much. Mainly they're hitting the reverse slope of the southern ridge." That was where the fake bunkers were, and the concrete lures were fulfilling their passive mission. This line of defenses had been set up contrary to published Russian doctrine, because whoever had set them up had known that all manner of people can read books. Komanov's own position covered a small saddle-pass through two hills, fit for advancing tanks. If the Chinese came north in force, if this was not just some sort of probe aimed at expanding their borders—they'd done that back in the late 1960s—this was a prime invasion route. The maps and the terrain decided that.

"That is good, Lieutenant. Now listen: Do not expose your positions unnecessarily. Let them in close before you open up. Very close." That, Komanov knew, meant a hundred meters or so. He had two heavy machine guns for that eventuality. But he wanted to kill tanks. That was what his main gun had been designed to do.

"Can we expect more artillery support?" he asked his commander.

"I'll let you know. Keep giving us target information."

"Yes, Comrade Colonel."

For the fighter planes, the war began when the first PLAAF crossed over the Amur. There were four Russian fighter-interceptors up, and these, just like the invaders, were Sukhoi-27. Those on both sides had been made in the same factories, but the Chinese pilots had triple the recent flight time of the defending Russians, who were outnumbered eight to one.

Countering that, however was the fact that the Russian aircraft had support from the USAF E-3B Sentry AWACS aircraft, which was guiding them to the intercept. Both sets of fighters were flying with their target-acquisition radars in standby mode. The Chinese didn't know what was out there. The Russians did. That was a difference.

"Black Falcon Ten, this is Eagle Seven. Recommend you come right to new course two-seven-zero. I'm going to try an' bring you up on the Chinese from their seven o'clock." It would also keep them out of Chinese radar coverage.

"Understood, Eagle. Coming right to two-seven-zero." The Russian flight leader spread his formation out and settled down as much as he could, with his eyes tending to look off to his left.

"Okay, Black Falcon Ten, that's good. Your targets are now at your nine o'clock, distance thirty kilometers. Come left now to one-eight-zero."

"Coming left," the Russian major acknowledged. "We will try to start the attack Fox-Two," he advised. He knew American terminology. That meant launching infrared seekers, which did not require the use of radar, and so did not warn anyone that he was in harm's way. The Marquis of Queensberry had never been a fighter pilot.

"Roger that, Falcon. This boy's smart," the controller commented to his supervisor.

"That's how you stay alive in this business," the lieutenant colonel told the young lieutenant at the Nintendo screen.

"Okay, Falcon Ten, recommend you come left again. Targets are now fifteen kilometers . . . make that seventeen kilometers to your north. You should have tone shortly."

"Da. I have tone," the Russian pilot reported, when he heard the warble in his headset. "Flight, prepare to fire . . . Fox-Two!" Three of the four aircraft loosed a single missile each. The fourth pilot was having trouble with his IR scanner. In all cases, the blazing rocket motors wrecked their night vision, but none of the pilots looked away, as they'd been trained to do, and instead watched their missiles streak after fellow airmen who did not yet know they were under attack. It took twenty seconds, and as it turned out, two missiles were targeted on the same Chinese aircraft. That one took two hits and exploded. The second died from its single impact, and then things really got confusing. The Chinese fighters scattered on command from their commander, doing so in a preplanned and well-rehearsed maneuver, first into two groups, then into four, each of which had a piece of sky to defend. Everyone's radar came on, and in another twenty seconds, a total of forty missiles were flying, and with this began a deadly game of chicken. The radar-homing missiles needed a radar signal to guide them, and that meant that the firing fighter could not switch off or turn away, only hope that his bird would kill its target and switch off his radar before his missile got close.

"Damn," the lieutenant observed, in his comfortable controller's seat in the E-3B. Two more Chinese fighters blinked into larger bogies on his screen and then started to fade, then another, but there were just too many of the Chinese air-to-air missiles, and not all of the Chinese illumination radars went down. One Russian fighter took three impacts and disintegrated. Another one limped away with severe damage, and as quickly as it had begun, this air encounter ended. Statistically, it was a Russian win, four kills for one loss, but the Chinese would claim more.

"Any chutes?" the senior controller asked over the intercom. The E-3 radar could track those, too.

"Three, maybe four ejected. Not sure who, though, not till we play the tape back. Damn, that was a quick one."

The Russians didn't have enough planes up to do a proper battle. Maybe next time, the colonel thought. The full capabilities of a fighter/AWACS team had never been properly demonstrated in combat, but this war held the promise to change that, and when it happened, some eyes would be opened.

CHAPTER 51

Falling Back

Senior Lieutenant Valeriy Mikhailovich Komanov learned something he'd never suspected. The worst part of battle—at least to a man in a fixed emplacement—was knowing that the enemy was out there, but being unable to shoot at him. The reverse slopes of the ridge to his immediate south had to be swarming with Chinese infantry, and his supporting artillery had been taken out in the first minutes of the battle. Whoever had set up the artillery positions had made the mistake of assuming that the guns were too far back and too shielded by terrain for the enemy to strike at them. Fire-finder radar/computer systems had changed that, and the absence of overhead cover had doomed the guncrews to rapid death, unless some of them had found shelter in the concrete-lined trenches built into their positions. He had a powerful gun at his fingertips, but it was one that could not reach over the hills to his south because of its flat trajectory. As envisioned, this defense line would have included leg infantry who'd depend on and also support the bunker strongpoints—and be armed with mortars which could reach over the close-in hills and punish those who were there but unseen behind the terrain feature. Komanov could only engage those he could see, and they—

"There, Comrade Lieutenant," the gunner said. "A little right of twelve o'clock, some infantry just crested the ridge. Range one thousand five hundred meters."

"I see them." There was just a hint of light on the eastern horizon now. Soon there would be enough light to see by. That would make shooting easier, but for both sides. In an hour, his bunker would be targeted, and they'd get to see just how thick their armor protection really was.

"Five Six Alfa, this is Five Zero. We have infantry eleven hundred meters to our south. Company strength and moving north toward us."

"Very well. Do not engage until they are within two hundred meters." Komanov automatically doubled the shooting range at which he'd been trained to open fire. What the hell, he thought, his crews would do that in their own minds anyway. A man thinks differently when real bullets are flying.

As if to emphasize that, shells started landing on the crest immediately behind his position, close enough to make him duck down.

"So they see us?" his loader asked.

"No, they're just barraging the next set of hills to support their infantrymen."

"Look, look there, they're on top of false bunker One Six," the gunner said. Komanov shifted his glasses—

Yes, they were there, examining the old KV-2 gun turret with its vertical sides and old 155-mm gun. As he watched, a soldier hung a satchel charge on the side and backed away. Then the charge went off, destroying something that had never worked anyway. *That would make some Chinese lieutenant feel good,* Komanov thought. Well, Five Six Alfa would change his outlook somewhat, in another twenty or thirty minutes.

The bad part was that now he had perfect targets for his supporting artillery, and those old six-inch guns would have cut through them like a harvester's scythe. Except the Chinese were *still* hitting those positions, even though the Russian fire had stopped. He called Regiment again to relay his information.

"Lieutenant," his colonel answered, "the supporting battery has been badly hit. You are on your own. Keep me posted."

"Yes, Comrade Colonel. Out." He looked down at his crew. "Don't expect supporting fire." The weapons of World War III had just destroyed those of World War I.

"Shit," the loader observed.

"We'll be in the war soon, men. Be at ease. The enemy is now closer . . ."

"Five hundred meters," the gunner agreed.

"Well?" General Peng asked at his post atop Rice Ridge.

"We've found some bunkers, but they are all unoccupied," Colonel Wa reported. "So far, the only fire we've taken has been indirect artillery, and we've counterbatteried that to death. The attack is going completely to plan, Comrade General." They could see the truth of that. The bridging engineers were rolling up to the south bank of the Amur now, with folded sections of ribbon bridge atop their trucks. Over a hundred Type 90 main-battle tanks were close to the river, their turrets searching vainly for targets so that they could support the attacking infantry, but there was nothing for them to shoot at, and so the tankers, like the generals, had nothing to do but watch the engineers at work. The first bridge section went into the water, flipping open to form the first eight meters of highway across the river. Peng checked his watch. Yes, things were going about five minutes ahead of schedule, and that was good.

Post Five Zero opened up first with its 12.7-mm machine gun. The sound of it rattled across the hillside. Five Zero was thirty-five hundred meters to his east, commanded by a bright young sergeant named Ivanov. *He opened up too early,* Komanov thought, reaching for targets a good four hundred meters away, but there was nothing to complain about, and the heavy machine gun could easily reach that far . . . yes, he could see bodies crumpling from the heavy slugs—

—then a crashing *BOOM* as the main gun let loose a single round, and it reached into the saddle they defended, exploding there amidst a squad or so.

"Comrade Lieutenant, can we?" his gunner asked.

"No, not yet. Patience, Sergeant," Komanov replied, watching to the east to see how the Chinese reacted to the fire. Yes, their tactics were predictable, but sound. The lieutenant commanding them first got his men down. Then they set up a base of fire to engage the Russian position, and then they started maneuvering left and right. Aha, a section was setting up something . . . something on a tripod. An anti-tank recoilless rifle, probably. He could have turned his gun to take it out, but Komanov didn't want to give away his position yet.

"Five Zero, this is Five Six Alfa, there's a Chinese recoilless setting up at your two o'clock, range eight hundred," he warned.

"Yes, I see it!" the sergeant replied. And he had the good sense to engage it with his machine gun. In two seconds, the green tracers reached out and ripped through the gun section once, twice, three times, just to be sure. Through his binoculars, he could see some twitching, but that was all.

"Well done, Sergeant Ivanov! Look out, they're moving to your left under terrain cover."

But there wasn't much of that around here. Every bunker's field of fire had been bulldozed, leveling out almost all of the dead ground within eight hundred meters of every position.

"We shall see about that, Comrade Lieutenant." And the machine gun spoke again. Return fire was coming in now. Komanov could see tracers bouncing off the turret's thick armor into the sky.

"Regiment, Five Six Alfa here. Post Five Zero is under deliberate attack now from infantry, and—"

Then more artillery shells started landing, called in directly on Five Zero. He hoped Ivanov was now under his hatch. The turret had a coaxial machine gun, an old but powerful PK with the long 7.62-mm cartridge. Komanov let his gunner survey the threat to his bunker while he watched how the Chinese attacked Sergeant Ivanov's. Their infantry moved with some skill, using what ground they had, keeping fire on the exposed gun turret—enough artillery fell close enough to strip away the bushes that had hidden it at first. Even if your bullets bounced off, they were still a distraction to those inside. It was the big shells that concerned the lieutenant. A direct hit might penetrate the thinner top armor, mightn't it? An hour before, he would have said no, but he could see now what the shells did to the ground, and his confidence had eroded quickly.

"Comrade Lieutenant," his gunner said. "The people headed for us are turning away to attack Ivanov. Look."

Komanov turned around to see. He didn't need his binoculars. The sky was improving the light he had, and now he could see more than shadows. They were man shapes, and they were carrying weapons. One section was rushing to his left, three of them carrying something heavy. On reaching a shallow intermediate ridgeline, they stopped and started putting something together, some sort of tube . . .

. . . it was an HJ-8 anti-tank missile, his mind told him, fishing up the information from his months of intelligence briefings. They were about a thousand meters to his left front, within range of Ivanov . . .

. . . and within range of his big DshKM machine gun. Komanov stood on his firing stand and yanked back hard on the charging handle, leveling the gun and sighting carefully. His big tank gun could do this, but so could he . . .

So, you want to kill Sergeant Ivanov? his mind asked. Then he thumbed the trigger lever, and the big gun shook in his hands. His first burst was about thirty meters short, but his second was right on, and three men fell. He kept firing to make sure he'd destroyed their rocket launcher. He realized a moment later that the brilliant green tracers had just announced his location for all to see—tracers work in both directions. That became clear in two minutes, when the first artillery shells began landing around Position Five Six Alfa. He only needed one close explosion to drop down and slam his hatch. The hatch was the weakest part of his position's protection, with only a fifth of the protective thickness of the rest—else he'd be unable to open it, of course—and if a shell hit *that,* he and his crew would all be dead. The enemy knew their location now, and there was no sense in hiding.

"Sergeant," he told his gunner. "Fire at will."

"Yes, Comrade Lieutenant!" And with that, the sergeant loosed his first high-explosive round at a machine-gun crew eight hundred meters away. The shell hit the gun itself and vaporized the infantrymen operating it. "There's three good Chinks!" he exulted. "Load me another!" The turret started turning, and the gunner started hunting.

Getting some resistance now," Wa told Peng. "There are Russian positions on the southern slope of the second ridge. We're hitting them now with artillery."

"Losses?"

"Light," the operations officer reported, listening in on the tactical radio.

"Good," said General Peng. His attention was almost entirely on the river. The first bridge was about a third complete now.

Those bridging engineers are pretty good," General Wallace thought, watching the "take" from Marilyn Monroe.

"Yes, sir, but it might as well be a peacetime exercise. They're not taking any fire," the junior officer observed, watching another section being tied off. "And it's a very efficient bridge design."

"Russian?"

The major nodded. "Yes, sir. We copied it, too."

"How long?"

"The rate they're going? About an hour, maybe an hour ten."

"Back to the gunfight," Wallace ordered.

"Sergeant, let's go back to the ridge," the officer told the NCO who was piloting the UAC. Thirty seconds later, the screen showed what looked like a tank sunk in the mud surrounded by a bunch of infantrymen.

"Jesus, that looks like real fun," Wallace thought. A fighter pilot by profession, the idea of fighting in the dirt appealed to him about as much as anal sex.

"They're not going to last much longer," the major said. "Look here. The gomers are behind some of the bunkers now."

"And look at all that artillery."

A total of a hundred heavy field guns were now pounding Komanov's immobile platoon. That amounted to a full battery fixed on each of them, and heavy as his buried concrete box was, it was shaking now, and the air inside filled with cement dust, as Komanov and his crew struggled to keep up with all the targets.

"This is getting exciting, Comrade Lieutenant," the gunner observed, as he loosed his fifteenth main-gun shot.

Komanov was in his commander's cupola, looking around and seeing, rather to his surprise, that his bunker and all the others under his command could not deal with the attackers. It was a case of intellectual knowledge finally catching up with what his brain had long proclaimed as evident common sense. He actually was *not* invincible here. Despite his big tank gun and his two heavy machine guns, he could not deal with all these *insects* buzzing about him. It was like swatting flies with an icepick. He reckoned that he and his crew had personally killed or wounded a hundred or so attackers—but no tanks. Where were the tanks he yearned to kill? He could do that job well. But to deal with infantry, he needed supporting artillery fire, plus foot soldiers of his own. Without them, he was like a big rock on the sea coast, indestructible, but the waves could just wash around him. And they were doing that now, and then Komanov remembered that all the rocks by the sea *were* worn down by the waves, and eventually toppled by them. His war had lasted three hours, not even that much, and he was fully surrounded, and if he wanted to survive, it would soon be time to leave.

The thought enraged him. Desert his post? *Run away?* But then he remembered that he had orders allowing him to do so, if and when his post became untenable. He'd received the orders with a confident chuckle. Run away from an impregnable mini-fortress? What nonsense. But now he was alone. Each of his posts was alone. And—

—the turret rang like an off-tone bell with a direct impact of a heavy shell, and then—

—*"Shit!"* the gunner screamed. "Shit! My gun's damaged!"

Komanov looked out of one of his vision slits, and yes, he could see it. The gun tube was scorched and . . . and actually bent. Was that possible? A gun barrel was the sturdiest structure men could make—but it was slightly bent. And so it was no longer a gun barrel at all, but just an unwieldy steel club. It had fired thirty-four rounds, but it would fire no more. With that gone, he'd never kill a Chinese tank. Komanov took a deep breath to collect himself and his thoughts. Yes, it was time.

"Prepare the post for destruction!" he ordered.

"Now?" the gunner asked incredulously.

"Now!" the lieutenant ordered. "Set it up!"

There was a drill for this, and they'd practiced it. The loader took a demolition charge and set it among the racked shells. The electrical cable was in a spool, which he played out. The gunner ignored this, cranking the turret right to fire his coaxial machine gun at some approaching soldiers, then turning rapidly the other way to strike at those who'd used his reaction to the others' movement for cover to move themselves. Komanov stepped down from the cupola seat and looked around. There was his bed, and the table at which they'd all eaten their food, and the toilet room and the shower. This bunker had become home, a place of both comfort and work, but now they had to surrender it to the Chinese. It was almost inconceivable, but it could not be denied. In the movies, they'd fight to the death here, but fighting to the death was a lot more comfortable for actors who could start a new film the next week.

"Come on, Sergeant," he ordered his gunner, who took one last long burst before stepping down and heading toward the escape tunnel.

Komanov counted off the men as they went, then headed out. He realized he hadn't phoned his intentions back to Regiment, and he hesitated, but, no, there wasn't time for that now. He'd radio his action from the moving BTR.

The tunnel was low enough that they had to run bent over, but it was also lit, and there was the outer door. When the reserve gunner opened it, they were greeted by the much louder sound of falling shells.

"You fucking took long enough," a thirtyish sergeant snarled at them. "Come on!" he urged, waving them to his BTR-60.

"Wait." Komanov took the twist-detonator and attached the wire ends to the terminals. He sheltered behind the concrete abutment that contained the steel door and twisted the handle once.

The demolition charge was ten kilograms of TNT. It and the stored shells created an explosion that roared out of the escape tunnel with a sound like the end of the world, and on the far side of the hill the heavy turret of the never-finished JS-3 tank rocketed skyward, to the amazed pleasure of the Chinese infantrymen. And with that, Komanov's job was done. He turned and followed his men to board the eight-wheeled armored personnel carrier. It was ensconced on a concrete pad under a grass-covered concrete roof that had prevented anyone from seeing it, and now it raced down the hill to the north and safety.

Bugging out," the sergeant told the major, tapping the TV screen taking the feed from Marilyn Monroe. "This bunch just blew up their gun turret. That's the third one to call it a day."

"Surprised they lasted this long," General Wallace said. Sitting still in a combat zone was an idea entirely foreign to him. He'd never done fighting while moving slower than four hundred knots, and he considered that speed to be practically standing still.

"I bet the Russians will be disappointed," the major said.

"When do we get the downlink to Chabarsovil?"

"Before lunch, sir. We're sending a team down to show them how to use it."

The BTR was in many ways the world's ultimate SUV, with eight driving wheels, the lead four of which turned with the steering wheel. The reservist behind that wheel was a truck driver in civilian life, and knew how to drive only with his right foot pressed to the floor, Komanov decided. He and his men bounced inside like dice in a cup, saved from head injury only by their steel helmets. But they didn't complain. Looking out of the rifle-firing ports, they could see the impact of Chinese artillery, and the quicker they got away from that, the better they'd all feel.

"How was it for you?" the lieutenant asked the sergeant commanding the vehicle.

"Mainly we were praying for you to be a coward. What with all those shells falling around us. Thank God for whoever built that garage we were hidden in. At least one shell fell directly on it. I nearly shit myself," the reservist reported with refreshing candor. They were communicating in face-to-face shouts.

"How long to regimental headquarters?"

"About ten minutes. How many did you get?"

"Maybe two hundred," Komanov thought, rather generously. "Never saw a tank."

"They're probably building their ribbon bridges right now. It takes a while. I saw a lot of that when I was in Eighth Guards Army in Germany. Practically all we practiced was crossing rivers. How good are they?"

"They're not cowards. They advance under fire even when you kill some of them. What happened to our artillery?"

"Wiped out, artillery rockets, came down like a blanket of hail, Comrade Lieutenant, *crump,*" he replied with a two-handed gesture.

"Where is our support?"

"Who the fuck do you think we are?" the sergeant asked in reply. They were all surprised when the BRT skidded to an unwarned stop. "What's happening?" he shouted at the driver.

"Look!" the man said in reply, pointing.

Then the rear hatches jerked open and ten men scrambled in, making the interior of the BTR as tight as a can of fish.

"Comrade Lieutenant!" It was Ivanov from Five Zero.

"What happened?"

"We took a shell on the hatch," he replied, and the bandages on his face told the truth of the tale. He was in some pain, but happy to be moving again. "Our BTR took a direct hit on the nose, killed the driver and wrecked it."

"I've never seen shelling like this, not even in exercises in Germany and the Ukraine," the BTR sergeant said. "Like the war movies, but different when you're really in it."

"Da," Komanov agreed. It was no fun at all, even in his bunker, but especially out here. The sergeant lit up a cigarette, a Japanese one, and held on to the overhead grip to keep from rattling around too much. Fortunately, the driver knew the way, and the Chinese artillery abated, evidently firing at random target sets beyond visual range of their spotters.

It's started, Jack," Secretary of Defense Bretano said. "I want to release our people to start shooting."

"Who, exactly?"

"Air Force, fighter planes we have in theater, to start. We have AWACS up and working with the Russians already. There's been one air battle, a little one, already. And we're getting feed from reconnaissance assets. I can cross-link them to you if you want."

"Okay, do that," Ryan told the phone. "And on the other issue, okay, turn 'em loose," Jack said. He looked over at Robby.

"Jack, it's what we pay 'em for, and believe me, they don't mind. Fighter pilots live for this sort of thing—until they see what happens, though they mainly never do. They just see the broke airplane, not the poor shot-up bleeding bastard inside, trying to eject while he's still conscious," Vice President Jackson explained. "Later on, a pilot may think about that a little. I did. But not everyone. Mainly you get to paint a kill on the side of your aircraft, and we all want to do that."

Okay, people, we are now in this fight," Colonel Bronco Winters told his assembled pilots. He'd gotten four kills over Saudi the previous year, downing those poor dumb ragheaded gomers who flew for the country that had brought biological warfare to his own nation. One more, and he'd be a no-shit fighter ace, something he dreamed about all the way back to his doolie year at Colorado Springs. He'd been flying the F-15 Eagle fighter for his entire career, though he hoped to upgrade to the new F-22A Raptor in two or three more years. He had 4,231 hours in the Eagle, knew all its tricks, and couldn't imagine a better aircraft to go up in. So, now he'd kill Chinese. He didn't understand the politics of the moment, and didn't especially care. He was on a Russian air base, something he'd never expected to see except through a gunsight, but that was okay, too. He thought for a moment that he rather liked Chinese food, especially the things they did to vegetables in a wok, but those were American Chinese, not the commie kind, and that, he figured, was that. He'd been in Russia for just over a day, long enough to turn down about twenty offers to snort down some vodka. Their fighter pilots seemed smart enough, maybe a little too eager for their own good, but friendly and respectful when they saw the four kills painted on the side panel of his F-15-Charlie, the lead fighter of the 390th Fighter Squadron. He hopped off the Russian jeep—they called it something else that he hadn't caught—at the foot of his fighter. His chief mechanic was there.

"Got her all ready for me, Chief?" Winters asked, as he took the first step on the ladder.

"You bet," replied Chief Master Sergeant Neil Nolan. "Everything is toplined. She's as ready as I can make her. Go kill us some, Bronco." It was a squadron rule that when a pilot had his hands on his aircraft, he went only by his call-sign.

"I'll bring you the scalps, Nolan." Colonel Winters continued his climb up the ladder, patting the decorated panel as he went. Chief Master Sergeant Nolan scurried up to help him strap in, then dropped off, detached the ladder, and got clear.

Winters began his start-up procedures, first of all entering his ground coordinates, something they still did on the Eagle despite the new GPS locator systems, because the F-15C had inertial navigation in case it broke (it never did, but procedure was procedure). The instruments came on-line, telling Winters that his Eagle's conformal fuel tanks were topped off, and he had a full load of four AIM-120 AMRAAM radar-guided missiles, plus four more of the brand-new AIM-9X Sidewinders, the super-snake version of a missile whose design went back to before his mom and dad had married in a church up on Lenox Avenue in Harlem.

"Tower, this is Bronco with three, ready to taxi, over."

"Tower, Bronco, you are cleared to taxi. Wind is three-zero-five at ten. Good luck, Colonel."

"Thank you, Tower. Boars, this is lead, let's get goin'." With that, he tripped his brakes and the fighter started moving, driven by its powerful Pratt & Whitney engines. A bunch of Russians, mainly groundcrewmen, but judging by the outfits, some drivers as well, were out on the ramp watching him and his flight. *Okay,* he thought, *we'll show 'em how we do things downtown.* The four taxied in pairs to the end of the runway and then roared down the concrete slabs, and pulled back into the air, wingman tucked in tight. Seconds later, the other two pulled up and they turned south, already talking to the nearest AWACS, Eagle Two.

"Eagle Two, this is Boar Leader in the air with four."

"Boar Leader, this is Eagle Two. We have you. Come south, vector one-seven-zero, climb and maintain flight level three-three. Looks like there's going to be some work for ya today, over."

"Suits me. Out." Colonel Winters—he'd just been deep-dip selected for his bird as a full bull colonel—wiggled a little in his seat to get things just right, and finished his climb to 33,000 feet. His radar system was off, and he wouldn't speak unnecessarily because someone out there might be listening, and why spoil the surprise? In a few minutes, he'd be entering the coverage of Chinese border radar stations. Somebody would have to do something about that. Later today, he hoped, the Little Weasel F-16s would go and see about those. But his job was Chinese fighter aircraft, and any bombers that might offer themselves. His orders were to remain over Russian airspace for the entire mission, and so if Joe Chink didn't want to come out and play, it would be a dull day. But Joe had Su-27s, and he thought those were pretty good. And Joe Chink Fighter Pilot probably thought he was pretty good, too.

So, they'd just have to see.

Otherwise, it was a good day for flying, two-tenths clouds and nice clean country air to fly in. His falcon's eyes could see well over a hundred miles from up here, and he had Eagle Two to tell him where the gomers were. Behind him, a second and third flight of four Eagles were each taking off. The Wild Boars would be fully represented today.

The train ride was fairly jerky. Lieutenant Colonel Giusti squirmed in his upright coach seat, trying to get a little bit comfortable, but the Russian-made coach in which he and his staff were riding hadn't been designed with creature comforts in mind, and there was no sense grumbling about it. It was dark outside, the early morning that children sensibly take to be nighttime, and there wasn't much in the way of lights out there. They were in Eastern Poland now, farm country, probably, as Poland was evolving into the Iowa of Europe, lots of pig farms to make the ham for which this part of the world was famous. Vodka, too, probably, and Colonel Giusti wouldn't have minded a snort of that at the moment. He stood and walked down the aisle of the car. Nearly everyone aboard was asleep or trying to be. Two sensible NCOs were stretched out on the floor instead of curled up on the seats. The dirty floor wouldn't do their uniforms much good, but they were heading to combat operations, where neatness didn't really count all that much. Personal weapons were invariably stowed in the overhead racks, in the open for easy access, because they were all soldiers, and they didn't feel very comfortable without a usable weapon close by. He continued aft. The next coach had more troopers from Headquarters Company. His squadron sergeant major was in the back of that one, reading a paperback.

"Hey, Colonel," the sergeant major said in greeting. "Long ride, ain't it?"

"At least three more days to go, maybe four."

"Super," the senior non-com observed. "This is worse'n flying."

"Yeah, well, at least we got our tracks with us."

"Yes, sir."

"How's the food situation?"

"Well, sir, we all got our MREs, and I got me a big box of Snickers bars stashed. Any word what's happening in the world?"

"Just that it's started in Siberia. The Chinese are across the border and Ivan's trying to stop 'em. No details. We ought to get an update when we go through Moscow, after lunchtime, I expect."

"Fair 'nuff."

"How are the troopers taking things?"

"No problems, bored with the train ride, want to get back in their tracks, the usual."

"How's their attitude?"

"They're ready, Colonel," the sergeant-major assured him.

"Good." With that, Giusti turned and headed back to his seat, hoping he'd get a few hours anyway, and there wasn't much of Poland to see anyway. The annoying part was being so cut off. He had satellite radios in his vehicles, somewhere on the flatcars aft of this coach, but he couldn't get to them, and without them he didn't know what was happening up forward. A war was on. He knew that. But it wasn't the same as knowing the details, knowing where the train would stop, where and when he'd get to offload his equipment, get the Quarter Horse organized, and get back on the road, where they belonged.

The train part was working well. The Russian train service seemingly had a million flatcars designed expressly to transport tracked vehicles, undoubtedly intended to take their battle tanks west, into Germany for a war against NATO. Little had the builders ever suspected that the cars would be used to bring American tanks east to help defend Russia against an invader. Well, nobody could predict the future more than a few weeks. At the moment, he would have settled for five days or so.

The rest of First Armored was stretched back hundreds of miles on the east-west rail line. Colonel Don Lisle's Second Brigade was just finishing up boarding in Berlin, and would be tail-end Charlie for the division. They'd cross Poland in daylight, for what that was worth.

The Quarter Horse was in the lead, where it belonged. Wherever the drop-off point was, they'd set up perimeter security, and then lead the march farther east, in a maneuver called Advance to Contact, which was where the "fun" started. And he needed to be well-rested for that, Colonel Giusti reminded himself. So he settled back in his seat and closed his eyes, surrendering his body to the jerks and sways of the train car.

Dawn patrol was what fighter pilots all thought about. The title for the duty went back to a 1930s Errol Flynn movie, and the term had probably originated with a real mission name, meaning to be the first up on a new day, to see the sun rise, and to seek out the enemy right after breakfast.

Bronco Winters didn't look much like Errol Flynn, but that was okay. You couldn't tell a warrior by the look of his face, though you could by the look *on* his face. He was a fighter pilot. As a youngster in New York, he'd ride the subway to La Guardia Airport, just to stand at the fence and watch the airplanes take off and land, knowing even then that he wanted to fly. He'd also known that fighters would be more fun than airliners, and known finally that to fly fighters he had to enter a service academy, and to do that he'd have to study. And so he'd worked hard all through school, especially in math and science, because airplanes were mechanical things, and that meant that science determined how they worked. So, he was something of a math whiz—that had been his college major at Colorado Springs—but his interest in it had ended the day he'd walked into Columbus Air Force Base in Mississippi, because once he got his hands on the controls of an aircraft, the "study" part of his mission was accomplished, and the "learning" part really began. He'd been the number-one student in his class at Columbus, quickly and easily mastering the Cessna Tweety Bird trainer, and then moving on to fighters, and since he'd been number one in his class, he'd gotten his choice—and that choice, of course, had been the F-15 Eagle fighter, the strong and handsome grandson of the F-4 Phantom. An easy plane to fly, it was a harder one to fight, since the controls for the combat systems are located on the stick and the throttles, all in buttons of different shapes so that you could manage all the systems by feel, and keep your eyes up and out of the aircraft instead of having to look down at instruments. It was something like playing two pianos at the same time, and it had taken Winters a disappointing six months to master. But now those controls came as naturally as twirling the wax into his Bismarck mustache, his one non-standard affectation, which he'd modeled on Robin Olds, a legend in the American fighter community, an instinctive pilot and a thinking—and therefore a very dangerous—tactician. An ace in World War II, an ace in Korea, and also an ace over North Vietnam, Olds was one of the best who'd ever strapped a fighter plane to his back, and one whose mustache had made Otto von Bismarck himself look like a pussy.

Colonel Winters wasn't thinking about that now. The thoughts were there even so, as much a part of his character as his situational awareness, the part of his brain that kept constant track of the three-dimensional reality around him at all times. Flying came as naturally to him as it did to the gyrfalcon mascot at the Air Force Academy. And so did hunting, and now he was hunting. His aircraft had instrumentation that downloaded the take from the AWACS aircraft a hundred fifty miles to his rear, and he divided his eye time equally between the sky around him and the display three feet from his 20-10 brown eyes . . .

. . . there . . . two hundred miles, bearing one-seven-two, four bandits heading north. Then four more, and another flight of four. Joe Chink was coming up to play, and the pigs were hungry.

"Boar Lead, this is Eagle Two." They were using encrypted burst-transmission radios that were very difficult to detect, and impossible to listen in on.

"Boar Lead." But he kept his transmission short anyway. Why spoil the surprise?

"Boar Lead, we have sixteen bandits, one-seven-zero your position at angels thirty, coming due north at five hundred knots."

"Got 'em."

"They're still south of the border, but not for long," the young controller on the E-3B advised. "Boar, you are weapons-free at this time."

"Copy weapons-free," Colonel Winters acknowledged, and his left hand flipped a button to activate his systems. A quick look down to his weapons-status display showed that everything was ready to fire. He didn't have his tracking/targeting radar on, though it was in standby mode. The F-15 had essentially been designed as an appendage to the monstrous radar in its nose—a design consideration that had defined the size of the fighter from the first sketch on paper—but over the years the pilots had gradually stopped using it, because it could warn an enemy with the right sort of threat receiver, telling him that there was an Eagle in the neighborhood with open eyes and sharp claws. Instead he could now cross-load the radar information from the AWACS, whose radar signals were unwelcome, but nothing an enemy could do anything about, and not directly threatening. The Chinese would be directed and controlled by ground radar, and the Boars were just at the fuzzy edge of that, maybe spotted, maybe not. Somewhere to his rear, a Rivet Joint EC-135 was monitoring both the radar and the radios used by the Chinese ground controllers, and would cross-load any warnings to the AWACS. But so far none of that. So, Joe Chink was coming north.

"Eagle, Boar, say bandit type, over."

"Boar, we're not sure, but probably Sierra-Uniform Two-Sevens by point of origin and flight profile, over."

"Roger." Okay, good, Winters thought. They thought the Su-27 was a pretty hot aircraft, and for a Russian-designed bird it was respectable. They put their best drivers into the Flanker, and they'd be the proud ones, the ones who thought they were as good as he was. *Okay, Joe, let's see how good you are.* "Boar, Lead, come left to one-three-five."

"Two." "Three." "Four," the flight acknowledged, and they all banked to the left. Winters took a look around to make sure he wasn't leaving any contrails to give away his position. Then he checked his threat receiver. It was getting some chirps from Chinese search radar, but still below the theoretical detection threshold. That would change in twenty miles or so. But then they'd just be unknowns on the Chinese screens, and fuzzy ones at that. Maybe the ground controllers would radio a warning, but maybe they'd just peer at their screens and try to decide if they were real contacts or not. The robin's-egg blue of the Eagles wasn't all that easy to spot visually, especially when you had the sun behind you, which was the oldest trick in the fighter-pilot bible, and one for which there was still no solution . . .

The Chinese passed to his right, thirty miles away, heading north and looking for Russian fighters to engage, because the Chinese would want to control the sky over the battlefield they'd just opened up. That meant that they'd be turning on their own search radars, and when that happened, they'd spend most of their time looking down at the scope instead of out at the sky, and that was dangerous. When he was south of them, Winters brought his flight right, west, and down to twenty thousand feet, well below Joe Chink's cruising altitude, because fighter pilots might look back and up, but rarely back and down, because they'd been taught that height, like speed, was life. And so it was . . . most of the time. In another three minutes, they were due south of the enemy, and Winters increased power to maximum dry thrust so as to catch up. His flight of four split on command into two pairs. He went left, and then his eyes spotted them, dark flecks on the brightening blue sky. They were painted the same light gray the Russians liked—and that would be a real problem if Russian Flankers entered the area, because you didn't often get close enough to see if the wings had red stars or white-blue-red flags painted on them.

The audio tone came next. His Sidewinders could see the heat bloom from the Lyul'ka turbofan engines, and that meant he was just about close enough. His wingman, a clever young lieutenant, was now about five hundred yards to his right, doing his job, which was covering his leader. *Okay,* Bronco Winters thought. He had a good hundred knots of overtake speed now.

"Boar, Eagle, be advised these guys are heading directly for us at the moment."

"Not for long, Eagle," Colonel Winters responded. They weren't flecks anymore. Now they were twin-rudder fighter aircraft. Cruising north, tucked in nice and pretty. His left forefinger selected Sidewinder to start, and the tone in his earphones was nice and loud. He'd start with two shots, one at the left-most Flanker, and the other at the right-most . . . right about . . .

"Fox-Two, Fox-Two with two birds away," Bronco reported. The smoke trails diverged, just as he wanted them to, streaking in on their targets. His gunsight camera was operating, and the picture was being recorded on videotape, just as it had been over Saudi the previous year. He needed one kill to make ace—

—he got the first six seconds later, and the next half a second after that. Both Flankers tumbled right. The one on the left nearly collided with his wingman, but missed, and tumbled violently as pieces started coming off the airframe. The other one was rolling and then exploded into a nice white puffball. The first pilot ejected cleanly, but the second didn't.

Tough luck, Joe, Winters thought. The remaining two Chinese fighters hesitated, but both then split and started maneuvering in diverging directions. Winters switched on his radar and followed the one to the left. He had radar lock and it was well within the launch parameters for his AMRAAM. His right forefinger squeezed the pickle switch.

"Fox-One, Fox-One, Slammer on guy to the west." He watched the Slammer, as it was called, race in. Technically a fire-and-forget weapon like the Sidewinder, it accelerated almost instantly to mach-two-plus and rapidly ate up the three miles between them. It only took about ten seconds to close and explode a mere few feet over the fuselage of its target, and that Flanker disintegrated with no chute coming away from it.

Okay, three. This morning was really shaping up, but now the situation went back to World War I. He had to search for targets visually, and searching for jet fighters in a clear sky wasn't . . .

. . . there . . .

"You with me, Skippy?" he called on the radio.

"Got you covered, Bronco," his wingman replied. "Bandit at your one o'clock, going left to right."

"On him," Winters replied, putting his nose on the distant spot in the sky. His radar spotted it, locked onto it, and the IFF transponder didn't say friendly. He triggered off his second Slammer: "Fox-One on the south guy! Eagle, Boar Lead, how we doing?"

"We show five kills to this point. Bandits are heading east and diving. Razorback is coming in from your west with four, angels three-five at six hundred, now at your ten o'clock. Check your IFF, Boar Lead." The controller was being careful, but that was okay.

"Boar, Lead, check IFF now!"

"Two." "Three." "Four," they all chimed in. Before the last of them confirmed his IFF transponder was in the transmit setting, his second Slammer found its target, running his morning's score to four. *Well, damn,* Winters thought, *this morning is* really *shaping up nice.*

"Bronco, Skippy is on one!" his wingman reported, and Winters took position behind, low, and left of his wingman. "Skippy" was First Lieutenant Mario Acosta, a red-haired infant from Wichita who was coming along nicely for a child with only two hundred hours in type. "Fox-Two with one," Skippy called. His target had turned south, and was heading almost straight into the streaking missile. Winters saw the Sidewinder go right into his right-side intake, and the resulting explosion was pretty impressive.

"Eagle, Boar Lead, give me a vector, over."

"Boar Lead, come right at zero-nine-zero. I have a bandit at ten miles and low, angels ten, heading south at six-hundred-plus."

Winters executed the turn and checked his radar display. "Got him!" And this one also was well within the Slammer envelope. "Fox-

One with Slammer." His fifth missile of the day leaped off the rail and rocketed east, angling down, and again Winters kept his nose on the target, ensuring that he'd get it on tape . . . yes! "That's a splash. Bronco has a splash, I think that's five."

"Confirm five kills to Bronco," Eagle Two confirmed. "Nice going, buddy."

"What else is around?"

"Boar Lead, the bandits are running south on burner, just went through Mach One. We show a total of nine kills plus one damage, with six bandits running back to the barn, over."

"Roger, copy that, Eagle. Anything else happening at the moment?"

"Ah, that's a negative, Boar Lead."

"Where's the closest tanker?"

"You can tank from Oliver-Six, vector zero-zero-five, distance two hundred, over."

"Roger that. Flight, this is Bronco. Let's assemble and head off to tank. Form up on me."

"Two." "Three." "Four."

"How we doing?"

"Skippy has one," his wingman reported.

"Ducky has two," the second element leader chimed in.

"Ghost Man has two and a scratch."

It didn't add up, Winters thought. Hell, maybe the AWACS guys got confused. That's why they had videotape. All in all, not a bad morning. Best of all, they'd put a real dent in the ChiComm Flanker inventory, and probably punched a pinhole in the confidence of their Su-27 drivers. Shaking up a fighter jock's confidence was almost as good as a kill, especially if they'd bagged the squadron commander. It would make the survivors mad, but it would make them question themselves, their doctrine, and their aircraft. And that was good.

So?"

"The border defenses did about as well as one could reasonably expect," Colonel Aliyev replied. "The good news is that most of our men escaped with their lives. Total dead is under twenty, with fifteen wounded."

"What do they have across the river now?"

"Best guess, elements of three mechanized divisions. The Americans say that they now have six bridges completed and operating. So, we can expect that number to increase rapidly. Chinese reconnaissance elements are pushing forward. We've ambushed some of them, but no prisoners yet. Their direction of advance is exactly what we anticipated, as is their speed of advance to this point."

"Is there any good news?" Bondarenko asked.

"Yes, General. Our air force and our American friends have given their air force a very bloody nose. We've killed over thirty of their aircraft with only four losses to this point, and two of the pilots have been rescued. We've captured six Chinese pilots. They're being taken west for interrogation. It's unlikely that they'll give us any really useful information, though I am sure the air force will want to grill them for technical things. Their plans and objectives are entirely straightforward, and they are probably right on, or even slightly in advance of their plans."

None of this was a surprise to General Bondarenko, but it was unpleasant even so. His intelligence staff was doing a fine job of telling him what they knew and what they expected, but it was like getting a weather report in winter: Yes, it was cold, and yes, it was snowing, and no, the cold and the snow will probably not stop, and isn't it a shame you don't have a warm coat to wear? He had nearly perfect information, but no ability to do anything to change the news. It was all very good that his airmen were killing Chinese airmen, but it was the Chinese tanks and infantry carriers that he had to stop.

"When will we be able to bring air power to bear on their spearheads?"

"We will start air-to-ground operations this afternoon with Su-31 ground-attack aircraft," Aliyev replied. "But . . ."

"But what?" Bondarenko demanded.

"But isn't it better to let them come in with minimal interference for a few days?" It was a courageous thing for his operations officer to say. It was also the right thing, Gennady Iosifovich realized on reflection. If his only strategic option was to lay a deep trap, then why waste what assets he had before the trap was fully set? This was not the Western Front in June of 1941, and he didn't have Stalin sitting in Moscow with a figurative pistol to his head.

No, in Moscow now, the government would be raising all manner of political hell, probably calling for an emergency meeting of the United Nations Security Council, but that was just advertising. It was his job to defeat these yellow barbarians, and doing that was a matter of using what power he had in the most efficient manner possible, and that meant drawing them out. It meant making their commander as confident as a schoolyard bully looking down at a child five years his junior. It meant giving them what the Japanese had once called the Victory Disease. Make them feel invincible, and *then* leap at them like a tiger dropping from a tree.

"Andrey, only a few aircraft, and tell them not to risk themselves by pressing their attacks too hard. We can hurt their air force, but their ground forces—we let them keep their advantage for a while. Let them get fat on this fine table set before them for a while."

"I agree, Comrade General. It's a hard pill to swallow, but in the end, harder for them to eat—assuming our political leadership allows us to do the right thing."

"Yes, that is the real issue at hand, isn't it?"

CHAPTER 52

Deep Battle

General Peng crossed over into Russia in his command vehicle, well behind the first regiment of heavy tanks. He thought of using a helicopter, but his operations staff warned him that the air battle was not going as well as the featherheads in the PLAAF had told him to expect. He felt uneasy, crossing the river in an armored vehicle on a floating bridge—like a brick tied to a balloon—but he did so, listening as his operations officer briefed him on the progress to this point.

"The Americans have surged a number of fighter aircraft forward, and along with them their E-3 airborne radar fighter-control aircraft. These are formidable, and difficult to counter, though our air force colleagues say that they have tactics to deal with them. I will believe that when I see it," Colonel Wa observed. "But that is the only bad news so far. We are several hours ahead of schedule. Russian resistance is lighter than I expected. The prisoners we've taken are very disheartened at their lack of support."

"Is that a fact?" Peng asked, as they left the ribbon bridge and thumped down on Russian soil.

"Yes, we have ten men captured from their defensive positions—we'll see them in a few minutes. They had escape tunnels and personnel carriers set to evacuate the men. They didn't expect to hold for long," Colonel Wa went on. "They *planned* to run away, rather than defend to the last as we expected. I think they lack the heart for combat, Comrade General."

That information got Peng's attention. It was important to know the fighting spirit of one's enemy: "Did any of them stand and fight to the end?"

"Only one of their bunker positions. It cost us thirty men, but we took them out. Perhaps their escape vehicle was destroyed and they had no choice," the colonel speculated.

"I want to see one of these positions at once," Peng ordered.

"Of course, Comrade General." Wa ducked inside and shouted an order to the track driver. The Type 90 armored personnel carrier lurched to the right, surprising the MP who was trying to do traffic control, but he didn't object. The four tall radio whips told him what sort of track this was. The command carrier moved off the beaten track directly toward an intact Russian bunker.

General Peng got out, ducking his head as he did so, and walked toward the mainly intact old gun turret. The "inverted frying pan" shape told him that this was off an old Stalin-3 tank—a very formidable vehicle, once upon a time, but now an obvious relic. A team of intelligence specialists was there. They snapped to attention when they saw the general approach.

"What did we kill it with?" Peng asked.

"We didn't, Comrade General. They abandoned it after firing fifteen cannon shots and about three hundred machine gun rounds. They didn't even destroy it before we captured it," the intelligence captain reported, waving the general down the tank hatch. "It's safe. We checked for booby traps."

Peng climbed down. He saw what appeared to be a comfortable small barracks, shell storage for their big tank gun, ample rounds for their two machine guns. There were empty rounds for both types of guns on the floor, along with wrappers for field rations. It appeared to be a comfortable position, with bunks, shower, toilet, and plenty of food storage. Something worth fighting for, the general thought. "How did they leave?" Peng asked.

"This way," the young captain said, leading him north into the tunnel. "You see, the Russians planned for everything." The tunnel led under the crest of the hill to a covered parking pad for—probably for a BTR, it looked like, confirmed by the wheel tracks on the ground immediately off the concrete pad.

"How long did they hold?"

"We took the place just less than three hours after our initial bombardment. So, we had infantry surrounding the main gun emplacement, and soon thereafter, they ran away," the captain told his army commander.

"I see. Good work by our assault infantry." Then Peng saw that Colonel Wa had brought his command track over the hill to the end of the escape tunnel, allowing him to hop right aboard.

"Now what?" Wa asked.

"I want to see what we did to their artillery support positions."

Wa nodded and relayed the orders to the track commander. That took fifteen minutes of bouncing and jostling. The fifteen heavy guns were still there, though the two Peng passed had been knocked over and destroyed by counter-battery fire. The position they visited was mainly intact, though a number of rockets had fallen close aboard, near enough that three bodies were still lying there untended next to their guns, the bodies surrounded by sticky pools of mainly dried blood. More men had survived, probably. Close to each gun was a two-meter-deep narrow trench lined with concrete that the bombardment hadn't done more than chip. Close by also was a large ammo-storage bunker with rails on which to move the shells and propellant charges to the guns. The door was open.

"How many rounds did they get off?" he asked.

"No more than ten," another intelligence officer, this one a major, replied. "Our counter-battery fire was superb here. The Russian battery was fifteen guns, total. One of them got off twenty shots, but that was all. We had them out of action in less than ten minutes. The artillery-tracker radars worked brilliantly, Comrade General."

Peng nodded agreement. "So it would appear. This emplacement would have been fine twenty or thirty years ago—good protection for the gunners and a fine supply of shells, but they did not anticipate an enemy with the ability to pinpoint their guns so rapidly. If it stands still, Wa, you can kill it." Peng looked around. "Still, the engineers who sited this position and the other one, they were good. It's just that this sort of thing is out of date. What were our total casualties?"

"Killed, three hundred fifty, thereabouts. Wounded, six hundred twenty," operations replied. "It was not exactly cheap, but less than we expected. If the Russians had stood and fought, it could have been far worse."

"Why did they run so soon?" Peng asked. "Do we know?"

"We found a written order in one of the bunkers, authorizing them to leave when they thought things were untenable. That surprised me," Colonel Wa observed. "Historically, the Russians fight very hard on the defense, as the Germans found. But that was under Stalin. The Russians had discipline then. And courage. Not today, it would seem."

"Their evacuation was conducted with some skill," Peng thought out loud. "We ought to have taken more prisoners."

"They ran too fast, Comrade General," operations explained.

"He who fights and runs away," General Peng quoted, "lives to fight another day. Bear that in mind, Colonel."

"Yes, Comrade General, but he who runs away is not an immediate threat."

"Let's go," the general said, heading off to his command track. He wanted to see the front, such as it was.

"So?" Bondarenko asked the lieutenant. The youngster had been through a bad day, and being required to stand and make a report to his theater commander made it no better. "Stand easy, boy. You're alive. It could have been worse."

"General, we could have held if we'd been given a little support," Komanov said, allowing his frustration to appear.

"There was none to give you. Go on." The general pointed at the map on the wall.

"They crossed here, and came through this saddle, and over this ridge to attack us. Leg infantry, no vehicles that we ever saw. They had man-portable anti-tank weapons, nothing special or unexpected, but they had massive artillery support. There must have been an entire battery concentrated just on my one position. Heavy guns, fifteen-centimeter or more. And artillery rockets that wiped out our artillery support almost immediately."

"That's the one surprise they threw at us," Aliyev confirmed. "They must have a lot more of those fire-finder systems than we expected, and they're using their Type 83 rockets as dedicated counter-battery weapons, like the Americans did in Saudi. It's an effective tactic. We'll have to go after their counter-battery systems first of all, or use self-propelled guns to fire and move after only two or three shots. There's no way to spoof them that I know of, and jamming radars of that type is extremely difficult."

"So, we have to work on a way to kill them early on," Bondarenko said. "We have electronic-intelligence units. Let them seek out those Chink radars and eliminate them with rockets of our own." He turned. "Go, on. Lieutenant. Tell me about the Chinese infantry."

"They are not cowards, Comrade General. They take fire and act properly under it. They are well-drilled. My position and the one next to us took down at least two hundred, and they kept coming. Their battle drill is quite good, like a soccer team. If you do *this,* they do *that,* almost instantly. For certain, they call in artillery fire with great skill."

"They had the batteries already lined up, Lieutenant, lined up and waiting," Aliyev told the junior officer. "It helps if you are following a prepared script. Anything else?"

"We never saw a tank. They had us taken out before they finished their bridges. Their infantry looked well-prepared, well-trained, even eager to move forward. I did not see evidence of flexible thinking, but I did not see much of anything, and as you say, their part of the operation was preplanned, and thoroughly rehearsed."

"Typically, the Chinese tell their men a good deal about their planned operations beforehand. They don't believe in secrecy the way we do," Aliyev said. "Perhaps it makes for comradely solidarity on the battlefield."

"But things are going their way, Andrey. The measure of an army is how it reacts when things go badly. We haven't seen that yet, however." *And would they ever?* Bondarenko wondered. He shook his head. He had to banish that sort of thinking from his mind. If he had no confidence, how could his men have it? "What about your men, Valeriy Mikhailovich? How did they fight?"

"We *fought,* Comrade General," Komanov assured the senior officer. "We killed two hundred, and we would have killed many more with a little artillery support."

"Will your men fight some more?" Aliyev asked.

"Fuck, yes!" Komanov snarled back. "Those little bastards are invading *our* country. Give us the right weapons, and we'll fucking kill them all!"

"Did you graduate tank school?"

Komanov bobbed his head like a cadet. "Yes, Comrade General, eighth in my class."

"Give him a company with BOYAR," the general told his ops officer. "They're short of officers."

Major General Marion Diggs was in the third train out of Berlin; it wasn't his choosing, just the way things worked out. He was thirty minutes behind Angelo Giusti's cavalry squadron. The Russians were running their trains as closely together as safety allowed, and probably even shading that somewhat. What *was* working was that the Russian national train system was fully electrified, which meant that the engines accelerated well out of stations and out of the slow orders caused by track problems, which were numerous.

Diggs had grown up in Chicago. His father had been a Pullman porter with the Atcheson, Topeka, and Santa Fe Railroad, working the Super Chief between Chicago and Los Angeles until the passenger service had died in the early 1970s; then, remarkably enough, he'd changed unions to become an engineer. Marion remembered riding with him as a boy, and loving the feel of such a massive piece of equipment under his hands—and so, when he'd gone to West Point, he'd decided to be a tanker, and better yet, a cavalryman. Now he owned a lot of heavy equipment.

It was his first time in Russia, a place he certainly hadn't expected to see when he'd been in the first half of his uniformed career, when the Russians he'd worried about seeing had been mainly from First Guards Tank and Third Shock armies, those massive formations that had once sat in East Germany, always poised to take a nice little drive to Paris, or so NATO had feared.

But no more, now that Russia was part of NATO, an idea that was like something from a bad science-fiction movie. There was no denying it, however. Looking out the windows of the train car, he could see the onion-topped spires of Russian Orthodox churches, ones that Stalin had evidently failed to tear down. The railyards were pretty familiar. Never the most artistic examples of architecture or city planning, they looked the same as the dreary yards leading into Chicago or any other American city. No, only the train yards that you built under your Christmas tree every year were pretty. But they didn't have any Christmas trees in evidence here. The train rolled to a stop, probably waiting for a signal to proceed—

—but no, this looked to be some sort of military terminal. Russian tanks were in evidence off to the right, and a lot of sloped concrete ramps—the Russians had probably built this place to ship their own tracked vehicles west, he judged.

"General?" a voice called.

"Yo!"

"Somebody here to see you, sir," the same voice announced.

Diggs stood and walked back to the sound. It was one of his junior staff officers, a new one fresh from Leavenworth, and behind him was a Russian general officer.

"You are Diggs?" the Russian asked in fair English.

"That's right."

"Come with me please." The Russian walked out onto the platform. The air was fresh, but they were under low, gray clouds this morning.

"You going to tell me how things are going out east?" Diggs asked.

"We wish to fly you and some of your staff to Chabarsovil so that you can see for yourself."

That made good sense, Diggs thought. "How many?"

"Six, plus you."

"Okay." The general nodded and reached for the captain who'd summoned him from his seat. "I want Colonels Masterman, Douglas, Welch, Turner, Major Hurst, and Lieutenant Colonel Garvey."

"Yes, sir." The boy disappeared.

"How soon?"

"The transport is waiting for you now."

One of theirs, Diggs thought. He'd never flown on a Russian aircraft before. How safe would it be? How safe would it be to fly into a war zone? Well, the Army didn't pay him to stay in safe places.

"Who are you?"

"Nosenko, Valentin Nosenko, general major, Stavka."

"How bad is it?"

"It is not good, General Diggs. Our main problem will be getting reinforcements to the theater of action. But they have rivers to cross. The difficulties, as you Americans say, should even out."

Diggs's main worry was supply. His tanks and Bradleys all had basic ammo loads already aboard, and two and a half additional such loads for each vehicle were on supply trucks sitting on other trains like this one. After that, things got a little worrisome, especially for artillery. But the biggest worry of all was diesel fuel. He had enough to move his division maybe three or four hundred miles. That was a good long way in a straight line, but wars never allowed troops to travel in straight lines. That translated to maybe two hundred miles of actual travel at best, and that was not an impressive number at all. Then there was the question of jet fuel for his organic aircraft. So, his head logistician, Colonel Ted Douglas, was the first guy he needed, after Masterman, his operations brain. The officers started showing up.

"What gives, sir?" Masterman asked.

"We're flying east to see what's going on."

"Okay, let me make sure we have some communications gear." Masterman disappeared again. He left the train car, along with two enlisted men humping satellite radio equipment.

"Good call, Duke," LTC Garvey observed. He was communications and electronic intelligence for First Tanks.

"Gentlemen, this is General Nosenko from Stavka. He's taking us east, I gather?"

"Correct, I am an intelligence officer for Stavka. This way, please." He led them off, to where four cars were waiting. The drive to a military airport took twenty minutes.

"How are your people taking this?" Diggs asked.

"The civilians, you mean? Too soon to tell. Much disbelief, but some anger. Anger is good," Nosenko said. "Anger gives courage and determination."

If the Russians were talking about anger and determination, the situation must be pretty bad, Diggs thought, looking out at the streets of the Moscow suburbs.

"What are you moving east ahead of us?"

"So far, four motor-rifle divisions," Nosenko answered. "Those are our best-prepared formations. We are assembling other forces."

"I've been out of touch. What else is NATO sending? Anything?" Diggs asked next.

"A British brigade is forming up now, the men based at Hohne. We hope to have them on the way here in two days."

"No way we'd go into action without at least the Brits to back us up," Diggs said. "Good, they're equipped about the same way we are." And better yet, they trained according to the same doctrine. *Hohne,* he thought, their 22nd Brigade from Haig Barracks, Brigadier Sam Turner. Drank whiskey like it was Perrier, but a good thinker and a superior tactician. And his brigade was all trained up from some fun and games down at Grafenwöhr. "What about Germans?"

"That's a political question," Nosenko admitted.

"Tell your politicians that Hitler's dead, Valentin. The Germans are pretty good to have on your side. Trust me, buddy. We play with them all the time. They're down a little from ten years ago, but the German soldier ain't no dummy, and neither are his officers. Their reconnaissance units are particularly good."

"Yes, but that is a political question," Nosenko repeated. And that, Diggs knew, was that, at least for now.

The aircraft waiting was an Il-86, known to NATO as the Camber, manifestly the Russian copy of Lockheed's C-141 Starlifter. This one had Aeroflot commercial markings, but retained the gun position in the tail that the Russians liked to keep on all their tactical aircraft. Diggs didn't object to it at the moment. They'd scarcely had the chance to sit down and strap in when the aircraft started rolling.

"In a hurry, Valentin?"

"Why wait, General Diggs? There's a war on," he reminded his guest.

"Okay, what do we know?"

Nosenko opened the map case he'd been carrying and laid out a large sheet on the floor as the aircraft lifted off. It was of the Chinese-Russian border on the Amur River, with markings already penciled on. The American officers all leaned over to look.

"They came in here, and drove across the river . . ."

How fast are they moving?" Bondarenko asked.

"I have a reconnaissance company ahead of them. They report

in every fifteen minutes," Colonel Tolkunov replied. "They are moving in a deliberate manner. Their reconnaissance screen is composed of WZ-501 tracked APCs, heavy on radios, light on weapons. They are on the whole not very enterprising, however. As I said, deliberate. They move by leapfrogging half a kilometer at a bound, depending on terrain. We're monitoring their radios. They're not encrypted, though their spoken language is deceptive in terminology. We're working on that."

"Speed of advance?"

"Five kilometers in an hour is the fastest we've seen, usually slower than that. Their main body is still getting organized, and they haven't set up a logistics train yet. I'd expect them to attempt no more than thirty kilometers in a day on flat open ground, based on what I've seen so far."

"Interesting." Bondarenko looked back at his maps. They'd start going north-northwest because that's what the terrain compelled them to do. At this speed, they'd be at the gold strike in six or seven days.

Theoretically, he could move 265th Motor Rifle to a blocking position . . . here . . . in two days and make a stand, but by then they'd have at least three, maybe eight, mechanized divisions to attack his one full-strength unit, and he couldn't gamble on that so soon. The good news was that the Chinese were bypassing his command post—*contemptuously?* he wondered, *or just because there was nothing there to threaten them, and so nothing to squander force on?* No, they'd run as fast and hard as they could, bringing up foot infantry to wall off their line of advance. That was classic tactics, and the reason was because it worked. Everyone did it that way, from Hannibal to Hitler.

So, their lead elements moved deliberately, and they were still forming up their army over the Amur bridgehead.

"What units have we identified?"

"The lead enemy formation is their 34th Red Banner Shock Army, Commanded by Peng Xi-Wang. He is politically reliable and well-regarded in Beijing, an experienced soldier. Expect him to be the operational army group commander. The 34th Army is mainly across the river now. Three more Group A mechanized armies are lined up to cross as well, the 31st, 29th, and 43rd. That's a total of sixteen mechanized divisions, plus a lot of other attachments. We think the 65th Group B Army will be next across. Four infantry divisions plus a tank brigade. Their job will be to hold the western flank, I would imagine." That made sense. There was no Russian force east of the breakthrough worthy of the name. A classic operation would also wheel east to Vladivostok on the Pacific Coast, but that would only distract forces from the main objection. So, the turn east would wait for at least a week, probably two or three, with just light screening forces heading that way for the moment.

"What about our civilians?" Bondarenko asked.

"They're leaving the towns in the Chinese path as best they can, mainly cars and buses. We have MP units trying to keep them organized. So far nothing has happened to interfere with the evacuation," Tolkunov said. "See, from this it looks as if they're actually bypassing Belogorsk, just passing east of it with their reconnaissance elements."

"That's the smart move, isn't it?" Bondarenko observed. "Their real objective is far to the north. Why slow down for anything? They don't want land. They don't want people. They want oil and gold. Capturing civilians will not make those objectives any easier to accomplish. If I were this Peng fellow, I would be worried about the extent of my drive north. Even unopposed, the natural obstacles are formidable, and defending his line of advance will be a beast of a problem." Gennady paused. Why have any sympathy for this barbarian? His mission was to kill him and all his men, after all. But how? If even marching that far north was a problem—and it was—then how much harder would it be to strike through the same terrain with less-prepared troops? The tactical problems on both sides were the kind men in his profession did not welcome.

"General Bondarenko?" a foreign voice asked.

"Yes?" He turned to see a man dressed in an American flight suit.

"Sir, my name is Major Dan Tucker. I just flew in with a downlink for our Dark Star UAVs. Where do you want us to set up, sir?"

"Colonel Tolkunov? Major, this is my chief of intelligence."

The American saluted sloppily, as air force people tended to do. "Howdy, Colonel."

"How long to set up?"

The American was pleased that this Tolkunov's English was better than his own Russian. "Less than an hour, sir."

"This way." The G-2 led him outside. "How good are your cameras?"

"Colonel, when a guy's out taking a piss, you can see how big his dick is."

Tolkunov figured that was typical American braggadocio, but it set him wondering.

Captain Feodor Il'ych Aleksandrov commanded the 265th Motor Rifle's divisional reconnaissance element—the division was supposed to have a full battalion for this task, but he was all they had—and for that task he had eight of the new BRM reconnaissance tracks. These were evolutionary developments of the standard BMP infantry combat vehicle, upgraded with better automotive gear—more reliable engine and transmission systems—plus the best radios his country made. He reported directly to his divisional commander, and also, it seemed, to the theater intelligence coordinator, some colonel named Tolkunov. That chap, he'd discovered, was very concerned with his personal safety, always urging him to stay close—but not too close—not to be spotted, and to avoid combat of any type. His job, Tolkunov had told him at least once every two hours for the last day and a half, was to stay alive and to keep his eye on the advancing Chinese. He wasn't supposed to so much as injure one little hair on their cute little Chink heads, just stay close enough that if they mumbled in their sleep, to copy down the names of the girlfriends they fucked in their dreams.

Aleksandrov was a young captain, only twenty-eight, and rakishly handsome, an athlete who ran for personal pleasure—and running, he told his men, was the best form of exercise for a soldier, especially a reconnaissance specialist. He had a driver, gunner, and radio operator for each of his tracks, plus three infantrymen whom he'd personally trained to be invisible.

The drill was for them to spend about half their time out of their vehicles, usually a good kilometer or so ahead of their Chinese counterparts, either behind trees or on their bellies, reporting back with monosyllabic comments on their portable radios, which were of Japanese manufacture. The men moved light, carrying only their rifles and two spare magazines, because they weren't supposed to be seen or heard, and the truth was that Aleksandrov would have preferred to send them out unarmed, lest they be tempted to shoot someone out of patriotic anger. However, no soldier would ever stand for being sent out on a battlefield weaponless, and so he'd had to settle for ordering them out with bolts closed on empty chambers. The captain was usually out with his men, their BRM carriers hidden three hundred or so meters away in the trees.

In the past twenty-four hours, they'd become intimately familiar with their Chinese opponents. These were also trained and dedicated reconnaissance specialists, and they were pretty good at their jobs, or certainly appeared to be. They were also moving in tracked vehicles, and also spent a lot of their time on foot, ahead of their tracks, hiding behind trees and peering to the north, looking for Russian forces. The Russians had even started giving them names.

"It's the gardener," Sergeant Buikov said. That one liked touching trees and bushes, as though studying them for a college paper or something. The gardener was short and skinny, and looked like a twelve-year-old to the Russians. He seemed competent enough, carrying his rifle slung on his back, and using his binoculars often. He was a Chinese lieutenant, judging by his shoulderboards, probably commander of this platoon. He ordered his people around a lot, but didn't mind taking the lead. So, he was probably conscientious. *He is, therefore, the one we should kill first,* Aleksandrov thought. Their BRM reconnaissance track had a fine 30-mm cannon that could reach out and turn the gardener into fertilizer from a thousand meters or so, but Captain Aleksandrov had forbidden it, worse luck, Buikov thought. He was from this area, a woodsman of sorts who'd hunted in the forests many times with his father, a lumberjack. "We really ought to kill him."

"Boris Yevgeniyevich, do you wish to alert the enemy to our presence?" Aleksandrov asked his sergeant.

"I suppose not, my captain, but the hunting season is—"

"—closed, Sergeant. The season is closed, and no, he is not a wolf that you can shoot for your own pleasure, and—down," Aleksandrov ordered. The gardener was looking their way with his field glasses. Their faces were painted, and they had branches tucked into their field clothing to break up their outlines, but he was taking no chances. "They'll be moving soon. Back to the track."

The hardest part of their drill was to avoid leaving tracks for the Chinese to spot. Aleksandrov had "discussed" this with his drivers, threatening to shoot anyone who left a trail. (He knew he couldn't do that, of course, but his men weren't quite sure.) Their vehicles even had upgraded mufflers to reduce their sound signature. Every so often, the men who designed and built Russian military equipment got things right, and this was such a case. Besides, they didn't crank their engines until they saw the Chinese doing the same. Aleksandrov looked up. Okay, the gardener was waving to those behind him, the wave that meant to bring their vehicles up. They were doing another leapfrog jump, with one section standing fast and providing over-watch cover for the next move, should something happen. He had no intention of making anything happen, but of course they couldn't know that. Aleksandrov was surprised that they were maintaining their careful drill into the second day. They weren't getting sloppy yet. He'd expected that, but it seemed that the Chinese were better drilled even than his expectations, and were assiduously following their written doctrine. Well, so was he.

"Move now, Captain?" Buikov asked.

"No, let's sit still and watch. They ought to stop at that little ridge with the logging road. I want to see how predictable they are, Boris Yevgeniyevich." But he did trigger his portable radio. "Stand by, they're jumping again."

The other radio just clicked on and off, creating a whisper of static, rather than a spoken reply. Good, his men were adhering to their radio discipline. The second echelon of Chinese tracks moved forward carefully, at about ten-kilometer speed, following this opening in the forest. Interesting, he thought, that they weren't venturing too far into the adjoining woods. No more than two or three hundred meters. Then he cringed. A helicopter chattered overhead. It was a Gazelle, a Chinese copy of the French military helicopter. But his track was back in the woods, and every time it stopped, the men ran outside to stretch the camo-net around it. His men, also, were well-drilled. And *that,* he told his men, was why they didn't dare leave a visible trail if they wanted to live. It wasn't much of a helicopter, but it did carry rockets—and their BRM was an armored personnel carrier, but it wasn't *that* armored.

"What's he doing?" Buikov asked.

"If he's looking, he's not being very careful about it."

The Chinese were driving up a pathway built ages ago for an unbuilt spur off the Trans-Siberian Railroad. It was wide, in some places five hundred meters, and fairly well-graded. Someone in years past had thought about building this spur to exploit the unsurveyed riches of Siberia—enough to cut down a lot of trees, and they'd barely grown back in the harsh winters. Just saplings in this pathway now, easily ground into splinters by tracked vehicles. Farther north, the work was being continued by army engineers, making a path to the new gold find, and beyond that to the oil discoveries on the Arctic Coast. When they got that far, the Chinese would find a good road, ready-made for a mechanized force to exploit. But it was a narrow one, and the Chinese would have to learn about flank security if they kept this path up.

Aleksandrov remembered a Roman adventure into Germany, a soldier named Quintilius Varus, commanding three legions, who'd ignored his flanks, and lost his army in the process to a German named Armenius. Might the Chinese make a similar mistake? No, everyone knew of the Teutonenberg Forest disaster. It was a textbook lesson in every military academy in the known world. Quintilius Varus had been a political commander, given that command because he'd been beloved of his emperor, Caesar Augustus, obviously not because of his operational skill. It was a lesson probably better remembered by soldiers than by politicians. And the Chinese army was commanded by soldiers, wasn't it?

"That's the fox," Buikov said. This was the other officer in the Chinese unit, probably the subordinate of the gardener. Similar in size, but he had less interest in plants than he had in darting about. As they watched, he disappeared into the tree line to the east, and if he went by the form card, he'd be invisible for five to eight minutes.

"I could use a smoke," Sergeant Buikov observed.

"That will have to wait, Sergeant."

"Yes, Comrade Captain. May I have a sip of water, then?" he asked petulantly. It wasn't water he wanted, of course.

"Yes, I'd like a shot of vodka, too, but I neglected to bring any with me, as, I am sure, you did as well."

"Regrettably, yes, Comrade Captain. A good slug of vodka helps keep the chill away in these damp woods."

"And it also dulls the senses, and we need our senses, Boris Yevgeniyevich, unless you enjoy eating rice. Assuming the Chinks take prisoners, which I rather doubt. They do not like us, Sergeant, and they are not a civilized people. Remember that."

So, they don't go to the ballet. Neither do I, Sergeant Buikov didn't say aloud. His captain was a Muscovite, and spoke often of cultural matters. But like his captain, Buikov had no love for the Chinese, and even less now that he was looking at Chinese soldiers on the soil of his country. He only regretted not killing some, but killing was not his job. His job was watching them piss on his country, which somehow only made him angrier.

"Captain, will we ever get to shoot them?" the sergeant asked.

"In due course, yes, it will be our job to eliminate their reconnaissance elements, and yes, Boris, I look forward to that as well." *And, yes, I could use a smoke as well. And I'd love a glass of vodka right now.* But he'd settle for some black bread and butter, which he did have in his track, three hundred meters to the north.

Six and a half minutes this time. The fox had at least looked into the woods to the east, probably listened for the sound of diesel engines, but heard nothing but the chirping of birds. Still, this Chink lieutenant was the more conscientious of the two, in Buikov's opinion. *They should kill him first, when the time came,* the sergeant thought. Aleksandrov tapped the sergeant on the shoulder. "Our turn to leapfrog, Boris Yevgeniyevich."

"By your command, Comrade Captain." And both men moved out, crouching for the first hundred meters, and taking care not to make too much noise, until they heard the Chinese tracks start their engines. In five more minutes, they were back in their BRM and heading north, slowly picking their way through the trees, Aleksandrov buttered some bread and ate it, sipping water as he did so. When they'd traveled a thousand meters, their vehicle stopped, and the captain got on his big radio.

Who is Ingrid?" Tolkunov asked.

"Ingrid Bergman," Major Tucker replied. "Actress, good-lookin' babe in her day. All the Dark Stars are named for movie stars, Colonel. The troops did it." There was a plastic strip on the monitor top to show which Dark Star was up and transmitting. Marilyn Monroe was back at Zhigansk for service, and Grace Kelly was the next one up, scheduled to go in fifteen hours. "Anyway"—he flipped a switch and then played a little with his mouse control—"there's the Chinese lead elements."

"Son of a bitch," Tolkunov said, demonstrating his knowledge of American slang.

Tucker grinned. "Pretty good, ain't it? Once I sent one over a nudist colony in California—that's like a private park where people walk around naked all the time. You can tell the difference between the flat-chested ones and the ones with nice tits. Tell the natural blondes from the peroxide ones, too. Anyway, you use this mouse to control the camera—well, somebody else is doing it now up at Zhigansk. Anything in particular that you're interested in?"

"The bridges on the Amur," Tolkunov said at once. Tucker picked up a radio microphone.

"This is Major Tucker. We have a tasking request. Slew Camera Three onto the big crossing point."

"Roger," the speaker next to the monitor said.

The picture changed immediately, seeming to race across the screen like a ribbon from ten o'clock down to four o'clock. Then it stabilized. The field of view must have been four kilometers across. It showed a total of what appeared to be eight bridges, each of them approached by what looked like a parade of insects.

"Give me control of Camera Three," Tucker said next.

"You got it, sir," the speaker acknowledged.

"Okay." Tucker played with the mouse more than the keyboard, and the picture zoomed in—"isolated"—on the third bridge from the west. There were three tanks on it at once, moving at about ten kilometers per hour south to north. The display showed a compass rose in case you got disoriented, and it was even in color. Tolkunov asked why.

"No more expensive than black-and-white cameras, and we put it on the system because it sometimes shows you things you don't get from gray. First time for overheads, even the satellites don't do color yet," Tucker explained. Then he frowned. "The angle's wrong, can't get the divisional markings on the tanks without moving the platform. Wait." He picked up the microphone again. "Sergeant, who's crossing the bridges now?"

"Appears to be their Three-Oh-Second armored division, sir, part of the Twenty-Ninth Group-A Army. The Thirty-Fourth Army is fully across now. We estimate one full regiment of the Three-Oh-Second is across and moving north at this time," the intel weenie reported, as though relating the baseball scores from yesterday.

"Thanks, Sarge."

"Roger that, Maj."

"And they can't see this drone?" Tolkunov asked.

"Well, on radar it's pretty stealthy, and there's another little trick we have on it. Goes back to World War II, called Project Yehudi back then, you put lights on the thing."

"What?" Tolkunov asked.

"Yeah, you spot airplanes because they're darker'n the sky, but if you put lightbulbs on 'em, they turn invisible. So, there are lights on the airframe, and a photo sensor dials the brightness automatically. They're damned near impossible to spot—they cruise at sixty thousand feet, way the hell above contrail level, and they got no infrared signature at all, hardly—even if you know where to look, and they tell me you can't hardly *make* an air-to-air missile lock onto one. Pretty cool toy, eh?"

"How long have you had this?"

"I've been working on it, oh, about four years now."

"I've heard of Dark Star, but this capability is amazing."

Tucker nodded. "Yeah, it's pretty slick. Nice to know what the other guy's doing. First time we deployed it was over Yugoslavia, and once we learned how to use it, and how to coordinate it with the shooters, well, we learned to make their lives pretty miserable. Tough shit, Joe."

"Joe?"

"Joe Chink." Tucker pointed at the screen. "That's what we mainly call him." The friendly nickname for Koreans had once been Luke the Gook. "Now, Ingrid doesn't have it yet, but Grace Kelly does, a laser designator, so you can use these things to clobber targets. The fighter just lofts the bomb in from, oh, maybe twenty miles away, and we guide it into the target. I've only done that at Red Flag, and we can't do it from here with this terminal, but they can up at Zhigansk."

"Guide bombs from six hundred kilometers away?"

"Yeah. Hell, you can do it from Washington if you want. It all goes over the satellite, y'know?"

"Yob tvoyu maht!"

"Soon we're going to make the fighter jocks obsolete, Colonel. Another year or so and we'll be doing terminal guidance on missiles launched from a coupla hundred miles away. Won't need fighter pilots then. Guess I'll have to buy me a scarf. So, Colonel, what else do you want to see?"

The Il-86 landed at a rustic fighter base with only a few helicopters on it, Colonel Mitch Turner noted. As divisional intelligence officer, he was taking in a lot of what he saw in Russia, and what he saw wasn't all that encouraging. Like General Diggs, he'd entered the Army when the USSR had been the main enemy and principal worry for the United States Army, and now he was wondering how many of the intelligence estimates he'd help draft as a young spook officer had been pure fantasy. Either that or the mighty had fallen farther and faster than any nation in history. The Russian army wasn't even a shadow of what the Red Army had been. The "Rompin', Stompin' Russian Red Ass" so feared by NATO was as dead as the stegosaurus toys his son liked to play with, and right now that was not such a good thing. The Russian Federation looked like a rich family of old with no sons to defend it, and the girl kids were getting raped. Not a good thing. The Russians, like America, still had nuclear weapons—bombs, deliverable by bombers and tactical fighters. However, the Chinese had missiles to deliver theirs, and they were targeted at cities, and the Big Question was whether the Russians had the stones to trade a few cities and, say, forty million people for a gold mine and some oil fields. Probably not, Turner figured. Not something a smart man would do. Similarly, they could not afford a war of attrition against a country with nine times as many people *and* a healthier economy, even over this ground. No, if they were to defeat the Chinese, it had to be with maneuver and agility, but their military was in the shitter, and neither trained nor equipped to play maneuver warfare.

This, Turner thought on reflection, *was going to be an interesting war.* It was not the sort he wanted to fight. Better to clobber a dumb little enemy than mix it up with a smart powerful one. It might not be glorious, but it was a hell of a lot safer.

"Mitch," General Diggs said, as they stood to walk off the airplane. "Thoughts?"

"Well, sir, we might have picked a better place to fly to. Way things look, this is going to be a little exciting."

"Go on," the general ordered.

"The other side has better cards. More troops, better-trained troops, more equipment. Their task, crossing a lot of nasty country, is not enviable, but neither is the Russian task, defending against it. To win they have to play maneuver warfare. But I don't see that they have the horsepower to pull it off."

"Their boss out here, Bondarenko. He's pretty good."

"So was Erwin Rommel, sir, but Montgomery whupped his ass."

There were staff cars lined up to drive them into the Russian command post. The weather was clearer here, and they were close enough to the Chinese that a clear sky wasn't something to enjoy anymore.

CHAPTER 53

Deep Concerns

So, what's happening there?" Ryan asked.

"The Chinese are seventy miles inside Russia. They have a total of eight divisions over the river, and they're pushing north," General Moore replied, moving a pencil across the map spread on the conference table. "They blew through the Russian border defenses pretty fast—it was essentially the Maginot Line from 1940. I wouldn't have expected it to hold very long, but our overheads showed them punching through fairly professionally with their leading infantry formations, supported by a lot of artillery. Now they have their tanks across—about eight hundred to this point, with another thousand or so to go."

Ryan whistled. "That many?"

"When you invade a major country, sir, you don't do it on the cheap. The only good news at this point is that we've really given their air force a bloody nose."

"AWACS and -15s?" Jackson asked.

"Right." The Chairman of the Joint Chiefs nodded. "One of our kids made ace in a single engagement. A Colonel Winters."

"Bronco Winters," Jackson said. "I've heard the name. Fighter jock. Okay, what else?"

"Our biggest problem on the air side is going to be getting bombs to our airmen. Flying bombs in is not real efficient. I mean, you can use up a whole C-5 just to deliver half the bombs for one squadron of F-15Es, and we've got a lot of other things for the C-5s to do. We're thinking about sending the bombs into Russia by train to Chita, say, and then flying them up to Suntar from there, but the Russian railroad is moving just tanks and vehicles for now, and that isn't going to change soon. We're trying to fight a war at the end of one railroad line. Sure, it's double-tracked, but it's still just one damned line. Our logistical people are already taking a lot of Maalox over this one."

"Russian airlift capacity?" Ryan asked.

"FedEx has more," General Moore replied. "In fact, FedEx has a lot more. We're going to ask you to authorize call-up of the civilian reserve air fleet, Mr. President."

"Approved," Ryan said at once.

"And a few other little things," Moore said. He closed his eyes. It was pushing midnight, and nobody had gotten much sleep lately. "VMH-1 is standing-to. We're in a shooting war with a country that has nuclear weapons on ballistic launchers. So, we have to think about the possibility—remote maybe, but still a possibility—that they could launch at us. So, VMH-1 and the Air Force's First Heli at Andrews are standing-to. We can get a chopper here to lift you and your family out in seven minutes. That concerns you, Mrs. O'Day," Moore said to Andrea.

The President's Principal Agent nodded. "We're dialed in. It's all in The Book," she said. That nobody had opened that particular book since 1962 was beside the point. It was written down. Mrs. Price-O'Day looked a little peaked.

"You okay?" Ryan asked.

"Stomach," she explained.

"Try some ginger?" Jack went on.

"Nothing much works for this, Dr. North tells me. Please excuse me, Mr. President." She was embarrassed that he'd noticed her discomfort. She always wanted to be one of the boys. But the boys didn't get pregnant, did they?

"Why don't you drive home?"

"Sir, I—"

"Go," Ryan said. "That's an order. You're a woman, and you're pregnant. You can't be a cop all the time, okay? Get some relief here and go. Right now."

Special Agent Price-O'Day hesitated, but she did have an order, so she walked out the door. Another agent came in immediately.

"Machismo from a woman. What's the goddamned world coming to?" Ryan asked the assembly.

"You're not real liberated, Jack," Jackson observed with a grin.

"It's called objective circumstances, I think. She's still a girl, even if she does carry a pistol. Cathy says she's doing fine. This nausea stuff doesn't last forever. Probably feels like it to her, though. Okay, General, what else?"

"Kneecap and Air Force One are on hot-pad alert 'round the clock. So, if we get a launch warning, in seven minutes or less, you and the Vice President are on choppers, five more minutes to Andrews, and three more after that you're doing the takeoff roll. The drill is, your family goes to Air Force One and you go to Kneecap," he concluded. Kneecap was actually the National Emergency Airborne Command Post (NEACP), but the official acronym was too hard to pronounce. Like the VC-25A that served as Air Force One, Kneecap was a converted 747 that was really just a wrapper for a bunch of radios flying in very close formation.

"Gee, that's nice to know. What about my family?" POTUS asked.

"In these circumstances, we keep a chopper close to where your wife and kids are at all times, and then they'll fly in whatever direction seems the safest at the moment. If that's not Andrews, then they'll get picked up later by a fixed-wing aircraft and taken to whatever place seems best. It's all theoretical," Moore explained, "but something you might as well know about."

"Can the Russians stop the Chinese?" Ryan asked, turning his attention back to the map.

"Sir, that remains to be seen. They *do* have the nuclear option, but it's not a card I would expect them to play. The Chinese *do* have twelve CSS-4 ICBMs. It's essentially a duplicate of our old Titan-II liquid fuels, with a warhead estimated to be between three and five megatons."

"City-buster?" Ryan asked.

"Correct. No counterforce capability, and there's nothing we have left to use against it in that role anyway. The CEP on the warhead is estimated to be plus or minus a thousand meters or so. So, it'd do a city pretty well, but that's about all."

"Any idea where they're targeted?" Jackson asked. Moore nodded at once.

"Yes. The missile is pretty primitive, and the silos are oriented on their targets because the missile doesn't have much in the way of cross-range maneuverability. Two are targeted on Washington. Others on LA,

San Francisco, and Chicago. Plus Moscow, Kiev, St. Petersburg. They're all leftovers from the Bad Old Days, and they haven't been modified in any way."

"Any way to take them out?" Jackson asked.

"I suppose we could stage a mission with fighter or bomber aircraft and go after the silos with PGMs," Moore allowed. "But we'd have to fly the bombs to Suntar first, and even then it'll be rather a lengthy mission for the F-117s."

"What about B-2s out of Guam?" Jackson asked.

"I'm not sure they can carry the right weapons. I'll have to check that."

"Jack, this is something we need to think about, okay?"

"I hear you, Robby. General, have somebody look into this, okay?"

"Yes, sir."

Gennady Iosifovich!" General Diggs called on entering the map room.

"Marion Ivanovich!" The Russian came over to take his hand, followed by a hug. He even kissed his guest, in the Russian fashion, and Diggs flinched from this, in the American fashion. "In!"

And Diggs waited for ten seconds: "Out!" Both men shared the laugh of an insider's joke.

"The turtle bordello is still there?"

"It was the last time I looked, Gennady." Then Diggs had to explain to the others. "Out at Fort Irwin—we collected all the desert tortoises and put them in a safe place so the tanks wouldn't squish 'em and piss off the tree-huggers. I suppose they're still in there making little turtles, but the damned things screw so slow they must fall asleep doing it."

"I have told that story many times, Marion." Then the Russian turned serious. "I am glad to see you. I will be more glad to see your division."

"How bad is it?"

"It is not good. Come." They walked over to the big wall map. "These are their positions as of thirty minutes ago."

"How are you keeping track of them?"

"We now have your Dark Star invisible drones, and I have a smart young captain on the ground watching them as well."

"That far . . ." Diggs said. Colonel Masterman was right beside him now. "Duke?" Then he looked at his Russian host. "This is Colonel Masterman, my G-3. His last job was as a squadron commander in the Tenth Cav."

"Buffalo Soldier, yes?"

"Yes, sir," Masterman confirmed with a nod, but his eyes didn't leave the map. "Ambitious bastards, aren't they?"

"Their first objective will be here," Colonel Aliyev said, using a pointer. "This is the Gogol Gold Strike."

"Well, hell, if you're gonna steal something, might as well be a gold mine, right?" Duke asked rhetorically. "What do you have to stop them with?"

"Two-Six-Five Motor Rifle is here." Aliyev pointed.

"Full strength?"

"Not quite, but we've been training them up. We have four more motor-rifle divisions en route. The first arrives at Chita tomorrow noon." Aliyev's voice was a little too optimistic for the situation. He didn't want to show weakness to Americans.

"That's still a long way to move," Masterman observed. He looked over at his boss.

"What are you planning, Gennady?"

"I want to take the four Russian divisions north to link up with the 265th, and stop them about here. Then, perhaps, we will use your forces to cross east through here and cut them off."

Now it wasn't the Chinese who were being ambitious, both Diggs and Masterman thought. Moving First Infantry Division (Mechanized) from Fort Riley, Kansas, to Fort Carson, Colorado, would have been about the same distance, but it would have been on flat ground and against no opposition. Here that task would involve a lot of hills and serious resistance. *Those factors* did *make a difference,* the American officers thought.

"No serious contact yet?"

Bondarenko shook his head. "No, I'm keeping my mechanized forces well away from them. The Chinese are advancing against no opposition."

"You want 'em to fall asleep, get sloppy?" Masterman asked.

"Da, better that they should get overconfident."

The American colonel nodded. That made good sense, and as always, war was as much a psychological game as a physical one. "If we jump off the trains at Chita, it's still a long-approach march to where you want us, General."

"What about fuel?" Colonel Douglas asked.

"That is the one thing we have plenty of," answered Colonel Aliyev. "The blue spots on the map, fuel storage—it is the same as your Number Two Diesel."

"How much?" Douglas asked.

"At each fuel depot, one billion two hundred fifty million liters."

"Shit!" Douglas observed. "*That* much?"

Aliyev explained, "The fuel depots were established to support a large mobile force in a border conflict. They were built in the time of Nikita Sergeyevich Khrushchev. Huge concrete-and-steel storage tanks, all underground, well hidden."

"They must be," Mitch Turner observed. "I've never been briefed on them."

"So, we evaded even your satellite photos, yes?" That pleased the Russian. "Each depot is manned by a force of twenty engineers, with ample electric pumps."

"I like the locations," Masterman said. "What's this unit here?"

"That is Boyar, a reserve mechanized force. The men have just been called up. Their weapons are from a hidden equipment-storage bunker. It's a short division, old equipment—T-55s and such—but serviceable. We're keeping that force hidden," Aliyev said.

The American G-3 arched his eyebrows. Maybe they were outmanned, but they weren't dumb. That Boyar force was in a particularly interesting place . . . if Ivan could make proper use of it. Their overall operational concept looked good—theoretically. A lot of soldiers could come up with good ideas. The problem was executing them. Did the Russians have the ability to do that? Russia's military theorists were as good as any the world had ever seen—good enough that the United States Army regularly stole their ideas. The problem was that the U.S. Army could apply those theories to a real battlefield, and the Russians could not.

"How are your people handling this?" Masterman asked.

"Our soldiers, you mean?" Aliyev asked. "The Russian soldier knows how to fight," he assured his American counterpart.

"Hey, Colonel, I am not questioning their guts," Duke assured his host. "How's their spirit, for one thing?"

Bondarenko handled that one: "Yesterday I had to face one of my young officers, Komanov, from the border defenses. He was furious that we were unable to give him the support he needed to defeat the Chinese. And I was ashamed," the general admitted to his guests. "My men have the spirit. Their training is lacking—I just got here a few months ago, and my changes have barely begun to take effect. But, you will see, the Russian soldier has *always* risen to the occasion, and he will today—if we here are worthy of him."

Masterman didn't share a look with his boss. Diggs had spoken well of this Russian general, and Diggs was both a good operational soldier and a good judge of men. But the Russian had just admitted that his men weren't trained up as well as they ought to be. The good news was that on the battlefield, men learned the soldier's trade rapidly. The bad news was that the battlefield was the most brutal Darwinian environment on the face of the planet. Some men would learn, but others would die in the process, and the Russians didn't have all that many they could afford to lose. This wasn't 1941, and they weren't fighting with half their population base this time around.

"You're going to want us to move out fast when the trains drop us off at Chita?" Tony Welch asked. He was the divisional chief of staff.

"Yes," Aliyev confirmed.

"Okay, well, then I need to get down there and look over the facilities. What about fuel for our choppers?"

"Our air force bases have fuel storage similar to the diesel depots," Aliyev told him. "Your word is infrastructure, yes? That is the one thing we have much of. When will they arrive?"

"The Air Force is still working that out. They're going to fly our aviation brigade in. Apaches first. Dick Boyle's chomping at the bit."

"We will be very pleased to see your attack helicopters. We have all too few of our own, and our air force is also slow delivering them."

"Duke," Diggs said, "get on the horn to the Air Force. We need some choppers right the hell now, just so we can get around and see what we need to see."

"Roger," Masterman replied.

"Let me get a satellite radio set up," Lieutenant Colonel Garvey said, heading for the door.

Ingrid Bergman was heading south now. General Wallace wanted a better idea for the Chinese logistical tail, and now he was getting it. The People's Republic of China was in many ways like America had been at the turn of the previous century. Things moved mainly by rail. There were no major highways as Americans understood them, but a lot of railroads. Those were efficient for moving large quantities of anything over medium-to-long distances, but they were also inflexible, and hard to repair—especially the bridges—and most of all the tunnels, and so that was what he and his targeting people were looking at. The problem was that they had few bombs to drop. None of his attack assets—mainly F-15E Strike Eagles at the moment—had flown over with bombs on their wings, and he had barely enough air-to-mud munitions for an eight-ship strike mission. It was like going to a dance and finding no girls there. The music was fine, and so was the fruit punch, but there really wasn't anything to do. Perversely, his -15E crews didn't mind. They got to play fighter plane, and all such people prefer shooting other airplanes down to dropping bombs on mud soldiers. It just came with the territory. The one thing he had going now was that his scarf-and-goggles troops were playing hell with the PRC air force, with over seventy confirmed kills already for not a single air-to-air loss. The advantage of having E-3B AWACS aircraft was so decisive that the enemy might as well have been flying World War I Fokkers, and the Russians were learning rapidly how to make use of E-3B support. Their fighters were good aerodynamic platforms, just lacking in legs. The Russians had never built a fighter with fuel capacity for more than about one hour's flight time. Nor had they ever learned how to do midair refueling, as the Americans had. And so the Russian MiG and Sukhoi fighters could go up, take their instructions from the AWACS, and participate in one engagement, but then they had to return to base for gas. Half of the kills his Eagle drivers had collected so far were of Chinese fighters that had broken off their fights to RTB for gas as well. It wasn't fair, but Wallace, like all Air Force fighter types, could hardly have cared less about being fair in combat.

But Wallace was fighting a defensive war to this point. He was successfully defending Russian airspace. He was not taking out Chinese targets, not even attacking the Chinese troops on the ground in Siberia. So, though his fighters were having a fine, successful war, they just weren't accomplishing anything important. To that end, he lifted his satellite link to America.

"We ain't got no bombs, General," he told Mickey Moore.

"Well, your fellow Air Scouts are maxed out on taskings, and Mary Diggs is screaming to get some trash haulers to get him his chopper brigade moved to where he needs it."

"Sir, this is real simple. If you want us to kill some Chinese targets, we have to have bombs. I hope I'm not going too fast for you," Wallace added.

"Go easy, Gus," Moore warned.

"Well, sir, maybe it just looks a little different in Washington, but where I'm sitting right now, I have missions, but not the tools to carry those missions out. So, you D.C. people can either send me the tools or rescind the missions. Your call, sir."

"We're working on it," the Chairman of the Joint Chiefs assured him.

Do I have any orders?" Mancuso asked the Secretary of Defense.

"Not at this time," Bretano sold CINCPAC.

"Sir, may I ask why? The TV says we're in a shooting war with China. Am I supposed to play or not?"

"We are considering the political ramifications," THUNDER explained.

"Excuse me, sir?"

"You heard me."

"Mr. Secretary, all I know about politics is voting every couple of years, but I have a lot of gray ships under my command, and they're technically known as *war*ships, and my country is at war." The frustration in Mancuso's voice was plain.

"Admiral, when the President decides what to do, you will find out. Until then, ready your command for action. It's going to happen. I'm just not sure when."

"Aye, aye, sir." Mancuso hung up and looked at his subordinates. "Political ramifications," he said. "I didn't think Ryan was like that."

"Sir," Mike Lahr soothed. "Forget 'political' and think 'psychological,' okay? Maybe Secretary Bretano just used the wrong word. Maybe the idea is to hit them when it'll do the most good—because we're messing with their heads, sir, remember?"

"You think so?"

"Remember who the Vice President is? He's one of us, Admiral. And President Ryan isn't a pussy, is he?"

"Well . . . no, not that I recall," CINCPAC said, remembering the first time he'd met the guy, and the shoot-out he'd had aboard *Red October.* No, Jack Ryan wasn't a pussy. "So, what do you suppose he's thinking?"

"The Chinese have a land war going on—air and land, anyway. Nothing's happening at sea. They may not expect anything to happen at sea. But they are surging some ships out, just to establish a defense line for the mainland. If we get orders to hit those ships, the purpose will be to make a psychological impact. So, let's plan along those lines, shall we? Meanwhile, we keep getting more assets in place."

"Right." Mancuso nodded and turned to face the wall. Pacific Fleet was nearly all west of the dateline now, and the Chinese had probably no clue where his ships were, but he knew about them. USS *Tucson* was camped out on *406,* the single PRC ballistic-missile submarine. It was known to the west as a "Xia" class SSBN, and his intelligence people disagreed on the sub's actual name, but "406" was the number painted on its sail, and that was how he thought of it. None of that mattered to Mancuso. The first shoot order he planned to issue would go to *Tucson*—to put that missile-armed sub at the bottom of the Pacific Ocean. He remembered that the PRC had nuclear-tipped missiles, and those in his area of responsibility would disappear as soon as he had authorization to deal with them. USS *Tucson* was armed with Mark 48 ADCAP fish, and they'd do the job on *that* target, assuming that he was right and President Ryan wasn't a pussy after all.

And so, Marshal Luo?" Zhang Han San asked.

"Things go well," he replied at once. "We crossed the Amur River with trivial losses, captured the Russian positions in a few hours, and are now driving north."

"Enemy opposition?"

"Light. Very light, in fact. We're starting to wonder if the Russians have any forces deployed in sector at all. Our intelligence suggests the presence of two mechanized divisions, but if they're there, they haven't advanced to establish contact with us. Our forces are racing forward, making better than thirty kilometers per day. I expect to see the gold mine in seven days."

"Is anything going badly?" Qian asked.

"Only in the air. The Americans have deployed fighters to Siberia, and as we all know, the Americans are very clever with their machines, especially the ones that fly. They have inflicted some losses on our fighter aircraft," the Defense Minister admitted.

"How large are the losses?"

"Total, over one hundred. We've gotten twenty-five or so of theirs in return, but the Americans are masters of aerial combat. Fortunately, their aircraft can do little to hinder the advance of our tanks, and, as you have doubtless noted, they have not attacked into our territory at all."

"Why is that, Marshal?" Fang asked.

"We are not certain," Luo answered, turning to the MSS chief. "Tan?"

"Our sources are not certain, either. The most likely explanation is that the Americans have made a political decision not to attack us directly, but merely to defend their Russian 'ally' in a pro forma way. I suppose there is also the consideration that they do not wish to take losses from our air defenses, but the main reason for their restraint is undoubtedly political."

Heads nodded around the table. It was indeed the most likely explanation for the American lack of action, and all of these men understood political considerations.

"Does this mean that they are measuring their action against us in such a way as to cause us minimal injury?" Tong Jie asked. It was so much the better for him, of course, since the Interior Ministry would have to deal with the internal dislocations that systematic attacks might cause.

"Remember what I said before," Zhang pointed out. "They *will* do business with us once we've secured our new territory. So, they already anticipate this. It seems plain that they will support their Russian friends, but only so much. What else are the Americans but mercenaries? This President Ryan, what was he?"

"He was a CIA spy, and by all accounts an effective one," Tan Deshi reminded them.

"No," Zhang disagreed. "He was a trader in stocks before he joined CIA, and then he was a stock trader again after he left—and whom does he bring into his cabinet? Winston, another hugely rich capitalist, a trader in stocks and securities, a typical American rich man. I tell you, money is the key to understanding these people. They do business. They have no political ideology, except to fatten their purses. To do that, you try not to make blood enemies, and now, here, with us, they do not try to anger us too greatly. I tell you, I understand these people."

"Perhaps," Qian said. "But what if there are objective circumstances which prevent more aggressive action?"

"Then why is their navy not taking action? Their navy is most formidable, but it does nothing, correct, Luo?"

"Not to this point, but we are wary of them," the marshal warned. He was a soldier, not a sailor, even though the PLAN did come under his command. "We have patrol aircraft looking for them, but so far we have not spotted anything. We know they are not in harbor, but that is all."

"They do nothing with their navy. They do nothing with their land forces. They sting us slightly with their air forces, but what is that? The buzzing of insects." Zhang dismissed the issue.

"How many have underestimated America, and this Ryan fellow, and done so to their misfortune?" Qian demanded. "Comrades, I tell you, this is a dangerous situation we are in. Perhaps we can succeed, all well and good if that comes to pass, but overconfidence can be any man's undoing."

"And overestimating one's enemy ensures that you will never do anything," Zhang Han San countered. "Did we get to where we are, did our country get to where we are, by timidity? The Long March was not made by cowards." He looked around the table, and no one summoned the character to argue with him.

"So, things go well in Russia?" Xu asked the Defense Minister.

"Better than the plan," Luo assured them all.

"Then we proceed," the Premier decided for them all, once others had made the real decisions. The meeting soon adjourned, and the ministers went their separate ways.

"Fang?"

The junior Minister-Without-Portfolio turned to see Qian Kun coming after him in the corridor. "Yes, my friend?"

"The reason the Americans have not taken firmer action is that they act at the end of a single railroad to move them and their supplies. This takes time. They have not dropped bombs on us, probably, because they don't have any. And where does Zhang get this rubbish about American ideology?"

"He is wise in the ways of international affairs," Fang replied.

"Is he? Is he really? Is he not the one who tricked the Japanese into commencing a war with America? And why—so that we and they could seize Siberia. And then did he not quietly support Iran and their attempt to seize the Saudi kingdom? And why? So that we could then use the Muslims as a hammer to beat Russia into submission—so that we could seize Siberia. Fang, all he thinks about is Siberia. He wishes to see it under our flag before he dies. Perhaps he wishes to have his ashes buried in a golden urn, like the emperors," Qian hissed. "He's an adventurer, and those men come to bad ends."

"Except those who succeed," Fang suggested.

"How many of them succeed, and how many die before a stone wall?" Qian shot back. "I say the Americans will strike us, and strike us hard once their forces are assembled. Zhang follows his own political vision, not facts, not reality. He may lead our country to its doom."

"Are the Americans so formidable as that?"

"If they are not, Fang, why does Tan spend so much of his time trying to steal their inventions? Don't you remember what America did to Japan and Iran? They are like the wizards of legend. Luo tells us that they've savaged our air force. How often has he told us how formidable our fighters are? All the money we spent on those wonderful aircraft, and the Americans slaughter them like hogs fattened for market! Luo claims we've gotten twenty-five of theirs. He *claims* only twenty-five. More likely we've gotten one or two! Against over a hundred losses, but Zhang tells us the Americans don't want to challenge us. Oh, really? What held them back from smashing Japan's military, and then annihilating Iran's?"

Qian paused for breath. "I fear this, Fang. I fear what Zhang and Luo have gotten us into."

"Even if you are right, what can we do to stop it?" the minister asked.

"Nothing," Qian admitted. "But *someone* must speak the truth. *Someone* must warn of the danger that lies before us, if we are to have a country left at the end of this misbegotten adventurism."

"Perhaps so. Qian, you are as ever a voice of reason and prudence. We will speak more," Fang promised, wondering how much of the man's words was alarmism, and how much was good sense. He'd been a brilliant administrator of the state railroads, and therefore was a man with a firm grasp on reality.

Fang had known Zhang for most of his adult life. He was a highly skilled player on the political stage, and a brilliantly gifted manipulator of people. But Qian was asking if those talents translated into a correct perception of reality, and did he *really* understand America and Americans—and most of all, this Ryan fellow? Or was he just forcing oddly-shaped pegs into the slots he'd engraved in his own mind? Fang admitted that he didn't know, and more to the point, didn't know the answers to the implicit questions. He did not know himself whether Zhang was right or not. And he really should. But who might? Tan of the Ministry of State Security? Shen of the Foreign Ministry? Who else? Certainly not Premier Xu. All he did was to confirm the consensus achieved by others, or to repeat the words spoken into his ear by Zhang.

Fang walked to his office thinking about all these things, trying to organize his thoughts. Fortunately, he had a system for achieving that.

It started in Memphis, the headquarters of Federal Express. Faxes and telexes arrived simultaneously, telling the company that its wide-body cargo jets were being taken into federal service under the terms of a Phase I call-up of the Civilian Reserve Air Fleet. That meant that all freight-capable aircraft that the federal government had helped to finance (that was nearly all of them, because no commercial bank could compete with Washington when it came to financing things) were now being taken, along with their crews, under the control of the Air Mobility Command. The notice wasn't welcome, but neither was it much of a surprise. Ten minutes later came follow-up messages telling the aircraft where to go, and soon thereafter they started rolling. The flight crews, the majority of them military-trained, wondered where their ultimate destinations were, sure that they'd be surprising ones. The pilots would not be disappointed in this.

FedEx would have to make do with its older narrow-body aircraft, like the venerable Boeing 727s with which the company had gotten started two decades earlier. That, the dispatchers knew, would be a stretch, but they had assistance agreements with the airlines, which they would now activate in order to try to keep up with the continuing shipment of legal documents and live lobsters all over America.

Just how inefficient is it?" Ryan asked.

"Well, we can deliver one day's worth of bombs in three days' worth of flying—maybe two if we stretch things a little, but that's as good as it's going to get," Moore told him. "Bombs are heavy things, and getting them around uses up a lot of jet fuel. General Wallace has a nice list of targets to service, but to do that he needs bombs."

"Where are the bombs going to come from?"

"Andersen Air Force Base on Guam has a nice pile," Moore said. "Ditto Elmendorf in Alaska, and Mountain Home in Idaho. Various other places. It's not so much a question of time and distance as of weight. Hell, the Russian base he's using at Suntar is plenty big for his purposes. We just have to get the bombs to him, and I've just shunted a lot of Air Force lifters to Germany to start loading First Armored's aviation assets to where Diggs is. That's going to take four days of nonstop flying."

"What about crew rest?" Jackson asked.

"What?" Ryan looked up.

"It's a Navy thing, Jack. The Air Force has union rules on how much they can fly. Never had those rules out on the boats," Robby explained. "The C-5 has a bunk area for people to sleep. I was just being facetious." He didn't apologize. It was late—actually "early" was the correct adjective—and nobody in the White House was getting much sleep.

For his part, Ryan wanted a cigarette to help him deal with the stress, but Ellen Sumter was home and in bed, and no one on night duty in the White House smoked, to the best of his knowledge. But that was the wimp part of his character speaking, and he knew it. The president rubbed his face with his hands and looked over at the clock. He had to get some sleep.

It's late, Honey Bunny," Mary Pat said to her husband.

"I never would have guessed. Is that why my eyes keep wanting to close?"

There was, really, no reason for them to be here. CIA had little in the way of assets in the PRC. SORGE was the only one of value. The rest of the intelligence community, DIA and NSA, each of them larger than the Central Intelligence Agency in terms of manpower, didn't have any directly valuable human sources either, though NSA was doing its utmost to tap in on Chinese communications. They were even listening in on cell phones through their constellation of geosynchronous ferret satellites, downloading all of the "take" through the Echelon system and then forwarding the "hits" to human linguists for full translation and evaluation. They were getting some material, but not all that much. SORGE was the gemstone of the collection, and both Edward and Mary Patricia Foley were really staying up late to await the newest installment in Minister Fang's personal diary. The Chinese Politburo was meeting every day, and Fang was a dedicated diarist, not to mention a man who enjoyed the physical attractions of his female staff. They were even reading significance into the less regular writings of WARBLER, who mainly committed to her computer his sexual skills, occasionally enough to make Mary Pat blush. Being an intelligence officer was often little different from being a paid voyeur, and the staff psychiatrist translated all of the prurient stuff into what was probably a very accurate personality profile, but to them it just meant that Fang was a dirty old man who happened to exercise a lot of political power.

"It's going to be another three hours at best," the DCI said.

"Yeah," his wife agreed.

"Tell you what . . ." Ed Foley rose off the couch, tossed away the cushions, and reached in to pull out the foldaway bed. It was marginally big enough for two.

"When the staff sees this, they'll wonder if we got laid tonight."

"Baby, I have a headache," the DCI reported.

CHAPTER 54

Probes and Pushes

Much of life in the military is mere adherence to Parkinson's Law, the supposition that work invariably expands to fill the time allocated for it. In this case, Colonel Dick Boyle arrived on the very first C-5B Galaxy, which, immediately upon rolling to a stop, lifted its nose "visor" door to disgorge the first of three UH-60A Blackhawk helicopters, whose crewmen just as immediately rolled it to a vacant piece of ramp to unfold the rotor blades, assure they were locked in place, and ready the aircraft for flight after the usual safety checks. By that time, the C-5B had refueled and rolled off into the sky to make room for the next Galaxy, this one delivering AH-64 Apache attack helicopters—in this case complete with weapons and other accoutrements for flying real missions against a real armed enemy.

Colonel Boyle busied himself with watching everything, even though he knew that his troops were doing their jobs as well as they could be done, and would do those jobs whether he watched and fussed over them or not. Perversely, what Boyle wanted to do was to fly to where Diggs and his staff were located, but he resisted the temptation because he felt he should be supervising people whom he'd trained to do their jobs entirely without supervision. That lasted three hours until he finally saw the logic of the situation and decided to be a commander rather than a shop supervisor, and lifted off for Chabarsovil. The flying was easy enough, and he preferred the medium-low clouds, because there had to be fighters about, and not all of them would be friendly. The GPS navigation system guided him to the right location, and the right location, it turned out, was a concrete helipad with soldiers standing around it. They were wearing the "wrong" uniform, a state of mind that Boyle knew he'd have to work on. One of them escorted Boyle into a building that looked like the Russian idea of a headquarters, and sure enough, it was.

"Dick, come on over," General Diggs called. The helicopter commander saluted as he approached.

"Welcome to Siberia, Dick," Marion Diggs said in greeting.

"Thank you, sir. What's the situation?"

"Interesting," the general replied. "This is General Bondarenko. He's the theater commander." Boyle saluted again. "Gennady, this is Colonel Boyle, who commands my aviation brigade. He's pretty good."

"What's the air situation, sir?" Boyle asked Diggs.

"The Air Force is doing a good job on their fighters so far."

"What about Chinese helicopters?"

"They do not have many," another Russian officer said. "I am Colonel Aliyev, Andrey Petrovich, theater operations. The Chinese do not have many helicopters. We've only seen a few, mainly scouts."

"No troop carriers? No staff transport?"

"No," Aliyev answered. "Their senior officers prefer to move around in tracked vehicles. They are not married to helicopters as you Americans are."

"What do you want me to do, sir?" Boyle asked Diggs.

"Take Tony Turner to Chita. That's the railhead we're going to be using. We need to get set up there."

"Drive the tracks in from there, eh?" Boyle looked at the map.

"That's the plan. There are closer points, but Chita has the best facilities to off-load our vehicles, so our friends tell us."

"What about gas?"

"The place you landed is supposed to have sizable underground fuel tanks."

"More than you will need," Aliyev confirmed. Boyle thought that was quite a promise.

"And ordnance?" Boyle asked. "We've got maybe two days' worth on the C-5s so far. Six complete loads for my Apaches, figuring three missions per day."

"Which version of the Apache?" Aliyev asked.

"Delta, Colonel. We've got the Longbow radar."

"Everything works?" the Russian asked.

"Colonel, not much sense bringing them if they don't," Boyle replied, with a raised eyebrow. "What about secure quarters for my people?"

"At the base where you landed, there will be secure sleeping quarters for your aviators—bombproof shelters. Your maintenance people will be housed in barracks."

Boyle nodded. It was the same everywhere. The weenies who built things acted as if pilots were more valuable than the people who maintained the aircraft. And so they were, until the aircraft needed repairs, at which point the pilot was as useful as a cavalryman without a horse.

"Okay, General. I'll take Tony to this Chita place and then I'm going back to see to my people's needs. I could sure use one of Chuck Garvey's radios."

"He's outside. Grab one on your way."

"Okay, sir. Tony, let's get moving," he said to the chief of staff.

"Sir, as soon as we get some infantry in, I want to put security on those fueling points," Masterman said. "Those places need protecting."

"I can give you what you need," Aliyev offered.

"Fine by me," Masterman responded. "How many of those secure radios did Garvey bring?"

"Eight, I think. Two are gone already," General Diggs warned. "Well, there'll be more on the train. Go tell Boyle to send two choppers here for our needs."

"Right." Masterman ran for the door.

The ministers all had offices and, as in every other such office in the world, the cleanup crews came in, in this case about ten every night. They picked up all sorts of trash, from candy wrappers to empty cigarette packs to papers, and the latter went into special burn-bags. The janitorial staff was not particularly smart, but they had had to pass background checks and go through security briefings that were heavy on intimidation. They were not allowed to discuss their jobs with anyone, not even a spouse, and not *ever* to reveal what they saw in the wastebaskets. In fact, they never thought much about it—they were less interested in the thoughts or ideas of the Politburo members than they were in the weather forecasts. They'd rarely even seen the ministers whose offices they cleaned, and none of the crew had ever so much as spoken a single word to any of them; they just tried to be invisible on those rare occasions when they saw one of the godlike men who ruled their nation. Maybe a submissive bow, which was not even acknowledged by so much as a look, because they were mere furniture, menials who did peasants' work because, as peasants, that was all they were suited for. The peasants knew what computers were, but such machines were not for the use of such men as they were, and the janitorial staff knew it.

And so when one of the computers made a noise while a cleaner was in the office, he took no note of it. Well, it seemed odd that it should whir when the screen was dark, but why it did what it did was a mystery to him, and he'd never even been so bold as to touch the thing. He didn't even dust the keyboard as he cleaned the desktop—no, he always avoided the keys.

And so, he heard the whir begin, continue for a few seconds, then stop, and he paid no mind to it.

Mary Pat Foley opened her eyes when the sun started casting shadows on her husband's office wall, and rubbed her eyes reluctantly. She checked her watch. Seven-twenty. She was usually up long before this—but she usually didn't go to bed after four in the morning. Three hours of sleep would probably have to do. She stood and headed into Ed's private washroom. It had a shower, like hers. She'd make use of her own shortly, and for the moment settled for some water splashed on her face and a reluctant look in the mirror that resulted in a grimace at what the look revealed.

The Deputy Director (Operations) of the Central Intelligence Agency shook her head, and then her entire body to get the blood moving, and then put her blouse on. Finally, she shook her husband's shoulder.

"Out of the hutch, Honey Bunny, before the foxes get you."

"We still at war?" the DCI asked from behind closed eyes.

"Probably. I haven't checked yet." She paused for a stretch and slipped her feet into her shoes. "I'm going to check my e-mail."

"Okay, I'll call downstairs for breakfast," Ed told her.

"Oatmeal. No eggs. Your cholesterol is too high," Mary Pat observed.

"Yeah, baby," he grumbled in submissive reply.

"That's a good Honey Bunny." She kissed him and headed out.

Ed Foley made his bathroom call, then sat at his desk and lifted the phone to call the executive cooking staff. "Coffee. Toast. Three-egg omelet, ham, and hash browns." Cholesterol or not, he had to get his body working.

You've got mail," the mechanical voice said.

"Great." The DDO breathed. She downloaded it, going through the usual procedures to save and print, but rather more slowly this morning because she was groggy and therefore mistake-prone. That sort of thing made her slow down and be extra careful, something she'd learned to do as the mother of a newborn. And so in four minutes instead of the usual two, she had a printed hard copy of the latest SORGE feed from Agent SONGBIRD. Six pages of relatively small ideographs. Then she lifted the phone and punched the speed-dial button for Dr. Sears.

"Yes?"

"This is Mrs. Foley. We got one."

"On the way, Director." She had some coffee before he arrived, and the taste, if not the effect of the caffeine, helped her face the day.

"In early?" she asked.

"Actually I slept in last night. We need to improve the selection on the cable TV," he told her, hoping to lighten the day a little. One look at her eyes told him how likely that was.

"Here." She handed the sheets across. "Coffee?"

"Yes, thank you." His eyes didn't leave the page as his hand reached out for the Styrofoam cup. "This is good stuff today."

"Oh?"

"Yeah, it's Fang's account of a Politburo discussion of how the war's going . . . they're trying to analyze our actions . . . yeah, that's about what I'd expect . . ."

"Talk to me, Dr. Sears," Mary Pat ordered.

"You're going to want to get George Weaver in on this, too, but what he's going to say is that they're projecting their own political outlook onto us generally, and onto President Ryan in particular . . . yeah, they're saying that we are not hitting them hard for political reasons, that they think we don't want to piss them off too much . . ." Sears took a long sip of coffee. "This is really good stuff. It tells us what their political leadership is thinking, and what they're thinking isn't very accurate." Sears looked up. "They misunderstand us worse than we misunderstand them, Director, even at this level. They see President Ryan's motivation as a strictly political calculation. Zhang says that he's laying back so that we can do business with them, after they consolidate their control over the Russian oil and gold fields."

"What about their advance?"

"They say—that is, Marshal Luo says—that things are going according to plan, that they're surprised at the lack of Russian opposition, and also surprised that we haven't struck any targets within their borders."

"That's because we don't have any bombs over there yet. Just found that out myself. We're having to fly the bombs in so that we can drop them."

"Really? Well, they don't know that yet. They think it's deliberate inaction on our part."

"Okay, get me a translation. When will Weaver get in?"

"Usually about eight-thirty."

"Go over this with him as soon as he arrives."

"You bet." Sears took his leave.

Bedding down for the night?" Aleksandrov asked.

"So it would seem, Comrade Captain," Buikov answered. He had his binoculars on the Chinese. The two command-reconnaissance vehicles were together, which only seemed to happen when they secured for the night. It struck both men as odd that they confined their activities to daylight, but that wasn't a bad thing for the Russian watchers, and even soldiers needed their sleep. More than most, in fact, both of the Russians would have said. The stress and strain of keeping track of the enemies of their country—and doing so *within* their own borders—were telling on both of them.

The Chinese drill was thorough, but predictable. The two command tracks were together. The others were spread out, mainly in front of them, but one three hundred meters behind to secure their rear. The crews of each track stayed together as a unit. Each broke out a small petrol stove for cooking their rice—*probably rice,* the Russians all thought. And they settled down to get four or five hours of sleep before waking, cooking breakfast, and moving out before dawn. Had they not been enemies, their adherence to so demanding a drill might have excited admiration. Instead, Buikov found himself wondering if he could get two or three of their BRMs to race up on the invaders and immolate them with the 30-mm rapid-fire cannons on their tracked carriers. But Aleksandrov would never allow it. You could always depend on officers to deny the sergeants what they wanted to do.

The captain and his sergeant walked back north to their track, leaving three other scouts to keep watch on their "guests," as Aleksandrov had taken to calling them.

"So, Sergeant, how are you feeling?" the officer asked in a quiet voice.

"Some sleep will be good." Buikov looked back. There was now a ridgeline in addition to the trees between him and the Chinks. He lit a cigarette and let out a long, relaxed breath. "This is harder duty than I expected it to be."

"Oh?"

"Yes, Comrade Captain. I always thought we could kill our enemies. Baby-sitting them is very stressful."

"That is so, Boris Yevgeniyevich, but remember that if we do our job properly, then Division will be able to kill more than just one or two. We are their eyes, not their teeth."

"As you say, Comrade Captain, but it is like making a movie of the wolf instead of shooting him."

"The people who make good wildlife movies win awards, Sergeant."

The odd thing about the captain, Buikov thought, *was that he was always trying to reason with you.* It was actually rather endearing, as if he was trying to be a teacher rather than an officer.

"What's for dinner?"

"Beef and black bread, Comrade Captain. Even some butter. But no vodka," the sergeant added sourly.

"When this is over, I will allow you to get good and drunk, Boris Yevgeniyevich," Aleksandrov promised.

"If we live that long, I will toast your health." The track was where they'd left it, and the crew had spread out the camouflage netting. *One thing about this officer,* Buikov thought, *he got the men to do their duty without much in the way of complaint. The same sort of good comradely solidarity my grandfather spoke about, as he told his endless tales of killing Germans on the way to Vienna, just like in all the movies,* the sergeant thought.

The black bread was canned, but tasty, and the beef, cooked on their own small petrol heater, wasn't so bad as to choke a dog. About the time they finished, Sergeant Grechko appeared. He was the commander of the unit's #3 BRM, and he was carrying . . .

"Is that what I think it is?" Buikov asked. "Yuriy Andreyevich, you are a comrade!"

It was a half-liter bottle of vodka, the cheapest "ВОДКА" brand, with a foil top that tore off and couldn't be resealed.

"Whose idea is this?" the captain demanded.

"Comrade Captain, it is a cold night, and we are Russian soldiers, and we need something to help us relax," Grechko said. "It's the only bottle in the company, and one slug each will not harm us, I think," the sergeant added reasonably.

"Oh, all right." Aleksandrov extended his metal cup, and received perhaps sixty grams. He waited for the rest of his crew to get theirs, and saw that the bottle was empty. They all drank together, and sure enough, it tasted just fine to be Russian soldiers out in the woods, doing their duty for their Motherland.

"We'll have to refuel tomorrow," Grechko said.

"There will be a fuel truck waiting for us, forty kilometers north at the burned-down sawmill. We'll go up there one at a time, and hope our Chinese guests do not get overly ambitious in their advance."

That must be your Captain Aleksandrov," Major Tucker said. "Fourteen hundred meters from the nearest Chinese. That's pretty close," the American observed.

"He's a good boy," Aliyev said, "Just reported in. The Chinese follow their drill with remarkable exactitude. And the main body?"

"Twenty-five miles back—forty kilometers or so. They're laagering in for the night, too, but they're actually building campfires, like they want us to know where they are." Tucker worked the mouse to show the encampments. The display was green-on-green now. The Chinese armored vehicles showed as bright spots, especially from the engines, which glowed from residual heat.

"This is amazing," Aliyev said in frank admiration.

"We decided back around the end of the 1970s that we could play at night when everybody else can't. It took a while to develop the technology, but it by-God works, Colonel. All we need now is some Smart Pigs."

"What?"

"You'll see, Colonel. You'll see," Tucker promised. Best of all, this "take" came from Grace Kelly, and she *did* have a laser designator plugged in to the fuselage, tooling along now at 62,000 feet and looking down with her thermal-imaging cameras. Under Tucker's guidance, the UAV kept heading south, to continue the catalog of the Chinese units advancing into Siberia. There were sixteen ribbon bridges on the Amur River now, and a few north of there, but the really vulnerable points were around Harbin, well to the south, inside Chinese territory. Lots of railroad bridges between there and Bei'an, the terminus of the railroad lifeline to the People's Liberation Army. Grace Kelly saw a lot of trains, mainly diesel engines, but even some old coal-burning steam engines that had come out of storage in order to keep the weapons and supplies coming north. Most interesting of all was the recently built traffic circle, where tank cars were unloading something, probably diesel fuel, into what appeared to be a pipeline that PLAA engineers were working very hard to extend north. That was something they'd copied from America. The U.S. and British armies had done the same thing from Normandy east to the front in late 1944, and *that,* Tucker knew, was a target worthy of note. Diesel fuel wasn't just the food of a field army. It was the very air it breathed.

There were huge numbers of idle men about. Laborers, probably, there to repair damaged tracking, and the major bridging points had SAM and FLAK batteries in close attendance. So, Joe Chink knew that the bridges were important, and he was doing his best to guard them.

For what good that would do, Tucker thought. He got on the satellite radio to talk things over with the crew up at Zhigansk, where General Wallace's target book was being put together. The crunchies on the ground were evidently worried about taking on the advancing People's Liberation Army, but to Major Tucker, it all looked like a collection of targets. For point targets, he wanted J-DAMs, and for area targets, some smart pigs, the J-SOWs, and then Joe Chink was going to take one on the chin, and probably, like all field armies, this one had a glass jaw. If you could just hit it hard enough.

The Russians on the ground had no idea what FedEx was, and were more than a little surprised that any private, nongovernment corporation could actually own something as monstrous as a Boeing 747F freighter aircraft.

For their part, the flight crews, mainly trained by the Navy or Air Force, had never expected to see Siberia except maybe through the windows of a B-52H strategic bomber. The runways were unusually bumpy, worse than most American airports, but there was an army of people on the ground, and when the swinging door on the nose came up, the ground crews waved the forklifts in to start collecting the palletized cargo. The flight crews didn't leave the aircraft. Fueling trucks came up and connected the four-inch hoses to the proper nozzle points and started refilling the capacious tanks so that the aircraft could leave as soon as possible, to clear the ramp space. Every 747F had a bunking area for the spare pilots who'd come along for the ride. They didn't even get a drink, those who'd sleep for the return flight, and they had to eat the boxed lunches they'd been issued at Elmendorf on the outbound flight. In all, it took fifty-seven minutes to unload the hundred tons of bombs, which was scarcely enough for ten of the F-15Es parked at the far end of the ramp, but that was where the forklifts headed.

Is that a fact?" Ryan observed.

"Yes, Mr. President," Dr. Weaver replied. "For all their sophistication, these people can be very insular in their thinking, and as a practical matter, we are all guilty of projecting our own ways of thinking into other people."

"But I have people like you to advise me. Who advises them?" Jack asked.

"They have some good ones. Problem is, their Politburo doesn't always listen."

"Yeah, well, I've seen that problem here, too. Is this good news or bad news, people?"

"Potentially it could be both, but let's remember that we understand them now a lot better than they understand us," Ed Foley told those present. "That gives us a major advantage, if we play our cards intelligently."

Ryan leaned back and rubbed his eyes. Robby Jackson wasn't in much better shape, though he'd slept about four hours in the Lincoln Bedroom (unlike President Lincoln—it was called that simply because a picture of the sixteenth President hung on the wall). The good Jamaican coffee helped everyone at least simulate consciousness.

"I'm surprised that their Defense Minister is so narrow," Robby thought aloud, his eyes tracing over the SORGE dispatch. "You pay the senior operators to be big-picture thinkers. When operations go as well as the one they're running, you get suspicious. I did, anyway."

"Okay, Robby, you used to be God of Operations across the river. What do you recommend?" Jack asked.

"The idea in a major operation is always to play with the other guy's head. To lead him down the path you want him to go, or to get inside his decision cycle, just prevent him from analyzing the data and making a decision. I think we can do that here."

"How?" Arnie van Damm asked.

"The common factor of every successful military plan in history is this: You show the guy what he expects and hopes to see, and then when he thinks he's got the world by the ass, you cut his legs off in one swipe." Robby leaned back, holding court for once. "The smart move is to let them keep going for a few more days, make it just seem easier and easier for them while we build up our capabilities, and then when we hit them, we land on them like the San Francisco earthquake—no warning at all, just the end of the fuckin' world hits 'em. Mickey, what's their most vulnerable point?"

General Moore had that answer: "It's always logistics. They're burning maybe nine hundred tons of diesel fuel a day to keep those tanks and tracks moving north. They have a full five thousand engineers working like beavers running a pipeline to keep up with their lead elements. We cut that, and they can make up some of the shortfall with fuel trucks, but not all of it—"

"And we use the Smart Pig to take care of those," Vice President Jackson finished.

"That's one way to handle it," General Moore agreed.

"Smart Pig?" Ryan asked.

Robby explained, concluding: "We've been developing this and a few other tricks for the last eight years. I spent a month out at China Lake a few years ago with the prototype. It works, if we have enough of them."

"Gus Wallace has that at the top of his Christmas list."

"The other trick is the political side," Jackson concluded.

"Funny, I have an idea for that. How is the PRC presenting this war to its people?"

It was Professor Weaver's turn: "They're saying that the Russians provoked a border incident—same thing Hitler did with Poland in 1939. The Big Lie technique. They've used it before. Every dictatorship has. It works if you control what your people see."

"What's the best weapon for fighting a lie?" Ryan asked.

"The truth, of course," Arnie van Damm answered for the rest. "But they control their news distribution. How do we get the truth to their population?"

"Ed, how is the SORGE data coming out?"

"Over the 'Net, Jack. So?"

"How many Chinese citizens own computers?"

"Millions of them—the number's really jumped in the past couple of years. That's why they're ripping that patent off Dell Computer that we made a stink about in the trade talks and—oh, yeah . . ." Foley looked up with a smile. "I like it."

"That could be dangerous," Weaver warned.

"Dr. Weaver, there's no safe way to fight a war," Ryan said in reply. "This isn't a negotiation between friends. General Moore?"

"Yes, sir."

"Get the orders out."

"Yes, sir."

"The only question is, will it work?"

"Jack," Robby Jackson said, "It's like with baseball. You play the games to find out who the best is."

The first reinforcing division to arrive at Chita was the 201st. The trains pulled into the built-for-the-purpose offloading sidings. The flatcars had been designed (and built in large numbers) to transport tracked military vehicles. To that end, flip-down bridging ramps were located at each end of every single car, and when those were tossed down in place, the tanks could drive straight off to the concrete ramps to where every train had backed up. It was a little demanding—the width of the cars was at best marginal for the tank tracks—but the drivers of each vehicle kept their path straight, breathing a small sigh of relief when they got to the concrete. Once on the ground, military police troops, acting as traffic cops, directed the armored vehicles to assembly areas. The 201st Motor Rifle Division's commander and his staff were there already, of course, and the regimental officers got their marching orders, telling them what roads to take northeast to join Bondarenko's Fifth Army, and by joining it, to make it a real field army rather than a theoretical expression on paper.

The 201st, like the follow-on divisions, the 80th, 34th, and 94th, were equipped with the newest Russian hardware, and were at their full TO&E. Their immediate mission was to race north and east to get in front of the advancing Chinese. It would be quite a race. There weren't many roads in this part of Russia, and what roads there were here were unpaved gravel, which suited the tracked vehicles. The problem would be diesel fuel, because there were few gas stations for the trucks which ran the roads in peacetime pursuits, and so the 201st had requisitioned every tanker truck its officers could locate, and even that might not be enough, the logisticians all worried, not that they had much choice in the matter. If they could get their tanks there, then they'd fight them as pillboxes if it came to that.

About the only thing they had going for them was the network of telephone lines, which enabled them to communicate without using radios. The entire area was under the strictest possible orders for radio silence, to deny all conceivable knowledge to the enemy; and the air forces in the area, American and Russian, were tasked to eliminate all tactical reconnaissance aircraft that Chinese would be sending about. So far, they'd been successful. A total of seventeen J-6 and -7 aircraft, thought to be the reconnaissance variants of their classes, had been "splashed" short of Chita.

The Chinese problem with reconnaissance was confirmed in Paris, of all places. SPOT, the French corporation which operated commercial photosatellites, had received numerous requests for photos of Siberia, and while many of them came from seemingly legitimate western businesses, mainly news agencies, all had been summarily denied. Though not as good as American reconnaissance satellites, the SPOT birds were good enough to identify all the trains assembled at Chita.

And since the People's Republic of China still had a functioning embassy in Moscow, the other concern was that their Ministry of State Security had Russian nationals acting as paid spies, feeding data to Russia's new enemy. Those individuals about whom the Russian Federal Security Service had suspicions were picked up and questioned, and those in custody were interrogated vigorously.

This number included Klementi Ivanovich Suvorov.

"You were in the service of an enemy country," Pavel Yefremov observed. "You killed for a foreign power, and you conspired to kill our country's president. We know all this. We've had you under surveillance for some time now. We have this." He held up a photocopy of the one-time pad recovered from the dead-drop on the park bench. "You may talk now, or you may be shot. It is your life at risk, not mine."

In the movies, this was the part where the suspect was supposed to say defiantly, "You're going to kill me anyway," except that Suvorov had no more wish to die than anyone else. He loved life as much as any man, and he'd never expected to be caught any more than the most foolish of street criminals did. If anything, he'd expected arrest even less than one of those criminals, because he knew how intelligent and clever he was, though this feeling had understandably deflated over the last few days.

The outlook of Klementi Ivan'ch Suvorov was rather bleak at the moment. He *was* KGB-trained, and he knew what to expect—a bullet in the head—unless he could give his interrogators something sufficiently valuable for them to spare his life, and at the moment even life in a labor camp of strict regime was preferable to the alternative.

"Have you truly arrested Kong?"

"We told you that before, but, no, we have not. Why tip them off that we've penetrated their operation?" Yefremov said honestly.

"Then you can use me against them."

"How might we do that?" the FSS officer asked.

"I can tell them that the operation they propose is going forward, but that the situation in Siberia wrecked my chance to execute it in a timely fashion."

"And if Kong cannot leave their embassy—we have it guarded and isolated now, of course—how would you get that information to him?"

"By electronic mail. Yes, you can monitor their landlines, but to monitor their cellular phones is more difficult. There's a backup method for me to communicate with him electronically."

"And the fact that you haven't made use of it so far will not alert them?"

"The explanation is simple. My Spetsnaz contact was frightened off by the outbreak of hostilities, and so was I."

"But we've already checked your electronic accounts."

"Do you think they are all written down?" He tapped the side of his head. "Do you think I am totally foolish?"

"Go on, make your proposal."

"I will propose that I can go forward with the mission. I require them to authorize it by a signal—the way they set the shades in their windows, for example."

"And for this?"

"And for this I will not be executed," the traitor suggested.

"I see," Yefremov said quietly. He would have been perfectly content to shoot the traitor right here and now, but it might be politically useful to go forward with his proposal. He'd kick that one upstairs.

The bad part about watching them was that you had to anticipate everything they did, and that meant that they got to have more sleep, about an hour's worth, Aleksandrov figured, and no more than that only because they were predictable. He'd had his morning tea. Sergeant Buikov had enjoyed two morning cigarettes with his, and now they lay prone on wet dew-dampened ground, with their binoculars to their eyes. The Chinese had also had soldiers out of their tracks all night, set about a hundred meters away from them, so it seemed. *They weren't very adventurous,* the captain thought. He would have spread his sentries much farther out, at least half a kilometer, in pairs with radios to go with their weapons. For that matter, he would have set up a mortar in the event that they spotted something dangerous. But the fox and the gardener seemed to be both conservative and confident, which was an odd combination of characteristics.

But their morning drill was precise. The petrol heaters came out for tea—*probably tea,* they all figured—and whatever it was that they had for breakfast. Then the camouflage nets came down. The outlying sentries came in and reported in person to their officers, and everyone mounted up. The first hop on their tracks was a short one, not even half a kilometer, and again the foot-scouts dismounted and moved forward, then quickly reported back for the second, much longer morning frog leap forward.

"Let's move, Sergeant," Aleksandrov ordered, and together they ran to their BRM for their first trek into the woods for their own third installment of frog leap backwards.

There they go again," Major Tucker said, after getting three whole hours of sleep on a thin mattress four feet from the Dark Star terminal. It was Ingrid Bergman up again, positioned so that she could see both the reconnaissance element and main body of the Chinese army. "You know, they really stick to the book, don't they?"

"So it would seem," Colonel Tolkunov agreed.

"So, going by that, tonight they'll go to about here." Tucker made a green mark on the acetate-covered map. "That puts them at the gold mine day after tomorrow. Where do you plan to make your stand?" the major asked.

"That depends on how quickly the Two Zero One can get forward."

"Gas?" Tucker asked.

"Diesel fuel, but, yes, that is the main problem with moving so large a force."

"Yeah, with us it's bombs."

"When will you begin to attack Chinese targets?" Tolkunov asked.

"Not my department, Colonel, but when it happens, you'll see it here, live and in color."

Ryan had gotten two hours of nap in the afternoon, while Arnie van Damm covered his appointments (the Chief of Staff needed his sleep, too, but like most people in the White House, he put the President's needs before his own), and now he was watching TV, the feed from Ingrid Bergman.

"This is amazing," he observed. "You could almost get on the phone and tell a guy where to go with his tank."

"We try to avoid that, sir," Mickey Moore said at once. In Vietnam it had been called the "squad leader in the sky" when battalion commanders had directed sergeants on their patrols, not always to the enlisted men's benefit. The miracle of modern communications could also be a curse, with the expected effect that the people in harm's way would ignore their radios or just turn the damned things off until they had something to say themselves.

Ryan nodded. He'd been a second lieutenant of Marines once, and though it hadn't been for long, he remembered it as demanding work for a kid just out of college.

"Do the Chinese know we're doing this?"

"Not as far as we can tell. If they did, they'd sure as hell try to take the Dark Star down, and we'd notice if they tried. That's not easy, though. They're damned near invisible on radar, and tough to spot visually, so the Air Force tells me."

"Not too many fighters can reach sixty thousand feet, much less cruise up there," Robby agreed. "It's a stretch even for a Tomcat." His eyes, too, were locked on the screen. No officer in the history of military operations had ever had a capability akin to this, not even two percent of it, Jackson was sure. Most of war-fighting involved finding the enemy so that you knew where to kill him. These new things made it like watching a Hollywood movie—and if the Chinese knew they were there, they'd freak. Considerable efforts had been designed into Dark Star to prevent that from happening. Their transmitters were directional, and locked onto satellites, instead of radiating outward in the manner of a normal radio. So, they might as well have been black holes up there, orbiting twelve miles over the battlefield.

"What's the important thing here?" Jack asked General Moore.

"Logistics, sir, always logistics. Told you this morning, sir, they're burning up a lot of diesel fuel, and replenishing that is a mother of a task. The Russians have the same problem. They're trying to race a fresh division north of the Chinese spearhead, to made a stand around Aldan, close to where the gold strike is. It's only even money they can make it, even over roads and without opposition. They have to move a lot of fuel, too, and the other problem for them is that it'll wear out the tracks on their vehicles. They don't have lowboy trailers like ours, and so their tanks have to do it all on their own. Tanks are a lot more delicate to operate than they look. Figure they'll lose a quarter to a third of their strength just from the approach march."

"Can they fight?" Jackson asked.

"They're using the T-80U. It would have given the M60A3 a good fight, but no, not as good as our first-flight M1, much less the M1A2, but against the Chinese M-90, call it an even match, qualitatively. It's just that the Chinese have a lot more of them. It comes down to training. The Russian divisions that they're sending into the fight are their best-trained and -equipped. Question is, are they good enough? We'll just have to see."

"And our guys?"

"They start arriving at Chita tomorrow morning. The Russians want them to assemble and move east-southeast. The operational concept is for them to stop the Chinese cold, and then we chop them off from their supplies right near the Amur River. It makes sense theoretically," Mickey Moore said neutrally, "and the Russians say they have all the fuel we'll need in underground bunkers that have been there for damned near fifty years. We'll see."

CHAPTER 55

Looks and Hurts

General Peng was all the way forward now, with the leading elements of his lead armored division, the 302nd. Things were going well for him—sufficiently well, in fact, that he was becoming nervous about it. *No opposition at all?* he asked himself. Not so much as a single rifle round, much less a barrage of artillery. Were the Russians totally asleep, totally devoid of troops in this sector? They had a full army group command section at Chabarsovil, commanded by that Bondarenko fellow, who was reported to be a competent, even a courageous, officer. But where the hell were his troops? Intelligence said that a complete Russian motor-rifle division was here, the 265th, and a Russian motor-rifle division was a superbly designed mechanized formation, with enough tanks to punch a hole in most things, and manned with enough infantry to hold any position for a long time. Theoretically. But where the hell was it? And where were the reinforcements the Russians had to be sending? Peng had asked for information, and the air force had supposedly sent photo-reconnaissance aircraft to look for his enemies, but with no result. He had expected to be mainly on his own for this campaign, but not *entirely* on his own. Fifty kilometers in advance of the 302nd Armored was a reconnaissance screen that had reported nothing but some tracks in the ground that might or might not have been fresh. The few helicopter flights that had gone out had reported nothing. They should have spotted *something,* but no, only some civilians, who for the most part got the hell out of the way and stayed there.

Meanwhile, his troops had crewed up this ancient railroad right-of-way, but it wasn't much worse than traveling along a wide gravel road. His only potential operational concern was fuel, but two hundred 10,000-liter fuel trucks were delivering an adequate amount from the pipeline the engineers were extending at a rate of forty kilometers per day from the end of the railhead on the far bank of the Amur. In fact, that was the most impressive feat of the war so far. Well behind him, engineer regiments were laying the pipe, then covering it under a meter of earth for proper concealment. The only things they couldn't conceal were the pumping stations, but they had the spare parts to build plenty more should they be destroyed.

No, Peng's only real concern was the location of the Russian Army. The dilemma was that either his intelligence was faulty, and there *were* no Russian formations in his area of interest, or it was accurate and the Russians were just running away and denying him the chance to engage and destroy them. But since when did Russians *not* fight for their land? Chinese soldiers surely would. And it just didn't fit with Bondarenko's reputation. None of this situation made sense. Peng sighed. *But battlefields were often that way,* he told himself. For the moment, he was on—actually slightly ahead of—schedule, and his first strategic objective, the gold mine, was three days away from his leading reconnaissance element. He'd never seen a gold mine before.

I'll be damned!" Pavel Petrovich said. "This is *my* land. No Chink's going to chase me off of it!"

"They are only three or four days away, Pasha."

"So? I have lived here for over fifty years. I'm not going to leave now." The old man was well to the left of defiant. The chief of the mining company had come personally to drive him out, and expected him to come willingly. But he'd misread the old man's character.

"Pasha, we can't leave you here in their way. This is their objective, the thing they invaded us to steal—"

"Then I shall *fight* for it!" he retorted. "I killed Germans, I've killed bears, I've killed wolves. Now, I will kill Chinese. I'm an old man, not an old *woman,* comrade!"

"Will you fight against enemy soldiers?"

"And why not?" Gogol asked. "This is *my* land. I know all its places.

I know where to hide, and I know how to shoot. I've killed soldiers before." He pointed to his wall. The old service rifle was there, and the mining chief could easily see the notches he'd cut on the stock with a knife, one for every German. "I can hunt wolves and bear. I can hunt men, too."

"You're too old to be a soldier. That's a young man's job."

"I need not be an athlete to squeeze a trigger, comrade, and I know these woods." To emphasize his words, Gogol stood and took down his old sniper rifle from the Great Patriotic War, leaving the new Austrian rifle. The meaning was clear. He'd fought with this arm before, and he was quite willing to do so again. Hanging on his wall still were a number of the gilded wolf skins, most of which had single holes in the head. He touched one, then looked back at his visitors. "I am a Russian. I will fight for my land."

The mining chief figured he'd buck this information up to the military. Maybe they could take him out. For himself, he had no particular desire to entertain the Chinese army, and so he took his leave. Behind him, Pavel Petrovich Gogol opened a bottle of vodka and enjoyed a snort. Then he cleaned his rifle and thought of old times.

The train terminal was well-designed for their purposes, Colonel Welch thought. Russian engineers might have designed things clunky, but they'd also designed them to work, and the layout here was a lot more efficient than it looked on first inspection. The trains reversed direction on what American railroaders called a wye—Europeans called it a turning triangle—which allowed trains to back up to any one of ten off-loading ramps, and the Russians were doing it with skill and aplomb. The big VL80T electric locomotive eased backwards, with the conductors on the last car holding the air-release valve to activate the brakes when they reached the ramp. When the trains stopped, the soldiers jumped from their passenger coaches and ran back to their individual vehicles to start them up and drive them off. It didn't take longer than thirty minutes to empty a train. That impressed Colonel Welch, who'd used the Auto Train to take his family to Disney World, and the off-loading procedure in Sanford, Florida, usually took an hour and a half or so. Then there was no further waiting. The big VL (Vladimir Lenin) engines immediately moved out for the return trip west to load up another ten thousand tons of train cars and cargo. It certainly appeared as though the Russians could make things happen when they had to.

"Colonel?" Welch turned to see a Russian major, who saluted crisply.

"Yes?"

"The first train with your personnel is due in four hours twenty minutes. We'll take them to the southern assembly area. There is fuel there if they need it, and then we have guides to direct them east."

"Very good."

"Until then, if you wish to eat, there is a canteen inside the station building."

"Thank you. We're okay at the moment." Welch walked over to where his satellite radio was set up, to get that information to General Diggs.

Colonel Bronco Winters now had seven red stars painted on the side panel of his F-15C, plus four of the now-defunct UIR flags. He could have painted on some marijuana or coca leaves as well, but that part of his life was long past, and those kills had been blacker than his uncle Ernie, who still lived in Harlem. So, he was a double-ace, and the Air Force hadn't had many of those on active duty in a very long time. He took his flight to what they had taken to calling Bear Station, on the western edge of the Chinese advance.

It was an Eagle station. There were now over a hundred F-16 fighters in Siberia, but they were mainly air-to-mud rather than air-to-air, and so the fighting part of the fighter mission was his department, while the -16 jocks grumbled about being second-class citizens. Which they were, as far as Colonel Winters thought. Damned little single-engine pukes.

Except for the F-16CGs. They were useful because they were dedicated to taking out enemy radars and SAM sites. The Siberian Air Force (so they now deemed themselves) hadn't done *any* air-to-mud yet. They had orders not to, which offended the guys whose idea of fun was killing crunchies on the ground instead of more manly pursuits. They didn't have enough bombs for a proper bombing campaign yet, and so they were coming up just to ride guard on the E-3Bs in case Joe Chink decided to go after them—it was a hard mission, but marginally doable, and Bronco was surprised that they hadn't made the attempt yet. It was a sure way to lose a lot of fighter planes, but they'd lost a bunch anyway, and why not lose them to a purpose . . . ?

"Boar Lead, this is Eagle Two, over."

"Boar Leader."

"We show something happening, numerous bandits one-four-five your position, angels three-three, range two hundred fifty miles, coming north at six hundred knots—make that count thirty-plus bandits, looks like they're coming right for us, Boar Lead," the controller on the AWACS reported.

"Roger, copy that. Boar, Lead," he told his flight of four. "Let's get our ears perked up."

"Two." "Three." "Four," the rest of his flight chimed in.

"Boar Leader, this is Eagle Two. The bandits just went supersonic, and they are heading right for us. Looks like they're not kidding. Vector right to course one-three-five and prepare to engage."

"Roger, Eagle. Boar Lead, come right to one-three-five."

"Two." "Three." "Four."

Winters checked his fuel first of all. He had plenty. Then he looked at his radar display for the picture transmitted from the AWACS, and sure enough, there was a passel of bandits inbound, like a complete ChiComm regiment of fighters. The bastards had read his mind.

"Damn, Bronco, this looks like a knife fight coming."

"Be cool, Ducky, we got better knives."

"You say so, Bronco," the other element leader answered.

"Let's loosen it up, people," Colonel Winters ordered. The flight of four F-15Cs separated into two pairs, and the pairs slipped apart as well so that each could cover the other, but a single missile could not engage both.

The display between his legs showed that the Chinese fighters were just over a hundred miles off now, and the velocity vectors indicated speeds of over eight hundred knots. Then the picture dirtied up some.

"Boar Lead, looks like they just dropped off tanks."

"Roger that." So, they'd burned off fuel to get altitude, and now they were committed to the battle with full internal fuel. That would give them better legs than usual, and they had closed to less than two hundred miles between them and the E-3B Sentry they clearly wanted to kill. There were thirty people on that converted 707, and Winters knew a lot of them. They'd worked together for years, mainly in exercises, and each controller on the Sentry had a specialty. Some were good at getting you to a tanker. Some were good at sending you out to hunt. Some were best at defending themselves against enemies. This third group would now take over. The Sentry crewmen would think this wasn't cricket, that it wasn't exactly fair to chase deliberately after a converted obsolete airliner . . . just because it acted as bird-dog for those who were killing off their fighter-pilot comrades. *Well, that's life,* Winters thought. But he wasn't going to give any of these bandits a free shot at another USAF aircraft.

Eighty miles now. "Skippy, follow me up," the colonel ordered.

"Roger, Lead." The two clawed up to forty thousand feet, so that the cold ground behind the targets would give a better contrast for their infrared seekers. He checked the radar display again. There had to be a good thirty of them, and that was a lot. If the Chinese were smart, they'd have two teams, one to engage and distract the American fighters, and the other to blow through after their primary target. He'd try to concentrate on the latter, but if the former group's pilots were competent, that might not be easy.

The warbling tone started in his headphones. The range was now sixty miles. *Why not now?* he asked himself. They were beyond visual range, but not beyond range of his AMRAAM missiles. Time to shoot 'em in the lips.

"Going Slammer," he called on the radio.

"Roger, Slammer," Skippy replied from half a mile to his right.

"Fox-One!" Winters called, as the first one leapt off the rails. The first Slammer angled left, seeking its designated target, one of the enemy's leading fighters. The closure speed between missile and target would be well over two thousand miles per hour. His eyes dropped to the radar display. His first missile appeared to hit—yes, the target blip expanded and started dropping. Number Eight. Time for another: "Fox-One!"

"Fox-One," his wingman called. Seconds later: "Kill!" Lieutenant Acosta called.

Winters's second missile somehow missed, but there wasn't time for wondering why. He had six more AMRAAMs, and he pickled four of them off in the next minute. By that time, he could see the inbound fighters. They were Shenyang J-8IIs, and they had radars and missiles, too. Winters flipped on his jammer pod, wondering if it would work or not, and wondering if their infrared missiles had all-aspect targeting like his Sidewinders. He'd probably find out soon, but first he fired off two 'winders. "Breaking right, Skippy."

"I'm with you, Bronco," Acosta replied.

Damn, Winters thought, *there are still at least twenty of the fuckers.* He headed down, speeding up as he went and calling for a vector.

"Boar Lead, Eagle, there's twenty-three of them left and they're still coming. Dividing into two elements. You have bandits at your seven o'clock and closing."

Winters reversed his turn and racked his head against the g-forces to spot it. Yeah, a J-8 all right, the Chinese two-engine remake of the MiG-21, trying to get position to launch on him—no, two of the bastards. He reefed the turn in tight, pulling seven gees, and after ten endless seconds, getting his nose on the targets. His left hand selected Sidewinder and he triggered two off.

The bandits saw the smoke trails of the missiles and broke apart, in opposite directions. One would escape, but both the heat-seekers locked on the guy to the right, and both erased his aircraft from the sky. But where had the other one gone? Winters' eyes swept a sky that was both crowded and empty at the same time. His threat receiver made its unwelcome screeching sound, and now he'd find out if the jammer pod worked or not. Somebody was trying to lock him up with a radar-guided missile. His eyes swept around looking for who that might be, but he couldn't see anyone—

—Smoke trail! A missile, heading in his general direction, but then it veered and exploded with its target—friend or foe, Winters couldn't tell.

"Boar Flight, Lead, check in!" he ordered.

"Two." "Three." A pause before: "Four!"

"Skippy, where are you?"

"Low and right, one mile, Leader. Heads up, there's a bandit at your three and closing."

"Oh, yeah?" Winters yanked his fighter to the right and was rewarded with an immediate warbling tone—but was it friend or foe? His wingman said the latter, but he couldn't tell, until—

Whoever it was, it had launched at him, and so he triggered a Sidewinder in reply, then dove hard for the deck while punching off flares and chaff to distract it. It worked. The missile, a radar seeker, exploded harmlessly half a mile behind him, but his Sidewinder didn't miss. He'd just gotten another kill, but he didn't know how many today, and there wasn't time to think things over.

"Skippy, form up on me, we're going north."

"Roger, Bronco."

Winters had his radar on, and he saw at least eight enemy blips to the north. He went to afterburner to chase, checking his fuel state. Still okay. The Eagle accelerated rapidly, but just to be safe, he popped off a string of chaff and flares in case some unknown Chinese was shooting at him. The threat receiver was screeching continuously now, though not in the distinctive chirping tone that suggested lock-up. He checked his weapons board. Three AIM-9X Sidewinders left. Where the hell had this day gone to?

"Ducky is hit, Ducky is hit!" a voice called. "Aw, shit!"

"Ghost Man here, got the fucker for you, Ducky. Come right, let me give you a damage check."

"One engine gone, other one's running hot," the second element leader reported, in a voice more angry than afraid. He didn't have time for fear yet. Another thirty seconds or so and that would start to take hold, Winters was sure.

"Ducky, you're trailing vapor of some sort, recommend you find a place to set it down."

"Eagle Two, Bronco, what's happening?"

"Bronco, we have six still inbound, putting Rodeo on it now. You have a bandit at your one o'clock at twenty miles, angels three-one, speed seven-five-zero."

"Roger that, Eagle. I'm on him." Winters came a little right and got another acquisition tone. "Fox-Two!" he called. The smoke trail ran straight for several miles, then corkscrewed to the left as it approached the little dot of gray-blue and . . . yes!

"Rodeo Lead," a new voice called. "Fox-One, Fox-One with two!"

"Conan, Fox-One!"

Now things were really getting nervous. Winters knew that he might be in the line of fire for those Slammers. He looked down to see that the light on his IFF was a friendly, constant green. The Identification Friend or Foe was supposed to tell American radars and missiles that he was on their side, but Winters didn't entirely trust computer chips with his life, and so he squinted his eyes to look for smoke trails that weren't going sideways. His radar could see the AWACS now, and it was moving west, taking the first part of evasive action, but its radar was still transmitting, even with Chinese fighters within . . . twenty miles? Shit! But then two more blips disappeared, and the remaining ones all had friendly IFF markers.

Winters checked his weapons display. No missiles left. How had all that happened? He was the United States Air Force champ for situational awareness, but he'd just lost track of a combat action. He couldn't remember firing all his missiles.

"Eagle Two, this is Boar Lead. I'm Winchester. Do you need any help?" "Winchester" meant out of weapons. That wasn't entirely true. He still had a full magazine of 20-mm cannon shells, but suddenly all the gees and all the excitement were pulling on him. His arms felt leaden as he eased his Eagle back to level flight.

"Boar Lead, Eagle. Looks like we're okay now, but that was kinda exciting, fella."

"Roger that, Eagle. Same here. Anything left?"

"Negative, Boar. Rodeo Lead got the last two. I think we owe that major a couple of beers."

"I'll hold you to that, Eagle," Rodeo Lead observed.

"Ducky, where are you?" Winters called next.

"Kinda busy, Bronco," a strained voice replied. "I got a hole in my arm, too."

"Bronco, Ghost Man. Ducky's got some holes in the airframe. I'm going to shepherd him back to Suntar. Thirty minutes, about."

"Skippy, where you be?"

"Right behind you, Leader. I think I got four, maybe five, in that furball."

"Any weapons left?"

"Slammer and 'winder, one each. I'll look after you, Colonel," Lieutenant Acosta promised. "How'd you make out?"

"Two, maybe more, not sure," the squadron commander answered. The final tally would come from the AWACS, plus a check of his own videotape. Mainly he wanted to get out of the aircraft and take a good stretch, and he now had time to worry about Major Don Boyd—Ducky—and his aircraft.

So, we want to mess with their heads, Mickey?" Admiral Dave Seaton asked.

"That's the idea," the Chairman of the Joint Chiefs told the chief of naval operations.

"Makes sense. Where are their heads at?"

"According to what CIA says, they think we're limiting the scope of operations for political reasons—to protect their sensibilities, like."

"No foolin'?" Seaton asked with no small degree of incredulity.

Moore nodded. "Yep."

"Well, then it's like a guy holding aces and eights, isn't it?" the CNO thought aloud, referring to the last poker hand held by James Butler—"Wild Bill"—Hickok in Deadwood, South Dakota. "We just pick the mission that's sure to flip them out."

"What are you thinking?" Moore asked.

"We can slam their navy pretty hard. Bart Mancuso's a pretty good operator. What are they most afraid of . . . ?" Seaton leaned back in his swivel chair. "First thing Bart wants to do is take out their missile submarine. It's at sea now with *Tucson* in trail, about twenty thousand yards back."

"That far?"

"It's plenty close enough. It's got an SSN in close proximity to protect it. So, *Tucson* takes 'em both out—zap." Moore didn't get the terminology, but Seaton was referring to the Chinese ships as "it," meaning an enemy, a target worthy only of destruction. "Beijing might not know it's happened right away, unless they've got an 'I'm Dead' buoy on the sail. Their surface navy's a lot easier. That'll be mainly aircraft targets, some missiles to keep the surface community happy."

"Submarine-launched missiles?"

"Mickey, you don't sink ships by making holes that let air in. You sink ships by making holes that let water in," Seaton explained. "Okay, if this is supposed to be for psychological effect, we hit everything simultaneously. That'll mean staging a lot of assets, and it runs the risk of being overly complicated, having the other guy catch a sniff of what's happening before we do anything. It's a risk. Do we really want to run it?"

"Ryan's thinking 'big picture.' Robby's helping him."

"Robby's a fighter pilot," Seaton agreed. "He likes to think in terms of movie stuff. Hell, Tom Cruise is taller than he is," Seaton joked.

"Good operational thinker. He was a pretty good J-3," Moore reminded the senior sailor.

"Yeah, I know, it's just that he likes to make dramatic plays. Okay, we can do it, only it complicates things." Seaton looked out the window for a second. "You know what might really flip them out?"

"What's that?" Moore asked. Seaton told him. "But it's not possible for us to do, is it?"

"Maybe not, but we're not dealing with professional military people, are we? They're politicians, Mickey. They're used to dealing with images instead of reality. So, we give them an image."

"Do you have the pieces in place to do that?"

"Let me find out."

"This is crazy, Dave."

"And deploying First Armored to Russia isn't?" the CNO demanded.

Lieutenant Colonel Angelo Giusti was now certain that he'd be fully content never to ride on another train as long as he lived. He didn't know that all of the Russian State Railroad's sleeper cars were being used to transport Russian army forces—they'd never sent any of the cars as far west as Berlin, not to slight the Americans, but because it had simply never occurred to anyone to do so. He took note of the fact that the train veered off to the north, off the main track, thumping over various switches and interlockings as it did so, and then the train came to a halt and started going backwards slowly. They seemed to be in the yard alone. They'd passed numerous westbound trains in the past two hours, all with engines dragging empty flatcars, and the conductor who appeared and disappeared regularly had told them that this was the approximate arrival time scheduled, but he hadn't really believed it, on the premise that a railroad with such uncomfortable seats probably didn't adhere to decent schedules either. But here they were, and the off-loading ramps were obvious for what they were.

"People, I think we're here," the commander of the Quarter Horse told his staff.

"Praise Jesus," one of them observed. A few seconds later, the train jolted to a stop, and they were able to walk out onto the concrete platform, which, they saw, stretched a good thousand meters to the east. Inside of five minutes, the soldiers of Headquarters Troop were out and walking to their vehicles, stretching and grousing along the way.

"Hey, Angie," called a familiar voice.

Giusti looked to see Colonel Welch and walked up to him with a salute.

"What's happening?" Giusti asked.

"It's a mess out east of here, but there is good news."

"What might that be?"

"There's plenty of fuel stashed for us. I've been flying security detachments out, and Ivan says he's got fuel depots that're the size of fuckin' supertankers. So, we're not going to run out of gas."

"That's good to know. What about my choppers?" Welch just pointed. There was an OH-58D Kiowa Warrior sitting not three hundred yards away. "Thank God for that. What's the bad news?"

"The PLA has four complete Group-A armies in Siberia and heading north. There hasn't been any heavy contact yet because Ivan's refusing combat at the moment, until they can get something big enough to meet them with. They have one motor-rifle division in theater and four more heading up there. The last of 'em just cleared this railyard an hour and a half ago."

"That's, what? Sixteen heavy divisions in the invasion force?"

Welch nodded. "Thereabouts."

"What's my mission?"

"Assemble your squadron and head southeast. The idea is First Armored will cut off the bottom of the break-in and interrupt their supply line. Russian blocking force will then try to stop them about two hundred miles northeast of here."

"Can they do it?" Four Russian divisions against sixteen Chinese didn't seem especially favorable odds.

"Not sure," Welch admitted. "Your job is to get out and establish lead security for the division. Advance to and secure the first big fuel depot. We'll play it from there."

"Support?"

"At the moment, the Air Force is mainly doing fighter work. No deep strikes yet because they don't have enough bombs to sustain any kind of campaign."

"What about resupply?"

"We have two basic loads for all the tracks. That'll have to do for a while. At least we have four units of fire for the artillery." That meant four days' worth of shells—based on what the Army computed that a day of combat required. The supply weenies who did those calculations weren't stingy on shells to shoot at the other guy. And in the entire Persian Gulf war, not a single tank had completely shot out its first basic load of shells, they both knew. But that was a different war. No two were ever the same, and they only got worse.

Giusti turned when he heard the first engine start up. It was an M3A2 Bradley Scout track, and the sergeant in the commander's hatch looked happy to be moving. A Russian officer took over as traffic cop, waving the Brad forward, then right toward the assembly area. The next train backed up to the next ramp over. That would be "A" or Avenger Troop, with the first of Quarter Horse's really heavy equipment, nine of the M1A2 main battle tanks.

"How long before everything's here?" Giusti asked.

"Ninety minutes, they told me," Welch answered.

"We'll see."

What's this?" a captain asked the screen in front of him. The E-3B Sentry designated Eagle Two was back on the ground at Zhigansk. Its crew was more than a little shaken. Being approached by real fighters with real blood in their eyes was qualitatively different from exercises and postmission analysis back stateside. The tapes of the engagement had been handed off to the wing intelligence staff, who viewed the battle with some detachment, but they could see that the PLAAF had thrown a full regiment of first-line fighters at the AWACS, and more than that, done it on a one-way mission. They'd come in on burner, and that would have denied them a trip back to their base. So, they'd been willing to trade over thirty fighters for a single E-3B. But there was more to the mission than that, the captain saw.

"Look here," he told his colonel. "Three, no, four reconnaissance birds went northwest." He ran the tape forward and backward. "We didn't touch any of them. Hell, they didn't even see them."

"Well, I'm not going to fault the Sentry crew for that, Captain."

"Not saying that, sir. But John Chinaman just got some pictures of Chita, and also of these Russian units moving north. The cat's out of the bag, Colonel."

"We've got to start thinking about some counter-air missions on these airfields."

"We have bombs to do it?"

"Not sure, but I'm taking this to General Wallace. What's the score on the air fight?"

"Colonel Winters got four for sure and two probables. Damn, that guy's really cleaning up. But it was the -16 guys saved the AWACS. These two J-8s got pretty damned close before Rodeo splashed them."

"We'll put some more coverage on the E-3s from now on," the colonel observed.

"Not a bad idea, sir."

Yes?" General Peng said, when his intelligence officer came up to him.

"Aerial reconnaissance reports large mechanized formations one hundred fifty kilometers west of us, moving north and northeast."

"Strength?" the general asked.

"Not sure. Analysis of the photos is not complete, but certainly regimental strength, maybe more."

"Where, exactly?"

"Here, Comrade General." The intelligence officer unfolded a map and pointed. "They were spotted here, here, and from here to here. The pilot said large numbers of tanks and tracked vehicles."

"Did they shoot at him?"

"No, he said there was no fire at all."

"So, they are rushing to where they are going . . . racing to get to our flank, or to get ahead of us . . . ?" Peng considered this, looking down at the map. "Yes, that's what I would expect. Any reports from our front?"

"Comrade General, our reconnaissance screen reports that they have seen the tracks of vehicles, but no visual sightings of the enemy at all. They have taken no fire, and seen nothing but civilians."

"Quickly," Aleksandrov urged.

How the driver and his assistant had gotten the ZIL-157 to this place was a mystery whose solution didn't interest the captain. That it had gotten here was enough. His lead BRM at that moment had been Sergeant Grechko's, and he'd filled up his tanks, and then radioed to the rest of the company, which for the first time broke visual contact with the advancing Chinese and raced north to top off as well. It was dangerous and against doctrine to leave the Chinese unseen, but Aleksandrov couldn't guarantee that they'd all have a chance to refuel otherwise. Then Sergeant Buikov had a question.

"When do *they* refuel, Comrade Captain? We haven't seen them do it, have we?"

That made his captain stop and think. "Why, no, we haven't. Their tanks must be as empty as ours."

"They had extra fuel drums the first day, remember? They dropped them off sometime yesterday."

"Yes, so maybe they have one more day of fuel, maybe only half a day, but then someone must refill them—but who will that be, and how . . . ?" the officer wondered. He turned to look. The fuel came out of the portable pump at about forty liters or ten gallons per minute. Grechko had taken his BRM south to reestablish contact with the Chinese. They were still sitting still, between frog-leap bounds, probably half an hour away if they stuck with their drill, from which they hadn't once deviated. And people had once said that the Red Army was inflexible . . .

"There, that's it," Aleksandrov's driver said. He handed the hose back and capped the tank.

"You," the captain told the driver of the fuel truck. "Go east."

"To where?" the man asked. "There's nothing there."

That stopped his thinking for a few seconds. There had been a sawmill here once, and you could see the wide swaths of saplings left over from when whoever had worked here had cut trees for lumber. It was the closest thing to open ground they'd seen in over a day.

"I came from the west. I can get back there now, with the truck lighter, and it's only six kilometers to the old logging road."

"Very well, but do it quickly, corporal. If they see you, they'll blast you."

"Farewell then, Comrade Captain." The corporal got back into the truck, started up, and turned to the north to loop around.

"I hope someone gives him a drink tonight. He's earned it," Buikov said. There was much more to any army than the shooters.

"Grechko, where are you?" Aleksandrov called over his radio.

"Four kilometers south of you. They're still dismounted, Captain. Their officer seems to be talking on the radio."

"Very well. You know what to do when they remount." The captain set the radio microphone down and leaned against his track. This business was getting very old. Buikov lit a smoke and stretched.

"Why can't we just kill a *few* of them, Comrade Captain? Would it not be worth it to get *some* sleep?"

"How many times must I tell you what our fucking mission is, Sergeant!" Aleksandrov nearly screamed at his sergeant.

"Yes, Captain," Buikov responded meekly.

CHAPTER 56

March to Danger

Lieutenant Colonel Giusti started off in his personal HMMWV, the new incarnation of the venerable Jeep. *Using a Bradley would have been more comfortable, even more sensible, but overly dramatic,* he thought, *and there wouldn't be any contact anytime soon.* Besides, the right front seat in this vehicle was better for his back after the endless train ride. In any case, he was following a Russian UAZ-469, which looked like a Russian interpretation of an American SUV, and whose driver knew the way. The Kiowa Warrior helicopter he'd seen at the railyard was up and flying, scouting ahead and reporting back that there was nothing there but mostly empty road, except for some civilian traffic being kept out of the way by Russian MPs. Right behind Giusti's command vehicle was a Bradley flying the red-and-white guidon of the First of the Fourth Cavalry. The regiment had, for American arms, a long and distinguished history—its combat action had begun on July 30, 1857, against the Cheyenne Indians at Solomon River—and this campaign would add yet another battle streamer to the regimental standard . . . and Giusti hoped he'd live long enough to attach it himself. The land here reminded him of Montana, rolling foothills with pine trees in abundance. The views were decently long, just what a mechanized trooper liked, because it meant you could engage an enemy at long range. American soldiers especially preferred that, because they had weapons that could reach farther than those of most other armies.

"DARKHORSE SIX to SABRE SIX, over," the radio crackled.

"SABRE SIX," LTC Giusti responded.

"SABRE, I'm now at checkpoint Denver. The way continues to be clear. Negative traffic, negative enemy indications, over. Proceeding east to checkpoint Wichita."

"Roger that, thank you, out." Giusti checked the map to be sure he knew exactly where the chopper was.

So, twenty miles ahead there was still nothing to be concerned about, at least according to the captain flying his lead helicopter. *Where would it start?* Giusti wondered. On the whole, he would have preferred to stand still and sit in on the divisional commander's conference, just to find out what the hell was happening, but as cavalry-screen commander, it was his job to go out forward and find the enemy, then report back to IRON SIX, the divisional commander. He really didn't have much of a mission yet, aside from driving up to the Russian fuel depot, refueling his vehicles there, and setting up security, then pulling out and continuing his advance as the leading elements of the First Armored's heavy forces got there. It was his job, in short, to be the ham in the sandwich, as one of his troop commanders liked to joke. But this ham could bite back. Under his command were three troops of armored cavalry, each with nine M1A2 Abrams main-battle tanks and thirteen M3A2 Bradley cavalry scout vehicles, plus a FISTV track for forward observers to call in artillery support—somewhere behind him, the First Armored's artillery would be off-loading soon from its train, he hoped. His most valuable assets were D and E troops, each with eight OH-58D Kiowa Warrior helicopters, able both to scout ahead and to shoot with Hellfire and Stinger missiles. In short, his squadron could look after itself, within reasonable limits.

As they got closer, his troopers would become more cautious and circumspect, because good as they were, they were neither invincible nor immortal. America had fought against China only once, in Korea nearly sixty years earlier, and the experience had been satisfactory to neither side. For America, the initial Chinese attack had been unexpected and massive, forcing an ignominious retreat from the Yalu River. But for China, once America had gotten its act together, the experience had cost a million lives, because firepower was always the answer to raw numbers, and America's lasting lesson from its own Civil War was that it was better to expend *things* than to expend *people.* The American way of war was not shared by everyone, and in truth it was tailored to American material prosperity as much as to American reverence for human life, but it was the American way, and that was the way its warriors were schooled.

"I think it's about time to roll them back a little," General Wallace observed over the satellite link to Washington.

"What do you propose?" Mickey Moore asked.

"For starters, I want to send my F-16CGs after their radar sites. I'm tired of having them use radar to direct their fighters against my aircraft. Next, I want to start going after their logistical choke points. In twelve hours, the way things are going, I'll have enough ordnance to start doing some offensive warfare here. And it's about time for us to start, General," Wallace said.

"Gus, I have to clear that with the President," the Chairman told the Air Force commander in Siberia.

"Okay, fine, but tell him we damned near lost an AWACS yesterday—with a crew of thirty or so—and I'm not in a mood to write that many letters. We've been lucky so far, and an AWACS is a hard kill. Hell, it cost them a full regiment of fighters to fail in that mission. But enough's enough. I want to go after their radar sites, and I want to do some offensive counter-air."

"Gus, the thinking here is that we want to commence offensive operations in a systematic way for maximum psychological effect. That means more than just knocking some antennas down."

"General, I don't know what it looks like over there, but right here it's getting a little exciting. Their army is advancing rapidly. Pretty soon our Russian friends are going to have to make their stand. It'll be a whole lot easier if the enemy is short on gas and bullets."

"We know that. We're trying to figure a way to shake up their political leadership."

"It isn't politicians coming north trying to kill us, General. It's soldiers and airmen. We have to start crippling them before they ruin our whole damned day."

"I understand that, Gus. I will present your position to the President," the Chairman promised.

"Do that, will ya?" Wallace killed the transmission, wondering what the hell the lotus-eaters in Washington were thinking about, assuming they were thinking at all. He had a plan, and he thought it was a pretty good systematic one. His Dark Star drones had given him all the tactical intelligence he needed. He knew what targets to hit, and he had enough ordnance to do the hitting, or at least to start doing it.

If they let me, Wallace thought.

Well, it wasn't a complete waste," Marshal Luo said. "We got some pictures of what the Russians are doing."

"And what's that?" Zhang asked.

"They're moving one or two—probably two—divisions northeast from their rail assembly point at Chita. We have good aerial pictures of them."

"And still nothing in front of our forces?"

Luo shook his head. "Our reconnaissance people haven't seen anything more than tracks in the ground. I have to assume there are Russians in those woods somewhere, doing reconnaissance of their own, but if so, they're light forces who're working very hard to keep out of the way. We know they've called up some reserves, but they haven't shown up either. Maybe their reservists didn't report. Morale in Russia is supposed to be very low, Tan tells us, and that's all we've really seen. The men we captured are very disheartened because of their lack of support, and they didn't fight all that well. Except for the American airplanes, this war is going extremely well."

"And they haven't attacked our territory yet?" Zhang wanted to be clear on that.

Another shake of the head. "No, and I can't claim that they're afraid to do it. Their fighter aircraft are excellent, but to the best of our knowledge they haven't even attempted a photo-reconnaissance mission. Maybe they just depend on satellites now. Certainly those are supposed to be excellent sources of information for them."

"And the gold mine?"

"We'll be there in thirty-six hours. And at that point we can make use of the roads their own engineers have been building to exploit the mineral finds. From the gold mine to the oil fields—five to seven days, depending on how well we can run supplies up."

"This is amazing, Luo," Zhang observed. "Better than my fondest hopes."

"I almost wish the Russians would stand and fight somewhere, so that we could have a battle and be done with it. As it is, my forces are stringing out somewhat, but only because the lead elements are racing forward so well. I've thought about slowing them down to maintain unit integrity, but—"

"But speed works for us, doesn't it?" Zhang observed.

"Yes, it would seem to," the Defense Minister agreed. "But one prefers to keep units tightly grouped in case there is some contact. However, if the enemy is running, one doesn't want to give him pause to regroup. So, I'm giving General Peng and his divisions free rein."

"What forces are you facing?"

"We're not sure. Perhaps a regiment or so could be ahead of us, but we see no evidence of it, and two more regiments are trying to race ahead of us, or attack our flank, but we have flank security out to the west, and they've seen nothing."

Bondarenko hoped that someday he'd meet the team that had developed this American Dark Star drone. Never in history had a commander possessed such knowledge as this, and without it he would have been forced to commit his slender forces to battle just to ascertain what stood against him. Not now. He probably had a better feel for the location of the advancing Chinese than their own commander did.

Better yet, the leading regiment of the 201st Motor Rifle Division was only a few kilometers away, and the leading formation was the division's steel fist, its independent tank regiment of ninety-five T-80U main-battle tanks.

The 265th was ready for the reinforcement, and its commander, Yuriy Sinyavskiy, proclaimed that he was tired of running away. A career professional soldier and mechanized infantryman, Sinyavskiy was a profane, cigar-chomping man of forty-six years, now leaning over a map table in Bondarenko's headquarters.

"This, this is my ground, Gennady Iosifovich," he said, stabbing at the point with his finger. It was just five kilometers north of the Gogol Gold Field, a line of ridges twenty kilometers across, facing open ground the Chinese would have to cross. "And put the Two-Oh-First's tanks just here on my right. When we stop their advance guard, they can blow in from the west and roll them up."

"Reconnaissance shows their leading division is strung out somewhat," Bondarenko told him.

It was a mistake made by every army in the world. The sharpest teeth of any field force are its artillery, but even self-propelled artillery, mounted on tracks for cross-country mobility, can't seem to keep up with the mechanized forces it is supposed to support. It was a lesson that had even surprised the Americans in the Persian Gulf, when they'd found their artillery could keep up with the leading tank echelons only with strenuous effort, and across flat ground. The People's Liberation Army had tracked artillery, but a lot of it was still the towed variety, and was being pulled behind trucks that could not travel cross-country as well as the tracked kind.

General Diggs observed the discussion, which his rudimentary Russian could not quite keep up with, and Sinyavskiy spoke no English, which really slowed things down.

"You still have a lot of combat power to stop, Yuriy Andreyevich," Diggs pointed out, waiting for the translation to get across.

"If we cannot stop them completely, at least we can give them a bloody nose" was the belated reply.

"Stay mobile," Diggs advised. "If I were this General Peng, I'd maneuver east—the ground is better suited for it—and try to wrap you up from your left."

"We will see how maneuver-minded they are," Bondarenko said for his subordinate. "So far all they have done is drive straight forward, and I think they are becoming complacent. See how they are stretched out, Marion. Their units are too far separated to provide mutual support. They are in a pursuit phase of warfare, and that makes them disorganized, *and* they have little air support to warn them of what lies ahead. I think Yuriy is right: This is a good place for a stand."

"I agree it's good ground, Gennady, just don't marry the place, okay?" Diggs warned.

Bondarenko translated that for his subordinate, who answered back in machine-gun Russian around his cigar.

"Yuriy says it is a place for a fucking, not a wedding. When will you join your command, Marion?"

"My chopper's on the way in now, buddy. My cavalry screen is at the first fuel depot, with First Brigade right behind. We should be in contact in a day and a half or so."

They'd already discussed Diggs's plan of attack. First Armored would assemble northwest of Belogorsk, fueling at the last big Russian depot, then leap out in the darkness for the Chinese bridgehead. Intelligence said that the PLA's 65th Type-B Group Army was there now, digging in to protect the left shoulder of their break-in. Not a mechanized force, it was still a lot for a single division to chew on. If the Chinese plan of attack had a weakness, it was that they'd bet all their mechanized forces on the drive forward. The forces left behind to secure the breakthrough were at best motorized—carried by wheeled vehicles instead of tracked ones—and at worst leg infantry, who had to walk where they went. That made them slow and vulnerable to men who sat down behind steel as they went to battle in their tracked vehicles.

But there were a hell of a lot of them, Diggs reminded himself.

Before he could leave, General Sinyavskiy reached into his hip pocket and pulled out a flask. "A drink for luck," he said in his only words of broken English.

"Hell, why not?" Diggs tossed it off. It was good stuff, actually. "When this is all over, we will drink again," he promised.

"Da," the general replied. "Good luck, Diggs."

"Marion," Bondarenko said. "Be careful, comrade."

"You, too, Gennady. You got enough medals, buddy. No sense getting your ass shot off trying to win another."

"Generals are supposed to die in bed," Bondarenko agreed on the way to the door.

Diggs trotted out to the UH-60. Colonel Boyle was flying this one. Diggs donned the crash helmet, wishing they'd come up with another name for the damned thing, and settled in the jump seat behind the pilots.

"How we doing, sir?" Boyle asked, letting the lieutenant take the chopper back off.

"Well, we have a plan, Dick. Question is, will it work?"

"Do I get let in on it?"

"Your Apaches are going to be busy."

"There's a surprise," Boyle observed.

"How are your people?"

"Ready" was the one-word reply. "What are we calling this?"

"CHOPSTICKS." Diggs then heard a laugh over the intercom wire.

"I love it."

Okay, Mickey," Robby Jackson said. "I understand Gus's position. But we have a big picture here to think about."

They were in the Situation Room looking at the Chairman on TV from the Pentagon room known as The Tank. It was hard to hear what he was muttering that way, but the way he looked down was a sufficient indication of his feelings about Robby's remark.

"General," Ryan said, "the idea here is to rattle the cage of their political leadership. Best way to do that is to go after them in more places than one, overload 'em."

"Sir, I agree with that idea, but General Wallace has his point, too. Taking down their radar fence will degrade their ability to use their fighters against us, and they still have a formidable fighter force, even though we've handled them pretty rough so far."

"Mickey, if you handle a girl this way down in Mississippi, it's called rape," the Vice President observed. "Their fighter pilots look at their aircraft now and they see caskets, for Christ's sake. Their confidence has got to be gone, and that's all a fighter jock has to hold onto. Trust me on this one, will ya?"

"But Gus—"

"But Gus is too worried about his force. Okay, fine, let him send some Charlie-Golfs against their picket fence, but mainly we want those birds armed with Smart Pigs to go after their ground forces. The fighter force can look after itself."

For the first time, General Mickey Moore regretted Ryan's choice of Vice President. Robby was thinking like a politician rather than an operational commander—and that came as something of a surprise. He was seemingly less worried about the safety of his forces than of . . .

. . . *than of what the overall objective was,* Moore corrected himself. And *that* was not a completely bad way to think, was it? Jackson had been a pretty good J-3 not so long before, hadn't he?

American commanders no longer thought of their men as expendable assets. That was not a bad thing at all, but sometimes you had to put forces in harm's way, and when you did that, some of them did not come home. And that was what they were paid for, whether you liked it or not. Robby Jackson had been a Navy fighter pilot, and he hadn't forgotten the warrior ethos, despite his new job and pay grade.

"Sir," Moore said, "what orders do I give General Wallace?"

Cecil B. goddamned DeMille," Mancuso observed crossly.

"Ever wanted to part the Red Sea?" General Lahr asked.

"I ain't God, Mike," CINCPAC said next.

"Well, it *is* elegant, and we *do* have most of the pieces in place," his J-2 pointed out.

"This is a political operation. What the hell are we, a goddamned focus group?"

"Sir, you going to continue to rant, or are we going to get to work on this?"

Mancuso wished for a *lupara* to blast a hole in the wall, or Mike Lahr's chest, but he *was* a uniformed officer, and he *did* now have orders from his Commander-in-Chief.

"All right. I just don't like to have other people design my operations."

"And you know the guy."

"Mike, once upon a time, back when I had three stripes and driving a submarine was all I had to worry about, Ryan and I helped steal a whole Russian submarine, yeah—and if you repeat that to anyone, I'll have one of my Marines shoot your ass. Sink some of their ships, yeah, splash a few of their airplanes, sure, but 'trailing our coat' in sight of land? Jesus."

"It'll shake them up some."

"If they don't sink some of my ships in the attempt."

Hey, Tony," the voice on the phone said. It took Bretano a second to recognize it.

"Where are you now, Al?" the Secretary of Defense asked.

"Norfolk. Didn't you know? I'm on USS *Gettysburg* upgrading their SAMs. It was your idea, wasn't it?"

"Well, yeah, I suppose it was," Tony Bretano agreed, thinking back.

"You must have seen this Chinese thing coming a long way off, man."

"As a matter of fact, we—" The SecDef paused for a second. "What do you mean?"

"I mean, if the ChiComms loft an ICBM at us, this Aegis system does give us something to fall back on, if the computer simulations are right. They ought to be. I wrote most of the software," Gregory went on.

Secretary Bretano didn't want to admit that he hadn't really thought about that eventuality. Thinking things through was one of the things he was paid for, after all. "How ready are you?"

"The electronics stuff is okay, but we don't have any SAMs aboard. They're stashed at some depot or something, up on the York River, I think they said. When they load them aboard, I can upgrade the software on the seeker heads. The only missiles aboard, the ones I've been playing with, they're blue ones, exercise missiles, not shooters, I just found out. You know, the Navy's a little weird. The ship's in a floating dry dock. They're going to lower us back in the water in a few hours." He couldn't see his former boss's face at the moment. If he could, he would have recognized the *oh, shit* expression on his Italian face.

"So, you're confident in your systems?"

"A full-up test would be nice, but if we can loft three or four SAMs at the inbound, yeah, I think it oughta work."

"Okay, thanks, Al."

"So, how's this war going? All I see on TV is how the Air Force is kicking some ass."

"They are, the TV's got that right, but the rest—can't talk about it over the phone. Al, let me get back to you, okay?"

"Yes, sir."

In his office, Bretano switched buttons. "Ask Admiral Seaton to come in to see me." That didn't take very long.

"You rang, Mr. Secretary," the CNO said when he came in.

"Admiral, there's a former employee of mine from TRW in Norfolk right now. I set him up to look at upgrading the Aegis missile system to engage ballistic targets."

"I heard a little about that. How's his project going?" Dave Seaton asked.

"He says he's ready for a full-up test. But, Admiral, what if the Chinese launch one of their CSS-4s at us?"

"It wouldn't be good," Seaton replied.

"Then how about we take our Aegis ships and put them close to the likely targets?"

"Well, sir, the system's not certified for ballistic targets yet, and we haven't really run a test, and—"

"Is it better than nothing?" the SecDef asked, cutting him off.

"A little, I suppose."

"Then let's make that happen, and make it happen right now."

Seaton straightened up. "Aye aye, sir."

"*Gettysburg* first. Have her load up what missiles she needs, and bring her right here," Bretano ordered.

"I'll call SACLANT right now."

It was the strangest damned thing, Gregory thought. This ship—not an especially big ship, smaller than the one he and Candi had taken a cruise on the previous winter, but still an oceangoing *ship*—was in an elevator. That's what a floating dry dock was. They were flooding it now, to make it go down, back into the water to see if the new propeller worked. Sailors who worked on the dry dock were watching from their perches on—whatever the hell you called the walls of the damned thing.

"Weird, ain't it, sir?"

Gregory smelled the smoke. It had to be Senior Chief Leek. He turned. It was.

"Never seen this sort of thing before."

"Nobody does real often, 'cept'n those guys over there who operate this thing. Did you take the chance to walk under the ship?"

"Walk *under* ten thousand tons of metal?" Gregory responded. "I don't think so."

"You was a soldier, wasn't you?"

"Told you, didn't I? West Point, jump school, ranger school, back when I was young and foolish."

"Well, Doc, it's no big deal. Kinda interesting to see how she's put together, 'specially the sonar dome up forward. If I wasn't a radar guy, I probably woulda been a sonar guy, 'cept there's nothing for them to do anymore."

Gregory looked down. Water was creeping across the gray metal floor—*deck?* he wondered—of the dry dock.

"Attention on deck!" a voice called. Sailors turned and saluted, including Chief Leek.

It was Captain Bob Blandy, *Gettysburg*'s CO. Gregory had met him only once, and then just to say hello.

"Dr. Gregory."

"Captain." They shook hands.

"How's your project been going?"

"Well, the simulations look good. I'd like to try it against a live target."

"You got sent to us by the SecDef?"

"Not exactly, but he called me in from California to look at the technical aspects of the problem. I worked for him when he was head of TRW."

"You're an SDI guy, right?"

"That and SAMs, yes, sir. Other things. I'm one of the world's experts on adaptive optics, from my SDI days."

"What's that?" Captain Blandy asked.

"The rubber mirror, we called it. You use computer-controlled actuators to warp the mirror to compensate for atmospheric distortions. The idea was to use that to focus the energy beam from a free-electron laser. But it didn't work out. The rubber mirror worked just fine, but for some reason we never figured out, the damned lasers didn't scale up the way we hoped they would. Didn't come up to the power requirements to smoke a missile body." Gregory looked down in the dry dock again. It certainly took its time, but they probably didn't want to drop anything this valuable. "I wasn't directly involved in that, but I kibitzed some. It turned out to be a monster of a technical problem. We just kept bashing our heads against the wall until we got tired of the squishy sound."

"I know mechanical engineering, some electrical, but not the high-energy stuff. So, what do you think of our Aegis system?"

"I love the radar. Just like the Cobra Dane the Air Force has up at

Shemya in the Aleutians. A little more advanced, even. You could probably bounce a signal off the moon if you wanted to."

"That's a little out of our range gate," Blandy observed. "Chief Leek here been taking good care of you?"

"When he leaves the Navy, we might have a place for him at TRW. We're part of the ongoing SAM project."

"And Lieutenant Olson, too?" the skipper asked.

"He's a very bright young officer, Captain. I can think of a lot of companies who might want him." If Gregory had a fault, it was being too truthful.

"I ought to say something to discourage you from that, but—"

"Cap'n!" A sailor came up. "Flash-traffic from SACLANT, sir." He handed over a clipboard. Captain Blandy signed the acknowledgment sheet and took the message. His eyes focused very closely.

"Do you know if the SecDef knows what you're up to?"

"Yes, Captain, he does. I just spoke to Tony a few minutes ago."

"What the hell did you tell him?"

Gregory shrugged. "Not much, just that the project was coming along nicely."

"Uh-huh. Chief Leek, how's your hardware?"

"Everything's a hundred percent on line, Cap'n. We got a job, sir?" the senior chief asked.

"Looks like it. Dr. Gregory, if you will excuse me, I have to see my officers. Chief, we're going to be getting under way soon. If any of your troops are on the beach, call 'em back. Spread the word."

"Aye aye, sir." He saluted as Captain Blandy hustled back forward. "What's that all about?"

"Beats me, Chief."

"What do I do? Getting under way?" Gregory asked.

"Got your toothbrush? If not, you can buy one in the ship's store. Excuse me, Doc, I have to do a quick muster." Leek tossed his cigarette over the side and went the same way that the captain had.

And there was precisely nothing for Gregory to do. There was no way for him to leave the ship, except to jump down into the flooding floating dry dock, and that didn't look like a viable option. So, he headed back into the superstructure and found the ship's store open. There he bought a toothbrush.

Bondarenko spent the next three hours with Major General Sinyavskiy, going over approach routes and fire plans.

"They have fire-finder radar, Yuriy, and their counter-battery rockets have a long reach."

"Can we expect any help from the Americans?"

"I'm working on that. We have superb reconnaissance information from their movie-star drones."

"I need the location of their artillery. If we can take that away from them, it makes my job much easier."

"Tolkunov!" the theater commander yelled. It was loud enough that his intelligence coordinator came running.

"Yes, Comrade General!"

"Vladimir Konstantinovich, we'll be making our stand here," Bondarenko said, pointing to a red line on the map. "I want minute-to-minute information of the approaching Chinese formations—especially their artillery."

"I can do that. Give me ten minutes." And the G-2 disappeared back out to where the Dark Star terminal was. Then his boss thought about it.

"Come on, Yuriy, you have to see this."

"General," Major Tucker said by way of greeting. Then he saw a second one. "General," he said again.

"This is General Sinyavskiy. He commands Two-Six-Five. Would you please show him the advancing Chinese?" It wasn't a question or a request, just phrased politely because Tucker was a foreigner.

"Okay, it's right here, sir, we've got it all on videotape. Their leading reconnaissance elements are . . . here, and their leading main-force units are right here."

"Fuck," Sinyavskiy observed in Russian. "Is this magic?"

"No, this is—" Bondarenko switched languages. "Which unit is this, Major?"

"Grace Kelly again, sir. *To Catch a Thief* with Cary Grant, Hitchcock movie that one was. The sun'll be down in another hour or so and we'll be getting it all on the thermal-imaging systems. Anyway, here's their leading battalion, all look like their Type-90 tanks. They're keeping good formation discipline, and they just refueled about an hour ago, so, figure they're good for another two hundred or so kilometers before they stop again."

"Their artillery?"

"Lagging behind, sir, except for this tracked unit here." Tucker played with the mouse some and brought up another picture.

"Gennady Iosifovich, how can we fail with such information?" the division commander asked.

"Yuriy, remember when we thought about attacking the Americans?"

"Madness. The Chinks can't see this drone?" Sinyavskiy asked, somewhat incredulously.

"It's stealthy, as they call it, invisible on radar."

"Nichevo."

"Sir, I have a direct line to our headquarters at Zhigansk. If you guys are going to make a stand, what do you want from us?' Tucker asked. "I can forward your request to General Wallace."

"I have thirty Su-25 attack bombers and also fifty Su-24 fighter bombers standing by, plus two hundred Mi-24 helicopters." Getting the last in theater had been agonizingly slow, but finally they were here, and they were the Ace of Diamonds Bondarenko had facedown on the card table. He hadn't let so much as one approach the area of operations yet, but they were two hundred kilometers away, fueled and armed, their flight crews flying to practice their airmanship and shooting live weapons as rehearsal—for some, the first live weapons they'd ever shot.

"That's going to be a surprise for good old Joe," Tucker observed with a whistle. "Where'd you hide them, sir? Hell, General, *I* didn't know they were around."

"There are a few secure places. We want to give our guests a proper greeting when the time is right," Gennady Iosifovich told the young American officer.

"So, what do you want us to do, sir?"

"Take down their logistics. Show me this Smart Pig you've been talking to Colonel Tolkunov about."

"That we can probably do, sir," Tucker said. "Let me get on the phone to General Wallace."

So, they're turning me loose?" Wallace asked.

"As soon as contact is imminent between Russian and Chinese ground forces." Mickey Moore then gave him his targets. "It's most of the things you wanted to hit, Gus."

"I suppose," the Air Force commander allowed, somewhat grudgingly. "And if the Russians ask for help?"

"Give it to them, within reason."

"Right."

LTC Giusti, SABRE SIX, got off the helicopter at the Number Two fueling point and walked toward General Diggs.

"They weren't kidding," Colonel Masterman was saying. "This *is* a fuckin' lake." One and a quarter *billion* liters translated to more than three hundred million gallons, or nearly a million tons of fuel, about the carrying capacity of four supertankers, all of Number Two Diesel, or close enough that the fuel injectors on his tanks and Bradleys wouldn't notice the difference. The manager of the site, a civilian, had said that the fuel had been there for nearly forty years, since Khrushchev had had a falling-out with Chairman Mao, and the possibility of war with the *other* communist country had turned from an impossibility into a perceived likelihood. Either it was remarkable prescience or paranoid wish fulfillment, but in either case it worked to the benefit of First Armored Division.

The off-loading facilities could have been better, but the Soviets evidently hadn't had much experience with building gas stations. It was more efficient to pump the fuel into the division's fuel bowsers, which then motored off to fill the tanks and tracks four or six at a time.

"Okay, Mitch, what do we have on the enemy?" General Diggs asked his intelligence officer.

"Sir, we've got a Dark Star tasked directly to us now, and she'll be up for another nine hours. We're up against a leg-infantry division. They're forty kilometers that way, mainly sitting along this line of hills. There's a regiment of ChiComm tanks supporting them."

"Artillery?"

"Some light and medium, all of it towed, setting up now, with fire-finder radars we need to worry about," Colonel Turner warned.

"I've asked General Wallace to task some F-16s with HARMs to us. They can tune the seekers on those to the millimeter-band the fire-finders use."

"Make that happen," Diggs ordered.

"Yes, sir."

"Duke, how long to contact?" the general asked his operations officer.

"If we move on schedule, we'll be in their neighborhood about zero-two-hundred."

"Okay, let's get the brigade commanders briefed in. We party just after midnight," Diggs told his staff, not even regretting his choice of words. He was a soldier about to go into combat, and with that came a different and not entirely pleasant way of thinking.

CHAPTER 57

Hyperwar

It had been rather a tedious couple of days for USS *Tucson.* She'd been camped out on *406* for sixteen days, and was holding station seventeen thousand yards—eight and a half nautical miles—astern of the Chinese boomer, with a nuclear-powered fast-attack camped out just to the south of it at the moment. The SSN, at least, supposedly had a name, *Hai Long,* the intelligence weenies said it was. But to *Tucson*'s sonarman, *406* was Sierra-Eleven, and *Hai Long* was Sierra-Twelve, and so they were known to the fire-control tracking party.

Tracking both targets was not demanding. Though both had nuclear power plants, the reactor systems were noisy, especially the feed pumps that ran cooling water through the nuclear pile. That, plus the sixty-hertz generators, made for two pairs of bright lines on the waterfall sonar display, and tracking both was about as difficult as watching two blind men in an empty shopping mall parking lot at high noon on a cloudless day. But it was more interesting than tracking whales in the North Pacific, which some of PACFLT's boats had been tasked to do of late, to keep the tree-huggers happy.

Things had gotten a little more interesting lately. *Tucson* ran to periscope/antenna depth twice a day, and the crew had learned, much to everyone's surprise, that Chinese and American armed forces were trading shots in Siberia, and *that* meant, the crew figured, that *406* might have to be made to disappear, and *that* was a mission, and while it might not exactly be fun, it was what they were paid to do, which made it a worthwhile activity.

406 had submarine-launched ballistic missiles aboard, twelve Ju Lang-1 CSS-N-3s, each with a single megaton-range warhead. The name meant "Great Wave," so the intelligence book said. It also said they had a range of less than three thousand kilometers, which was less than half the range needed to strike California, though it could hit Guam, which was American territory. That didn't really matter. What did matter was that *406* and *Hai Long* were ships of war belonging to a nation with which the United States was now trading shots.

The VLS radio fed off an antenna trailed off the after corner of *Tucson*'s sail, and it received transmissions from a monstrous, mainly underground transmitter located in Michigan's Upper Peninsula. The tree-huggers complained that the energy emanating from this radio confused migrating geese in the fall, but no hunters had yet complained about smaller bags of waterfowl, and so the radio remained in service. Built to send messages to American missile submarines, it still transmitted to the fast-attacks that remained in active service. When a transmission was received, a bell went off in the submarine's communications room, located aft of the attack center, on the starboard side.

The bell *ding*ed. The sailor on watch called his officer, a lieutenant, j.g., who in turn called the captain, who took the submarine back up to antenna depth. Once there, he elevated the communications laser to track in on the Navy's own communications satellite, known as SSIX, the Submarine Satellite Information Exchange, telling it that he was ready for a transmission. The reply action message came over a directional S-band radio for the higher bandwidth. The signal was cross-loaded into the submarine's crypto machines, decoded, and printed up.

TO: USS TUCSON (SSN-770)
FROM: CINCPAC

1. UPON RECEIVING "XQT SPEC OP" SIGNAL FROM VLS YOU WILL ENGAGE AND DESTROY PRC SSBN AND ANY PRC SHIPS IN CONTACT.
2. REPORT RESULTS OF ATTACK VIA SSIX.
3. SUBSEQUENT TO THIS OPERATION, CONDUCT

UNRESTRICTED OPERATIONS AGAINST PRC NAVAL UNITS.

4. YOU WILL NOT RPT NOT ENGAGE COMMERCIAL TRAFFIC OF ANY KIND.

CINCPAC SENDS

END MESSAGE

"Well, it's about goddamned time," the CO observed to his executive officer.

"Doesn't say when to expect it," the XO observed.

"Call it two hours," the captain said. "Let's close to ten thousand yards. Get the troops perked up. Spin up the weapons."

"Aye."

"Anything else close?"

"There's a Chinese frigate off to the north, about thirty miles."

"Okay, after we do the subs, we'll Harpoon that one, then we'll close to finish it off, if necessary."

"Right." The XO went forward to the attack center. He checked his watch. It was dark topside. It didn't really matter to anyone aboard the submarine, but darkness made everybody feel a little more secure for some reason or other, even the XO.

It was tenser now. Giusti's reconnaissance troopers were now within twenty miles of the expected Chinese positions. That put them inside artillery range, and that made the job serious.

The mission was to advance to contact, and to find a hole in the Chinese positions for the division to exploit. The secondary objective was to shoot through the gap and break into the Chinese logistical area, just over the river from where they'd made their breakthrough. There they would rape and pillage, as LTC Giusti thought of it, probably turning north to roll up the Chinese rear with one or two brigades, and probably leaving the third to remain in place astride the Chinese line of communications as a blocking force.

His troopers had all put on their "makeup," as some called it, their camouflage paint, darkening the natural light spots of the face and lightening the dark ones. It had the overall effect of making them look like green and black space aliens. The advance would be mounted, for the most part, with the cavalry scouts mostly staying in their Bradleys and depending on the thermal-imaging viewers used by the driver and gunner to spot enemies. They'd be jumping out occasionally, though, and so everyone checked his PVS-11 personal night-vision system. Every trooper had three sets of fresh AA batteries that were as important as the magazines for their M16A2 rifles. Most of the men gobbled down an MRE ration and chased it with water, and often some aspirin or Tylenol to ward off minor aches and pains that might come from bumps or sprains. They all traded looks and jokes to lighten the stress of the night, plus the usual brave words meant as much for themselves as for others. Sergeants and junior officers reminded the men of their training, and told them to be confident in their abilities.

Then, on radioed command, the Bradleys started off, leading the heavier main-battle tanks off to the enemy, moving initially at about ten miles per hour.

The squadron's helicopters were up, all sixteen of them, moving very cautiously because armor on a helicopter is about as valuable as a sheet of newspaper, and because someone on the ground only needed a thermal-imaging viewer to see them, and a heat-seeking missile would snuff them out of the sky. The enemy had light flak, too, and that was just as deadly.

The OH-58D Kiowa Warriors had good night-vision systems, and in training the flight crews had learned to be confident of them, but people didn't often die in training. Knowing that there were people out there with live weapons and the orders to make use of them made everyone discount some of the lessons they'd learned. Getting shot down in one of those exercises meant being told over the radio to land, and maybe getting a tongue-lashing from the company commander for screwing up, which usually ended with a reminder that in real combat operations, he'd be dead, his wife a widow, and his children orphans. But they weren't, really, and so those words were never taken as seriously as they were now. Now it could be real, and all of the flight crews had wives or sweethearts, and most of them had children as well.

And so they moved forward, using their own night-vision equipment to sweep the ground ahead, their hands a little more tingly than usual on the controls.

Division Headquarters had its own Dark Star terminal set up, with an Air Force captain running it. Diggs didn't much like being so far in the rear with his men going out in harm's way, but command wasn't the same thing as leadership. He'd been told that years before at Fort Leavenworth's Command and General Staff School, and he'd experienced it in Saudi Arabia only the previous year, but even so, he felt the need to be out forward, close to his men, so that he could share the danger with them. But the best way for him to mitigate the danger to them was to stay back here and establish effective control over operations, along with Colonel Masterman.

"Cookstoves?" Masterman asked.

"Yep," the USAF captain—his name was Frank Williams—agreed. "And these bright ones are campfires. Cool night. Ground temperature's about forty-three degrees, air temperature is forty-one. Good contrast for the thermal viewing systems. They seem to use the kind of stoves we had in the Boy Scouts. Damn, there's a bunch of 'em. Like hundreds."

"Got a hole in their lines?"

"Looks thin right here, 'tween these two hills. They have a company on this hilltop, and another company here—I bet they're in different battalions," Williams said. "Always seems to work that way. The gap between them looks like a little more 'n a kilometer, but there's a little stream at the bottom."

"Bradleys don't mind getting a little wet," Diggs told the junior officer. "Duke?"

"Best bet for a blow-through I've seen so far. Aim Angelo for it?"

Diggs thought about that. It meant committing his cavalry screen, and that also meant committing at least one of his brigades, but such decisions were what generals were for. "What else is around?"

"I'd say their regimental headquarters is right about here, judging by the tents and trucks. You're going to want to hit it with artillery, I expect."

"Right about the time QUARTER HORSE gets there. No sense alerting them too soon," Masterman suggested. General Diggs thought it over one more time and made his first important decision of the night:

"Agreed. Duke, tell Giusti to head for that gap."

"Yes, sir." Colonel Masterman moved off toward the radios. They were doing this on the fly, which wasn't exactly the way they preferred, but that was often the world of real-time combat operations.

"Roger," Diggs called.

Colonel Roger Ardan was his divisional artillery commander—GUNFIGHTER SIX on the divisional radio net—a tall thin man, rather like a not-tall-enough basketball player.

"Yes, sir."

"Here's your first fire mission. We're going to shoot Angelo Giusti through this gap. Company of infantry here and here, and what appears to be a regimental command post here."

"Enemy artillery?"

"Some one-twenty-twos here, and what looks like two-oh-threes, eight inch, right here."

"No rocket-launchers?"

"None I've seen yet. That's a little odd, but they're not around that I can see," Captain Williams told the gunner.

"What about radars?" Colonel Ardan asked.

"Maybe one here, but hard to tell. It's under some camo nets." Williams selected the image with his mouse and expanded it.

"We'll take that one on general principles. Put a pin in it," Ardan said.

"Yes, sir. Print up a target list?"

"You bet, son."

"Here you go," Williams said. A command generated two sheets of paper out of the adjacent printer, with latitude-longitude positions down to the second of angle. The captain handed it across.

"How the hell did we ever survive without GPS and overheads?" Ardan wondered aloud. "Okay, General, this we can do. When?"

"Call it thirty minutes."

"We'll be ready," GUNFIGHTER promised. "I'll TOT the regimental command post."

"Sounds good to me," Diggs observed.

First Armored had a beefed-up artillery brigade. The second and the third battalions of the First Field Artillery Regiment had the new Paladin self-propelled 155-mm howitzer, and the 2nd Battalion, 6th

Field Artillery, had self-propelled eight-inch, plus the division's Multiple Launch Rocket System tracks, which ordinarily were under the direct order of the divisional commander, as his personal shotgun. These units were six miles behind the leading cavalry troops, and on order left the roads they were on and pulled off to firing positions north and south of the gravel track. Each of them had a Global Positioning Satellite, or GPS, receiver, and these told them where they were located down to an accuracy of less than three meters. A transmission over the Joint Tactical Information Distribution System, or J-TIDS, told them the locations of their targets, and onboard computers computed azimuth and range to them. Then they learned the shell selection, either "common" high-explosive or VT (for variable-time). These were loaded and the guns trained onto the distant targets, and the gunners just waited for the word to pull the strings. Their readiness was radioed back to the divisional HQ.

All set, sir," Colonel Ardan reported.

"Okay, we'll wait to see how Angelo's doing."

"Your screen is right here," Captain Williams told the senior officers. For him it was like being in a skybox at a football game, except that one team didn't know he was there, and didn't know the other team was on the field as well. "They're within three kicks of the enemy's first line of outposts."

"Duke, tell Angelo. Get it out on the IVIS."

"Done," Masterman replied. The only thing they couldn't do was cross-deck the "take" from the Dark Star drone.

Sabre Six was now in his Bradley instead of the safer Abrams main-battle tank. He could see better out of this one, Giusti judged.

"IVIS is up," the track commander called. Colonel Giusti ducked down and twisted around the gun-turret structure to see where the sergeant was sitting. Whoever had designed the Bradley hadn't considered that a senior officer might use it—and his squadron didn't have one of the new "God" tracks yet, with the IVIS display in the back.

"First enemy post is right over there, sir, at eleven o'clock, behind this little rise," the sergeant said, tapping the screen.

"Well, let's go say hi."

"Roger that, Colonel. Kick it, Charlie," he told the driver. For the rest of the crew: "Perk it up, people. Heads up. We're in Indian Country."

How are things up north?" Diggs asked Captain Williams.

"Let's see." The captain deselected Marilyn Monroe and switched over to the "take" from Grace Kelly. "Here we go, the leading Chinese elements are within fifteen klicks of the Russians. Looks like they're settled in for the night, though. Looks like we'll be in contact first."

"Oh, well." Diggs shrugged. "Back to Miss Monroe."

"Yes, sir." More computer maneuvers. "Here we are. Here's your leading cavalry element, two klicks from John Chinaman's first hole in the ground."

Diggs had grown up watching boxing on TV. His father had been a real fan of Muhammad Ali, but even when Ali had lost to Leon Spinks, he'd known the other guy was in the ring with him. Not now. The camera zoomed in to isolate the hole. There were two men there. One was hunched down smoking a cigarette, and that must have ruined the night vision of one of them, maybe both, which explained why they hadn't seen anything yet, though they ought to have heard something . . . the Brad wasn't all that quiet . . .

"There, he just woke up a little," Williams said. On the TV screen, the head turned abruptly. Then the other head came up, and the bright point of the cigarette went flying off to their right front. Giusti's track was coming in from their left, and now both heads were oriented in that general direction.

"How close can you get?" Diggs asked.

"Let's see . . ." In five seconds, the two nameless Chinese infantrymen in their hand-dug foxhole took up half the screen. Then Williams did a split screen, like the picture-in-picture feature of some television sets. The big part showed the two doomed soldiers, and the little one was locked on the leading Bradley Scout, whose gun turret was now turning a little to the left . . . about eleven hundred meters now . . .

They had a field phone in the hole, Diggs could see now, sitting on the dirt between the two grunts. Their hole was the first in the enemy combat outpost line, and their job would have been to report back when something evil this way came. They heard something, but they weren't sure what it was, were probably waiting until they saw it. *The PLA didn't have night-vision goggles, at least not at this level,* Diggs thought. That was important information. "Okay, back it off."

"Right, sir." Williams dumped the close-up of the two grunts, returning to the picture that showed both them and the approaching Brad. Diggs was sure that Giusti's gunner could see them now. It was just a question of when he chose to take the first shot, and that was a call for the guy in the field to make, wasn't it?

"There!" The muzzle of the 25-mm chain gun flashed three times, causing the TV screen to flare, and there was a line of the tracers, streaking to the hole—

—and the two grunts were dead, killed by three rounds of high-explosive incendiary-tracer ammunition. Diggs turned.

"GUNFIGHTER, commence firing!"

"Fire!" Colonel Ardan said into his microphone. Moments later, the ground shook under their feet, and a few seconds after that came the distant sound of thunder, and more than ninety shells started arcing into the air.

Colonel Ardan had ordered a TOT, or time-on-target barrage, on the regimental command post behind the small pass that the Quarter Horse was driving for. An American invention from World War II, TOT was designed so that every round fired from the various guns targeted on the single spot on the map would arrive at the same instant, and so deny the people there the chance to dive for cover at the first warning. In the old days, that had meant laboriously computing the flight time of every single shell, but computers did that now in less time than it took to frame the thought. This particular mission had fallen to 2nd/6th and its eight-inchers, universally regarded as the most accurate heavy guns in the United States Army. Two of the shells were common impact-fused high-explosive, and the other ten were VT. That stood for "variable time," but really meant that in the nose of each shell was a tiny radar transponder set to explode the shell when it was about fifty feet off the ground. In this way, the fragments lancing away from the exploding shell were not wasted into the ground, but instead made an inverted cone of death about two hundred feet across at its base. The common shells would have the effect of making craters, immolating those who might be in individual shelter holes.

Captain Williams switched Marilyn's focus to the enemy command post. From a high perspective the thermal cameras even caught the bright dots of the shells racing through the night. Then the camera zoomed back in on the target. By Diggs's estimation, all of the shells landed in less than two seconds The effects were horrific. The six tents there evaporated, and the glowing green stick figures of human beings fell flat and stopped moving. Some pieces separated from one another, an effect Diggs had never seen.

"Whoa!" Williams observed. "Stir-fry."

What was *it about the Air Force?* General Diggs wondered. *Or maybe it was just the kid's youth.*

On the screen, some people were still moving, having miraculously survived the first barrage, but instead of moving around (or of running away, because artillery barrages didn't arrive in groups of only one) they remained at their posts, some looking to the needs of the wounded. It was courageous, but it doomed most of them to death. The only one or two people in the regimental command post who were going to live were the ones who'd pick winning lottery tickets later in life. If there were going to be as many as two, that is. The second barrage landed twenty-eight seconds after the first, and then a third thirty-one seconds after that, according to the time display in the upper right corner of the screen.

"Lord have mercy," Colonel Ardan observed in a whisper. He'd never in his career seen the effect of fire in this way. It had always been a distant, detached thing to the cannon-cocker, but now he saw what his guns actually did.

"Target, cease fire," Diggs said, using tanker-talk for *It's dead, you killed it, find another one.* A year before in the sands of Saudi Arabia, he'd watched combat on a computer screen and felt the coldness of war, but this was infinitely worse. This was like watching a Hollywood special-effects movie, but it wasn't computer-generated animation. He'd just watched the command section of an infantry regiment, perhaps forty people, erased from the face of the earth in less than ninety seconds, and they had, after all, been human beings, something this young Air Force captain didn't seem to grasp. To him it was doubtless some sort of Nintendo game. Diggs decided that it was probably better to think of it that way.

The two infantry companies on the hilltops north and south of the little pass were clobbered by a full battery each. The next question was what that would generate. With the regimental CP down, things might get a little confusing for the divisional commander. Somebody would hear the noise, and if someone from regiment had been on the phone, the disconnect first of all would make people think, *huh,* because that was the normal human reaction, even for soldiers in a combat zone; bad phone connections were probably the rule rather than the exception, and they'd probably use phones rather than radios because they were more secure and more reliable—except when shellfire killed the phone and/or cut the lines. So, the enemy division commander was probably just waking up with a tug on his shoulder, then he'd be a little confused by what he was told.

"Captain, do we know where the enemy's divisional CP is yet?"

"Probably right here, sir. Not completely sure, but there's a bunch of trucks."

"Show me on a map."

"Here, sir." The computer screen again. Diggs had a sudden thought: This young Air Force officer might eat his meals off it. More to the point, the CP was just in range of his MLRS batteries. And it had a lot of radio masts. Yeah, that was where the ChiComm general was.

"GUNFIGHTER, I want this hit right now."

"Yes, sir." And the command went out over JTIDS to the 2nd/6th Field Artillery. The MLRS tracks were already set up awaiting orders, and the target assigned was well within the slewing angle for their launchers. The range, forty-three kilometers, was just within their capability. Here also the work was done by computer. The crewmen trained the weapons on the correct azimuth, locked their suspension systems to stabilize the vehicles, and closed the shutters on their windows to protect against blast and the ingress of the rocket exhaust smoke, which was lethal when breathed. Then it was just a matter of pushing the red firing button, which happened on command of the battery commander, and all nine vehicles unleashed their twelve rockets each, about a second apart, every one of which contained 644 grenade-sized submunitions, all targeted on an area the size of three football fields.

The effect of this, Diggs saw three minutes after giving the order, was nearly seventy *thousand* individual explosions in the target area, and as bad as it had been for the regimental CP, that had been trick or treat compared to this. Whatever division he'd been facing was now as thoroughly decapitated as though by Robespierre himself.

After the initial fire, Lieutenant Colonel Giusti found that he had no targets. He sent one troop through the gap while holding the north side of it himself, taking no fire at all. The falling 155s on the hills to his front and rear explained much of that, for surely it was a storm of steel and explosives. Someone somewhere fired off a parachute flare, but nothing developed from it. Twenty minutes after the initial barrage, the leading elements of First Brigade came into view. He waited until they were within a hundred meters before pulling off to the east to rejoin his squadron in the shallow valley. He was now technically inside enemy lines, but as with the first good hit in a football game, the initial tension was now gone, and there was a job to be done.

Dick Boyle, like most aviators, was qualified in more than one sort of aircraft, and he could have chosen to fly-lead the mission in an Apache, which was one of the really enjoyable experiences for a rotary-wing pilot, but instead he remained in his UH-60 Blackhawk, the better to observe the action. His target was the independent tank brigade which was the organizational fist of the 65th Type B Group Army, and to service that target he had twenty-eight of his forty-two AH-64D Apache attack helicopters, supported by twelve Kiowa Warriors and one other Blackhawk.

The Chinese tank force was twenty miles northwest of their initial crossing point, agreeably sitting in open ground in circular formation so as to have guns pointing in all directions, none of which were a matter of concern to Dick Boyle and his men. It had probably made sense to laager them that way forty years ago, but not today, not in the night with Apaches nearby. With his OH-58Ds playing the scout role, the attack formation swept in from the north, down the valley. Whatever colonel was in command of this force had selected a place from which he could move to support any of the divisions in the 65th Army, but that merely concentrated his vehicles in a single spot, about five hundred meters across. Boyle's only worry was SAMs and maybe flak, but he had Dark Star photos to tell him where that all was, and he had a team of four Apaches delegated to handle the threat first of all.

It was in the form of two missile batteries. One was composed of four DK-9 launchers very similar to the American Chaparral, with four Sidewinder-class heat-seekers mounted on a tracked chassis. Their range would be about seven miles, just a touch longer than the effective range of his Hellfire missiles. The other was their HQ-61A, which Boyle thought of as the Chinese version of the Russian SA-6. There were fewer of these, but they had ten miles of range and supposedly a very capable radar system, and also had a hard floor of about a hundred meters, below which they couldn't track a target, which was a good thing to know, if true. His tactic would be to detect them and take them out as quickly as possible, depending on his EH-60 electronic-intelligence helicopter to sniff them out. The code for one of these was HOLIDAY. The heat-seekers were called DUCKS.

The Chinese soldiers on the ground would also have simple man-portable heat-seekers that were about as capable as the old American Redeye missile, but his Apaches had suppressed exhausts that were expected to defeat the heat-seekers—and those who had voiced the expectations weren't flying tonight. They never did.

There were more air missions tonight, and not all of them were over Russian territory. Twenty F-117A Stealth fighters had deployed to Zhigansk, and they'd mainly sat on the ground since their first arrival, waiting for bombs to be flown over, along with the guidance package attachments that changed them from simple ballistic weapons to smart bombs that went deliberately for a special piece of real estate. The special weapons for the Black Jets were the GBU-27 laser-guided hard-target penetrators. These were designed not merely to hit objects and explode, but to lance inside them before detonating, and they had special targets. There were twenty-two such targets tonight, all located in or near the cities of Harbin and Bei'an, and every one was a railroad bridge abutment.

The People's Republic depended more on its rail transportation than most countries, because it lacked the number of motor vehicles to necessitate the construction of highways, and also because the inherent efficiency of railroads appealed to the economic model in the heads of its political leaders. They did not ignore the fact that such a dependence on a single transportation modality could make them vulnerable to attack, and so at every potential chokepoint, like river crossings, they'd used the ample labor force of their country to build multiple bridges, all of heavily-built rebarred concrete abutments. *Surely,* they'd thought, *six separate crossing points at a single river couldn't* all *be damaged beyond timely repair.*

The Black Jets refueled from the usual KC-135 tanker aircraft and continued south, unseen by the radar fence erected by the PRC government along its northeastern border, and kept going. The heavily automated aircraft continued to their destinations on autopilot. They even made their bombing runs on autopilot, because it was too much to expect a pilot, however skilled, both to fly the aircraft and guide the infrared laser whose invisible grounded dot the bomb's seeker-head sought out. The attacks were made almost simultaneously, just a minute apart from east to west at the six parallel bridges over the Songhua Jiang River at Harbin. Each bridge had major pier abutments on the north and south bank. Both were attacked in each case. The bomb drops were easier than contractor tests, given the clear air and the total lack of defensive interference. In every case, the first set of six bombs fell true, striking the targets at Mach-1 speed and penetrating in for a distance of twenty-five to thirty feet before exploding. The weapons each had 535 pounds of Tritonal explosive. Not a particularly large quantity, in tight confinement it nevertheless generated hellish power, rupturing the hundred of tons of concrete around it like so much porcelain, albeit without the noise one would expect from such an event.

Not content with this destruction, the second team of F-117s struck at the northern abutments, and smashed them as well. The only lives directly lost were those of the engineer and fireman of a northbound diesel locomotive pulling a trainload of ammunition for the army group across the Amur River, who were unable to stop their train before running over the edge.

The same performance was repeated in Bei'an, where five more bridges were dropped into the Wuyur He River, and in this dual stroke, which had lasted a mere twenty-one minutes, the supply line to the Chinese invasion force was sundered for all time to come. The eight aircraft left over—they'd been a reserve force in case some of the bombs should fail to destroy their targets—headed for the loop siding near the Amur used by tank cars. This was, oddly enough, not nearly as badly hit as the bridges, since the deep-penetrating bombs went too far into the ground to create much of surface craters, though some train cars were upset, and one of them caught fire. All in all, it had been a routine mission for the F-117s. Attempts to engage them with the SAM batteries in the two cities failed because the aircraft never appeared on the search-radar screens, and a missile launch was not even attempted.

The bell went off again, and the ELF message printed up as EQT SPEC OP, or "execute special operation" in proper English. *Tucson* was now nine thousand yards behind Sierra-Eleven, and fifteen from Sierra-Twelve.

"We're going to do one fish each. Firing order Two, One. Do we have a solution light?" the captain asked.

"Valid solutions for both fish," the weapons officer replied.

"Ready Tube Two."

"Tube Two is ready in all respects, tube flooded, outer door is open, sir."

"Very well, Match generated bearings and . . . shoot!"

The handle was turned on the proper console."Tube Two fired electrically, sir." *Tucson* shuddered through her length with the sudden explosion of compressed air that ejected the weapon into the seawater.

"Unit is running hot, straight, and normal, sir," Sonar reported.

"Very well, ready Tube One," the captain said next.

"Tube One is ready in all respects, tube is flooded, outer door is open," Weps announced again.

"Very well. Match generated bearings and shoot!" This command came as something of an exclamation. The captain figured he owed it to the crew, which was at battle stations, of course.

"Tube One fired electrically, sir," the petty officer announced after turning the handle again, with exactly the same physical effect on the ship.

"Unit Two running hot, straight, and normal, sir," Sonar said again. And with that, the captain took the five steps to the Sonar Room.

"Here we go, Cap'n," the leading sonarman said, pointing to the glass screen with a yellow grease pencil.

The nine thousand yards' distance to *406* translated to four and a half nautical miles. The target was traveling at a depth of less than a hundred feet, maybe transmitting to its base on the radio or something, and steaming along at a bare five knots, judging by the blade count. That worked out to a running time of just under five minutes for the first target, and then another hundred sixty seconds or so to the second one. The second shot would probably get a little more complicated than the first. Even if they failed to hear the Mark 48 ADCAP torpedo coming, a deaf man could not miss the sound of 800 pounds of Torpex going off underwater three miles away, and he'd try to maneuver, or do something more than break out the worry beads and say a few Hail Maos, or whatever prayer these people said. The captain leaned back into the attack center.

"Reload ADCAP into Tube Two, and a Harpoon into Tube One."

"Aye, Cap'n," the Weapons Officer acknowledged.

"Where's that frigate?" he asked the lead sonarman.

"Here, sir, Luda-class, an old clunker, steam-powered, bearing two-one-six, tooling along at about fourteen knots, by blade count."

"Time on Unit Two," the skipper called.

"Minute twenty seconds to impact, sir." The captain looked at the display. If Sierra-Eleven had sonarmen on duty, they weren't paying much attention to the world around them. That would change shortly.

"Okay, go active in thirty seconds."

"Aye, aye."

On the sonar display, the torpedo was dead on the tone line from *406*. It seemed a shame to kill a submarine when you didn't even know its name . . .

"Going active on Unit Two," Weps called.

"There it is, sir," the sonarman said, pointing to a different part of the screen. The ultrasonic sonar lit up a new line, and fifteen seconds later—

—"Sierra-Eleven just kicked the gas, sir, look here, cavitation and blade count is going up, starting a turn to starboard . . . ain't gonna matter, sir," the sonarman knew from the display. You couldn't outmaneuver a -48.

"What about—Twelve?"

"He's heard it, too, Cap'n. Increasing speed and—" The sonarman flipped his headphones off. "Yeow! That hurt." He shook his head hard. "Unit impact on Sierra-Eleven, sir."

The captain picked up a spare set of headphones and plugged them in. The sea was still rumbling. The target's engine sounds had stopped almost at once—the visual display confirmed that, though the sixty-hertz line showed her generators were still—no, they stopped, too. He heard and saw the sound of blowing air. Whoever he was, he was trying to blow ballast and head for the roof, but without engine power . . . no, not much of a chance of that, was there? Then he shifted his eyes to the visual track of Sierra-Twelve. The fast-attack had been a little more awake, and was turning radically to port, and really kicking on the power. His plant noise was way up, as was his blade count . . . and he was blowing ballast tanks, too . . . why?

"Time on Unit One?" the captain called.

"Thirty seconds for original plot, probably a little longer now."

Not much longer, the skipper thought. The ADCAP was motoring along on the sunny side of sixty knots this close to the surface . . . Weps went active on it, and the fish was immediately in acquisition. A well-trained crew would have fired off a torpedo of their own, just to scare their attacker off, and maybe escape if the first fish missed—not much of a play, but it cost you nothing to do it, and maybe got you the satisfaction of having company arrive in hell right after you knocked on the door . . . but they didn't even get a decoy off. They must have all been asleep . . . certainly not very awake . . . not very alert . . . didn't they know there was a war going on . . . ? Twenty-five seconds later, they found out the hard way, when another splotch appeared on the sonar display.

Well, he thought, *two for two. That was pretty easy.* He stepped back into the attack center and lifted a microphone. "Now hear this. This is the captain speaking. We just launched two fish on a pair of ChiComm submarines. We won't be seeing either one of them anymore. Well done to everybody. That is all." Then he looked over at his communications officer: "Prepare a dispatch to CINCLANT. 'Four Zero Six destroyed at . . . Twenty-Two-Fifty-Six Zulu along with escorting SSN. Now engaging Frigate.' Send that off when we get to antenna depth."

"Yes, sir."

"Tracking party, we have a frigate bearing two-one-six. Let's get a track on him so we can Harpoon his ass."

"Aye, sir," said the lieutenant manning the tracking plot.

It was approaching six in the evening in Washington, where everybody who was somebody was watching TV, but not the commercial kind. The Dark Star feeds were going up on encrypted satellite links, and being distributed around Washington over dedicated military fiber-optic lines. One of those, of course, led to the White House Situation Room.

"Holy God," Ryan said. "It's like some kind of fucking video game. How long have we had this capability?"

"It's pretty new, Jack, and yeah," the Vice President agreed, "it is kind of obscene—but, well, it's just what the operators see. I mean, the times I splashed airplanes, I got to see it, just I was in a G-suit with a Tomcat strapped to my back. Somehow this feels dirtier, man. Like watching a guy and a gal go at it, and not in training films—"

"What?"

"That's what you call porno flicks on the boats, Jack, 'training films.' But this is like peeking in a window on a guy's wedding night, and he doesn't know about it . . . feels kinda dirty."

"The people will like it," Arnie van Damm predicted. "The average guy out there, especially kids, to them it'll be like a movie."

"Maybe so, Arnie, but it's a snuff film. Real lives being snuffed out, and in large numbers. That division CP Diggs got with his MLRS rockets—I mean, Jesus Christ. It was like an act of an angry pagan god, like the meteor that got the dinosaurs, like a murderer wasting a kid in a schoolyard," Robby said, searching for just how dirty it felt to him. But it was business, not personal, for what little consolation that might be to the families of the departed.

"Getting some radio traffic," Tolkunov told General Bondarenko. The intelligence officer had half a dozen electronic-intelligence groups out, listening in on the frequencies used by the PLA. They usually spoke in coded phrases which were difficult to figure out, especially since the words changed on a day-to-day basis, along with identifying names for the units and personalities involved.

But the security measures tended to fall by the wayside when an emergency happened, and senior officers wanted hard information in a hurry. In this case, Bondarenko had watched the take from Grace Kelly and felt little pity for the victims, wishing only that he'd been the one inflicting the casualties, because it was *his* country the Chinks had invaded.

"The American artillery doctrine is impressive, isn't it?" Colonel Tolkunov observed.

"They've always had good artillery. But so do we, as this Peng fellow will discover in a few hours," CINC-FAR EAST replied. "What do you think he'll do?"

"It depends on what he finds out," the G-2 replied. "The information that gets to him will probably be fairly confusing, and it will concern him, but less than his own mission."

And that made sense, Gennady Iosifovich had to agree. Generals tended to think in terms of the missions assigned to them, leaving the missions of others to those others, trusting them to do the jobs assigned to *them.* It was the only way an army could function, really. Otherwise you'd be so worried about what was happening around you that you'd never get your own work done, and the entire thing would quickly grind to a halt. It was called tunnel vision when it didn't work, and good teamwork when it did.

"What about the American deep strikes?"

"Those Stealth aircraft are amazing. The Chinese rail system is complete disrupted. Our guests will soon be running short of fuel."

"Pity," Bondarenko observed. The Americans were efficient warriors, and their doctrine of deep-strike, which the Russian military had scarcely considered, could be damned effective if you brought it off, and if your enemy couldn't adapt to it. Whether the Chinese could adapt was something they'd have to see about. "But they still have sixteen mechanized divisions for us to deal with."

"That is so, Comrade General," Tolkunov agreed.

FALCON THREE to FALCON LEADER, I see me a SAM track. It's a Holiday," the pilot reported. "Hilltop two miles west of the CLOVERLEAF—wait, there's a Duck there, too."

"Anything else?" FALCON LEAD asked. This captain commanded the Apaches tasked to SAM suppression.

"Some light flak, mainly two-five mike-mike set up around the SAMs. Request permission to fire, over."

"Stand by," FALCON LEAD replied. "EAGLE LEAD, this is FALCON LEAD, over."

"EAGLE LEAD copies, FALCON," Boyle replied from his Blackhawk.

"We have SAM tracks in view. Permission to engage, over."

Boyle thought fast. His Apaches now had the tank laager in sight and surrounded on three sides. Okay, Falcon was approaching the hill overlooking the laager, code-named CLOVERLEAF. Well, it was about time.

"Permission granted. Engage the SAMs. Out."

"Roger, engaging. FALCON THREE, this is LEAD. Take 'em out."

"Take your shot, Billy," the pilot told his gunner.

"Hellfire, now!" The gunner in the front seat triggered off his first missile. The seven-inch-wide missile leaped off its launch-rail with a flare of yellow light, and immediately tracked on the laser dot. Through his thermal viewer, he saw a dismounted crewman looking that way, and he immediately pointed toward the helicopter. He was yelling to get someone's attention, and the race was between the inbound missile and human reaction time. The missile had to win. He got the attention of someone, maybe his sergeant or lieutenant, who then looked in the direction he was pointing. You could tell by the way he cocked his head that he didn't see anything at first, while the first one was jerking his arm like a fishing pole, and the second one saw it, but by that time there was nothing for him to do but throw himself to the ground, and even that was a waste of energy. The Hellfire hit the base of the launcher assembly and exploded, killing everything within a ten-meter circle.

"Tough luck, Joe." Then the gunner switched over to the other one, the Holiday launcher. This crew had been alerted by the sound, and he could see them scurrying to light up their weapon. They'd just about gotten to their places when the Duck launcher blew up.

Next came the flak. There were six gun mounts, equally divided between 25- and 35-mm twin gun sets, and those could be nasty. The Apache closed in. The gunner selected his own 20-mm cannon and walked it across every site. The impacts looked like flashbulbs, and the guns were knocked over, some with exploding ammo boxes.

"EAGLE LEAD, FALCON THREE, this hilltop is cleaned off. We're circling to make sure. No coverage over the CLOVERLEAF now. It's wide open."

"Roger that." And Boyle ordered his Apaches in.

It was about as fair as putting a professional boxer into the ring against a six-year-old. The Apaches circled the laagered tanks just like Indians in the movies around a circled wagon train, except in this one, the settlers couldn't fire back. The Chinese tank crewmen were mainly sleeping outside, next to their mounts. Some crews were in their vehicles, standing guard after a fashion, and some dismounted crewmen were walking around on guard, holding Type 68 rifles. They'd been alerted somewhat by the explosions on the hilltop overlooking the laager. Some of the junior officers were shouting to get their men up and into their tanks, not knowing the threat, but thinking naturally enough that the safe place to be was behind armor, from which place they could shoot back to defend themselves. They could scarcely have been more wrong.

The Apaches danced around the laager, sideslipping as the gunners triggered off their missiles. Three of the PLA tanks used their thermal viewers and actually saw helicopters and shot at them, but the range of the tank guns was only half that of the Hellfires, and all of the rounds fell well short, as did the six handheld HN-5 Sams that were fired into the night. The Hellfires, however, did not, and in every case—only two of them missed—the huge warheads had the same effect on the steel tanks that a cherry bomb might have on a plastic model. Turrets flew into the air atop pillars of flame, then crashed back down, usually upside-down on the vehicles to which they'd been attached. There'd been eighty-six tanks here, and that amounted to three missiles per helicopter, with a few lucky gunners getting a fourth shot. All in all, the destruction of this brigade took less than three minutes, leaving the colonel who'd been in command to stand at his command post with openmouthed horror at the loss of the three hundred soldiers he'd been training for over a year for this very moment. He even survived a strafing of his command section by a departing Apache, seeing the helicopter streak overhead so quickly that he didn't even have time to draw his service pistol.

"EAGLE LEAD, FALCON LEAD. The CLOVERLEAF is toast, and we are RTB, over."

Boyle could do little more than shake his head. "Roger, FALCON. Well done, Captain."

"Roger, thank you, sir. Out." The Apaches formed up and headed northwest to their base to refuel and rearm for the next mission. Below, he could see the First Brigade, blown through the gap in Chinese lines, heading southeast into the Chinese logistics area.

Task Force 77 had been holding station east of the Formosa Strait until receiving orders to race west. The various Air Bosses had word that one of their submarines had eliminated a Chinese boomer and fast-attack submarine, which was fine with them, and probably just peachy for the task force commander. Now it was their job to go after the People's Liberation Army Navy, which, they all agreed, was a hell of a name for a maritime armed force. The first aircraft to go off, behind the F-14Ds flying barrier combat air patrol, or BARCAP, for the Task Force, were the E-2C Hawkeye radar aircraft, the Navy's two-engine prop-driven mini-AWACS. These were tasked to finding targets for the shooters, mainly F/A-18 Hornets.

This was to be a complex operation. The Task Force had three SSNs assigned to "sanitize" the area of ChiComm submarines. The Task Force commander seemed especially concerned with the possibility of a Chinese diesel-powered SSK punching a hole in one of his ships, but that was not an immediate concern for the airmen, unless they could find one tied alongside the pier.

The only real problem was target identification. There was ample commercial shipping in the area, and they had orders to leave that entirely alone, even ships flying the PRC flag. Anything with a SAM radar would be engaged beyond visual range. Otherwise, a pilot had to have eyeballs on the target before loosing a weapon. Of weapons they had plenty, and ships were fragile targets as far as missiles and thousand-pound bombs were concerned. The overall target was the PLAN South Sea Fleet, based at Guangszhou (better known to Westerners as Canton). The naval base there was well-sited for attack, though it was defended by surface-to-air missile batteries and some flak.

The F-14s on the lead were guided to aerial targets by the

Hawkeyes. Again since there was commercial air traffic in the sky, the fighter pilots had to close to visual range for a positive ID of their targets. This could be dangerous, but there was no avoiding it.

What the Navy pilots didn't know was that the Chinese knew the electronic signature of the APD-138 radar on the E-2Cs, and therefore they also knew that something was coming. Fully a hundred Chinese fighters scrambled into the air and set up their own combat air patrol over their East Coast. The Hawkeyes spotted that and radioed a warning to the advancing fighters, setting the stage for a massive air engagement in the predawn darkness.

There was no elegant way to go about it. Two squadrons of Tomcats, twenty-four in all, led the strike force. Each carried four AIM-54C Phoenix missiles, plus four AIM-9X Sidewinders, The Phoenixes were old—nearly fifteen years old for some of them, and in some cases the solid-fuel motor bodies were developing cracks that would soon become apparent. They had a theoretical range of over a hundred miles, however, and that made them useful things to hang on one's airframe.

The Hawkeye crews had orders to make careful determination of what was a duck and what was a goose, but it was agreed quickly that two or more aircraft flying in close formation were not Airbuses full of civilian passengers, and the Tomcats were authorized to shoot a full hundred miles off the Chinese mainland. The first salvo was composed of forty-eight. Of these, six self-destructed within five hundred yards of their launching aircraft, to the displeased surprise of the pilots involved. The remaining forty-two streaked upward in a ballistic path to a height of over a hundred thousand feet before tipping over at Mach-5 speed and switching on their millimeter-band Doppler homing radars. By the end of their flight, their motors were burned out, and they did not leave the smoke trail that pilots look for. Thus, though the Chinese pilots knew that they'd been illuminated, they couldn't see the danger coming, and therefore could not see anything to evade. The forty-two Phoenixes started going off in their formations, and the only survivors were those who broke into radical turns when they saw the first warheads go off. All in all, the forty-eight launches resulted in thirty-two kills. The surviving Chinese pilots were shaken but also enraged. As one man, they turned east and lit up their search radars, looking for targets for their own air-to-air missiles. These they found, but beyond range of their weapons. The senior officer surviving the initial attack ordered them to go to afterburner and streak east, and at a range of sixty miles, they fired off their PL-10 radar-guided air-to-air missiles. These were a copy of the Italian Aspide, in turn a copy of the old American AIM-7E Sparrow. To track a target, they required that the launching aircraft keep itself and its radar pointed at the target. In this case, the Americans were heading in as well, with their own radars emitting, and what happened was a great game of chicken, with the fighter pilots on either side unwilling to turn and run—and besides, they all figured that to do so merely guaranteed one's death. And so the race was between airplanes and missiles, but the PL-10 had a speed of Mach 4 against the Phoenix's Mach 5.

Back on the Hawkeyes, the crewmen kept track of the engagement. Both the aircraft and the streaking missiles were visible on the scopes, and there was a collective holding of breath for this one.

The Phoenixes hit first, killing thirty-one more PLAAF fighters, and also turning off their radars rather abruptly. That made some of their missiles "go dumb," but not all, and the six Chinese fighters that survived the second Phoenix barrage found themselves illuminating targets for a total of thirty-nine PL-10s, which angled for only four Tomcats.

The American pilots affected by this saw them coming, and the feeling wasn't particularly pleasant. Each went to afterburner and dove for the deck, losing every bit of chaff and flares he had in his protection pods, plus turning the jamming pods up to max power. One got clean away. Another lost most of them in the chaff, where the Chinese missiles exploded like fireworks in his wake, but one of the F-14s had nineteen missiles chasing him alone, and there was no avoiding them all. The third missile got close enough to trigger its warhead, and then nine more, and the Tomcat was reduced to chaff itself, along with its two-man crew. That left one Navy fighter whose radar-intercept officer ejected safely, though the pilot did not.

The remaining Tomcats continued to bore in. They were out of Phoenix missiles now, and closed to continue the engagement with Sidewinders. Losing comrades did nothing more than anger them for the moment, and this time it was the Chinese who turned back and headed for their coast, chased by a cloud of heat-seeking missiles.

This bar fight had the effect of clearing the way for the strike force.

The PLAN base had twelve piers with ships alongside, and the United States Navy went after its Chinese counterpart—as usually happened, on the principle that in war people invariably kill those most like themselves before going after the different ones.

The first to draw the wrath of the Hornets were the submarines. They were mainly old Romeo-class diesel boats, long past whatever prime they'd once had. They were mainly rafted in pairs, and the Hornet drivers struck at them with Skippers and SLAMs. The former was a thousand-pound bomb with a rudimentary guidance package attached, plus a rocket motor taken off obsolete missiles, and they proved adequate to the task. The pilots tried to guide them between the rafted submarines, so as to kill two with a single weapon, and that worked in three out of five attempts. SLAM was a land-attack version of the Harpoon anti-ship missile, and these were directed at the port and maintenance facilities without which a naval base is just a cluttered beach. The damage done looked impressive on the videotapes. Other aircraft tasked to a mission called IRON HAND sought out Chinese missile and flak batteries, and engaged those at safe distance with HARM anti-radiation missiles which sought out and destroyed acquisition and illumination radars with high reliability.

All in all, the first U.S. Navy attack on the mainland of East Asia since Vietnam went off well, eliminating twelve PRC warships and laying waste to one of its principal naval bases.

Other bases were attacked with Tomahawk cruise missiles launched mainly from surface ships. Every PLAN base over a swath of five hundred miles of coast took one form of fire or another, and the ship count was jacked up to sixteen, all in a period of a little over an hour. The American tactical aircraft returned to their carriers, having spilled the blood of their enemies, though also having lost some of their own.

CHAPTER 58

Political Fallout

It was a difficult night for Marshal Luo Cong, the Defense Minister for the People's Republic of China. He'd gone to bed about eleven the previous night, concerned with the ongoing operations of his military forces, but pleased that they seemed to be going well. And then, just after he'd closed his eyes, the phone rang.

His official car came at once to convey him to his office, but he didn't enter it. Instead he went to the Defense Ministry's communications center, where he found a number of senior- and mid-level officers going over fragmentary information and trying to make sense of it. Minister Luo's presence didn't help them, but just added stress to the existing chaos.

Nothing seemed clear, except that they could identify holes in their information. The 65th Army had seemingly dropped off the face of the earth. Its commanding general had been visiting one of his divisions, along with his staff, and hadn't been heard from since 0200 or so. Nor had the division's commanding general. In fact, nothing at all was known about what was happening up there. To fix that, Marshal Luo ordered a helicopter to fly up from the depot at Sunwu. Then came reports from Harbin and Bei'an of air raids that had damaged the railroads. A colonel of engineers was dispatched to look into that.

But just when he thought he'd gotten a handle on the difficulties in Siberia, then came reports of an air attack on the fleet base at Guangszhou, and then the lesser naval bases at Haikuo, Shantou, and Xiachuandao. In each case, the headquarters facilities seemed hard-hit, since there was no response from the local commanders. Most disturbing of all was the report of huge losses to the fighter regiments in the area—reports of American naval aircraft making the attacks. Then finally, worst of all, a pair of automatic signals, the distress buoys from his country's only nuclear-powered missile submarine and the hunter submarine detailed to protect her, the *Hai Long,* were both radiating their automated messages. It struck the marshal as unlikely to the point of impossibility that so many things could have happened at once. And yet there was more. Border radar emplacements were off the air and could not be raised on radio or telephone. Then came another phone call from Siberia. One of the divisions on the left shoulder of the breakthrough—the one the commanding general of 65th Type B Group Army had been visiting a few hours before—reported . . . that is, a junior communications officer said, a subunit of the division reported, that unknown armored forces had lanced through its western defenses, going east, and . . . disappeared?

"How the hell does an enemy attack successfully *and disappear*?" the marshal had demanded, in a voice to make the young captain wilt. "Who reported this?"

"He identified himself as a major in the Third Battalion, 745th Guards Infantry Regiment, Comrade Marshal," was the trembling reply. "The radio connection was scratchy, or so it was reported to us."

"And who made the report?"

"A Colonel Zhao, senior communications officer in the intelligence staff of 71st Type C Group Army north of Bei'an. They are detailed to border security in the breakthrough sector," the captain explained.

"I know that!" Luo bellowed, taking out his rage on the nearest target of opportunity.

"Comrade Marshal," said a new voice. It was Major General Wei Dao-Ming, one of Luo's senior aides, just called in from his home after one more of a long string of long days, and showing the strain, but trying to smooth the troubled waters even so. "You should let me and my staff assemble this information in such a way that we can present it to you in an orderly manner."

"Yes, Wei, I suppose so." Luo knew that this was good advice, and Wei was a career intelligence officer, accustomed to organizing information for his superiors. "Quick as you can."

"Of course, Comrade Minister," Wei said, to remind Luo that he was a political figure now rather than the military officer he'd grown up as.

Luo went to the VIP sitting room, where green tea was waiting. He reached into the pocket of his uniform tunic and pulled out some cigarettes, strong unfiltered ones to help him wake up. They made him cough, but that was all right. By the third cup of tea, Wei returned with a pad of paper scribbled with notes.

"So, what is happening?"

"The picture is confused, but I will tell you what I know, and what I think," Wei began.

"We know that General Qi of Sixty-fifth Army is missing, along with his staff. They were visiting 191st Infantry Division, just north and west of our initial breakthrough. The 191st is completely off the air as well. So is the 615th Independent Tank Brigade, part of Sixty-fifth Army. Confused reports talk of an air attack on the tank brigade, but nothing precise is known. The 735th Guards Infantry Regiment of the 191st division is also off the air, cause unknown. You ordered a helicopter out of Sunwu to take a look and report back. The helicopter will get off at dawn. Well and good.

"Next, there are additional reports from that sector, none of which make sense or help form any picture of what is happening. So, I have ordered the intelligence staff of the Seventy-first Army to send a reconnaissance team across the river and ascertain what's happening there and report back. That will take about three hours.

"The good news is that General Peng Xi-Wang remains in command of 34th Shock Army, and will be at the gold mine before midday. Our armored spearhead is deep within enemy territory. I expect the men are waking up right now and will be moving within the hour to continue their attack.

"Now, this news from the navy people is confusing, but it's not really a matter of consequence. I've directed the commander of South Sea Fleet to take personal charge of the situation and report back. So say about three hours for that.

"So, Comrade Minister, we will have decent information shortly, and then we can start addressing the situation. Until then, General Peng will soon resume his offensive, and by evening, our country will be much richer," Wei concluded. He knew how to keep his minister happy. His reward for this was a grunt and a nod. "Now," General Wei went on, "why don't you get a few hours of sleep while we maintain the watch?"

"Good idea, Wei." Luo took two steps to the couch and lay down across it. Wei opened the door, turned off the lights, then he closed the door behind himself. The communications center was only a few more steps.

"Now," he said, stealing a smoke from a major, "what the hell is happening out there?"

"If you want an opinion," a colonel of intelligence said, "I think the Americans just flexed their muscles, and the Russians will do so in a few hours."

"What? Why do you say that? And why the Russians?"

"Where has their air force been? Where have their attack helicopters been? We don't know, do we? Why don't we know? Because the Americans have swatted our airplanes out of the sky like flies, that's why."

"We've deluded ourselves that the Russians don't want to fight, haven't we? A man named Hitler once thought the same thing. He died a few years later, the history books say. We similarly deluded ourselves into thinking the Americans would not strike us hard for political reasons. Wei, some of our political leaders have been off chasing the dragon!" The aphorism referred to opium-smoking, a popular if illegal pastime in the southern part of China a few centuries before. "There were no political considerations. They were merely building up their forces, which takes time. And the Russians didn't fight us because they wanted us to get to the end of the logistical string, and then the fucking Americans cut that string off at Harbin and Bei'an! General Peng's tanks are nearly *three* hundred kilometers inside Russia now, with only *two* hundred kilometers of fuel in their tanks, and there'll be no more fuel coming up to them. We've taken over two *thousand* tanks and turned their crews into badly trained light infantry! That is what's happening, Comrade Wei," the colonel concluded.

"You can say that sort of thing to me, Colonel. Say it before Minister Luo, and your wife will pay the state for the bullet day after tomorrow," Wei warned.

"Well, I know it," Colonel Geng He-ping replied. "What will happen to you later today, Comrade General Wei, when you organize the information and find out that I am correct?"

"The remainder of today will have to take care of itself" was the fatalistic reply. "One thing at a time, Geng." Then he assembled a team of officers and gave them each a task to perform, found himself a chair to sit in, and wondered if Geng might have a good feel for the situation—

"Colonel Geng?"

"Yes, Comrade General?"

"What do you know of the Americans?"

"I was in our embassy in Washington until eighteen months ago. While there, I studied their military quite closely."

"And—are they capable of what you just said?"

"Comrade General, for the answer to that question, I suggest you consult the Iranians and the Iraqis. I'm wondering what they might try next, but thinking exactly like an American is a skill I have never mastered."

They're moving," Major Tucker reported with a stretch and a yawn. "Their reconnaissance element just started rolling. Your people have pulled way back. How come?"

"I ordered them to collect Comrade Gogol before the Chinese kill him," Colonel Tolkunov told the American. "You look tired."

"Hell, what's thirty-six hours in the same chair?" *A helluva sore back, that's what it is,* Tucker didn't say. Despite the hours, he was having the time of his life. For an Air Force officer who'd flunked out of pilot training, making him forever an "unrated weenie" in Air Force parlance, a fourth-class citizen in the Air Force pecking order—below even helicopter pilots—he was earning his keep more and better than he'd ever done. He'd probably been more valuable to his side in this war than even that Colonel Winters, with all his air-to-air snuffs. But if anyone ever said such a thing to him, he'd have to *aw-shucks* it and look humbly down at his shoes. *Humble, my ass,* Tucker thought. He was proving the value of a new and untested asset, and doing so like the Red Baron in his red Fokker Trimotor. The Air Force was not a service whose members cultivated humility, but his lack of pilot's wings had compelled him to do just that for all ten of his years of uniformed service. The next generation of UAVs would have weapons attached, and maybe even be able to go air-to-air, and then, maybe, he'd show those strutting fighter jock-itches who had the real balls in this man's Air Force. Until then, he'd just have to be content gathering information that helped the Russians kill Joe Chink and all his brothers, and if this was Nintendo War, then little Danny Tucker was the by-God cock of the by-God walk in *this* virtual world.

"You have been most valuable to us, Major Tucker."

"Thank you, sir. Glad to help," Tucker replied with his best little-boy smile. *Maybe I'll grow me a good mustache.* He set the thought aside with a smile, and sipped some instant coffee from a MRE pack—the extra caffeine was about the only thing keeping him up at the moment. But the computer was doing most of the work, and it showed the Chinese reconnaissance tracks moving north.

Son of a bitch," Captain Aleksandrov breathed. He'd heard about Gogol's wolf pelts on state radio, but he hadn't seen the TV coverage, and the sight took his breath away. Touching one, he halfway expected it to be cold and stiff like wire, but, no, it was like the perfect hair of a perfect blonde . . .

"And who might you be?" The old man was holding a rifle and had a decidedly gimlet eye.

"I am Captain Fedor Il'ych Aleksandrov, and I imagine you are Pavel Petrovich Gogol."

A nod and a smile. "You like my furs, Comrade Captain?"

"They are unlike anything I have ever seen. We have to take these with us."

"Take? Take where? I'm not going anywhere," Pasha said.

"Comrade Gogol, I have my orders—to get you away from here. Those orders come from Headquarters Far East Command, and those orders will be obeyed, Pavel Petrovich."

"No Chink is going to chase me off my land!" His old voice thundered.

"No, Comrade Gogol, but soldiers of the Russian Army will not leave you here to die. So, that is the rifle you killed Germans with?"

"Yes, many, many Germans," Gogol confirmed.

"Then come with us, and maybe you can kill some yellow invaders."

"Who exactly are you?"

"Reconnaissance company commander, Two-Six-Five Motor Rifle Division. We've been playing hide-and-seek with the Chinks for four long days, and now we're ready to do some real fighting. Join us, Pavel Petrovich. You can probably teach us a few things we need to know." The young handsome captain spoke in his most reasonable and respectful tones, for this old warrior truly deserved it. The tone turned the trick.

"You promise me I will get to take one shot?"

"My word as a Russian officer, Comrade," Aleksandrov pledged, with a bob of his head.

"Then I come." Gogol was already dressed for it—the heat in his cabin was turned off. He shouldered his old rifle and an ammunition pack containing forty rounds—he'd never gone into the field with more than that—and walked to the door. "Help me with my wolves, boy, will you?"

"Gladly, Grandfather." Then Aleksandrov found out how heavy they were. But he and Buikov managed to toss them inside their BRM, and the driver headed off.

"Where are they?"

"About ten kilometers back. We've been in visual contact with them for days, but they've pulled us back. Away from them."

"Why?"

"To save you, you old fool," Buikov observed with a laugh. "And to save these pelts. These are too good to drape over the body of some Chinese strumpet!"

"I think, Pasha—I am not sure," the captain said, "but I think it's time for our Chinese guests to get a proper Russian welcome."

"Captain, look!" the driver called.

Aleksandrov lifted his head out the big top hatch and looked forward. A senior officer was waving to him to come forward more quickly. Three minutes later, they halted alongside him.

"You are Aleksandrov?"

"Yes, Comrade General!" the young man confirmed to the senior officer.

"I am General Sinyavskiy. You've done well, boy. Come out here and talk to me," he ordered in a gruff voice that was not, however, unkind.

Aleksandrov had only once seen his senior commander, and then only at a distance. He was not a large man, but you didn't want him as a physical enemy in a small room. He was chewing on a cigar that had gone out seemingly hours before, and his blue eyes blazed.

"Who is this?" Sinyavskiy demanded. Then his face changed. "Are you the famous Pasha?" he asked more respectfully.

"Senior Sergeant Gogol of the Iron and Steel Division," the old man said with great dignity, and a salute which Sinyavskiy returned crisply.

"I understand you killed some Germans in your day. How many, Sergeant?"

"Count for yourself, Comrade General," Gogol said, handing his rifle over.

"Damn," the general observed, looking at the notches, like those on the pistol of some American cowboy. "I believe you really did it. But combat is a young man's game, Pavel Petrovich. Let me get you to a place of safety."

Gogol shook his head. "This captain promised me one shot, or I would not have left my home."

"Is that a fact?" The commanding general of 265th Motor Rifle looked around. "Captain Aleksandrov, very well, we'll give our old comrade his one shot." He pointed to a place on the map before him. "This should be a good spot for you. And when you can, get him the hell away from there," Sinyavskiy told the young man. "Head back this way to our lines. They'll be expecting you. Boy, you've done a fine job shadowing them all the way up. Your reward will be to see how we greet the bastards."

"Behind the reconnaissance element is a large force."

"I know. I've been watching them on TV for a day and a half, but our American friends have cut off their supplies. And we will stop them, and we will stop them right here."

Aleksandrov checked the map reference. It looked like a good spot with a good field of fire, and best of all, an excellent route to run away on. "How long?" he asked.

"Two hours, I should think. Their main body is catching up with the screen. Your first job is to make their screen vehicles disappear."

"Yes, Comrade General, that we can do for you!" the captain responded with enthusiasm.

Sunrise found Marion Diggs in a strangely bizarre environment. Physically, the surroundings reminded him of Fort Carson, Colorado, with its rolling hills and patchy pine woods, but it was unlike America in its lack of paved roads or civilization, and that explained why the Chinese had invaded here. With little civilian population out here, there was no infrastructure or population base to provide for the area's defense, and that had made things a lot easier for John Chinaman. Diggs didn't mind it, either. It was like his experience in the Persian Gulf—no noncombatants to get in the way—and that was good.

But there were a lot of Chinese to get in the way. Mike Francisco's First Brigade had debauched into the main logistics area for the Chinese advance. The ground was carpeted with trucks and soldiers, but while most of them were armed, few were organized into cohesive tactical units, and that made all the difference. Colonel Miguel Francisco's brigade of four battalions had been organized for combat with the infantry and tank battalions integrated into unified battalion task groups of mixed tanks and Bradleys, and these were sweeping across the ground like a harvesting machine in Kansas in August. If it was painted green, it was shot.

The monstrous Abrams main-battle tanks moved over the rolling ground like creatures from Jurassic Park—alien, evil, and unstoppable, their gun turrets traversing left and right—but without firing their main guns. The real work was being done by the tank commanders and their M2 .50 machine guns, which could turn any truck into an immobile collection of steel and canvas. Just a short burst into the engine made sure that the pistons would never move again, and the cargo in the back would remain where it was, for inspection by intelligence officers, or destruction by explosives-carrying engineer troops who came behind the tanks in their HMMWVs. Some resistance was offered by the Chinese soldiers, but only by the dumb ones, and never for long. Even those with man-portable anti-tank weapons rarely got close enough to use them, and those few who popped up from Wolfholes only scratched the paint on the tanks, and usually paid for their foolishness with their lives. At one point, a battalion of infantry did launch a deliberate attack, supported by mortars that forced the tank and Bradley crews to button up and reply with organized fire. Five minutes of 155-mm fire and a remorseless advance by the Bradleys, spitting fire from their chain guns and through the firing ports for the mounted infantry inside, made them look like fire-breathing dragons, and these dragons were not a sign of good luck for the Chinese soldiers. That battalion evaporated in twenty minutes, along with its dedicated but doomed commander.

Intact enemy armored vehicles were rarely seen by the advancing First Brigade. Where it went, Apache attack helicopters had gone before, looking for targets for their Hellfire missiles, and killing them before the ground troops could get close. All in all, it was a perfect military operation, totally unfair in the balance of forces. It wasn't the least bit sporting, but a battlefield is not an Olympic stadium, and there were no uniformed officials to guard the supposed rules of fair play.

The only exciting thing was the appearance of a Chinese army helicopter, and two Apaches blazed after it and destroyed it with air-to-air missiles, dropping it in the Amur River close to the floating bridges, which were now empty of traffic but not yet destroyed.

"What have you learned, Wei?" Marshal Luo asked, when he emerged from the conference room he'd used for his nap.

"The picture is still unclear in some respects, Comrade Minister," the general answered.

"Then tell me what is clear," Luo ordered.

"Very well. At sea, we have lost a number of ships. This evidently includes our ballistic missile submarine and its escorting hunter submarine, cause unknown, but their emergency beacons deployed and transmitted their programmed messages starting at about zero-two-hundred hours. Also lost are seven surface warships of various types from our South Sea Fleet. Also, seven fleet bases were attacked by American aircraft, believed to be naval carrier aircraft, along with a number of surface-to-air missile and radar sites on the southeastern coast. We've succeeded in shooting down a number of American aircraft, but in a large fighter battle, we took serious losses to our fighter regiments in that region."

"Is the American navy attacking us?" Luo asked.

"It appears that they are, yes," General Wei answered, choosing his words with care. "We estimate four of their aircraft carriers, judging by the number of aircraft involved. As I said, reports are that we handled them roughly, but our losses were severe as well."

"What are their intentions?" the minister asked.

"Unclear. They've done serious damage to a number of bases, and I doubt we have a single surface ship surviving at sea. Our navy personnel have not had a good day," Wei concluded. "But that is not really a matter of importance."

"The attack on the missile submarine is," Luo replied. "That is an attack on a strategic asset. That is something we must consider." He paused. "Go on, what else?"

"General Qi of Sixty-fifth Army is missing and presumed dead, along with all of his senior staff. We've made repeated attempts to raise him by radio, with no result. The 191st Infantry Division was attacked last night by heavy forces of unknown identity. They sustained heavy losses due to artillery and aircraft, but two of their regiments report that they are holding their positions. The 735th Guards Infantry Regiment evidently took the brunt of the attack, and reports from there are fragmentary.

"The most serious news is from Harbin and Bei'an. Enemy aircraft attacked all of the railroad bridges in both cities, and all of them took damage. Rail traffic north has been interrupted. We're trying now to determine how quickly it might be reestablished."

"Is there any good news?" Marshal Luo asked.

"Yes, Comrade Minister. General Peng and his forces are getting ready now to resume their attack. We expect to have the Russian gold field in our control by midday," Wei answered, inwardly glad that he didn't have to say what had happened to the logistical train behind Peng and his 34th Shock Army. Too much bad news could get the messenger killed, and *he* was the messenger.

"I want to talk to Peng. Get him on the phone," Luo ordered.

"Telephone lines have been interrupted briefly, but we do have radio contact with him," Wei told his superior.

"Then get me Peng on the radio," Luo repeated his order.

"What is it, Wa?" Peng asked. Couldn't he even take a piss without interruption?

"Radio, it's the Defense Minister," his operations officer told him.

"Wonderful," the general groused, heading back to his command track as he buttoned his fly. He ducked to get inside and lifted the microphone. "This is General Peng."

"This is Marshal Luo. What is your situation?" the voice asked through the static.

"Comrade Marshal, we will be setting off in ten minutes. We have still not made contact with the enemy, and our reconnaissance has seen no sizable enemy formations in our area. Have you developed any intelligence we can use?"

"Be advised we have aerial photography of Russian mechanized units to your west, probably division strength. I would advise you to keep your mechanized forces together, and guard your left flank."

"Yes, Comrade Marshal, I am doing that," Peng assured him. The real reason he stopped every day was to allow his divisions to close up, keeping his fist tight. Better yet, 29th Type A Group Army was right behind his if he needed support. "I recommend that 43rd Army be tasked to flank guard."

"I will give the order," Luo promised. "How far will you go today?"

"Comrade Marshal, I will send a truckload of gold back to you this very evening. Question: What is this I've heard about damage to our line of supply?"

"There was an attack last night on some railroad bridges in Harbin and Bei'an, but nothing we can't fix."

"Very well. Comrade Marshal, I must see to my dispositions."

"Carry on, then. Out."

Peng set the microphone back in its holder. "Nothing he can't fix, he says."

"You know what those bridges are like. You'd need a nuclear weapon to hurt them," Colonel Wa Cheng-Gong observed confidently.

"Yes, I would agree with that." Peng stood, buttoned his tunic, and reached for a mug of morning tea. "Tell the advance guard to prepare to move out. I'm going up front this morning, Wa. I want to see this gold mine for myself."

"How far up front?" the operations officer asked.

"With the lead elements. A good officer leads from the front, and I want to see how our people move. Our reconnaissance screen hasn't detected anything, has it?"

"Well, no, Comrade General, but—"

"But what?" Peng demanded.

"But a prudent commander leaves leading to lieutenants and captains," Wa pointed out.

"Wa, sometimes you talk like an old woman," Peng chided.

There," Yefremov said. "They took the bait."

It was just after midnight in Moscow, and the embassy of the People's Republic of China had most of its lights off, but not all; more to the point, three windows had their lights on, and their shades fully open, and they were all in a row. It was just as perfect as what the Americans called a "sting" operation. He'd stood over Suvorov's shoulder as he'd typed the message: *I have the pieces in place now. I have the pieces in place now. If you wish for me to carry out the operation, leave three windows in a row with the lights on and the windows fully open.* Yefremov had even had a television camera record the event, down to the point where the traitor Suvarov had tapped the ENTER key to send the letter to his Chink controller. And he'd gotten a TV news crew to record the event as well, because the Russian people seemed to trust the semi-independent media more than their government now, for some reason or other. Good, now they had proof positive that the Chinese government was conspiring to kill President Grushavoy. That would play well in the international press. And it wasn't an accident. The windows all belonged to the Chief of Mission in the PRC embassy, and he was, right now, asleep in his bed. They'd made sure of that by calling him on the phone ten minutes earlier.

"So, what do we do now?"

"We tell the president, and then, I expect, we tell the TV news people. And we probably spare Suvarov's life. I hope he likes it in the labor camp."

"What about the killings?"

Yefremov shrugged. "He only killed a pimp and a whore. No great loss, is it?"

Senior Lieutenant Komanov had not exactly enjoyed his last four days, but at least they'd been spent profitably, training his men to shoot. The reservists, now known as BOYAR FORCE, had spent them doing gunnery, and they'd fired four basic loads of shells over that time, more than any of them had ever shot on active duty, but the Never Depot had been well stocked with shells. Officers assigned to the formation by Far East Command told them that the Americans had moved by to their south the previous day, and that their mission was to slide north of them, and do it today. Only thirty kilometers stood between them and the Chinese, and he and his men were ready to pay them a visit. The throaty rumble of his own diesel engine was answered by the thunder of two hundred others, and BOYAR started moving northeast through the hills.

Peng and his command section raced forward, calling ahead on their radios to clear the way, and the military-police troops doing traffic control waved them through. Soon they reached the command section of the 302nd Armored, his leading "fist" formation, commanded by Major General Ge Li, a squat officer whose incipient corpulence made him look rather like one of his tanks.

"Are you ready, Ge?" Peng asked. The man was well-named for his task. "Ge" had the primary meaning of "spear."

"We are ready," the tanker replied. "My leading regiments are turning over and straining at the leash."

"Well, shall we observe from the front together?"

"Yes!" Ge jumped aboard his own command tank—he preferred this to a personnel carrier, despite the poorer radios, and led the way forward. Peng immediately established a direct radio connection with his subordinate.

"How far to the front?"

"Three kilometers. The reconnaissance people are moving now, and they are another two kilometers ahead."

"Lead on, Ge," Peng urged. "I want to see that gold mine."

It was a good spot, Aleksandrov thought, *unless the enemy got his artillery set up sooner than expected,* and he hadn't seen or heard Chinese artillery yet. He was on the fairly steep reverse side of an open slope that faced south, rather like a lengthy ramp, perhaps three kilometers in length, not unlike a practice shooting range at a regimental base. The sun was starting to crest the eastern horizon, and they could see now, which always made soldiers happy. Pasha had stolen a spare coat and laid his rifle across it, standing in the open top hatch of the BRM, looking through the telescopic sight of his rifle.

"So, what was it like to be a sniper against the Germans?" Aleksandrov asked once he'd settled himself in.

"It was good hunting. I tried to stick to killing officers. You have more effect on them that way," Gogol explained. "A German private—well, he was just a man—an enemy, of course, but he probably had no more wish to be on a battlefield than I did. But an officer, those were the ones who directed the killing of my comrades, and when you got one of them, you confused the enemy."

"How many?"

"Lieutenants, eighteen. Captains, twelve. Only three majors, but nine colonels. I decapitated nine Fritz regiments. Then, of course, sergeants and machine-gun crews, but I don't remember them as well as the colonels. I can still see every one of those, my boy," Gogol said, tapping the side of his head.

"Did they ever try to shoot at you?"

"Mainly with artillery," Pasha answered. "A sniper affects the morale of a unit. Men do not like being hunted like game. But the Germans didn't use snipers as skillfully as we did, and so they answered me with field guns. That," he admitted, "could be frightening, but it really told me how much the Fritzes feared me," Pavel Petrovich concluded with a cruel smile.

"There!" Buikov pointed. Just off the trees to the left.

"Ahh," Gogol said, looking through his gunsight. "Ahh, yes."

Aleksandrov laid his binoculars on the fleeting shape. It was the vertical steel side on a Chinese infantry carrier, one of those he'd been watching for some days now. He lifted his radio. "This is Green Wolf One. Enemy in sight, map reference two-eight-five, nine-zero-six. One infantry track coming north. Will advise."

"Understood, Green Wolf," the radio crackled back.

"Now, we must just be patient," Fedor Il'ych said. He stretched, touching the camouflage net that he'd ordered set up the moment they'd arrived in this place. To anyone more than three hundred meters away, he and his men were just part of the hill crest. Next to him, Sergeant Buikov lit a cigarette, blowing out the smoke.

"That is bad for us," Gogol advised. "It alerts the game."

"They have little noses," Buikov replied.

"Yes, and the wind is in our favor," the old hunter conceded.

Lordy, Lordy," Major Tucker observed. "They've bunched up some."

It was Grace Kelly again, looking down on the battlefield-to-be like Pallas Athena looking down on the plains of Troy. And about as pitilessly. The ground had opened up a little, and the corridor they moved across was a good three kilometers wide, enough for a battalion of tanks to travel line-abreast, a regiment in columns of battalions, three lines of thirty-five tanks each with tracked infantry carriers interspersed with them. Colonels Aliyev and Tolkunov stood behind him, speaking in Russian over their individual telephones to the 265th Motor Rifle's command post. In the night, the entire 201st had finally arrived, plus leading elements of the 80th and 44th. There were now nearly three divisions to meet the advancing Chinese, and included in that were three full divisional artillery sets, plus, Tucker saw for the first time, a shitload of attack helicopters sitting on the ground thirty kilometers back from the point of expected contact. Joe Chink was driving into a motherfucker of an ambush. Then a shadow crossed under Grace Kelly, out of focus, but something moving fast.

It was two squadrons of F-16C fighter-bombers, and they were armed with Smart Pigs.

That was the nickname for J-SOW, the Joint Stand-Off Weapon. The night before, other F-16s, the CG version, the new and somewhat downsized version of the F-4G Wild Weasel, had gone into China and struck at the line of border radar transmitters, hitting them with HARM antiradar missiles and knocking most of them off the air. That denied the Chinese foreknowledge of the inbound strike. They had been guided by two E-3B Sentry aircraft, and protected by three squadrons of F-15C

Eagle air-superiority fighters in the event some Chinese fighters appeared again to die, but there had been little such fighter activity in the past thirty-six hours. The Chinese fighter regiments had paid a bloody price for their pride, and were staying close to home in what appeared to be a defense mode—on the principle that if you weren't attacking, then you were defending. In fact they were doing little but flying standing patrols over their own bases—that's how thoroughly they had been whipped by American and Russian fighters—and that left the air in American and Russian control, which was going to be bad news for the People's Liberation Army.

The F-16s were at thirty thousand feet, holding to the east. They were several minutes early for the mission, and circled while awaiting word to attack. Some concertmaster was stage-managing this, they all thought. They hoped he didn't break his little baton-stick-thing.

Getting closer," Pasha observed with studied nonchalance.

"Range?" Aleksandrov asked the men down below in the track.

"Twenty-one hundred meters, within range," Buikov reported from inside the gun turret. "The fox and the gardener approach, Comrade Captain."

"Leave them be for the moment, Boris Yevgeniyevich."

"As you say, Comrade Captain." Buikov was comfortable with the no-shoot rule, for once.

How much farther to the reconnaissance screen?" Peng asked.

"Two more kilometers," Ge replied over the radio. "But that might not be a good idea."

"Ge, have you turned into an old woman?" Peng asked lightly.

"Comrade, it is the job of lieutenants to find the enemy, not the job of senior generals," the division commander replied in a reasonable voice.

"Is there any reason to believe the enemy is nearby?"

"We are in Russia, Peng. They're here somewhere."

"He is correct, Comrade General," Colonel Wa Cheng-gong pointed out to his commander.

"Rubbish. Go forward. Tell the reconnaissance element to stop and await us," Peng ordered. "A good commander leads from the front!" he announced over the radio.

"Oh, shit," Ge observed in his tank. "Peng wants to show off his *ji-ji.* Move out," he ordered his driver, a captain (his entire crew was made of officers). "Let's lead the emperor to the recon screen."

The brand-new T-98 tank surged forward, throwing up two rooster tails of dirt as it accelerated. General Ge was in the commander's hatch, with a major acting as gunner, a duty he practiced diligently because it was his job to keep his general alive in the event of contact with the enemy. For the moment, it meant going ahead of the senior general with blood in his eye.

Why did they stop?" Buikov asked. The PLA tracks had suddenly halted nine hundred meters off, all five of them, and now the crews dismounted, manifestly to take a stretch, and five of them lit up smokes.

"They must be waiting for something," the captain thought aloud. Then he got on the radio. "Green Wolf here, the enemy has halted about a kilometer south of us. They're just sitting still."

"Have they seen you?"

"No, they've dismounted to take a piss, looks like, just standing there. We have them in range, but I don't want to shoot until they're closer," Aleksandrov reported.

"Very well, take your time. There's no hurry here. They're walking into the parlor very nicely."

"Understood. Out." He set the mike down. "Is it time for morning break?"

"They haven't been doing that the last four days, Comrade Captain," Buikov reminded his boss.

"They appear relaxed enough."

"I could kill any of them now," Gogol said, "but they're all privates, except for that one . . ."

"That's the fox. He's a lieutenant, likes to run around a lot. The other officer's the gardener. He likes playing with plants," Buikov told the old man.

"Killing a lieutenant's not much better than killing a corporal," Gogol observed. "There's too many of them."

"What's this?" Buikov said from his gunner's seat. "Tank, enemy tank coming around the left edge, range five thousand."

"I see it!" Aleksandrov reported. ". . . Just one? Only one tank—oh, all right, there's a carrier with it—"

"It's a command track, look at all those antennas!" Buikov called.

The gunner's sight was more powerful than Aleksandrov's binoculars. The captain couldn't confirm that for another minute or so. "Oh, yes, that's a command track, all right. I wonder who's in it . . . "

There they are," the driver called back. "The reconnaissance section, two kilometers ahead, Comrade General."

"Excellent," Peng observed. Standing up to look out of the top of his command track with his binoculars, good Japanese ones from Nikon. There was Ge in his command tank, thirty meters off to the right, protecting him as though he were a good dog outside the palace of some ancient nobleman. Peng couldn't see anything to be concerned about. It was a clear day, with some puffy white clouds at three thousand meters or so. If there were American fighters up there, he wasn't going to worry about them. Besides, they'd done no ground-attacking that he'd heard about, except to hit those bridges back at Harbin, and one might as well attack a mountain as those things, Peng was sure. He had to hold on to the sill of the hatch lest the pitching of the vehicle smash him against it—*it was a track specially modified for senior officers, but no one had thought to make it safer to stand in,* he thought sourly. He wasn't some peasant-private who could smash his head with no consequence . . . Well, in any case, it was a good day to be a soldier, in the field leading his men. A fair day, and no enemy in sight.

"Pull up alongside the reconnaissance track," he ordered his driver.

Who the hell is this?" Captain Aleksandrov wondered aloud. "Four big antennas, at least a division commander," Buikov thought aloud. "My thirty will settle his hash."

"No, no, let's let Pasha have him if he gets out."

Gogol had anticipated that. He was resting his arms on the steel top of the BRM, tucking the rifle in tight to his shoulder. The only thing in his way was the loose weave of the camouflage netting, and that wasn't an obstacle to worry about, the old marksman was sure.

"Stopping to see the fox?" Buikov said next.

"Looks that way," the captain agreed.

"Comrade General!" the young lieutenant called in surprise.

"Where's the enemy, Boy?" Peng asked loudly in return.

"General, we haven't seen much this morning. Some tracks in the ground, but not even any of that for the past two hours."

"Nothing at all?"

"Not a thing," the lieutenant replied.

"Well, I thought there'd be something around." Peng put his foot in the leather stirrup and climbed to the top of his command vehicle.

"It's a general, has to be, look at that clean uniform!" Buikov told the others as he slewed his turret around to center his sight on the man eight hundred meters away. It was the same in any army. Generals never got dirty.

"Pasha," Aleksandrov asked, "ever kill an enemy general before?"

"No," Gogol admitted, drawing the rifle in very tight and allowing for the range. . . .

"Better to go to that ridgeline, but our orders were to stop at once," the lieutenant told the general.

"That's right," Peng agreed. He took out his Nikon binoculars and trained them on the ridge, perhaps eight hundred meters off. Nothing to see except for that one bush . . .

Then there was a flash—

"Yes!" Gogol said the moment the trigger broke. Two seconds, about, for the bullet to—

They'd never hear the report of the shot over the sound of their diesel engines, but Colonel Wa heard the strange, wet thud, and his head turned to see General Peng's face twist into surprise rather than pain, and Peng grunted from the sharp blow to the center of his chest, and then his hands started coming down, pulled by the additional weight of the binoculars—and then his body started down, falling off the top of the command track through the hatch into the radio-filled interior.

That got him," Gogol said positively. "He's dead." He almost added that it might be fun to skin him and lay his hide in the river for a final swim and a gold coating, but, no, you only did that to wolves, not people—not even Chinese.

"Buikov, take those tracks!"

"Gladly, Comrade Captain," and the sergeant squeezed the trigger, and the big machine gun spoke.

They hadn't seen or heard the shot that had killed Peng, but there was no mistaking the machine cannon that fired now. Two of the reconnaissance tracks exploded at once, but then everything started moving, and fire was returned.

"Major!" General Ge called.

"Loading HEAT!" The gunner punched the right button, but the autoloader, never as fast as a person, took its time to ram the projective and then the propellant case into the breech.

Back us up!" Aleksandrov ordered loudly. The diesel engine was already running, and the BRM's transmission set in reverse. The corporal in the driver's seat floored the pedal and the carrier jerked backward. The suddenness of it nearly lost Gogol over the side, but Aleksandrov grabbed his arm and dragged him down inside, tearing his skin in the process. "Go north!" the captain ordered next.

"I got three of the bastards!" Buikov said. Then the sky was rent by a crash overhead. Something had gone by too fast to see, but not too fast to hear.

"That tank gunner knows his business," Aleksandrov observed. "Corporal, get us out of here!"

"Working on it, Comrade Captain."

"GREEN WOLF to command!" the captain said next into the radio.

"Yes, GREEN WOLF, report."

"We just killed three enemy tracks, and I think we got a senior officer. Pasha, Sergeant Gogol, that is, killed a Chinese general officer, or so it appeared."

"He was a general, all right," Buikov agreed. "The shoulder boards were pure gold, and that was a command track with four big radio antennas."

"Understood. What are you doing now, GREEN WOLF?"

"We're getting the fuck away. I think we'll be seeing more Chinks soon."

"Agreed, GREEN WOLF. Proceed to divisional CP. Out."

"Yuriy Andreyevich, you will have heavy contact in a few minutes. What is your plan?"

"I want to volley-fire my tanks before firing my artillery. Why spoil the surprise, Gennady?" Sinyavskiy asked cruelly. "We are ready for them here."

"Understood. Good luck, Yuriy."

"And what of the other missions?"

"BOYAR is moving now, and the Americans are about to deploy their magical pigs. If you can handle the leading Chinese elements, those behind ought to be roughly handled."

"You can rape their daughters for all I care, Gennady."

"That is *nekulturniy,* Yuriy. Perhaps their wives," he suggested, adding, "We are watching you on the television now."

"Then I will smile for the cameras," Sinyavskiy promised.

The orbiting F-16 fighters were under the tactical command of Major General Gus Wallace, but he, at the moment, was under the command—or at least operating under the direction—of a Russian, General-Colonel Gennady Bondarenko, who was in turn guided by the action of this skinny young Major Tucker and Grace Kelly, a soulless drone hovering over the battlefield.

"There they go, General," Tucker said, as the leading Chinese echelons resumed their drive north.

"I think it is time, then." He looked to Colonel Aliyev, who nodded agreement.

Bondarenko lifted the satellite phone. "General Wallace?"

"I'm here."

"Please release your aircraft."

"Roger that. Out." And Wallace shifted phone receivers. "EAGLE ONE, this is ROUGHRIDER. Execute, execute, execute. Acknowledge."

"Roger that, sir, copy your order to execute. Executing now. Out." And the colonel on the lead AWACS shifted to a different frequency: "CADILLAC LEAD, this is EAGLE ONE. Execute your attack. Over."

"Roger that," the colonel heard. "Going down now. Out."

The F-16s had been circling above the isolated clouds. Their threat receivers chirped a little bit, reporting the emissions of SAM radars somewhere down there, but the types indicated couldn't reach this high, and their jammer pods were all on anyway. On command, the sleek fighters changed course for the battlefield far below and to their west. Their GPS locators told them exactly where they were, and they also knew where their targets were, and the mission became a strictly technical exercise.

Under the wings of each aircraft were the Smart Pigs, four to the fighter, and with forty-eight fighters, that came to 192 J-SOWs. Each of these was a canister thirteen feet long and not quite two feet wide, filled with BLU-108 submunitions, twenty per container. The fighter pilots punched the release triggers, dropped their bombs, and then angled for home, letting the robots do the rest of the work. The Dark Star tapes would later tell them how they'd done.

The Smart Pigs separated from the fighters, extended their own little wings to guide themselves the rest of the way to the target area. They knew this information, having been programmed by the fighters and were now able to follow guidance from their own GPS receivers. This they did, acting in accordance with their own onboard mini-computers, until each reached a spot five thousand feet over their designated segment of the battlefield. They didn't know that this was directly over the real estate occupied by the Chinese 29th Type A Group Army and its three heavy divisions, which included nearly seven hundred main-battle tanks, three hundred armored personnel carriers, and a hundred mobile guns. That made a total of roughly a thousand targets for the nearly four thousand descending submunitions. But the falling bomblets were guided, too, and each had a seeker looking for heat of the sort radiated by an operating tank, personnel carrier, self-propelled gun, or truck. There were a lot of them to look for.

No one saw them coming. They were small, no larger, really, than a common crow, and falling rapidly; they were also painted white, which helped them blend in to the morning sky. Each had a rudimentary steering mechanism, and at an altitude of two thousand feet they started looking for and homing in on targets. Their downward speed was such that a minor deflection of their control vanes was sufficient to get them close, and close meant straight down.

They exploded in bunches, almost in the same instant. Each contained a pound and a half of high-explosive, the heat from which melted the metal casing, which then turned into a projectile—the process was called "self-forging"—which blazed downward at a speed of ten thousand feet per second. The armor on the top of a tank is always the thinnest, and five times the thickness would have made no difference. Of the 921 tanks on the field, 762 took hits, and the least of these destroyed the vehicles' diesel engine. Those less fortunate took hits through the turret, which killed the crews at once and/or ignited the ammunition storage, converting each armored vehicle into a small man-fabricated volcano. Just that quickly, three mechanized divisions were changed into one badly shaken and disorganized brigade. The infantry carriers fared no better, and it was worst of all for the trucks, most of them carrying ammunition or other flammable supplies.

All in all, it took less than ninety seconds to turn 29th Type A Group Army into a thinly spread junkyard and funeral pyre.

Holy God," Ryan said. "Is this for-real?"

"Seeing is believing. Jack, when they came to me with the idea for J-SOW, I thought it had to be something from a science-fiction book. Then they demo'd the submunitions out at China Lake, and I thought, Jesus, we don't need the Army or the Marines anymore. Just send over some F-18s and then a brigade of trucks full of body bags and some ministers to pray over them. Eh, Mickey?"

"It's some capability," General Moore agreed. He shook his head. "Damn, just like the tests."

"Okay, what's happening next?"

Next" was just off the coast near Guangszhou. Two Aegis cruisers, *Mobile Bay* and *Princeton,* plus the destroyers *Fletcher, Fife,* and *John Young,* steamed in line-ahead formation out of the morning fog and turned broadside to the shore. There was actually a decent beach at this spot. There was nothing much behind it, just a coastal-defense missile battery that the fighter-bombers had immolated a few hours before. To finish that job, the ships trained their guns to port and let loose a barrage of five-inch shells. The crack and thunder of the gunfire could be heard on shore, as was the shriek of the shells passing overhead, and the explosions of the detonations. That included one missile that the bombs of the previous night had missed, plus the crew getting it ready for launch. People living nearby saw the gray silhouettes against the morning sky, and many of them got on the telephone to report what they saw, but being civilians, they reported the wrong thing, of course.

It was just after nine in the morning in Beijing when the Politburo began its emergency session. Some of those present had enjoyed a restful night's sleep, and then been disturbed by the news that came over the phone at breakfast. Those better informed had hardly slept at all past three in the morning and, though more awake than their colleagues, were not in a happier mood.

"Well, Luo, what is happening?" Interior Minister Tong Jie asked.

"Our enemies counterattacked last night. This sort of thing we must expect, of course," he admitted in as low-key a voice as circumstances permitted.

"How serious were these counterattacks?" Tong asked.

"The most serious involved some damage to railroad bridges in Harbin and Bei'an, but repairs are under way."

"I hope so. The repair effort will require some months," Qian Kun interjected.

"Who said that!" Luo demanded harshly.

"Marshal, I supervised the construction of two of those bridges. This morning I called the division superintendent for our state railroad in Harbin. All six of them have been destroyed—the piers on both sides of the river are totally wrecked; it will take over a month just to clear the debris. I admit this surprised me. Those bridges were very sturdily built, but the division superintendent tells me they are quite beyond repair."

"And who is this defeatist?" Luo demanded.

"He is a loyal party member of long standing and a very competent engineer whom you will *not* threaten in my presence!" Qian shot back. "There is room in this building for many things, but there is *not* room here for a *lie!*"

"Come now, Qian," Zhang Han Sen soothed. "We need not have that sort of language here. Now, Luo, how bad is it really?"

"I have army engineers heading there now to make a full assessment of the damage and to commence repairs. I am confident that we can restore service shortly. We have skilled bridging engineers, you know."

"Luo," Qian said, "your magic army bridges can support a tank or a truck, yes, but not a locomotive that weighs two hundred tons pulling a train weighing four thousand. Now, what else has gone wrong with your Siberian adventure?"

"It is foolish to think that the other side will simply lie down and die. Of course they fight back. But we have superior forces in theater, and we will smash them. We will have that new gold mine in our pocket before this meeting is over," the Defense Minister promised. But the pledge seemed hollow to some of those around the table.

"What else?" Qian persisted.

"The American naval air forces attacked last night and succeeded in sinking some of our South Sea Fleet units."

"Which units?"

"Well, we have no word from our missile submarine, and—"

"They sank our only missile submarine?" Premier Xu asked. "How is this possible? Was it sitting in harbor?"

"No," Luo admitted. "It was at sea, in company with another nuclear submarine, and that one is also possibly lost."

"Marvelous!" Tong Jie observed. "Now the Americans strike at our strategic assets! That's half our nuclear deterrent gone, and that was the *safe* half of it. What goes on, Luo? What is happening now?"

At his seat, Fang Gan took note of the fact that Zhang was strangely subdued. Ordinarily he would have leaped to Luo's defense, but except for the one conciliatory comment, he was leaving the Defense Minister to flap in the wind. What might that mean?

"What do we tell the people?" Fang asked, trying to center the meeting on something important.

"The people will believe what they are told," Luo said.

And everyone nodded nervous agreement on that one. They *did* control the media. The American CNN news service had been turned off all over the People's Republic, along with all Western news services, even in Hong Kong, which usually enjoyed much looser reins than the rest of the country. But the thing no one addressed, but everyone knew to worry about, was that every soldier had a mother and a father who'd notice when the mail home stopped coming. Even in a nation as tightly controlled as the PRC, you couldn't stop the Truth from getting out—or rumors, which, though false, could be even worse than an adverse Truth. People *would* believe things other than those they were told to believe, if those other things made more sense than the Official Truth proclaimed by their government in Beijing.

Truth was something so often feared in this room, Fang realized, and for the first time in his life he wondered why that had to be. If the Truth was something to fear, might that mean they were doing something wrong in here? But, no, that couldn't be true, could it? Didn't they have a perfect political model for reality? Wasn't that Mao's bequest to their country?

But if that were true, why did they fear having the people find out what was really happening?

Could it be that they, the Politburo members, could handle the Truth and the peasantry could not?

But then, if they feared having the peasantry get hold of the Truth, didn't that have to mean that the Truth was harmful to the people sitting in this room? And if the Truth was a danger to the peasants and workers, then didn't *they* have to be wrong?

Fang suddenly realized how dangerous was the thought that had just entered his mind.

"Luo, what does it mean to us strategically," the Interior Minister asked, "if the Americans remove half of our strategic weapons? Was that done deliberately? If so, for what cause?"

"Tong, you do not sink a ship by accident, and so, yes, the attack on our missile submarine must have been a deliberate act," Luo answered.

"So, the Americans deliberately removed from the table one of our only methods for attacking them directly? Why? Was that not a political act, not just a military one?"

The Defense Minister nodded. "Yes, you could see it that way."

"Can we expect the Americans to strike at us directly? To this date they have struck some bridges, but what about our government and vital industries? Might they strike directly at *us*?" Tong went on.

"That would be unwise. We have missiles targeted at their principal cities. They know this. Since they disarmed themselves of nuclear missiles some years ago—well, they still have nuclear bombs that can be delivered by bombers and tactical aircraft, of course, but not the ability to strike at us in the way that we could strike at them—and the Russians, of course."

"How sure are we that they are disarmed?" Tong persisted.

"If they have ballistic arms, they've concealed it from everyone," Tan Deshi told them all. Then he shook his head decisively. "No, they have no more."

"And that gives us an advantage, doesn't it?" Zhong asked, with a ghoulish smile.

USS *Gettysburg* was alongside the floating pier in the York River. Once the warheads for Trident missiles had been stored here, and there must still have been some awaiting dismantlement, because there were Marines to be seen, and only Marines were entrusted to guard the Navy's nuclear weapons. But none of those were on the pier. No, the trucks that rolled out from the weapons depot were carrying long square-cross-sectioned boxes that contained SM-2 ER Block-IVD surface-to-air missiles. When the trucks got to the cruiser, a traveling crane lifted them up to the foredeck of the ship, where, with the assistance of some strong-backed sailors, the boxes were rapidly lowered into the vertical launch cells of the forward missile launcher. It took about four minutes per box, Gregory saw, with the captain pacing his wheelhouse all the while. Gregory knew why. He had an order to take his cruiser right to Washington, D.C., and the order had the word "expedite" on it. Evidently, "expedite" was a word with special meaning for the United States Navy, like having your wife call for you from the baby's room at two in the morning. The tenth box was duly lowered, and the crane swung clear of the ship.

"Mr. Richardson," Captain Blandy said to the Officer of the Deck.

"Yes, sir," the lieutenant answered.

"Let's get under way."

Gregory walked out on the bridge wing to watch. The Special Sea Detail cast off the six-inch hawsers, and scarcely had they fallen clear of the cleats on the main deck when the cruiser's auxiliary power unit started pushing the ten thousand tons of gray steel away from the floating pier. And the ship was for sure in a hurry. She was not fifteen feet away when the main engines started turning, and less than a minute after that, Gregory heard the *WHOOSH* of the four jet-turbines taking a big gulp of air, and he could *feel* the ship accelerate for the Chesapeake Bay, almost like being on a city transit bus.

"Dr. Gregory?" Captain Blandy had stuck his head out the pilothouse door.

"Yeah, Captain?"

"You want to get below and do your software magic on our birds?"

"You bet." He knew the way, and in three minutes was at the computer terminal which handled that task.

"Hey, Doc," Senior Chief Leek said, sitting down next to him. "All ready? I'm supposed to help."

"Okay, you can watch, I suppose." The only problem was that it was a clunky system, about as user-friendly as a chain saw, but as Leek had told him a week before, this was the flower of 1975 technology, back when an Apple-II with 64K of RAM was the cat's own ass. Now he had more computing power in his wristwatch. Each missile had to be upgraded separately, and each was a seven-step process.

"Hey, wait a minute," Gregory objected. The screen wasn't right.

"Doc, we loaded six Block-IVD. The other two are stock SM-2 ER Block IIIC radar-homers. What can I tell you, Cap'n Blandy's conservative."

"So I only do the upgrade on holes one through six?"

"No, do 'em all. It'll just ignore the changes you made to the infrared homing code. The chips on the birds can handle the extra code, no sweat, right, Mr. Olson?"

"Correct, Senior Chief," Lieutenant Olson confirmed. "The missiles are current technology even if the computer system isn't. It probably costs more to make missile seeker-heads with current technology that can talk to this old kludge than it would to buy a new Gateway to upgrade the whole system, not to mention having a more reliable system overall, but you'll have to talk to NAVSEA about that."

"Who?" Gregory asked.

"Naval Sea Systems Command. They're the technical geniuses who won't put stabilizers on these cruisers. They think it's good for us to puke in a seaway."

"Feathermerchants," Leek explained. "Navy's full of 'em—on land, anyway." The ship heeled strongly to starboard.

"Cap'n's in a hurry, ain't he?" Gregory observed. *Gettysburg* was making a full-speed right-angle turn to port.

"Well, SACLANT said it's the SecDef's idea. I guess that makes it important," Mr. Olson told their guest.

I think this is imprudent," Fang told them all.

"Why is that?" Luo asked.

"Is fueling the missiles necessary? Is there not a danger of provocation?"

"I suppose this is a technical matter," Qian said. "As I recall, once you fuel them, you cannot keep them fueled for more than—what? Twelve hours?"

The technocrat caught the Defense Minister off guard with that question. He didn't know the answer. "I will have to consult with Second Artillery for that," he admitted.

"So, then, you will not prepare them for launch until we have a chance to consider the matter?" Qian asked.

"Why—of course not," Luo promised.

"And so the real problem is, how do we tell the people what has transpired in Siberia?"

"The people will believe what we tell them to believe!" Luo said yet again.

"Comrades," Qian said, struggling to keep his voice reasonable, "we cannot conceal the rising of the sun. Neither can we conceal the loss of our rail-transport system. Nor can we conceal the large-scale loss of life. Every soldier has parents, and when enough of them realize their son is lost, they will speak of it, and the word will get out. We must face facts here. It is better, I think, to tell the people that there is a major battle going on, and there has been loss of life. To proclaim that we are winning when we may not be is dangerous for all of us."

"You say the people will rise up?" Tong Jie asked.

"No, but I say there could be dissatisfaction and unrest, and it is in our collective interest to avoid that, is it not?" Qian asked the assembly.

"How will adverse information get out?" Luo asked.

"It frequently does," Qian told them. "We can prepare for it, and mitigate the effect of adverse information, or we can try to withstand it. The former offers mild embarrassment to us. The latter, if it fails, could be more serious."

"The TV will show what we wish them to show, and the people will see nothing else. Besides, General Peng and his army group are advancing even as we speak."

What do they call it?"

"This one's Grace Kelly. The other two are Marilyn Monroe and—can't remember," General Moore said. "Anyway, they named 'em for movie stars."

"And how do they transmit?"

"The Dark Star uploads directly to a communications satellite, encrypted, of course, and we distribute it out of Fort Belvoir."

"So, we can send it out any way we want?"

"Yes, sir."

"Okay, Ed, the Chinese are telling their people what?"

"They started off by saying the Russians committed a border intrusion and they counterattacked. They're also saying that they're kicking Ivan's ass."

"Well, that's not true, and it'll be especially untrue when they reach the Russian stop-line. That Bondarenko guy's really played his cards beautifully. They're pretty strung out. We've chopped their supply line for fair, and they're heading into a real motherfucker of an ambush," the DCI told them. "How about it, General?"

"The Chinese just don't know what's ahead of them. You know, out at the NTC we keep teaching people that he who wins the reconnaissance battle wins the war. The Russians know what's happening. The Chinese do not. My God, this Dark Star has really exceeded our expectations."

"It's some shiny new toy, Mickey," Jackson agreed. "Like going to a Vegas casino when you're able to read the cards halfway through the deck. You just can't hardly lose this way."

The President leaned forward. "You know, one of the reasons we took it on the chin with Vietnam is how the people got to see the war every night on Huntley-Brinkley. How will it affect the Chinese if their people see the war the same way, but *live* this time?"

"The battle that's coming? It'll shake them up a lot," Ed Foley thought. "But how do we—oh, oh, yeah . . . Holy shit, Jack, are you serious?"

"Can we do it?" Ryan asked.

"Technically? It's child's play. My only beef is that it really lets people know one of our capabilities. This is sensitive stuff, I mean, right up there with the performance of our reconnaissance satellites. It's not the sort of thing you just let out."

"Why not? Hell, couldn't some university duplicate the optics?" the President asked.

"Well, yeah, I guess. The imagery systems are good, but they're not all that new a development, except some of the thermal systems, but even so—"

"Ed, let's say we can shock them into stopping the war. How many lives would it save?"

"Quite a few," the DCI admitted. "Thousands. Maybe tens of thousands."

"Including some of our people?"

"Yes, Jack, including some of ours."

"And from a technical point of view, it's really child's play?"

"Yes, it's not technically demanding at all."

"Then turn the children loose, Ed. Right now," Ryan ordered.

"Yes, Mr. President."

CHAPTER 59

Loss of Control

With the death of General Peng, command of 34th Shock Army devolved to Major General Ge Li, CG also of 302nd Armored. His first task was to get himself clear, and this he did, ordering his tank off the long gun-range slope while one of the surviving reconnaissance tracks recovered Peng's body. All of those tracked vehicles also pulled back, as Ge figured his first task was to determine what had happened, rather then to avenge the death of his army commander. It took him twenty minutes to motor back to his own command section, where he had a command track identical to the one Peng had driven about in. He needed the radios, since he knew the field phones were down, for whatever reason he didn't know.

"I need to talk to Marshal Luo," he said over the command frequency, which was relayed back to Beijing via several repeater stations. It took another ten minutes because the Defense Minister, he was told, was in a Politburo meeting. Finally, the familiar voice came over the radio.

"This is Marshal Luo."

"This is Major General Ge Li, commanding Three-On-Second Armored. General Peng Xi-Wang is dead," he announced.

"What happened?"

"He went forward to join the reconnaissance section to see the front, and he was killed by a sniper bullet. The recon section ran into a small ambush, looked like a single Russian personnel carrier. I drove it off with my own tank," Ge went on. It was fairly true, and it seemed like the sort of thing he was supposed to say.

"I see. What is the overall situation?" the Defense Minister asked.

"Thirty-fourth Shock Army is advancing—well, it was. I paused the advance to reorganize the command group. I request instructions, Comrade Minister."

"You will advance and capture the Russian gold mine, secure it, and then continue north for the oil field."

"Very well, Comrade Minister, but I must advise you that Twenty-ninth Army, right behind us, sustained a serious attack an hour ago, and was reportedly badly hit."

"How badly?"

"I do not know. Reports are sketchy, but it doesn't sound good."

"What sort of attack was it?"

"An air attack, origin unknown. As I said, reports are very sketchy at this time. Twenty-ninth seems very disorganized at the moment," Ge reported.

"Very well. You will continue the attack. Forty-third Army is behind Twenty-ninth and will support you. Watch your left flank—"

"I know of the reports of Russian units to my west," Ge said. "I will orient a mechanized division to deal with that, but . . ."

"But what?" Luo asked.

"But, Comrade Marshal, we have no reconnaissance information on what lies before us. I need such information in order to advance safely."

"You will find your safety in advancing rapidly into enemy territory and destroying whatever formations you find," Luo told him forcefully. "Continue your advance!"

"By your command, Comrade Minister." There wasn't much else he could say to that.

"Report back to me as necessary."

"I will do that," Ge promised.

"Very well. Out." Static replaced the voice.

"You heard him," Ge said to Colonel Wa Cheng-gong, whom he'd just inherited as army operations officer. "Now what, Colonel?"

"We continue the advance, Comrade General."

Ge nodded to the logic of the situation. "Give the order."

It took hold four minutes later, when the radio commands filtered down to battalion level and the units started moving.

They didn't need reconnaissance information now, Colonel Wa reasoned. They knew that there had to be some light Russian units just beyond the ridgeline where Peng had met his foolish death. *Didn't I warn him?* Wa raged to himself. *Didn't Ge warn him?* For a general to die in battle was not unexpected. But to die from a single bullet fired by some lone rifleman was worse than foolish. Thirty years of training and experience wasted, lost to a single rifleman!

There they go again," Major Tucker said, seeing the plume of diesel exhaust followed by the lurching of numerous armored vehicles. "About six kilometers from your first line of tanks."

"A pity we can't get one of these terminals to Sinyavskiy," Bondarenko said.

"Not that many of them, sir," Tucker told him. "Sun Micro Systems is still building them for us."

That was General Ge Li," Luo told the Politburo. "We've had some bad luck. General Peng is dead, killed by a sniper bullet, I just learned."

"How did that happen?" Premier Xu asked.

"Peng had gone forward, as a good general should, and there was a lucky Russian out there with a rifle," the Defense Minister explained. Then one of his aides appeared and walked to the marshal's seat, handing him a slip of paper. He scanned it. "This is confirmed?"

"Yes, Comrade Marshal. I requested and got confirmation myself. The ships are in sight of land even now."

"What ships? What land?" Xu asked. It was unusual for him to take an active part in these meetings. Usually he let the others talk, listened passively, and then announced the consensus conclusions reached by the others.

"Comrade," Luo answered. "It seems some American warships are bombarding our coast near Guangszhou."

"Bombarding?" Xu asked. "You mean with guns?"

"That's what the report says, yes."

"Why would they do that?" the Premier asked, somewhat nonplussed by this bit of information.

"To destroy shore emplacements, and—"

"Isn't that what one does prior to invading, a preparation to putting troops on the beach?" Foreign Minister Shen asked.

"Well, yes, it could be that, I suppose," Luo replied, "but—"

"Invasion?" Xu asked. "A direct attack on our own soil?"

"Such a thing is most unlikely," Luo told them. "They lack the ability to put troops ashore in sufficiently large numbers. America simply doesn't have the troops to do such a—"

"What if they get assistance from Taiwan? How many troops do the bandits have?" Tong Jie asked.

"Well, they have some land forces," Luo allowed. "But we have ample ability to—"

"You told us a week ago that we had all the forces required to defeat the Russians, even if they got some aid from America," Qian observed, becoming agitated. "What fiction do you have for us now, Luo?"

"Fiction!" the marshal's voice boomed. "I tell you the facts, but now you accuse me of that?"

"What have you *not* told us, Luo?" Qian asked harshly. "We are not peasants here to be told what to believe."

"The Russians are making a stand. They have fought back. I told you that, and I told you this sort of thing is to be expected—and it is. We fight a war with the Russians. It's not a burglary in an unoccupied house. This is an armed contest between two major powers—and we will win because we have more and better troops. They do not fight well. We swept aside their border defenses, and we've pursued their army north, and they didn't have the manhood to stand and fight for their own land! We will *smash* them. Yes, they will fight back. We must expect that, but it won't matter. We will *smash* them, I tell you!" he insisted.

"Is there any information which you have not told us to this point?" Interior Minister Tong asked, in a voice more reasonable than the question itself.

"I have appointed Major General Ge to assume command of the Thirty-fourth Shock Army. He reported to me that Twenty-ninth Army sustained a serious air attack earlier today. The effects of this attack are not clear, probably they managed to damage communications—and an *air* attack cannot seriously hurt a large mechanized *land* force. The tools of war do not permit such a thing."

"Now what?" Premier Xu asked.

"I propose that we adjourn the meeting and allow Minister Luo to return to his task of managing our armed forces," Zhang Han Sen proposed. "And that we reconvene, say, at sixteen hours."

There were nods around the table. Everyone wanted the time to consider the things that they'd heard this morning—and perhaps to give the Defense Minister the chance to make good his words. Xu did a head count and stood.

"Very well. We adjourn until this afternoon." The meeting broke up in an unusually subdued manner, without the usual pairing off and pleasantries between old comrades. Outside the conference room, Qian buttonholed Fang again.

"Something is going badly wrong. I can feel it."

"How sure are you of that?"

"Fang, I don't know what the Americans have done to my railroad bridges, but I assure you that to destroy them as I was informed earlier this morning is no small thing. Moreover, the destruction inflicted was deliberately systematic. The Americans—it must have been the Americans—deliberately crippled our ability to supply our field armies. You only do such a thing in preparation to smashing them. And now the commanding general of our advancing armies is suddenly killed—stray bullet, my ass! That *tset ha tset ha* Luo leads us to disaster, Fang."

"We'll know more this afternoon," Fang suggested, leaving his colleague and going to his office. Arriving there, he dictated another segment for his daily journal. For the first time, he wondered if it might turn out to be his testament.

For her part, Ming was disturbed by her minister's demeanor. An elderly man, he'd always nonetheless been a calm and optimistic one for the most part. His mannerisms were those of a grandfatherly gentleman even when taking her or one of the other office girls to his bed. It was an endearing quality, one of the reasons the office staff didn't resist his advances more vigorously—and besides, he *did* take care of those who took care of *his* needs. This time she took her dictation quietly, while he leaned back in his chair, his eyes closed, and his voice a monotone. It took half an hour, and she went out to her desk to do the transcription. It was time for the midday meal by the time she was done, and she went out to lunch with her co-worker, Chai.

"What is the matter with him?" she asked Ming.

"The meeting this morning did not go well. Fang is concerned with the war."

"But isn't it going well? Isn't that what they say on TV?"

"It seems there have been some setbacks. This morning they argued about how serious they were. Qian was especially exercised about it, because the American attacked our rail bridges in Harbin and Bei'an."

"Ah." Chai shoveled some rice into her mouth with her chopsticks. "How is Fang taking it?"

"He seems very tense. Perhaps he will need some comfort this evening."

"Oh? Well, I can take care of him. I need a new office chair anyway," she added with a giggle.

Lunch dragged on longer than usual. Clearly their minister didn't need any of them for the moment, and Ming took the time to walk about on the street to gauge the mood of the people there. The feeling was strangely neutral. She was out just long enough to trigger her computer's downtime activation, and though the screen was blank, in the auto-sleep mode, the hard drive started turning, and silently activated the onboard modem.

Mary Pat Foley was in her office, though it was past midnight, and she was logging onto her mail account every fifteen minutes, hoping for something new from SORGE.

"You've got mail!" the mechanical voice told her.

"Yes!" she said back to it, downloading the document at once. Then she lifted the phone. "Get Sears up here."

With that done, Mrs. Foley looked at the time entry on the e-mail. It had gone out in the early afternoon in Beijing . . . what might that mean? she wondered, afraid that any irregularity could spell the death of SONGBIRD, and the loss of the SORGE documents.

"Working late?" Sears asked on entering.

"Who isn't?" MP responded. She held out the latest printout. "Read."

"Politburo meeting, in the morning for a change," Sears said, scanning the first page. "Looks a little raucous. This Qian guy is raising a little hell—oh, okay, he chatted with Fang after it and expressed serious concerns . . . agreed to meet later in the day and—oh, shit!"

"What's that?"

"They discussed increasing the readiness of their ICBM force . . . let's see . . . nothing firm was decided for technical reasons, they weren't sure how long they could keep the missiles fueled, but they were shook by our takeout of their missile submarine . . ."

"Write that up. I'm going to hang a CRITIC on it," the DDO announced.

CRITIC—shorthand for "critical"—is the highest priority in the United States government for message traffic. A CRITIC-flagged document must be in the President's hands no less than fifteen minutes after being generated. That meant that Joshua Sears had to get it drafted just as quickly as he could type in his keyboard, and that made for errors in translation.

Ryan had been asleep for maybe forty minutes when the phone next to his bed went off.

"Yeah?"

"Mr. President," some faceless voice announced in the White House Office of Signals, "we have CRITIC traffic for you."

"All right. Bring it up." Jack swung his body across the bed and planted his feet on the rug. As a normal human being living in his home, he wasn't a bathrobe person. Ordinarily he'd just pad around his house barefoot in his underwear, but that wasn't allowed anymore, and he always kept a long blue robe handy now. It was a gift from long ago, when he'd taught history at the Naval Academy—a gift from the students there—and bore on the sleeves the one wide and four narrow stripes of a Fleet Admiral. So dressed, and wearing leather slippers that also came with the new job, he walked out into the upstairs corridor. The Secret Service night team was already up and moving. Joe Hilton came to him first.

"We heard, sir. It's on the way up now."

Ryan, who'd been existing on less than five hours of sleep per night for the past week, had an urgent need to lash out and rip the face off someone—anyone—but, of course, he couldn't do that to men who were just doing their job, with miserable hours of their own.

Special Agent Charlie Malone was at the elevator. He took the folder from the messenger and trotted over to Ryan.

"Hmm." Ryan rubbed his hand over his face as he flipped the folder open. The first three lines jumped into his consciousness. "Oh, shit."

"Anything wrong?" Hilton asked.

"Phone," Ryan said.

"This way, sir." Hilton led him to the Secret Service upstairs cubbyhole office.

Ryan lifted the phone and said, "Mary Pat at Langley." It didn't take long. "MP, Jack here. What gives?"

"It's just what you see. They're talking about fueling their intercontinental missiles. At least two of them are aimed at Washington."

"Great. Now what?"

"I just tasked a KH-11 to give their launch sites a close look. There's two of them, Jack. The one we need to look at is Xuanhua. That's at about forty degrees, thirty-eight minutes north, one hundred fifteen degrees, six minutes east. Twelve silos with CCC-4 missiles inside. This is one of the newer ones, and it replaced older sites that stored the missiles in caves or tunnels. Straight, vertical, in-the-ground silos. The entire missile field is about six miles by six miles. The silos are well separated so that a single nuclear impact can't take out any two missiles," MP explained, manifestly looking at overheads of the place as she spoke.

"How serious is this?"

A new voice came on the line. "Jack, it's Ed. We have to take this one seriously. The naval bombardment on their coast might have set them off. The damned fools think we might be attempting a no-shit invasion."

"What? What with?" the President demanded.

"They can be very insular thinkers, Jack, and they're not always logical by our rules," Ed Foley told him.

"Great. Okay. You two come on down here. Bring your best China guy with you."

"On the way," the DCI replied.

Ryan hung up and looked at Joe Hilton. "Wake everybody up. The Chinese may be going squirrelly on us."

The drive up the Potomac River hadn't been easy. Captain Blandy hadn't wanted to wait for a river pilot to help guide him up the river—naval officers tend to be overly proud when it comes to navigating their ships—and that had made it quite tense for the bridge watch. Rarely was the channel more than a few hundred yards wide, and cruisers are deepwater ships, not riverboats. Once they came within a few yards of a mudbank, but the navigator got them clear of it with a timely rudder order. The ship's radar was up and running—people were actually afraid to turn off the billboard system because it, like most mechanical contrivances, preferred operation to idleness, and switching it off might have broken something. As it was, the RF energy radiating from the four huge billboard transmitters on *Gettysburg*'s superstructure had played hell with numerous television sets on the way northwest, but that couldn't be helped, and probably nobody noticed the cruiser in the river anyway, not at this time of night. Finally, *Gettysburg* glided to a halt within sight of the Woodrow Wilson bridge, and had to wait for traffic to be halted on the D.C. Beltway. This resulted in the usual road rage, but at this time of night there weren't that many people to be outraged, though one or two did honk their horns when the ship passed through the open drawbridge span. Perhaps they were New Yorkers, Captain Blandy thought. From there it was another turn to starboard into the Anacostia River, through another drawbridge, this one named for John Philip Sousa—accompanied by more surprised looks from the few drivers out—and then a gentle docking alongside the pier that was also home to USS *Barry*, a retired destroyer relegated to museum status.

The line handlers on the pier, Captain Blandy saw, were mainly civilians. Wasn't that a hell of a thing?

The "evolution"—that, Gregory had learned, was what the Navy called parking a boat—had been interesting but unremarkable to observe, though the skipper looked quite relieved to have it all behind him.

"Finished with engines," the CO told the engine room, and let out a long breath, shared, Gregory could see, by the entire bridge crew.

"Captain?" the retired Army officer asked.

"Yes?"

"What is this all about, exactly?"

"Well, isn't it kinda obvious?" Blandy responded. "We have a shooting war with the Chinese. They have ICBMs, and I suppose the SecDef wants to be able to shoot them down if they loft one at Washington. SACLANT is also sending an Aegis to New York, and I'd bet Pacific Fleet has some looking out for Los Angeles and San Francisco. Probably Seattle, too. There's a lot of ships there anyway, and a good weapons locker. Do you have spare copies of your software?"

"Sure."

"Well, we'll have a phone line from the dock in a few minutes. We'll see if there's a way for you to upload it to other interested parties."

"Oh," Dr. Gregory observed quietly. He really should have thought that one all the way through.

This is RED WOLF FOUR. I have visual contact with the Chinese advance guard," the regimental commander called on the radio. "About ten kilometers south of us."

"Very well," Sinyavskiy replied. Just where Bondarenko and his American helpers said they were. Good. There were two other general officers in his command post, the CGs of 201st and 80th Motor Rifle divisions, and the commander of the 34th was supposed to be on his way as well, though 94th had turned and reoriented itself to attack east from a point about thirty kilometers to the south.

Sinyavskiy took the old, sodden cigar from his mouth and tossed it out into the grass, pulling another from his tunic pocket and lighting it. It was a Cuban cigar, and superb in its mildness. His artillery commander was on the other side of the map table—just a couple of planks on sawhorses, which was perfect for the moment. Close by were holes dug should the Chinese send some artillery fire their way, and most important of all, the wires which led to his communications station, set a full kilometer to the west—that was the first thing the Chinese would try to shoot at, because they'd expect him to be there. In fact the only humans present were four officers and seven sergeants, in armored personnel carriers dug into the ground for safety. It was their job to repair anything the Chinese might manage to break.

"So, comrades, they come right into our parlor, eh?" he said for those around him. Sinyavskiy had been a soldier for twenty-six years. Oddly, he was not the son of a soldier. His father was an instructor in geology at Moscow State University, but ever since the first war movie he'd seen, this was the profession he'd craved to join. He'd done all the work, attended all the schools, studied history with the manic attention common in the Russian army, and the Red Army before it. This would be his Battle of the Kursk Bulge, remembering the battle where Vatutin and Rokossovskiy had smashed Hitler's last attempt to retake the offensive in Russia—where his mother country had begun the long march that had ended at the Reich Chancellery in Berlin. There, too, the Red Army had been the recipient of brilliant intelligence information, letting them know the time, place, and character of the German attack, and so allowing them to prepare so well that even the best of the German field commanders, Erich von Manstein, could do no more than break his teeth on the Russian steel.

And so it will be here, Sinyavskiy promised himself. The only unsatisfactory part was that he was stuck here in this camouflaged tent instead of in the line with his men, but, no, he wasn't a captain anymore, and his place was here, to fight the battle on a goddamned printed map.

"Red Wolf, you will commence firing when the advance guard gets to within eight hundred meters."

"Eight hundred meters, Comrade General," the commander of his tank regiment acknowledged. "I can see them quite clearly now."

"What exactly can you see?"

"It appears to be a battalion-strength formation, principally Type 90 tanks, some Type 98s but not too many of those, spread out as though they went to sub-unit commanders. Numerous tracked personnel carriers. I do not see any artillery-spotting vehicles, however. What do we know of their artillery?"

"It's rolling, not set up for firing. We're watching them," Sinyavskiy assured him.

"Excellent. They are now two kilometers off by my range finder."

"Stand by."

"I will do that, Command."

"I hate waiting," Sinyavskiy commented to the officers around him. They all nodded, having the same prejudice. He hadn't seen Afghanistan in his younger years, having served mainly in 1st and 2nd

Guards Tank armies in Germany back then, preparing to fight against NATO, an event which blessedly had never taken place. This was his very first experience with real combat, and it hadn't really started yet, and he was ready for it to start.

"Okay, if they light those missiles up, what can we do about it?" Ryan asked.

"If they launch 'em, there's not a goddamned thing but run for cover," Secretary Bretano said.

"That's good for us. We'll all get away. What about the people who live in Washington, New York, and all the other supposed targets?" POTUS asked.

"I've ordered some Aegis cruisers to the likely targets that are near the water," THUNDER went on. "I had one of my people from TRW look at the possibility of upgrading the missile systems to see if they might do an intercept. He's done the theoretical work, and he says it looks good on the simulators, but that's a ways from a practical test, of course. It's better than nothing, though."

"Okay, where are the ships?"

"There's one here now," Bretano answered.

"Oh? When did that happen?" Robby Jackson asked.

"Less than an hour ago. *Gettysburg.* There's another one going to New York—and San Francisco and Los Angeles. Also Seattle, though that's not really a target as far as we know. The software upgrade is going out to them to get their missiles reprogrammed."

"Okay, that's something. What about taking those missiles out, before they can launch?" Ryan asked next.

"The Chinese silos have recently been upgraded in protection, steel armor on the concrete covers—shaped like a Chinese coolie hat, it will probably deflect most bombs, but not the deep penetrators, the GBU-27s we used on the railroad bridges—"

"If they have any left over there. Better ask Gus Wallace," the Vice President warned.

"What do you mean?" Bretano asked.

"I mean we never made all that many of them, and the Air Force must have dropped about forty last night."

"I'll check that," SecDef promised.

"What if he doesn't?" Jack asked.

"Then either we get some more in one big hurry, or we think up something else," TOMCAT replied.

"Like what, Robby?"

"Hell, send in a special-operations team and blow them the fuck up," the former fighter pilot suggested.

"I wouldn't much want to try that myself," Mickey Moore observed.

"Beats the hell out of a five-megaton bomb going off on Capitol Hill, Mickey," Jackson shot back. "Look, the preferred thing to do is find out if Gus Wallace has the right bombs. It's a long stretch for the Black Jets, but you can tank them going and coming—and put fighters up to protect the tankers. It's complicated, but we practice that sort of thing. If he doesn't have the goddamned bombs, we fly them to him, assuming there are any. You know, weapons storage isn't a cornucopia, guys. There's a finite, discrete number for every item in the inventory."

"General Moore," Ryan said, "call General Wallace and find out, right now, if you would."

"Yes, sir." Moore stood and left the Situation Room.

"Look," Ed Foley said, pointing to the TV. "It's started."

The wood line erupted in a sheet of flame two kilometers across. The sight caused the eyes of the Chinese tankers to flare, but most of the front rank of tank crews didn't have time for much more than that. Of the thirty tanks in that line, only three escaped immediate destruction. It was little better for the personnel carriers interspersed with them.

"You may commence firing, Colonel," Sinyavskiy told his artillery commander.

The command was relayed at once, and the ground shook beneath their feet.

It was spectacular to see on the computer terminal. The Chinese had walked straight into the ambush, and the effect of the Russian opening volley was ghastly to behold.

Major Tucker took in a deep breath as he saw several hundred men lose their lives.

"Back to their artillery," Bondarenko ordered.

"Yes, sir." Tucker complied at once, altering the focus of the high-altitude camera and finding the Chinese artillery. It was mainly of the towed sort, being pulled behind trucks and tractors. They were a little slow getting the word. The first Russian shells were falling around them before any effort was made to stop the trucks and lift the limbers off the towing hooks, and for all that the Chinese gunners worked rapidly.

But theirs was a race against Death, and Death had a head start. Tucker watched one gun crew struggle to manhandle their 122-mm gun into a firing position. The gunners were loading the weapon when three shells landed close enough to upset the weapon and kill more than half their number. Zooming in the camera, he could see one private writhing on the ground, and there was no one close by to offer him assistance.

"It is a miserable business, isn't it?" Bondarenko observed quietly.

"Yeah," Tucker agreed. When a tank blew up it was easy to tell yourself that a tank was just a *thing*. Even though you knew that three or four human beings were inside, you couldn't see them. As a fighter pilot never killed a fellow pilot, but only shot down his aircraft, so Tucker adhered to the Air Force ethos that death was something that happened to objects rather than people. Well, that poor bastard with blood on his shirt wasn't a *thing*, was he? He backed off the camera, taking a wider field that permitted godlike distancing from the up-close-and-personal aspects of the observation.

"Better that they should have remained in their own country, Major," the Russian explained to him.

Jesus, what a mess," Ryan said. He'd seen death up-close-and-personal himself in his time, having shot people who had at the time been quite willing to shoot him, but that didn't make this imagery any the more palatable. Not by a long fucking shot. The President turned.

"Is this going out, Ed?" he asked the DCI.

"Ought to be," Foley replied.

And it was, on a URL—"Uniform Resource Locator" in 'Netspeak—called http://www.darkstarfeed.cia.gov/siberiabattle/realtime.ram. It didn't even have to be advertised. Some 'Net crawlers stumbled onto it in the first five minutes, and the "hits" from people looking at the "streaming video" site climbed up from 0 to 10 in a matter of three minutes. Then some of them must have ducked into chat rooms to spread the word. The monitoring program for the URL at CIA headquarters also kept track of the locations of the people logging into it. The first Asian country, not unexpectedly, was Japan, and the fascination of the people there in military operations guaranteed a rising number of hits. The video also included audio, the real-time comments of Air Force personnel giving some perverse color-commentary back to their comrades in uniform. It was sufficiently colorful that Ryan commented on it.

"It's not meant for anyone much over the age of thirty to hear," General Moore said, coming back into the room.

"What's the story on the bombs?" Jackson asked at once.

"He's only got two of them," Moore replied. "The nearest others are at the factory, Lockheed-Martin, Sunnyvale. They're just doing a production run right now."

"Uh-oh," Robby observed. "Back to Plan B."

"It might have to be a special operation, then, unless, Mr. President, that is, you are willing to authorize a strike with cruise missiles."

"What kind of cruise missiles?" Ryan asked, knowing the answer even so.

"Well, we have twenty-eight of them on Guam with W-80 warheads. They're little ones, only about three hundred pounds. It has two settings, one-fifty or one-seventy kilotons."

"Thermonuclear weapons, you mean?"

General Moore let out a breath before replying. "Yes, Mr. President."

"That's the only option we have for taking those missiles out?" He didn't have to say that he would not voluntarily launch a nuclear strike.

"We could go in with conventional smart bombs—GBU-10s and -15s. Gus has enough of those, but not deep penetrators, and the protection on the silos would have a fair chance at deflecting the weapon away from the target. Now, that might not matter. The CSS-4 missiles are delicate bastards, and the impact even of a miss could scramble their guidance systems . . . but we couldn't be sure."

"I'd prefer that those things not fly."

"Jack, nobody wants them to fly," the Vice President said. "Mickey, put together a plan. We need *something* to take them out, and we need it in one big fuckin' hurry."

"I'll call SOCOM about it, but, hell, they're down in Tampa."

"Do the Russians have special-operations people?" Ryan asked.

"Sure, it's called Spetsnaz."

"And some of these missiles are targeted on Russia?"

"It certainly appears so, yes, sir," the Chairman of the Joint Chiefs confirmed.

"Then they owe us one, and they damned well owe it to themselves," Jack said, reaching for a phone. "I need to talk to Sergey Golovko in Moscow," he told the operator.

The American President," his secretary said.

"Ivan Emmetovich!" Golovko said in hearty greeting. "The reports from Siberia are good."

"I know, Sergey, I'm watching it live now myself. Want to do it yourself?"

"It is possible?"

"You have a computer with a modem?"

"One cannot exist without the damned things," the Russian replied.

Ryan read off the URL identifier. "Just log onto that. We're putting the feed from our Dark Star drones onto the Internet."

"Why is that, Jack?" Golovko asked at once.

"Because as of two minutes ago, one thousand six hundred and fifty Chinese citizens are watching it, and the number is going up fast."

"A political operation against them, yes? You wish to destabilize their government?"

"Well, it won't hurt our purposes if their citizens find out what's happening, will it?"

"The virtues of a free press. I must study this. Very clever, Ivan Emmetovich."

"That's not why I called."

"Why is that, *Tovarisch Prezidyent*?" the SVR chairman asked, with sudden concern at the change in his tone. Ryan was not one to conceal his feelings well.

"Sergey, we have a very adverse indication from their Politburo. I'm faxing it to you now," he heard. "I'll stay on the line while you read it."

Golovko wasn't surprised to see the pages arrive on his personal fax machine. He had Ryan's personal numbers, and the Americans had his. It was just one way for an intelligence service to demonstrate its prowess in a harmless way. The first sheets to come across were the English translation of the Chinese ideographs that came through immediately thereafter.

Sergey, I sent you our original feed in case your linguists or psychologists are better than ours," the President said, with an apologetic glance at Dr. Sears. The CIA analyst waved it off. "They have twelve CSS-4 missiles, half aimed at you, half at us. I think we need to do something about those things. They may not be entirely rational, the way things are going now."

"And your shore bombardment might have pushed them to the edge, Mr. President," the Russian said over the speakerphone. "I agree, this is a matter of some concern. Why don't you bomb the things with your brilliant bombs from your magical invisible bombers."

"Because we're out of bombs, Sergey. They ran out of the sort they need."

"*Nichevo*" was the reaction.

"You should see it from my side. My people are thinking about a commando-type operation."

"I see. Let me consult with some of my people. Give me twenty minutes, Mr. President."

"Okay, you know where to reach me." Ryan punched the kill button on the phone and looked sourly at the tray of coffee things. "One more cup of this shit and I'm going to turn into an urn myself."

The only reason he was alive now, he was sure, was that he'd withdrawn to the command section for 34th Army. His tank division was being roughly handled. One of his battalions had been immolated in the first minute of the battle. Another was now trying to maneuver east, trying to draw the Russians out into a running battle for which his men were trained. The division's artillery had been halved at best by

Russian massed fire, and 34th Army's advance was now a thing of the past. His current task was to try and use his two mechanized divisions to establish a base of fire from which he could try to wrest back control of the battle. But every time he tried to move a unit, something happened to it, as though the Russians were reading his mind.

"Wa, pull what's left of Three-Oh-Second back to the ten o'clock start-line, and do it now!" he ordered.

"But Marshal Luo won't—"

"And if he wishes to relieve me, he can, but he isn't here *now* , is he?" Ge snarled back. "Give the order!"

"Yes, Comrade General."

With this toy in our hands, the Germans would not have made it as far as Minsk," Bondarenko said.

"Yeah, it helps to know what the other guy's doing, doesn't it?"

"It's like being a god on Mount Olympus. Who thought this thing up?"

"Oh, a couple of people at Northrop started the idea, with an airplane called Tacit Rainbow, looked like a cross between a snow shovel and a French baguette, but it was manned, and the endurance wasn't so good."

"Whoever it is, I would like to buy him a bottle of good vodka," the Russian general said. "This is saving the lives of my soldiers."

And beating the living shit out of the Chinese, Tucker didn't add. But combat was that sort of game, wasn't it?

"Do you have any other aircraft up?"

"Yes, sir. Grace Kelly's back up to cover First Armored."

"Show me."

Tucker used his mouse to shrink one video window and then opened another. General Diggs had a second terminal up and running, and Tucker just stole its take. There were what looked like two brigades operating, moving north at a measured pace and wrecking every Chinese truck and track they could find. The battlefield, if you could call it that, was a mass of smoke columns from shot-up trucks, reminding Tucker of the vandalized Kuwaiti oil fields of 1991. He zoomed in to see that most of the work was being done by the Bradleys. What targets there were simply were not worthy of a main-gun round from the tanks. The

Abrams just rode herd on the lighter infantry carriers, doing protective overwatch as they ground mercilessly forward. The major slaved one camera to his terminal and went scouting around for more action . . .

"Who's this?" Tucker asked.

"That must be BOYAR," Bondarenko said.

It was what looked like twenty-five T-55 tanks advancing on line, and these tanks were using their main guns . . . against trucks and some infantry carriers . . .

Load HEAT," Lieutenant Komanov ordered. "Target track, one o'clock! Range two thousand."

"I have him," the gunner said a second later.

"Fire!"

"Firing," the gunner said, squeezing the trigger. The old tank rocked backwards from the shot. Gunner and commander watched the tracer arcing out . . .

"Over, damn it, too high. Load another HEAT."

The loader slammed another round into the breech in a second: "Loaded!"

"I'll get the bastard this time," the gunner promised, adjusting his sights down a hair. The poor bastard out there didn't even know he'd been shot at the first time . . .

"Fire!"

"Firing . . ."

Yet another recoil, and . . .

"Hit! Good shooting Vanya!"

Three Company was doing well. The time spent in gunnery practice was paying off handsomely, Komanov thought. This was much better than sitting in a damned bunker and waiting for them to come to you . . .

What is that?" Marshal Luo asked.

"Comrade Marshal, come here and see," the young lieutenant colonel urged.

"What is this?" the Defense Minister asked with a trailing-off voice . . . *"Cao ni ma,"* he breathed. Then he thundered: *"What the hell is this?"*

"Comrade Marshal, this is a web site, from the Internet. It purports to be a live television program from the battlefield in Siberia." The young field-grade officer was almost breathless. "It shows the Russians fighting Thirty-fourth Shock Army . . . "

"And?"

"And they're slaughtering our men, according to this," the lieutenant colonel went on.

"Wait a minute—what—how is this possible?" Luo demanded.

"Comrade, this heading here says *darkstar.* 'Dark Star' is the name of an American unmanned aerial vehicle, a reconnaissance drone, reported to be a stealth aircraft used to collect tactical intelligence. Thus, it appears that they are using this to feed information, and putting the information on the Internet as a propaganda tool." He had to say it that way, and it was, in fact, the way he thought about it.

"Tell me more."

The officer was an intelligence specialist. "This explains the success they've had against us, Comrade Marshal. They can see everything we do, almost before we do it. It's as though they listen to our command circuit, or even listen into our staff and planning meetings. There is no defense against this," the staff officer concluded.

"You young defeatist!" the marshal raged.

"Perhaps there is a way to overcome this advantage, but I do not know what it is. Systems like this can see in the dark as well as they can in the sunlight. Do you understand, Comrade Marshal? With this tool they can see everything we do, see it long before we approach their formations. It eliminates any possibility of surprise . . . see here," he said, pointing at the screen. "One of Thirty-fourth Army's mechanized divisions is maneuvering east. They are here—" he pointed to a printer map on the table— "and the enemy is here. If our troops get to this point unseen, then perhaps they can hit the Russians on their left flank, but it will take two hours to get there. For the Russians to get one of their units to a blocking position will take but one hour. That is the advantage," he concluded.

"The Americans do that to us?"

"Clearly, the feed on the Internet is from America, from their CIA."

"This is how the Russians have countered us, then?"

"Clearly. They've outguessed us at every turn today. This must be how they do it."

"Why do the Americans put this information out where everyone can see it?" Luo wondered. The obvious answer didn't occur to him. Information given out to the public had to be carefully measured and flavored for the peasants and workers to draw the proper conclusions from it.

"Comrade, it will be difficult to say on state television that things are going well when this is available to anyone with a computer."

"Ahh." Less a sound of satisfaction than one of sudden dread. "Anyone can see this?"

"Anyone with a computer and a telephone line." The young lieutenant colonel looked up, only to see Luo's receding form.

"I'm surprised he didn't shoot me," the officer observed.

"He still might," a full colonel told him. "But I think you frightened him." He looked at the wall clock. It was sixteen hours, four in the afternoon.

"Well, it is a concern."

"You young fool. Don't you see? Now he can't even conceal the truth from the Politburo."

Hello, Yuri," Clark said. It was different to be in Moscow in time of war. The mood of the people on the street was unlike anything he'd ever seen. They were concerned and serious—you didn't go to Russia to see the smiling people any more than you went to England for the coffee—but there was something else, too. Indignation. Anger . . . determination? Television coverage of the war was not as strident and defiant as he'd expected. The new Russian news media were trying to be even-handed and professional. There was commentary to the effect that the army's inability to stop the Chinese cold spoke ill of their country's national cohesion. Others lamented the demise of the Soviet Union, whom China would not have dared to threaten, much less attack. More asked what the hell was the use of being in NATO if none of the other countries came to the aid of their supposed new ally.

"We told the television people that if they told anyone of the American division now in Siberia, we'd shoot them, and of course they believed us," Lt. Gen. Kirillin said with a smile. That was something new for Clark and Chavez to see. He hadn't smiled much in the past week.

"Things looking up?" Chavez inquired.

"Bondarenko has stopped them at the gold mine. They will not even see that, if my information is correct. But there is something else," he added seriously.

"What's that, Yuriy?" Clark asked.

"We are concerned that they might launch their nuclear weapons."

"Oh, shit," Ding observed. "How serious is that?"

"It comes from your president. Golovko is speaking with President Grushavoy right now."

"And? How do they plan to go about it? Smart bombs?" John asked.

"No, Washington has asked us to go in with a special-operations team," Kirillin said.

"What the hell?" John gasped. He pulled his satellite phone out of his pocket and looked for the door. "Excuse me, General. E.T. phone home."

"You want to say that again, Ed?" Foley heard.

"You heard me. They've run out of the bombs they need. Evidently, it's a pain in the ass to fly bombs to where the bombers are."

"Fuck!" the CIA officer observed, out in the parking lot of this Russian army officers' club. The encryption on his phone didn't affect the emotion in his voice. "Don't tell me, since RAINBOW is a NATO asset, and Russia's part of NATO now, and since you're going to be asking the fucking Russians to front this operation, in the interest of North Atlantic solidarity, we're going to get to go and play, too, right?"

"Unless you choose not to, John. I know you can't go yourself. Combat's a kid's game, but you have some good kids working for you."

"Ed, you expect me to send my people in on something like that and I stay home and fucking knit socks?" Clark demanded heatedly.

"That's your call to make. You're the RAINBOW commander."

"How is this supposed to work? You expect us to jump in?"

"Helicopters—"

"Russian helicopters. No thanks, buddy, I—"

"Our choppers, John. First Armored Division had enough and they're the right kind . . ."

They want me to do *what*?" Dick Boyle asked.

"You heard me."

"What about fuel?"

"Your fueling point's right about here," Colonel Masterman said, holding the just-downloaded satellite photo. "Hilltop west of a place called Chicheng. Nobody lives there, and the numbers work out."

"Yeah, except out flight path takes us within ten miles of this fighter base."

"Eight F-111s are going to hit it while you're on the way in. Ought to close down their runways for a good three days, they figure."

"Dick," Diggs said, "I don't know what the problem is exactly, but Washington is really worried that Joe is going to launch his ICBMs at us at home, and Gus Wallace doesn't have the right bombs to take them out reliably. That means a special-ops force, down and dirty. It's a strategic mission, Dick. Can you do it?"

Colonel Boyle looked at the map, measuring distance in his mind . . . "Yeah, we'll have to mount the outrigger wings on the Blackhawks and load up to the max on gas, but, yeah, we got the range to get there. Have to refuel on the way back, though."

"Okay, can you use your other birds to ferry the fuel out?"

Boyle nodded. "Barely."

"If necessary, the Russians can land a Spetsnaz force anywhere through here with additional fuel, so they tell me. This part of China is essentially unoccupied, according to the maps."

"What about opposition on the ground?"

"There is a security force in the area. We figure maybe a hundred people on duty, total, say a squad at each silo. Can you get some Apaches out there to run interference?"

"Yeah, they can get that far, if they travel light." *Just cannon rounds and 2.75-inch rockets*, he thought.

"Then get me your mission requirements," General Diggs said. It wasn't quite an order. If he said it was impossible, then Diggs couldn't make him do it. But Boyle couldn't let his people go out and do something like this without being there to command them.

The MI-24s finished things off. The Russian doctrine for their attack helicopters wasn't too different from how they used their tanks. Indeed, the MI-24—called the Hind by NATO, but strangely unnamed by the Russians themselves—was referred to as a flying tank. Using AT-6 Spiral missiles, they finished off a Chinese tank battalion in twenty minutes of jump and shoot, sustaining only two losses in the process. The sun was setting now, and what had been Thirty-fourth Shock Army was wreckage. What few vehicles had survived the day were pulling back, usually with wounded men clinging to their decks.

In his command post, General Sinyavskiy was all smiles. Vodka was snorted by all. His 265th Motor Rifle Division had halted and thrown back a force more than double its size, suffering fewer than three hundred dead in the process. The TV news crews were finally allowed out to where the soldiers were, and he delivered the briefing, paying frequent compliments to his theater commander, Gennady Iosefovich Bondarenko, for his cool head and faith in his subordinates. "He never lost his nerve," Sinyavskiy said soberly. "And he allowed us to keep ours for when the time came. He is a Hero of Russia," the division commander concluded. "And so are many of my men!"

Thank you for that, Yuriy Andreyevich, and, yes, for that you will get your next star," the theater commander told the television screen. Then he turned to his staff. "Andrey Petrovich, what do we do tomorrow?"

"I think we will let Two-Six-Five start moving south. We will be the hammer, and Diggs will be the anvil. They still have a Type-A Group army largely intact to the south, the Forty-third. We will smash it starting day after tomorrow, but first we will maneuver it into a place of our choosing."

Bondarenko nodded. "Show me a plan, but first, I am going to sleep for a few hours."

"Yes, Comrade General."

CHAPTER 60

Skyrockets in Flight

It was the same Spetsnaz people they'd trained for the past month or so. Nearly everyone on the transport aircraft was a commissioned officer, doing sergeants' work, which had its good points and its bad ones. The really good thing was that they all spoke passable English. Of the RAINBOW troopers, only Ding Chavez and John Clark spoke conversational Russian.

The maps and photos came from SRV and CIA, the latter transmitted to the American Embassy in Moscow and messengered to the military airfield out of which they'd flown. They were in an Aeroflot airliner, fairly full with over a hundred passengers, all of them soldiers.

"I propose that we divide by nationalities," Kirillin said. "Vanya, you and your RAINBOW men take this one here. My men and I will divide the rest among us, using our existing squad structures."

"Looks okay, Yuriy. One target's pretty much as good as another. When will we be going in?"

"Just before dawn. Your helicopters must have good range to take us all the way down, then back with only one refueling."

"Well, that'll be the safe part of the mission."

"Except this fighter base at Anshan," Kirillin said. "We pass within twenty kilometers of it."

"Air Force is going to hit that, they tell me, Stealth fighters with smart bombs, they're gonna post-hole the runways before we drive past."

"Ah, that is a fine idea," Kirillin said.

"Kinda like that myself," Chavez said. "Well, Mr. C, looks like I get to be a soldier again. It's been a while."

"What fun," Clark observed. Oh, yeah, sitting in the back of a helicopter, going deep into Indian Country, where there were sure to be people with guns. Well, could be worse. Going in at dawn, at least the gomers on duty would be partly asleep, unless their boss was a real prick. *How tough was discipline in the People's Liberation Army?* John wondered. Probably pretty tough. Communist governments didn't encourage back talk.

"How, exactly, are we supposed to disable the missiles?" Ding asked.

"They're fueled by a ten-centimeter pipe—two of them, actually—from underground fueling tanks adjacent to the launch silo. First, we destroy the pipes," Kirillin said. "Then we look for some way to access the missile silo itself. A simple hand grenade will suffice. These are delicate objects. They will not sustain much damage," the general said confidently.

"What if the warhead goes off?" Ding asked.

Kirillin actually laughed at that. "They will not, Domingo Stepanovich. These items are very secure in their arming procedures, for all the obvious reasons. And the sites themselves will not be designed to protect against a direct assault. They are designed to protect against nuclear blast, not a squad of engineer-soldiers. You can be sure of that."

Hope you're right on that one, fella, Chavez didn't say aloud.

"You seem knowledgeable on this subject, Yuriy."

"Vanya, this mission is one Spetsnaz has practiced more than once. We Russians have thought from time to time about taking these missiles—how you say? Take them out of play, yes?"

"Not a bad idea at all, Yuriy. Not my kind of weapons," Clark said. He really did prefer to do his killing close enough to see the bastard's face. Old habits died hard, and a telescopic sight was just as good as a knife in that respect. Much better. A rifle bullet didn't make people flop around and make noise the way a knife across the throat did. But death was supposed to be administered one at a time, not whole cities at once. It just wasn't tidy or selective enough.

Chavez looked at his Team-2 troopers. They didn't look overtly tense, but good soldiers did their best to hide such feelings. Of their number, only Ettore Falcone wasn't a career soldier, but instead a cop from the Italian Carabinieri, which was about halfway between military and police. Chavez went over to see him.

"How you doing, Big Bird?" Ding asked.

"It is tense, this mission, no?" Falcone replied.

"It might be. You never really know until you get there."

The Italian shrugged. "As with raids on mafiosi, sometimes you kick the door and there is nothing but men drinking wine and playing cards. Sometimes they have *machinapistoli,* but you must kick the door to find out."

"You do a lot of those?"

"Eight," Falcone replied. "I am usually the first one through the door because I am usually the best shot. But we have good men on the team there, and we have good men on the team here. It should go well, Domingo. I am tense, yes, but I will be all right. You will see," Big Bird ended. Chavez clapped him on the shoulder and went off to see Sergeant-Major Price.

"Hey, Eddie."

"Do we have a better idea for the mission yet?"

"Getting there. Looks like mainly a job for Paddy, blowing things up."

"Connolly's the best explosives man I've ever seen," Price observed. "But don't tell him that. His head's swollen enough already."

"What about Falcone?"

"Ettore?" Price shook his head. "I will be very surprised if he puts a foot wrong. He's a very good man, Ding, bloody machine—a robot with a pistol. That sort of confidence rarely goes bad. Things are too automatic for him."

"Okay, well, we've picked our target. It the north- and east-most silo. Looks like it's on fairly flat ground, two four-inch pipes running to it. Paddy'll blow those, and then try to find a way to pop the cover off the silo or otherwise find an access door—there's one on the overhead. Then get inside, toss a grenade to break the missile, and we get the hell out of Dodge City."

"Usual division of the squad?" Price asked. It had to be, but there was no harm in making sure.

Chavez nodded. "You take Paddy, Louis, Hank, and Dieter, and your team handles the actual destruction of the missile. I take the rest to do security and overwatch." Price nodded as Paddy Connolly came over.

"Are we getting chemical gear?"

"What?" Chavez asked.

"Ding, if we're going to be playing with bloody liquid-fueled missiles, we need chemical-warfare gear. The fuels for these things—you don't want to breathe the vapor, trust me. Red-fuming nitric acid, nitrogen tetroxide, hydrazine, that sort of thing. Those are bloody corrosive chemicals they use to power rockets, not like a pint of bitter at the Green Dragon, I promise you. And if the missiles are fueled and we blow them, well, you don't want to be close, and you *definitely* don't want to be downwind. The gas cloud will be bloody lethal, like what you chaps use in America to execute murderers, but rather less pleasant."

"I'll talk to John about that." Chavez made his way back forward.

Oh, shit," Ed Foley observed when he took the call. "Okay, John, I'll get hold of the Army on that one. How long 'til you're there?"

"Hour and a half to the airfield."

"You okay?"

"Yeah, sure, Ed, never been better."

Foley was struck by the tone. Clark had been CIA's official iceman for close to twenty years. He'd gone out on all manner of field operations without so much as a blink. But being over fifty—had it changed him, or did he just have a better appreciation of his own mortality now? The DCI figured that sort of thing came to everybody. "Okay, I'll get back to you." He switched phones. "I need General Moore."

"Yes, Director?" the Chairman of the Joint Chiefs said in greeting. "What can I do for you?"

"Our special-operations people say they need chemical-warfare gear for their mission and—"

"Way ahead of you, Ed. SOCOM told us the same thing. First Armored's got the right stuff, and it'll be waiting for them at the field."

"Thanks, Mickey."

"How secure are those silos?"

"The fueling pipes are right in the open. Blowing them up ought not to be a problem. Also, every silo has a metal access door for the maintenance people, and again, getting into it ought not to be a problem. My only concern is the site security force; there may be as much as a whole infantry battalion spread out down there. We're waiting for a KH-11 to overfly the site now for a final check."

"Well, Diggs is sending Apaches down to escort the raiding force. That'll be an equalizer," Moore promised. "What about the command bunker?"

"It's centrally located, looks pretty secure, entirely underground, but we have a rough idea of the configuration from penetrating radar." Foley referred to the KH-14 Lacrosse satellite. NASA had once published radar photos that had shown underground tributaries of the Nile that emptied into the Mediterranean Sea at Alexandria. But the capability hadn't been developed for hydrologists. It had also spotted Soviet missile silos that the Russians had thought to be well camouflaged, and other sensitive facilities, and America had wanted to let the Russians know that the locations were not the least bit secret. "Mickey, how do you feel about the mission?"

"I wish we had enough bombs to do it," General Moore replied honestly.

"Yeah," the DCI agreed.

The Politburo meeting had gone past midnight.

"So, Marshal Luo," Qian said, "things went badly yesterday. How badly? We need the truth here," he concluded roughly. If nothing else, Qian Kun had made his name in the past few days, as the only Politburo member with the courage to take on the ruling clique, expressing openly the misgivings that they'd all felt. Depending on who won, it could mean his downfall, either all the way to death or simply to mere obscurity, but it seemed he didn't care. That made him unusual among the men in the room, Fang Gan thought, and it made him a man to be respected.

"There was a major battle yesterday between 34th Shock Army and the Russians. It appears to have been a draw, and we are now maneuvering to press our advantage," the Defense Minister told them. They were all suffering from fatigue in the room, and again the Finance Minister was the only one to rise to his words.

"In other words, a battle was fought, and we lost it," Qian shot back.

"I didn't say that!" Luo responded angrily.

"But it is the truth, is it not?" Qian pressed the point.

"I told you the truth, Qian!" was the thundering reply.

"Comrade Marshal," the Finance Minister said in a reasonable tone, "you must forgive me for my skepticism. You see, much of what you've said in this room has turned out to be less than completely accurate. Now, I do not blame you for this. Perhaps you have been misinformed by some of your subordinates. All of us are vulnerable to that, are we not? But now is the time for a careful examination of objective realities. I am developing the impression that objective reality may be adverse to the economic and political objectives on whose pursuit this body has sent our country and its people. Therefore, we must *now* know what the facts are, and what also are the dangers facing us. So, Comrade Marshal, now, what is the military situation in Siberia?"

"It has changed somewhat," Luo admitted. "Not entirely to our benefit, but the situation is by no means lost." He'd chosen his words a little too carefully.

By no means lost, everyone around the table knew, was a delicate way of saying that a disaster had taken place. As in any society, if you knew the aphorisms, you could break the code. Success here was always proclaimed in the most positive terms. Setbacks were brushed aside without admission as something less than a stunning success. Failure was something to be blamed on individuals who'd failed in their duty—often to their great misfortune. But a real policy disaster was invariably explained as a situation that could yet be restored.

"Comrades, we still have our strengths," Zhang told them all. "Of all the great powers of the world, only we have intercontinental missiles, and no one will dare strike us hard while we do."

"Comrade, two days ago the Americans totally destroyed bridges so stout that one would have thought that only an angry deity could so much as scratch them. How secure can those missiles be, when we face a foe with invisible aircraft and magical weapons?" Qian asked. "I think we may be approaching the time when Shen might wish to approach America and Russia to propose an end to hostilities," he concluded.

"You mean surrender?" Zhang asked angrily. *"Never!"*

It had already started, though the Politburo members didn't know it yet. All over China, but especially in Beijing, people owning computers had logged onto the Internet. This was especially true of young people, and university students most of all.

The CIA feed, http://www.darkstarfeed.cia.gov/siberiabattle/realtime.ram, had attracted a global audience, catching even the international news organizations by surprise. CNN, Fox, and Europe's SkyNews had immediately pirated it, and then called in their expert commentators to explain things to their viewers in the first continuous news coverage of an event since February of 1991. CIA had taken to pirating CNN in turn, and now available on the CIA website were live interviews from Chinese prisoners. They spoke freely, they were so shocked at their fates—stunned at how near they'd come to death, and so buoyantly elated at their equally amazing survival when so many of their colleagues had been less fortunate. That made for great verbosity, and it was also something that couldn't be faked. Any Chinese citizen could have spotted false propaganda, but equally, any could discern this sort of truth from what he saw and heard.

The strange part was that Luo hadn't commented on the Internet phenomenon, thinking it irrelevant to the political facts of life in the PRC, but in that decision he'd made the greatest political misapprehension of his life.

They met in college dorm rooms first of all, amid clouds of cigarette smoke, chattering animatedly among themselves as students do, and like students everywhere they combined idealism with passion. That passion soon turned to resolve. By midnight, they were meeting in larger groups. Some leaders emerged, and, being leaders, they felt the need to take their associates somewhere. When the crowds mingled outside, the individual leaders of smaller groups met and started talking, and super-leaders emerged, rather like an instant military or political hierarchy, absorbing other groups into their own, until there were six principal leaders of a group of about fifteen hundred students. The larger group developed and then fed upon its own energy. Students everywhere are well supplied with piss and vinegar, and these Chinese students were no different. Some of the boys were there hoping to score with girls—another universal motivation for students—but the unifying factor here was rage at what had happened to their soldiers and their country, and even more rage at the lies that had gone out over State TV, lies so clearly and utterly refuted by the reality they saw over the Internet, a source they'd learned to trust.

There was only one place for them to go, Tian'anmen Square, the "Square of Heavenly Peace," the psychological center of their country, and they were drawn there like iron filings to a magnet. The time of day worked for them. The police in Beijing, like police everywhere, worked twenty-four-hour days divided into three unequal shifts, and the shift most lightly manned was that from 2300 to 0700. Most people were asleep then, and as a direct result there was little crime to suppress, and so this shift was the smallest in terms of manning, and also composed of those officers loved the least by their commanders, because no man in his right mind prefers the vampire life of wakefulness in darkness to that in the light of day. And so the few police on duty were those who had failed to distinguish themselves in their professional skills, or were disliked by their captains, and returned the compliment by not taking their duties with sufficient gravity.

The appearance of the first students in the square was barely noted by the two policemen there. Their main duties involved directing traffic and/or telling (frequently inebriated) foreign tourists how to stumble back to their hotels, and the only danger they faced was usually that of being blinded by the flashes of foreign cameras held by oafishly pleasant but drunken *gwai.*

This new situation took them totally by surprise, and their first reaction was to do nothing but watch. The presence of so many young people in the square *was* unusual, but they weren't *doing* anything overtly unlawful at the moment, and so the police just looked on in a state of bemusement. They didn't even report what was going on because the watch captain was an ass who wouldn't have known what to do about it anyway.

"What if they strike at our nuclear arms?" Interior Minister Tong Jie asked.

"They already have," Zhang reminded them. "They sank our missile submarine, you will recall. If they also strike at our land-based missiles, then it would mean they plan to attack us as a nation, not just our armed forces, for then they would have nothing to hold them back. It would be a grave and deliberate provocation, is that not so, Shen?"

The Foreign Minister nodded. "It would be an unfriendly act."

"How do we defend against it?" Tan Deshi asked.

"The missile field is located far from the borders. Each is in a heavily constructed concrete silo," Defense Minister Luo explained. "Moreover, we have recently fortified them further with steel armor to deflect bombs that might fall on them. The best way to add to their defense would be to deploy surface-to-air missiles."

"And if the Americans use their stealthy bombers, then what?" Tan asked.

"The defense against that is passive, the steel hats we put on the silos. We have troops there—security personnel of Second Artillery Command—but they are there only for site security against intruders on the ground. If such an attack should be made, we should launch them. The principle is to use them or lose them. An attack against our strategic weapons would have to be a precursor to an attack against our nationhood. That is our one trump card," Luo explained. "The one thing that even the Americans truly fear."

"Well, it should be," Zhang Han Sen agreed. "That is how we tell the Americans where they must stop and what they must do. In fact, it might now be a good time to tell the Americans that we have those missiles, and the willingness to use them if they press us too hard."

"Threaten the Americans with nuclear arms?" Fang asked. "Is that wise? They know of our weapons, surely. An overt threat against a powerful nation is most unwise."

"They must know that there are lines they may not cross," Zhang insisted. "They can hurt us, yes, but we can hurt them, and this is one weapon against which they have no defense, and their sentimentality for their people works for us, not them. It is time for America to regard us as an equal, not a minor country whose power they can blithely ignore."

"I repeat, Comrade," Fang said, "that would be a most unwise act. When someone points a gun at your head, you do not try to frighten him."

"Fang, you have been my friend for many years, but in this you are wrong. It is *we* who hold that pistol now. The Americans only respect strength controlled by resolve. This will make them think. Luo, are the missiles ready for launch?"

The Defense Minister shook his head. "No, yesterday we did not agree to ready them. To do so takes about two hours—to load them with fuel. After that, they can be kept in a ready condition for about forty-eight hours. Then you defuel them, service them—it takes about four hours to do that—and you can refuel them again. We could easily maintain half of them in a ready-launch condition indefinitely."

"Comrades, I think it is in our interest to ready the missiles for flight."

"No!" Fang countered. "That will be seen by the Americans as a dangerous provocation, and provoking them this way is madness!"

"And we should have Shen remind the Americans that we have such weapons, and they do not," Zhang went on.

"That invites an attack on us!" Fang nearly shouted. "They do not have rockets, yes, but they have other ways of attacking us, and if we do that now, when a war is already under way, we guarantee a response."

"I think not, Fang," Zhang replied. "They will not gamble millions of their citizens against all of ours. They have not the strength for such gambling."

"Gambling, you say. Do we gamble with the life of our country? Zhang, you are mad. This is lunacy," Fang insisted.

"I do not have a vote at this table," Qian observed. "But I have been a Party member all of my adult life, and I have served the People's Republic well, I think. It is our job here to build a country, not destroy it. What have we done here? We've turned China into a thief, a highway robber—and a *failed* highway robber at that! Luo has said it. We have lost our play for riches, and now we must adjust to that. We can recover from the damage we have done to our country and its people. That recovery will require humility on our part, not blustering defiance. To threaten the Americans now is an act of weakness, not strength. It's the act of an impotent man trying to show off his *gau.* It will be seen by them as a foolish and reckless act."

"If we are to survive as a nation—if *we* are to survive as the rulers of a powerful China," Zhang countered, "we must let the Americans know that they cannot push us farther. Comrades, make no mistake. Our lives lie on this table." And that focused the discussion. "I do not suggest that we launch a nuclear strike on America. I propose that we demonstrate to America our resolve, and if they press us too far, then we will punish them—and the Russians. Comrades, I propose that we fuel up our missiles, to place them in a ready posture, and then have Shen tell the Americans that there are limits beyond which we cannot be pushed without the gravest possible consequences."

"No!" Fang retorted. "That is tantamount to the threat of nuclear war. *We must not do such a thing!*"

"If we do not, then we are all doomed," said Tan Deshi of the Ministry of State Security. "I am sorry, Fang, but Zhang is correct here. Those are the only weapons with which we can hold the Americans back. They will be tempted to strike at them—and if they do . . ."

"If they do, then we must use them, because if they take those weapons away from us, then they can strike us at will, and destroy all we have built in sixty years," Zhang concluded. "I call a vote."

Suddenly and irrationally, Fang thought, the meeting had struck out on a path with no logic or direction, leading to disaster. But he was the only one who saw this, as for the first time in his life he took a stand against the others. The meeting finally broke up. The Politburo members drove directly home. None of them passed through Tiananmen Square on the way, and all of them fell rapidly asleep.

There were twenty-five UH-60A Blackhawks and fifteen Apaches on the ramp. Every one had stubby wings affixed to the fuselage. Those on the Blackhawks were occupied with fuel tanks. The Apaches had both fuel and rockets. The flight crews were grouped together, looking at maps.

Clark took the lead. He was dressed in his black Ninja gear, and a soldier directed him and Kirillin—he was in the snowflake camouflage used by Russian airborne troops—to Colonel Boyle.

"Howdy, Dick Boyle."

"I'm John Clark, and this is Lieutenant General Yuriy Kirillin. I'm RAINBOW," John explained. "He's Spetsnaz."

Boyle saluted. "Well, I'm your driver, gentlemen. The objective is seven hundred sixteen miles away. We can just about make it with the fuel we're carrying, but we're going to have to tank up on the way back. We're doing that right here"—he pointed to a spot on the navigation chart—"hilltop west of this little town named Chicheng. We got lucky. Two C-130s are going to do bladder drops for us. There will be a fighter escort for top cover, F-15s, plus some F-16s to go after any radars along the way, and when we get to about here, eight F-117s are going to trash this fighter base at Anshan. That should take care of any Chinese fighter interference. Now, this missile base has an associated security force, supposed to be battalion strength, in barracks located here"—this time it was a satellite photo—"and five of my Apaches are going to take that place down with rockets. The others will be flying direct support. The only other question is, how close do you want us to put you on these missile silos?"

"Land right on top of the bastards," Clark told him, looking over at Kirillin.

"I agree, the closer the better."

Boyle nodded. "Fair enough. The helicopters all have numbers on them indicating the silo they're flying for. I'm flying lead, and I'm going right to this one here."

"That means I go with you," Clark told him.

"How many?"

"Ten plus me."

"Okay, your chem gear's in the aircraft. Suit up, and we go. Latrine's that way," Boyle pointed. It would be better for every man to take a piss before the flight began. "Fifteen minutes."

Clark went that way, and so did Kirillin. Both old soldiers knew what they needed to do in most respects, and this one was as vital as loading a weapon.

"Have you been to China before, John?"

"Nope. Taiwan once, long ago, to get screwed, blued, and tattooed."

"No chance for that on this trip. We are both too old for this, you know."

"I know," Clark said, zipping himself up. "But you're not going to sit back here, are you?"

"A leader must be with his men, Ivan Timofeyevich."

"That is true, Yuriy. Good luck."

"They will not launch a nuclear attack on my country, or on yours," Kirillin promised. "Not while I live."

"You know, Yuriy, you might have been a good guy to have in 3rd SOG."

"And what is that, John?"

"When we get back and have a few drinks, I will tell you."

The troops suited up outside their designated helicopters. The U.S. Army chemical gear was bulky, but not grossly so. Like many American-issue items, it was an evolutionary development of a British idea, with charcoal inside the lining to absorb and neutralize toxic gas, and a hood that—

"We can't use our radios with this," Mike Pierce noted. "Screws up the antenna."

"Try this," Homer Johnston suggested, disconnecting the antenna and tucking it into the helmet cover.

"Good one, Homer," Eddie Price said, watching what he did and trying it himself. The American-pattern Kevlar helmet fit nicely into the hoods, which they left off in any case as too uncomfortable until they really needed it. That done, they loaded into their helicopters, and the flight crews spooled up the General Electric turboshaft engines. The Blackhawks lifted off. The special-operations troops were set in what were—for military aircraft—comfortable seats, held in place with four-point safety belts. Clark took the jump seat, aft and between the two pilots, and tied into the intercom.

"Who, exactly, are you?" Boyle asked.

"Well, I have to kill you after I tell you, but I'm CIA. Before that, Navy."

"SEAL?" Boyle asked.

"Budweiser badge and all. Couple years ago we set up this group, called RAINBOW, special operations, counter-terror, that sort of thing."

"The amusement park job?"

"That's us."

"You had a -60 supporting you for that. Who's the driver?"

"Dan Malloy. Goes by 'BEAR' when he's driving. Know him?"

"Marine, right?"

"Yep." Clark nodded.

"Never met him, heard about him a little. I think he's in D.C. now."

"Yeah, when he left us he took over VMH-1."

"Flies the President?"

"Correct."

"Bummer," Boyle observed.

"How long you been doing this?"

"Flying choppers? Oh, eighteen years. Four thousand hours. I was born in the Huey, and grew up into these. Qualified in the Apache, too."

"What do you think of the mission?" John asked.

"Long" was the reply, and Clark hoped that was the only cause for concern. A sore ass you could recover from quickly enough.

I wish there was another way to do this one, Robby," Ryan said over lunch. It seemed utterly horrid to be sitting here in the White House Mess, eating a cheeseburger with his best friend, while others—including two people he knew well, Jack had learned—were heading into harm's way. It was enough to kill his appetite as dead as the low-cholesterol beef in the bun. He set it down and sipped at his Coke.

"Well, there is—if you want to wait the two days it's going to take Lockheed-Martin to assemble the bombs, then a day to fly them to Siberia, and another twelve hours to fly the mission. Maybe longer. The Black Jet only flies at night, remember?" the Vice President pointed out.

"You're handling it better than I am."

"Jack, I don't like it any more than you do, okay? But after twenty years of flying off carriers, you learn to handle the stress of having friends in tight corners. If you don't, might as well turn in your wings. Eat, man, you need your strength. How's Andrea doing?"

That generated an ironic smile. "Puked her guts out this morning. Had her use my own crapper. It's killing her, she was embarrassed as a guy caught naked in Times Square."

"Well, she's in a man's job, and she doesn't want to be seen as a wimp," Robby explained. "Hard to be one of the boys when you don't have a dick, but she tries real hard. I'll give her that."

"Cathy says it passes, but it isn't passing fast enough for her." He looked over to see Andrea standing in the doorway, always the watchful protector of her President.

"She's a good troop," Jackson agreed.

"How's your dad doing?"

"Not too bad. Some TV ministry agency wants him and Gerry Patterson to do some more salt-and-pepper shows on Sunday mornings. He's thinking about it. The money could dress up the church some."

"They were impressive together."

"Yeah, Gerry didn't do bad for a white boy—and he's actually a pretty good guy, Pap says. I'm not sure of this TV-ministry stuff, though. Too easy to go Hollywood and start playing to the audience instead of being a shepherd to your flock."

"Your father's a pretty impressive gent, Robby."

Jackson looked up. "I'm glad you think so. He raised us pretty good, and it was pretty tough on him after Mom died. But he can be a real sundowner. Gets all pissy when he sees me drink a beer. But, what the hell, it's his job to yell at people, I suppose."

"Tell him that Jesus played bartender once. It was his first public miracle."

"I've pointed that out, and then he says, if Jesus wants to do it, that's okay for Jesus, boy, but *you* ain't Jesus." The Vice President had a good chuckle. "Eat, Jack."

"Yes, Mom."

This food isn't half bad," Al Gregory said, two miles away in the wardroom of USS *Gettysburg*.

"Well, no women and no booze on a ship of war," Captain Blandy pointed out. "Not this one yet, anyway. You have to have some diversion. So, how are the missiles?"

"The software is fully loaded, and I e-mailed the upgrade like you said. So all the other Aegis ships ought to have it."

"Just heard this morning that the Aegis office in the Pentagon is having a bit of a conniption fit over this. They didn't approve the software."

"Tell 'em to take it up with Tony Bretano," Gregory suggested.

"Explain to me again, what exactly did you upgrade?"

"The seeker software on the missile warhead. I cut down the lines of code so it can recycle more quickly. And I reprogrammed the nutation rate on the laser on the fusing system so that I can handle a higher rate of closure. It should obviate the problem the Patriots had with the Scuds back in '91—I helped with that software fix, too, back then, but this one's about half an order of magnitude faster."

"Without a hardware fix?" the skipper asked.

"It *would* be better to increase the range of the laser, yes, but you can get away without it—at least it worked okay on the computer simulations."

"Hope to hell we don't need to prove it.'

"Oh, yeah, Captain. A nuke headed for a city is a *bad* thing."

"Amen."

There were five thousand of them now, with more coming, summoned by the cell phones that they all seemed to have. Some even had portable computers tied into cellular phones so that they could tap into the Internet site out here in the open. It was a clear night, with no rain to wreck a computer. The leaders of the crowd—they now thought of it as a demonstration—huddled around them to see more, and then relayed it to their friends. The first big student uprising in Tiananmen Square had been fueled by faxes. This one had taken a leap forward in technology. Mainly they milled around, talking excitedly with one another, and summoning more help. The first such demonstration had failed, but they'd all been toddlers then and their memory of it was sketchy at best. They were all old and educated enough to know what needed changing, but not yet old and experienced enough to know that change in their society was impossible. And they didn't know what a dangerous combination that could be.

The ground below was dark and unlit. Even their night-vision goggles didn't help much, showing only rough terrain features, mainly the tops of hills and ridges. There were few lights below. There were some houses and other buildings, but at this time of night few people were awake, and all of the lights were turned off.

The only moving light sources they could see were the rotor tips of the helicopters, heated by air friction to the point that they would be painful to touch, and hot enough to glow in the infrared spectrum that the night goggles could detect. Mainly the troops were lulled into stuporous lassitude by the unchanging vibration of the aircraft, and the semi-dreaming state that came with it helped to pass the time.

That was not true of Clark, who sat in the jump seat, looking down at the satellite photos of the missile base at Xuanhua, studying by the illumination of the IR light on his goggles, looking for information he might have missed on first and twenty-first inspection. He was confident in his men. Chavez had turned into a fine tactical leader, and the troops, experienced sergeants all, would do what they were told to the extent of their considerable abilities.

The Russians in the other helicopters would do okay, too, he thought. Younger—by eight years on average—than the RAINBOW troopers, they were all commissioned officers, mainly lieutenants and captains with a leavening of a few majors, and all were university graduates, well educated, and that was almost as good as five years in uniform. Better yet, they were well motivated young professional soldiers, smart enough to think on their feet, and proficient in their weapons.

The mission should work, John thought. He leaned to check the clock on the helicopter's instrument panel. Forty minutes and they'd find out. Turning around, he noticed the eastern sky was lightening, according to his goggles. They'd hit the missile field just before dawn.

It was a stupidly easy mission for the Black Jets. Arriving overhead singly, about thirty seconds apart, each opened its bomb bay doors and dropped two weapons, ten seconds apart. Each pilot, his plane controlled by its automatic cruising system, put his laser dot on a preplanned section of the runway. The bombs were the earliest Paveway-II guidance packages bolted to Mark-84 2,000-pound bombs with cheap—$7.95 each, in fact—M905 fuses set to go off a hundredth of a second after impact, so as to make a hole in the concrete about twenty feet across by nine feet deep. And this all sixteen of them did, to the shocked surprise of the sleepy tower crew, and with enough noise to wake up every person within a five-mile radius—and just that fast, Anshan fighter base was closed, and would remain so for at least a week. The eight F-117s turned singly and made their way back to their base at Zhigansk. Flying the Black Jet wasn't supposed to be any more exciting than driving a 737 for Southwest Airlines, and for the most part it wasn't.

"Why the hell didn't they send one of those Dark Stars down to cover the mission?" Jack asked.

"I suppose it never occurred to anybody," Jackson said. They were back in the situation room.

"What about satellite overheads?"

"Not this time," Ed Foley advised. "Next pass over is in about four hours. Clark has a satellite phone. He'll clue us in."

"Great." Ryan leaned back in a chair that suddenly wasn't terribly comfortable.

"Objective in sight," Boyle said over the intercom. Then the radio. "BANDIT SIX to chicks, objective in sight. Check in, over."

"Two." "Three." "Four." "Five." "Six." "Seven." "Eight." "Nine." "Ten."

"COCHISE, check in."

"This is COCHISE LEADER with five, we have the objective."

"Crook with five, objective in sight," the second attack-helicopter team reported.

"Okay, move in as briefed. Execute, execute, execute!"

Clark was perked up now, as were the troops in the back. Sleep was shaken off, and adrenaline flooded into their bloodstreams. He saw them shake their heads and flex their jaws. Weapons were tucked in tight, and every man moved his left hand to the twist-dial release fitting on the belt buckle.

COCHISE flight went in first, heading for the barracks of the security battalion tasked to guard the missile base. The building could have been transported bodily from any WWII American army base—a two-story wood-frame construction, with a pitched roof, and painted white. There was a guard shack outside, also painted white, and it glowed in the thermal sights of the Apache gunners. They could even see the two soldiers there, doubtless approaching the end of their duty tour, standing slackly, their weapons slung over their shoulders, because *nobody* ever came out here, rarely enough during the day, and never in living memory at night—unless you counted the battalion commander coming back drunk from a command-staff meeting.

Their heads twisted slightly when they thought they heard something strange, but the four-bladed rotor on the Apache was also designed for sound suppression, and so they were still looking when they saw the first flash—

—the weapons selected were the 2.75-inch-diameter free-flight rockets, carried in pods on the Apaches' stub wings. Three of the section of five handled the initial firing run, with two in reserve should the unexpected develop. They burned in low, so as to conceal their silhouettes in the hills behind them, and opened up at two hundred meters. The first salvo of four blew up the guard shack and its two sleepy guards. The noise would have been enough to awaken those in the barracks building, but the second salvo of rockets, this time fifteen of them, got there before anyone inside could do more than blink his eyes open. Both floors of the two-story structure were hit, and most of those inside died without waking, caught in the middle of dreams. The Apaches hesitated then, still having weapons to fire. There was a subsidiary guard post on the other side of the building; COCHISE LEAD looped around the barracks and spotted it. The two soldiers there had their rifles up and fired blindly into the air, but his gunner selected his 20-mm cannon and swept them aside as though with a broom. Then the Apache pivoted in the air and he salvoed his remaining rockets into the barracks, and it was immediately apparent that if anyone was alive in there, it was by the grace of God Himself, and whoever it was would not be a danger to the mission.

"COCHISE Four and Five, Lead. Go back up Crook, we don't need you here."

"Roger, Lead," they both replied. The two attack helicopters moved off, leaving the first three to look for and erase any signs of life.

Crook flight, also of five Apaches, smoked in just ahead of the Blackhawks. It turned out that each silo had a small guard post, each for two men, and those were disposed of in a matter of seconds with cannon fire. Then the Apaches climbed to higher altitude and circled slowly, each over a pair of missile silos, looking for anything moving, but seeing nothing.

BANDIT SIX, Colonel Dick Boyle, flared his Blackhawk three feet over Silo #1, as it was marked on his satellite photo.

"Go!" the co-pilot shouted over the intercom. The RAINBOW troopers jumped down just to the east of the actual hole itself; the "Chinese hat" steel structure, which looked like an inverted blunt ice cream cone, prohibited dropping right down on the door itself.

The base command post was the best-protected structure on the entire post. It was buried ten meters underground, and the ten meters was solid reinforced concrete, so as to survive a nuclear bomb's exploding within a hundred meters, or so the design supposedly promised. Inside was a staff of ten, commanded by Major General Xun Qing-Nian. He'd been a Second Artillery (the Chinese name for their strategic missile troops) officer since graduating from university with an engineering degree. Only three hours before, he'd supervised the fueling of all twelve of his CSS-4 intercontinental ballistic missiles, which had never happened before in his memory. No explanation had come with that order, though it didn't take a rocket scientist—which he was, by profession—to connect it with the war under way against Russia.

Like all members of the People's Liberation Army, he was a highly disciplined man, and always mindful of the fact that he had his country's most valuable military assets under his personal control. The alarm had been raised by one of the silo-guard posts, and his staff switched on the television cameras used for site inspection and surveillance. They were old cameras, and needed lights, which were switched on as well.

What the fuck!" Chavez shouted. "Turn the lights off!" he ordered over his radio.

It wasn't demanding. The light standards weren't very tall, nor were they very far away. Chavez hosed one with his MP-10, and the lights went out, thank you. No other lasted for more than five seconds at any of the silos.

We are under attack," General Xun said in a quiet and disbelieving voice. "We are under attack," he repeated. But he had a drill for this. "Alert the guard force," he told one NCO. "Get me Beijing," he ordered another.

At Silo #1, Paddy Connolly ran to the pipes that led to the top of the concrete box that marked the top of the silo. To each he stuck a block of Composition B, his explosive of choice. Into each block he inserted a blasting cap. Two men, Eddie Price and Hank Patterson, knelt close by with their weapons ready for a response force that was nowhere to be seen.

"Fire in the hole!" Patterson shouted, running back to the other two. There he skidded down to the ground, sheltered behind the concrete, and twisted the handle on his detonator. The two pipes were blown apart a millisecond later.

"Masks!" he told everyone on the radio . . . but there was no vapor coming off the fueling pipes. That was good news, wasn't it?

"Come on!" Eddie Price yelled at him. The three men, guarded now by two others, looked for the metal door into the maintenance entrance for the silo.

"Ed, we're on the ground, we're on the ground," Clark was saying into his satellite phone, fifty yards away. "The barracks are gone, and there's no opposition on the ground here. Doing our blasting now. Back to you soon. Out."

Well, shit," Ed Foley said in his office, but the line was now dead.

What?" It was an hour later in Beijing, and the sun was up. Marshal Luo, having just woken up after not enough sleep following the worst day he'd known since the Cultural Revolution, had a telephone thrust into his hands. "What is this?" he demanded of the phone.

"This is Major General Xun Qing-Nian at Xuanhua missile base. We are under attack here. There is a force of men on the ground over our heads trying to destroy our missiles. I require instructions!"

"Fight them off!" was the first idea Luo had.

"The defense battalion is dead, they do not respond. Comrade Minister, what do I do?"

"Are your missiles fueled and ready for launch?"

"Yes!"

Luo looked around his bedroom, but there was no one to advise him. His country's most priceless assets were now about to be ripped from his control. His command wasn't automatic. He actually thought first, but in the end, it wouldn't matter how considered his decision was.

"Launch your missiles," he told the distant general officer.

"Repeat your command," Luo heard.

"*Launch your missiles!*" his voice boomed. "*Launch your missiles NOW!*"

"By your command," the voice replied.

Fuck," Sergeant Connolly said. "This is some bloody door!" The first explosive block had done nothing more than scorch the paint. This time he attached a hollow-charge to the upper and lower hinges and backed off again. "This one will do it," he promised as he trailed the wires back.

The crash that followed gave proof to his words. When next they looked in, the door was gone. It had been hurled inward, must have flown into the silo like a bat out of—

—"Bloody hell!" Connolly turned. "Run! *RUN!*"

Price and Patterson needed no encouragement. They ran for their lives. Connolly caught them reaching for his protective hood as he did so, not stopping until he was over a hundred yards away.

"The bloody missile's fueled. The door ruptured the upper tank. It's going to blow!"

"Shit! Team, this is Price, the missiles are fueled, I repeat the missiles are fueled. Get the fucking hell away from the silo!"

The proof of that came from Silo #8, off to Price's south. The concrete structure that sat atop it surged into the air, and under it was a volcanic blast of fire and smoke. Silo #1, theirs, did the same, a gout of flame going sideways out of the open service door.

The infrared signature was impossible to miss. Over the equator, a DSP satellite focused in on the thermal bloom and cross-loaded the signal to Sunnyvale, California. From there it went to NORAD, the North American Aerospace Defense Command, dug into the sub-basement level of Cheyenne Mountain, Colorado.

"Launch! Possible launch at Xuanhua!"

"What's that?" asked CINC-NORAD.

"We got a bloom, a huge—*two* huge ones at Xuanhua," the female captain announced. "Fuck, there's another one."

"Okay, Captain, settle down," the four-star told her. "There's a special op taking that base down right now. Settle down, girl."

In the control bunker, men were turning keys. The general in command had never really expected to do this. Sure, it was a possibility, the thing he'd trained his entire career for, but, no, not this. No. Not a chance.

But someone was trying to destroy his command—and he did have his orders, and like the automaton he'd been trained to be, he gave the orders and turned his command key.

The Spetsnaz people were doing well. Four silos were now disabled. One of the Russian teams managed to crack the maintenance door on their first try. This team, General Kirillin's own, sent its technical genius inside, and he found the missile's guidance module and blew it apart with gunfire. It would take a week at least to fix this missile, and just to make sure *that* didn't happen, he affixed an explosive charge to the stainless steel body and set the timer for fifteen minutes. "Done!" he called.

"Out!" Kirillin ordered. The lieutenant general, now feeling like a new cadet in parachute school, gathered his team and ran to the pickup point. As guilty as any man would be of mission focus, he looked around, surprised by the fire and flame to his north—

—but more surprised to see three silo covers moving. The nearest was only three hundred meters away, and there he saw one of his Spetsnaz troopers walk right to the suddenly open silo and toss something in—then he ran like a rabbit—

—because three seconds later, the hand grenade he'd tossed in exploded, and took the entire missile up with it. The Spetsnaz soldier disappeared in the fireball he'd caused, and would not be seen again—

—but then something worse happened. From exhaust vents set left and right of Silos #5 and #7 came two vertical fountains of solid white-yellow flame, and less than two seconds later appeared the blunt, black shape of a missile's nosecone.

"Fuck," breathed the Apache pilot coded Crook Two. He was circling a kilometer away, and without any conscious thought at all, lowered his nose, twisted throttle, and pulled collective to jerk his attack helicopter at the rising missile.

"Got it," the gunner called. He selected his 20-mm cannon and held down the trigger. The tracers blazed out like laser beams. The first set missed, but the gunner adjusted his lead and walked them into the missile's upper half—

—the resulting explosion threw Crook Two out of control, rolling it over on its back. The pilot threw his cyclic to the left, continuing the roll before he stopped it, barely, a quarter of the way through the second one, and then he saw the fireball rising, and the burning missile fuel falling back to the ground, atop Silo #9, and on all the men there who'd disabled that bird.

The last missile cleared its silo before the soldiers there could do much about it. Two tried to shoot at it with their personal weapons, but the flaming exhaust incinerated them in less time than it takes to pull a trigger. Another Apache swept in, having seen what Crook Two had accomplished, but its rounds fell short, so rapidly the CSS-4 climbed into the air.

"Oh, fuck," Clark heard in his radio earpiece. It was Ding's voice. "Oh, fuck."

John got back on his satellite phone.

"Yeah, how's it going?" Ed Foley asked.

"One got off, one got away, man."

"What?"

"You heard me. We killed all but one, but that one got off . . . going north, but leaning east some. Sorry, Ed. We tried."

It took Foley a few seconds to gather his thought and reply. "Thanks, John. I guess I have some things to do here."

"There's another one," the captain said.

CINC-NORAD was trying to play this one as cool as he could. Yes, there was a spec-op laid on to take this Chinese missile farm down, and so he expected to see some hot flashes on the screen, and okay, all of them so far had been on the ground.

"That should be all of them," the general announced.

"Sir, this one's moving. This one's a launch."

"Are you sure?"

"Look, sir, the bloom is moving off the site," she said urgently. "Valid launch, valid launch—valid threat!" she concluded. "Oh, my God . . ."

"Oh, shit," CINC-NORAD said. He took one breath and lifted the Gold Phone. No, first he'd call the NMCC.

The senior watch officer in the National Military Command Center was a Marine one-star named Sullivan. The NORAD phone didn't ring very often.

"NMCC, Brigadier General Sullivan speaking."

"This is CINC-NORAD. We have a valid launch, valid threat from Xuanhua missile base in China. I say again, we have a valid launch, valid threat from China. It's angling east, coming to North America."

"Fuck," the Marine observed.

"Tell me about it."

The procedures were all written down. His first call went to the White House military office.

Ryan was setting down to dinner with the family. An unusual night, he had nothing scheduled, no speeches to give, and that was good, because reporters always showed up and asked questions, and lately—

"Say that again?" Andrea Price-O'Day said into her sleeve microphone. "What?"

Then another Secret Service agent bashed into the room. *"Marching Order!"* he proclaimed. It was a code phrase often practiced but never spoken in reality.

"What?" Jack said, half a second before his wife could make the same sound.

"Mr. President, we have to get you and your family out of here," Andrea said. "The Marines have the helicopters on the way."

"What's happening?"

"Sir, NORAD reports an inbound ballistic threat."

"What? China?"

"That's all I know. Let's go, right now," Andrea said forcefully.

"Jack," Cathy said in alarm.

"Okay, Andrea." The President turned. "Time to go, honey. Right now."

"But—what's happening?"

He got her to her feet first, and walked to the door. The corridor was full of agents. Trenton Kelly was holding Kyle Daniel—the lionesses were nowhere in sight—and the principal agents for all the other kids were there. In a moment, they saw that there was not enough room in the elevator. The Ryan family rode. The agents mainly ran down the wide, white marble steps to the ground level.

"Wait!" another agent called, holding his left hand up. His pistol was in his right hand, and none of them had seen *that* very often. They halted as commanded—even the President doesn't often argue with a person holding a gun.

Ryan was thinking as fast as he knew how: "Andrea, where do I go?"

"You go to KNEECAP. Vice President Jackson will join you there. The family goes to Air Force One."

At Andrews Air Force base, just outside Washington, the pilots of First Heli, the USAF 1st Helicopter Squadron, were sprinting to their Bell Hueys. Each had an assignment, and each knew where his Principal was, because the security detail of each was reporting in constantly. Their job was to collect the cabinet members and spirit them away from Washington to preselected places of supposed safety. Their choppers were off the ground in less than three minutes, scattering off to different preselected pickup points.

Jack, what is this?" It took a lot to make his wife afraid, but this one had done it.

"Honey, we have a report that a ballistic missile is flying toward America, and the safest place for us to be is in the air. So, they're getting you and the kids to Air Force One. Robby and I will be on KNEECAP. Okay?"

"Okay? Okay? What is this?"

"It's bad, but that's all I know."

On the Aleutian island of Shemya, the huge Cobra Dane radar scanned the sky to the north and west. It frequently detected satellites, which mainly fly lower than ICBM warheads, but the computer that analyzed the tracks of everything that came into the system's view categorized this contact as exactly what it was, too high to be a low-orbit satellite, and too slow to be a launch vehicle.

"What's the track?" a major asked a sergeant.

"Computer says East Coast of the United States. In a few minutes we'll know more . . . for now, somewhere between Buffalo and Atlanta." That information was relayed automatically to NORAD and the Pentagon.

The entire structure of the United States military went into hyperdrive, one segment at a time, as the information reached it. That included USS *Gettysburg*, alongside the pier in the Washington Navy Yard.

Captain Blandy was in his in-port cabin when the growler phone went off. "Captain speaking . . . go to general quarters, Mr. Gibson," he ordered, far more calmly than he felt.

Throughout the ship, the electronic gonging started, followed by a human voice: "General Quarters—General Quarters—all hands man your battle stations."

Gregory was in CIC, running another simulation. "What's that mean?"

Senior Chief Leek shook his head. "Sir, that means something ain't no simulation no more." *Battle stations alongside the fucking pier?* "Okay, people, let's start lighting it all up!" he ordered his sailors.

The regular presidential helicopter muttered down on the South Lawn, and the Secret Service agent at the door turned and yelled: *"COME ON!"*

Cathy turned. "Jack, you coming with us?"

"No, Cath, I have to go to Kneecap. Now, get along. I'll see you later tonight, okay?" He gave her a kiss, and all the kids got a hug, except for Kyle, whom the President took from Kelley's arms for a quick hold before giving him back. "Take care of him," he told the agent.

"Yes, sir. Good luck." Ryan watched his family run up the steps into the chopper, and the Sikorsky lurched off before they could have had a chance to sit and strap down.

Then another Marine helicopter appeared, this one with Colonel Dan Malloy at the controls. This one was a VH-60, whose doors slid open. Ryan walked quickly to it, with Andrea Price-O'Day at his side. They sat and strapped down before it lumbered back into the air.

"What about everybody else?" Ryan asked.

"There's a shelter under the East Wing for some . . ." she said. Then her voice trailed off and she shrugged.

"Oh, shit, what about everybody else?" Ryan demanded.

"Sir, I have to look after *you.*"

"But—what—"

Then Special Agent Price-O'Day started retching. Ryan saw and pulled out a barf bag, one with a very nice Presidential logo printed on it, and handed it to her. They were over the Mall now, just passing the George Washington Monument. Off to the right was southwest Washington, filled with the working- and middle-class homes of regular people who drove cabs or cleaned up offices, tens of thousands of them . . .there were people visible in the Mall, on the grass, just enjoying a walk in the falling darkness, just being people . . .

And you just left behind a hundred or so. Maybe twenty will fit in the shelter under the East Wing . . . what about the rest, the ones who make your bed and fold your socks and shine your shoes and serve dinner and pick up after the kids—what about them, *Jack?* A small voice asked. *Who flies* them *off to safety?*

He turned his head to see the Washington Monument, and beyond that the reflecting pool and the Lincoln Memorial. He was in the same line as those men, in the city named for one, and saved in time of war by another . . . and he was running away from danger . . . the Capital Building, home of the Congress. The light was on atop the dome. Congress was in session, doing the country's work, or trying to, as they did . . . but he was running away . . . eastern Washington, mainly black, working-class people who did the menial jobs for the most part, and had hopes to send their kids to college so that they could make out a little better than their parents had . . . eating their dinner, watching TV, maybe going out to a movie tonight or just sitting on their porches and shooting the bull with their neighbors—

—Ryan's head turned again, and he saw the two gray shapes at the Navy Yard, one familiar, one not, because Tony Bretano had—

Ryan flipped the belt buckle in his lap and lurched forward, knocking into the Marine sergeant in the jump seat. Colonel Malloy was in the right-front seat, doing his job, flying the chopper. Ryan grabbed his left shoulder. The head came around.

"Yes, sir, what is it?"

"See that cruiser down there?"

"Yes, sir."

"Land on it."

"Sir, I—"

"Land on it, that's an order!" Ryan shouted at him.

"Aye aye," Malloy said like a good Marine.

The Blackhawk turned, arcing down the Anacostia River, and flaring as Malloy judged the wind. The Marine hesitated, looking back one more time. Ryan insistently jerked his hand at the ship.

The Blackhawk approached cautiously.

"What are you doing?" Andrea demanded.

"I'm getting off here. You're going to KNEECAP."

"NO!" she shouted back. "I stay with you!"

"Not this time. Have your baby. If this doesn't work out, I hope the kid turns out like you and Pat." Ryan moved to open the door. The Marine sergeant got there first. Andrea moved to follow.

"Keep her aboard, Marine!" Ryan told the crew chief. "She goes with you!"

"NO!" Price-O'Day screamed.

"Yes, sir," the sergeant acknowledged, wrapping his arms around her.

President Ryan jumped to the nonskid decking of the cruiser's landing area and ducked as the chopper pulled back into the sky. Andrea's face was the last thing he saw. The rotor wash nearly knocked him down, but going to one knee prevented that. Then he stood up and looked around.

"What the hell is—Jesus, sir!" the young petty officer blurted, recognizing him.

"Where's the captain?"

"Captain's in CIC, sir."

"Show me!"

The petty officer led him into a door, then a passageway that led forward. A few twists and turns later, he was in a darkened room that seemed to be set sideways in the body of the ship. It was cool in here. Ryan just walked in, figuring he was President of the United States, Commander-in-Chief of the Army and Navy, and the ship belonged to him anyway. It took a stretch to make his limbs feel as though they were a real part of his body, and then he looked around, trying to orient himself. First he turned to the sailor who'd brought him here.

"Thanks, son. You can go back to your place now."

"Aye, sir." He turned away as though from a dream/nightmare and resumed his duties as a sailor.

Okay, Jack thought, now what? He could see the big radar displays set fore and aft, and the people sitting sideways to look at it. He headed that way, bumping into a cheap aluminum chair on the way, and looked down to see what looked like a Navy chief petty officer in a khaki shirt whose pocket—well, damn—Ryan exercised his command prerogative and reached down to steal the sailor's cigarette pack. He lifted one out, and lit it with a butane lighter. Then he walked to look at the radar display.

"Jesus, sir," the chief said belatedly.

"Not quite. Thanks for the smoke." Two more steps and he was behind a guy with silver eagles on his collar. That would be the captain of USS *Gettysburg*. Ryan took a long and comforting drag on the smoke.

"God damn it! There's no smoking in my CIC!" the captain snarled.

"Good evening, Captain," Ryan replied. "I think at this moment we have a ballistic warhead inbound on Washington, presumably with a thermonuclear device inside. Can we set aside your concerns about secondhand smoke for a moment?"

Captain Blandy turned around and looked up. His mouth opened as wide as a U.S. Navy ashtray. "How—who—what?"

"Captain, let's ride this one out together, shall we?"

"Captain Blandy, sir," the man said, snapping to his feet.

"Jack Ryan, Captain." Ryan shook his hand and bade him sit back down. "What's happening now?"

"Sir, the NMCC tells us that there's a ballistic inbound for the

East Coast. I've got the ship at battle stations. Radar's up. Chip inserted?" he asked.

"The chip is in, sir," Senior Chief Leek confirmed.

"Chip?"

"Just our term for it. It's really a software thing," Blandy explained.

Cathy and the kids were pulled up the steps and hustled into the forward cabin. The colonel at the controls was in an understandable hurry. With Three and Four already turning, he started engines One and Two, and the VC-25 started rolling the instant the truck with the steps pulled away, making one right-angle turn, and then lumbering down Runway One-Nine Right into the southerly wind. Immediately below him, Secret Service and Air Force personnel got the First Family strapped in, and for the first time in fifteen minutes, the Secret Service people allowed themselves to breathe normally. Not thirty seconds later, Vice President Jackson's helicopter landed next to the E-4B National Emergency Airborne Command Post, whose pilot was as anxious to get off the ground as the driver of the VC-25. That was accomplished in less than ninety seconds. Jackson had never strapped in, and stood to look around. "Where's Jack?" the Vice President asked. Then he saw Andrea, who looked as though she just miscarried her pregnancy.

"He stayed, sir. He had the pilot drop him on the cruiser in the Navy Yard."

"He did *what?*"

"You heard me, sir."

"Get him on the radio—*right now!*" Jackson ordered.

Ryan was actually feeling somewhat relaxed. No more rushing about, here he was, surrounded by people calmly and quietly going about their jobs–outwardly so, anyway. The captain looked a little tense, but captains were supposed to, Ryan figured, being responsible in this case for a billion dollars' worth of warship and computers.

"Okay, how are we doing?"

"Sir, the inbound, if it's aimed at us, is not on the scope yet."

"Can you shoot it down?"

"That's the idea, Mr. President," Blandy replied. "Is Dr. Gregory around?"

"Here, Captain," a voice answered. A shape came closer. "Jesus!"

"That's not my name—I know you!" Ryan said in considerable surprise "Major—Major . . ."

"Gregory, sir. I ended up a half a colonel before I pulled the plug. SDIO. Secretary Bretano had me look into upgrading the missiles for the Aegis system," the physicist explained. "I guess we're going to see if it works or not."

"What do you think?" Ryan asked.

"It worked fine on the simulations" was the best answer available.

"Radar contact. We got us a bogie," a petty officer said. "Bearing three-four-niner, range nine hundred miles, speed—that's the one, sir. Speed is one thousand four hundred knots—I mean fourteen *thousand* knots, sir." *Damn*, he didn't have to add.

"Four and a half minutes out," Gregory said.

"Do the math in your head?" Ryan asked.

"Sir, I've been in the business since I got out of West Point."

Ryan finished his cigarette and looked around for—

"Here, sir." It was the friendly chief with an ashtray that had magically appeared in CIC. "Want another one?"

"Why not?" the President reasoned. He took a second one, and the senior chief lit it up for him. "Thanks."

"Gee, Captain Blandy, maybe you're declaring a blanket amnesty?"

"If he isn't, I am," Ryan said.

"Smoking lamp is lit, people," Senior Chief Leek announced, an odd satisfaction in his voice.

The captain looked around in annoyance, but dismissed it.

"Four minutes, it might not matter a whole lot," Ryan observed as coolly as the cigarette allowed. Health hazard or not, they had their uses.

"Captain, I have a radio call for the President, sir."

"Where do I take it?" Jack asked.

"Right here, sir," yet another chief said, lifting a phone-type receiver and pushing a button.

"Ryan."

"Jack, it's Robby."

"My family get off okay?"

"Yeah, Jack, they're fine. Hey, what the hell are you doing down there?"

"Riding it out. Robby, I can't run away, pal. I just can't."

"Jack if this thing goes off—"

"Then you get promoted," Ryan cut him off.

"You know what I'll have to do?" the Vice President demanded.

"Yeah, Robby, you'll have to play catch-up. God help you if you do." *But it won't be* my *problem,* Ryan thought. There was some consolation in that. Killing some guy with a gun was one thing. Killing a million with a nuke . . . no, he just couldn't do that without eating a gun afterward. *You're just too Catholic, Jack, my boy.*

"Jesus, Jack," his old friend said over the digital, encrypted radio link. Clearly thinking about what horrors he'd have to commit, son of a preacher-man or not . . .

"Robby, you're the best friend any man could hope to have. If this doesn't work out, look after Cathy and the kids for me, will ya?"

"You know it."

"We'll know in about three minutes, Rob. Get back to me then, okay?"

"Roger," the former Tomcat driver replied. "Out."

"Dr. Gregory, what can you tell me?"

"Sir, the inbound is probably their equivalent of one of our old W-51s. Five megatons, thereabouts. It'll do Washington, and everything within ten miles—hell, it'll break windows in Baltimore."

"What about us, here?"

"No chance. Figure it'll be targeted inside a triangle defined by the White House, the Capitol Building, and the Pentagon. The ship's keel might survive, only because it's under water. No people. Oh, maybe some really lucky folks in the D.C. subway. That's pretty far underground. But the fires will suck all the air out of the tunnels, probably." He shrugged. "This sort of thing's never happened before. You can't say for sure until it does."

"What chances that it'll be a dud?"

"The Pakistanis have had some failed detonations. We had fizzles once, mainly from helium contamination in the secondary. That's why the terrorist bomb at Denver fizzled—"

"I remember."

"Okay," Gregory said. "It's over Buffalo now. Now it's reentering the atmosphere. That'll slow it down a little."

"Sir, the track is definitely on us, the NMCC says," a voice said.

"Agreed," Captain Blandy said.

"Is there a civilian alert?" Ryan asked.

"It's on the radio, sir," a sailor said. "It's on CNN, too."

"People will be panicking out there," Ryan murmured, taking another drag.

Probably not. Most people don't really know what the sirens mean, and the rest won't believe the radio, Gregory thought. "Captain, we're getting close." The track crossed over the Pennsylvania/New York border—

"System up?" Blandy asked.

"We are fully on line, sir," the Weapons Officer answered. "We are ready to fire from the forward magazine. Firing order is selected, all Block IVs."

"Very well." The captain leaned forward and turned his key in the lock. "System is fully enabled. Special-Auto." He turned. "Sir, that means the computer will handle it from here."

"Target range is now three hundred miles," a kid's voice announced.

They're so cool about this, Ryan thought. *Maybe they just don't believe it's real . . . hell, it's hard enough for me . . .* He took another drag on the cigarette, watching the blip come down, following its computer-produced velocity vector right for Washington, D.C.

"Any time now," the Weapons Officer said.

He wasn't far off. *Gettysburg* shuddered with the launch of the first missile.

"One away!" a sailor said off to the right. "One is away clean."

"Okay."

The SM2-ER missile had two stages. The short booster kicked the assembly out of its silo-type hole in the forward magazine, trailing an opaque column of gray smoke.

"The idea is to intercept at a range of two hundred miles," Gregory explained. "The interceptor and the inbound will rendezvous at the same spot, and—zap!"

"Mainly farmland there, place you go to shoot pheasants," Ryan said, remembering hunting trips there in his youth.

"Hey, I got a visual on the fucker," another voice called. There was a TV camera with a ten-power lens slaved into the fire-control radar, and it showed the inbound warhead, just a featureless white blob now, like a meteor, Ryan thought.

"Intercept in four—three—two—one—"

The missile came close, but exploded behind the target.

"Firing Two!" *Gettysburg* shook again.

"Two away clean!" the same voice as before announced.

It was over Harrisburg, Pennsylvania, now, its speed "down" to thirteen thousand miles per hour . . .

Then a third missile launched, followed a second later by a fourth. In the "Special-Auto" setting, the computer was expending missiles until it saw a dead target. That was just fine with everyone aboard.

"Only two Block IVs left," Weps said.

"They're cheap," Captain Blandy observed. "Come on, baby!"

Number Two also exploded behind the target, the TV picture showed.

"Three—two—one—now!"

So did Number Three.

"Oh, shit, oh, my God!" Gregory exclaimed. That caused heads to snap around.

"What?" Blandy demanded.

The IR seekers, they're going for the centroid of the infrared source, and that's *behind* the inbound."

"What?" Ryan asked, his stomach in an instant knot.

"The brightest part of the target is *behind* the target. The missiles are going for *that*! Oh, fuck!" Dr. Gregory explained.

"Five away . . . Six away . . . both got off clean," the voice to the right announced again.

The inbound was over Frederick, Maryland, now, doing twelve thousand knots . . .

"That's it, we're out of Block IVs."

"Light up the Block IIIs," Blandy ordered at once.

The next two interceptors did the same as the first two, coming within mere feet of the target, but exploding just behind it, and the inbound was traveling faster than the burn rate of explosive in the Standard-2-ER missile warheads. The lethal fragments couldn't catch up—

"Firing Seven! Clean." *Gettysburg* shook yet again.

"That one's a radar homer," Blandy said, clenching his fist before his chest.

Five and Six performed exactly as the four preceding them, missing by mere yards, but a miss in this case *was* as good as a mile.

Another shudder.

"Eight! Clean!"

"We have to get it before it gets to five or six thousand feet. That's optimal burst height," Gregory said.

"At that range, I can engage it with my five-inch forward," Blandy said, some fear in his voice now.

For his part, Ryan wondered why he wasn't shaking. Death had reached its cold hand out for him more than once . . . the Mall in London . . . his own home . . . *Red October* . . . some nameless hill in Colombia. Someday it would touch him. Was this the day? He took a last drag on the smoke and stabbed it out in the aluminum ashtray.

"Okay, here comes seven—five—four—three—two—one—now!"

"Miss! *Fuck!*"

"Nine away—Ten away, both clean! We're out of missiles," the distant chief called out. "This is it, guys."

The inbound crossed over the D.C. Beltway, Interstate Highway 695, now at an altitude of less than twenty thousand feet, streaking across the night sky like a meteor, and so some people thought it was, pointing and calling out to those nearby. If they continued to look at it until detonation, their eyes would explode, and they would then die blind . . .

"Eight missed! Missed by a cunt hair!" a voice announced angrily. Clear on the TV, the puff of the explosion appeared mere inches from the target.

"Two more to go," the Weapons Officer told them.

Aloft, the forward port-side SPG-62 radar was pouring out X-band radiation at the target. The rising SM-2 missile, its rocket motor still burning, homed in on the reflected signal, focusing, closing, seeing the source of the reflected energy that drew it as a moth to a flame, a kamikaze robot the size of a small car, going at nearly two thousand miles per hour, seeking an object going six times faster . . . two miles . . . one mile . . . a thousand yards . . . five hundred, one hun—

—On the TV screen the RV meteor changed to a shower of sparks and fire—

"Yeah!" twenty voices called as one.

The TV camera followed the descending sparks. The adjacent radar display showed them falling within the city of Washington.

"You're going to want to get people to collect those fragments. Some of them are going to be plutonium. Not real healthy to handle," Gregory said, leaning against a stanchion. "Looked like a skin-skin kill. Oh, God, how did I fuck up my programming like that?" he wondered aloud.

"I wouldn't sweat it too bad, Dr. Gregory," Senior Chief Leek observed. "Your code also helped the last one home in more efficient-like. I think I might want to buy you a beer, fella."

CHAPTER 61

Revolution

As usual, the news didn't get back quickly to the place where it had actually started. Having given the launch order, Defense Minister Luo had little clue what to do next. Clearly, he couldn't go back to sleep. America might well answer his action with a nuclear strike of its own, and therefore his first rational thought was that it might be a good idea for him to get the hell out of Beijing. He rose, made normal use of his bathroom, and splashed water on his face, but then again his mind hit a brick wall. What to do? The one name he knew to call was Zhang Han Sen. Once connected, he spoke very quickly indeed.

"You did—*what* happened, Luo?" the senior Minister Without Portfolio asked with genuine alarm.

"Someone—Russians or Americans, I'm not sure which—struck at our missile base at Xuanhua, attempting to destroy our nuclear deterrent. I ordered the base commander to fire them off, of course," Luo told his associate minister, in a voice that was both defiant and defensive. "We agreed on this in our last meeting, did we not?"

"Luo, yes, we discussed the possibility. But *you fired them without consulting with us*?" Zhang demanded. Such decisions were always collegial, never unilateral.

"What choice did I have, Zhang?" Marshal Luo asked in reply. "Had I hesitated a moment, there would have been none left to fire."

"I see," the voice on the phone said. "What is happening now?"

"The missiles are flying. The first should hit their first targets,

Moscow and Leningrad, in about ten minutes. I had no choice, Zhang. I could not allow them to disarm us completely."

Zhang could have sworn and screamed at the man, but there was no point in that. What had happened had happened, and there was no sense expending intellectual or emotional energy on something he could not alter. "Very well. We need to meet. I will assemble the Politburo. Come to the Council of Ministers Building at once. Will the Americans or Russians retaliate?"

"They cannot strike back in kind. They have no nuclear missiles. An attack by bombers would take some hours," Luo advised, trying to make it sound like good news.

At his end of the connection, Zhang felt a chill in his stomach that rivaled liquid helium. As with many things in life, this one—contemplated theoretically in a comfortable conference room—was something very different now that it had turned into a most uncomfortable reality. And yet—was it? It was a thing too difficult to believe. It was too unreal. There were no outward signs—you'd at least expect thunder and lightning outside the windows to accompany news like this, even a major earthquake, but it was merely early morning, not yet seven o'clock. Could this be real?

Zhang padded across his bedroom, switched on his television, and turned it to CNN—it had been turned off for most of the country, but not *here,* of course. His English skills were insufficient to translate the rapid-fire words coming over the screen now. They were showing Washington, D.C., with a camera evidently atop the CNN building there—wherever that was, he had not the faintest idea. It was a black American speaking. The camera showed him standing atop a building, microphone in hand like black plastic ice cream, speaking very, very rapidly—so much so that Zhang was catching only one word in three, and looking off to the camera's left with wide, frightened eyes.

So, he knows what is coming there, doesn't he? Zhang thought, then wondered if he would see the destruction of the American capital via American news television. That, he thought, would have *some* entertainment value.

"Look!" the reporter said, and the camera twisted to see a smoke trail race across the sky—

—*What the hell is that?* Zhang wondered. Then there was another . . . and more besides . . . and the reporter was showing real fear now . . .

. . . it was good for his heart to see such feelings on the face of an American, especially a black American *reporter.* Another one of those *monkeys* had caused his country such great harm, after all . . .

So, now he'd get to see one incinerated . . . or maybe not. The camera and the transmitter would go, too, wouldn't they? So, just a flash of light, maybe, and a blank screen that would be replaced by CNN headquarters in Atlanta . . .

. . . more smoke trails. Ah, yes, they were surface-to-air missiles . . . could such things intercept a nuclear missile? *Probably not,* Zhang judged. He checked his watch. The sweep hand seemed determined to let the snail win this race, it jumped so slowly from one second to the next, and Zhang felt himself watching the display on the TV screen with anticipation he knew to be perverse. But America had been his country's principal enemy for so many years, had thwarted two of his best and most skillfully laid plans—and now he'd see its destruction by means of one of its very own agencies, this cursed medium of television news, and though Tan Deshi claimed that it was not an organ of the American government, surely that could not be the case. The Ryan regime in Washington must have a very cordial relationship with those minstrels, they followed the party line of the Western governments so fawningly . . .

. . . two more smoke trails . . . the camera followed them and . . . what was that? Like a meteor, or the landing light of a commercial aircraft, a bright light, seemingly still in the sky—no, it was moving, unless that was the fear of the cameraman showing—oh, yes, that was it, because the smoke trails seemed to seek it out . . . but not quite closely enough, it would seem . . . *and so, farewell, Washington,* Zhang Han Sen thought. Perhaps there'd be adverse consequences for the People's Republic, but he'd have the satisfaction of seeing the death of—

—what was that? Like a bursting firework in the sky, a shower of sparks, mainly heading down . . . what did *that* mean . . . ?

It was clear sixty seconds later. Washington had not been blotted from the map. *Such a pity,* Zhang thought . . . *especially since there would be consequences* . . . With that, he washed and dressed and left for the Council of Ministers Building.

"Dear God," Ryan breathed. The initial emotions of denial and elation were passing now. The feelings were not unlike those following an auto accident. First was disbelief, then remedial action that was more automatic than considered, then when the danger was past came the whiplash after-fear, when the psyche started to examine what had passed, and what had almost been, and fear after survival, fear *after* the danger was past, brought on the real shakes. Ryan remembered that Winston Churchill had remarked that there was nothing more elating than rifle fire that had missed—"to be shot at without result" was the exact quote the President remembered. If so, Winston Spencer Churchill must have had ice water in his cardiovascular system, or he enjoyed braggadocio more than this American President did.

"Well, I hope that was the only one," Captain Blandy observed.

"Better be, Cap'n. We be out of missiles," Chief Leek said, lighting up another smoke in accordance with the Presidential amnesty.

"Captain," Jack said when he was able to, "every man on this ship gets promoted one step by Presidential Order, and USS *Gettysburg* gets a Presidential Unit Citation. That's just for starters, of course. Where's a radio? I need to talk to KNEECAP."

"Here, sir." A sailor handed him a phone receiver. "The line's open, sir."

"Robby?"

"Jack?"

"You're still Vice President," SWORDSMAN told TOMCAT.

"For now, I suppose. Christ, Jack, what the hell were you trying to do?"

"I'm not sure. It seemed like the right idea at the time." Jack was seated now, both holding the phone in his hand and cradling it between cheek and shoulder, lest he drop it on the deck. "Is there anything else coming in?"

"NORAD says the sky is clear—only one bird got off. Targeted on us. Shit, the Russians still have dedicated ABM batteries all around Moscow. *They* probably could have handled it better than us." Jackson paused. "We're calling in the Nuclear Emergency Search Team from Rocky Mountain Arsenal to look for hot spots. DOD has people coordinating with the D.C. police . . . Jesus, Jack, that was just a little intense, y'know?"

"Yeah, it was that way here, too. Now what?" the President asked.

"You mean with China? Part of me says, load up the B-2 bombers on Guam with the B-61 gravity bombs and send them to Beijing, but I suppose that's a little bit of an overreaction."

"I think some kind of public statement—not sure what kind yet. What are you gonna be doing?"

"I asked. The drill is for us to stay up for four hours before we come back to Andrews. Same for Cathy and the kids. You might want to call them, too."

"Roger. Okay, Robby, sit tight. See you in a few hours. I think I'm going to have a stiff one or two."

"I hear that, buddy."

"Okay, POTUS out." Ryan handed the phone back. "Captain?"

"Yes, Mr. President?"

"Your entire ship's crew is invited to the White House, right now, for some drinks on the house. I think we all need it."

"Sir, I will not disagree with that."

"And those who stay aboard, if they feel the need to bend an elbow, as Commander in Chief, I waive Navy Regulations on that subject for twenty-four hours."

"Aye, aye, sir."

"Chief?" Jack said next.

"Here, sir." He handed his pack and lighter over. "I got more in my locker, sir."

Just then two men in civilian clothes entered CIC. It was Hilton and Malone from the night crew.

"How'd you guys get here so fast?" Ryan asked.

"Andrea called us, sir—did what we think happened just happen?"

"Yep, and your President needs a bottle and a soft chair, gentlemen."

"We have a car on the pier, sir. You want to come with us?"

"Okay—Captain, you get buses or something, and come to the White House right away. If it means locking the ship up and leaving her without anyone aboard, that's just fine with me. Call the Marine Barracks at Eighth and I for security if you need to."

"Aye, aye, Mr. President. We'll be along shortly."

I might be drunk before you get there, the President thought.

The car Hilton and Malone had brought down was one of the black armored Chevy Suburbans that followed the President everywhere he went. This one just drove back to the White House. The streets were suddenly filled with people simply standing and looking up—it struck Ryan as odd. The thing was no longer in the sky, and whatever pieces were on the ground were too dangerous to touch. In any case, the drive back to the White House was uneventful, and Ryan ended up in the Situation Room, strangely alone. The uniformed people from the White House Military Office—called Wham-O by the staff, which seemed particularly inappropriate at the moment—were all in a state somewhere between bemused and stunned. And the immediate consequence of the great effort to whisk senior government officials out of town—the scheme was officially called the Continuation of Government—had had the reverse effect. The government was at the moment still fragmented in twenty or so helicopters and one E-4B, and quite unable to coordinate itself. Ryan figured that the emergency was better designed to withstand a nuclear attack than to avoid one, and that, at the moment, seemed very strange.

Indeed, the big question for the moment was *What the hell do we do now?* And Ryan didn't have much of a clue. But then a phone rang to help him.

"This is President Ryan."

"Sir, this is General Dan Liggett at Strike Command in Omaha. Mr. President, I gather we just dodged a major bullet."

"Yeah, I think you can say that, General."

"Sir, do you have any orders for us?"

"Like what?"

"Well, sir, one option would be retaliation, and—"

"Oh, you mean because they blew a chance to nuke us, we should take the opportunity to nuke them for real?"

"Sir, it's my job to present options, not to advocate any," Liggett told his Commander-in-Chief.

"General, do you know where I was during the attack?"

"Yes, sir. Gutsy call, Mr. President."

"Well, I am now trying to deal with my own restored life, and I don't have a clue what I ought to do about the big picture, whatever the hell that is. In another two hours or so, maybe we can think of something, but at the moment I have no idea at all. And you know, I'm not sure I want to have any such idea. So, for the moment, General, we do nothing at all. Are we clear on that?"

"Yes, Mr. President. Nothing at all happens with Strike Command."

"I'll get back to you."

"Jack?" a familiar voice called from the door.

"Arnie, I hate drinking alone—except when there's nobody else around. How about you and me drain a bottle of something? Tell the usher to bring down a bottle of Midleton, and, you know, have him bring a glass for himself."

"Is it true you rode it out on the ship down at the Navy Yard?"

"Yep." Ryan bobbed his head.

"Why?"

"I couldn't run away, Arnie. I couldn't run off to safety and leave a couple of million people to fry. Call it brave. Call it stupid. I just couldn't bug out that way."

Van Damm leaned into the corridor and made the drink order to someone Jack couldn't see, and then he came back in. "I was just starting dinner at my place in Georgetown when CNN ran the flash. Figured I might as well come here—didn't really believe it like I should have, I suppose."

"It was somewhat difficult to swallow. I suppose I ought to ask myself if it was our fault, sending the special-operations people in. Why is it that people second-guess everything we do here?"

"Jack, the world is full of people who can only feel big by making other people look small, and the bigger the target, the better they feel about it. And reporters love to get their opinions, because it makes a good story to say you're wrong about anything. The media prefers a good story to a good truth most of the time. It's just the nature of the business they're in."

"That's not fair, you know," Ryan observed, when the head usher arrived with a silver tray, a bottle of Irish whiskey, and some glasses with ice already in them. "Charlie, you pour yourself one, too," the President told him.

"Mr. President, I'm not supposed—"

"Today the rules changed, Mr. Pemberton. If you get too swacked to drive home, I'll have the Secret Service take you. Have I ever told you what a good guy you are, Charlie? My kids just plain love you."

Charles Pemberton, son and grandson of ushers at the White House, poured three drinks, just a light one for himself, and handed the glasses over with the grace of a neurosurgeon.

"Sit down and relax, Charlie. I have a question for you."

"Yes, Mr. President?"

"Where did you ride it out? Where did you stay when that H-bomb was coming down on Washington?"

"I didn't go to the shelter in the East Wing, figured that was best for the womenfolk. I—well, sir, I took the elevator up to the roof and figured I'd just watch."

"Arnie, there sits a brave man," Jack said, saluting with his glass.

"Where were you, Mr. President?" Pemberton asked, breaking the etiquette rules because of pure curiosity.

"I was on the ship that shot the damned thing down, watching our boys do their job. That reminds me, this Gregory guy, the scientist that Tony Bretano got involved. We look after him, Arnie. He's one of the people who saved the day."

"Duly noted, Mr. President." Van Damm took a big pull on his glass. "What else?"

"I don't *have* a what-else right now," SWORDSMAN admitted.

Neither did anyone in Beijing, where it was now eight in the morning, and the ministers were filing into their conference room like sleepwalkers, and the question on everyone's lips was "What happened?"

Premier Xu called the meeting to order and ordered the Defense Minister to make his report, which he did in the monotone voice of a phone recording.

"You ordered the launch?" Foreign Minister Shen asked, aghast.

"What else was I to do? General Xun told me his base was under attack. They were trying to take our assets away—we spoke of this possibility, did we not?"

"We spoke of it, yes," Qian agreed. "But to do such a thing without our approval? That was a political action without reflection, Luo. What new dangers have you brought on us?"

"And what resulted from it?" Fang asked next.

"Evidently, the warhead either malfunctioned or was somehow intercepted and destroyed by the Americans. The only missile that launched successfully was targeted on Washington. The city was not, I regret to say, destroyed."

"You regret to say—you *regret* to say?" Fang's voice spoke more loudly than anyone at the table could ever remember. "You fool! If you had succeeded, *we would be facing national death now*! You *regret*?"

At about that time in Washington, a mid-level CIA bureaucrat had an idea. They were feeding live and taped coverage from the Siberian battlefield over the Internet, because independent news coverage wasn't getting into the People's Republic. "Why not," he asked his supervisor, "send them CNN as well?" That decision was made instantaneously, though it was possibly illegal, maybe a violation of copyright laws. But on this occasion, common sense took precedence over bureaucratic caution. CNN, they decided quickly, could bill them later.

And so, an hour and twenty minutes after the event, http://www.darkstarfeed.cia.gov/siberiabattle/realtime.ram began to cover the coverage of the near-destruction of Washington, D.C. The news that a nuclear war had been begun but aborted stunned the students in Tiananmen Square. The collective realization that they themselves might be the targets of a retaliatory strike did not put fear so much as rage into their young hearts. There were about ten thousand of them now, many with their portable laptop computers, and many of those hooked into cell phones for Internet access. From overhead you could tell their positions just by the tiny knots of pressed-together bodies. Then the leaders of the demonstration got together and started talking fast among themselves. They knew they had to do something, they just didn't know exactly what. For all they knew, they might well all be facing death.

The ardor was increased by the commentators CNN had hurriedly rushed into their studios in Atlanta and New York, many of whom opined that the only likely action for America was to reply in kind to the

Chinese attack, and when the reporter acting as moderator asked what "in kind" meant, the reply was predictable.

For the students, the question now was not so much life and death as saving their nation—the thirteen hundred *million* citizens whose lives had been made forfeit by the madmen of the Politburo. The Council of Ministers Building was not all that far away, and the crowd started heading that way.

By this time, there was a police presence in the Square of Heavenly Peace. The morning watch replaced the night team and saw the mass of young people—to their considerable surprise, since this had not been a part of their morning briefing. The men going off duty explained that nothing had happened at all that was contrary to the law, and for all they knew, it was a spontaneous demonstration of solidarity and support for the brave PLA soldiers in Siberia. So, there were few of them about, and fewer still of the People's Armed Police. It would probably not have mattered in any case. The body of students coalesced, and marched with remarkable discipline to the seat of their country's government. When they got close, there were armed men there. These police officers were not prepared to see so many people coming toward them. The senior of their number, a captain, walked out alone and demanded to know who was in charge of this group, only to be brushed aside by a twenty-two-year-old engineering student.

Again, it was a case of a police officer totally unaccustomed to having his words disregarded, and totally nonplussed when it took place. Suddenly, he was looking at the back of a young man who was supposed to have stopped dead in his tracks when he was challenged. The security policeman had actually expected the students to stop as a body at his command, for such was the power of law in the People's Republic, but strong as the force of law was, it was also brittle, and when broken, there was nothing behind it. There were also only forty armed men in the building, and all of them were on the first floor in the rear, kept out of the way because the ministers wanted the armed peasants out of sight, except in ones and twos. The four officers on duty at the main entrance were just swept aside as the crowd thundered in through the double doors. All drew their pistols, but only one fired, wounding three students before being knocked down and kicked into senselessness. The other three just ran to the main post to find the reserve force. By the time they got there, the students were running up the wide, ceremonial stairs to the second floor.

The meeting room was well soundproofed, a security measure to prevent eavesdropping. But soundproofing worked in both directions, and so the men sitting around the table did not hear anything until the corridor was filled with students only fifty meters away, and even then the ministers just turned about in nothing more than annoyance—

—the armed guard force deployed in two groups, one running to the front of the building on the first floor, the other coming up the back on the second, led by a major who thought to evacuate the ministers. The entire thing had developed much too quickly, with virtually no warning, because the city police had dropped the ball rather badly, and there was no time to call in armed reinforcements. As it played out, the first-floor team ran into a wall of students, and while the captain in command had twenty men armed with automatic rifles, he hesitated to order opening fire because there were more students in view than he had cartridges in his rifles, and in hesitating, he lost the initiative. A number of students approached the armed men, their hands raised, and began to engage them in reasonable tones that belied the wild-eyed throng behind them.

It was different on the second floor. The major there didn't hesitate at all. He had his men level their rifles and fire one volley high, just to scare them off. But these students didn't scare. Many of them crashed through doors off the main corridor, and one of these was the room in which the Politburo was sitting.

The sudden entrance of fifteen young people got every minister's attention.

"What is this!" Zhang Han Sen thundered. "Who are you?"

"And who are *you?*" the engineering student sneered back. "Are you the maniac who started a nuclear war?"

"There is no such war—who told you such nonsense?" Marshal Luo demanded. His uniform told them who he was.

"And you are the one who sent our soldiers to their death in Russia!"

"What is this?" the Minister Without Portfolio asked.

"I think these are the people, Zhang," Qian Kun observed. "*Our* people, Comrade," he added coldly.

Into the vacuum of power and direction, more of the students forced their way into the room, and now the guard force couldn't risk shooting—too many of their country's leadership was right there, right in the field of fire.

"Grab them, grab them! They will not shoot these men!" one student shouted. Pairs and trios of students raced around the table, each to a separate seat.

"Tell me, boy," Fang said gently to the one closest to him, "how did you learn all this?"

"Over our computers, of course," the youngster replied, a little impolitely, but not grossly so.

"Well, one finds truth where one can," the grandfatherly minister observed.

"So, Grandfather, is it true?"

"Yes, I regret to say it is," Fang told him, not quite knowing what he was agreeing to.

Just then, the troops appeared, their officer in the lead with a pistol in his hand, forging their way into the conference room, wide-eyed at what they saw. The students were not armed, but to start a gunfight in this room would kill the very people he was trying to safeguard, and now it was his turn to hesitate.

"Now, everyone be at ease," Fang said, pushing his seat gently back from the table. "You, Comrade Major, do you know who I am?"

"Yes, Minister—but—"

"Good, Comrade Major. First, you will have your men stand down. We need no killing here. There has been enough of that."

The officer looked around the room. No one else seemed to be speaking just yet, and into that vacuum had come words which, if not exactly what he wanted to hear, at least had some weight in them. He turned and without words—waving his hands—had his men relax a little.

"Very good. Now, comrades," Fang said, turning back to his colleagues. "I propose that some changes are needed here. First of all, we need Foreign Minister Shen to contact America and tell them that a horrible accident has occurred, and that we rejoice that no lives were lost as a result, and that those responsible for that mistake will be handled by us. To that end, I demand the immediate arrest of Premier Xu, Defense Minister Luo, and Minister Zhang. It is they who caused us to embark on the foolish adventure in Russia that threatens to bring ruin to us all. You three have endangered our country, and for this crime against the people, you must pay.

"Comrades, what is your vote?" Fang demanded.

There were no dissents; even Tan and Interior Minister Tong nodded their assent.

"Next, Shen, you will immediately propose an end to hostilities with Russia and America, telling them also that those responsible for this ruinous adventure will be punished. Are we agreed on that, comrades?"

They were.

"For myself, I think we ought all to give thanks to Heaven that we may be able to put an end to this madness. Let us make this happen quickly. For now, I will meet with these young people to see what other things are of interest to them. You, Comrade Major, will conduct the three prisoners to a place of confinement. Qian, will you remain with me and speak to the students as well?"

"Yes, Fang," the Finance Minister said. "I will be pleased to."

"So, young man," Fang said to the one who'd seemed to act like a leader. "What is it you wish to discuss?"

The Blackhawks were long on their return flight. The refueling went off without a hitch, but it was soon apparent that almost thirty men, all Russians, had been lost in the attack on Xuanhua. It wasn't the first time Clark had seen good men lost, and as before, the determining factor was nothing more than luck, but that was a lousy explanation to have to give to a new widow. The other thing eating at him was the missile that had gotten away. He'd seen it lean to the east. It hadn't gone to Moscow, and that was all he knew right now. The flight back was bleakly silent the whole way, and he couldn't fix it by calling in on his satellite phone because he'd taken a fall at some point and broken the antenna off the top of the damned thing. He'd failed. That was all he knew, and the consequences of this kind of failure surpassed his imagination. The only good news he could come up with was that no one in his family lived close to any likely target, but lots of other people did. Finally the chopper touched down, and the doors were opened for the troopers to get out. Clark saw General Diggs there and went over to him.

"How bad?"

"The Navy shot it down over Washington."

"What?"

"General Moore told me. Some cruiser—*Gettysburg,* I think he said—shot the bastard down right over the middle of D.C. We got lucky, Mr. Clark."

John's legs almost buckled at that news. For the past five hours, he'd been imagining a mushroom cloud with his name on it over some American city, but God, luck, or the Great Pumpkin had intervened, and he'd settle for that.

"What gives, Mr. C?" Chavez asked, with considerable worry in his voice. Diggs gave him the word, too.

"The Navy? The fuckin' Navy? Well, I'll be damned. They are good for something, eh?"

Jack Ryan was about half in the bag by this time, and if the media found out about it, the hell with them. The cabinet was back in town, but he'd put off the meeting until the following morning. It would take time to consider what had to be done. The most obvious response, the one talking heads were proclaiming on the various TV stations, was one he could not even contemplate, much less order. They'd have to find something better than wholesale slaughter. He wouldn't order that, though some special operation to take out the Chinese Politburo certainly appealed to his current state of mind. A lot of blood had been spilled, and there would be some more, too. To think it had all begun with an Italian cardinal and a Baptist preacher, killed by some trigger-happy cop. Did the world really turn on so perverse an axis as that?

That, Ryan thought, *calls for another drink.*

But some good had to come from this. You had to learn lessons from this sort of thing. But what was there to learn? It was too confusing for the American President. Things had happened too fast. He'd gone to the brink of something so deep and so dreadful that the vast maw of it still filled his eyes, and it was just too much for one man to handle. He'd bounced back from facing imminent death himself, but not the deaths of millions, not as directly as this. The truth of the matter was that his mind was blanked out by it all, unable to analyze, unable to correlate the information in a way that would help him take a step forward, and all he really wanted and needed to do was to embrace his family, to be certain that the world still had the shape he wanted it to have.

People somehow expected him to be a superman, to be some godlike being who handled things that others could not handle—*well, yeah,* Jack admitted to himself. Maybe he had shown courage by remaining in Washington, but after courage came deflation, and he needed something outside himself to restore his manhood. The well he'd tapped wasn't bottomless at all, and this time the bucket was clunking down on rocks . . .

The phone rang. Arnie got it. "Jack? It's Scott Adler."

Ryan reached for it. "Yeah, Scott, what is it?"

"Just got a call from Bill Kilmer, the DCM in Beijing. Seems that Foreign Minister Shen was just over to the embassy. They have apologized for launching the missile. They say it was a horrible accident and they're glad the thing didn't go off—"

"That's fucking nice of them," Ryan observed.

"Well, whoever gave the order to launch is under arrest. They request our assistance in bringing an end to hostilities. Shen said they'd take any reasonable action to bring that about. He said they're willing to declare a unilateral cease-fire and withdraw all their forces back to their own borders, and to consider reparations to Russia. They're surrendering, Jack."

"Really? Why?"

"There appears to have been some sort of riot in Beijing. Reports are very sketchy, but it seems that their government has fallen. Minister Fang Gan seems to be the interim leader. That's all I know, Jack, but it looks like a decent beginning. With your permission, and with the concurrence of the Russians, I think we ought to agree to this."

"Approved," the President said, without much in the way of consideration. *Hell,* he told himself, *you don't have to dwell too much on* ending *a war, do you?* "Now what?"

"Well, I want to talk to the Russians to make sure they'll go along.

I think they will. Then we can negotiate the details. As a practical matter, we hold all the cards, Jack. The other side is folding."

"Just like that? We end it all just like that?" Ryan asked.

"It doesn't have to be Michelangelo and the Sistine Chapel, Jack. It just has to work."

"Will it work?"

"Yes, Jack, it ought to."

"Okay, get hold of the Russians," Ryan said, setting his glass down.

Maybe this was the end of the last war, Jack thought. If so, no, it didn't have to be pretty.

It was a good dawn for General Bondarenko, and was about to get better. Colonel Tolkunov came running into his command center holding a sheet of paper.

"We just copied this off the Chinese radio, military and civilian. They are ordering their forces to cease fire in place and to prepare to withdraw from our territory."

"Oh? What makes them think we will let them go?" the Russian commander asked.

"It's a beginning, Comrade General. If this is accompanied by a diplomatic approach to Moscow, then the war will soon be over. You have won," the colonel added.

"Have I?" Gennady Iosifovich asked. He stretched. It felt good this morning, looking at his maps, seeing the deployments, and knowing that he held the upper hand. If this was the end of the war, and he was the winner, then that was sufficient to the moment, wasn't it? "Very well. Confirm this with Moscow."

It wasn't that easy, of course. Units in contact continued to trade shots for some hours, until the orders reached them, but then the firing died down, and the invading troops withdrew away from their enemies, and the Russians, with orders of their own, didn't follow. By sunset, the shooting and the killing had stopped, pending final disposition. Church bells rang all over Russia.

Golovko took note of the bells and the people in the streets, swigging their vodka and celebrating their country's victory. Russia felt like a great power again, and that was good for the morale of the people. Better yet, in another few years they'd start reaping the harvest of their resources—and before that would come bridge loans of enormous size . . . and maybe, just maybe, Russia would turn the corner, finally, and begin a new century well, after wasting most of the previous one.

It was nightfall before the word got out from Beijing to the rest of China. The end of the war so recently started came as a shock to those who'd never really understood the reasons or the facts in the first place. Then came word that the government had changed, and that was also a puzzling development for which explanations would have to wait. The interim Premier was Fang Gan, a name known from pictures rather than words or deeds, but he looked old and wise, and China was a country of great momentum rather than great thoughts, and though the course of the country would change, it would change slowly so far as its people were concerned. People shrugged, and discussed the puzzling new developments in quiet and measured words.

For one particular person in Beijing, the changes meant that her job would change somewhat in importance if not in actual duties. Ming went out to dinner—the restaurants hadn't closed—with her foreign lover, gushing over drinks and noodles with the extraordinary events of the day, then walked off to his apartment for a dessert of Japanese sausage.